Heather Graham

THREE COMPLETE
NOVELS

Heather Graham

THREE COMPLETE NOVELS

Sweet Savage Eden

A Pirate's Pleasure

Love Not A Rebel

WINGS BOOKS

NEW YORK
AVENEL, NEW JERSEY

This omnibus was originally published in separate volumes under the titles:

SWEET SAVAGE EDEN, copyright © 1989 by Heather Graham Pozzessere
A PIRATE'S PLEASURE, copyright © 1989 by Heather Graham Pozzessere
LOVE NOT A REBEL, copyright © 1989 by Heather Graham Pozzessere

This edition contains the complete and unabridged texts of the original editions. They have been completely reset for this volume.

This 1994 edition is published by Wings Books,
distributed by Outlet Book Company, Inc., a Random House Company,
40 Engelhard Avenue, Avenel, New Jersey 07001,
by arrangement with Dell Publishing, a division of Bantam Doubleday Dell Publishing Group, Inc.

Random House
New York • Toronto • London • Sydney • Auckland

BOOK DESIGN BY SIGNET M DESIGN, INC.

Printed and bound in the United States of America

Library of Congress Cataloging-in-Publication Data

Graham, Heather.
    [Novels. Selections]
    Heather Graham : three complete novels.
        p.   cm.
    Contents: Sweet savage Eden—A pirate's pleasure—Love not a rebel.
    ISBN 0-517-10171-8
    1. Man-woman relationships—United States—Fiction. 2. Marriage—United States—Fiction.
3. Historical fiction, American. 4. Domestic fiction, American. 5. Love stories, American.
I. Title. II. Title: Three complete novels.
PS3557.R198A6 1994   93-45732
813'.54—dc20   CIP

8 7 6 5 4 3 2 1

CONTENTS

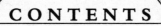

SWEET

SAVAGE

EDEN

NORTH AMERICAN
WOMAN
1

To Scarlet & Joe Rios

with lots of love

1

WHILE THE COLD WIND WHISTLED AND RAGED, threatening to tear asunder the rafters of the tiny attic bed-chamber, Jassy clenched her hands into fists at her sides. She didn't feel the cold as she stared down at the frail beauty on the bed cocooned in threadbare blankets. The woman drew in a rattling breath, and suddenly Jassy became aware of her surroundings, the unpainted rafters that barely held the walls together, the smut from the candles, the ancient trunk at the foot of the bed holding their few belongings, the cold that ever seeped in upon them. Jassy swallowed and her jaw locked tightly as tears pricked her eyes.

She'll not die like this! she swore to herself. *I'll not let her! I shall beg, borrow, or steal, but so help me God, I shall not let her die like this!*

But even as Jassy silently made her vows, old Tamsyn was staring at her sadly, shaking his head just slightly, in a way not meant to be seen, and certainly not understood. But Jassy understood the motion all too well; Tamsyn had already given up all hope on Linnet Dupré.

"Quinine, girl. Quinine might help to ease her misery some, but that be all I can tell you."

Tears welled anew in her eyes; she could not allow them to fall. Impatiently she brushed her small, work-roughened hands across her temple, raising her chin.

Tamsyn was wrong, she assured herself. He had to be wrong. What was Tamsyn but another beaten-down drunk to have found his livelihood with the rest of them at the Crossroads Inn? He claimed to have once been a physician who had even studied long ago at Oxford, but perhaps that was a lie. A lie like the dreams he had spun for her of a new day to come, of distant lands and faraway places, exotic voyages and emerald seas.

Her mother was dying. She had no time for dreams, and she dared not fall prey to despair.

"Quinine," Jassy said briskly.

"Quinine," Tamsyn repeated. "But ye may as well wish for the moon, Jassy, lass. The cost of a dose . . ."

His words trailed away, and Jassy gnawed bitterly into her lower lip. The cost for anything was dear when her mother's wages at the inn came to no more than one gold coin and a bolt of cloth a year.

And when she was paid nothing herself, as well. Nothing, since she apprenticed to the cook and her endeavors would not be considered worthy of coin until she had completed five years of service.

She lowered her head suddenly, whispering in desperation, "I can beg Master John—"

"Save your breath, girl," Tamsyn warned her. "Master John will give you naught."

And she knew that he was right. The customers ate great platters of meat with rich gravy, they drank tankards of ale and imported French wines. Master John was quick to buy a round of drinks, generous to all his customers.

To his servants he was mean and cheap.

And, Jassy thought was a little sigh, they had stayed, anyway, knowing that he was stingy and even cruel at times. They had stayed, for Linnet had always been fragile, not cut out to work, and only here, where they could share this little attic hovel and Jassy could do the majority of her mother's work could they hope to survive.

A slight whimpering sound came from the bed. Jassy rushed to her mother's side, kneeling down beside her, grasping her frail hand in her own. Her tears almost spilled then. Linnet did not appear real at all, but as some fairy queen. Even now she was fine and beautiful—now, when death lay a claim upon her. Nay, not death! Jassy swore. She would be hanged before she would see her mother die here, beautiful, beautiful Linnet, never intended for such a life in such a horrid, squalid place.

Linnet's eyes opened, glazed with fever, all the more beautiful for that glaze. They were truly violet eyes, not blue, not gray, but deep, beautiful violet. A violet as lovely as the gold of her hair and the parchment-pale, but perfect, oval of her face.

A face not old in years but made to appear so by years of care and struggle.

"Mama!" Jassy gripped her hand warmly. "I am here!"

Then panic struck her, for Linnet did not recognize her. She spoke to the past, to people no longer present. "Is that you, Malden? Tell Sheffield that the curtain must be held, for I am feeling poorly, and that twit of a girl is no understudy to take on the role of Lady Macbeth!"

Again tears burned beneath Jassy's lids, and dark despair seized hold of her. Linnet, she saw, was losing her slender grip upon reality, upon life. She reverted quickly to days gone by. To a tender past, a far grander place than the present. For Linnet Dupré had not always been cast into such a lowly state in life—nay, she had most oft been cast as a princess or an heiress. She had reigned as a queen, a queen in the London theatrical community. She had traveled to Paris and Rome; she had been welcomed and applauded throughout the Christian world.

In those days she had been courted by dukes and earls, by nobility and grandeur.

Somewhere among that grandeur she had produced Jassy.

And for many, many years Jassy had lived in grandeur too. Her mother had housed a multitude of servants—and treated them kindly! There had been Remington to answer the bell and look after the house; old Mary to cook; Sally Frampton from nearby Waverly to bathe her mother in rich lotions and dress her hair in the latest styles. There had been Brother Anthony to teach Jassy French and Latin, Miss Nellie to teach her to dance, and Herr Hofinger to teach her all about the world at large, the oceans and the rivers, the Romans and the Gauls. He, too, had filled her head with fantasy; stories about the explorer, Columbus; about the New World, the Colonies, the Americas and the Indians. He had told her tales about the Spaniards and the great defeat of the Armada, and how the English still met and tangled with the Spaniards on the sea, claiming pieces of the New World. And he had told her stories about the great houses and mansions and castles within England, and in her dreams she had been swept off her feet by a golden knight and taken to a glorious castle to reign evermore as its mistress. In those dreams Linnet would never be exhausted or overburdened. She would sit at ease and elegantly pour tea from a silver server, and she would be dressed in silk and velvet and fur.

That had all been a dream, in a far distant and different life.

There had come that long dry spell when Linnet had not been able to obtain a role in the theater. And Linnet had never bothered with her own finances, so she was in complete shock and distress to learn that not only did she not have the money to take a smaller house, but also was so far in debt that the gaping jaws of Newgate Prison awaited her eagerly as her fate.

Some godsend fell upon them then; miraculously a mysterious "donor" kept them discreetly from distress. Linnet knew what had occurred; she would not tell Jassy, as Jassy was but a nine-year-old child.

But by the age of ten, Jassy understood servants' gossip. They all whispered about the Duke of Somerfield having "done something fair" for her mother at long last.

And then they stared at her, and through little George, the cook's son, she learned that she was "illy-gitmit" and that everyone thought that the duke, who had had "illy-cit" relations with her mother, should have surely pulled them out of trouble long before.

Such rumors were lovely dreams to Jassy at first; she imagined that her father would be a great, handsome man in his prime; that one day she should appear in his great hall and that he would instantly think her beautiful and accomplished and love and adore her above all his legitimate offspring. Then he, of course, could introduce her to the handsome golden knight who would sweep her away to her own castle.

It wasn't to be. At the little kitchen breakfast table they could then afford, Linnet jumped up one morning, screamed, and fell to the floor in a dead faint.

Jassy rushed to help her, as did Mary. Mary muttered, wondering what could have caused such a thing. But Jassy then picked up the paper, being able to read as Mary could not, and quickly perused the page, learning then that the duke had been killed most ingloriously in an outlawed duel.

There was no one to pay the rent on the small house. One by one the servants went. Then the house went, and then the very last of their precious hoard of gold coins and pounds sterling. Linnet could not find work in the London theater again—the duke's vicious duchess was busy seeing that no establishment would have her.

Jassy quickly realized that they must find work. In time Linnet knew, too, that menial work would be their hope of survival, Newgate awaiting any man or woman who did not meet their obligations.

She also discovered that she was singularly talentless when it came to working for a living, and in the end she was forced to become the scullery maid at the inn, work totally unsuited to her lovely, fragile form.

Master John hired them on only because Jassy was twelve by then, in the peak of health, easily able to work the full fourteen-hour day that her mother could not.

Jassy was jerked back to the present as Linnet moved fretfully on the bed, speaking again.

"Tell them—tell them that the curtain must be held," Linnet whispered softly. The glaze left her eyes and she frowned, then soft tears fell from her eyes to her cheeks.

"Jassy . . . Jassy, Jasmine. 'Twas he who named you, for he loved the scent of Jasmine. You were beautiful, too, a babe like a flower, a blossom . . . so very sweet. And I did have such dreams! He loved us. He did love us. You were to be a lady, loved and coveted. And still . . . your hands. Oh, Jassy! What have I done to you? To leave you here in this awful place . . ."

"Nay, Mother, nay! I am fine, and I shall get you well, and we . . ." She paused, a lie coming to her from nowhere. "Mother, we shall get out of here as soon as you are well. I have heard from my half sister, one of the duke's children, and we are to travel to his estates. Her—her mother has died, and she is anxious to make reparation. We shall live in splendor, I swear it, Mother, only first you must get well." She had sworn out a lie. Would God understand such a thing? Would he forgive her? Her heart hardened, for she could not care. God had deserted her. He had left her to survive on her own, and that she must do. Linnet, though, would be horrified, for her belief in her religion was great.

But Linnet hadn't even heard the quickly spoken and desperate lie. "Ah, yes! None has ever done Juliet with such poise and innocence! That is what the critics said; that is what I shall do again."

She stared straight at Jassy, releasing her hand with a flourish. "Go now! Tell them that the curtain shall be held!"

The door to the attic loft suddenly swung open.

"Tamsyn!"

Master John stood in the doorway, seeming to bark out his man's name. " 'Tis docked pay you'll get, me man!" he continued. "I need two kegs in the taproom, and I need them now! Jassy, if she's not up and working by morning, it's out on your arses, you are. The two of you."

Suddenly a great laugh bellowed from him, and he bowed to her. "My lady!"

He sent a curt blow reeling against Tamsyn's head. "Hurry, man, hurry! The coach has just come in from Norwood! And you—my lady attic rat," he told Jassy sternly, "had best get down to serve tonight."

"I can serve no one! I must care for her!"

Jassy quickly regretted her temper—she needed to placate Master John. She stood quickly, lowering her eyes and facing him. "In fact, Master John, I meant to come to you for help! I am desperate, sir, for coin. My mother needs quinine and—"

She broke off, for he had come before her, raising her chin with his finger so that her eyes met his. He smiled, and she saw his blackened teeth and felt overwhelmed by his foul breath.

"I've told you before, girl, if you want extra coin from me, you know how to earn it."

The room seemed to spin, and she actually feared that she would throw up her meager dinner if he came any nearer.

She knew what he meant. She thought that she knew a good deal about the private things that went on between men and women. Molly, who worked the taps, engaged in affairs quite frequently. With a cheery wink she had often told Jassy that it was a hideous business with the man grunting and panting and placing, well . . . part of his person into, well . . . parts of her person. It all sounded quite horrid, and made Jassy flinch.

"Ah, with a young and 'andsome one it ain't so bad. In fact, there's some what thinks 'tis heaven! But mark my words, lass, it's a lot of sweat and pumping. And if it were with one who was a lout, well, I think as like I'd prefer death, I do!"

Molly had her standards.

But she continued to see the " 'andsome ones"; she was very fond of the money that could be had that way.

Jassy gritted her teeth and kept her eyes lowered. Her mother was dying. Linnet was everything that she had in this world. Everything.

She stiffened her back. She would do anything to keep her mother alive.

And one day, one day! she vowed, she would kill Master John!

"John!"

The shrill cry came up from below, and Master John seemed to shrink before them. He was afraid of his goodwife, as well he should be, for she was two hundred pounds if she was a single one, and she worked quite well with a rolling pin when she was in a temper.

"Alas, girl! No coin have I this night!" he mumbled suddenly, and turned. He looked at Tamsyn and decided the man needed another blow to the head, and then he departed, wrinkling his nose at the attic odor.

Tamsyn caught his head and jumped to his feet. He was a little man, slim, graying, but strong in his wiry fashion. He caught Jassy's shoulders.

"Jassy, for the love of God! Don't ever, ever think of such a thing! Your mother will d—" He stopped. That her mother would die soon no matter what was what he meant. He had no doubt that Linnet was dying, and that there was very little if any hope at all that she could survive more than another day. But he hadn't the heart to say it so bluntly. "Jassy, your mother would rather die than have you give yourself to such a stinking oaf!"

Tears dampened her lashes and threatened to spill to her cheeks. She looked at Tamsyn, and he shuddered, for what the girl did not know was that even here, even in rags and squalor, she was twice the beauty that Linnet had ever been. She had the same fine, fragile features and more, for her beauty went deeper than anything that could be seen or touched. Hers was a fighting spirit, one that rebelliously challenged and dared from the depths of her eyes. Eyes that tilted just slightly at the corners, intriguing and exotic. Eyes that were so clear and deep and crystal a blue that they might have been violet. And they were framed by lashes so thick and dark, they might have been fashioned against the rose and cream of her young complexion by an artist with India ink.

"I must—I will do something!" she swore, shaking away his touch. She straightened her shoulders and stiffened her spine, so regally.

Tamsyn swallowed, wishing he had not, long ago, come to be such a worthless drunk that he had lost all in life except for a rather worthless instinct to survive.

"I've got to get down, girl. Bathe her face, talk to her, be with her. When she sleeps comfortable, get down to work before mean old John sets you both out in the street!"

Jassy lowered her head and nodded with understanding. Tamsyn squeezed her shoulders and left her, and she knelt back at her mother's side, trying to ease the fever that raged through her.

"Oh, Mother!" she whispered softly, not caring now that they were alone that tears slid down her cheeks and dropped upon the blanket. "Mother, we shall get out of this! I'll make you well, I swear it!"

She swallowed painfully. At the moment Linnet slept, as ethereal, as beautiful, as a hummingbird.

Jassy rose slowly. She kissed Linnet's hot cheek and then hurried out of the room.

Down below, the coach was already in. Jassy hurried to the kitchen to help the cook, but Jake, John's obnoxious doorman, bellowed out that she was to work in the taproom, serving ale.

The inn was dense with smoke, rowdy with talk. Each of the planked tables was full, some with common folk, some with gentry.

Jassy hated the taproom. It seemed always to be filled with a score of Master Johns—louts who grinned lasciviously and tried to pinch some part of her anatomy. Nor was she allowed to slap the wandering hands that touched her; Master John would have booted her out on the steps.

It seemed that she moved from the kitchen to the bar to the tables endlessly, carrying great trays of roast beef and duckling with savory gravies, and scores of tankards. Her shoulders and sides ached from the heavy work. At one point during the night Molly passed her in the hallway from the kitchen to the taproom and gave her cheek a friendly pinch.

"Ah, luv, you look pale, you do! I know yer worryin' 'bout your ma, luv.

Don't you fret, now. Cook just slipped me a bit of good wine and some soup; it's hid by the sideboard. You can get it up to her soon.'' '

"What's this!"

Master John was suddenly behind them. "Ah, her majesty, the Lady Jasmine!" He bowed mockingly. "Missy—I see you off this floor once again and yer ma's in the street!" he warned Jassy, waggling one of his fingers before her face.

"Ah, Master John!" Molly batted her lashes at their taskmaster, pleading nicely. "Please, sir, the girl but—"

"The girl shirks work!" John roared. "If she's off this floor before midnight, she can look for her supper elsewhere!"

He physically turned Jassy about, pushing her forward. Jassy almost screamed. She thought that she might well have stabbed her mother, and then herself, before she could have abided his touch. She clenched her teeth tightly together. She was still so desperate.

Molly, with her red country cheeks and snapping dark eyes, caught up with her again.

"I'll get up there and feed her the soup and the wine, Jassy, I swear it. You just keep out of the way of mean ol' John, eh?"

Gratefully Jassy nodded. "Bless you, Molly!"

It was then that Jake told her she must bring another round of good ale to the two gents nearest the fire.

"And no uppity nose-turning from you, miss!" Jake warned in a growl. "Them two are class, they are! You serve them right!"

She knew what "serve them right" meant, and she wondered with a rush of hostility why he hadn't sent Molly to serve the two. If they laughed and pinched Molly, she would blush and say just the right things.

Jassy walked quickly to the table. The two men, she noted, definitely were "class." More than gentry, she thought, by the quality and cut of their breeches and coats and hose.

Despite herself, she discovered that her heart fluttered just a bit as she neared them, for the gentleman on the right of the fire was handsome, very handsome indeed. He was blond and as light as dreams of heaven, with a wonderfully slim and genteel face and bright, sparkling blue eyes. He glanced up as Jassy set the first tankard down, and he bestowed upon her a smile that actually made her feel as if her senses reeled.

"Ah, and lass, where have you been all my life?" he teased.

Jassy flushed; he was kind, he was gentle. He was the type of man that once she might have dreamed of loving—in a very vague way, of course. A man to sweep her upon a mighty steed, the very knight of her dreams. He would take her back to the world she had once known, or onward to the shining castle of her imagination. It would be a new world. A world where servants moved to the slightest whim, where sheets were clean, where food was plentiful. And he would be the man she had imagined, a man to be a husband, a father, a golden, shining defender in every hour. . . .

She lowered her lashes again and stiffened her spine. What in the Lord's name was the matter with her? Men of stature did not come here to flirt with serving wenches to sweep them away to lives of dignity and grandeur. They wanted what Molly called a "dashing roll in the hay" and nothing more.

She raised her head again proudly. One day she would escape this bondage. She would escape poverty, she would travel where it was wild and free and where she would disdain all those who thought themselves above her.

"Thank you," he told her, referring to his ale. He watched her somewhat gravely, and it seemed that he flirted no more. She liked his eyes; she liked the way that he looked at her, as if he saw far more than a wench or a servant.

And she smiled slightly in return, for he was genuinely kind, and she barely noted what she was doing as she set the other tankard down. His fingers grazed against her hand, holding her there as he watched her. Still, what ensued next was not her fault.

"Robert! Quit ogling the lass and listen well, for this is not a matter that can be dealt with lightly."

The blond man smiled at her with such a touch of admiration that Jassy barely heard the other man's words and therefore could not be offended.

"Be that as it will, Jamie, we're just setting to dinner now, and you're telling me about the Injuns, as it were!"

"Robert!"

With that explosive sound he sent a hand waving with such energy that it caught Jassy unaware. She moved, startled, and the tankard she had not set down properly was caught in the movement. Ale spewed and then fell all around them.

"Damn, girl! Look to what you're doing!"

It wasn't her shining golden knight who came out with the impatient curse but the man across from him. The man that Jassy had barely even noticed as yet.

She did now, for he was on his feet, glaring at her. She had spilled ale not only over his elegant laced white shirt, but also on the documents he had been studying.

He was tall, she noted at first. Very tall, which was hard to miss, since she was slender and small. In his anger he was towering over her. Beneath the deceiving elegance of his shirt, she noted next, his shoulders were very broad, and though his hips were lean, his thighs, tightly hugged by his breeches, were as muscled and powerful as his boots were high and shiny.

His hair was as black as his boots, nearly indigo with its sheen, barely darker than his flashing eyes, cast into a rugged face that was tanned from much exposure to the sun. He was probably not much older than the handsome blond man who had been so kind; somehow he seemed the fiercer man, alive with a striking tension and a volatile energy that seemed to exude from him. He therefore appeared older, more the hardened and arrogant man than his smiling, handsome companion.

He did not stare upon her with admiration. His dark eyes smoldered with annoyance, and something that wounded her pride even worse—a total dismissal and disregard.

Without thinking about her position, she lashed out at this man who had attacked her so unfairly.

"Sir! 'Twas your arm that jolted me! The accident was not my fault."

"Jamie!" the golden man protested softly. "Take a care, please! 'Tis a tyrant runs this place; 'tis likely he'll beat the girl."

Jamie seemed to ignore him. He did not appear to care about his shirt, but he was eager to save his documents, and heedlessly he dragged Jassy to him by her skirts as he sought to use that means to dry the parchments.

"Leave me be!" Jassy cried, as indignation and rage rose within her. She pummeled against his shoulder in sudden, wild fear, for those strange, dark eyes had fallen upon her again—and lingered this time.

"Stop!"

He halted her assault simply, catching her wrists, dragging her down to the bench beside him. He might have been a devil, she thought, he was so very dark, so arrogant, so supremely confident of himself. He did not think that she would dare to fight him.

"Bastard!" she hissed in a soft, sure warning. "Let go of me!"

He laughed in amusement. She longed to move her hands, but his hold on her carried an unearthly strength, and she was suddenly quite certain that his air of total confidence had not come to him without just cause. He was a powerful man; she could feel it in the vibrant heat that passed from his thighs through her skirts; she could feel it in his very hold upon her. It meant nothing. He did not strain. But he held her fast and studied her boldly, frowning curiously as his deadly dark, satanic eyes came to her own, fell to encompass her features, her lips . . . her breasts and hips.

Something warm seemed to sizzle through her. Her heart began to thunder; she tried to jerk away from him, wanting only to do battle, thinking of nothing but his touch upon her and her desperate desire to escape him.

But then her heart sank.

Master John was bearing down upon them.

"My lords, my lords! What is the problem here? Forgive the girl—she's new. And I warrant that she will be well punished for her clumsiness!"

He was about to drag Jassy from the bench, but the beautiful golden-blond man came to her rescue. "Master John! I'd not hurt the girl."

Master John looked at Jassy as if he'd like to beat her flat down to the floor.

"Indeed, sir," the gallant blond man continued with a hauteur that could only belong to the nobility, "I should find myself in a position to see that all my friends and acquaintances were to avoid this place were I to believe that you chastised your servants too severely."

The dark-haired man finally looked at John after it seemed that the blond had kicked him beneath the table.

He sighed impatiently. "Indeed, sir, I should feel compelled to warn many from this place! Alas—and I had so enjoyed the ale and the fire!"

John appeared quite near to apoplexy. For several seconds he just stood there, his face growing redder and redder.

The dark-eyed man spoke again, this time with a deadly authority. He rose to his full height again, hands on his hips, towering over them all. "Should I hear that any harm has befallen the girl, I swear I shall return and break both your legs. Do you understand?"

"Aye!" John said quickly, barely breathing.

"Good!" The man sat again, eyeing John.

"Get back to work, girl!" John commanded Jassy.

And she did so—swiftly. She was eager not just to escape her horrid master, but also longed with all her heart to escape the dark-haired stranger.

John caught up with her quickly, whispering into her ear. "You think you're something, eh, Lady Jasmine of the Attic? Not to me, you're not!" Her heart catapulted downward as he laughed bitterly. "So I can't touch you! Well, I'll tell you this! You're docked, girl, you and her up them stairs!"

Docked! Less money when they were paid a pittance to begin with! And all over that lout of a stranger!

"Just leave me be!" she said gratingly.

"To the kitchen!" Jake ordered. "Bring out the platters of food for His Majesty's soldiers just arrived."

She headed for the kitchen. Molly crossed by her quickly there. "I reached yer ma, luv. She drank some broth."

"Bless you!" Jassy murmured, and even as the cook loaded the heavy trenchers onto her shoulders, her episode with the gentlemen faded from her mind and worry came back to it. Tamsyn's one word flooded her thoughts.

Quinine.

Linnet needed quinine to combat the fever.

She could buy some from the chemist across the lane—if she only had the coin to do so.

The cook was gossiping with one of the newly arrived coachmen even as she burdened down Jassy's great tray. The coachman, seated at the big kitchen table, tipped his hat to Jassy and offered her a friendly grin. She smiled vaguely in return, balancing her tray. Cook flashed her a quick smile, too, but gave her attention to the visiting coachman.

"Lord love us, I don't believe a word of it, Matthew!" she said, but she laughed delightedly.

"Well, 'tis true! Jassy, you should hear this one!"

"Matthew, she's a sweet young thing!" Cook protested sternly.

"But it's a great story! All about Joel Higgins, who worked in the London livery. He was such a handsome, strapping youth! He told me about this old woman, see, and she was willing to pay for his services—but he weren't that hard up! So he made her think he were willing to give when he weren't, and when the old battle-ax had her clothing a-gone, he took her purse and disappeared, saying he just had to wash up. Imagine her—a-laying there waiting while he stole away her purse!" He laughed heartily, enjoying his own story. "A good comeuppance for the old girl, eh?"

"Ah, and Joel will meet up with the hangman, that he will!" Cook prophesied dourly. "And, Matthew, you watch your mouth around my young help. Hmmph! Jassy, I be needin' you in here, I am, and he's got you out on the floor. Well, damn the man, then, if his sides of beast ain't roasted the way he'd have 'em! Sorry, girl, 'bout your ma."

"Thank you," Jassy murmured, gritting her teeth against the weight of the tray balanced on her shoulder. She paused, though, when she should have turned with her burden and hurried. "Cook, have you by any chance—"

"Lord love ye, girl! I'd gladly loan ye a coin if I had me one! I sent me last money home for me own old mother! You've my prayers, though, girl. The Lord God will provide, you just look to Him!"

The coachman sniggered. "Aye! The Lord God provides—more'n likely He helps those what help themselves!"

Jassy had already given up on the Lord, and she would fall beneath the weight of the tray soon. She gave Cook a smile and hurried out.

The night wore on. She felt that endless hours passed. At long last she was released to go back to the attic.

She ran instantly to Linnet's side, then put her forehead against the bed, crying softly as she heard her mother's great rasping attempts to draw breath.

Quinine. Tamsyn said it might ease her.

There was a soft rapping at her door. " 'Tis me—Molly, Jass."

Jassy came back to her feet and hurried to the door, throwing it open. Molly studied her ravaged face.

"Is she no better, then?"

"No better at all."

"Ah, lass!" She paused for a moment, hesitating, studying Jassy.

The girl should have had more, Molly thought. All of them had thought it. Cook, her, the upstairs maids. The girl was better than this life. Better than endless scrubbing of cold stone floors. Better than her raw, ragged hands, better than her rag of a dress. They'd all had dreams for her. She was their prize—more lovely than a human had a right to be, even if it was hard to see that loveliness, clad as she was in rags, her glorious golden hair all trussed up in an ugly net. She was fine. A rose among thorns, a blossom of spring against the dead of winter.

She was doomed. To this life; to hell on earth.

Molly sighed. "Jassy, I know your ma never much wanted you falling to our ways, but, well, that tall handsome lord was asking questions about you. He said that his lodgings were at the Towergate, across the row, and that he meant to stay up late."

Jassy inhaled sharply. An illness seemed to sweep through her stomach.

The blond man. The kind, handsome blond man had wanted her.

She stiffened. As kind as he had been, he wanted a whore for the night. She could have created an entire daydream around him; she could have envisioned him as all that life had to offer.

Her shoulders dropped. Linnet rasped away behind her. She clenched her fists together.

"Jassy!" Linnet called out.

"Mother!" She swung around and fell down by the bed. "I am here!"

Linnet's head tossed about. Jassy touched her forehead and discovered that it burned. Linnet's eyes opened for a moment, but they were glazed. She did not see her daughter. "Help me," she whispered feverishly. "Oh, help me, please . . ."

Her voice faded away; her eyes closed.

"Oh, God!" Jassy cried out. She caught her mother's hands and held them tightly, then she stood and whirled about, almost blinded by her tears.

No! she thought, and it was a silent scream of agony. *I will not let her die here! I will beg, borrow—or steal.*

And that was when the idea caught hold of her.

Steal . . . yes.

Surely God would understand, and He was her only true judge. She had turned her back on Him, but maybe now He was helping her to help herself.

She could steal the money that she needed. And keep her daydream. If the blond man did not suspect her of a foul deed, she could suddenly cry innocence and escape him. He was so kind. He would understand.

And if he caught her in the lie . . . well, again she would depend upon his kindness.

And if that didn't work . . .

She swallowed bitterly. She could go through with the bargain. She could not let Linnet die.

"Ah—thank you, Molly. Thank you for so much."

Molly cleared her throat. "He's an exciting one, he is!" she said, trying to sound cheerful. She flushed slightly. "I—I tried to exchange myself for you; I'd have gladly given you the coin. But he wanted you, he did, were he to have any at all."

"Thank you."

"Shall I stay with her for you?"

"Oh, bless you, Molly! Will you?"

Molly nodded.

Jassy hurried to the washbowl, poured out the remaining water, and tried to scrub her face. She was shaking so badly!

Molly wandered in and sat down. "Best hurry, child," she said tonelessly.

Jassy knelt down by her mother's side once again and picked up her frail hand. It burned to the touch, and there was no response.

"Mama, I love you very much! I'll not let you die this way."

She swore it out loud, passionately. Then she was on her feet, slipping into her worn cloak, on her way out the attic door.

One last time she paused, her beautiful features tense and dark with torment.

"Nay, I'll not let you die this way! Not if I have to beg, borrow—or steal!"

2

HE SAVAGE COLD STRUCK JASSY AS SOON AS SHE set out on the path from the inn to the Towergate. The two establishments were not far apart, for in this town where the road ran south from London, there was continual commerce and travel, and even a third innkeeper might have fared very well. The general consensus was that Master John set the better table, while the Towergate offered more amiable rooms—more private rooms, at that. The gentry and nobility tended to spend their nights at the Towergate even if they did sup at Master John's, while common folk enjoyed fewer amenities—and lower prices—at Master John's.

Jassy's teeth chattered. Her nearly threadbare cloak provided scant protection against the winter wind, and the ground snow—where it had not turned to muck from the countless carts and carriages passing by—had frozen to ice. She was somewhat glad of the cold, for it seemed to have frozen over her mind and her thoughts. When she stood before the door of the Towergate, she was trembling from the cold and from fear of what she was about to do.

The wind blustered behind her as she entered, drawing the door quickly closed. She leaned against it and noted that hounds and hands dozed about the dying fire alike, that there was very little commerce at this late hour, only one pair of fellows still seeming to be engaged in quiet conversation near the wall.

One of the Towergate's serving wenches came forward, and Jassy found herself furiously swallowing her pride and pulling the hood of her cloak lower about her forehead.

"What do you want, girl?" the wench demanded, and Jassy feared that she would be sick. The tavern wench was young, with well-rounded bosom and hips, and she moved with an explicit sway that brought new horror to Jassy. This . . . this was what she would become.

Quinine! She reminded herself desperately, and the thought gave her courage. "I have been asked here," she said simply.

"Oh," the wench said, smiling slyly and eyeing her curiously. She shrugged and cast a glance toward the stairway. "Here for his lordship, eh? Well, well. Aye, he'd be expectin' you. Third door. Best room in the house."

Jassy nodded. As she moved toward the stairs the wench sauntered over to the barkeep and whispered quite loudly to him, "Why, 'tis Jassy Dupré. Imagine! Her what thinks she's better than the rest of us! Whorin' up to him that's rich and fine, same as any other lass!" She laughed delightedly.

The barkeep chuckled, and Jassy could feel his eyes boring into her back. "So 'tis her, ain't it, now? Maybe she won't be so high-flyin' in the days to come, eh?''

They both burst into crude laughter. The malicious mockery followed her all the way up the stairs and along the hallway.

Jassy reached the door and desperately threw it open, not thinking to knock. She closed the door tightly behind her and leaned against it, gasping for breath. Here she was in a man's bedchamber—as the hired entertainment for the evening.

Not any man's, she reminded herself. Robert's. The kind, golden-haired gentleman. She would not die at his touch; she would come away with coin—bartered or stolen—and with her virginity intact.

Instinct forced her first to appreciate the warmth of the room. Then she noted that it was very dark, for the fire in the hearth that provided the warmth had burned down very low, to glowing embers. The room seemed empty, and as her eyes adjusted to the dim light she stiffened, biting into her lower lip with perplexity.

Before the softly glowing embers of that fire sat a deep metal hip bath, from which steam wafted. It was definitely empty. Awaiting . . . her.

Bitterly she wondered how she would manage to scan his clothing when it appeared that she was to doff her own first. Nor could she make any attempt at playing the seductress, and then the innocent, until she had crawled into that tub, for it was understandable that such a gentleman would not want a serving girl until that girl had bathed.

Uneasily she stepped into the room, softly treading nearer the tub, wondering what had become of the man she had been summoned to . . . serve.

She gasped, her heart seeming to beat like thunder, when large hands fell upon her shoulders from behind. She did not spin around but stood like a deer, poised for flight, yet achingly aware that she dare not run.

"Your cloak, mistress," came a husky male voice from the darkness that loomed all around her. "May I?"

Panic seized her. He was behind her, it was so terribly unnerving to feel him there. The room seemed to blacken still further, and then spin, and she braced herself. Slowly the dizzy sensations faded.

She lowered her head, nodding. She tried to remind herself that this was the golden-blond, shining knight who had championed her in the public room when his towering, dark friend had so cruelly cast her into trouble.

She closed her eyes tightly, the better to remember his light, gentle eyes. So admiring.

"You are cold. As cold as ice. The bath and the fire will warm you." He spoke very quietly. His words were nearly whispers, and yet they, too, unnerved her. Soft, they were different somehow. They held a curious tension, a certain fever. He was a man, she reminded herself. A man who had hired a harlot for the evening.

He touched her. . . .

Her cloak was gone. His hands fell to her shoulders, and she tried not to shiver at the feel of those long male fingers there.

She stepped forward, eluding those fingers.

"The bath. It is for me, then?"

There seemed to be a slight, ironic pause. "Aye, mistress. For you." Then once again those fingers settled upon her shoulders, moving with expertise to the buttons on her simple woolen gown. She willed herself to remain still. She had not expected this feeling. This feeling that he should tower so behind her, seem to sear her with his hands, with the promise of his length and breadth behind her.

She narrowed her eyes, seeing the mist rise from the tub, the embers glow in the hearth. If she could just see it all like this! A red and glowing mist sheathed in darkness!

His fingers moved on down her back and skimmed the fabric from her shoulders. Once again she nearly gasped, nearly screamed out loud, for he lowered his head and pressed his lips to her nape. She felt that touch as if it were a brand of fire sweeping through her, riddling her to awful panic, yet waking her too. As if it had given her some special substance to her blood, to her veins, to her body. She felt alive, where before she had been numb. Trembling, yet aware anew that she must play this game oh so carefully to escape with her pride, her chastity—and the money she so badly needed.

His hands caressed her shoulders, and the gown fell down her arms even as she thought and planned. The wool fell over her meager petticoat, and she instinctively found herself stepping from it—and away from his grasp once again.

Her eyes lit upon the armchair just behind the tub and the fire. His frock coat lay across the top of it, neatly folded. So close to the tub. One could just reach out—and search the pockets.

If only she could escape his scrutiny long enough.

Ah, unlikely! For though she dared not look, she heard a soft sound as he whisked her dress away—and came a step closer to her once again, this time finding the hook to her petticoat, releasing it, watching it fall. In her shift she felt the cold once again. _Turn,_ she warned herself. _Turn and slip into his arms. He is blond and golden and gentle, and you must woo him with a smile if you hope to leave him as a lady._

But she could not turn. She longed to do so, but she could not. Not even to stare into those gentle eyes. Not now, not yet, for she was suddenly ashamed to be here before him in her shift and stockings alone.

Again she shivered. She felt the tension and vitality of his movement behind her, the whisper of his breath. She inhaled and felt dizzy, for she breathed in the subtle scent of him, dangerously male and potent. He clutched her shoulders, bringing her back against him, and she felt all the muscled hardness of his body.

And the growing desire within it.

She saw his hands, long-fingered and bronzed and powerfully broad as he swept his arms around her, pulling her close. She felt dizzy again, nearly overwhelmed.

And once again, ever so near to a scream, for those hands cradled around her breasts, cupping the weight, thumbs lightly flicking against her nipples through the material of her shift, so sheer that it might not have been there. She ground down hard on her jaw to keep silent, and she mentally braced herself so that she would not bolt and fly from his touch.

Then some ragged, heavy sound came to his breathing, and his fingers moved to the pins in her hair. Her hair fell from its heavy braid down her neck in a massive coil, and she inched forward again, lowering her head.

"Please . . . I cannot get it wet. I should freeze when I left here."

She heard the softest laugh and almost wished that he did not lurk in the darkness behind her, that he would step forward, smile upon her with his soft, expressive eyes.

And yet she did not really wish to see him. Not now. Not when she must forget all inhibition, all strict teachings of a lifetime. She must forget about the whispers going on downstairs, whispers about how the arrogant Miss Dupré was, after all, no untouchable thing, no ice maiden, but a whore to the highest bidder.

"I shall not touch your hair, though I long to see it free. Please, go. Take your leisure in the bath."

She bit her lip, wishing she might ask him to turn from her as she further disrobed.

She knew that she could not.

And so she was glad that he lingered in the darkness as she stepped forward, trembling, trying her best to whisk her stockings from her legs with some grace and poise, pausing uncertainly before she could step from the shift, and unwittingly performing it all in a most sensual manner.

All Jassy could think was that it was quite important to let her shift lie close to his frock coat so that she might reach the latter in pretense of seeking the first. And once that garment was gone, she was in all haste to reach the hip bath, for never in her life had she felt her own nakedness so keenly.

She sank into the water, closed her eyes, and tried to keep her teeth from chattering, though the water still steamed.

Something fell before her. Her eyes sprang open, yet she saw nothing, for once again he was behind her.

"Soap, love," he murmured, still so husky, still so low, yet there was the slightest irony there, and she wondered if he were truly as kind as she had thought him. All the better if he could be crude, she thought, for then it would be easier to deceive him, to take from him what she had no desire to earn.

A cloth followed the soap into the tub. She nervously grasped both, wishing fervently that he would not hover behind her so. He must move! He must! And she was not so sure anymore that he would gladly hand over his coin were she not to perform her services, and therefore she must reach his frock coat.

He paced behind her; she wondered if he grew impatient. She grew desperate, gnawing upon her lip as she sought a way to move him.

Mercifully it was he who moved himself, in a most obliging fashion.

"Would you like a drink?" he asked her softly.

"Aye, that I would," she whispered in reply, and he strode quickly to the door, throwing it open to call down for service.

Jassy dropped soap and towel and lunged over the edge of the tub swiftly, delving her fingers into his pocket, discovering it loaded with coins. Bitterly she realized he would surely not miss one, and it was a sorry world indeed that a man of means could purchase a woman and not even notice the cost of all that she had to give. Quickly she returned to the bath.

She heard him thanking someone curtly at the door, returning with a tray. She risked a glance at him as he set it upon the table and poured out two glasses, but she could not see him at all, for he lingered in shadow. She knew only that he had stripped down to shirt and breeches, that in bare feet he was soundless and sleek, and that he was truly a tall man, broad and trim.

Robert . . .

If she could but see his gentle eyes . . .

Ah, and good that she could not, for his coin was caught in the palm of her hand, and she dare not let him find it there!

She lowered her face into the water and started violently when she raised it, for he was hunched down behind her, one arm cast around her shoulder. He offered her a glass of amber liquid.

"Rum," he said briefly. "Caribbean rum, golden and pure. 'Twas this or weak ale."

She took the glass and drained it, gasped and coughed, and heard his laughter as he patted her damp back. "I should have taken the ale," he murmured apologetically.

"Nay, nay, 'tis fine," she responded. And indeed it was, for it burned like a sustaining fire as she swallowed, and it eased all that seemed so rough and jagged and terrible about the night.

"You would try more?"

"I would," she murmured, her eyes downcast, and again reckoned bitterly that the cost of the rum was probably greater than that of the common whore.

It did not matter now! she assured herself, for the coin was in her palm—soon she could turn to him, then start to cry, and plead forgiveness. She would prove herself the daughter of the great actress Linnet Dupré with a convincing and magnificent performance.

Then she would leave.

And in leaving, save the dream. That in life she could come upon this golden man again, all honor intact. And by some miracle she would be rich and beautiful in silks and satins, and he would fall madly in love with her. And then . . .

He handed her the glass again. And knelt down behind her. His finger caressed her neck, from the slope of her shoulder to the lobe of her ear.

It was not so bad, it was not so bad. She had the rum.

She swallowed down that second glass and felt its hearthlike warmth and amber glow.

"You are quite rare," he said curiously. "Too slim and yet so elegant. The face of an aristocrat and, alas, the hands of a charwoman. The body of a temptress and eyes that warn of the cunning vixen, proud and sly."

She wondered at his words. That he should sound so entranced and so acidic —all in one.

And she shivered, for he suddenly did not sound at all like that gentle man with the golden head and appealing eyes.

"Mistress . . ."

The word was a whisper that was like a strange wind, quiet and yet savage, touching her flesh, filling her with a feeling of fire. Husky, it rose from the depths of him, like the deep caress of a warm summer's wind. The soap was in his hands. She could not protest him, for she held the empty glass of rum in one palm—his coin in the other. She trembled and blinked and held herself immobile. She felt the soap and cloth sweep over her, over her breasts. Slowly . . . his hands moved with an easy leisure. They moved upon her as if they had some right. As if they had known each other a long time. And she sat there and allowed the shocking intimacy. The soap and cloth coursed over her. Touching her nape, stroking against her throat, and then her shoulders, and then . . .

Her breasts once again. She shivered and trembled, shocked and staggered by sensation, feeling much as a cornered hare. The power in that touch was mesmerizing. Her eyes fell closed in confusion, and then she felt him move, move around, and touch his lips to hers.

Ah, so hot, coercive, persuasive. Consuming and expert, casting that trembling throughout her body. She felt her mouth part, the pressure of his tongue sweeping through it. And as she struggled against the overwhelming feel of it all, she was heartily sorry that she had swallowed the rum so quickly, since what had been sustaining warmth was now a rush that added to her panic and confusion. She was engulfed! Terrified suddenly at the absolute power of the man, terrified that it was all racing along in a heedless, reckless fashion and that she was quite near to losing all control.

She had never been kissed before. And this . . .

He seemed suddenly to be over her and around her, his lips upon her own, upon her throat. And his hands . . . delving into the water, sliding along her thighs, folded so crudely within the confines of the tub. Oh, now, now! She screamed inwardly. Now! She had to end it, else all would be lost.

His arms swept around her, lifting her from the tub. She let out a great startled gasp, instinctively clinging to him lest she should fall, yet somehow sure from his laughter that her weight was as nothing against his strength. His laughter . . . against the steam, against the mist, was neither light nor amused but still ironic, adding to her sense of panic.

"Please, please, sir," she murmured, and her voice, though breathless, carried the right amount of quivering pathos. Yet she discovered herself upon the vastness of the bed, the hardness of his form atop her, his dark head bowed over her breast. . . .

His hot, demanding kisses falling there.

She dug her fingers into his hair, trying to stop him. "No!" she whispered, for his mouth opened over the dusky rose of her nipple, drawing upon it, suckling it, and causing a searing to pierce into the very length of her. She could not bear it; she convulsed and trembled with the stunning sensation of it. Her flesh blazed and burned crimson as she felt that hot, liquid touch upon her, entering deep within her, shooting straight to her womb.

"No, please!" she said, fighting for coherency. "Please, gentle sir, kind sir! I thought that I could come here for you were ever so fair, yet I have discovered that I—"

She broke off in a gasp, for though her head spun with the rum and other shocking sensations and a growing panic, she had just realized her own thoughts. She stared at the hair she held, at the head of the man who so intimately used her.

Dark head. Dark . . .

"Oh! Oh, stop! By God . . ."

His face lifted to hers. No kind, light eyes with a gentleman's civility surveyed her. Dark eyes stared down at her. Dark, cynical eyes that matched the tension of his whisper. Eyes like Satan's own. Sharp and piercing, tearing into her with a scalding contempt. They were not even black or brown, as she had imagined. They were indigo and gray. Surely the devil's own. Oh, surely . . . 'twas not Robert at all, she realized in awful horror, but the rude and arrogant Jamie who held her—naked—in his grasp!

"You!"

She forgot that she had actually toyed with the idea that to gain the money she had needed, she'd have even bedded Master John. Or perhaps it seemed that this was worse—this bronzed, indigo-eyed stranger who had already treated her with such scorn. Perhaps it was his hated body upon her; his breath still scalding the dampness he had left upon her breast, his hand upon her hip.

"You!" she gasped out again in awful horror, and he smiled, a mocking curl of the lip, tight-lipped and grim, and he gazed upon her from narrowed eyes.

"Aye, yes, me. You thought to snare Robert in your little trap, eh, love? Why, you mewling little petty thief. It's a pretty game, I must say. Come like a seductress, pick a man's pocket, then cry innocence!" He made a ticking sound of disgust. "Curious. I had thought there was something special about you. I'm disappointed. You're nothing but a common whore and a thief."

"I am no thief!" she said, refuting him desperately. Dear God, she wanted to die.

"Not a thief?" His arrogant head tilted to one side.

"Get off me!" she cried. She tried to twist but found that his leg was cast over her own. She tried to strike him, but her hands were too quickly caught. She could not dislodge him from her naked body. "I'm not a thief—"

"The money, mistress, in your palm. I saw you delve your dainty little hands into my pocket. Alas! And you haven't earned it yet! Of course, I will give you that opportunity."

"No! No!"

Madly, with a strength and energy born of fury and desperation, she fought him. She struggled, swearing, to free her wrists. She arched but managed only to come closer, more surely against him. She kicked and flailed and managed to draw more than a grunt from him, but nothing else. His fingers were like steel bands, his body was immovable. It was hard as rock but hot, like the summer sun, and she could feel all his strength too keenly as she lay there naked. Vulnerable. And caught in the act of robbery. She could not win. She could only touch him more and more. Know more and more about him, as a man.

In the end she lay panting, vowing not to cry, deadly still beneath him, her wrists secured by his left hand, his right leg cast over her thigh, pinning her beside him.

She did not look at him. This was not the kind, gentle, shining, golden man of her dream. This was the other, hard and ruthless, and she would give him nothing. She would not plead. She would not tell him that she was desperate. She could not act out any charade, for he had already called her bluff. There was nothing to do but lie there and withdraw, despise him, and think herself far, far away—and pray that he did choose to call the magistrate.

He stared at her. She could not withdraw so completely that she could escape the fact that he stared at her. She was too aware of his muscular body, clad yet somehow savage to her, and her own nudity. If one could die of humiliation, she thought, she would surely perish then. Yet hatred, she had heard, was a sustaining reason to live. Perhaps she did not die because she hated him so. More determined, she stared straight into the night and waited, quivering despite herself.

He moved suddenly and she cried out, but he ignored her, securing her wrists with one of his own. He leaned over her and with his free hand opened up her palm.

And found his money within it.

She did not respond but stared straight ahead.

"Have you no excuse?"

She did not reply, and he laughed harshly.

"Ah, if I were but Robert! You would turn to me with tears in those lovely eyes and swear out your innocence. Or perhaps I should hear some story about a child needing a meal, or some other such rot! But I'm not Robert—and you did seem wise enough to know that."

"You are a despicable, ruthless bastard," she said smoothly, still addressing the ceiling. Oh, God. She had nothing, and she was in his power. If he called the hangman, she didn't think that she would give a damn. She had failed miserably.

"Ah, my love, I do protest! I tend to be fond of your fair kind, ladies and whores. 'Tis thieves alone I abhor!"

He spoke with a certain edge, and though she had just convinced herself that she did not care what came, be it death itself, she emitted a strangled gasp when she discovered him moving against her. Curtly, roughly, brusquely, rebalancing his weight—forcing her thighs apart with blunt and unyielding force.

She had thought that nothing could humiliate her any further, yet this did. She strained against him in renewed fury, swearing out her hatred, as his hand touched her, as his fingers probed her with a ruthless intimacy. She twisted her head; color and a profusion of heat filled her; mortified, she longed for death.

"I shall scream. I shall scream rape—"

"A whore who knowingly came to me?" he inquired with a certain amusement.

"Oh—God! Stop!"

The plea came from her in a ragged gasp. She could not escape him, could not escape his touch. She tried to twist, to hide, yet he surveyed her mercilessly as he examined her so insolently, ignoring her protest. Had she only had a weapon, she'd have surely slain him. He gave her no quarter, no compassion. It was not that he hurt her; it was simply that he explored where he would, his touch entering even inside her.

And then . . . his touch was gone. He still held her prisoner; still clamped her to the bed. But the terrible intimate exploration of his long bronze fingers was gone, and she was terrified to breathe.

"A virgin?" he inquired. The sound of his voice was curiously polite and distant, as if they were discussing the weather.

"Oh, for the love of God and all the saints—!"

"Mistress, do cease," he said, interrupting her. "You came to me, remember? I made my intent quite clear when I spoke to the other bar whore."

"I'm not a whore!"

"So it seems. You are a thief."

"And you are a despicable, arrogant bastard, a vile defiler of women, a—"

"Have you as yet been defiled, little thief?"

"You're touch has defiled me!"

"Ah, mistress! There is so much more that can be shared between a man and a woman!" he assured her. "Shall we explore the possibilities?"

"No!"

"So you did come with the sole purpose to rob me blind. Ah, no. My mistake. You came to rob poor Robert blind."

"Yes, and I have failed. So let me go."

She lay there trembling in desperate fear. He was so casual, and so at ease! His hand rested very low upon her belly, his leg still blocking her escape. She might as well have been in chains beneath him. She should cry, she should act out some sweet penance. But she could not act before him. She had already discovered that. And any minute now he would take what he wanted from her. He surely would enjoy taking her brutally, for he truly seemed to hate her and he had already proven that he had no compassion.

"You think that I should let you go?" he asked quietly. His knuckles grazed her belly and she bit hard into her lip, praying that he would not delve within her again. Her flesh burned anew. She swore against him and breathed a silent prayer.

He laughed dryly, rolling from her, resting his weight upon an elbow to stare at her. For a moment she could not believe that she was really free. She returned his glare and saw fully his face. The bronzed, rugged planes, the indigo eyes—the long, arrogant nose. The lips, full and sensual, twisted into a mocking sneer. Dark hair, tumbling over his forehead. His throat, bronze against his shirt, his shirt caught tight against the corded muscles of his shoulders and chest. A medal, a golden St. George slaying the dragon, lay cast against the darkly haired section of his chest where his shirt lay open in a vee.

"Are you reconsidering, wench? Shall you stay? Ah, I see, you are enamored of me, after all. You are free, and still you remain at my side!"

Free . . . he had released her. What did she care if he stared at her so? "Oh!"

She bolted from the bed like a hawk in flight, nearly tripping over herself to procure her clothing. She ignored her shift, petticoat, and stockings, stumbling into the harsh wool of her gown with nothing beneath, barely slipping into her shoes before she was grasping for the door. "Enamored of you! I shall hate and loathe and detest you until my dying day! Were I a man, I would slay you. Had I the chance and ability, I'd slay you, anyway, so beware, sir, lest we ever meet upon the road!" With that, she spun for the door. Hot tears were burning behind her lashes.

"Girl!" he thundered suddenly, and despite herself, she stopped, her back to him. She obeyed the raw command in his voice, and she hated herself for doing so.

Something struck the door. The coin she had taken.

"You went through quite a bit for it. Take it."

She swallowed. Oh, how she wanted to refuse that coin! How she longed to spit in his face!

She could not. Her mother was dying.

She stooped, shoulders slumping wearily, to retrieve it. She vowed in wretched silence that someday, someday she would come into affluence, and so help her, she would find and repay this man for the awful humiliation he had heaped upon her.

She jerked the door open and went stumbling out. For a moment she was totally disoriented. She stood there, desperate just to breathe, and then she rushed down the stairs mindless of the hussy Megan watching her, and of the ogling stare of the barkeep.

She rushed out of the Towergate's front door, then stopped, glad, oh so glad, of the snow that cast her into chills, of the cold breeze that seemed somehow to cleanse her.

She walked a few steps, stumbling, then stopped to stare at the money in her hand. She need only get back to the attic. Blessed Tamsyn—he would find the chemist and buy her the quinine. Any humiliation would be worth the price, for Linnet would live, and she could quickly scorn that atrocious black-hearted man!

She started to walk again.

"Mistress! Mistress Dupré!"

She stopped again, in awful pain. How had she missed the voice! Oh, how had she been such a fool? For she knew his voice now—gentle Robert's voice—beckoning her to stop.

She turned, and the red of a summer rose stained her cheeks. The gallant, handsome blond was rushing toward her, her cloak, petticoat, and stockings cast over his arm. He knew. He knew where she had been. She thought that she would die of the shame.

"Mistress! Jamie bid me catch you, as you shall need these!"

Nearly choking on the tears she tried desperately to swallow, she stared up into his sympathetic light eyes. She shook her head vehemently, unable to speak. He stuffed the things into her arms, and in horror she turned to run.

"Mistress . . . Jassy! Please, wait! If there is some problem, I would help!"

Help! Ah, too late! She could not bear to see him again. Not now, not ever.

She kept running. Running, heedless of ice and snow and wetness and cold until she reached the kitchen entrance of Master John's. Cook, by the fire, let her in, pressing a finger to her lips. Jassy gave her a grateful nod and went tearing up the servants' stairway.

She quickly went through the attic door and saw that Tamsyn was back in the room, by her mother's bed.

"I've got it, Tamsyn. Money. Please, will you get the quinine for me? I feel I must stay by her side."

"Jassy—"

Molly caught her arm. She shrugged off her friend's touch. Tamsyn stood quickly and caught her.

"Jassy, lass. Your mum's at peace now."

"Peace?"

She stared at him uncomprehendingly. Then his words began to sink in to her mind, and she shook her head in fierce denial.

"No. *No!* You must get the quinine, Tamsyn! Surely she just sleeps!"

Neither Tamsyn nor Molly could stop her. She fell to her knees at her mother's side, grasping the frail white hand. A hand as cold as the blustering wind outside. Stiff, lifeless.

"Oh, no! Oh, God, please, no!" She screamed out her anguish, then she cried, and she tried to kiss her mother, to warm her with her body. She stared down at her beautiful face and saw that indeed the Master Johns of the world could touch her mother no more. Linnet was gone.

Jassy laid her head upon the bunk and sobbed.

Molly came to her and took her in her arms. And still Jassy sobbed, on and on, until there were no more tears to cry.

" 'Tis all right, luv, 'tis all right," Molly said, soothingly.

And at last Jassy looked at her, eyes glazed but wildly determined.

"Molly! I shall not live like this, and so help me—I shall not die like this!"

"There, there," Molly said with a soft sigh of resignation.

And Jassy discovered that after all, her tears were not all spent. Because she caught her mother's cold, delicate hand once again and warmed it with a new flood of sobbing.

3

SHALL BE GOING BACK," JAMIE CAMERON SAID to Robert. "And you should be coming with me."

The stableboy had saddled his horse, a bay stallion called Windwalker, but Jamie felt compelled to check the girth himself.

"I don't know," Robert said doubtfully, watching Jamie as he mounted the prancing stallion at last. They were both dressed elegantly for their travel, for by nightfall they would reach Jamie Cameron's family home, Castle Carlyle, near Somerfield. Jamie was to meet with his father on business, and he was dressed today as his noble sire would wish him to, in a fine white shirt with Flemish lace at the collar and cuffs, slashed leather doublet, soft brocade breeches, a fur-lined cloak, high black leather riding boots, and a wide-brimmed, plumed hat. He was the perfect cavalier. Robert thought with a mild trace of bitterness that his friend could deck himself in any apparel and still appear negligent of it all, masculine and rugged.

Though Jamie was not his father's heir, but rather a third son, he admired his father greatly, and they were business partners, both greatly enthusiastic about their joint venture.

"I'm starting to think that you are mad!" Robert said.

"Oh? And why is that?"

"Well, Jamie Cameron, perhaps you will not be the next Duke of Carlyle. But nevertheless, were you not the son of an extremely wealthy and powerful noble, you have used your own trust funds well. You have fought on the seas, and you have met with the savages in Virginia. Any one of them might well have skewered you through. And for what? A company that much more often fails than prospers, and a plot of land given you directly by the king. When you've so many acres here in England that I find it doubtful any of your family has ever ridden over them all!"

Jamie laughed and stared westward, almost as if he could see the New World, where it seemed his heart so often lay, even when he was home. "I don't know myself, Robert. But there is a draw. I feel it always. It is a passion that grows in my blood, in my heart. I love the land and the river and the endless forests. There are places of such beauty and quiet!"

"I've seen the sketches brought back of the Indian attacks, and of the 'starving time' in 1609, my friend. The Indians are savage barbarians. It is a savage land, so they say. Bitterly cold, then humid and hot."

"The Indians are of a different culture," Jamie mused. "But they are men and women, just as we."

Robert laughed out loud. Jamie cast him a quick glance and shrugged. He'd had the pleasure of meeting the colonizer John Rolfe and his wife, the Indian princess Pocahontas, both in Virginia, and at King James's royal court. It was said that she had saved the life of John Smith when her father would have taken his head, and the lady did not deny the story. Jamie had been saddened to hear that she had died in England. And recently, her father, the great Powhatan, the big chief of many tribes, had died too. It was as if an era were already over, when so much had just begun.

When the London Company had first sent its men sailing across the sea, and when they had first established their settlement at Jamestown on the James River in Virginia, the days had been dreary indeed. They had left England in 1606. King James had sat upon the throne then, but it was just three years after the death of Elizabeth, and three years after a tempestuous age. The age of explorers, of Sir Francis Drake, of Sir Walter Raleigh, of the Spanish Armada. Entering into Virginia, they were aware that there was a constant threat of invasion from the Spaniards, of attacks by the Indians. Many things had hindered the growth of the colony. Supplies hadn't always arrived, as planned, from England. Men had looked for profits, and they had planted too much tobacco and not enough food. They had starved, they had clashed with the Indians, the Pamunkies, the Chick-ahominies, the Chesapeakes.

But much had improved since then. Though Pocahontas and Powhatan were dead, the peace formed at the time of her marriage to John Rolfe seemed to have lasted. There had been few women in the colony; now married men brought their wives, and the Company had made arrangements for young ladies of good character to cross the ocean, and the colony and the various "hundreds" surrounding it were beginning to flourish and prosper. From the Old English hundred, established before the Norman Conquests. A great swath of land where a hundred families could live.

On his last trip to Virginia, Jamie had staked out his own land. He and his father were heavy investors in the London Company, but Carlyle Hundred, as he was calling his land, came to him directly from the king in recognition of the services he had rendered there.

His land was directly upon the James River, in a far more fortuitous spot than Jamestown, so he thought, for his land was higher and not so dank and infested as the Jamestown acreage. It was beautiful, high land, with a small natural harbor. The pines and grass grew richly, so profuse that the area seemed a blue-green. By the water there was a meadow, and as Jamie had stood there, alone with the sound of the sea and the very quiet of the earth, he had felt anew his passion for the land. It would be great. The country stretched forever. It was where he would dig his roots, and it was where his children would be born, where they would grow, where they would flourish. The Carlyle Hundred. "It seems to be a land of endless opportunity," he said aloud.

"I'd enjoy any of your opportunity," Robert replied with a sigh. He had gambled away much of his own inheritance and, indeed, traveled with Jamie now in the hopes of meeting a lady of fortune who would appreciate his fine lineage and ignore his lack of a purse.

"If you choose to come with me, I will deed you a thousand acres of your own."

"Acres covered with savages and pines!"

"It is an Eden, Robert. Raw and savage, yes, but with the promise of paradise." He pulled up on his bay suddenly, for they had come to the outskirts of town, and they could no longer pass easily on the road, for there was a funeral procession passing by. People stepped out of the way. An old crone looked up at the two of them and whistled softly. " 'Tis nobility! Best we give way!"

"Nay, woman!" Jamie said. "Hold your peace. All men are holden unto God, and we would not disturb those who grieve." The woman stared at him and nodded slowly. Windwalker pawed the cold earth, impatient to be on, but Jamie held him still. He watched as a bony nag dragged a cart forward. There was a gable-roofed wooden coffin upon the cart, but Jamie saw that it was constructed so that the foot of the coffin would give way.

Apparently the family had not been able to afford the cost of a permanent coffin. When the final words had been spoken, the shrouded corpse would be cast into the earth, and the coffin retrieved.

The day was nearly as cold as the night had been. But behind the cart with the coffin walked a black-swathed woman. Slim but very straight, she did not cry; she made no noise and held herself with the greatest pride. Yet in the very stiffness of her spine, Jamie sensed something of her grief. Pain so great that she dared not give way to it.

"Who has died?" Robert queried softly.

The old crone snorted. "Linnet Dupré. Her Majesty, the actress. Though were ye to ask me, my fine lord, I'd say that Master John as well as killed her, for he is a mean one. She never had no strength. Were it not for that girl of hers, she'd have languished in Newgate long ago."

Listening, Jamie frowned. A gust of wind caught the black hood on the woman's head at last, causing it to fall about her shoulders. It was Jassy, the wench who had so fascinated him the night before. The thief.

His jaw hardened for a moment, then he relaxed, and he almost smiled. Well, her fascination had been for Robert. And perhaps she had been stealing for a reason. Perhaps she had longed to buy a proper coffin.

Or perhaps her mother had even lived and needed medication.

"Why, look, 'tis the beautiful tavern wench!" Robert exclaimed.

"Indeed," Jamie agreed.

"Perhaps we could help her. Perhaps we could be of service."

Jamie thought dryly of the night gone past and determined that she would not want any help from him. And yet she had taken the coin he had tossed her. He would never forget her eyes, though. They had burned like sapphires in the night, blue fire filled with hatred and a fierce, fighting spirit.

There was more about her he might not forget, he reminded himself. She was beautiful, of course. She had all her teeth, and they were straight and good. Her skin was achingly soft. Her face was fragile and fine, high-boned, exquisite. She seemed like a fragile flower, and yet there was that tremendous strength to her. No one would ever hold her down, he thought with amusement. Then he felt a flash of heat, for he had held her, and that, too, would take time to forget. She might have been created with the hottest sensual pleasure her entire purpose, for though she was overly slim, she was sweetly lush, with wonderful, firm breasts, rose-crested, beautiful. Her back was long and sleek, her legs long and shapely. Her stomach dipped and her hips flared, and she had been mercury to touch. She had left him aching in every conceivable way.

She had wanted Robert, he reminded himself. Women never seemed to realize where true strength lay, for Robert could not provide what she had needed. He hadn't the purse for it. Nor, for that matter, Jamie decided—with a certain arrogance, he was ready to admit—could his friend have provided what she needed in other ways. She was an innocent maid, but there was something about her that reminded him of his raw, untamed land. There was a promise of something wonderful and tempestuous and passionate about her. It was in her eyes; aye, even in the hatred she felt so wholeheartedly for him.

"She will not want any help from me," he said softly. He turned to Robert, reaching into his doublet for the pounds sterling he carried there. "Robert, follow her. When you are able, see that she receives these. Insist that her mother be buried in the coffin if she fights you."

"But, Jamie—"

"Please, Robert, do as I say."

Robert shrugged and smiled. "My pleasure. Perhaps it will enamor me to the lass. You should take care."

"We shall probably—neither of us—see her again, so what does it matter? Charm her into taking enough to get by on. Enough to find a new position away from such a one as Master John."

"Aye." Robert nodded. "Were that oaf to touch such beauty, it would indeed be a sacrilege."

"Aye, that it would. Go on now, the funeral party moves onward."

Robert dismounted his horse and wedged his way forward through the crowd.

She had not brought the black hood back up about her head, and from his position Jamie could see her face. No tears touched her cheeks, and her magnificent eyes were open wide upon the world. Yet she moved like some ice princess of a fantasy, forever frozen, forever made cold. No heart could beat within her breast, no warmth could thaw her. Her hair, a flow of golden silk, lifted and fluttered about her cheeks, and she seemed not to notice it. She walked straight forward, ever forward. She did not smile, and she did not crack. She was as beautiful as ice.

The wagon moved on; the crowd moved on. Jamie followed at a discreet distance, and he wondered vaguely why he took the time, and why he would bother with a maid with a temper like hers. She had tried to rob him and she had been blatantly disappointed—no, horrified!—to discover that he was Jamie, and not Robert.

It was her circumstance, he thought. Pity; had she come straight to him, he gladly would have eased her way and asked naught of her. He could be a hard man and he was aware of it, but those who knew him and those who served him knew that he was always fair and, in times of need, generous. What was his he claimed wholeheartedly, yet what was his he by rights could give, and he would have given the girl the money she needed without a thought.

He shrugged against the cold. What difference could it make?

They walked, against the winter chill, a good distance from the town. The crowd thinned. All who followed the girl now were a wizened little man and the plump, pretty barmaid who had also served them the night before.

Jamie realized that they had come to the common folks' cemetery.

No great monuments rose to the dead here. He thought of the chapel at Castle Carlyle, of the great monuments sculpted to his ancestors. Here there was earth, and the occasional poor cross, or a death's-head riding an angel. Mostly there was nothing but the barren winter earth.

A large hole awaited the cart. A mutual grave. Other shrouded corpses had been cast into it already, and more would join it before the day was done.

The priest stepped down from the cart. He waved a pot of incense, and his words rose high. God forgave all mortal sins, and Christ welcomed his own into his fold. Dust to dust. Ashes to ashes. Linnet Dupré had found a haven in the arms of the Lord Jesus.

Jamie watched Jassy, watched her standing tall and proud, the wind moving the sheaths of black gauze all about her. The priest's words fell like clods of earth, burying her mother with finality. And still she did not move, did not whisper, did not speak.

The swift service came to an end. The girl stepped forward to press a small coin into the open palm of the priest, and at last Robert stepped forward. The girl started. Her enormous blue-violet eyes opened wide, and emotion came to her at last: dismay, surprise, and a pale hint of shame.

Jamie felt his lip curl into a grim line. He hadn't known why, but he had asked Robert to return her things with a certain purpose. He hadn't known that he had such a cold streak of maliciousness, but it had seemed important that she know Robert had been aware of her activity. Perhaps she had wounded his pride. Perhaps it seemed that she believed Robert could give her more. Maybe he was just annoyed that she fawned so over his friend, believing there could be a future for her. Perhaps she dreamed of a fine house, of a title, of precious things. Perhaps he was the one who could draw the fire from her eyes and into the heart of her body.

Perhaps she even believed he was so soft of heart that he would marry her. She had misjudged her man. Robert needed wealth, and he would marry for wealth, no matter how great the beauty of a golden-blond barmaid.

As Jamie watched, Robert paid the priest for the coffin, and the toothless driver of the cart—apparently the owner of the coffin—came around, his ugly face gnarled up with interest.

The girl protested. She murmured something, and Robert turned to her and explained that she must let her mother rest in the coffin for eternity; it was a very small thing for him. The priest, who had been tipped well by now, assured her that it was important for Linnet's mortal remains to rest well in the wood.

The girl pulled the black gauze from about her and draped it lovingly over the coffin. Robert took her by the shoulders and led her away from it.

The cart was lifted and lowered.

The coffin made a thump as it landed in the ground. Only then did Jamie see the emotion that touched her face, a crippling anguish. It touched her for just a second, and then it was gone, and the ice was back about her, the crystal-cold control.

They came from the cemetery, and she saw him then, sitting high upon Windwalker. He saw her stiffen, and he saw the hatred enter into her eyes. She pulled away from Robert's hold, but Robert was talking and pretended not to notice.

The girl's eyes remained locked on Jamie's.

He dismounted from his horse. As they came closer, Molly and the wizened little man bobbed to him, murmuring, "Milord!" Jassy said nothing. She did not bow, and she offered him no title. She stood like stone against the cold and the wind. Behind them, the cart and the priest rode by, and the grave diggers hurried on with their task.

"Ah, there you are, Jamie!" Robert said. "I was telling her she must not return to Master John's, but she has said she has no intent to do so, anyway. She has a bit of money on her now, and she plans to travel southward to find her family."

"Does she?" Jamie said.

"Aye, that she does."

They were all standing out in the snow-packed road. Windwalker snorted loudly, and the breeze picked up with a vengeance.

"I've got to get back, luv," Molly told Jassy. "He'll have a strip of my skin if I don't."

"Oh, Molly!" Jassy whispered. The two women hugged each other. Jamie was treated to another glimpse of the warmth she was capable of expressing when she chose.

"And I, Jassy," the wizened little man said. "God go with you, child! Remember, we will always be here, should you need us!"

Jassy hugged him too. Fervently. He and the woman Molly bobbed to Robert and Jamie again, then swiftly departed.

"You were planning to walk to your family? Alone?" Jamie said skeptically.

"Aye," she snapped back. "And what is it to you, sir?"

"Lord Cameron, Miss Dupré," he said, correcting her with a slight bow. "Mistress, the question is of some importance to me, for my father's estates are not far, and he would be gravely distressed to hear of a young serving wench accosted and set upon and perhaps even left for dead."

"Should I be accosted and left for dead, Lord Cameron, I shall ask my Maker to see that your father does not hear of the event," she retorted. With a sweet smile she turned to Robert. "Thank you, sir, for all your kindness."

"Jassy, let us take you to the town ahead at least. We've an . . ." He paused, looking at Jamie with a shrug. "We've an extra horse. Ah, mistress! Truly the way is rough and ragged and littered with misfits and vagabonds, and I would be your escort."

Jassy smiled slightly and nodded, then looked Jamie's way. "And tell me, kind sir, is Lord Cameron accompanying you?"

"Aye, that he is," Robert said uncomfortably.

"Then I should prefer the misfits and vagabonds," Jassy said quietly.

Jamie forgot that she was a young woman, forgot that she had just lost her mother, and his infamous Cameron temper came into play. He clamped his hands down hard upon her shoulders, swirling her about. His face was darker than ever with the depth of his anger, his jaw clenched tight with the strength of it.

"Mistress, I believe you're forgetting that I might well have set the law upon you. Thievery of your type is punishable by hanging."

"Jamie!" Robert protested.

Jamie ignored him, staring into the hate-filled eyes of the woman before him. "What, madame, were you planning on stealing—a horse? Or are you so very cunning then, or is it a matter of sheer stupidity?"

"Don't touch me!"

He swore out something in absolute fury. He released her shoulders but caught her waist. Before she could protest, he set her upon Windwalker's back. He leapt up behind her, grasping the reins with some difficulty, for she was swearing then, with the penchant of a dockhand. She tried to shift, tried to dislodge herself. Robert stood in the road, laughing.

"Well, there's one not dying to be a Cameron heir!" Robert chuckled. "Excuse me, Jassy." He bowed very low to her. "Please, do excuse me if I enjoy myself. You see, in London the ladies throw themselves all over him and he barely notices. It's nice for a change to see Lord Cameron at a loss!"

"Robert, mount up, will you?"

Jassy twisted against him. Beneath her threadbare cloak she was wearing the same garments she'd worn the night before. She tried silently to dislodge his arms from about her.

"Let me—"

"There is no extra horse, mistress. You may ride this one. Have you left anything behind?"

"I am most eager to leave you behind!" Was he mistaken, or was there a hint of desperation about her? Did the threat of tears hover in her eyes? Did her blood truly run warm, like that of other women?

"Mistress, you are a wretched witch, and in all honesty I do not know why we don't drop you here in the road!" Why in God's name was he bothering with her? She had annoyed him yesterday; he had been engrossed with his Royal

Charter, his plans and his sketches, and he had sorely lost his temper when she had interrupted him. But then she had attracted his attention, and he wasn't at all sure why he should give a damn, or even if he truly did.

There's the lie, he realized. And there's the rub. He was worse than Robert, for he wanted her with an obsession. He wanted to find that thing about her which he could not see, and could not touch. He wanted the fire beneath the ice.

Her fingernails suddenly curved over his hands where they lay upon the reins, digging in. She spoke, her voice grating from her clenched teeth. "Lord Cameron, you vile heap of rodent compost—"

"Mistress, enough!" he roared. Her nails hurt. He should have been wearing his gloves. He swore, and with that, he set his heels to the bay. Windwalker took flight, sending her reeling hard against him. He heard a slight gasp. She clung desperately to the saddle pommel, and he was glad, for at least she had the instinctive sense to value her own life.

Hoofbeats sounded as Robert followed behind them. The winter wind blew about them, and though it seemed they rode the clouds, they rode hard, and it was cold.

Jassy was glad of it, for she quickly became numb. She had no adequate covering for this wild ride, nor did she know how she had found herself cast upon it. Perhaps it was all a nightmare. Within a day her life had changed so drastically. That morning she had broken all ties with the past. Linnet was gone. There was no reason for her to remain with a brute like Master John. She was young, she was very strong, she could not only read and write but also could teach geography or Latin and even history. There had to be a better place in life for her.

First, however, there was a matter of vengeance.

She was going to her father's house. She wanted nothing from anyone. All she wanted to do was to meet the duchess—and to spit upon her and let her know that she had brought about the destruction of Linnet Dupré, and that somehow, somewhere in time, she would pay for her cruelty. When that was done, Jassy could live again. She would find a better life.

She didn't want to admit that it was thanks to the gold coin that Jamie Cameron had so carelessly thrown her way that she could possibly make the long journey to Somerfield.

Jamie Cameron! she thought with scalding fury. Jassy's mother was gone, she was lost and bereft, and this dark son of Satan did not seem to care. He had no manners, no chivalry, but still insisted upon being there—ever a memory of her deepest humiliation!

She longed to throw herself from the horse! But she could not, and so she clung tight.

The wind stayed with them. They rode hard, passing frozen fields and ice-covered forests. The cold wrapped her and filled her, and at the least, it kept her from thinking of her loss. Her mind was upon him, for with each great movement of the bay's legs she was pressed against his chest. She felt his arms about her as he held the reins, and she felt the pressure of his thighs against her. How could he? she wondered bleakly. After the things that had passed between them, how could he imagine that she could bear the sight of him?

Suddenly the landscape changed, or what she could see of it, for her hair continued to lash against her face, stinging her eyes. The trees thinned, and they passed more of the barren fields of winter. There were barns and stables and cottages to the left of the road, and a frozen brook to the right. Within minutes they came upon a village.

Only then did Jassy realize that the bay had slowed, and that their wild ride had come to an end. Nor had he run the horses too wickedly, for they had come no more than twenty or twenty-five minutes from the Crossroads Inn. Suddenly they stopped. Lord Cameron leapt down from his mount and turned to reach for her. She ignored his arms at first, but though his eyes were enigmatic, they carried some curious warning or demand, and she allowed him to help her down. She hated the impact of his touch. She hated the strength of his arms and the feel of his hands upon her.

"From here, Mistress Dupré, we shall have to know where it is that you want to go."

"I want to go alone," she said quietly.

Robert came up behind them then, and two young stableboys came running out of the single tavern in the small place. Both seemed awed by the sight of Jamie and Robert, and Jassy quickly ascertained that the nobility and gentry seldom rode along this path. But the boys were quick to serve, and the horses were led away to the warmth of the stable. The tavern keeper came to the wooden steps of his establishment and stared at the lot of them with equal awe.

"Shall we dine?" Robert asked Jassy with a smile. He offered her his arm, and she gladly accepted it. Jamie followed them at a distance, then climbed up the steps and came into the establishment.

They were the only ones there, and the tavern keeper urged them into a private room with a bar and tap in the corner and a cheery fire burning in the grate. Robert brought Jassy forward while Jamie discussed the offerings with the cheery man. Robert sat Jassy down upon a bench. He knelt at her side and took her ragged hands into his own, rubbing them, warming them. She looked into his gentle eyes and saw his rueful smile, and the ever-present admiration he bestowed so kindly upon her. "You're dreadfully cold," he murmured.

"You're making me warmer," she said softly. She watched him, and she appreciated the fire's sure warmth, for she was flushing. This was what Molly meant by a handsome man. If a woman could but be his wife, maybe it would be easy to lie with him. Perhaps she would not feel the humiliation and the crimson heat. Perhaps she could endure it all and return soft kisses to his gentle lips. Lips so different from those that curled with such scorn from the bronzed face of Lord Jamie Cameron. Oh, God! She would never forget that night. She prayed that he would fall off the face of the earth!

He ruined everything for her. He ruined the fact that Robert had cared, that he had come so gallantly to pay for a coffin for her mother, that he had offered her a horse that her journey might be with him, and be safe.

But he knew. He knew that she had gone to Jamie Cameron's room as a hired whore. And there was no way for her to tell him that nothing had happened, that she was still free to love where she would.

Her fantasies were taking hold of her. She could not marry him, no matter what. Men of his class did not marry women of her own.

She smiled and quickly drew her hands away. Then she realized that Jamie Cameron had long since ceased to speak with the tavern keeper, that he was staring at her with his relentless dark eyes. In silence he had watched Robert hold her hands, had watched her tender smile to his friend.

Robert stood up. "It is viciously cold, isn't it?" He warmed his hands before the fire, then turned around and warmed his backside. The tavern keeper had taken their cloaks. Jassy was still shivering.

Jamie swore softly and rudely touched her skirt. "Is that all that you have?"

She wrenched her skirt from his touch. "Aye!"

"Did your mother leave you nothing?"

"Oh, she had a dress, aye! Would you have had me set her naked in her shroud?"

Jamie took a step nearer the fire, rested his booted foot upon the stone hearth before it. He eyed her critically. "You cannot survive without warmer clothing."

"I will have warmer clothing," she said, staring at the flames.

"Perhaps this man's wife has some heavier cloak she'll no longer use," Robert said cheerfully. "I shall see."

"No, please!" Jassy swung around on the bench. "You must not spend your money on me. No more. I shall survive on my own. Honestly, I have made my way before, and I shall do so now."

"Then you'll excuse me a moment for private reasons," Robert said, and left them.

Jassy watched him go. Jamie frowned, looking down at her work-roughened hand where it lay against the wood of the bench. She wore a ring. A ruby ring with the emblem of a falcon upon it.

Jassy heard his movement, heard it like the wind, but she was not quick enough to stop his touch, nor had she the strength to battle against his sudden attack.

"You *are* a bloody thief!" he swore, catching her hand, wrenching her to her feet, and studying the ring.

"Stop it!" She tried to retrieve her hand. She could not. He sat upon the bench himself, dragging her down beside him. Then his indigo eyes found hers with seething fury, causing him to pierce into her like forks of lightning.

"Where did you get this?"

"My mother—"

"You liar! Who did you con for this ring?"

"I conned no one!"

"Who did you seduce and rob blind for this? What a fool I was! That is your act, is it not? You don't care if you are caught or not—you cry prettily—"

"I never cried before you!"

"You did not need to. I set you free. But with others you have cried! What a pity that I did not make you earn your income this time, but rather fell prey like all the others! Perhaps we should remedy the situation!"

"There were no others!" Jassy hissed furiously. "And I will never, never put myself in a position to be—to be so much as touched by you again!" Of course, he was touching her, and she hated herself for bothering with a reply. But he was on the bench beside her, and she was aware that he was no gentleman and that his touch was that of hardened steel. His hold upon her hand was brutal; the warmth of his breath touched her cheek. She could not escape him.

She gritted her teeth and went very still, but his hold did not ease. He jerked hard upon her hand again. "Who?" he demanded.

"I seduced no one!" she cried in fury. She tried to stand, and he dragged her back.

"Where did you get this ring?"

"It is none of your business!"

His eyes narrowed upon her, hard and without mercy, without a trace of compassion. "You may tell me now, Jassy, or so help me, this time I shall call the law down upon you and they will hang you by your very pretty little neck."

"You will not!"

"Test me, then, mistress."

She hesitated. She didn't know whether to believe him or not, and then, looking at his hard and implacable bronze features, she realized that he despised her and that he might do anything.

"It's my father's ring!" she snapped.

"What?"

Again she tried to wrench her hand away. "It is the crest of the Duke of Somerfield."

"Aye," she said gratingly.

"Do forgive me," he said mockingly, "but I know the children of the late Duke of Somerfield and a Crossroads serving wench is not among them."

She stared at him with the calmest loathing she could summon. "As a bastard child, she is, my lord!"

He released her hand suddenly. He was still and silent for several seconds, and then he began to laugh. "The old duke's daughter?"

"Aye, and not by choice!"

"You did not wear the ring the other night!"

"Nay, I did not, for it was on my mother's finger then. He always said that she must keep it, and she did. For this—and the taint of his 'nobility'—are my inheritance!"

He was still laughing. She hated the sound of it.

"Stop it! Oh, please, God!" Jassy groaned. "Will you not get out of my life!"

"Nay, not today, girl. I've brought you this far; I shall bring you the rest of the way."

"The rest of the way?"

"My father's lands border those of the new duke—your brother, Henry. I shall be glad to bring you to a loving reunion."

"I want no loving reunion!" She jumped up off the bench and whirled away from him. She faced him from near the fire. "I haven't come for a reunion, I have come to tell the duchess that she is guilty of murder!" She bit her lip to keep from crying out; her loss was still so close to her heart. The laughter had left him. He was watching her gravely. "She is guilty of murder! She killed my mother. I wanted nothing from him. I never saw him and I never wanted to see him. But she—his duchess! My mother was no serving wench. She was an actress, a fine one. But the duchess saw to it that she could never find work upon the stage. The duchess saw to it that she was worn into the very ground, that her health failed, that—oh, God, why am I telling you this? I hate you! I loathe you almost as much as I loathe her!"

Her words hung upon the air. The fire crackled, and he continued to survey her unblinkingly, insolent, arrogant, and ever superior. Then he smiled coldly and rose, and he towered over her, lean and hard, and suddenly she was afraid.

But he did not touch her.

"I'm afraid, my dear, that you will have to vent all that hatred upon me."

"What do you mean?" she asked quickly, backing away from him.

"The duchess is dead. She died two years ago. Well, the old duchess, I should say. There is a Duchess of Somerfield. Your brother has married."

Jassy's hand fluttered to her throat. "She . . . is dead?"

"Aye. Dead and buried."

Jassy turned away from him and studied the flames. "There is no reason for me to go there, then."

"No reason? Why, my girl! Knowing your ways, mistress, I would think that you might be most eager. Your brother is extremely rich." He paused a moment, and a curious softness touched his eyes. "And your sister is charming. Elizabeth. You should meet her."

"I will not go there."

He leaned casually against the mantel. "Then what will you do? Settle into scrubbing floors and peeling potatoes again?" He grabbed her hand again, lifting it high for her to see its work-roughened flesh. "Is this what you want for your life? To live and die in servitude?"

She snatched her hand away. "What I do or do not do with my life is none of your concern."

"I am simply trying to help. If you are so interested in scrubbing floors, I might speak with my father. He pays his servants very well, and feeds them even better."

"Thank you, no. I would not care to serve any relation of yours any more than I would ever care to serve you."

"I see. The tavern life suits you. There are always men about to seduce into parting with income for the mere promise in your eyes."

"Any man, my lord. Any five, any ten, any twenty—rather than you."

They stared at each other, and then the door swung open and Robert reentered the room. "Ah, Jassy, see what we have found!" He had an armful of garments and came to the bench, spreading them out to be surveyed by the other two. "It seems that Lady Tewesbury came through here not long ago. Do you know the story about Lady Tewesbury? I shall tell you. Her first husband died and she married a man who had pined for her for years. Well, this was a stop on their honeymoon tour, a reckless lovers' tryst in the forest. Anyway, her new husband could bear nothing of her old husband, and so he forced her to leave all her things here!" He glanced at Jamie. "The tavern keeper is willing to dispose of it all at a very modest cost." Jamie nodded slightly, and Robert went on. "I think that they shall fit you quite well!"

"Oh, but I can't—" Jassy said.

"Oh, but you must," Jamie said, interrupting smoothly. "Robert, you can't imagine what I have just discovered. Jassy is the . . ." He paused, and she wondered what he had first intended to say. "Jassy is the half-sister of the Duke of Somerfield."

"What?"

The garments fell from Robert's hands, and he stared at Jassy with renewed and keen interest.

"Alas," Jamie said, "I wonder if the duke knows of her existence."

"I wonder," Robert murmured.

"I had thought," Jamie said casually, "that we should find out. I shall hire a messenger to hurry to my father's house, and we shall take Jassy straight to Somerfield."

"Of course," Robert agreed. He was still staring at her. His breathing had gone very shallow. He smiled fully, then he let out a little cry of joy. "Somerfield, eh!" He laughed, then he reached for her hands and began to dance her around the room. Jassy thought that he had lost his mind, but he was so handsome and appealing and young and light with his laughter that she discovered herself joining in. If only Jamie Cameron weren't over by the fire, watching her with his dark, brooding gaze!

"Oh, our supper has come at last!" Robert said. He stopped dancing but still held her fingers, and the feeling was delightful. The tavern keeper entered the room with a kitchen boy at his side. He brought a feast of fish, poultry, and meat swimming in a pool of thick gravy. He brought a huge platter of bread and a dried apple tart and tankards of ale. For once, Jassy realized, she was not serving it. She was being invited to dine.

"Is it all to your liking, Jassy?" Robert asked her, and his blue eyes danced.

"It is lovely, thank you."

She managed to seat herself beside Robert, but Jamie Cameron was still there, across the table from her. And as always, he stared at her, condemning her, his dark gaze piercing into her, making her feel naked to the soul. She tried to ignore him, and she was somewhat successful, for she had never known just how hungry she was. She couldn't remember eating food that tasted this good, that was served so deliciously.

Then she looked up and found him still staring at her, and her pleasure in the meal dimmed. She did not know which of the men was paying the cost of the meal.

Jamie Cameron refilled her tankard with ale. She took it from him, sipping it, nervously meeting his eyes. Robert was talking about the fine flavor of the tart. She barely heard him, for she felt Jamie Cameron's eyes. Felt them, just as she had when they had fallen on her naked flesh, searching into her.

"Eat," Jamie said softly, "but go carefully."

"I have eaten too much," she murmured.

"Nay, it is good to see you so thoroughly enjoy that which I have taken far oft for granted. Take care, lest it be too much for your stomach."

She nodded and set down the bread upon which she had chewed. He stood up and walked to the window and watched the winter wind. "Master John should be hanged," he muttered suddenly, savagely.

Then he turned back to the two of them. "Hurry, now. Jassy, you must change. And we must be under way. I'd reach Somerfield before dark if at all possible."

"I'll see about the horses," Robert said. He squeezed Jassy's hand and strode out of the room. Jassy rose. She stared over at the clothing, and she knew that she could not go on. It wasn't right; it was making her the woman she had sworn she would not become.

"I am not going," she said.

"You are."

She shook her head. "Robert has been kind to me, but I can accept no more. I want nothing from the Somerfields, and I am certain that they will not welcome me. I wish to go on, alone."

He walked over to the bench. He plowed through the clothing there, to find a dress in dark green velvet with tiers of black lace over white lace at the bodice and sleeve. The underskirt was beige silk, daintily embroidered. There were no corsets among the things, and no petticoats. Those that she had would have to do. "Thank God you are small, and the same size. This is the one you will wear now." He came to her with the dress.

She shook her head. "You are not listening—I am not going with you."

His brow arched tauntingly. "Are you such a coward, then?"

"I am not a coward! I have no desire to be with you!"

"Ah, but I shall leave you at Somerfield."

"No!"

He thrust the dress toward her. "Do take this. I will leave you alone to dress."

"I will not—"

"I will," he said, interrupting her softly. "And I think that you know that I will, so please, change on your own. You have no secrets from me, you know. None at all."

Totally exasperated, she stamped her foot on the ground. "I am not going with you! You may have wealth and power, Lord Cameron, but I am not a slave! You cannot make me!"

"Then what will you do? You have nothing."

"You forget. I have your coin from last night. And believe me, Lord Cameron, I have earned it!"

He smiled slowly, shaking his head. "Ah, but you *don't* have the coin I gave you last night."

"Threw at me."

"Whatever. You have it no longer."

He spoke with quiet assurance. She plunged her hand into her pocket and discovered that he was right—her one gold coin was gone.

He bowed low to her. "I'm afraid, Mistress Jassy, that you have taught me your tricks."

"Give it back to me!"

"But it is mine."

"No!"

"You performed no service. Did you intend to alter that fact?"

"Oh!" She dropped the dress and tried to strike him. He caught her arm, and she fell against him, breathing heavily. He pulled her close and their eyes met. "Now—"

"Give it back!"

"Gladly. But you earn it here and now."

"Oh! You are a toad!"

"Perhaps, but, mistress, you are no princess! Now—"

"You gave it to me!"

"Threw it, or so you say. What matters that? It is mine now. I possess it. And I will not lose it again. I try very hard to keep all that is mine."

"Possessions, all!" she cried.

"Aye—possessions, all. Now change and come along." He released her at last. She staggered for balance and he offered her his hand again, but she eschewed it scathingly.

"I do pray by the hour that the earth shall open and swallow you whole! Nay, a bear should lay claim to you! A sea monster should seize you. Indians should roast and consume your flesh—"

"Jassy, I understand your meaning, thank you."

He strode to the door, fully assuming that she would do as he told her. And she would. She knew that he would carry out any threat, and she dared not take the chance that he would touch her again.

"Why are you doing this to me?" she called out.

He swung around and looked at her with a certain surprise. "I don't really know. Aye, maybe I do. Believe it or not, Miss Dupré, I'd just as soon not see you wind up a tavern whore or a common thief. That neck is too pretty to be broken by a noose." He smiled suddenly, and it was a surprisingly gentle smile for the man.

"You remind me of Virginia," he said softly, and then he left her, closing the door tightly behind him.

4

ASSY WAS SOON GLAD THAT SHE HAD DRESSED quickly, for it seemed that Jamie Cameron had barely gone before he returned. Smoothing the velvet down over her stomach, she stepped back as the man entered, Robert following close behind him.

"A vision!" Robert swore. He came to her and fell to his knees, then swept his hat from his head and cast it over his heart. "My lady, you are a vision, indeed!"

"And no lady, Robert, but you are very kind."

She flushed and glanced at Jamie Cameron. He didn't say a word. He studied her with his dark gaze.

"Will it do?" she demanded.

"Aye, it will do. Let's be on our way."

He stepped toward Lady Tewesbury's things once again and quickly selected a fur-trimmed cloak. He tossed it to Robert, who set it around her shoulders, then he called to the tavern keeper and asked that the rest of the things be wrapped for them. A curious silence reigned among them all the while they waited. When the clothing was wrapped, Jamie took the bundle. Apparently he had already paid the tavern keeper, and paid him well, for he was all smiles as they left. Outside in the cold again, Jassy was startled to see that a third horse was being held by the stableboy.

Jassy looked to Robert, who grinned with pleasure. "Well, she's a decent enough filly, I think."

"No bloodlines," Jamie murmured.

"She's beautiful, Robert. I thank you for letting me use her."

"She is yours," Robert said.

"No, I cannot accept her, but she is very fine, and I thank you for her use."

Robert looked sheepishly to Jamie, and Jamie firmly shook his head. "Let me help you mount."

He set his arms about her. Jamie watched as he lifted her high, setting her upon the mare's back.

"What is her name?" Jassy asked.

"I don't know." Robert looked to the stableboy. "Lad, what is her name?"

The lad blushed a furious red. " 'Tis Mary, sir." He hesitated. "Virgin Mary."

"Oh?" Robert lifted a brow in laughter.

"Ye see, me ma yelled at me pa when he bought her, she did. Said that this was a hauling place and that we needed such a filly just as a brothel might need the Virgin Mary."

"That's blasphemous!" Jassy gasped, trying hard not to laugh.

"Ah, so, 'tis an Anglican country now, thanks to good Bess." Robert chuckled and waved to the blushing boy. Jamie tossed him a coin, and the three of them started out.

For most of the journey she rode with Robert, and Jamie rode ahead in silence. They talked of the trail, and they talked about new modes of French fashion, and about the great discoveries in the world. She realized that he kept talking to keep her mind off her mother's death, and it seemed impossible that it was still so near.

Later in the day they stopped along a great forest in order to water the horses, and Robert left them alone, seeking the privacy of the trees. Jassy listened to the brook as it rippled, and the slurping sounds made by the horses as they sought water. She was sore; she was not accustomed to riding but to scouring floors and peeling potatoes.

She looked up and discovered that Jamie Cameron was staring at her as ever with his dark and enigmatic eyes. She looked over at the filly, then challenged him. "Bloodlines mean so very much to you, then, Lord Cameron?"

He shrugged. "In a horse, mistress? Often. Certain animals are bred for racing, some for stamina, and others for strength."

"Ah, yes, and in people, too, I would imagine! For certain, nobility breeds grace!"

He was still for a moment, then he shook his head slowly. "Nay, mistress. In beasts, as in people, one must be very careful. Bloodlines can be overbred and thus weakened. If you have brought in too fragile a dam for a stud, your colts will be tiny, and brittle in their bones. Sometimes it is best to go outside of the bloodlines and add new excitement to the line."

He spoke casually, yet there was that timbre to his voice, the way he looked at her, that made her feel as if hot tremors racked her inside. She turned away from him, wishing that she had never met him. There had surely been nothing wrong with *his* bloodlines. He was tall, he was powerful. He was as graceful as a big cat, as sure of his movement, as confident . . . as arrogant. He didn't have Robert's beautiful face, but surely some would consider it a handsome face, for it was well defined and cuttingly strong, the jaw so determined, the nose hard and long, his eyes so dark and sharp, and his mouth so fully mobile and finely shaped. She imagined he might fight off the women in a place like London, for perhaps those ladies were fascinated by his dark appeal, and perhaps even his very disdain enchanted them. They were welcome to him. She truly hated him.

"This is absurd," she told him. "You are going to drag me to my brother's house, and he will not have me there. Is this to further humiliate me?"

"He will have you."

"And why is that?"

"Because I will bring you there."

"But—"

"You will see," he told her, and that was all, for Robert had returned. She escaped into the trees herself, and then they mounted up again. It was growing dark, and thus it was growing colder.

Then a full moon began to rise, and in time the sky was blanketed in velvet, with the ivory cast of that moon rising high above them. Jamie urged them to hurry onward, and soon, though she sat shivering, Jassy had her first sight of Somerfield Hall.

It was magnificent, she thought. It was a palace, not a castle. It stretched across the land on the other side of a little river that glittered beneath the moon. It was built of stone, there were windows of paned glass, the front of it was built in a full arc for carriages to come and go, and there were endless steps to reach the entryway.

"It's beautiful!" she said quietly. It was her father's home. It could have been her heritage.

Her father was the man who had loved and left her mother, who had left them the legacy of poverty.

Jamie Cameron watched her curiously. Even now, even in the darkness and the cold, his scrutiny seemed always upon her.

"Come, let's reach it, shall we? The night is cold."

"Fine," she said. She dreaded reaching the manor. She was certain that he had forced her along to heap torture after torture upon her in some bizarre form of revenge. She was a fool. She didn't have to be here. She should have asked Robert for a loan. She could have sworn to have paid him back, and one day she would have done so. She meant to be a survivor.

She heard the baying of hounds, and then the circular entryway was filled with noise. A servant came to the top of the steps with a lantern and held it high, and the hounds wiggled their tails at his feet, baying again and again.

"Who comes here?" came his cry.

" 'Tis Jamie Cameron, Lydon. Tell the duke and duchess that I have come."

"Aye, milord, right away! Welcome, sir, welcome home!"

Jassy cast him a quick glance and wondered briefly where he had been. They walked their horses over the bridge that spanned the brook, and when they reached the courtyard, there was a multitude of grooms waiting to take their mounts. Jamie lifted her from her horse, not waiting for a by-your-leave, and certainly not asking for one. He set her down upon the ground and eyed her critically. He smoothed back a strand of her hair, then nodded. "You will do."

"How very kind of you!" she whispered in return. She tried to take a step, but her legs suddenly would not hold her. She could barely feel them. She nearly fell. "Robert!" she gasped. But Robert did not come quickly enough to her aid. Jamie reached her and caught her. "What is the matter with you?"

"My legs . . . the horse . . ."

"I thought you could ride," he said with impatience.

"Well, I can. Obviously I have ridden here! But I had not ridden in years and years. . . . Master John did not give us Saturday mornings for jaunts in the park, you know!"

"Hold on to me. After a few steps it will be better. You will hurt for a few days, for it cannot be helped."

He took her elbow and started up the steps with her while the man named Lydon queried him relentlessly about someplace called the Carlyle Hundred. Robert followed behind them and easily joined into the conversation, which made no sense to her at all. Then Jamie thought to introduce her. "Ah, Jassy Dupré, this is Lydon, the duke's valet and his most trusted employee. Lydon, Mistress Jasmine Dupré."

Old Lydon's eyes lit up like a freak fire, and he swallowed so fiercely that his Adam's apple jiggled. "Dupré?" he queried in a small squeak.

"Yes," Jamie said with amusement. "Miss Dupré. Have you informed the duke and duchess that we are here?"

"Aye, milord, I have, but I . . ."

"But what, Lydon?"

"Oh, nothing, milord. Do please come in. Welcome to Somerfield Hall, Miss —Dupré."

He pushed open double doors that opened upon a beautiful marble rotunda. There was a broad, sweeping staircase to the left side. To the right were double doors that Lydon hurried ahead to open, displaying a large tea room with molded ceilings, brocade drapes, upholstered chairs, and a shining wood table with an elegant silver service and crystal glasses upon it.

The family was awaiting them there.

At least she assumed they were the "family"—a group of richly dressed women and one man. He was in light silk breeches and a matching doublet with fine silk hose and buckled shoes. She gasped when she saw him, for she had always considered her coloring to be her mother's, but this man was very much like her, except for being taller and very broad about the shoulders. But his eyes were the same shade of blue; his hair, worn to his collar, was every bit as blond, and though his features were broader and heavier and very masculine, there was no mistaking the fact that they were related. And two of the women behind him were golden blondes, one the same height as she, and one taller and very slim.

The world seemed to churn and simmer. Blackness rushed upon her. She was certain that both Jamie and Robert stepped far out of the way, and that they left her alone there, like a lamb to the lions. They stared at her—the man, the blond women, and the pretty, dark-haired woman who stepped forward curiously, slipping her arm through the man's.

"Jamie! Robert! How wonderful to see you both! Henry, what is the matter with you? Lenore, Elizabeth?" She stepped forward, smiled broadly, and hugged Jamie Cameron with true, uninhibited affection, then kissed Robert on the cheek. "And who is this young lady?" she inquired sweetly.

"Jane, this is Jasmine Dupré."

"Dupré!"

The sound came out in an explosion of horror. Jane turned around and spoke sharply. "Lenore, where are your manners! Your papa would be shocked. Miss

Dupré, please, you must come in and join us. Shall you have some wine? Or would you prefer ale?"

She wouldn't prefer anything. She could not talk, and she could not move, and she hated Jamie Cameron with an ever greater passion.

Suddenly the man, Henry Somerfield, stepped forward with long strides. Beneath the foyer chandelier, he grabbed and lifted Jassy's chin and stared deeply into her eyes, inspecting her. She found life at last. She stepped back and slapped his hand away. "How dare you!"

He spun around on his heels and stared at Jamie. "What is the meaning of this? I demand to know."

"Careful, Henry," Jamie said softly. "I do not much care for demands. If you care to step into the study, perhaps you and I shall discuss it."

"Why bother stepping into the study?" Jane Somerfield inquired flatly. "She knows who she is, and we all know who she is. Why not discuss it openly?"

"She is a bastard!" one of the blond women hissed.

"Lenore, I will not have it!" Jane said.

"You are not my mother—"

"I am the duchess, your brother's wife, and lady of this house. You will obey me."

"Henry—"

"You will obey Jane!" he snapped. He was still watching Jamie, and Jamie was watching him. Henry smiled slowly. "Where did you discover this little gutter wench? Is this some grand joke upon me, Jamie? What is going on?"

"I stumbled upon her the other night. She is your sister, isn't she, Henry. How can I ask such a thing? I had not realized until I saw your father's ring, but now that you are together, the resemblance is uncanny. And she is no gutter wench, Henry. She is more of an abused child."

"I am no child—"

"Jassy, shut up and stay out of this. I found her in extremely unfortunate circumstances—"

"You were the unfortunate circumstance!"

"Jassy, shut up. Your father recognized her, Henry. Your father recognized her, and your mother is gone now. There is no one left to be hurt—no one but this girl."

"This . . . bastard!" the taller blond girl hissed again.

"Lenore!" Jamie snapped this time.

"Lenore, please—" Robert repeated.

"For God's sake!" Jassy exploded. "Will you please quit speaking about me as if I were not here? Lenore, your manners are the worst I have ever seen."

"I'm not about to split a copper farthing of my inheritance with you, you little fortune digger!"

"I want nothing from you!" Jassy cried.

"I will gladly share with you!" the smaller blonde claimed suddenly. She cut through everyone and came up to Jassy and reached for her hand. She blushed. "Well, actually, I'm the youngest, and I haven't much of an inheritance. Just a dowry. But I'm very happy that you're here. We knew about you, of course. Poor Mama hated the very thought of you and your mother. I think, though, that my papa loved you very much, and I'm glad that you're here."

The kindness was what Jassy could not bear. She had expected the insults; she had expected to be reviled, to be hated. She had not expected this gamine creature with her soft, radiant smile and shy touch.

Tears instantly welled behind her eyes. She blinked furiously to keep from shedding them.

"Thank you," she could barely whisper. Then she found her strength and backed away. "I did not wish to come here." She cast an acidic glance Jamie's way. "Lord Cameron insisted."

Henry stared at Jamie, and Jamie laughed. "Well, I could hardly take her home with me!"

"I think I'll have some wine," Jane said. "Let's do please quit gawking in the entryway like common folk. Oh. I am sorry. I didn't mean—oh, never mind. Lydon, wine for me, please. Girls? Henry, Robert? Jamie, a drink?"

"I'll have Scots whiskey—five fingers, please," Henry said. He was still staring at Jassy. She had walked into the room with them. She did not sit; she longed to run, but she would not do so. She would not so entertain her brother Henry or her sister Lenore, nor so please them.

"She can have the maid's room off mine," Elizabeth said.

"She'll have to. Lord, Jamie, I can't bring a bastard into this house and try to pawn her off as legal issue! I can see that she is fed and clean—"

"Oh, she is quite clean," Jamie said, interrupting. Jassy longed to slap him. Just once. Solidly across his bronze cheek.

Jane spoke up softly. "Neither can you turn her out on the streets, Henry. She is your blood."

"And she would rather not be," Jassy said coolly.

Henry stared at her, then he laughed. "She certainly has some of Papa in her, hasn't she?"

"She has, indeed," Jassy murmured. "Her teeth are very good, you see, and her hooves are quite sound."

"We are discussing her as we might a horse," Elizabeth said.

"Lydon, the drinks, please," Jane reminded their servant.

"No dowry. I cannot afford it. She may have the room off Elizabeth's, and if she cares to help with the domestic chores, then she may stay. When there is no company, she may dine with the family."

They were still discussing her as if she were not among them. She wanted to scream and she wanted to cry, and most of all she wanted to escape. Robert Maxwell was still among them, listening to it all with amusement. He gave her a kindly smile, but her heart sank at the things he had to hear. She was coming to care so greatly for him. He was still a dream that she coveted deep inside her breast.

"Where did you find her, Jamie? In a brothel?"

"Lenore, I do believe that I could be tempted to drag you out to the stables with a switch myself," Jamie said coolly. Lenore flushed, and opened and closed her mouth. But she didn't dispute him. "I found her at her mother's funeral, having labored for many years to keep the woman alive."

"Oh, dear!" Jane said softly. "Well, we can keep you from that fate at the very least! Isn't that true, Henry?"

"I have already said that she should stay."

"Well," Jassy spoke up, "I do not care to stay, thank you!" She turned, hoping to make a graceful exit. She did not manage it, for her legs gave out beneath her. She wavered and then fell. Her head struck the mantel and she cried out. She fell and fell and fell in a strange darkness, and still she did not reach the floor. She was caught in strong arms and lifted high. "Jassy!"

She could not answer. The darkness caught hold of her.

She woke up upon something very soft, and the light that gently glowed around her seemed to come from a single candle. She had never known such sweet comfort. She was clad in a clean white gown, and she lay upon clean white sheets, and the softest wool blanket she could imagine lay over her.

It took her a few minutes to discover these things, for they were hazy at first. Instinctively she touched her temple where it still throbbed, but there was a bandage there now.

The face of a woman wearing a bed cap hovered over her. It, too, was hazy, then it cleared. It was her sister, Elizabeth.

"Hello," Elizabeth said very softly. "Can you hear me?"

"Yes."

"That's a very good sign," Elizabeth said gravely.

"Is it?" She had to smile. "Where am I? How did I get here?"

Elizabeth sat back on the side of the bed and extended both her hands. "This is the small maid's room off my own." She frowned. "We've better rooms in the house, of course, but well, I suppose that they can't really give you the status of a legitimate child. Oh, I don't mean that cruelly. Do you understand?"

Jassy nodded. Her head was beginning to pound. "Really, I didn't want to come here. I will leave—"

"Oh, no! Please don't leave! I wondered about you for years and years. Papa and Mama had horrible rows about you. You are just wonderful. Please, stay. Jane is a darling, but then she and Henry are the duke and duchess. And Lenore, well, you've met Lenore. I have no one."

"But surely you've friends!" Jassy tried to sit up. It was very difficult to do, and her head began to pound all over again.

"Shush, and be careful! You've quite a gash upon your head. I'm afraid I haven't really friends, not as you think. Father preferred to go to London alone, I was never allowed to play with the servants, and Jane and Jamie were our nearest neighbors. Lenore is not as bad as she sounds, honestly, but still . . . please, say that you will stay awhile."

She couldn't say it. She wasn't certain that she could stay in this house very long, not when there was so much hostility directed against her.

"The room is lovely. It is by far the grandest that I have ever known," she assured Elizabeth. It was a beautiful room. It contained the wonderfully soft bed she lay upon and the fresh clean sheets and the warm wool blanket. There were drapes at the window and small, elegant tapestries on the walls. There was a trunk at the foot of the bed and a heavy oak dressing table. "How did I come here?"

"Jamie brought you up."

"Oh," she murmured, and she tried to hide her disappointment. She had hoped it had been Robert. She lowered her lashes swiftly.

Elizabeth giggled. "Take care if you've set your mind on Lord Robert Maxwell, for Lenore is taken with him. Ah, well, she is in love with Jamie, too, but he can be so very exasperating."

"That he can."

"Lenore is so demanding, and of course, no one shall ever demand things of Jamie. He barely stays within the realms of courtesy as it is. She gets so very angry with him. Then he leaves and she cries and frets for nights, and then it all happens again."

"Really." Jassy couldn't imagine caring in the least if Jamie Cameron determined to stay away forever. But Robert Maxwell was another matter. It seemed horrible to her that a woman like her sister Lenore might very well marry Robert—while she could not. Even now she would remain a poor relation. The sister from the wrong side of the sheets. It was foolish to be bitter. Molly had always told her so. It was a waste of time. But she was bitter, and she could not help it.

Elizabeth was staring at her with grave concern. They really did not look so much alike, after all, Jassy decided. Oh, the resemblance was there, but Elizabeth had a rounder face, a turned-up nose, and far more innocent eyes. She smiled, studying her sister. She had never expected to find someone like her.

"And what about you, Elizabeth? Who shall you marry?"

"Oh, no one!" she cried. "Unless, of course, Henry forces me. He shan't, I'm certain. Jane is a dear, and she will not let him force me into a marriage. I had thought for a while that I would join with the sisters of St. Francis, but I discovered that I did not have the vocation, after all."

"Then perhaps you will fall in love."

"No, I don't think so. I'm too shy. Oh, I have known Jamie all my life, and Robert is so sweet and funny. But I am no good with strangers. I love this house, but I hate it, too, for it has also been my prison. It can become a prison, you shall see! But now, tell me about your life. I am so anxious to hear."

Jassy felt a new rush of tears come to her eyes as she finished telling her story and turned her head into her pillow. *Mother,* she cried silently as she buried her face within the bedding, *I loved you. I would do anything to have you back. I still cannot believe that you are gone, that I will wake and you will not be with me.*

Elizabeth was there beside her, and it was all right that she saw Jassy's tears. They hugged each other and rocked back and forth, and Jassy tried to explain. "You buried her this morning!" Elizabeth said, shocked. "You poor, poor dear.

Oh, Jassy, you must stay! They'll give you a hard time, but you must stay. The world will treat you cruelly if you do not! It will break you, as it broke your mother! The pain fades, Jassy, and in time you remember what was good and what was sweet. I promise."

———

The next morning Jassy was summoned by the Duke of Somerfield. When she entered his office, he was sitting behind his desk. He rose but did not invite Jassy to sit. He walked around her, observing her carefully. Then he backed away. She stared at him, not speaking, for she had not been spoken to. He was many years older than she, she determined, but was still a young man. He was elegantly dressed in wide breeches and a heavily embroidered doublet with wide, fashionable sleeves.

"You've no humility," he said at last. "None at all. You need some, you know."

She lowered her eyes and her head, remembering that she had decided she did want to stay at Somerfield Hall. For a time, at least—until she could fathom a way to reach her own destiny, to acquire her own wealth. A dream perhaps, but a dream that sustained her.

"You are not a legitimate member of this household!" he said sharply.

"No," she agreed softly.

"And I will not treat you like legitimate issue."

She said nothing but waited.

His voice softened. "And yet you are my sister, and very beautiful. More beautiful than Lenore, and probably more clever than us all. Your position here is a difficult one. I do not care to have a member of my bloodline living in abject poverty, so I would keep you here. We must give you a task. I imagine that you have been well educated?"

She nodded. "I had tutors until I was twelve."

"The duchess is with child. When the babe is born, you shall be the Lady Jane's nursemaid, and you must keep a stern eye on the wet nurse, for I've found only a country lass who is slow for the task. When my son is able to talk and comprehend, you will begin his lessons until he comes of such an age that I hire proper tutors. Can I trust you with such a position?"

She raised her eyes again. She had expected worse from him, much, much worse. "Thank you. I love children, and I promise that I will tend yours well."

"Then that is all. Oh, except for this: If you ever mention your birth to anyone again, I shall ask you to leave." His eyes traveled over her slowly. "Everyone will know who you are. But you are my hired governess, and that is to be that, do you understand?"

"Clearly."

"For the time you may help Jane with her correspondence."

"Thank you."

"You may go. She will call you when she wants you."

Jassy fled from the room and returned to her own, where both Elizabeth and Kathryn, the kindly ladies' maid, eagerly awaited the outcome of her interview.

She told them quickly, and they both laughed happily, and the three of them decided that it was the very best that could have been expected.

Soon after that the duchess sent for Jassy. In a beautiful solar she kept an elegant secretary, and her stationery and seal. She smiled at Jassy when she arrived, and though she wasn't as effusive as Elizabeth, Jassy felt that she had another friend.

"I think that this will work out very well, don't you?" Jane asked after she had had Jassy write out a letter of condolence to a friend on the death of her husband. "What lovely penmanship! I think that we shall get along very well. Oh, and Jassy . . ." She paused, picking up Jassy's small hand. "I've some cream we must try. It will take away the redness, and in time, perhaps, heal the skin altogether. I'll have Kathryn bring it to you tonight."

"Thank you. You are very kind."

The duchess smiled and sat at the chair behind the secretary. She sighed. "I am glad you will be tending the babe. He will be your nephew, you know, even if we aren't allowed to say."

"Yes. I promise you I will tend him or her with all my heart and soul."

"Yes, I believe that you will." She smiled but appeared tired. "Heavens! In the commotion last night I forgot to tell my brother that I am enceinte."

"Your brother?" Jassy murmured warily.

"Why, yes. Jamie is my brother. That globe-trotting pirate. Why he will not sit still in this good country . . . Castle Carlyle is big enough for a dozen families, ten times larger than Somerfield Hall. And Jamie has built his own home on land my mother left him. But then my papa, too, is obsessed with the Virginia colonies, so I suppose it is understandable that Jamie thinks it fine to sail that ocean again and again." She shivered. "You'd not get me onto one of those miserable ships for a three-month voyage. But Jamie will do as he chooses; he has always done so and he always will, and heaven help the man or woman who tries to stand in his way. I think that that is all for now. If I need you this afternoon, I will send for you."

Jassy nodded, still somewhat stunned by the news that the duchess was Jamie Cameron's sister, although why, she wasn't sure. The Camerons and the Somerfields had all grown up together. Their lands adjoined.

"Oh, Jassy!"

"Yes, Your Grace."

Jane flushed. "You need not call me that, unless my husband is present. You may call me Jane, please. When you are at leisure, I will appreciate your spending time with Elizabeth. She is terribly shy, you know, and has no real friends."

"It is a pleasure to be with Elizabeth."

"Good." Jane grinned and waved a hand in the air. "Is there anything that you need?"

"Nothing."

Jane told her what her wages would be, and Jassy gritted her teeth not to cry out. In one month she would earn what she had slaved a year for at Master John's.

When she left Jane, she was dreaming already. She would diligently save her wages. She would buy land, or she would buy a tavern. She would become her own mistress. It would take time. So much time. But she would never be poverty-stricken again.

"Ah, my sister, the well-dressed bastard!"

Jassy was rudely jolted out of her daydream. Lenore stood before her in the hallway. Jassy said nothing but waited.

Lenore grinned suddenly. "Thank God that he has made you a servant! You would be stiff competition if you had any type of dowry whatsoever."

Jassy arched a brow, wondering just what Lenore meant.

"Oh, I'm really not so terrible. I mean, I don't wish to drown you like an unwanted litter of kittens or anything. I just want you out of my way. All right?"

"I hardly see how I could be in your way."

"Then you are blind to your own image," Lenore said flatly. "You will eat in your room tonight; Kathryn will bring you a tray. I am having company, and alas, we want you seen as little as possible."

"Fine," Jassy said, and she stepped by Lenore.

Curiously, that first day set the tone for many of the days to follow. In the morning Kathryn woke her. Elizabeth improved her wardrobe with cast-off pieces from Jane and Lenore. And strangely, Lenore did not seem to mind. "As long as you have the secondhand pieces, I do not care at all," she said airily.

Until noon she worked on correspondence with Jane, and in the afternoons she was at leisure to read or walk with Elizabeth, and even to ride. On her third day there she discovered that the horse, Mary, was in the Somerfield stables. "She is yours, of course," Jane told her, "and you must take her out whenever you choose."

"But I told Robert that I could not keep her!" Jassy protested, distressed.

Jane watched her curiously. "Jamie left her for you. And she is your horse. Speak with Jamie if you do not want her."

"I will," Jassy said. But she could not leave the docile creature with no attention, and so she began to ride her, and each time she rode her, she remembered the conversation she'd had with Jamie about bloodlines.

Lenore was always catty, and Henry was always cold, blunt, and upon occasion, cruel, but Jane was charming and Elizabeth was sweet. As winter melted into spring she was pleased with the turn her life had taken. Things were so different here. There was so much of beauty about the Hall. There were sculptures from France and Italy, and the table was set with silver, gold, crystal, and painted Dutch plates. The Hall itself was a thing of beauty, and she discovered despite herself that she was bitter still, for she coveted the fine house and all the beautiful things within it. Her sweetest pastime was dreaming, and in that she frequently indulged.

She was so engaged late one afternoon when Elizabeth came running into her room. "Jassy! We are to have company tonight, and you are to come down to dinner as well!"

"I am? Why?" Her dreams were ever with her now. Some young squire had seen her riding about the place. He was a friend of Henry's, and he had insisted that the hidden sister be presented before him when he came for a meal. He would be fabulously wealthy, and she would fall in love with him. He would smile like Robert, sweep her away, and she would be mistress of her own castle or magnificent mansion.

"We're to discuss the May Day dance." She giggled. "Think! It's but a month away. Anyway, Jamie will be here—"

"Oh," Jassy murmured disappointedly.

"And Robert. They always come to help plan the theme. Well, it's the Duke of Carlyle who plans the event with the Duke of Somerfield, but his father has no interest in such things, and his elder brothers are in London this year, so Jamie must represent the duke. And Robert is still his guest, so they will both come. It will be fun, and very casual."

"Yes, it sounds like wonderful fun." She would see Robert again. That, in itself, was exciting.

"The May Day dance is even more fun. Lenore is in a complete tizzy."

"Oh, why?"

"Oh, well, you don't know, I guess. It's May Day. They set up a huge pole. It's really supposedly a pagan rite. The pole is actually a"—Elizabeth paused, and though they were alone, she moved very close to whisper in Jassy's ear—"a phallic symbol! But oh, the day is wonderful. And at the end of it there is a dance, a very swift and wild dance, and when the dance is over, a woman is supposed to find her mate for life, her beloved. Oh, Jassy, perhaps you will find a husband! Not that it is legal, of course, but usually lovers are able to find each other. Weddings do follow! That is why Lenore is in such a state. She doesn't know whether she will try to catch Jamie or Robert. Jassy, you look so pale. Are you listening?"

"Yes, yes, I'm listening."

"Isn't it exciting?"

"Oh, yes. Very exciting."

"Then hurry! We must dress for dinner! Kathryn will come and do our hair, and it will be very special."

Elizabeth was still talking, but a tingling sensation rippled along Jassy's spine, and she could not really hear her any longer. Lenore could not decide whether she wanted Robert or Jamie Cameron. A maid was to set out to capture her husband. . . .

Henry would probably refuse to allow her to be a part of it.

She would go, anyway, she determined. Somehow she would manage to capture Robert Maxwell. And then she would have everything; she would have him—charming, kind, tender Robert. She would be a wife and no longer a mistress, no longer a servant. She would have a house and a home of her own, and she would have realized her greatest dream.

All that she had to do was plan, very, very carefully.

5

ROM THE START IT PROMISED TO BE A GRAND evening.

As Jamie and Robert were to be the only company, Elizabeth was pleased and in a fine mood. Jane was anxious to see her brother, and even Henry seemed to be in a rare good disposition. Lenore was highly intrigued with another chance to study both men, and to determine who she would prefer to have as a husband.

For Jassy it was her first real chance to dress up, and she felt like a princess preparing for a ball. She wore one of Elizabeth's gowns that evening, a wonderful creation of crimson velvet and soft mauve silk. The half-sleeves were ribboned and the stomacher was embroidered with gilt. Kathryn thread silver and gold ribbons through her hair, and when she was done, Jassy was ecstatic. She preened and swirled before Elizabeth and Kathryn, and laughed with nervous gaiety. For the first time she felt as if she could really play a lady. For the first time she was aware that she could appear beautiful.

"Will I do?" she asked.

Elizabeth laughed. "Lenore shall be green with envy."

Jassy didn't really want to make Lenore green with envy, but she did want to sweep Robert Maxwell off his feet. He did care something for her, she was certain that he did, and if only she could make him see that she could stand among the most refined and cultured young ladies. She knew now from Elizabeth that he was the second son of the Earl of Pelhamshire, but like Jamie, he was not his father's heir. Perhaps it was a dream, but she had halfway convinced herself that he would be willing to cast convention to the wind, if he could be made to love her deeply enough. She had to make him fall in love with her. Surely he could not love Lenore with her rapier-sharp tongue!

"Shall we go down?" Elizabeth suggested.

"Oh, yes!"

Kathryn straightened her skirts one last time, and then Elizabeth and Jassy started for the sweeping stairway. Jassy had never felt so marvelously alive and excited, her senses attuned to everything around her. She felt the rich material of her gown against her skin, and the very air as it touched her. Her blood seemed to dance within her, and her breath came short and quick.

"Oh, they've come!" Elizabeth whispered excitedly behind her. "Jamie and Robert are here, and Lenore has already gone down, and Jane and Henry are there too. You must let me go first, and then you follow and make a wonderfully grand entrance!"

Elizabeth gave Jassy no chance to protest; she raced down the stairway, greeting their guests effusively. Jassy hesitated and felt the fierce beat of her heart as she started down the stairway.

She could hear the sound of voices coming from the landing, and then they all ceased. She watched as all eyes rose to her. Her brother Henry's were startled then guarded and thoughtful. Elizabeth's were sparkling. Jane's were intrigued. Lenore's were hard and wary. Robert Maxwell's were filled with pleasure and wicked admiration. Those were the eyes that mattered. The eyes that she sought to please, and she met them gladly. But even as she smiled in return, she felt a curious draw, and she met the piercing gaze of Jamie Cameron.

He betrayed no pleasure and no surprise. Indeed, it was as if he expected her to appear no less finely attired and groomed. His dark gaze was as fathomless as ever, and he stood as still as a rock himself, striking in a white laced shirt and dark navy jerkin and trousers, white hose and buckled shoes. She thought then, though, that it would not have mattered what he wore. He had been born the aristocrat, and it was apparent in the very way he stood, in his unyielding and ever-present confidence in himself. It was in the way that he held his head, in the way he observed all things with insolence. It was in the mocking curve of his lip, and in the nonchalant way he crossed his arms over his broad chest. In rags he would appear the proud lord, the master of his world, and so his elegant attire mattered little.

She could not draw her eyes from his, and she felt her flesh grow warm. The way he looked at her was unnerving. He stripped her naked with his eyes, and easily he could, for he knew what lay beneath her clothing. She was certain that he was condemning her, laughing at her attempts to join society.

Robert Maxwell was not laughing. He did not scorn her. All the bright and wonderful admiration he felt was apparent in his eyes. He stepped forward as she reached the landing, caught her hand, and laughed. "Why, this blossom we plucked and planted here is no weed but a radiant flower for certain! Jassy, you are beautiful beyond belief. Henry, you have proven yourself a great benefactor."

"Yes, she has come along quite well," Henry said impatiently. "We are all here now. Shall we hurry along to the dining room? I admit to being famished."

There were murmurs of assent all about. Lenore, as beautiful as a snow queen in white brocade and fox fur, stepped forward swiftly, slipping her arm through Robert Maxwell's. "Robert, we are paired for the meal. Will you escort me?"

He gave Jassy a quick look of pained regret with a promise of a future meeting, then he turned with all his charm to Lenore. "It is always my greatest pleasure to be at your side."

They began to file from the entryway to the dining room, through great double doors. Thrilled with Robert's response to her, Jassy felt as if she walked on clouds.

Then she was dragged back to earth by a vise upon her elbow.

Jamie Cameron held her.

"What do you want?" she demanded sharply.

"Merely to view this creation of mine," he replied. She did not want to make a scene, and so she stood impatiently still, feeling the heat rise in her again as his sharp eyes raked over her from head to toe.

"I am not your creation."

"Ah, but you are."

"Stop it. Stop looking at me as if you know what lies beneath my clothes."

"Ah," he murmured softly, "but I do know what lies there. I have a wonderfully clear memory of it all."

"You are hateful, and far from gallant."

"And you may wear ribbons and gold thread and all the adornment that you please, and you shall still be the gold-digging little thief I carried away from the tavern."

"Carried away! Your creation! You are an insolent son of a bitch!"

"And there comes the tongue of the tavern wench."

She jerked hard upon her elbow; he did not let go. He touched her hair instead, smoothing back a strand. Seething, she gritted her teeth and prayed that he would release her soon. She smiled. "Well, then, my Lord Cameron, what is your opinion of the adornment? Shall I suffice to grace this hallowed hall?"

His dark eyes met hers. "The adornment is wonderful. You are quite beautiful, and you know it well. But I do suggest that you take care. You are giving yourself airs, and no one here has forgotten the fact that you are the child born on the wrong side of the sheets. Don't fool yourself. It matters."

"I shall do my best to remember your warnings!"

This time when she jerked upon her elbow, he released her. With a toss of her head and a flounce of her skirts, she hurried on into the dining room.

Her place was in the middle of the table. The duchess sat at one end of the long table, and the duke sat at the other. To Jassy's annoyance, Robert was across the table from her, while Jamie was seated to her right. He smiled apologetically as he drew out his chair. She ignored him. She concentrated instead on the beauty of the table, and of the night. Not a month ago she was a wretched servant carrying tankards of ale to lascivious louts. Now she sat here, sipping fine wine from crystal, dining with a silver fork, on a table covered in white linen and lace. She would not let Jamie Cameron ruin it all.

The meal began with a toast to the duchess, in honor of the child she would soon bear the duke. Jassy was as enthusiastic as the others as she raised her glass to Jane, for she had become very fond of the no-nonsense woman.

Then she watched as Jamie rose and kissed her, and a little knot began to form in her stomach, for then the duke rose, too, and she saw the deep affection that passed between them all. The duke's fingers fell over Jane's shoulders with tenderness, and much love was apparent in his gaze. How very sweet it seemed. In those moments Jassy envied Lady Jane with a deep and startling anguish. That was what she wanted. The knowledge that she was needed, that she was loved and cherished.

She bit her lip and stared at her plate, and then she raised her chin again. She would have Robert. She would win him and she would love him, and he would cherish her with tenderness, as she had just witnessed. And he would make her mistress of her own home.

Conversation went on to the May Day ball, with Lenore enthusiastically leading it, and Robert joining in. Lenore charmed Robert and then swept Jamie with the radiance of her warmth and smile too. She pretended to draw Jassy into her circle, for not to do so would have appeared rude. Yet Jassy occasionally felt her sister's gaze, and thought there did not seem to be hatred behind it. There was an assurance, as if she had a card to play which Jassy knew nothing about. Perhaps she did. Jassy couldn't really care.

Then Jamie no longer discussed details with them, for Henry had drawn him into a discussion on the Jamestown colony in the New World. Jassy had little interest in such a faraway and savage land. She ignored his bronze hand when it brushed hers, and she ignored the heat of his body, so close to her own. She listened while Lenore described the Maypole, and how someone was always Queen of the May, and how there was a table set for the servants, and one for the gentry and nobility. She paused and smiled, and Jassy was sure that Lenore was thinking that Jassy would definitely sit with the servants on that day. "But the meal, of course, comes after the dance of the May." She giggled and cast Robert a flirtatious glance. "It's all in costume, of course, but single maidens may seek out their true love, and if they can hold him until the music ends, then he must marry her."

"Is it legal?"

"Oh, of course not! But it is terribly romantic. Even among the poorer folk, marriage is a matter of grave concern. And when it comes to men and women of family, well, of course, there are grave details to be worked out. Dowries and contracts and the like. But I tell you, many a free maid has made her choice, and it has been honored through such play! Why, any man is honor-bound to offer the maid marriage, you see."

Honor-bound. Robert Maxwell was a most honorable young man. Jassy still could not tell if Lenore would seek out Robert or Jamie when the time came. She hoped that Lenore would seek Jamie. The two of them deserved each other, in Jassy's opinion.

"No, Henry, I think that you are wrong," Jamie said emphatically at her side, interrupting her dreams of things to come. "The first charter given to the Company in 1606 left a nebulous question of authority—the king and his council held much power, and they were across an ocean, too far away. There have been many new charters since."

"Governors have come and gone, and the Company fares no better," Henry said. His liveried servants moved about the room in practiced silence as he spoke, offering up the various platters of food prepared for the meal. A plate of fish beautifully molded to resemble a swimming flounder came Jassy's way, then a plate of parsley-sprigged lamb, and a kidney pie, and then a serving platter with a cooked pheasant, feathers surrounding the body upon the tray. It was all delicious, and Jassy gave but scant attention to the conversation as she concentrated upon the food. Sometimes it was difficult to remember that she was not starving anymore, and that she had far more than thin soup and watery gruel to fill her stomach these days.

"I beg to differ," Jamie told Henry, drawing Jassy's attention once again. "Matters have improved. The Indians and the white men are at peace. Men are learning to grow food, as well as tobacco. And there are many women in the colony now, and on the various hundreds surrounding it. And my land is an individual grant from the king. I am the authority upon it."

"I doubt not that you will grow rich on tobacco, Jamie," Henry agreed, "for what you touch turns to gold. But must you spend so much time in such a heathen land?"

"Especially when you have just built such a stunning new manor here!" Lenore said.

Jassy quickly looked over at her sister. Lenore's eyes were warm and sparkling, and they stayed upon Jamie as she smiled deeply. "It is one of the most beautiful places I have ever seen, Jamie. That you keep wandering away is a crime. It is a palace."

"It is not a palace, Lenore."

"It is grander than many a royal residence," Henry said wryly. "And still you travel on to the heathen wilderness. What is the draw?"

Jamie shrugged. "The very wilderness, I suppose. There is a pagan beauty there, raw and untamed. I am fascinated by the spirit of it. I would fight the elements, I suppose, and by God, I would win."

"And what if you lose?" Jassy asked, challenging him.

His dark indigo gaze fell to her. "I do not lose, Miss Dupré. Ever. What I set out to do is done, and what I wish to acquire is mine."

"Not every time, surely."

"Surely, yes, but it is so."

"There will come a time when it is not so."

He was no longer looking at her, but he stared across the table at Lenore, who returned his gaze. "I do not think I need to worry," he said simply. Lenore flushed, her lips parted slightly, and she seemed entranced. It seemed that Jamie had decided on her, and that in the end, no matter how she teased and pouted and tormented, Lenore would have him. It would be just as he had said—he would have what he wanted.

Robert laughed. "That is Jamie. He must win, and he will have that which he chooses."

"I should much rather talk about the dance than a heathen land," Lenore said, and shivered. "The talk of those Indians—"

"Oh, but the stories about John Smith and Pocahontas were so wonderful! She befriended our people then, and married Mr. John Rolfe, and so the colony survived. That is wondrous."

"Wondrous! Why, the pagans slice hair and flesh from men's heads!" Jane said. "The wars have been dreadful. Jamie can tell you. He fought the Indians there."

"They paint their bodies in hideous designs!" Lenore said.

"They paint their bodies in beautiful designs," Jamie said, "and the wars have been over for a long time now. When British colonists were starving in 1609, it was the Indians who fed them."

"Why, Jamie, I think that you actually admire those red devils," Lenore admonished.

"I do. Many of them. They have a sense of honor, and though many of their values differ greatly from our own, many are the same. They love their children as we love our own. They revere a man who is honest and trustworthy, and they will fight to defend what is theirs. Powhatan was a very great chief, and Pocahontas was a lady I considered myself privileged to know."

"I do suppose she was fascinating," Lenore said politely. "But not nearly so fascinating as your lovely new manor."

Elizabeth trembled suddenly at Jassy's side. "I should hate it! I should just hate the new land. It is damp, with mosquitoes and pests. And the Indians are hideous beasts, no matter what you say, Jamie. I have read about the Lost Colony, and Sir Walter Raleigh, and the poor, poor infant, Virginia Dare. The Indians carried them off and killed them, and perhaps even ate them! It is a dreadful new world."

"Elizabeth," Jamie said gently, "it is not a dreadful world, I promise. There are acres and acres for cattle to graze, acres where deer roam in plenty and where there is an endless supply of pheasant. Sometime, little one, you must come with me. You will see. But enough for now, if we distress you. Who will you come as to the ball? A Greek maiden? Helen of Troy? A fairy-tale princess, perhaps?"

Elizabeth's eyes widened. "Why, I shall not dress at all. I do not wish to capture a husband!"

They all laughed. Then Robert stared across the table at Jassy.

"And who, Miss Dupré, shall you come as?"

Caught unaware, Jassy hesitated. Henry spoke up sharply for her. "Jassy will not attend this year. She is too new to this house and needs time to adjust before indulging in such games."

Jassy felt as if an ocean of icy water had been cast over her dreams. She had to go to the ball!

Perhaps her disappointment was betrayed in her face, for Jane spoke quickly, saying that as the meal was completed, they should move into the solar, for she had hired a puppeteer to entertain them for the night.

As Jassy blindly rose, trying to swallow down her rage and disappointment, a warm breath touched her nape, and she heard Jamie Cameron's whisper. "Don't be too distressed. Occasions such as the ball are purely for show and mean little. Alas, you shall have to capture a rich husband elsewhere."

She managed to discreetly cast her elbow into him but knew little satisfaction, for he barely seemed to note the intended torment. He caught her elbow to lead her from the room. "Please don't fret. I shan't attend the ball, either. I find such charades far more savage than the practices of the North American Indians."

"A pity!" Jassy snapped in return. "You've come to plan an event in which you'll not participate?"

"It is the responsibility of the Dukes of Somerfield and Carlyle. I merely represent my father."

"I'm sure that Lenore shall be heartily disappointed. What, then, have you no interest in marriage? Why, Lenore is there, milord, quite for the taking."

"Ah, but there is Robert to consider."

"Do you really consider any man or woman in your quest for what you desire, my Lord Cameron?"

"But I don't know quite what I desire," he said. "Marriage is a most serious step. A wife must not only be winsome to the eye but a capable lass."

"Capable? Why, Lord Cameron, you need but a showpiece, or so it seems. Someone to grace your illustrious mansion, to give you illustrious children, and serve wine and comfits—illustriously, of course. Why, Lenore should charmingly fit such a bill of needs."

"You underestimate what I seek in a mate, Miss Dupré," he told her, and bowed, releasing her arm.

He moved to Lenore's side then, whispering something in her ear. Lenore laughed delightedly, turned to him, and set her elegant hand upon the frilled lace that spilled over his doublet at his chest. He seemed very tall and dark then, as striking as a prince, and Lenore, with her blond beauty, looked well with him. She sighed softly and trembled, and Jassy thought that her sister wasn't at all immune to the oft-aloof charm of Lord Cameron.

Robert was engaged in conversation with Elizabeth, and Elizabeth was laughing happily. The duke was bowed over his duchess as the puppet master prepared his show. Jassy suddenly felt very much alone—very much the bastard child, the poor, unwanted relation from the wrong side of the sheets. Her temple thundered with a sudden pain, and she hated Henry with all the venom she could muster. He could not stop her! She would go to the ball, and she would marry well. She would not know poverty again, but she would leave this hall where she was so unwelcome and become mistress of her own destiny.

None of them noticed her, and no matter how brave her imaginings, she was, at the moment, unnoticed, unneeded. She turned around and fled, leaving the solar, running on Elizabeth's soft satin slippers out through the dining room and the back of the house toward the stables beyond. Her way was well lit, for there was a full moon, and stars dotted the sky, and the house was well supplied with lanterns for the evening, as were the stables. There she raced along the length of stall until she found Mary, the poor little mare with the faulty bloodline, and slid beside her. She patted the animal's velvet nose and crooned to her softly.

"I care not that your pedigree is weak, my dear, for your heart is very valiant, and you are faithful and good and true. Wherever I go, I promise that I will see to you! They will not cast you out for not being a good worker, or a beautiful horse for the hunt, or a great breeding mare. I swear, I shall bring you with me wherever I shall go." She hesitated. "And I shall pay that bastard for you first, so that you will truly be mine."

She started then and fell silent, for she heard some sound at the door to the stables. She thought that it was late for the young grooms to be about, for they all lived in the cottages that surrounded the estate, and none of them lived in the stable. Not even old Arthur, in charge of the horses and grooms, slept here, for his pallet lay in the little room next to the tack house.

"Jassy?"

It was Robert's voice. She smiled with a rush of pleasure and came around the mare's rump. He had left the puppet show to come to her. "Robert, I am here."

"Jassy!" Wearing a charming, crooked smile, he came her way. "I was worried when I realized that you were gone."

"I felt like an intruder."

"An intruder?" he murmured. He was before her by then. He took both her hands in his own and laced her fingers with his. The light seemed to waver, the room to spin. "You could never be an intruder, Jassy."

"I do not think that my brother would agree with you," she said. She might have added that her sister Lenore would not agree with him, either, but just then, as they stood there alone in the lamplight, she didn't want to breathe Lenore's name.

"Your brother has seen this night that you have an uncanny beauty, and that your grace came inborn, and that there is a fire inside of you that fascinates and beckons."

"Has he seen this?" she whispered. Perhaps there was fire in her eyes, and she did feel beautiful, for he allowed her to feel so. Excitement crackled around her, and her dreams seemed to find full measure once again.

He pulled her closer and closer, holding their laced fingers down by his side. She stared into his light, dancing eyes, and her heart fluttered at the things she saw within them.

Then he kissed her.

His mouth was soft and persuasive. It formed over hers, and she parted her lips instinctively to his. He released her fingers, wrapped his arms around the small of her back, and pressed her hard against him. His lips moved then, wetly and sloppily over hers, and she didn't really care. She threaded her fingers into his hair and felt their hearts pounding together. He groaned against her, their lips broke, and he whispered with agony, "How I have wanted you."

"I am here!" she whispered with little thought, for her imaginings had not gone far beyond this point. But her words were a fuel to him, and his lips pressed against her throat and lowered to the rise of her breasts. Then he arched her tightly against him, feverishly kissing her. Her mind whirled, and she felt his hands upon her, here and there, and then his lips again, and his fingers, plucking at the ties to her stomacher.

No, he must not. Yet she could not find the words or the will to stop him. He loved her, she was certain. Yet she knew, too, that she could let him go no farther. Not unless he married her.

"Robert . . ." she whispered.

Her breasts were spilling from the gown, and she could neither stop nor dislodge him. He caught her lips in a kiss again. It was a sweet kiss, soft, tender. She closed her eyes and held tight to him. Then they were both interrupted by the loud sound of someone clearing his throat.

Robert abruptly straightened. He still held Jassy about the waist. He stared toward the first stall. Jassy, her eyes glazed with fascination, was slower to realize the interruption. Then she, too, stared down the length of the stables to the first stall.

Jamie was there, casually leaning against the hayrack, arms crossed over his chest, one booted foot atop a bale of hay. "Excuse me, but the Lady Lenore has been seeking you, Robert, to question you about your costume."

"Damn!" Robert muttered. "Love, forgive me." He set Jassy straight, leaving her to deal with the disarray of her gown. He thanked Jamie and strode on out of the stables.

Jamie remained. He didn't move. He watched her with dark and condemning eyes.

Trying to ignore him, Jassy lowered her eyes. She tried to adjust the gown's stomacher and retie the ribbons, but her fingers were trembling horribly.

He strode toward her, and when she looked up, there was such a dark fire to his gaze that she had to bite her lip to keep from crying out. He brushed her hands aside.

"Stop it!" she protested.

"Would you be found here as you are?" he demanded roughly. With practiced fingers he retied the ribbons. He brushed her bare flesh with his touch again and again, and she wanted to scream. He was in no way gentle. He was nearly brutal. Standing before her, he seemed ablaze with tension, so vibrant and hot that heat emanated from him and washed upon her in great waves.

"How much were you paid for that endearing scene, Mistress Dupré? Had I realized that you were still in the market for a lover, I'd have put in a higher bid."

She shrieked in fury and tore away from him, then came for him again, lashing out for his face, his chest, whatever she could strike. She caught him, as she had longed to do, with one good cut across the jaw, but he was swift with his reprisal, capturing her wrists, twisting them harshly behind her back. She was tightly pressed to him, still alive with fury, and she tried to kick him. He easily slipped his foot behind hers, and she fell to ground, dragging him down upon her. She heard the grate of his teeth, and when she stared into his eyes, they seemed black, and the tension that gripped his features in a steel-hard rage was merciless. And still she twisted and fought against him, heedless that her hair was falling, that her beautiful gown was being torn and dirtied. "You insufferable oaf, I have had it with you—I hate you and I loathe you and I despise you—and I will never let you touch me, not for any price! I cannot bear your touch—"

"No? You are a liar, Jassy, for you are no hothouse flower but the wildest of roses, made for a tempest. You fool! You would hate Robert in a matter of months were you to have him, for indeed, you would twist him to your will. But you cannot have him. You won't see that, will you? But I will prove to you that you were not meant for him."

"No!"

He ignored her completely. He pressed his lips to hers, and they were neither soft, nor gentle, nor persuasive in the least. They were a brand, demanding, hot and searing. They forced her mouth apart beneath him, and his tongue savagely ravaged the fullness of her mouth, hot and hard. She could barely draw breath, she could not move, and she could not fight him. She could feel him only. The wild, rugged tempest that raged inside of him seemed to sweep inside of her. She did not want him, she hated his touch, she despised him . . . and still, it was as if he had drugged her. It was as if he filled her with fire and rage, and with a slow, beating tempo and hot, liquid fury. He kissed her and kissed her, and the tempo beat throughout her, and she could fight him no longer. The tempo had entered her head. She dared not move, for she could feel his body through the layers of clothing between them. She could feel the savage power in him. She shuddered, for it swept from him to her, cascaded down the length of her. His hand was upon her, upon the ribbons at her bodice, and they were untied once more. She was freed from the stomacher of her gown, and his palm swept over her nipple while he curved his hand and cupped her breast where it mounded over the lace and bone of her corset. His thumb teased the nipple through the gauze. A thread of silver sensation shot through her from that touch. She squirmed and wiggled, and merely felt his body more fully, and still she could not escape the pressure of his kiss. His heat became a part of her. She could no longer fight. She was dazed by his power, and by his touch. She lay still. The savagery of his assault slackened instantly. His hand barely touched her breast. His lips barely fell against hers, and the tip of his tongue rimmed her mouth and her inner lip, and curiously, she lay there still, allowing it all to happen.

Then, abruptly, he lifted his head. Her lips were surely bruised and damp, and they lay parted, for she was desperate to breathe. Her hair was in disarray, loosed from its ribbons. Her breast was bare, except for the sheer lace of the corset that did not cover it at all.

He smiled down at her sardonically. "A position as my mistress remains open, Jasmine, and I do assure you, my financial assets far exceed Robert's expectations."

She stared at him, longing for the words to tell him how she hated him, longing to be freed from his touch. She shrieked out something and tried to strike him again. He caught her hands and twisted them behind her back. Laughing, he lowered his head, and his tongue touched her nipple through the lace, and then he lowered his head still farther, bringing the whole of it into his mouth. She swore again, yet she shuddered as the ribbon of sensation leapt from her breast to the innermost part of her. Slowly he released her, gently easing the high peak of her breast and the lace of her corset from the graze of his teeth.

She raged against him, jerking and twisting and pelting him with her fists, but her only reward was the sound of his harsh laughter. Then he climbed from her at last and caught her hands and pulled her to her feet. She jerked from his touch, tears spilling from her eyes. She blinked them away. Her fingers still trembled when she tried to right her clothing, but when he roughly said, "Here, let me help!" she swore with ever greater menace and turned away from him.

"Leave me!" she demanded, turning her back upon him. "After all that you have done, can you not at least go!"

"Nay, I shall not go. I shall walk you back into the house when we are certain that you look none the worse for wear."

"I will never walk anywhere with you! You are untrustworthy! I cannot bear you to—"

He swung her around, staring at her with a curious passion, and the tension was ever about him. "No, don't say it again, for we both know that it is a lie. You are no Lady Lenore, and indeed, you are no lady I have ever known, for you are real, alive, and breathing, and with a heart that pounds fiercely and eyes that are full of a feminine promise." He clutched her hands and drew them between them. "Look! Look here at the unladylike calluses upon these hands! Mistress, they are admirable hands to my eyes, for they have known work and toil. Jassy, your quest is for life, you little fool! It is for life and for passion, and you cannot be made to see it, though you feel it! How long will you lie to yourself? You can bear my touch, you can bear it very well. It is what you need, it is what you require, it is what you crave! I know you. I know your strengths, and I know your weaknesses, and I know the workings of your cunning little mind and your greedy little heart! You are playing a dangerous game, you are playing it all wrong, and you are ignoring the rules—"

"Just get away from me!" she insisted, wrenching her hands from his grasp. Ah, but they were a sore spot with her! They were a reminder that she had been a cook's apprentice and a scullery maid. They were rough and reddened, and though Jane's lotion had helped, they betrayed her at every turn, no matter how she dressed in silks and fur. She cast them behind her back, lifted her chin, squared her shoulders, and cared not how disheveled her gown was as she faced and challenged him. "You play your games, Lord Cameron, and I shall play mine. And if I don't know the rules, all the better, for then I may just ignore them. Like you, I play to win, and so help me, milord, I *will* win! I will never be your mistress, and you are wrong! I crave nothing from you!"

He reached out to her. She screamed in fury, stamping a foot, and he laughed. "There is hay in your hair now, mistress. May I remove it for you?"

"No!"

"Come here, for you shall never redress yourself—"

"I don't trust you!"

"Then don't trust me. But if you ever wish to return to the house, you need my help."

"I don't need—"

"Oh, shut up!"

He dragged her close and she kicked him, but he grunted and pulled the hay from her hair. In a no-nonsense manner he spun her around, set the stomacher straight, and began lacing it into her bodice. In seconds it was properly tied, and he was no more intimate with her than a ladies' maid might have been. Once again he swirled her around, straightening her skirt, and she tried to walk away from him. "Don't!"

"Get over here."

He caught her arm, wrenched her back around, and turned her. Once again, his hands were on her hair. She gritted her teeth, amazed that fingers that could touch with such force could move so surely upon her hair.

"This is a service it seems you have performed many times!" she said gratingly.

"Enough, I suppose." She tried to move away from him.

"Stand still!" he commanded.

"Oh, I suppose that your mistresses usually do."

"And you are the unusual mistress."

"I am not your mistress at all."

"Ah, more's the pity. I thought that you had just agreed to the position."

"Never!"

"You'll dream about me," he promised.

"Only in my darkest nightmares!"

"I promise, you will yearn for my touch."

"I will yearn for your demise upon some heathen Indian spear."

"There. Now, let me see."

Without the least gentleness he pushed her from him and spun her about to face him. He critically scanned her hair and costume. "I think that the damage has been repaired."

"The damage can never be repaired!"

"How rude. After all I have done to repair your appearance."

" 'Twas your touch that destroyed it!"

"Ah, but I was not the first to touch! I merely ventured where another man had already explored."

"Oh!" She raised her hand to slap him, but he laughed and brought her back hard against his chest again.

"Shall I prove to you again that the day will come when you pine for the mere mention of my name? Alas, when we have just taken such pains to assure the demure chastity of your costume!"

"You have proven nothing, except that you are a rude and insolent rodent! Robert is your friend, yet you demean him! You laugh at his intentions, but what of your own? You must take what I would willingly give to him—"

"Fool!" he swore. She had yet to see him so darkly angry, so lacking in control. He shoved her from him and she staggered back. "So be it! Find Robert Maxwell! Give to him what you will. I cannot stop you. I can only warn you that he has nothing, and that no matter how enamored of you he is, there is nothing at all that he can give you. You dream of marriage. It will never be. Spin your dreams. You are blind, even unto yourself!"

He bowed very low to her, spun about, and left her. Jassy watched him go, her breasts heaving, her teeth grating, her mind in a tempest. "Good riddance!" she swore.

But she was shaking very badly and couldn't stand. She lowered herself down to the balls of her feet on the floor, trying to draw steady breaths. God! But how she loathed him!

Her fingers flew to her mouth, and she felt that her lips were still swollen from his touch. She still trembled but maintained some vague feeling of burning restlessness within her. She hated him with a blinding passion.

But she could not get him out of her mind, and when she slipped back into the hall at last and escaped to the haven of her own small room, it was the searing blaze of his kiss that haunted her, while the soft touch of Robert's lips faded annoyingly from her memory.

6

JASSY EXPECTED THE SUMMONS THAT CAME from her brother the next day.

Henry never forgot that he was Duke of Somerfield, especially when he dealt with her. He did not speak with her casually, and when he passed her in the hall he expected a submissive curtsy from her. Like a feudal lord, he wanted those under his roof to be under his strict domination.

"Jane tells me that you serve her well."

"Then I am glad," she said, and she winced as she added, "Your Grace."

"I am not a cruel man, Jasmine."

"No, milord. Pray, tell me, have I indicated that you were?"

He shook his head, and she wondered if their father had looked like him when he had first seduced her mother, tall and very golden, and certainly splendid in his brocade and silk.

Henry walked to the window and looked out on the great curving drive before the Hall. "Let me give you a history lesson, little sister. In the late 1400s, men suspected that Richard III slew his own nephews, mere boys, in the Tower. In the next century Queen Mary had executed her legitimate cousin, Lady Jane Grey, for seizure of her throne, and for refusing to accept her Popish faith. Later, our great lady, Queen Elizabeth, had her cousin Mary Queen of Scots slain for plots against the throne. The Wars of the Roses were great, fratricidal battles. But then, you do know your history, don't you? Jane tells me that it seems your education was well taken in hand."

"Yes, I know my history," Jassy said.

"Then you will understand that blood ties mean little in this world, especially when that blood tie is tarnished by the stain of your bastardy. I have done the best that I can for you. You are not a true member of this family, and you will not participate in events of importance as if you were. Jane likes you; Elizabeth dotes upon you. But I find you a fortune-digging little temptress like your mother, and you will not step upon my back to secure your fortune. You are my wife's serving girl, and nothing more. You will not attend the ball. Lenore will find her husband then, and you will not interfere."

Jassy locked her teeth and lifted her chin. "Your Grace, how could I, a bastard, possibly interfere?"

He returned to his desk and picked up a quill and a parchment of accounts. "You know, Jasmine, exactly how you might interfere. You are like your mother, a woman men lust for. You cause trouble by your very nature. I shall do my best to see that Christian and godly ways are instilled in you. Defy me and you will be beaten. Now, I am busy. You are excused."

She didn't leave. She ran to the desk, kneeling down before him. "Your Grace! Elizabeth tells me that the lowliest milkmaid is allowed to attend—"

"But you are not. Go now! You are disturbing me."

"But your Grace—"

"If you disobey me, ever, I will strip you naked, lay welts upon your back by my own hand, and send you back to the slop alley from which you came."

She rose, and she swore to herself that she would never forgive him. Blood meant nothing to him; it meant nothing to her.

She fled from the room then, terrified that she would burst into tears. In her room she paced the floor. Robert would come to the ball and Jamie would not. Lenore would find herself in Robert's arms, and it would be right, and it would be perfect, and the honorable thing would be for them to marry.

No! It wasn't fair!

She threw herself on top of her bed and stared at the ceiling. She should be grateful for her comfort and seek no more! she told herself. But Henry's words gnawed at her. She was living by the grace of another, and it was frightening. If she offended him now, two years from now or five years now, he would send her back out into the streets. Back to abject poverty.

There had to be a way.

Kathryn came to summon her again; Jane needed her services. Jassy swallowed down her hatred for her brother and went to serve his wife. Jane dictated her letters, many of which were to stockholders in the Virginia Company. Jane, like her father and brother, had invested heavily with the Company, and with a similar venture, the Bermuda Company. When they were done with the correspondence, Jane sighed and leaned back on her bed. "I feel so weary so quickly. And so fat! Like a house."

"Milady, one can barely tell that you are with child."

"You are a diplomat, along with your other talents!" Jane laughed. "And smart," she added softly. She indicated the pile of correspondence. "Tell me, what do you think of this venture?" she asked.

"Milady?"

Jane laughed. "The Virginia Company. Jamie is so enthused. There have been many failures, but now, you see, I am determined to invest in my brother. The company travails for lack of organization. The leaders quibble with one another. Still, much has happened since 1606. Jamie tells me that there are many families in Jamestown. And in the various hundreds on the James. I think that Jamie will make us all prosper with that new land of his."

"I'm sure he shall," Jassy said politely. Her fingers tightened around her quill.

"He is an adventurer, Jamie is. He loves the wind and the sea and faraway lands. Though truly the manor he has built is amazing. Oh, well, perhaps he will settle down now with Lenore, and she will convince him to remain at home. I don't know. Perhaps it would be a bad match. He is determined to go where and when he pleases, and Lenore is no wanderer." She shrugged. "It is between the two of them. And Henry, of course, but he is quite determined that Lenore will be married this year. She must make her choice."

"And what if she chooses Robert Maxwell?" Jassy could not help but ask.

"Oh, then I can see it all very easily. They are both frivolous flirts, and they shall have to take great care that they learn some sense of responsibility!"

Jassy hesitated. "And what of you?" she queried softly. "How do you and Henry manage?"

Jane smiled slowly. "Well enough. You find him cruel, I'm certain, but you must remember that he was always taught that he would be the duke, 'His Grace,' and that he was very nobly born. Jassy, it is true, most men would not even allow you in their house."

"I am a burden to him. Perhaps, if he allowed me to go to the ball, I would no longer have to be a burden."

Jane laughed. "He wants Lenore married. When that has come about, you shall see, he will discover that you are worthy of his attention. There will always be another ball. And in time I'm certain that Henry will decide upon a proper match for you, perhaps with a prospering merchant." She smiled and winced. "Jassy, if you'll forgive me, I'm getting a terrible headache."

Jassy leapt to her feet. "If you've some mineral water, perhaps I could help. My mother used to get such headaches."

Jane arched a brow but directed Jassy to her dressing table and the mineral water. Jassy came behind Jane and dampened her fingers and set them gently upon Jane's temple. She began to move them in a lulling motion, and after several moments Jane sighed contentedly. "You are marvelous, a gift from God!" Jane proclaimed. Jassy demurred, but in a few minutes Jane was sleeping. Jassy slipped quietly from the room.

She left the house and came out to the stables and asked one of the grooms to saddle Mary for her. While she waited, Elizabeth came down and decided to ride with her. Elizabeth laughed and chatted about the ball—she loved to prepare things! And, of course, before the ball they would fast for Lent, and then celebrate Easter; there would be much for everyone to do.

Jassy brooded and listened just vaguely. She did not pay attention to their path but allowed Elizabeth to lead. Then suddenly she reined in, for they had followed an unfamiliar trail and had come to a new and gleaming residence grander than any palace Jassy had ever imagined. A high wall encircled numerous cleared acres and groves, and beyond the wall, a whitewashed palace rose against the green of the new spring grass, a tall, imposing structure in brick with symmetrical outbuildings and fascinating turrets and towers. She had once seen Hampton Court as a child; this seemed grander than that royal residence taken from Cardinal Wolsey by Henry VIII.

"What is it?" Jassy said, awed.

Elizabeth laughed. "It is Jamie's new manor. He has traveled much, you know. The symmetry is from the Italians, or so he told me. The balance is

French, but we are Englishmen and Englishwomen here, and so the design is Tudor. It is wonderful, is it not?"

"Yes, it is wonderful."

"Come, we'll see it."

"Oh, we cannot! I don't wish—"

"Don't worry. Jamie is in London now. The king's council is in session, and the Duke of Carlyle is in council, and Jamie is with his father, advising him. Lymon Miller is the steward of the estate; he will take us through it."

Jassy could protest no more, for Elizabeth nudged her mount forward and they raced together to the grand wall and the massive wrought-iron entry with its emblem of the lion and the hawk. A gatekeeper recognized Elizabeth and welcomed her with respect, letting them through. Then they approached the steps to the manor itself. Grooms appeared quickly to take their horses, and even as they removed their gloves a spry bald man in handsome dark livery came hurrying down the many steps. "Lady Elizabeth!" he said with delight. "Welcome. Lord Cameron will be so sorry he missed you. He's not at Castle Carlyle, no, I'm sorry to say. They've gone on to London."

"Oh, I know that, Lymon. This is my sister, Jasmine. I wanted to show her the manor. May I?"

Lymon cast Jassy a quick and curious stare, and she knew that the entire region must have heard of her sudden appearance from a sordid past. "Miss Jasmine," Lymon said. "You must do as you wish, Lady Elizabeth. Will you have coffee? Lord Cameron has just acquired some from his ships in the Mediterranean."

"Yes, Lymon, thank you. In the blue room, I think."

Jassy followed Elizabeth up the grand stone stairway and past the concrete lions guarding the double doorway. There was a rich red runner sweeping down the length of a grand hallway, so wide and huge that it could easily accommodate a hundred guests. Portraits lined the walls, and doorways opened on either side to various other rooms. A great curving stone stairway rose from the rear of the hall, and it, too, was covered in the rich red velvet runner that came to the door. Elizabeth smiled as Jassy gaped. "It is lovely, isn't it?"

"Yes. It is exquisite."

"And imagine. He is hardly ever here. When he returns from his journeys, he spends time with his father. He keeps his belongings here, and that is it, so it seems." She laughed. "Ah, well, if Lenore has her way, they will marry, and he will have to come home more often, don't you agree?"

Jassy nodded, but she didn't want to agree. She didn't want to think of Lenore in the manor, she wanted to imagine that it belonged to her. It was fun to close her eyes and see herself in silks and furs, walking down the stairway greeting her guests. They would toast her; they would say that she was the grandest hostess in all of King James's realm, the poor little bastard serving wench who had pulled herself up and proved that a commoner could rise above her lot to grace the society of nobles and gentry.

The house belonged to Lord Cameron, she reminded herself.

"Shall we have coffee? The blue room." Elizabeth directed her to the left, where the walls were covered with light blue silk and the floor by a braided rug. Shining wooden chairs were pulled before a low-burning fire. The ceiling was molded and the mantel was made of marble. A cart that held a silver service was pulled before the fire.

"Sit. I shall pour." Elizabeth indicated a seat. Jassy bit her lower lip and smiled.

"Please, Elizabeth, may I pour?" Jassy said. She'd never had coffee before. It was an Eastern drink, and only the very wealthy were beginning to import it from places in southern Europe.

"Why, milady, do go right ahead!"

And as Jassy poured their coffee she discovered herself every bit the actress that her mother had been. She spoke about Lord so-and-so's day on the floor at Parliament, and how Lady da-de-da had been presented before the king and queen. "And where was it? Oh, they were at the Tower, I believe. And did I tell you that Lady Cauliflower stayed there recently—the queen insisted, of course— and claimed that the Tower Green was definitely haunted? Well, it is Catherine Howard who screams along the corridors of Hampton Court, but it is Anne Boleyn who carried her head about the Tower Green!"

Elizabeth convulsed with laughter. "Oh, Jassy! You would make a great lady. A very great lady, indeed!"

"Oh, indeed, she would," came a sudden, masculine voice from the doorway.

Jassy jumped up, spilling her coffee. Elizabeth dropped her cup. They both stared at Jamie Cameron. He entered the room, stripping away his gauntlets. Lymon followed after him, ready to accept the gauntlets and take his black cloak as he cast it off. Beneath the cloak he was clad in knee-high riding boots, crimson breeches, a slashed doublet, and a fine white shirt. He handed his plumed hat to his steward, too, thanking Lymon cordially for the service.

Then he was staring at the two of them again, and though he greeted Elizabeth warmly enough, he seemed to view them with displeasure.

"Do forgive me—" Elizabeth began, but he interrupted her with a kiss on the cheek.

"Elizabeth, you are always welcome in my home."

Jassy had not said a word. She clenched her teeth and held her hands folded before her. She hated that he had come upon them. Always! Always! He destroyed her dreams. He broke into them with harsh reality, and with his ever-present mockery and scorn. Nor could she forget when they had parted. Seeing him brought back a wave of emotion, and she trembled inside. He stared at her now with polite inquiry, and without a word of welcome to her.

"I did not expect you back."

"Matters in London were solved much more quickly than I expected. Are you —er, ladies having coffee? Forgive me if I indulge in a whiskey." He went to the sideboard and poured himself an amber drink from a crystal decanter. He turned, leaned against the sideboard, and watched them both again, yet Jassy felt his acute gaze fall her way, and his lips curled into a mocking smile.

"Elizabeth, I think that we should be leaving," Jassy said.

"Yes, perhaps—" Elizabeth said, but as she spoke, she turned, catching her fragile coffee cup with her skirt, and the contents spilled upon it. "Oh, dear! Henry has so recently bought this fabric from Flanders, he will be furious with me—"

"I'm sure that Lymon can quickly catch the stain, Elizabeth, and I'm equally certain that Henry could not be distressed with you." He called for Lymon. "See, Elizabeth, it is just this bit, here, that is stained."

"If you'll come with me, Lady Elizabeth, we shall solve the problem in moments."

"Jassy, I shall be right back."

"Oh, Elizabeth, perhaps I can help—"

"I'm sure, Miss Dupré, that they can manage," Jamie Cameron said. He smiled and blocked her way when she might have followed the two of them out. She did not try to barge past him. She turned with a rustle of fabric and wandered to the rear of the room, ostensibly studying the wall cloth.

"You're good, Jassy. Very good," he said softly.

"Am I?" It seemed better to face him then. She was distinctly uneasy with her back to him. "At what?"

"At all of it. At aping your betters."

"I have no betters, Lord Cameron."

He started to laugh, and then he inclined his head slightly to her. "Perhaps you don't, 'milady.' Perhaps you don't. Your mother was an actress. You have her talent. I believe that I would dare to take you to Court upon my arm, and have little fear that your manners would be anything but perfectly correct. But you are dreaming still, Jassy."

"Do you think so?"

He approached her, and she backed away from him nervously, but then there was nowhere left to go, and so she stood her ground. He cornered her. He placed his hands on either side of her head, and he smiled, his face very close to hers. "May I tell you exactly what I read in the beautiful, cunning, and oh so betraying eyes? You love the elegance of this house, and you imagine yourself mistress here. Ah, but the house would not come with someone so loathsome as me. Oh, no! It would be Robert Maxwell's estate, and of course, he would not dishonor you with any kind of licentious proposal, but he would forget fortune and class and the society of princes and kings to make you his wife. And you and he would rule here forever and forever."

"Maybe someone will shoot you in a duel," Jassy said sweetly. "And maybe Robert Maxwell cares more than you might think."

He turned away from her, negligently returned to the sideboard, and sat before the fire with a casual air, dangling one leg over the side of the chair. He smiled, watching her where she still stood against the wall. "Robert will never marry you. He must marry elsewhere, and quickly. He needs the income. He has gambled away a great deal of his income."

"You are a liar. You are rude and uncouth and as savage as the heathens in that godforsaken land that so excites you. You are determined to drag Robert Maxwell down at every opportunity."

He shook his head slowly. "No, Jassy. Robert is my friend. I do not seek to hurt him. I was just in London to bail him out of difficulty."

"You were there to meet your father."

"Have it as you will."

"I should be better off to come and sleep with you, right?" she said scornfully.

"Actually, yes. You could indulge in great fantasy. You could imagine that you had done away with me yourself, that the manor was entirely your own, and that you could reign here as a gracious queen forever."

"I should dearly love to do away with you," she replied.

"But then, I'm afraid that the fantasy couldn't last forever. You see, I intend to marry soon."

"The great and wondrous Lord Cameron deigns to take a wife. I hope that you shall make each other entirely miserable for a lifetime."

"No one shall make me miserable for a lifetime, mistress," he advised her. "You see, a wife has certain functions. To bear heirs, to be her lord's hostess, and his supporter in all things. And above all, of course, she is to obey him, and follow him wherever he shall choose to lead. Then again, if she should prove not so gentle and not so kind and not so pretty as she seemed before the binding words were spoken, she may be left at one estate while her lord travels on to another."

"Then the man has married himself a fool," Jassy said. "And, my Lord Cameron, you do deserve one."

His laughter followed her as she left the room at last, determining that she would wait for Elizabeth outside. A servant opened the door for her and she fled down the steps. Even as she reached the ground, the grooms were hurrying out with the horses. Elizabeth did come right along. She said good-bye to Jamie at the steps. Jassy was mounted when Elizabeth reached her. A groom quickly helped Elizabeth upon her mount.

"It's a glorious place, isn't it?" Elizabeth demanded.

"Glorious. Let's please do go!"

That night Jassy had the first of her nightmares. She saw the attic room at Master John's again, and she saw the blond figure lying there. She came toward the bed, knelt beside it, and touched the covers. Linnet turned to her, and Jassy began a long, silent scream, for her mother's flesh had rotted from her face, and she touched her upon the breast with a bony finger. Then she fell back against the pallet, and when Jassy looked again, it was not Linnet lying there at all, it was her, and she was dying just as her mother had died, in filth and poverty. For days the nightmare haunted her.

But a week later the flowers came from Robert Maxwell, and she forgot the horror, for fantasy was awakened inside of her once again.

She was at the stables when the boy arrived, a young lad with a limp and a wool cap pulled low over his forehead. He carried a handful of roses, and he came to her swiftly, nervous that someone else might be about.

"Jasmine Dupré?"

"Yes?"

He thrust the flowers to her. "Compliments of Robert Maxwell, with his greatest regard."

And that was it. The boy turned and ran away, but Jassy was left with the flowers, and they seemed the greatest gift that any woman could receive.

She brought them back to her room and laid them out on her pillow. She breathed in their sweet scent, thinking that winter was indeed gone, and spring had come. Perhaps the cold had gone from her life forever, for Robert loved her, she was certain.

She carefully pressed the flowers into the one true gift her brother had given, a copy of the King's new Bible.

The days began to rush by; they fasted for Lent, and they atoned for their sins on Maundy Thursday and Good Friday. Easter was soberly celebrated with a long Mass, and when that day came to an end, the household began to plan for May Day with exuberance.

Even Elizabeth was excited, though she had no intention of being part of the dance. The tenants were raising a giant Maypole with brightly colored streamers to hang from it. For them it would be a grand holiday. They would all receive a measure of rum, a silver coin, and a bolt of cloth. A village girl would be proclaimed Princess of the May, while the title of Queen belonged indisputably to Lenore.

The family and the invited nobility and gentry would sup in the dining room, while a banquet for the servants and tenants would take place in the courtyard area between the hall and the stables. To attend, the duke's dependents were all to bring him a gift, and so he would hold court outside, since the gifts would most oft consist of little piglets.

"You needn't fret that you're not actually dancing," Elizabeth told Jassy. "You shall enjoy it. There's ever so much activity. Henry has hired an animal keeper with a dancing bear and ever so many musicians. There will be numerous puppeteers, and all manner and sort of entertainment!"

"Yes, I'm sure it will be wonderful," Jassy told her.

Lenore announced that she would be dressed in white, and that she would attend as a white dove. She didn't wish to leave her suitors with any doubt as to who she was.

One afternoon as the day neared, Lenore summoned Jassy to her rooms. "I have the most hateful headache," she complained. "Jane tells me that you can soothe the pain."

Jassy had little desire to soothe any of Lenore's pain. She shrugged. "I am not so talented."

"Would you try, please? I am in agony."

While she rubbed her sister's temples with mineral water, Jassy remained silent. Lenore leaned back in her chair and sighed. "Oh, Jassy, you are very good! Sometimes I wish that you were my true sister—you'd have been fun, I'm certain. Not like Elizabeth, who is too timid ever to defy Henry! Then I am glad that you are the bastard child, for you might have been some wicked competition." She laughed openly and honestly, then twisted around. "If Henry makes life too unbearable for you, you shall come and live with me when I have married. I shall keep you merely to cure headaches!"

"That's quite kind, I'm sure."

"Jassy, you shall never be meek and mild. No matter what your words say, your eyes flash."

"Who do you think you will marry?" Jassy asked.

Lenore sighed. "Well, Jamie Cameron has claimed that he isn't coming to the dance—he does not like such things. Of course, he never wanted to marry. Not before this year. I do not know what has changed him so." She hesitated. "I do adore Jamie!" she whispered, almost with awe. "When he is near, I feel that I am hot, that I cannot breathe. He is as dashing as the devil himself, so tall and dark and cynical in all things! His eyes, his whisper, make me quiver. But then, he frightens me sometimes too. He will never do as a wife asks. He will never bow down before any man or woman. He is terribly demanding. I am oft surprised that he has managed to be friends with King James." She laughed. "The king is oft so dour, and convinced that witches are after him! But that is neither here nor there—Jamie is a strong man. Too strong, perhaps. I think that Robert would be the easier match. He is quick to laugh, and to flirt, and still . . . I feel perhaps he would be the more loyal husband, for his needs are not so great. Jamie would demand both flesh and soul. Oh, but he is so handsome with his marvelous eyes. Just the way that he looks at a woman . . . but here I go, on and on. You really mustn't look so unhappy. Henry will arrange a marriage for you."

"I do not want an arranged marriage."

"No," Lenore said shrewdly. "You want to join the dance."

Jassy shrugged. Lenore suddenly leapt up. "I'll help you."

"What? Why should you?" she asked suspiciously.

"Oh, come now, I am not so awful a person as you may think! We did have the same father—even if your mother was a strumpet—"

"My mother was not—"

"Well, you are the bastard, right? Let's not quibble. We shall both go, and we shall both wear white. Henry will never know that you are there, for we are so alike that if he sees you about the room, he will think that you are me."

"He has threatened me with grave consequences, you know."

"Oh, pooh. Henry is really not such a monster, either. It will be all right. But we must plan now carefully, and in secrecy. And if we play our cards right, perhaps you will capture some handsome young knight!"

Jassy lowered her head. She could not tell Lenore that she slept with the Bible with Robert Maxwell's flowers pressed into it, nor that she had already chosen the knight that she wanted. She raised her eyes to Lenore's and could not hide the excitement in them. "Let's do it!"

When May Day came, the very air was filled with such excitement that Jassy could not be afraid of the possibly dire consequences of her deception. She heard the horses and carriages arriving, and she heard the tenants and servants playing down in the courtyard. She could hear them from her window, and when she looked down from it, she could see all manner of gaiety. Maids and youths already danced around the Maypole. The man with the bear had the animal doing circles upon his hind feet, and a marionette show was already in progress. A flutist was playing, and, in honor of King James, a group of Highlanders played the bagpipes. There was a great deal of noise and confusion. The day was bright and clear and blue and beautiful. Spring was indeed with them.

Jassy rushed along the corridors until she reached Lenore's door. She tapped, and Lenore drew her in, giggling. "Hurry!"

An hour later both girls were dressed alike. Jassy was delighted. Her hose were white silk, and her little leather slippers were white and decorated with glass stones. She wore a soft silk shift next to her flesh, and over it a binding corset, and three different petticoats. The dresses themselves were white brocade, with stomachers in a tougher velvet, low-cut bodices, and half sleeves with scores of white lace. Their face masks were covered with feathers and plumes. A little bit of a heel had been added to Jassy's slippers to make her as tall as Lenore, and they had flattened her breasts as best they could with the corset. They had both done their golden hair up in ringlets, tied through with white satin ribbons.

When they were done, they stared at each other and both burst out laughing. "We are wonderful!" Lenore insisted.

Jassy spun about and peered into her sister's mirror. She felt beautiful and as innocent as a bride. She paused, hoping that Lenore would not hate her too much if she managed to capture Robert Maxwell. No, for Lenore would be equally happy with Lord Cameron. After all, he was immensely wealthy, and Lenore had known him all her life. They would fare well enough together.

And if not, it would not be Jassy's fault. Lenore did not know what poverty was. She did not understand hunger and want. Jassy had to capture Robert.

"Come on, let's slip down together."

"Together!"

"Just to the landing. Then you must sneak outside, and I will go into the dining room. When the meal is halfway through, I will think of an excuse and change places with you. Now remember, you don't have to admit anything to anyone, or say anything at all if you don't want. This is a masked ball."

"But to come down together—"

"The excitement is in the risk!"

Certainly, Jassy thought sourly. Henry would speak firmly to Lenore if they were caught—he would whip Jassy, then cast her out.

"Let's go, then!" she hissed.

Amazingly, there was no mishap as they came down the stairway. Jassy quickly found the front entrance, came through it, and ran down the steps, encircling the massive building to come around the back. By then she was passing many people. The duke's friends, his guards, his fighting men, the farmers, and some of the merchants with their wives and daughters. The gentry mixed with the common folk. Where the pipers played a fling, a guard in half leather armor danced with a barefoot farmer's lass, and Jassy thought that many weddings were sure to follow.

She stopped before the marionette show. The puppets were beautifully crafted, and the stage scenery in the small box was excellent. Watching it, Jassy had a sense of a deep forest, and a wide ocean before it. Log buildings stood about, and houses made of wattle and daub. An Indian puppet cast herself over the body of a white man, and the white man was spared.

"There you are, minx!"

It was Robert. He caught her by the shoulders and turned her around. He was dressed in Italian Renaissance fashion, with short ballooned breeches, long hose, and pointed toe-shoes. His mask barely covered the area of his eyes. He looked briefly around, then brushed her lips with a quick, stolen kiss. "The queen of the May! You are beautiful, my love. Tell me, will you come to my arms this day?"

It did not occur to her that he might think she was Lenore. She nodded, certain that he was aware of their deception. He laced his fingers with hers. "That you insist upon this silly charade! But, love, I am besotted. I shall come where you lead me!"

Delighted, Jassy smiled. She did not speak; she did not wish to impose upon the magic. She indicated the Maypole, and with their hands laced together they came to it. Some goodwife handed them each a ribbon, and they joined the revelers singing and dancing around it. The goodwife claimed they would all be fertile, and bear many children, like the seeds of the harvest.

Looking toward the house, Jassy was alarmed to see that Lenore had made her appearance. She loosed her ribbon and ran. Lenore saw her and started in the opposite direction. Jassy raced for the house. She heard Robert as he caught up with Lenore. "Vixen! Come here!" And he laughed with the good fun of it. Lenore's laughter tinkled along with his.

It was not so amusing for Jassy. She came into the dining room and took Lenore's seat. To her great dismay she discovered that she was between Henry and Jamie Cameron. When she seated herself, Jamie poured her more wine from a silver chalice and whispered in her ear. "I had wondered when you were returning."

"I—I have returned."

Henry lowered his head to her and spoke softly. "I shall not tolerate such rudeness. Don't disappear again until this meal has come to an end."

Upon her lap and beneath the snowy tablecloth, Jamie Cameron's fingers curled around her own and squeezed. She wanted to scream. Their hands rested together upon her thigh. She felt too warm, and her heart was thundering. Jamie was staring at her. He always knew what lay beneath the coverings. He was always capable of stripping her down to the heart and soul and bare flesh.

"Lenore! Lady Renwig has just asked you about the duke's ball at Northumberland."

The duke's ball at Northumberland. She had no idea what Lady Renwig wanted. Lady Renwig wore a headpiece that resembled a giant hedgehog.

"The ball . . . was lovely," she said. Henry would note the difference in their voices. No, she was her mother's daughter, she was an actress, she could carry it off. "The weather was divine, and we danced beneath the moon. Even the king enjoyed it all tremendously."

"To James I!" someone cried. "King of England and king of the Scots! Uniting us at last!"

Then someone else said that they really didn't want to be united with the heathen Scots, and there was a whisper that such words could be treasonous. Jassy didn't care. It had taken the pressure away from her.

"Are you all right?" Henry whispered to her.

"I don't think that she is all right at all. I think that she is flushed beneath that mask," Jamie said.

"I need air, please!"

"Perhaps I should take her out, Henry," Jamie suggested. "They are crowning the princess of the May right now; Lenore shall need to be in the ceremony soon."

Henry lifted his hand with dismissive annoyance. Jassy mustered up the courage to graciously excuse herself.

Jamie's hand was on her arm. He did not lead her outside but through the door to the entryway and out to the front of the estate where there was no activity. "You've the heart of a true flirt, Lenore. The people were too much for you?" He spoke in a husky whisper. She found herself pressed against the house, and his lips touched down on hers.

"No," she protested.

"Lenore, half an hour ago you were devouring me. Now you are playing the coy maid. What shall it be?"

Her heart was thundering. "I must get out back." She hesitated, then stood on her toes and kissed him quickly. She mustn't forget that she was Lenore. "I promise to devour you again, my Lord Cameron!" she whispered. Then she fled. Her knees were weak and her flesh was aflame, and she could still taste his lips upon her. She tried to wipe away the touch as she fled around to the gaiety in the back.

She came around the house just in time to see Lenore mounting a dais. Jassy, catching her breath, tore into the open doorway of the tack house. Desperately gasping for breath, she watched as Lenore was made queen of the May by her brother, the duke. Jane, now noticeably with child, stood at his side. They all laughed and kissed one another. It was a pretty scene. Pretty pageantry for the poor people, Jassy thought. But then, she promised herself, from this day onward she would never be poor again. She would love Robert and support him in all things. She would check his gambling—if he really had such a habit!—and make him eternally happy and proud.

Henry stood before his people, and they cheered him. He raised his hands—the magnanimous landlord!—and the crowd fell silent. With a flourish he announced the dance of the May.

The musicians began to play. The beat was slow. Men and women moved into one another's arms.

Lenore disappeared into the crowd.

Jassy saw Robert Maxwell. He was far across the crowd, on the other side of the dais. She had to reach him. She slipped from the doorway of the barn and began threading her way through the costumed dancers.

She walked into Henry and Jane and froze. "Choose carefully!" Henry told her affectionately. She nodded, breathed again, and started through the crowd once again. The tempo of the music picked up. Laughter rose, and the slow, staid dance became wilder. She saw Robert. He was just ahead of her.

A hand clamped down upon her shoulder. She was whisked into strong arms and swirled about with startling force. Stunned, she looked up into Jamie Cameron's eyes. They began to circle and circle. Jassy tried to jerk free. "No!" she said in panic.

She felt faint. She twisted and saw that the real Lenore was now in Robert Maxwell's arms. They were swirling to the furious beat with its pagan thunder of drums. They were laughing in each other's arms.

She looked into Jamie Cameron's eyes. She saw their hated dark indigo depths, tearing into her soul. She felt the force of his arms around her, felt her dreams plummeting to the bottom of the deepest ocean.

"Now!" the duke commanded, and the music ceased.

She tried to pull away, to free herself. Jamie Cameron ripped her mask from her face. "Jasmine," he said.

She turned around, dazed. She still could not free herself from his hold. She saw Lenore, and Lenore was with Robert, and he was kissing her tenderly, and they were both laughing.

Then she saw her brother, Henry, and she saw the raw fury in his face as he came toward her.

"Please, God, have some pity! Let me go!" she told Jamie Cameron, and she wrenched away from him at last and ran.

7

ASSY FLED AROUND TO THE FRONT OF THE
house, running like a cornered fox. When she reached the
entryway, she didn't know what to do or where to go. She had
to flee. Henry would carry out his threat, she knew. She
would be best off if she left by herself.

Her fear was little greater than her disappointment. She was still stunned that
Lenore and Robert could be together, and so very happy in each other's arms.

Jassy heard voices, and men running behind her. She ducked into the house—
and ran straight into her brother's arms. He was still red with rage. As if he might
have an attack of apoplexy at any moment.

"I'll leave!" she cried.

"When I'm ready for it, mistress! You disobeyed the one edict that I gave
you!"

"Henry!" Jane came hurrying up behind him. "Henry, please, have some
mercy—"

"The girl disobeyed a direct order! Haven't I been kind, haven't I been
decent? I have done more for her than our father did, and still she defies me."

"Henry—"

"No, my God, woman, leave me be!"

He had Jassy by the wrists, and he dragged her along with him up the stairway.
"You have made a fool of me before my guests, girl, and this you will pay for!"

"Please, I have told you I will leave!"

He ignored her, and in minutes they reached his study. He threw her into the
room, then closed the door behind them, but he did not bother to lock it. Jassy
prayed that Jane would try to intervene again. No one came. Henry stared at her
for a minute then came after her and caught her wrists again. She struggled
against him. He was far too powerful. He threw his desk chair into the center of
room and forced her down upon her knees before it. He tied her hands to the
back of it, having wrenched the satin ribbon from her hair for his bond. He
grasped a quill-sharpening blade from his desk, and Jassy, so tightly bound to the
chair, cast back her head and screamed in terror, certain that he meant to slay
her. He did not. He came around and slashed the fabric of her gown and
wrenched it down her back, leaving it bare. From a hook upon the wall he
snatched a riding crop, and he flourished it before her, slapping it against his
palm. "You want all things due the legal heirs of our father, Jasmine? This he
called judgment, and we were all privy to it! Perhaps it is just that if you would
come here, you would feel the mark of his anger."

She did not know if she was more afraid of the bite of the whip, or more mortified by her position, for her torn garments hung from her and she was nearly naked from the waist up, and forced upon her knees, and desperate with her hands so brutally tied. She wanted to speak to him, to reason with him, but she dared not open her mouth, for she was so afraid that she would cry. "You see, my dear, the bastard children do find certain benefits!" He stroked her bare back with the crop of the whip.

"Your Grace—" she began, and then she screamed, for he brought the whip down upon her naked back with a violent force that was shattering. She had never known such agony. Tears stung her eyes, and she didn't know how many more she could bear.

The door opened, but she was barely aware of it through her haze of pain. She wanted to brace herself, to prepare for the next, but Henry knew how to punish, and how to extend the pain.

"How many lashes, Jasmine? How many do you think before you would obey me? You see, I fear that I could tear your flesh to ribbons, and still it would help little. Still, I must try."

"Henry, no!" came a commanding male voice.

The lash fell again, and she could not help herself; she cried out with the agony of it.

"Henry, stop!" came the command again. There were footsteps before her. A man approached her brother and wrenched the crop from his hands.

"Damn you, Cameron, what right have you to stop me! You brought me this chit to harbor, and she has defied me! It is my right to punish her as I see fit. She deserves what I give her."

Jassy tried to blink back her tears. She wanted to die. Now Jamie Cameron was witness to this humiliation too.

Her gown was completely awry, her breasts were bare, tears stung her eyes, and she prayed only that the tall, towering, dark man who had brought her a respite would disappear into thin air. She would rather bear the whip than the damning glare of his indigo eyes.

"By God and all that is holy, Jamie, we are friends, but this is my business now. Do not interfere!"

"I have the right!" Jamie declared. He knelt down before Jasmine. She wished he would go away. He untied the ribbon that held her. She had no strength left. She fell from her knees to the floor. He came around to her side, lifting her. She cried out, for the cuts on her back stung painfully, and she cried out in protest, for she was so exposed and vulnerable and didn't want him witnessing her in this state. He stripped off his doublet and wrapped it around her gently, taking care when she flinched as the fabric hit her back.

"Damn you, Jamie Cameron!" Henry swore.

"It is my right, for I will marry her."

"What?" Henry said, astounded.

There were others in the room then, Jassy realized, for they all repeated Henry's exclamation.

"But that's foolish, man! Think of your position. You will have to have a special dispensation. You cannot marry this common—"

"Take care!" Jamie warned. "It is my betrothed you speak of now!"

"Jamie, you have lost your mind!" It was Jane speaking. She was kind, but she had a strong sense of propriety. "Think of who and what you are, and think of your life and your life-style—"

"That is exactly what I am thinking of," Jamie said curtly. He scooped Jassy into his arms. Instinctively she clung to him. He whirled around to face Henry. "Where is her room? Where shall I take her?"

"I'll show you!" Elizabeth said. Jassy saw her sister's pretty face dance before her. "Come, Jamie, I will show you."

"This is madness, Jamie!" Henry called after him.

"I held her when the dance ended, did I not?"

"I would never hold you to a marriage with a bastard!"

"I hold myself to the bargain," Jamie replied, and he followed Elizabeth out into the hallway.

"Jamie Cameron, you'll not interfere with me this way! You cannot mean this! You don't want the girl punished, though God knows why. I do not maim her!"

"I play no game," Jamie said softly. "I have decided. I will marry her."

They walked along the hallway. Dazed with pain, Jassy stared up at him. His neck seemed very bronze and powerful, and his jaw was hardened with determination. He glanced down at her, and his eyes were dark and menacing.

"I won't marry you," she said.

"No? Not even for all that money I've got?"

She shook her head. "I hate you. I'll never marry you. You should have let Henry whip me."

"Perhaps I should have," he said.

"Here, this way," Elizabeth said before them.

He entered into her room, and he laid her down upon her bed. He set her upon her side, then rolled her to her stomach, freeing his doublet from her and baring the strokes of the whip.

"Please, go away!" Jassy said breathlessly.

"Some salve will heal them. Henry does care something for you; I saw him lash a groom for thievery once, and there was little flesh left," Jamie said flatly. "Elizabeth, my sister has a lotion that will be soothing. Other than that, the marks should fade in a few weeks."

"Please, go away," Jassy implored him again, her face in her pillow. He didn't go away. He sat at her side and continued to study her back.

She didn't turn around and she didn't look his way; she felt him pick up her hand. He slid a ring onto her small finger. "This will be the mark of my betrothal. It will keep you safe from . . ." He paused. Jassy thought that he meant to say she would be safe from her brother, but he did not. "You will be safe from all harm," he finished.

"I will never marry you," she said dully. "And you do not mean this. You needn't continue the charade."

"But I do mean it," he said very quietly, and she felt the whisper of his voice against the bare flesh at her nape. "I do mean it, with all of my heart." Something hot and frightening filled her as the fever of his words touched her again. She turned suddenly, seeking his eyes. Her torn bodice and shift fell, and flushing, she retrieved them, staring at him in amazement. "Why? Why would you want to do this thing? Henry is right. No one will hold you to it! I am a bastard, and you are the son of a duke. Why?"

He shrugged. His eyes were dark and dusky, and his face was hard set. He crossed his arms over the breadth of his chest and rose, and she trembled, watching him. She remembered Lenore's words. He would bow to no man. He would do what he chose with his life: he had asked her to be his mistress and now he was willing her to be his wife.

"Why? Well, because I do desire you, I suppose. I want you, and marriage seems to be one kind of a price to pay. You do demand your price, don't you?"

She couldn't speak. She burned beneath his gaze and felt as if they had barely scratched the surface of things, as a tempest brewed between them both. She was afraid but swore that she would not be afraid. Lenore knew him, and the strength of his will. Jassy swore then that she would fight it.

"Excuse me, love, till we meet again," he said. He kissed her forehead and bowed to Elizabeth, and Jassy still hadn't spoken when she realized that he had left the room.

"I will not do it!" she said in panic. "Elizabeth, I will not do it! He saved me from Henry's wrath, yes, but if he were in a temper or if he had been defied, I would fear him far more than I would Henry! He can't mean it, it will never happen—oh, why did he have to step out in front of me! He meant to catch Lenore, and Lenore meant to have him—"

"Oh, don't worry about Lenore!" Elizabeth said happily. "Lenore has Robert!"

"Oh!" Jassy said, and suddenly she burst into tears. Elizabeth, distressed, tried to comfort her. "You're in pain. I shall get the lotion. Kathryn will come. We'll clean you up and get you a hot drink laced with rum. Then you'll sleep, and it will all look so much better in the morning."

In the morning it looked even worse. Jassy woke to find Lenore beside her. Lenore kissed her cheek effusively. "Oh, Jassy, but you do carry incredible luck with you! I had thought that we were all doomed, and what happens? Of all men, Jamie Cameron determines to marry you! You! A commoner and a bastard! Henry would have whipped you and ordered me to my room until my marriage, but he is so bemused, he doesn't know what to do! Jassy, I had thought at first that I begrudged you so very much. But I am happy. Honestly, I am so very happy! And we must be friends. Oh, you needn't worry about the London snobs, either. I shall handle them. And the king will accept you for Jamie's sake, so you've really nothing to fear at all. It will be wonderful! We'll all be very close. You, me, and Elizabeth!"

"I cannot marry him," Jassy said.

"Don't be absurd. Oh! I had thought that you might trap yourself a young soldier or a merchant, and now . . . now you shall be Lady Cameron!"

"I cannot marry him."

"Oh, you're jittery, that's all. I suppose I might be a little afraid myself if I were to wed Jamie. He does have the devil of a temper and the will to match. But he is so handsome, and so very rich. Robert isn't nearly so rich, you know. Thankfully there is my trust fund, which is my dowry. We shall do very well, for we love each other dearly. Well, I'll admit, I had decided on Jamie at the beginning of the day. He kissed me and I could scarce stand. Or perhaps I kissed him. I don't remember. But it is quite all right that you marry him. It is fate, I think."

"No. I cannot marry him."

Lenore did not believe her; neither did Jane, who came to see her later in the afternoon. "He wishes the wedding to take place by the first of June, for he will have to leave shortly afterward for his holdings in Virginia. Naturally he wants some time with his new bride. I have spoken with him at length, all to no avail. I have wondered myself if you are not completely a scheming and fortune-hunting little strumpet, but none of it means a thing to Jamie. You do not know my brother; when he sets his mind on something, there is simply no stopping him."

"I will stop him. I will not marry him."

"What are you, a complete fool? One might take you for many things, my dear, but never a fool. He brought you out of a gutter; now he is willing to marry you. He is one of the richest men in the country. And you say that you will not marry him. Fine, then, return to your gutter! Wallow in it."

Still, for the rest of that day she lay in bed, and she shivered and swore to herself and to anyone else who came near that she would not marry him. Then, that night, Kathryn came to her room and told her that she must get up and dress, Lord Cameron was waiting to see her in her brother's office.

When she entered Henry's office and saw Jamie, her heart began to beat too fast, and trembling sensations seized her. She could not cast herself to his mercy. He knew that she hated him. This was some great and final mocking joke on his part. It had to be.

Nor did he act much like the loving husband-to-be. He eyed her critically when she entered, and in silence. Then he spoke at last. "I have made arrangements for a dressmaker to come here. You will be available to her at all times. You must have a completely new wardrobe, for my wife must not wear hand-me-downs, no matter how fine. You will need much in wool, and I suggest that you have her fashion you warm woolen stockings and pantalets, for winters can be harsh. Also, see to it that you are supplied with ball gowns, for one never knows. Henry has seen that the church has cried the banns, and we will be married on the first of June."

Her throat was dry, and she could barely move her parched lips. "No. I have said that I will not marry you."

He arched a brow, and his mouth curled into a smile. "You mean it?"

"Yes."

"Well, then, the offer has been made."

He stepped by her. She stared up at the powerful breadth of his back and his dark head, and she shivered.

The door closed behind him. She opened it and ran, returning to her room. She asked Kathryn to pick her a few warm things, things given to her by Elizabeth, her one true friend. Henry would have her leave in the morning, she was certain.

"Relax, love, it will work out!" Kathryn assured her. "I'll give you warm milk and you'll sleep, and it will look better by morning."

The morning did look better, for by night she had slept, and in sleeping, she had dreamed. She was back in the awful attic, and the wind was raging. It was dark and dreary and cold and filthy, and she was approaching the bed, for Linnet was dying. She had to reach her, she had to touch her, warm her. She reached out for the threadbare blanket covering her mother, and it was awful, for even before the figure turned, Jassy knew what she would see.

She would see death.

And still she had to touch the figure. And the figure turned, and indeed she saw the death's-mask, awful, pitiable, horrible. It was the face of starvation and misery and age come by wear, not by years. It was the ravaged, torn face of disease and hunger and desperation.

She started to scream. It was not her mother's face. It was her own.

"Jassy! Wake up!" Elizabeth was there, shaking her. The dream had been so horrible, it was hard to come from it. Elizabeth shook her again. "Jassy! It is a nightmare, nothing more."

Jassy looked around her. She saw by the windows that it was nearly dawn. She threw off her covers and ran to her wardrobe.

"Jassy! Where are you going, what are you doing?"

"Is he still there, do you know?"

"Who? Where?"

"Jamie Cameron. Is—is he staying at his house?"

"Yes, I believe so. He is not due to sail until the middle of June."

Jassy dressed quickly. She was barely aware of what clothing she wore. She started for the door, then she came back and kissed Elizabeth's cheek. "I love you," she whispered. Then she ran out the door and down the steps.

The servants were barely awake. She had to call for a groom to come and saddle Mary for her. Impatiently she mounted with no help, and she kicked the little horse with much more vigor than was needed, then she apologized to the faithful mare as she raced along. The sun still had not risen completely when she came to the gates of Jamie Cameron's magnificent estate. She had to wait for a gatekeeper to come, and as she waited, she stared at the house. It would not be so bad. Nothing would be so bad, for this would be her home; she would be mistress of this magnificent mansion. If she married him, she would never want again for anything.

She would have to lie with Jamie Cameron, she reminded herself. Night after night, into eternity. That would be her payment for security and riches. She started to tremble, and she almost turned around to ride back. She could remember his bronze fingers on her flesh all too clearly. She could remember his kiss, and the hot way it made her feel. She could not do it.

She nearly turned the mare about, but then the gate opened, and she rode through. Lymon was waiting to greet her on the steps. A groom took the mare, and she started up the steps. "Is—is Lord Cameron awake as yet?" she asked him.

"He is, mistress, and is aware that you have come. I'll take you to him."

She hadn't been up the grand staircase yet. As she mounted it, her heart hammered and she breathed with great difficulty. She tried to look at the finely carved wood, and on the second floor she looked over the fine portrait gallery, the silver sconces on the wall, and the superb deacons' benches that lined the alcoves of the hallway. Lymon came to great double doors, and he pushed them open for her. "Lord Cameron awaits you, mistress."

He ushered her into the room. The doors closed behind her.

She was in his bedchamber. It was a huge room with a canopied four-poster bed to the right of a large stone mantel. Huge Elizabethan chairs faced the fire around a circular, inlaid table. By the windows was a large desk, angled so as to make the most of the sunlight. There were brocade drapes tied away from the window. There was another door, which stood ajar and led to a dressing room and privy. It was fine; it was a palace. She could be mistress of it all! she told herself.

Then her eyes wandered to the bed, for there would lie the crux of it all. To marry him gave him the right to have her. To touch her whenever he chose. A shiver ran down her spine.

He was seated casually upon the thick carved windowsill, staring out at the day. He wore only a white shirt, plain brown breeches, and his high boots. He stared at the sun, and his arms were crossed over his chest. He did not turn to face her.

"Mistress Dupré, to what do I owe this honor?"

She tried very hard to speak, but no sound came. "I—"

He turned to her, and his eyes fell upon her sharply. "Come, come, speak up! You can do much better than that. I cannot believe that the cat could have gotten the better of your very adroit tongue!"

Anger smoldered within her.

"You could make things easier!"

"What things? I have no idea what you're talking about."

"You do!"

He arched a brow. He leapt from the windowsill and walked around her, smiling. "You want me to help you, mistress? Well, then, I shall try. Have you come, perhaps, to see if my marriage proposal still remains open?"

She couldn't go through with it. She hated the way he scorned her with his simple words.

She had to go through with it. She would not live as her mother had, nor would she die that way. She lowered her head and nodded.

"I thought so. Now, let me guess." He strode around her again, slowly, rubbing his jaw. "You awoke in the middle of the night with the sudden and amazing vision that you were deeply and desperately in love with me, and you could hardly bear another night without me. No? Ah, alas, I did not think so. Let's try again. You woke up in the middle of the night with the sudden and startling realization that you would never get such an offer again. That you would be a lady—not that I think titles matter to you much. Ah, but you would be a rich lady. A very rich lady. Money. That is it, isn't it?"

She kept her head lowered. She locked her jaw and remained silent.

"Isn't it!" he snapped, and he came before her and jerked her chin up.

"Yes! Yes, that is it exactly!" she cried, wrenching from his hold. "I never pretended to love you—I never pretended to like you! This has been a bizarre accident and nothing more!"

"But you are determined now that you will marry me. A man whom you hate."

The passion left her. She lowered her head. "Yes."

He was silent. She lifted her eyes at last, and she could read nothing from his harsh, dark gaze. "I don't always hate you," she said. Then she emitted an impatient oath. "Why offer, then? You have no love for me. Why do you make this proposal?"

"I, at least, want you," he said softly. He grabbed her hand suddenly and pulled her over to the canopied bed, and he cast her upon it. He clutched the canopy rod and stared down upon her. "This is my bed, mistress. If you go through with this, you will have no room of your own, you will join me here. Nightly. You will not have headaches, nor will you suffer distress. And you are still willing to marry me?"

She furrowed her brow. The image of the dirty attic room and the death's-head rose before her.

"Yes," she said coldly.

He laughed then, and pulled her up. "You are a whore," he told her.

She lunged at him furiously, and he caught her wrist. He did not pull her close but just held her. "If you would engage in battle, my love, be assured that I will ever be ready to enjoin it. Take care, lest the injury you would inflict upon me fall home upon you. I saved you from Henry's wrath only because I had made up my mind that I would wed you. I think a few more lashes would have stood you well, but should they ever be administered, I think I would prefer to raise the rod myself."

"Let go of me!" she raged, jerking her wrist.

He quirked his brow. "Come, love! Are those the words of a tender fiancée?" He held her a moment longer, then released her. He returned to his window seat, and she saw then that he had a number of documents there and had been studying them before her arrival. He had dismissed her, she thought. And she was all too glad. She was ready to turn and flee.

"The wedding will be on the first of June, as I have said. I shall send the dressmaker today, for there is very little time. Tell her that she is free to hire as many seamstresses as she deems necessary to finish your wardrobe by June. Jane and Lenore have excellent taste if you wish advice, though I wonder if you are not as talented with style as you are with accent and manner. I shall send a purse to Henry for anything else you might require before the wedding."

"There is nothing that I will require."

"What? You are marrying me for money, and you are shy about taking it?"

She did not know how to tell him that she was marrying him not so much for money as she was for the mere security of steady meals, a soft bed, and a sturdy roof over her head. For heat against the chill of winter and bread against the bite of hunger.

"There is nothing that I require," she said simply.

He was silent for a moment. She wondered what he thought as he watched her. "That will be to your discretion," he said at last, and he turned his attention back to his documents.

Jassy didn't move. Now that the arrangement had been made and she had refused his purse, she thought of a few things she might have done with it. She cleared her throat, and then was annoyed with herself for her manner. When he looked up at her again, clearly irritated by the interruption this time, she spoke sharply. "There are a few things that I would—that I would like done."

"You will be mistress of the house. You may do as you please."

She lowered her head. "Molly . . . the girl at the tavern. She was very good to me. Always. May I bring her here?"

"You may. I'll have her sent for. She can be here for the wedding."

"And . . . and Tamsyn too?"

"Tamsyn?"

"He was a doctor once, I believe. He works at the tavern."

"That old drunk—"

"He is not an old drunk. He is a man down upon his luck. I can make him work well. He will be sober, I swear it!"

Jamie shrugged. "The servants are your domain. I have vast holdings, and we shall need many of them. Hire whom you will. If this Tamsyn can be found with Molly at Master John's tavern, then I will see to it that he comes here with Molly. Is there anything else?"

She shook her head. He waited. She moistened her lips.

"Thank you," she managed to say to him, and then she fled.

———

The dressmaker came that afternoon, and the afternoon after, and the afternoon after that. Her small room became filled with velvets, taffetas, silks, laces, linens, and brocades. She was fitted for day dresses and evening dresses, warm dresses and summer wear. She was to have several warm muffs, jewelry, caps, elegant hats, and fashionable purses. Jane and Lenore were very much into the spirit of things. Jane produced numerous fashion dolls from Paris. "One must be careful, though, for the king was raised by strict Presbyterians. Alas, fashion hasn't changed much! At least the ruffs are gone. I remember as a little child that we had to wear them. So uncomfortable!"

"The queen is very fashionable," Lenore protested.

"Anne of Denmark adds jewels to old styles!" Jane complained.

Jassy barely heard them. She watched her wardrobe grow around her. Sometimes she would touch the soft fur that rimmed a collar or a sleeve, and she would marvel that such beautiful, costly things could be hers. Then she would realize that the cost of a single muff might have saved her mother's life and she would be morose again. The days were rushing forward. May passed in a blaze of glory.

On the twentieth of the month, Jamie came to dinner. He and Henry were cordial friends again. Henry, in fact, considered himself the extreme benefactor. Thanks to his good graces, Jassy had been given the opportunity to rise above her station in life.

The meal was good, duckling and early vegetables, but Jassy could barely eat. She could hardly lift her glass to her lips. Robert was with Jamie, and he and Lenore were planning their own wedding. It would take place two weeks after Jassy's.

Jassy was seated next to Jamie. She could not speak to him, nor could she join into the other conversations. Lenore laughed and said that it was nerves. Jamie commented that it certainly was.

When the meal was over, Jassy fled outside. She went to the stables, and to her mare. Robert found her there again. Bitterly she remembered the first time he had met her there.

He kissed her soundly on the cheeks. "Ah, Jassy, it has come well for you, hasn't it? Had I but had Jamie's resources, it might have been different. You are so beautiful."

"And you are a man betrothed to my sister," she said to him.

"The sister with the dowry," he murmured.

"Be good to her," Jassy warned.

He laughed. "Oh, I will be. Lenore is a beauty too. There's something about you, though, Jassy. Alas, it is my best friend to wed you. You've come so very far. Who would have imagined this of the wench in the tavern?"

"The wench in the tavern makes her own way, Robert," Jamie said, entering the barn. Jassy did not like the sizzle in his eyes. It was harder than usual.

"Robert was congratulating me," she said.

"So he was."

"I'm happy for both of you," Robert said, and grinned. "Ah, a haystack! I shall leave you two young lovers alone."

Jamie remained at one end of the stables. Jassy nervously stroked the mare at the other.

"Strange, how it comes to mind the way that I found you two together the last time I was here."

"There was no contract between us then," she said.

"Ah, but there is a contract now. I've even the king's blessing upon my endeavor."

Jassy held quiet for a moment. He was still; he had not raised his voice. Yet she sensed the leashed fury of him down the length of the stalls, and she spoke defensively. "There was nothing between us."

"Did I say that there was? I accused you of nothing."

"Because there is nothing to accuse me of."

"I came quickly."

"You are absurd."

"You claimed to be in love with him once. I am merely hoping that you have curbed the emotion."

"Don't threaten me."

"My love, this is no threat. This is a deep and grave promise. If I ever find you so close with any man again, you will find the lashing you received from your brother to have been a tap on the hand, and nothing more, compared with what you shall receive from me."

Jassy urged Mary back into her stall with all the control that she could summon, then she started walking down the length of the stable. He was between her and the doorway. She tried to walk around him. He blocked her.

She tried again. This time he caught her shoulders. She cast her head back and stared at him coldly.

"Please, milord, take your hands from me."

"You are something!" he murmured. "Airs and graces lie all about you."

"You are about to marry me. I thought that you wished me to play the part of a lady."

He shook his head. "Not in front of me, mistress. Not in front of me. For I swear, I will strip those airs and graces from you."

"Never, milord. Now, may I step by you?"

His hand moved. It traveled from her shoulder to her throat. He cupped her chin and she held still. She willed herself not to shiver, not to betray the rampant tempest that played throughout her like a storm, hot and windswept. His fingers moved down her throat. He spoke to her harshly.

"Aye, mistress, you are beautiful." He lowered his face to hers. His lips touched hers. They were gentle enough at first, then they moved with force. She was in his arms, her mouth was parted, and he played within it easily and with leisure, with the wet blade of his tongue. She clung to him, for she could not stand. The weakness seized her, and the shivering came violently.

She tore away from him, afraid of the volatile emotions and sensations inside her.

"Please! Let me by. We—"

"We what?"

"We are not married yet."

He smiled with humor, with the patient grace of a stalking tiger.

"Alas. We are not married—yet. But that is soon to be rectified, isn't it?"

She started to run by him. He caught her arm once again. "No cold feet, milady?"

She looked from his hand upon her to his eyes and back down to his hands again. "No cold feet, my Lord Cameron."

"You haven't forgotten that I shall expect everything from you. And that I am not a patient man."

"I have forgotten nothing."

"It is all an unfortunate price that must be paid."

"Yes, yes! What difference does it make?"

For the briefest of moments she thought that he appeared disappointed in her. Then he seemed nothing more than hard and cold and ruthless again.

"There is no difference to any of it, Jassy. No difference. We both know what we want, and we are going for it. You are the adventurer, as much as I. The savage heart, my love." He released her. "Go. Run. You've only a matter of days left now. Oh, my father will be coming by in the next few days. Be cordial to him."

"Why? Shall he command you not to marry me? Shall he stop your allowance?"

He touched her again, his fingers digging into her arm cruelly. "I do as I choose, mistress, in all things. You had best remember that. And my fortune is my own, I receive an allowance from no man. You will be decent to him, at your most courteous best, because he is a fine old man, and I would have him think that I chose a beauty for her spirit, rather than that I made a deal with a harlot, my money for her person."

She jerked away from him, blinking furiously at the tears that stung her eyes. "May I go now, my Lord Cameron?"

"You may. Oh, I have your friends. They are already situated at the manor."

"Molly? And Tamsyn?"

"Yes. Both of them are with me."

She hesitated and lowered her head. "Thank you. Thank you very much," she told him. Then she ran back to the house.

Three days later his father, the Duke of Carlyle, arrived in a magnificent coach. Jane and Henry sat with her in the receiving room while she greeted him.

He was a wonderful man. She had trembled before meeting him, wondering if he would despise her as a strumpet who had ensnared his son. He greeted her as if Jamie had chosen a grand duchess for his bride. As tall as his son, with the same dark, flashing eyes, he reached out his arms to her and stood on no ceremony. "Welcome, Daughter," he told her, and he took her into his arms.

She nearly burst into tears but managed to avoid them. He did not speak of her past, he spoke of the future. Jane teased him and they all laughed, and when the duke had departed, Jassy tried to run out of the room. Jane called her back. "Jassy, whatever is wrong? Papa was not so bad, was he?"

She shook her head. She was going to burst into tears. "Your father is wonderful," she said. And then she ran, and Jane did not try to stop her.

The wedding came too soon. The morning dawned ominously dark, with rumbles of thunder and lightning. Kathryn, Elizabeth, Jane, and Lenore ignored the weather. They all met in Jassy's room early, decking her out in her wedding gown. It was in ivory satin, with pearls and glass beads sewn throughout it. The bodice was low, and lined with white fox. She wore a tiara of diamonds that held her veil in place, and the veil, too, was embroidered and studded with pearls and little sapphires.

Jassy stood still the entire time they dressed her. She could eat nothing, she could drink nothing. She clenched her hands nervously, and released them again and again.

At one o'clock it was time to go down. Henry called for the carriage, and she was handed into it. They arrived at the old Norman church in the village within minutes, and she was handed out of the carriage. Thunder cracked and rolled. "Get in, get in!" Henry urged her impatiently.

He would give her away. Robert was to stand as Jamie's witness, and Jane as her own. Jane and Elizabeth walked down the aisle before her, and then Henry tugged on her arm. "Jasmine!" he urged her. "Now!"

She started to walk. Jamie was at the end of the aisle, resplendent in black breeches and doublet and a red silk shirt and silk hose, his hair just curling over the lace at his collar. He watched her as she came down the aisle, and he betrayed neither impatience nor pleasure. As usual, she did not know at all what he was thinking.

Suddenly she was there, beside him, and she was handed over to him. She felt his touch, his hand hot, his fingers a vise upon her own. She felt the startling heat of him, as he was close. She saw his clean-shaven cheeks and breathed in the scent of him. She was trembling again before the service ended. She could not speak her vows, and the priest had to prompt her twice. Jamie stared at her curiously, a smile curving his mouth. She managed to answer.

He spoke his own firmly, with no hesitation.

Then it was over. He kissed her, and kissed her freely, and the young men in the pew called to him with laughter. Robert cleared his throat, and told Jamie that they must depart; the wedding feast awaited them.

She left the church in her husband's carriage, suddenly very aware of the band of gold on her middle finger. She moved it nervously, aware that he stared at her while they rode, that he assessed and studied her with curiosity. He moved the curtain on the carriage. "Your prize, milady. Your manor looms before us."

The carriage moved through the gates. When he lifted her down from it, she stared at the beautiful mansion, and a thrill rippled through her. He had called her "milady," and it was her rightful title now; he had made it so. And this was her home.

If she could just keep from thinking that the night must come!

"Come, love," he whispered to her. The other carriages were arriving. He lifted her off her feet and into his arms, and he carried her over the threshold of the house for luck. Applause followed them, and then the manor came alive. Liveried servants were everywhere, supplying guests with plates and crystal glasses of wine and ale in the hallway. Her father-in-law kissed her, and Jane kissed her, and Elizabeth gushed, and even Henry kissed her. She was introduced to nobility and gentry, for she was a lady now, the wife of Lord Jamie Cameron.

It was a fairy tale. She was the bountiful mistress of this. She had become a princess, and this was her palace.

"You should have taken your bride to Paris," Lenore told him good-naturedly. "I should have demanded it."

"Ah, but my bride could have demanded and demanded, and it couldn't have been, for I sail in two weeks. No . . ." He paused, and his gaze lingered as it fell over Jassy. "In the time we have as newlyweds, I shall seek the comfort of my bed, the service of my trusted friends here."

Jassy turned away. Her head was pounding. Musicians began to play, and she was happy to dance. She even laughed when she danced with Robert, for he was always funny, and he was able to lift her mood. Until she discovered Jamie watching her again. Still, she wanted the music to go on and on. But, of course, it couldn't.

And finally the last carriage rolled away. Lymon announced that he would seek her council about the household in the morning.

Lymon left them at opposite ends of the hallway. Jamie lifted his wineglass to her.

"I shall give you thirty minutes, Jassy. No more."

She could not breathe. The time of her reckoning had come. She could not set down her own glass and turn to the stairs.

"Thirty minutes. No more," he told her again.

She gripped her glass more tightly and turned to the stairs. She fled up them. She knew the way to his room. She ran into it and closed the door. Leaning against it, she closed her eyes. She swallowed down the last of her wine, and in a sudden pique, she sent the glass flying across the room and into the fire.

"Jassy!"

She looked up, and there stood Molly, all beautifully dressed, her eyes bright and her cheeks rosy. "Molly!" Jassy hurtled herself across the room and into her friend's arms.

"Lord luv you, girl, but you've married a lord! Oh, bless you, lass, and you remembered me and old Tam. Oh, Jassy! We're together again. I cannot believe me own eyes! This fine place is yours!"

She swallowed. Yes, this fine place was hers. The crystal and the silver and the silk and the marble. Fine things, and they were all hers.

Molly mattered more than any of them. "Oh, Molly! How are you? Tell me, how have you been? You look wonderful. I've missed you so. Tell me—"

"Lord luv you, lass! But 'tis your wedding night, and I've no mind to be here when your handsome groom appears. Come, let's undress you. I've laid out your nightgown; now let's get all this off!"

She was tempted to cling to her clothing. Panic was setting in on her again.

Molly set to work. She carefully removed Jassy's veil and gown. Then she made her sit, and she removed Jassy's shoes and stockings and untied the constraining corset. Jassy was down to her shift, and suddenly she turned and clung to Molly.

"I can't do it. I can't go through with it."

"Why, Jassy! It will be nothing. He's a fine, striking man. Many a lass would trade years off her life for the opportunity of one night with such a one! And you're so very beautiful. He will love you with all his heart."

No, he hates me, she thought, but she could not bring herself to say that to Molly.

Molly reached for her shift, and she was suddenly naked and shivering. Then the soft silk nightdress was falling over her shoulders. It was high about her neck, and long to the floor, and the sleeves were long, too, but there was nothing modest about the gown, for it was almost entirely sheer.

There was a knock upon the door. "Oh!" Jassy cried. She tumbled into the big bed beneath the canopy, crawling beneath the sheets and blankets and pulling them tight to her chin. Molly hurried, stuffing her shift into the trunk at the foot of the bed. She raced to the door then, and threw it open, grinning in her broad, country, good-natured way. "Evening, milord!" she said. And then she hurried by him and Jassy was alone.

He entered the room and closed the door. He moved into the room, casting off his doublet and casually allowing it to fall on the trunk at the foot of the bed. Heat coursed to Jassy's face and she watched him with a growing panic. He went on over to his desk, where he poured himself a large measure of some liquor, then sank negligently into the chair before it. His eyes sliced like indigo steel into her soul as he stared pointedly upon her and sipped his drink.

He lifted the glass to her and spoke softly. "So. Here we are, my love, together, alone, at last." He smiled, and his brow arced. "And we are married now, aren't we, milady?" He set his drink down upon the table, and he stood, and there was nothing negligent or casual about him anymore. He strode toward her with purpose and wrenched the covers from her fingers. "Let's see if this bargain is worth its measure, shall we?"

8

ASSY CRIED OUT AT HIS TOUCH. SHE HAD NOT
meant to, but he startled her so when he wrenched upon the
sheets that the sound escaped her. She tried to retrieve her
covers, but they remained tight in his hands while his eyes
condemned her. A dark cast of annoyance tightened his features, and she tried
very hard not to gasp out again. She was no coward, and she didn't fear his anger,
she assured herself. She was indebted to him; he had made her his wife. He had
made her mistress of this glorious house, and he had given her crystal and silver
and silks and gems. But those things meant nothing to him. They were not given
out of love or regard, but as a matter of course. As his horses were well shod, so
would be his wife.

He smiled slowly, cynically, as if he read her mind again. She would have run,
had there been a place to go. But there was nowhere to go. Nowhere but the
streets or the gutter. She was his wife, and she had married him willingly.

"What? Second thoughts, love?"

If only he didn't smile so hatefully, knowing her every thought, reading her
mind! Locking her jaw, she released the covers and fell back against her pillow.
She crossed her arms over her chest, and her eyes snapped with the glow of the
fire as she stared at him.

"I have no second thoughts."

"I see. You have been breathlessly anticipating this moment for many a lonely
night?"

"I have no second thoughts."

"Good." His smile faded. He wrenched the covers from the bed, dropping
them upon the floor. Then he moved away from her, sitting at the foot of the
bed. He cast off his fine buckled shoes, pulled his shirt from his breeches, and cast
it over his head.

Before he had come, the room had been cast in the shadows of the night.
Now it seemed that there were candles everywhere, burning from the desk, from
the trunk at the foot of the bed, from the mantel. The fire that had seemed to
burn low in the grate had cast out only a pale glow, but now the logs snapped
and crackled and hissed, sending out a fierce light. The draperies were pulled
against the night sky, and the massive room seemed very small, for they were
encapsulated within it, just the two of them. Light played and flickered over his
bare back and chest, over muscle and sinew. His shoulders were very broad, and
his back and breast were as bronze as his features, from constant exposure to the
sun. She wondered briefly how he had come to such dark color upon his chest.

She bit softly into her lower lip to keep from shivering as she watched him. The muscles in his arms were very large; they tightened and flexed naturally with his every movement, like those across his chest. They were the arms of a blacksmith, she thought, and not of a lord. All together, he seemed like some heathen then, so paganly bronzed and built, like one of the strange red men he so frequently defended from the new land across the Atlantic.

His shirt fell on top of the covers on the floor. He stood in his breeches and hose. A profusion of short, dark hair grew upon his chest, narrowing to a thin line as it tapered to his waistband, forcing her to wonder what lay beneath the band. She wound her fingers together tightly, praying for some miraculous salvation. She burned one moment and lay cold the next. She willed herself not to bolt, for she was certain he would merely drag her down. She had only to imagine herself somewhere else and she could endure this. She had to endure it, for she had married him.

Paying her scant attention, he walked to his desk, moving silently, with a curious grace and ease, like a great cat in the night. With his thumb he smothered the candle there. He repeated the action with the candle upon the trunk.

And still, Jassy thought, the light blazed too brightly, and Jamie knew too well how to draw out torture. With each second that passed, she trembled more fiercely. She grew more aware of his strength and his manhood, and of one irrefutable fact—that she had married him. She had done so for a life of fine things, and in doing so she had given him the right to her.

He walked to the mantel, his footsteps silent, and smothered out the flame there.

And still, light poured from the hearth. From the dying fire lit against the chill rain of the day, sparks flamed and glowed, casting their glaze upon him. He rubbed the back of his neck, and for a moment Jassy actually thought that he had forgotten all about her.

He had not.

Standing there before the fire, he stripped away his breeches, and then his hose, and they lay where he had dropped them. He turned then to Jassy and came around to where she lay, again his stride so silent, as if she were being stalked, and indeed, she believed that she was. She longed to run. She had to keep reminding herself that she had nowhere to go. She wondered if there was anything that she could say or do to put the moment off, if she could not plea or beg or seek some gentle spot within his heart. She wanted to keep her eyes level with his, but she could not. They fell against the length of him, and her cheeks burned. His stomach was flat and hard, with the delineation of tight muscles. His thighs were long and as hard as his arms, his calves shapely. The trail of dark hair that tapered to his waist tapered below it, too, then flared again to a thick nest, and from that nest his male shaft protruded like a blade—strong, bold, and sure. He approached her with no hesitance and no modesty, but with firm and unfaltering purpose.

He did not smile. There was no mockery to him then, and neither was there humor. He planted his hands upon his hips and stared down upon her coldly. "Off with the gown."

She backed herself against the bed as best she could. She willed her fingers to cease trembling, but they would not. She hated his proprietary tone of voice, and she was suddenly determined that she would fight him.

"If you had the least bit of care, milord, you would not force the issue this evening."

"What?"

"Perhaps in time—"

"Get the gown off, milady. Now."

"Robert Maxwell would never have behaved so crudely! He'd have given his bride the time to know him."

"Madame, you know me, and you do know me well! So your dreams are of Robert Maxwell still. Then know this, Jassy. I am not Robert Maxwell, and if naught else at the end of this evening, you will know that for a certainty." His words were clipped; a pulse ticked in his throat. She thought that she had seen him angry before, and yet this sudden wrath he unleashed seemed more terrible than any ire she had provoked in him before. In fear, she lashed out.

"You have the manners and finesse of a wild boar," she told him scathingly.

There was no challenging him. "And you, my dear," he said, leaning over her, his palms upon the headboard on either side of her head, "have the scruples, manners, and morés of a London slut."

Jassy cried out, lifting her hand against him in fury. She caught his cheek, and the mark of her fingers burned brightly against it. His lip tightened, and in a split second he wrenched her to her feet. She was barely standing before the bodice of her sheer white gown was caught between the power of his strong bronze hands and ripped asunder. She swore as the soft material fell to her feet and they were left naked together. She slammed her hands against his chest, as he lifted her into his arms, and the ruthless darkness of his eyes blazed into her own as he walked the few steps back to the canopied bed.

"You bastard!" she cried out to him. "So this is nobility! This is the behavior of a lord!"

"You play the grande dame well, Jassy, very well. But in our particular circumstance I find your modesty a jest, and though your airs are very pretty and will certainly have their place, I promise that you'll not bring them into this bed with you." So saying, he tossed her upon it. There was nothing to grab to shield her from his relentless gaze, for the covers were gone. There was nothing, nothing at all. No barrier against his slow, critical scrutiny of every inch of her body. She lay still and miserable beneath his gaze.

"Have you no mercy whatsoever?" she demanded, "Are you forgetting that I —that I—"

"That you are innocent, my love? Oh, it is a strange form of innocence, but I do not forget it."

"We could wait—"

"Preferably until I leave? Alas, no, love. I get little enough from this contract as it is. No wealth, no riches, no titles. Your dowry lies in the verdant field before me, and as it is all, I would avail myself now. So come. You are the consummate actress! Welcome your lord and husband, lady."

"Oaf!"

Tears stung her eyes. She swore that she would not shed them. Then he came down upon her, once again moving as silently, as powerfully, as sleekly as a great cat. He stretched out his naked length upon her, taking her into his arms. She struggled against him in silence, her fingers upon the hot, muscled feel of his arms, her legs trapped beneath the casual curve of his own. She could not move him; she could only feel him more fully, his chest against her breasts, his limbs entangled with hers; his sex, hard and prominent, seemed ablaze against the apex of her thighs. She went very still. He was all steel. He did, for a moment, let his indigo eyes blaze above her, then his fingers threaded into the hair at her nape, and his lips fell upon hers.

He did not hurt her. His mouth molded slowly over her own, and when his lips had possessed hers, he pried them open and filled her mouth with his tongue. A curious warmth filled her. The heat that he always brought about was like a fire that rippled and cascaded along her spine, but it entered into her, and it came from within her too. It swept from the liquid warmth of his tongue to her lips, and it came from the encompassing and volatile heat of his body, pressed hard to hers. It came from the pulsing masculine blade of him, as insinuative as the stroke of his tongue within her mouth. In and out and sweeping, and deep within her again, until she was breathless. He freed his hand from her hair. He cupped her breast as he kissed her, his fingers winding around the firm weight of it. His thumb grazed over the rose crest of it, and he rubbed that peak between his thumb and forefinger. She shuddered at the streak of sensation that bolted through her, from that touch, to the very core of her. A streak like a sizzle of lightning, so very hot.

She was terrified of that heat, frightened that it might seize her completely, and if it did, then she would have no defense against him ever again. He did not love her, he scorned her, he called her whore. She could not give anything to him. Nothing.

She twisted her lips from his and drew in a ragged breath. His face was over hers again, hard and taut and relentless, "Please!" she hissed. "Do what you will, but must . . . must you kiss me?"

He went dead still, then she felt the furious shudder that rippled through his hard body, and she saw the dark contortion of his features. She had wounded him, and for a moment she was glad, for she often hated his smugness.

Then she cried out, for as his eyes locked with hers, he caught her knee, and with swift and brutal determination he parted her legs, and his weight fell between them. "We shall have it your way . . . milady," he told her. "But have you this evening, I shall."

His hand moved down the length of her, along her thigh. He lifted her legs high against him, and she swallowed sharply when she felt the touch of his hand intimately upon her. His eyes remained hard upon hers. She knew then that she could have cried out, that she could have whispered a single word, just one plea, and he would have taken her differently, more gently, tenderly, even. Perhaps. But she could not whisper that single word; she could not plead, and she could admit to nothing, give nothing. She would not ask for mercy. She clenched her teeth, her lashes fell over her eyes, and she shivered against the raw honesty of their bodies together, terribly aware of all of him, of the naked sexuality that lay between them. Still, she would beg no quarter, would seek no mercy.

And she would receive none. She felt the hard, pulsing shaft of his sex against her, then thrusting, plunging, deep, deep, within her. Blatant and bold and with no hesitation, he claimed her. Then she choked and screamed, and stretched and struggled to free herself, like a trapped and panicked animal, for she had never imagined such a searing pain. The size and breadth of him were too much; he would tear her apart.

Instantly he went still. She trembled, choking on her tears, wishing that she could free herself from him. He swore, and she did not know if it was at her, or at himself.

"Easy," he told her softly.

"You are—killing me!" she told him brokenly. The intimacy was unbearable. He was a part of her. He lay atop her and within her. All that was personal and vulnerable lay naked and open to him. His breath mingled with her own, and their heartbeats were one upon the other.

"You will not die, I assure you. Women have been accommodating men since the beginning of time," he said wryly. She met his eyes again. He held himself very still, staring at her, and still he was there. She could barely meet his gaze, and neither could she look away. "Part your lips," he told her.

"I—"

"Part your lips to mine. Part your lips, and lay still to my touch. Cease to fight me."

He dipped his head, and the tip of his tongue flicked over her mouth and delved into it. Then the blaze of his kiss ran a path down the length of her throat. His tongue laved over the valley between her breasts, then circled the nipples, and then the full weight of each of her breasts. And all the while she felt him within her, still but pulsing with life, so alien, so ferociously alight with fire and promise. The pain was keen, and she lay still herself, with each new intimate assault upon her senses, with the practiced play of his mouth and hands upon her.

The pain began to fade. The warmth filled her. She parted her lips to his command, and she did not protest his hands upon her body. He stroked her breasts until she cried out, and still she was aware of the hardness of him inside her, achingly aware of the sexual intimacy. And acutely aware of the combustile warmth. She could not give in to it. She must never give in to it. . . .

Suddenly he withdrew from her. The burning was still all about her. She wondered with rising hope if he meant to leave her be now, if that was all . . .

It was not. It was to be worse. His eyes upon her, he stroked the length of her torso with his hands. He covered her breasts, came down to her waist, and lifted her buttocks. He raised her high. She gasped and cried out, burning crimson that he should look at her so, then she realized his design, and she cried out in protest. "Nay, oh, please—"

"Lie still, madame. I will ease your pain."

"No! No—"

But the complete, intimate invasion had begun. Her fingers wound into the bed sheet, and she tossed her head, continuing to protest. It stood her no stead, for he took his leisure. She tried not to think, but she had never felt anything more keenly in her life, not the pangs of hunger, not the fear of death, not the promise of heaven. With a touch of sizzling, wet fire he stroked her and laved her, and she burned with a terrible ache, felt a crimson tide threaten to seize her. She twisted and writhed and begged him to cease. He touched and probed and laved her again. She wanted to die and felt that she could.

Then he released her. He crawled over her and thrust deep inside of her once again, and when he was there, the feel of him was absurdly right. He filled her still, a massive blade that cut inside her, but her body gave to his. Where her heart could not give, her form surrendered, and she yielded to his command.

When he began to move, she gasped. Her fingers dug into his hair and into his back. He moved slowly at first. His whisper touched, brushed her cheek. "Do I hurt you?"

She shook her head. She could never look at him again. She would never be able to face him. She burned still from that very first thrust, but he caused her no new pain. She buried her face against his shoulder. The scent of him was not unpleasant. It was clean and masculine, and somehow it was better than to be against him.

She shuddered suddenly, fiercely, as a surge of power seized him. It was a storm, a tempest, come upon him. Nothing was slow and nothing was easy, and she clung to him tightly, lest she be lost to the storm. On and on it raged, a tempest of power, of driving thrusts and strokes, of tension, terrible and sweet. She lay there, aware of the rising fire all around her, vaguely aware that something sweet lay within her reach, something that made this wild storm the tempest that it had become for him. She could give in to it, she thought, as he moved against her again and again, indomitable. She could give in to it, to the strength of the arms that held her, to the curious promise of glory.

No, no! She must never . . .

He rose above her high, and he came into her again, shuddering and rigid. He fell against her. Something honeyed entered into her, a warm liquid seeping from his body into hers.

His arm lay over her breasts; his fingers touched her nipple with absolute possession. Jassy felt the burning between her legs, and his casual and negligent touch with his complete assumption of right. It was over. He had taken what he wanted, and now she had no secrets from him. She had been, she was certain, as well used as a woman could be.

She swore savagely. She tossed his arm from her, and she turned and crawled to the far corner of the bed, her back to him. To her dismay, tears spilled down her cheeks.

He never let her be! He touched her shoulder and pulled her back.

"Stop, please, leave me be now, for God's sake!" she demanded.

But he ignored her. His indigo eyes pierced her as thoroughly as his body had done. "I did not seek to hurt you."

"I am not hurt!" she lied.

"I told you that if you married me, you would lie here. You were in agreement."

Her lashes fell over her eyes. She felt his fingers again, light, idly stroking her breasts. "Please!"

"It is never easy the first time, so they say. Damn you! I did not seek to hurt you! 'Tis your tongue; it is a vicious thing, a weapon few men could withstand."

"Does it matter?" She looked up. She did not protest his touch. She gritted her teeth against it, and his hand stopped its movement.

"Nay, madame, perhaps it does not."

He turned away from her. Jassy rolled again to the far side of the bed and curled into a ball. She shivered, but she dared not reach over him to the covers on the floor. She tightened into herself as much as she could. She closed her eyes and tried to imagine being mistress of the house. She thought of the graceful pillars and the beautiful lines, of the crystal and the silver and the gold.

It did not work. All that she could see was the passion in his dark eyes as he moved over her. It still seemed that he was with her. It seemed as if he would always be a part of her from now, until forever. She would never free herself of the feel of him. She had sold her soul and would never find peace.

But she did find it. In time she heard his even breathing. She lay awake, aware of him there. She thought that she would move, that she would find the remnants of her gown, that she would sleep in a chair. But she did not move; exhaustion claimed her and she found the peace she so desperately sought.

———

The instant Jamie awoke, he longed to touch her. He did not, no more so than he did already, for the cold of the night had sent her against him. She lay, beautiful and naked and sleek, against his side. She was at a half curve, her back to him, her arm cast out, her knee curled high. Her breast peeked out from a tangle of hair and the crook of her elbow, and it was such a temptingly ripe fruit, he barely restrained himself.

Yet he did. He stared at her, and he bitterly mocked himself. He had been certain that when he had her in his arms, he could make her come alive! That he could touch a fire and ignite the spirit within her.

He was a fool who had been taken in by a fortune-hunting piece of baggage. He had seen a sensuality in her that did not exist; he had sought a promise that had never been given.

He sighed softly to himself. Well, it was done. He had married her, despite the protest of friend and foe alike, and even the king. She had never pretended not to hate him.

Yet, he thought gravely, it might have been better. Had she not turned from his kiss, and by God, had she not brought Robert's name into their bed, he would have taken a far greater care before touching her in violence. He wondered if it could ever be rectified now, and then he thought of the years and years before them, and it was a chilling thought.

No, he promised himself, he had not made a mistake. She was what he wanted. She was strong and willful, and if she despised him, perhaps that was well, for she would need the power of her emotions to endure the hardships ahead. And all the better for him. He wanted a wife, he needed a wife to complete his life in the New World, and he was determined to have children, many of them. She was young and strong. She could detest every single minute of her duty, but she would accustom herself to it, and she would give him sons.

He wondered what had driven him with such determination to marry her. She was beautiful, but it was not her beauty. Lenore had much of her look—in fact, he had decided that he would marry Lenore, as he desired a wife. But from the beginning Jassy had bewitched him. It was something that he could not touch, not even now, now that he had married her, that he had bedded her at last. It was elusive; he still could not touch it. It was her will, it was her determination, it was the very strength of her hatred and determination. It was the spark in her eyes, the fire . . . fire that he could not tap. . . .

She sighed. Her lips parted, and they were soft and beguiling. By God, he would find it. He would reach for the fire, until it blazed to an inferno, for him.

He touched the tangle of her golden hair, and he drew his finger down the length of her spine and over her buttock. Still sleeping, she stretched, sleek and lovely and sensual. Her breasts jutted out then, and she sighed softly again.

He came behind her. He wrapped his arms around her, pressed his lips against her nape, and filled his hands with the full, round firmness of her breasts. He had never seen a woman more beautiful naked. Her skin was silken, her waist was tiny, and her hips held a fascinating, sensual flare. Her legs were long and very shapely, and her nipples were large and an exquisite deep rose color. It was there! he was certain. It was there, a deep and sultry passion! He tightened his jaw, and he swore savagely to himself that he would find it—and if he did not, he would tame her still. She could vent her rage all she chose—she would learn that it would do her no good.

She sighed softly again in her sleep. He cupped her breast, curved his body to hers from behind, and flicked her nipple with his thumb. She moved against him, awakening. He pressed his lips against her shoulders and ran his hand down her flanks. She arched, then awoke, stiffening.

"Lie still," he commanded her.

"It's morning—"

"Lie still."

"It's light—"

"I like the light."

She swore softly. He ignored it and ran his hands over her buttocks again, lifting her thigh slightly and urging it forward. She turned her head away from him again, some sound escaping her, and he stroked her inner thigh, again and again, roaming every higher. He kissed her nape, bit lightly into her shoulder, and moved his tongue over her upper vertebrae. She lay very still, as he had commanded, and he wondered at her eyes, if they would be filled with fire and hatred, if she would fight him at the end, or if she had determined to honor her bargain. He slipped his thumb into her and felt her stiffen and shudder, but she did not protest, and to his surprise she was even sweetly wet and ready. He entered her from behind, pulled her close, and felt the blind, driving passion seize him. He swept into her stronger and deeper, and then with a raging abandon.

When it was over, she did not cry, scream, or protest. She lay on the bed and stared up at the ceiling, her beautiful sky-blue eyes blank. Entirely irritated, Jamie pulled the bell cord. Jassy came alive then, leaping from the bed. Curiously, after the evening and morning was spent, she still tried to hide herself from him. She sought her gown, and when it came up in shreds, she swore. He did not help her. He sought his wardrobe and donned a robe, and while she was still searching in her trunk for something, there came a knock on the door.

She cast him a scathing glance. He smiled. "Get back into bed. I'll give you the covers. Come in, please, Lymon."

She hurried back into bed. As he had promised, he threw her the covers and she hid herself beneath them. The door opened and Lymon entered. Jamie bid him good morning cheerfully, then asked for milk, coffee, and rolls to be served in the room. "And the hip bath, too, Lymon. With lots of hot water."

Lymon cast a quick glance at the figure beneath the rumpled covers, then promised that it would be done right away. Jamie thanked him. When Lymon was gone, he walked back over to the bed and wrenched the covers from her hold again. "Madame, you are supposed to be found in my bed by morning, you know. You are my wife."

She grabbed for the covers again, coming to her knees, leaping up and seizing the sheets. He watched her movement. He watched the spill of her golden hair over her back, curling to her rump, and he watched the tendrils that fell over her breasts and curled around them. He watched the spark in her eyes, and the angry purse of her lips, and he watched the graceful sway of her hips and the movement of her legs. His eyes wandered to the juncture of her thighs, and he felt his loins tighten and harden.

He wanted her again. He took her and exploded with the force of it, and then he wanted her all over again. He didn't know quite what it was, but he vowed to himself that he would discover it.

"May I have the first bath?" she asked him, tossing back her head of golden curls.

"Certainly. But you cannot wash away this marriage, you know."

"It is not the marriage that I wish to wash away."

"Ah, that's right. Marriage is the manor and the servants and the estate. 'Tis only me you wish to wash away."

"Those are your words."

"Well, think of it. In two weeks I shall be gone."

"Across the ocean," she agreed.

"A perilous trip. Storms plague ships at sea. One never knows when one will meet up with a Spanish pirate."

"I shall pray for you."

He cast back his head and laughed. "I daresay that you shall be praying. But take heed, milady. Unless you bear me an heir, my estates will revert to my father. So perhaps you should pray that I do live for a while."

"Have I no widow's compensation?" she asked him sweetly.

"You do."

"Well, then, that, I imagine, should be sufficient."

He curved his lip into a smile and inclined his head toward her. "Alas, the emotion within you wrings my heart."

"You know I have no feelings for you," she said suddenly, passionately. Her eyes were very wide, somehow frightened, and very blue. "You chose to marry me. Would you have me pretend now?"

"No, love," he said wearily, "we will have no pretense. If nothing else lies between us, let it be honesty."

"You do not care for me!"

"But I do want you. More noble than mere marriage for money, I think."

"I see. Lust is preferable," she said grandly.

"You are an adventuress, Jassy. Perhaps we shall make out very well."

He hesitated, for there was a knock on the door. He raised his voice and said that the caller must enter, and the door opened. Lymon entered with a half score of serving boys. He carried food, while the servants brought the carved wood hip bath and buckets of hot water. The household was very efficient, for while Lymon set out the milk, coffee and rolls, the boys brought more water. They all bowed to Jassy in her nest of covers. She colored and nodded an acknowledgment.

Then they were gone. Jamie poured two cups of coffee and brought her one. She accepted it with a soft "Thank you."

"Breakfast is usually in the dining room," he told her, "and usually much more substantial. In good weather we eat in the back, on the terrace."

She sipped her coffee, then she set down her cup. Jamie watched her broodingly as she suddenly streaked from the bed and into the tub. She howled at the heat of the water, and, he was certain, had he not been standing there, she'd have jumped back out of the water. She sat, though, winding her hair above her head to keep it dry. She realized then that she hadn't the soap or a cloth.

Jamie brought her both, still sipping his coffee. He dropped the cloth and the soap upon her and moved to the mantel, where he had a wonderful view of her. She lifted a long leg and scrubbed it, and then she remembered that he was there. With a scowl she slipped back into the tub.

"Please, don't let me disturb you."

"You do disturb me."

"Do I?"

He set his cup upon the mantel. Her breasts were level with the height of the water, her nipples even with it. She saw the intent in his eyes as he approached her, and she let out a little sound of protest. He barely heard her. A rush of desire raged in his head, and he heard nothing but the driving wind of it. He knelt by the tub and took the soap and cloth in his hands. He laved her breasts with the suds and the piece of linen. "Don't!" she whispered, leaning back, swallowing. He stretched his hand downward and between her legs, and she cried out, but he ignored her. She brought her hands against him, but then they went limp, and she lay back in the tub. Her lips were slightly parted, her eyes closed. Her head rolled back and forth. "Don't . . . please, don't."

He lifted her out of the tub. He laid her down upon the sheets, and when she tried to twist away, they both saw the stains on the sheets where her virginity had been lost. She twisted again and met his eyes. "No . . ."

He unbelted his robe and let it fall to the floor. She closed her eyes again and started to roll away. He straddled her, stopping her, whirling her around to face him.

"I just washed *you* away!" she cried.

He arched a brow. "No, madame. You washed for my pleasure and convenience."

"*Oh!*" She tried to sit. He caught her shoulders and led her back. Her eyes were wild and somewhat panicked as she stared at him then. "Lie still!" he commanded her impatiently. "It should not be loathsome, and you should not feel pain. You should lie there, seeking me, as I seek you."

"No!"

"But you will in time, I swear it."

"You are an insolent pest!"

"Lie still, madame. I will prove it." He took his hands off her. She bit into her lip and tried to squirm from beneath him. "Uh-uh, milady. Still. Unless, of course, you wish to scream and weep and writhe with passion."

She swore again. He laughed, caught her wrists, and pressed her back to the bed. "I will kiss you whenever and wherever I choose, Jasmine," he whispered, and then he set out to prove it.

She did not protest, twist, or fight. Her lips parted easily beneath his, and he kissed her deeply, feeling the rise of passion, of haunting, desperate desire. At last he raised his lips from hers. They remained parted, moist, and her breath came from her in little gasps. Her eyes, glazed and wide, met his. He smiled. Thunder and lightning raged through him, demanding he take her there and then, but he did not. He met her gaze, and his smile was wicked. He held her eyes while touching and playing with her breasts, and moved his hands ever lower and more intimately upon her. She tried to close her eyes. "Look at me!" he told her, and for a moment she did. But then he moved from her and parted her thighs. She closed her eyes again. "No!" she protested in a weak whisper. "No, no . . ."

He caught her foot, kissed the sole of it, and ran his tongue over her toes. He parted her thighs wider. When she tried to bring them back together, he spread them with his shoulders, allowing her no retreat. He stroked her thighs, and then he gave deliberate and piercing attention to the golden triangle of her sex. He took his leisure, touching, exploring, savoring the honey taste of woman and soap, and leaving her drenched. And still she gave nothing to him. She remained as still as he had commanded her to be.

He crawled over her. Her eyes were open and glazed over, and her fingers were knotted into the sheets. She tried too hard to deny him! He swore in silence and caught her knees, then brought them high over his shoulders. He swept into her with a single stroke, and she encapsulated him easily with the sleek, sweet feel of honey. He placed his hands on her shoulders and thrust farther, and she tossed her head to the side. He drove harder into her. She cried out once, and then she was silent. He gritted his teeth, and the storm of his passion swept over him. The explosion of it was violent, and he fell against her, gasping for breath. She curled quickly away from him.

Furious, he caught her shoulder and swirled her back around. "Why? Why, damn you, must you fight me?"

"I did not fight you!" she cried.

"Nay, lady," he said scornfully, "you did not claw or beat me, or try to run, but you fight what you feel yourself. You do not give yourself to me; you deny me every step of the way."

She was trembling. She wanted to escape him. He was so achingly familiar with the beautiful naked length of her now that he could not bear it. He held her hard and fast. "Why?"

"Because I feel nothing!"

"You are a liar!"

"You take what you want; that is all there is!"

He let out a furious oath and moved away from her, stepped into the now-cold bath, and loved it. He washed with a vengeance, aware that she lay immobile on the bed, afraid to move. When he finished, he grabbed a towel and dried himself harshly.

He ignored her while he dressed. His tastes were simple that day, dark breeches and a white shirt and a leather jerkin and his high black riding boots. While he tugged them on, he spoke to her coldly, not glancing her way.

"I am sorry to leave you so, my dear, on the first day of our wedded bliss, but I'm certain that you'll find it in your heart to forgive me. I have to see a man about the supplies for the ship."

He stood. She was on the bed, in a cocoon of covers. She was, he thought, a whore who had married him with no pretense for his money. Well, it was a bargain well met. A bargain crafted in hell. He had married her for her youth and her health and her strength.

And her beauty. Even now, even in his raw anger, he saw that beauty. Her golden hair was completely tangled, and a tempest about her. She was swathed in the covers, but her shoulders were sloping and bare, and the rise of the sheets barely covered the full slopes of her breasts. She looked very young then, and lost and alone and vulnerable. He almost wanted to offer her some assurance.

Vulnerable! he thought with a snort. She was as vulnerable as one of the sharp-toothed barracuda that lurked in the warm southern waters off the American coast. She was hard, as hard as stone. She didn't even play at gratitude.

He did come by her, and run his fingers over the top of her hair. "Take heart, madame. Two weeks is not such a terribly long time. Then you shall not see me for a minimum of four months." He walked on by her, heading for the door.

"Four months!" she said in surprise. "But I thought it took three months to cross the ocean? And three months to come back again. And surely you intend to spend time there—"

"More time than I had thought at first," he told her. He watched her, curious to her reaction. "Much more time. That is why I have decided that you must sail, too, as soon as possible."

"What?" She gasped. She must have been truly stunned, taken completely by surprise, for she forgot her nudity and leapt from the bed, running after him. She seemed small as she grabbed his hand. But then, he was booted and clad, and she was like a golden Eve, naked, with her hair tumbling down about her.

He smiled wickedly; he could not help himself. "Aye, lady. My pinnace, *Sweet Eden,* will leave the London dock on the twentieth of July. You will be upon it with whatever supplies and servants you shall require. My love, you will follow me to the New World."

"No!" She cried with horror.

He tapped her chin closed for her. "Yes, my love."

She shook her head violently. "No! I will not leave England! I will not come to that savage land full of Indians and insects! You have said yourself that it is dangerous. That Spanish pirates roam the seas! That there may be tempests at sea—"

"You will come, madame. And you will come when I command, for you are my wife."

"No—"

"And you will come when I command, milady, because if you don't, then I shall come back for you. And if you force me to do such a thing, then I swear, heaven will need to help you, for you cannot imagine what violent paths my wrath may take, and what tempest it is that you should truly fear."

His smile deepened; he shook himself free of her touch and exited the room, slamming the door sharply behind him.

9

TEN DAYS LATER, AT HER FIRST CHANCE TO EN-
tertain in grand style, Jassy still turned pale at the very mention
of the word *Virginia*.

Robert and Lenore and Henry and Jane and the Duke of
Carlyle and, of course, Elizabeth came for their first visit. Jassy should have found
it her greatest triumph, for she, an illegitimate child of the streets, had come to
reign in grandeur on an estate far grander than her brother's. She was dressed in
the finest fabric, in the newest style, and she entertained with the Venetian
crystal, the Dutch plates, and the English sterling flatware, in the room where the
walls were covered in silk. She had everything that she had coveted within her
hands.

And the man she had married was telling her that she should leave it all behind
and follow him to the savage wilds of a new country inhabited by wild men.

The day had not been without its triumphs. Her father-in-law the duke had
greeted her with warmth and pleasure, telling her that she graced his son's fine
house. Jane had laughed; Henry had muttered that there was, after all, much of
their father within her. Elizabeth had whisked her into a corner where she had
giggled delightedly. "Oh, Jassy! Remember the day when we came here and it
was all pretense? And now it is real. Oh, truly, you are the grand lady!"

Not for long, she thought, but she refrained from speaking, for if this was to be
her one shining moment, she wanted to cling to it. "Come, Elizabeth. What will
you have? some wine?"

"Oh, yes, please! Wine will be grand."

Conversation was casual as they gathered in the blue room, much of it regarding Lenore's coming nuptials. Jassy often felt Robert Maxwell looking her way.
Once she caught him doing so, and he raised his glass to her. She flushed and
quickly looked away, but then, when he found her alone for a moment, she felt a
bitter pleasure in his company. He caught her hands and kissed them both, and
his admiration was unmistakable. "I have never seen you so beautiful. Marriage
becomes you. Or *something* becomes you. You are radiant. I should have swept
you away when I had the chance."

Yes! she wanted to cry. You should have done so!

She remained silent, but she felt her heart pound. A new excitement filled her,
and the day was fun once again. She could forget that she had married a dark,
demanding man who gave no quarter, ever, and even now watched her from his
stance at the mantel. He rested an elbow upon the mantel, but lifted his brandy

snifter to her sarcastically as he caught her eye. Her smile and enthusiasm faded, and she quickly turned away. Still, she felt his eyes upon her.

Their days of newlywed "bliss" had been fraught with tension. Most of the day Jamie was gone, and at night Jassy went up to the room alone. She dressed in the plainest gowns, and feigned sleep the moment she heard his footsteps near their door. And every night he laughed at her attempts to avoid him, and it mattered little what she had chosen to wear, for she did not wear it for long.

She did not fight him, ever. She willed herself to lie still, and she realized that it was herself she had come to fight. He was not cruel to her, nor was he brutal, though she knew that he would have brooked no resistance from her. Every night and each time he touched her, she grew more sensitive to him. Sometimes she ached for his hand before it came to her flesh, and she despised herself for the weakness. She bit into her lip when she would cry out at some sudden sensation, and she forced herself to remain still and impassive. She knew that he watched her, and she knew that he was vastly disappointed in her. She had to resist him. There was so little that was hers, and hers alone, to give.

So it had been . . . she thought pensively, until the last two nights had passed them by. On the first she had pretended sleep, and he had allowed her the deception, lying on his side of the bed, staring up at the canopy. To her surprise, she had lain awake very late, stunned that he had not touched her.

Then last night he had said wearily that she should snuff out the candles when she crawled into bed. And again he had ignored her, and again she had lain awake a long, long time.

To add fuel to the fires of discord, Jamie's mind was on his coming voyage. Jassy was determined not to join him, and she argued with him at every opportunity. And at every opportunity he argued back, and informed her that she would do as she was told. If she wasn't careful, he would demand that she come with him on the *Hawk* when he left on the fifteenth.

"Truly, Jassy, you look marvelous today. The lady born and bred. More noble than any of us!" Robert said, laughing ruefully and drawing her from her introspection.

"Thank you, Robert," she said.

"And you, Jamie. How do you find marriage, now that you have succumbed to the state at long last?"

Jassy felt Jamie's eyes upon her. "I find it deeply rewarding," he said. "Infinitely . . . rewarding. And intriguing."

They were spared further conversation on the subject, for Lymon came to the door, announcing that Captain Hornby was there.

"He begs not to disturb a private party," Lymon said, addressing Jamie.

Jassy was somewhat startled when Jamie deferred to her. "My love, what an unexpected guest, a man of esteemed character." He watched her still, and she wondered if he tested her. She wondered if he ever spoke with Robert and told him what a disappointment he really considered her to be. She did not believe so, but neither could she be grateful for the fact that if his marriage was less than he hoped, he gave no hint of such a thing in public. He was a proud man and would never admit to defeat.

"Good old Hornby?" Robert said. "Is he really here?"

"You must invite him in, Lymon," Jassy said. Lymon bowed to her and left them.

"A wonderful old soul," Robert said cheerfully to Jassy.

"Robert, really! What a way to refer to the poor man!" Lenore protested, but she smiled, taking the sting from her words. Maybe she really was in love with him, Jassy thought. She had grown far more gentle as of late.

"Well, love, he is old. He was old when Jamie first sailed with him in '08. He must be ancient now."

"And the finest mariner I have ever met," Jamie said. Then Lymon was back with the man in question.

He *was* old, Jassy thought. His hair was snow white, as were the whiskers at his chin, and his face was heavily lined. He had bright green eyes, though, and he walked with the agility of a man half his age.

Captain Hornby apologized for the interruption, and assured Jamie that they could speak later. Jassy insisted he sit and have a drink, and he chose whiskey. She was glad that Lymon served the drink, for with Jamie's next words, her fingers trembled in sudden spasms.

"Captain Hornby sails the *Sweet Eden,* my love. He will bring you to me in the Virginia colony."

"Oh!" Lenore cried suddenly, looking at Jamie. "So Jassy is to come?"

"Aye, Jassy is to come."

Lenore turned to her. "Oh, I'm ever so glad."

"Why?" Jassy asked.

"Oh, well, you see, Robert has determined that we must sail too. He wishes to take his chances with Jamie, and seek his fortune in Virginia."

Jassy shook her head, forgetting her husband. "But, Robert, you are a fool! The land is full of warring heathens—"

"Oh, lady, nay, not so much as before!" the good captain said, interrupting her.

"No, it is not so bad as it once was," the Duke of Carlyle told her, gazing affectionately at his son. He took Jassy's hand in his own. "There were bad times, of course. When Captain Smith and the others arrived in 1607, the Indians were hostile. Some of the party believed that Powhatan's people might have been responsible for the annihilation of the Roanoke colony at the end of last century. There have been reports of curiously light boys among their number, so perhaps the survivors were taken in by the confederation tribes."

"The Indians had some good reason for hostility," Jamie said from his stance at the mantel. "They had seen French and Spanish and English ships in the Chesapeake by the time the Jamestown settlers arrived. In 1524 Giovanni da Verrazano, Gomez the year after, and in 1560, Pedro Menendez de Aviles, who captured and enslaved the son of a werowance."

"A heathen spiritual leader," Captain Hornby informed Jassy.

"They all came with their guns blazing ceremonially, and few came in peace."

"Ah, Lord Cameron!" Captain Hornby said. "You should know that the heathens are not so peaceful themselves!" He looked at Jassy. "He knows, milady, your husband does! On his first voyage he went with Captain John Smith up the peninsula to find Powhatan. It was the starving time, and the men were desperate to secure food. Powhatan tricked Captain Smith. Pocahontas warned them of the trick, and they survived. And the heathens are savage to their captives. Why, they mutilate their prisoners. They dismember them and throw the body parts into the fire to burn while they still live and breathe, and then they disembowel them."

"Captain Hornby!" Jamie said sharply.

"I believe I'm going to faint!" Lenore gasped.

"Elizabeth *has* fainted!" Jassy cried. She was quickly on her feet, and she managed to catch her sister before she could fall. Then Jamie was beside her, lifting Elizabeth, carrying her to the massive chair before the fire. Her eyes flickered and opened. Someone had brought water for her. She looked about.

"Oh, I am sorry! So very sorry."

"Nay, milady!" Captain Hornby apologized. "It is I who am sorry. I am not accustomed to the company of ladies. Forgive me."

"You are forgiven, and gladly," Elizabeth said. She looked up at Jassy and smiled wanly. "Well, don't you see? If you go, and Lenore goes, then I must go too."

"Don't be mad!" Jassy said harshly. "You have a beautiful home here. You needn't risk any of it. You won't be alone. Jane and Henry will be here. And—and we will be back as soon as possible."

No one said anything. Jassy realized that the silence was for her sake. Jamie was demanding that she come, because he knew that he would be gone for a very long time.

"I want to come with you," Elizabeth said, and she squeezed Jassy's hand.

"You are a wonderful, brave girl," Jamie told her, "and we will be delighted to have you."

Elizabeth smiled radiantly.

Jassy glanced quickly at her husband. She had always struggled too desperately through life to pay much heed to the news of distant lands, but men in the tavern had often spoken of the Jamestown colony. She had heard of the "starving time." Over nine hundred settlers had traveled to Jamestown by that time. After Indian raids, disease, and starvation, only sixty or so had survived. She couldn't imagine that a man of Jamie Cameron's means could have risked his life on such a foolish quest.

She still hated him for even contemplating such a thing now.

"Other than the Indians, it was still a bad time, the starving time," Captain Hornby said. "Why, white men, good English men, feasted upon the dead of their own kind."

"Captain!" Robert warned, "the ladies!"

"If the ladies are to travel to Virginia, perhaps they had best hear it all," Jane said softly. "Are you all right now, Elizabeth?"

"Oh, yes, I—I am fine."

"They ate Indians that year too," Captain Hornby said cheerfully. "One fellow went mad and murdered his wife. Then he salted and ate her."

"Captain, enough!" Jamie warned.

"And we call the Indians the savages," Henry commented with disgust. "I am glad that you are the lot that has chosen to go." He affectionately touched his wife's protruding belly. "My son will be born on this land, as a good Englishman should be born."

"A good Englishman? Henry, we've all heard of an instrument called the Earl of Exeter's daughter, a good English torture device named for the charming man who invented it." Jamie smiled at Jassy. "The rack, my love. The good, civilized, English rack. We disjoint and cripple and maim more slowly than the savages, perhaps."

"Powhatan was a crafty old warrior," Captain Hornby warned.

"Powhatan is dead."

"That is true, and when his brothers, Opitchapan and Opechancanough, shared the rule of the Powhatan Confederation, it seemed that peace might be assured. But I am not so sure. Now Opechancanough rules alone. He is a crafty one, I'll wager. Much like his brother."

"Thank God I'm not having my child there!" Jane said, and shuddered.

Jassy's stomach churned. She couldn't imagine bearing a child in the wretched wilderness in which her husband was determined she would live. The child would die, she would die, they would all die.

"It sounds like a horrible place," Jassy said aloud.

"Oh, no, milady, that it is not!" Captain Hornby protested. "I'll grant you, milady, that there was confusion at the first. A profusion of leaders. There was Edward Wingfield, who was unpopular for his Catholicism, Captain Newport, and John Smith himself. Lord de la Warr made it just in time to save the colony when the survivors were leaving in '09. He was a harsh man, but he saved the colony, he did. There have been a number of charters." He hesitated, looking at Jamie. "The Company did not always make the right decisions, and the king did not always judge the situation well, being here while the colony was there. With the lottery disbanded, one of the principal means of income has been lost, but now the tobacco crop flourishes, and the colony is making money of its own. Not that any of it will matter to you, milady," he told Jassy. "The hundred is not Jamestown."

Jassy stared reproachfully at Jamie.

He shrugged. "The hundred is my own land, and we are not subject to the rule of Jamestown. We will abide by the laws of England there. At the Carlyle Hundred we will be self-sustaining. We've already many families living there. Five carpenters, three gentlemen of means, fifteen farmers, ten laborers, two bricklayers, two tailors, two blacksmiths, and three masons, and all their diverse servants and so on. I interviewed them all myself before they sailed, and I am certain that we shall prosper."

Why did he care? She wanted to scream it, to demand it. She wanted to cry and rail that he was a fool, but she could not do so, not here, not now. She had company, and her company, all but Elizabeth, still watched her for some flaw in the porcelain mask of her manner. She would not let them find a flaw. She stood. "I'm sure that our dinner is served. Shall we adjourn to the dining hall?"

With murmurs they all rose and left the room for the hall. Jassy realized that Jamie hung behind, that he watched her until the room had emptied. She paused. "Well, have I passed inspection? Do I manage well enough?"

"You manage well enough. You know it."

"Not that it will matter. An actress's bastard child can surely greet a heathen tribe of Indians as well as a grand lady."

"I'm sure that you will do well, my pet, whichever and whomever you choose to be." Calmly he strode by her. She hesitated, breathing hard, hating him.

He waited for her before the doors to the dining room. He took her hand. "You do sparkle today."

"Do I?"

"Is it because Robert Maxwell is here?"

"You must think what you will, milord."

"And you may think what you will, but I have determined that I will find the woman with the sparkling eyes tonight. When the company has gone, when we are alone."

"She is the same woman you're standing beside."

"She is not. But so help me, lady, I will meet her, in my bed, this very night."

"This is a crude conversation. We've guests."

"I will crush those airs, lady, mind you." He did not lead her into the dining room but propelled her there with a hard shove upon the back. No one noticed them, though, for Lenore was busy chuckling, demanding to know what clothing was worn in the wilds.

"Oh, it's all very civilized," Captain Hornby assured her. "Men wear what is proper, as prescribed by Parliament in the days of good Queen Bess. For laborers, homespun linen or canvas jerkins, breeches, and hose. On Sundays they wear their best, with their flat caps, while the gentry, and nobility, milady, deck themselves out in their finest, in their taffetas and satins, decorated with embroidery and slashes and pinking. You needn't fear. None has forgotten that it is a God-fearing, English community! There are some concessions, of course, to the wilderness. But I believe you will be heartily pleased with the goodness of the colonial manners and ways."

"Well, that is encouraging, isn't it, Jassy?" Lenore said. Jassy offered her a halfhearted smile and wondered how Lenore could be so cheerful about the prospects of their lives. Lenore had never known anything but comfort. She knew very little about the lives of the common man in England, much less across the distance of an ocean. She didn't know that people starved. She didn't know that there were game laws, that men could be hanged for stealing a loaf of bread because they starved. She had no true conception of dirt, let alone a life of hardship and travail. No matter what Captain Hornby said, Jassy was certain that Virginia must be a grim place indeed.

Jassy took her place at the head of the table, her husband seating her. And when the lord himself was seated, the meal was served: soft, flaky flounder; baby eels; roasted pheasants; new potatoes; and fresh summer vegetables. It was a wonderful and elegant feast.

Tears pricked her eyes. There was so very much! The cost of this meal alone might have saved her mother's life. It could have spared her two months of scrubbing floors.

She realized that Josh, one of the kitchen lads, all decked out in Cameron livery, was standing beside her with the steaming platter of fish. She smiled, took a helping, and thanked him softly. She could not eat the fish. She looked down the table, her beautiful table, with its chandeliers and cloth and crystal and silver. The Duke of Carlyle was engaged in heavy conversation with Captain Hornby. Elizabeth laughed at something Henry said, and Jane, smiling bemusedly, paid them both heed. Robert whispered to Lenore, and Lenore smiled radiantly.

She felt Jamie's eyes upon her long before she met his gaze. He had noted the way that she watched Lenore and Robert.

He lifted his glass to her. She lowered her eyes.

Later that afternoon they danced. The grand hallway was cleared, and musicians sat up in the minstrel's gallery and played. Even Jane, so very pregnant, joined in the fun, for though she had protested that it was entirely improper, Jamie insisted that they were all related by blood or marriage, except for Captain Hornby, of course, and the good captain promised not to notice. The Duke of Carlyle brought his daughter out on the floor. Henry danced with his sister, Lenore. Elizabeth turned to Jamie, and he escorted her to the floor, leaving Jassy alone for Robert. And while they whirled around the floor, Robert, who knew her misgivings, made her laugh about the trials and tribulations of a long sea voyage. He told her cheerfully that they would chew upon plenty of lemon peel and thus avoid scurvy. "And we shall hang a ring of sachets about our necks, and thus avoid the odor of those who have not chewed upon their lemon peel!"

He spun her about, and she was laughing again, but her laughter faded and the light fled her eyes, for he spun her into her husband's arms, and the dark brooding she discovered in Jamie's eyes was grim, foreboding worse to come.

"May I take my wife, Robert?"

"Aye, but of course!"

And so she was swept away into rigid arms of steel, and his eyes pierced into her. "Where is it, milady? Where is the laughter? Where is the smile that animates, the glow that comes to you so seldom?"

"I don't know what you mean," she said sullenly.

"You know exactly what I mean."

"We are being rude. Captain Hornby is standing alone."

"Don't play the grande dame with me. I want to know. Where is the girl with the laughter, with the sparkling eyes?"

"She does not exist for you!" Jassy snapped, and thankfully the Duke of Carlyle chose that moment to claim her, and Jamie cordially acquiesced to his father.

But he watched her still.

Jassy avoided her husband for the rest of the afternoon, but when night fell, their company left them. Thankfully Captain Hornby was the last to leave. He required a few moments business with Lord Cameron, and Jassy was given a certain respite. She was certain that he had not forgotten his irritating determination to plague her.

She stood in the hallway while the men entered Jamie's study to the left of the hall, behind the dining room. She could hear their voices droning on and on, as Jamie gave the captain requisitions for supplies. Four more cannon, twenty-five muskets, a thousand feet of match, barrels of black powder, ramrods, balls, twenty-five suits of half-armor, breast- and backplates, and helmets. Captain Hornby should also bring five more ewes, five good Hereford cows, twenty chickens, and a rooster.

"The weapons are necessary," Captain Hornby said. "But bear in mind, the muskets will stand you well in hunting, milord, but they are not much good against the Pamunkee. You will need swords and knives. Not even pikes are much good against a Pamunkee lying in wait in the grass."

"Yes, you're right," Jamie said. There was a rustling sound; she heard the clink of glass and she knew that the men were pouring drinks.

"You know them better than most men," Captain Hornby said.

"Yes, I know them, and we should be at peace. Powhatan's brothers are not as powerful as he was; the confederacy has loosened. Many of the Indians are interested in trade with the white men. And still . . ."

"Still?"

"They can be a savage lot. I traveled with Captain Smith often when I was a lad, when Father decided that a third son must see the world and seek his place. I have been to their camps. I have seen them prepare for their torture rites. They are renowned cooks among the Indians. The women prepare great feasts. They cover themselves with tattoos, and they eagerly await their entertainment. When a man is not dismembered and disemboweled, he is beaten to death. So was the case, Smith told me, when Pocahontas saved his life. She was just a child, but the great Powhatan's favorite, though the lord alone knows how many children he sired, for he had many, many wives. The girl laid her head over Smith's so that none would beat him."

"But you seem to like them, Lord Cameron."

"Call me Jamie, we are alone. I like the Indians, yes. They have a sense of honor, and many of them are peaceful. I simply never forget that our cultures differ. That they worship first Okeus, a dark demon, and that they sacrifice their own children to this god."

"Well, the Carlyle Hundred will be well prepared to meet with any threat," Hornby promised. "Now tell me, Jamie, is there anything else you would have brought aboard the *Sweet Eden*?"

Jamie seemed to hesitate. "Aye, Captain. Buy me a fine bed, with a good down mattress, in London."

"And shall I see to the silks and draperies for it?"

"In the colony?" Jamie said, and laughed. Then he hesitated again. "Aye. See to it. Women like that sort of thing, don't they?"

"Her ladyship will surely appreciate it, aye."

"Will she?" Jamie mused, and Jassy sensed the bitterness in his words.

"You married wisely, milord. She is a beautiful lady, and sure to do you proud in the New World. She has the spirit for it."

"So I had thought," Jamie said.

"She does not wish to come?"

"She does not, but she will do so."

"Ah, milord, can you be sure?"

"If she does not willingly step aboard the pinnace, then you will have your orders to see that she comes aboard it trussed in a canvas bag. I care not how you bring her. Perhaps I shall send her back in time." He suddenly sounded weary, very weary. "Perhaps life will prove more palatable without her. Time alone will tell."

Jassy stood in the hallway, her face burning. She had frozen when they spoke of the Indians. She had frozen, and then felt ill. Then they had spoken of her, and the burning glow had slowly come to her cheeks. She still could not move.

The men spoke for a few more minutes, then the captain took his departure. Jasmine, aware then that she had been eavesdropping, shrank against the wall. The captain did not notice her. He walked on out the entrance. Lymon closed the door, bidding the captain good night.

She heard Jamie's glass clink down upon his desk, and she realized that he would soon be up to the bedroom—to join her. To finish what he had begun during the day.

She turned in a sudden panic and fled up the steps. She dared not be in the room, and yet she still clung to the belief that she might one day convince him that she slept, and slept too deeply to disturb, when he arrived.

She had difficulty with the fasteners upon her dress. She kicked off her shoes and thought of calling for Molly, then decided that it would take too much time, and she had so little left. She tried to calm herself and find the hooks, but she could not. She was trembling fiercely. She grasped the bedpost and tried to breathe slowly, but she could not, for all that she could see was a horde of Indians before her, naked and tattooed and leaping before a fire and dismembering some poor captive. . . .

The door opened. She whirled in dismay and stared across the room to it. Jamie was there. He arched a brow to her, and his slow, mocking smile as he looked from her to the bed indicated his surprise that she was not already in it.

"You are still up?"

"My hooks have caught—"

"You should have sent for Molly."

"Yes, perhaps. I shall do so now."

"Never mind." He strode across the room. She tried to turn away from him.

"I can manage."

"No, you cannot. Stand still."

Quickly he unhooked her dress. Then he walked over to his desk and poured himself a snifter of amber liquid, propping his feet up on the desk and watching her. Jassy stared at him awkwardly.

"Please," he told her, "do go on."

"If you were in the least the cavalier, you would exit the room until I—"

"I am not the least bit cavalier, and you are my wife. If you need more assistance, I am eager and willing to oblige."

She wondered what it was about him that could make her temper flare so quickly. She swore softly and turned her back on him, and still she felt his eyes, and still she felt awkward, and her fingers trembled. At last she drew her fine dress over her shoulders and tossed it carelessly on the floor. She stepped from her petticoat and saw that Molly had laid out one of her nightgowns, but one of Molly's choosing, of course, in peach silk with satin ribands at the sleeves and at the low-cut bodice and hem. She grabbed the gown, aware that there was no other she could find easily, and then tried to hold it as she struggled with the ties of the corset she wore. It was then that Jamie moved. He came behind her and deftly worked the strings, and the garment fell free. She muttered a curt "Thank you," and he returned to his desk and his drink, and she felt his burning gaze again as he continued to watch her. She halfway dropped her shift and slipped into the nightgown, then let the shift fall. She forgot her garters and hose and got into the bed, drawing to her own side of it, her heart pounding in a fury. She was there for several seconds before she heard him rise. His fine doublet and shoes hit the floor, and she tried not to listen; she tried to close her eyes and feign sleep.

She heard nothing more. Cautiously she opened her eyes. He was standing above her, staring down at her, waiting for her to do so. He smiled, and his hand fell upon the valley of her breast, and they both felt the frantic beat of her heart. "Sleeping?" he inquired pleasantly enough. He carried his drink in his hand. He was barefoot and bare-chested, and clad only in his breeches.

She didn't answer him. She didn't like his mood at all that evening. It was cynical, and he had been consuming a great deal of liquor.

He touched her chin. He moved it backward and forward, studying her eyes. "Where is she?" he whispered.

"I think that you are drunk," she said haughtily.

"The brandy? My love, it helps to make life palatable. You must have some."

"I don't want any."

"You are refusing to drink with me?"

If he poured her a brandy, he would go away, she decided. "I will drink with you."

"Good." He walked back to the desk and poured her drink. Warily she kept her eyes upon him. She leapt out of bed then, thinking that it was a dangerous place to be. But her movement might have been more dangerous, she realized too late, for her gown was far more revealing than concealing, and as soon as Jamie turned to her and his eyes moved over her, she saw her mistake.

But he did not touch her. He handed her the snifter. Still, he studied her eyes. She turned away from him and walked to the window seat. The windows were open to the warm summer breeze. It wafted in upon her, touching her hair, lifting it.

She didn't hear or feel him coming up behind her. She cried out, startled, when he touched her. He lifted her from the waist and set her upon the window seat. She clenched her teeth, for his hands moved upon her calf to her thigh, discovering her garter and loosening it and her stocking. He peeled the silk stocking from her leg, the rough pads of his fingers brushing over the soft tender skin of her inner thigh, and she was shocked by the strength of the sensation it evoked. Her eyes met his, and the indigo depths within them burned.

"Where is she?" he murmured tensely. "Can I reach her?"

Frightened, she tensed. He ignored her, his hands slipped up the length of her other leg, and his fingers tarried upon the flesh of her inner thigh again. She bit into her lip and swallowed fiercely, but his eyes were keenly upon her, and his touch did not cease when he reached the height of the garter upon her leg. His fingers moved higher and higher, teasing her. She swallowed down the brandy in a single instant. It burned down her throat and into her belly, and then lower, where the sensation met with his fingers and seemed to explode in aching heat.

"Stop," she whispered, but he paid her no heed.

He studied her eyes. "Where is the spirit, the passion, the life? The fire . . . I saw it today again but only briefly."

"Perhaps you haven't the fuel to ignite it!" she cried out.

He shook his head slowly. "No, no, I do not believe that, and so help me, lady, this evening we will discover it, no matter what it takes."

"No . . ."

He plucked the brandy glass from her hand and pressed her back against the enclosure. His lips met hers, and they were fierce and hungry and demanding. His one hand rounded the curve of her breast while he held the other beneath the silk of her gown, between her thighs, teasing, probing.

His tongue entered her mouth again and again. She wanted to twist away. She could not. The pressure of his naked arms and chest were too much.

Suddenly he pulled her down, and she lay across the window seat. She stared up at him, at the dark, demanding passion in his eyes. She gasped when he tore open the soft peach gown, and she lifted a hand to draw the gaping sides together.

"No," he told her firmly.

"It was one of my favorites," she complained.

"You may buy another." Their eyes met, and she remained silent. He caught her hands and drew them high above her, and he kissed her lips again. He drew his lips and the tip of his tongue down the valley of her breasts, and then he circled each nipple. Then he touched her with that wet fire again, down to her navel and below. The June breeze came in the window and brushed over her naked flesh where the dampness of his lips and tongue remained, and she quivered. The heat of the brandy seemed to touch her everywhere, and the feel of the air upon her was curiously fascinating . . . delicious. His lips traveled to her belly, below her navel. His breath was warm. His dark head moved upward again. His lips seared her, and his tongue laved her flesh. He came to her breasts, and he played with one while he sucked lightly, then passionately, upon the other. She caught her breath, swallowed, and held rigid, and then his mouth wandered upon her again, and his tongue plundered into her navel, and then below. He caught her thighs, spread them apart, then bit lightly upon their inner flesh, rising higher and higher to the tender, intimate flesh at her apex.

And it was then that the fire bit fiercely into her, seeming to explode throughout her. Her body trembled, she gasped, and she thought to stop him while the myriad sensations cascaded down upon her. The feeling was so good and so sweet that it was unbearable. She arched and she twisted, and the steaming, sweet ache and hunger remained with her, and to her astonishment she did not seek to escape him but to avail herself more fully to him. Starlight and the black velvet of the night and the June breeze all played over her, and she burned, sizzled, and craved from the inside out. She was barely aware of the intimacy between them; she desired the wet, encompassing hunger of him, and the rugged feel of his hands upon her body. She cried out, twisted, and yearned. She trembled and arched to him mindlessly.

Sensations exploded and burst inside of her again, and she reached a curious peak of ecstasy and splendor, and she felt her body shudder and convulse and give. In awe, she gasped out, and felt the honeyed liquid inside of her flow like a river, and she was washed again in little spasms of ecstasy and delight.

And then she met his eyes, triumphant, over hers.

"Oh!" she gasped in horror, and she yearned desperately to escape him, to escape his eyes, but she could not, for he wouldn't free her. He caught her lips, and she heard him tugging upon his breeches, and then he stepped away to free himself from the restriction of them. In the starlight he was extraordinary, like an Adonis, bronzed and created of nothing but muscle and sinew and the long, hard staff of his desire. He lifted her high in his arms, she flushed with the embarrassment of her actions, and he was still triumphant with his throaty laughter. "Please . . ." she said to him, and she hadn't the faintest idea of what she meant by it. He laid her down upon the bed and crawled atop her, driving into her as he took her breast deep into his mouth again. She gasped, for it was all with her again so easily, the sweet need, the ache deep inside of her, the desperate, undulating desire to have more and more of him.

And that he was willing to give. He held himself above her, and his face was strained with the harsh fever of desire, dark and striking. She did not look at him long; she could not meet his eyes. Her breath came in quick, desperate pants, and she moved with him rhythmically, accepting his every thrust with fervor, feeling the sensations rise in splendor and beauty, knowing what she reached for, and the cascading climax of it all. She was as wet and sleek as he, and achingly aware.

Then she felt the explosion burst upon her again, the glorious, sweet answer to her need. She felt the sudden, shuddering ferocity with which he thrust within her, again and again. He cast his head back, a guttural groan escaped him, and he fell down beside her.

She lay in silence. Even as the breeze cooled her, her face flamed, and she wondered if a lady was supposed to behave so wantonly. She wanted to burrow into the pillows, she wanted to hide herself away somewhere, curl into a little ball in a hole deep in the darkness of the earth.

It wasn't to be. Just seconds passed when she felt his hands upon her again. They were light and idle, his fingers just brushing over her naked flesh.

Then he pounced over her and caught her chin, and she hated the victory and the laughter she saw in his eyes.

"So she does exist!" he said. "The woman of passion, the creature of fire."

"No . . ."

She closed her eyes and tried to deny him. She heard his husky laughter again, and felt his lips upon her throat, and then upon her breast, and she was so sensitive to his lightest touch by then that she cried out and shuddered and instinctively reached out, digging her fingers into his shoulder.

"No more!" she whispered. "Oh, no more!"

His dark eyes swam before her own. "I must have more while I have this woman of fire," he told her, "lest I lose her when I shall seek her again."

And he would have more. Nor could she deny him, or the miraculous new sensations she had discovered. There was little difference in her surrender to him when he made love to her again and again that night. . . .

Except that instinct took over completely, and she was not aware herself that she made love in return, that her fingers moved sensually up and down his back, that she bit into his shoulders and laved each little hurt with the tip of her tongue. . . .

She was not aware of it, but Jamie was, and for the splendor of that evening he gloried in her every abandoned breath and movement. He bitterly rued the fact that he was due to leave her soon.

And so he used the evening well, determined that she would not forget him, nor their marriage, when the time came that he must sail away. The dawn had long broken when he let her sleep at last, and even then he brooded upon her. He stroked the long, golden strands of hair that lay across his pillow like a sunburst, and he followed the elegant lines of her features to the slender and beautiful curves of her body.

Was he a fool, he wondered, to whisk her away, across a treacherous ocean?

She sighed, and smiled in her sleep, and he wondered of whom she dreamt. He had touched her passions. At long last he had reached inside of her, and he had found the deep sensuality he had been certain must lie beneath her sizzling eyes. But he was truly a fool, bewitched and besotted, if he didn't realize that it meant little between them. When morning came, she would despise him anew, and perhaps ever more so, for he had proven himself the victor on this curious battleground.

No . . . he was right. His dream of the hundred had always been his true passion. He had married her, aye, because he had wanted her, and because he was his own master, and he had chosen to do so. But he had done it, too, because there was about her an innate strength. Her passion was for life. He would not live without her. Happy or not, she would come, and she would be his wife in all things.

Already he missed her. Already he longed for her again. There was so little time left. . . .

He rolled her over. Her sleepy gaze widened to his, and she whispered in protest.

"Nay, Jasmine, no words and no pretense, for I want you, and I will have you!"

She gasped, and the world spun into splendor again. When it was ended that time, he rose, quickly washed and dressed, then exited the room. A new day had dawned.

And she was left alone, small and spent, naked and tangled in the covers of their huge bed, and suddenly aware that she had given in to him. She had submitted, surrendered, and given away all.

She cursed, she cried, and she threw a pillow across the room with a vengeance, and then she lay back and cried violently into her pillow.

10

AMIE HAD BARELY LEFT THE ROOM WHEN JASSY heard the sound of horses' hooves and the clatter of carriage wheels on the cobblestones below the open window to their room.

Shouts and commotion assured her that someone of import had arrived. Drawing the sheets about her, she rushed to the window, crawled upon the seat, and stared down to the ground.

There was, indeed, a carriage below, drawn by four perfect bays and bearing the crest of King James I. Jassy gasped and shivered slightly, and her eyes widened. She suddenly realized the importance of the man she had married, that a royal messenger would come to him from the king.

A portly man with a set of lush, dark curls stepped down as the footman ran down the velvet-clad ladder. By the time he stood upon solid ground, Jamie himself had appeared below to greet him. The visitor was dressed in green taffeta with red stockings and ribbons upon his doublet, and he wore a richly plumed hat. Jamie was in simple black breeches that morning, and a loose linen shirt, and his high black boots. He stood tall, whipcord-hard and lean beside the stranger. No elegance worn by another could ever diminish the nobility of his bearing, Jassy thought, and she startled herself. She bit into her lip and realized that he was an extraordinary man. From the proud carriage of his head to the sharp intelligence of his eyes, he was striking. There was much about him that was extremely fine. He had the grace of a cat, and its sleek power. He was always vital, even in stillness, even in silence. Like the sun, he radiated heat; like a forest blaze, he swept in an indomitable fury against any opposition. His passions were hungry ones; his demands he saw as law. And yet he was strikingly sensual, and that morning she at last saw the raw magnetism of him as a man, and understood that London might well be filled with women who had coveted her husband's touch. He could stir and elicit the wild winds of the heart with a touch, with a breath, with the pressure of his lips upon naked flesh. . . .

He greeted the newcomer like an old friend, and received a rolled parchment from him. Then, as if he sensed some scrutiny, he looked up and saw her there, her hair tumbled all about her face, her fingers clutching the covers to her throat. He stared at her long and hard, with a curious cast to his eyes. Then he smiled slowly, and it was a smile that acknowledged not his own demanding sexuality, but hers. It was his smile of triumph, and it was a sensual invitation all its own. Then his smile faded as he heard something that the portly man said. He paid

Jassy no more heed, but a dark, annoyed frown fell over his features, and he was hard and unapproachable.

Jassy gritted her teeth, flushed, and drew back inside. She found the pitcher and bowl and hurriedly washed. She quickly dug into her chest for a clean linen shift, slipped it over her head, and found her petticoats upon the floor, where she had discarded them the night before. She paused, picking up her gown, running her hands over the silk. She pressed it to her face. She was seldom so careless with things of value. She had traded the value of her life for the value of a fine bed and a strong roof, and silk against her flesh.

Her fingers started to shake, color rushed to her face, and she felt nearly faint and very warm. The previous night had been no part of a contract, no deception. Thoughts of it still made her long to bury her face from the world, and yet they made her feel as if her bones melted inside of her, and she wondered now if the shattering ecstasy could have been real. She was shamed to realize that deep inside herself she yearned to discover it all anew.

No! She would not think about it; she could not admit to the exquisite pleasure, nor allow herself such abandonment again. She was certain that a true lady would not do so, and that when he'd looked up at her from the cobblestones below, with her hair awry and tumbling down, he'd determined that he had indeed married a whore.

She bit her lip and straightened, realizing that Molly would come and cheerfully straighten the room. She was the lady of the manor, and as such, she must hurry down and greet the royal messenger. But standing there in her petticoats and shift, she was startled when the door to their room burst inward. With her eyes very wide, she watched Jamie as he purposefully strode back into the room, a fierce scowl tightening his features.

"What—what has happened?" she said.

He cast her an irritated glare, striding toward his desk and jerking open the drawer. "God rot his Royal Majesty!" he swore in what was surely a treasonous statement.

"What—"

"The King is inconstant. The man was four hundred thousand pounds in debt when he inherited the crown from Elizabeth; five years later he is seven hundred thousand pounds in debt! He and Anne provide masque after masque for their own entertainment, when what income he has could so better be used to support his colony. One day he supports his bishops and swears that he will prosper in the New World, that he will see the Virginia colony grow and expand and fight the Catholic cloak of the Spaniards. Then he is apologizing for his colonists to the Spaniards, eager for the alliances of his children to the nobles of Europe. He is inconstant, I tell you, and seldom knows his own mind. He creates havoc by mere whim."

"I thought that he was your friend."

"He is the king, madame, and as such, I serve him. Yet he is part of the very reason I hunger for the new land, for though it is the king's dominion, it is far away, and a man is judged far more for his measure than he is for his title."

"But what is wrong?"

He cast her a sharp gaze. "You will be delighted, madame, I am sure. I have been summoned by the king to receive and deliver some of his correspondence to the Jamestown colony. I leave earlier than expected. I leave now."

He found what documents he sought and slammed the drawer shut. He strode across the room to the door. "Lymon!" he called.

Jassy, standing there in her shift and petticoat, gasped in protest. "Don't you dare call Lymon, and don't think to vent your wretched temper upon me. I'm not decently clad, and I tell you, I will not have it—"

"You!" he seemed to growl, coming to her quickly and setting his finger upon her chin to lift it. "You, my grand lady, will not tell me anything. You will sit still and await my convenience." He lifted her up by the waist and cast her in a flurry of her petticoats upon the bed. Tears stung her eyes, and she swore at him, and she wondered how, after the previous night, he could still be so carelessly rude to her. By then Lymon had reached the room, and she backed against the head-board, pulling the covers to her. She sat in brooding silence as Lymon assisted Jamie with the final touches to his packing, for he had been nearly prepared for the voyage. More servants arrived to carry down the heavy trunks, and when they were gone, Jamie at last turned to her. He leaned upon his desk and crossed one booted foot over the other, and his arms across his chest. "I had thought to have more time to express the vehemence of my determination. Lymon will see to it that a coach is prepared to bring you to London with your immediate household in time for the *Sweet Eden* to sail. You are free to bring your horse, Mary, if you desire, for you will definitely need a mount in Virginia, and as you seem attached to the creature, you may bring her. I know that you are still totally against the voyage, but I stress to you, my love, should you not arrive upon the *Sweet Eden,* you had best pray that your remains rest at the bottom of the sea, for I swear it will be a better end than what I shall have in mind."

She did not know if it was his words, or the insolent way in which he said them, but her temper seemed to burst and shatter, and she'd have gladly torn every last hair from his dark, arrogant head. She leapt from the bed in a blur of motion and flurry and catapulted herself against him, her fists flying, her words incomprehensible, her nails bared. She came in such distraught passion that he was unprepared, and her palm and nails caught his chin and drew blood. She was scarcely aware of it, though, or of the leashed rage that grimly tautened his flesh over his features. He caught her hands and dragged them behind her back, and she swore on in a vengeance, suddenly very lost and confused, and hating him fiercely. "How dare you, how dare you speak to me this way, how dare you continue to abraid and abuse me—"

"Abuse you, madame? You know nothing of the word! Alas, perhaps I do abuse you! I drag you away from the china and the crystal, and the elegance of the manor. And you do covet fine things, do you not, milady?" He pressed her ever backward as he spoke. She stared up into the smoldering blue fire in his eyes, and the battle was still with her.

"Yes! Yes!" she cried. "You thought that if you married a tavern wench, she would not care that you brought her to a barbaric mud pit! Well, you are a fool, for I shall hate it with every breath in my body, just as I hate you—"

"Despise it, Jasmine, but find yourself there. And you may despise me, madame, but so help me, you will not forget me, or that I command your life, ever."

"No? I have forgotten you already!" she swore violently.

He had reached the foot of the bed, and she was startled when he suddenly cast her free, shoving her upon it. He loomed over her, and she had been a fool not to realize the tempest of anger, or that the blaze in his eyes had come from anger to something more. Stunned and dazed, she struggled up to her elbows.

"Lady, we shall see that you do not forget me!"

"No!"

She struggled fiercely, slamming him hard in the chin with her elbow. He grunted in acknowledgment of the pain, and it was then that she saw the blood she had drawn upon him. She cried out, in a fury to avoid him, to twist away from him. His mouth ground down hard upon hers, and his body pinned her to the bed. There was nothing tender about his kiss, it was brutal and punishing, and still, it was searing in its heady passion. She felt a warm rush about her, the male scent of him, the unyielding strength of his arm. The pressure of his knee increased. She freed her lips from his, breathing in ragged gasps. He caught tendrils of her hair, golden in the sunlight, and wound his fingers into them, then found her lips again. She twisted from him, tears stinging her eyes. "No, you will not! You cannot order me about and have me at your whim. You will not—"

"But I will, madame," he said grimly, "and when I am done, you will never dare jest that you have forgotten me, not for a single moment."

"Bastard!"

"Nay, I married the bastard, you will recall. The scheming, grasping little wench who yearned for my money. How ironic! But, madame, think of it! None in the New World will know you as anything but a very grand lady, indeed. You may reign over the savages supreme!"

"Get off me!" Jassy raged. "I have paid for this bargain, and dearly. I hate you, and I hate you—I hate you atop me, and—"

"Do you? Last night I was convinced otherwise."

"You, sir, are the one who called me a magnificent actress! Get off me!"

"Never, madame, for you will give me my due—"

"I owe you nothing—"

"At my leisure, my dear wife. The bastard, the actress, the whore—you have come to perform very well. Let's see if we can draw such a performance again!"

"No!" She clawed at him anew, but he was in command, and she was pushed back, back—into the softness of the down mattress. It was quick, it was violent, and it was shattering. He secured her wrists as she swore and struggled, pushed up her petticoats and the linen of her shifts, and fumbled with the draw of his breeches. She didn't think that she had ever despised him so fiercely. . . .

And yet when he took her, the fire had never been so brightly lit within her. Her struggles ceased, her hands were free, and she was sinking endlessly into the soft clouds of the bed. She cried out at the fierce impact of his thrust, and she shuddered. He paused, and then his lips lowered and took hers, and his tongue came warm into her body, as did his sex. She came alive, wild and desperate, and dug her fingers into his shoulders. She wanted him, more than she had ever learned to want him the night before. She arched for the feel of his hand upon her breast through the linen of her shift, and her hips shifted and moved and undulated in a fever. So much came so quickly. The soaring rise of sweet need, the thunderous beat of his deep strokes. She wound her limbs around him and held tight, straining against his body. His dark eyes loomed above her, and with a sob she pulled his face to hers, and her lips, curiously wet with the salt of tears, demanded something of his. He kissed her deeply, raggedly, and then tore from her, an anguished, shuddering groan escaping him. Fulfillment raged through her, cascading like a warm blanket of liquid sunshine, seeping through her limbs and into her womb. Little tremors seized her again and again, and then she fell down to earth once again, down to the tangle of sheets and linen and petticoats, and the man who still lay heavy upon her.

Wordlessly he pushed himself from her and rose. He straightened his breeches. She lay still, dead still, spent and dazed.

Jamie stared at her for one minute. She did not meet his eyes but stared at the canopy above her. He swore softly, vehemently, then turned from her. She heard him sweep up his hat and his doublet from his desk, and then his long strides bore him swiftly across the room. The door slammed in his wake.

She lay there a long, long time. She heard the coach departing below, and she heard the grooms and the milkmaids and the servants as they set about the business of the day.

She realized that she lay in dishevelment and shame, her shift and petticoats pushed up high to her waists, the sheets beneath her twisted and dislodged. Her limbs were so sore, she scarcely could move them. She drew them together, and she rolled over, and despite the June day, she began to shiver. He was gone, she thought dully. He was gone, and it would be many months before she saw him again.

She could run away, she thought, but she did not want to. She liked being Lady Cameron; she *needed* to be Lady Cameron.

No matter what it entailed.

She would not be on the ship, the *Sweet Eden,* she decided. He could rage and protest and swear and thunder all he liked, but he would be three months away on another continent. She would not go; that was all there was to it. She would not go.

She shivered, remembering his conversation with Hornby. She would be dragged aboard the ship if she did not walk upon it. Not if they couldn't find her, not if she disappeared . . .

She lay there miserably with her arms curled about her chest, cold, her teeth chattering, despite the June sunlight streaming in. As time passed, she realized that she would be on the ship. Even across the vast distance of time and an ocean, she hadn't quite the nerve to defy him. He would hunt her down, she was certain, and he would find her.

Three days later, Robert and Lenore were duly married. Jassy sat in misery through the ceremony, then smiled brightly for them both.

That night she lay awake a long, long time, tossing and turning. As dawn came, she realized with horror that she missed her husband beside her. She missed the startling rapture he had taught her to feel. She missed the strength of his arms.

The next morning, she was summoned to her brother's house. Jane was in labor. After fourteen hours, a beautiful little girl was born. Jassy came home exhausted, but happy.

A week later her happiness faded when morning sickness began to plague her. She lay in bed in terror, looking about her beautiful room. It would be one thing to bear a babe here. . . .

But hers would be born in the wilderness, with savages.

She hated Jamie fiercely.

But still, she was missing him. Every bit as passionately.

11

HEIR CROSSING WAS ONE OF THE FIERCEST JAMIE had ever endured. Storms beset them across the Atlantic and continued to plague them as they neared the American coastline. Heavy crosscurrents pressed the flagship of his four-pinnace fleet, the *Hawk,* ever northward. Jamie stood with Captain Raskin at the bow, his glass in his hand as he observed the distant shore beneath a gray day and a dripping rain.

" 'Tis what happened to the Separatists, the 'Pilgrims' who left London late last summer," Captain Raskin said morosely. "They meant to settle somewhere southward, in the land chartered as North Virginia. But the currents swept them northward to the point that John Smith had drawn as Plymouth on his map, and there they stayed."

Jamie cast Raskin a quick stare. He wouldn't have minded a side trip to the Puritan community under normal circumstances. He would liked to have seen how the men and women of the Plymouth colony were faring now that their first brutal winter was over and they had learned something of survival. In London he had heard that the death toll had been tremendous. He hoped that they were surviving well.

The death toll in the Jamestown colony and its surrounding hundreds had often been tremendous, he reminded himself. And yet Jamestown had survived thus far, and with the plantations and hundreds arising along the peninsula on the James, the area seemed destined to endure.

The Pilgrims were escaping religious persecution, while the Jamestown settlers had come for more commercial reasons.

He had come for the adventure himself—and because his father had deemed it appropriate for a young man of his situation to see the world and seek his place. When he had first seen the land before the starving time of 1609, he had felt its draw. Within the Chesapeake Bay lay hundreds of fine natural harbors. The bay was fertile, and the Indians had proven that the fields were rich. The forests were verdant, and he had thought he had never seen a more natural state of the earth, nor a more beautiful one. The very loneliness, the very wildness of the land had excited him.

By 1613, he had turned twenty-one and taken over the trust his mother had left him. Wise investments, backing hardworking London merchants, had tripled his income. He had invested in the ships then, and his little fleet had carefully traveled the Caribbean, avoiding the Spaniards, who liked to claim the whole of the New World, and moving onward to the Bermuda colony and then back to England again.

He needed no more commercial gain. He was well set for life, and he had built his beautiful home in England. He didn't know why he felt the obsession to build here in Virginia. It was as if the land was a comely mistress, a tart who flirted and laughed and seduced, and in the end, would have her way. Like a woman, the land was unpredictable. To reach it, one challenged dangerous shoals. And once upon it, a man faced starvation and the hazards of hurricanes and Indians' arrows and knives. But to Jamie Cameron the rewards were endless. To touch the land, to build upon it, to create a new world. He could not deny the fascination. It was like something that stirred in his blood, ever driving him. It was like the passion and obsession that had seized him when he had first seen Jasmine. . . .

"Let's move inward and anchor for the evening," Jamie said. He handed the glass to Captain Raskin. "I don't want to lose a month's time by being forced northward. My wife will be arriving by the start of fall, and there are things that I would have prepared."

"Aye, aye, milord!" Captain Raskin said, and he called out orders to his men.

Jamie stood on deck while the sails were furled against the treacherous power of the wind of the dreary gray day. Though his cloth was finer, his clothing that day was much like that which the sailors wore: loose breeches and a simple jerkin of tough leather. He was known to take the wheel of his own ships, and to pitch in with the men when a heavy wind threatened, or when any decisive, demanding change of course was commanded. He liked to sail. He liked the wind and the tempest of the sea. One of his mistresses had told him once that he was hot-blooded, that he loved anything that demanded challenge or fever or high passion. He wondered idly if it was true.

He watched as the mainsail came down, then he turned away and headed toward the aft, and his cabin, which rode high above the waterline and was graced starboard and port with paned windows and heavy damask drapes. It was an elegant cabin with a velvet interior. There was a cherrywood desk and a big bunk and a wardrobe, and all were well nailed into the floorboards against the whims of the waves.

The difficulty with it now was that he sailed alone.

Inside the cabin, he drew open a desk drawer and pulled out a bottle of whiskey. He swallowed some, plopped down upon his bunk, and closed his eyes.

He should have made her come with him, he thought, and wondered why he had not commanded her to do so.

He had married her under false circumstances, he mused. He had known from the beginning that he was determined to come here, and that was why he had determined to take a wife. For the first time he had been seized with the concept of destiny, of future years and future generations. This was where he wanted to build, and this was where he wanted to raise a family. He wanted to see his sons cutting down the forest, and he wanted to see the day when a fine brick government house might rise in the wilds. In a hundred years when Virginia flourished, he wanted his grandsons to be a part of it, a part of the founding of the New World.

He swallowed again on the whiskey, and he winced against the burning sensation that trailed down his throat. He should have made her come with him. He wanted her, now, beside him. Perhaps she would not have been so dismayed by the savage rawness of the new community if she had accustomed herself to life with him upon the ship. Perhaps she would have believed that they could one day create a home as elegant as the cabin. Perhaps he could have inflamed her with his own enthusiasm and passion for the land.

He swallowed again upon the whiskey, and the fire of it all seized him, and he gritted his teeth and shuddered. He had believed in the promise in her eyes, and at last he had discovered that there was, indeed, a steaming sensuality that lay beneath the genteel airs with which she had cloaked herself. He had married her because he had wanted her—and more. He had married her because of the fire and spirit with which she had challenged him that very first night at the Crossroads; he had married her for the very sizzle of her hatred. He had married her because he had longed to take her between his two hands and force her to turn around and see him, to tame her, to live a life in a raw Eden with a savage passion and a never-ending flame of life and desire. . . .

He had married her, he admitted bitterly to himself at last, because he had fallen in love with her.

He swallowed down more of the whiskey, and he wondered if he hadn't been wrong to force so much upon her. Perhaps he could have won her heart in a more gentle fashion. He remembered that last time between them with a surge of shame, for she had so seared his temper that his violence had surpassed all tenderness and care. He could remember her now . . . the sight of her sprawling in the tangle of covers upon the bed was forever etched in his mind. She had never seemed more vulnerable to him, more soft and fragile and feminine, her hair splayed in soft, golden tendrils and tangles across the pillow, her eyes so wide open and glazed. . . .

He had touched her at long last. He had grown weary of seeking a response from her. He had believed that he had been wrong, that he had indeed been a fool. That he had married a cunning little wench with no warmth, no heart, no soul whatsoever. That he had doomed them both to a life of bitterness and hatred.

And then had come their last night together, when she had come alive, like kindling set to a sudden flame, like a fierce blaze raging through a forest. He had found the passion within her; he had discovered that the warmth, indeed, existed. And in the aftermath of his violence and fury, she had met him again in a rage of desire, and remembering her, even now, locked him in an anguish of longing once again. She detested him still. But he had at least discovered that her blood ran as hot as his. He twisted and hardened his jaw, and he thought of the eager young ladies, the daughters of dukes and earls, who had batted their lashes his way, and he thought of the eager mamas who had longed to wed their girls to the Duke of Carlyle's third son. Women had teased his senses before, and he'd known many of them. But none of them had so swept into his heart as the one he had married, the bastard waif who had despised and defied him at every turn. It was ironic and painful to love her. He, the proud Lord Cameron, brought low by the waif.

He laughed aloud, and the sound was dry. They were cast to their fate now. Perhaps he never could make her love him, but he would be damned if she would continue to crave another. She could rue the day that she had met him every moment of her life, but she would be his wife in all ways, at all times. That was the bargain, the covenant they had made. Perhaps he could be a bit more like Robert Maxwell and offer her the laughter and the courtesy she so craved. After all, she would spend two to three months upon the *Savage Eden* with Robert. Robert Maxwell was his friend, but he knew his friend's faults. Jamie once had saved him from Newgate for indebtedness. He was a charmer, but one with little sense of responsibility. The New World was his last chance at respectability, and Jamie had promised Robert land when his father had sworn that he had washed his hands of his son and his careless ways.

He tensed, remembering the time he had come upon the two locked in an embrace. She would not deceive him now. Surely even she would not go so far. Still, the thought plagued him, as it had a number of times. The pinnace was not so large. Robert would be aboard ship with his own wife, and certainly Jassy would be in Elizabeth's company.

He rolled over, clenching his teeth. He had seen passion in her; he had never known her laughter. An ugly vision reared its head, of his wife riding upon his best friend, her breasts firm and beautiful and dancing above him as her eyes shimmered and her mouth curved with laughter. Rage came so sharply to his mind that he nearly blacked out with it, and then it subsided. Robert was his friend, and in his debt, and though he might covet Jassy, he would not touch her. Jamie knew it. And still, the vision haunted him. He had found her passion; he had never seen her laughter. Not for him.

Maybe he could try to woo her. Maybe he could attempt a more tender approach. If he could just dispel the haunting image and the anger, he could give the laughter a chance.

There was a fierce pounding upon his cabin door. "What is it?" he said.

Captain Raskin, with a broad smile splitting his bewhiskered mouth, entered. "The wind, milord! The wind turns in our favor!"

Jamie leapt up, corking the whiskey bottle and slamming it down upon his desk. He followed Captain Raskin out. Indeed, the wind was in their favor. It had picked up from the northeast, and it would drive them homeward.

Homeward. Aye, the Carlyle Hundred was his home.

———

Three weeks later they came upon the natural harbor of the hundred. From the deck of the ship Jamie stared toward land, and his heart swelled with pride and pleasure. When he had left last fall, his plans had been drawn and his instructions clearly set out, but little had stood then, except for the wall and the palisade and the few small houses where the farmers and laborers had lived, the kiln, the chapel, and the storehouse.

Now, as he looked, the homes had already spilled beyond the palisade. The cannons he had sent in the spring were mounted upon the wooden palisade in four places, three facing inland and one facing the sea. Though he doubted that the Spaniards would invade this late in the game, it seemed only wise to be prepared. The fields to the right and left of the hundred center had been cleared. Cattle and sheep and goats grazed close to the coast, while farther inland, he could see the summer growth of tobacco and corn and grain. Dead center of the palisade, he could see his own home.

Once it had been a hastily constructed creation of logs and wattle and daub. Now, though the materials remained much the same, the house had grown. Though there were no glass panes for them, Jamie could see that the windows he had drawn had been cut and completed, and that a second story had been added to the structure, and two long els on either side.

"She's grown, eh, milord?" Captain Raskin said.

"Aye, and finely so!" Jamie replied. "Captain, let's get her berthed, then see to the unloading of the vessel. Give the sailors double rations. We've come home again, and I'm eager to touch foot upon the soil!"

Twenty minutes later the pinnace had been drawn to her deepwater dock. Before the slips were tied, Jamie leapt onto the wooden dock and strode toward its end. It was a hot day, with the sun fiercely shining down, and it was late summer and glorious. At the end of the dock he met with Sir William Tybalt, sergeant at arms of the ten trained fighting men he had in his employ, and governor of the community in Jamie's absence. They were old friends, having fought Indians together as lads, and an occasional Spaniard upon the sea. William rode a bay gelding and led a mount for Jamie. William dismounted and greeted Jamie with a firm handshake, then the two men mounted together and rode toward the palisade.

"How fare things here?" Jamie asked.

"Well!" William assured him with a broad grin. He was a man of thirty years with dark brown eyes and sandy hair and a quick grin. Like Jamie, he had found a fascination with the land. He had not cared for the Jamestown community life itself, with its ever-changing authority, but he had well liked Jamie's determination to build a new hundred.

William grinned. "We are working diligently here, and I think that we will have plenty of grain for the winter ahead. And young Tom Lane has become an expert marksman, and brings down wild turkeys with little effort. We've carefully planted food and gardens as well as tobacco, and still the tobacco does well. Come, let's hurry onward, for the men have arranged a display of arms, Father Steven is eager to greet you, and when the good father is gone, I've arranged a surprise for you myself."

They came before the palisade. The gates were open, for no danger threatened, and the people came and went. The wives of the laborers, hurrying along footpaths with their water buckets or laundry or produce, stopped to greet him, bowing low, and hailing him with true enthusiasm. He responded to all of them with nods and a deep smile as he rode into the palisade and saw that the soldiers were lined up before his house, dressed in their steel helmets and half-armor, front- and backplates, and prepared for an exercise with their pikes. William rode to the end of the line of men and began to shout out his commands. The men assembled impenetrable formations with their sharp, long shafts, went at ease, and grouped formation again. Jamie applauded their efforts, and William excused them from their ranks. Jamie informed them all that there would be a feast that night; they would slay one of the huge hogs that had come with him on the ship and roast the pork over a spit throughout the afternoon. Cheers went up, and he was glad of it.

"There's some business to attend to," William cautioned him. "A few cases on which we've awaited your judgment."

"It will wait until I've seen the house," Jamie told him. Dismounting from his horse, he cast the reins down and hurried the few steps to the heavy wooden door and pushed it open.

There had been vast changes in the dwelling. The floor was laid with boards, and the carpenters had fashioned a sweeping staircase that led up to a gallery. The entryway stretched into a long hallway like his house in England; at the end was a large, beautifully oiled, polished dining table, with a bowl of flowers atop it. To either side lay the els, and up the stairs, he knew, were the family bedrooms.

He took the stairs two at a time and found that the right side of the upper floor, behind the gallery, was intended for his use. An arched opening broke the long room into two, one a bedroom—where the bed he had ordered in London would lie but now held a lumpy pallet on a boxed wood frame—and one where his desk was set, and where the walls were lined with shelving for his books. A stone hearth lay to the side, which he had specifically requested. He did not care for the colonial habit of building open fires beneath flues.

Jamie left the bedroom and looked across the hall and found two more bedrooms, then he came back down the stairs. To the right he found a row of small rooms, sleeping quarters for household servants. To the left of the hallway was a large room that held a dais to the rear and had numerous chairs. It could be a ballroom or a courtroom, and certainly would be used as both.

The house in no way compared to the magnificent manor in England, but Jamie was pleased with it. It had been hewn from a raw wilderness, and it was a beginning. Each ship that came would bring more comforts, and eventually it *would* be a grand manor.

When he came to the entryway, William was there. "Well?"

"It looks fine."

William exhaled with pleasure, then grinned. "Well, the hog is about to sizzle. The sailors have come ashore and are causing havoc with the unmarried servant girls and the daughters of the laborers. But, as I said, Lord Cameron, there is business."

After Jamie settled a few disputes among people living in the hundred and William introduced him to the new house servants they came out to the hallway and sat around the dining table. Jamie stretched out his legs upon the table and cast his plumed hat over his head.

"An order of rum sounds in good standing," Jamie declared, and William laughed, approving heartily. Jamie called for Mrs. Lawton, the housekeeper, and the woman brought them a bottle and small glasses, and then discreetly departed again. The men filled their glasses, and William talked more about the events of the time passed—four infants had been born, but two of them had died soon after birth and were buried in a plot of hallowed earth outside the compound. A group of men from Jamestown and the surrounding hundreds had visited with Opechancanough, and they believed that the Indians were as pleased with the peace that lay between them all, as the white men were.

Jamie frowned. "I don't know. He is a warlike man. Clever, like Powhatan." He shrugged. "But I am for peace. It is productive. And my wife will be here soon. She has glorious golden hair, and I'd not like to see it worn upon a warrior's mantle."

"A wife!" William said. "Ah, so one of the fawning London beauties caught you at last!" He chuckled.

"She is not from London," Jamie said. The day lay upon him hard; the prospect of a hanging was not a pleasant one. He wondered what William would think if he told him that he had married a bastard scullery wench who had once come to him as a whore and a thief. He said nothing but swallowed more rum. "She is from the outskirts and travels with at least one of her sisters, Robert Maxwell, and a few serving maids, no doubt."

William arched a brow with a bit of a smirk. "You'd bring a lady here, milord? From your fine marble-and-brick manor to a house of wood and daub?"

"I have done so," Jamie said simply. He stood. The room was growing dark with the shadows of the late afternoon. "Come, William, I can smell the roasted pork, and I am famished."

In the center of the compound, the pork was indeed nearing completion. The people were gathering around the fire with contributions of their own: fresh Indian corn, bread, summer peas swimming in rich butter. The laborers, artisans, and gentry gathered together, and though Jamie and Sir William were given respect accordingly, there was a camaraderie here that could not exist in England. The men who served him welcomed him. Daughters were shyly introduced to him; wives came to offer him bounty from their kitchens. He sat cross-legged upon woven mats on the ground with them. Rum flowed along with the good food. Instruments appeared in the compound, fiddles and trumpets and drums and even a spinet, and soon there was dancing on the grass and dirt. Jamie was soon pulled to his feet by a group of giggling girls, and he gallantly bowed to each and, one by one, danced with each girl beneath the moonlight. When the night lay full upon them at last, he excused himself to the remaining revelers, found his own door, and stumbled up the stairs. Exhausted, he stripped, then cast himself down upon his pallet, and was startled to hear a soft giggling sound. He moved his hand across the bedding and encountered bare flesh.

"What's this?" he said. Groping for a candle, he carried it to the low-burning hearth and lit it.

A girl lay within his bed, as naked as he, propped up on an elbow and staring at him with huge green eyes. He had danced with her that evening, he realized. Her name was Hope, but it had once been something else, though she did not remember what. She was a Pamunkee Indian who had been taken in at Jamestown, since her green eyes had convinced him that she was a descendant of some white settler from the lost Roanoke colony. She was a bewitching child, no more than seventeen, with glowing copper skin, fascinating eyes, and full breasts with huge brown nipples. He did not resist the temptation to look at the length of her, for from the tip of her coal-dark hair to her dusty feet she was sensual and fascinating.

"What are you doing here?" he asked her.

"I have come to serve you."

Jamie paused for a moment. Now his eyes had adjusted to the darkness and the candlelight, and a soft glow played over both of them. He had missed the heady passion he had discovered so briefly with his wife, and he was a man with heavy appetites. He had never refrained from such an invitation before, and his body ached to accept the girl now. It was a novelty to be wanted so. It would be interesting to lay with a woman he needn't fight. Especially this exotic creature from two worlds.

He knelt down beside her, and he took her hands between his palms. He smiled ruefully, because something inside of him revolted at the idea. She wasn't Jassy. She had sultry, beautiful eyes, but not eyes that burned with crystal-blue spirit. She had wide, sensual lips, but not Jassy's defined mouth with the lovely color and pouting lower lip. Her breasts were tempting, but they did not cause the breath to leave his body, his fingers to itch with anticipation, his mouth to water for the sweet taste of their crests.

"I am married," he told her.

She frowned, and Jamie smiled, because she was apparently accustomed to men who gave the matter little thought. Perhaps he was a fool to do so. If he had any sense, he would lay with the little white Indian again and again and cleanse his ever-grasping, calculating, but exquisite wife from his system.

"Married?"

"I have a wife. A woman of my own."

"Where is she?"

"She is coming. She sails across the sea."

"But she is not here now."

"No. And still, she is my woman."

Hope smiled. "Sir Tybalt said that I was to be a surprise for you."

So that was what William had been planning. He had probably sent the girl still, leaving the matter to his own discretion.

"You are a beautiful surprise."

Her eyes lit straight upon his loins, caressing a certain part of his anatomy. She stared at him with pleasure and triumph. "You are pleased with me. I will stay." She snuggled down into the pallet.

Jamie laughed and lifted her up, and set her on her feet. "Hope, you are a sweet surprise, but I must wait for my wife."

"You are ready for Hope."

Her hands came upon him, encompassing his shaft. He caught her wrists. "Hope, no. You will meet her soon."

"She is so beautiful?"

"Yes, she is beautiful."

"And you—you love her so very much?" Her green eyes were wide, questioning. She was a precocious girl, and she had lived several years with the settlers in Jamestown, but she still seemed something of the pagan with her long, thick dark hair and demanding, uninhibited gaze.

"I—she is my wife," he insisted. "Now come, dress. I have had a very long day and I must sleep."

He paused then. "Hope, you speak the Powhatan language well, don't you?" She nodded.

The language the tribes of the Powhatan Confederacy spoke was a derivative of the Algonquin family, the Indians many of the explorers had met in the northern regions while searching for a northwest passage. Jamie knew many words himself, but he preferred having an interpreter when he traveled into the Powhatan lands.

"If you want to help me, Hope, you may come with me on a trip. I wish to find Opechancanough and offer him some things. You will come with me?"

"When?"

"Oh, maybe a week. I have a few things to settle here, and then we will go. I must bring letters and documents from the king to Jamestown on the ship, and from there we will travel inland."

"Oh, yes!" she said. "I will love the ship. I will take great care of you."

"I don't need great care," he said. "But I would be glad if you will sail on the ship."

He found her simple homespun dress upon the floor. He handed it to her. Unabashedly she slipped it over her head. "I will still serve you, anyway."

"Thank you. But I am married."

"You can handle more than one woman."

He laughed. "In some ways, maybe, but then, I'm not so terribly sure. I will have you work for me, very soon."

Hope left him at last. He lay down on his pallet, and her image haunted him. He should have kept her with him and snuffed out all the light.

It would have done no good. In pitch blackness he would know his wife; he would know her scent. He would know the softness of her hair. He would know the shape of her, and the sound of her, and he would know the feel of her breast and the undulation of her hips beneath him. He would know her forever. He had sworn that she would not forget him. He would not forget her.

At long last he closed his eyes and slept.

A week later, with the pinnace loaded for the journey home, the supplies settled, Jamie boarded the ship again with Captain Raskin and the crew. He left Sir William at the palisade with five of the men-at-arms, and he took Father Steven, the chapel's young Anglican priest, and two of the laborers with him—along with Hope—in the ship on a sail up the peninsula.

The wind was with them, and the afternoon brought them to Jamestown Island. It, too, had grown, with houses spilling in row after row around the wooden palisades of the town. His ship had been seen coming in, and the royal governor was there to greet him, quick to ask about the most recent affairs in London, and determined that Lord Cameron join him for supper. Jamie stayed, and while he listened to the governor, he thought of the years gone by, of the many mistakes of the London Company of Virginia, of the confusion and mis-management—and still the colony was thriving. There had been very few white women before 1619, and now there were many wives and sisters and daughters. He assumed the white population—including the various hundreds, bought by subsidiary companies or parceled out by King James—had to have reached three thousand. And in the governor's house he ate off fine plates with silver, and he saw that the governor's mantel had been decorated with delft tiles. He would try to remember to order similar pieces, thinking that Jassy would like them.

Jassy . . . he could never push the haunting image of her dazed blue eyes and her spread of golden hair far from his mind.

That afternoon, though he was encouraged to stay, he determined to set out. Opechancanough was at Rasawrack, he had been told, one of the Indian capitals. In Jamestown, he bought several horses accustomed to the overgrown trails and started out.

That night they slept in the wilderness. Jamie heard the owls and the night creatures and looked through the spidery branches of the trees to the sky. He felt the cool air of late summer, and was curiously at peace. He heard new sounds in the night, but the others slept, and he refrained from bolting up to call out an alarm. Though the footsteps in the night were furtive, he didn't believe that he was under attack. Nor was it Hope, determined to find him. She knew Father Steven, it seemed, and had already discovered the young priest's penchant for long sermons on the proper behavior for young women.

In the morning he discovered footprints, and he knew that the Indians were watching him and allowing him to come forward. He wondered if the chief had sent out the scouting party. The Pamunkees, the Paspaheghs, the Kecoughtans, the Nansemonds, and the Chesapeakes were all under the rulership of the Pow-hatan Confederacy, and in neighboring areas lived the Chickahominies and the Potomacs and the Monacans. Jamie did not know who followed them, but he sensed they would not be harmed. Still, as he packed up their gear, he was careful to see that his sword was belted at his waist, and that his knife was sheathed at his ankle. Muskets and pikes were little good in forest fighting. To be aimed, the muskets had to set upon rests. One had to carry several feet of burning match to assure that the black powder could be lit when the time was right. Loading a musket was a slow process—load the powder, ram in patch and ball. Though skilled men could fire off four rounds in a minute, it was still a tricky business at best, and near impossible when a lithe Indian leapt down upon a man from the shadow of the trees. Swords and knives were far more useful weapons here.

It took them three days to reach Rasawrack. Before they came upon the Powhatan capital, warriors came rushing out to greet them. Barely clad and heavily tattooed, they danced and let out curious cries but offered the party no harm. John Smith had once warned Jamie never to give up his weapons to the Indians. They asked him to, but he refused, and they let it be.

Jamie was taken to the chief's house, a long, arborlike structure created by implanting double rows of saplings and bending the tops to make the arched roof. The roof was thatched, with a smoke hole in the center. The other houses in the community were much like it, but Opechancanough's house was larger. They were brought into the large center room, and the chief came out to greet Jamie.

He seemed pleased, and reminded Jamie that he had been a very small lad when they had first met. What words Jamie did not understand, Hope filled in for him. Jamie was glad to see him, and to hear of his power. Opechancanough smiled slyly, and Jamie again worried that trouble was in the offing. The chief was a very tall man, ten years Jamie's senior at least, and strongly built, with very handsome features. His eyes were dark, his nose long and flat, his cheekbones very high and proud.

He invited them to a feast, and Jamie said that he would be glad to attend—as long as it was not a torture feast. The chief laughed and assured them it was not. It was a feast of creation.

Outside the chief's house, cooking fires raged, and men in breechclouts danced around long poles. Father Steven appeared frightened and appalled, and Jamie mischievously whispered that it reminded him of May Day.

"This is creation," Opechancanough told them. "The Powhatan were created by a giant hare, and he kept us prisoners for many years, while old women battled him for his prisoners. Finally he determined to let us be earth dwellers, and he gave us down to the soil and the forest."

Women moved about with bowls of food. Father Steven seemed leery; Jamie knew that the Powhatan were good cooks. For their celebration they had made a tasty stew of rabbit meat. It was eaten with the fingers, with flat bread to sop up the juices.

The men danced, then naked women in blue paint with leaves about their loins joined the men. They sang and moved with erotic abandon. The men-at-arms enjoyed it thoroughly, Father Steven looked as if he would have apoplexy, and Hope moved back and forth to the music, her lips parted.

They stayed with the Powhatan that night, and for the two nights following. Father Steven tried to tell the Indians about Christ, and they were quick to tell him about their gods, Okeus and Ahone. The chief and Jamie spoke affectionately about Pocahontas, and Jamie reminded him that John Rolfe was back living in Virginia, and that he was assuring a future for the princess's son. Jamie tried to explain the king, and Opechancanough told him about Powhatan's funeral, about the temples of feathered mantles and war paint and copper and jars that had been prepared for his death.

When their stay came to an end, Jamie saw that Opechancanough was given a large supply of glass beads in radiant colors, two ivory-handled knives, and a blue linen shirt with inserts of cloth of gold. The chief seemed very pleased, and insisted that Jamie return with numerous bags laden with dried fruits and grains.

It had gone well, Jamie thought. He and Opechancanough had made a vow of friendship, and he was certain that the Powhatan chief remembered and respected him. But something about the chief was crafty, and made Jamie wary.

They were longer coming back to the hundred, for they could not make the distance between Jamestown and the Carlyle Hundred by ship. When they came through the trail in the woods to the clearing of the fields and the palisades at last, Jamie was stunned to see that a ship lay out at harbor.

It was the *Sweet Eden*.

Jamie calculated swiftly. It was only the fifth of October. He had not expected the ship for at least another two weeks, but there she lay, in the harbor.

A thunder came to his head, and to his great irritation his palms went damp, and his fingers trembled where they locked around the bore of his musket.

He urged his mount forward, galloping hard over the fields to reach the dock. His heart thundered, his loins ached, and his mouth grew dry. He was about to see her again.

He was properly clad in a silk shirt, leather doublet, fawn breeches, and his high boots, for the Indians understood such things as the proprieties of English dress. He was even clean-shaven, for Hope had performed that barber's function for him not with a razor but with the Powhatans' method of a sharp, honed shell. He was clean, for the Powhatan bathed daily in the rivers, and he found it a very palatable custom. Still, he had not planned to meet her this way. He had wanted to see the house, to assure himself that it was ready. He had wanted to have time to think . . .

And to dream. But then, he had dreamed of her often, and always it had been the same. He had seen her lying as he had left her, disheveled and spent and curiously beautiful and also . . .

Hurt.

"Milord, the ship is in!" someone called as he raced by the palisade. But that was evident. The *Sweet Eden* had already pulled to the deepwater dock. Sir William had come down in his absence, to greet his wife.

Racing pell-mell upon his mount, he felt his body heat and churn, and he gritted his teeth, swearing that he would behave the noble lord and husband and not wrench her into his arms to soothe his loneliness. He would not take her brusquely, or in anger.

But neither could he forget in those moments that her passions could be reached, that though she denied him in her heart, she could not do so with her body, and his appetites that day were sorely whetted and keen. He had missed her and she was his wife.

And perhaps she had missed *him*. Perhaps she would come down the dock and stare at him, and at long last there would be a radiant smile upon her face, and the spark in her eyes would blaze for him.

The horse's hooves thundered beneath him, but already the passengers were beginning to disembark. He saw her; he could not miss the golden glow of her hair. She was dressed in soft blue, with a darker velvet cloak thrown over her shoulders and encompassing the length of her. She had seen Sir William, but she had not yet seen the rider racing toward the dock.

She looked over the hundred. He could see her pale, beautiful face, her sapphire eyes . . . her soft red lips.

Aye, he could see her face.

She stared upon the wooden palisade and the wood-and-thatch-and-daub houses with horror. Sir William spoke, and she tried to smile, but it was a lame effort.

"Jamie!"

It was Elizabeth, walking behind her, who called out with such joy. He reined in upon his horse and dismounted quickly. William saw him at last, and grinned.

Then all the others seemed to drift away, or perhaps in that moment, they simply didn't matter at all. His wife stood before him after the long months apart, and they stared at one another.

She did not smile, and her eyes did not come alive. She was so pale that it worried him, and she was thin. Her flesh seemed nearly translucent, and she was even the more beautiful for it, ever more a crystal goddess. He ached to touch her. He ached to shake her and grab her down from the pedestal of her aloofness. He longed to strike her down to her knees and demand that she cease to hate him so.

He locked his jaw tightly, for what he wanted truly was to take her into his arms and hear her cry with joy, and that was not going to happen, either. He had not realized that a hum had filled his whole being, that words and other sounds had escaped him, that he had been aware of nothing but her, until he heard her voice again. He walked down the dock, his strides long. He reached her, and the sweet scent of her washed over him as she cast back her head to stare up into his eyes.

"Welcome to Carlyle Hundred, milady," he said. He bent and would have kissed her, but she moved her face so that his lips brushed her cheek.

"Jamie!" Elizabeth cried. His eyes remained coldly on Jassy as Elizabeth stepped forward, hugging and kissing him warmly. "Elizabeth . . ." he kissed her back, and then he ignored his wife. Robert came up, shaking his head industriously, and then Lenore met him, cheerfully railing against him for having missed her wedding.

William spoke up, and Jamie introduced him around. By then Captain

Hornby was on the dock, and Jamie applauded the time he made across the Atlantic.

"Fortuitous winds," the captain said, pleased.

Then Jassy spoke softly but with an undercore of bitterness that startled him. "It was a very long and horrible trip."

Some agony touched her beautiful eyes, but then it was gone.

"Come to the palisade and the house," Jamie said. He reached for her hand, and she cringed. His temper snapped. "Come, Jassy, you will ride with me quickly to open your own door to your guests," he said. "They will follow in the wagon."

"No—" she began, but he did not allow that rebuttal. His good intention fell from him with the chill river of her disdain, and he caught her hand firmly and dragged her along. She struggled, but his grip was so firm that none could see. Halfway down the dock he paused, spinning her about and lifting her into his arms. Holding her so, in a grim silence, he hurried toward his horse. He set her firmly upon it and leapt up behind her.

She was trying to dismount from the creature already.

"Don't!" He jerked her so that she sat still, and then his whisper fell against her neck. "I have done everything that I can think to do for you, madame. I have hired on your friends, I have given you clothing and jewels, and even here, in the wilderness, you will have servants aplenty. And still, madame, at every turn you attempt to humiliate me. May I warn you, madame, don't ever, ever do it again!"

"If you would do anything for me," she cried, "free me!"

"Free you?"

Her head lowered. "I—I hate this place. I cannot be your wife here. I cannot."

He nudged the horse, swallowing down a bitter, bitter disappointment. His arms around her, he lifted the reins and guided the horse toward the palisade that meant so much to him.

"Jasmine, you will be my wife here. Tonight. I promise you."

His heels touched the bay, and the lathered horse broke into another gallop, bringing them quickly onto the palisade, and their new home in the wilderness.

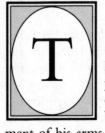

12

HE WIND RUSHED OVER HER FACE, THE HORSE pounded its mighty legs beneath her, and Jassy could hear cheers all around her. But most of all she was aware of Jamie behind her—the hard, vibrant wall of his chest; the entrapment of his arms, warm and unyielding as they came around her to hold the reins. She felt absurdly giddy, as if she might pass out at any moment. She felt a rush of warmth within her, because he touched her. She didn't want this . . . this gruesome place, and she didn't want to sail again, not when infants died and were cast, tiny and pitiless, into the sea. Not when even sailors sickened and died, and weevils chewed into the food. Not when storms raged and buffeted a vessel until not even the screams of the passengers could challenge the moaning of the wind.

From the moment they had boarded the *Sweet Eden,* things had gone badly. A scream had brought Jassy down to the hold where she discovered Joan Tannen, the wife of one of Jamie's men, in the midst of a cruel labor. A day later, Joan had borne a dead, blue-faced baby, swearing her loyalty to her husband and Jamie even then.

The wind howled; the rain slashed. Jassy divided her time among the sick children and Joan, trying not to leave her side for long. It did no good.

Two weeks after the baby had been cast into the sea, Joan had followed. She had bled to death, begging Jassy to give her husband the very last of her love.

She didn't want to be a part of this place. . . .

There was nothing here, just the log palisade and the looming cannons that warned of further death, and the little houses made of wood and wattle and daub. Beyond that, beyond the fields, there seemed to be nothing but the endless forests. By night it would black, as dark as any true pit of hell.

She didn't want to be with child. She didn't want to bear a child, not here in the wilderness.

But even as she longed to escape the voyage and the land, she again felt her husband's touch, the sweet dizziness; the rush of warmth encompassed her, and she lowered her head, feeling her body grow warm, for she was stunned to realize how she had missed him, how she had wanted to feel him beside her again. . . .

And how she had longed for the expertise of his intimate touch. Even if that touch had cast her into her present, frightening predicament, she longed for it. She had even lain awake at night aboard the wretched ship and thought that perhaps, had he been there, had she been able to turn to him and cry out her loss and her fear and her anguish, it might have been better. If he had been there to hold her and soothe her, to take her into his arms.

He had never taken her into his arms, not to be tender, or to gently soothe her, she reminded herself. And he probably never would, for she had seen the stark disappointment in his face when she had spoken on the dock, and even now she felt the harsh power of his anger.

They rode through the palisade and followed a trail through thatched-roof houses and structures that brought them to the largest of the buildings. Jamie reined in, leapt down to his feet, and reached for her. His eyes were dark and cold and fathomless. His face was more bronzed than ever, and he loomed taller than she had remembered, and when she placed her hands upon his shoulders while his hands wrapped around her waist, she thought that he seemed more tightly muscled, more savagely and perfectly honed, than ever before.

He set her down before him. "Milady?" He indicated the house. She held tight to her cloak and preceded him up a stone path. The door opened before she reached it. A plump, middle-aged lady bowed to her quickly, then offered her a cheerful smile, then nearly fell back upon herself with another courtly bow.

"Amy Lawton, my dear," Jamie said behind her, and she didn't know if the wry tone of his voice was for her, or for their very respectful servant. "She will be in charge of the household, and, I'm sure, eagerly awaits whatever commands you might have."

"Oh, yes, milady."

Jassy took her hand. "Amy, I am glad to have you, and as I know nothing about living here at all, I will be grateful for your guidance."

Amy flushed with pleasure. Someone giggled behind her, and Jassy was introduced to the two young maids, Charity and Patience. A youth, bobbing and nervously twirling his flat cap in his hands, stepped forward next. He was Simm Tyler, the groom. Jassy gave him a smile and asked him if he would be especially good to her little horse Mary, for the mare had not liked the crossing one bit. The young man, with freckles and ears too big for his slender face, promised that he would see to the poor creature.

The last of the servants was Jonathan Hayes. Jamie introduced him as their cook, and she looked at him with special interest, for she never forgot that she had been apprenticed to Master John for just such a position. He was a very skinny man for one who spent his time in the kitchen, but he had nice, warm eyes, sunk into the near cadaverous hollows of his face, and Jassy decided that she liked him very much. There were others about. Men arrived, bearing supplies from the ship.

They smiled to her; they bobbed to her with respect. She liked them all very much.

It was Virginia that she did not like. It was the wilderness, the savage threat of the forest beyond them.

"My dear, you had best release Jonathan and the girls to their duties," Jamie said, his hands upon her shoulders. "We've guests coming along shortly, as weary as you are yourself from the voyage, no doubt."

"Of course," Jassy murmured.

Jamie started to take her cloak. She pulled it back around her, wrapping it tight. She heard his teeth grate, and she whirled from him defensively. "Milord, I am still chilled."

"Then we shall stoke the fire," Jamie said. He left her, walking down the hallway to the huge brick hearth that burned halfway down the length of the room.

"Ah, milady, I shall pour you some warm mead with a good shot of cinnamon in it. 'Tis warming, it is!" Amy Lawton assured her. She urged Jassy into a chair by the hearth while she sent Charity Hume to the kitchen for the mead. Seconds later a crude mug was in her hand, and Amy was telling her with pride that it had been crafted there, in the hundred, in their own kiln.

She sipped the mead and gasped, for it was potent, but it was good, and after the trip she felt that she could drink many, many cups of Mrs. Lawton's mead. She looked up and saw Jamie where he stood by the mantel, one elbow resting upon it, his eyes pensive but giving away nothing in his thoughts. Even as he looked at her they heard a commotion in the front and knew that the others had arrived in the wagon. Amy Lawton smoothed her skirts and hurried to the door. In seconds they were all filing into the house, Robert and Lenore and Elizabeth, and behind them, Tamsyn and Molly and Kathryn, and then Captain Hornby and Sir William Tybalt. "Oh, how quaint, how crude!" Lenore proclaimed.

Jamie smiled indulgently at her, and Jassy wondered what his response would have been had she uttered the statement.

"We're very proud of this house," Jamie told her.

"Oh, dear, you mean it goes downhill from here?"

"I'm afraid we have a one-room hovel," Robert said ruefully, "and for that, my love, we must be grateful."

"You've no hovel, Robert. I'm afraid that the two of you are guests in this house for now. I was not sure that I could convince you to come, and so your house is not yet built. But we shall get our carpenters working upon it immediately, and it will not take long. Now, drinks all about, I think. Amy, Patience, if you will. Whiskey for the gentlemen, I think, and more mead for the ladies."

"Me, too, milord, I'm hoping!" Molly piped in, and Jamie laughed, in good humor again. "You, too, Molly. And Kathryn. And Tamsyn. Be assured, today you've no duties but to acquaint yourselves with your new home."

Jassy watched him covertly. He was good with servants, she thought, with men—and with women. With servants he was gentle, with his peers he was knowledgeable and determined, and with women he was not gentle, but there was something about his dark good looks and very indifference that seemed to seduce them all. Molly was taken with him, as was Kathryn. Lenore had once admitted her fascination with him. And Jassy, herself, had learned the heady lesson that he had promised—she never forgot him, not ever. He entered into her dreams, he touched her by the coolness of dawn, and by the darkness of the night, ever in her imagination.

"Jamie, I do love it!" Elizabeth cried with sudden enthusiasm. They all stared at her. She flushed, then came to sit beside Jassy. "Oh, did you see the colors in the trees! Fall is coming, and the forest is lush now in yellow and green, and I can imagine that in a number of weeks it will be radiant with red and orange . . . it is so raw, a beginning. Like a Garden of Eden!"

"Serpents stalked the Garden of Eden," Jassy reminded her.

Captain Hornby laughed gruffly, then once again there was a certain amount of commotion, for their traveling trunks and the new four-poster bed that had been specially purchased in London had arrived, though in a number of pieces. Again Jassy was struck by not only the respect but also the affection with which these people viewed her husband, and how eagerly and cheerfully they served. The men who had come to lift and carry bobbed to her with real pleasure, and if they cast her a sly glance here and there and grinned to one another, they still did so with such good humor that it was difficult to be offended. She wondered if Jamie had seen the glances, and turning to look at him, she found his eyes upon her. He had. But the way that he stared at her disturbed her, for it was not with the lust she had expected but with some deeper emotion, and she realized that once again she had disappointed him heartily.

She tossed her head. To the devil with him! She despised this place, and longed to go home. She did not want to have her child in this savage wilderness. Still, tears stung her eyes, and she wondered why, and then she knew that she wanted him to look at her with pride, and with respect, and with . . . tenderness.

"When things are set, milady, we will see that our guests are comfortably settled, then we shall gather once again for supper," Jamie said.

Time passed with them all together, but for Jassy, things were set too quickly. Captain Hornby said he would return to his ship, and Sir William had business to attend to as well. The workers finished with the upstairs, and departed. Amy quickly showed Kathryn, Mary, and Tamsyn to their rooms in the servants' wing, and Charity led Lenore and Robert and Elizabeth up the beautifully carved and polished stairway to their rooms at the left of the second floor, while Patience brought Jassy to the suite of rooms she would share with her husband.

Alone, at last, she stared down at the desk and then at the bookcases, and she saw that her husband had brought many of his fine leather-bound books to his new home. There were candles in copper holders upon the mantel, brick in these rooms too. There was a screen, and behind it she discovered a washstand and pitcher and bowl and the chamber pot. A huge armoire was in the corner of the room, and her traveling trunks were aligned at the foot of the bed, by the window, and near the door. There was also a beautiful dressing table beside the bed, and then there was the bed itself.

It seemed very large, and was grander even than the one in Jamie's room at the manor in England. Four simple, straight posts held up heavy draperies, secured by loops at every post. It was piled high with pillows and covered in a tapestry-woven blanket. She walked over to it, gingerly placed her hand upon the down mattress, and discovered that it was very soft. She knew Jamie had ordered it in England, that men had worked quickly to assemble it for her comfort.

"It is much like the one that King James once sent to Powhatan, the gift of a king to a king. I hope you like it."

Jassy spun around. Jamie had silently entered the room and stood with his back to the door, leaning against it. His dark eyes fell broodingly upon her, and still she had little clue to his thoughts.

"It's—fine."

"Is it?" He walked on into the room, his arms crossed over his chest, circling her but not touching her. She felt him with every breath of her, and she wondered that he did not touch her, for they had been so long apart that they were nearly strangers, and yet it was as if the flesh and blood of her had lived in wait to know his touch again.

"It is the finest of all the colony, madame. As is this house. I believe it is even grander than the house in which the Jamestown governor resides. Alas—it still is not grand enough for the scullery maid from the Crossroads."

She stiffened as if he had slapped her. "If you are disappointed in me, then it is your own fault, milord. I did not wish to wed you, and I made it amply clear that I had no desire to come here."

"Then why did you come?"

Suddenly he was closer. His hands were on her shoulders, and his fingers bit into her arms ruthlessly. She cried out softly and tried to free herself, and he shook her so that her head fell back and her eyes met his.

"Why?"

"Because you commanded that I must!"

"You are a talented woman, in many ways. You could have eluded my men, if not me, and I was traveling an ocean."

"You said that you would come for me and that I—"

"Ah, but it would have taken me months to realize that you did not come, and months to retrieve you. And perhaps by that time I would have decided that you were not worth the bother. So why did you come?"

His eyes were fire and his touch was steel, and she was desperate to escape him. She twisted to bite his hand, and he hissed out in surprise. then suddenly he lifted her and sent her flying onto the mattress of the beautiful new bed. He joined her there, catching her shoulders again.

"Let me go! I shall scream!"

"Enjoy yourself."

"We've guests in the house."

"Then let them wonder if you are screaming from pleasure or pain; this is my room in my house, and you are my wife." For a moment she thought that he meant to lean over her, to kiss her with the same savage passion that glittered in his eyes. She felt the heat of his body, cast beside hers, and breathed in the subtle, seductive male scent of him. She was dizzy again, filled with a aching rush that left her trembling. It was wrong, and it had to be shameful, for they were such bitter enemies, but she wanted him desperately. She wanted even the anger, so long as it came with the explosion of passion. She wanted his hands against her bare flesh, his lips burning into her, and the flame of his body warming hers.

His fingers bit tightly into her shoulders again. "Why are you here?" he demanded.

"Let me go!" she shrieked, for she had to fight him, and fight this place, this wilderness. He held her so tightly, his breath came in raw and ragged anger, and everything about his hard body seemed vital and alive, streaked with lightning. The very room seemed alive with it, with combustible sparks, with tension that ripped the air between them. He would touch her, he would take her, and she could fight no more, for she could not . . .

"Answer me!" He shook her again.

"No! No! I have answered you! I mean that I want you to let me go!" Her eyes, wide and sapphire blue and sparkling with the hint of tears behind them, met the savage indigo of his. "Let me go home."

"Your true home is in the gutter, milady."

"An *English* gutter, milord, and I believe that I should prefer it!"

"Bitch!" he swore suddenly. And then, to her astonishment, he was gone.

He left her, and she was cold and alone in the beautiful new bed that might have been made for a king, encompassed in her royal-blue cloak. Bereft, she moved her fingers over the bed and cried softly. She hadn't even told him about the baby. She hadn't told anyone, because she did not want the baby to exist. She did not want her baby to be born in the primitive wilds.

She did not want to be so alone. So terribly alone. She had her sisters . . . she had Molly and Kathryn and Tamsyn. But she did not have Jamie, and she was alone, hurt, and frightened. If even the passion had left them, then there was nothing remaining at all, except for a bleak life of bitter hatred.

She curled her fingers into a fist, for she still longed to touch him. She wanted to run her fingers over the strong lines of his face and down to the slope of his shoulder. She wanted to see him prowling naked and supremely confident and graceful again, and she wanted his arms around her, safe and secure. She wondered if he would come back. He did not. She closed her eyes in misery, and she still felt as if she experienced the rocking of the ship. She closed her eyes and slept.

In the end he did return. She felt him shaking her shoulders and calling to her, as if from some great distance. She was so exhausted, and so very weary. She tried to awaken and she tried to smile, to show him that she was glad to see him.

But he tossed her over curtly and spoke with blunt, commanding words. "Get up. Dinner is being served, and you have many guests. Wear something very grand—we would show our friends and family and the people that we can have elegance here in the wilderness." He pulled open her various trunks and began pulling clothing out and tossing it upon the bed. "Get up!"

She didn't move; she was exhausted. He grasped both her hands and dragged her to her feet and tugged upon the tie to her blue cloak. It fell to the floor, and she instinctively touched her stomach. No one could tell, as yet. She could feel the hard swelling in her stomach and the fullness of her breasts, but no one else had fathomed her secret, except for Molly, perhaps, and Molly wasn't telling. But Jassy didn't want Jamie touching her this way. If he had come to her gently, or even with passion, she could have coped. But she would not have him discover it so.

"Leave me alone!" She turned away.

"I said—"

"Oh, yes, milord! And I will obey! Yes, milord, no, milord, whatever your whim, milord. You did take me from a gutter to a primitive forest, and I must be forever grateful and at your command!"

She didn't like the set of his jaw when he took a firm step toward her, and she moved away again. "I will dress in whatever you have chosen!"

"I will send Molly—"

"No. You said that they have no duties today. I will manage if you will just please let me!"

She watched the pulse tick at his throat, and she wanted to burst into tears. Apparently he had changed while she slept, and she had never seen him appear more masculine and exciting. His shirt was white against the bronze of his throat, his breeches were royal-blue satin, and his doublet was black. His hose hugged the muscles of his calves, and he wore buckled black shoes. His hair was long, curling far over his collar, and though he was clean-shaven, he had some of the rugged look of the place about him, and it was very appealing.

"Five minutes, milady."

He turned and left her.

———

She didn't manage to make it downstairs in five minutes, but in ten. Elizabeth had come before her and was sitting with Jamie before the hearth, listening with enchantment to some tale he was telling her. Elizabeth looked up when she arrived. Jamie stood and greeted her with a proper murmur.

"Jamie has been telling me about a delightful stream, not far from here." She flushed, bringing her hand to her mouth. "The Indian maidens swim naked, and so do many of the white women now, because the water is so wonderfully clear and cool."

"The Indian maidens seek to catch husbands," Jamie said.

Elizabeth laughed. "Do they? So things are not so different among peoples, after all."

"No, they are not," Jamie said, watching Elizabeth with tender admiration.

Robert and Lenore arrived then, breathlessly. Jamie said that he would call Mrs. Lawton to prepare their drinks, and then they might sit to dinner. Amy brought French wine that had arrived with them upon the *Sweet Eden,* and when they were all served a glass, they gathered around the table. Lenore giggled and apologized for being late, and she looked at Robert and said sweetly, "Oh, but it was nice to . . ." She paused, realizing what she had said, and blushed prettily. "It was nice to be upon solid ground again."

Everyone burst into laughter except for Jassy. Lenore stared at her with innocent eyes. "Wasn't it nice, Jassy?"

She gazed down at her plate, because the innuendo was there, and of course everyone was assuming that she and Jamie couldn't wait to make love once they were alone. She could not bear to say that her husband had not wanted her, nor could she look across the table to where he sat. She felt his eyes upon her.

"The ship was tiresome," she said.

"Milady?"

Jonathan—dressed now in Cameron livery—stood beside her, offering her a huge silver trencher. He lifted the cover, and the sweet aroma of the food made her mouth water. "Venison, milady." She nodded. "Jonathan, it looks wonderful. Thank you so much. If you will serve Lady Maxwell first, please."

Jonathan served the meat, Amy Lawton served buttered squash and beans, and the girls came after them with breads and puddings and slabs of wild turkey. The meal was delicious, and there was plenty, and it was difficult to believe that there had been a starving time here. Sir William Tybalt arrived when they were halfway finished; and apologized for being late, explaining to Jamie that one of the little children had wandered into the woods.

Jamie frowned. "Why didn't you call me?"

"It is your first day back—with your wife."

"I know the woods well," Jamie said. "In the future you must summon me immediately."

"She is back, alive and well," William said.

Robert looked at Jamie. "Your responsibility here seems heavy, Jamie. You are the lord of the manor, do you not rest?"

Jamie shook his head. "No, Robert. Here we all toil with the earth, you will see. No man rests easily. There is always forest to clear, homes to be made, land to be plowed. Our ships come sporadically, and we must become as independent as possible if we are to survive. I can buy many things, but if the ship they are due upon is caught by a storm and swept astray, then my money is as worthless as the goods I have imported. We are not so savage as you might imagine, and still we pull together. Candles must be made, and soap, and the animals must be attended. I hunt food with the men when I am here, and I saw logs, and I think, Robert, that you might come to enjoy it."

"Well, we shall see," Robert agreed pleasantly. He smiled at Jassy. "You should fare well enough, milady. You were a regular angel aboard the ship."

"Down below, administering to the common folk," Lenore said. " 'Tis a wonder she caught no diseases or creatures from them!"

"Lenore, really—"

"Jassy, you must be more careful. You could infect us all."

"The woman who died bled to death from childbirth, Lenore," Jassy said softly. She looked up. Jamie's eyes were on her again. He was silent, and yet she felt that he did not stare at her so condemningly as he had before.

Jonathan cleared his throat at the head of the table, and Jamie turned to him. The man whispered discreetly to Jamie, and Jamie rose. "Bring her in."

"Excuse me," he said to his company. "I will return as quickly as possible."

Elizabeth asked Sir William about his customary day; and Sir William politely answered her, promising that he would teach them all the proper use of the matchlock musket. Jassy listened vaguely, but her curiosity got the better of her, and she excused herself, too, hurrying down the length of the hallway to the front where Jamie spoke with a soldier in half-armor and a woman.

The woman was unlike anyone Jassy had ever seen before. Her hair was incredibly long and sleek and black, her skin the color of honey, and her eyes bright green. She wore a simple homespun dress with no petticoats or corset, and the pendulous size of her breasts seemed indecently evident.

"You must see that the chief is thanked, and is assured that my bride will value the gift greatly—" Jamie was saying. He broke off, realizing that Jassy stood behind him. He brought her forward. "Jasmine, Lyle Talbot of our patrol, and Hope. Lyle, Hope, this is my wife, the Lady Jasmine."

Lyle knelt before her and handsomely offered her his service.

Hope did not stir at all. She studied Jassy with her eyes, then bobbed a bit. "Lady," she said. She looked over Jassy's head to Jamie with a glitter in her eyes. "I will convey your message."

"Thank you."

Hope smiled. "I shave you well, yes?"

"What?" Instinctively Jamie lifted his hand to his cheek. He had forgotten Hope's administrations with her honed oyster shell. "Yes, you did well. Thank you."

Before him, Jassy stiffened. Lyle Talbot hurried Hope out the door, and Jamie closed it tightly. Jassy stared at him until he turned about, and it was her opportunity to stare at him with condemning eyes.

"Jassy—"

"The meal grows cold," she said, and swung about with great dignity.

She prayed that he didn't see that she was trembling and seething as she walked. It had not occurred to her that he might do to other women what—what he had done to her. She was dismayed at the rage that swept through her, and the pain. He could not! He could not desire that curious heathen over her! He would never, never touch her again; she would not allow it.

Her teeth were grating when she returned to the table. Then she did not know what struck her, but it was wanton and wicked, and she set out with sudden cheer to charm both the other men at the table. She grew animated and bright, and she asked endless questions of Sir William, and when the voyage across the sea was mentioned again, she took Robert's hand. "Robert has ever been the most gentle man and the best of friends. Why, I should not have borne the voyage at all, were not for his every assistance. The loneliness would have been unbearable—except that he was there."

Lenore, who had known that her husband had been at her own side during the voyage, thought nothing of her sister's sweet words of praise.

On the other hand, Jamie, who knew full well that his friend had once deeply desired his wife, knew nothing of the kind. Jassy saw the wrath that tightened the muscles in his throat, sending a blue fire to his eyes. She delighted in it. How dare he touch the heathen girl and bring her into their house!

They moved downward to the hearth when the meal was finished for whiskey and pipes and mulled wine, but Elizabeth wearily declined any substance at all, and Lenore quickly yawned and excused herself too. Sir William was explaining the musket to Jassy, and she listened avidly to his every word, widened her eyes, and said that he must teach her. He stumbled over his promise to do so.

"Jassy, hadn't you best go up too?" Jamie said, irritated.

"Oh, no! I am not tired at all. I am desperately eager to meet the challenge of this new world!" she claimed innocently.

His gaze then frightened her, and she dared only flirt with Sir William a moment longer. Then she fled up the stairs.

She would undress like mercury, she determined, don her nightgown, and plummet into the bed. And if he thought to waylay her this evening, she would send him to his Indian harlot. He would not dare touch her, she swore it.

The plan went awry from the beginning, for he entered the room, closing and bolting the door, while she was struggling to bring her dress over her forehead. She felt his presence as he remained by the door, watching her, then he stepped forward and pulled the gown from over her head.

Pins loosened from her hair and fell to the floor, and she met his eyes. He tossed her dress to the side and stared at her as she stood there, her shoulders bare, the soft, white mounds of her breasts rising high over her corset, her eyes liquid blue pools, and her petticoats streaming from her waist. Soft tendrils of golden hair curled over her shoulders and around the fullness of her laced breasts, and blue veins pulsed against the slender column of her throat. He had never seen her more desirable. Longing seared through him with the vigor of a shot. He shuddered with the stark heat of it. "Come here," he told her, his voice caught in a rasp.

"You have lost your mind!" she said gratingly. "You will never touch me again, you savage."

"The hell I will not—milady!" he told her, and he wrenched her into his arms.

Her fists pelted against his chest, but he held her tight and lowered his mouth upon hers, forcing it open, taking her lips with a bruising passion. His fingers threaded into her hair, and he dragged back her head as his lips traveled downward to the pulse at her throat, and onward to her shoulders.

"Don't you dare!" she gasped, shoving hard against him.

He ceased his motion and held her still, his eyes blazing into hers with fury. "What, milady? You played the whore tonight for Sir William, and now, in this room, you would be the nun?"

"I was polite and nothing more to Sir Tybalt."

"The grande dame! Your performances are so fine, milady. Tell me, what of Robert Maxwell?"

"For him, milord, I play the dedicated friend! What he has given me, I seek to give to him."

"In this room, milady," Jamie insisted, sweeping her from the floor, "you will play my wife!"

She fought him with a fury she had not known she possessed that evening, for imbedded in that fury was anguish. She could not bear that he had turned to another. Especially when he had forced her here and she was terrified that she would die with the birth of his child.

She was flung upon the bed, and he was quickly atop her. She lashed out for his face, but he secured her wrists. She kicked at him savagely, and he cast his weight over her.

"I will scream."

"Scream loudly, then. I'll not have you taking half measures."

"Go to your Indian whore!"

"What?"

"Take your stupid, panting lust to your Indian whore!"

"Are you jealous, love?" He paused, arching a dark brow, comfortably situated as he held both her wrists in his one hand and held her down with one leg cast over her thighs.

"Never, milord. I am humiliated."

He moved his free hand over her cheek. She wrenched away from his touch. His fingers wandered down her throat and fell upon the laces to her stays. He deftly untied them. His gaze and his fingers roamed freely, lightly, over her shoulders and her breasts, teasing her. His thumb and forefinger paused over an achingly sensitive nipple, rubbing it to a long, darkened peak. Jassy tossed her head, twisted, and looked away, and she wondered if he had held the Indian girl so, and if he took more pleasure from the honey-colored flesh than from her own.

He lowered his mouth against her. "I hate you!" she choked out. His hand cupped her breast, his lips and teeth encompassed her nipple, and she cried out at last, shuddering at the searing rage of deep, molten desire that swept through her. "Stop it, I hate you, I hate you, I hate you—"

He had stopped. He held her wrists in a fierce, merciless grasp and tore at her petticoats and shift with a sudden, startling violence. Frightened, Jassy writhed to be free of him, wondering at his intent. She swore, she twisted, but in seconds she lay entirely naked, with her petticoats and shift a pile of debris beneath her, only her garters and stockings covering her legs.

His hand fell heavily over her abdomen, large, his fingers nearly covering the entire area of it. He inhaled sharply, and his eyes found hers once again.

He knew. He knew about the child.

"You're pregnant," he said crudely.

"It is scarcely my fault!"

He stiffened like steel. His fingers bit into her wrist, and his hand tensed upon her abdomen. "Whose is it?" he asked in a deceptively pleasant voice.

It took her several seconds to realize the accusation of his question, and when she did, she exploded with fury and broke his grip upon her. The tears she had held back, and all the desperate fear of the ocean voyage, surged into her, and she became a wild thing, crying, screaming, tearing at him, striking out with her fists and her feet and barely coherent words.

"Jassy!"

She didn't hear him. She managed to rise to her knees, and he rose to meet her, but she slammed her fists against his breast with such a vengeance that he grunted in pain. She leapt from the bed and started to run in her stockings and little blue satin shoes, but he caught her hair and spun her back. She slammed back against the bed again, and he was on top of her.

"Jassy!"

"No, no, no!" She tossed her head in furious distress while he straddled her. "You will not speak to me so, treat me so, and think that we can do . . . this!"

"Jassy, shush!"

"Go to her, go to your Indian mistress!"

"She is not my mistress, I have never touched her."

"But she serves you so well!"

"She shaved me this morning, that is all. While you—"

"You hateful, loathsome snake! It is your baby, but that doesn't matter to me. I don't care whose baby it is, I don't want it! I want to go home! I do not want to die here—"

"Jassy, you're not going to die!"

Silent tears streamed down her face. "Why not? The baby died upon the ship. It was born blue. They wrapped it up and they threw it overboard, and the fish have surely eaten it. And then Joan died too. She bled to death. She lay there and she bled to death, and there was nothing—nothing!—that could be done for her."

She hadn't realized that he had freed her hands until she saw that she was pounding them with little strength against his chest. He was dead still, tense, watching her, and ignoring her blows. Finally he caught her hands. He held them between his own. "Jassy, you are not going to die. You are a very healthy young woman."

"I don't want this child!"

"I do."

She opened her eyes wide and stared at him. "Why did you marry me?"

"What?" he said wearily.

She started to laugh. "You did not want me. You wanted a vessel who you could force here. You wanted someone who could survive childbirth in this place. You—"

"Stop it, Jassy."

"No!"

"Stop it!"

"No!"

She opened her mouth to speak again, but this time he found a more direct route to stop her. He closed her mouth with a kiss.

It was a deep, searing . . . and tender kiss.

His tongue delved into her mouth again and again. It filled her mouth insinuatively, and then withdrew, and each time her lips parted more fully in anticipation, and then she met his tongue with her own, and their mouths met again and again. He began to stroke her body, and she had never known such care from his hands, such a tenderness. He touched her so lightly that she arched, aching to feel more his palm against her breast. He breathed and nibbled against her earlobes, and his tongue drew a fiery trail down her throat and over her collarbones and into the deep, shadowed valley between her breasts. And again she writhed and arched to meet him when his mouth fell full and wide over her breasts and sucked upon her slowly and completely. His hands wandered and roamed and found the moist center of her, and she cried out and pressed him there too. Trembling from head to toe, she closed her eyes and writhed, awaiting him. Suddenly he was gone.

And she had what she had wanted, what she had longed for.

He stripped impatiently.

She watched him through half-closed eyes. He moved toward her, bronzed and sleek and powerfully muscular. She admitted as she lay there with the air caressing her body that she loved the proud, leonine quality of his head, the indigo of his eyes, the rich, dark hair upon his head, his chest, and nesting the protruding manhood of him. She wanted him. . . .

He crawled atop her and caught her palm and brought it to his lips. He kissed it and brought her hand downward.

"Touch me," he whispered.

"No . . ."

"Touch me."

"No . . ."

"Touch me."

"Yes . . ."

He cast back his head and let out a male groan of pleasure and triumph that might have shattered the house. Jassy did not care. She was fascinated by the powerful shaft of him, by the seething pulse, the massive life. His lips found hers, and he kissed her, and he touched her, too, and in the end she was nearly delirious. He groaned out again and twisted her and turned her, and there was nowhere upon her that his lips did not brush her flesh. His teeth nipped against her buttocks and his tongue ran hot and wild over her spine, and she was seeking access to him, too, all the while. She indulged herself in her whims, and in her dream, and she stroked the fine muscles of his chest, she played the touch of her fingers over his tightly muscled rear, and she teased his earlobes with her teeth and bathed his shoulders with her kisses. She was half sobbing when he rose above her at last, and she screamed with incredible pleasure when he plunged deep, deep within her, burying himself.

She screamed again when it was over, the sensation was so strong and so volatile. Embarrassed, she buried herself against the slick dampness of his chest and tried not to think of all the very wanton things she had done.

His arms wrapped tightly around her. His chin rested on her forehead, and he stroked her hair. He was as silent as she.

The fire in the hearth burned low. Jassy thought that perhaps he slept. She turned slightly, but he held her still, his hand beneath her breast, his fingers very lightly splayed upon it. She felt the length and warmth and strength of his body, curled flush to hers.

"Jassy . . ." he whispered. His fingers moved from her breast to her belly. "Don't be afraid. You are not going to die. I want my son. I will be with you."

"I—"

"What?"

"I want to go home," she said.

He stiffened, and his arm went still. She trembled and caught his hand when he turned away from her. She was suddenly terrified that he would spurn her.

"Jassy," he said, and he held her again. "This is your home."

"You will not let me go?" she whispered.

"No."

Another tremor ripped through her, and she was not sure if his answer distressed her, or made her sweetly pleased. Her fingers tightened around his, and he paused and laced his slowly and carefully with hers. "You are my wife, for better or worse, and I will never allow you to leave me."

"You accused me of lying with Robert!" she said.

"I do not think that you would."

"And why not?"

"Because you know that I would be forced to slay Robert."

She shivered, suddenly, violently, because it was certainly true. She wished that he had told her that he knew that she would not because she would not dishonor him, her sister, or herself.

But then, Jamie certainly did not think the best of her, or of her motives.

He had gone silent. He held her still, warm and secure against him, and for that she was glad. But she could not bear her life here if he were to turn from her.

"What of the Indian girl?" she persisted.

"She is an interpreter. Nothing more."

"Would you swear it to me?"

He released her suddenly, rising above her to study her eyes in the darkness. "What?"

She swallowed, meeting his eyes with a mixture of determination and innocence in her own. "Please, I want you to swear it to me."

He smiled slowly. "This once, milady, but I am not a man accustomed to having his word doubted, so do not think to challenge me so again. I swear— Hope is an interpreter, and nothing more. We think that she is a descendant of a white hostage from Roanoke, the lost colony. I have never touched her, I promise. Is that all?"

"Yes," Jassy said complacently. She hesitated and added a prim "Thank you."

"You're welcome."

He lay down beside her. His arm did not come around her until she nudged her buttocks against him and sighed softly. Then he turned, holding her against him once again, his hips to her derriere, his hand resting upon and below her breast.

It was a very comfortable way to rest, Jassy determined.

"One more thing, milady."

"Yes?"

"I shall teach you how to fire a musket; you need ask no other man."

"No, milord," Jassy said sweetly. "I will need to ask no other man."

"For anything."

"For anything."

Her fears had receded remarkably, and to her amazement she quickly closed her eyes and very quickly drifted into a sound and dreamless sleep.

13

ASSY AWOKE WHEN A FIRM HAND MADE SOUND
contact with her derriere. She jerked up in indignation and
discovered that Jamie was already dressed, and staring down
upon her like a tyrant. The fire had burned very low and the
room was cold. Adding insult to injury, he pulled her covers away. " 'Tis morning, love. And we've things to do. Up."

It wasn't morning, not at all. There was only the palest flicker of soft pink light
finding its way into the room. Jassy stared at him with sure hostility, reprocured
her covers, and burrowed back within them. She had not risen so early in a very
long time. Not since she had scrubbed floors before dawn to save her mother the
labor at Master John's.

"Come, milady—up!"

The covers were swept away again. Jassy cried out in protest, coming to her
knees to retrieve them. She came flush against Jamie, who was laughing at her, a
wicked gleam to his dark gaze. Men, she decided, were impossible. She had
submitted and surrendered to him, answered his every demand in life, and he was
behaving like the devil's own autocrat.

"I'm freezing!" she said.

"Then dress quickly and you will not be so cold. Wear something warm, for it
seems we have an early cold snap."

"Fine!" she promised him. He started to turn, and she snatched back her
covers and sank back into the down of the bed. She was startled to hear the
sound of his laughter, and then feel the weight of his body as he leapt down
beside her. Her eyes opened wide upon his, and the mischievous glare within
them.

"If I cannot get you up, then I suppose that I must come down."

She gasped softly and rolled quickly from the bed, just evading the grasp of his
fingers. Shivering, she landed upon the floor but quickly leapt up and snatched
the covers around her nakedness. She frowned, seeing the good humor in his
face as he propped upon an elbow to watch her. He was completely dressed,
down to high boots and greatcoat and plumed hat.

"You've been out already?" she said.

"Aye, madame, I have. The hunting is best in the very early morning, when
the creatures of the forest awake to break their own fasts of the eve."

"You might have let me sleep—"

"Nay, love, though I'd a mind to, in appreciation for the wondrous quality of
the night."

She flushed and bit into her lower lip. He was amused; she wished that she did not so easily betray her ardor, for she was certain that it gave him good cause to reflect upon her background. "If there is a certain time—"

"There is, and it is now. The day begins early, at dawn. We hunt, and the farmers take in the first hours of the day to work the fields, for with winter almost upon us, darkness comes early. And now is the time when we dine, and since the days are so busy, it is best if we all dine at one time."

"I will dress."

He sighed with drama, and his eyes fell fleetingly over the length of her. "Be damned with a meal!" he declared, pushing off from the bed and striding toward her. She let out a little gasp, but he was upon her, taking her hard into his arms. "Be damned with a meal, and with time, and with schedules. I cannot bear it. I fear that I must sweep you into my arms. . . ."

He kissed her, sweetly and deeply and tenderly, and though she knew that he was teasing her and being entirely dramatic, the kiss was sweet and enflaming and entirely decadent, and quickly sent a surging stream of molten flame streaking through her. His lips left hers to land against the pulse at her throat, and she whispered to him in sudden panic. "No, Jamie, it is morning! People will expect us downstairs, we must go down. I'll dress quickly, Jamie, they will be waiting for us—" She choked off, catching her breath, for he pulled the sheet away from her in an instant, baring her body to the cool air of the morning.

"Let them wait," he said, and he was teasing her no longer. His eyes were hungry, and they ravaged her with no uncertainty. She was indeed freezing now, for the room was chilly, and she had no sheet about her, nor did he touch her to warm her. Her teeth chattered, goose pimples broke out on her flesh, and her hair streamed out over her breasts where the peaks of them teased through golden strands, hardened by the chill, and fascinatingly enlarged by her pregnancy.

"Jamie . . ."

He came back to her, laughing. He took her into his arms and kissed her again, then his laughter faded and his lips found her shoulder blades and collarbone, and he very slowly lowered his length against her. Her fingers fell upon his well-clad shoulders and she could have pushed him away, but she did not. "I am cold—"

"Nay, lady you are hot as fire."

And soon she was. The light of day was upon them, and it seemed dangerous and sinful and very exciting. She shivered still against the cold of the room, but where his lips touched her and where his hands fell upon her, she was aflame. He traveled the length of her, and she gasped and bit back a scream when he touched her searingly and intimately, and she cast back her head to the abandon of it, her fingers moving over his shoulders and then into his hair, her body alive with trembling. She could not think, but only feel the sheer, sweet assault upon her senses.

She was not cold. . . .

No, not cold at all. The molten fire raged the whole of her, like sunlight streaking from the center of her being, wherever he touched and ravaged and laved. She gasped and cried out, incoherently mouthing his name, pleading that he stop. But he did not, and the sunfire did burst and explode and cascade throughout her, and then she heard his pleased, husky laughter, and flamed crimson as the nectar of her ecstasy escaped from her body.

She thought that she would fall, but he quickly swept her into his arms. He laid her upon the end of the bed, adjusted no more than his breeches, knelt down, and swept into her with the driving velocity of a sudden summer storm. He held tight to her shoulders and met her eyes, until she cried and twisted so that he could not stare at her eyes and see the betraying and forbidden things that were surely alive within them.

The storm spent, he lay against her, his dark head just below her breasts. She was tempted to run her fingers through his hair, but she bit into her lower lip and held back, suddenly afraid of the very depths of the thing that raged between them. She must not give *so* much, *so* freely. She could hold nothing back, nothing at all, and it was frightening, when he still held so very much of himself away from her.

He shifted slightly, and his hand moved over her abdomen. She stiffened; she could not resist, for no matter what his words, the thoughts of the child brought new horrors to her.

"What is the matter?"

"Nothing," she lied quickly.

He swore slightly, turning away from her. "I wish I knew what it was that could unlock your mind!"

"Unlock my mind!" she cried. "You have everything! You have even that which I would hold away from you—"

"That's it, my love. Exactly. You try to hold back."

"But I am the daughter of a whore and unable to do so?" she whispered bitterly.

He caught her shoulders, pulling her up. "Jassy, you are my wife, and a beautiful and passionate woman, and nothing else beyond that matters."

"Because we are in this wilderness."

"Because I have said that it is so."

She flushed and lowered her eyes, for she thought that he was in earnest, and that he did not mock her. He rose and adjusted and tied his breeches, and before she could curl away from him, he was beside her again, his hand lightly upon the swell of her abdomen. His fingers rose and encircled her breasts, and she bit her inner lip, staring toward the door.

"You frighten me," he said softly.

She stared at him, amazed for one that anything could frighten Jamie Cameron. "Why?"

"Because you do not want the child and you are capable of impetuous and dangerous measures. Tell me, is it because it is my child?"

She didn't understand his question at first, and therefore she hesitated, then hoped she had not hesitated too long. "No," she said quickly. "I—"

"Never mind. I don't want to hear it. But you will hear me out, and hear me out well. If you think to avoid this pregnancy, you could very seriously be risking your own life."

She stared at him for a minute blankly before she realized what he meant. Then she tried to twist away from him, only to be dragged firmly back. "Jassy?"

"Had I thought to do something, milord, I would have done so long ere now!"

He stared down at her, apparently satisfied. "Joan Tannen might have died in her own bed," Jamie said, "in England."

"But she didn't. She died on the ship, trying to reach this pagan land." Her eyes came to his once again. "I must see the laborer John Tannen. I—"

"He has been told about his wife and child."

She shook her head, and she was afraid that she was going to cry. She had to see the man herself. No one else knew as she did how Joan had loved him, and he deserved to be told. "I must see him!"

"Jassy—"

"Please!"

Startled, he hesitated, watching her curiously. Then he shrugged. "After breakfast I intend to give you your first lesson with the musket. Supper is at four; you may find John Tannen between the two, if you are so determined."

"I am. Please."

He nodded, and still he watched her, holding her still. She felt a flush rising to her face again, and she lowered her lashes over her eyes. "What is it? We will be very late if you do not let me rise and dress. You are ready rather easily," she said with a certain resentment edging her tone.

He laughed again, and she liked the sound of it; she even liked the look of him when she dared meet his eyes again. His hat had fallen, and rich tendrils of dark hair fell in disarray over his forehead, and his eyes blazed their deep, rich blue from the bronze hues of his well-structured face. He was startlingly appealing then, ever more so with his laughter.

"You used my Christian name," he said.

"What?"

He leaned down very close to her and whispered above her lips. "When we made love, my dear. You called out to me and used my name. You have never done so before." He kissed her lips lightly, her forehead, her left breast, and her belly, then rose quickly. "Come on! We are frightfully late."

"Late!"

"Aye!"

He pulled her to her feet. She ran, freezing and naked once more, behind the screen to the washstand. There was a discreet knock upon the door, Jassy heard footsteps behind the screen, and then Jamie cast the door open. She heard his deep, well-modulated words to the caller who had come for them. "Good morning, Molly, did you sleep well enough in your new bed?"

"Aye, my Lord Cameron, that I did!"

"Are we so late, then?"

"Well, milord, Amy is fretting—"

"There is no need. I shall talk to her right now. And, Molly, your timing is wonderful, for your mistress is just this moment in need of your services."

The door shut, and Jassy heard a rustle of skirts as she doused her face and hands with water from the pitcher on the washstand. "Jassy!" Molly called.

"Aye!"

"What'll you be needing?"

"Everything!" Jassy said, and in a moment a shift appeared over the screen and she slipped it on and came around. Molly, her eyes bright and her cheeks flushed, awaited her in high good humor. "Late night, love?"

"Molly!" Jassy said, stepping into her petticoats.

Molly laughed delightedly, then hugged her. "I'm just so very happy for you, love. I always did think that he was the one for you. There's a grain of strength in him, not like the blond—"

"Robert Maxwell?"

"Aye, that one." Molly came around with her corset and tied up the ribbons as Jassy adjusted the stays.

"Robert is a wonderful man."

"And you, no doubt, were in love with him when you snared this one, eh? Well, mark my words, love, and I know men, that I do. You acquired the better of the two."

Jassy's head popped out of the plain blue wool she had chosen from her trunk. "You're mad, Molly. Robert is very gentle and caring, a fine man."

Molly narrowed her eyes. "So that's the way it is!"

"It is no special way," Jassy retorted. And it was true, she thought. She liked Robert more and more, like a brother. She was not in love with him. She could not be in love with him, for she could never forget her husband's hands upon her, nor the power of his being, the possession in his eyes. Whether she hated him or nay, he had encompassed something of her, and she no longer envied her sister Lenore her husband. She was too busy grappling with her own, in her dreams and in her flesh.

"Take care, love—"

"I am late, Molly. Thank you for your concern."

Jassy was angry, and so she quickly departed the room, leaving Molly and the mess within it behind.

Everyone else was already downstairs at the table: Lenore and Elizabeth and Robert and Jamie. The men rose when she approached the table, and Lenore offered her a wistful smile. Jassy apologized for being late. Robert Maxwell looked at her with knowing eyes, and she flushed. Jamie noted her reaction to his friend. She saw his jaw harden and his eyes grow dark. She tossed back her head. She was innocent of any wrongdoing, and she would be damned before she spent her life tiptoeing about his suspicions.

She sat and complimented Amy Lawton on the good breakfast of fish and bread and fresh milk and cheese. When the meal was finished, Jamie was the first to rise, pulling back his wife's chair. "I shall start with Jassy on musketry. Tomorrow, if you are so inclined, Elizabeth, I will bring you too."

"I—I don't think that I could fire a gun," Elizabeth said.

"It is your choice."

Jassy added to her sister's sentiment. "Jamie, I don't know if I will be at all capable myself—"

"Jassy, come on. Now." He had picked up his musket, resting on the wall by the hearth. He procured a length of match from a roll beside it and lit it from the fire at the hearth. Then he came back for her. He led her out by the hand, and they left the others sitting at the table. At the front door Amy met them, handing Jamie a leather bag of powder, a small satchel of balls, and a long stick with a forked end, a "rest," as Jamie murmured to Jassy. He thanked Amy. Jassy forced out a smile and told the housekeeper good morning, that she would be back soon.

As they walked through the buildings in the palisade, the housewives about their business and the occasional workman they encountered all greeted Jamie with respect and pleasure, and bobbed prettily to Jamie's wife.

"The lord and master, eh?" Jassy breathed sweetly.

"Aye, my love. Remember that."

"Did you think I might forget?"

"I think that I like not the sparkle in your eyes—that I see for other men."

"You are imagining things."

"I am not."

"But you know that I would not tarry with Robert Maxwell, for you would slay him, and then me, too, surely. I have not forgotten."

"Oh, I would not slay you, love. I would allow my son to be born, then I should lay your tender flesh black and blue and lock you away in a high tower where you could repent at leisure."

He mocked her, she thought, casting him a covert cast. Or did he? She knew him so intimately, and she didn't know the deep corners of his heart or mind at all.

They walked through the gates of the palisade, and he kept her hand held tightly in his own. They kept walking. The morning, Jassy decided, was beautiful. The sun was rising full and bright against the coolness of autumn, and already more of the leaves on the trees in the forests were changing colors. A few crimsons splashed against the golds and yellows and greens, and even the river seemed exceptionally blue and calm. In the distance Jassy could see the fields where the men were working, harvesting their spring crops. "Tobacco, our cash crop," Jamie told her, seeing the direction of her gaze.

She smiled, ignoring his words. "You would not dare beat me," she told him.

He laughed pleasantly. "Don't try me, love," he warned her.

"I cannot help that you see what is not there."

He stopped suddenly, and the humor was not about him, but something serious and tense. "What do I see? And what *is* really there, milady?"

"I—I don't know what you mean," she murmured, moving back, and wishing she had not spoken so cockily.

He advanced on her, not touching her, but towering dark and powerful over her. "Yes, you do, madame. You do not love me. That is established. Am I to believe that you have fallen *out* of love with our dashing and illustrious friend?"

Her heart leapt and careened, and she stared with a dangerous fascination at the pulse that leapt with a furious beat at the base of his throat. "*You* do not love me," she reminded him. "So what may I take that to mean?"

"Ah, madame, but I desire no other woman as I desire you. Answer me."

She lowered her head, suddenly very afraid of him, afraid also of the powerful range of his temper. "I—I love no man," she said, and lifted her eyes to his again. "It is money I cherish, remember, milord?"

His jaw tightened, but he said nothing more. He caught her hand and jerked her along again until they came to a cleared place with a single line of wooden fencing.

He took the long stick. "This is the rest," he said matter-of-factly. "The musket is heavy and difficult to aim. The rest will hold the weight and help to keep your hand steady. Do you understand?"

Icily she repeated his words. He slammed the rest into the ground. "That," she said, indicating the firearm, "is the musket. Black powder and balls. And you've an incredible amount of match." The match hung from the musket, one end burning.

"Milady, if the match is not long enough, a hunter finds his prey and discovers he has no firepower, or worse. A scout meets up with a feisty Indian and discovers that he is weaponless. Never leave without a good length of match. You do not know when you will need your weapon."

"Never leave without a good length of match," she repeated between clenched teeth. "Even though you have repeatedly assured me that the Indians are peaceful these days."

"I have never assured you so."

"You like the Indians."

"I respect their right to their own way of life," he said, drawing up the gun. "I have never suggested that a man need not take grave care around them. There are many tribes and many rulers, and a man may never know whose temper has been sparked when. Now take heed. This compartment is for the powder." He sprinkled from the bag into the powder dish, showing her how much. "Take care that the burning end of your match is away, lest you blow your fingers to ribbons," he warned her. "Close the compartment. Drop your ball and your packing, and then ram both down the barrel. Now you are ready to aim."

"And by now your feisty Indian has surely slit my throat."

"You will gain speed when you become adept. Aim low. The musket will kick back."

He fired off a shot, hitting a target upon a distant tree dead center. He reloaded, showing her how quickly all of the separate acts could be performed. Then he set the musket upon the rest for her. She aimed, low as he had suggested. The match ignited the powder, which shot off the ball. There was a tremendous roar and a mighty recoil. It sent her flying backward, and she would have fallen had he not caught her.

"You will get used to it," he said, setting her firmly upon her feet. "Now, let's do it again. You do all the steps this time."

She was exhausted when he at last determined that she should have a rest. The musket was monstrously heavy and difficult to manage. He yelled at her when she forgot to close the powder dish, and he yelled at her again when the long match dangled too close to her skirts. She yelled back and tried again, sweat beading upon her brow and trickling between her breasts. She determined that she would come to fire the damned thing better than he could. On her last effort she did very well. She loaded, aimed, and fired in a matter of a minute or two, and she did not fall back with the kick of the firepower. Triumphantly she handed him the heavy musket.

"Have I passed for the day, milord?"

"You have," he said calmly. "But then, I expected you to do very well indeed."

"Oh, yes. That is why you married me."

He stared at her hard. "You know why I married you. Let's go. You wish to see John Tannen. Now is the time to do so."

Silently they walked back to the palisade. Jamie knew his way about. He wound through the rows of houses and buildings until he came to one of the small wattle-and-daub thatched-roof homes with a smoke hole in the center. He started to knock upon the door, but the door opened and a young bearded blond man stood there, his thin face ravaged and weary but a surprised smile coming quickly to his features. "Lord Cameron, 'tis a pleasure."

"John Tannen, this is my wife, Lady Cameron. She has something she wishes to tell you."

The man looked very awkward. He pulled his flat cap from his head and squeezed it between his hands, then indicated that they should come in. "I'm so sorry, milady, milord. I'm in a bit of upheaval. I was awaiting me Joan, ye know, and, well, I'm not much of a housekeeper. And I've the older boy with me, and Joan's little sister, and we don't seem to be able to keep up much."

The small house was something of a sty, Jassy thought, for there was clothing everywhere, and the pots and pans and trenchers and jugs from many a meal were strewn about a rough wood table. A dirty little girl with huge, brown, red-rimmed eyes stared at her dolefully from the center of the room, and a boy of about ten watched her from the table where he tried to mend a pair of hose with a needle and thread and brass thimble.

Jassy looked from the boy to John Tannen. "I—I wanted to say that I was with your wife at the . . . at the end, Mr. Tannen. She spoke of you with a great deal of love, and I wished to convey that to you. I thought it important."

He suddenly took her hand in both of his great, rough worker's hands and knelt down upon the rough floor of his dwelling. He bowed humbly over her hand.

"Milady, I have heard of your tender care of my wife, and as God is my witness, you've my eternal gratitude."

Jassy stepped back, reddening. She hadn't thought much of a man who had allowed his wife to travel to meet him, especially in Joan's condition, but John Tannen seemed a sincere individual, bereft, and doing his best to stumble through the trying time. She tugged upon his hand. "Mr. Tannen, please get up. I did nothing, really."

He nodded, not really hearing her words, and he did not rise. "Mr. Tannen." She looked helplessly to Jamie. He was watching her with curious eyes, and he shrugged, leaving the situation to her.

"Mr. Tannen, get up! Now, I know that you are in pain, but indeed, this place is a hovel, and Joan would have been sorely disappointed in it." She pulled her hand away from him and looked to Jamie again, but Jamie intended to give her no help. She felt a slight quivering in her chin, wondering if the action she was contemplating would assure him that he had married beneath his class, but then she didn't care. He had cast her out to sink or swim, and so she would do as she chose.

She walked over to the table. "What's your name, boy?"

"Edmund, milady." He jumped up quickly. He was growing fast, Jassy saw. Too fast for his clothing, so it seemed.

"Edmund, fetch a good bucketful of water and heat it for me over the fire. Have you had your meal yet? Jamie will send some venison from the house, and he will send Molly over, too, and we will shortly have this place to rights."

"But you must not, milady!" John Tannen had stumbled to his feet at last. Aghast, he looked from Jassy to Jamie, back to Jassy, and then to Jamie once more. "Lord Cameron, you must explain to her that I am a common laborer and that she is your wife, and that it—that I am grateful, but . . ." He paused, talking to Jassy. "I am ever so grateful, but . . . Lord Cameron, please help me."

Jassy looked to Jamie too. If he denied her, she knew that she would defy him. This man needed help. Jamie was his master, and John Tannen had lost his wife in Jamie's service.

And she wanted to help. She *needed* to help. She held her breath and lifted her chin high.

Jamie watched her with his dark, fathomless gaze, then replied slowly to John Tannen. "I am afraid that she is determined, John, and there is little that I can say to her. You cannot deny that you need the help, and I promise you, my wife will see to it that you are quickly in some state of repair. I will send her maid, as she has suggested, along with a side of venison. Edmund, see that you escort her home after dinner."

His eyes fell upon Jassy one last time. She watched him in return, and she could not tell for sure, but he did not seem to be judging her or condemning her. If she sensed anything at all in his gaze, it was pride, and it was a good feeling. It warmed her deeply.

"Edmund! Come along now, these things must be done. What is your sister's name?"

"She is Ma's sister, not mine," Edmund said. "Her name is Margaret."

"Margaret." Jassy lifted the girl off the floor and set her upon the table. She found a mop cloth on the table and a bowl of water, and began dabbing at the little girl's face. "Ah! There is a child beneath the dirt! And truly a girl. A very pretty little girl. Come now, let's move along. There's much to do."

Molly soon arrived with the venison. She reviled poor John Tannen for the state of his house, and when he tried to explain that it was the harvest season, she found fault with something else. Jassy ignored them both and set about making a good and palatable meal. With Margaret's help she found vegetables for a stew and a bit of salt for seasoning, and cooked it all in a pot above the hearth. With Molly in charge, the place quickly became more habitable. She had everyone moving about, including John Tannen. She had the poor man so befuddled that when he at last sat down to eat, he did so with a sigh of great impatience. "Woman!" he muttered to Molly, "you do make a body long for solitude!"

Molly rapped him on the hand with her serving spoon. "John Tannen, get your filthy fingers off that bread. You will wash for this meal, or you will not consume it!"

With a quick oath he threw the bread down and rose. Then he looked at Jassy and apologized profusely. "Milady, she could make the good Lord rise and shudder himself, she could!"

"I've no doubt," Jassy said, laughing at Molly's quick look of frustration. "Now run along and wash. She is right about your hands at least."

He went along and did as he was told. When the meal was over, he went back to work, his son coming along at his heels. Jassy determined to bathe Margaret and dress her in a clean gown. She only had one other, but it was better than the first. With her face and body scrubbed, Margaret was a very pretty little girl, and she very much resembled her sister Joan. "I am going to make you another dress," Jassy promised her. "From one of my own. Would you like that?"

"Oh, yes, milady!" Margaret said. Jassy looked at Molly and found that her friend and servant was studying her solemnly.

Promising a gown to this little waif . . . it was another of those things that she was able to do because she had been swept from the gutter by Lord Cameron.

She stood and kissed Margaret's little cheek. "I hear John and Edmund coming back. Edmund will walk Molly and me home, but we shall come see you tomorrow. All right?"

Shyly Margaret nodded. John and Edmund were inside the door. John Tannen tried to speak, but Molly interrupted him. "We shall finish tomorrow. Until then, Mr. Tannen, you keep from destroying all that has been set right, eh?"

Jassy grinned and shrugged. It was the most fun she had had in a very long time. She had done something for someone that day, and it seemed that it had even worked out right.

Jamie was awaiting her in the hall when she returned. He sat at the table sipping wine, and he offered both her and Molly something to eat and drink while they spoke about the day. Molly was more verbal, tsking and telling him about John's slovenly ways.

"But he's a very good worker," Jamie said. He poured Jassy a glass of wine and held the earthenware jug above a third glass.

"Milord, I don't mind if I do at all," Molly said, and Jamie laughed and poured out the glass. The fire was still burning in the hearth, and Molly sat right beside them at the table.

"John will have his own acres soon enough," Jamie told Molly. "He labors in the township, and he works in the field. He is a man who will prosper, and I am heartily sorry that he lost his wife and child."

"Well, in another day or two he shall be set!" Molly said firmly. She drained her wine, then seemed to realize that she sat between the lord and lady of the house. She stood quickly. "Good night, Lord Cameron, Jass—er, I mean, Lady Cameron."

"Good night, Molly," Jamie said.

Jassy echoed his words, then nervously finished the wine that her husband had poured her. She wanted to show her gratitude in some measure, not so much for any material thing that he had given her but because he had bestowed his faith upon her.

She stood up, then yawned unintentionally. It had been a very long day, and she had worked very hard. "Excuse me!" she murmured self-consciously.

"You're excused," he said gravely.

"I . . . I wish to thank you."

"For what?"

"I suppose my behavior today was not the best. Perhaps I should not have insisted I stay in the house and work. I realize that I did not appear the lady at all—"

He stood, taking her glass from her hand, cutting her off. "On the contrary, love. I think that you appeared a very grand lady today. A very grand lady, indeed. Now, come to bed. It is late, and the morning will come early."

She meant to respond to him that night. She meant, with all her heart, to respond to him fully and willingly.

But he had some business to attend to at his desk, and as soon as her head hit the pillow, she fell asleep, soundly exhausted and very comfortable. In the night she felt an even greater comfort, for his arms came around her. And in the morning she was awakened by the soft pressure of his hands caressing her breasts, moving over her buttocks. She started to speak, to turn to him. His whisper touched her earlobe. "Sh . . ."

Then she gasped, startled with the pleasure as he slipped into her erotically from behind. She had been barely awake, and it all had the magical quality of a dream, yet he was real enough, very real, and the sensations that erupted over her were the same.

Then he rose quickly, kissed her cheek, and reminded her that breakfast was early.

———————

Her first weeks in the township went much the same. Molly quickly had the Tannen home in good order, but she and Jassy continued to spend time there, for Jassy had become very attached to little Margaret. And when she finished helping out at the Tannen home, she discovered that there was much to do in her own home. They could not depend upon supplies from England. Nor could any lady be idle, for there was not just the management of the household to be kept in order, but also there was always some food to be dried and stored for winter, meat to be smoked or salted, candles and soap to be made, bread to be baked, and so forth. Having servants was one thing, Jassy quickly discovered, but here, it meant having someone to share the work, not having someone to do it all. Monday through Saturday were workdays, and Sunday was a day of worship, and everyone from Lord and Lady Cameron and their noble guests to the lowliest laborer or serving wench attended services at the church. They wore their best clothes, and they celebrated the day with grace and good humor.

Jassy had been in the hundred for nearly a month when Jamie left her for a week, traveling into the interior at the request of Opechancanough. She was startled at the distress his departure caused her, and she tried to talk him out of going. So far, the only Indian she had met was Hope, and she wasn't sure that Hope would count as a representative of the Powhatan Confederation. She had seen some of the Indians, walking along or riding by the palisade. She had even seen Jamie pause to speak with the wildly tattooed men and children, but Jamie had been high atop his horse with his knife at his calf, his musket upon his saddle.

She did not like the idea of his going into the interior.

"Do you care so much, then, my love?" he asked that night, teasing her. She brushed her hair, and he lay in bed watching her.

"I think that you are being foolish."

"I have been invited. For the sake of the settlement, I must go."

"Someone else should go. I have heard what these Indians can do to white men."

"If I am slain, milady, think of the benefits that will come your way. You carry my heir, and so all of my property will rest in your hands. You can return to England, if you so wish. You can do whatever you will."

"Stop it!" she hissed to him. "They *do* kill white men, you know. *Savagely*. They mutilate and burn them and skin them alive, or so I have heard."

"*Do* you care, then?" Jamie said softly.

Jassy kept her eyes from him and concentrated upon the length of her hair. "I should hate to think of you overly bloodied."

"I shall ask them to kill me quick."

She threw the brush at him. He laughed and leapt out of bed, naked and sleek and graceful, and swept her up into his arms. He dropped her down upon the bed, and he stared at her a long time, holding her tight, feeling their hearts thud together and smiling at the sizzle of anger in her eyes. "I think that you do care, my love. Just a little bit. So kiss me. Let me bring the feel of you, the scent of you, the taste of you, into the heart of the fray."

"There is no fray—" she began, but his lips had found hers, and in a matter of moments she was caught up in a tempest again. He kissed her everywhere and swore that he would remember her taste, just as he would recall, in the cold and lonely nights to come, the fullness of her breasts and the curve of her hip, the musky perfume of her soap mingled with what was all woman about her. His words, his kisses, inflamed her again and again. She was amazed that he could leave her so sated one moment and be back to touch her again even as she sighed and closed her eyes. It was a long and tempestuous night, and in the morning she could barely awaken. Jamie rose, left her, and came back again. He kissed her lips. "I leave in an hour. You must come down."

To her own surprise she clung to him, her arms about his neck, her bare breasts crushed to his chest. She buried her face against his neck until he slowly released her. "You must come down," he repeated huskily, and then he was gone.

She awoke fully at last, stretching her hand across the bed and finding that it was cold where Jamie had been.

She crawled out of bed, shivering. The November morning was brisk and cold. She thought about calling for Molly or Kathryn. The fire had died out in the hearth, and she would have dearly loved a long, hot bath. But she was very cold, so she quickly washed, pouring water from the pitcher to the bowl, and scrubbing with the cloth neatly folded on the stand. She dressed in one of the warm wool gowns she had made, and came out on the landing.

She ran into Robert Maxwell, who was just coming from his bedroom. He offered her a wry smile, rubbing his freshly shaven chin. "Good morning, Jassy. You're up and about."

"Yes. Jamie is leaving soon."

"Lenore is still sleeping. I should awaken her."

"Let her sleep, then."

"Ah, but this is the New World, and a new way, and I believe that we all must get accustomed to it."

He was still very handsome, Jassy thought. He had always had his quick smile ready, and he was ever courteous. Sometimes he could still make her heart flutter, and he could make her laugh when she was low. But something about the way she felt about him was changing, and it had been doing so for a long time now. She wondered it it was because Jamie more and more filled her thoughts. Whether she was hating him or longing for him, he was always on her mind, a strong, definitive presence, and one that she could not shake.

"I suppose we must," she said softly. "But then, you can go home if you choose, Robert. I cannot."

"I cannot go home," he assured her, "for I have no home." He laughed suddenly and touched her cheek with gentle affection. "Ah, Jassy, you are the best of the lot of us, do you know that? They would label you a bastard, but you've inherited the best of the nobility, and the very finest of the common lass.

You will survive, and survive well, and put the rest of us to shame. We shall flounder, as we did on the ship, and you shall lead the way."

"I did nothing—"

"You did. You were brave and determined, and we admired you very much, with all of our hearts."

His tone was earnest and his voice was soft, and it was a calming salve against the fears that had lived with her so long. She stretched up on her toes to kiss him. It was not with passion of any kind, but with nothing more than the deep, sisterly affection she was coming to know for him.

"Good morning, Jassy, Robert."

The startling sound of her husband's voice drew Jassy back to her solid feet, and she spun upon the landing. Jamie stood at the foot of the carved stairway, a curious smile twisting his lips, his dark eyes hard upon them.

"Good morning, Jamie," Robert said heartily. "And you are off, so I hear. I wonder what I shall do without your leadership."

Robert offered Jassy his hand, and she took it. She was innocent, and she was not going to let Jamie's hot eyes condemn her. At the base of the stairway Robert handed her over to Jamie very properly, and Jamie accepted her hand from his friend. She felt the simmering ire within him. She lifted her chin, ignoring it.

"Robert, I imagine that you shall do fine in my absence," Jamie said dryly. "See to your house, man, for it is almost completed, and I find that the workmen have done very well. Let's sit to breakfast, shall we, for then I must take my leave."

He led them down the vast hallway to the table at the rear of it. Here the fire in the hearth burned healthily, and a cauldron of something simmered above it. Amy was there, stirring the stuff inside. She smiled happily at Jassy. Jassy smiled back, aware of Jamie's fingers, a burning vise upon her.

"A Scottish porridge," Amy advised her. "Good against the cold and damp here, milady."

"It smells wonderful."

"Of course, we've game too. His Lordship is a fine hunter, and we never lack for fowl or venison. There's cold meat atop the table already, and bread and milk."

Jassy freed herself from her husband's touch and found her place at the table. Robert and Jamie joined her, and she gave her attention to the meal, complimenting Amy, who admitted that she had prepared the porridge as Jonathan was busy plucking the wild turkeys that Lord Cameron had brought in that morning.

Jassy cast her husband a quick glance and found that his eyes were upon her speculatively. He smiled. "The day always starts early here, my love."

"You've been hunting already?" Robert demanded. "*Today?*"

"Aye, that I have."

"On a day that you will leave? And imagine, you could sleep late and be damned with labor back home in England."

"Perhaps."

"Well," Robert said, "it is the life that I would choose."

"And you, Jassy?" Jamie inquired, his tone light, "I believe that you would have preferred such a life."

Things had gone so well between them for so long. Had it all been illusion? That morning he was angry and mocking, and it infuriated her and cut deeply. She did not wish to fight that morning, but he had seen her kissing Robert, and his temper had flamed, no matter how he attempted to conceal it. He did not trust her. What had they between them, then?

She replied to him bitterly. "I did not come from such a life, milord," she reminded him, aware that Amy Lawton heard her every word. "But I was not given a choice, if I recall. Besides, my home, sir, is the gutter, as you deem important to remind me at times."

Amy, about to set down a bowl of porridge, stiffened. Jamie's eyes glittered, his temper rising. He idly drew his finger upon the back of Jassy's hand. She did not dare draw away.

He smiled above her head to Amy, his dark eyes alight, his mouth curved into a sardonic, wickedly appealing grin. "She married me for my money, you see. It has been a grave disappointment for my lady to discover that she had married not for silver and crystal, but for a raw log home in the wilderness."

Amy flushed crimson. Jassy longed to kick Jamie beneath the table. Robert laughed uneasily.

Jassy stood. "How dare you, Jamie Cameron—"

"I only ended what you chose to begin, my love," Jamie said, his eyes narrowing. He used his foot to pull in her chair, causing her to fall back into it. "Sit, my lady. You have not dined as yet. And you must. Mustn't she, Mrs. Lawton? It is cold and hard here, and she must keep up her strength."

"Milord, I am sure—" Amy Lawton began.

"That it is none of your affair. Quite right, Mrs. Lawton. You are the very soul of discretion, and we are well pleased with you." He stood suddenly, impatiently. "Lady Cameron is with child, Amy. Our babe will be born in February, though she conceals her state well in those voluminous skirts. You will, I trust, see to her welfare while I am gone?"

Amy gasped softly, staring at Jassy. "Milady, I did not realize—"

"So you are with child," Robert breathed, startled.

Jassy kept her furious eyes pinned upon her husband. "Yes."

"You said nothing on the ship," Robert said. "None of us knew. Even now you did not tell us—"

"There was little reason to do so."

"We should have been taking greater care of you."

Jassy stood again and smiled down at Robert ruefully. "Why? Joan Tannen received no special care. They sent her down to the common quarters. Her baby died and she died. And no one thought a thing of it. She was a commoner, as I am myself." She turned to leave.

Jamie caught her arm. "You are my wife," he reminded her softly, "and for that reason alone, madame, you will take care."

She pulled away from him, wondering just what his words meant, if he thought that she should take care for her health's sake, or for their child's sake . . . or if she should take very special care that he not discover her again as close to Robert Maxwell as he had that morning.

Tears suddenly stung her eyes as she lowered her head and rued the argument that had sprung up between them. He was entering the Indians' territory, and they were at tragic odds.

They had always been at tragic odds, she told herself. The change had been an illusion.

"Jassy—" Jamie said, catching her arm again.

"I do intend to take the greatest care, milord!" she said, raising her lashes at last, and meeting his eyes with her own, glazed with tears. "And may I suggest, milord, that you do the same yourself?"

He smiled suddenly, tensely. He pulled her against him, there at the table. "Kiss me good-bye," he whispered to her.

She did not need to kiss him. He kissed her. Passionately, forcefully, violently . . . then tenderly. Her heart thundered, she could scarcely breathe, and she could taste him and all the salt of her tears. When he released her at last, she was dizzy, and she could barely see, for she was blinded with her tears.

"Good-bye, milord, take heed!" she said, and she pushed away from him, ran for the stairs, and fled up the length of them.

14

JASSY SAW HER FIRST INDIAN BRAVE ON THE tenth of December, when Jamie had already been gone for almost two weeks.

She was beyond the palisade with Sir William Tybalt as her escort, and she was covered with soot and smudge, industriously studying the art of musketry. Elizabeth was at her side, shivering with each recoil of the weapon, and warning Jassy that she could bring harm to her child.

"Elizabeth, this is very important—" Jassy was saying when she saw the curious red-skinned man upon the pinto pony.

He was perhaps fifty yards away from them, observing them. There were a half dozen men behind him, but none of them was noticeable, not when the startlingly proud figure sat before them on his horse.

"It is Powan," Sir William said, standing between the women and the warrior. Jassy peeked around Sir William, fascinated.

Even atop the pony it was evident that Powan was a tall man. His buckskin-clad legs were very long, and dangled far below the horse's belly. He was not so much red as he was a deep, deep bronze, and his eyes were the darkest mahogany color Jassy had ever seen. He carried his head with the air of a king, and his features were somehow noble, too, high-boned and broad, long-nosed and square-jawed. He looked at them with a penetrating gaze, an autocrat who wore a cloak of blue-and-white plumes over broad, heavily muscled shoulders. Despite the growing December chill, he wore no shirt beneath the cloak, and Jassy could see tattoos of primitive hunting scenes upon his arms.

"Powan?" she murmured.

He carried a feathered and sharpened shaft, some kind of a spear, but he held it more like a scepter than a weapon. He nudged his pony and advanced upon them. Despite the fact that they were basically alone with Sir William by the fencing, Jassy was more curious than frightened. Perhaps it was a dangerous fascination, brought on by the endless stories she had heard of the Algonquin family savages. But surely there could be no real danger. The men were busy collecting the last of the winter harvest from the fields, and carpenters and laborers worked on various dwellings within and without the palisade. Nearer the river, a number of the women were busy with candlemaking, dipping and stringing their tallow. Powan had come with only a handful of braves. Jassy was aware that her knowledge of the Indians was limited, but instinct told her that this was a peaceful venture.

"Powan!" Sir William said, and he lifted his hand in a gesture of friendship.

The Indian dismounted and came forward. He was very tall, as Jassy had suspected. As tall as Jamie at least. And there were other curious resemblances between the men, she thought. They were built much the same, lean but tightly muscled, graceful, and supremely confident in their silent movement.

"Good day, William Tybalt," the Indian said, and Jassy started at his use of the king's good English. His eyes fell upon her and, in a leisurely and insolent fashion, traveled up and down the length of her. Jassy flamed beneath the pagan regard and wondered at the red man's thoughts, for in a month the pregnancy she had concealed for so long in the pure volume of her petticoats and skirts had become quite evident. Still, he seemed to find her as fascinating as she found him.

"Powan, it is always good to wish you good day," Sir Tybalt said. "This is the Lady Cameron, Jamie's woman, his wife."

A curious flicker of emotions passed over the Indian's strong features. "Jamie's wife?"

"Yes."

"Good day, Jamie's wife," Powan said.

"Good day, Powan," Jassy said. Impulsively she stepped forward. She took his hand and shook it. He watched her with a mixture of amusement and pleasure, then laughed and looked at Sir William. "She is a fine woman for my friend, Jamie. She grows heavy with his seed. It is good."

Elizabeth still cringed behind Jassy. Jassy dragged her sister around. "This is Elizabeth. Lady Elizabeth. She is my sister."

Elizabeth could not speak. Powan looked her up and down with a certain contempt and spat on the ground. He muttered something in his native tongue, then lifted his hand, and one of his men came forward, carrying a broken musket. The firing mechanism had disjoined from the wooden barrel.

Powan moved on to matters of business. "Where is Jamie? I would like this fixed."

"Jamie has gone to see Opechancanough," Sir William informed Powan, "at the chief's request. In his stead I will give you this musket . . ." He paused. Jassy was leaning upon the weapon. She smiled quickly and lifted up the heavy weapon to give to Powan. He took it from her and laughed. "She is a strong woman. Good for Jamie. She will work hard in his fields and give him many children."

Then Powan had nothing else to say. He shouldered the musket and lifted his feathered shaft in a gesture of farewell. He leapt upon his saddleless pony, lifted the gun and the shaft again, then whirled the horse around and headed for the forest, his men jogging along after him.

Elizabeth let out a gasp of relief, then started to fall in a swoon. "Oh, catch her!" Jassy cried, and Sir William did so, lifting Elizabeth into his arms. Elizabeth's blue eyes opened, wide and dazed. "Oh, he could have killed us!"

"Nay, nay, lady!" Sir William said assuringly. "We are at peace with the Indians."

"Let's go back to the house and have some warmed mead, shall we?" Jassy suggested. She didn't want Elizabeth to see it, but she was still shaking herself, and she didn't know if it was with fear or excitement.

Sir William carried Elizabeth, but near the palisade she determined that she could walk; she did not want someone making a fuss over her. At the house Jassy quickly searched the wooden shelves behind the big table for a ceramic jug of mead and, finding it, poured out a glass for Elizabeth. Elizabeth choked it down, then smiled dazedly at Jassy. "Oooh, he was so frightening!"

"Nonsense, Elizabeth, he did nothing frightening at all!" Jassy protested.

"Powan is a friend," Sir William assured her. "Jamie is his *good* friend. In the winter of 1608 to 1609, Jamie was here with Captain John Smith. The whites were nearly betrayed by Powhatan, and a ruthless killing started up between the two sides. Powan and Jamie were just lads, but Powan stumbled upon a group of bitter Jamestown settlers on the river. They meant to string up Powan, but Jamie let him go, telling the men that the king's good Englishmen did not murder children. They have never forgotten each other. Powan is a chief of his people now. Opechancanough is still the final law upon the Confederation, but Powan does have a certain authority."

"He is a savage!" Elizabeth insisted, shivering. She swallowed more mead.

"Savage, yes, but a part of this land," Sir William said. He smiled ruefully to Jassy. "You handled yourself very well, Lady Cameron. Jamie would have been proud."

Sir William bowed low to her and Elizabeth, then took his departure. Jassy watched his retreating back and wondered just what her husband would think about his Indian friend's approval. She made a good wife—she would work hard in Jamie's fields and give him many children. Well, it was what Jamie had wanted.

That night when she lay in bed, she thought about her husband, as she had every night since he had left. She ran her fingers over the bed where he usually lay, and she was swept through with a curious shivering and anguish. She missed him sorely. Even hating the way that they had parted, she missed him. She did not care if they fought, if they came together in tempest or in anger. She wanted him beside her, touching her. She liked the security of lying with him, and she was anxious for the deep sound of his voice. And now she missed the laughter, too, and the tenderness that they had shared so many times. No matter what she tried to hold from him, she gave all of herself too easily. She lay down upon the bed, and he swept her to new heights. He touched her if she feigned sleep, and he awoke her with the dawn. Sometimes he was fierce and impatient, and sometimes he was achingly slow and gentle, and yet she could never lie still, never pretend that he did not unlock the deepest secrets and passion within her, for he would always persist, and in the end she would submit to the overwhelming sensation. Now, with him gone, she had only her dreams, and they were usually sweet. She dreamt of him, of his indigo eyes, naked in their intent and purpose. She awaited him in a bed of white down, and he strode toward her, bronzed and savage and beautiful, and she lifted her arms out to him.

That night the dream changed. It began the same way, but then it changed.

Jamie was coming to her. Tall and towering and muscled and sleek and bronzed and blatantly sexual in his sure, silent approach. She awaited him, aching for him. But then he was no longer purely naked; he wore a cloak of white feathers, and his look had been altered, until he was coming upon her like one of the pagan Indians. It was Jamie still, but then it was not, and she was afraid. He caught her ankles within his hands and wrenched her down toward him, brutally parting her legs. She started to scream, but no sound would come, and she was drowning in a sea of white feathers. . . .

The feathers were lifted into mist. She was walking now, approaching a bed. She didn't want to lift the covers, but she had to do so. She started to scream again. There were corpses there, a line of them. Her mother's emaciated body was riddled with worm holes. Jamie, in the white feather cloak, lay beside Linnet, and an ax protruded from his heart. Beside him she lay herself, white and wide-eyed, the head of her scalped infant child cradled in her arms.

She bolted up and discovered that she was not alone. Elizabeth and Lenore were in her doorway. Robert was at her side.

"It—it was a dream," Jassy said. She was trembling still. Robert took her into his arms, and she started to sob. He soothed her, smoothing back her hair.

"It is all right. It is all right," Robert said.

"It was the Indian," Elizabeth said bluntly. She looked at Lenore. "She had ceased the nightmares, and now she has them again. It was the Indian, I know it."

"We shall all be slain in our beds!" Lenore said, distressed.

Listening to them, Jassy realized her own weakness. She pushed away from Robert, quickly and ruefully wiping the tears from her cheeks with her knuckles. "I'm sorry. I'm such a fool, really. I do have dreams now and then. It's all right. I'm all right. Lenore, we will not be slain. Powan is Jamie's friend. We have a good guard about the hundred. I am so sorry that I disturbed you. Please go back to sleep, and don't be alarmed."

By then Amy Lawton had come up the stairs, and she stared at Robert and Jassy together. "What is it?"

"A dream, Mrs. Lawton, nothing more. I am so very sorry," Jassy said.

Robert kissed her forehead. She rose quickly, hugged both her sisters, and offered Mrs. Lawton another apology. "Please, forgive me. Go to sleep."

When she was alone again, she did not think. She lay awake, not dreaming, but imagining her husband. She saw his dark eyes, his tall, proud build, powerful, exciting, arresting. She respected him, she knew. The dream had reminded her that he was his own man, and that he made his own rules. He had defied propriety and class and had married her. He had swept her from poverty and starvation, and the cruel grip of a life of labor. He had quickly demanded her respect. But there was more to it now. She might be angry, but she did not detest him. She wanted him, she desired him, with a fever that was surely indecent. She was afraid to fathom what she felt, but she promised herself that night that when he came home, she was going to be a good wife to him in all ways.

The next day, another of her husband's ships appeared on the river. It was the *Lady Destiny,* and her captain, Roger Stewart, quickly sought out Jassy. The *Lady Destiny* had brought many gifts from England. Jamie had ordered Jassy a wool-and-ermine cloak for the winter, and a whole assortment of fur muffs. Crate after crate of soft silks and laces and taffetas and brocades was delivered to the house. There was also a set of gold-plated chalices, and a multitude of ceramic jars and vases from Italy and Spain. The finest of the gifts was a delicate filigree necklace from which suspended a fine blue sapphire surrounded by diamond chips. With her sisters about her to help her, she laughed joyously as they opened box after box. Jamie, she thought, was very good to her. She would quit complaining about this place, she thought, and she would strive to like it. Perhaps it would not be so hard. More and more, the hundred became a complete community. There were now two kilns, and two talented potters at work. Another weaver and a metalsmith had arrived from England.

Mr. and Mrs. Donegal had opened a trading center where the artisans sold their crafts. Even John Tannen was doing well, with Molly more frequently with him than with Jassy and the household.

Tamsyn was no longer an old drunk. He was clean-shaven and neat in appearance and never imbibed too much liquor these days. He was not even so old, Jassy realized, and she enjoyed his company often in the afternoons. She would come out to the large stable built off the back of the house, and while he worked upon the horses, he would spin tales for her about things he had learned during his days at Oxford. He opened the world to her, and once, when he realized that she was brooding, he reminded her that he had been a good physician once, and that he would readily die himself before letting anything happen to her in childbirth.

Aye . . . the days were growing good, and far less grim than Jassy had imagined. Tamsyn had regained his soul and his strength, and Molly might well become the wife of a free man with a fine future. Little Margaret looked happier and prettier by the day, and it was all a magic *she* had created . . . by her husband's largesse, she admitted. A husband who now haunted her dreams and inflamed her senses.

For the first time Jassy realized she might do more than survive. She might also have a chance to be happy.

With her palm upon the bed where Jamie should be, she smiled, and at last she slept, in peace.

————

Jamie and his party, Father Steven among them, arrived home in the early-dawn hours of December seventeenth. The first soft snow of the winter season came floating down to the ground, and though the day was cold, it promised to be beautiful too.

Jamie was weary and confused as he rode. Opechancanough had been behaving very strangely, he thought. He had invited—summoned—Jamie to his home; he had assured Jamie that he liked him well, and then he had suggested that he go home. Not to the hundred, but home, to England.

Jamie—alone with his ten men in the midst of hundreds of Pamunkees—had promised the chief that he would think about it, but he had expressed his confusion. Sharing a pipe with the chief, he had told him, "But if I leave this place, what benefit will it be to our people? The Englishman has come here to stay, Opechancanough."

"The land belongs to the Powhatan. My brother fought to bring the tribes here to order. Order will remain."

Jamie had left laden down with gifts once again, with dried meat and bags of grain and maize corn, and he had left Opechancanough with several scores of old buttons with the Tudor rose emblemed upon them. The chief had seemed pleased. And still, the entire visit had disturbed Jamie. He intended to take care in the months that followed.

He had not realized the extent of his worry until he left the forests and came upon the clearing for the fields of the hundred. He looked toward home, and the palisade still stood, with the cannons rising westward in the shadows. He let out a pleased cry that brought laughter to his men, then he nudged his horse and shot like a bolt ahead of them. The palisade gate opened as he approached it, and he was glad and relieved again, for it meant that an armed man was on duty, keeping careful watch.

Few people were about as he hurried his way to his house. The man Tamsyn was up, and he sleepily took Jamie's horse. "How fares my wife?" Jamie asked him.

The man smiled and answered him with an articulate tongue. "The lady fares very well, Lord Cameron. She blossoms daily."

Jamie laughed and hurried for the house, pulling off his gauntlets. At the door to the hallway he paused.

He had not thought of their parting argument since the early days of his departure, when the words they had exchanged had haunted him nightly. He was wrong, he knew, and he had no right to taunt and bait her about Robert Maxwell. Robert had his faults, but he was a trusted friend. And Jassy . . .

She had never lied to him. She had married him with the truth of her feelings upon her lips, and yet she had never really given him reason to believe that she would betray him.

It was his temper, he thought, his damnable temper, and the jealousy that soared from his heart—and his loins—when he saw the sparkle in her eyes when she spoke to another. Aye, it was bitter medicine, but he loved her, and he must hide the emotion from her. Anger was easier than betraying his heart. If often seemed that she had none, and therefore a wise man would build a careful shield around his own. He was, perhaps, a man possessed, but proud nevertheless, and he'd not let his heart or his loins rule his mind. He would be master of his own house despite the minx, and if she never learned to *love* him, she would come to *obey* him.

He wondered bleakly if she would ever cast aside the barriers that she had set before him. If she would ever come to him with husky laughter on her lips and the bright fire of passion in her sapphire eyes. That was what she kept from him, he realized. That was what she held away, like some sacred prize.

It was a prize, he thought, for he longed to obtain not her submission but her partnership.

He inhaled and exhaled, and a hot shudder swept his body, piercing his loins. For the time being, he thought, he could live with submission. He had thought of nothing but her soft, creamy, naked flesh during all the nights of his journey. He had thought of her sky-colored eyes, of her hair tumbling about the fragile structure of her face, and he had thought of the evocative swell of her breasts and the darkened shade of her nipples, and he had imagined the curves of her body as she lay awaiting him. He had seen her lips, parted, damp, and he had awakened many times in a cold sweat, wanting her. She would be further along now . . . but not too far along.

He had to see her.

He pushed open the door impatiently. Amy Lawton, in her nightcap with her long gray braid streaming down her back, hurried out with a candle to meet him.

"My Lord Cameron! Welcome home." She looked at him a bit askance—he was dressed in soft, warm buckskins given him by the chief, and his head was bare. He might well have resembled a savage himself.

"Thank you, Mrs. Lawton, I am glad to be home." He spoke softly, for it seemed that it was still night in the house. He had ridden through the darkness, anxious to be here. The days of Christmas were almost upon them, and he wanted to be among his own people for the Christian celebration. No . . . he wanted to be back with his wife. He wanted to know if she was still angry for the way they had parted, or if she had forgiven him. He had just wanted to touch her again. If she did not give in to him, he wanted the passionate, frenzied response that he could draw from her, he wanted to see her lips parted and damp, and slightly swollen by his kiss, her eyes open and blue and heavy-lidded with desire. . . .

And he had wanted to assure himself that their child grew well in her womb. "Is all well?"

Amy Lawton seemed distressed, and so he moved to the fire with a frown, warming his hands. "Is all well?"

"Well enough, milord. But . . ."

"But? Speak up."

"Lady Cameron had some horrid dreams, I think, while you were gone. One night I awoke and came to her, but she did not need me, for her brother-in-law was already with her. The poor lady! I was heartily sorry, for she seemed so distressed."

"Really?" He did not want to feel it, but the dark anger cascaded over him again. Robert! Always she was reaching to Robert!

He gritted his teeth. He reminded himself of the anguish he had endured, wanting her through the long nights. He tried to remind himself that his jealousy was invalid, for though she might still feel some draw to Robert, she would not act upon it. Surely she would not.

But no logic worked upon him. Robert Maxwell had soothed Jassy in the bed she shared with him, and the thought of it infuriated him. What else had happened there?

"Milord, shall I get you something?" Amy said.

"No, I think that I will see to my wife."

"Oh, she slept peacefully and well last night, milord, I do believe. She bathed late in the outhouse and drank warm milk before bed, and I am certain that she did not awake distressed. Oh, and, milord, the *Lady Destiny* arrived with your gifts, and your lady was quite pleased."

"Was she?" Aye, Jassy would be pleased. She was like a child with a present. She had married him for his wealth and position, he reminded himself. The lady could be bought.

"Thank you, Amy," he told his servant, and headed for the stairs. "See that Sir William is informed that I will speak with him later. And tell Captain Stewart that I will see him too. I am sure that he is anxious to sail southward before winter comes upon us any more viciously."

"Yes, milord," Amy told him, but he barely heard her, for his attention was already upon the door at the top of the stairs. Still, when he reached it, he paused again. He stood there, his palms growing damp, his heart beating too quickly and too hard. She was a harlot, he reminded himself. She had sold herself into marriage, but it had been a payment, nonetheless. She was his wife and was honor-bound to obey him. He did not need to tremble like a lad in the schoolroom.

He pushed open the door and stepped into his room.

She slept, and she slept as sweetly and as innocently as a child. He could smell the soft rose scent of French perfumed soap upon her body even as he stood over her. She was clad from head to toe in a soft white gown, laced and beribboned on the bodice, entirely chaste. The covers were swept over her to her waist, but her gown dipped precariously from her shoulder, exposing a fascinating expanse of clear ivory flesh. Her hair was a profusion of sunshine splayed upon the pillow, and her lips were as he had so often dreamed of them, softly parted as she breathed evenly with her sleep. He ached to touch her; he burned to touch her. His loins ached, and only the tightness of his buckskin breeches kept his naked desire from showing as clearly as the king's flag upon a pinnace.

He reached to touch her naked shoulder, and then he drew away. He ground down hard on his teeth and walked around to his desk. He sat and plopped his feet upon it. He stared at her, then searched for the jug of rum in the bottom drawer of his desk. It was early morning, and he did not need his mind fogged. He drew deeply on the rum, anyway.

In a matter of moments she began to stir. Like a cherished child, she stretched, and a soft, smug smile touched her lips. And well she should be pleased, Jamie decided sardonically, for she thought him still gone, while his gifts lined her trunks. Robert slept across the hall and could come at her first call of distress. Robert, who she had planned to trap in her matrimonial web. . . .

Robert would sleep across the hall no longer, Jamie determined. The Maxwell house would be hurried along. He did not wish to fight the urge to smash his friend's pleasant features every time they chanced to meet.

Her eyes opened suddenly, falling full upon him. Then they widened and she sat up, and to his chagrin he thought that she was about to scream.

"Is my appearance so distressing, then?" he said harshly.

"Jamie!"

"Yes, my love, returned alive and well," he said.

"Oh!" She placed her hand over her heart. Her gown spilled farther down, and her breasts rose and fell in tempting agitation. Her hair, tousled by sleep, was a wild glory about her. He fought to remain still at his desk. "Who were you expecting?"

She pointed to him, indicating his clothing. She smiled ruefully and beautifully, and it did seem that her face was alive with welcome. "I—I—your outfit. It frightened me."

"Oh?" He stared down blankly at the buckskins. "Forgive me, love. Were you about to scream for Robert?"

The welcoming smile quickly faded from her features. "I don't know what you're talking about."

He wished that he hadn't spoken, but he couldn't take the words back now. He leaned deep into his chair, watching her through a bare slit in his eyes. "I have heard, madame, that your distress in the night is eased by Robert Maxwell."

She stiffened and did not reply. She sat there like a queen, entirely regal and disdainful in her silence. His throat grew dry, and again he longed to take back his words, but they had already been spoken and could not be taken back. More than ever, he ached to touch her, to slide his trembling fingers over the naked expanse of her shoulder so displayed to him. He wanted to move but could not. At last she did so. With her head proudly carried and her hair tumbling about her, she slipped her legs over the side of the bed, discreetly adjusting her gown to stand. But when she stood, he saw the startling change in her, and a hoarse sound of surprise escaped him. She whirled to him in alarm.

His boots landed on the floor and he was upon his feet. She was back toward the wall, her eyes wide with sudden alarm, her hands splayed protectively over the swell in her abdomen.

"Come here!" he whispered. She ignored him, and he swore vehemently. "Do you think that I would harm you, madame?" Impatiently he strode to her, and she backed away again.

"You *have* threatened grave harm!" she reminded him.

"Only under damning circumstances, madame, and you've done nothing damning, have you?" His strides brought him to her. She choked back a gasp and seemed to brace herself, but he offered her no force or violence. He came down upon one knee before her and cast his hands upon the swell of her belly.

Fascinated, he felt the hardness of the child growing within her. He swept his palms slowly over the swell again and again. He reached higher and encompassed her breasts with tenderness, then he rose, pulling the gown up and over her head.

"No!" she protested in distress.

"I have ached for the sight of you," he said.

She tried to elude his arms. "I am large and awkward of a sudden, and not much to see," she murmured.

He could not see her eyes or her face, for she had lowered her lashes and her head against him, and since she could not escape his hold, she had pressed against him. He caught her chin, and when he lifted it, there was the slightest glaze of tears touching the exquisite sapphire of her eyes. He felt suddenly as if they had never parted. Tension filled him, and he wondered what was truth about her, and what was pretense and lies.

"Give me the gown!" she implored him.

"No."

"Please. I am so . . . fat!"

He had expected anger or denial, and not this. A smile touched his lips, and he whispered, "To me, madame, you are more exquisitely beautiful than ever."

He threaded his fingers through her hair and tilted her face to his. He kissed her deeply, the fire in his loins exploding again with the searing hot contact of their lips. He lay hold upon the ache that plagued him, for he had determined that he would be gentle now, and so he would. He knelt before her and explored again the hard curve of her belly where his child found life. Her fingers curled into his hair. Distressed, she tugged upon him, but he ignored that pain and pressed his cheek against her flesh.

"Jamie . . ." she said, tugging upon him. But then she ceased the effort, and her knees began to tremble, and when he looked up at her, she had her head cast back, her lips were slightly parted, and her breath came in ragged pants. He rose and swept her into his arms and then onto the bed. He tugged off his boots and hose and buckskin breeches and jerked his leather doublet over his head. He shook with the fever to have her, but even as hunger swamped him he took a tender care with her, greater than any he had exercised before. And still, when it was over, he knew a satisfaction like nothing he had ever known before. She reached for the sheet, and he stopped her, lethargically propping himself up on an elbow and running his fingers with idle abandon over her belly. He paused, his heart slamming against his chest, for he felt a sudden movement. He looked to her. She was flushed with embarrassment, and he laughed with sudden joy. "The babe?"

She nodded.

Holding his weight upon his knees, he straggled over her. He cupped her abdomen again with his hands and smiled as he felt the sudden power of a kick against his hand. "He is strong."

"*She* is not so fond of you this morning either."

"Alas, did you not miss me?" he said tauntingly.

Her lashes fell quickly over her eyes. "Milord, I had Robert Maxwell, don't you recall?"

His jaw tightened, and the movement of his hands ceased. "This is a wound into which you rub salt, my love. Take care."

Her lashes flew open, and her eyes met his again. She was so achingly beautiful that he wanted to shake her. He wanted her to swear that she was loyal, that she had been a fool . . . that she loved him.

She did not do so, but she swallowed and answered softly with an admirable dignity. "I have done nothing but suffer your slings and arrows, milord, for what is a friendship with the man who is my sister's husband—and your dear companion, or so the past has claimed. If you would taunt me, milord, than you must expect my ridicule on the subject."

He lowered his face, taut with emotion, until it hovered over hers. "*Did* you miss me, madame?"

She hesitated a long time, then her dignity was lost in an angry cry, and she tried to wrest him from her person. "Aye! My Lord Cameron, I have missed you. I have felt the snow of winter and the chill of frost coming upon us, and I have ached for the searing fire that you can bring against the cold."

His breath caught; he had not expected such an admission from her. Slowly, slowly, he lowered himself beside her, his eyes locked upon hers. She swallowed again, nervously lowering her lashes. "Have *you* missed *me,* milord?"

"More than I have ever yearned for water to drink, or air to breathe. With every fiber and drop of blood within me, milady, I ached to hold you in my arms again."

A smile touched her lips. He pulled her close, and he pulled the covers over them both. It was good to be home.

In seconds he was sleeping.

When he awoke that afternoon, Molly was in the room straightening up, and his wife was nowhere to be seen. He frowned to Molly, who was painfully cheerful. He had a splitting headache from the rum he had drunk with the dawn.

"Where is Jassy?"

"Why, milord!" Molly said innocently, "Jassy is about business. One cannot sleep late and tarry here, sir. This *is* the New World. Nay, milord, not even nobility and gentry can while away precious time here."

"Molly, where is my wife?"

"Why, she is seeing that the meat in the smoke shed is coming along properly. The game has been slim of late, as you can imagine, I am certain. But Powan and his men were by recently. Jassy made him a satin shirt from some of the fabric that arrived upon the *Lady Destiny,* and he was quite pleased with it. He has brought up many rabbits, and a great deal of pumpkin bread in turn."

Jamie shot up, then remembered that he was naked, and jerked the covers up. "Powan?" he demanded.

"Oh, yes, the chief has been around often, as have many of the Indians. Lord Newbury was in from Jamestown, and everyone seems to be getting along very well. The Indians are often helping the settlers these days. Isn't it wonderful?"

"Wonderful," Jamie murmured. Powan was an old friend, but he had not expected to see him this far south upon the peninsula at this time of the year.

And he had certainly never expected Jassy to make the Indian a shirt. Wryly he realized that he had not expected Jassy ever to speak to an Indian, much less form the facsimile of a friendship. He would be curious to hear more about the affair.

A man could never fathom what might happen in his absence, he determined.

"Has anything else happened which I should know about?" he asked Molly, crossing his arms over his chest.

"No, milord."

"Did you know that Jassy has distressing nightmares?"

Molly's eyes lowered quickly. "We are all plagued by dreams now and then."

Molly wasn't going to say any more. Jamie grunted. He noted the warm, luxurious fox fur that stretched out at the foot of the bed. "So the *Lady Destiny* arrived with her cargo."

"Oh, yes!" Molly was all animation again. "Jassy—Lady Cameron—was so pleased with the things!"

So pleased . . . oh, yes, his wife could be purchased.

"Milord, is there anything else?"

Jamie scowled. "Yes, Mistress Molly, I would like you out of my room so that I might dress. Now!"

Molly jumped and fled. Jamie rose and folded his buckskins and sought out his good Englishwear. In satin breeches, silk shirt, and a woolen doublet he set out for the day, anxious for the business at hand.

He met with Sir William, and William told him about the day when Powan had come and first met Jassy. William grinned. "He told her that he thought she was a good choice for you—she would work hard in your fields and bear you many children."

"That must have gone over well," Jamie murmured.

Sir William was amused.

"She handled herself most admirably."

"I am sure that she did," Jamie said. Then he told William about his visit to Opechancanough, warning Sir William that he was worried, though he could not pinpoint the danger. "We must keep up a careful eye," Jamie warned, and Sir William agreed.

Later that day he met with Captain Stewart and gave him his sailing orders. The captain's cargo of tobacco for England was loaded. He chewed on his pipe, enjoying the Virginia tobacco himself while he watched the loading with Jamie on the dock. He would return in the spring with the supplies ordered from the mother country.

Late in the afternoon Elizabeth found him, and she proudly showed him that she had not only learned to carry one of the heavy muskets but to load and fire it, and actually to hit a tree as well. "Jassy taught me," she told him proudly.

Jamie wasn't sure why, but he was further irritated.

Then Jassy did not appear at the dinner table—she was still engaged in some task or another, Lenore told him. Jamie liked Lenore well enough, and he was very fond of Elizabeth, and Robert was his friend. But they needed to be in their own home, and he would see that they moved quickly, he vowed to himself.

Still weary from his all-night ride to reach home, he climbed the stairs to his room, his temper seething as he wondered about the whereabouts of his wife.

He was not to wonder long.

She was seated upon the foot of the bed, her legs curled beneath her. She was dressed in a diaphanous gown that clearly delineated every full, sensual, and sexual curve of her body. She brushed her hair into silky strands. Her movements were slow and sensual, and the mere sight of her sent him floundering into a stream of desire. He took care, though, walking to his desk, sitting behind it and folding his hands and watching her thoughtfully.

He wondered at her motive.

He did not see the hurt in her eyes as he ignored her; he only saw that she was playing at seduction, the actress again. He did not want an act, and he did not want a game.

"Why weren't you at dinner?" he asked her.

She stretched, graceful, entirely feline, feminine, and exciting. The deep rouge crests of her swelling breasts strained against the silk gauze of her gown, and she smiled lazily. "I looked after the meat we are still preparing for the winter today. I seemed to be filled with the scent of smoke, and so I bathed and washed my hair, and then I needed to dry before the fire.

The fire . . . the firelight played all over her. It enhanced the curves that teased him beneath the evocative gown. It made her hair gleam like goldleaf, and her skin, too, seemed to gleam golden. He gritted his teeth and watched her from narrowed, suspicious eyes.

She yawned deliciously, and stretched again. Graceful, unbearably sensual. He rose and walked over to her. He took the brush from her fingers and leaned over her with twisted tension that forced her back upon the bed. He planted his palms on either side of her head. "What is this display, madame?"

Her eyelashes flickered uncertainly. "I did not get to thank you this morning for the many gifts you sent aboard the *Lady Destiny*—"

She did not finish speaking; he swore with a startling violence and pushed away from her. "You really are a whore, milady, aren't you? Determined to pay your debts."

Shock registered on her features, a look of naked pain that passed by so quickly that he might have imagined it, and then a look of raw fury and hatred. She lashed out in rage, railing against him, trying to strike him. He caught her wrists, and to his astonishment she fought on, kneeing him curtly in the groin. Stunned and in agony, he fell from her.

She leapt up and swept her new furred cloak around her and stared down at him scathingly. "You needn't worry, milord, you haven't the price to pay any more, ever!"

"Jasmine . . ." he began in a growl. He meant to catch her. He was in pain and his temper was seething, and he meant to have it out then and there. She was too quick for him. She was gone. In her sheer gown and her furred cloak, she was gone.

————

Of all the people that Jassy did not want to see at the moment, the half-breed girl, Hope, might surely have topped her list.

No one else was about when she reached the downstairs hall, but the beautiful, honey-colored girl sat at the table eating stew with her fingers. She saw Jassy and smiled at her agitation.

"What are you doing here?" Jassy asked her.

Hope licked her fingers very slowly and completely. "I am eating my dinner. I traveled with Lord Jamie, and so now I am here, in his hall." She stared pointedly at Jassy, then looked up the stairway and rolled her eyes. "What are you doing here, lady?"

Jassy fought back the temptation to slap the girl's face.

"It is my house, Hope. I belong here."

"You belong up there, with him. It is *his* house."

She stiffened, because the girl was right. And she had to sit, suddenly feeling very ill because she should have been with him, but she should have never, never made such a fool of herself. She was incapable of being a temptress, and now she hated her husband all over again because . . .

He had spurned her advance; he had called her a whore. And here was this half-pagan strumpet instructing her about duty!

Hope began to chuckle. "So you do not please him so much anymore. You should try harder. He is a man to be cherished." She seemed to purr the last words, and the sound scraped along Jassy's back. She gritted her teeth together hard.

"Hope, you are an insolent creature. *I* am none of *your* business, and neither is Lord Cameron."

"Lord Cameron might well be my business." Smiling, Hope sat back. Then she leaned toward Jassy, and it was evident that she wore no stays beneath her simple gown; her large breasts swayed with her every movement. To Jassy's amazement, Hope spread out her hands, making an imaginary measurement. "If you do not care for Lord Jamie, I will, lady. He is the finest man I have ever seen."

Jassy realized that Hope was measuring the most masculine part of her husband's anatomy. Anger flared within her so hotly that she seemed to see red. Dizziness swept her.

She stood. "How dare you!" she grated out. Without much thought she set her hands firmly upon the girl's shoulders, wrenching her like a little child from the table. She set her down upon her feet and turned her toward the door. "Out! And do not come back!"

By that time, Jassy heard footsteps hurrying down the stairs. Jamie—she had forgotten him in the depths of her rage.

His hair was mussed, and he was barefoot and clad only in a pair of breeches. As soon as he appeared, Hope set up a wail. She raced for him, throwing herself against his chest when he reached the landing. She set up a horrible wailing.

"What in the Lord's name—" Jamie looked from Hope to Jassy. Jassy stood silent in rage, and Hope began to cry. "She beats me, she sets her hands upon me and beats and throws me out into the snow—"

"Jassy, is this—"

Jassy didn't let him finish speaking. She came up to the two of them, slapped him across the face with a stunning blow, and headed for the door. "No, I did not beat her. And I will not throw her out into the snow. *I* am going!"

She didn't realize until she stepped outside and bitter cold knifed into her that she wasn't wearing shoes. She had walked at least twenty feet before it registered in her mind that she had nowhere to go, and *had* she had somewhere to go, she could not make it there barefoot.

It didn't matter. By then, Jamie was behind her. He ran like light, sweeping her into his arms, catapulting her into the snow. She gasped and sputtered the white flakes from her mouth and looked up to see that he was bare-chested and shivering and furious.

"Madame, once we are both back in that house and thawed, I intend to wring your neck."

"My neck! You bloody, lying knave!"

"What? Never mind!"

He rose, wincing, swearing once again that if they both lived with all their limbs and extremities intact, she would pay dearly. He pulled her up, lifted her into his arms, and, looking straight ahead, carried her back to the house.

Hope was gone and the hall was empty, but were it not, she was certain that her husband would have behaved in the same heedless manner. He thundered up the steps, tearing into her verbally, swearing that she was a fool, and a fool risking the life and health of an innocent child as well as her own.

She fought his hold. Once they had reached the harbor of their room, he freely let her go, setting her before the fire while he came close to singeing his hand and feet, trying to warm them. "I should beat you—" he began, his teeth chattering, but Jassy was already on her feet.

"Beat me? Nay, milord, you snake! You cast doubt upon an innocent friendship while you lie in my face!"

"What are you talking about?" he said, exploding.

Her cloak was tangled about her and falling. Jassy impatiently tossed it down and leaned forward as Hope had done, displaying the fullness of her breasts temptingly before him. "What am I talking about?" she repeated, mimicking Hope. "I am talking about you—and the piece of your anatomy that rules your heart and stupid mind!" She put her hands out as Hope had done, showing him an extremely accurate measurement of size.

"What?" he repeated.

She swung, intending to strike him again. He wouldn't allow it. He caught her arm, she spun into his arms, and he held her tight. "Let me go!" she demanded, wild with fury.

Suddenly he was laughing. "You're jealous."

"You will never touch me again, I do not care about marriage vows or—"

"Jassy, I never touched her!"

"She has seen you—bare. I know it!"

He whirled her around and looked into the wild tempest of her eyes, and it made the pulse of desire within him shoot and sear like gunfire. He carried her over to the bed and set her down, and when she tried to rise, he cast the weight of his leg over hers, taking care of the babe but pinning her down. He started to untie his breeches, and she went wild, tossing like a wild pony beneath him. "You will not—"

His breeches were free. He leaned over her, pinning her wrists with his hand, finding her body unbearably evocative beneath the gauzy gown. He caressed the full, firm weight of her breast while she squirmed and swore, and when she tired, he spoke again. "She saw me, yes. But I never lay with her, Jassy, never, and I will swear it upon the Bible before Father Steven. She appeared here one night, determined on seduction, but I did not touch her."

She went still, watching him suspiciously. He bent his head and sucked her breast over the gauze of the gown. He felt her grow taut beneath him. "Why not?" she whispered.

"You were on my mind," he murmured, lightly closing his teeth over her nipple. Her head twisted and her body suddenly surged against his, and he slipped his hand between her thighs, and then rolled suddenly, dragging her around. His eyes heavy-lidded and sultry, he smiled at her vulnerability. "I swear!" he repeated, tugging her gown high. "Love me, wife. I've no need for any woman—nay, any life or sustenance!—but you."

He tugged up her gown, caught her hips, and brought her slowly down upon him. When he began to fill her, she suddenly resisted.

"I tried!" she choked out. "You—"

"You tied my heart and mind and loins all in a knot together, and I humbly beg your forgiveness!" he claimed. He caught her hips and brought her fully down, and he watched the beauty of her face as the passion caught hold of her. Moments later he found the hem of her gown, tossed it over her head, and he was swamped with the heady passion that possessed him as she moved, fluid as a river, graceful and sweet, her back arching, her breasts full and bouncing before him. In the end he caught her to him, and she was soaked and exhausted and completely sated. She didn't speak. She fell silent beside him.

He waited, and smiled. Then he kissed her forehead. "Jassy, it is the truth. I never touched her. I will be glad to swear it."

She was quiet for a moment. Her eyes remained closed, and he thought that she slept, but then she answered him. "And I, milord, swear that what I feel for

Robert Maxwell is a deep friendship; he is my brother, my sister's husband, and nothing more."

Her eyes opened and met his.

"It will be a long, cold winter, my love. Truce?" he said.

Her eyes fell closed again.

"Truce," she agreed.

15

S CHRISTMAS NEARED, WINTER CAME UPON them in full, cold and hard and brutal. Jamie left very early each morning in search of game and came back later every afternoon. Jassy quickly realized that there could be little class distinction here, for the settlers were forced to band together to survive. Jamie had managed to bring many supplies from England, but they must be shared, and being a "lady" here—especially Lord Cameron's wife—was a matter of responsibility and not leisure.

She did have help, for their household servants had come to the New World for a new life, and were willing to work hard to survive the rigors of the winter. It wasn't, however, England. There were no major social obligations for nobility or gentry, and though Jassy did spend time writing a letter to Jane and Henry to be taken back on the next ship to arrive, it was her only correspondence. The settlement did not yet provide the customary activities for ladies of means. Jamie assured her that in the spring they would entertain the governor of the Jamestown colony, and that they would ride to the other settlements. But on the whole, she certainly had no demanding social schedule; she didn't need to prepare to travel to Court, nor was she expecting any royal visitors. She did have a busy household, with constant tasks, and if she occasionally mourned for the grand manor in which she had reigned so briefly in England, she was also quick to forget the elegance when engaged in some necessary chore. The days were short, and the nights were long and cold. Men of all classes cut trees and stacked wood; women sewed, salted and smoked and preserved meat and foodstuff, made candles and soap, and engaged in the endless task of laundry.

The Indians began appearing more frequently. They came to the palisade to trade; they came in friendship. In winter they wore buckskin, the men *and* the women. Jassy did not see Powan again. She was fascinated by the Indians but also wary, and she tended to keep a careful distance from them. A few of the settlers who had been with the hundred since Jamie had first chosen the site knew some of the Indians' language and managed to communicate with them effectively. Jamie knew enough of it to get by very well, and she saw him greeting various of the Indians many times. He knew them by name, welcomed them, and encouraged Jassy to get to know them. But even then he warned her that she must take care around them too.

"Why?" she asked him one night. She was bundled into a long blue nightgown, and he was at his desk, setting the last of some entry for the day into his calendar. He looked up at her, startled.

"Why?" he repeated.

"*You* seem to like them very much, but you warn *me* away."

"I do not warn you away. As my wife, I expect you to greet them always with courtesy."

"I am courteous," she told him, her temper simmering at his indication that she had not.

He shrugged, then set down his pen. "I have seen you near them, madame, upon occasion. You are stiff, and careful not to come too close. That is not exactly courtesy."

"I met Powan and—"

"You did well, yes. It seems that you are deeply fascinated, but I think, too, that you forget that they are men and women just as we are. They are made of flesh and blood, and they are born with hopes and fears and emotions."

"I am aware of that," Jassy said coolly. "I did not think that you had complaints about my demeanor as your wife."

"The little actress," he said softly. "I do always wonder what you are *really* thinking or feeling."

"I would assume, milord, that you expect me to do better here, with savages and farmers, than with your friends of the nobility and gentry back home."

"I assume, milady, that you will do just fine, no matter with whom you are cast."

"So, have I done well here?" she demanded, her chin high. She knew that he watched her often; she never knew what he *thought*.

"You know that you have done very well. You need not seek a compliment. In fact, you have done exceptionally well, considering your hatred for the voyage, and for leaving England. I think you hated it all enough to regret the marriage, no matter what it brought to you." He watched her pensively. "Tell me, milady, have you regretted it?"

She kept her eyes upon his, and her throat went strangely dry. Her eyes lowered. "I—I have regretted nothing," she murmured. "You forget, I could still be a servant in my brother's house."

"You are an ingenious woman, milady. I'm rather sure that you'd not have stayed there long."

She ignored his words and pleated the sheets beneath her fingers. "Tell me, milord, have *you* regretted your marriage?"

He took a long time to answer, sitting back in the chair. He stared at her so long that she flushed, and very deeply regretted the question.

"My passion for you has not died, milady," he said at last.

"That does not mean you do not regret the marriage," she murmured, her cheeks aflame.

"I do not regret the marriage," he said. He looked back to his paper but continued speaking to her, returning to the subject of the Indians. "Remember, Jassy, that you are to take care with the Powhatans. In their beliefs they are very different. They did not spring from Adam and Eve but from the pouch of a giant hare. They fear their evil god more than they love their benevolent one, and they have sacrificed their own infants and children to that god. They have little mercy for their enemies."

"Are we their enemies?"

He set his pen down and walked over to the hearth, stopping to watch the fire burn. "If Opechancanough's brother still lived, I would have felt more secure. He was a man of peace, while Powhatan earned his great power by violence, and Opechancanough is a man who is quick to violence too. They have at times befriended us; they have never really accepted us."

Despite herself, she was shivering. "Why are we here, then?"

Annoyed, he stared at her. "Madame, we are here because I choose it so." He walked over to the bed, and she flushed, realizing the intent in his eyes. He tilted her chin so that their eyes met. "And *you* will take grave care, milady, because I have commanded that you do so, will you not?"

She was not sure what he meant, but she nodded to the dark demand in his eyes, and she trembled then, for his arms came around her with every bit as much demand as stoked his eyes. This she could not regret, this magical flame that leapt between them.

But later, when she lay by his side and heard the even whisper of his breath as he slept, she wondered uneasily of the future. Her fascination for him grew daily. But would the time come when the passion he felt for her died, when the flame ran its course? If so, she would be lost, and she would not even have the strength of her hatred to sustain her.

She was his wife, she reminded herself. She was about to bear his child. But was that enough?

For the first time she realized that she wanted his love.

On the twentieth of December, Robert and Lenore moved into their new home. The entire settlement had worked upon the finishing of the house, including Robert and Jamie. They were all very excited, as the house was nearly as grand as Jamie's, and put together very quickly but very well. Jassy was somewhat startled by Lenore's enthusiasm, for her sister was often very conscious of class, and the house did not compare to the home she had known growing up.

"That was always our brother's home, Jassy," Lenore explained. "This is the very first home I shall have of my own."

The three sisters worked hard upon a set of tapestries to keep the cold out. "Ladies' work, and very proper!" Lenore assured Jassy. She had never approved of Jassy's involvement with John Tannen and his pathetic little family, but Jassy had shrugged aside her objections. It was surprising, though, to realize as they worked together on the last day that she would miss Lenore. And when night fell and the men came back to tell them that it was time to move, she embraced Lenore warmly, and Lenore hugged her fiercely in return. Then Robert kissed her and smiled at her. "Good-bye, little sister. Take care."

"We will not be so far," she said.

"Merely a stone's throw," he agreed.

"It is a very small community," Jamie said dryly. "I daresay that we will see as much of one another as we always have. We shall merely . . . sleep in different places." He drew Jassy away from Robert and back to his side. He seemed tense and somewhat irritable. He did not seem to mind, however, kissing Lenore very warmly before it was time for them to depart.

Jamie was to see them to their new home. Jassy assumed that she would accompany them, too, but when she asked Molly to fetch her cape, Jamie whirled her around, shaking his head. There was a curious fever about his eyes. "Madame, it is late and bitterly cold for you to come out in your condition. Your good-byes have been said, and you can take a walk to the new house in the morning with Elizabeth."

She wanted to argue with him. She longed to see the new house, with the last of it completed. And she didn't like being left alone when surely they all would have a welcome toast and Jamie would probably stay very late while she sat upstairs alone.

"Jamie, there is no reason—"

His jaw twisted and set. "There is every reason."

She lowered her head, then tossed her hair back, ready to challenge him. "Jamie—"

His hands fell upon her shoulders, his eyes burning. "It is not a good night. The snow has iced over, and you might trip or stumble, and fall. Would you risk my child so readily?"

"We shall all get together in the morning," Robert said cheerfully. "Well, maybe not." He grimaced. Robert was learning the way of the settlement. He was accompanying Jamie on his morning hunting trips outside the palisade. "I shall be out with Lord Cameron, but then you ladies shall probably enjoy each other's companionship well enough."

"To bed," Jamie told Jassy firmly.

She set her jaw, kissed Lenore, and then Robert once again, and hurried for the stairs. Jamie nodded to Molly, and Molly nodded gravely in return, and followed Jassy.

Jassy fumed to Molly about her ill treatment, and Molly, setting out one of her bed gowns and folding the lace ruff Jassy had worn fashionably about her neck, cheerfully ignored her. "Women do get temperamental in your state, so they say, pet! Oh, I do hope that I shall find out soon enough! Crawl into bed now."

Curious, Jassy obediently crawled beneath the covers. "Now what does that mean, Molly?"

"John Tannen has suggested that we should marry." Molly was trying very hard to subdue her excitement. "He is asking Father Steven if we might marry before Christmas Day."

"So quickly!" Jassy gasped.

"And more proper than not," Molly murmured. "Jassy, I spend so much time there with the children and . . . all. Oh, Jassy, I am so excited! I am getting on, you know. And once I felt so old and worn and I thought that no man would ever have me . . . I have been honest with John, he knows all about my past, and he cares nothing of it. He says that all that matters is what lies between the two of us. He said that I was a whirlwind of giving energy, and that he cannot help but love me, for he has watched me with his son and his little sister-in-law, and thinks that they could have no finer a stepmother, nor could he choose a more tender bride."

"Oh, how beautiful!" Jassy cried. "I am so very pleased for you, Molly."

"It is all thanks to you, Jassy."

"Molly! I did not make you kind and good and loving!"

"You gave me a new life. You and Lord Cameron."

And Lord Cameron, Jassy silently acknowledged. She lowered her eyes and bit into her lower lip. He had made life good. He had made it a tempest, and he was still a horrible autocrat, but she could no longer imagine a life without him. He infuriated her, he stimulated and excited her to sheer abandon, and he was the force of her life.

She kissed Molly warmly. "I wish you the very, very best."

"Oh, thank you, Jassy. I will need your blessing, and Lord Cameron's."

"He will give it freely." That much she thought, she could say with confidence. Jamie would be pleased for Molly and John. In many aspects these were his people, far more so than their loyalty or lives belonged to any king. He was the governor here, the law, the only king that any of them knew, or could touch, reach, or recognize.

Both women started suddenly, for they heard Jamie's footsteps upon the stairs. He was coming to the room, long-strided, swift and, sure. "Good night!" Molly told Jassy, and slipped away quickly. Jassy listened, curious, as Molly and Jamie greeted each other, and then Molly scurried down the stairs. The door to the room opened, and he was there, his heavy cloak covered in snowflakes. He cast it carelessly aside, his eyes still hot, curiously excited, and fevered as they fell upon her. He stumbled out of his boots, watching her all the while. She kept a wary eye upon him in return. Was he angry over Robert again? He had snatched her quickly enough from his friend, and he had ordered her upstairs. . . .

He wrenched off his doublet, and practically tore off his shirt in his haste to get it over his head. Approaching the bed, he pulled away his hose and garters but went no further. With some kind of a barbaric cry he leapt upon the bed, seized her to his side, and kissed her with a dizzying passion. She struggled against him at first, then gave way to the honeyed sensations that swept warmly and deliciously through her. His hands gently ravaged her, and when he broke away at last, a blazing and devilish smile touched his eyes and curved his lips.

Jassy moistened her lips. "What is it?"

"It? It is passion, and an obsessive desire, and I can bear it no longer, and, madame, we are so much more *alone* in our house!"

"Jamie, how can you be so crude—"

"Not crude, madame," he said, shimmying from his trousers. "Delighted."

"Robert is your friend."

"Um. And your friend, too, milady. Tell me, do you ever think of him?"

"What?" she demanded, startled.

He cupped and cradled her breast and brought his body, naked and hard, flush to hers. "Do you still think of him? Wishing that you had not been so rudely caught within my arms on May Day?"

She went very pale, wondering at the tension within him. "What do you want from me?" she asked harshly. "I am huge with your child, and still you would taunt me so! What do you want?"

He gazed at her a long time, his eyes indigo fire, so dark and enigmatic that they seemed black. "Your very soul, perhaps, milady. That which I do not hold."

"No man should hold everything of a woman!" she cried. For then the woman, she thought silently, would be so sadly at his mercy.

"And what of the woman, milady? Should she hold everything of a man?"

"You are talking in riddles, and I do not understand you. You have whatever you choose you take."

"What I choose to take . . ." he repeated savagely. His head lowered to hers, his lips seizing upon her mouth, and he filled her with the potent surge of his desire. He made love to her with tenderness, and with a searing and shattering sensuality. She rode the wild wind of the reckless emotion that haunted him, and she was cast higher into a realm of abandon and ecstasy than she had ever gone before. She had once thought that this thing between them could know no higher bounds, yet he taught her again and again that she could soar farther into distant heavens. When he had finished with her, she felt entirely sated and spent, somewhat awed, and thoroughly dazed. Exhausted, she curled against him and felt his hand sweep around what had once been her waist. She expected some arrogant comment from him, some taunting assurance that she was *his* possession and she would learn not to think of another.

He was silent for a very long time, then she heard him sigh, and he touched her gently. "Alas, my love, my fiendish pleasure comes too late. I should not have had you this night, fiercely or otherwise. Feel? The babe kicks. He protests his father's rudeness. Did I hurt you, Jassy?"

She was glad of the darkness, for she flushed crimson. "No, you did me no harm."

He kissed her forehead. "Well, milady, my wife, you will be free of me now, for some months to come." Again he was silent. He teased her breasts with the idle play of his fingers, just touching the tip with his tongue. He hovered over her in the night. "Tell me, Jassy, will you be glad? Or will you not miss this . . . just a bit?"

"Jamie, please . . ."

He rolled away from her and got up from the bed. "Go to sleep, Jassy," he said harshly.

"Jamie—"

"Go to sleep."

She watched him miserably as he moved across the room, his naked back and buttocks tightly muscled and sinewed, and beautiful in a curious manner. He did not gaze back to her but stood before the fire.

She wanted to cry out to him, but she could not. The words would have tumbled from her lips fast and desperately, and she would have given away more than her soul; she would have cast her naked heart before him, and that she dared not do. She closed her eyes, and exhaustion overwhelmed her.

———

The house was very different in the morning. Lenore and Robert had taken Kathryn with them, and Charity had left to serve in their house, too, if only for a week or so, or until some girl was found to help with the household tasks. Elizabeth had opted to stay with Jamie and Jassy, if Jamie didn't mind. Jamie didn't mind Elizabeth at all—it was only Robert he had wanted gone. With Elizabeth, Jassy set out to see her sister's new home, and Lenore was glad to greet them both, showing them about as if she had acquired a palace.

"This," she said, showing them a little loft, "will be for the baby."

"Oh, Lenore, you too!" Elizabeth cried with pleasure. "How far along are you?"

Lenore giggled. "Well, I am not yet. Except that I think that maybe last night . . . well, Robert was quite determined." She gave Jassy a smug, conspiratorial smile. "Men . . . Mostly he is so courteous, and not at all demanding. Last night he said that we must have children too. He has pointed out how very well you manage in your condition. He also pointed out how quickly you arrived in your condition." She idly curled a lock of hair around her finger, studying Jassy. "But then you married Jamie Cameron, and he must be the devil himself in—in private."

"Lenore!" Elizabeth gasped.

"Oh, don't be such a little church mouse!" Lenore laughed. "Honestly. I was the one Jamie intended to marry. Sometimes I do wonder."

Jassy was pink by then, but Lenore didn't intend to let the matter drop. "It isn't a 'duty,' is it? It is exciting and decadent and—"

"Lenore!" Elizabeth said entreatingly. "You're making Jassy very uncomfortable."

Jassy smiled suddenly. "Lenore, I am quite content."

Lenore laughed good-naturedly. "Jassy, *I* am quite content. *You* are something more, I think."

Perhaps she was, but in the next few days it seemed that a breach widened between her and Jamie. He was gone long in the morning, and had much to do in the afternoons, and he started working at his desk until very late at night.

As Jamie had expected, Lenore and Robert were still with them almost as much as they were not. It was an evening only three nights after they had left the house when they returned for dinner. Jassy learned from Molly that Father Steven had approved her immediate marriage to John Tannen. With all of them present, Jassy broached the subject to Jamie.

Jamie was thoughtful at first, arching a brow to the very suggestion. In England, such a marriage would have been a breach of morality, for poor Joan was barely dead and cast to the sea for six months. In the hundred, it was a matter of good sense, for John Tannen needed Molly, and it seemed that Molly's temper had been a matter of her mixed emotions.

"Father Steven has approved this?" Jamie asked Jassy.

"He has. . ." She hesitated. "I would like to have a reception for them here, following the ceremony."

Silence greeted her suggestion.

Then Lenore spoke up, quickly and certainly. Such an event would have been an outrageous breach of society had they been home in England, she was quick to point out. But they weren't in England, Jassy was just as quick to counter. And, standing by the mantel, her hands lightly resting upon her rounded abdomen, Jassy quietly reminded her sister that at home, in England, Jassy could barely muster into the ranks of society herself. "And you are forgetting one thing," she reminded her sister, her head held high. "Molly is not just my servant; she is my friend. Her circumstances are much the same as my own. She was always at my side when I needed her, and I wish to do for her now what I can."

Lenore stared at her sister, shaking her head, then turned to Jamie. "Can't you stop this? Life is certainly different here, but . . ."

Jamie, paying little heed as he scoured his musket barrel, looked up at last, shrugging to Lenore. "Jassy must do as she chooses. It is her home."

The matter was settled, and Molly was duly married, and amid the white snow of winter and with everyone in attendance, from the maids and carpenters and laborers to Sir William and Lenore and Robert and Father Steven, Jassy held her first party for her friend. It was fun, and it was a relief from the rigors of the weather and the dampness that could so easily chill the bones. Jassy danced happily with Sir William, the groom, and Robert. It was then that her husband cut in upon her. His eyes were grave, and she stiffened, wary lest he have some comment about Robert. He did not. He swept her around himself, saying merely, "I think it is time that you rested. In England, my lady, a damsel so far enceinte would not be so gaily upon a dance floor." He hesitated. "You could harm the babe, love. Or yourself."

Flushing, she dutifully left the floor and set herself the task of handing out warmed mead and ale. And when the party came to an end, she was filled with pleasure as Molly kissed and hugged her, promising her that she would forever serve her, and do so with love.

She was grateful to Jamie that night, but she was hesitant about making any overtures to him, for she still could not forget that she had attempted either to please or seduce him once, and had failed miserably in the attempt. He had said that he would not touch her again, but she did miss him. Still, she might harm the babe, and she grew more awkward daily. She was very heavy with the child, and she wondered sometimes with dismay how she could have grown so large so quickly. And so she did not attempt to seduce him; she crawled into bed and watched him as he disrobed. Even in the shocking cold he slept naked, and—in the days before his determination not to touch her—she had usually wound up so herself. After her first protests he had laughed and assured her that the warmth they generated together was the greatest form of heat they could achieve. She could not tell him, but she did not mind. She liked the feel of his hard body flush to hers while they slept. She liked the possessive splay of his hands upon her, and the tickle of the hairs upon his chest against her back. It was exciting—all of it, just as Lenore had suggested—it was comfortable, and there was also a soft and pleasant intimacy about it that caused her to yearn for more, for something she could not quite see, and for which she was afraid to reach.

With the covers about her, she watched Jamie as he finished some notation at his desk, stretched with his hands upon his lower back, and stood pensively before the fire, his elbow resting upon the mantel, idly stroking his cheek. He looked at her at last, and her cheeks burned, for he caught her scrutiny of him, and he smiled slowly, his brow arching.

"Did you mind the party so much?" she asked him.

"I did not mind it at all. And you enjoyed it."

"Ah, but *you* did not come from the gutter," she said, and as a scowl darkened his features she quickly repented her words. She looked down quickly at her hands, wanting to apologize, but not at all sure how to do so.

"This is a new world, indeed, milady. And I'm not at all sure that it matters where one was born to excel here."

He turned away from the mantel and started across the room for his cloak. Jassy was startled, realizing that he intended to go out. Once she would have been inordinately pleased to have him leave her alone in their bed. Now her heart quickened, and she wondered if she hadn't finally become so misshapen that she could no longer hold his interest, and she couldn't help but wonder where he was going.

"Jamie?"

He paused, then came back by the bed. He lifted her chin and studied her eyes. "Go to sleep," he told her softly. "I won't be long. I feel a certain restlessness and want to see that the gates are locked, and that the guard is awake."

Once he was gone, she lay awake, foolishly fighting a wave of tears. She didn't know what she was feeling, except that she was in a tempest. She would never sleep. But as seemed usual of late, she was exhausted, and she fell into a restless sleep.

Somewhere in the night, he crawled in beside her. She sensed his presence, and her rest became more peaceful.

On Christmas Eve, Father Steven held church services, and the settlement crowded into the small chapel. They sang English carols, and despite the cold and the hardships, the night was one of revelry. Even Elizabeth was in good spirits, and she spent much time with Sir William Tybalt, which intrigued Jassy and gave her hope for her sister's future. She would love to see Elizabeth happy and wed.

The family exchanged small gifts in the hall when the services were over. Jassy had muffs for her sisters, and for Robert and Jamie she had sewn soft leather jerkins. She was anxious to see Jamie with his gift, and when he had lifted the doublet, she showed him the shirt beneath. It was made from the best of the silk that had come to them on the *Lady Destiny*. He sat across from the fire, and Jassy was pleased that they were a certain distance from the others. She was anxious to see his reaction to the gift.

He looked at her quickly and curiously, fingering the cloth. "It is probably the best piece brought over. And you've certainly used the best of the lace upon the sleeves and collar. I had thought that you would have wanted a dress made from this."

She shrugged, fingering the pendant that lay against her breast, his gift to her. It was a gold medallion, engraved with the Cameron crest and studded with precious jewels. "Do you not like the shirt?"

He studied her carefully. "I like it very much. Who made it?"

"I did."

"I never saw you work upon it."

"I meant for it to be a surprise. I worked when you were out of the house. Are you surprised?"

"Very. The cloth is rich, madame. You did not take it for yourself. If you do not take care, I will begin to imagine that you did not marry me entirely for my money. I thought that you craved the best of everything, my love."

Jassy flushed, still fingering the precious golden medallion. He taunted her, but it was Christmas, and she did not care.

"I never craved the best of anything . . . material, milord. I did seek not to starve, I admit. And I did seek . . . ."

"What?"

"Never mind," she said, swiftly turning aside. He would not let her go. He stood, catching her arm, pulling her back to him. "You did seek what, milady? Tell me."

"Jamie, it is Christmas. We have guests—"

"And may God bless them. Answer me. You did seek what?"

She lifted her head and met his demanding stare gravely. "I sought not to die, nor to live, like my mother. Please, could you be so good as to release me now?"

His hand fell away from her arm. She lowered her eyes quickly from his and hurried back to the fire. Tamsyn sat upon the hearth, playing a rousing melody upon a flute. Lenore and Robert were dancing to the curious tune, while Kathryn, the Hume girls, and Mrs. Lawton laughed and applauded. Breathless at last, Lenore fell into a chair before the blaze. "Alas, if only it were England!"

"Are you so homesick, then?" Elizabeth asked her.

"Sometimes," Lenore admitted. "I should love just to see London this night! London, with her busy streets and carefree revelers and her churches, with the bells all pealing merrily. I should love to see Hampton Court; I would cherish a visit to Oxford. I would even love to walk the streets among the people. I *am* homesick, I suppose. I should not like to see the palisade—I should like to see Westminster Abbey and the shops—"

"Shops!" Robert groaned.

"Oh, come!" Lenore said, pouting. "I do not want to smoke meat and worry if we've enough candles and wood for the winter. Look at my hands! Alas, they are almost as bad as Jassy's. I have stooped to the making of candles and soap!"

They all laughed. Jassy was startled by her husband's touch when he picked up her small hand and smoothed his large fingers over it. The fire flickered, and it seemed that the room grew silent—even Tamsyn ceased to play—and Jamie studied her hand very carefully. "This is not a bad hand, as I see it, Lenore. It came to me rough and worn in the service of others, and now it stays rough and worn in the service of my dream. It is a fine hand. It holds great strength, yet it can touch with tenderness. I am quite fond of it, really. Tell me, Jassy, are you so homesick too? Do you still abhor the Carlyle Hundred?"

She could not snatch her hand away, nor could she understand the curious tone of voice with which he softly spoke, then so abruptly demanded. "I am here, milord, for you commanded it so. Remember?"

"Ah. You, too, would prefer London."

"You forget yourself, Lord Cameron. Where you go, I am thither commanded. And you choose to be here."

"Is it really so simple, then?"

"You have seen that it is so," Jassy replied demurely. She was trembling, and she didn't know why. She tugged lightly upon her hand and freed it at last. She looked about at their company and mumbled out some excuse about being exhausted. Then she fled them all, seeking the sanctuary of her room. Jamie would come soon enough, but he would not touch her. He would crawl into his side of the bed, keep his careful distance, and not disturb her.

Molly was not with her, and so she quickly disrobed alone and crawled into bed, shivering. She did not remove her pendant but held it between her fingers. *Cameron*. It was her name. Jassy Cameron. She had never stopped to realize it before, and now it suddenly meant very much. Holding the pendant, she closed her eyes and quickly drifted off to sleep.

It was not, however, a restful sleep. Of all strange times, her nightmares returned. And soon she started to scream again. To scream, and scream, and scream . . .

"Jassy!"

She awoke drenched in sweat, shaking convulsively. She was not alone. Jamie was back, and he held her tightly against himself. "Jassy, shush, it's over now. It's a dream, it's a nightmare. That's all. It is nothing real, nothing that can hurt you!"

She stared into his eyes. Against the soft light of the fire they were very blue and gentle. He touched her cheek and smoothed away the tears that she had shed in her sleep. "Jassy!" he repeated.

She had been as taut as steel, she realized. She went limp in his arms. It had been a dream. No specters haunted their bedroom, no corpses.

"I'm . . . sorry," she whispered. "I'm sorry that I disturbed you."

"And that I am here, not Robert Maxwell?" he said sharply.

She stared quickly into his eyes again, wondering if he was angry. He did not appear to be so, but the question was still intense, and she felt herself shivering again.

"I am sorry," she said softly, "that I disturbed you, milord, and nothing more."

"There is nothing that can hurt you here, Jassy. You are safe with me. You are safe." He smoothed back her hair and held her gently in his arms. "Are you all right?"

Her heart kept beating hard, but the pace was beginning to subside. The light of the fire had bathed the room in a soft glow, and she was leaving behind the shadowed world of her nightmarish terror. She nodded to him. He rose, shivering against the chill as he moved to the hearth to stoke the dying blaze with the poker. Then he returned to her, slipping beneath the covers and pulling her against him. She rested with her cheek upon his naked chest. Her hand also rested upon it, and her fingers were teased by the crisp mat of dark hair beneath them. He lay with his arm crooked beneath his head, stroking her hair, staring up at the canopy of their bed.

"Tell me about it. Tell me about the dream," he said.

She tensed, wondering if she could do so. He must have felt the new fear within her, for he reached for her chin and tilted her head so that she could meet his eyes. "No demons lie in wait for you here, Jassy. Tell me what torments you, and perhaps you will be freed from it."

She lowered her head against him again, rubbing her cheek against the sleek warmth of his chest. "It—it always starts with my mother," she whispered.

"And she is ill?"

"She is dying. I can see her: She is lying on the pallet in Master John's attic, and there is a sheet covering her, and I know what I will find, but I must go to her, anyway. I come closer and closer, and then I pull away the covers and she is there, but she is dead, and she has been dead for a very long time, for her eyes are nothing but dark, empty sockets, and it is as if the carrion and wormshave preyed upon her. I stare at her and I stare at her and . . ."

"And, my love?"

"As I watch her, she becomes me, and I am in terror then that . . ."

"That what, Jassy?"

"I . . . do not want to die as she did," Jassy mumbled against his flesh.

He was silent for several long seconds. "She died the night that we first met."

"Yes."

"And you were trying to buy her some medication, or the services of some physician?"

"Yes," she barely whispered. The sound was a ragged breath of warmth that touched his flesh. Her fingers curled suddenly against him. "You must understand . . . Robert was very kind to me that day. She would not even lie in a coffin had he not insisted on paying the cost of it."

Jamie grunted. His voice took on a slight edge. "And that is it? The extent of the dream?"

She shuddered again, violently. "Sometimes . . . sometimes it is different."

"And tonight?"

"Tonight it was worse. I watched her, and even as I stared at her, she became me. I saw myself lying there, and I knew that I was dead. I was dead . . . as my mother had been."

"Was I there?"

She recalled the dream, Jamie staring down upon her, Hope sidling around him. She remembered holding the baby, the blue, pinched, stillborn baby.

"Yes, you were there."

"And what was I doing?"

"You were watching me. Very gravely, very sadly."

"Why?"

"Because . . . because the babe was laid upon me, and it was dead too."

"Jassy! Jassy!" He set his hands upon her and sat up, sweeping her into his arms and cradling her within them. His chin rested atop her head, and he held her close. He took her hand and stretched out her fingers, then laid her hand against the swell of her stomach. "Feel him! He kicks even now. He is strong and you are strong, and both of you will survive. I will not let anything happen to you."

She twisted against him, burying her face against his neck. He continued to hold her tight.

"Trust in me," he told her. He threaded his fingers through hers and laced them together over the bulge of their child. "Trust in me; I will be beside you, and I will never let you starve or want for anything."

Jassy had never known such a wondrous feeling of security.

Of being cherished . . .

She laid her head against him, savoring the sensation. She yawned, exhausted again, certain that her dreams would no longer be haunted.

"Was there more to it?" he asked.

"What, milord?" she asked in sleepy contentment.

"The dream. Was there any more to it?"

"Oh . . . yes. Hope was beside you as you watched me."

He laughed suddenly, and with good humor. "You are a jealous little minx."

She started to stiffen against him. "Milord, I most certainly am not."

"You are."

"I am not . . ." She hesitated, for the baby was moving in great ripples against her stomach. "I . . . have grown so very large," she murmured.

He chuckled softly, nuzzling her head with his chin. "It will not be long now, madame. Not long at all. The end of February, the beginning of March."

"It will not be long," she agreed. She trembled, for she could not quite shake the fear. He held her closer. "I will be with you," he promised her. "I will be with you, and no harm will come to you."

She believed him. She gazed up at him with a tender, dazzling smile, and then she closed her eyes, and in a matter of minutes she was sleeping again, softly and easily this time.

Jamie laid her down, smoothed the hair from her brow, and studied her features, gentle with sleep, a smile still curved about her lips. She grew more beautiful daily, he thought, and he grew evermore beneath the shadow of her spell. He felt like a lovesick boy at times, watching her movements, watching her laughter, watching her when she frowned, concentrating intently upon some task or another.

Regrets . . . *He* had none.

He had determined to have her, and he had determined to marry her, and he had known that she had the passion and the spirit to rival his, to meet and challenge this brave new land. He had known that he had the power to make her his wife, and he even had had the sure confidence to believe that he could awaken the passion and sensuality that had lain behind the vehemence of her hatred and the volatility of her spirit. He had, in his arrogance known that he could claim her and awaken her, and command her here, to his side.

But he could not make her *love* him.

She was his wife. Soon they would have a child, and there was no reason that he should lose her.

No reason . . . except that he might well let her go. He could not love like this and keep silent. Nor could he lay his heart before her feet and lose his soul. She had wanted Robert. She dreamed of a man full of flattery and laughter. Someone gentle, easily led and maneuvered.

He clenched his jaw, hard and tight. He could not be a half-wit fool for her entertainment. If she could not love the man that he was, then he would have to let her go.

Misery clamped down upon him hard, and his muscles constricted, taut and painful. They would know soon enough, he thought. When the child came, there would be a time of reckoning. He would demand it.

And he would have it.

16

THEY WERE NOT TO WAIT AS LONG AS ANY OF them had anticipated for Jassy's baby to be born.

The doctor from Jamestown had promised to make it down to the hundred by the twenty-fifth of February, but it was only the fifteenth of that month when she felt the first startling pain.

She was out in the kitchen with Jonathan when she felt the constriction come around her, like a steel band tightening around her lower back. She had been bending over a pot of stew, and at first she felt as if she had merely stood over it too long. The last weeks had been wretched for her. She could find no such thing as a comfortable position, not to sit in, stand in, or sleep in. Rising was difficult, and walking had its annoyances, and she was ever in need of a chamber pot. She had grown very anxious and longed for the birth.

Straightening, Jassy held her hands upon her hips and stretched, and in a few moments the pain faded. Jonathan Hayes looked at her worriedly. "We can take stock of the spices later, milady."

She shook her head, smiling. "We don't know when the next ship is due, and I believe that we are running low on salt. Let's continue."

Jonathan went onward to assess the cloves, and Jassy listened to him as he droned on, marking down the amounts of various herbs and spices in Jamie's ledger. Suddenly she could hear Jonathan speak no more, for the constriction came again, and no little twinge, but an agonizing knot about her. She jumped to her feet, gasping with it, squeezing her eyes tightly shut.

"Milady—"

"I am all right," she said, but the band constricted tighter and tighter. She fell back into the chair and looked at Jonathan. "I am *not* all right."

"I'll get help." Jonathan grabbed his cloak from the peg and went racing out into the yard. The pain began to ebb again, and Jassy worried that she might have given poor Jonathan a false alarm. She started to rise again, then felt a flood of water cascade from her, drenching her skirts and petticoats. She gripped hard to the table, for the cascade came with another pain, this one more fierce than ever before.

The door burst inward, and a cold gust of wind followed Tamsyn into the kitchen. He came hurriedly over to her.

"It is the baby," he said.

"It is too early!" Jassy protested.

Tamsyn smiled at her. "Jassy, girl, there's none can tell a babe eager to enter the world that it's too early. They will come when they choose to do so, and that's a fact. You need to get up to your bed, like a good lass."

"Then what?"

"Then, lass, you wait. Come, I'll help you." He set an arm about her shoulders. The door burst inward again, and Jamie was there. He stood, framed by the doorway, very tall and dark and forbidding. He looked at Tamsyn, and then his wife. He drew off his gloves as he came into the kitchen, tossing them upon the table. "Move aside, man!" he told Tamsyn, stooping low to sweep Jassy into his arms.

"No!" she cried, and she looked anxiously to Tamsyn. "Jamie, he studied at Oxford, please . . ." She hooked her arms around his neck, shivering. The birth water had made her very cold. "I am soaking you," she added in distress.

Jamie gave no heed to her sodden condition but stared hard at Tamsyn. He was not the same man he had once urged from the Crossroads Inn. He was clean-shaven, and he often smoked upon a clay pipe, but he seldom inbibed in anything stronger than ale, and he was frugal in that taste. Now, as he looked at the man, Jamie hesitated only briefly. He could not be sure of the man's credentials, but Jassy trusted in him, and perhaps that was the most important thing. "Come along, then," Jamie said.

Jassy whispered her thanks against his shirt.

He strode through the breezeway from the kitchen to the house, coming in by the dining room. The cold February wind struck them hard, and he felt her shiver anew. He saw Amy Lawton sweeping the hallway as he entered the main house, and he called to her quickly. "Go to the Tannen house. Fetch Molly. Where is Elizabeth?"

"I'm here!" Elizabeth called from the stairway.

"The babe comes," Jamie said briefly. He strode on up the stairs with Jassy in his arms. In their room he set her down and instantly set upon the hooks and eyes upon her gown. She looked up at him, shivering miserably. He tried to pull the gown over her head.

"You shouldn't be here," she whispered. "I am a disaster."

"Let's get this off." He pulled the gown over her head. She wore no corset or stays but only a shift and two loose petticoats. With the dress gone, she stood and backed away from him. "I can manage, Jamie, honestly."

"Get over here!" he commanded her gruffly. "You cannot manage."

"Jamie—"

Elizabeth had followed them into the room by then. She cleared her throat softly. "I'll find a new gown," she said.

Another pain seized upon Jassy hard, and she gritted her teeth as tears stung her eyes and she doubled over. "Little fool!" Jamie chastised her. He caught hold of her, taking her hands in his own. She gripped hard in return. Harder and harder. "Easy!" he whispered to her. "Breathe deep, Jassy. Easy, love, easy . . ."

The band of agony eased, and she went limp against him. He took the opportunity to strip her of her petticoats and shift, and Elizabeth came quickly over to assist him, and to slide the clean, dry nightgown over her head. By then Tamsyn, too, was standing in the doorway. Jamie stared at him hard. "All right, then, man. What now?"

"Now she must lie down and wait, milord."

"That's all?"

"That is all that can be done," Tamsyn replied. Elizabeth drew back the sheets, and Jamie swept Jassy up and laid her out upon the bed.

Jassy caught his hand. "Jamie," she whispered. "It's too early."

"Not so very early," he told her encouragingly. He glanced at Tamsyn. He wished that he knew more about the birth process. He had learned so much in life. He could sail a ship, tramp his way through any wilderness, and survive off the land or the sea, but he didn't know how to ease a single furrow of pain from Jassy's brow, and he didn't have any idea if the babe was really too early, if it could survive at all.

"Two weeks," Tamsyn said, "if my old eyes don't deceive me. I'm a-thinking this lad might have found his roots on the very night of your wedding, milord, and therefore he has chosen to come just a mite too soon. Things should come well enough." He looked at Elizabeth. "Lady Elizabeth, if you would find Molly when she comes, have her tend to the water we need, and the cloths to wipe up his little lordship when he arrives, and for Jass—milady."

"What can I do?" Jamie said.

"Why, milord, perhaps you should go and smoke a pipe and have a whiskey. It will be a while."

Jamie shook his head. "I promised her that I would stay with her."

"Then stay with her, milord," Tamsyn said, and smiled ruefully. "Cool her brow, hold her hand, and be at her side."

It was exactly what he did.

The man, Tamsyn, seemed awkward at first about touching Jassy in Jamie's presence. Then he seemed to shrug, realizing that Lord Cameron was in the birth room to stay, and that was that. Jamie knew that Tamsyn was aware of his doubt, and in the end Tamsyn squared his shoulders and spoke to Jamie as he worked over Jassy. Jassy winced and clung to her husband's hand. Jamie's flesh went white where she gripped against him, but he made no sound.

"We are in good stead," Tamsyn said cheerfully. "She has come far already, and the babe is in the proper position."

A sigh of relief escaped Jassy. Jamie looked at her pained features and knew that she was thinking of Joan Tannen aboard the *Sweet Eden,* and of the babe stillborn upon the vessel.

Her features screwed up into a curious mask. Jamie lay his hand upon her abdomen and felt the tremendous tightening in her womb. Her fingers shook, then dug into his hand again. "They come so fast!" she cried piteously.

And they did come fast. Elizabeth and Molly came back with the water and the cloths. Jamie wiped her face, and he spoke to her reassuringly each time that the pains subsided, but they came again and again, faster and faster.

She pleaded with him once to leave, but he met Molly's eyes over her form, and Molly shook her head. A second later Jassy's fingers crunched down upon his, and he held her, trying to take some of the pain away, trying to give to her some of his strength. At one point she seemed to sleep. Her grip eased from his. He stood, stared at Tamsyn, and paced the room, his hands locked behind his back. Elizabeth and Molly looked on.

Jamie threw his hands into the air. "Do something!"

"Do what, Lord Cameron?"

"Hurry this along. She cannot stand so much pain."

Molly, Tamsyn, and Elizabeth all gazed at one another. Elizabeth stepped forward, reaching for Jamie's hand. "It is not so very long, Jamie. It has been just a matter of hours. Many more hours may go by before the babe comes; it is nature's way. You do not understand so much about babes coming into the world."

"And you do?" Jamie said.

Elizabeth flushed. "I was there when your sister bore your niece, My Lord Cameron, so, yes, I know something of it!"

Jamie lowered his head in acknowledgment. Elizabeth trembled slightly. She had never seen him even remotely humble before. She touched his arm. "I know that everything will be well, Jamie."

Jassy screamed suddenly from the bed, awakened by the ferocity of another pain. Jamie flew back to her side, his face dark, his hands shaking. "Easy, Jassy, easy."

"I cannot bear this—"

"You will bear it. Breathe."

"I cannot—"

"I command it, love. Breathe and hold my hand, and let loose of my son, madame."

"Let loose of your son!"

Her eyes opened in a flash of temper, and Jamie laughed. "Aye, lady, come now. You dally here!"

She lay back, telling him that he was a vile knave. When the next pain seized her, she swore like a dockhand and dug her nails into his hand, but she did not cry or weaken or scream. The pains were coming very, very fast.

Tamsyn realized that they would not be waiting hours and hours. The babe was coming before nightfall.

Lord Cameron's face was ashen as he watched over his wife. Tamsyn lightly touched his arm. "The babe comes soon."

Jamie started, sitting up. Molly awaited the child with swaddling, and Tamsyn talked to Jassy. "You never could wait for anything, lass. You never did learn patience, and you never could do things in half measures. You couldn't marry a merchant, but you had to have a fine lord, and that, lass, you did in a hurry too. Seems that this little lad will be one like his mother. Now push, Jassy, love. Give him a push."

"I cannot!" She fell back in exhaustion. Jamie caught her shoulders and pressed her forward. "Jassy, 'tis Tamsyn talking to you, and you must give him heed."

"Oh!" she cried out, and she tried to escape his hold and give up. He would not release her, and she was forced to bear down.

"I see a very dark head!" Molly cried enthusiastically.

"Again!" Tamsyn persisted.

"No!"

"Jassy, I will have my son now!"

"A daughter," Jassy said argumentatively.

"Push!" Jamie said gratingly.

And the baby came from her. It was the greatest relief that Jassy had ever known. Life spilled from her in a great, heavy gush, and the pain was numbed. . . .

And she heard the cry, the sharp, plaintive wail that came from her newborn infant. Sharp, plaintive, and very lusty.

"A son, at that!" Tamsyn laughed. "And very much alive and well."

"Oh!"

A son . . .

Just as Jamie had commanded.

The squalling infant passed from Tamsyn's hands to Molly, who quickly and tenderly swept him into swaddling and began to clean his little face. Jamie quickly and vehemently kissed Jassy fully upon the lips, running his knuckles over her cheeks. She was dazed, but still she thought that he looked upon her with great tenderness. But he was up then, and demanding his child from Molly. He stood in the candlelight and stared down upon the tiny new life, lifting away the covering and inspecting every bit of the child. He smiled, and he looked striking when he turned back to his wife with pleasure and exuberance.

"Perfect, my love. Ten fingers, ten toes, a stubborn chin, blue eyes, and very dark hair, I *believe*. It's quite sodden."

The new Cameron howled, and Jassy saw a tiny fist protrude from the coverings. A sharp sensation stung her breasts, and she felt them swell. "May I see him?" she whispered. She tried for the strength to sit up but was exhausted. Despite the cold of winter, sweat trickled through her hair and dampened her forehead.

"Jassy, one more time," Tamsyn said to her, and she looked at him in confusion. "One last time, love. The birth sac must come now. Push for me, lass."

It was not so hard that time. She was so anxious to see her son. She gritted her teeth and bore down, and again she felt the most wonderful sensation of relief. She fell back, closed her eyes, and breathed in exhaustion, but when she opened her eyes again, Jamie was hovering over her, and he very carefully placed the baby into her arms.

The love that swelled in her heart was instant and total. He seemed very tiny, but he was perfect. His mouth was open and his screaming was probably quite horrible, but it was delightful to her ears. His eyes *were* blue, a dark blue, like Jamie's, though she knew they might change and take on her lighter hue. His cap of hair was all Jamie's, though, very dark and rich and in startling plenty for a newborn. She loved his little gnome's face, wrinkled and pink and knotted up in the effort that drew forth his lusty howls. She, too, pushed the swaddling back. He *was* quite perfect. He was long and was very certainly a little boy, and though he wasn't chubby, he didn't seem to have suffered the loss of the extra weeks he should have spent in the womb.

She started to shake. Her nightmare vision was really at rest. Her son had been born alive, and he was beautiful.

"Oh, Jamie!" she whispered, and she was afraid she was going to burst into tears. "He is . . . fine."

"He is magnificent," Jamie corrected her. He gently touched his son's cheek with his finger, his hand seeming huge against the tiny face. Then he brushed her lip with his thumb, and she looked into his eyes. "He is magnificent," Jamie repeated.

Tears were welling in her eyes. Molly stepped forward very matter-of-factly. "Let him nurse, love. He won't get too much nourishment yet, but he needs to pull the milk in." Molly hesitated suddenly, looking from Jamie to Jassy. "That is, if you want it in. Ladies don't always nurse their own, do they, Lord Cameron?"

Jassy's breath caught. Did they not nurse their children out of choice? she wondered. She wanted nothing more than to have the baby as close to her as possible. She wanted to explore every angle of this new thing called motherhood, and she hoped desperately that Jamie would not deny her. Perhaps husbands chose wet nurses so that their wives would not be overly occupied with their newborns.

"We haven't a tremendous supply of wet nurses around," Jassy murmured.

"I'm sure that someone can be found—" Molly began.

"Jassy will nurse the babe," Jamie said firmly.

She gazed at him, grateful for his response. Beside her, he was every bit as fascinated with the infant, and he smiled at her and gently pulled upon the lace of her gown. Awkwardly, for her fingers trembled, Jassy set the baby to her nipple, and then laughed, her nervousness easing as he rooted about her breast, finding his hold upon her. He latched on hard at last, and a shaft of lightning seemed to streak through her. Love, as intense as the blaze of the sun, filled her with the strange new sensation. He began to suck hard upon her, sounding much like a little pig. Molly and Elizabeth laughed. "There's a hungry one for you," Molly said.

"Like his father," Jassy murmured, and then she realized what she had said, and looked up, reddening with embarrassment. But Jamie laughed then, too, and Tamsyn joined in, and it was one of the nicest moments of her life. She held the baby against her breast for a few minutes more, then Jamie took him from her again. He kissed her lips once more. "Molly says she's going to bathe you and set the bed right. Then you need to sleep. I'll come to you later."

Her eyes were already closing. She was dimly aware that Molly asked for the baby back, that he might be bathed. Jamie turned the baby over to Molly and left the room. Jassy awoke somewhat when Molly moved her about to change the sheets and her gown, wiping her down with a wet cloth.

Then she slept, and slept hard, with no dreams or nightmares to disturb her.

Later that night she awoke, ravenous, and achingly aware of the howls and sniffles that aroused her from her slumber. She opened her eyes and found that Jamie was with her again, pulled up to the bed in the large captain's chair from his desk. The baby, now clean and swaddled anew in soft linen, lay upon his lap. He smiled when he saw her open eyes, then lay the baby at her side. The aching sensation seared her breasts, and she turned to her side and led the baby to nurse. He latched quickly and fiercely, and her eyes met Jamie's with delight. "I must do it right."

He chuckled. "Certainly so, madame. I never doubted you for a moment, and neither did he, so it seems."

She smiled, pleased and warmed. Jamie moved forward, stroking the babe's cheek, lightly brushing his fingertips over her breast. "He must be baptized first thing in the morning. What shall we call him?"

"First thing?" she repeated with a frown, and panic seized her. "Jamie, he is all right? There is no need to fear—"

"Jassy, he is in good health. Tamsyn assured me that it is so. It is only right to baptize him as soon as possible."

She nodded, lowering her head and wishing that she didn't betray her fears so quickly all of the time.

"Jassy, he needs a name."

"Don't—don't fathers usually insist upon naming their sons?"

"He is your son, too, madame. I had thought that after this morning you'd be quite loath to give me any of the credit."

She flushed, thinking that indeed it seemed far the easier measure to be a sire than a dam. "James," she said out loud.

"For the king?"

"Nay, for his sire. He is the firstborn."

"Is that a promise for an army to come?"

"Nay, it is no promise!" Jassy said vehemently, and he laughed.

"If you wish it, he will be James. James Daniel Cameron, if that suits you, and we might, for the moment, call him Daniel to avoid confusion."

"James Daniel Cameron," Jassy murmured. "I like it." James Daniel opened his eyes wide to her. "James Daniel Cameron," she repeated. She bent down and kissed his impossibly soft and downy head. "I love you, James Daniel."

The baby's eyes closed. She stroked his soft skull with wonder, then she saw that Jamie was watching her. She stared at him and he smiled ruefully. "It is customary for a lord to present his lady with a gift upon such an occasion. I admit, were we home, I would have given you a rope of pearls, but alas, I have no such thing—"

"It does not—"

"I do have something else which I think is very fine." He produced a narrow string of rawhide, upon which was a striking and unusual amulet. The fingers of a man and a woman were etched primitively upon a pink shell. A sun burst above the two of them, casting rays about them both. A god seemed to peer down benevolently from the rays of the sun. With the baby asleep at her breast and his mouth half opened upon it, Jassy studied the amulet. She looked at Jamie and smiled slowly. "It is lovely."

"It was given to me once by a little girl."

"A little girl?"

He smiled. "The first time that I was here, I met Pocahontas. She had saved John Smith, but she was just an eleven-year-old child, and her fascination and generosity to the settlers was astounding. I was young myself, into my teens. She and Powan and I came together, first when the whites would have slain Powan, and second when the warring Powhatans might have gotten their hands upon me. I have always cherished it, and I hope that it will mean something to you, if it is only a symbol of the pearls that I will one day come to find."

He did not look in her eyes. He gently disengaged their sleeping son from her breast, then set him upon his shoulder.

"Jamie."

"Yes?"

"It is beautiful. I will cherish it, I swear it." She slipped it over her neck. He smiled at her.

"Molly has stayed. She will bring you something to eat in a minute. You must eat, and you must sleep, and—"

"I will be up soon, I promise."

"Milady, you will not. You will not rise for more than an hour or two for at least a week. Tamsyn has said so, and I will see that it is so." He smiled again, taking the sting from his words.

The door closed in his wake. Jassy pulled the covers close to her chin, and she smiled to herself.

She had never known that it was possible to be so radiantly happy.

―――――

In the days that followed, Jassy was absorbed with the baby. They never did call him James or Jamie; from the beginning he was Daniel.

He delighted Jassy, for he seemed stronger by the minute. He quickly lost his wizened appearance, and she liked to stare at him for hours, and compare every one of his little features to those of his father. He was remarkably like Jamie. Even being an infant, Daniel had certain ways of looking at her that pulled strongly upon her heart, for they were so similar to the very ways that Jamie could look at her. He could be silent and grave, and howl like the very north wind. She was certain that he had already learned to smile, although Molly assured her that it was a "wee bit of the air in his belly"—Daniel was too young to smile. Jassy didn't believe it for a second. He had come into the world determined, and now that he was within it, he was ingenious and precocious. She was certain of it. When she held him in her arms. she felt complete, as she had never been complete before. Something that she had done in life was right, and special, and entirely unique.

Her one unhappiness in those days was that it seemed that she saw less and less of Jamie.

He did not sleep with her the night that Daniel was born, nor the night after. Molly had determined to stay for a few days, and so Jamie had ordered that a cot be brought up for her comfort. A group of the laborers from the settlement had come with a gift for Jassy, and Jamie had brought them up to the room. She had greeted them from her bed, and she had been delighted with their gift, a cradle that had been lovingly carved from the best of the wood, and engraved upon the side with the Cameron crest. From the bottom of her heart she had thanked them, and John Tannen, who had led the group of them, was the one to speak to her, twirling his flat cap in his hands as he was so wont to do.

"Milady, if our gift pleases you, we are most humbly grateful. We were many of us a-fearing your arrival, for we thought that Lord Cameron's lady might be a harsh and cold mistress, demanding her distance from us all. But you came to us, lady, like a sweet angel of mercy, and we are, one and all, grateful. Molly and me are grateful, and I know that my Joan and our infant went to the Maker from a gentle touch. Lady, the best to you, and to the bonny boy!"

"Thank you, John," Jassy said. "Thank you all so much. We will keep the cradle forever, I promise you, and it will be cherished for the craftsmanship, and for the heart with which it was given."

She could not look at Jamie, who stood silently in the corner of the room. Emotions were churning too deeply within her. She had not wanted to come here, yet no place had ever been so much like home. She had married for gain, and if her driving desire had been a life without hunger, poverty, and want, she *had* accepted Jamie, knowing that he offered a life of much more, a life of luxury. There was little enough luxury to be found here, but that had long ago ceased to matter. It seemed so long ago now. All that mattered to her now was Daniel, and the welfare of her family and her dear friends and servants, and . . .

Her husband.

"Come down and warm yourselves with some ale, for it still blows cold beyond the doors," Jamie said, inviting the men. They left her with good cheer. Jamie's eyes remained upon her until he had left the room, but she could not tell what he was thinking.

Molly stayed for the week, and then she returned to her own newly acquired family. Jassy missed her, but she had Elizabeth with her, and Mrs. Lawton, and Charity and Patience.

She still didn't have Jamie.

The first night she hadn't questioned his disappearance. Then Molly had been there. But when Molly had gone home, he still avoided his own bed, sleeping across the hall in the room where Lenore and Robert had stayed. He did not wish to disturb her or the babe, he told her awkwardly one morning, slipping in to find more pairs of his hose. She needed her sleep.

Jassy, hurt, did not argue with him. She wondered if perhaps he did not want his own sleep disturbed, since the winter hung on and he was busy with survival.

But sometimes she heard him late at night, pacing the floor. At those times she hugged the baby to her, whether Daniel slept or not, and she bit deep into her lip, hoping that he had not ceased to care. She knew that they could not resume marital relations for some time, but they had not been together in that way for some time before Daniel had been born, and it had not mattered; it had been good to sleep beside him, to feel his heartbeat beneath her chin, to feel his arms around her. Tamsyn had told her that she must wait a month, a full month, and go carefully then. She did not know if Tamsyn had spoken to Jamie, too, or if Jamie simply had been aware of the ways of women and childbirth. Or if Jamie simply had ceased to care.

The nights when he paced disturbed her. The nights when he did not pace disturbed her more. She didn't know where he was, or who he was with, or where his thoughts and yearnings might have wandered.

Hope was about too. When the snow melted, a group of the Indians came to the house, bearing gifts from Opechancanough. The great chief sent the baby a small amulet much like the one that the princess Pocahontas had given to Jamie, and that Jamie had given to her. She seldom took hers off, and though she was afraid that the baby might strangle on his, she tied it over his cradle. She wasn't sure why. She had sometimes lost faith in her own God, but she certainly felt nothing for the peculiar and demanding gods of the Algonquin peoples in the Powhatan Confederacy. Still, she felt that it was important the baby be protected by the amulet. The Christian God was just gaining a foothold here. The Indian gods had been around much longer.

To placate Father Steven, she also asked John Tannen to make her a crucifix to rest at the foot of the cradle. Father Steven objected to the amulet. Jamie was amused by it all. "Father, we acknowledge no craven images, so it seems to matter little what decoration we choose to use upon the lad's cradle. I'm sure that it will not sway him from growing up in the proper ways of the Church of England."

Father Steven threw up his arms and offered no further protest. Jassy cast her husband a grateful glance, but he didn't seem to notice. In his mind he was already away from her, anxious to attend to more important business.

Jassy was glad of his support in many things. If the question involved her in those days, he always deferred to her.

And still he stayed away. Jassy saw less and less of him.

When Daniel was two weeks old, the last of the fallen snow melted. Jonathan, who had been in the Jamestown settlement before he had come to work for Jamie in the hundred, told Jassy that maybe there would be no more snow that year.

February turned to March.

Tamsyn was no longer working in the stables. Jassy had been startled to discover that he had been set up in a small house of his own, and that the care of their medical supplies had been put in his hands. Little by little the people turned to him for help with their various woes and ailments.

" 'Tis your husband's doing," Tamsyn was quick to tell her. "When Daniel was born, he bid me follow him to the great room to the left of the hallway, and

I near thought that he meant to say, 'Off with this man's head.' But he asked me about Oxford and my studies, and he was heartily angry, so it seemed, that I had let my life come to this over an indulgence in drink. I swore to him that I had no more difficulty, and he told me that it was a new world, a new life, and that he could not afford for me to waste my education and knowledge here. He gave me the house, and he sent the people to me. They came slowly at first. But I cured Mrs. Danver's stomach colic, and set Timothy Hale's broken arm, and they seem to have confidence in me now."

Jassy was glad for Tamsyn, and she offered her gratitude to Jamie that night. "I did nothing, madame," he told her impatiently, "but advise the man to use skills which we have grave need of here."

He dismissed her quickly and curtly, and she said no more.

March came blustering in with wind and rain, but by the fifteenth, on the day that Daniel became a month old, it seemed that spring was on its way. It was a beautiful day with a rich promise of warmth and a clear blue sky. The land had never seemed more verdant beyond the palisade. The farmers were preparing for their planting, everything seemed sweetly alive and awakened, and everyone seemed aware that it was almost spring, a season for warmth and laughter and gaiety.

Everyone but Jamie.

There were times when Jassy thought that he hated her, and there were times, too, when she thought that he had grown completely indifferent to her. He was very quick to anger, and he was almost constantly curt to her. He avoided her, staying out late at night, leaving the house by day.

And still sometimes she caught him watching her with a grave and brooding darkness to his features and his eyes, watching her as if he sought something. If she came to him, he would deny that he stared at her, and impatiently he would leave her.

Puzzled, hurt, and growing very frightened, Jassy watched him in turn. He loved Daniel, she was certain of it. He asked every evening that the child be brought to him, and Jassy would pensively hand her son over to Amy or Charity or Patience so that he could be brought to his father. Daniel did not return until he was squalling to be fed, and needed his mother.

On the fifteenth Jassy determined that she would have her husband back in her bed. She had not lost the least bit of her absorbing interest in her child, but she craved Jamie. She was young and in good health, and she missed him desperately, the way that he held her . . . the way that he loved her.

She dressed with special care, in a gown with a low-cut bodice and soft lace ruff that spilled over her breasts. She had spent the morning, once Daniel had been fed, washing and drying her hair, and it fell down her back like a cascade of sunshine. Anxiously pinching her cheeks, she sought out Jamie in the great room off the hall.

He and Sir William were involved in the business of charting out an area up the river they wished to map. Charts and quills were strewn over a large table in the center of the room.

The men looked up at her arrival. Sir William was quick to greet her with a smile of admiration and a quick bow. Jamie's eyes upon her were his only indication that he knew she had come.

"Good day, Sir William," she said. She looked at her husband. "I see that you are busy."

"Never so busy that it is not a pleasure for an interruption as beautiful as you, milady," Sir William said.

"What do you want?" Jamie asked curtly.

Even Sir William stared at him, shocked by his tone of voice. Then it seemed Sir William decided upon a hasty retreat, for he mumbled something about forgetting to see to the late guard. "I will return quickly, milord," he promised Jamie.

Then Jassy and Jamie were left alone in the space of the large room with a silence resting between them. Jamie stared at her hard, then issued a sound of impatience.

"What, madame, is so important that you must interrupt work and create a scene?"

"Create a scene?" Jassy repeated, her temper flaring.

"And disturb Sir William."

"Sir William did not seem at all disturbed."

"Ah, yes, you like compliments and admiration, and that he gives you willingly."

"Which you do not."

"I am not accustomed to fawning. Now, what do you want?"

"Neither are you accustomed to common courtesy, so it seems, my most noble lord! And what do I want from you? Nothing, nothing at all from you, but that which I have always craved—my freedom!" She spun around in a fury. She could barely see or hear she was so blinded with her anger and the surge of pain that his coldly spoken words had brought.

He caught her arm, pulling her back. She hated the power in his hold at that moment. She hated the vise-like grip he held about her arm, and she hated the way that he towered over her and stared down at her with his eyes so dark and speculative. "Is that what you truly want, milady?"

"What?" she cried.

"Freedom?"

She hesitated, her lips gone dry, her tongue frozen. She ached to cry out, to pitch herself into his arms and let go with a flood of tears. She wanted to tell him the truth, that freedom from him would be misery. One word from him . . . a smile . . . a gentle touch . . . and she would do so.

She received nothing from him. Just his demanding, hard blue stare and the tense rigor in his muscles. Life had become so ironic, ah, yes, life, always the jest. She had despised him so. And now, when she had come to love him with all the heart and passion and aching need that lay within her, he had come to despise her.

"I have asked you a question, Jassy."

"I—" she began, but the door burst open, and Sir William came rushing back in.

"She's come, Jamie! The *Lady Destiny* ventures into the bay and will soon find her dockage in our deep harbor. She has come, ah, at last! Surely it *is* spring!"

Sir William hadn't seemed to notice the way that Jamie held Jassy, or the tangible tension that had riddled the air.

Jamie released her. "Let's hurry to greet the *Lady Destiny,* shall we?"

He walked out of the room, leaving Jassy to stare after him, feeling as if he had centered his sword well within her heart.

The pinnace came with supplies, with beautifully created clothing for Daniel, with guns and swords and ammunition, and with company too. Sirs Allen Wethington and Cedric Aherne arrived along with a cartographer, a metalsmith, and wives and children of the established settlers, and with new carpenters and laborers and craftsmen to make their homes within the hundred.

Jassy was pleased with their company.

Sirs Allen and Cedric were to stay in an empty house across the compound, but that was only to sleep. They dined in grand style that night at Lord Cameron's house, and Jassy was glad to be a hostess, she performed her duties with a fever.

If her husband no longer wanted her, she could prove that other men might.

Lenore and Robert came, and Elizabeth joined them shyly too. There was an abundance of fresh wild turkey for the meal, brought to them just that morning by a few of the Indians. There were meat pies and berries and corn bread, and the *Lady Destiny* had brought over a supply of coffee—becoming so very popular a drink in Italy now—and the fragile little cups for it so like the set Jamie had in the manor in England. When the meal was over, the men lit pipes, and still the party went on, for even Jamie was eager for news from England, and they were all soon laughing at Sir Allen's descriptions of the staid court of their dear King James and his Anne of Denmark.

Jassy realized quickly that Jamie had known Allen and Cedric in London; they had shared certain tutors at various times. They were all of an age, Allen reminding her much of Robert, for he was blond and blue-eyed and quick to smile. Cedric was a dashing redhead with a mustache and full beard, a bit of a portly girth, but great shoulders and heavy thighs to match. They were both charming to her, and she was delighted and on fire with the evening. Some sweet devil had entered into her, she knew. She wished, with all her heart, to provoke her husband's temper. She knew how to do it too. Not quickly, not with some overt action. But slowly. Too deep a smile for one man, too long a laughing touch upon another's arm. He never could have complained that his tavern wench of a wife did not have the manners of a lady, for she was soft-spoken and charming throughout the evening. She had gained their hearts upon a string, and she knew it.

"We'd heard that you'd run off and married, Jamie," Allen said. "And if you didn't find the loveliest demoiselle in all England. Where did he find you, my dear? Locked away in some north county tower? How is it that we missed you?"

Jassy held silent, her heart beating. She looked at Jamie, but he stood by the mantel, his elbow resting upon it, resplendent with dark good looks and subdued finery. His eyes fell upon her and he shrugged. "My wife and I met by sheer chance, gentlemen, upon the road, as it was. She was traveling to her family's home, conveniently close to my own. I was able to escort her, and as luck would have it, she came into my arms at precisely the right time."

Jassy's eyes fell. She was surprised that he hadn't denounced her in his present mood. "She is a tavern wench, gentlemen, and I met her in truth when she came to my room as a whore."

Perhaps appearances meant something to him, after all, she thought bitterly, and she lifted her chin. She rose swiftly to her feet and asked if she might get them something else to drink. She offered Robert Maxwell her most winning smile and refilled his glass with wine.

Charity came down the stairs then, excusing herself, and whispering to Jamie. He stared across the room at Jassy and smiled with a taut satisfaction.

"My dear, I believe that you need to excuse yourself for the evening." He looked to Sir Cedric. "My son is but a month old today, and still awakens in the eve, wanting his mother."

The men stood. Sir Allen came to her, taking her hand. "Surely, Jamie, you could have arranged for some assistance for your wife. That you could take her away from us . . ." His voice faded away with a tone of deep regret.

"But motherhood is quite a talent with my lady, gentlemen. She would have it no other way. *Good night,* my love."

Motherhood . . . it was her *only* talent, so it seemed, and Jamie was glad to order her from the party. She was eager to fight him, eager to assure the gentlemen that she would be right back. But then she heard Daniel, snuffling in Patience's arms up the stairway. Her breasts tingled and she was ashamed that she could forget her son—even in her vengeance against her husband.

She said good night and started up the stairway. Then she could not help but pause and call down to the company, sweetly assuring the men that she would see them on the morrow. Jamie's eyes touched hers briefly. She had angered him. She had taunted and teased and flirted very carefully, and surely her husband's friends would lie awake, wondering about her.

And perhaps her husband would come to her. . . .

He did come, and not twenty minutes later. She lay with Daniel. His tiny fist rested against her breast while he rooted at it. She had not changed but lay with her bodice apart, cradling her son to her.

She started at Jamie's appearance. He did not knock, he threw open the door to their room. She started and pulled away from the baby, holding her bodice together.

"You might have knocked." She gasped, stunned.

He stood tall in the doorway, implacable and unyielding. "You forget, madame, I am the *least* courteous man you know. And this is my bedroom, milady. I will never knock upon the door."

"You sleep across the hall, milord," she said, her heart thundering.

"I sleep across the hall. I will still enter here whenever I choose."

Daniel, interrupted from his meal, started to cry. Jamie's gaze fell upon his son, and he entered into the room, closing the door behind him. "Your son, madame," he said to her.

"If you have something to say to me, please do so, then I may return to my *talent* of motherhood. Tell me, milord, do you consider it my only talent?"

"You've many talents, Jasmine. Feed the babe. I am not leaving."

She bit her lip, quickly lowering her eyes. She flushed and burned, and heady, potent excitement filled her. She turned her back on him and brought Daniel back to her breast. He would stay. He was angry, but she had brought him back, and he would stay.

But he was silent, silent so long that she spoke herself.

"What an interesting reply you gave your friends about the acquisition of your wife."

"What would you have had me say, my love? 'I married a tavern wench. You can see by the way that she whores and flirts about you'?"

"I did nothing of the kind!" Jassy snapped.

He was nearer to her. She had not heard him, but he hovered at her back. He leaned over and touched Daniel's cheek, his long, dark finger moving over the softness of the child. Jassy froze. His finger moved onward, stroking over the fullness of her breast. She did not care if they battled. Only that he came to her, that he lay beside her. She cared not if he took her violently, only that he did so.

He drew his hand away. "Take care, madame. I have decided that you may travel back on the *Lady Destiny,* if you so seriously crave your freedom. But while you are here, take care."

"What?" Jassy gasped.

"You may leave me. I am giving you permission to do so. Daniel stays, though. He is my son and my heir, and he will stay."

Daniel, the point of discussion, was forgotten. Jassy bolted up, her breasts spilling from her gown, her eyes a tempest. "I will never leave him! He is *my* son! I carried him and I bore him, and he needs me, he needs to nurse—"

"Don't fret, love. A woman can be hired to provide, I am certain. Good night."

"No!"

"We will discuss it, madame, in the morning."

"Jamie—"

"If you are so concerned about Daniel, Jassy, see to him now. He screams again that you should be so careless of his needs. Good night."

The door closed softly in his wake. Jassy bit hard into the back of her hand to silence the scream that threatened to erupt from her.

Daniel bellowed out loudly.

She swept him into her arms in stark panic. Jamie could not make her go away; she was his wife. He could not take Daniel away from her. He could not, he could not . . .

"Shush, shush, my little love!" she whispered to the baby. "I am here, I am with you, I love you, I love you so much. I will never leave you, I will never leave . . . him."

She lay down with the babe, and in moments his howls faded to the sound of his greedy suckling. Jassy's eyes were open in shock. Tears began to trickle down her cheeks, and then, in time, she turned her head into her pillow to muffle her sobs.

Then they dried. She would not leave. She would have her husband back. She was a fighter and a survivor.

Hadn't he always told her so?

She would fight him, and she would win. So help her.

17

 THEY DIDN'T SPEAK IN THE MORNING. JAMIE HAD to leave.

Lent had brought them to Palm Sunday, and with Easter coming early that year, the settlers began to plan for the holy day, and for the feasts they would all have within their homes.

The Cameron house was no different in that aspect, except that it was even busier than the others. Jamie had matters of government to attend to, and he had to spend two days in the Jamestown settlement. A legislative body was already at work in the colony, and Jamie, though he held his land directly from the king rather than the Company, was still a part of it. The laws in the Virginia colony were very much like those in England, and they were also maintained in much the same manner. Murder was a crime punishable by death, as was the stealing of an animal such as a horse or an ass or a cow, the type of beast that could mean a man's survival. There was very little crime in the hundred, despite the fact that some settlers had come to the New World to avoid fates in Newgate.

On the nineteenth, three days before Easter, Jamie returned. Jassy was perfectly cordial to him. She was warm to Robert and to their guests.

Jamie did watch her. He watched her, and the glow in her eyes, and the striking beauty that it gave her. He watched her come alive for the other men, and despite his best intentions, his temper slowly simmered and seethed.

At dinner she laughed and flirted and played the perfect hostess. She was quick to suggest music, and she had certainly planned her entertainment, for she had musicians ready at her behest. He did not dance with her, nor did she carry the child any longer, and so he had no excuse to send her from the floor. He stared at her as she swirled in some man's arms, and he told himself bitterly that she was a hussy, had always been one, and that he had been a fool to marry her. Then he would remember that he had been the one to teach her what she knew about passion, and his throat would tighten and his stomach knot, and everything within him would burn. He had told her that he would set her free. He would do so.

Furious and anguished, he had but one avenue open to him. He left the house.

On Easter morning he rose early and looked into her room. Daniel slept sweetly in his cradle, but Jassy was nowhere to be seen. Anxious, Jamie ran out of the house and leapt upon his horse without hailing a groom. Bareback, he rode with a vengeance from the compound and out of the open gates of the palisade.

He found Jassy with Sir Cedric, far beyond the walls of the palisade. She was laughing delightedly and pretending a sweet innocence when it came to the use of firearms.

She was dressed in royal-blue velvet over a softer shade of linen. The gown was ruffed with white lace over black, and her breasts seemed to press quite dangerously against the bodice.

She was more beautiful that day than he had ever seen her, her eyes alive with laughter, the sound of that laughter like a melody of spring. Her cheeks were flushed, and she was as lithe and slender as a little wood nymph. She held the musket then, and flashed Sir Cedric her stunning smile as she looked to him for advice on the right position in which to hold the musket. A group of Indians came from the far western woods. Jamie raised a hand in acknowledgment, but other than that, he barely noticed them, for his eyes were on his wife. The Indians knew that the settlers were preparing for a Christian holy day. The Powhatans were probably bringing food and gifts, and they were certainly interested in the things that would take place. He should probably go greet them, but most of the Indians had good friends among the settlers and would be all right.

He was *not* all right himself.

Some invisible line in his temper stretched taut as wire, and then snapped.

He had done everything he could. He had made her his wife, and he had fallen in love with her. He had offered her freedom. . . .

And she seemed keen on taking him up on the offer. She was behaving as if she were free right now. No, she was behaving worse than that. She was a flirt, a tease. She was slowly and carefully cultivating and charming and possessing every man she met.

His head reeled with a jagged ache, as if it had exploded with a charge of black powder. Barely in control, he nudged his horse and came nearer the pair, watching as Sir Cedric helped Jassy align the musket upon the rest.

He paused at last behind the two of them. Jassy fired the musket and laughed with pleasure as her ball struck the target.

"Milady, you're a natural!" Sir Cedric congratulated her.

"Do you think so, really?" she asked, dimpling prettily, and flushing a lovely shade of rose. Her lips seemed like a shade of wine that day. Her hair was pulled back from her forehead with ribbon but spilled down her back and caught the glow of the coming sun. She was radiant and fascinating. Jamie's loins thundered along with his head, and he thought that it had been an endless time since he had touched her. It had been since he had realized how deeply and irrevocably he had fallen in love. Since he had worried about endangering their babe.

Daniel was over a month old now. And she was certainly behaving like a woman in the finest health.

"A perfect shot, my love. Alas, poor Cedric! She cons you, I'm afraid. Jassy *is* a natural, and has been for some time. Her accuracy is frightening. She aims her barbs, and they do strike, swift and sure."

Jassy spun around, looking at him. Cedric, at a loss, and yet aware of the terrible tension suddenly around him, laughed nervously. "Lady Cameron! You *have* had lessons before."

"Yes," she murmured sweetly. She kept a hostile and wary eye upon Jamie. "But none so gently given, Sir Cedric. You are a wonderful marksman, and a superb teacher."

"But the lesson is over," Jamie said, looking down at her from atop his mount.

"I rather thought that we had just begun," Jassy told him.

"You have thought wrong," he said softly. He dismounted from his horse and strode toward her. "I think we should go for a ride, madame."

"I do not care for a ride."

"And I do not care what *you* care for, milady. Come—now."

She stood stubbornly, hesitating for just a moment too long. Jamie stepped forward again and furiously swept her off her feet, striding back to his horse and tossing her rudely upon it. Her hair flew and tossed about her in a sudden disarray as she scrambled for her balance. Looking at her, Jamie knew what he wanted from her at that moment. He knew exactly what he wanted.

"Jamie Cameron, you—"

"Excuse us, Cedric, will you please?" Jamie said politely. He leapt up behind Jassy, nudging his heels hard into the horse's flanks. They took flight, southwestward, toward the deep forest.

Her hair slapped against his face with the force of the wind. He inhaled the clean, perfumed scent of her, the blond locks, and of her flesh. The wind seemed to rage, and the earth to churn beneath him, and all the while the violence and anger seemed to burn in his loins, to thunder in his head. Her body was rigid before his, and she gripped on to the horse's mane. His thighs locked against hers as they rode the animal bareback, coming closer and closer to the dense thicket of trees.

He at last slowed the horse, and when he entered into a trail that led to a copse of trees, he reined in. Visible through the pines and hemlocks was a brook, trickling softly and beautifully and white-tipped through the forest. Below them lay a bed of soft fallen pines, and all about them came the chirp and song and melody of birds.

Jamie did not notice much of nature. He dismounted, casting his leg over her, leaping to the ground. He turned around and stared at her while he reached for her. Her eyes were dusky, unreadable, in the green light of the forest, but he sensed that a spark of cold fury burned brightly within her.

"Come on, get down!" he snapped.

"You are the rudest individual I have ever met."

"Get down here."

"Make me."

"I damned well intend to!"

He wrenched her down from the horse and onto her feet before him. The vixen! She cast back her head and glared at him with a raw challenge. He held on to her shoulders, and he was tempted to shake her until she begged for forgiveness, until she fell to her knees before him.

She wasn't about to beg for anything, or so it seemed. Her hair was wild, and her breasts heaved excitingly with the flame of her exertion. "What do you think you're doing?" she spat out.

"Me?" He slipped a foot behind her ankle, causing her to cry out and fall to the earth, yet held in his arms, she came down gently upon the bed of pines. He came atop her, and then she swore, suddenly and furiously, struggling against him.

"You, *Lord* Cameron! You—"

"Me, milady, your husband. Alas, I am not the gentle teacher that Sir Cedric is! I haven't Robert Maxwell's flattering phrases, and God alone knows what else I lack. *Constraint.* I have offered you freedom aboard the *Lady Destiny,* but you can't even wait the time to board her to taunt other men before me."

"I have taunted no one!"

"You have swayed your hips and laughed and spoken and charmed and seduced. And, madame, you have done so well. God damn you, lady, for I meant to give you what you craved; you so despised this place that I meant to let you leave it, and—that scourge of your life—me, madame. But it seems that I have left you lacking, that I have perhaps been overly kind, for you only play the whore."

She tried to slap him. No, she tried to scratch his face. Then she tried to lift her knee and kick him, but he slammed his weight down hard upon her, and she cried out.

"Poor, innocent, demoiselle!"

"Savage jackal! Let me up. You fool. You—"

He ground his lips down upon hers. They punished and bruised. She fought him, and still the taste of her lips was wet and sweet and more potent than wine. He delved deeper and deeper into the dark recesses of her mouth. It had been too long since he had kissed her so. The memories reborn of the taste and feel and scent of her were so enticing that he shook with it. She twisted from him, trying to shove him aside. Her eyes were wild, and her hair was a halo about her, spilling over the pines. Her lips were damp and parted and bewitching. Her face was beautiful, beguiling, and filled with pride and hatred and the spirit of her fight.

"You fool! You will not do this on the ground in the dirt—"

"Nay, lady, you will not deny me, not today. Not this morning. Tomorrow you may do as you please. For today, madame, you have swished your tail one too many times in my direction, and I will have what I want. Nay, lady, what I *demand*!"

He forced his lips upon her again and caught her hands against the pines, palm to palm. He laced his fingers with her struggling ones and felt the pressure she wielded against him. He ignored it. He kissed her, drinking her in, tasting and seeking, and . . . gentle now. There was no more brutality to his kiss. She was open to him.

Her fingers curled against his.

He lifted some of his weight and removed his hand from hers. He pulled at the ribbons of her bodice, and then at her chemise, watching her eyes. She did not fight him but stared directly at him. He had no patience. The thunder rose painfully in his groin, driven by the weeks of waiting, and the nights of longing, and the anguished moments when he thought about her in the arms of another man.

He cast back his head and let out a loud groan. He buried his face against the spill of her breasts and thought of his son. He pressed his mouth to her flesh and felt her shudder. He would have pulled away, but she let out a soft, choking sigh, and when he released her hands, she held him there, against her. He tasted her as Daniel would taste her, and he filled himself with the feel and texture of her breasts, the thunder pounding ever more fiercely. He caught her skirts, pushed them up against her, and released the ties on his breeches. She still looked at him, her sapphire eyes glimmering in the green darkness. He touched her thighs and eased the stroke of his fingers against them. And still she looked at him with her luminous eyes and her beautiful face, defying him.

He nearly rammed into her but in time remembered that their child had not been born so long ago. He moved gently . . . but she spoke no protest, and he cast back his head, encased and shuddering, and groaned out the anguish in his heart and in his loins. She seemed to burst forth with a mercury, arching against him. He forgot everything else but the force of his desire, and he felt the thunder burst free from him, tear across the heavens and the earth, the blue sky and the verdant pines, and into her.

He cried out, and the sound of her voice rose with his own. The end came to him explosively, fiercely. He arched hard and held, and then fell upon the earth beside her, drained of his lust and his temper all in one, and suddenly, uncomfortably ashamed. He had raped his wife in the forest, upon the pines.

She was silent beside him, breathing hard, staring now at the sky. She made no attempt to adjust her clothing but lay so still that it frightened him.

"Jassy!"

She turned to look at him. There was a soft glaze of tears in her eyes. He swore, furious with himself. Pulling down her skirts, he rose, desperate to be away from her.

"Damn you!" he whispered, his voice shaking. He turned away from the striking and terrible innocence in her crystal-blue eyes, adjusting his breeches. He wanted to explain that she had pushed him to the limit, that no man could watch his wife with other men so long without going over some brink and landing his soul in a pool of dragons. He wanted to say so many things to her. He wanted to say that she had bested him in every way, that he loved her beyond measure. It would sound so very hollow now. . . .

He leapt to his feet. He did not help her up; he did not think that she was ready to rise.

"I'll leave you the horse," he said huskily. "When the *Lady Destiny* sails, I will give you my leave to take Daniel with you to England too."

"Jamie—" she began.

"I will not force you to stay, madame." He hesitated briefly. "Good day, milady. I am heartily sorry for my bad manners."

He left her, disappearing into the woods.

Jassy lay there, feeling the prick of the pines beneath her, for a long time. She listened to the ripple of the brook and felt the sun touch her cheeks through the trees. She brought her fingers to her face and discovered that her face was damp with her silent tears. How could she have failed so miserably?

She realized numbly that he had given her Daniel. He didn't even care if he kept their child anymore, he just wanted her to leave.

She closed her eyes, cast her elbow over them, and swallowed hard. He couldn't have ceased to want her so completely; he could not hate her so vehemently. She had wanted him so badly; she loved him. Loving was worse than the pain of hunger; it was worse than the fear of poverty. It was more painful than anything she had ever known.

She would *not* go. She had to talk to him. She had to make him stand still and listen to her. If she told him that she loved Virginia, that she loved the forest, primeval and so rich and dark, and the river and the Chesapeake Bay and the oysters that they pulled out of it. She loved the palisade, and the way of life, and she never had wanted to return to England. Even if he did not love her, he had to let her stay. She wouldn't go. She simply wouldn't do so.

Slowly, painfully, she came to her feet. She adjusted her clothing and tried to smooth down her hair and rid it of the forest floor. He had left her the horse, and he had gone off on foot—where, she did not know.

Wearily she looped her skirts together, took a handful of the horse's mane, and leapt onto the animal. At a very slow pace she started back toward the palisade. She was young and she was strong, and whatever came, she vowed silently to herself, she would survive. But she could not give up on her husband so easily. She could not.

When she broke slowly from the verdant foliage of the forest, she saw the palisade rising before her in the sunlight. No, it was not London, it was not Oxford, it was not even the Crossroads Inn. No grand Gothic or Renaissance buildings rose in mighty splendor against the coming of the morning. Yet what stood there was finer in its way, for what it was, was what men had built from a raw wilderness, and it was composed of blood and sweat and dreams of the future. The palisade was strong, and beyond it lay the church and her house and the potter's kilns and the blacksmith's shop and the homes of them all.

The gates of the palisade were open, welcoming visitors on the holy day. By the outer wall, one of the young farmers was cutting wood. A Pamunkee Indian was at his side, stacking the logs as the farmer cut them.

Then, suddenly, the Pamunkee snatched the ax from the young farmer and sank the sharp-bladed instrument right into the man's skull.

Jassy opened her mouth in horror, but her astonishment caused her to choke on her cry. Shocked, she reined in on the horse, disbelieving what she had seen with her own eyes.

The farmer clutched his head, fell to his knees, then fell flat, the ax still imbedded in his head. The Pamunkee calmly stepped over him to retrieve the ax, and looked toward the open palisade.

Jassy's limbs seemed to freeze, inch by inch. The cold and numbness overcame her, then struck pure icy terror into the very center of her heart.

"No!" At last her scream tore from her, and Jassy kicked the horse hard into a gallop, her mind racing. It was not just the horror of the murder she had witnessed. It had been the way in which it had taken place. The Pamunkee had stood with the farmer as his friend. They had been laughing, and then the Indian had grabbed the weapon and slain the man . . . then retrieved the weapon and looked toward the palisade.

How many of the Pamunkees were already inside the gates? They had been coming all morning—in friendship. Was it an isolated incident? Had the Indian gone mad?

Earth churned and flew as Jassy sped toward the gates. The Indian who had accomplished the murder was just nearing the palisade. He swung around, the ax in his hand dripping blood, and stared at her.

"Help! Sound the alarm!" she screamed. The blade looked lethal. She tried not to stare down at the dead body of the farmer. She urged the skittish horse around the body and kept her eyes upon the Indian. "Sound the alarm!" she screamed, hoping someone would hear her.

From somewhere deep within the compound came the sound of a scream. She and the Indian stared at each other warily. Jassy jammed her heels into the horse's flanks, and the animal reared, then bolted past the Pamunkee. She heard the sound of another scream, then she saw one of the soldiers come out of the guardhouse. He was wearing his helmet and his half-armor. He wore a look of wide-eyed shock as he stumbled out before Jassy, clutching his stomach. She realized that he held the shaft of a knife there. He had been skewered with his own weapon.

Jassy screamed herself. Another of the guards came out of the little house. "The alarm!" she shouted.

It was too late, for the two Indians had set upon the guard already. He battled them with a vengeance.

Still atop the nervous and rearing horse, Jassy looked toward the inner working steps of the palisade, those leading to the bell alarm and the cannon facing westward.

The cannon would do them little good. The enemy had come at them from within.

She had to reach the steps, and she had to sound the alarm.

Then she had to get home; she had to get back to her house. Daniel lay sleeping there. Elizabeth was there, and Amy Lawton and the girls. She had to get home, and she had to find a way to warn Lenore and Robert.

A man wearing a hastily donned shirt of chain mail came bursting wildly out of the guardhouse. Jassy saw that it was Robert Maxwell.

"Robert!"

He didn't hear her at first. He was looking sickly at the dead man with the knife protruding from his gut, below his half-armor. He stared at him, the knife he carried himself held in a white-knuckled grip, his features as pale as new snow.

"Robert!" she called again. He still didn't hear her. He was in shock, she realized. "Robert!" Jassy urged the horse over to him. Still, he did not look up. She leapt down and shook him. "Robert! We have to sound the alarm. People have to know; they have to prepare. They have to fight back. We have to reach our houses. . . . Robert, the *alarm*!"

She slapped him, hard. He looked at her at last. "Oh, Jassy!" He was falling apart, she realized. He would be no help to her. She gave him a fierce shove. "Go, hurry! Warn them at my house, and hurry on to your own. I'm going to sound the alarm."

At last he moved. He looked back and saw the single guard still trying to fight off the two Indians. Jassy wondered if she should help him first, then she realized with a curious numbness that she might be killed, and if she were killed, she could never sound the alarm. She pushed away from the horse and went racing to the steps. She tore up them to the roof tower.

Just beyond the top step, at the tower door, stood one of the Indians. His chest was naked, and his well-muscled arms were laden with various tattoos. He wore only a breechclout, white goose feathers in his hair, and a necklace with a rawhide cord. He looked at Jassy and smiled slowly, awaiting her. She looked beyond him. Another of their armed men lay dead. He had been bashed on the head with a cannonball.

The murders were certainly not isolated incidents, Jassy thought furiously. The Indians had come to kill the white men. They were killing the settlers with their own weapons. They were killing them with anything at all that they could find at hand.

And the man at the tower meant to kill her.

Screams were rising now, near the gate. Soon everyone would know. Soon they would all realize the treachery . . . soon, as they lay dying.

"No!" Jassy screamed in a frenzy. She hurtled herself at the Indian with all her strength, and they toppled to the ground together.

Her attack upon the man had been a mistake. The warm, brown body that fell over hers was hard and powerful and relentless. She bit and she kicked and she struggled fiercely, but to little avail. The Indian was young and wire-sinewed, proud of his health and strength and entirely in his prime. She was strong, too, she knew. She clawed and scratched and caused him some injury, but she really had no chance, not from the very beginning.

He pressed his knee into her midriff, and all the air went out of her. Almond-dark eyes met hers with a glitter of amusement, and she knew that her fight was such a feeble one that he was enjoying the whole of it. He reached to his ankle, producing a knife from a rawhide sheath. He took hold of a strand of Jassy's hair and stared upon it for a moment, bemused. Jassy realized that she was about to be scalped.

She screamed, twisting and fighting in renewed fury.

Suddenly there was the soft and curious sound of a sickening thud. Blood spilled over Jassy's beautiful spring dress.

The amusement left the brave's eyes. He stared at her blankly, and she saw that a knife shaft protruded from the center of his bare chest. He grasped for it, his fingers convulsed, and then he went dead still and toppled over on her. She screamed, shoving him aside, and then she looked down the length of the ladder.

Jamie was there. His booted foot rested upon one of the steps, from where he had so swiftly and accurately sent the knife flying to kill the Indian. His eyes met hers, and despite the bloodshed, she trembled. He was solid like rock, as agile and stealthy as the Indians who knew their land so well. He was there for her, tall upon the steps, dark and fierce. He would never panic; he would always meet what came his way with dignity and undauntable courage. She had come to recognize and love the man that he was . . . perhaps *really* too late.

He moved and came racing up the steps toward her. He wrenched her to her feet. "What are you doing? What the *hell* are you doing! You should be back at the house, safe with Daniel!" His voice thundered; he was shaking with anger. He bent and retrieved his knife from the dead brave. He wiped the blade on his trousers and shoved the knife back into the sheath at his calf.

She was stunned, Jassy realized. As slow and as worthless as Robert. "The alarm! Someone has—"

He stepped by her and pulled hard on the bell cord. The sound began to peal, loud and strong. "Come on!" Jamie urged.

He dragged her down the steps into the compound. Three of the Indians were at the foot of the ladder. Like the Indian at the tower, these men were barely clad. They did not notice the cool breezes of the spring morning. One of them wore paint over his cheeks. They all stared at Jamie, tensing and bracing themselves for the fight.

It would be with knives. Twisting their blades in their hands, they stared at Jamie.

Jamie, warily keeping his eyes upon the Indians, shoved Jassy behind him.

"Get away! Hide! Find somewhere safe and stay there!"

"No—"

"Jamie!" came a booming male voice behind them. Sir William! It was Sir William Tybalt, alerted by the alarm! Jamie would no longer face their enemies alone.

"William!" Jamie said. He shoved Jassy quickly toward his friend. "Get her out of here."

"No! He must fight with you—" Jassy protested.

"William, take her. You are sworn to obey me, and I order you to take her out of here." He stared hard at Jassy. "When it starts, run from behind me. Get to the house. Get Daniel and Elizabeth and the others and make your way to the church. It's the only building of brick, and it is fortified. There are muskets in the back pews, and swords in the deacon's benches."

"I can't leave you."

"Come, my lady—" Sir William began. He had a firm grip upon her. He was Jamie's man, and would defend and obey him until the very end, that much she knew.

"I can't leave you!" she screamed again to Jamie.

"You have to leave me!"

"Jamie!"

She tried to hold on to his arm as they faced the Indians. Sir William pulled her away. Wetness streamed down her cheeks. She wanted to talk to Jamie. They were facing death, and there was no time to say anything, and she was choking on the tears that tasted of blood and metal in her mouth.

"Jamie—"

"Go!" he screamed to her. "For God's sake, Jassy! Do you think that I can concentrate on a fight with you behind me? Get out of here, get Daniel, *now*! William, for the love of Christ. . . !"

Sir William tugged hard upon her hand. Staring at Jamie, Jassy swallowed down hard on a sob, and blindly led by Sir William, she turned and ran at last. They stumbled along a fair distance, then, blinking furiously, Jassy pulled back and stopped.

"My lady!" Sir William urged her.

"Please, wait!"

"He knows what he is doing, Lady Cameron!"

Still, she had to see. The first Indian had already rushed Jamie. Jamie moved as quick as light, his knife blade reflecting the sun. The Indian came up taut against Jamie. He had been met with the knife in his loin. The two of them were face-to-face. The Indian breathed his last and fell. Now there were only two of the warring Pamunkees left. It was a far more even fight.

Jassy heard a scream behind her. She whirled around. Mary Montgomery, the blacksmith's stout wife, was laying a fire poker upon an Indian who had attempted to attack her with her own bread board.

Sir William rushed to help her, but Mary, on her own, did all right. She laid the poker flat upon the brave's head, and he fell without a sound. She looked at Jassy with satisfaction. "Another heathen gone to hell." She stared at the blood covering Jassy. "Lady Cameron, are you all right? Come in, Geoffrey and me will see to your protection. Sir William, you may well leave her with us."

"Thank you, good woman," Sir William said, but he didn't need to go any farther, for Jassy was shaking her head.

"I cannot stay. Daniel . . . my son. I have to get my child." She was already moving. Men were rushing by her. They were grim-faced and determined, trying to reach the gates where Jamie had fought alone. There were bodies strewn all about. Some of them belonged to the white men. And women. And many of them belonged to the Pamunkees. She stepped gingerly over the open-eyed corpse of an older brave. "I have to find my son!"

"He'll be all right, milady. Bless us! Those treacherous devils! We'd all be dead if the alarm hadn't sounded!"

Jassy nodded, and kept stumbling along the muddy streets to her house. The sounds of the fighting continued. Sir William followed behind her.

Then suddenly an Indian jumped down from a thatched roof before them. Jassy screamed, and Sir William pushed her forward. "Go, milady, you are almost home. Run!"

The Indian fell upon him. Sir William drew his sword, and battle was engaged. "Run!" he shouted again to Jassy.

Daniel. Her innocent, vulnerable child lay at her house. Elizabeth and Amy and the other women waited there. Sir William would fare well enough without her. She nodded jerkily, and then she turned and ran once again. She could smell smoke. Some of the houses were on fire.

Bodies continued to line the way. Blindly choking, sobbing, she stepped over and around them.

She reached her own door at last and shoved it open. "Amy! Elizabeth!" No one answered her. She came tearing up the stairs and burst into her own room, where she had left Daniel in his cradle.

She stopped short in the doorway, her hand flying to her open mouth.

Daniel was still there, fast asleep. Elizabeth, ashen and terrified, was backed into a corner, held there at knifepoint by a young Indian. Another of the Pamunkees stood over the cradle, shaking his head. He looked at Jassy, then he fingered the little amulet that Opechancanough had sent the baby as a gift. It looked as if he meant to touch the baby next.

"No!" Jassy screamed. She tore into the room and swept the baby up from beneath his eyes. She held him tightly against her. "No, no, no!" She narrowed her eyes and said the Indian chief's name. "Opechancanough! Opechanca-nough!"

The two Indians looked at one another, and then at her. Jassy flipped out her own amulet, the gift once given to Jamie by Pocahontas. Both Indians paused, then the first Indian indicated that she must put the baby back in his cradle. Daniel, awakened and sniffing his mother's scent, began to cry.

"No!" she screamed. She cradled her son closer to her. The Indian came to her. She stared into his eyes, but like Elizabeth, she found herself backed to the wall. "No! Opechancanough."

He came to her at last. He pressed the blade of his knife threateningly against Jassy's throat. She lifted her chin, tears stinging her eyes. Where was Jamie now? Was he alive or dead? Had Robert ever come to warn them here? Sir William! Surely he would come to her rescue at any moment.

There was a sudden sound of movement in the doorway, and Jassy quickly looked there with fervent prayers of rescue.

It was no rescue. It was Hope who stood there. Jassy wondered bitterly if she had known about the attack all along. Had she slain the whites who had taken her in?

Hope stepped warily into the room. She was dressed in European fashion, with a mass of petticoats holding out her skirts. She looked at Jassy with her curious green eyes, then spoke to the Indians in their own tongue. She was very quiet and very calm. The brave moved his knife away from Jassy's throat and spoke to Hope insistently.

"He says," Hope told her, "that the baby has Opechancanough's protection. He may stay. You are to come with him."

"What?" Jassy repeated. "But I am protected. . . ."

Hope looked at her with wide, greedy eyes. "But you are a woman. You are to come with them. You, and her"—she pointed to Elizabeth—"are his hostages, and you will get him out of the fort. You should leave your son." She hesitated. "They sacrifice their own sometimes. It would be wise to leave him. You must come."

Jassy shook her head. She glanced quickly at Elizabeth in the corner. Her sister seemed to be in shock, her blue eyes wide, open, and staring.

"I will not come," she said firmly.

Hope spoke to the Indian, and the Indian shook his head firmly, flashing a white, malicious smile. He spoke to her, and Hope looked to Jassy again. "If you do not come, he will slice out her heart and make you watch, and then he will kill you. He will do so immediately. It is your decision."

Elizabeth gasped and sank against the wall.

Jassy trembled, feeling the blood seep from her face. It took her several attempts to form words with her dry lips and speak. "Tell him that I will come."

"Both of you," Hope murmured. She offered Jassy a peculiar smile, and Jassy realized that it was one of concern. "I will come with you too. Do not be afraid. I will not let them kill you."

Jassy wasn't sure that anyone could stop this Indian from killing anyone. Still, ironically, she was very grateful to Hope. "Thank you," she whispered. She kept her eyes upon the lethal brave. "Hope, please take Daniel and put him in his cradle."

Hope shook her head. "I will carry him out. They might fire the house."

Hope took the baby from Jassy. He was screaming in raw fury then, his face mottled and red, his little fists waving. Her breasts burst forth in an aching reply, but she dared not touch him again. Tears threatened to spill from her in hysterical measure, but she braced her jaw and held stubbornly to a show of bravado. She edged against the wall, watching the brave, and sinking down by Elizabeth. "Come on, Elizabeth. We must go. We will be all right."

Elizabeth stared at her hopefully, her cheeks wet and stained with tears. "Jamie will come for us," she said.

"Jamie will come for us," Jassy agreed. He would come, if he did not already lay dead in the spring mud of the complex. "Come, Elizabeth. We will move slowly. Hope is coming too."

Hope lowered her head over Daniel's forehead. She turned around and started down the stairway.

The house seemed painfully silent as Jassy followed Hope, feeling the point of the Indian's blade at the small of her back. She held Elizabeth's arm, trying to give her sister strength. Elizabeth trembled, and silent tears fell down her cheeks, but she kept moving.

At the bottom of the stairway Jassy nearly lost control. A sharp cry escaped her as she saw that Amy Lawton lay upon the floor, the victim of an attack made with the dish of an English garden spade. Jassy fell to her knees beside the woman, rolling her over and seeking life.

Amy's eyes were open and seemed to mirror the final terror she had witnessed. There was no life left within her.

The brave behind Jassy growled out some warning and wrenched her back to her feet. They all heard a snuffling sound coming from the servants' wing. The second Indian started off that way, but Hope caught his arm, and pleaded with him violently, showing him the baby. At length the Indian nodded. Hope gazed at Jassy encouragingly, and hurried down the hallway. She appeared again a moment later, pulling along Charity Hume, who now held the screaming Daniel. "Tell her, Lady Cameron, that she will be all right. She must take the baby and go. They will burn the house."

Charity looked numb, and deeply in shock. She saw the Indians and started to shrink away. She was going to drop Daniel, Jassy thought.

"Charity!" she lashed out, and she knew that she had never spoken before with so much authority as Lady Cameron. "Charity! They are not going to hurt you. But if you harm Daniel in any way, so help me, I will! Take him quickly. Go to the church."

Charity stared at her for a moment, hardly believing her good luck that she might escape. She clutched the baby more tightly to her. "I will keep him, lady. I will keep him well. I will keep him—"

The first Indian was already setting fire to the tapestries and draperies about the hallway. The material caught the blaze quickly and hungrily.

"Charity, go!"

The young woman sped from the house. Tears burst from Jassy's eyes as they filled with smoke, and as her heart was torn raggedly apart by the pathetic wails of her son, slowly fading in the distance.

She had no more chance for tears or worry or emotion. The first Indian caught her by the hair and dragged her hurriedly from the house. He was taking no more time.

The streets outside were empty, except for a few strewn bodies. The Indian did not head for the gateway to the palisade but pulled her along toward the rear of the structure. She could hear Elizabeth choking and panting and sobbing behind her, and she knew that her sister was being dragged at the same frantic pace. Her scalp pained her mercilessly, the brave's hold upon it so strong. But at least, she reminded herself, it was still attached to her body.

They came to the rear wall. Jassy tried to stagger back. There were other Indians waiting there, about eight of them. When they saw Jassy and Elizabeth and their captors arriving, they began a rush up one of the rear stairways to the parapets and towers.

The Indian said something to her, jerking hard upon her hair. She was dragged up the stairs. Upon the parapet, she looked over the log wall. A hay cart lay beneath them. The Indian pushed her forward.

"No!" she cried in panic.

He lifted her up and tossed her over. Jassy screamed as she fell. She landed upon the hay, the breath knocked from her. She heard an echo of her scream.

Elizabeth landed beside her. Jassy tried to sit. She tried to help her sister. Some of the Indians were scaling the wall with ropes; three of them landed in the hay wagon too. Jassy desperately sought balance, but the vehicle suddenly jolted and started moving.

The wagon made it to the entrance of the forest, where the trails suddenly narrowed. The Indians had been prepared, Jassy realized. A group of horses waited in the clearing. She was lifted, struggling and fighting, from the wagon. She was thrown atop a horse, and a brave leapt up behind her. She tried to bite his hand. He slapped her across the cheek, a stinging blow.

Dimly she realized that she could no longer hear Elizabeth.

She did hear a soft whisper. It was Hope. "Don't fight him. This is Poca-nough, and he will hurt you."

"Elizabeth," she murmured, dazed.

"Your sister has fainted. It is best for her."

Jassy swallowed and went silent. The Indian nudged the horse, and the animal leapt high and began a frantic race into the forest.

Jassy leaned back and felt the wind and the slick nakedness of the brave's chest, and she wished with all her heart that she, too, could pass out.

Jamie would come for her. Jamie would come . . .

If he did not lay dead in a pool of his own blood.

No, she could not believe it. He could not be dead. He could not. She would not be able to bear it if he was.

Tears spilled again from her eyes to her cheeks, but they went unnoticed, for the wind dried them even as they fell. She never would be able to lay down her pride and tell him that she loved him. She had been given everything in the world, and she had cast her heart to Robert Maxwell instead. And now she had lost even the opportunity to reach with all her heart for the things that once had been given to her so very freely. . . .

She closed her eyes against the wind, and in misery she endured the long and wretched ride.

It was all over but the burying, Jamie thought at last.

His white shirt was soaked in blood; his knife was caked with it. Indians lay about his feet in huge heaps, and his own men lay there too. How many had died? he wondered. Ten, twenty, maybe more?

He looked up at the spring sky, and he swore with a sudden vehemence. He had known! He had known not to trust Opechancanough! The wily chief had sent men slowly to befriend them, and then to murder and decimate those friends.

"My God! You have slain them all!"

It was Sir Cedric talking to him. Allen came rushing up at his side, cleaning the blade of his sword. He was glad that the knights had been with him during the bloodbath. They were brave fighters, and trained to the challenge. The Indians had attacked so stealthily that many would not have stood a chance against them.

Jamie looked down at the ground again. How many men had he killed himself? Ten, twenty? He did not know. Somewhere in the fierce struggle he had lost all sense of humanity. He had fought blindly, and with a blood lust of his own. They had attacked his home. They had attacked his palisade, and God help them, they had attacked his wife.

Suddenly he smelled smoke. He pulled Cedric close to him. "There are more of them. More of them, in the complex!"

"Come on!" Allen cried.

Men—the last of the trained and armed soldiers, the artisans and laborers forced into being warriors—followed behind as they all raced through the streets. The place was alive once again with survivors crawling about the streets, wailing over their dead, seeking out the wounded. The blacksmith's wife assured them that the Indians were gone from the compound. "There were but few who made it this deep, Lord Cameron."

That encouraged Jamie. He wanted to see Jassy. He wanted to take her into his arms and shudder and tell her that it was terrible, that he had seen so much death, that he had killed so much himself. He wanted to assure her first. He wanted to swear that he would take her home. He wanted to beg her forgiveness and ask humbly if they might have a chance to start all over again. He would bring her back to the manor in England, and even when he felt the urge to come back to this land, he would never expect it of her. Mostly he just wanted to hold her, and he wanted to hold his son.

"Lord Cameron!" a man cried. " 'Tis Sir William!"

"What?" Jamie cried. He hurried forward toward the man and knelt down upon one knee. His heart congealed. It *was* Sir William, slain. He had died fighting, for even as the blood had seeped from his great heart, he had brought down his opponent with him. A brave, with Sir William's blade through his gut, lay atop him.

Jamie quickly crossed himself. Prayer eluded him, but he knew that God would welcome such a brave spirit as Sir William. He clenched his teeth together tightly in pain for his good friend, then he came quickly to his feet, a new anguish searing through him.

"My wife. My God, he was escorting my wife!"

He tore down the street, and then he realized from where the smell of fire came. His whole street had been set to the torch.

His stomach lurched, and he stared at the flaming buldings. Behind him, someone called out orders to squelch the fire.

Jamie started to run again. He raced through the heat and the smoke for the church. As he reached it the doors opened, and Father Steven led his flock out to greet him.

"Lord Cameron, have we come through our test in the wilderness?"

"It is over," Jamie said curtly, staring into the crowd, into the smudged faces that met his. He saw Lenore and Robert. They were huddled together. There were many people there, many, many people. Jassy had saved them, he thought. She had remembered the alarm, and the people had surged into the church. The death toll would stand at twenty or thirty, he was certain, but most of the people had survived the attack, thanks to his wife's quick thinking—and courage.

"Where is she?" he said aloud. He gripped Father Steven's arms, and the man paled and did not answer him. He stepped forward into the church, reaching Lenore and Robert. "Where is she?" he repeated.

Then he heard the cry. Daniel's cry. He turned around, hope filling his breast, and he was instantly grateful to see his son.

But it was not Jassy holding the boy. It was the servant girl, Charity.

"Where is Jassy?" he demanded in a rage.

Charity shuddered. Jamie pulled the child from the girl's arms, holding him close. Daniel continued to cry, the sound echoing the howl in Jamie's heart. "Where in God's name is my wife!" he demanded.

It was Charity who answered him at last. She stumbled forward and sobbed out her story. They had come to the house, the Indians had, two men. They had come with gifts of pumpkin bread, and they had found Amy in the garden. Amy had brought them in, and one had taken the spade and killed her with it, and the other had taken the fire poker and slain Charity's sister, and then they had gone up the stairs. Charity had hidden, and she had stayed beneath her bed until the girl, Hope, had come and pulled her out. And then she had seen Lady Cameron, all covered in blood, her hair tumbling around her in awful disarray, but still very calm, her chin high and her shoulders straight.

"She had me take the babe, and she ordered me to bring him out, and she warned me that she'd have my hide were he hurt. Oh, milord! I ran, I was so scared. She made me. She said that they were going to burn the house. She knew it. She was holding up her sister, for Lady Elizabeth, she was so scared."

Lenore started crying softly. She fell into one of the pews. "They will slay them, they will kill them both! Oh, my God, Jamie, I have heard what they do with their captives—oh, dear God!"

Jamie stood very still, holding his screaming son. He cast back his head and let out a single cry of anguish, a sound more savage than any heard from the primitive tribes.

Then he clenched his teeth and drew his son to him tightly. He held him that way for a long moment, then he gave the child into Lenore's arms. "Care for him with Charity."

"As I would my own," Lenore mumbled, cradling the baby. Daniel continued to cry. Jamie turned away, ripping open the pews and carefully arming himself.

Robert stepped forward. "Jamie, what are you doing?"

Jamie looked at him. "I am going after my wife."

"Wait. Wait until help has come from Jamestown, or from the Bermuda Hundred, or—"

"We do not know that there is any help to come," Jamie said.

Robert swallowed in fear. "I will come with you," he managed to gasp out at last. Jamie looked at his friend and slowly shook his head. "No, stay here. And you, too, Cedric, Allen. We haven't the power to fight the entire Powhatan Confederacy. If I am to get Jassy and Elizabeth back, it will be by stealth or negotiation. I am best off alone, and you are best off repairing our lives here, and mourning what we have lost."

He gathered what weapons he wanted, then turned away. People followed him from the church as he left it.

Thankfully the stables had not been burned. The house, and all the fine riches that Jassy had so cherished, were nothing but ashes. He stepped past the burning refuse and entered the stable and chose his own horse, Windwalker. He leapt upon the nervous stallion and started out of the complex.

"Jamie!"

As he urged his mount forward Sir Allen caught up with him, offering him a clean shirt and an unstained leather jerkin. He paused, taking them, and changed. When he was done, he smiled to his friend. "Thank you."

The people followed in turn. They offered him a water flask, and dried beef, and whatever else they could find that he might need. Sir Allen brought him a strong bow and a quiver of arrows.

At the gate to the palisade he turned and looked upon the smudged, bloodied, and anxious faces. They were all his friends, he thought. His people, his friends, and even before assessing their own losses, they were eager to minimize his. He looked over the tired and weary faces, and in them he saw strength. They would build again, they would build anew. They would bury their dead, but they would stay, and they would make the land theirs, make it good.

He lifted a hand to them all in acknowledgment, then turned Windwalker around and nudged the stallion into a gallop, westward, toward the forest, toward the Indian nations of the Powhatan Confederacy.

18

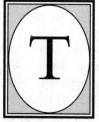

T HEY TRAVELED ALL THROUGH THE DAY AND into the darkness, and when the rugged journey ended at last, Jassy was close to unconsciousness. She could not stand when the brave dismounted from his horse, and despite herself, she fell into his arms. She was lifted and carried along, until they came to the largest of their curious, long, arched-roof houses. There were many, many Indians there. They followed along behind her, laughing and making derisive noises. Thankfully she was oblivious of them. They spat toward the ground, but they did not touch her. The brave pushed them away, and she was brought into the house, and Elizabeth was carried in behind her. There was a sudden and curious silence. Someone spoke, and she was laid down. She heard a rustle of movement, and then an Indian was staring down at her. She tried very hard to focus upon him. He was nearly naked, dressed like the others in a breechclout, and wearing a strand of beads and shells about his neck. Dark hair fell to his shoulders and was parted neatly in the center of his head. His eyes were incredibly dark, and the very strength of his features was arresting. Startled, Jassy dampened her lips and tried to speak. "Powan!" she whispered.

"Cameron's woman," he said in acknowledgment. His face wavered before her, then disappeared. He came back to her, shoving a water bowl into her hands. Gratefully she tried to drink, having little strength left. He lifted her head for her. The water was good. He let her sink back to the floor.

He rose then, walked to the entrance to his house, and spoke sternly to his people. Jassy was then dimly aware that he was arguing fiercely with the brave who had brought her in, the Indian Pocanough.

While the argument went on, Jassy heard a rustling, and then someone came close to her. She opened her eyes again. It was Hope.

"Pocanough says that you are *his* hostage. He took you. It is for him to decide if you should be tortured and killed, and if not, you should be his captive, his slave."

Jassy shivered uncontrollably. She was miserable and exhausted, and her breasts pained her mercilessly, swollen terribly because she had not nursed Daniel since early morning. Her head hurt and her thighs hurt, and her body seemed alive with agony, and still she didn't want to die.

And certainly not the way that the Pamunkees brought about death. Bashing their victim's skulls in upon their sacrificial rocks or altars. Or dismembering them and roasting their limbs one by one, disemboweling them while they lived . . .

"Oh, God!" she whispered. She tried to sit up. Hope helped her. Elizabeth was on a pallet, not far away. She inched over toward her sister. Elizabeth was still pale, her eyes closed. Jassy felt for her wrist and found that her heart was still beating. It was better this way. Elizabeth was being spared the awful agony of not knowing their plight.

"Powan comes back!" Hope whispered. "They will do nothing to you tonight. They will let you sleep."

Jassy came back to where they had lain her. She stretched out and closed her eyes. She sensed the presence of the Pamunkee chief as he came over to her, staring down at her. He said something to Hope, and Hope answered him softly in return. He made a sniffling sound and turned away from her. He sat before the open fire with the smoke hole above it in the center of his house. He snapped out some order—a command for Hope to come forward, for that was what she did. Something was cooking, and Jassy thought that he ordered Hope to prepare him a dish of food, for she did that too.

For the longest time Jassy lay awake, listening. She thought about escaping, but she knew that she hadn't the strength, and that she could bring Powan's wrath down upon her when he seemed to be her only chance of survival.

Finally Powan stretched out.

Soon she heard even breathing. He slept.

Looking back over the day, Jassy longed to rise, find his knife, and slit his throat. She trembled with the thought, aching to do so. But someone would come and slay her in turn. And they would slay Elizabeth, too, and maybe even Hope for good measure.

She didn't want to die. She wanted to live to return to her son, and to Jamie. If he lived.

If he lived.

She rolled over in a horrible agony. She had never wanted him so badly in her life. She wanted to pray, but she wasn't even able to do so.

Finally, restlessly, tears damp upon her cheeks, she slept.

———

The morning began with pure terror.

She awakened to the sound of raucous screaming. Opening her eyes, she saw a dozen Indian women staring down at her. They laughed at her, pulled at her hair, and spit at her dress. They were doing the same to Elizabeth. She heard her sister cry out in distress.

Her temper flared and exploded. Jassy leapt to her feet, snarling, and hurtled herself at the young woman who attempted to remove her hair from her head. She managed to bring the Indian maid down to the ground before Powan returned to the tent, and the women all fell silent. Powan came to her, dragging her off the maiden.

"Cameron's woman, you will behave," he told her.

"Tell *her* to behave!" Jassy snapped. Then she remembered that her life hung in the balance, and she locked her jaw. She still met his eyes. He smiled and shoved her back at the women.

"They will not hurt you. You wear the blood of our warriors, and that offends them. You will be bathed and cleansed, and that is all."

"That is all?" she whispered hopefully.

"For now," he said forebodingly. But she was to get no more from him. He left his house, and the women latched on to her arms. Elizabeth, too, was escorted from the house on the arms of the women.

They were taken past a village center. There was an interesting circle of poles and ashes there, and a large rock. The rock was red, bloodstained. Jassy paled, knowing what the rock was—the "altar" where men's heads were caved in. The sickening smell of fire and ash was still on the air.

She almost fell, buckling over with such strength that the women had to jerk her back to her feet. They had not been the only prisoners of the Pamunkee the previous night. Some captives had already met their fates upon the rock, and in the tortuous flames.

"Oh, God!" Elizabeth gasped.

"Come on, quickly, move, don't look!" Jassy urged her. She screwed up her own eyes until they entered into a trail of trees, and from there they came to a brook. Jassy shook herself free from the woman who held her, anxious to reach Elizabeth. She was too late. Elizabeth was violently sick, right into the bushes. Jassy held her up, smoothing back her hair, waiting for the spasm to die.

"It's all right, it's all right—" Jassy said.

"No, no, it's not. It is what they're going to do to us! I read John Smith's reports of the murder of John Calvin. They were in your house. I read them . . . I read about the Indians. They are going to torture and kill us just the same—"

"No, no, they're not. Powan won't let them."

"Powan will light the fires," Elizabeth said.

"Jamie will come," Jassy said.

She was wrenched away from Elizabeth. The women set upon them both, tearing and ripping at their clothing until they were both left shivering and naked and panting from the fight they had waged. They were shoved into the water then. The cold was shocking. Jassy rose, gasping for air. They were quickly joined by the women, who did not seem to feel the cold of the brook. Then they were set upon again, and scrubbed thoroughly with handfuls of sand and stones. Jassy hated every touch. Her breasts were in agony that morning, overflowing. No matter how she screamed and fought, they, too, were viciously scrubbed.

Finally, exhausted and panting, she and Elizabeth were left upon rocks to dry beneath the sun. Then they were given short, leather, apronlike dresses to wear, like the other women. They were not given shoes. Jassy thought that they were kept barefoot to hinder escape attempts, since most of the women did wear soft leather moccasins.

They were brought back to Powan's house then, and given bowls of meat in gravy. Jassy looked at the food suspiciously, but she was ravenous, and when she tasted the stew, it was delicious. Hope came back to them soon and told them that the meal had been rabbit, and that they needn't fear eating—the Pamunkees did not poison their captives; when they meant to kill them, they did so with a feast and lots of entertainment so that the deaths could be enjoyed.

"What is happening?" Jassy asked Hope.

"They are talking about you again in a council. Pocanough says that he wants you, and that he will have you. Powan says no, that he is the chief, that he will wait and see if your husband lived through the massacre and if he will come for you."

Elizabeth was poking at her stew. Jassy glanced at her quickly, then looked at Hope again. "Someone will come. They will come from the other hundreds—"

"Maybe. Eventually. But it was not only the Carlyle Hundred that was attacked. We came off very lightly, they are saying. The Indians managed to kill only twenty or thirty whites in a population of over two hundred. At Martin's Hundred, half were killed. It is the same at many of the others. Jamestown was spared, for the people were warned. Jamie saved many by being prepared; they say that *you* saved many by sounding the alarm."

"The entire Virginia colony was attacked?" Elizabeth whispered in horror.

Hope nodded gravely. "Opechancanough ordered it so."

"Why?" Jassy breathed.

"He wants his land back, I suppose," Hope said.

Jassy touched her hand suddenly. "Thank you, Hope. Thank you for coming with us. Why—why did you do it? You did not have to."

Hope shrugged. She lowered her head. "I lied to you. I was jealous. I wanted your husband, and I told you that I knew him to make you mad. He loves you. It was wrong."

Jassy inhaled softly. "I—I don't think that he loves me."

"Yes, yes, he does. He loves you very much." She smiled. "If he can come, he will. Powan expects him. He says that Jamie will come alone. Pocanough thinks that Jamie should be slain, but Powan says that Jamie is fair, and he will be fair too. If Pocanough wants to fight Jamie for you, that will be all right. Whichever man lives will have you, and if both are killed, you will belong to Powan. That is what I think that they are deciding."

Jassy shivered, then she looked at Elizabeth again. She couldn't tell what her sister had heard, and what she had comprehended. Elizabeth had never looked more fragile, or more beautiful. Her soft blond hair curled softly about her face and her flower-blue eyes. The leather apron exposed a great deal of her fair, silky skin, enhancing the fullness of her breasts and the long, shapely length of her legs. Jassy looked at Hope. Hope shook her head and left them quickly.

In the afternoon one of the women came back with a bag of grain and a mortar and pestle, trying to show them that they must work. Jassy shook her head, and Elizabeth stubbornly followed suit. The young woman looked at them angrily, then returned with one of the matrons with a long reed. The older woman began with Jassy, lashing out at her with hard, stinging blows. Jassy screamed and covered her face and fell to the ground so that the blows could be deflected by the leather upon her back.

Suddenly the blows stopped.

"Stop it! Stop it!" she heard Elizabeth shrieking.

Her sister—her sweet, shy sister—was on top of the Indian woman, wrenching the reed from her hands and wrestling her in a fury. Jassy staggered to her feet, hurrying to Elizabeth's aid. Just then, Powan came back into the house.

In a fury, he tugged up both her and Elizabeth by the hair. The older woman —with a bleeding lip, thanks to Elizabeth's tender touch—began to rant and rail and lash out at the white woman again. Powan thundered out in fury and pushed the two of them to the far rear of the house. He sent the woman away.

Jassy held still, watching the tall, muscled Indian pick up the reed. He came over to them and waved it in front of them. "Everyone works. You work too. Next time I will let them beat you until the blood flows from your flesh."

He dropped the reed and turned and left them. Hope returned with the wheat they were to grind. Looking at Elizabeth's smudged face, Jassy had to smile. "You *are* a fighter!" She laughed.

Elizabeth flushed. "She was beating you. I could not stand by and watch it."

Impulsively Jassy hugged her. Hope cleared her throat and told them that they must finish their work. "Everyone works to eat. It is the way that it is done," she said, looking at them anxiously.

Jassy and Elizabeth looked at each other and shrugged, and then set forth on their task. If it could remain so, if they could grind wheat by day and have Powan's protection by night, then they could survive until . . .

Until Jamie came, if he was alive to do so.

And if he could survive Pocanough.

If things could just stay the same . . .

But things were not to stay the same. That night, when Powan came back to his house, he dragged them both to their feet. He stared at Jassy and pulled on the amulet she wore around her neck so that it hung low over her breasts. His mere touch upon them caused her to wince, and he smiled, slowly and curiously. She gasped, stunned, when he ripped open her garment, baring her to the waist. Her breasts, so heavy and painful now, surged forth. She tried to cover herself, and he grabbed her hands, wrenching them around behind her back and holding her tautly to his chest with just one hand to imprison her. "You tempt me, Cameron's woman." She gritted her teeth against the humiliation and pain as he moved his fingers over the full globes of her breasts, pausing to flick the nipples and see them fill with milk. She wanted to lash out at him; she was afraid that she would fall, and she hadn't the strength to free herself from his powerful hold. "You tempt me, yes . . . but James Cameron is a man I will give a chance."

She opened her eyes wide upon his, aware that Powan was taunting her but that she would even be spared rape because of the man her husband was.

She heard a sudden hissing noise, and then fists slammed against Powan's back. Elizabeth! She was even daring to attack the Indian brave in Jassy's defense.

"Elizabeth!" she cried, but it was too late. Powan had already shoved her aside and clutched Elizabeth to him. He smiled, looking down at Elizabeth. He had her wrist and pulled her inexorably closer. "No!" Elizabeth murmured, shaking her head.

"Powan! Please—" Jassy began. She raced back to him, trying to swing the solid brave around. "Please don't. She is Jamie's sister-in-law! She is afraid of you, she will hate you—"

He started to laugh, and his eyes swept over her, lingering on her naked breasts and slim waist. "She is not his wife, and a captive need not love a captor."

"You can't!" Jassy cried, flinging herself against him.

She scratched, she raked, she sobbed, and she fought him very bitterly, but he was quickly on top of her, despite Elizabeth's harrying him from behind. Powan got Jassy down upon her stomach, and he laced her wrists together with a strip of rawhide, then dragged her to a corner where he tied the rawhide to a stake.

"Leave her alone!" Elizabeth cried, thundering upon his back. "Leave her alone!"

He tied Jassy securely.

"Leave her alone!" Elizabeth cried again. Jassy saw his jaw harden as Elizabeth's nails raked his bare flesh. He ignored the attack, and his dark eyes found Jassy's. "Don't make me forget who you are, Cameron's woman," he warned her.

"You can't—" she said, but he had already spun around and seized Elizabeth.

Jassy strained against her bonds in agony. She heard her sister scrambling away, gasping, sobbing, no longer seeking to attack but trying with all her heart to escape.

Bracing herself, she strained against the pole as she heard the frantic fight that ensued, a fight that was quickly ended.

She heard Elizabeth's piercing scream.

And she heard the sounds of Powan moving over her sister, breathing raggedly, ramming his body again and again. She heard the Indian's emission of a pleased grunt. She heard it all, burning inwardly and outwardly, wishing she could scream and scream and scream, just so that she would not have to hear what went on.

But she could hear. She heard Powan fall from Elizabeth, and then she heard her sister sobbing through the night. She could not go to her; she could not even talk to her. Elizabeth slept with the Indian brave. In the dim firelight Jassy could see that her sister was imprisoned by a strong brown arm. Elizabeth had gone silent, still and silent. Jassy wondered if she slept. She did not sleep again herself that night.

In the morning Powan slit the ties that bound Jassy to the pole before he left the house. Jassy stared at him with hard reproach, but he impassively ignored her. As soon as he had stepped from the doorway, she crawled over to Elizabeth. Elizabeth flinched from her touch and looked, dazed, into her eyes. "Oh, Jassy!" Tears welled within the deep blue pools. "Oh, Jassy, it was awful!"

Jassy held her and rocked her.

Then Elizabeth began to swear. She talked about how she hated the Indian and how she would one day cut his heart out and toss it into a fire while he still lived. Jassy finally encouraged Elizabeth to get up, and she worked on adjusting both of their outfits so that they might decently make it to the brook. People watched them as they walked, but no one tried to stop them. Jassy kept a sharp lookout, desperate now that they might find a way to escape. But although no one impeded their way, there were Indians everywhere, the men and the women, watching them. Escape would be difficult.

"He'll do it again!" Elizabeth stormed at the brook.

There was nothing that Jassy could say to reassure her. She could not fight and save her. Powan didn't give a damn about either of them, but in his curious way he did care about Jamie, and if she wanted just to spare Elizabeth, Powan still would not take her in her sister's stead.

"We'll escape," she promised. "We'll escape."

But they didn't escape that day, and by night, Powan seized Jassy and brought her, screaming and thrashing, to be tied to the pole again.

And he seized upon Elizabeth again. The only difference was that Elizabeth no longer cried when it was over.

They *had* to escape.

But two weeks later they had not.

They were coming to know the Pamunkee way of life. Powan was the chief of this tribe, and he spent much of his time in council meetings and debate. He was also a hunter and a warrior, and he expected his woman to serve him. A Pamunkee could take as many wives as he could provide for, so it was natural that he had laid claim to the women hostages, and that he held them for whatever trade it might take to return them.

After the initial torture by the other women, Jassy and Elizabeth were fairly much left alone. Hope continued to be their friend, and to keep them advised of what was happening.

In the morning they bathed and were set to work, either with grain or mending, or with plucking a wild turkey, or skinning or tanning. Neither of them took easily to the tasks, for although they were accustomed to days of work, preparing skins for clothing was hard and arduous. They were corrected many times by the Indian women when they stretched and scraped and cleaned and dried the skins. Jassy didn't mind the days. She came to like the mornings and bathing in the cool brook. She didn't mind the labor because it kept her mind busy.

She hated the nights. There was no way to avoid hearing Powan and her sister, and there was no way to avoid lying there and wondering if Daniel was all right, if he missed her, if he was being loved and cared for, if he was being fed and tended gently. And there was no way not to wonder about Jamie. If he was alive, he would come for her. He would have to. Whether he cared for her or not, he would have to come. It would be part of his code of honor. He would have to save her from the Indians . . . just so that he could send her home to England. Alone.

Somewhere in the third week of their captivity, things took on a subtle change, and Jassy was never quite sure just when it had happened. The noises she heard at night began to change. Powan had apparently determined to seduce rather than ravage. Jassy heard Elizabeth panting and gasping and emitting soft moans and whimpers, and then startling cries. Realizing what she heard now, Jassy closed her eyes in mortification and turned to the wall of saplings, gritting her teeth through the night. Once she had twisted to awaken and see in the firelight the two of them standing together, gleaming and golden, and Powan tenderly stroking her sister's nakedness. Ashamed, Jassy closed her eyes and rolled again, keeping her eyes tightly closed. She heard whispers that meant nothing, yet meant everything. She tried not to listen, but she could not help feeling an anguished longing deep inside and wishing that time could be erased, that she could be lying with her husband as Elizabeth lay with the Pamunkee.

Powan called Elizabeth his golden bird. He was coming to care for her very deeply, and Elizabeth was coming to blush when the Indian's name was spoken.

Jassy was growing desperate to escape.

On the twenty-fifth day of their captivity, she realized that by mid-morning there were few braves about. The women were busy and were accustomed to Elizabeth and her being busy too. If they came back from bathing, then calmly walked away into the forest, they might not be missed for several hours, enough time to give them a good head start.

Elizabeth argued with Jassy. "We don't know where we are!"

"The James River lies to the south of us. I need only find the river and follow it. I would have to find Jamestown. I can do it, Elizabeth, I can lead us home. I know it."

"We will run on foot. They will come after us on horses."

"We will hide. They will give up. And we might find white men in the forest, looking for us."

At last Elizabeth agreed.

The sounds in the darkness lasted longer than usual the night before they were to escape. Jassy thought that Elizabeth was telling her lover good-bye.

With the dawn, they went to the brook as usual. Hope brought them a turkey to pluck that morning, and Jassy whispered that they were going to escape. "Will you come?"

Hope thought about it for a minute. "No. If I am caught helping you, they will punish me as a traitor."

Jassy did not ask what they would do to Hope. She didn't want to know. She hugged the girl fiercely and promised her that they would meet again.

She waited another half hour or so, then tapped Elizabeth on the shoulder. They came out together and stretched, as if taking a brief break from their labors. No one paid them any heed. Jassy motioned toward the trail that had brought them to the village, and they calmly started walking along the dirt.

"I can't believe we're doing this," Elizabeth whispered. "We will probably perish. We will be consumed by insects. What if we are struck by a venomous snake?"

"Save your breath and walk," Jassy commanded her.

They had walked about an hour when they came upon the horses. Jassy grasped Elizabeth and pulled her into the bushes. One of the horses was a spotted mare. Jassy had seen it before. She had ridden upon it when Pocanough had abducted her to the village. "It is a hunting party!" she told Elizabeth.

"What will we do?"

"Just stay silent until they have passed us by."

Even as she whispered, the Indians returned to their horses, leaping upon them. Jassy saw Pocanough. He wore rawhide boots up to his ankles, his breech-clout, a band with feathers across his forehead, and nothing more. He was with five other men. He already had several pheasants tied over his horse's haunches, brought down with his arrows.

The men all mounted. They laughed and joked, ready to ride on.

Suddenly Elizabeth gasped. Jassy heard the soft sound of a rattle. She looked around and saw that a snake, posing to strike, lay within range of the bushes where they hid. They must have disturbed the creature or its nest.

"Damn!" she cried in anguish, wrenching Elizabeth from their position and rolling with her far from the snake's possible strike zone . . . and right into the path of the Pamunkee warriors.

When Jassy looked up, Pocanough had stopped his mount right before her, the animal's hooves so close that he could crush her head any second.

He started to dismount. Jassy saw the malicious pleasure in his eyes. She leapt to her feet and ran.

She didn't care about snakes or brambles or the insects or anything else; she ran in panic into the trees and through them. She heard Pocanough thrashing behind her.

She ran until her heart hurt and her lungs burned and her legs were in agony. She ran until she felt that her insides were bursting, and that she would die if she took another step. Still she kept running.

But the Indian knew his way, and suddenly he was in front of her in a copse instead of behind her. Gasping, clutching her heart, and inhaling desperately, Jassy reeled back. Pocanough smiled, leapt upon a fallen tree, and sprang for her, knocking her to the ground with the impetus of his pounce.

She screamed and twisted beneath him. He tried to subdue her, catching her hands. She escaped his hold and rent a long scratch down his cheek. That angered him. He slapped her hard, and she caught her breath, dizzy from the blow. He lifted his hand to slap her again, and she thought that that was it; she could fight no more. Her strength was deserting her.

Then suddenly, out of the clear blue, a pair of bronze hands set themselves upon the warrior's shoulders, and Pocanough was wrenched cleanly and clearly away from her.

———

Jamie had been despairing, aware that he could never give up, but sinking lower into depression day by day.

Jamie had combed the peninsula. He had gone to Opechancanough, despite the massacre of the whites, and he had walked into the great chief's village with such arrogance that the chief had let him live. Opechancanough had told him that Powan had his wife and her sister but that he did not know where Powan was. Jamie would have to find him. It would be treacherous. Yes, he had ordered the whites attacked. All of the whites. He'd had a vision. They would keep coming and coming, and there could be no peace. The Indians would be absorbed into the earth, and the great Powhatan Confederacy would be no more. "The English must leave. My people know this. If they find you in the forest, James Cameron, they will probably kill you."

"You forget, Opechancanough, that I learned from the Powhatan how to move in the forest. I must have my wife. You know that. A man must do this thing."

Opechancanough agreed with him. He gave him supplies.

But the days passed, and he could not find the village where Powan was residing. He came upon tribes of Chickahominies, and though the Indians were not hostile to him, they could tell him nothing. Finally, the day before, he had ridden Windwalker into the domain of a curious old medicine man, and the medicine man had suggested that he try deep in the woods.

He had been riding since then. With the noon sun high overhead, Jamie had rested by a stream, tossing rocks into the water and torturing himself with his imagination. Opechancanough had ordered whites killed, men and women. The Powhatans did not mind taking female prisoners, but even then, it was possible that they would grow angry and kill the prisoners. And if they had not killed her . . .

He had learned that it was a warrior named Pocanough who had taken Jassy and Elizabeth. Powan was his chief, but Pocanough was a wily and temperamental young brave, and it was possible that he had demanded his way, that he had demanded the hostages he had taken.

His face contorted with pain, his body tensed rigidly, and he fought the piercing wave of agony that assailed him as he imagined her with the Indian brave. If she fought him, he would hurt her. If he lusted after her, he would take her brutally. If she kept fighting, he would beat her, until he broke her or killed her, one or the other.

Self-reproach paralyzed him, then he forced himself to breathe, knowing that it would stand him little good now. He had to find Jassy and Elizabeth.

And if nothing else, he had to kill Pocanough. He could not bear what the man had done to his house and his home. He had slain his housekeeper, had taken his wife. Jamie went rigid again with the pain of it.

It was then that he heard the scream.

He did not know at first if his fears and dreams had collided and he had imagined the sound of the scream. Then it came again, closer, and he leapt to his feet, pulling out his knife. He looked around, and he heard the sound of foliage snapping and breaking. He stepped back, into the shadow of wild berry branches.

Then he saw the Pamunkee burst into the clearing. Grinning with an evil leer, the warrior waited in silence.

Then Jassy appeared.

Jassy . . .

Not as he remembered her.

Her eyes were incredibly blue against the soft tan glowing on her face. She was clad in buckskin, in an Indian maiden's dress, short and sleeveless, tied at the bodice with rawhide. Her hair was free and flew out behind her like a golden pendant as she ran. She was as wild and panicked as a pursued doe, beautiful and sure and lithe, and he ached from head to toe the moment he saw her, and he longed to call out her name.

The Pamunkee brave laughed and leapt from a fallen tree to accost her, bearing her down to the ground.

She screamed and screamed again, clawing him. And he struck her.

Jamie saw red. His temper split and flew, and he saw the red of the blood that had stained his home. He saw the hot red of the noonday sun, and of the fury that threatened to blind him. He sheathed his knife at his calf and leapt forward, placing his bare hands upon the brave and dragging him from his wife. The young buck was no coward, and no weakling. Jamie's anger was a powerful force, and he had been proven in many a battle. He slammed the Indian down to the ground and landed upon him. Again and again he drove his fist into the proud face. Then the Indian bucked in a frenzy beneath him, sending Jamie flying.

"Jamie!"

He heard the cry of alarm in her voice, and the concern in it was as sweet as nectar. He wanted to look at her. He wanted to sweep her into his arms, to touch her, to hold her. He could not. He needed to concentrate on the battle before him.

Jamie landed hard, but he quickly regained his footing, balancing upon the balls of his feet while the Indian charged him. He ducked, letting the Pamunkee use his own force to crash hard against a tree. Then Jamie came at him again with a rain of blows, to his lean, hard gut, to his face, to his gut again, to his chin, to his eye. The Pamunkee struck back. As Jamie reeled, the Indian pulled his knife. Jamie raised his own, and they faced each other, circling warily in the small clearing. The Indian smiled through a slit, half-closed eye. "Cameron," he said. "Cameron." Then he continued slowly in his native tongue, and Jamie understood every word. The white woman had defied Powan and escaped, and so now Pocanough could have her. He had found her again. And Jamie would be dead.

Pocanough lunged forward. Jamie met the drive and smashed down hard on the buck's shoulders. He fell forward on his knee, and Jamie brought his knife to the Indian's throat.

Suddenly a shot was fired.

"No!" A voice said firmly.

Jamie stiffened, holding still. He straightened and turned around but kept his knife flush with the Indian's throat.

Powan had come among them. He had ridden his big bay into the clearing, and he had ordered one of his men to fire off a musket round.

He had Jassy seated before him. With wide, blue, tempestuous eyes she stared down at Jamie in anguish.

"I have come for my wife, Powan, and the mother of my son."

"It must be done where men of the Pamunkee can see it," Powan said. He looked with distaste at Pocanough. "She belongs to neither of you now. She is mine. If you both die in battle, she will remain mine. If one of you slays the other in a fair fight before witnesses, she will then belong to the victor." He looked to his men. "Take them both. They will fight tomorrow."

Jamie dropped the knife. He could have killed Pocanough then, and he wanted to. But then they would have killed him. His only chance of getting Jassy back was to do it Powan's way. When the Indian escort came for him, he walked along willingly. He did not look at Jassy as he passed her by. He felt her eyes upon him and wondered at her thoughts.

That night the Pamunkees prepared for their entertainment. They danced erotically before the fire, and many of the women, with designs drawn upon their bodies with berry juice, danced naked and enticingly, reminding him of the time that he had traveled with Captain Smith in his youth. It had been so long ago now.

Then he had been a guest. Now he was part of the entertainment.

They had taken him to the brook to bathe, and then they had dressed him in a breechclout. He sat before the fire at Powan's side, across from Pocanough. They watched the dancing, and when the women had disappeared, the chief rose and told his people that in the morning there would be a fight, unto the death. If the white man survived, he was to take his woman and walk away unmolested. It was his, Powan's, word, and it would be obeyed.

Then he and Pocanough were taken and tied to posts. Two men, naked and heavily tattooed, began to dance around them, carrying claws of the brown bear. Suddenly the men raked the claws down the backs of the men who would fight. Jamie felt his flesh tear, and he ground down hard on his teeth, determined to make no sound. A Pamunkee would not cry out, and he, too, had to win this fight as a guest-member of the great Powhatan Confederacy. Inwardly he screamed, for the claws started at his shoulders and tore down to the small of his back. He felt the blood surge from the gashes.

When they untied him, he nearly fell, nearly blacked out. He balanced himself against the pole, and he was glad to see that Pocanough was staggering too.

Jamie was led to one of the small houses near that of the chief's. He entered in and fell to his knees. He crawled to his pallet, and as he lay there the pain began to ease. They had left something to drink by the pallet in a gourd, and he rose and swallowed the mixture. He knew it was some drug against the pain, and to help him sleep.

Still, somewhere in the night, he awoke. He did not know what had awakened him at first. The fire in the center of the sapling house had burned down very low, and the light within was eerie. He felt something, some cool, sweet breeze. He looked up and started. He came up on an elbow and stared at the apparition before him.

It was Jassy.

Jassy, with her hair soft and nearly white-gold in the firelight. Jassy, with her eyes tender and wide and seductive upon him.

Jassy . . . erotically naked, her skin very bronzed over the length of her body, her breasts large and firm and provocatively swaying, the nipples very large and dark. He looked at her, and he saw that her buckskin had been tossed in the corner. He wondered if she was a drug-induced dream, or if his wife could really stand so before him, inviting his thirsting eyes.

"Jassy . . ."

She brought her finger to her lips. Then, miraculously, she came closer. She stepped over him, her legs apart. Then very, very slowly, she lowered herself over him. She sat upon his loins, and her hair trailed over his chest as she pressed her lips against his flesh, over and over again, moving against him sinuously. He felt the hot, sensual love of her tongue, and thought that he had lost his mind. Desire burst upon him in a flood, and he rose hard and swift and tried to sweep her beneath him. Her head rose. She stared at him with her hair trailing upon him.

"No," she said softly.

He hesitated.

Then she moved against him again.

All of her body moved and rubbed against him. She used her teeth upon his nipples and then licked them. She swept the softness of her hair over him and shimmied lower and lower against him. When she reached the fullness of his arousal, she took him into her mouth, until he did nearly lose his mind. He sank his fingers into her hair, and he pulled her against him. He brought them both to their knees, and he kissed her until she whimpered softly, then he drew his lips in drunken desire over her throat and shoulders, and he fondled her breasts and teased them with his lips and tongue and sucked them hard into his mouth. He worked upon her with a fascination, until her head fell back and she whimpered out whispers and cried of need and longing and desire . . . for him. Her milk spilled back onto her breasts, and he stood, dragging her to her feet. Then he did to her as she had done to him . . . kissing and caressing the length of her, forcing her to stand still while he ravaged her with the hunger of his lips and tongue. When she fell against him, he brought them together at long last.

And the night burst into splendor.

Nothing had ever been like this—the beauty of her seduction, the loveliness of her long, supple body in the firelight. If he dreamed, then he would gladly die in dreaming, for he had never known her touch to be so tender, so sensual, so impassioned.

And she had come to *him*. . . .

He moved upon her and within her, gentle and fierce, slow, and with impassioned fever. They soared to a summit together and plummeted softly back to earth in the shadow of each other's arms. and still the fire burned softly, and the darkness cloaked them, and it was real. They were together.

She rolled against him, sobbing softly. He tugged upon her hair, bringing her around to face him. "Why are you here?" he demanded. "Has . . . has Powan let you come?"

"Yes."

"Has Powan . . . touched you?"

"No. He has—he has taken Elizabeth." She shuddered and buried her face against him. "I am so frightened, Jamie. I'm so very, very frightened."

His heart hammered, and he tried to make her face him again. "Why? I swear, if I die, he will die with me."

A shattering sob escaped her. "Oh, God, Jamie! I do not want you to die for me! I have brought you nothing but misery and—"

He gripped her hair so fiercely that she cried out, but he had silenced her, and he spoke swiftly and vehemently. "You have brought me everything. You have given me Daniel—"

"Daniel!"

"Rest easy, he is loved and well. Jassy, if I die, I swear that Pocanough will die too. Appeal to Powan as the child's mother and he will let you go to Daniel. I know him well."

She sobbed against the sleek, bare dampness of his chest. "And he knows you, too, for you are here. Oh, Jamie . . ."

He lifted her above him and spoke, his passion naked in his taut features and in his voice. "Love me again, Jassy. Love me before the dawn threatens and you must go back."

She did. Again and again. Until the first pink light of dawn rose and she slipped back into her buckskin dress and tiptoed back into Powan's sapling house. Jamie did not sleep that night. He did not need to.

———

In the morning he was brought to bathe again. The Indians would all eat their breakfast, and then they would gather for the fight. Jamie did not see Jassy, not until he was led out before the crowd, barefoot, bare-chested, and unarmed.

She was seated on the ground before Powan and beside Elizabeth. The chief's hands rested on the two blond heads. Elizabeth tried to smile encouragingly. Jassy did not try. Her eyes were in torment.

Hope came up to him. She smiled, too, and Jamie knew that the half-breed girl believed in him with all her heart. He smiled in return. Hope gave him the short-bladed knife with which he was to fight. The blades were short, to make the battle longer—it would not be easy to give a mortal blow.

Then he faced Pocanough across the circle. A chanting rose on the air. Powan stood and spoke again. Then he dropped his arm, and the fight was on.

Pocanough did not wait a second. Snarling like a bear, he burst for Jamie, casting him off-balance. Both men came down to the ground, writhing and rolling and viciously attempting to stab each other. Pocanough's knife skimmed Jamie's back where the wounds from the night before lay open and vulnerable. Jamie nearly screamed. He kicked and bucked and sent Pocanough flying across the circle. He leapt to his feet and followed the brave. Falling upon him again.

Both had been smeared with bear grease, and it was impossible to get a hold upon the Indian. Jamie decided to break away, and regain his footing. He did so, and balancing carefully on the balls of his feet, he awaited the Indian's next move.

Pocanough leapt high and came down upon Jamie, smashing both of his feet against his chest. The air went out of him, and he fell, stunned and dazed, unable to move.

Then he heard her scream.

He looked up and saw that Pocanough was coming upon him now with the sure fire of triumph in his eyes, his knife raised and aimed directly for Jamie's heart.

In a split second Jamie rolled. The Indian smashed into the earth. Without a second thought Jamie swirled after him, implanting his blade with force between the cleft of the warrior's shoulder blades.

Pocanough raised his head back in a dying scream of rage and agony that ended in a peculiar gurgling sound.

Then he fell face forward into the dirt.

Jamie staggered over to the chief. He fell to his knees. He looked Powan in the eyes. "I claim my wife and her sister," he said. Then he pitched forward, too, exhausted, wondering numbly if the very blackness of death itself was not seeping into him.

"Jamie!"

She called his name and fell down beside him, cradling his head into her lap. He opened his eyes and saw the tears in hers, and he smiled. Then he closed his eyes, and the darkness claimed him.

He slept until nightfall, and in his restless sleep he wondered again what had been real and what had been a dream.

When he opened his eyes again, she was there.

She was real.

He came up quickly on an elbow. He reached out to touch her. "Jassy . . ."

"You need rest. You need to sleep."

He shook his head, rising quickly. He was naked, he quickly realized, but his own European trousers were near his head. He quickly stumbled into them. "I don't want to sleep. I want to go home. I want to take you away from here."

"Jamie—"

"I want to go now." He caught her slender chin within his hands, wondering if the love and the tenderness and the passion could possibly be real too. "I am all right, Jassy, I swear it. I want to mount Windwalker and go home. Get Elizabeth."

Jassy left him and went into Powan's house, looking for her sister. She noticed that her palms were trembling and damp, now that it was over. The trial was over. . . .

Life was yet to be lived.

She found that Elizabeth was sitting before the chief's fire, studying the flames. Jassy hugged her. "We can go home now, Elizabeth. We can go."

Elizabeth studied her curiously, then shook her head ruefully, her blue eyes filling with tears. "I'm not going with you, Jassy."

"What?"

"I'm going to have Powan's baby. I don't think that they would care for my child back at the settlement."

"Don't be absurd. They will love your child! I will love your child and—"

Elizabeth laughed, touching her hand. "Yes, Jassy, you have so much wonderful passion and strength, and if you demanded it, no doubt, the people would all come to love my child. But . . ." She hesitated and spoke in a bare whisper. "I was always so afraid of men, and the world, and everything and anything at all. And now I am not afraid anymore. Jassy, don't laugh. Please don't laugh. I think that I love him. He will marry me, and he says that he will not need any other wives. Jassy, I am home. Please, please try to understand, and try to love me, anyway."

"Oh, Elizabeth, I will love you forever!" Jassy promised her. They cast themselves into each other's arms and hugged and cried. Jamie and Powan found them so together, and neither of the men had a word to say.

An hour later it was growing dark, but Jamie and Jassy were on the trail, mounted together upon Windwalker. Jassy had thought busily for the last hour of a way to start speaking. Jamie had cleared his throat a dozen times.

At last he found words. "Are you sure that you're all right?"

"I was never harmed," she promised him. She leaned back against him. She savored the warm strength of his chest, and she found incredible comfort in his arms, wrapped around her.

"Jassy . . ." He paused, and he sounded humble. She had not thought that he could ever sound so. "Jassy, if you wish it, I will take you home."

"But we are going home."

"I will take you to England. I will have to leave again, but I will never force *you* to stay here again. I had never imagined anything such as this massacre. . . ." His voice trailed away. They both knew then that hundreds of the English settlers had been slain throughout the Virginia colony. One of the greatest tragedies was that John Rolfe, the widower of the Princess Pocahontas, had been slain by his wife's own people. Thankfully their young son remained behind in England and had come to no harm. "I don't want you to have to be afraid again," he whispered to her. "I don't want you to be in danger again."

She twisted around, looking up at him. She touched his cheek, growing dark with the growth of beard. "I am not afraid," she said.

"I will see you safely home."

She hesitated, then pulled in on Windwalker's reins herself. She threw her leg over the horse's haunches, leapt to the ground, and stared up at him indignantly.

"Why did you come after me, my great Lord Cameron, just to get rid of me?"

"I said that—"

She smiled suddenly, thinking of her sister's words, and she interrupted him curtly. "You married me, Cameron, and you'll not get rid of me so easily. I *am* home!"

"What?" He raised a doubtful brow and stared down at her. To his amazement she cast a wicked blow against his thigh. "I am your *wife*. I have a right to stay, and I intend to." She hesitated and added more softly. "I am home, Jamie, *I am home.*"

He leapt down from the horse, taking her by the shoulders, the fires of hope leaping into his eyes. "We have no house!" he said harshly. "Except for the brick cornerstone foundations, we have nothing left. Nothing at all."

She bit her lip, aware that tears threatened to spill from her eyes. "If we have the foundation, haven't we really got everything that we need?"

His fingers clasped her arms so tightly that the grip was painful, but she did not cry out or protest. She studied the burning heat and tension in his eyes, and she began to tremble beneath his hold.

"You really would stay?"

"Yes."

"Why?"

"Why?" she repeated.

"Why?" he thundered, and there was no mercy in him. He was as hard and ruthless as she had ever seen him. She wrenched away from him, the tears spilling from her eyes at last. Her nails dug into her palms, and she shouted back, "Because I—because I love you, you stupid, arrogant knave!"

"What?" he thundered again, coming toward her. She gasped, wondering if he meant to shake the insolence from her, but when she would have fled, he caught her about the waist and spun her around. She struggled against his hold, and they both landed hard upon the dirt. He straddled her and caught her wrists, then pulled them high above her head, laughing. "Tell me. Tell me again!"

"Stupid, arrogant—"

"No!"

"You told me—"

"The other. Tell me the other. Damn it, say!"

The tears were in her eyes again. She wanted to shout. She whispered, "I love you, Jamie."

"Again."

"I love you."

His lips fell upon hers. Sweet, hungry, exciting, evocative. He kissed her with a fascinating leisure for their curious position upon the forest trail. He kissed her as if nothing else in the world mattered, and maybe, beneath the green shadows of the forest, nothing else did. And when he ended the kiss, his smile so tender and gentle, she cried out and threw her arms around him again. He held her so for a long time without speaking, then he ran his thumb softly over her cheek and whispered to her at last. "Can you really love me?"

"I do," she vowed. "Oh, Jamie, please don't send me away."

"I never wanted to send you away. I only wanted to give you the freedom you wanted. Jassy!" He held her close, and his voice was filled with passion. "I did not marry you to survive this place, or to have a woman who could be dragged to a wilderness. I married you because of the spirit and fervor and passion in your soul, in your eyes. I married you to touch those things, and when I did touch them, I was not appeased but floundering ever further beneath your spell. Jassy, I fell in love with you so long ago—"

"I could not tell!" she interrupted in awe and reproach, and he laughed.

"Well, you were pining after Robert Maxwell. I am a proud man."

"I had not noticed!" Jassy laughed, but then she sobered and reached out, brushing the hair from his forehead. "Oh, Jamie, I was so wrong! It was you all along, wasn't it? You paid for my mother's coffin, not Robert."

He held silent, and she smiled. She would never tell him of Robert's lack of valor on the day of the massacre. It wasn't necessary. The truth was. "I fell out of love with Robert long, long ago, milord."

"How so?"

"He could not fill my heart or mind once you had set your claim upon me. Never, from the very beginning, milord, have I managed to forget you, as you promised me that I would not. And when you turned from me, I did not think that I would be able to bear it."

He groaned, burying his face against her throat. "I thought that you despised me still, and I could not love you and force you to remain any longer."

"Oh, Jamie! Could you not tell! When you touched me and I fell so swiftly to your command . . ."

"We are both proud and stubborn. It almost cost us so much. Oh, Jassy, I knew that I had your passion. I wanted your love."

"You have it all, all of me, Lord Cameron."

The trees rustled above them, a soft breeze moving over the land. He kissed her again, slowly and deeply, and the fires of spring came alight within them both, radiant and as beautiful as the burst of the sun, for their whispers were of love.

Jamie looked up and saw where they lay, in the dirt, in the road. He rose and swept her into his arms, carrying her into the brush, into the verdant leaves. He laid her down upon a field of green earth beneath the swaying branches of an oak, and he spread her hair against the earth. Then he laid himself against her, and he made love to her as he never had before, for her whispers of love filled his senses to bursting, and his passionate vows and promises urged her on to ever greater heights. And when it was over, they both lay in the wilderness, watching the canopy of the trees, naked and content in the green darkness of the forest.

He whispered again and again that he loved her. And she responded with awe, touching his cheek, adoring him.

At last he helped her dress, and they journeyed onward again. It was a long trip home but a good one for them both. During all of the journey they touched each other, talked of their pasts, and spoke of the future.

At last they came to the Carlyle Hundred, and when they were spotted, the people came milling out to greet them, waving excitedly. Jassy leaned back against her husband, trembling.

"Jamie, we are home."

"Home, love, is that burned-out shell."

She twisted to meet his cobalt stare, darkened with amusement and a curious tenderness. "The foundation is good. And upon that foundation we can build."

"We can build, my love. In this wilderness we shall build."

He smiled and laced his fingers with hers, and they both knew that the foundation was not within the bricks in the ground but within their own hearts.

Jamie urged Windwalker forward at a greater pace, and then the horse sped into an easy gallop. Home lay before them, and their infant son, and the sweet golden promise of tomorrow.

A
PIRATE'S
PLEASURE

NORTH AMERICAN
WOMAN
2

To Shery Woods

always an inspiration

and a friend

Prologue

April 4, 1718
Cameron Hall
Tidewater, Virginia

IRATES! DAMNED PIRATES!"

The explosive words rocked the apparent serenity of the coming night. It was sunset along the James River. Soft hues of orange and tawny yellow were falling against the moss-touched oaks and the gentle sloping grasses leading to the river. Someone hummed somewhere as they worked, and birds sang melodic songs.

"Pirates!" came the resounding thunder once more, and it seemed that a hush fell upon the day.

Lieutenant Governor Alexander Spotswood of Virginia slammed his hand upon the polished pine side table by his chair on the porch to further emphasize his fury and displeasure. Lord Cameron leaned idly against one of the massive pillars and glanced at his friend with a wry smile. Alexander was obsessed. A bright and reasonable man, attractive in his person, dress, and manner, he was quite popular among the colonists, from the lords and ladies to the scullery maids. His eyes were intelligent and grave, and outraged though he was, he still appeared the aristocrat—from his fine white wig, the ends of it neatly curling over his shoulders, to his peach brocade frockcoat to his soft mustard knee breeches and silver buckled shoes. At the moment, though, he was lacking his customary oratorical prowess. He was fixed upon one word.

"Pirates! I say," Spotswood repeated. He did not slam his hand against the table again, but preferred to rescue his glass of sherry before his own vitality sent it crashing to the floor. "Pirates, pirates, pirates! They will be the bane of me yet!" His eyes narrowed sharply upon his host, Petroc Cameron, Lord Cameron of Cameron Hall, and "Roc" to his friends and relations. Cameron was sharp, and like his father before him, he was a tall man, young, striking, with strong, handsome features and some indomitable presence about him that instantly attracted the eye and commanded respect. Like many Camerons, he possessed sharp gray eyes that could sizzle silver by certain light. His hair was dark when he disdained to wear a wig; this late afternoon, with the falling sun upon it, the color seemed like jet.

Even in stillness he was vital.

Now, casually leaning against the pillar and looking out to the James River, he still emitted some energy that belied his nonchalance. Humor touched his eyes, but more. If there were danger, then danger be damned. He was a man to meet a challenge.

"Sir," he reminded his friend, "you cannot single-handedly do away with them. But I swear it, sir, we shall do our best to cast the worst of them into gibbets."

"Bah!" Spotswood protested impatiently. "I would chain them all in gibbets by the docks as warning. A pity that chains and gibbets cost so much money, I cannot afford to display the more petty offenders!" He leaned back and looked down the broad slope of grass to the river. It was a beautiful place, this, the Cameron estate. Strategically planned, it combined the best of an English country manor with the wild beauty of the colony. Because of the depth of the river, ships could come to the Cameron docks as if they came to Lord Cameron's very front door. The house itself was both practical and elegant. Spotswood had been friends with this young Cameron's father in the days when he had planned the governor's mansion in Williamsburg, and he had often thought of Cameron Hall when he spoke with the architects. The house had been begun in late 1620s. There had been just the main hall and upstairs bedrooms then. There was a brick in the cellar in the foundation attesting to the date of the building. "With these bricks we build our house, Jamie and Jassy Cameron, the Year of Our Lord 1627. The foundation will be strong, and God granting, our house and our family will stand the test of time."

The family had, so far, stood strong with the best and the worst of times. The eldest son always grew to be a member of the Governor's Council. To Spotswood, they were proving to be very fine friends, indeed. None so staunch as Roc Cameron.

"Sir," Cameron said now, "you do well against the hordes."

Was he teasing him? Spotswood never knew. He swept out a hand indicating the paper he had just been reading and had tossed down with an incredible flourish just before he had banged the table. "There's another article in there by a so-called wife of that Edward Thatch, Teach, Tech—whatever his bloody name is! The man marries women right and left!"

"And they live to tell of it," Roc Cameron said gravely. Teach was a pirate who was beginning to draw attention to himself. Blackbeard, they called him, because of his ferocious facial hair. It was rumored that he hailed from Bristol, and that he had served in Queen Anne's War, and that he had gone on to be tutored beneath the pirate Hornigold to learn a new trade as a scavenger upon the high seas. But he wasn't the worst of the lot. "Logan is running around out there. And One-Eyed Jack. Those are the two who not only steal cargo, but are heinously careless with human life."

Spotswood looked at him with a slow, curious nod. He sat back, lacing his fingers together, watching his younger friend. "And then there's the Silver Hawk."

"And then there's the Silver Hawk," Cameron agreed flatly.

"We need new commissions," Spotswood complained. "Queen Anne lies dead, and that German upon the throne—"

Roc's laughter interrupted him and the lieutenant governor flushed. "Well, the man is a German! He's the King of England, and he doesn't even speak the king's good English! What is this world coming to? Pirates ever plaguing the seas, and a king who can't even speak his country's English!"

"Better than a papist, sir, or so, it seems, the country decided." Roc Cameron considered himself a Virginian. The affairs of the mother country were of concern to him only when they concerned Virginia. He was passionately in love with his land. The ultimate gentleman farmer, and a fine merchant, despite his title. That was the way with the New World, or so it seemed. A man could make great riches here, but only if a man were hard and bright and willing to work.

Spotswood loved Virginia himself. But he was an Englishman, appointed by the Crown. He might mutter about the king being a German, but still he bowed to England in all things. Queen Anne, the last of the Stewart monarchs, had died in 1714. That poor lady's many children had all died before her, and rather than accept her half-brother—a papist—on the throne, the English were willing to look to Germany for a Protestant king. The religious issue was a crucial one. In the colonies, men tended to be more tolerant of religious differences. But even here, every man of property or means belonged to the Church of England, and he kept his vows to the church as sacred.

Spotswood sighed. Always a challenge! The Indians had beset men a century ago. Now it was the damned pirates.

"Roc—" the governor began, leaning forward. But he was suddenly cut off by a huge commotion coming from the house.

The porch lay off the grand central hallway. It was situated so that the river breeze swept from the open hallway doors in the back to the open hallway doors at the front, when the weather was hot. Now the governor and Lord Cameron heard a bellowing voice and the clump of heavy footsteps. The governor frowned. Roc Cameron grinned and shrugged. "Lord Kinsdale, I believe," he said dryly.

Peter Lumley, Lord Cameron's butler and valet, appeared first. A man of about forty, he was lean and small, but straight and stiff with indignation.

"Sir, I did tell his lordship that you were engaged, and with the lieutenant governor! But he insisted—"

"That's quite fine, Peter," Roc said, pushing away from his pillar. He thrust back the folds of his fawn-colored frockcoat to plant his hand upon his hips. He waited. A second later a small portly man with blue eyes and wild wisps of gray hair appeared.

"Cameron! Have you heard of it! More and more debauchery upon the open seas!" He held the very newspaper that the governor had allowed to fall to the floor.

"Yes, Theodore, I have heard of it," Roc said. Lord Theodore Kinsdale paused to bow in acknowledgment to the governor. Spotswood nodded and met Cameron's eyes above the little man. They both smiled. Theodore Kinsdale was a good man, a fine man. He supported the governor in all things, and held many a merry ball. He owned vast sugar estates in the islands, but preferred to live in

Williamsburg. He did, in fact, despise the three-hour drive out to Cameron Hall, and so, for him to have arrived here unannounced, he must be flustered and upset indeed.

"Alexander, what do you intend to do about all of this!" Theodore demanded.

Spotswood glared at him. "I have ships all over the coast! I am doing things, man!"

"Have a drink, Theo," Roc Cameron suggested.

"Don't mind if I do, don't mind if I do. Scotch!"

He sat in one of the handsome twined chairs upon the porch and mopped his face with a scarf. He stared from Roc to Alexander Spotswood, and then back again. "My daughter sails," he moaned.

"When?" Roc Cameron said.

"Her ship has left this very day."

Spotswood cleared his throat. "There's no reason to believe that your ship will be attacked."

"There is every reason to believe that the *Silver Messenger* will be taken! I am a wealthy man. The ship sails with a tremendous cargo. Why, her jewels alone are worth a fortune." He stared straight at Roc Cameron. Cameron stiffened. The two gentlemen were engaged in a running feud. Roc Cameron's father and Theo had betrothed their children at birth.

Roc now found such an arrangement barbaric. He preferred to choose his own bride, at his own time. And rumor had reached him, even from England. The girl wanted nothing to do with him. He didn't consider himself unduly proud, but admittedly, her rumored refusal annoyed him. Still, it made matters easy for him. He had vowed to his father upon his deathbed to uphold his every promise. To keep his honor.

"I'm sure that she will be safe—" Alexander began, trying to mollify Theo.

But Theo would have none of it. He jumped up, staring at Lord Cameron. "Roc, please! Your father was my dearest friend. You can make sure that she is safe! You have friends among the pirates—"

"Friends!" Roc Cameron exploded.

Theo lowered his voice just a shade, clamping his hands together, trying to hide his agitation. "She is my life!" he whispered. "She is all that I have left! I ordered her to return home to marry you! Now she sets sail. All right. You have not friends among the pirates, you have relations—"

"I do not claim pirates as relations!" Roc said firmly. He knew that the lieutenant governor was staring at him, and he cast the man a warning glare, then returned his attention to Kinsdale. "Sir! You would make it sound as if I fraternize with the likes of pirates."

Governor Spotswood grinned at Roc, sitting back, preparing to enjoy the promised show. Roc Cameron frowned to him darkly but the governor's grin widened.

"They say," Theo said, his fists clenched by his side, "they say that the Silver Hawk is a Cameron—"

"He is no Cameron!"

"That the silver eyes give him away. They say, too, that out of some curious respect for the family name, he is willing to negotiate with you. It is rumored that he is quick to seize your ships, and quick to return them for a reasonable fee. They say that you have some power, that you have even been to that island of his and negotiated with him. By God, Petroc! You must help me!"

Cameron threw up his hands. "So, milord, this pirate comes from some ill-begotten and illegal branch of my family! So he is a bit less willing to cut my throat than yours. What would you have of me?"

Theo was silent for a long moment. Then he drew a scroll from within his pocket. "Marry her. Now."

"What?" Cameron exploded incredulously.

"Marry my daughter now. Fulfill the vow you made to your father."

"The girl isn't even here—"

"I have proxy papers. I acquired them when I was in London."

"But your daughter—"

Theo waved a hand in the air. "She has signed them. Oh, I grant you, she doesn't know what she signed, she was arguing with me—speaking with me, that is—about other matters. But it is all well and legal, I assure you. Marry her now—"

"Why?"

"Because the Silver Hawk is your cousin. Because he might find my ship, and my daughter. And even if he does not, many of the others will respect his relationship with you, they will fear what he may do if they seize that particular ship."

"This is insane!"

"No! Cameron, you do not understand!" The man's voice trembled, his countenance had gone white with emotion. "It's the darkness, you see. She cannot stand the darkness."

Kinsdale was losing his mind.

Roc Cameron wasn't prone to rudeness, but he threw up his hands, turned around, and started walking down the slope of the estate toward the water. Kinsdale! The man was too much. Roc could not agree to the insanity.

Nearing the bottom of the slope, he turned away, not wanting to see the workers on the docks. He stared down at his ship, the gunned sloop the *Lady Elena,* named for his mother. It would be time to sail again soon. Very soon.

Inhaling sharply, he turned away and strode back toward the eastern side of the house. The outbuildings were there. Neat cottages for the servants, the smokehouse, the kitchen, the stables, the blacksmith's shop, the cooper's work-house, the laundry. Far below them, enveloped by trees, lay the graveyard.

He walked there and paused. His mother and father and an infant child lay closest to the new fence. A hundred years of Camerons lay beyond them.

He walked back to the slate headstones that his father had ordered re-etched just before his death. They belonged to his great-grandparents, Jassy and James. He touched the cool stone and thought of the pair. They had endured. They had come here and created a dynasty, and they had endured. They had braved the Indians and remained despite the annihilating attack of 1622. Their heirs had populated a large part of Virginia. And the Carolinas and New York and the eastern states, he thought with some amusement.

Then his smile faded slightly and he turned around again, leaving the cemetery behind him. He strode back toward the house. Spotswood and Kinsdale were no longer on the porch. He heard their voices coming from the formal dining room. Peter would have seen to it that his guests were fed, he knew.

He hesitated then strode up the wide, sweeping stairway that seemed to climb to lofty heights from the expanse of the hall.

At the top of the stairway was the portrait gallery.

Camerons were always painted. The practice had begun with Jamie and Jassy, and continued to Roc's mother and father. He passed by his parents' pictures briefly. They were wonderful portraits. She was beautiful and dark and shyly smiling; he was proud and dignified, and the strange silver color of his eyes had been well captured by the artist. Still, Roc did not pause long. He walked down past his grandparents and great-grandparents. Then he paused, before Jassy Cameron.

She had been a fighter, so he had heard, and the sizzle of fire was captured in her gaze, while laughter was captured upon her lips. She had been a beautiful woman, stunning, and with fine and delicately chiseled features. Her eyes had been painted so that they seemed to fall upon him. Even as a child, he had often come to the portrait, fascinated by it.

He glanced at Jamie. Lord Cameron. Dignified, proud, young. Roc owed them something. Camerons peopled the New World and the Old, and yet he was the heir to their legacy.

Jassy Cameron's glance seemed to remind him so.

"All right, milady," he said softly to the picture, "I have long been a man, and I do realize that three decades is considered a sufficient age. And perhaps my life is haphazard and reckless. But, you see, I'd had in mind to choose the mother of my children myself. This girl could be cross-eyed or quite insane, you know. She could bring in some horrible disease. . . ."

His words trailed away. His eyes fell over the length of the portrait hall. To every Cameron pictured here, honor had been sacred. He cast his hands upon his hips and walked back to his parents' pictures. "I am against this, sir. Totally. You taught me to be my own man in all things, but you have left me with this vow! For the record, sir, I am totally against the marriage. But"—he paused— "as you wish it, Father. I will do my very best for her." He started to walk away, then he turned back, wagging a finger at the portrait. "Sir, I do hope that she is not cross-eyed or hunchbacked!"

He burst into the dining room. Spotswood and Kinsdale were just picking up tender bits of venison. Startled, they looked at Roc.

"Let's have done with this thing, then," he told Kinsdale.

Kinsdale leaped to his feet. "Peter, Peter! You must run quickly to the rectory and bring back Reverend Martin. And his daughter, Mary. She may stand for Skye."

Roc nodded. "Do it, Peter, please. Sir—" he addressed the governor. "You will stand witness to the legality of this rite?"

"If Lord Kinsdale's papers are in order, and it is your wish."

"It is my wish," he said.

The governor sighed, staring at the table. "And it was such a delectable dish!"

In a matter of minutes, the flustered Reverend Martin arrived with his blushing young daughter.

Words were said, and papers were signed and witnessed, and then the deed was done.

Kinsdale was no longer interested in dinner. Indeed, he no longer had a wish to remain. "I intend that everyone shall know that you have wed her, and the Cameron name will keep her safe."

"Lord Kinsdale—"

Roc tried to stop the man, but Kinsdale was in a hurry, asking Peter to call his coachman and valet so that he might start back, despite the fall of darkness.

"Theo! Listen to me. There are no guarantees upon the open sea! Can't you see, man—"

His new father-in-law clutched his hands. "Thank you. Thank you! Remember, sir, that she fears the darkness above all else. Keep her from it! I left a locket with her picture in it on the table." Kinsdale pumped his hand. Lord Cameron escorted his guest to the doorway. His coach, the lanterns swinging from the driver's canopy, awaited him. "Cameron, I will trust in God Almighty, and in your fine name and honor!"

With that, Kinsdale was gone.

Roc Cameron wandered into the house and into the dining room. Spotswood had sat back down to venison freshly warmed for him.

"Eat up! 'Tis your wedding feast!" Spotswood said, holding the locket in his hands.

Roc Cameron scowled sharply and laughed.

"Don't you care to see your bride?"

"Is she cross-eyed?"

"No. She is quite beautiful."

"What can you tell from a tiny portrait?"

Spotswood closed the locket with a snap and pocketed it. He smiled. "I know the lady. I haven't seen her in years, but the child gave great promise."

"Wonderful," Lord Cameron muttered darkly.

"She has a will of steel, my friend. A fine temper to match, and she is bold and quite intelligent and—"

"She will come here and mind her own affairs and that shall be that," Roc said flatly.

The governor smiled, looking at his plate. "I think not," he said softly.

"Your pardon, sir?"

"I said, 'So, it seems that you will sail sooner than expected.' "

"Yes, so it seems." Lord Cameron stood and poured himself a fair measure of whiskey. "To my cousin, Governor! To the Silver Hawk. May we negotiate the very best of terms."

"To the Silver Hawk." The governor raised his glass.

Roc Cameron slammed his glass down upon the table and left the room in a controlled fury. Lieutenant Governor Alexander Spotswood lowered his glass more slowly. He pulled the locket from his pocket and snapped it open and smiled down at the delicate and beautiful features that looked his way.

"And to you, Lady—Cameron!" he said softly. "Skye, it will be good to see you home. It will be most intriguing to see the sparks and feathers fly when you meet your new lord. Ah, if I wasn't the governor, I would set sail myself, for this promises to be high adventure!"

He snapped the locket shut and nearly set it upon the table. After all, Kinsdale had left it for Roc Cameron.

A slow mischievous grin came to his features. He pocketed the locket again. Let him imagine that his bride was slack-jawed and cross-eyed!

His smile faded slowly. Pirates *would* go after Lord Kinsdale's ship if they heard that she had sailed. She would carry not only his daughter, a valuable hostage, but her personal belongings, and God alone knew what else. Of course, she could cross the ocean unmolested.

She could . . .

But it was doubtful. The world was indeed in sad shape.

"Pirates!" he swore vehemently.

Indeed, it was sometimes a sorry world. Pirates were plaguing the coast, and a German was sitting upon the throne of England.

He patted his pocket where the locket lay within it. "Take care, milady!" he said softly. "I'm afraid that for you the tempest has already begun."

1

THE JOLLY ROGER! 'TIS THE JOLLY ROGER, THE death's-head, the skull and crossbones, bearing down upon us!"

Skye Kinsdale reached the helm in time to hear the lookout's panicked words. She came, teetering and floundering, just as a streak of lightning lit up the heavens, sizzling through the sky and the sea. It illuminated the ship that had been following the *Silver Messenger* like a ghostly echo through the night. Already the crew fought to trim the sails against the storms that plagued the Atlantic; now, new terror was offered as the phantom ship displayed her true colors, those of the bleached white bones against the black of eternal night, rogue's colors, a pirate's colors.

"Captain! She waves the Jolly Roger!" the lookout repeated.

"The skull and crossbones!" Skye said in dismay, now standing by Captain Holmby's side. The beleagered lookout, high atop the crow's nest, stared down upon her. He was Davy O'Day of County Cork, recently hired onto the *Silver Messenger,* her father's ship.

Davey looked down upon Skye, and his fear for himself lessened as his heart took flight with the sight of her fiery gold hair, her fine, delicate, and intelligent features, and her eyes of fierce and compelling aquamarine. Her cape whipped around her feminine form, and the wind that tore upon it seemed to make tendrils of her beautiful hair dance upon the very air. In danger, in fear, in laughter, she seemed to shimmer and sizzle with vibrance and life, perhaps a very part of the storm and tempest.

He had adored her since she had first stepped foot aboard the ship, smiling and laughing, always a lady, and always with her keen interest about everything and everyone around her. He was in love with her, as much in love as a scrap of an Irish boy could be, and he vowed in those moments that he would die gladly to save her. Pirates! Mother of God!

Captain Holmby was impatiently staring up at him. Davey found his tongue again, wondering if the captain had comprehended his words.

"Sir! The Jolly Roger! The flag she waves is the Jolly Roger. 'Tis a pirate vessel! We're under attack!"

"I know that, boy! Mr. Gleason!" The captain called out to his first mate. "My glass, sir!"

Skye watched with a curious mixture of dread and excitement as the captain's first officer came forward and handed the spyglass to the captain. The weather was more than rough that morn, with the ship pitching and swaying upon the whitecaps that rode the Atlantic. The scent of a storm was strong upon the air, for the heavens were darkened by a curious gray and the day was cool, growing cold, and the wind was fierce and salt-laden.

It was a day to fear storms and the wrath of God, but no man sailed the seas these days without some fear of the bloody pirates laying waste to unwary vessels upon the Atlantic Ocean and the Caribbean Sea. Indeed, there were great bounties being offered for the likes of Blackbeard and Anne Bonny, One-Eyed Jack and the Silver Hawk.

It was not the proper weather for a pirate attack. The rogues, Captain Holmby had assured her just last night, did not like to attack when they might receive more harassment from King Neptune than from any guns at sea. Nay, Captain Holmby had said, they would have safe sailing, even though the winds might blow and tempest rage, and their journey across the Atlantic would soon be at an end. She would be delivered to her father in Williamsburg, and soon enough, her lucky beau would be blessed with his glorious bride. The last had been accompanied by a wink, and since the captain had proven to be such a sweet and delightful old man, Skye had smiled sweetly in return.

Whether or not she would be a bride was another matter altogether. Her father had decreed that she would marry a man she had never set eyes upon, and though she knew the arrangement was customary and proper, she was not about to accept it. Perhaps the Camerons had built the finest plantation in all of Tidewater Virginia, and perhaps Lord Cameron was a great gentleman, but Skye was determined that she would not be an object to be bartered and sold and possessed, no matter what. No, she'd never had any intention of arriving in Virginia to be a bride. She'd had every intention of escaping marriage someway.

This, however, had not been the way!

There would be a way, of course, a legitimate way. She was all that her father had, just as her father was all that she had. Since her mother had been killed when she was a child, she had clung to him, and he to her. She had always known his very mind and had been able to wheedle from him anything she wanted.

Until six months ago when he had come to her school in London to tell her that she was coming home. She had been so thrilled. Then he had told her that she was coming home to marry and she had been stunned. She had been careful at first, soft-spoken and respectful. Then she had wheedled, and then she had grown furious. He was being so stubborn. Some silly betrothal had been agreed upon before she could even walk, and since she was supposed to marry Lord Petroc Cameron, her father had no intention of seeing reason. She had talked and cried and stamped her feet, and none of it had done her a bit of good. Lord Theodore Kinsdale had hugged her fiercely and told her he'd be awaiting her at their home in Williamsburg when her term at Mrs. Poindexter's School for Refined Ladies was done, and that was that. She was eager to leave Mrs.

Poindexter's, so she determined that she would continue her fight in the New World. She would get out of it!

Yes, because a pirate ship was coming straight at them.

Suddenly, from out of the bleak gray sky and sea came a startling flash of color, of fire, of gold and sizzling red against the day.

The pirate vessel was firing upon them.

"One-Eyed Jack!" the captain stormed. He raised his glass to point across the sea. "He means to ram and grapple us! Mr. Gleason! All hands on deck! Call the men to their battle stations!"

The missile did not strike the ship, but water blew nearby them, as if sent to the surface by a great whale, spewing forth foam.

"Is it One-Eyed Jack?" Skye asked, cold fear lacing her insides despite her best efforts at courage. She had heard tales about the man. He kept hostages only if the fancy struck him. He slew good men as he swatted flies. And women . . .

She did not dare think. Her fear would steal her will to reason, and to fight.

"Aye, 'tis One-Eyed Jack!" the captain said. "See the flag, milady. Even his skull lacks the eyehole." He patted her hand absently. "Bring her about! Call the gunners to their stations, Mr. Gleason." Captain Holmby's blue eyes fell upon Skye. "Lady Kinsdale, I shall have you escorted to your quarters," he told her.

"But, sir—"

"Ah, nay, lady, you must stay in my cabin—less danger in case of fire—" He stopped speaking abruptly and swallowed hard with a certain guilt. "I did not mean—"

"I am not a child, Captain," Skye said. Nor would she sit meekly and be slain if the heathens came aboard. She knew how to fight well, and she would do so.

"Boy, come down!" the captain called to Davey, atop the crow's nest. "Take Lady Kinsdale to my cabin."

"Aye, aye, sir!" the lad replied, and quickly shimmied down.

"Don't be afraid, my lady! We will prevail."

"I am not afraid of the danger, Captain, but of the cabin—" Skye began, but she had lost his attention. He gave his orders to his first officer, who then boomed them out to the crew over the sound of the coming storm and the waves, and over the sounds of the fire that now began, cannon to vie with the thunder.

"Come, me dear lady!" Davey encouraged her, grasping her hand. He began to run over the hull. They dodged grim-faced sailors and the rigging and they came to the door of the captain's cabin. It was an elegant place, finely set with a huge oak desk, damask draperies, and a deep-set bunk surrounded by bookshelves hewn into the very body of the vessel. The elegant china tea service reserved for the captain's use still sat atop his desk. Presumably he had been at tea when the call had come that the weather worsened and an unidentified ship approached.

"May God be with you, lady!" Davey cried to her. "I will lock you in, milady, and—"

"No!" she protested in a sharp scream. Then she smiled apologetically. She would be all right as long as there was light, as long as the door was not locked. "Please, Davey, I would not be trapped. Do not lock me in."

"No, milady, if that is your wish."

"Thank you. Go on now, and God be with you!" she said quickly, for already he was pulling the door shut behind him. Skye picked up her skirts and ran behind him, placing her hands upon the door and leaning against it. She could hear the footsteps pounding over the deck; she could hear the captain's first officer raging out his orders. She screamed suddenly, thrown back with such vengeance that she fell hard against the desk. She heard the fine china rattle and fall. A ball, she surmised, had struck the ship somewhere.

She heard a man scream, scream with such pain and agony that she could feel his anguish deep inside. Then she felt a deep and terrible shuddering within the ship.

The pirate vessel was upon them. She could hear grappling hooks being tossed and thrown, catching and sinking into the wood of the hull like the giant fangs of some evil monster. Aye, a monster it was.

Rubbing her shoulder where she had struck the deck, she carefully rose. The skirt to her new gold-threaded gown had caught and torn upon the carved foot of the desk and she wrenched at it with all speed. Smoke was seeping into the cabin now. Smoke from the fires caused by the cannonballs, fires that surely blazed now within canvas sails. Men were screaming and shouting, and the clash of steel and the horrible scent of powder and flame were all about.

It was stifling; she could not breathe. She flew to the door and angled behind it, opened it enough that she could see.

Dread filled her heart, and swept through her blood, and congealed as ice in her soul.

The good captain lay dead before her very feet. Though officers and sailors still gave battle about the deck, it was painfully obvious that the pirates were the victors of this particular battle upon the sea.

Skye clutched her heart, then set her hands against her ears as the clash of steel continued. She closed her eyes, sick with anguish for the poor gallant captain, and for his men.

Then her eyes flew open once again. She heard the rise of female screams, and she realized that her young maids, fresh from the Irish countryside, had been discovered down in the hold. Bessie was screaming desperately; Tara was gulping out little squawking sounds.

And even as Skye watched, the two women were dragged to midships, beneath the mainsail. All around them tinder burned and the small fights continued. But there was no gallant knight to come to the girls' defense; all the officers and men were well occupied in their own skirmishes.

"No!" Skye whispered aloud, biting into her lower lip.

But there was no denial.

Despite the gray of the day and the thunder and the lightning and the awful smell of charred wood and charred flesh and the threat of rain, certain of the buccaneers were determined. Tara with her soft blue eyes and snow white skin was being tossed soundly upon the deck. With the pitch and sway and tempest of the ocean, she was thrown hard against the water bucket, and none of the riotous rogues seemed to notice her cry of pain. It was a party of four that attacked the girls, one a youth with a scraggly white-blond beard, one missing a tooth, a graybeard, and a nasty, evil dark-haired fellow with yellow, tobacco-stained teeth.

Skye closed her eyes and leaned back against the door. She could not let this happen.

Yet what could she do? The ship was alive with beasts, and the force of good was surely losing to evil.

And still, eventually, they would find her. Was it not better to go down fighting than to be cornered and caught like a fox?

She was not terrified of fighting for her life. She was only afraid of small dark places from which she could not escape.

She looked above the captain's desk, where a fine pair of Damascus swords were hung, one upon the other. The ship pitched dangerously, as if they would all be swept up by the storm, swallowed, and taken to the bottom of the sea.

She prayed briefly. She asked God to forgive her a multitude of sins, pride not the least of them.

Then she sprang forward, leaped upon the desk itself, and wrested a sword from its scabbard against the paneling.

She felt the steel in her hand. She slashed the sword carefully through the air, testing its weight. Then she swirled about, hurriedly leaving the safety of the cabin before she could lose her nerve and cower in terror in some dark corner.

Skye carried her blade in one hand, sweeping her skirts up behind her with the other. The horrible smells of battle were even worse on deck. So much charred flesh! Broken timber, broken limbs, and canvas that continued to burn. She swallowed hard, fighting an urge to faint at the sight of the still-staring—but sightless—captain. She steeled herself and stepped over the man. So far, she hadn't been noticed in the melee.

They would notice her soon enough.

She flew forward in a burst of courage and strength, flying toward the men who held down Tara and Bess.

"Leave them be!" she commanded, waving her sword toward the graybeard who tore at Tara's skirts.

He paused, staring at her. All of them paused, in surprise. The graybeard slowly smiled, licking his lips. "Well, lookee here, will you now! We've found the crème de la crème, eh, boys?" He started to laugh, rising, tossing down Tara's skirt and adjusting his breeches. "How-de-do, mee-lady. Old Samuel, here, and indeed, mum, I do intend to show you a good time."

"Shut your mouth and step aside, Samuel. And you!" she said sharply to the blond youth who was nearly upon poor Bess. "I suggest you return your pro-truding anatomy to your breeches, boy, lest I find myself tempted to lop it off!"

Samuel burst into a loud guffaw. The blond boy did not find the threat so amusing. He quickly stumbled to his feet, drawing the cord on his breeches tight.

"A feisty wench, this one!" Samuel called happily. "Toss me a sword; this bird I shall quickly best, and have."

"And share!" the boy said.

"Let's see how the lady does. I think perhaps that the prize might first be mine," a voice called out, and Skye quickly turned about.

She didn't need to be told that she had come face-to-face with the man known as One-Eyed Jack. A black patch covered his one eye. He smiled an evil leer and she saw yellowed, rotting teeth beneath the curve of his lip. He was a small, sinewy man with whiskers.

Her stomach heaved. The idea of fighting to the very death gained new appeal for her.

"Captain!" cried Old Samuel. "I killed the captain of this here ship—she's a prize, and mine! Give me a sword!"

"Take on the fight, Sam, and we will judge the lady," One-Eyed Jack agreed. He tossed a sword the man's way. He smiled at Skye, displaying his rotten teeth again. 'Twould be prettier, she thought, to bed a warthog.

She would die first, she vowed to herself.

Which was a growing possibility!

She quickly bemoaned the warning she had given the man—she should have slain him while he attacked Tara unarmed. He was a pirate, an animal, but she had not been able to slay an unarmed man. Now it seemed that she would pay for her morality—and stupidity.

"Sir!" she snapped out, tossing her skirts behind her, finding her position.

And it seemed that Old Samuel was soon as dismayed as she, for the fight went on. Skye knew that he had assumed her threats were idle; he could not know that before her father had shipped her off to Mrs. Poindexter's School for Refined Ladies, he had sent to France to hire her a world-renowned instructor when she had determined to learn the art of swordplay. Samuel had learned the art upon the sea. He was strong, but he knew no finesse.

She could best Samuel. She knew that she could.

But when that was done, there would still be another twenty to fifty pirates . . . perhaps more . . . to fight off.

"Methinks you are no lady!" Samuel called to her. A mean look crossed his face. He was not fighting for a prize anymore; he was fighting for his life, and he knew it. He tried to shatter her strength, slamming down upon her blade. She was too quick. She parried, and feinted, and eluded his anger. She leaped high upon a charred sail beam, and when he slammed downward, she ducked, and flew into a pirouette, and brought her blade slicing through his midsection.

Samuel died, staring at her in rage and disbelief until the fire left his eyes to be replaced by the cold glaze of death.

She swirled around. She realized suddenly that the ship had grown silent. There were no more small skirmishes being fought upon the deck. The officers who'd survived had swords cast against their throats. And they, like the pirates, stared at her.

One-Eyed Jack slowly clapped his hands together, eyeing her with a new respect. "Madame, in the end, it is me that you will meet."

There was little that she could do; nothing that she could say.

She raised her sword. Her eyes lit upon the lot of them, and she backed against the mast, looking to her left and to her right, awaiting her next opponent.

It was to be the youth. He rose and spat upon the deck. Someone tossed him a sword. He bowed mockingly.

"Milady?"

Then he lunged forward.

He was an easy opponent, too easy. He hadn't the strength or barbaric skill of the older man. Soon Skye saw sweat beading his brow. They moved across the deck, and men gave way.

"Lady Skye!"

For a second, a mere second, Davey's anguished cry distracted her. He warned her that a second man had drawn a sword to come up behind her. A balding pirate with a red kerchief about his head popped Davey hard on the head with the butt of his pistol, and the boy sank silently to the deck.

She started instinctively for his side. The blond youth made a swipe toward her, slicing through her skirt. She swung about just in time to save her flesh from the tip of the blade.

"Go ahead, milady, skewer the young hearty!" the balding pirate encouraged. "The boy's not dead; 'e sleeps!"

"No more interference!" One-Eyed Jack called out. "If she's as feisty beneath the covers, I want her alive!"

This was a game to them, she realized, this fight, this murder, this death. And until they drowned in a pool of their own blood, they would play it.

Until she fell. Until she was at the mercy of the one-eyed creature who watched the savagery with such gusto, and waited.

"On guard, monsieur," she told the youth. "To the death."

"Or . . . other." The boy laughed.

Skye stepped forward. Then she fell forward, stumbling along with the others. Suddenly, out of the grayness of the day, came another monster.

The ship was rammed from portside. Pirates and officers alike teetered and grasped for balance and looked about in dismay.

No one had seen the ship that had come upon them out of the murk and tempest of the day. None had seen her ghostly shape or her haunting form as she came upon them, a wraith from the sea.

None had seen her. . . .

Until she rammed the injured ship.

And now, Skye's duel was interrupted, for new screams filled the air. Skye had hoped in an instant that it might be rescue.

That hope was quickly dashed, like the deck beneath a cannon's fire, for it was not rescue that had come.

It was a second pirate ship.

Muskets flared; screams rose. The screech and thunder of grappling hooks was heard again, and from the rigging of the newcomer, men leaped down upon the decks, and battle was joined once more.

"'Tis the Silver Hawk!" someone called. "In the rigging! 'Tis the Hawk himself! Lay down your arms, and he'll do no murder!"

"Bah, you coward!" another man called out. "One-Eyed Jack is me captain, and I'll not grovel before the Hawk."

"There, there upon the ropes! See him, he comes!"

Skye forgot her own opponent. Her sword rested upon her torn skirts as she stared upward.

Indeed, he was coming. The Silver Hawk, as they called him.

He was clad in black from head to toe, his shirt seemed to be of black silk; his frockcoat, silver-threaded, was black brocade. His boots, thigh high, were black, as were his skintight breeches. A black hat with silver eagle plumes rested upon his head. A full set of neatly trimmed silver-and-black whiskers covered his chin. A black mustache curled stylishly upon his lip.

And for all of his elegance of dress, he moved upon the ropes with skill and speed and uncanny ease. In seconds, he was upon the deck, and before his boots struck wood, he was engaged in battle.

"Surrender, me hearties, and leave me the prize. Your choice, messieurs, to die!" he called, his deep voice a thunder that challenged the sky, that challenged the very tempest of the day.

Pirates stepped back, and pirates stepped forward. The proud old-timer met and defied him first, and lay down so quickly and silently to die that Skye barely saw the battle.

She saw his blade, the silver blade of the Silver Hawk, and she saw the striking, magical grace with which he leaped and danced and moved then upon the deck. No man challenged him alone. They came against him in groups, a pair first, a trio when they fell. And through it all, Skye watched in amazement, unaware of her danger.

Until more of his men came upon the deck. Until fighting erupted all around her once again.

"Take hostages of the crew!" came a shout, and Skye was aware that the deep, commanding voice belonged to the pirate, the Silver Hawk.

"Hawk, I'll kill you!" One-Eyed Jack roared out.

"Valiant words, Jack! Match the action to them!" the Hawk retorted.

And the men met with a vicious clash of steel. The fighting, all around Skye, was suddenly fast and furious once again.

The blond youth swung around abruptly, his face a mask of fury. Skye, startled, raised her sword to parry his lethal blow without a second to spare. She could watch no one else, for she was suddenly thrust into a violent struggle for her own life. The blond furiously lunged toward her. She leaped aside and parried, and caught his throat with the tip of her sword. With a peculiar whishing sound, he fell before her. She gasped, staggering. She could hear the clang of steel around her.

And then, suddenly, she could not.

The deck had fallen silent once again.

And even the wind had died.

Gray rose around her. The gray of the storm that teased and threatened, the gray from black powder and shot, from battle and burning. It rose like a curious fog, as if she had been cast upon the London stage.

And all those around her were curious players.

Once again, pirates ranged about the ship's deck. The crew, she saw, had been ushered toward the aft cabin and were being held there at sword's point.

The second officer held young Davey, and Davey, coming to, held his own head.

One-Eyed Jack would never leer her way again. He lay dead in a pool of blood by the mizzenmast.

And resting upon the fine teak balustrade leading to the helm was the pirate, Silver Hawk.

Silver Hawk, standing well over six feet tall, with his elegantly plumed hat, his black-gloved hands resting upon the hilt of his sword, the point of that sword scarring the deck. He stared at Skye, and her fallen, blond-haired opponent.

"Bravo, milady. Now be a good girl and cast down your sword."

He had taken the ship, that much was obvious. But she had not surrendered to the first set of pirates; she was not about to surrender to this new rogue.

She shook her head. He cocked his own in curious surprise and pushed away from the balustrade, coming toward her.

"You'll not surrender, milady?"

"Never," she said softly.

A hysterical cry came her way. "Throw it down! Milady, throw it down, he'll let you live!" It was Bess. She'd been thrust into the arms of one of the new pirates, a young fellow with dark eyes and striking features. "Mother of God, milady, he'll let us live, he'll—"

"Shush now, ye hussy!" the dark-haired man interrupted her, squeezing her tight about the middle. "Captain," he complained. "What'll we do with these 'uns here?"

The Silver Hawk shook his head, his eyes never leaving Skye's. "Whatever you so desire, Peter. Whatever you so desire."

A boisterous cry went up among the men.

And then young Davey suddenly broke away from the young ship's officer who held him. He lunged toward the Silver Hawk.

The pirate moved back with the speed and agility of a tiger. Davey would die, and Skye knew it.

"No!" she screamed. She cast herself between the pirate and the lad. Davey flew against her and fell to the deck. Sprawled in her petticoats and torn skirts, Skye tried to rise. The pirate stood before her, reaching down a hand.

She ignored it.

She managed to roll, and she leaped to her feet, angling back, her blade wagging before her.

The pirate paused, laughing. He bowed to her very deeply. "As you wish it, milady." He cast his left hand behind his back, and raised his sword. "Someone get the lad. He seems to offer his lady a foolish loyalty, and I'd not want to slay him for it!"

A man came forward for Davey. The boy struggled fiercely, but Skye could pay him no more mind. The Silver Hawk stepped toward her, his blade flashed.

The clash was terrible. She could barely keep her hand upon the hilt of her sword.

She had asked for death. She could not fight this man. Yet if she did not fight, didn't she face a fate worse than death at his hands? She did not know, she only knew that the battle was engaged, and that if she turned to run, he would probably cleave her into two pieces. The man reeked of his bloody strength, of his fascinating agility, of a masculinity so strong that it caused her to quake as well as shiver, to falter when she should have found courage.

"Milady!" he acknowledged, dipping back, allowing her to regain her grip upon her sword.

"Sir!" she said, and rallied.

The dark-haired man holding Bess suddenly tossed her to another, stepping forward. "Captain, the lady's at a disadvantage! Her skirts!"

"Shed them!" the Silver Hawk ordered.

Skye nearly screamed. The handsome young pirate raised his sword and it slashed through the air. She was not struck at all, but her cumbersome skirts and petticoats were sheared from her form, and she was left to fight with her hose and sheer shift protruding from the tattered remnants of her gown. Crimson flooded her face, but she raised her chin and did not gaze upon the humiliating exposure of her form. None of it could matter now. She could cling to her pride, for it was all she had left, and if she could find courage, he could not take it from her.

"Milady?"

"Sir, as you have ordered, I am ready."

"I give you leave to attack, Lady . . ."

"Kinsdale."

"Kinsdale!"

She thought that he gave pause then, that she had startled him with her name, that he did, indeed, know it well. Whatever, his pause did seem to give her an advantage, and so she did attack, thrusting forward, seeking his heart.

Deftly, quickly, he parried her thrusts. She feinted again, he parried. He backed to the balustrade and leaped up upon it. Caught up in the fray of battle, Skye followed him. He did not attack at all, she realized too late. He merely watched her with his eyes alive, silver gray like the day, like the color of his blade, like the mist of the tempest about them.

A cry went up. Laughing, applauding, the pirates followed along behind them. There was no escape, Skye realized, but that didn't seem to matter anymore. Her arm felt like lead; it was so tired, she thought that it might drop right off with the sword. Now each clang of steel seemed to echo and reverberate throughout her body. She shuddered with each thrust, and she kept driving faster and faster, seeking some vulnerability.

The man had none.

A dark and sleekly savage beast, he barely breathed hard as he caught and fended off her every thrust and parry. Surely, she seemed the wild one, for her cape was lost, her skirts torn and shredded, and her hair flew about her in disarray.

He was deadly calm, a smile twisted into his features beneath the display of mustache and beard. His accent had been English, she thought, or was it? He was whipcord lean and hard-muscled, and the more she realized that she could not win, the more she became determined that she should do so.

"Watch her now, Hawk, they say she knows how to threaten the right part of a man, or the wrong part, depending on a way of thinking."

"Can't imagine the captain with a high voice!"

"She'll never touch him with steel!"

"Never in a coon's age!"

"She's desperate, Captain!"

She was desperate, very. And so she was trying for desperate measures. She allowed her sword to drop, and when he stepped near, she sliced upward with all her strength, just missing the length of his thigh. He leaped back. Laughter rose. His eyes met hers, burning silver with the challenge, burning silver with stark warning.

"Mam'selle, I begin to think that you are no lady," he said, coming to the same conclusion as her previous opponent.

"You, sir, are most certainly no gentle knight."

"Alas, I am a pirate."

"And I, sir, your victim. And therefore, I will fight you with any means at my disposal."

"Is that so?"

"It is." She had warned him. She swirled with her sword, slicing the air. And she was nearly victorious. With any other man, her thrust would have been lethal. She would have slit him cleanly from his groin to the gullet.

But the Silver Hawk moved too quickly. He sensed her movement and responded to it, fighting with uncanny grace and strength, and it was a combination she feared that she could not match.

"Eh, Captain, we warned you!" someone called out.

"That you did!" he replied pleasantly, his voice loud. Then he dropped his tone and spoke to her softly. "Careful, mam'selle, lest I discover the same wicked rules of swordplay."

"Have you rules, monsieur, of your own? I had not thought that you knew the meaning of rules, or of fair play."

"You receive fair play right now, milady."

"Sir, you are a bastard knave, and give me nothing. What man honors himself to fight a lady?"

She thought that she had found his weakness, for he paused, and it seemed that he mused over the question. She had to best him, she had to! And she had to do so soon, for her strength was waning.

She thrust forward with all of her strength.

He parried with a single, swift blow. The staggering strength of it caught her unaware. So far, all that he had done was tease her, play with her. He hadn't used a tenth of his power, or skill.

Now he did.

And the force threatened to break her arm. She cried out, falling as her sword was sent flying high, until it blended with the silver and gray of the day, soaring in the sky . . . then splashing softly into the water.

Skye, cast down upon the deck, gasped desperately for breath, her arm aching, her head spinning.

He smiled down at her. "The man who is challenged by a lady must fight her, mam'selle," he said, replying to her at last. "She gives him no choice." He looked up and called out in his deep, ringing voice, " 'Tis all over now, me lads!"

His dark-haired lackey called out. "All over but the cleanup."

The cleanup. And what was that? Skye wondered. She came up upon her elbows, her gaze upon the pirate's glittering, silver-blue eyes. He returned her stare.

"The hostages—" someone called.

The pirate Silver Hawk crossed his arms over his chest. His full, sensual mouth curved into a curious smile.

He stepped forward.

Skye inched away upon her haunches, never turning from him, never losing his silver gaze.

"Take the officers down below. Send One-Eyed Jack's men down to the hold."

"The women—"

"You know what to do with them," he said softly.

The dark-haired man strode forward. "I shall take the Lady Kinsdale—"

"Oh, no," the Silver Hawk said. And he stepped forward. He planted one booted foot on either side of Skye, catching the tattered remnants of her once-beautiful gown and strands of her golden hair beneath his boots. She tried to wriggle away, but cried out as her hair pulled. She stopped, gritting her teeth and looking up past the long, steel-muscled length of his legs to the breadth of his chest and onward to his rock-hard features.

He lowered himself slowly over her, imprisoning her between his powerful thighs.

Their eyes met in a sizzling tempest of fire.

"Get away, me mates," he said very softly. "This one is mine."

And he reached for her, just as a jagged flash of lightning tore across the heavens once again.

His touch was no less powerful than that fire.

2

EFORE SHE KNEW IT, SKYE WAS STANDING AGAIN upon her own feet. He had drawn her up against him. Contact with his hard muscular body caused her eyes to widen, and he smiled satanically at her betrayal of alarm. Furiously, she tried to squirm from his hold. The sea even seemed to play to his dictate, for a swell took hold of the ship, careening her ever more tightly against him. He held his stance well, riding the sea as an accomplished horseman might ride a wild mount. He laughed aloud, seeing the combination of fear and anger in her delicate features.

"Why, milady! You met my steel with such admirable courage. Would you meet the man himself with anything less?"

"I would not meet the man at all," she retorted, which only served to amuse him further and bring out a burst of laughter from his rowdy crew. He laughed, too, as he held her. Then another bolt of lightning lit up the heavens as if it threatened to strike the main mast. Thunder burst in a furious roar, and the pirate quieted his laughter to a curious smile. "Alas, milady, but you will have to wait, I fear. The gods of wind and water seek to keep us apart."

"May the gods let you choke—" Skye began, but she never finished, for she cried out as she found herself lifted and cast over his shoulder with determined force. He had played with her, she realized, but he played no more. The day had made him sober. She struggled against him, but he ignored her, holding her firmly with ease, and striding across the deck, shouting commands. "Fenwick, you will captain our prize—"

"Let me down!" Skye screamed, pummeling furiously against his shoulders. "Let me—"

"Milady, shut up!" he commanded, and she discovered herself choking out a humiliated cry, for his hand landed upon her rump with a fearsome power, bringing tears to her eyes. She was momentarily silenced, and he continued speaking to his men, striding for the rigging as he did so. "Take care with our prisoners, for we will demand ransoms. One-Eyed Jack's men to the brig if they choose to surrender. Take the guns and any prizes from his ship, then send her to the bottom of the sea."

"Aye, aye, Captain!" came a dozen replies.

"Get your hands off me!" Skye swore, straining against him. It was a futile effort. With his left hand he caught hold of the mainmast rigging and crawled upon it. The ship pitched and swayed violently again. He was a madman, she decided. The sea was a whirlpool, the wind was vicious, and he ignored them

283

both. Like a wraith he took his ease with the rigging. Rather than fighting him, Skye suddenly discovered herself clinging to him as he crawled high upon the rigging to catch hold of a free-swinging rope. She screamed in sheer terror as she realized his intent.

"Relax—Lady Kinsdale. Relax, and hold tight," he advised her, but otherwise he gave her fear no consideration.

Then a moment later, it seemed that they were flying. They fell against the coolness of the wind and the soft gray of the sky. She didn't know if she was plunging to her death or soaring to the heavens.

She did neither, for in seconds he had made an easy leap to the deck of his own ship. Dizzy, Skye struggled to see around herself, and became aware of more of his crew, most of them barefoot, clad only in cotton shirts and knee breeches and many of them whiskered and bearded. They seemed to be of all ages, and to a man, they smiled and waved at her with good humor. It seemed they were loyal to their captain. A cheer went up as he landed nimbly upon the deck with her. Skye thought that they would both tumble at last upon the wooden decking, for the ship swayed starboard as if it would capsize.

Silver Hawk did not fall or falter. His men, too, held their ground, and raised their voices once again in a loud salute. Their captain lifted a hand to acknowledge them, then swung about with her, his prize, in his arms still.

Skye pressed against his back, seeking to plead with his crew of cutthroats.

"I'm worth a fortune!" she cried suddenly. "See that he leaves me be this instant, and my father will reward you greatly!"

"Will he now?" a graybeard called pleasantly.

"Good night, milady!" said another, and they all bowed to her deeply, ignoring her plight.

She cried out in rage again, once more struggling to free herself from her ignominious position upon the pirate's shoulder.

He spun around again, seeing her eyes as she raised herself upon his shoulders. "What is this!" he said in mock protest. "Why, gents, I swear to you that just seconds ago, she held on to me like an adoring mistress. Women are fickle, are they not?" He did not desire a reply, nor did he get one, and the humor fell from his voice as he spoke again. "I'll be at the helm, me lads. The wind is howling ever louder. Like a woman."

"Which is more deadly, Cap'n, do you think? The lady wind that rages upon the sea, or the Lady Kinsdale, shrieking upon your back?"

More laughter rose. "Why," replied the captain, "the lady upon my back, of course!"

He turned about and strode with her now upon his own ship, past the mainmast and forward. A set of handsome, intricately carved double doors lay before them. He set his hand upon a brass knob and pushed inward. Barely a moment later Skye found herself falling hard upon the large carved bunk in the far starboard corner of the cabin. She gasped for breath, realizing suddenly that the remains of her petticoats and gown were rising precariously to her hips and that she was lying before him nearly naked. She had no doubts as to his intent, but she planned to fight him to the very death if need be. She might lose, but she would fight.

He stood above her, shadowed by the sudden darkness in the cabin, and she rolled as best she could against the wall, pulling the fine-knit bed covering over her exposed limbs as she did so. She tried to meet his eyes in the sudden shadow to dare him to protest, but she could read nothing of his gaze, and fear set into her once again even as she assured herself that she would fight forever.

If she could only see his face now!

But she could not. She could see only the hard, lean length of the man, a silhouette before her. He would pounce upon her, she thought. He was like a hawk indeed, circling his prey, waiting only for the precise right moment to pounce down upon her.

Fear seized her, and in panic she thought to bolt, not knowing where she would run. She tried to leap from the bunk, but landed instead within his arms.

"Bastard!" she hissed, near tears as his arms wound around her.

"Alas, lover, I do apologize!" he said, pressing her back. "That you are so eager to consummate this affair, but I must leave you, milady!"

"Eager! I loathe you, I long to skewer you through—"

His laughter cut her off. She could see his eyes suddenly, or something of their deep blue flame and searing humor. "Take care!" he warned her, and there was a razor's edge to the sound of his voice. "Lest you be the one . . . skewered through!"

She knew not if he meant that he would slay her, or if his words carried a more intimate meaning, but his laughter and the soft touch of his breath against her cheeks made her tremble once again, and she braced hard against the steel power of his arms and chest. She could never fight this man, she realized. He was in the prime of life, muscular, powerful, and skillful. She could not best him with a sword, and she would never best him with her fists. She waged her war with a vengeance, and he merely smiled at her futile efforts. He laughed. He gloated. He was completely assured of his triumph in all things. He held her steady against the continual rock and sway of the ship.

"Let me go!" she cried, and she sought to rake her nails over his bearded cheek, but he caught her hand, and the pressure he grimly set against it caused her to cry out, and give up, sagging against him. She became acutely aware of him then as a man, for the black material of his shirt and breeches was thin, and her own clothing gave her no barrier. He was strikingly warm and alive, vibrant. Energy as hot and powerful as the lightning that lit up the heavens beyond them seemed to surround him. To leap from him.

To touch her.

"Please!" she gasped out.

He pulled her closer, and his words curiously seemed to caress the softness of her face. "Where would you go, milady? Would you race out and join the crew, and entertain them, one and all? Or had you thought of the sea? A watery tomb, cold and eternal? I think not." He released her suddenly. She fell back upon the bed, and his eyes were captured once again by the shadows. She did not think of fighting. She did not think of anything. She did not even think to shrink from his gaze as she lay in dishevelment, her shirts and bodice torn, so very much of her flesh bared to him. She lay back, barely daring to breathe.

She did not even move when he reached out to touch her. His fingers brushed lightly over the rise of her breasts as they spilled from her corset.

She did not even scream, for the touch was brief and gentle, and so quickly gone it might not have been.

"Do not fear, Lady Kinsdale, I will be back."

She came up upon an elbow then, a certain courage returning to her as he whispered out her name.

"You will pay for this treatment of me!" she cried. "My father will see that you pay, my fiancé will see that you pay—"

"Will he, mam'selle?" he inquired. Hands on his hips, he cocked his head to the side.

"Of course!" Her voice only faltered slightly. "I am to marry Lord Cameron. He will see that you hang!"

"How intriguing. Well, I hope that he is a man of selfless honor, lady, for all of Williamsburg knows that you have spurned your betrothed and sworn that you will not marry."

Skye gasped, amazed that such gossip could have reached the colony before she had arrived there herself. Then she was furious with herself because her reaction had given away so very much.

"He—he is a man of honor!" she swore quickly.

"And then again," the pirate captain mused, ignoring her words, "I have heard that Lord Cameron is no more eager for this marriage than you are, but out of respect for your father he has not—as yet—opposed the promises made by his father when he was but a lad of ten and you were within your cradle."

"How dare you—" she began, her voice low and shaking.

"Oh, mam'selle, I am afraid that you will soon discover that I am a man to dare anything. But for the moment, if you will be so kind as to excuse me—"

"Sir, there is no excuse for your vile existence, none at all!"

He merely smiled. "Adieu, milady."

"Wait!" she cried.

He paused, arching a brow. "What, mam'selle?"

"You can't—you can't leave me in here!"

He gazed at her in startled surprise. "Lady Kinsdale, it is the finest cabin on the ship, I assure you. You will be safe."

"Safe!" she screeched.

He grimaced at her with casual humor. "Safe—from the storm, milady. Until later," he said. He bowed with courtly gallantry, and then he was gone. Skye heard his long strides take him to the doors. They closed behind him, and she heard the sure sound of a bolt sliding home. She was locked in, alone and wretched, and surrounded by darkness, and by fear.

She couldn't bear it. The darkness pressed in upon her. The walls seemed to press closer and closer.

She had been trapped within the cabin on her own ship, she reminded herself. But there had been light then. Not this terrible darkness.

It seemed that endless moments passed in which she just lay there, listening to the wind. It shrieked, it groaned, it screamed. It rose over the sounds of the slashing rain that had begun, and like a woman, it seemed to cry. The ship did not stay still for a second, but rolled and tossed and pitched and spun, and in time Skye realized that she was clinging to the sheets and knit coverlet. She lay there quaking, and when she wasn't fearing the awful darkness, she feared the man. She shouldn't be fearing the man, she told herself, not at that moment. She should be praying that they survive the storm, for she had never seen a night so savage.

Lightning flashed, illuminating the cabin. It was a vast space, she thought, for a ship, set high upon the top deck of his fleet ship. The cabin! She needed to think about the cabin. It was large enough for his bunk and shelves and tables and chairs and a stove, trunks, and a built-in armoire. The high square windows probably looked out on the churning sea by day, Skye thought, but now they were covered by rich velvet maroon drapes.

The glow of lightning no longer illuminated the cabin, but Skye continued to register in her mind the things that she had seen. The shelves were lined with books, the desk was polished mahogany, and the chairs were heavy oak, upholstered in brocade. It was an elegant cabin, a cabin for a captain of prestige and means and manners, not the cabin of a savage pirate.

He'd seized the ship from some poor suffering fool! she reminded herself. Indeed, he was a thief of the vilest sort, a rapist, a murderer, a scourge upon the seas.

And he would come back to this cabin.

Unless she lay trapped forever in the darkness.

Growing more and more agitated, she tried to rise. The sway of the ship sent her flying back down to the bunk. She tried again. She moved carefully this time, holding to the wooden bunk frame, then plunging toward the doors. She slammed against them, and nearly gave way to a flurry of tears. They were bolted tight. There was no way out for her.

She sank against the doors, fearful that the ship would sink, and that she would be caught within the cabin.

Skye brought her fingers pressing against her temples. Fear came against her in great, suffocating waves then. It was worse than facing the pirates, it was worse than facing ruthless steel. She could not stand darkness; she could not bear it. Ever since she had been a child, on the awful day that her mother had died, she had feared being locked away in the darkness.

She leaped back to her feet. She beat against the door, screaming, crying until she was hoarse. Tears streamed down her face, and her voice rose higher and higher, rivaling the cries of the wind. She beat against the wood until her hands were raw. Her voice grew hoarse, and she sank to the floor, nearly delirious.

Then suddenly the door was thrown open. A man, young, dark-haired and clad in nothing but knee breeches, stood there. Rain dripped from his features and sluiced down his chest.

"Lady, what ails thee—" he began, but he was never able to go further for she sprang to her feet and leaped past him, straight into the riveting rain, into the tempest of the wind. She heard the shouts of the men as they fought to stabilize the ship. She heard the waves, lashing hard against the bow. The force of the wind seemed terrible. She didn't realize its strength until it whipped her bodily about, and she was cast to the deck as if by a heavenly hand.

An oath was suddenly roared out above her. She moved her hand over her eyes, shielding them from the onslaught of wind and rain. Hands were reaching for her and she was plucked back up and sheltered by broad, strong arms.

"What is she doing here?" Silver Hawk demanded.

"She raced by me. I'd no idea, Captain—"

"Get to the helm!" His eyes lowered to her. "I'll take you back to the cabin."

"No!" she whispered, but he had already brought her there with his long, determined strides. He shoved the door open with his foot and cast her down to the floor with a vengeance.

"Fool!" he swore to her.

She ignored him, and sat there in a spill of tattered, damp clothing and wind-tossed hair, cold and wet and shivering.

Lightning scorched the night and created a golden backdrop for the darkness of his form. It shone in upon Skye where she knelt upon the floor in her tatters of velvet and lace, her hair free and tangled and spilling all around her.

He stood before her and she stared upon his black boots. They glistened with the glow of the rain that had drenched him. She looked up slowly. His shirt and breeches were skintight against his body, plastered to his form.

Skye drew in a quivering breath that sounded like a sob.

"No! Don't go!"

She was hurt! he thought, and he strode quickly toward her, hunkering down by her side and lifting her chin. She trembled. From head to toe she trembled. But as he looked at her he saw that though her eyes were wide and dilated, she showed no injury.

"What in God's name are you up to?" he demanded.

"Let me out of here!" she told him.

"Nay, lady!" he said harshly. "You've seen the storm!" Her words were a ploy. The fool girl meant to flee him at any cost.

"Please!" she whispered, and despite his better judgment, the curious plea tore at his heart. He had never seen a woman fight as she had earlier. Perhaps she was as good at acting as she was at swordplay.

He shook his head with impatience. "Lady Kinsdale, the storm is lessened, but it has not ended. You must remain here." He stood, and headed toward the doors.

"No!" she cried, leaping to her feet. She caught his hand. "Take me with you! Please, take me with you—"

"You are mad!"

"No, I—"

"The winds nearly swept you over, Lady Kinsdale. And you are worth far too much for such a fate."

"Don't leave me!" she pleaded.

He paused, looking at her hands, small and delicate, upon his own. They were as pale as cream and as soft as velvet. Her nails were long as were her fingers, and they spoke of a genteel elegance. Amazed, he looked into her eyes.

She wasn't looking at him. She was, but her eyes went through him, and beyond him.

He took her hand, freeing his own. "I cannot take you out there."

"Then give me a light."

"Milady—"

"Please!" He stared at her, trying to fathom this woman, and she took his hesitation as a denial. "Please!" she repeated. Her voice lowered and cracked. "Leave me with a light, sir, and I swear that I shall . . ."

Intrigued, he paused, watching her carefully. "You shall what, mam'selle?"

"I shall—" She paused, but went on then. "I shall repay the kindness."

"You shall repay . . . the kindness?"

"Yes!" she screamed.

He arched a brow, inclining his head, taking his time. "Milady, my apologies, but I would that you be a bit more specific. We pirates are known for being dim-witted."

She wanted to kick him. She might well have done so except that he seemed to sense her intent and carefully caught her by the shoulders, drawing her against him. His eyes bored into hers. She felt his breath once more against her cheeks, against her lips. Curiously, his breath was sweet. It smelled of mint. His teeth were good, his own, and clean and white and straight and handsome, flashing with his every dangerous smile. His beard covered most of his face, but she thought that it was probably a striking face beneath the dark mat, ruthless perhaps, and formidable, but striking nonetheless.

She was thinking this of a pirate. A man who intended to rape her, and barter her back to her father or fiancé.

And worse, she was ready to promise him anything, just so long as he didn't leave her in the darkness again.

"What are you saying, Lady Kinsdale?" he demanded softly.

"I will do anything you want!" she lashed out. "Just so long as you don't leave me again in the darkness." She hesitated again and then whispered desperately, "I promise!"

He stared at her long and hard. Rather than being pleased by her promise, he seemed to be furious. He shoved her away from him. She stumbled, but she did not fall. He strode across the room to the bookcase and she saw that there was a lantern there, protected from falling off the shelf by wooden laths, just as the books were protected from being thrown about the cabin.

Watching her with that same curious fury, he found a striker and flint and went to the stove first, lighting the coals. As the glow rose around him, Skye realized just how cold she had been. He must have been freezing, too, she thought, for he was drenched. Despite herself, she found her eyes wandering over him. Muscle and sinew were delineated clearly.

His eyes fell upon her and she found herself shivering. With great deliberation he found a length of match and lit the lamp from the fire in the Dutch stove. He set the lamp back in its place. "Don't touch it or the stove," he said harshly. "I would not survive the storm to burn to a crisp upon the sea."

"I won't let anything burn. I promise."

"You are quick to hand out promises, Lady Kinsdale," he commented.

She shrugged, staring at the warmth of the fire, ignoring him. He kept watching her. She shivered anew with the warning tone of his next words.

"You will keep any promises you make to me, milady."

She nodded, playing only for the moment. Light and warmth flooded the room, and courage began to seep back into her along with the warmth. Then he took two steps toward her and she knew that he meant to touch her then and there. Despite herself she screamed. He ignored her, catching her shoulders, dragging her close. "No!" she gasped, seeking to stop his hands as they fell upon her bodice. Little was left of her gown; he found the ties of her corset and tugged upon them.

"Wait!"

"Your promise, milady!"

"You said you were going back out! The storm! The wind, it still rages, stop, please, you must—stop!"

"Be damned with the ship, mam'selle!"

"We'll drown!"

"Happily shall I die in your arms!"

Her bodice came free and her breasts spilled forth. Color bathed her face, but he barely glanced at her, swinging her around and plucking her torn wet gown over her head. Desperately she flailed against him, but managed only to entangle herself in her clothing. Then suddenly she was naked, shorn of her gown and corset and even her shift, and left only in her stockings and garters. She stared from the pool of her clothing cast upon the floor to his face, and his eyes so cold upon her, denying his taunting words. He took stock of her in a calculating assessment. His gaze was so icily cold that she did not even think to cover herself, to draw her arms about her. He did not in the least seem to appreciate what he saw; indeed, it was almost with disdain that he swept his eyes over her body. He hated her, she thought. But then he took a step toward her again and she screamed with pure primal dread.

He did not touch her. He wrenched the knit coverlet from the bed and tossed it upon her nakedness. She stumbled to her knees as she caught it, sweeping it around her shoulders and hovering there, her eyes lowered.

"You'll die of pneumonia and be worthless to me, mam'selle, if you do not dry off," he said curtly. She did not answer him. She saw his boots before her lowered eyes. His gleaming black boots. She did not look up.

The boots moved. He turned around and strode toward the door. He paused there and spoke very softly. "Don't deceive yourself, Lady Kinsdale. I have not forgotten your promise. You do give your oath freely, mam'selle. And with little meaning, so it appears. What you promise to me, you will give."

She heard the slam of the doors against the wind, and then he was gone.

Skye pulled the cover more tightly around herself. The cabin slowly became warm, and it was bright and comfortable.

And she slowly ceased to shiver, and when she did, she hated herself. The fear! It was so awful, and so ridiculous. She had humiliated herself before the very dregs of the earth because of it. She had made a promise to a pirate!

Suddenly she was shivering again, remembering the way that he had looked at her, as if he hated her. As if he knew her, or knew something about her, deep inside, and hated her for it. What?

Why should she care?

She should cling desperately to every moment that kept her away from him.

He teased her now. He taunted her. He would come back, and it would be all the worse for her because he hated her, too. . . .

At least he had all of his teeth. And he didn't smell bad. His husky whispers carried the scent of mint. . . .

What was she thinking?

Skye bolted to her feet and raced to his desk. She tore open drawer after drawer. He was a pirate, wasn't he? He had to be carrying about some kind of grog.

But his desk was empty. As she stood there perplexed, the ship took a sudden harsh keel and she landed flat upon her derriere. She swore softly and wished heartily she were back in London. London! Suddenly she loved it. There was so much there! Not the struggling new city of Williamsburg. In London there were balls and there was the theater and the opera and the elegance of court. In London there were rakes and rogues, of course, but they were of the civil kind, and a lady could not fall from virtue unless it was her choice. In London, there were no pirates!

She had loved her home in Williamsburg before she had left it. She had loved the beautiful streets, so carefully laid out when it had been determined to move the capital of the Virginia Colony from Jamestown to the place that they had previously called Middle Plantation. She had loved the College of William and Mary, and the capitol building they had built. The homes were clean and bright with white picket fences, and sometimes it seemed a raw place, and sometimes it seemed incredibly exciting to watch it grow. When she had been a child they had begun the grand mansion for the governor, and now, so father had written, Governor Spotswood was moving in. At one time, it had been so beautiful to her. . . .

But now she was being forced to return home to marry a stranger who lived out in one of the godforsaken plantations.

No. She was a pirate's captive. A plaything. And the pirate didn't think that her fiancé would avenge her honor. Perhaps, the pirate had suggested, Lord Petroc Cameron would not even offer to pay a ransom.

Her eyes fell upon a rosewood caddy, that she hadn't noticed earlier, by the side of his desk. There was a decanter of brandy and four stemmed glasses there, held in place by brass racks. Skye quickly stumbled to her feet and filled a glass with the brandy. It was hot and it burned, and it was the most delicious drink she had ever tasted.

She coughed and sputtered, and filled another glass.

The light, the warmth, and the alcohol quickly restored her courage. She railed at herself for having been such an awful coward, but the moment was past now, and the damage done. She had to look to the future. Setting her glass down once again, she began to search through the desk. There had to be a weapon here, somewhere.

There wasn't. All she could find were ledgers and maps. Frustrated, she slammed the drawers.

She paused for a moment. The ship was not swaying so violently anymore. The storm was breaking.

He could come back at any moment.

Inspired with renewed energy, Skye dove toward one of his handsome traveling trunks. She cast it open and came upon an array of stockings and breeches and vests and shirts and coats. They were in differing styles and fabrics, but they shared one common trait. All were in the color black.

"Damn!" she swore softly, despairing that she could find some help for herself. Then she lifted the last of the shirts and discovered a blade at the bottom of the trunk.

She gasped, for she had come upon a short broadsword, a two-foot weapon honed to a razor's sharpness on both edges. She held it in her hands, dreaming of freedom. Then the blood drained from her face as she wondered how she would manage once she had slain the captain.

His men would slice her to ribbons.

She could capture him. She could hold him hostage and demand that his men bring them into the Chesapeake Bay, and down the James. Perhaps she could capture the entire ship.

She sighed, shuddering. She would not capture the ship. But neither would this pirate, the Silver Hawk, ever touch her again and live to tell of it.

There were footsteps beyond the door, coming very close to it. She froze for a moment, then they moved away. She heard laughter now. Voices rising over the sound of the wind.

They had bested the storm.

Skye hurried toward the bunk. Wrapping herself, she put the evil blade close within the coverlet, then scurried as close to the wall as she could. Her heart raced furiously. What should she do? If she feigned sleep, perhaps she could buy herself more time. He would have to be exhausted when he returned. He had battled the other pirates, he had battled her, and he had battled the storm.

She heard footsteps again. And again, they paused before the double doors. She had just begun to relax, thinking that the footsteps would move away again, when the doors flew open.

And the Silver Hawk stepped into the cabin.

Skye closed her eyes and hoped that she appeared very small.

And very pathetic. Then she wished that she had not curled so completely toward the wall, for her back was exposed to him.

Every fool knew not to expose his or her back to the enemy!

But she dared not turn, lest he suspect that she was awake. And so she strained to listen, hoping desperately that he would leave her be.

She heard him close and bolt the doors, and she heard the sounds of his boots against the wood as he moved into the cabin. He paused before the stove, and she could imagine him warming his hands. Seconds later, she nearly screamed, for the bunk shifted as he sat down upon it. His boots clunked to the floor. Then she could hear little, but she was horribly aware of what he was doing. His sodden shirt struck the floor to be followed by his breeches and hose. She heard the curious smacking sounds as the wet fabric slapped against the floorboards.

She waited for him to touch her, or to stretch out beside her.

He did not.

He rose and silently padded across the cabin. She heard a tinkle of glass and knew that he had gone for the brandy. His soft laughter assured her that he realized that she had been into the liquor already.

He poured himself a drink, and then there was absolute silence for so long that Skye feared she would scream and slit her own throat with the double-edged blade.

She heard nothing else.

She felt his touch. Soft, light, and subtle. It came against her so suddenly that she barely refrained from jerking away.

His fingers ran over her blanketed shoulder, and down the length of her back. He paused, then ran his hand over the protruding curve of her derriere.

She bit into her mouth to keep her silence, and she waited, praying.

His weight came down beside her, and he touched her no more.

She would wait, she thought. She would wait, and he would fall asleep, and she would have him at her mercy.

But it didn't work out that way. Skye tried to listen for his even breathing. It was late, and he had worked hard, surely. No, it was no longer late, but early. The sun was rising. The fire in the stove still warmed the cabin, but light from outside glowed against the draperies. It was day again.

And still, he moved restlessly. He did not sleep.

Skye waited. . . .

At some point she ceased to wait. Exhaustion, perhaps, or betrayal by the brandy. He did not sleep; she did so, in truth.

Moments later—or was it hours?—she awoke. Her eyes flew open and she remembered that she lay in a pirate's bunk with only her hose and garters and a coverlet and a twin-sided blade. She needed to roll and face the pirate and plan her strategy.

She was already staring straight at the pirate, she realized.

She had rolled during the night, or so it seemed. She lay on her side facing him.

He lay upon his back. His eyes were closed, his deep dark hair was tossed about his forehead. His nose, she thought, was long, and very straight, and his whiskers were far more curly than the hair upon his head. He should shave, she found herself thinking. He probably had a handsome face.

He was a deplorable pirate!

But this morning there was definitely no denying that he was a pirate in his prime. Even in sleep his stature was imposing. His shoulders seemed to stretch the width of the bed, and like his arms they were heavily laden with muscle. He was deeply bronzed from the sun, and his flesh glistened and rippled even as he slept. His chest was furred with crisp dark hair that narrowed at his waist. Below his waist it flared and thickened again and formed a neat nest for . . .

Her face flamed and her eyes widened and jerked from the grandly protruding piece of his anatomy back to his eyes.

They were open. He was staring at her.

He smiled at her pleasantly. "Ready to keep your promise, Lady Kinsdale?"

She flushed furiously, wishing there were a way to instantly escape life itself. He rolled swiftly to his side and stroked her cheek, and though she tried not to, she slapped his hand away. She tried not to stare into flashing blue eyes, but to keep her gaze fixed upon the ceiling.

His laughter was quick and easy, as if his earlier anger had dissipated. But his face came nearer hers and he caught her chin between his thumb and forefinger. "You were warned, mam'selle."

"I am exhausted."

"Are you?"

"Utterly. How can one possibly fulfill such a promise in such a state?"

"You're a liar. Why, Lady Kinsdale, I believe that you do not intend to keep your promise at all."

Her eyes sizzled with a fury she could not suppress. "You are a pirate, sir. You are the scum of the earth. No decent man or woman would begin to imagine that such a vow need be upheld."

"The very scum of the earth?" he said. "Mam'selle, how offensive!"

"You are offensive!"

"But I am not, milady. . . ." he whispered softly, his voice trailing away in a haunting whisper. His knuckles brushed over her cheek and his fingers whispered against the length of her throat. She stared at him, unable to move or protest, compelled to silence by the silver-blue command of his eyes. Compelled, perhaps, by more.

"Ah, lady, think! It might have been One-Eyed Jack with his gruesome pitted face, decaying teeth, and lice-ridden body. You've done quite well, I daresay."

"You conceited oaf!" she spat, regaining her composure. He laughed, catching her wrists with one hand, straddling her squirming form. "Conceited, mam'selle? Nay, I offer you cleanliness and sound teeth, and you scoff at the lot of it."

"Bastard!"

"Ummm!" he agreed, and the touch of his free hand and fingers traveled lower, teasing the mound of her breast. She gritted her teeth, preparing to scratch and rail and fight and find some way to reach the blade at her side. His fingers fell lower and lower, rounding her breast, grazing her nipple. She screamed out with protest, but before she could fight him, he laughed, and his touch was gone.

He had released her. His feet swung over the side of the bed and she lay in ardent misery as he moved about, completely naked and completely comfortable with his state. Skye drew her covers close and felt the cold steel of the blade against her arm. She had wanted to put him at a disadvantage. He was awake now. Awake, aware, and rested.

There was a knock upon the door. With a slight oath he reached for one of the linen sheets upon the bunk, ripping it free and wrapping it about his waist. Skye, aware that he meant to open the door, drew her coverlet more securely over her breasts and bit her lip in consternation.

The handsome young pirate who had encouraged her fight the previous afternoon stood there with a tray. "Coffee, Captain. Sorry that there's no cream for the lady, but it's been a bit since we've seen a cow. There's sugar, though, and Cookie's sent some fine dark rolls."

"Thank you, Arrowsmith. Have you heard of the lady's ship?"

"Aye, it's sailing along behind us just fine. We all weathered the storm just fine."

"We'll see that she's repaired in New Providence."

"What?" Sky shrieked from the bed. Startled, they both turned to her. "Wh—where? We're not headed for the James?"

They smiled to one another. "Why, nay, milady!" the Silver Hawk assured her. "Would you have me hang so quickly? I dare not sail straight up the James! I have no wish to see Virginia."

"But I have!"

"And so you shall—when your ransom is met. And frankly, my dear, I am in no great hurry for that." His eyes roamed over her quite differently. They touched her with a shimmering heat. They seemed to stroke her, as if she were a possession, already known, and cherished.

A cry of rage escaped her and the pirate turned to his man with a shrug. He took the tray of coffee and rolls. "Women. You never can please them, Arrowsmith."

Arrowsmith laughed and cleared his throat. He inclined his head in Skye's direction and saluted his captain. Then he took his leave, closing the doors in his wake.

Silver Hawk set the tray down upon his desk. He munched upon a roll and sipped his coffee, black and steaming. "You've one hell of a temper, milady Kinsdale," he noted.

"You made him think—"

"Precisely."

"You are despicable!"

"Am I? I have merely made you my possession, mam'selle, and that keeps you safe from the others—until, such time, of course, that you do see fit to keep your promise."

"Never!" she vowed to him, her eyes narrowing.

"Another 'promise'? Then I've little to fear."

She didn't reply. She stared at him while he watched her, and she felt suddenly very warm inside, wondering at his thoughts. Then she swiftly lowered her eyes, wondering at his mercy. He had wanted her that morning, and easily could have raped her. He teased, he taunted, but he did not move against her in violence. But how long would his behavior remain that way?

"We sail . . . where?" she inquired, gathering her coverlet and the broadsword within it. She came to the edge of the bed, and then she stood, looking at him innocently.

"To the Caribbean, Lady Kinsdale. To New Providence, and beyond."

"And I?" she murmured, stepping forward.

He smiled and shrugged, then turned and deliberately spooned jam upon a roll. His back was to her as he answered.

"I think that you will remain in my company."

"And I think not!" Skye cried, leaping toward him. Her strategy had been planned, and before he could turn she had reached him, dragging her coverlet in one hand, slipping the other about his shoulder to bring the broadsword against his throat.

He did not flinch, nor blink. Despite the sharp blade against his throat, he offered her a slow smile.

"I have the upper edge!" Skye hissed. "Cease your silly grin lest you would die with it upon your face."

"And why not, mam'selle? What better way to die?"

"I do not tease or taunt, sir, as is your way. When I threaten, I carry out the threat."

"Lady, beware, when I threaten, for I, too, carry out the threat."

Skye swore with the vengeance of a fishwife. "Cease! Now you will summon your men and order them to make haste for the James River!"

"I think not."

"What?"

He ducked and swirled with such swift agility that her quick reaction still offered nothing but a scratch to his throat. He caught her coverlet, and as his arm cracked down upon hers, sending the broadsword flying. He jerked upon the cloak she had fashioned for herself, and caught within the folds, she went sprawling down upon the ground facefirst.

She quickly rolled, grasping for the covers again, aware of his bare feet, set firm upon them. He did not release the covers to her fevered grasp.

She did not want to see his eyes, but her own were drawn to them, and she had no choice.

Cobalt and dark, they danced with fury. Beneath the fur of his beard his jaw was twisted and set, his lips were grim.

Slowly, slowly, he crouched down beside her. She gritted her teeth as he caught her chin. She tossed back her hair, defying him.

"That was foolhardly, my love. If you ever bring a weapon against me again, you will pay dearly. That is a threat. Is it clear?"

She hesitated, then she clamped down hard on her teeth and nodded. She didn't want to shiver or show fear today. Not after her performance yesterday. But her teeth were chattering, and when her mouth opened, she softly spoke words that she abhorred. "You will not . . . you will not hurt me?"

He shook his head, watching her. She flushed and lowered her eyes.

She raised them again in alarm, for he was reaching for her, lifting her. She felt his arms around her naked flesh, and panic filled her. "You said that you would not hurt me!"

"I said that I would not hurt you. I didn't say that I wouldn't touch you . . . or . . . er, entertain you!" he whispered.

She cast back her head to scream. She did so and he watched with amusement.

Then he seated her before the tray of coffee and rolls.

"Breakfast, Lady Kinsdale. Do you always scream blue blazes when you are offered a cup of coffee?"

3

HEN SHE WAS SETTLED IN THE SEAT BEHIND HIS
desk, he retrieved her coverlet, tossing it over her shoulders.
Skye grasped at the garment and sat there stiffly. He moved
across the room to his trunk and drew out clothing. He looked
her way, arching his brows, and she flushed furiously, turning aside as he dressed.
She felt his eyes upon her as he buttoned his shirt and tied his breeches, then sat
to pull on his high black boots.

"So, tell me, milady, why is it that you are so afraid of the dark?"

"I am not afraid of the dark," she lied ridiculously.

"You are not?"

"No."

"That's a lie."

She shrugged. "A gentleman would allow a lady the lie."

"But I'm not a gentleman. I'm a pirate, remember."

"Oh, yes. A nasty, brutal beast, and I've nothing to say to you upon any
account."

He rose. She still did not look his way, but shivers claimed her despite her best
efforts as he moved around behind her. He did not touch her, but his hands fell
upon the back of the chair where she sat and his head lowered so that she could
hear and feel his whisper. "Nasty and brutal, Lady Kinsdale? Alas! I fear that if I
keep my distance, I will dearly disappoint you! You've suffered no beatings as yet,
mam'selle. The only violence that has come your way has been that given in
retribution for your own intent of murder. Bear this in mind."

Skye stiffened, her fingers curling into the handsomely carved arms of the
chair, her gaze remaining straightforward. How she hated this man! she thought.
Hated his laughter and his mockery, hated his power. Just as she hated the
haunting sound of his whispers and the curve of his smile, and the fine, taut
musculature of his body. He was an animal! she thought. A pirate. A vile knave, a
beast.

But a striking beast, bold, determined, and blunt. If she were not his prisoner,
she might very well find him charismatic, his form alluring, his less-than-subtle
innuendo exciting. . . .

Dear God, she was a captive losing her mind! He was young enough, perhaps,
despite the silver that tinted his hair and beard. And his speech was cultured, his
manner sometimes even inoffensive. But he was a cutthroat, no more, no less,
and she would still fight him and hate him until her dying breath.

"Nothing to say, my love?" He plucked up a tendril of her hair. His fingers brushed her shoulder where the coverlet had fallen away and she was startled by the searing sensation that swept through her. She slapped his hand away, still staring forward, trembling. "Nothing but the obvious, sir. Your teeth may be better than One-Eyed Jack's, but you are still the same monster as he was. No better."

He laughed, straightening, and going for the broadsword that lay upon the floor. "I do beg to differ, milady. Had he lived, and had you spent the night in his cabin, I think you would have discovered a vast difference twixt the two of us."

"Really? Perhaps were I tavern slut, I might have managed to say, 'what a wonder! The man has his teeth, and for garbage, his stench is not too severe.' But I am no tavern wench, sir, and from where I sit, refuse is refuse, and all to be abhorred."

His laughter was swift and genuine. "Ah, from your lofty heights, mam'selle! I don't wish to disturb such noble ideals, but I tell you this in all truth, a woman is a woman, and a man must be judged by his measure, and not by his position upon this earth. The finest lady, the most noble duchess, tumbles upon the mattress much the same as the tavern wench. She learns to long and ache and desire in the same fashion, to whisper her lover's name, to curl to his caress and strain to his form." He came back behind her, bending over her. "And she learns so much more quickly when he still has all of his teeth!"

"Your conceit is extraordinary."

He faced her and lifted her chin. "That you can doubt my words, mam'selle, lends credence to the very truth of them. There is a grave difference. Had you spent your night in Jack's cabin, you'd not have awakened thinking there could be no difference in men."

She wanted to wrench from him. He held his grip. "I did not say men, sir. I spoke of refuse—pirates."

"Such harsh words, milady! When I carry still in the boundaries of my heart your sweet promise to please me in any way, to offer any diversion I might desire."

"Diversion!"

His lip began to curl with humor. She did twist her chin from his grip. She raised her hand with a vengeance, halfway rising, determined to strike him. She just barely caught his cheek before his fingers wound around her wrist. He twisted his jaw and she was pleased that she had hurt him, then she was suddenly frightened, for a pulse ticked against his throat and she did not care to be hurt in return, and she had definitely angered him as well. She sank slowly back into the chair, her eyes locked with his. She already knew that when the soft silver darkened to a cobalt blue, his temper was flaring. But he did not strike out at her in return. He swallowed, as if he clamped down on his temper. His smile returned. "Were you aware, milady, that you've splendid breasts?"

"What?" she gasped. Her eyes fell downward where the coverlet had fallen from her and where her flesh now lay bare to him. She must have been cold, for her nipples protruded like hardened rosebuds against the mounds.

"Oh!" she swore, and she sought, clumsily, to strike him again and retrieve her covering at the same time. He was not about to be struck again and caught her wrist quickly and easily. "Madame, I am patient, but I do have my limits. So far you've tried to slice my throat and dislodge my jaw. Do take care!" His husky laughter irritated her to no end, but she lowered her head, seeking desperately to free her hand, to recover herself. She glanced up at him quickly and went still, for the color of his eyes had changed again. They had gone to a warm, smoke color, and they remained upon her person, then slowly met hers. She did not quite understand the message in his eyes, but her breath caught in her throat and her blood surged throughout her limbs with a sizzling force. Something in her abdomen coiled tightly and she desperately moistened her lips. "Please!" she gasped out, unaware of just what it was that she requested.

He freed her wrist. She lowered her eyes, drawing the coverlet about her. She sought desperately for something to say.

"I, er, I did not promise—diversion!"

"Ah, but you did promise me . . . what was it . . . ? Anything! I do believe that is what you said," he reminded her, laughing. He turned from her and picked up his hat and set it upon his head. "I shall be waiting, mam'selle. Thank God that I am a patient man!" He paused just a moment longer, belting his scabbard and cutlass to his side, and taking the broadsword beneath his arm. He took a dirk from the bookcase and cast her a wry glance. "I wonder if it is safe to leave you with the serving tray. Ah, yes, bless Cookie, he is a man of rare good sense. He has sent a spoon and not a knife for the jam. Take care, my dear, until we meet again."

With a sweeping flourish of his hat, he left her. She sat still until she heard the bolts slide into place at the doors. Then she leaped up, led by instinct, slamming against them.

She was locked in once again.

She swore violently and was overcome with a sense of panic and desolation. Shrieking aloud, she stormed about and sent the tray with the coffee and rolls flying. The porcelain cups shattered and the jam jar cracked in two, spilling out blood red strawberry preserves. Skye stood still looking upon the havoc she had wreaked, the coverlet still wrapped about her shoulders. She was startled when the doors burst open again and she discovered that the Silver Hawk had returned.

He stood in the doorway, exceptionally tall in his plumed hat and high boots. His eyes sizzled silver and blue and they fell upon her with a shimmering anger.

"Brat!" he exploded.

And he was striding her way with purpose.

Skye gasped out and turned to run, but there was nowhere to go. She collided with the bookshelves and too hastily turned from them, and tripped. In a tangle of covers she fell facedown on the bunk. Gulping for air, she tried to twist and turn, but he was upon her by then, his weight falling hard upon hers. His arms stretched out and his hands fell upon hers, his fingers lacing with her own.

"Let me go!" she cried out fiercely.

But she had no effect upon him at all at that moment. She kicked, she flailed, she bit at him, catching his arm so savagely with her teeth that he let out a roar. To her vast dismay she realized that he was sitting then and that she was being dragged relentlessly over his lap. Her coverlet was stripped away with every twist and movement and she was both swearing and sobbing in her desperation to elude him. But at that moment, he was ruthless.

"Nearly sliced, broken, and now bitten!" he grated out furiously. "Cups shattered, property destroyed—"

"Property destroyed! Those words from a pirate!" she cried.

The irony of it eluded him. He held her in a vise against him and she could not even twist to see his face, to brush her hair from its tangle over her eyes and mouth.

"Mam'selle, I have had it!" he said. "Act like a child and you'll be treated as one!"

A shriek exploded from her as his hand fell with a searing force upon the exposed and tender curve of her derriere. Tears stung her eyes from both the startling pain of his blow and the humiliation of it. Wretchedly she stretched over the burning muscles of his thighs, her face in the covers as she struggled to be free. She could not bear it. She twisted, crying out again. She hated him! She wanted to take whatever he dished out to her with dignity and silence. She wanted to bear any pain.

And she could not. She could not stand this awful indignity.

His hand was rising again. "Please! Stop!" she sobbed out.

And to her amazement, he did.

His teeth clenched together, his hand slowly fell. He shoved her from his lap and she went to the floor in a disheveled pile of covers and tousled hair. She landed hard on her rump and she nearly screeched again, for he had injured her sorely, and she imagined then that it would be a number of days before she managed to sit comfortably again.

"Damn you!" he muttered darkly.

He stood, stepping over her. She didn't see him look back her way because her head had fallen and her hair hid her eyes. "Pick up this mess!" he ordered her succinctly, each word enunciated slowly.

She tossed back her hair, heedless that her eyes were filled with tears. She opened her mouth to tell him that although he was pirate and she was his prisoner, she would never, never obey him. But he spoke first.

"You will do it, Skye, whether I am a bastard pirate or not! You will do it because I have ordered you to do so, and because I promise you that you will rue the day if you do not, and because that is a threat, and as I have warned you, I carry out all threats. If you find it prudent to defy me over jam, then you are truly a fool, and deserve whatever fate awaits you!"

His hands were on his hips, his long legs were outstretched, and his boots were firmly cast upon the floor. His silver eyes sizzled and burned a startling dark silver, and she knew how he had gotten his name. The line of his mouth was grim against the curl of his mustache and the dark fur of his beard, and in that particular moment, she had no more will to fight him.

"Mam'selle! Do you comprehend me?"

"Yes!"

She saw the expression in his eyes soften and he moved his hand, as if he would touch her, almost as if he wanted to reach out to her. Then he swore and snorted, and spun around.

Then he was gone. The doors slammed and the bolts slid in his wake. Skye stared after him, not breathing.

Then she gulped in air and cast herself against the floor and gave way to a flood of tears.

An hour later, after a great deal of reflection, she determined that she would clean the mess she had made. She brooded long and hard over the action, but in the end, she had to agree that the pirate had made one good point—a jar of jam was not worth this awful humiliation.

She picked up the tray and the shattered porcelain and glass and cleaned the floorboards with a linen napkin. When she was done, she approached the windows and pulled back the drapes. She was startled to see that the sun was already fallen. They must have slept very late into the day. Night was coming again already.

She tied the draperies by their cords, eager for the light that remained. The lamp had gone out and the stove had issued its last warmth and light. Skye knotted her fingers into her fists.

He would leave her here again, she thought. Locked in as darkness fell. He would see her reduced to a groveling fool once again, and he would laugh all the while. He would assume that she deserved it.

There was a knock upon the door. Startled, she whirled. She did not think that the Silver Hawk would be knocking. She pulled the coverlet tightly around her shoulders. "Yes?" she called softly.

The door opened and the handsome young man the pirate had called Arrowsmith walked in, somewhat burdened by the weight of one of her traveling trunks.

"This is yours, I believe?" he said.

"Yes," Skye said.

"Then you'll excuse me if I put it down. 'Tis heavy! What on earth is it that you women carry?"

"I'm sure you've taken plunder enough to know the answer to that!" she retorted.

He grimaced. "No, milady. We ransom off our plunder, just as we do our hostages."

"You'll swing by the neck for it, just the same."

"Perhaps." He grinned, setting down her trunk next to his master's trunk at the foot of the bed. "I'm afraid we'll have to wait until we reach the Caribbean for me to bring you the rest of your trunks," he said apologetically. "The captain went through this one and thought that it offered all that you might require for the next few days of travel."

"The captain—went through it?"

"Yes, milady."

She thought that she would scream her outrage, but she kept silent. Her clothing and jewels were valuable plunder. She was probably lucky that he had decided to clothe her.

"I shall take this away," Arrowsmith said. He smiled and picked up the tray with the broken cups without blinking. He turned to leave the room.

"Wait, please!" Skye said. He was a pirate, too, she reminded herself. Even if he was young and handsome and even gentle in his way. He stopped, looking to her.

"Could you . . . light a lamp for me, please? It is growing dark."

"I shall take care of it, Robert."

Startled, they both looked to the doorway. The Silver Hawk had returned.

"Aye, Captain, as you wish it." Robert Arrowsmith inclined his head toward Skye and exited the room, brushing by his captain. The Silver Hawk came into the room, turning his back to her and, with slow purpose, closing the doors. He turned around again, leaning against them. He looked over the floor, and over Skye, and to the foot of the bunk where her trunk now lay.

"I came to light the lamp for you, milady," he said softly.

She said nothing, standing still and awaiting his next move. It was a long time in coming. He strode across the room and lit the wick of the lamp. The glow filled the room. Skye lowered her head in a turmoil. She had thought that he would exploit her fear, that he would purposely leave her to her terror of the darkness.

He had not.

And yet it wouldn't be proper to thank the vile pirate for the kind gesture, would it? Not after all that he had done to her.

He set the lamp into its protected niche. "We head south with a good wind. It will be too warm for the fire, I believe, but the light should be good enough."

Skye swallowed and nodded.

"I had thought to find you dressed by now."

"The trunk just arrived."

"Yes. Find something. I will help you don your clothing, and you can come on deck for an hour or so."

Her eyes widened and she bit into her lip. "I can dress myself, thank you."

"Shall I choose for you?"

There was an edge to his voice. They were engaging in battle again.

Eventually, she thought with a shiver, he would wear her down. Their strange encounters were unnerving her completely.

"Sir, I tell you—"

"I shall choose then." He strode toward her trunk. She found herself running after him, catching his arm, then was dismayed by her action. She gazed at her hand where it rested upon him and recoiled swiftly, startled by the blood that had hardened upon his shirt. She stared at him in horror.

"You're—bleeding."

"I was bleeding, milady. A shrew with sharp teeth caught hold of my flesh."

She swallowed, her eyes locked with his.

"It is no matter, Lady Kinsdale. If you'll excuse me—"

"No! You needn't go into my things again. You had no right to do so before. Sir, I tell you—"

"Milady, I tell you. You had no difficulty riffling through my belongings to find that wretched broadsword. I found no difficulty in disturbing your belongings for a far more gentle mission, that of seeing you clad!"

He was already upon his knees, casting back the unlocked lid of her chest. He found a corset and tossed it back down, then procured a simple shift and a linen gown with short sleeves. It was a soft, cool blue with white lace trim and she had purchased it with thoughts of the long hot Virginia summers in mind.

"This one," he muttered.

She flushed furiously that his hands should be upon her apparel. She tried to shove him aside, taking up the corset he had dropped. "If you will just leave me—"

"I will not. And drop that whalebone torture creation. You don't need stockings, either. Even with the breeze, it is warm this evening."

"Mr. Hawk!" she snapped in exasperation. "Is it Hawk? Or is it Mr. Silver? I mean, really, sir, just how does one address you?" she demanded irritably.

He sat back on his haunches and his slow grin curled into his lip. "I think that I might like the sound of 'milord,' from your lips, Lady Kinsdale. Or perhaps, 'my dear lord.'"

"Never," Skye said flatly.

"Then 'Hawk' will do, milady. Come, let's see you clad in this piece of summer's frivolity."

Skye straightened to her full height. "Sir, this will be done by violence only."

"If that's the way you choose it," he said with a shrug, rising and taking a step toward her. "The manner is of no difference to me."

"Stop!" Skye pleaded, backing away from him. She hadn't the energy for the fight. Her flesh still burned from his earlier, less than tender touch. She promised herself that she hated him still with a vengeance, but for the moment, she needed to lick her wounds and recoup her energy.

He stood still, watching her. She lifted her arms and dropped the coverlet from about her shoulders. She meant to keep her eyes on his but she could not, and her eyes fell in shame.

"Oh, you will quit playing Ophelia!" he said in harsh exasperation. He stepped forward, but took his time easing her plight, raising her chin and meeting her eyes. His gaze passed quickly over the length of her. "Milady, the silk stockings must go. Clad only in them, you are most provocative."

If she had thought to shame him, she had sadly miscalculated, and her own temper flew back to a new high as he lifted her from the floor and tossed her nonchalantly upon the bed to strip away her stockings, all that remained of her clothing from the previous day.

Skye swore, she flailed at him. He avoided her pummeling with amusement and quickly did away with the offending garments. "Calm down!" he charged

her. And capturing her shoulders, he straddled her. She wasn't aware at first that
he had her shift, and that he was trying to slip it over her shoulders. "Lady
Kinsdale, I do swear, it is far more difficult to dress you than it has ever been to
charm and unclothe any tender maid in all of my days."

"I daresay you've never known a tender maid!" Skye retorted. She quickly
slipped her arms into the silken straps of the garment and faced him again,
flushed and furious. He stood by the bed, watching her with a curious expression, his eyes the color of fog and steel, a pallor seeming to touch his face. She
noted that his fists were clamped hard at his sides. He did not rise to her retort. It
occurred to Skye that her shift defined more than it concealed, that her breasts
were pressed strainingly against the bodice of the gossamer undergarment, and
that the line of her hip and the soft triangle at the juncture of her thighs were
hauntingly evident.

"Why do you humiliate me like this!" she cried suddenly. "Why this slow
torture—"

"Milady, I promise," he interrupted her dryly, "the torture I do is to myself."

"Then . . ."

"Then what?"

"Then . . . stop it!" she whispered.

"Alas," he murmured, and the word carried a tender and wistful sound, "I
have discovered that I cannot." He turned swiftly away from her, finding the
dress. "Come, Skye, let's set this upon your shoulders and ease both our souls."

Skye . . .

He had used her given name. He had used it with the ease of a friend or
relation, or of a lover. She should have despised the sound of it upon his tongue,
but she did not. She should have ignored his command, but she could not. She
crawled from the bed and stepped to him slowly. She reached up as he deftly set
the yards of muslin over her head and arms. He twirled her around and set to the
twenty-one tiny buttons that closed the dress. He was deft with his movement, as
if he was well-acquainted with women's fashion. She began to tap a bare toe as
his fingers brushed her back.

"Are you done?" she inquired.

"Umm. You intended to do this alone?"

"The intent of such a gown is to have one's maids along. But since those poor
lasses have fallen prey to your men . . ."

He was undaunted. "That is why, mam'selle, you must be grateful for my
assistance."

"Grateful!" She pulled away, and whirled about. "May we go?"

"If you wish." But he reached down into her trunk again and plucked from it
her silver initialed brush. "Your hair resembles an ill-kept bird's nest."

"That is hardly my fault."

"But if you don't care, lady, then I must. Come to me, and I'll make some
semblance of golden curls from that thatch yet."

"I care!" Skye cried quickly. On her bare feet she hurried forward, snatching
the brush from his fingers. She tried to work through the length of her thick

tendrils quickly, but she was nervous and tugged and tore far more than she cared to admit. He emitted some impatient sound and stepped forward with purpose, snatching the brush away again. "Turn!" he ordered her. Gritting her teeth, she did so.

Again, his fingers were deft. There was no tenderness to his touch, but he was apt and able, and with little pain to her, the dreadful knots caused by the wind and tempest of the storms outside and inside the captain's cabin were quickly untangled. Her hair fell about her back and shoulders in soft, shimmering waves.

"It is an unusual color," he commented almost idly. "It is neither gold nor red."

She turned around, smiling succinctly. "It is the color of thatch, so you said."

"Ah, yes, thatch," he agreed, and smiled. Her eyes narrowed and she swung around again, waiting for the door to open. He came around and opened it for her. He offered her his arm. She chose to ignore it, staring straight ahead.

"Skye, take my arm, else resign yourself to this cabin for the length of the voyage."

He spoke the truth, and she knew it. She took his arm and he politely opened the door.

Sunset was coming. The very sight of the spectacular colors streaking across the heavens gave a curious thrill to her heart. The world had fallen apart. She had fallen prey to the true monsters that roamed the seas. Her own captain lay dead and surely floated in some watery grave. Crew had fought and died, and infamy had ensued. She had spent the night in the company of one of the four most notorious pirates about . . . and still, the sunset spoke of hope.

It was glorious. It was red and gold and all the shades in between. The sun itself was a glorious orb falling slowly into the cobalt and azure of the sea. The colors seemed to stretch into eternity.

"Now I know the color," he murmured suddenly behind her.

"What?" she said, turning to him.

His eyes, smoke now, fell upon hers. "Your hair. It is the color of this sunset." He was silent only a moment. "Come on. I am taking the helm. You may stay at my side for a while."

He gave her no choice but to come, holding her tightly as they walked across the decking from his cabin past huge cleats and piles of rigging and canvas sail until they came to the carved steps that led to the wheel. Men saluted, doffing their caps to her, smiling their knowing smiles. She felt her cheeks grow warm and she did not respond, but she tried to raise her chin.

"Evening, Captain!" came a cry from the crow's nest.

"Evening, Jacko. Is she clear?"

"Clear as the sound o' my sweet mother's voice, captain! It seems we've weathered the storms, and moved into clear weather."

"That's fine to hear, Jacko."

"Milady, you're looking well!" the man called.

Skye did not reply to him. The Hawk laughed and answered in her stead.

"Perhaps, Jacko, the lady, too, has weathered the storm of the previous night and seeks calm seas this eve!"

Jacko laughed. Skye was certain that she heard subtle sneering sounds from all about her, but then maybe she had imagined them. The Hawk's men seemed more cheerful than licentious. They were a well-disciplined lot for scourges of the sea, she thought. And they were clean for pirates. And neatly garbed.

Hawk led her around to a carved wood seat that curved around the wheel, built into the superstructure of the ship. The man at the wheel saluted Hawk, nodded very properly to her, and gave over the helm. "The course is set south, southeasterly, sir!"

"Fine, Thompkins. We'll keep her so. You are at leisure, Mr. Thompkins."

"Thank you, sir," Thompkins responded. He saluted again and left the helm. The Hawk took the huge wheel, legs spread firm and apart as he stood and surveyed the sea from behind it. They might have been alone in the world, Skye thought, for the sea and sky seemed so very vast. The sunset falling portside was still a sight of crystalline beauty and the wind was gentle and balmy.

She drew her bare toes up beneath her and leaned her head back, feeling the wind. She should be thinking of some new way to slay him, she thought. She should not let another night pass by. She desperately needed to find a way to salvage life and dignity and honor from this fiasco.

But she was weary and unarmed and the air was gentle and soft. She needed to regain her strength, to find the will and energy and way to defy him.

She opened her eyes, and discovered that he was no longer watching the sea. He was watching her.

"What!" she cried irritably. "What is it that you want out of me!"

He shrugged and glanced toward the sea once again. "I am curious, Lady Kinsdale, and that is all."

"Curious, why?"

"That a woman raised as you have been—a God-fearing lass, born into the peerage—can take her vows so lightly."

She stiffened. "I do not take promises lightly, sir. Not unless they are given to the rodents and snakes."

"A promise, milady, is a promise."

"Not—"

"Yes, milady, a promise, even given to me, is a promise."

"You are a rake and a rogue and a—"

"Pirate! It is a most noble profession, milady! Why that dear great lady, Queen Elizabeth herself, encouraged the profession. Sir Francis Drake was a pirate, you know. Anytime that England has been at war with the Spanish or French, pirating has been called noble!"

"Drake was a privateer—"

"Pirate!" he claimed, laughing. "Or, to be a thief is fine—as long as we steal from other nations!"

Skye turned away, looking westward toward the sunset. "You would compare One-Eyed Jack with Sir Francis Drake."

"No, I would compare One-Eyed Jack with Attila the Hun, for both were cold-blooded murderers."

"Oh? Are there good pirates and bad?"

"Of course. There are the good and the bad in all peoples."

"You are scum," she said sweetly.

"And you are changing the subject. Consider then that we have established that I am scum. Let's return to you."

"Let's not."

He ignored her words. "To promises."

"I have already told you—"

"That you are not beholden to keep a promise to me. Because I am scum. But what of your fiancé?"

"What?"

"You intend to breech your promise to him."

"I never voiced any such promise!" Skye declared. Then, furious that she had replied to him, she turned again. "It is none of your business, you—"

"Cease. I tire of the barbs in your tongue."

"I tire of your presence."

"That can easily be rectified. Come, I will return you to your prison."

"Can't you please let me be! Have you no mercy within you?"

"I am afraid, milady, that you cannot expect 'scum' to come equipped with mercy."

"Oh!" she cried, frustrated. "What is all this to you anyway?"

"I am curious."

"Why?"

"Pure and simple, milady. I wonder if the dear fellow will or will not be willing to pay for your return."

Skye drew her knees up beneath her, folded her hands upon them, and rested her chin there. "It matters not if he pays or not. My father will ransom me."

"But what if your father has had a bad year? Most of his fortune comes from his holdings on the islands. It's been a bad year for the sugar plantations."

"Lord Cameron will pay!" she snapped.

"He will pay for you, even tarnished as you are?"

"I am not tarnished!" she snapped. Then she lowered her eyes slightly, for it was by a curious mercy on his part that she was not, and she did not wish to test that mercy. Then she remembered his touch and his eyes, and the fact that sitting was still difficult because of a certain placement of his hand upon her bare anatomy. "I am only slightly tarnished," she amended, and he laughed softly.

"I think you are right," he said. "I think that Cameron will pay for you, no matter how tarnished you should become. You see, he is a man who knows how to keep a promise. He was pledged as a child, but from respect for his deceased father's wishes, I am sure that he will pay."

She glanced at him sharply. He was watching the sea once again. She cried softly, "You know him! You know the man to whom I am engaged."

He did not reply for a moment.

"You know him!" Skye cried once again.

"Aye, I know him."

"How!" She hadn't realized that she had stood, or that she had moved, until she saw that her hand rested upon his where it lay against the mighty wheel. She flushed and quickly drew away her touch. "How do you know him?"

He shrugged. "He intercedes sometimes when I return hostages. We meet on Bone Cay. I have—holdings—there."

"Then—then I will not be a prisoner long?" she whispered.

A lazy smile touched his lips and one of his dark brows arched. "Long enough, milady."

She drew away from him and turned about. "What is he like?"

"Petroc Cameron?"

"Yes."

"He is like me."

"What!" she stormed, whirling around with great indignation.

His laughter was deep and husky and seemed to fill the night, and his eyes sparkled a fascinating silver. "At least you are quick to leap to his defense!"

"He is a gentleman. You are—"

"Un-uh. Watch it, lady. I am weary."

"You are a—pirate," she said. She meant "scurvy rodent," and they both knew it. His jaw twisted, but he was still amused. She was, after all, she admitted ruefully, broken down to a certain control.

"He is like me," the Hawk said, "because he is my cousin."

She gasped so awfully that she choked. He patted her firmly upon the back and quickly apologized. "Milady, please do not have apoplexy upon me! You needn't fear the future so intensely upon my account. He is a second cousin of sorts. And I, of course, poor slime, am from the wrong side of the sheets several generations back. The Camerons do not like to speak of it, of course, and they admit nothing. But when you meet your dear betrothed, you will see that there can be no real denial, for the Lord Cameron and I do bear a certain resemblance to one another."

Skye sank back into her seat, staring at him dismally. "And you would tarnish your own cousin's fiancée?" she demanded.

"There is no love lost between us."

"But—"

"And remember, milady, as of this moment, you are only 'slightly' tarnished. And if rumor stands correct, you intend to dishonor your bethrothal anyway."

"That is mere speculation."

"To many. You forget. I know you."

"You do not know me at all!"

"I am learning more about you with each passing hour, Lady Kinsdale."

"Again, you show your conceit."

She crossed her arms over her chest and looked away. "Governor Spotswood hates pirates! He will catch you one day and he will hang you high, and I will make you one promise now that I will keep. The day that they hang you I will be there with bells on. I will watch with the greatest glee."

"Bloodthirsty wench," he said.

"In your case, Sir Rogue!"

He laughed, letting go the wheel, turning to her. She wished to escape his nearness but it was too late. He caught her hands and bowed low so that their faces nearly touched and he all but whispered into her lips. "Milady, one day I promise—a promise that will be kept!—you will call me 'lord' and you will bow to my command!"

"Never!" she promised, but the cry was but a whisper, too, and that against his lips. He so nearly brushed her flesh! So nearly met his mouth to hers. A hammering came to her, and it was the sound of her heart. She heard the rush of the ocean, then realized that it was her blood, cascading and steaming within her. Surely, he saw how she trembled. He would know . . .

Know what? she demanded desperately of herself.

She did not find the answer for someone nearby cleared his throat and the Hawk straightened. Robert Arrowsmith stood with one foot upon the first step to the helm.

"I've laid the lady's supper out in your cabin, Captain."

The Hawk reached for her hand, drawing her to her feet, his eyes deep and hard upon hers. "Mr. Arrowsmith will escort you to the cabin." His voice lowered. "You needn't fear. The lanterns are already lit."

He did not wait for a reply but handed her over to Robert. Robert escorted her past the rigging and to the cabin door. "Good night, milady," he said to her.

And the doors were closed and bolted. But as the Hawk had promised, two lanterns burned brightly, illuminating the water left for her to wash and the meal left for her upon the Hawk's desk. She would never eat, she thought. But it had been endless hours since she had last eaten and she quickly realized that she was famished and that the stew left for her smelled wonderful.

She sat down. It was a fresh fish stew, she quickly realized, thick with potatoes and carrots. The bread at her side was fresh, too, and vermin free. With less than ladylike manners she set into it, and when she paused at last, she realized that she had consumed it all.

She hadn't even bothered to pour herself some of the burgundy left for her. She did so then, reflecting on the night.

He would not hurt her. He had told her so. If she took care, she would be rescued soon enough.

If her father had the ransom, she thought dully.

Or if Lord Cameron was still willing to come to her aid.

She was only slightly tarnished. . . .

Restlessly, she stood. The food had been wonderful. It had left her with a sense of well-being. The wine was good, too. It went down well, and it eased away the fear and the pain. She was still so very tired.

She looked from the washbowl and French soap and sponge to the door, wondering when he would burst back in upon her. Nervously she dug into her trunk for a substantial nightdress, and even more nervously she set to the endless task of trying to undo her buttons. She let her dress fall to her waist and scrubbed her upper torso.

No one came to the door.

She slipped her nightdress over her shoulders and soaped and sponged her lower half, finishing with her feet. Then she breathed a sigh of relief, for no one had come.

She sat down and finished the wine. Still, no one disturbed her. The lanterns burned brightly, and she was at ease. She leaned back and closed her eyes.

Later, she tried to move, and she struck wood. Panic seized her. She was surrounded by darkness. She was locked into a small wooden space, and darkness surrounded her.

She could hear the screams. . . .

Stay! She had to stay!

But she could not. She could not remain in her prison and listen to the horrible screams!

She tried to scream herself, but the sound would not come. They had warned her not to make a sound, not to make a sound. . . .

It burst from her, the awful sound of her dream. There were hands upon her. They had found her. They had come for her, too. She scratched and fought furiously. They would kill her, without a second thought.

"Skye!"

There was light again, she realized. She blinked furiously, looking about herself. She was in his bed, beside him. She had banged against the paneling at the side of the bunk.

"It went out!" she cried. "The light went out."

"Hush, I'm sorry."

He held her, very tenderly. He was naked beneath the covers, she knew. His shoulders were bare and the hair upon his chest teased her cheek. He was a pirate, and she couldn't care, she couldn't even think about it. She lay against him, trembling and dazed. His hands soothed her, touching her hair, stroking her cheek. "It's all right. I won't let the light go out again. Ever."

She kept trembling. His arms came more tightly against her and she buried her face against the strength of his broad chest.

"Don't fight me, Skye. Lie still, lie easy. I won't leave you and I won't hurt you. Don't fight me. . . ."

She had no thought to fight him that night. None at all. With a soft sob she curled against him. Slowly, her trembling eased. He whispered to her still. In time, her eyes closed. Then she slept, a dreamless, easy sleep.

He waited until that time. Then he uncurled the fingers that still tore into his flesh with terror. He smoothed them out, softly massaging her palms.

He gazed down upon her tearstained face, so fine in the web of her sunset hair.

He admitted that she was beautiful.

And he admitted, too, that he was playing a losing game. He had made her his prisoner.

But now, he was the one in chains. He would never be able to just release her.

Before it all ended, he would have to have her.

And leave her very, very tarnished indeed.

4

KYE AWOKE WITH A START, ONLY TO DISCOVER that she was alone. She looked quickly about the cabin, assuring herself that the Silver Hawk was nowhere about, then she winced and leaned back again, thoroughly despising herself for her weakness and more perplexed than ever by the pirate. At certain times he was ruthless beyond measure; he didn't bend, break, or give the slightest quarter.

But he could also be gentle, sensitive beyond measure to the terrors of darkness that plagued her heart.

None of that mattered, she told herself flatly. She had lain in bed with a pirate and set her cheek against his chest and her hands against his flesh and she had clung to the very scourge of the seas.

A lamp was lit, but the drapes were still closed against the sunshine. Skye crawled from bed and walked to the starboard windows, pulling back the velvet to look out. It was a beautiful day. All blue and golden. The sea was calm, stretching endlessly beneath the powder blue horizon.

There was a knock upon the door. She wasn't exactly decently clad, Skye decided, but her nightgown did cover her chastely from throat to toe. "Come in," she called out.

The doors opened and Robert Arrowsmith entered with a breakfast tray. "Good morning, milady." She nodded his way as he set the tray upon the table. He seemed pleased with himself that morning as he removed the silver warmer from the plate upon the tray. "I've a surprise for you. Fresh milk and eggs and a ham steak, milady."

She couldn't resist the food, nor her curiosity. "Fresh milk?"

"We met with a sister ship this dawn coming out of Charleston, milady." He hesitated. "The captain had a hip bath brought aboard, too, and he bought a supply of French milled soap. Now I warned him that you might not care to immerse the whole of your body into the water and take a chance with disease, but the captain's regularly into bathing himself, so he thinks as how you might want the opportunity, too."

"I would dearly love a bath," she said. Where was her pride? she wondered. She should scoff at every offer given her by the wretch of a pirate. She wasn't terribly certain if her pride could be salvaged by remaining sticky and dirty and she scoffed at the idea that evil spirits and diseases entered into the body when it was submerged. She had grown up in a hot climate and had learned to love to bathe.

"Fine, then, some of the lads and I will be back with the tub and water. You can heat more yourself, of course, if you wish. I shall light the stove and leave you a kettle."

Skye thanked him and sat behind the desk. He set forth lighting the stove and she watched him as she delicately cut into the ham on the plate before her. She chewed reflectively. "Charleston," she murmured. "And we sail for New Providence?" She knew the general vicinity of the island. And she knew that it was a pirate's haven, a true den of iniquity. The small swift pirate ships were able to manuever the reefs and shoals about her while the warships and merchantmen too often cracked up upon the treacherous coral rock. The English proprietors of the island seemed not to have the energy to deal with the pirate problem, and so, Skye had heard, the only law there came to be that based on the will of the strongest rascal who happened to be present.

Robert hesitated, jabbing at the coals in the stove. "Aye, we sail for New Providence," he said, looking her way. "You know of it?"

"Too well."

"You needn't fear. The Hawk does not intend for you to leave the ship. We won't stay long. Then we'll move on to Bone Cay. The Hawk is the law there. He will see that you are kept safe."

"Safe?" she said sweetly.

"Quite safe," he said. "Until some arrangement is made."

Skye gave him a beautiful smile. "Tell me, Robert, what happens if my father cannot pay the sum of money that the Hawk demands?"

"Surely, Lord Cameron—"

"But what if Lord Cameron does not choose to pay?"

"He will," Robert insisted.

"But if he does not?"

"He will."

"But what if he does not?"

"Milady, you are insistent!" he said, standing.

"Yes, I am."

"Well then . . . ." He threw his arms up in the air. "Well, then you will like Bone Cay, I suppose. I don't know. I am quite certain that you will be ransomed quickly."

"How long till we reach New Providence? Two days, three?"

"Yes, depending upon the wind."

She stared at him hard and he shuffled his feet uneasily. He was a striking young man, much like his master. His speech was cultured and his manner refined.

Perhaps, she mused, he was not so horrible a pirate. He treated her like a lady despite the circumstances. He seemed to admire her, and she was not without a certain confidence in her ability to charm. He might be persuaded to help her.

She smiled at him, sadly.

"You must cease this horrible life, you know," she told him. She pushed up from her chair and hurried around to touch his shoulder. She was so intent upon her pursuit that she did not see the doors swing open, or the Hawk enter into the cabin behind them. "Mr. Arrowsmith, if you could, perhaps, help me to escape, I could speak to the governor on your behalf. Oh, he is a man who wretchedly hates pirates, but he is quick to see remorse, and ever ready to give a man a chance! Robert, can't you see? You will hang if you persist in this life! I could help you, truly I could. And oh, sir! I would despair to see you swinging from a rope!"

Her fingers fell upon his sleeve. He flushed, for they were very close, and her gown, though sedate, was made of thin cotton. "Milady—" he began.

"Yes, milady!" came a long drawl from the doorway. Robert jerked and jumped away from her. He stared blankly at the Hawk. The pirate smiled his slow sardonic smile. "That's all, Robert."

"Aye! Aye, aye, sir!" Robert sped on out of the cabin. Skye remained before the desk, her heart sinking as she watched the thunder of a pulse against his throat. He was dressed, as usual, in black corded by silver threads. His shirt was open and much of his bronze chest was displayed. She felt a nervousness leap into the pit of her belly and it was difficult to remain where she was. She wanted to run from him, and from the feeling inside of her. His eyes touched hers with dark and shimmering power, and to her eternal shame, she did not think to be furious or indignant. She thought instead of the night. She thought of her dreadful fear, and of how secure she had felt once his arms had come around her. They were like steel. They were bronze and hard and vibrant. Like the beat of his heart.

The blood began to drain from her face as she remembered their first morning together, and seeing him fully naked. Tremors shook her and she swallowed, trying to keep her eyes wide open and upon his. She did not wish to let them fall. Indeed, she did not wish to recall his anatomy one bit, and yet she did, and the very memory caused her to heat and burn inside. His sexual drive seemed as potent as his fighting force, and yet . . .

He had let her be.

"Alas, love!" he murmured softly, coming in and walking around to take the seat she had vacated. He picked up her coffee cup and sipped the warm brew, sighing with satisfaction as he raised his booted feet to clunk upon his desk. He folded his hands over his chest. "So you were trying to charm poor Robert into mutiny."

"I was telling him rationally what would happen if he persisted in this life of infamy."

"You lie, milady. But then, that is your way."

"I am not lying. I would hate to see him hang."

"And what of me, love?"

"I have told you, I will cheer the loudest when you swing by the neck!"

He watched her for a long moment, his eyes fathomless, his smile implacable. "Yes, I believe that you would. But they will have to catch me first, you know."

"Perhaps Robert will betray you."

"Fallen to your charms!"

"I did not intend to charm him, nor did I do so."

"Be glad then that you did not, mam'selle, for then I should have been forced to slay him."

Skye gasped. *He* was lying now! she thought. But how could she know? The man was an enigma. He leaned toward her then, speaking softly. "Indeed, I warn you, Skye, take care with my men. Any who touches you will die, and I will come to think that I do not give you adequate attention if you must seek out others."

"I seek escape!"

"You will be free soon enough," he said flatly. He started to rise, and she was glad, for she was sure that he meant to leave, and she was trembling terribly. But there was a knock upon the door and it opened and Robert was there again. He looked at the Hawk, who waited expectantly. "We've the hip bath, Captain."

"Bring it in."

Skye looked at him in horror, swirling to the far corner of the cabin quickly. She sought to hide, she realized, but there was nowhere to go. Two sailors walked in with the wooden tub between them and it seemed that a score of others followed with buckets of water.

And they all saw her. Every man saw her there in his quarters like a common . . . harlot.

She locked her jaw but didn't make a move. The men filed out, one after the other, until only Robert remained, explaining that he had set a kettle within the stove and that towels and soap were set upon her trunk. Then he, too, was gone, and she was left alone with the Hawk and her steaming tub.

Still, she remained dead still. Steam wafted above the tub and silence hung heavy upon the air. It dragged on and on. Then the Hawk idly lifted a hand. "Your bath is ready."

"Well, I am not."

"The men worked long and hard to prepare this water for you, milady. I suggest that you use it."

"I see. And I don't suppose that you might consider leaving so that I might do just that?"

"No, I will not consider leaving."

"Sea slime!" she hissed.

"A previously established fact, milady."

"Oh, stop it, will you!"

"Why?" he inquired innocently. "Stop what? I am trying to be a gentleman sea slime and refrain from arguing with a lady."

"This is absurd. I will not get into that tub with you here."

He arched a brow, and she saw that he was not at all in a good humor, no matter how light his words. "How cold, Lady Kinsdale, how very cruel! I bear the burning tortures of the flesh by night to offer comfort and nothing more, and for my pains I return to my cabin—where I strive to keep you in comparative comfort and ease—to find you casting yourself into the arms of my second mate! Then, when I find my own leisure from the travail of captaining the ship, it is only for you to suggest I leave! Have pity, milady."

"You should have sought a career upon the stage, sir," Skye told him curtly. "It would have been a legal profession, and one at which I am quite sure you would have excelled."

"Skye, I will not leave my cabin."

"And I will not crawl into that bath."

"I can make you, you know."

"So you can. But it will be against my will."

"Then is it your will that we clash by flesh again?"

She flushed, grating her teeth. Was she insane? He spoke the truth. It would be easier to move of her own accord. But that would be surrendering to his command, and she could not bring herself to do so.

"I will not crawl into that tub," she repeated.

"By all the saints!" He swore with such vehemence and fury, leaping to his feet, that she cried out and backed further against the wall. She'd been a fool. He would touch her and with violence. He would rip the gown from her and toss her into the steam and . . .

She didn't know what came after the "and."

"Wait!" she pleaded, but he ignored her. With deadly menace he walked around his desk, his hands upon his hips. He stared at her hard, and his voice rang out with a deep tenor that caused a tremor in her heart and made surrender seem a most viable possibility. "Well, milady, if you will not get into that tub—" He paused, and she was halfway certain that he was about to do her severe bodily harm. But he twisted around instead, starting upon his own buttons. "If you will not get in, Lady Kinsdale, then I shall do so myself."

"What?" she gasped, stunned.

He tossed his shirt to the floor and pulled off one of his boots. "I'm not about to waste that water."

"But you can't just—" She broke off. His other boot fell to the floor. He paused.

"I can't just what?" he demanded politely.

"Take a bath in front of me!"

He cast his head back and his husky laughter held a dangerous note. "Milady, I beg to differ. I can. And I intend to."

His hands were at the back tie of his knee breeches. She turned her back to him and stared at the wall. He ignored her. She heard him sink into the hot water with a self-satisfied sigh.

"You have the morals of . . . of . . ."

"Sea slime?" he asked politely.

"Of a gutter rat!"

"We cannot all play the grand hypocrite, milady. Be a love, will you? Yell out to Robert. This soap will not do at all."

"I will not call out to Robert!" Skye protested.

"But then," he said indignantly, "I shall smell like a French whorehouse. Oh, that will not do! It will not do at all. Come now, Lady Kinsdale, lend a hand here."

"You're out of your mind!" she said, staring at the paneling and shelves. Damn him! His sigh had been highly irritating. He was enjoying her bath.

"Will you call the man for me, or not?"

She didn't hear that his tone had changed. "No!"

"Then I shall have to call him myself!"

She heard the water roll and sluice as he stood. Despite herself, she twisted slightly. Whipping up the massive cotton towel that Robert had left for her use, the Hawk strode to the doors and pulled them open. "Mr. Arrowsmith! I need you, please!"

Robert must have been accustomed to running quickly to his master's call, for he appeared momentarily and listened to the Hawk's command for a more gentlemanly soap. Then the Hawk waited at the doors, tapping his foot.

Robert returned and gave him the soap. The Hawk then returned to his bath, humming. He had closed the doors, Skye realized, but he had not bolted them.

"You don't need to peek, Lady Kinsdale. I am here for the asking, you know. Alas, awaiting your gentle promise."

"You will rot in an unmarked grave, you know," she said sweetly.

"Perhaps, but until then . . . oh, this is frustrating. Come here, will you? I need help with my back."

"You will die of a horrible case of insanity," she assured him, "and then rot in an unmarked grave."

"I don't think so. I think that you will come over here and give me the small comfort of your sweet assistance."

"Sir, I would not spit your way if you died of thirst."

"You press Lady Luck, mam'selle."

"Do I?" she murmured uneasily. She did not like having her back to him, but she did not intend to move, and she was not going to rise to any of his taunts or obey a single command.

The doors, she recalled, were open.

Perhaps she just might pretend to obey a command. . . .

"Lady Kinsdale—" he began, but broke off when she spun around. She stared hard at him. He looked absurdly comfortable in the tub, the steam matching the mist of his eyes, his long legs drawn up beneath him, his arms draped comfortably over the sides. A pleased smile curved his mouth as he watched her. "How nice, mam'selle! If you just soap and scrub the upper shoulder?"

She smiled sweetly in return. She strode toward the tub, and then straight by it. She just caught sight of his smile as it faded, then she reached the doors.

But just as she cast them open and started to flee, she felt a tug upon her gown and then heard the awful rending sound as it split down her back. She cried out, swinging around. Naked and dripping, he stood behind her, a large part of her gown in his hands. A strangled sound escaped her as she realized that her lower body was bared to the wind. "Oh!" she railed.

She nearly ran anyway, to jump into the sea if need be. But he was quick. He dropped the fabric in his hands and caught hold of her arm, wrenching her back into the cabin. He slammed the doors shut with a vengeance. And this time he slid the bolt.

He turned around, staring at her. Her gaze fell against his body, then her eyes jerked back to his with growing alarm. He smiled. Like a hawk with a field mouse within its claws. Then his smile faded and he stared at her somberly. His voice was deep, menacing in its very quiet. "End of play time, my love. There is one serious thing here that you have failed to realize. It is imperative that you follow my orders. And from now on, Skye, I promise that you will."

Her lower lip was trembling despite her staunchest efforts to remain calm. She clutched the remnants of her gown to her, gritted her teeth, and backed away, vowing to herself that she would not falter. But her resolve fled from her when he took his first step toward her. She panicked, shrieked, and leaped away. He caught her arm, pulling her back to face him. He wrenched the gown from her, his eyes so dark they were like burning coals upon hers. A breath of air and no more separated their bodies. She could feel him with the length of her. A whisper of space and she would be crushed against him . . . she would know all the hard-muscled coils and planes of his body, she would know the feel of the dark hair that curled over his chest, just as she knew the searing pulse that protruded from him and did touch her body, brushing like a living flame against her belly.

She could not swallow, she could not breathe. His lips were close, so close. He was wet and sleek and all the more menacing for it, the bulge of his shoulders and arm and chest muscles glistening in the sunlight that streamed in from the open window. She wanted to scream, but she could not, for she still couldn't even draw breath. The world would fade. She would fail, she would sink to the floor in a dead faint and he would surely know nothing of mercy. . . .

"Your bath awaits you," he said, his words falling like a touch of mist against her lips. Then he was touching her completely, sweeping her up into his arms.

And he deposited her firmly within the tub.

Instinctively she drew her knees as close to her chest as she could. He rescued her hair, winding it into a knot. The water was steaming hot and delicious. She shivered uncontrollably in spite of it.

"Let's see . . . it's quite all right if *you* smell like a French whorehouse," he muttered. He was behind her. She tried to twist and rise and elude him, but his hands were already upon her. He held a cloth fragrant with the sweet-smelling soap and he moved it over her neck and shoulders and down the length of her arms. Her movement of protest worked well against her, for his hand slipped down, and cloth and soap and man came in startling contact with the full curve of her breast. She gasped, startled and desperate, for the brush of his fingers against the peak of her breast made it swell and harden, and horror filled her, just as the sensation of lightning swept with a vengeance into the whole of her being. Their eyes met. She was caught in some strange hypnotism again, unable to move. She felt the ferocity of her heartbeat and she knew that he saw the pulse that throbbed against her throat. She hardly dared to look at him, and yet she could not help herself, and when her eyes fell upon his body again, panic seized her. He had dropped the cloth. His bare hand lay against her breast. He was as still as she, his eyes burning, the whole of him gone rigid. Her lips were dry despite the steam. She fought to moisten them. To draw breath to speak.

"Please!" she managed to cry out.

She heard the grate of his teeth. He shoved away from the tub with the frightening thunder of an oath upon his lips. Skye sank further into the tub, hugging her knees once again. She heard him jerk on his breeches. He clothed himself no more thoroughly, but barefoot and bare-chested slammed his way out of his cabin.

He did not even pause to bolt her in from the outside. Nor did Skye dare to move at first. She waited, frozen there.

Seconds later, she heard the bolt slide home. Robert Arrowsmith had come, she thought. Always his master's man, tying up whatever loose ends the Silver Hawk might leave.

She came to life then. She scrubbed herself quickly and furiously, then leaped from the tub and dried as quickly as she could manage with the one towel that had been left between them. It carried a hint of his scent, she thought. Of the more masculine soap he demanded that Robert bring him. Of something deeper. Of something that was curiously pleasant and deeply primal, the subtle scent that was uniquely his.

She threw the towel from her and hurriedly searched her trunk for a clean shift. She dressed carefully and completely in hose and shift and corset and petticoats and gown, but it wouldn't have mattered what she had chosen to wear.

He did not come back to the cabin. Not that day. Not that night. Robert came with men to clear away the tub and breakfast tray, and he came again later to bring her supper.

She fell asleep at his desk.

Later, she awoke in his bed, and wondered how she had come there. Had she walked? She was still clad in her gown and petticoats. All that had been stripped from her body were the soft leather slippers she had worn upon her feet.

Had he come back?

He was not within the cabin. Two lanterns burned brightly, and she was not left to the darkness.

Skye lay back down, deeply disturbed. She hugged one of his pillows tightly against her, horrified to realize that she missed the man beside her, and missed the way that he had held her, making her feel secure against each and every terror of the night.

He did not come the next day. Robert Arrowsmith arrived bright and early with her breakfast. He promised that he would return to walk her about the ship.

She did not ask about the Hawk, nor did she seek to "rehabilitate" his second mate.

The Hawk had said that he would kill any man who betrayed him, and Skye believed that he did not make idle threats.

By noon Robert took her out on deck. Every man jack was courteous to her, tipping his hat or cap or inclining his bare head her way. They sailed with a good wind.

The Silver Hawk was nowhere to be seen. Skye leaned against the portside hull and felt the wind whip through her hair and caress her face. Robert pointed out the distant shores of Florida, and she nodded, then gazed at him pensively.

"What has happened to Bess and Tara?" she asked him. "The young Irish maids. Do they . . . live?"

She thought that he quickly hid a smile, but he spoke to her gravely. "Aye, lady. They live. They will be returned with you, no doubt, to Virginia."

"Yes, yes! Please see that it is so. My father will pay for them, I promise."

"I will inform the Hawk about your concern," he said.

"Where is the Hawk this morning?" she said, then despised herself for the query. What did she care? She was grateful for his absence, no matter what had caused it, or what it meant.

"He, er, is busy. He will be busy for quite some time. Probably until we reach New Providence."

"How . . . nice," Skye said flatly.

Robert looked at the sky, then cleared his throat. "I'm afraid it's time for you to return to the cabin. Can I bring you anything?"

She shook her head, then she changed her mind. "Er, I'd have another bath if I might." What a lovely opportunity. She would have the sweet-scented soap and the wonderfully steaming water without any fear of his arrival.

"Another bath?" Robert said disbelievingly. "You expose your pores, milady, to heaven knows what maladies!"

She was surprised to discover that she could smile at his very real concern. "So far, Mr. Arrowsmith, I have been quite lucky with my health, despite the bathing. Is this a problem?"

"No, no! Your wish is my command, Lady Kinsdale."

How ironic! she thought bitterly. It was such a pity that her wishes didn't seem to mean a damned thing to his master.

"Thank you," she murmured.

He returned her to the cabin. Restlessly she studied the books in the shelves. They were many and varied. He had texts by Bacon and Shakespeare and Sir Christopher Wren. Greek classics lined one shelf and there were tomes on not only warfare and naval maneuvers but also philosophy and medicine and the astrological sciences.

The Silver Hawk was a well-read man.

Else he had privateered the ship of some well-read gent! That, too, was a possibility. He was a thief. He had probably stolen the books just as he had everything else.

Robert and two sailors brought the tub to her again and the crew filed in and out with their buckets of water. Again, she thought they seemed too decent a lot to be pirates.

She had been locked in the room for four days, going on five, and she was losing her mind.

Nervously she disrobed and hopped in the tub. She expected him to arrive the very second her clothes were shed, but he did not. In a matter of moments, she leaned back. She let the steam enter deep into her and soothe her muscles and her aching spirits. The water began to lose its heat after a while. She had lingered too long.

Had she waited for him? she wondered.

No!

But perhaps she had. Perhaps she had waited to feel the explosive sensation of lightning tearing into the very core of her body, as she'd felt when his fingers had curved over her breast.

"Never!" she whispered aloud, shamed and humiliated. She leaped out of the tub, grabbing her towel, wrapping it around herself.

That was when the doors opened.

Fully clad in his boots and a handsomely trimmed frockcoat, he was holding a ledger in his hands and he seemed preoccupied with it. When he came full upon her, he stopped in surprise. Skye hugged the end of the towel to her chest and stared at him, her eyes wide, and did not say a word.

Nor did he speak. He tossed the ledger upon his desk. For the longest time he watched her, and she felt her blood begin to race within her.

"You like to bathe," he said politely.

"Yes," she managed to reply. He was very grave.

"Did you sleep well, mam'selle?"

"Yes."

He went silent for a moment. "Robert came and took you about the deck?"

"He—he did."

He ran out of small talk then. He took the two steps that brought him before her. She didn't try to run. She didn't even think to do so. His silver-blue eyes held hers in a curious grip, and she scarce had breath in her body. Her flesh burned, and she felt rooted to the floor.

She could not run.

He paused before her and his fingers very slowly threaded through her hair. He tilted her head back, and then he slowly lowered his lips to hers.

His touch brought the lightning to her again, and a sweet fever seemed to rage through her body. His beard and mustache teased her flesh as his lips pressed against hers with a consuming force that swept all thought from her mind. His tongue teased the edge of her mouth, causing her lips to part to the provocative demand. His tongue filled her, and the kiss was planted deeper and deeper.

No longer was he content with the sweetness of her mouth. His hands fell to the small of her back, bringing her flush against him. Then his fingers fell against her cheeks, along the slender column of her throat, to the rise of her breasts.

Not once did she think to fight him.

Not even when his hand closed over the full naked curve of her breast and she dimly realized that her towel had fallen. Not even then did she fight him. She did not think to fight, for thought eluded her completely, and the shattering sensations ruled her heart and soul. The liquid heat of his kiss swept into the length of her, the sensual stroke of his callused fingertips brought a peculiar sob to her throat. . . .

It was the sound of that sob, wanton and hungry, that shocked her from her paralysis. She pressed hard upon his chest, but he held her there tightly. She beat against him desperately, but he did not free her. Her head fell back and she met his eyes. They were dark with a brewing tempest, frightening to behold. "Don't play with me, girl, so help me!"

"Play!"

"Don't tempt, lady, and for the love of God, don't tease!"

"I have not! You are the puppet master here, pulling the strings like an almighty god! You seized me! You imprisoned me, and you give out orders like a tyrant king. You are a master of torture. You taunt until I am insane. I fear rape, I fear death, and you play with me like a cat with a mouse!"

He touched her cheek, his eyes still stormy, his features tense. She strained against him, but his thumb fell over her damp and swollen lips.

"Was that, milady, a threat of rape?"

"Please . . ."

"You made a promise. Perhaps you do mean to fulfill it."

She jerked from him, falling to her knees, reaching for the towel. He came down beside her, resting upon the balls of his feet. "It seems that I am the plaything, lady. You cling to me in the night, and trust in my goodness. In the darkness I could take whatever I desired, couldn't I, Lady Kinsdale?" Her head was down, but he lifted her chin.

"I was kidnapped—"

"Answer my question."

"All right!" she shouted. "It would be easy for you then. So easy. I've oft wondered why you didn't . . ."

"Rape you as you clung to me in terror?" he demanded sharply.

"Yes!" she whispered. Tears came to her eyes, glazing them. He would not let her free.

He shook his head slowly. "I will never have you that way, milady. Coming to me in fear of the darkness. I will have you only when you turn to me because desire, not fear, guides you."

Her eyes widened.

"I will never desire a pirate!"

A slight smile touched his features. His finger rode slowly, sensually over the bare slope of her shoulder.

"If I willed it, you could be coerced into desiring me this very moment," he said softly. Then he rose abruptly, and she felt very small as he spoke down to her. "You are right, milady, on one account. I am a master of torture, and it is myself that I so abuse. I will depart, until you are safely clad."

He turned smartly upon a heel and left her. Slowly she rose, her body on fire, her limbs quaking. She was lethargic at first. She could scarce will herself to move.

She touched her lips with her fingers, and she started shaking all over again. She could feel his lips still, she could feel his hands upon her. . . .

He was coming back. He had said so.

She dove into her trunk. She had one nightgown left within it. Soft blue flowered cotton with satin ribands about the puffed sleeves and waist. The cotton was gossamer, sheer but strong.

She plunged quickly into the gown, and none too soon. There was a sharp rap upon the door, then the Hawk entered once again. For a pirate, he was absurdly regal, striking in his outfit of black, from his elegantly cut coat to the plume that danced upon his hat. Robert entered behind him, and the pirate captain gave his mate the ledger. "Care will be taken, the gravest care," he said.

Robert looked her way and nodded. Then he smiled nervously, finding her eyes meeting his. "Supper comes, my lady," he told her.

She didn't care. She wanted only to escape the presence of the Hawk.

"I am not hungry," she whispered. Robert nodded vaguely, watching her, then his eyes narrowed as he looked at the Hawk again. The pirate captain had taken his chair behind his desk, and seriously studied figures within a second book.

Skye crawled into the bunk, far against the wall. The two men continued to talk about cargo to be bartered, bought, or taken. She closed her eyes. Their voices droned on.

She drifted to sleep, hearing their conversation like some lulling sound. Sleep was sweet, and sleep was good, until the darkness suddenly intruded upon it.

She was trapped. She pushed and shoved and she could not escape. It had come to choke her, the darkness. She could not breathe, she could not swallow, she could not summon the air to scream. . . .

"Skye!"

His voice fell upon her like a gentle ray of sunlight. Her eyes flew open.

His face was above hers. Light filled the room; there had never been any darkness.

"Oh!" she cried, and she tried to cover her face with her hands. The fear had seized her, and would not let go.

He must have come to bed with her that night meaning to sleep, for his chest was bare, and though the coverlet spread over his lower torso, she assumed that his legs would be bare as well. It was the way that he slept.

His arms came around her and the gentle touch of his fingers led her cheek to rest against his chest. He stroked her hair. "What is the terror?" he asked her softly.

She shook her head. He sighed.

At last, her shaking began to ease. She pressed against him, her face rising upon his chest to meet his eyes.

"You—you needn't comfort me."

"It's all right."

"But you say that I crawl to you . . . and taunt you."

"It's all right."

"I do not mean to do so."

He caught her hands, and eased them from his chest. Her hair spilled over the golden breadth of it. His features seemed tense, for all of the gentle tenor of his words.

"Truly, you do not have to comfort me!" she whispered.

He sighed very deeply. "Milady, it is all right. It is my pleasure, Skye Kinsdale, I swear it. Lie still, and sleep once more."

She closed her eyes, and felt his body shudder.

My pleasure! he thought.

And truly, torture beyond all earthly reason.

5

HE SILVER HAWK STOOD HIGH ATOP THE FOR-
ward deck of his ship, legs firmly planted, his hands upon his
hips. The breeze rushed by him as he surveyed the channel
they so carefully navigated. They were clear, he knew. Robert
was at the helm while certain of his sailors climbed the rigging with the agility of
monkeys, leaving them enough sail to catch the breeze, but cutting in deftly for
speed and maneuverability. They were coming upon the island of New Providence, to the lusty port town where rogues held sway and thieves and butchers
ruled.

He knew the port well. He had come here often enough.

Some curious little tremor seized him suddenly, as if he had stepped from a
hot bath into the chill of a winter's day. He shook away the feeling with a shrug
of his shoulders. There was danger here still, he thought.

But there was always danger. He had entered into this devil's pact of his
knowing that danger abounded.

Still, this was different.

It was the girl, he knew.

He should have gone on to Bone Cay, he thought, even if it increased his
travel time. He couldn't have done that, not plausibly so, but it was from this den
of thieves that he would send his messages out and strike his bargains for the
return of the ship and the hostages. And he had to come here now, for this was
where the captains all came to plot their courses and pick their prizes. It was
imperative that he come.

It was just the girl, damn her hide!

She would be safe. He would leave her carefully bolted within her room. They
would take the long boats in, and he would leave her in the care of Jacques
DuBray. That mammoth Frenchman was a master with a rapier. No harm would
come her way.

He took his glass from his pocket and surveyed the scene they came upon. He
could see the shanties of the town, the ribald colors and patterns that made up
the pirates' haven. Kegs of gunpowder and salt fish lay on a wharf. A dark-haired
whore stretched atop the bow of a small cutter, her skirts high against her thigh,
her legs bronzed from the sun. She waved a fan in a leisurely fashion, idly
listening to the talk of the two men who straightened fishing nets nearby.
Further into town, there were more decent structures that resembled houses, but
most of the place was beach and shanty . . . and warehouse for ill-gotten gains.

It was not a place for a lady. . . .

He scowled suddenly and leaped down from the bow peak. He waved to Rutger Gunnan at the wheel and nodded out his satisfaction at their course. They would cast anchor soon. "Tell Robert we will set to shore within the hour!" he called.

Rutger nodded his assent. "Aye, Captain!"

The Hawk turned and approached the door to his cabin. To his great annoyance he paused before sliding the bolt and entering his own realm. He'd been a fool to ever bring her here. She'd been such a challenge with her lightning speed with a sword that it had seemed necessary to cast the very fear of demons into her soul.

He had not suspected that they resided there already, nor that it would be he who would suffer the torment of the damned rather than she.

Impatiently he shoved the doors open and entered his cabin.

She was perched upon the window seat. The drapes were back and daylight streamed in. Her legs curled beneath her; she wore a soft white muslin with a brocade bodice, which was fashionably low cut to display the rising curves of her breasts. The skirt spilled out over a volume of petticoats in a soft burst of snow white and soft pastel. She worked on some piece of mending for him, which brought another scowl to his lips. Her hair was free.

The color of a sunset.

Cascading and waving over her shoulders and breast like a web of radiant silk.

He itched to run his fingers through it. Actually, he itched to do much, much more. When she looked up at him, a soft smile on her lips, her aquamarine eyes shimmering like the most glorious Caribbean sea, he wanted to stride right to her and wrench her into his arms. He wanted to play the pirate in the most heinous fashion, rip her beautiful gown to shreds, and leave her with no doubt as to his rapacious desires and determination.

She looked so damned comfortable! And assured. Even domestic.

He clenched down hard upon his jaw and swallowed the force of his emotion, watching her as he walked around to take his seat behind his desk. He cast his booted feet upon the desk and laced his fingers behind his head. She held his shirt, he saw. The full-sleeved shirt he had worn the evening of their first encounter. She mended a tear near the throat. Her fingers, long and elegant, lay still over the material.

Just as they lay by night, long and elegant, over his bare chest.

"You will make a wonderful wife," he found himself snapping out at her with a startling hostility.

She arched a brow. A flicker of amusement curled her lip. "Why, Mr. Silver Hawk," she taunted, "I strive to be the very best of hostages, and still I do not please you! I no longer toss about jam and coffee cups, but spend my endless time pursuing the best interests of your wardrobe!"

He wagged a finger at her. "Beware, lady, you do play with fire."

She lowered her head, smiling. Damn her! She trusted him. Six days and nights with him now and she thought that she had discovered his true measure. Something made a snapping sound. He looked down to see that he had picked up a quill, and crushed it between his fingers.

He dropped the pieces and walked around to her. She barely skipped a beat with her task. She did not look up, nor did her fingers cease to move.

He reached down to her, cupping her chin with his fingers, raising her eyes to meet his. She was, indeed, a startling beauty. No artist could ever capture the blues and greens that mingled within her eyes, nor find the glorious reds and golds of her hair among oils or paints. The greatest sculptors of the Renaissance could not have duplicated the fine and delicate structure of her face, the regal position of her cheekbones, the determined set of her jaw. No man could mold what God had created of her form, an Eve cast upon him from the sins of Eden, slender in the waist, long-limbed, with delicate ankles and lush firm breasts, ripe and provocative beyond measure. To touch her was to stroke silk.

And she smiled . . . in complete comfort in his presence.

She needed to fear him somewhat. It was essential.

He plucked the mending from her hands, casting it aside. A look of startled alarm came into her eyes, and she struggled against him as he drew her inexorably to her feet.

"We come to the island," she said breathlessly.

"So I see," he told her, but he saw nothing at all at that moment, nothing but her eyes.

"Shouldn't you be—"

"Do you know, my lady, that you are one of the most beautiful creatures ever to walk this earth? Perhaps you do know. You are not a woman who lacks confidence."

Her breath came quickly. Her lips were dry and she moistened them. She strained against his firm hold upon her upper arms, but he did not release her. Her gaze wavered, then returned to his. "What do you want?" she cried.

He smiled slowly, assessing her. "I'm not quite sure as yet. I think I've decided that I could tame you. Perhaps I shall not ransom you at all. Perhaps I shall take you with me and have you reside with me forever."

"Don't tease me!" she pleaded, her eyes very wide upon his as she sought some truth from him.

What did plague him? he wondered. His fingers bit more forcefully into her arms. "Indeed, why should you think that I tease you, Skye Kinsdale? We pirates revel in debauchery and conquest. It would be most natural to return the ship . . . but not the maiden."

He lowered his lips as he spoke until his words fell like a warm breeze upon her parted lips. Then his mouth formed to the sweet curve of hers. She gasped but he drew her closer, seized by the dark power of a sweeping desire. Her lips were sweet; the clamor of her heart was sweeter still. He plundered her mouth with his tongue. He ravished and he laid bare. He tasted her until drums beat explosively in his head, and he knew that he would lose not only control, but his very soul in the bargain.

His lip moved from hers. He seared a trail down her throat with the damp heat of his parted lips, teasing her flesh with the tip of his tongue. He swept her collarbone, and the rise of her breasts above the haunting décolletage of her gown.

She had been still through it all. Then, as his kiss touched her breast, she let out a shriek of rage. He no longer held her with force, and she wrenched from him, shaking, wiping her lips with the back of her hand as if she had tasted evil.

It was less than complimentary, he decided wearily.

"Bastard!" she screamed, and she flew forward, her fists flailing. He barely protected his face and beard, catching her clawing fingers in the nick of time and bringing her back into his hold.

Damn her, he thought, then, and damn himself, for his desire for her remained, or perhaps it burned more fiercely. She was energy there in his arms, she was the power of the sun and the rhythm of the sea. She loathed him so . . . but it had taken her a long, long time to protest against the intimacy of his kiss, and she seemed ablaze. Was it hatred? Certainly, but it was a passionate hatred, alive, searing. It caused her to sizzle, to tremble, to stare at him with eyes afire. She swept into the very core of his being, heating him anew with her fire. In silence he swore against himself, and he swore against her.

He was captain. He could do what he chose. He was a pirate. The dread pirate Silver Hawk. He could sweep her across the room to his bunk, tear her clothing asunder, have her, sink into her, die within her . . . and it would but enhance his reputation.

He was losing his mind. He struggled with his heart, with his soul, and with the searing piece of his anatomy that was sweeping away his senses. Then he smiled at her, crookedly.

"Good, Lady Skye. Your kiss is good, your lips are sweet, your body is sound. You would not make a bad companion for the while, except that your temper is quite a thorn. But then again, perhaps your father or Lord Cameron will offer a high enough price for your head. No woman is worth too much a sum of silver or gold. And you do seem to lack experience."

"Oh!" she cried, and swore again with vengeance. Her eyes snapped and sparked their luminous aquamarine and he was ever more tempted by her.

"Milady, I have not heard such language from the rogues who sail with me. Take care. I may well tame you yet."

She spat out an explicit oath, struggling fiercely.

"Maybe you sit too easily today. Perhaps you need to be reminded that my touch is not always so gentle and tenderly given."

"Gentle!" she gasped. "Tenderly given!" But she went still then, her eyes very round, her features ashen. She had not forgotten their encounter the day when she had wreaked havoc upon his tableware.

No, she had not forgotten, nor did she sit so easily yet. Skye gritted her teeth and kept her eyes hard upon him. She fought no more, for she was suddenly certain that the words were more of a warning than she could imagine, that he was truly at some brink, as if his temper burned on some very short fuse. But oh, she longed to hurt him! How she longed to have the power to taunt and humiliate! She despised him with every breath within her, she was infuriated. . . .

With herself, as well as with him.

She stood so still before the very onslaught of his lips. She did not hate and decry his kiss, she felt it, she savored it. She allowed it! He startled her so, he took her so quickly. . . .

There was no excuse, for in her heart she knew that she had allowed it. Fascination had held her still, and a simmering curiosity had swept her into its grip while his heat had seeped into her, leaving her without sense or reason and scarce able to breathe.

He was a pirate, a cur. Then what was she, she wondered with humiliation, that she could so easily crave his touch, rather than despise it?

She stiffened her shoulders and raised her chin. "Do it!" she snapped out. "If you intend to rape me, then do it now! Let's end this torment!"

A single dark brow shot up and his lip curled into a rogue's smile, a quick, handsome smile that caused a new shimmering to take hold deep within her. She would shame him! She would make him feel less than a man, and surely he would leave her be!

"Pardon?" he said politely.

"I said do it! If you intend—" He stared at her so boldly! The words began to falter on her lips. "Do it! I have had it with this constant torment!"

"You're inviting me to rape you?" he said pleasantly.

"Yes! No!" she cried in dismay, and it didn't matter at all, because suddenly he did sweep her off her feet, and with long strides he bore her toward the waiting bunk where they had lain together so many nights now.

She fell upon her back, and he was over her. Her heart thundered and her breath came too quick and panic seized her. She hadn't shamed him in the least!

"No!" she cried, struggling fiercely. But his thighs, hot and strong as steel, locked around her, and laughing, he grabbed her wrists. She tossed, she writhed and arched, until she realized that her movement brought them into close contact. She railed against him with a new assertion that he was the absolute worst of the sea slime, but then she realized that he wasn't moving anymore at all, that his bold rogue's smile still touched his features.

"Alas! And I thought that I had disappointed you!" he cried passionately. "How would you have it now? Clothed, or unclothed. It can be done either way, I assure you. Shall I rent and tear fabric? How shall I manage this?"

"What?" she gasped.

"Ah, such a quandary, my dear love!" He adjusted his weight, straddling over her firmly. With one hand he pulled her wrists high atop her head, leaving the other free to taunt her. He touched her cheek and she twisted her head, trying to bite him. "Ah, careful, love!" he growled out, his smile fading, tension riding high within his features as he lowered his face close to hers once again. "Careful, careful love!" Then he cupped her breast, the heat of his hand defying the fabric that lay between his hand and her flesh. She spat out an oath and he laughed, taking his leisure, amused as she writhed and thrust against him. "Shall I take it slow, my dear? Tease and taunt and relish every movement you make against me?" His fingers found her nipple and she gasped and swore again, yet felt a rush of color flood her cheeks as she felt the peaks of her breasts grow pebble-hard to his touch. It was not the man, it was not an attraction, it was surely a response just like—

"Stop!" she hissed.

"How *shall* it be? There's fast, there's brutal. I could thrust you up against the wall and lift your lovely thighs about me and have done with it all in a matter of minutes!"

He no longer stroked her breast. His weight shifted again and he was leaning atop her, his fingers tugging upon the hem of her skirt and bringing it high against her thighs. His touch roamed intimately against her and she cried out, squirming to escape him, yet bringing herself intimately against his touch. Her cry suddenly changed to one of desperation as she felt the total heat and power and strength of the man. His heart was thunder, his pulse ticked mercilessly. She had perhaps asked for rape, and he now seemed obliged to have it all as she had challenged him.

"Please . . . !"

"Please? Please shall I continue? Shall it be rough and tumble? Or shall we try seduction?"

She closed her eyes, gritting her teeth, and trembled suddenly. "I shall see you hang!" she whispered.

She heard a curious sound. She opened her eyes carefully. He was laughing again, watching her. "You are a challenge, love. A definite challenge." He leaned close to her. "But I promised you once, lady, that it will not be this way, though I am ever more convinced that the time will come when we will lie together."

His face was so near, his whisper touched her. His eyes sought out hers with such a startling silver glimmer that she felt her protest die within her throat. She wanted him away, and that was all. For whatever else he might be, the Silver Hawk was an exceptional man. Honed and muscled and bronzed and fine, and able to awaken her from a maiden's innocence. She could deny it, but it was true.

Even though he had told her that no woman was worth much in silver or gold.

Yet he was going to let her go, she realized. He was not going to rape her. He had never intended to do so. He had merely meant to taunt and torture and tease her and provide himself with vast amusement.

"Oh!" she cried, squirming furiously against him again. "I, sir, will never come to you!" she promised him. His eyes flickered a silver warning and her voice fell to a quiet tone, but still, her words did not falter, and she was glad of it.

He said no more but released her and climbed off the bunk. He walked to his desk and searched through some papers there, speaking to her with his back to her. Skye lay still for a moment, afraid to move. Then she rolled to the edge of the bunk and sat there, smoothing back her hair and keeping a very wary eye upon him.

"I will be gone for some hours, probably late into the night. You will not be alone." He swung around suddenly. "New Providence is a dangerous place. Keep the drapes closed while we are here. Do not seek the deck, for no man will take you there."

She did not respond to him. He spoke to her sharply, very sharply.

"Do you understand me?"

Her eyes flashed angrily but she answered him very sweetly. "Why, Captain, your every wish is my command."

"Lady, trust me, you do not begin to know the depths of my temper, but I promise that you will know my wrath and know it well if you do not heed my warnings."

"What is there to heed!" she cried, leaping to her feet. "You will lock me in here, and your men will not let me out! Why bother to threaten me!"

He strode the few steps toward her, pulling her back into his arms. His lip curled as she jerked upon her wrists to free herself from his touch. He shook her suddenly, fiercely. "I know you, my love!" he said curtly, his eyes meeting hers as her head fell back and her hair cascaded around them both. "I know you, and I am never quite sure how I should be dealing with you. Warnings are no good—only threats seem to avail."

She stamped on his foot as hard as she could. For a moment she was vastly pleased, for the taunting smile left his lips and his face paled with the pain. Then she screamed, for he quickly sat down upon the bunk, dragging her along with him—over his knee.

"I've thought all along that you really need a good thrashing!" he swore.

"No!" Skye screeched, straining to raise herself from his lap. She bit his thigh. His hand landed harshly upon her posterior section and she cried out, tears stinging her eyes with the humiliation. She twisted around in time to see his hand rise again. "Stop, please!"

"You bit me! You stomped on me, and then you bit me! Apologize!"

"I can't!"

He was about to pull her skirt up for more intimate contact with her flesh. Crimson, Skye squirmed her way from him so that she fell to the floor at his knees. She stared up at him, dazed. "Please, stop!"

"Apologize!"

"All right! I'm sorry that I bit you!"

She lowered her head, despising herself for having apologized to a pirate. He stood up, and she saw his boots as he walked by her.

"I'm sorry I bit you!" she cried out, adding softly, "I wish that I could have boiled you in oil."

He was back beside her, lifting her chin. The silver in his eyes danced and the devil's smile was back upon his lips, so sensual that she trembled with warmth even as she swore that she hated him.

"I cannot wait to return," he told her very softly. "We can explore all of these secret yearnings of yours."

She opened her mouth to reply, but he had already turned away and was gathering his papers again. He swung back to her, his eyes narrowed. "Behave, Skye. I am warning you." His long strides brought him to the door. He swung about and stared at her hard one more moment, and then he turned to leave. She never heard the doors close with such a shattering force before.

Despite his warning, or forgetting it, Skye leaped up and raced to the window seat at the port side of the ship which faced the island. She hesitated there, wondering why he was so determined that she not open the drapes, then she set her hand upon the material, just to peek out. She shivered slightly. They were close to the shore, and she could see a great deal very clearly. All manner of persons lined the docks! Fishermen hawked their catches while a curious array of men and women walked the streets. Two scantily clad women looked down from a shanty balcony to beckon laughingly to a tall lad below. Barrels lined the steps before the thatch-roofed dwelling. Arm in arm, a man and woman lumbered along, then fell, drunk, upon each other in the street. Dandies strutted about in brocades and velvets. They wore knee breeches and silver-buckled shoes and silken hose and scarves and magnificent plumed hats. And yet some of these very dandies walked with near-naked seamen. They wore eye patches, and many a man had a stump for a leg.

She gasped suddenly, realizing that the finery was most probably ill-gotten gain. These were not gentlemen that she observed, but pirates, and probably the very worst of the lot. The Silver Hawk had come here to do business.

Just as the thought passed her mind, she drew back quickly, letting the drapery fall.

A longboat was moving out, away from the ship. The Silver Hawk was within it along with a dozen or so of his men. She had no desire to be caught by the man. She did not know quite what he would do to her, but she did not care to discover what it might be. Not after everything that had just passed between them. He would do anything, she thought. Dare anything . . .

He would come back. To her. No matter what she did. And she did not know how long she could bear the emotions and sensations that he brought raging within her.

She inhaled deeply, thinking of the island.

The lure of the place fascinated her. She waited impatiently, biting her lip, until she was sure that the longboat had reached the docks. Then she looked out again.

A second longboat had left the pirate ship. There were a good forty or so of the Hawk's men going to shore. She didn't think that he sailed with a crew of more than fifty or so. Few men would have been left aboard.

The Silver Hawk must have believed that no man would molest his property in the pirate haven.

Skye drew the drapery once again. The sun was setting, and the shantytown did not appear so tawdry or so dangerous. Someone was lighting flares to line the docks and the distant beach.

The longboats had reached shore. Someone came up to the Silver Hawk, offering him a silver horn to drink from. There was suddenly a burst of revelry upon the shore and men crowded around him.

She let the drapery slide back into place. A slow, burning heat had set fire deep inside of her, and she longed to leave the Hawk's cabin. Leave this atmosphere dominated by his presence. Her cheeks flamed as she remembered his words that he might decide to keep her. Then he had told her that no woman was worth much in silver or gold.

Perhaps all pirates felt that way. Somewhere here she could strike a deal. She could promise a sailor a huge quantity of money for her safe passage to Williamsburg.

But she couldn't even leave the cabin! she reminded herself. She was locked in. But she wasn't alone. Someone was with her. She knew it. Robert Arrowsmith? She hoped fervently that it was that young man left behind to guard her.

She was being absurdly reckless! she warned herself. She was waltzing into danger. The island was not populated by gentlemen. It was inhabited by cutthroats and rakes. They might not offer her help, but only the gravest danger!

But what danger could be greater than this she already faced? Lying with a man who threatened her with much more than the sins of the flesh as night after night passed by. Oh, indeed, he threatened her very belief in herself, he threatened her dignity and her pride, and assuredly, her very soul.

She leaped to her feet and paused a bare second. Then she hurried to the door and knocked strenuously upon it.

She would see him hang! she swore to herself. Indeed, she would see the Silver Hawk dance from a rope, so help her God!

———

The pub was called the Golden Hind in honor of a man that many of their brotherhood deemed to be the greatest pirate of them all, Sir Francis Drake. It sat far back from the market; to the left lay the sands of the beach and to the right were the docks where a man could purchase almost anything he desired. A ship could be repaired here, knives could be honed, weapons acquired. Flesh could be bought as easily as a fillet of fish, and even a murder could be negotiated if a man so desired. But there was honor among thieves, for the men here had their own twisted code of ethics, and upon the island, a pirate's property—stolen though it might be—was sacred.

Usually. But private wars did arise.

And this night, since his adventures with One-Eyed Jack, Silver Hawk knew he might be called upon to defend himself. He had, however, made his intent to take the *Silver Messenger* clear, and so he was the man with the right to the spoils. Jack was the offender, and a man was expected to slay an offender.

Tonight the Golden Hind was in raucous full swing. Fiddlers played upon a dais, rum flowed freely, and it seemed that the best names in the business were all in attendance. An up-and-coming man who was rumored to hail from Bristol— Edward Teach, who was known more notoriously as Blackbeard—held court at a far rear table. A man nearing forty, or so the Hawk determined, he was known for being ruthless, though not so deadly as the late Captain Kidd. Anne Bonny, her youth fast fading, sat nearby with her own grouping of louts. Whores freely strode about, pocketing the loot tossed about by the drunken pirates.

William Logan, a lean, mean bastard with blackened front teeth and a steel claw for a right hand, sat at a table with a few of his henchmen. A dark-haired whore perched upon the arm of his chair, but Logan gave her little attention. He stared broodingly at the Hawk.

"There's one to give us trouble," Robert Arrowsmith murmured as he entered at the Hawk's side.

The Hawk shrugged and took his place at a center table along with his men. He frowned, noticing that a man hastily entered the establishment and came up to William Logan, stopping by his side and speaking hastily. It disturbed the Hawk, though he wasn't sure why. Some sixth sense of danger sounded an alarm, but he held his ground.

What was going on? The question would have to wait.

Captain Stoker, sometimes called the "governor" of the island, sat before him and his men. He was an older man, bearded and graying, but he was built like an old Saxon warrior, and had a body to reckon with in a fight. He was grave as he spoke to the Hawk.

"There's some as don't like the idea o' Jack bein' dead, and you know that rightly. We're not out to murder our own number, Hawk, and that's a fact, it is."

The Hawk leaned across the table, skewering a piece of roasted lamb from a trencher in the center. His eyes met those of Captain Stoker. "Jack was well aware that the *Silver Messenger* was mine. I laid claim to her back here in March, the very day we learned that she had set sail from England!"

"Jack spoke of it first—"

"Jack mentioned the ship, sir. He was interested in the Spaniard, *La Madonna,* out of Cartagena, at that time!"

"Still—"

The Hawk slammed his knife, meat and all, into the table, and stood. "Listen to me well, me hearties!" he called, his voice ringing out. The music ceased. In seconds, the room came silent. Every man and woman looked at him, some with trepidation, and some, the Hawk knew, like Blackbeard, with interest. Some would respect his stand, and some would whisper behind his back. "One-Eyed Jack is dead, that is a fact, and that he died by my sword I do not deny! But I did not seek his death, he desired the fight, for he disturbed what he knew to be my intention, my prize. He died in combat with me, and me alone. He died by the very rules we all know here within our hearts. If any man here—or woman"— he interrupted himself, bowing to Anne Bonny—"cares to dissent with my words, I am ready to listen. Face me now, for whisperers will know my wrath!"

A fist slammed against the table. William Logan stood. The Hawk faced Logan. They had grappled once before, in this very room. Logan had wanted an English ship, and the Hawk had seized it first. They had dueled here with cutlasses.

And Logan had lost a hand before Captain Stoker had stepped in to end it all.

Logan wanted blood now.

"The ways that I sees it," Logan said, "Jack was already aboard the *Silver Messenger*. He had claimed the ship for his own. He had done battle, and he had taken the prize."

The Hawk planted a boot atop a bench and leaned forward casually. "He knew the prize was mine. The ship was not secured when I came aboard. Jack could have given way, and sailed clean and free. He chose to fight. And he died."

"So you're saying, Captain Hawk, that one of our brotherhood has the right to another prize?"

"It was my prize."

"His prize—that you seized from him."

"The overfine logic is yours, sir."

"What's logic?" a drunken whore whispered, and hiccuped.

Logan bowed low to the Hawk. "Logic, sir! As you will have it!" He turned, and with his men in tow, he exited the establishment.

No one else moved for quite some time. Then a young pirate, an Englishman, rose and spoke quietly. They said that his name was Richard Crennan, but whether that was true or false, no one knew. Men left their homes to seek their fortunes, dreaming of riches. Most of them thought to return to their homes one day, and so they seldom used true names, or gave out true facts regarding the towns from which they had hailed.

The Hawk liked young Crennan. He was a gentleman pirate, so they said, and hailed from a good family somewhere. Like the Hawk, he made money on his hostages, and disdained murder.

"I say that this matter is well and done!" Crennan called out. He raised a pewter mug. "We all know the Silver Hawk. He laid claim to the *Silver Messenger* out of England, I know well, for I was here, in this very room, when he did so. He did not betray our articles of brotherhood! He fought a fair fight. I say, gents, that that is that!"

"Here, here!" came a voice. It was Blackbeard, the Hawk saw. The man was a bloody cutthroat, but a strong ally nonetheless.

Hawk turned to Anne Bonny. "Madame, I crave your opinion?"

She smiled. Once, he thought, she had been a young thing. With dreams similar to those dreams that haunted other young maidens. He did not know what had drawn her here.

"I saw, Captain, that you have presented yourself well. The matter is done, and the facts established."

"I thank you, Mistress Bonny!"

He sat again. The proprietor made an appearance again, bringing wine and bread and more lamb to the table. "Hiding out lest there be trouble, eh, Ferguson?" the Hawk inquired, amused.

"Captain Hawk, I tell you, the roof is thatch, since you fine sirs do continually see fit to duel and set fires. My tables are ramshackle, easily replaced. My hide, though tough, is not so easy to replace, and so, good sir, yes! I disappear at the slightest hint of trouble."

The Hawk laughed and poured more wine for Captain Stoker. "Ease up, Cap'n! The matter is settled now, and peacefully at that."

"Logan will not let it lie. Already, he seeks to carve your heart from your body, you know!"

The Hawk waved a hand in the air. The musicians began to play again. A harlot shrieked with glee as a seaman poured a trickle of wine into the valley of her breasts. Laughter rose, and the night was made merry once again.

The Hawk picked up a pewter goblet of wine. "He will simply never have a piece of me, Captain, you needn't fear."

"I fear this warfare among us, for it will bring destruction down upon us."

Robert Arrowsmith glanced quickly at the Hawk. "How?" the Hawk asked with an easy smile. "Why, I hear tell that the governor of North Carolina is in league with a certain one of us! A man to be bribed, so they say. We, in this our Golden Age, shall reign forever."

Stoker shook his great head broodingly. He shrugged. "In the Carolina waters, perhaps, we find a certain safety. But in Virginia that damned Lieutenant Governor Spotswood seeks us out like bloodhounds!"

"So they say."

Stoker smiled, finding some amusement in the matter. "He will have to intrude upon Carolina to destroy us, though, eh?"

He started to laugh. The Hawk glanced at Robert, and then he started to laugh, too. He patted Stoker strongly upon the back. "Aye, Captain, he'll have to do just such a thing!" He sobered. "Now, to business, sir. I need canvas, needles, coffee, and fresh meat. And rum. Can you see to it all?"

Captain Stoker raised a hand, calling to one of his clerks. A little man hurried to them with an inkpot, quill, and paper, and sat down to take the orders.

For the moment, peace and laughter reigned.

———

It was not Robert who had been left aboard the ship to guard her. When she slammed upon the door, it was soon opened, but it was opened by a huge, burly Frenchman.

"Mademoiselle!" he cried, looking at her warily. He was like Samson out of the Bible, she decided. He had a head of dark curls and warm brown eyes. His size was intimidating; his eyes were not.

"Monsieur! Forgive me! I feel so ill of a sudden. I must have some air!"

"Ah, but my lady! *Sacrebleu!* The captain would have my head. You are to remain here."

"Ooooh!" she started to moan, doubling over. "I feel so very ill, I must have air. . . ."

"D'accord! I will take you out. Come, lean on me!"

She offered him a sweet, pathetic smile and leaned heavily against him. He led her out to the deck. She inhaled deeply, gasping, bringing in air. This was easy. Much, much easier than she had imagined.

He brought her to the railing. She leaned over, clinging to him, gulping for air. She also looked around herself. The ship was almost empty. She looked up.

There was a man in the crow's nest. She looked across the water. There were still men upon the dock. Someone was pointing their way. She felt a shiver seize her. Night was coming on quickly. Darkness was falling. Perhaps this plan of hers was not so well advised.

She looked down. The ladder was still in place from the deck to the water, and a longboat waited there, tied in place should it be needed. The temptation was too great to be resisted.

"Mademoiselle! Speak to me, are you better?"

The Frenchman's attention was entirely for her, and he was desperately worried. She felt a twinge of guilt, but ignored it. She sank down upon one of the barrels near the rail. "Oh, monsieur, I am much better, truly!" she said. He was by her side. She offered him a flashing smile, for it was then or never.

She reached down and drew his cutlass quickly from the scabbard that laced around his waist. Before he could move, she had brought the point to his very chin.

"Monsieur, forgive me, but I will be free this night!" she told him.

"Mademoiselle!" he said, and he tried to move. She pressed the point against him, drawing blood, and he went still. "Now, come, sir!" she said softly. "We will take the longboat to shore. If you cross me, I will skewer you through. I will do so unhappily, for you appear to be too kind a man for this life you have chosen, but I swear that I will gladly slice you open, nonetheless."

He said nothing. She pressed her point still further.

"Am I understood?"

"*Mais oui,* mademoiselle—" the Frenchman began, but he broke off as the sound of an explosion suddenly burst through the night.

Skye leaped to her feet, backing away from the Frenchman. There was a huge thud and she screamed as she saw that the sailor in the crow's nest had fallen to the deck, his shirt crimson with the spill of his blood.

"*Mon Dieu—*" the Frenchman said, ignoring her and spinning around to see from where death had sprung.

A man was halfway over the railing. He tossed a still-smoking pistol to the deck and drew forth a second flintlock weapon, aiming it their way.

He was a hideous soul, Skye thought, her heart hammering. He was dark and surly; a scar marred his right cheek. He wore a hat pulled low over his forehead, but it did not hide his eyes. They were pale and cold. He smiled, and his mouth seemed a black cavern, and his teeth looked awful and fetid. The leer gave him such a bearing of cruelty that she trembled.

Then she saw his left hand, or the very lack thereof. A deadly-looking hook protruded from his coat sleeve.

He aimed his pistol straight at the Frenchman. Without a sound or a word of warning, he fired.

Skye screamed with horror as the Frenchman went down in a pool of blood. She stared at the fallen man, frozen.

The hook-armed pirate crawled aboard. She had the Frenchman's cutlass. She needed to lunge quickly and fight. She needed to make the attack. It was her only hope. She raised her sword.

The hook-handed pirate looked past her, allowing his smile to deepen. "My pet, but you are sweeter than gold!" he said softly, and then he nodded.

Skye swung around, but too late. She barely saw the man who had come up behind her. There was a blur, and then nothing more. She was struck upon the head, and the world faded as she fell. The last thing she saw was the blood seeping over the deck. Then it all went black.

She heard the sound of waves lapping nearby. She became aware that she was rolling backward and forward herself, and that oars were striking against water. She opened her eyes. Darkness still surrounded her and she realized that she was wrapped in a suffocating, rough wool blanket. She struggled to free herself from its confines. The blanket fell away and she faced the pirate with the hook again. He aimed his sword with deadly accuracy against her throat and she sat still, watching him. "So the Silver Hawk sought the *Silver Messenger*," he mused. "I do wonder if you were the prize he sought all along. He was careless to let you be seen, my love. Very careless. Had Brice here not seen you peeking through the window, I'd never have thought to find you. And then, my dear, you came straight to the deck, making the whole thing so very easy for me. I do thank you." Behind her, his accomplice continued to stroke the water with his oars. She said nothing, and he idly picked up a golden curl with the point of his sword. "My dear, I am so very pleased to have found you! Not only shall I have my opportunity to slay the Hawk now, but I shall enjoy you as I'm sure you can't even begin to imagine."

"Over my dead body!" she whispered vehemently.

He leaned toward her. "Yes, my dear, that is quite possible, too."

Skye quickly changed her tactics. "I'm worth a fortune. If you keep me safe and return me—"

"I'm so sorry, my dear. This is vengeance, not finance. Brice! Row more quickly. I would not have the Hawk leave the Golden Hind before I can show him that I hold his prize."

He was deadly, Skye realized with a sinking heart. He was cold, as if no blood flowed through his veins.

And he was revolting; from his fetid breath to his icy eyes, he made her skin crawl. She had sought to flee one knave only to stumble into the arms of a monster. Her teeth chattered.

She wanted to die.

She leaped to her feet suddenly, praying that the boat would tip. She could swim, but she would rather drown than go any further with the horrid monster who sat before her.

"Grab her, Brice!" he roared, leaping to his feet. The longboat teetered precariously. It careened over.

She pitched downward into the warm, aquamarine sea. They were almost to the dock. If she could just swim . . .

But she could gather no speed, for her skirts were dragging her down.

A hand grabbed her hair, tugging painfully. She screamed, and drew in water. Coughing and sputtering, she fought only to breathe. She was being dragged along through the water. Light wavered before her eyes. She was wrenched upon a wooden dock, surrounded by voices and kissed by the balmy warmth of the night. She closed her eyes and opened them.

And stared into the evil glare of the hook-handed pirate.

She spat at him, struggling to rise. He swore, and tossed a new blanket over her face. She was being smothered again, but she could still fight with her limbs, kicking and scratching.

But she was dragged up and cast over his shoulder and held there forcibly.

"Don't fret, my dear. You will see blood run soon enough," he promised her.

––––––––

They drank, they laughed, they ate. The whores flirted, and they laughed at their antics. A buxom blonde promised Hawk the finest night of his life, and he told her that her words were a challenge indeed, but all the while he was thinking of another woman. One who was young and fresh and radiant and possessed the most glorious eyes.

And somehow she was able to touch him in a way he had never imagined. Touch him with her innocence, and yet evoke the most pagan and sensual thoughts that had ever come to plague him, to burn him. The whore whispered something, and he laughed. Then his laughter faded as the front doors to the establishment were suddenly cast wide open again.

He leaped to his feet. The whore fell to the floor, ignored. His hand lay upon his sword hilt where it rested within its scabbard upon his hip.

Logan had returned.

And he wasn't alone. He swaggered into the building, a blanket-draped, struggling figure held over his shoulder, his pistol raised in his free hand.

"Hawk!" he called. "You say it's just to seize one another's prizes? Well, sir, I have seized one from you, and in honor of our late brother, One-Eyed Jack, I demand of the brotherhood that this prize shall be mine in your stead!"

And with that, he cast his struggling bundle upon the floor, wrenching the blanket away.

To the Hawk's eternal horror, the Lady Skye Kinsdale appeared, scrambling frantically to her feet, pausing only when she saw the assemblage of rogues before her. Her hair was a tousled sunburst, damp and curling to her face and shoulders. Her gown was ragged, drenched, and torn, and her beautiful eyes were wide and brilliant with horror. She stood before them like a shimmering star in the horizon. Disheveled, she was still the lady, tall and straight, her pride radiating from her in the beautiful colors of life that separated her from the riffraff that filled the room. Her very beauty separated her from it all.

She was, indeed, a prize.

God in heaven, how in hell had she come to be there? the Hawk wondered in fury. He had to save her, he determined.

Just so that he could throttle her himself!

She spun to flee suddenly. Logan pushed her forward. Laughter broke out. A seaman rose to stop her when she lunged anew. And then another man rose, and another, and she was nearly encircled.

It was time for him to step into it. She lunged anew, and he left his table. The next time she lunged, she fell to the floor at his feet. She was quick. She braced her palms against the floor to rise, then paused, seeing his boots.

She looked up. Her eyes met his. She inhaled and gasped. He did not know if she trembled to see him, or if the dazzling liquid in her eyes was meant as a plea to save her. His heart leaped and careened to his stomach. They were in deadly danger now.

She had betrayed him somehow. Despite his threats, his words of warning, she had betrayed him.

He smiled icily. "Well, milady, do not say that you were not warned!" he whispered furiously. But there was no more that he could do then.

Logan had drawn his cutlass, and was stepping toward him.

6

SKYE WATCHED IN DEEP DREAD AS THE HAWK stepped over her to meet the instant clash of Logan's steel.

With a gasp she swiftly rolled to avoid being trampled. She came up beneath a table, and with a certain, horrified fascination, she watched the fighting men.

It was a fair fight; one well met. They might have engaged in a macabre dance, so graceful, yet so deadly, were their movements. Their left arms remaining behind their backs, they met and clashed, and parted again, their swords ripping the very air, so that it seemed the night itself whispered and cried. Cheers rose within the room, some claiming for Logan, some for the Hawk, and all of them urging on the fight with merriment and blood lust.

The men broke apart. Logan jumped upon a table. Leaping into flight, the Hawk followed behind him. The table crashed to the floor. Wine and ale spilled freely and pewter clanked upon the floor. Skye's hand fluttered to her throat, for she saw no movement. If he had died, then it seemed that she had best pray for death. What madness had brought her here? she wondered. But her thoughts were fleeting, for both men were upon their feet again. The duel was reengaged.

A hand clamped upon her shoulder of a sudden. She choked upon a scream as she was dragged to her feet.

She looked into the eyes of a man with thick dark hair, a stocky build, a sharp, cunning gaze, and the faint sign of pockmarks beneath the heavy growth of his beard. He wore a scarlet frockcoat with golden epaulets and fine soft mustard breeches. He hauled her up against him. She struggled fiercely, seeking to bite him. "Hold, lassie!" he warned her. "I'm not your enemy!" Swinging her before him, he called out to the fighting men. "Gents of the brotherhood! Cease this ghastly foray and listen! This fight is no longer over Jack, nor, I daresay, was it ever! Logan, you would have him dead. Hawk, you would have the woman. Let's put a price on her head. That's our business, is it not? Gaining riches? So what is she worth, gentlemen? In gold?"

"Here, here!" someone else cried, laughing. "Is it open bidding, then? I'll give a hundred pieces o' eight, Spanish gold, the best o' the lot!"

"One-fifty!"

"Two hundred!"

"A thousand gold doubloons!"

"A thousand!" It was the Hawk. He stared down the length of her, then looked to her captor. "Nothing that lies 'twixt a maiden's thighs could come so dear!"

"Dear me, and not hers!" chortled one of the whores, who waltzed by Skye, tweaking her cheek. Skye kicked her furiously. The woman screamed out, lunging toward her.

"Cease!" the Hawk yelled, catching the whore. She turned to him with huge dark eyes and her painted features, a pretty thing despite her paint, young and buxom.

"She kicked me, Hawk! Why, I'll claw her eyes out, I will!"

"She's not that easy, Mary, trust me. And she is to be ransomed, so keep clear of her, eh?" Gently, he thrust the whore far from himself, and far away from Skye.

"Is the bidding open again?" someone called.

"Aye, and think on this. She's a feisty piece of baggage!" the dark pirate called out.

Skye stared about herself in dismay. The Hawk was lost to a clang of steel once again while the others were all having a rollicking good time discussing her life in terms of the highest sum. The pirate holding her had a cutlass at his waist. She eyed it as another bid rang out. She itched to get her fingers upon it!

"A thousand! I've said a thousand! Someone top that, me friends!"

Skye heard something like the roar of a furious lion, and she saw that the Silver Hawk had come to the center of the room again, staring at her and her new captor, Teach, as Hawk had called him. "She is not public property, Teach! I took the prize, the prize is mine, and I will slay every man jack here who attempts to tell me otherwise!"

"What?" the pirate Teach said in dismay. "Why, I'd had in mind to bid upon this morsel meself! Can she be worth so very much then, Captain Hawk?"

The Hawk's eyes raked her with a careful disdain. Even there, before all others, the gaze seemed to strip her of her clothing, to lay her bare and naked before them all. A sizzle of mockery touched his eyes. "No woman is worth so much," he said, "and this one screams like a banshee and lies like a log. The equipment is there, but alas, she lacks the talent to use it."

She gasped out loud, despising him, despising the way that he had made her feel. She hated the cold steel in his eyes, and she hated the humiliation he caused her. Snickers of laughter rose up softly at his suggestion of their intimacy. "The point, sir," Hawk continued, "is that the prize is mine! What is mine, I shall keep!"

"But if she is of little use—"

"She will draw a good ransom."

"I would pay that ransom."

"Neverless, sir, I have begun a certain . . . er, contact with the lady, and I would continue where I have left off."

"You said—"

"Aye, Blackbeard, but I believe I could train her and tame her, and for the very measures, I would keep her now in my possession until I have chosen to make other arrangements."

Blackbeard! Skye shivered, aware then that she was being touched by another of the most notorious pirates in the Caribbean.

"Perhaps this could be settled with Captain Logan if you were to pay him the ransom," Blackbeard suggested.

"I'll not take money!" Logan cried.

"And I'll not buy back what is already mine!" the Hawk claimed.

Watching him in fury and amazement, Skye suddenly screamed. Logan had wasted little time, but had come up behind him, his sword raised and ready to swing in a wide arc. The Hawk ducked just in time, else the arc would have severed his neck and sent his head flying. The Hawk swirled about, striking out.

"Logan, you backstabbing refuse!" the Hawk roared.

"This is a fight!" Logan snarled back. "Not a bloody mincing court of civil law!"

The Hawk caught Logan's cutlass with his blade; the sword flew and clattered. The Hawk stepped back, but one of Logan's men leapt into the fray, charging for the Hawk.

"The plate!" A heavy-jowled man behind Skye and Blackbeard called out. "Save the plate!"

Skye quickly understood why. The fight was no longer one-on-one, but a melee. Men leaped about to join in with roars and cheers, and steel was soon clashing about the room.

"Look at this, at what you have caused!" Blackbeard hissed in her ear. "Alas, the law does not catch men, but mere women send them to their dooms. Perhaps I should let them all battle it out, mam'selle, and spirit you away myself."

She did not know if he taunted her or spoke the truth. The room had become terribly warm. Now screams arose, and injured men fell from the fray, crashing upon tables, falling to the floor.

Blood ran, mingling with the wine upon the sand and dirt.

Very likely, they would all long to slit her throat when it was over.

Skye acted on desperate impulse, reaching swiftly for the man's cutlass and jerking it from his hold. She wagged the sword beneath his nose. "Leave me be, sir, and I will leave you be!" she cried out.

"Why, a fighting maiden. Girl, give me back that sword!"

She shook her head. Blackbeard yelled out. "Mr. Clifford! Toss me a sword!"

A sword flew his way. He grinned at Skye. "Now give me that weapon, girl!"

She refused and he thrust toward her blade. She parried him with swift skill, but knew that his strength would be great.

"Blimey!" he cried. "She knows how to use it!"

Skye wanted no more of the man known as Blackbeard. She counted on her speed to bring her through the crowd of rioting men. At first, no one thought to strike her, only to stop her wild flight. Then, as more and more of the sailors came away from a brief encounter with pricks of blood upon their persons, cries of warning went up.

Three men came toward her.

There was a stack of wine barrels by the door. Skye instinctively tossed them over. They cracked and spilled, and it seemed that the earth was soaked with it.

"Dear God, dear God, I am ruined!" called out the proprietor. A straw-haired harlot in totally disreputable undress shook a fist toward Skye. "You've cost us all, girl!"

Skye ignored her, looking to greater danger. She was backed against a wall then, and more and more men were coming her way. They laughed no more. Their faces were grim.

"Get behind me!" she heard. White-faced, she dared to look around.

The Hawk was coming her way, fiercely challenging every man who sought to approach her. She was amazed again at the deftness of his swordplay. He leaped upon a bench and soared forward, taking with him three of her attackers. He spun about and caught one man at the knees, leaving him screaming, slicing a second man through the arm, and catching a third at the throat.

She nearly missed an opponent, watching him. She came to attention just soon enough and ducked a blow that struck the wall. Hawk was beside her then. His weapon, she saw, had taken a beating. The steel had cracked.

"Give me the sword!" he commanded her.

She stared at him, her eyes growing very wide. Did it matter? She had caused this fray. She had brought him to arms against his comrades. He had claimed that she wasn't worth any fortune in gold, that he would keep her just because he already had her. He was surely furious with her, and might very well plan to torture her near to death once he had his hands upon her.

She could not give her sword away.

Men were approaching them quickly.

"Give me the sword!" he roared once more.

Of course, if she didn't hand him the sword, they might very well perish at that very moment.

He lunged for it. She gasped, but released the steel to his grasp. He stared at her with a promise of fury, then turned to the sailors now ready to assault. He raised the weapon against them, and steel began to clang again.

He moved forward, maneuvering himself and Skye away from their disadvantaged position against the wall. Skye saw that they were slowly joined by the Hawk's men. She didn't know them all, but she suddenly realized that she was being shielded behind the Hawk and Robert Arrowsmith. They were fighting their way to the door.

Slowly, the attackers began to fall away. Only a few remained when they reached the entryway.

The Hawk paused, reaching into a pocket within his frockcoat. He drew out a number of gold coins.

"Mr. Ferguson! For the damage done, sir!" he shouted. Then he said to Robert, "Watch my back, Mr. Arrowsmith!"

"Aye, aye, sir!"

And with that, the Hawk grabbed hold of Skye's arm. He dragged her along the primitive road with him in a raw fury. They were not far from the sea. She could smell the salt and feel the breeze. The Hawk's men now raced behind them, like a giant wave, seeming to pitch them ever forward. She could still hear shouts of rage and fury from behind them. What had happened to Logan? She didn't know.

She stumbled.

"Move!" the Hawk shouted to her. Grasping his arm, she tried to do so. She apparently did not move fast enough for he swept her up into his arms. She struggled briefly. "I can walk—"

"By God, I should let them have you!" he thundered out. Caught by moonlight, his eyes glittered with a striking, chilling silver. She caught her lower lip between her teeth and went silent. He wasn't looking at her anymore, he was running with her held taut in his arms. "The longboats!" someone cried. "We're there! All men to the oars, and quickly."

Their boots fell heavy against the dock as they raced down to the longboats. Skye was tossed heavily within the first. The Hawk quickly landed by her side. He dropped his borrowed sword while his men crawled in with them and picked up the oars. Reaching to his waist he drew out a long flintlock pistol. Staring at him, Skye had not seen the shirtless man with the knife between his teeth reaching up to her from the water. The pistol flared. The man cried out, and the knife fell from his teeth as he crashed into the water.

The Hawk cast her a chilling stare. Her eyes fell upon the sword as the longboat shot away from the dock. Fear made her think to lunge for the sword. His booted foot fell upon her fingers before they could wind around the steel. She cried out and her eyes met his again, and this time the hostility in them ran deep, and far colder than she could have ever imagined.

"Aye, mistress! I should have left you to them!" he hissed, sinking down beside her.

Shouts were arising from the dock. The contingent from the tavern had followed them down to the sea.

"Are they coming, Mr. Arrowsmith?" the Hawk called to his man.

"I'm not sure, Captain. They seem to be hovering at the moment, sir, and nothing more."

The Hawk's eyes were upon her again. Skye felt them boring into her. She shivered with a dreadful cold. She looked to the shouting rogues upon the dock, and to the man beside her, and then to the water. The dark depths seemed absurdly inviting that evening.

His hand clamped hard upon hers and she started, meeting his fiery gaze. "No, milady, I think not! I did not haul you from that menacing crowd to lose you to the sea!"

She sat still and tried not to shiver. His eyes remained upon her. "What happened?" he demanded curtly. "What has come of Jacques DuBray and the men left with you."

She started to shake her head, unable to speak. His fingers dug into her damp hair, wrenching her head back. "What happened?"

"Jacques—the Frenchman is dead."

He swore violently, staring at her with a greater hatred. "A good man, and dead, on your behalf, milady! You still have not told me what happened!"

His hold upon her was fierce. His men, setting their oars upon the sea, also stared at her. In the darkness she could feel their eyes condemning her as the longboat skimmed the water, bringing them ever closer to his ship.

"Tell me!"

"Logan came! He came from the shore and snuck up on the ship. The man in the crow's nest saw him, but Logan shot him before he could cry out an alarm. Then he came topside and shot the Frenchman."

The Hawk swore violently. His hand fell from her hair and he looked toward his ship.

None of the men on the docks seemed to be coming in pursuit, Skye saw. She shivered, feeling very, very cold. The sea breeze seemed to glue her wet clothing to her and the little discomforts made her ever more wretched as she wondered about her fate.

The figurehead of his ship loomed into view. Skye had never noted it before. It was the proud figure of a woman, one of the Greek goddesses, she imagined. The breasts were bared, and a crown rode the head. Soft carved curls fell over the woman's shoulders and her face was strong and beautiful.

It was a fine and artistic piece of work, Skye thought. Of course. The ship had surely been seized.

Her teeth were chattering. Her mind was wandering to all sorts of avenues, because she was afraid.

The longboat came shipside. The ladder awaited them, hanging there in the darkness of the night.

"I shall go first," the Hawk told his men. He rose, clutching the rope, shimmying quickly upon it. He paused, pulling a knife from inside his boot, looking to Robert. "Mr. Arrowsmith, see to Lady Kinsdale."

"Aye, aye, sir!"

Skye sat in silence while the Hawk disappeared over the portside hull of his ship. She heard the water lapping against the longboat and felt the eyes of his men upon her. She had endangered them all.

I am your prisoner! she wanted to shout out to them. Had you let me be, I'd have offered you no harm!

But she didn't open her mouth. She waited in silence, and then she realized that they were all waiting with anxiety, and she, as well as the men, was worrying about the Hawk.

Worrying about a man who would probably flay every inch of her flesh from her bones . . .

"All clear!" he called suddenly from far above them. She nearly screamed, she was so startled. He held a lantern far above his head, and in the night he watched her, his eyes nearly fathomless within the curious shadows of his face.

"Come along, Lady Kinsdale," Robert told her gruffly. Numb and frightened, she obeyed, reaching for the ladder. She faltered nearing the top of the rope. The Hawk reached down to her, dragging her over the hull of the ship. She nearly fell. He held her up and pulled her against him.

The men climbed aboard the ship. The Hawk shoved her toward Robert. "See that she is locked in," he said briefly. Robert took her arm and started toward the captain's cabin.

She turned back, opening her mouth to speak. She didn't know what she meant to say and words caught in her throat. He was watching her. Watching her by moonlight, his hands upon his hips, his face now in the shadows.

Then he turned away from her.

Robert swung open the doors and thrust her into the darkened cabin. He didn't pause. He slammed the doors and bolted them without a thought.

The darkness closed around her.

Skye wrapped her arms around herself and closed her eyes tightly and sank to the floor. She tried to fight it. With all of her heart she tried to fight the fear that was overwhelming her. She felt as if the walls moved, as if they came around her, as if they would close upon her.

They wanted to hurt her, she reminded herself. Hawk and all his men were bitter against her for the havoc and death they believed she'd caused. She needed to be still, to be silent, to pray that they would forget her here within the cabin. . . .

Logic did her no good. The fear was not a rational fear, it was not something that she could control. The night seemed so black; she could not breathe, she could not see, she could not help the sensations that spilled upon her. Sweat broke out upon her brow and goose bumps rose all over her skin. It was sweeping over her, wave after wave of awful, terrible and primal fear. . . .

She wasn't aware at all of what she did. In total terror she cast back her head and started to scream as if she were encountering the very demons of hell.

The door burst open. Dimly she was aware of the light. Even more dimly, she was aware of the figure of the man silhouetted there within its glow.

He moved quickly, coming down upon the ground beside her. She didn't know how long she had been in the darkness, ensnared within the web of fear. She was aware that he held her, but she shook violently still. He rocked her, but she stared into the night with open eyes. His arms came more tightly around her and he lifted her, holding her close as he strode quickly about the room, lighting the lanterns.

He sat with her upon the bunk. He whispered to her, and she didn't hear the words, but the cadence of his voice worked its way into her heart. Slowly, the icy chill left her. She ceased to shiver, and shook only in an occasional spasm. She blinked, and then she was able to close her eyes, and then she leaned against him, sobbing softly.

His fingers moved over her hair. "It's all right, it's all right. I am here," he whispered.

Perhaps that was the very moment when things would forever change for her. No matter what was to come between them in the future, whether fear or anger or hatred burned in her heart, she would not be able to forget that moment.

"What is it?" he murmured. "What is it that you fear more deeply than death?"

"The darkness," she said softly.

"What of the darkness?" he said.

But that she could not answer, and he did not press her, but sighed. His muscles constricted suddenly as if he would move. Her fingers wound into his shirt. His own closed around them. "I told you that it was all right. That I am here."

He eased her fingers from him and stretched her out upon the bed. She bit into her lower lip, letting her lashes shield her eyes. He strode across the room and she heard the clink of glass. A moment later he was back, lifting her head. He teased her lips with the snifter of brandy and she swallowed. He crawled to the back of the bunk, leaning against the paneling and bringing her head down upon his lap. He sipped the brandy himself, then lifted her head once more, and this time she swallowed deeply. The brandy burned throughout her. It warmed her. She gasped and fell back again, her lashes heavy over her eyes.

He studied her, staring down at the perfect oval beauty of her face and the softness of her skin, ashen then. Even her lips remained pale. He traced them with his finger. Her eyes flew open. Glistening turquoise, they held fever and torment. Her lips trembled slightly. "I am sorry about your Frenchman," she said softly. "He was kind."

"I am sorry, too. He was a good man."

"He was a pirate," she said gravely. "At least, now, he shall not come to hang."

"As I shall?" he demanded softly.

Her lashes fell upon her eyes once more, covering them. "As you shall!" she whispered. But she did not say the words with venom, just with a terrible certainty.

The Hawk twirled the remaining brandy in its crystal snifter, watching the swirl of amber liquid. He smiled with a certain irony, then sighed and sat back. He needed to be on deck. He did not care to test the reefs by darkness—many a careless captain had lost his vessel and his life upon the deadly coral—and so they needed to keep a sharp guard until morning. Perhaps the trouble was over; perhaps it was not. He would wait until the morning to see if the business deals he'd negotiated with Stoker were still valid. Then he would ride the outgoing afternoon tide and hurry for Bone Cay.

He did not want to leave her, he realized.

His fingers fell upon her hair again. It was tousled and still sticky from her bout in the sea. It was still beautiful, still the color of a sunset.

She did not move beneath his touch. He waited a few moments longer, then eased her down upon a pillow. He rose carefully and walked back over to his desk. He poured out another two fingers of brandy and swiftly swallowed it down.

He stared at her pensively, then he forced himself to come about and return to his deck, and his command.

When Skye awoke, daylight was streaming into the cabin. The draperies were drawn far back.

She rose stiffly. She could feel the dried salt upon her body and her hair.

The ship was moving.

She leaped out of bed and hurried to the windows. Looking out, she saw that the ship sluiced swiftly through the water. They were leaving the island of New Providence behind.

Even as she sat upon the window seat, staring out, the door burst open. She swiveled quickly to face the Hawk as he entered the cabin, eyeing her as he carefully closed the door behind him. She almost offered him a wavering smile, but it faded before it ever came to her face. His tenderness and care of the night before were gone. She faced a cold taskmaster that morning, one who seemed without mercy.

He did not speak. He sat behind his desk and rubbed his bearded chin, staring at her.

"We have left the island," Skye said.

"Aye, milady, we left the island. You, mam'selle, made my position quite untenable there."

She rose, her fingers clenching by her side. Did he want her to feel guilty? By daylight, she was able to fight. "Sir, you have made my position quite untenable!"

"Have I?" he asked her. Dark lashes fell over his eyes, then his searing silver gaze swept her once again. "So untenable, mam'selle, that you would have preferred Logan?"

"Logan, One-Eyed Jack, the Silver Hawk, Blackbeard, pirates one and all."

He pushed his seat away from the desk and stood, walking around to lean upon the edge of it. "I was able to complete my business this morning despite your antics, Skye. Supplies were delivered to the ship along with a few offers. One fool fellow is still willing to pay me a thousand Spanish gold doubloons for you. Perhaps I should oblige him."

She gritted her teeth. "Perhaps you should."

"Tell, me, mam'selle, are you worth it?"

"What?"

"Are you worth a thousand gold doubloons?"

"According to you, sir, I have no more worth than any other woman, and as I saw last night, the tavern was crawling with women. Of course, I daresay that things do also crawl upon those women, but then, what is that to one of your . . . persuasion."

He crossed his arms slowly over his chest. "I may well have saved your life, you know."

"And I may well have saved yours."

He burst out laughing and came toward her, pulling her into his arms. "So you saved my life, did you?"

She pressed against his chest, seeking to free herself. "I cast you my sword—"

"You cast me your sword! Why even in the moment of greatest distress, I had to snatch it from you! Imagine, milady! I offer my throat to a dangerous murderer on your behalf—I find myself at odds with every man in the brotherhood—and you have the audacity to claim that you saved my life!"

She pressed more firmly against him. His smile faded. "We have just cast Jacques and Hornby to their graves within the sea, milady."

She swallowed, lowering her lashes. Her palms remained pressed against him. "I am your prisoner. I must attempt escape—"

An oath of such vehemence escaped him that her eyes flew to his. "You would escape me—into Logan's arms? Tell me, do I beat you? Starve you? Why is it, mam'selle, that you would escape to a man who would treat you with total disregard and violence?"

"Let me go!" she whispered feverishly.

He did not let her go. He fingered a lock of her hair, and then he moved against her, his lips searing her throat and touching her shoulder. She gasped, startled by the touch, stunned by the sensation.

He stepped away from her suddenly, and his eyes were bright. He swept his hand from his head and gave her a sweeping bow. "Perhaps, mam'selle, you are worth a thousand gold doubloons," he told her.

Her hand fluttered to her throat. His gaze swept her up and down in a fashion that left her feeling naked and afire inside. Then he arched a brow and scratched his bearded chin.

"Not as it stands, I think. Dear woman, you do, decidedly, need a bath."

With a vicious oath, she threw the pillow from the window seat at him. He caught the pillow, smiling.

"For your entertainment? No!" she snapped.

"We'll arrive at Bone Cay at nightfall," he told her softly. "Home."

"Should that please me?" she demanded.

"It pleases me. And who knows? Perhaps I shall seek to determine whether you are worth the trouble you have cost me."

"You, sir, have caused *me* the trouble!"

"Worth a thousand gold doubloons," he murmured.

"My father will pay—"

"Ah, but has he the purse?"

"If not, then my fiancé will pay. Lord Cameron is one of the wealthiest men in the Virginia Colony."

"But I do believe that he is aware of your feelings toward your impending nuptials, mam'selle. And, alas, all men are not so eager to pursue vixens who despise them."

"I do not despise Lord Cameron," she said coolly.

"Don't you? Well, I am sure that such words would truly warm his heart! Lady Kinsdale, this is enchanting, but you must excuse me. We come ever nearer Bone Cay, but I fear that Logan is either so enamored of you or hostile toward me that he may seek an engagement upon the sea. I am needed."

He bowed deeply and turned to leave her. At the door he paused and turned back, and amusement curled his lip. "I shall send men with the tub and water."

"You needn't. I rather like the way that I am since it does not please you!"

The smile stayed upon his lips. "Lady Kinsdale, I am giving you a direct order."

"And I—" She broke off, for he was returning to the room. He sat upon the edge of the desk, waiting. "What are you doing?" she cried.

"If you cannot obey a simple order, then I shall stay to assist you."

"You just said that you fear an attack!"

"Let Logan come with his guns blazing! If this is how you will have it be, then this is one war that I will wage first." He raised his voice. "Robert! Mr. Arrowsmith. I need you!"

Skye stared at him and knew that he meant every word, no matter how dramatically each was spoken. She stamped a foot upon the floor. "Go!" she breathed in fury. "Go! I shall just live and breathe, Captain, to obey your slightest order!"

He smiled. "Good," he said pleasantly, and jumped down from his desk. He turned at the door, and she saw the sizzle of amusement in his eyes, and she realized that more than anything, he taunted her. He'd offered the bath for her comfort, and not his own entertainment.

He had come to her against the terror of the night.

He was her enemy. Her deadly enemy. But he was a curious man, and she could not deny his courage, his determination. . . .

Or his strange tolerance and his even stranger tenderness. In her greatest hour of need, he had offered comfort.

"Mam'selle—" he said, nodding as he opened the door to leave her.

"Wait!" she cried.

He paused, a brow arched. She lowered her eyes.

"Yes, mam'selle?"

"Thank you."

"Thank you?" he repeated, amazed.

"For the lights," she whispered.

It seemed that he paused a very long time. "You are most heartily welcome, mam'selle," he said at last. Then he left her, and the door closed.

Robert came with coffee and rolls, and then he and a number of sailors trudged in with the hip bath and water. She felt the men watching her. Blue eyes, green, brown, and hazel, they all fell upon her. Old men, young men, thin and ruddy, they stared at her as they came and went. They despised her, she thought.

But when she dared to look up, she did not think that they hated her so. The last man to leave the cabin bowed her way. "You fought well last night, Lady Kinsdale!" he said. He smiled deeply. "A lady, and ye dared take Blackbeard's own sword against him!"

"Out, Rodgers!" Robert Arrowsmith commanded gruffly.

"Aye, sir, aye! Good day, Lady Kinsdale."

The door closed. Skye let out a long, uneasy breath.

She stood still for several seconds, then turned back to the window seat and stared out to sea. Would Logan really come for them? She shuddered. She had lied so deeply to the Hawk. She knew he was a better man than any of the others. A man to be respected.

And . . . were he not a pirate, she would have admired him.

As the long afternoon waned, Skye dozed in the window seat. She was awakened by a loud blast of one of the ship's cannons. Jerking up in terror, she stared out at the sea.

They had slowed their pace to a mere crawl and she could just see the shore. Far to her left stretched white sands and long grasses. To her right she saw towers, high brick towers rising on either side of a slender channel. They approached that channel.

She sank back, her heart thundering. Home, the Hawk had called this place.

A cannon fired in answer from one of the towers. Skye lay still as she felt the ship move through the channel. Then she bolted up again as she heard laughter and words of welcome.

They had come to rest against a long wooden dock, and the plank was being lowered. Men were teeming off of the ship, being greeted by their fellows. . . .

And by their women.

Skye gnawed her lip, straining to see. Many of the sailors were being hugged and caressed by women, old women, young women, pretty young barefoot girls, and somber-looking matrons.

There was a whole community here! she thought. Bone Cay. It seemed that the Hawk ruled his own little kingdom. The Hawk! There he was himself, tall, lean, and striking in an elegant black frockcoat and knee breeches. A small blond woman yelled something and he laughed to her, picking her up in greeting, swinging her about. He set her down and she stared up at him adoringly. Another sailor joined them, and another woman. Skye experienced a strange searing sensation that brought a flush to her features. She swallowed tightly against the pain. She hated him, she wanted nothing to do with him, and she was glad that he was back to his beloved mistresses.

She started, falling back from the window as the door opened. It was Robert Arrowsmith.

He bowed gravely. "Milady, if you will accompany me, please?"

"Where are you taking me?"

"To your room within the castle."

"The castle?" she inquired imperiously.

" 'Tis what we call the house, milady, for it is made soundly of stone, a fortress if you like. You will be safe there."

"I will be a prisoner there."

Robert paused. "A safe prisoner, mam'selle."

She accepted his arm, eager to quit the ship but determined that he would not know her mind. He led her from the cabin and across the deck. The sails were furled now, and the deck was silent and still.

Robert Arrowsmith led her over the gangplank. A hush fell over the dock. Men and women stared at her, and she stared in turn. Robert led her through the crowd that thronged around the ship.

The people gave way, parting to give them an open path.

Then she saw that the Silver Hawk was still there. Indeed, he awaited her. He sat mounted upon a huge white steed, his plumed hat low on his head.

Skye paused, ignoring the pressure of Robert's arm upon her.

"Come, Lady Kinsdale!" the Hawk shouted to her. "Welcome to the Hawk's Nest! Do hurry along."

"I'll not!" she shouted defiantly. It was the gravest pleasure to humiliate the man in turn.

But he was not humiliated. He cast his head back with a thunder of deep laughter, and she was left to gasp as the white horse thundered down upon her. She stood her ground.

She should have turned to flee.

She should have . . . but she did not. And upon his snow-white stallion, the Silver Hawk seemed to fly on the wind. And leaning from his seat, he plucked her from the ground, sweeping her before him, and racing toward the fortress that rose ahead of them.

And still the deep husky sound of his laughter rang against the coming of the night.

7

HEY DID NOT RIDE FAR. SKYE HAD JUST DUG HER fingers into the stallion's mane when she saw tall stone walls rising above her. The wind swept by them and the sandy earth churned as they came upon a set of wrought-iron gates, opened in expectation of the master's return, or so it seemed.

The horse unerringly turned and brought them through a courtyard to a high rising porte cochere. The Hawk reined in, setting Skye upon the ground. He touched his plumed hat. "Milady, my house is yours," he said simply.

Smiling, he turned the horse around. He led the animal around the side of the house. Skye watched him go, and then paused, staring about herself in ironic dismay. No one was near her; she was neither chained nor confined. But she had probably never been more of a prisoner, for there was absolutely nowhere to go. The Silver Hawk had chosen his base of operations well. The island was surrounded by coral atolls and shoals, deadly to the unwary sailor. His harbor was protected by the deep, natural U shape of his island. The channel was protected by the towers with their massive guns. It would take an army to come in here and clean out his rogue's den. And for a prisoner, there was very simply nowhere at all to go. The island was his. The people who lived upon it were his.

And she was his, she reminded herself. Worthless—or not worth any great sum, or so he had said. But still, his prize, and as such, he had fought for her, and he had kept her. And he had brought her here.

She shivered suddenly. Not because it was cold, and not because she feared him, but because she was afraid to be there, upon the island with him. She knew not why.

She turned about and followed the handsome brick path to the door of the imposing structure. She shouldn't be afraid. This was where she would wait for her father or her fiancé to rescue her. The Hawk would surely grant her some privacy here. It was a huge domicile.

She lifted her hand to knock, but the door opened before she could and to her surprise the Silver Hawk stood within the door frame. She frowned and he quickly arched a brow. "I left Samuel in his paddock, milady. You did take your sweet time to enter."

"Samuel?" she murmured. "Not the Silver Wind? Not the Hawk's Messenger, or some such. You named your horse Samuel?"

"Sam for short. He much prefers the abbreviation." He reached out and caught her hand, drawing her into his fortress. The entryway was in shadows, but she could see his eyes, smoke gray now, and haunting. "I'm sorry if I disappoint you, but I'm afraid that I was just a lad when Sam was born, and therefore I named him quickly. He's twenty-three now, and I'd not disturb his tranquillity with a change of name to suit my fancy."

"Twenty-three?" Skye said. The huge, sleek animal looked to be a young horse. "He has aged well."

The Hawk smiled slowly, and to her great distress, Skye felt her heart quiver as he drew her close. "I take very good care of all living creatures within my domain, milady. Alas, I tried take good care of you, but you are forever fighting my efforts."

"Perhaps, sir, it is because I am not your property to be cared for. I am neither pet, nor beast of burden, nor—yours."

A smile touched his lip. "Well spoken, milady, but then that is part of your appeal."

"Ah! But still a woman, and worth only so much!"

"Your worth is still debatable," he said. The words were simple and light, but the silence that followed them was not, for she felt both the warmth of his hands and the heat of his appraisal, and it seemed that a lingering question hung upon the air. She flushed and pulled from his grip, spinning to see the entryway.

It was grand. It was huge, with doors leading to rooms on either side. The walls and ceiling were paneled, and then lined handsomely with weapons of warfare, cutlasses, rapiers, scores of hunting rifles and muskets and brown Besses.

"Impressive," she muttered.

"Every man and woman on the island knows where to come in case of attack."

"And every one of them shall die with you?"

He shrugged. "They are here by choice. I force no one to live here."

"You have forced me."

"You, milady, are visiting, and naught more. Come along. I shall show you the rest of the house."

He took her hand into his own. To the right was a library with a guest bed, to the left was the butler's pantry—complete with butler. The man stood so silently awaiting their arrival that Skye gasped to see him living, alive and well. He was tall and strong of build, white-haired and immensely dignified. "Mr. Soames," the Hawk said in introduction, and Mr. Soames bowed to her very gravely. "What you need, he will give you."

"With the greatest pleasure, milady," Soames said, and bowed.

He might have graced the finest English manor! Skye thought, and she wondered how on God's good earth such a man had come to work in a pirate kingdom.

"All the pleasures of home," she murmured softly.

"What was that, Lady Kinsdale?" the Hawk said. She was certain that he winked to the butler, and that the butler winked in return. It was all a joke perhaps.

No, it was not joke. The cannons upon the protective towers were no joke.

The skill of the Hawk was hardly amusing to the men he had robbed of ships and plunder.

Soames excused himself and closed the door upon his domain. The Hawk was staring at her. "Well?"

"Quite remarkable."

"The house itself is remarkable, don't you agree? But not so difficult to construct as you might imagine. Brick makes wonderful ballast. I was able to have this all brought within the span of a few years." He walked her along the hall and paused, pushing open a set of doors. A long, claw-footed mahogany table stretched before them. It would seat at least twenty people, she thought. "The formal dining room."

"For those 'state' occasions?" she taunted.

"For negotiations," he corrected. "Your very worth might well be negotiated right here, milady."

"With whom do you negotiate?"

"No man fears to come here if he is invited, Lady Kinsdale. Your fiancé is well aware of the truth of those words. There is no safer haven upon the seas than this."

He drew her out and closed the doors. Pointing toward the rear of the house, he told her, "The ballroom, milady. And occasionally we do have balls."

He barely let her see the long room before he was whirling her around again and pulling her toward the stairway. It was big and broad with a velvet runner. A manservant polishing the banister bobbed to her and saluted the Hawk. "Sir, 'tis good to see you home, sir!"

"Mr. Tallingsworth, Lady Kinsdale. He, too, will be delighted to see to your every comfort."

"Yes, milady," Mr. Tallingsworth said.

She nodded skeptically and the Hawk continued to lead her upward. The second floor, too, seemed to stretch endlessly. He did not attempt to show her the length of it, but rather paused to the right side of the stairway, pushing open a door.

It was his room, she knew instantly. The dominant furniture within it was a huge four-poster bed in a dark walnut. Full-length windows lay open to the breeze coming off of the sea, making the room cool despite the heat of the day. There was a huge desk on the other side of the windows, and there were chairs and a daybed in front of a marble-manteled fireplace. In the center of the room was a fine cherrywood dining table, far more intimate than the large table downstairs.

"Your personal domain?" she inquired. She knew that he was watching her as she studied his room.

"Umm. Through here," he said, and he took her hand, leading her to the back of the room. He opened a doorway there and they entered a second chamber, not much smaller than the first. But whereas the larger room had been beyond a doubt decorated for a man, this room was softer. It might have been decorated to resemble a lady's chamber at Versailles. The delicate, white furniture appeared to be of French design. The drapes at the windows were sheer and trimmed with gold thread, and a gilded mirror hung over the fireplace. There was a card table and a huge wingback chair before the long windows, and the dressing table came complete with a set of silver combs and brushes. The chamber looked almost like a bride's room.

"I'm to stay in the room next to yours?" she said. She was not afraid of the situation. At least she did not think that she was afraid. She had spent nearly a week aboard ship in the arms of the man and he had not, in any serious way, brought harm to her.

Indeed, he had come to her time after time, a bastion against the terrors of the night. She might well miss the security and warmth of his arms. . . .

Never! she assured herself hastily. Never . . .

He smiled. "The door locks."

She cocked her head, meeting his eyes with a cynical smile. "And will I be able to lock you out, Captain Hawk?"

He did not answer right away, but took her hand within his. His fingers stroked it and his lips touched the back of it in the lightest caress. "Milady, locks lie within the heart or soul, and not upon the material earth."

He released her. "If you'll excuse me, I've things to attend to. I shall join you for supper, but it will be a late repast, I am afraid. Your belongings will be brought to you."

He paused because she was smiling. He arched a brow. "What is it, Lady Kinsdale, that you find so amusing?"

"You."

He stiffened. "Oh? And why is that?"

"Your manner, sir. You have dragged me about like a deer carcass at times, and now you are unerringly polite."

"One never knows—does she?" he said lightly.

Shivers danced along her spine as his eyes met hers. No, she never knew. He kept her off balance at every moment. He made her furious, he made her afraid, and then he would whisper to her or touch her and give her sweet comfort. This week he had become her very life, and every other moment before he had swept upon her from the sea paled and faded before him. But it was true; she never knew. She never, never knew. What would the evening bring? Laughter or fury. Would he treat her like fine porcelain, would he drag her mercilessly into his arms . . . ?

She backed away from him. He said no more, but turned and left her, going back through his own room. The door closed.

Skye sat upon the bed and trembled. How long would she be kept here in this prison? She was not cast into any dungeon, not beset with hardship.

This was far, far worse. . . .

She leaped to her feet and hurried to the door that connected her room to his. Apparently the door locked both ways, for she had been locked out of his chamber. Curious, she hurried to the hallway door. To her surprise, that door swung open to her touch. She stepped out, and then back in.

What was it of his that he did not want her to find? She wondered. She wandered to the windows and pondered the question.

She was a captive, she thought, in a most curious place.

———

He did not return for supper that night. Her trunks were delivered to her, all of them, and she saw that nothing of hers had been molested. Her jewels were still among her belongings, along with the finest of her gowns—velvets and brocades, gold-threaded linens, silks and satins, all were there. They were delivered by Mr. Tallingsworth and another man, under the direction of Mr. Soames. Later, Robert Arrowsmith came to see her, informing her that the Hawk would not return, much to his regret. Mr. Soames would see that supper was delivered to her room.

Skye thanked Robert Arrowsmith, keeping her eyes lowered. She was alarmed to discover that it was much to her regret, too, that the Hawk would not be returning.

Robert had been given careful orders, she thought. He walked about the room lighting lanterns until all was aglow. She thanked him quietly, and he left her.

She slept well that night.

In the morning she awoke to the sounds of laughter. Carefully opening her eyes, she gasped in astonishment. The pretty Irish lasses, Tara and Bess, were standing before her, and looking none the worse for wear.

"Bess! Tara!" she cried, pushing up in amazement.

Tara plopped a tray upon her lap. "Aye, Lady Kinsdale!" A shimmer of tears touched her eyes. "We're so grateful to ye, lady! Ye stepped in ta save us, ya know."

Skye blinked. "I didn't save you from anything! We're captives of a pirate. They dragged—"

"They dragged us into the second mate's cabin, and treated us with more kindness than many a mistress I've known," Tara said. Skye stared at the girl. She was very young, barely sixteen, but she spoke with a startling wisdom.

Skye's eyes narrowed. "You were not . . . you were not bothered in any way?"

Tara shook her head. "Not at all. Oh, we were deeply afraid when the commotion began at that other island! I thought that someone would come to burst down the doors! But nothing bad happened to us, and then we were brought here!"

"And it is paradise!" Bess cried.

Nibbling upon a piece of bread, Skye eyed her suspiciously. Her brow arched. "And how do you know that this is . . . paradise?"

Tara stared at Bess and shrugged. "Why, we've seen much of it, milady. Near the dock there's a few fine houses and stores and the like. Any seaman who chooses to do so may build himself a home. There's a freshwater lagoon inland, and deep into the cove there are soft sand beaches protected by rocks and shoals and the water is the most beautiful color you'd ever want to see, milady!"

"Oh?" Skye murmured.

Tara flushed crimson. "There's a man. A Mr. Roundtree, milady. He took us riding there in his little pony trap when we arrived."

"A man?" Skye said. "Oh, Tara. A pirate!"

Tara shrugged, then lowered her head in shame. She looked at Skye then with a sheepish smile. "Milady, there's even a chapel here! And a minister from the Church of England."

Skye swallowed some coffee then offered the tray back to Bessie. "I see. And when Mr. Roundtree was finished showing you this paradise, he took you to church services?"

Bessie flushed radiantly this time. "Well, no, but Lady Kinsdale, he did point out the chapel to us."

"A pirate's priest," Skye muttered. "What next?"

What next indeed?

Having given back her breakfast tray, she pattered to the pitcher and bowl left upon a small stand and washed her face, appreciating the coolness of the water against her flushed skin. While she toweled her skin she decided to test her freedom. She turned back to the girls. "Bessie, would you find my riding habit? I should like to view this—paradise."

Bessie and Tara obligingly set to work. It was fun to have them back. They chattered nonstop, and even if their chatter was all about Mr. Roundtree and his friend, Simon Greene, it brightened her spirits tremendously. That the girls were alive did not surprise her, for she knew that the Silver Hawk was not a blood-thirsty murdering pirate.

That they were happy as larks did startle her, however, for she could not forget those first moments when the Hawk had wrested the ship from One-Eyed Jack, claimed her for himself—and cast the girls to their fate among his men.

The Hawk was, indeed, a most exceptional man.

Dressed handsomely in a riding suit of brown velvet, Skye left Tara and Bessie. Her skirt was full and sweeping with yards of fabric, while the jacket much resembled a man's frock coat. She ran down the stairway, seeing no one, and when she came into the front hall, she heard voices. There was a group of men in the dining room, she realized. She headed for the doorway, but before she could peek in, Mr. Soames appeared, closing the door behind himself. "Good morning, Lady Kinsdale," he said.

"Good morning, Mr. Soames."

"Was your breakfast satisfactory, milady?"

"It was perfect, Mr. Soames." She smiled. There was something about the way that he guarded his master's door that reminded her that this was no English manor. "I would like to ride, Mr. Soames. Would that be possible?"

"But, of course, milady. We wish to afford you whatever pleasures you desire.

Come with me, please, I will take you to Señor Rivas. He is the horsemaster here at Bone Cay, and will be your delighted servant."

They left the house by the rear and came instantly to the stables, whereby Skye learned how the Hawk had made it back to the house so quickly the night before.

They entered into the shadows, but Skye quickly saw that there were at least twenty stalls, and that the stables were kept as neatly as the Hawk kept his ship. A tall, lean, dark-haired man stepped forward. He was Señor Rivas, and Mr. Soames quickly left her in his care. Skye realized that she was waiting for someone to leap out and stop her, to tell her that it was an absurd joke and she was insane to think that she might have the freedom to ride. But no one appeared and Señor Rivas drew a dapple gray mare from a stall and saddled and bridled her. He led her from the stables and to a block so that Skye might mount easily, then he stepped away. "Good day, Lady Kinsdale. Enjoy your ride."

His soft Spanish accent again reminded her that this was the New World, and that she was in a most uncivilized part of it at that. Spaniards and Englishmen mixed easily enough here now, for Spaniards and Englishmen had become pirates together, preying upon one another. The wars might be over now, but piracy was not.

Certain pirates were flourishing!

Skye turned the mare toward the docks and rode back the way that she had come. Barefoot children upon the sandy streets greeted her with bobs and curtsies. Small craft lay moored by the docks, too, and fishermen dragged in nets full of fish. Near the Silver Hawk's sleek dark pirate ship Skye paused. Some of the crew remained upon her, repairing rents in sails, unloading cargo, scrubbing down decks, running new lines. She watched for several moments. Men saluted her, but none of them spoke to her, and none questioned her. She turned the mare about at last, and in a fit of aggravation, set her to galloping.

She raced with the wind past the fine brick walls and the pirate's house. The land was nearly flat; sand and scrub fell away beneath her, and then the foliage began to thicken and it seemed that the trail began to rise over a mountainous terrain. At length, she reined in. She heard a rush of water, and she wandered further along a pine path and then came upon a startling and glorious sight. A deep blue pool lay before her with the water splashing over pebbles and rocks, and falling from a cliff high above in dazzling spurts of silver foam.

Skye dismounted from her horse and walked along the water's edge on the clean, hard-packed sand. She did not sit, but stared over the water. Flowers surrounded the small pool with a burst of color, which followed the route where the water trickled into a brook and disappeared into the trees. It was, she thought, a startling paradise.

Standing there, Skye at last looked across the water to the shore beyond. Her hand flew to her mouth and a gasp escaped her. He was there, the Hawk, upon his white horse, watching her from the foliage. He had not been hiding; he merely sat so still atop the snow-white stallion that she had not seen him in the profusion of color.

He lifted a hand to her and urged his mount forward. The white stallion stepped into the cool water without hesitation. The water rose higher and higher, past the stallion's flanks, and still he proceeded without fear. Like his master, the stallion moved purposefully. The water began to fall away, and the magnificent creature rose out from it, bearing the Hawk ever closer to her. She looked at the man. He was wearing a loose white shirt, black breeches, and his boots. His hat lay low over his eyes, the plume dancing, shadowing his eyes and whatever secrets lay within his heart. He looked like a true rogue, reckless, careless, ever the adventurer.

He came toward her, and she did not move, but held her position upon the shore. Still in the shallow water, he dismounted several feet from her. He was silent, watching her. She heard the soft music of the water as it cascaded from the cliffs and danced below in the sunlight. The breeze was light and soft and cool, and just whispered a tropical cadence as it rustled through the flowers and foliage.

For the longest moment, for eternity, Skye felt that her eyes were caught by his, and that his soul laid claim to her own. Locks lay upon the heart, he had told her. Not upon the material earth. Perhaps it was true. Perhaps there was no way to guard herself from the man.

He stepped back suddenly, casting a foot upon a rock, crossing his arms over his chest. "Good morning, milady," he said, his rakish gaze sweeping the length of her and breaking the curious spell. "How do you find this place?"

"A prison, sir, for all its beauty."

"I see," he murmured. "Well, perhaps I have not had the time to show it to you properly. This is a place of most exquisite beauty. And unique, although much of the island of Jamaica is similar."

"Why is this island so unique?"

"Why? Ah, Lady Kinsdale, this island is mine. That in itself makes it unique."

He caught her arm, drawing her forward. "This water is fresh, not brackish. We never want for pure sweet water to drink. See the cliff and the flowers, and the radiant burst of color. This is soft here, while not a mile away lies the tempest of the ocean. Storms rage here, wild and free, embroiling the ocean. Yet the reefs protect us, for only an accomplished sailor would dare to risk my shores!"

He stood beside her, his arm touching hers, and she felt keenly how very much alone they were, the delicate rhythms of the moving water and the whispering wind their only company beside that of the waiting horses. He smelled of cleanliness, of soap, and of polished leather, and beneath it all, she felt a haunting pulse, the essence of the man, calling upon something within her that had little to do with life as she knew it. In a place like this, it was easy to forget the boundaries she had always known.

Easy to forget innocence.

She pulled away from him, crying out hoarsely. "Why are you always here? Always near me! I came to ride alone, and you are here! I never turn that you are not there, endlessly, always, there! Leave me be! I cannot abide you! Don't be polite, don't be courteous! You are a pirate, sir, and I despise you!"

She flung around in such fury that she startled the mare. Skye set about to leap upon her, but the creature snorted and reared, frightened. Her hooves rose high, scraping the air. Skye watched in fascinated horror as they danced above her.

"Skye! Damn you!"

He was upon her in an instant, bearing her swiftly up and out of the way. The speed and the force with which he moved sent them both flying down to the soft sand.

The mare's hooves struck the earth, just inches away. Sand blew past them. Skye strained to sit up, but he was over her, his eyes on fire, his arms holding her tightly. Muscles clenched and unclenched within his face and throat and shoulders, and he railed against her. "Why, lady, are you always such a fool! You would cast yourself into any danger in order to get away from me! So you would not have me courteous, for I am a pirate still. Then, madame, let me play that pirate, and be damned with it all!"

"Bastard, let me up!" she cried. "You should have—"

"Aye, I should have! I should have given you free to One-Eyed Jack, and I should have let Logan take you and be damned with you then. Blackbeard could have been plagued with you as his prize, and I damned well should have let the horse mar your beauty forever, that you might haunt no other man with your glory and your fire. But you would have a pirate, lady, a rapist, a rogue, and never a gentleman. Then let's have it, for, lady, I am done skirting the thorns of your temper!"

She opened her mouth to scream and gasp in terror, for she had never seen him so angry. No sound left her, for his mouth ground hard upon hers with a punishing power. His tongue ravished her lips and teeth, forcing them apart. She gave way to breathe, and then felt the startling warmth as he filled her with the heat and lightning and intimacy of his kiss. She longed to fight, to twist. She had no power to do so. His fingers curled within hers, his weight bore her down upon the earth, and the passion and the savagery of his assault were stunning. She lay there and felt the ground, and it seemed to tremble beneath her. She heard the soft sound of the water, but it was no melody within her ears, it was a rush, a flow, a cascade. It mingled with the searing flow of her blood. She did not fight . . . she felt his lips, and the hardness of his body. She felt the sun, and the taste of the man, and the tempest of him.

And felt that tempest sweep into her being.

His hands were upon her, stroking the length of her, fire through fabric. They touched the bare flesh of her thighs, and she gasped, unable to breathe, for his lips burned their fiery path against her throat. They fell to the rise of her breasts, and still she did nothing but stare at the sky above her, beset by soft, flowing clouds. She felt the sun, but the sun had lost its heat, for fire burned deep, deep inside of her. It came where his lips seared her, where his fingers stroked her flesh, where the very hardness of his body drove her down to the earth.

His fingers tore upon the ribbons at her bodice, and the fabric gave way. Her breasts spilled above the bone of her corset and his lips found that tender flesh as his hand cupped the mound to the hungry desire of his teeth and tongue. A molten, demanding tug raked upon her nipple, and then it was laved by his tongue. The sweet, blinding sensation ripped into her like cannonshot, firing throughout her body. His beard teased her bare flesh with ever-greater intimacy.

"No!" she cried out suddenly, but he had seized her mouth again. She struggled, but fell limp as languor overcame her. The very earth continued to tremble. Perhaps it was not the earth. The trembling came from deep within her, a beat, a pulse, a sweet yearning need to know more. . . .

She was not a prisoner. Her hands were free and they were upon his shoulders, and it did not occur to her that he was a pirate, only a man, and a man who had shielded her against all enemies. Muscle rippled beneath her fingers, and in this strange paradise with the water rippling around them and the tropical breeze a tender touch upon them, he was all that she had ever desired in the deep secret shadows of her heart. The scent of him filled her; the force of his passion swept her into netherworlds where nothing mattered at all except for the sleek animal grace of him, and of his touch.

Suddenly he wrenched away. He stumbled to his feet. His back to her, he looked up at the sky. "God damn you!" he raged at her. He jerked around, caught her hands, and pulled her to her feet. "What would you have of me?" he shouted.

She jerked away from his touch, horrified that it was he, and not her own protest, that had put a stop to what they'd been doing. "I wish that you would leave me be! I wish that I could be away from this place!" she cried, wiping her mouth with the back of her hand. She could not erase the feel of his lips. She felt his eyes upon her, burning still, and she realized that her bodice was askew, her breasts bared and spilling forth. She blushed deeply, but she did not lower her head and fought for whatever control she possessed. Still her hands trembled as she brought her fingers to her laces. He tore his eyes from her breasts and looked directly into hers. "You will be gone soon enough, I swear it!" he told her heatedly.

She turned from him, running toward the offending mare. The frightened beast skittered away. An oath burst forth from him. "Don't ever run from me, you little fool. You would never manage it, and in each of your attempts you are hurt or cause havoc!" He caught hold of the mare's reins and brought her around. He reached for Skye's waist.

"I can manage, leave me be!"

"You cannot manage."

He set her firmly upon the horse. She picked up the reins and stared down at him. "I think, Captain Silver Hawk, that you are running from me."

His eyes narrowed. "Lady Kinsdale, I will never run from you, I swear it. I've tried to leave you be, as you so ardently wish. And even when you singe my soul with the heat of your flame, I do back away. Don't try me again, lady. In this battle I tell you, the gentleman is surely giving way to the rogue within me, and if next tempted, the pirate will prevail."

Hot shivers ran down her spine. She jerked the reins from his hand, nudged the mare, and turned to race away from the lagoon, and from the haunting, bitter laughter that played upon the air in her wake.

Skye returned to the stable in a tempestuous mood. She left the mare to Señor Rivas, and walked hurriedly into the house, ignoring Mr. Soames, who came to greet her by the stairway. She raced up to her room and slammed the door hard, then sent the bolts hammering into place at that door, and at the door that connected her room to the Hawk's. She paced the room in deep agitation, then glanced at the connecting door again. The lock wouldn't mean a thing to him if he wanted to reach her. A lock? Why the man fought battles upon the sea and had seized her very ship! What was a lock to such a man. . . .

A lock lay within the heart, or within the soul, or so he had told her. No man could hold the key to such a lock, unless it was given to him, and freely so. And this the Silver Hawk seemed to know, and know well.

She stiffened suddenly, aware of a door slamming below. The Hawk had returned, too, and it seemed that he, too, was not in the best of humor. His shouting could be heard throughout the house.

Skye raced to the hallway door. She could not make out the crisp words, only that it was his voice, deep and vibrant, commanding. She heard his footsteps upon the stairs, and then the door to his room opened and slammed, and she stood dead still, her hand cast to her throat. He would come to her then. He would ignore the door that lay between them, he would come to her in anger, seize her. . . .

Seconds ticked by. The door slammed again. The Hawk was gone. She breathed a deep sigh of relief and cast herself across the bed, then stared up at the canopy. Surely, he had business to attend to. And he had broken away, not she. . . .

She flamed with humiliation. He wanted her gone. This would not go on much longer. Perhaps, say what he might, he had his own sense of honor. She was his cousin's betrothed, despite the fact that that cousin be distant, and born on the right side of the sheets.

Betrothed . . .

She had no wish to meet such a man! Not when her lips remained swollen and her flesh burned from another's touch.

She sat up, pressing her temple between her palms. God help her, she did not know herself anymore.

She leaped from the bed and threw open the door to the hallway. Mr. Soames had said that he was there to serve her. Well, she wanted to be served. "Mr. Soames!" she called down the stairs.

"Milady!" Within seconds the elderly gentleman had climbed the stairs to reach her. "I'd have some brandy, if I may, please," she told him.

He arched a brow in surprise that she should ask for spirits, but quickly lowered his brow again. "Yes, milady," he said, and was quickly gone. She paced again as she awaited his return. He arrived with brandy and a single crystal glass upon a silver tray. She thanked him, and waited for him to leave.

"The Hawk will have supper with you, milady. He will knock for you at eight."

"Will he? You must tell the Hawk that I do not care to have supper with him," she said.

"But, milady—"

"You have heard me, Mr. Soames, and you have said that you will attend to my every wish. Well, I wish you to tell your master that I will not have supper with him."

"Yes, milady."

With no further display of emotion or opinion, Mr. Soames bowed to her and left her side.

She liked the brandy. It soothed her spirits and eased the tempest in her soul. She stared broodingly out the windows at the startling blue beauty of the island. Bone Cay. Such an ugly name for such a striking piece of paradise.

The day grew warm and she opened the windows to feel the breezes. She cast aside her jacket and tried to cease her endless pacing. What would his reaction be? He had come back in a state of anger to demand that she attend him for a meal. Would he accept her refusal with a casual shrug?

The afternoon was waning, but her spirits slowly rose and her confidence returned in direct proportion to the brandy she consumed. He would not break the lock; it would be against his very peculiar code of honor.

Feeling hot and sticky as sunset neared, she called down to Mr. Soames again. He ran back up the stairs. She asked him sweetly if she might have a bath. He stared at her blankly, and she knew that sending a half-dozen servants with a tub and water would be a hardship on him as head of the household staff at this particular hour of the afternoon. She wasn't terribly sorry. She didn't care to be there. If they didn't care to have her there, then they would hurry to see that she left. The Hawk had said that she would be gone soon. He had said it with a vengeance. Surely, Mr. Soames would help see to it that he kept that vow!

"I should like it very quickly, Mr. Soames!" she told him as innocently as she could.

"I shall do my best, milady."

"Perhaps you could send my own young lasses along, and spare your own staff."

"That won't be possible, milady."

"And why is that?"

"Well, they're at the fish market, milady."

"The fish market?"

"They wished to stay busy, and you had given them no word that you might require their service. . . ." His words trailed away. He had given the girls leave to go, she realized. She smiled. She had no rights here—except those given her by the Hawk, and it was the Hawk she longed to annoy.

"Whenever you can manage, Mr. Soames," she said very sweetly.

She was quickly obliged. Very little time had passed before Señor Rivas and one of his young grooms dragged up a brass tub, and then a stream of servants—household and estate men, so it seemed—arrived with water. She thanked them all charmingly. Mr. Soames himself came with towels and rose scents and a thick sponge. "If you require anything else . . ."

"Not a thing. Just my privacy," she said.

"Yes, milady." He bowed his way out. Skye stared after the closed door, suddenly sorry for making the elderly man miserable. His master had already screamed at him, and now poor Soames had the sorry task of telling the Hawk that his female prisoner had no intention of obeying his commands for the evening.

Her guilt faded away as she cast her clothing off in disarray. She had consumed way too much brandy, and she knew it. She didn't care. It had eased her torment, it had made her almost cheerful. Content and relaxed, she crawled into the tub. She coiled her hair on top of her head and lazily rubbed the sweet-smelling rose-scented soap over her body. She smiled. There were benefits to being the hostage of a prosperous pirate. He did supply the finest in luxury accommodations, fresh from Paris.

She set aside her sponge and soap and leaned back, basking in the warmth of the water. With one eye barely open, she saw that the sun was setting, sinking into the horizon beyond the windows. The colors of the coming night were breathtaking, strident red, shocking gold, so very bright, so very deep.

She allowed her eyes to close. It was so easy, so gentle, to be there. The water was warm, near tender in its touch. Her head was so delightfully at ease. . . .

She was aware of shadows upon the rippling bathwater, then she was aware of nothing at all. Then she thought that she dreamed, for she heard a fierce pounding, and it was as if her name was being called from a distance.

There was a sound of thunder, stark, strident. Skye bolted up just in time to hear wood crackle and split, and to hear the Hawk slamming into her room, the door falling flat to the floor. He stared at her, his hands on his hips, his eyes on fire.

She parted her lips and tried to speak. He sounded as if he was strangling.

"My God! I thought you were dead!"

"You said I might lock the door—"

"Did you hear me! I thought that you were dead! I knocked, I shouted!"

"I—"

She slipped within the tub, nearly going under. He exploded with a furious oath, and she heard a new thunder. It was the sound of his footsteps, falling upon the floor. Then his hands were upon her, wrenching her up, and into his arms.

She soaked him. Water sluiced from her body to his own, and dripped onto the floor. He paid no attention to it, but stared at her sharply. Alarm swept through her, as shocking as his hands upon her.

She struggled against him. "I did not care to come to dinner!" she cried.

"But I commanded that you should."

"I do not dine with thieves, with gentlemen rogues. Your manner does not save you from the truth! I will not sit to eat with a courteous—"

"Sea slime? Gentleman rogue, milady?" his eyes, flashing fire, fell upon hers.

"This night, lady, I am no gentleman rogue, and a rogue at the very least. You wish a pirate, you expect one—"

"Put me down, Hawk!" she cried, her panic growing. The soft brandy blur was deserting her. She was naked, and his touch upon her bare flesh was an excruciating sensation. She was in his arms, and he was vibrant, burning with the heat of anger. He was a flame that seemed to consume everything, her will, her heart. She had to escape him, to stand outside that flame. She did not so deeply fear his anger; she feared the tempest within him that so seduced and beguiled her.

She pressed fully against his silk-clad chest. "Now! I demand it!"

He shook his head slowly. "You do not like to be treated with courtesy, not by a pirate, so you say. Well, take heed then, lady. This night you have the pirate, the demon, the monster, the rogue. And trust well, lady, that this night, the rogue will have you. If you have thought to cry for mercy, now is the time to do so, milady."

8

ERHAPS WE *SHOULD* DINE FIRST," SKYE SAID softly.

He stared down upon her. "What?" he shouted in exasperation.

"Dinner!" she whispered desperately, meeting his silver gaze. "You wished to have dinner. It's . . . it's all right with me."

He was still stiff with anger, as hot and radiant as a winter's fire, but as hard as stone. "You're drunk," he said.

"What?"

"You're drunk!"

"I am not! Ladies of good breeding do not get drunk, sir!"

"I shudder to suggest, Lady Kinsdale, that your breeding is anything but the absolute best, so I must beg to differ upon the principle itself. You are drunk."

"Tipsy, perhaps."

"Sodden."

"Sir, you drive me to drink," she said woefully. Her fingers curled about his neck as she held him tightly rather than fall.

"I drive you to drink, lady! My God, but a sane man would have left you upon the sea!" He cast her down suddenly and with such vehemence that she gasped, for she was certain that her bones would shatter upon the floor. They did not, for he had come to the bed and cast her upon the soft down mattress. Like silver daggers, his eyes flashed upon her. "I drive you to drink? Lady, you would drive the very saints to despair!"

He whirled around and she clutched nervously at the bedclothes, dragging them around her. He seemed as explosive as a keg of powder, and though she had a reprieve, she wondered what his next action would be.

He wrenched open one of her trunks with a vengeance. Silks and satins and velvets went flying about. Then he tossed a soft green satin garment her way. She reached for the fabric as his footsteps cracked and thundered upon the floor and on the shattered door. "Dinner, milady, is already served."

For the longest time she lay there, her hand at her heart, feeling the frantic beat. He was gone again. But not far. He stood away from her, through a doorway that could no longer be closed or locked. It had never meant anything anyway. He had always known and she was discovering that the barriers lay within herself.

And within him.

Skye lay very still. Night was coming quickly. It would not matter, she realized. If darkness fell, he would come back to light up the night for her, whether she did or did not rise. If she stayed just as she was, she would need have no fear. He would not touch her, nor would he let blackness descend upon her.

She rose quickly, glancing nervously to the open doorway. She could not see him. She scrambled into the gown he had left her, a satin dinner gown with a laced bodice, high collar, and sweeping train. She came to the dresser, observed her pale image within the mirror, and mechanically picked up the silver brush he had provided and swept it through her hair. The golden locks fell like waves of sun and fire upon her shoulders. The high collar of the gown complemented the deep cleft of the bodice. Her eyes were grave then, for the tender embrace of the brandy was fast fading away, and it seemed that very much lay at stake that night.

Impulsively she turned from the dresser to dig about in her trunks. She found a delicate gold necklace with an emerald pendant that was surrounded by a sunburst of diamonds. She hooked it about her neck and it fell far below her throat to touch the valley of her breasts.

She walked over to the open doorway and paused there, watching him.

He stood by the windows, and seemed as pensive as she. The drapes were open, the breeze blew in. He looked the gentleman then, the striking young gentleman, more lordly than any man she knew, lost in thought, tall and undaunted against the coming night. He held a silver goblet in one hand. Across the room, Skye saw that the small dining table was laden with a meal, with silver flatware and fine plates upon a white cloth. Candles were burning, casting a gentle glow over the table.

"Lord Cameron comes for you any day now," Hawk said without turning to her.

"How can he?" she murmured. "How can he even know that I am here?"

"I sent your ship, the *Silver Messenger,* close in to Cape Hatteras as we traveled south. Her signalman sent messages to a merchantman. The *Silver Messenger* came here this afternoon, and my man assures me that his messages were received, and answers were sent."

"That is . . . good to hear," she said softly.

He turned around suddenly and his eyes swept over her from head to toe. They lingered upon the emerald that lay between her breasts, but he did not mention it. He bowed to her. "Milady, you wished to dine?" He indicated the table. She walked to it and he was quickly behind her, pulling out her chair. He poured her wine in a goblet before taking his own seat. The candles glowed softly between them, flickering occasionally, for the table lay before the open window, and both the colors of the sunset and the coolness of the twilight breeze rushed softly in upon them.

"Shall I serve you, milady?" he asked.

Skye nodded, sitting back, her fingers curving over the arms of her chair. She watched his dark head and the fine, brooding line of his features as he dished out food from the servers. She wasn't sure what touched her plate, for she studied him so earnestly. He caught her gaze at last. She flushed and picked up her wineglass. But she continued to study him.

"What? What now, milady?" he demanded acidly.

And she smiled very slowly. "What manner of pirate are you, sir? I sit before you unmolested. In my jewels." She leaned forward, fingering the emerald. "It's worth a small fortune, Sir Silver Hawk. Of that, I am sure you are aware."

"Perhaps, lady, I will receive a small fortune for your safe return."

"Perhaps." she murmured, but her smile remained. He swore softly and tossed down his serving implements. "Lady, I tell you, I am at the end of my resources. I am past being driven to mere drink, and I hunger for far more than dinner."

She picked up her fork and idly touched her food. She was scarcely hungry herself. She tasted some delicious fish, and steamed fresh carrots and potatoes and sweet toasted bananas. She could eat very little. Nor did he pay much attention to his food. He watched her, and a deep, dark tension remained with him. His brow continued to knit and a scowl played upon his lip beneath his mustache.

"He will come here?" she said. "Lord Cameron?"

"Aye."

"He will feel safe?"

"He will know himself safe."

She shoved about a piece of fish with her fork. He leaned toward her. "What is it, milady?" he snapped. "Who do you think you are, what sweet nobility sets you so confidently upon this golden crest of disdain you would cast down upon others? I am a pirate, yes, but you scorn a member of your own society, a man who is willing to sail a tempestuous sea for an unwilling bride?"

Her temper rose and her first impulse was to slap him. She smiled instead, holding her silver goblet, tracing its rim with her fingers. "I am my own mistress, sir, and that is all."

He sat back, his eyes narrowing. "And what precisely does that mean, lady?"

"I—I am graced with my own mind, sir. My mother"—she hesitated just briefly, swallowing—"my mother died when I was young, and I quickly ran my father's affairs. He sent me to school in London, and neglected to tell me about a promise given at my birth!"

"So the promise is not your concern."

"No."

"You do not choose to honor your father?"

"Not in this." She set her wine down and spoke to him earnestly. "One would think, sir, that daughters were created as slaves, to be cast to the highest bidder."

His eyes were smoke, concealing his thoughts. "Perhaps he cares for the security of your future."

She lowered her head suddenly. "He knows so little about me."

"About your fear of the dark?"

Her head jerked up like a marionette's. "I don't care to discuss any of this with you."

"Why not? Perhaps I can help."

"Help!"

He shrugged, sipping more wine. "He is a cousin, distant at that, proper, stoic, and all those gentlemanly things. I do know something of him. He is sailing to retrieve you. He is no ogre."

She smiled, touching her dangling pendant. "You are the ogre, right?"

"Don't test me," he warned her sternly.

"I have tested you time and again," she said softly. "You have proven yourself, sir."

"Have I? Lady, please, my mettle is in shatters. I promise you this, if I hold you again, I'll leave no questions in your mind as to my true nature."

She did not reply, but continued to smile. He reached over suddenly, grasping her wine goblet. He set it down upon the table with a small clunk. She arched a brow to him.

"I think you've had enough. How do you feel?"

"I feel very well. I dozed in the tub merely because of its comfort, and though I did consume a great deal of brandy, I did it throughout a very long day."

"Oh. Is that so?"

"It is."

He watched her for a long moment, his hands folded upon the table. "You are well and sober now?"

"I am, sir."

He stood and caught her hands, pulling her slowly up from the table and into his arms. She should resist. Something languorous stole over her with the gentle touch of the breeze. Draperies fluttered and the soft fragrance of the tropic night whirled around them. The moon had risen as the fiery colors of sunset gave way to shadow, and then darkness. Candleglow was soft, and gentle as the ethereal beams from the moon falling down upon them.

"Run!" he told her softly. "Run away, and embrace the darkness, for you enter here into greater peril." He clutched her hand and brought it to his chest, against his heart. "Feel the beat, lady, feel the pulse. Suffer the tempest, for I have been like a man long damned. Don't take comfort in my presence, and don't trust in my justice or honor, for by my justice you would lie with me now, and as I have warned you, what honor a rogue possesses ever dims within my heart. Run from me now, lady. And swiftly."

It was fair warning, and well she knew it. Her palm and fingers lay over an erratic pulse, and a wall of vibrant, living heat. They pressed so close together that a fever danced throughout her and cast her into a field of sweet confusion far greater than any spirit could bring. She wanted him. Shameful, horrid, and illicit as it might be, she wanted him. That such feelings should rage within her heart left her aware that she could be no true lady, but in the night breeze, she could not care. This world was real, and he was a beacon, shining ever more brightly to her tempest-tossed soul. Codes and society could not matter here, all that had meaning were the earth and sky, the breeze, the primal power of the man.

She parted her lips to whisper, but knew not what she would say. Rescue came for her any day now, blessed rescue to her home, to a land of safety. To a lord, a man of the peerage, the betrothed who would give her the proper place in society, a gracious home, wealth, servants, security, all that she could desire.

Her security lay here, she thought. And the wealth to be found in the arms of such a man were all the riches she might come to desire.

"Go! Go now, I warn you!" he growled to her.

She pulled away. She stared at him, thinking there were so many things that she would say to him, but none of them were things that words could convey. If she stayed, she would be damned. She turned and fled through the doorway, then paused, gasping, the tempo of her heart staccato, the very breath and soul of her in torment.

She did not think anew. She did not reason, nor pause to think that the morning light might bring regrets. She came back to the doorway and looked in once more.

He had come back to the window. He stood there, a tall and silent man, a powerful shadow in black silk shirt and breeches and boots, formidable and striking against the glow of the moon. She must have made some small sound, or else he sensed her there, that she had so swiftly returned. He came about, staring at her. She could not see his eyes, his features. She cried softly and raced toward him on her bare feet. She cast herself against him, and his arms swept around her with a staggering hunger. His lips found hers.

Captured there in the moonlight in his arms, she dared to kiss him in return. His tongue tempestuously seared her lips to plunder her mouth. She welcomed it, and daringly tasted, met, and matched his forays with her own. A sweet-honeyed surge burst forth from within her, swirling within her belly, rushing to fill her limbs. She sought to touch his hair, to tease it at his nape, to feel the power of his shoulders and arms, to come ever closer.

She gasped when his lips lifted from hers, and she stared up at him, framed as they were in the moonglow, in the windows opened to the night. He stared at her the longest time, and his ragged whisper rode hauntingly from his flesh. "You cannot run anymore," he said.

"No," she whispered, and her lashes did not flutter, nor did her eyes fall from his. His hands were upon her shoulders. Her lips parted in a soft gasp as he tore upon the fabric there and her gown swirled to a very soft heap of silk upon the ground. And still he stared at her, for the moonglow danced eloquently upon her body, outlining the firm fullness of her breasts and defining the dusky rouge peaks, touching shadow at the slender ribbon of her waist, glowing full on the flare of her hips. The moon seemed a master of temptation in itself, finding shadow again in the haunting juncture of her thighs.

A deep, guttural cry came from him, startling her, causing her to tremble. Then his hands were upon her again, pulling her close. She felt the fever of his mouth upon hers once more, and clung to him, stunned by this new ferocity of passion, yet willing to ride the soaring force of it. She met his lips again and again. He sought her mouth and tongue over and over, breaking away, finding her warmth once again. His hands began a bold foray upon her. As their lips met in searing fire, he stroked her shoulder and her breast, rounded her naked hip. His fingers grazed her belly and drew with startling purpose to the golden nest between her thighs.

She flinched, startled, but he drew her closer. He whispered against her lips as he explored her further. She gasped and shuddered, so weak that she fell against him as his touch surged intimately inside of her.

"I cannot, will not, let you go," he muttered.

She did not wish to be let go. She burrowed her head against him and she was swiftly swept off her feet and carried to his massive bed. Lying there without him, she was briefly cold, but he quickly returned to cover her with his warmth. His lips seared her all anew. He touched her with shattering liquid heat in intimate places, bringing gasps to her lips as he possessed her breasts with his touch and teeth and tongue, covering her belly with the ardent sweep of his mouth. The liquid fire was outside of her, and then inside of her. Sensation came to rule the night, for each new touch was shocking and evocative beyond measure, and she was barely able to register the one before the next began.

She knew that he was a practiced lover, and that did not matter to her. Not then. She knew, too, that a woman was seldom so carefully cherished with both tempest and tenderness when initiated into the realm of senses. He was with her because he had desired her, and tonight he could let hunger rage, for he had shown her long ago that he cared for her fears, and for her soul.

He moved from her, and she realized that he hovered over her, seeking out her eyes, his own ablaze with tension. Lightly he touched her breast, keeping his eyes upon her. He drew his fingers low over her ribs against her abdomen, down to her thighs. Her lashes fluttered. "No," he told her softly, and she lifted her gaze to his again as he invaded her more intimately. She drew her limbs together as the flame touched her features, but her body surged against his touch of its sweet desire and he laughed with sheer pleasure and triumph and his lips seized upon hers. "Moonglow," he told her. "Thank God, lady, that you crave the light, for I hunger for the very sight of you, and would die tonight for this touch!" His lips covered hers. In tempest and abandon they traveled to her breast. To her belly, ever downward. Brazenly he touched her. She cried out loud in stunned protest, writhing against him, reaching for him to draw him against her. He left her, stripping away his garments. And then it was he who was covered in the moonlight, and she was dizzy with anticipation, warmed by the beautiful bronze glow of his shoulders, frightened by the masculine force of him.

He did not let her know fear. He teased her no longer, but fell upon her with purpose, parting her thighs to his desire, cradling her gently into his arms.

The pain was astounding, wrenching her from the web of sweet desire that had wound within her. She cried out, she bit into his shoulders, she slammed against him and shrilled away in fury, tears stinging her eyes. He ignored her, holding her. Moving, moving against her. Thrusting harder and harder and tearing into her. "Pirate, bastard, rogue!" she choked out.

"Sea slime," he responded with a tender understanding, and she nearly laughed, and then the sweetness overrode the pain and she was astounded anew at herself. She had never known a hunger so great; she had never wanted so desperately. Her form shifted and writhed and arched on his own. She stroked his flesh and felt the constriction and heave of his muscle, and the ever-greater fury of his force. She swirled with it, she soared, she reached. Then it seemed as if the entire world exploded deep inside of her and that nothing had ever been so rapturous in her life. She was wrapped in clouds, cocooned among moonglow and stars, seared by the sun. Darkness nearly claimed her, the breath left her. She died, she thought. She touched the sun, and so she died.

She did not die. She closed her eyes perhaps, passed out, perhaps. But she did not die. She shuddered again and again and hot rapture tore through her. She opened her eyes to discover that she had not even left the earth, but lay within the bed still, drenched and slick, entwined with the Hawk. He lay atop her still, and quietly within her. He had not ravished or raped her or used violence against her in any way. She had come to him.

He pulled away from her, coming up on an elbow, smoothing the tangle of her hair away from her face. She wished suddenly that she did not so strenuously fear the dark, for she would have liked to hide her face in the shadows then.

"Regrets?" he asked her.

"No." Well, perhaps one, for now that ecstasy had quietly given way, she was sore and amazed at her own lack not only of virtue, but of anything resembling restraint.

"I warned you," he reminded her.

She nodded uneasily. She turned against him, burrowing against his chest. "Please, leave it be."

He touched her gently, letting her lie against him. She suddenly imagined that love was a grand and magical thing, for it was, perhaps, even more wonderful to lie against him so, to feel the ripple of his muscles and his soft touch upon her as he held her close. This seemed an even greater intimacy.

As did his easy stroke. He did not touch her then to enflame her, but just to idly feel her flesh and soothe her. He rested his bearded chin atop her head and sighed deeply.

"What shall you do now?" he asked her.

She shook her head against him, not knowing what he meant.

"Well, my love, you go to your betrothed. What shall you tell him?"

"The truth."

"The truth?"

Angry, Skye pushed away. "Tonight . . . this is not the truth. The truth has always been there, as you have been so quick to tell me! I will not marry him. I will not honor some silly pact made between his father and mine. He does not wish to marry me, either!"

"But he comes for you."

"What is this!" she charged him, pulling away, suddenly longing for her clothing and eager to be far, far away from him. Something terribly momentous had happened in her life. He had taken from her all that a woman had of her own to truly give, not so much the physical side of innocence, but the very heart of it, too. "Is your cousin your best friend that you must care for his concerns so deeply?"

"We are not friends at all. We are enemies. We respect one another and leave room for negotiation, but he would slay me in the open waters, and I would slay him in turn."

"Then leave me at peace! I shall deal with my own life." She tried to pull away in a sudden fury. He leaped atop her, smiling his buccaneer's leering smile, and pinning her beneath him. "Get off!" she insisted, flailing against him.

"No, lady, I cannot! And I gave fair warning. Forget the future, and answer to the sweet whispers of the night!"

"Nay—"

But her protest meant nothing. His lips seared hers, his body burned against her. She felt the hard swell of his sex and she gasped and strained to free herself, but he sank into her, filling her, and making her one with him. Tempest could not rise so swiftly again! she thought, and yet it did. Soaring, sweet, thundering, savage, it rose like a summer storm, brought her to a sweet and shattering climax, and cast her down softly and incredibly to earth once again. He gave her no quarter and no mercy, now that he possessed her. Still holding her, still entwined with her, he rose above her.

"Say the word, and I will rescue you from the trap of your betrothal. I will say that my hostage is not for sale, but my property and mine alone, now and forever."

She gasped, stunned by the ferocity of his words.

"I—I cannot!" she cried. She could not! She had discovered ecstasy here, and perhaps she had discovered a man of startling temper and curious honor upon the savage seas, but she could not stay here! Her mind would work but little then, but she knew that she could not be his mistress. She could not stay here.

"So you would marry Lord Cameron!"

"No! Yes, I mean that I could not stay here!" She could not, ever. Not while her father lived. As angry as she might become with him for charting her life, she adored him. He was all that she had in the world. All who really loved her, who needed her. Just as she needed him, and his love.

His eyes were fierce, they were silver, they probed her, they went past her nakedness and tore into her soul. "You little hypocrite!" he told her. "You deny the man, but you would have his position! You would dine at the governor's mansion and walk the streets in splendor. You cannot manage without your silks and velvets and jewels—"

"How dare you judge me!" she screamed, tearing at his chest. Suddenly she longed to escape him with such a fever she could scarce bear it. "It is not Lord Cameron! I tell you that I will not marry him—"

"You will not?" he taunted.

"I do not owe you an explanation!"

He wrenched back, still angry, and she wondered at the force of his explosion. He fell down beside her and she quickly sat up, searching for her gown to wrap around her nakedness. His eyes were scathing, telling her that she was a fool to cover herself from his eyes, ever again. She was furious with him, and furious with herself. Holding the covers tightly, she determined to get away from him.

She leaped to her feet. He rose, too, not coming after her, just watching her with his feet firm upon the floor, his arms crossed over his chest.

"And where are you going now, milady? I told you that you could not run any longer."

"I am going back to my own bed."

"Ah, but it is my bed, too, milady!"

"Nevertheless, you are not in it!"

She strutted through the doorway, regally clad in his bed covering. But she had scarce crossed the threshold into her own room when darkness descended upon her. The lanterns were not lit; he had not come there, for she had been with him.

God! How she despised the weakness! She claimed herself to be her own mistress, but the suffocating fear of the darkness came at her with talons to tear against her every time.

She cast her hands over her face, shuddering. Then she felt his hands upon her, gentle and tender. He lifted her, covers and all, into his arms, and strode with her back to his room, to where the candles flickered softly, and the moon-glow bathed them once again.

"When I am with you," he promised her softly, "I swear that there will always be light."

She slept then, in his bed, in his arms. Her last waking thought was that he had become her light, a searing sun ray, ever fierce against the darkness, ever strong against the night.

In the morning he was gone.

Skye slept very late, and when she awoke, she was alone. No one came to disturb her.

She left his bed to return to her own room, stepping upon the splintered door. Daylight did bring thoughts of the night crashing down upon her, but in truth she did not regret what had happened between them, although the consequences of what might come of it seemed to lie heavily upon her. Though she lived on the hope that she would elude her betrothal, breech of promise would not be smiled upon by many, and her father's position could well be jeopardized. No one could force her into anything.

But neither could she let her father be ruined.

Then, of course, there was the danger of the man himself. Were she to conceive a child . . .

She would not, she told herself hastily. She had no good reason to believe that she would not, but thought that God could not leave her with a pirate's child.

She had washed and dressed when this thought struck her. She cast herself back upon the bed and imagined that she held the Hawk's infant and watched while the pirate captain was led to the gallows on a spring day and hanged by the neck until dead. She shivered uncontrollably, hugging her arms about herself. He could die. He would die if he persisted in his dangerous calling!

There was a tap upon the door. She murmured uneasily, "Come in!" and Mr. Soames appeared with a breakfast tray. He was wonderfully impassive. He didn't even gaze toward the broken door. "The captain says if you've a mind, Lady Kinsdale, you might wish to meet him down by the lagoon this afternoon. He has business this morning, but will come soon after. He wants you to know that it will be his deepest pleasure."

"His deepest pleasure? Or his command?" she asked lightly.

"Milady, I am but a messenger—"

"Of course. Well, then, thank you, Mr. Soames, for the message."

He nodded uncomfortably and set her tray down upon the card table.

She didn't bother to ask about Tara and Bessie. They seemed to be making their own way upon the island, and making it well enough.

And besides, she reflected, with heart fluttering madly, she had every intention of riding out that afternoon.

She did. She waited until the sun rode high in the noon sky, then she went back to Señor Rivas. He saddled the same gray mare for her, and she rode slowly toward the lagoon.

When she arrived, he was not there. She looked anxiously about and saw his snow-white stallion grazing up the slope past the far bank. The water skipped and danced from the cliff, dazzling beneath the sun.

Skye dismounted and neared the water's edge. She let the horse nibble upon the plants there and sat upon the sandy slope. She edged nearer, feeling the water. It was cool and fresh.

Then her eyes rose slowly, for she discovered the Hawk's whereabouts.

He rose up out of the water. It sluiced from his body, the droplets catching the sun and burning like studded diamonds in the heat of the day. He was naked and bronzed from head to toe and he approached her with swift determination.

She came to her feet. She meant to speak, to say something. No words came to her.

She thought about the sun, high overhead. She thought about the breeze, and the gurgling waters of the brook. She could not shed her clothing here. She could not lie here, in the sand, in the soft grass.

He came closer to her. She could not speak, nor did he bother her with words. He slipped her riding coat from her shoulders, letting it fall to the grass. Then he spun her about, adroitly slipping each of the tiny hooks that lined her back. His fingers slid beneath fabric to touch her bare shoulders, and her gown fell low over her breasts and down to her waist. He lowered his head, and his lips and beard, wet and cool, touched her flesh. His tongue rimmed her shoulder and she started to shiver.

"I . . . I cannot!" she stuttered.

He spun her around. "You can," he assured her, and found her lips. His fingers fell upon the ties to her corset as his lips ravished and seduced. Her breasts were suddenly bare, and the sun warmed them. She was sinking down into a pile of her own clothing, and his weight and warmth were covering her.

He did not take her then. He touched and teased her and watched her as he slipped away her shoes and hose. She felt the fresh air touch her and she shivered and he drew her to him. They rolled upon the soft grasses, and he smiled as he caught her above him. "This is my domain, Lady Kinsdale, and none may enter here to come between us."

She smiled slowly to herself, enchanted by the beauty of the lagoon and by his whisper. There was some sweet madness there, and the excitement of it filled her. She could not be here, not so, not with him. She could not play in such a primitive Eden, laugh to the music of the bubbling water, dare to feel the breeze upon her flesh.

Her hair tumbled down upon him, covering his shoulders. His laughter faded and his eyes grew dark, and then he drew her head down to his, and his kiss entered and filled her, touching upon the newly lit flames of passion that stirred in her heart and body. His touch raked over her. He lifted her atop himself and she cried out in startled surprise as they came together instantly as one.

Sun touched her, whispers touched her, the trees and leaves shuddered over her. She felt the earth beneath her and the ragged breath of the man and her own reckless and abandoned cries as a sweet rush of satiation burst upon her. She felt the sand at her back and the tickle of the grass and the hard brush of male hair against her belly and thighs.

She felt his arms.

"Perhaps I will not let you go," he warned her. "Perhaps I shall do with you always what I will."

"You cannot," she told him firmly.

" 'Tis my domain," he reminded her. He lifted her high into his arms and she cried out in protest. "Wait! Where are you going! You cannot think to walk about like this!"

"I am not going far," he said, striding out into the water.

"Put me down."

"I will do as I choose with you, remember?"

She tossed her head back. "You will not do as you will with me, Captain Hawk. I will not allow it!"

"Oh?" He smiled with a sensual curl taking hold of the corner of his lip. His pirate's silver gaze sizzled. He dropped her flat, and she pitched into the cool fresh water.

She burst up, sputtering and protesting, and laughing. She tried to drag him under but she hadn't the strength. He caught her and brought them both beneath the cascade of the cliff, and then, as the cool water raged over them, he kissed her. A fervent flame beat against the cold. She felt his hands upon her breasts, between her legs, and she clung to him, stretching her fingers with sure fascination over his shoulders and back and hesitantly down to his buttocks.

It was madness. . . .

She cast her head back and his kiss consumed her throat until his mouth moved to close over her breast. He swept her beneath him and they came near shore, and as the cool water rushed over them, he made love to her there.

She felt the earth more keenly, never knew a touch so acutely, never imagined that a woman could know a man so completely. When she lay at rest, she had never known such a peace. He held her still, and the sun beat down upon the two of them and the water rushed over their limbs.

The sun created dazzling currents in the lagoon, and Skye narrowed her eyes against them. She spun a daydream as he held her, idly stroking her arm. Her father would come to this place. The Hawk would cast aside his buccaneer's ways and a pardon would be found. This madness could go on and on, forever. She could feel his strength and delight in his husky laughter and the fierce demand of his passion and desires. . . .

"What are you thinking?" he asked her.

"That you are a pirate," she said softly.

He stiffened. "A rogue—in a rogue's domain, milady."

"The seas will be cleared one day!" she said fervently.

He shifted, rising above her upon the sand. "That, milady, will take time. When your pious Lord Cameron comes for you, you must not travel the seas again. Do you understand me?"

Her eyes widened. "If I must do so—"

"There is no reason for you to do so."

"I am my own mistress!" she reminded him passionately.

"Are you? You forget yourself, lady. If I chose, I could keep you here. No man could storm this fortress. No pirate would think to come against me, and it would take the combined forces of several royal navies to destroy here. If I commanded it, you would stay."

She lay beneath him, trembling. If he chose, he could do so. She touched his cheek and whispered softly, "I am here because I knew no force from you. No man can force desire, sir. You said yourself that the lock upon the door did not matter, for locks lay within the heart. You could break the door, but you knocked gently upon my heart, and entered through there by the gentle care you gave me."

"And tell me, lady, shall I remain there, when you have gone on to a husband."

He mocked her. She bared her soul to him, and offered her heart. And he mocked her.

She pressed against him, maddened that he had the strength to hold her to his will. She tilted her chin proudly, but again, could not forget the hard naked feel of him against her. "I am my own mistress, sir."

"I shall miss you when you are gone, with all of my heart, Lady Skye. Tell me, will you miss me?"

"I think—quite highly of you," she said primly.

He laughed, and nuzzled her earlobe with a fascinating tenderness. "For sea slime, that is."

She met his eyes, silver with his laughter, touched by the charming rogue's curl of his lip. His arms were so strong about her. I have fallen in love with you! she thought with the deepest dismay and despair.

"You don't—you don't need to be sea slime forever," she told him.

"Alas," he said huskily, "there you are wrong, my dear, dear Lady Skye. The die has been cast."

Suddenly the natural quiet of the lagoon was split asunder. The sound of a single cannon rent the air.

The Hawk looked up. Some fiery light touched his eyes, and when he stared at her again, she thought that he did not know her at all.

She frowned. "What was that?"

He did not reply. He groaned deeply and shuddered and bent to take her lips. He kissed her deeply, and then more deeply. He held her fiercely, and still his lips assaulted hers with abandon. As if he drank from her to take his fill. As if he could not move away.

He moved sure and fleet, bringing his body against hers, and making love to her with a savage determination. She could not protest the driving force of it, for his hunger was so very deep, drawing upon the passion he had created within her. The day ceased to be, the fire of it was so swift, and so complete.

It was his world, his domain. He ruled here.

He had commanded her from the beginning, she realized. He had wanted her, and she had come to him, and in these blinding moments, it mattered not at all. He loved her with the force of a wild sweeping storm, he touched her as if his hands could hold the memory of her from everything. His palm closed upon her breast, and then his mouth, even as his body moved with arrogance and demand, knowing that he would stoke the flames with her. He reached to her womb, to her soul, she thought. His whispers cried out to her, and it was as if he cast the very force and life of himself into her, welding them into eternity. She rode a gale at sea, she thought, dangerous and beautiful. Or a fire storm. So very explosive . . .

She clung to him, and rode out the tempest, for her body gave so thoroughly to the impetus of his thrust. The sun upon their bodies was as radiant as the heat within them, the very ground beneath her back reminded her that this sweet and volatile binding of a man and woman was as old as the earth, as necessary. . . .

She cried out with the force and beauty of the shattering climax that fell upon her. He cast back his head, muscles tensed and the whole of him glimmering bronze with a sheen of perspiration, and cried out hoarsely. He fell upon her, and the raging force of him swept deep, deep inside of her like a liquid portion of the sun. She shuddered and fell back into his arms, awed and amazed anew, and certain that he would hold her then in tenderness.

He did not. He fell back against the earth, and a fierce oath exploded from him as he stared bleakly up into the powder-blue sky. He rolled and bounded to his feet. He stared down at her for a long moment. Her eyes were teal-blue and puzzled, her hair a damp splay of sunset over the earth.

He reached for her, offering her his hand.

"Get up," he said curtly.

She looked at him, hurt, her temper sizzling. "I do not obey commands, Captain Hawk."

"Don't you? We shall see."

"Shall we?"

He smiled, pulling her to her feet. His jaw was taut, his features strained as he spoke.

"The cannon, milady, is a signal. The ship has come, Lady Kinsdale. Your betrothed has come for you, slightly tarnished as you may be. I shall be heartily interested in the details of your nuptials."

She slapped him with such speed that he did not catch her until too late. Then he dragged her back against himself and bruised her lips with the hot demand of one last kiss. She jerked away from him, horrified. She would never, she thought, forget the mocking fire that burned so silver and so fierce within his eyes.

He turned away. She stared after him, blinded by sudden tears. "Wait!" she cried to him, and he turned back to her, and she wasn't even aware of what she did when she pitched herself into his arms.

He was stiff, cold. Then he held her more tightly and smoothed his fingers over her hair. A long, shuddering sigh escaped him and he kissed the top of her head. Then he freed himself from her hold and led her to the pile of her clothing. "Come, we must return before someone comes to look for us. No doubt, your fiancé is most eager to meet you."

9

ILADY, IT IS TIME."

Skye stood quickly at Robert Arrowsmith's words. She had been sitting restlessly in her room for what seemed like hours. It had not been so long, of course. At the lagoon the Hawk had helped her into her clothing—either the gentleman or the rogue until the very end—and then he had taken her into his arms one last time and cast upon her lips a kiss that would remain with her into eternity. She could still touch her mouth and feel the passion and pulse of it there now.

"You can stay," he had told her.

She shook her head desperately. She longed to tell him about her father, that there was more. That she could not bear to wait for the day when they would come and tell her that the Hawk lay dead. Nor could she bear to awaken and discover that there were many more women in his life, that he took them when he chose, and that they fell too easily to his rogue's smile and silver eyes, fell, just as she had done. . . .

"You can make me," she had whispered.

His laugh was curt and bitter. "Can I? Ah, yes! Demand a sum of Lord Cameron that is so high that all the nobility and honor of his fine house cannot pay it! Is that what you wish?" He brought his fingers to her lips. "Once you promised me everything. I brought you from the darkness of your dreams, and you promised me everything. And that is what I would require." They stared at one another, and he smiled wistfully and touched her cheek. "Perhaps we will meet again. I have never learned from you just what demon it is you fight in the darkness. I enjoyed slaying the dragons of your dreams, and I would have put them to rest forever, had I the power. Adieu, love." He dropped her fingers to her side. He brushed her forehead with his lips.

Then he disappeared into the water and crossed the lagoon, and she didn't think to turn away when he arose again, striking and noble in countenance and bearing. He had dressed with swift, deft movements and leaped upon the snow-white stallion. He looked her way and lifted a hand high.

Then he was gone, and she rode back alone.

"No hurry, milady!" Mr. Soames told her. Negotiation would take some time. That was well, she thought, for her hair was still sodden and dusted with sand as was her riding attire. A bath was in order and Mr. Soames did not mind at all; he suggested it.

And so it was, she thought when she was done, hair shampooed, her body newly attired in bone and elegant green muslin and brocade, that she would meet her betrothed in cleanliness of garb, even if she did not remain so pure in body or spirit.

She had no wish to meet this man! she thought. Reckless thoughts of breaking free upon his very deck filled her mind. Dreams of what went on below filled her thoughts. The Hawk would refuse to take ransom for her, claiming her for his own forever. And she might then protest this paradise, but remain in his arms nonetheless. . . .

It was a foolish dream. She could not bear not to see her father. He grew older with each passing year. He was precious to her, and he was surely worried and anxious beyond measure.

She stared down at her lace-gloved hands. They were trembling. A feeling of sickness surged in her stomach. She had to get out of here. She would forget. She was Lady Kinsdale, the very proud daughter of Lord Kinsdale, and she did not— by choice!—associate with pirates.

Aye, by choice, she had touched the Hawk, and been touched in turn.

By the time Robert came to the door, telling her, "Milady, it is time!" she felt as if they had come to take her to the executioner.

"It's time?" she repeated.

"Lord Cameron awaits you aboard his ship, the *Lady Elena*. He wishes to sail with the tide."

She swallowed quickly, trying to betray no emotion. "Will I see your master again?"

"I do not know, milady. Come along, please. Men will come for your trunks."

She left her room behind. Mr. Soames was waiting at the bottom of the stairs. She thanked him for his services and felt more and more like a maiden walking to the headman's block. She was being rescued, she reminded herself. Lord Cameron would expect her ardent thanks and appreciation.

Robert took her outside. Señor Rivas was waiting with a small pony trap to take her down to the dock. Robert helped her into the vehicle, then joined her. "I will see you safely to the *Lady Elena*," he said.

Skye looked back to the house. She stared up to the window at the master's bedroom. She thought that she saw the drapes fall back into place. Was he watching her leave?

She turned away from the window, feeling the fool. He had amused himself with her, then accepted payment to rid himself of her! She should despise him so very fiercely.

Tears welled within her throat. She knew that she would not shed them. She stiffened her shoulders and reminded herself that she was her father's daughter, and that she would not fail or falter now.

Before them lay the docks. She saw the two tall ships there, both tall and proud. The *Lady Elena,* and the *Silver Hawk.* She had never realized before that the pirate had drawn his name from his ship. She looked at the beautiful figure-head, a silent sentinel.

The *Lady Elena* lay with a woman's figure upon her bow, too. It was an Indian, Skye thought. An Indian maiden with long flowing hair and buckskin dress. What a curious choice for Lord Cameron, she thought.

The docks were busy. Men loaded supplies aboard the *Lady Elena;* seamen scrubbed deck and knotted rope. Skye saw all the hustle and bustle as the pony trap came to a halt and Robert Arrowsmith helped her down. Señor Rivas tipped his hat to her and Skye smiled, telling him good-bye. Then Robert led her along the broad plank that stretched from the dock to the *Lady Elena.*

She was a larger ship than the *Silver Hawk,* Skye thought. She seemed to carry fourteen guns, with a narrow and high-rising hull. She would be a fleet ship; if not quite so swift as the pirate ship, she was more heavily armed and could probably fight well upon the open sea. Lord Cameron was a merchant, she knew. His fields were filled with tobacco and cotton and corn, and his ships endlessly plied the routes between the mother country and the New World. He armed himself very well against pirates, she thought. And yet her father had thought that he had done the same, and still the *Silver Messenger* had been taken.

"There he is!" Robert said suddenly.

Skye's heart slammed hard against her chest and her breath seemed to catch within her throat. Her palms were damp. She was not afraid of Lord Cameron! she assured herself. But she was nervous about this first meeting. She did not yet know what she meant to say or do, or how she would manage her life from now on. Thoughts of this meeting had been difficult enough before she had come to know the Silver Hawk; now it seemed a travesty.

"Where?" she murmured uneasily.

"There," Robert said. "At the helm. He speaks with Mr. Morley, his quartermaster, and Mr. Niven, his first mate."

"He captains his own ship?"

"Always, milady, if he is aboard."

She could see only his back and his form, and nothing of his face. He was dressed in a fine fawn-colored brocade coat and soft brown knee breeches. His shirt was white beneath his waistcoat, laced and frilled, spilling from his cuffs and neck. He wore a cockaded hat with eagle plumes above a full powdered wig. He was a tall man, and seemed able.

"Milady?" Robert said.

She realized that she stood there, upon the plank. Robert took her hand and led her forward and helped her to leap down to the deck.

"Milord! Milord Cameron!" Robert cried.

The man paused, passing his ledger to the mate on his left. Robert urged Skye along, bringing her up the four steps to the high-rising helm. She stared downward, carefully holding her skirt lest she trip upon the stair.

"Milady, let me assist you."

The voice was low and well modulated. The hand that touched hers was gloved in soft leather. She accepted the assistance, and looked up slowly.

A startled gasp tore from her lips.

He was nothing like the Silver Hawk, nothing at all. He was clean shaven and his powdered wig was neatly queued, and he was dressed totally as the lord. He was young, and his features were striking and clean cut and strong.

It was his eyes . . .

Only his eyes . . .

They were the same as his distant cousin's, so very much the same. Silver-toned and arresting, perhaps more so on this man, for the very white of his powdered wig made the darkness of his lashes and brows all the more striking.

He arched a brow, stiffening at her look. "Milady, be not afraid! I am Petroc Cameron, sworn to defend you, and not that heathen cousin of mine. The eyes, I'm afraid, are an accident of birth. The resemblance has always been a matter of distress to me, but never so much as now, as it causes you discomfort!"

Discomfort . . . he did not know the depths of it!

"Sir!" she managed to murmur.

"Milady . . ." he said. She thought that there was warmth to his whisper. He held both of her hands and studied her swiftly. "You are well?" he said anxiously.

"Very."

"Thank God for that," he said, and turned to his men. "Mr. Morley, Mr. Niven, I give you my lady Skye. Skye, all and any of us are at your service, and we will strive to erase the horrors of the past days for you."

She could not speak. She nodded to Lord Cameron's mate and his quarter-master. Mr. Niven was young and blond and blue-eyed, and though his smile was as grave as the circumstances, his eyes were merry, and she thought that she might like him very well. Mr. Morley seemed more staid and strict; he was bewigged like Lord Cameron, and solid in posture.

"Mr. Morley will see you to your cabin, milady," Lord Cameron told her. "I will be with you as soon as possible; I'm afraid that I must now see to our embarkation."

She nodded, turning around to say good-bye to Robert. She would miss him. Robert was gone. He had left the deck without a word.

There was a touch upon her elbow. She turned again to see Mr. Morley standing there, a grave expression upon his heavy jowled face. "If you'll come with me, my lady?"

She nodded vaguely, but she had no desire to leave the deck. The plank was being pulled, and seamen were climbing into the rigging to half-hoist certain sails to catch a steady breeze and move them carefully down the channel. Small boats—the *Silver Hawk's* small boats—came to the bow, preparing to guide the *Lady Elena* away from the treacherous shoals.

"Milady?"

"Mr. Morley, I should like to stay on deck."

Mr. Morley shifted uncomfortably from foot to foot. "Lord Cameron has ordered that I take you to your chamber."

"I will not be ordered about by Lord Cameron, Mr. Morley."

"He thought that you would despise this island, this place of your imprisonment, and would be eager to see your last sight of it."

She smiled sweetly and with a tremendous guilt upon her heart. "I sail away, Mr. Morley, and the breeze is fresh and sweet."

The *Lady Elena* moved away from the dock. A command was shouted, and men scurried about. A sailor paused before Skye, bowed his head to her in flushing acknowledgment, and said, "Beg pardon, milady?"

"Oh, of course!" she murmured, and stepped aside. He cast his weight against the rigging for the mainsail, seemed to dangle upon it, and shouted for aid to pull up the canvas. Another of his fellows came along, and between them, the huge mainsail rose above them.

"Come, milady, please!" Mr. Morley urged her.

She sighed, but could not leave the deck. She pushed past him and hurried to the hull, looking backward to Bone Cay.

She saw a figure upon the pirate ship where it lay at berth, quiet and restful. Sunset was coming on. Sunset, and the tide. The island and ship and channel were bathed in color. Red draped beguilingly over the ship, the sand, the men and women milling upon the dock. She looked from the rise of the island to the outline of the house and walls back to the dock, and to the ship, an elegant lady in the sunset. Then she blinked back a sudden surge of tears.

He was standing aboard his ship, she thought. The *Silver Hawk* was floating there. The *Lady Elena* pulled swiftly away, but still, she knew that it was he. He stood tall upon the deck, his arms akimbo, his legs well spread apart as if he rode the waves, even though the ship lay at dock. He was dressed all in black, from his sweeping hat to his booted feet. The plume and brim fell well over his eyes, shielding his face from her view.

But it was he, she thought.

He lifted his hand to her in a final salute.

To her horror, a cry tore from her throat and she spun around to a very startled Mr. Morley. "Please! I'm ready. Take me from the deck to my quarters, now, please!"

She was half-blinded, she thought. He caught her arm and led her, and without him she would have tripped over the cleats and rigging. They came to a narrow passage of steps, and Mr. Morley warned her that she must take very grave care. She scarcely heard him.

They stepped below, and he led her quickly to the aft, throwing open a chamber door there. The cabin was huge, with windows stretching around the hull for her pleasure and ease. There was a large bunk, elegantly covered in white linen, and secured tight to the wall. There was a screen for her privacy, rows of books, a washstand and pitcher and bowl, a circular window seat, and a mirrored dressing table. It was all beautiful, all elegant, all well fit for a lady, one who was honored and cherished.

She could barely glance about herself.

"Thank you!" she told Mr. Morley.

"Lord Cameron will be with you soon. Supper will be served in his cabin as soon as we are clear of the shoals and reefs."

"Thank you. I shall look forward to our meeting." She dreaded their meeting with all of her heart. At the moment, though, she wished only to be free from Mr. Morley.

He bowed deeply to her and left. Skye swiftly closed her cabin door and cast herself down heavily upon her bunk. Tears suddenly fell swiftly and forcefully down her cheeks, and she found herself swearing aloud. "Damn him!"

Oh, but she had been a fool! To fall for a pirate, a knave, and now discover that her heart remained twisted within his callous hands.

What had she desired? she asked herself. To live with a pirate? To lose her father forever? To wonder day after day if the rake she had sold all honor and pride for would return from his latest venture? No! One day he was destined to hang, or he would die upon the sword of another, like Blackbeard or Logan. No . . .

But she didn't want to be here. Not aboard this ship. Not with the gentleman lord who had come to rescue her.

Her tears abated slightly. She needed time, and distance, she told herself. She needed to see her father, to cast herself into his arms, to cry her heart out and tell him that her world had been turned over, and she needed to learn to understand it, and herself.

It was going to grow dark, she told herself uneasily. And the Silver Hawk was no longer with her, a beacon against the night.

She rose, wiping her eyes. She saw no lanterns about the cabin, no candles. Beneath the washstand, though, she found a decanter of brandy. There were pewter mugs beside it but she did not bother with such a nicety. She pulled the stopper and drank heavily. The brandy burned throughout her. She felt somewhat better, somewhat stronger.

There was a knock upon her door. She threw it open and stared at the young man there in stunned surprise.

"Davey!"

It was the young, sweet lad from the *Silver Messenger*. She reached out and touched his shoulders, assuring herself that he was there. A smile of pleasure swept across her features. "Oh, Davey, you are alive and well!"

"And have been, Lady Skye," he assured her, flushing and grinning broadly. "He was not a cruel master, milady."

She gasped, drawing him into her cabin. "Tell me! Where have you been? What has happened?"

"Why, we've been at sea, milady. In your father's ship. We weathered the storm, then held off Hatteras. They were sending messages, I believe. We met with Lord Cameron's ship on the open water, and those of us who had been captured and sent to the hold were passed on over."

"Were you cared for, Davey?" she asked with a frown.

"Aye, milady, a surgeon was sent down to the lot of us. The Hawk, he said, did not care to see any seaman in chains, so if we promised good behavior, we were free. We were even brought on deck for good, fresh air. It was not so loathsome a time, milady." He paused, looked at her searchingly, then flushed. "And you, milady? I prayed for you daily. Are you well?"

She swallowed. "Aye, Davey, very well, thank you."

He nodded and flushed again, and stepped away from her. "I came to see if you might require anything, milady. Lord Cameron would probably not take too kindly to my talking with you."

"Lord Cameron has no right to tell me who I may or not speak with, Davey," Skye said flatly, standing. Then she paused, startled, and felt a peculiar sensation sweep along her spine. Her lips parted into a soft gasp, for she realized that the man had come up behind Davey, and stood, filling the doorway behind the lad.

Davey swung about, and whitened.

"Is your duty here done then, lad?" Lord Cameron inquired.

"Aye, sir!"

"Be gone with you then, son," Lord Cameron said, his eyes not upon Davey but looking over the young man's pale head, and finding Skye's. She started to tremble. She hated that silver color, and hated that he could appear so like the Hawk. . . .

And so entirely unlike his black-sheep cousin.

"We have left the shoals and reefs behind us, Skye. I have come to take you to dinner."

She folded her hands together tightly. "That is very kind of you, Lord Cameron. This is all . . . very kind of you. I do, however, find that I am very weary. If I could—"

"Lady Skye! I shall not keep you long at all, I promise. And I could not dream of allowing you to take to your cabin without a meal. I understand your distress, but please, I insist. You must come to dinner."

There was a note of steel to his voice. Like his distant cousin, he was accustomed to command. What was it with these men? she wondered irritably.

"Sir—"

"Milady," he said firmly, and offered her his arm.

She hesitated, then accepted, for short of total rudeness, she had no other choice, and whatever his feelings in the matter, he had risked life and limb to come for her.

He drew her arm within his and led her just down the hallway to the next door. "My cabin, milady. And should you need them, Mr. Morley and Mr. Niven share quarters just across. There are more officers down the hall, and the seamen's quarters are the deck below."

She nodded and tried to smile. When he pushed open the door, she entered quickly, eluding his touch. She looked around quickly and found it to be a more practical than elegant place, though all seemed to be in the best of taste. His desk was heavy and finely polished and heavily laden with charts. Warm velvet drapes fell over the windows in a deep sea blue, matching the simple coverlet that lay over the bunk against the far wall. A table had been brought to the room. A snowy white cloth lay atop it and a complete silver setting, and handsome plate with soft flowered designs.

Lord Cameron closed the door to his cabin behind him and walked behind one of the handsome high-backed chairs, pulling it out for her.

"Milady?"

"Thank you," she murmured, sliding into the chair.

He did not join her. He walked over to his desk, to a decanter there. "Wine, my dear?" He turned about to face her with a curious smile. "Or have you already been indulging?"

"What?" she gasped, staring his way. There was a look of steel about him that made her think that she had underestimated the man.

"Forgive my very bad manners, milady," he said apologetically. She avoided meeting his gaze. She could not bear to see the color of his eyes.

"You are forgiven."

"You have been through an awful ordeal. You are certainly entitled to—indulgence."

How did he manage to make the word sound so frightfully decadent?

He came to the table, setting a glass of deep red wine before her. She was tempted to grab it and swallow down the liquid in an instant. She could not let this man so unnerve her! He was no pirate, she reminded herself, but a lord of the peerage. He was sworn by honor to certain behavior, and she need not fear him.

She did not fear him. She picked up her wineglass and sipped upon it and forced herself to meet his eyes. "Yes, it has all been quite an ordeal."

He drew back his own chair and sat opposite her. "I heard wonderful things about your valor, Skye."

"Did you?"

He nodded to her gravely. "The crew rescued from your father's ship told us how you battled the pirates in defense of the Irish maids. They say you fought unbelievably well. They say that you won."

"I know something of swordplay."

"Yes, your father told me. You do not know something of it; you know it very well."

"Yes."

"So you bested the first pirates."

"Yes."

"But not the Silver Hawk."

Despite herself, she felt her eyes fall. "No."

He was silent, silent so long that she wished she could scream or meet his stare boldly and brazenly and shout out the truth of it all.

"But he did not injure you?"

"No, Lord Cameron, he did not injure me."

"Skye! We are soon to live together as man and wife. My given name is Petroc, a whim of my mother's, and those who are close to me call me Roc. I would hear that name from you."

She smiled stiffly and felt a chill sweep over her. As last she could meet his eyes, for he had ceased to plague her about her adventures. "Roc," she murmured obligingly.

"It sounds well upon your sweet lips, milady."

"Tell me, sir," she said, sitting forward. "How is my father."

"Well and good," he assured her. "He will meet us at Cameron Hall."

"Cameron Hall?" she said with dismay.

"What is wrong with that, milady?"

"Nothing. Why, nothing, of course. I had just thought that we would sail for Williamsburg."

"Ah." His dark lashes fell briefly over his eyes. He stood and moved away from her, sipping his wine and idly pulling back one of the drapes. It was nearly dark beyond the light from the cabin, Skye saw.

He dropped the curtain. "Williamsburg has vastly changed, you will discover. Governor Spotswood has moved into his new manor, and it is all but complete. He has hosted many an elegant ball there. The magazine is complete and filled with muskets and swords for the militiamen. The Bruton parish church has been rebuilt since you were home, and more and more merchants flock to the town daily. Even coming from London, my dear, I believe that you will be impressed with the growth of our capital city."

"I'm sure I shall."

"Not that we shall be so very close to Williamsburg."

"I beg your pardon."

"Cameron Hall, milady. It is a good three hours down the James. Closer to Jamestown, but on higher ground. We do, of course, come into the city now and then. You will not be so completely isolated."

She felt as if the bars of a new prison were falling quickly shut upon her.

"I wonder, milord—"

"Oh, you needn't fret so uncomfortably, milady. I have already heard that you are opposed to the marriage."

She stared at him, her eyes flashing. "Well, milord, I have heard that you, too, were opposed!"

He inclined his head, smiling. "Ah, but that was before I sailed the seas for you, milady!"

She flushed, and swallowed down the whole of her wine after all. Lord Cameron quickly stood, taking her glass to refill it. She watched him walk away. He was a tall man, too, with a long back and broad shoulders. She imagined that beneath his finery he was well muscled and toned. She shivered suddenly, and did not know why. He was unerringly polite, yet she sensed that his temper might be great when provoked.

"Milord—"

"Roc, Skye. Please, you must be comfortable with my given name."

"Roc—" She paused, gritting her teeth. He came around, facing her. He placed her wineglass down before her again and moved away, this time perching upon the corner of his desk. He waited expectantly. "Roc, I do with all my heart appreciate your trouble and valor in coming so swiftly to my rescue. And the expense, of course—"

"The expense?" He arched a brow.

"The—the expense," she repeated, faltering. "The ransom! I'm sure that he charged you dearly for my return."

"Why, not at all, milady."

"You are too polite and generous, milord."

"Not at all. I tell you the truth. The pirate didn't charge me a single farthing for your return."

She gasped out loud, coming to her feet. "He what?"

Lord Cameron's dark lashes flickered over his silver eyes. "Why the distress, milady? We paid for the seamen, the ship, and the maids, but you, my dear, were returned to us through goodwill."

"He did not even charge you for me!"

His brow flew up. She quickly tried to hide her distress, falling back into her chair, swallowing down her second glass of wine.

"I repeat, my dear, he did not charge for you."

She lowered her head quickly, but there came a knock upon the captain's door, and Lord Cameron quickly answered it. "Thank you, Mr. Monahan," he said, directing a hefty sailor with a huge serving tray to the table. "My dear, this is Mr. Monahan, the cook's assistant. Mr. Monahan, my Lady Skye."

"Lady," Mr. Monahan said, bowing deeply as he set the tray down with a flourish. He lifted the silver cover from the serving plate. "Pheasant, milady, stuffed with nuts and cornmeal and raisins. I hope that it will be to your pleasure."

"I'm sure that it shall, Mr. Monahan," she said sweetly. Then there was silence as Mr. Monahan prepared the plates. Skye waited uneasily until he was gone and cast a gaze toward Lord Cameron. Her heart catapulted when she discovered that he was staring at her deeply and intently. The cabin was too small for the two of them. She longed to escape him. She desperately, desperately needed to be alone.

"Do you feel ill?" he asked her when Mr. Monahan had left them. He took his place opposite from her.

She shook her head. "I—I'm fine." She wasn't fine. She didn't feel well at all. She picked up her fork and played idly with her food.

He was still watching her, paying no heed to his food. "The governor intends to clean out the pirates, you know. Lieutenant Governor Spotswood, that is. He is bold man, adventurous and determined. Where other men in power turn their heads, he stands strong. He will see all the pirates swept from the seas, skewered through or brought to trial. Then they may hang from the neck until dead."

She set her fork down.

"Skye, whatever is the matter?"

She shook her head, then she stared at him. "How can you be so callous? The man is your cousin."

"Cousin!" He shuddered. "Several times removed, milady, I do assure you. And lady, after all that has been done to you, I would think that you would rejoice to know that the scourge will be cleansed from the sea. Can you find the likes of pirates pleasant? Logan and his crew? The late One-Eyed Jack? Mr. Teach?"

"Of course not! I find them despicable. It's just that—"

"What?"

"You spoke of one who is your own blood, that is all."

"Barely, milady."

"Even your looks—"

"An accident of birth, and I don't care to be reminded of it."

"But you do know one another! You negotiate and speak, else I could not be here so swiftly."

"Bone Cay is the safest of the pirate havens, and the Hawk is perhaps the most dependable of the buccaneers; no more, milady. Aye, we speak. We come to agreements, that is all."

She lowered her head, still feeling queasy. "There is a precedent," she murmured.

"Pardon?"

"Sir Francis Drake," she said, and then she realized that she was repeating words she had heard from the Silver Hawk.

"Yes?" Lord Cameron arched a brow.

"He—he was a privateer. Men set sail against the Spanish, and even when we were not at war, Elizabeth turned her head while her Englishmen ravaged Spanish ships. When the Stuarts came to the throne, the mode continued. We created these men. And now they flourish. But where does the line come, Lord Cameron? Some were privateers, sanctioned by their governments. Some are cutthroats, and some simple thieves."

"Simple thieves have been known to hang. Trust me, the pirates will do so, too."

"Including the Silver Hawk?"

"I shall escort you myself to the execution."

She was silent. The pheasant was delicious; she had no appetite. The wine churned in her stomach.

"Let's not speak of this, milady. The past is over; you are safe with me. You do seem well. You were not harmed? In any way?"

A dark flush came quickly to her features. The question, she knew, was far more intimate than the words alone could convey.

"I was treated well enough," she said. She folded the corners of her napkin together in her lap. What did he know? Why did he stare at her so probingly, with his unusual eyes of silver, as riveting as the Hawk's? He could know nothing! she told herself.

"You're quite sure?" he asked.

"I was well treated!" she repeated.

"Tell me about it."

"What?" she gasped.

"Tell me what happened. I am most anxious to hear, and the governor will want information, too."

"I—"

"The ship was seized first by One-Eyed Jack and his men, is that right?"

"Uh—yes."

"But then the prize was stolen from one pirate by another, is that right?"

"Yes."

"The Hawk, of course, instantly knew your value."

"Yes, yes, of course."

He stroked his chin. "How strange. He then decided to release you, asking nothing for you." He leaned forward. "So you came to know him well."

"Well enough."

"And you were imprisoned separately from the others?"

"Yes."

"Where?"

The rapid, spitfire questions had her reeling, feeling deeply on the defensive. She leaped to her feet, allowing her chair to fall back. "Stop! I do not care to speak about it longer!"

"But you were treated well!" he reminded her.

"Lord Cameron!" She stared at him with all the icy reserve that she could summon. "I do not care to speak of it anymore! Not now, not ever! Governor Spotswood will seek out his pirates, and he will slay them all, no doubt! But I cannot go on tonight, do you understand me, sir?"

He came around, righting her chair. His hands fell upon her shoulders and she was startled by the strength of him. He spoke softly, his voice low, well modulated. He was a lord, a gentleman, yet more than ever she had the feeling that he was not to be underestimated, that a simmering anger lay deep within him, and that if it rose to the surface, it would be dangerous indeed.

"Sit, milady. I have not meant to distress you."

"I am not distressed."

"I am grateful to hear that. We will speak no more of it for now. The future lies before us, and we should not speak of the past."

She raised her eyes to his. "I am grateful, Lord Cameron. I am very grateful for your presence here, for the fact that you came so swiftly to my rescue. I will not marry you."

He arched a brow.

"You will not marry me?"

"No."

"Your father gave promise."

She shook her head impatiently. "I know, sir, that you did not wish to marry me—"

"Perhaps I have changed my mind."

She gritted her teeth. "I have not changed mine."

"I don't think that you understand. My will is very strong."

"I don't think you understand. I promise that my will can be of steel when I so choose."

"You cannot change what is."

"But I do not want—"

"You insult my family name, milady," he said pleasantly, but his eyes flashed their silver warning.

"This was a fool's bargain made by two doting fathers when we were just children. I was an infant. You cannot hold me to this." She pushed away from the table and stood. "If you will excuse me now, sir, I am very exhausted."

He stood, too, and came around the table, blocking her way to the door. He did not touch her, but he watched her, and she didn't know if his silver eyes danced with humor or fury.

"I'm afraid that I cannot excuse you as yet, milady."

"Oh, and why is that? Truly, Lord Cameron, you are not displaying the manners of a good gentle peer in the least!"

"My apologies, milady. But there is something that you must know before you quit this cabin."

She tossed back her head with her most imperious manner. "And what, pray tell, Lord Cameron, is that?"

"Only this, milady. Protest comes too late."

"What are you talking about?" She frowned. A certain dread came to settle over her. She longed to flee before he could speak. There would be no way. She could not barge past him. He was too tall, towering against the door. His shoulders, for all their elegant apparel, were too broad.

"I'm afraid that by the law, we are legally wed."

"What?"

"Your father was quite concerned even as you set sail from the English shore. We were wed by proxy the day you left London behind. You see, my dear, whether it pleases you or not, it is done."

He waited, allowing the words to settle over her. She was silent, stunned. Her father could not have done such a thing to her!

He sighed deeply, but spoke with a frightening edge to his voice.

"Madame, you are my wife, and that is that."

She shook her head, disbelieving. "No!"

"Yes."

"I will fight it."

"I will not allow you."

"You must! You cannot love me! You must let me go."

"No."

He said the word with such finality that she found herself shivering.

But then he stepped aside from the door, opening it for her. He bowed deeply. She stiffened, and walked by him. He caught her arm briefly.

"I will never let you go," he said. "You will become reconciled."

"I will never become reconciled. We will be wretched!"

"Then wretched, my love, we will be." He released her, bowing deeply. "Good night, my love."

The door closed, and she was left alone in the hallway.

10

KYE STORMED DOWN THE CORRIDOR TO THE door to her own cabin. She cast it open to step inside, and when she did, the darkness surrounded her.

She leaned against the door, swallowing, closing her eyes.

If only!

If only One-Eyed Jack had never spotted the *Silver Messenger,* if only the Silver Hawk had not come behind him. She had been mistress upon the *Silver Messenger,* her father's ship, and she had never needed to fear the darkness there, for she had always been surrounded by lamps and candles. Now, no matter what her feelings for the man, no matter what lay between them, she would have to go with him. The clammy hand of terror was already upon her. If she did not move swiftly . . .

She moved away from the door just as a tap came upon it. It opened, and she saw that Lord Cameron stood there, a lamp in his hands glowing cheerfully against the darkness. "Milady," he murmured, bowing to her and handing her the light.

Unnerved, she felt her fingers tremble as she took it from him. "How did you know!" she gasped out.

"It is my ship. That is why I knew that there was no lamp here," he told her.

He had known that there was no light, not that she was terrified beyond reason of the darkness.

"And," he added, "your father has warned me that you do not care for the darkness."

"Oh," she murmured, lowering her lashes. Drat father! she thought. What had he been doing to her? Giving away her every secret, and selling her, body and soul! "Er . . . thank you," she managed. Still, he hovered there in her doorway. Darkness hid his eyes and his features and she sensed him on different levels. Perhaps the Hawk had made her more attuned to the body. She felt the heat and energy of his presence, and breathed the scent of him. He smelled of very fine leather and good Virginia tobacco in a subtle and pleasant way. He was not at all, as a man, repulsive.

He was her husband, or so he claimed, she reminded herself, and was seized with a fierce shivering. He had given her a separate cabin, she quickly assured herself. He would not fall upon her, he would not demand his marital rights.

But perhaps he would!

He stepped through the doorway and looked about the cabin. "Is everything to your comfort?"

"Everything is fine!" she cried with vehemence. He looked her way, a smile curving into his lip. "You are very nervous, milady."

"I have been greatly unnerved by your comments."

"You mustn't despair." He came closer to her. She backed against the wall, turning her head from his, terrified that he meant to touch her. She had fallen from the arms of one charming rogue to another, she thought briefly, one a pirate and one a lord, and both far too arrogant and assured.

His knuckles grazed over her cheek. She barely held back a scream, and a soft gasp escaped her.

"You are my wife," he said.

"I am not your wife!" She stared at him again, her eyes sizzling. "And don't be so sure that all the pirates shall hang! I have come from London, sir, and I am far more abreast of certain news. I was in the mother country when Queen Anne died, when they reached over to Hanover for King George. The rights for trial upon men such as Hornigold and Blackbeard and—and the Silver Hawk—must come directly from the monarch. No new commissions have been granted by King George as yet. It was my understanding—"

"My dear lady, do tell me! Just what is your understanding, and from where do you draw upon it?"

"I do read the papers, Lord Cameron. And there was a great deal of talk in high places about the king offering a pardon to what pirates would surrender and swear an oath by a certain date. Perhaps these fellows will surrender, and there will be no need for murder."

"Murder! You call the death of a pirate murder?"

He spoke with a certain ferocity, but she sensed that he was smiling beneath it. Was he laughing at her? Was he furious with her? She didn't know.

"Bloodshed, Lord Cameron."

"You are opinionated."

"Yes! I am most opinionated, and very brash and outspoken, not at all ladylike, and surely not possessing qualities that you might want in a wife!"

"Ah! So you admit that you are my wife!"

"No!" she cried, alarmed, pressing ever backward against the paneling. She tried to straighten, to stand firm. He was a gentleman, a lord. He would not seize her, would he? "No! Why in God's name are you doing this! I had thought you opposed to this barbaric treatment of marriage, of—"

"I have discovered myself quite pleased—Lady Cameron," he said very softly. Chills swept along her spine. There was something about his speech . . . the soft, low, deeply modulated tone and cadence of it reminded her of the other. She was suddenly desperate for him to leave. She would have said anything just to be free of his presence then.

"Milord—" she whispered, but it was not necessary. He did not touch her, he moved away from her.

"There is ample oil for the lamp to burn until daylight," he said softly.

Then he left her, closing the door behind himself.

Skye remained against the paneling for a long time. Then she slowly exhaled and, in time, pushed away from the wall and sank down to her bed. She lay there fully clothed and thought wretchedly of the morning, and of the night that had passed before. She could not forget the Hawk. She could not stop thinking of everything that had passed between them, and she could not stop feeling as if her very heart bled. She could not love such a man; she could not even care for him! But she did. Heat washed over her with memory. Yet how carelessly, how callously, he had cast her aside! He spoke of money and ransom endlessly, yet she had, in the end, been worthless to him. He was a pirate; she had been a whim, an adventure, and the adventure was over now.

The adventure was over. . . .

And a tall bewigged stranger with silver eyes was telling her that she was his wife!

It was too much. Too much. She longed then for nothing but home. For Williamsburg. For market square with its endless fairs, for the bowling green where she had often played and laughed with the other children. Williamsburg, with her planned and beautiful, broad streets. With the College of William and Mary, her endless bustle of students and scholars, her law debates, her fashionable and tawdry taverns . . .

It was her home. It was where her father had built his house, just down from the governor's mansion begun when she had been a child. Alexander Spotswood had planned much of it himself. When she had been very little, she had watched the construction with him, and he had tousled her hair with affection. "See, child, the entry will be here, and I, your lieutenant governor, will greet most guests here. But if you are very important—and of course, Skye, you shall be that!—you may come up the steps and I will greet you in the hallway above. See here, I have shown your father. We will have the most fashionable leather to cover the walls in the hall. Then my bedchamber will be here, and our guests will be here. And as I've told your father, we will have the most fabulous wine cellar."

Home would be a haven, she thought.

But she was not going to be brought home. Lord Cameron was taking her somewhere down the peninsula to his Tidewater plantation. She swallowed fiercely, watching the lamplight waver over the walls of the ship.

He meant to keep her there. At some godforsaken manor in the wilderness. Surely, it would be horrible, it would be swampland. By summer the insects and heat would be unbearable.

She shuddered and reminded herself that she planned to fight Lord Cameron to the very end. A rising anxiety engulfed her. Could she fight him? There would be no help for her when she tried to fight a lord, a powerful landowner. No one would help her, for anyone would think that she was daft, trying to fight something so very right and proper.

Then there was Lord Cameron himself. . . .

She shivered, wondering how he would feel if he knew the truth about her. He would loathe her, she thought.

Perhaps . . . perhaps he would loathe her enough to disavow her. To annul the marriage himself. Proxy marriage! They could not do that to her, could they?

Perhaps . . .

But then again, perhaps, if he knew, he would show her no deference. He would hate her, but he would show her no deference at all. He would not leave her at peace in this cabin.

She turned over and tried to close her eyes, tried to find oblivion in sleep. It eluded her for a long, long time. Nor were her dreams restful. She imagined him coming to her. . . .

The Silver Hawk.

He came as he had come to her from the lagoon, rising up with the water sluicing from his body, coming to her with firm purpose, reaching for her. His eyes blazed, and suddenly he was not her lover, but the man who claimed to be her husband.

His arms closed around her and she struggled, but he was dragging her down, deep down into the sea. She heard him whispering to her, and she didn't hear the word. Then suddenly it came clear.

"Whore!"

She awoke with a jerk. She was fully clad and the light was bright around her and she was alone. She lay back, shivering. She did not sleep again that night.

———

Tara and Bess, cheerful and chattering, came to serve her in the morning. Skye was quiet, allowing Bess to talk on and on with grave excitement about the pirate's island while she brushed and braided her hair. Tara set up a breakfast tray for her, complete with fresh eggs, brown bread, and strong, sweet tea. The girls were excited, she knew, because they were heroines. They had survived an ordeal by fire, and when they spoke about the Bone Cay, they had a rapt audience among the young sailors. Skye kept a grip upon her tongue, determined not to ruin their happiness when she was bitter and frightened of the future herself.

Because a pirate continued to plague her dreams, and because Lord Cameron entered in upon them in moments of intimacy.

When her clothing had been straightened, her hair done, her cabin neatened, Bess asked permission to go on deck. Skye freely granted it.

She remained within the cabin herself for a long time, hoping to avoid Lord Cameron. But the walls seemed to close in upon her, and she soon came topside. He was at the helm. She stood far across the deck from him with crew and rigging and sails between them. He bowed to her, his hands upon the heavy wheel. She nodded curtly in return and came portside, staring out over the water. The day was beautiful, the water was very blue, and the sky was light and powdery. She could see a distant shoreline.

"Florida," he said softly behind her. She knew his voice, it was so like the Hawk's. His breath touched her nape and feathered along it. She turned. He wasn't looking at her, but at the land that lay off the hull of the ship. "A treacherous land, beautiful, and inhabited by all manner of creatures. It's fascinating." He smiled at her at last. "I have always loved it."

Something about his smile drew a response from her. "I have never seen it."

He shrugged, leaning over the helm. "Ah, but you've lived in London, and to many in our fair colony, London constitutes all of the world."

"And don't you feel that way, Lord Cameron?"

"More than anything, I love Virginia," he said, and she felt the curious intensity in his voice. He leaned against the wooden railing at the hull and studied her as he spoke. "I love Virginia, and Cameron Hall, and the acres that surround her. The house sits high atop a hill, and from the windows and porch you can look far down the slope and see the James flowing by. You can see when storms roll in and watch as the sun rises. You can see the ebb and flow of traffic upon the river. She runs deep. All manner of commerce come to us. Tenants work much of the land, and all of them come to the docks to send their produce to England, to buy their ribands and baubles and fine dish and plate and materials. The grass upon the slope is so green and verdant that at times it appears blue. The summers are hot, but the river sweeps away much of the heat. The winters are never too cold. It is endlessly beautiful."

"It sounds as if you speak of a paradise," she said softly, the last word catching in her throat, for she had found her own paradise, and that on a tropical isle with bright wildflowers and endless heat and the glow of the sun upon the earth. He could not know the secrets of her heart, she thought, and yet he looked at her with a slow, rueful smile that seized her heart. "Paradise? Perhaps. It is a realm we create ourselves, isn't it? Separate unto each and every one of us, and found where we choose to seek it."

She turned quickly from him, watching the shoreline.

"They say that there is endless treasure buried there, upon the sandy shores," he mused. "They've all played there, the buccaneers. Once it was Captain Kidd. Now Hornigold and Blackbeard and others." He looked at her once again. "Blackbeard and Hornigold have been wreaking havoc along the Carolinas this fall. Blackbeard fought a fierce battle with a ship of the Royal Navy. He is vastly admired among men. They stand in awe of his daring."

"Do they?" she murmured.

"It will be something to see, if this pardon proclamation of yours comes through."

"I imagine it will," she murmured.

"Thank God, my dear, that your adventuring days are over. Soon you will be at Cameron Hall . . . forever."

She looked to him quickly, and the gaze he gave her with his subtle curl of a smile sent rivulets of sensation coursing down her spine. Damn those silver eyes of his! The simple words seemed to carry the most satanish, underlying threat. Or promise. Or warning. It was a warning, she realized. On this ship, she was somewhat safe from him. But when they came to his house, his precious Cameron Hall, things were destined to change.

"Forever, sir? I think not. My father will be there when we come in, will he not? I must protest vehemently all that has been done without my consent."

"Nothing was done without your consent."

"But it was."

He shook his head gravely. Still she thought that he was enjoying her discomfort. "You signed all the appropriate papers when your father visited you in London."

"I—I did not!" she said, but her words tripped and faltered as she wondered just what she had signed. She had been arguing with her father, and therefore not paying much attention to what he required of her. Some of his holdings were in her name, too, for various business reasons. She often signed papers, and she had always hated to be bothered with the details of them. Especially in London, where so very much was going on at all times.

"We will see, milady," he said softly. He turned from her, heading back toward the helm. His absolute assurance ignited her fury. "Wait!" she demanded.

He turned back to her, arching a brow expectantly.

"You can't mean to keep an unwilling bride, Lord Cameron! Surely it would be far beneath your dignity."

He doffed his hat to her, bowing neatly. "Madame, I do intend to keep my bride, willing or no. Good afternoon, milady." He turned and walked again.

"Wait!" she cried again.

"What?" he demanded.

"I—I can't!"

"You can't what?"

She had to tell him that she couldn't possibly be his wife, but he was some distance from her then, and she didn't feel like shouting such news across the whole of the ship. He waited with definite exasperation. She moistened her lips, about to suggest a certain privacy, when suddenly the seaman atop the crow's nest shouted down to him. "Ship to the starboard, sir!"

Cameron turned around without another glance her way, striding with assurance and grace to leap up to the helm platform. "My glass, please!"

Skye, forgetting their dispute, raced toward him, lifting her skirts to hurry up to the helm. He ignored her, facing starboard. The seaman atop the crow's nest cried down to them. "She's changing her colors, sir! She was flying the English flag—now she gone a-pirate!"

"Gunners to your stations!" Cameron called. He brought the glass to his eye. "It isn't Logan," he muttered. "Nor Blackbeard, nor Hornigold . . ."

"Do you know them so well, sir?" Skye taunted softly.

"Blane!" he called to the hefty seaman at the wheel. "Bring her about sharp. We'll pretend to run, then ram straight toward her, all guns blazing then. Understood?"

"Aye, sir!"

He drew the glass from his eye, startled to see her beside him. "Go below," he told her curtly.

"No!" she said, backing away from him.

"I have ordered you—"

"You will not order me, sir! I have been through this before, and being ordered below will not save me, that I know well! Give me a sword, if you would be helpful, for I might defend myself where others might fail."

His eyes went very narrow and sharp, and for several seconds she did not see the anger blazing within them. "Mr. Blair, I shall return promptly!" he announced. He handed his glass to a seaman and took a step toward Skye. Too late she cried out in alarm and sought to escape him. Hands of iron set upon her, plucking her up.

"Sir! How dare you!" she protested in wild fury. She thundered her fists against his back to no avail. He came quickly to the steps leading below and ducked to bring her under. He walked the corridor with long even strides, ignoring her shouts and her fists. At her door he cast her down. It was daylight; there was nothing to fear. It was a test of wills that went on between them now, and they both seemed to realize it. Pretenses were stripped away as they stared at one another. How she hated those silver eyes! So like his cousin's in so many unfortunate ways. Their spark meant anger, and atrocious determination.

She didn't speak, but simply cried out in rage, casting herself upon him as if she could dislodge him from the doorway. He caught her wrists and pinned them to the small of her back. He was too like the Hawk! she thought in a growing panic, for his body was tall and heated against hers, too close, too masculine. She twisted savagely within his grasp, having no desire to meet his eyes. "Let me go!" she commanded him.

"Never, dear wife," he returned. She lifted her eyes to his. They were fire and smoke, a shield of secrets, and suddenly very dark as tension overcame him. His lip curled just slightly. He bent his head and his lips touched down upon hers, encompassing them, savoring them. The probe of his tongue parted her mouth and consumed her very breath. He touched all of her. The very movement, swift and deep and ravaging, seemed an ungodly insinuation of more. . . .

She writhed to free herself. She screamed deep within. She twisted free from him at last, twisting and shaking and appalled that he had been able to touch her so easily.

And appalled that he had touched her so deeply. She was trembling, she was hot and cold.

And all the things that she had learned in the arms of the Hawk were surging forward to wrap around her, and whisper softly to her of a desire that could exist.

Lord Cameron freed her suddenly, pushing her away. "This marriage may not be such a travesty, milady. I would love to explore it further, but I am afraid that pirates knock upon our doors. Will you excuse me?"

She cried out in fury, wiping her mouth with the back of her hand, wishing she could wipe the sight and sound and touch of him from her memory forever. Footsteps pounded overhead of them. The crew was preparing to go to battle.

"I must leave you—"

"Damn you! Leave me a sword!"

"So that you might use it against me later?" he mocked.

"Are you afraid that I might use it too well?"

He laughed, reached to his scabbard, and tossed her his sword. She meant to threaten him then and there and demand her freedom, but he was too quick for her, dodging behind the door and bowing deeply. "I should love to oblige you, my love, but I'm quite afraid that we are under attack. You will excuse me!"

The door slammed sharply, a lock twisted. Skye charged it, but too late. With an oath she slammed hard against it. He was gone, she knew, but she turned around to scream to the door anyway. "Men! You think to lock me in for protection, but if you fail, then the rogues will come so easily for me!"

There was no reply. She fell upon her bunk, holding his sword. It was rapier sharp. She bit her lip, and then she found herself hurtling across the cabin on the floor. The ship had come about at a startling, reckless speed.

Crushed amid her petticoats at the door, she stumbled to her feet just in time to fall again as the roar of the ship's cannons exploded all around her.

She came up and hurried to the window. She pulled back the draperies and gasped, for they were fast coming broadside against the buccaneer. The ships came together with a mighty crunch. There was an awful screeching sound as grappling hooks were tossed, and then the cries of a dozen men went up as they leaped from the rigging to the deck. The clash of steel could be heard above all else.

Skye scrambled for the sword and held it tight. She coughed, and her eyes started to water, and she realized that smoke was entering her cabin through the doorway.

She screamed, and hurled herself toward the door. It was not yet hot. She could still escape.

The door flew open. Young Davey stood there, his freckled face pale. "There's fire below, milady. They're fighting it, but I'll take you closer topside—"

Skye brushed past him. "Closer topside! I'd rather die by the sword than burn to death any day!" she assured him, starting along the narrow hallway.

"Milady, wait!" Davey wailed, scurrying to get before her. "All is under control, the rogues are just about bested! The ship is captured, she is!"

Skye ignored him and hurried up the steps, rushing up atop the deck. The air was not much better here, for it was thick with black powder from the cannons. She blinked, trying to get her bearings in the smoky shadows. She could hear no clash of steel; the day had gone silent, quickly, completely.

"Welcome, milady!"

Hands were upon her so suddenly and completely that she screamed, her wrist nearly crushed as a giant hairy paw fell upon it, shaking Lord Cameron's sword from her hand. She was jerked back against a burly, unwashed body and held tightly. A touch of sharp steel came against her throat and she gasped, then barely dared to breath. A long knife lay against her neck, and the slighted movement might well sever her very life.

"Lord Cameron, sir!" The man's laughter rang out. "Lookee what I've got here, sir! Perhaps this changes things just a bit, mee-lord! Now listen up, and listen real good! You want the girl back? Well, if you want her, you pay heed to my words. My men and I will nonchalantly return to our ship. I take her with me. When we're free of you, I'll send her back in a longboat with one of your own mates. What do ye think about that?"

There was no answer. Skye stood dead still as the powder began to clear.

Lord Cameron was perhaps twenty feet away. The deck was, indeed, filled with men in various positions. Bodies lay upon the deck, but mostly they seemed to be the pirates who had gotten the worst of it. Lord Cameron's men knew how to fight. The rogues had not surprised them; they had surprised the rogues.

She didn't allow her gaze to linger about the ship; it fell upon Cameron. He was coatless now; he had fought in fawn breeches and a white shirt. There was a small nick upon his cheek where a sword had touched him briefly, but other than that, he did not even seem to be breathing heavily. His one foot rested upon a coil of rope, a cutlass dangled from his right hand, and a pistol was gripped idly in his left. He smiled as he faced the pirate.

"Mr. Stikes," he said in answer to the pirate. "You are a rank amateur, sir!"

"Your pardon!" the pirate roared. He jerked upon Skye. "Amateur, indeed!" He started to laugh. "Drop your weapons, man, or she's mine, dead or alive, your choice!"

Roc Cameron shrugged casually. "She's a great deal of trouble."

"I'm what!" Skye cried out, gasping in amazement.

"What?" the pirates exploded in unison.

"You heard me!" Lord Cameron called out, ignoring Skye and addressing the pirate. "She's a great deal of trouble."

"Rumor has it that she's your wife!"

"Aye, my wife, and my headache!" Roc complained, adjusting his weight. "Go ahead! Take her. She's yours."

"Dear God!" Skye cried out in amazement. The scurvy coward! He meant to let her be taken by the likes of this man.

"Take her! If she was worth a halfpenny, she'd not have come topside in the midst of this! Take her!"

"Take her!" the pirate cried.

Cameron sighed. "All right. If you must, let her go."

"You're mad! You are absolutely mad!" the pirate said. "Back off! Just back off, I'm taking her with me!"

Skye felt that the grip upon her had been released just the slightest bit. He started to drag her forward. She came closer and closer to Petroc Cameron with his clean-shaven, hard aristocrat's features and smoldering silver eyes. Stikes drew by him.

Skye spat at Stikes. He flinched, startled. His eyes narrowed further as he wiped his face. They were straight before Cameron then, two feet away. The pirate Stikes began to speak. "Now listen to me, your lordship, one move—"

Roc Cameron moved. Skye stared aghast with horror as he drew his pistol upward with a startling speed, aimed, and fired.

The explosion of the bullet rent the air, and Skye was temporarily deaf. She screamed with horror, and she could not hear her own scream, but she felt the blood that sprayed from the pirate and onto her person, and then she was dragged down by the weight of the falling pirate. He fell, stone dead, atop her. She glanced at his face, and saw that it mostly gone, and she started to scream again, hysteria rising within her. She felt the body torn away from her, and she kept screaming.

Suddenly and rudely she was wrenched to her feet. She faced Cameron. His shook her fiercely and she gasped, ceasing to scream at last.

"Why, he's killed him! 'E's bloody killed Stikes!" someone shouted. Cameron continued to stare at her, and she stared back. Someone moved behind them and he swung around just in time to raise his cutlass and slay the cutthroat who had leaped toward him at Stikes's death.

There was movement again all about them. Skye dove for the sword that Stikes had knocked from her hand. Rising swiftly, she looked about herself, but she was safe. Cameron had her behind his back, and he was warily watching the men before him. His own crew had things in hand once again. There was silence. Slowly Cameron lowered his sword. "Mr. Blair! Take ten men. Put the rogues into the hold on the pirate ship. You'll take them straight to Williamsburg."

"Yes, sir!"

The danger, it seemed, was over.

Or else it was just beginning.

Skye stood braced against the mainmast as Cameron turned her way again, looking her up and down with a sweeping distaste. "You were told to stay below."

"There was a fire—"

"Davey was sent to bring you forward, not topside."

"I did not care to burn—"

"And how will you care, madame, when the lad receives a dozen lashes for failure to obey orders?"

"You wouldn't!" she gasped. But he would, she thought. A cold fury burned in his eyes. She stiffened, feeling the blood of the pirate upon her and longing for nothing more than to strip away her stained clothing and scrub the terror from her flesh. She raised her chin, frightened now for Davey, who was so ready to defend her always, no matter what punishment it brought upon him. She spoke as coldly as she could and with all the scathing dignity she could muster, hoping to shame him. "If you must mete out lashes, Lord Cameron, don't hurt an innocent boy. It was my fault, not his. Bring your whips against me."

"As you wish."

"What?"

"I said, as you wish. You or Davey. Someone must take the blame."

He turned from her as the body of the dead pirate was dragged away. They both stared as it was hoisted overboard. Then she stared at him again in amazement and shock.

"You wouldn't! You wouldn't dare tie me to the mast and bring a lash against me!"

He smiled very slowly. "With the greatest pleasure, milady."

Amazed, she gasped.

"Sir!" His attention was distracted as a seaman came to him, saluting sharply. "The fire is out, and it did no damage except within the hold. It is safe below."

"Very good," Lord Cameron said.

"Mr. Blair is prepared to toss the grappling hooks."

"Fine. Call the order, and we'll break away. I shall be at the wheel with all haste."

He turned back to Skye, but she had already intended to push past him. He stopped her, bringing his sword tip to her throat. She stood still, her chin raised, her temper soaring, and the whole of her quivering with outrage. His sword remained within her hand. She did not lift it. She intended to keep it within her own possession.

"This matter will wait," he said softly. His sword fell and she flinched anew, for his fingers came to her cheek, touching a spot where the blood of the pirate marred her pale flesh. "I'll see that you are brought water to bathe."

"You needn't bother—"

"Yes, I need bother," he said simply. "Do you need an escort, madame? Or can you manage on your own? I am afraid that I am growing shorthanded, so I would prefer—"

She swung away from him. At that moment, she was only too eager to reach the haven of her own cabin.

She hurried beneath the deck. The smell of smoke had faded away, and gunpowder no longer turned the air to gray. She heard commands shouted, and the heavy footsteps of men as they ran about. At the foot of the steps she paused, clutching her heart. She closed her eyes and listened. A mast had been hit and sailors hacked away at the wood and the canvas sail to cast the damaged pieces overboard. Other men raced about to raise the mainsail higher and catch the wind as they shoved away from the pirate vessel.

She made her way down the hall and hurried to her own cabin. She slammed the door. Once inside, she keenly felt the blood upon her. She started to tremble anew. Cameron! He had been so cold and cool and so damned competent! He had mocked and taunted, and she had been certain that he had meant to send her merrily upon her way with Stikes. But that had never been his intent. He had saved her with a swift and deadly cunning.

She sank down upon her bunk, but then she could not bear the clothes she wore. With a cry she rose and tore her gown in her haste to strip it away. She stood in her shift only, shivering, when there came a knock upon the door.

She grasped the coverlet from her bunk and wrapped it around herself, then threw the door open. It was not Davey who stood there or any man she knew. It was a graying and brawny seaman who carried a heavy brass tub of water. "Lady Cameron, may I?" He indicated the cabin, where he would set down his heavy load.

"Don't call me that!" she charged him.

He shrugged and came through the doorway, setting down the brass pot.

There was a sponge within it and steam rose high. It was a small bath, but she could just stand within it and sponge water over herself, and she could not help but long to do so.

"There you be, Lady Cam—" He hesitated with another shrug. "There you be, milady."

"Thank you," she told him. He left her. She stripped off her shift and found the sponge and soap within the water. She scrubbed herself as if she were covered in mud, and still she could feel the blood. She did so again, and again, until the water grew so cold that she stood there shivering.

There was another knock upon her door. She hastily dried and slipped into her shift and dragged the coverlet about herself again, then drew open her door. The graying seaman was back with a fine fluted glass dangling from his sausage-sized fingers and a bottle in his hand.

"Dark Caribbean rum, milady. His lordship thought as how you might need a swallow."

"His lordship is so right," Skye muttered. She heard the closing of a cabin door just down the hall. His lordship! She trembled, thinking of the man. Her temper burned, and her pride.

"Aye, and he'll see you soon, he says."

"Will he?" she muttered, and the shivering seized her again. Why was this man here? Why was he serving her? "Where is—where is young Davey?" she demanded.

The brawny man shook his head most sorrowfully. "Preparing to repent his ways, milady, if you know what I mean."

"No!" she gasped. He couldn't have! Cameron couldn't have taken that poor boy and lashed him for her appearance on the deck!

But he could have. She remembered the cool way that he had goaded Stikes and wrested her from the pirate, and she was convinced that the man calling himself her husband could do anything at all.

She forgot her state of undress and pushed past the seaman, heading down the hallway. She didn't knock, but shoved open Cameron's door and strode inside.

He was seated behind his desk. His legs were lifted upon it and he rubbed a sore muscle in his calf, wincing as he did so. Startled, he turned her way. His eyes quickly narrowed.

"You bastard!" she hissed.

The seaman came up behind her. "Sir, she slipped by me! I'm sorry, mi-lord—"

"It's all right, Mr. Whitehead. My wife is invited to join me in my cabin whenever she wishes." He smiled pleasantly, lifting his legs down to the floor.

"I am not visiting you in your cabin," Skye announced.

He arched a brow pleasantly, and stood. "That will be all, Mr. Whitehead."

"Yes, milord."

The burly seaman left them. The door closed sharply behind him. Skye realized that she was standing there barefoot and in her damp shift, with her bedcover upon her shoulders. She suddenly regretted the fury and impulse that had brought her here. Still, Davey had risked much for her. She would not allow him to be hurt.

"Where is Davey?" she demanded.

"Davey," he murmured. He came around his desk and sat upon its edge, watching her as he calmly crossed his arms over his chest. "Davey?"

"Davey! My man! He was a sailor aboard the *Silver Messenger,* and came into your service that way. You know exactly who I am talking about! And if you have offered him any harm—"

"Ah, yes, the lad! The one who deserves the stripes upon his back."

"He deserves nothing of the sort! I told you that it was my fault, my choice to come topside—"

"And did you realize, madame, that in coming topside you risked the lives of every man aboard this ship, not to mention your own?"

"You were quick enough to cast me to the wolves, milord!"

"Never, milady. There was not a single second when I did not prepare to slay the rogue."

"Then—"

"You endangered us all. Stikes was an amateur, madame. His crew was small, his vessel was faulty. We had bested him from the time that he raised his pirate colors over the flag of England."

"Then—"

"But you, madame," he interrupted again, his voice low and soft and still full of menace, "you could well have risked it all. To a man my crew would lay down their lives on your behalf. To see so much blood spilled unnecessarily would be a sorry crime before God. Discipline is mandatory upon a ship, especially in these waters. Davey must learn not to be conned by the wiles of a woman."

"He was not conned! I forced my way by him!"

"He should have suspected the trick."

"It was no trick!"

"Nevertheless, madame, your appearance on deck in the very arms of the pirate was disconcerting—"

"Disconcerting, indeed!" Seething, she approached him. She forgot her state of undress and the coverlet fell to the floor. Skye did not heed it as she slammed her fist upon the desk at his side. "Disconcerting! Well, then, sir, you should have let the pirate take me, trouble that I am! He was an honest rake, at that, while you! You claim to be a gentleman, a champion of justice! And you take that poor young boy—"

"Or yourself in his stead, madame."

She straightened, realizing how very close she had come to him and, at the same time, realizing her drastic state of undress. She had not dried thoroughly and her shift clung to her damp skin, outlining her breasts with a startling clarity. His eyes fell upon her with both amusement and fire and she tried to push away from the desk, determined to reach the coverlet. He caught her arm, dragging her back before him.

"Is it all bluff, milady? Tell me, are you willing to suffer for the lad? Is all that you say a lie or a taunt? Should you be stripped down to the bare truth of it all."

"No, it is not a lie!" she gasped, jerking upon his wrist. "Do it and be done with it! Call out your ship, if you so desire, and drag me in your chains! I will not protest!"

"No?"

She cried out, stunned, when he suddenly whirled her around, ripping the fragile material of her shift from her back. She fell to her knees, clinging to the damp material at the front of her shift, holding it to her breasts. What manner of man was this, she wondered, to behave in this fashion?

She stumbled up, ready to fight him on any level. But even as she held tight to her clothing and her dignity, he came behind her. The soft rush of his breath touched upon her bare flesh just as his arms wound around her, bringing her close.

"Nay, lady, I would not think to mar that beautiful flesh, ever, nor would I allow another man to bring harm to it!" She froze, then trembled fiercely as she felt the searing pressure of his lips against her naked back, blazing a trail of sensation to her nape and to her shoulder. "Nay, lady, I would not seek to harm you."

She swallowed, sinking swiftly into some netherworld. If he held too tightly to her, she would not be able to fight free.

But again, his words brushed against her earlobe, provocative in their sensual cadence.

"Lady, fear not. Your lad is below deck, punished with bread and water for the night, left alone, but well and unharmed, merely to reflect upon the foolishness of ever trusting a beautiful woman. Now, madame, as to you . . ." He paused, and it seemed that a fire ignited deep within her, flooding her limbs, causing her to tremble all anew.

With fear, with anger . . .

And, she realized with a startling horror . . .

With anticipation.

11

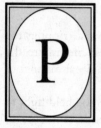

PETROC CAMERON STRODE ACROSS THE ROOM and plucked her coverlet from the floor. He returned to her, sweeping it around her shoulders while she stared at him in stunned silence. "As for you, madame, perhaps you would be so kind as to return to your own cabin. It has been a trying afternoon, and I've work to attend to."

Blankly, she stared at him. He smiled slowly. "Did you really think me so cruel? It's just that it is a very serious situation when a pirate flag flies, as you well know, and I must confess, my heart leaped to my throat when that ruffian had his filthy fingers upon you. Davey is a good lad; he will learn to be a fine sailor, And now, my love . . ."

She was silent still and he caught her arm, leading her to the door. He did not leave her in the hallway, but went with her down the few steps to her cabin. Someone had come back and cleared away the small tub, and several lamps burned brightly upon the dresser. He opened her door, bowed deeply, and left her, and she had still to say a single word.

He was a curious man, indeed.

She sat down upon her bunk, either bemused or completely in shock. In a while she curled up on it, drawing the covers high around her and shivering.

Perhaps she shouldn't have burst upon the deck so. It was just that she had not wanted to be trapped in the smoke and fire. It might have spread. A fire on shipboard was a frightening and serious matter. She walked right into the arms of the pirate, just as she walked straight into Logan's arms when she had been the Hawk's prisoner off of New Providence. . . .

She curled up and thought about the Hawk, and tried hard to cling to his memory. It was fading, and she could not allow it to do so. Fading . . . and becoming combined with the reality of his cousin. Her husband.

She burned suddenly where she lay, thinking of Cameron's intimate kiss. It had been no gentle caress, but something fierce and demanding. She thought of his casual display of disdain topside when the pirate had held her. Take her, she is trouble, he had said.

And he had bared her back, but not to the lash. Rather to the searing tenderness of his lips . . .

She tossed about. He could call himself "Lord" Cameron, but he was hard and could be callous. The tenderness was a facade, for they were already well cast into battle. She would not remain married to him—no, she would not accept that she was married to him! She would not. She owed him gratitude, perhaps, but no more.

She had just dozed when another seaman brought her dinner upon a silver tray. It was a delicious fresh fish seasoned with green peppercorns. She was weary and discouraged that night, though she knew not why. She didn't bother to dress for dinner, but cast aside her torn shift and donned a nightgown made of fine linen decorated with tiny embroidered daisies. She tied the delicate laces at the bodice and sat down in her nightdress and froth of covers to eat. The rum he had sent earlier sat upon the dressing table, and she dared to sip it. It was so potent a brew that her lips quivered before she could swallow, but she did manage to imbibe some. It burned down to the very heart, blazing a path from her throat to her stomach. She did not sip much, but she was glad of what she tasted, for it allowed her to lie down again and seek to sleep. In the midst of the night she dreamed of the beguiling paradise lagoon upon Bone Cay. Her lover rose from the water and came toward her, but with each step the man was different, depending on how the sunlight dappled on his naked shoulders. At one moment it the Silver Hawk, claiming her affections with gentle demand. Then the light would change, and it would be her lord husband, noble and imperious and bold and undaunted, and she would not know whether to run and to scream, or to wait until he came to her, and open her arms to him.

She awoke with a jerk. Her lamps were burning low, so she knew that morning was almost with them. Arising, she heard a soft oath in the hallway. Was someone coming her way?

She slipped out of bed and found Lord Cameron's sword upon the floor where she had left it the previous night. Footsteps were coming to her cabin. She leaped back into bed, carefully bringing the razor-sharp weapon along with her. Her heart thundered.

Her door was cast quietly open. For the longest time she lay there, barely daring to breathe. She opened her eyes a bare slit, allowing her lashes still to shield them. She feigned sleep, but looked to the doorway.

It was Lord Cameron. His white wig neatly queued, his shoulders broad upon his tall frame. He watched her in silence.

As she waited, he entered, closing the door. He came her way. The cover had slipped from her shoulders. She nearly screamed when he moved his hand to pull it more fully upon her. She could not help her eyes from flying open and falling upon his with grave alarm.

"There is nothing, madame. I apologize for disturbing you," he said softly, his words a breath of air in the night.

"You've no right in here!" she murmured nervously. He did not touch her, he just stood over her, and inwardly she came alive with hot, cascading shivers.

"I've every right in here, but we won't dispute that tonight. We'll come home soon enough."

"My home is Williamsburg."

"Milady, your home is a beautiful place upon the peninsula. Sweat and tears and blood went into the founding of it, and I do not take kindly to your insults."

"I've not insulted—"

"But you have. Good night."

She was not about to let him turn away. She sat up, drawing his sword from her covers with a blue flame rising in her eyes. She was quick and expert, bringing the tip of his own sword against his throat before he began to realize her intent.

"Skye—"

"No! No!" she admonished, holding the blade at his throat while she came up upon her knees and faced him. She dug slightly, forcing him to raise his head. It was her turn to smile. "Sir, I have had it with beginning and ending these conversations. Shall we go back to the beginning? You have no right here. You and my father played some trick and you think then that I am married. Well, I dispute that fact, so you do have no right here! Now, sir, you have rescued me from the grip of not one pirate, but two. However, sir, I find you little better than either of them! You fought today with the same sizzle of conquest in your eyes, and you are every bit as arrogant and disdaining of social custom as your cousin! I did not set out to make your life miserable, sir—you stumbled into my life!"

"I beg to differ. Your father—"

"My father!" She prodded the sword closer to his throat, forcing him to cease speaking. "My father! What is this about my father? Are you not a man, sir? Have you not heard the word 'no'?"

She pressed against his throat. He did not seem to care. His eyes grew narrower by the second and they seemed to blaze like the North Star. "Madame, there is nothing that I do not do by my will, and by my will alone. But I honor my father, and so I chose to honor his vows. If you have a disagreement about our present relationship, feel free to bring it up to your father, but know this! By the law you are my wife. By temperament I am afraid that your very hostility has made me bound and determined to keep what is mine. You are at my mercy, madame, and you'd best remember it!"

Skye laughed with sheer delight. She had him at the disadvantage; he was the one with the blade of honed steel against his throat, and he still thought to threaten her.

"I should slice and dice you!" she whispered.

"Yes, you should. And immediately," he said calmly. "Umm. I daresay that your best move would be to do murder this very second, because otherwise you will live to rue this moment with all of your heart."

"I don't think so. I think that you will leave my cabin this very second."

"Not without my sword."

"That will be difficult. I hold your sword."

"No, you do not."

Maybe he knew that she could not really murder him; maybe she had not been threatening enough, or maybe she had been so thrilled with her own moment of triumph that she had fallen prey to his speed and daring. He simply took the blade with both his hands and thrust it from him before snatching the hilt from her. And he did it with such speed and reckless bravado that the blade lay against her breast before she could so much as blink.

He smiled pleasantly. "I hold my sword, milady, as you see."

Skye sank down upon her haunches, keeping a very wary eye upon him. His smile remained. So did the blade. He very calmly drew it through the laces of her gown. Its honed edge slit the delicate ties soundlessly and effortlessly, and her gown spilled opened. His eyes fell upon her in the lamplight, but gave no clue to his thoughts. She could not have known if he desired her, or despised all that he saw. He moved the material away from her breast with practiced ease—the razor-edged blade did not so much as scratch her flesh. To her dismay, her body responded in an alarming fashion. Her breasts swelled, her nipples peaked and hardened. Her breath rasped too quickly and he surely saw the rise in her pulse as it beat against her veins. She saw his eyes then, and the satanic mischief in them. "Bastard!" she hissed to him, and shoved the sword away. With deep throaty laughter he allowed it to fall.

She clutched her bodice together. "This was a good gown!" she snapped to him.

"Since it is my duty to see you fed and clothed, I shall replace it, madame. May I say that it shall be well worth the cost."

"You may not!"

"Poor rogue who captured you, milady! So this is why the Hawk let you go without demanding a single farthing!" Chuckling softly, he turned. Had she been blessed with any good sense whatsoever, she would have let him go.

Good sense seemed to be the least of her virtues at the moment. Skye vaulted from the bed to slam against his back with both fists flying. "You are not amusing, and you are not my husband, and I absolutely insist that you—"

She broke off, for he had whirled around, and he held her very tightly in his arms. The sword had fallen to the ground, where he ignored it. He didn't speak for several seconds; she had gone dead still, for she sensed in his hold, in the heat of his body against hers, that now, more than ever, she had gone too far. He held her in a grip of steel, he held her without moving, barely breathing. Then at last he whispered very softly, "Unless you wish me to prove you my wife in every way this very night, this very moment, press me no further!"

She did not. She allowed her head to fall back and she watched him with a certain awe, trembling and trying not to do so. Her bodice gaped open and she felt the tremendous burning pressure of his body heat against her breasts. She could feel his hips, flush to her thighs.

She wanted to die. Shame and humiliation rushed into her, bringing a rose red flush to her cheeks. She did not want both men; she hadn't wanted either man, but the one had taught her about passion and the sweet dark secrets of desire, and now this stranger with the same silver touch seemed to be beckoning her anew. She could not allow it; she could not bear this of herself.

"Please! I am sorry, let me go!" she said.

He breathed out in a rasp, slowly releasing her. His fingers brushed her bare flesh as he brought the straying folds of her torn bodice together.

Then he turned again, and Skye was only too grateful to let him go. Alone at last, she sank back to her bunk, curved her legs taut to her stomach, and shivered anew. What in God's name was she going to do? She could not marry him; she could not be touched by him. . . .

She might well be carrying a rogue's child, she reminded herself.

And with that thought she leaped up once more, and drank down several swallows of the deadly potent rum.

––––––––

In his own cabin Petroc Cameron—captain of the *Lady Elena* and once master of his own destiny—sat and imbibed more than a few swallows of rum.

He sat at his desk and slammed down the bottle and swore with a startling velocity, then tossed back his head and drank even more deeply.

Damn Spotswood! Damn Blackbeard and Logan and Vane and every pirate who had ever sailed the Atlantic and Caribbean. "And most of all," he muttered aloud, "damn the Silver Hawk! Damn him to a hundred thousand different hells!"

He fell silent then and leaned his head back against his chair. The rum began to work its easing magic, pulling the pain and the tension, the ache and the desire, slowly from his constricted muscles, ligaments, and extremities. He closed his eyes, but he could not close his mind from the memories of her, nor could he cease to breathe in her scent, to imagine the silky softness of her flesh beneath his fingers, beneath his lips.

He could not forget her hair, spilling like sun rays over her breasts, wild and free and tempting him to touch. He could not forget her vows, or how like the Caribbean waters her eyes were, blue green, fascinating with their depths, their ever-changing color. . . .

He could not forget her form, and more than anything in the world, he wanted to drag her back into this cabin and feel her beneath him on his bunk that very night. Let the world be damned! Let any man come and blow them straight out of the water, he would sink and die happily, having her in his arms. . . .

She was his wife. He had the right.

The right . . .

But he had destroyed it all himself. In a surge of passion he had condemned himself to this hell, and so he would burn within it. He had no other choice.

He touched his clean-shaven cheeks and the nick where a blade had caught him that afternoon in the skirmish with pirates. He grimaced, duly noting that a bit closer and the blade might well have ended his days. His fingers ran down to his throat, where he could still feel the point of his sword. It was a mistake. He could see her face all over again, the fire in her eyes, the sweet triumph. She was always proud, he thought. She did not know how to surrender, no, she simply did not surrender, not even when she was bested. Even when he had wrested his throat away, even when he had slit the delicate ties to her gown, her eyes had battled him still. And surrender had lain within his own heart, for he had wanted with all of his heart to reach out and touch, to feel the fullness of her breast within his palm.

He swallowed more rum, groaning aloud. Had he any sense, he would keep away from her. He would bring her to Cameron Hall, deposit her there, see to business, and strike out again as soon as possible. Had he any sense. Sense did not always remain with him. One sight of her and he was challenged back to battle again. He could not leave well enough alone, he had to keep testing her.

He wanted the truth from her.

No, he wanted her. He wanted her with all the fire and flame within him, and he found it increasingly hard to endure the hell of his own creation. He could not seize her; he could not drag her here. He shouldn't have kissed her; he shouldn't have touched her. He should not be sitting here now, thinking of her. Of her hair brushing his naked flesh, of her eyes, liquid with passion, of her hips, moving beneath him. He should not. The hell was his, and his alone.

He would burn. . . .

With his bottle of rum, he thought wryly, and with his dreams.

During the next day it seemed that Lord Cameron quite purposely avoided her.

Davey was out and about again, and only slightly subdued as he served her. She was glad to have him and Bessie and Tara with her as she watched the ever-present shoreline.

The next day he did speak to her. He came to her where she stood by the railing, looking out. "North Carolina, madame. We near Virginia, and soon the Chesapeake Bay and the James River." He paused, and she felt his eyes falling over the length of her. "And Cameron Hall," he added.

"How nice. I shall see my father quickly, I imagine."

"I imagine that he will be at the house. I saw Spotswood before I sailed. He knew that your ship had been seized, and that I was to claim you from the Hawk. I am sure that he has had your father come to my home."

"We shall settle things quickly enough," she murmured.

"Perhaps," he said simply. He pointed to the shoreline. "Inlets and islands," he murmured. "Spotswood finds the government of North Carolina to be sorry indeed. But then he commands a fine militia himself. And he is a military man, you know."

She lifted her chin. "I know the lieutenant governor, Lord Cameron. I grew up not far from his new mansion."

"You haven't seen it yet, complete."

"No."

"It's a fine manor. His balls are famous." He smiled recklessly, widening his eyes like a rogue. "Be a good girl, and I shall take you to one."

"Behave, sir, and I shall see that you are still able to walk to reach one!"

He laughed softly. "Lady, you threaten so swiftly and so fiercely, when it is like a sparrow against a hawk!"

She looked away quickly at the word "hawk." Roc grated his own teeth, looking to the shore. "Madame," he said bluntly, "you will never best me. Cease to try, and we shall get along, I am sure. Truly, my every desire is to see to your comfort."

"My comfort—upon your bed!" she spat out, then flushed furiously, and looked about for someplace to escape him. She could not believe that she had said the words! He was laughing at her again, but his brow was arched and there was a cynical note to the sound. He came close to her.

"Tell me, my love, what do you know of such things?"

"Nothing!" she cried, and pushed away from the rail. She looked to the shore. "Father—er—Father says that Alexander is very suspicious of Governor Eden. He says that his government is not just poor, but perhaps corrupt. That he lets pirates seek safe havens in his waters—for a price."

"Many men have a price."

"Tell me—do you?" she demanded quickly.

He shook his head very slowly. "No, milady. I have my faults. I suppose you would say that arrogance is among them, no doubt."

"And a certain lack of humility?" she suggested sweetly.

"Maybe. But I cannot be bought. Not for any price. Remember that, milady. If you ever seek to—negotiate."

He turned away. She was left alone at the rail, shivering despite the balmy warmth of the day.

When she awoke the next morning, they were sailing the Chesapeake Bay. She quickly dressed and ate, and came topside, and by then they were coming down the James. There was tremendous energy and motion on board as seaman trimmed and drew in sails.

"Oh, how lovely, milady! Don't ye think so!"

She turned about. Arm in arm, Bessie and Tara were staring at the shoreline. There eyes were rapt, and Skye realized that this was a dream for them. They had left behind poverty and cramped spaces in the Old World, and they were looking to the New. She smiled, for they stood arm and arm, and in awe. Skye smiled at the two of them. "It is something indeed," she said agreeably.

She glanced to the helm. Lord Cameron himself was at the wheel, navigating the river. He did not look so much the seaman as the aristocrat. He was extremely proper in his queued wig, elegant brocade frockcoat, blue satin breeches, fawn hose, and silver buckled shoes. A dark velvet ribbon tied his queue while he wore an eagle-plumed three-cornered hat. Skye was not close to him, but yet she could sense the tension and energy about him. He stood so straight; he rode the ship so well. He looked to the land.

Then she felt him turn to her, as if by instinct. He stepped briefly from the wheel to bow to her.

Skye looked quickly back to the shoreline.

Not much later the order came down that a cannon should be fired.

Lord Cameron had come home.

Skye saw the house first. It was impossible to miss, for it sat high atop a hill.

Built of brick, it was both elegant and imposing. Tall pillars seemed to reach to the heavens, and the whole of the building was surrounded by a broad, sweeping porch. There were outbuildings all around it, making it appear more like a small village than a residence. The house seemed massive, and perhaps even more so because of the bounty of land that surrounded it. The hill commanded the area with majestic deep green grasses rolling down from it all of the way to the river and the docks. On either side Cameron Hall was surrounded by trees. Far beyond, she could see the fields.

"My great-great-grandparents claimed it from wilderness."

Startled, she swung around. The captain had left his helm to come by her side. "Jamie Cameron came as a lad first, sometimes exploring with John Smith. In 1621 he came over with his bride. There was a wooden palisade then, and his first home was built of wood. They were attacked by the Indians during the massacre at Easter in 1622. Jassy was kidnapped by the Indians."

Skye smiled, looking his way. "Sir, I am well aware that we have pushed the Indians far inland. Are you trying to frighten me?"

"Never, my love."

"I assume that your relative was rescued?"

"Of course. We Camerons love to rescue damsels in distress." He pointed upward to the house. "You can see the main hall, there. That was the first section built. King James died, and Charles the First came to the throne. Then came the English Civil War. Eion Cameron went home to fight as a Cavalier. He died there battling Cromwell's men. Some of our English holdings were lost, England was under the 'Protectorate,' and even our holdings in Virginia were in jeopardy. But then Cromwell died and good Charles the Second was invited to return to take up his crown. Eion's son went and retrieved his body and his property. Eion is buried upon our slopes. His son, another Jamie, added on the east wing." His grin deepened and he leaned toward her. "James the Second came to the throne upon his brother's death, and Jemmy, Duke of Monmouth, Charles's favorite bastard child, tried to take the throne, damning his uncle as a papist. Alas! Jemmy went to the block, and it's quite possible that his uncle did not blink an eye. Still, he was rumored to be handsome and gallant, and he had many supporters. Many of them came here, to Cameron Hall. There are secret passages within the walls, and tunnels run away to the sea."

"Ah! So the Camerons are known to harbor criminals!"

"Criminals? Never!" His eyes sparkled so that she discovered she had to smile in turn. "No criminals, madame, just those with visions different than some. Those passionate, and sometimes foolish, in their loyalties. There was little danger when he harbored Jemmy's revolutionaries. You see, James the Second did not last long upon his throne. William of Orange was a dour fellow, so they say, but extremely bright. With James's daughter Mary he started his own bloodless and 'glorious' revolution and between them and their very proper and Prostestant ways, they took the throne. And they were a tolerant pair. Alas, poor Mary died quickly, and then William, and then Queen Anne wore the crown, and now it is a German from Hanover. Meanwhile, over here, at Cameron Hall, we merely battle Indians and mosquitoes and disease, and we set sail from our coasts to battle the Spanish each time our reigning monarch declares us to be at war. We watched Jamestown burn, and burn again, and my father was delighted when they moved the capital to Williamsburg."

"And you, Lord Cameron, what do you delight in?"

It was a leading question; one she shouldn't have asked. He took her hand and kissed it slowly, meeting her eyes. "My love, I don't remember. Since I have seen your face, I delight in your presence."

There was a wicked gleam about his eyes. Skye snatched her hand away. "I believe, Lord Cameron, that since you have seen my face, you have delighted in taunting me!"

He bowed gracefully to her. "That, too, Lady Cameron. That, too."

He turned and strode back to the helm, shouting out orders as he did so. She did not miss his smile of amusement, despite his quick motion. He knows! she thought furiously. It was almost as if he knew the very truth of her heart, and taunted her mercilessly for it. She gritted her teeth and stared toward shore. The ship was coming about at the dock. She could see a throng of people there; it was like a holiday. Barefoot sailors cast ropes to the dock and the ship was soon brought to her berth. The sails were all furled and men worked to coil the rigging. Wives called to husbands, children to their fathers. It was a fascinating and colorful display. Tara and Bess were silent, in awe of the commotion. Skye was quiet, wondering at her future. She stared up the slope to the house. Her father would be there. And this fiasco would come to an end. She would go home and see her friends in Williamsburg. Mattie would be there, keeping house. Skye would be her father's hostess, planning parties and engagements with Mattie, discovering the gardens again, walking to the governor's new mansion for afternoon tea. It would be all right. She would pitch into her life with energy and fervor, and she would forget the pirate Silver Hawk, just as she would forget his noble cousin.

That was not to come so quickly, though. The plank was being stretched to the dock and Lord Cameron was coming her way once again. "My love?" He took her elbow, not allowing her to refuse his touch.

"I am not your love!"

"Come!" he commanded swiftly.

She had little choice. "Wait until I see my father!" she threatened him in a whisper.

"I wait with bated breath, madame," he assured her.

They stood upon the plank. Lord Cameron paused, smiling his charismatic smile. A cheer went up, and cries of welcome. He silenced them all. "My bride, Skye, Lady Cameron!" he announced. More cheers went up. Little urchins struggled from their mother's skirts to see her. Scarves were waved high in the air.

He led her across the plank and to the dock, and there he started making introductions so swiftly that her head began to ring. "My love, here's Mary, the rector's daughter. And Jeanne, his wife. Mr. Tibault, and Mr. Oskin—they are our tenants, my love, and farm the northern acres of the hundred. Mrs. Billings-gate—" He paused, brushing an old woman's face with a quick kiss that sent her to flushing like wildfire. "Her late husband sailed with me. She runs a wee store here at the docks for the men and their wives. She brews tea and ale and makes fine, sweet biscuits!"

Mrs. Billingsworth bobbed quickly to Skye, still blushing. Her eyes fell back to her lord, adoringly. He did have his charm, Skye admitted, and it seemed that his people were all a bit spellbound by it. He was a popular master.

"Ah, the carriage!" he said, and pulled her forward. With every step, there were more rapid introductions. She nodded here and there, meeting people whose names she would never remember. Everywhere she was greeted with warmth, and nowhere did she manage to say that she was not Lord Cameron's wife, nor would she ever be so.

He brought her to a handsome coach that would have been wonderfully appropriate for a fine English estate. The Cameron coat of arms was emblazoned upon the doorway. A footman opened the door while a coachman drove the fine team of four dapple grays. Skye entered the coach and he quickly followed her in. She sat back. It was luxurious indeed. A whip cracked in the air, and the horses started off. The ride was smooth, the upholstery was deep and cushiony and in an elegant teal velvet.

But even this ride had its price. He was watching her.

"What is it, madame, that dissatisfies you so?"

Skye moved against the door because he was leaning too close to her; his eyes were dark and probing, and she was suddenly afraid. He could be a brooding man, silent or eloquent as he chose. His temper could be great, she knew, soaring like flash fire before it became carefully leashed once more. "I don't know what you mean," she murmured. How long could this ride be? They were so near the house.

And he could be, at times, so like the Silver Hawk. He could reach inside of her. He could tease and evoke the same fevers, and make her feel as if she gasped for breath, as if she could forget the past, or remember it all too well.

"What is it, madame, that you do not like? My pride in my home is exorbitant, perhaps, but it is still one of the richest estates in all Tidewater Virginia—in all of the colony, I imagine. There is a certain prestige to be discovered here. The house has every luxury available, madame. We are a seafaring people, and acquire all manner of fine imports. Our table is always bountiful. So what is it, madame, that you do not like about being Lady Cameron?"

She smiled very sweetly. "*Lord* Cameron!" she told him, and turned quickly to look out the window. She did not know if she had ignited his temper, and she suddenly did not care to discover the truth of it if she had.

She heard his soft laughter, but it came with an edge. "We will see about that," he promised her.

"Aye, we shall!" she agreed.

The coach came to a halt. The door was swung open by the footman, whom Lord Cameron quickly thanked. Then he reached for Skye. She fell against him as he lifted her from the carriage to lower her to the ground. His eyes touched upon her. "Indeed, we shall see!" he promised her.

She was dismayed to discover that her heart raced frantically. Quickly she lowered her eyes and disengaged from him. He took her elbow, leading her quickly up the steps to the porch with its massive Greek columns. Doors to a massive hallway with a polished wood floor lay open to them and a very correct butler in handsome livery awaited them.

"Peter, how goes it, man?"

"Well enough, sir. A bit o' the gout in my leg, but that is all." The man swept a low bow to Skye. "We welcome you, milady, with all of our pleasure and very best wishes!"

Petroc Cameron stood away, and as Skye looked into the wide hallway, blinking against the sunlight, she saw that the household servants were all arrayed to meet her and offer her best wishes. She met the groom and the cook and the upstairs maids and the downstairs maid and the head groom and his staff. She smiled graciously, and seethed inside. She would not stay! And with every passing moment, she felt as if ties bound ever more tightly around her.

When she came to the end of the line, she discovered that her husband had disappeared. The butler Peter was waiting for her. He bowed again, offering a pleasant and eager smile. She thought that for all the very proper dress and appearance of the servants, things were very different here. Cameron was a lord, but he was a colonial, too. A Yankee, like herself. It was not England. Servants, tenants, and masters all depended upon one another, and so the lines of society were far less rigid here. Peter, she thought, was more Roc Cameron's friend than a mere servant. And he was eager to please her for his master's sake.

"Milady, if you'll be so good as to come along, I will show you to your room."

"Fine. Thank you. But, Peter, where is my father? Lord Cameron said that he would be here."

"Lord Kinsdale has not yet arrived, milady."

"Oh," Skye murmured, disappointed.

"If you will, please . . ." Peter indicated a graceful and sweeping stairway. She followed him along it, looking about. The manor was truly fine and gracious. The hallway loomed beneath her, while a fine gallery stood above her. She followed the curve of the banister and came at last to the landing, another hallway, leading to the main room, and to the two wings of the house, east and west.

She paused in the hallway. It was a portrait gallery, the type made popular during the reign of Elizabeth I. There was a fine array of Camerons portrayed there, beautiful women, handsome, provocative men.

Too many of them with the haunting, silver eyes! she thought, and shivered. They could be so much alike. The Hawk could just as easily have his portrait hung here as the rightful Cameron heir. Shave him and queue him neatly and dress him fashionably and—

"Milady, this way, please."

He took her through the hall to a more narrow corridor leading into the west wing. There he cast open a set of double doors to a large chamber.

Skye stepped inside.

The room was huge and handsome. Paned windows reached near to the floor on the far side, looking out upon the James River and the beautiful slope of the land. Skye walked to them first, and instinctively murmured with delight. Then her murmurs and delight faded as she slowly turned around to look at the room.

It was dominated by a huge four-poster bed with handsome blue velvet draperies. Far to the right were bookshelves, and far to the left was the fireplace with several wingback chairs brought near to the hearth. There was a huge trunk at the foot of the bed, and there were matching armoires in the two rear corners. Across from the fire and facing the windows was a large oak desk, and closer to the sunlight was a small round table covered simply in white linen. An open doorway led to a dressing room. Skye strode to the doorway and stepped through, bracing herself against the shadows there. There was a washstand and a pitcher and bowl and beyond it a huge brass hip tub and a necessary chair. To the far rear of this smaller room was a rack hung with coats and apparel.

Men's coats, men's apparel.

She stepped out from the dressing room. Her trunks were already arriving here. She didn't speak, but looked around once more. It was the master's room, beyond a doubt. It faced the river, and it caught the river breezes. It was a handsome and masculine room. It offered every amenity and elegance, but it retained something of a manly air.

"This—this cannot be my room!" she protested to Peter.

Peter, startled, looked her way. "Milady, this is Lord Cameron's room, of course. He instructed me to bring you here, Lady Cameron."

"But I'm not really—"

She broke off, not willing to argue with his servants. It would get her nowhere, she realized. Her trunks were already arriving, carried by grooms and houseboys, who all bowed to her again with shy and welcoming pleasure. If she protested, they would merely think that she had gone mad.

Her fight was with Lord Cameron. She had to stop him from this madness, and no one else.

She clenched her fists to her sides and approached Peter. "Where is your master, Peter."

"He's busy, Lady Cameron—"

"I did not ask you that. Where is he?"

"His office, milady. But I would not—"

"No, Peter, you should not—but I would, and I will interrupt him," she said sweetly. She left Peter and the servants and the wing behind, coming out upon the portrait gallery and clutching the banister to scamper down the length of the stairway. She felt all those pairs of blue and gray and silver eyes following her down to the landing in the lower hallway.

In his office . . .

She pushed open a door to the left and discovered the formal dining room.

Swords crossed over the fireplace, the table sat at least twenty, a Persian rug lay over the floorboards and beneath the table, and the Cameron coat of arms covered the far wall. Windows looked out upon the sloping lawns of the estate.

Skye slammed the door and went on. The next one entered to a music room with comfortable chairs and a beautiful rug and molded and corniced ceilings. She slammed that door and went on, discovering a parlor decorated to the Sun King's tastes. She slammed that door, too, and hurried across the hallway. She shoved open the first door and discovered Roc Cameron behind a massive, polished desk. There was a huge globe on the floor nearby, and every shelf there was lined with books. Again, it was a masculine room.

He had shed his coat and wore only his breeches and fine laced shirt. He pored over correspondence, a frown on his face that faded when he saw her standing there. He laid down the letter he was reading, and waited. He did not invite her in. He didn't even speak.

For a moment she panicked. She had rushed here, she had torn apart the house, and she wasn't even sure what she intended to say.

She should have just run, she thought. She should have very sweetly agreed to everything, and when the servants had all disappeared, she should have run for the stables and stolen a horse. She didn't know the peninsula well, but he had said that it was three hours to Williamsburg. Surely she could find her way!

"Are you coming in? Have you something to say? Or have you come merely to stare at me?"

"No, of course not."

Skye came in, closing the door behind her. She strode to his desk, then discovered herself tongue-tied. She pushed away from it and paced, then suddenly sat in the leather chair before his desk.

"You have put me in your room," she accused him.

He lifted his hands and shrugged. She sensed that a smile played beneath the bland and innocent stare that he gave her. "You are my wife," he said.

"I dispute that."

"You may dispute the sun, but when it rises, it is still daylight."

She slammed a fist against the table. "You said that my father would be here."

"I expected him, yes."

He was telling the truth, she thought. He seemed as puzzled as she that Theo had not yet arrived.

Skye sat back. "If my father were here," she told him with narrowed eyes, "you would not attempt to put me in your room!"

"Madame, if your father were here, and his father, and his father's father, I would still put you in my quarters. You are my wife."

"But—"

"I left you be upon the ship, milady, out of the delicacy of the situation. We are home now. Upon terra firma. I weary of the waiting, madame."

She stiffened, leaning back. He meant his words. She could not be his wife!

And unless she did escape him that very afternoon, there seemed little hope for it. Her stomach catapulted. He would discover her a liar in the very worst

way. What would he do to her then? What could he do, except release
her . . . ?

And yet, she didn't dare chance the discovery. Nor did she think that she
could bear his touch. She dreaded it; she felt the heat of it too keenly. She didn't
know if she despised the man, or if she was fascinated by him beyond all measure.
The tempest living inside of her was unbearable.

"I can't!" she said suddenly, certainly.

"Can't?"

She leaped up from the chair, walking about the room in a state of agitation.
Could she say what she intended about the Silver Hawk? What difference would
it make? If the Hawk were ever captured, he would hang pure and simple, and
her words could not make him die any more or less thoroughly.

For a moment, though, it seemed as if her heart itself sizzled, for she was
betraying something. It was love, she thought, for indeed, despite her later anger,
the tenderness and care of the pirate had drawn upon her every emotion. She
had, indeed, loved him with care as well as passion. Now she betrayed that very
love, but it seemed she had little choice.

"I cannot be your wife because . . ."

He sat back. "Because . . . ?" he prompted.

She turned her back to him, looking to the windows. If she was going to die,
she might as well do it dramatically, wholeheartedly.

She dropped her head in abject shame. "I cannot come to you as your wife.
Ever. I am not what I appear to be. I—"

She broke off.

"He—he raped me!" she claimed.

"He what?"

The chair fell back as Lord Cameron jumped to his feet in indignity. He came
behind her, grabbing her shoulders, spinning her around. "He—what?"

She kept her head lowered, willing a glaze of tears to her eyes. Slowly she let
her head fall back. "He is a pirate, you know! Scourge of the seas. A deadly,
horrible rogue."

"And he—raped you?" Lord Cameron repeated.

"Yes!" she cried, breaking away. He allowed her to go. She sat upon the edge
of his desk.

"My God," he whispered in what she was certain to be raw fury. "He used
horrific force against you? He dragged you—my very wife!—beneath him. Horribly and cruelly against your will?"

"Of course!"

"My God!"

She kept her head lowered. She brushed her cheek as if to take away tears of
shame.

"You did not tell me!"

"I could not—I could not speak of it at first. But now you have to know so
that you need not be saddled with me, or with this farce of a marriage. Lord
Cameron! I free you to find a proper and innocent bride."

"How ghastly!"

"Yes!"

"How very deplorable!"

"Yes!" She dared to turn, looking up at him at last. Shadows seemed to have fallen over the room, and she felt the silver probe of his eyes deeply upon her. She leaped up, lowering her head once again. "I shall see my things are moved. I will sign anything necessary to free you—"

"No, my love," he said very softly.

"What?" she gasped. He came toward her, taking her shoulders. Her head fell back. His eyes sizzled, and she wondered at his thoughts. "Your—honesty—is commendable, my love. But can you truly think so poorly of me? You are my wife, sworn to me before God. I will not cast you from my side, no matter what your generosity. So, go, my love, back to our room. When my business is done, I will join you there, and most gladly still!"

In disbelief she stared at him. His eyes danced in lamplight and shadow. He lowered his head slowly to hers, and she was too amazed to move. His mouth covered hers with passion and fire, his lips molding tight to hers, his tongue probing and ravaging past all barriers with fervent demand. Warmth filled her, as shocking as the invasion that seemed to fill the whole of her body. Laps of flame seemed to lick within her stomach and all along her spine, and spin and swirl to the very heart of her desire at the juncture of her thighs.

She wrenched away from him, gasping and desperate, despising herself, despising the very passion he could elicit and evoke within her. He watched her, his hands on his hips, his eyes knowing.

She backed away from him, trembling.

He smiled, and she felt as if she faced the very devil.

"Go to our room, love. To our bed. I will follow you swiftly, I swear it."

She wanted to deny him; she wanted to rage and tell him that she despised him completely.

But it wasn't the truth, and so she said nothing.

She no longer wished to fight; only to run.

And escape.

12

S KYE TURNED SWIFTLY AND FLED.

Outside Lord Cameron's door she knew that she had little choice left but to run. Where in God's name was her father?

She fled up the stairs and back to his room, frantically digging through her belongings until she found a skirt and jacket more serviceable than the gown she wore. She changed nervously, ever watching the door lest he should appear. He did not. Leaving all of her belonging behind, she left the room. She sped down the stairway, then backed against the wall, certain that she heard Roc Cameron talking with Peter. She ducked into the dining room, her heart thundering. Footsteps passed by on the hardwood floors. Their echo dimmed. Skye thrust open the door and checked out the hallway, then tore through the hallway and out to the porch.

The outbuildings stretched before her.

She had no difficulty locating the stables, for the building was large and impressive and the painted doors were open to the afternoon sun. She hurried along the path until she came there. A young groom, raking up hay, paused and bobbed her way.

"I need a mount, please, Reggie, is it?"

He smiled his vast pleasure and quickly nodded. "We've Lady Love, she mild and sweet—"

"Oh, no!" Skye allowed her eyes to flash with laughter. "I ride very well, Reggie, and would have a fleet mount to show me much of the property while it is still daylight."

"There's Storm then, milady. But he's Lord Cameron's stallion, and a wild one at that." His gaze was skeptical, and she felt sorry for the lad. He had long obeyed one master, but now he had a mistress, too, and he didn't seem to know if he should bow to the wishes of the one or worry about the other.

"Storm!" Skye said sweetly. "Wonderful. Reggie, fetch him for me, please, he sounds perfect for what I have in mind!"

Her smile convinced him. Reggie quickly returned with the animal in question. He was gray, and huge, prancing with his every movement and watching her with deep, dark wide-set eyes. He was one of the most handsome horses she had ever seen.

Except for the white, she thought. The great white animal she had seen upon Bone Cay. The Hawk's horse.

She bit her lip, unwilling to think further. She glanced nervously to the house, hoping that Lord Cameron's correspondence was holding his attention. She smiled a dazzling smile to young Reggie. "Thank you. Reggie, you are swift and sweet, and I promise that my husband will know how kind and helpful you have been."

Reggie, blushing furiously, brought the horse around to the mounting block and Skye quickly mounted upon him. She glanced around uneasily, getting her bearings. Northeastward along the river, and she would reach Williamsburg. Three hours, he had said.

Skye glanced anxiously toward the powder blue sky. She prayed briefly that the daylight would hold for her, then she gathered up the reins and nodded to young Reggie. "Thank you!" she cried swiftly, then she turned the huge horse about and swiftly nudged him. It was not difficult now, for a great sweeping drive beneath trails of oak led toward the main road.

She leaned against the stallion's neck, whispering to him. "Storm! Go! Race as you like, it cannot be too fast for me!"

The animal could race, she discovered. Earth thundered and tore beneath her, the trees and the world spun by. On the main road she loosened her rein and gave him his lead, ducking low against him and becoming as much one with him as she could. He was wonderfully powerful, and his muscles tautened and relaxed, tautened and relaxed. The wind whipped her face, and she loved it, for it was cool and fresh and it seemed to cry to her of freedom. She was nearly home. To her home. Away from the pirate, and away from the lord.

She let the stallion run for a good twenty minutes, then she pulled him in, afraid that she would injure such a noble beast. She still passed small wooden and thatch-roofed houses, farmhouses, and acre after acre of rich and verdant fields. Cows and horses grazed upon fields on the one side, and the forest stretched out on the other, deep and green and dark. Once, these had been the lands of the great Powhatan Confederacy. Now, there were few Indians left. War and disease had ravaged them, and the white man had pushed them ever further west.

Skye shivered anyway. Like the darkness, the thought of Indians never failed to bring new terror to her soul. She longed for courage but it was not to be hers.

She looked upward. Shadows were beginning to fall. She closed her eyes for a moment, beginning to feel dizzy. The daylight was fading fast, far more quickly than she had expected. When night came, it would come completely. She would be here, in the forest, with the darkness all around her. . . .

But she would not be caged, she assured herself. She would not be contained with the darkness in close quarters. A moon would rise, and stars would rise, and it would not be so awful.

"And I will have you!" she told Storm. His ears pricked as she spoke. "You handsome thing, you, I will not be alone. I will be free, and I will be fine. . . ."

Her voice faded away as she heard a rustling from the foliage. She looked toward the river and assured herself that there were other manors there, that Tidewater Virginia was coming to be very well populated. Indeed, her father's friend from Daniel Dridle's tavern, Lord Lumley, lived out here somewhere. She was not alone.

Shadows came deeper. She reined in, watching as the sun sank quickly to the west. There were no glorious colors of night, not that evening. Twilight came, shadowland, and then darkness.

Something rustled behind her in the brush. Panic seized upon her, pure and simple, and Skye dug her heels into the stallion's flanks. The animal took flight.

Skye's hair whipped before her, the stallion's mane flew back. Suddenly, a branch slapped against her, and she realized that they were no longer on the road, that the horse had raced into the thick and never-ending green darkness of the forest.

"No!" she shrilled, pulling back. And then she realized Reggie's hesitation in giving her the huge stallion, for she quickly discovered that the horse was more powerful than she. Desperately she tried to rein him in. She was a good rider, more than competent, she had ridden her entire life. It was just that the horse was stronger than she, and at the moment, every bit as panicked as she by the darkness.

"Storm!" she cried in dismay. The foliage tugged and tore at her clothing and scratched at her hands and face. She ducked lower, wondering when the horse would plow straight into an oak and kill them both. "Whoa, boy, whoa . . ."

There was another rustling sound. The horse reared straight up. Skye tried to hold her seat, but it was impossible. She screamed, letting go, frightened that he would fall and roll upon her. She hit the ground hard herself, and though stunned, she rolled into the brush, anxious to avoid the huge thrashing hooves of the stallion.

He fell to earth, rose and flailed the air, and fell back to the earth again.

Then he took flight, leaving her breathless and defenseless and totally alone in the darkness of the forest.

For several long moments she just lay there, paralyzed with fear. She heard the crashing sounds as the stallion rode away, far, far away from her. She began to hear the little rustlings all around her.

"Damn you, horse, oh, damn you!" she cried out softly. Her hands lay over her heart and she stared up at the sky, willing the moon to become more apparent.

There were insects all about her, she told herself. There could be snakes. She lay in the brush. She needed to move.

Carefully she stretched out her limbs. None was broken, and she closed her eyes and breathed quickly, then opened them to the night once again. She could not give way to fear. She could not!

She stumbled up and dusted the fragments of leaves and trees and dirt from her bodice and skirt.

The road! She needed to reach the main road, and walk swiftly, and not think of the darkness or the forest. She whirled around and looked up. There was a moon out. It offered a gentle glow. It was not so horribly dark. And there were stars in the heavens, too. She would be all right, she would be all right.

That way. She twirled around very slowly and repeated the words out loud. "That way. The road to Williamsburg is that way." She started to walk, tripping over fallen branches, feeling the slight sob in her each and every breath come just a little bit louder. The road was not that way at all. She was going deeper and deeper into the forest. An owl screeched over her shoulder suddenly and she screamed aloud, falling to her knees, breaking into sobs. She simply could not bear the awful darkness, not alone.

She fought for control and listened to the night. What, besides the horrible owl, lurked in the forest? The Indians were all gone—oh, God, please, it was true, they were gone, they were all gone!—but perhaps there were bears. Brown bears with long claws and a deadly hatred for men and women. . . .

What had ever caused the Camerons to come to such a godforsaken place! She hated it. She would never leave the city of Williamsburg again once she found it, she would never, never leave it again. But she had to find it first; she had to find it.

She stumbled to her feet. Her hand came to her throat as she heard movement behind her. She went dead still, the blood draining from her face, and listened. A bear. It had to be a bear, moving slowly but certainly, and with stealth. She opened her mouth to scream, but no sound would come from her. She turned blindly and started to run again.

Something was after her. Something in the darkness. It was stalking her, quietly, slowly, seeking her out. . . .

Then there was nothing.

Silence . . .

There was silence, but no, the forest wasn't silent at all, it was just that the rustling was drowned out by the rush of fear in her ears, by the awful pounding of her heart. The forest was not silent at all; it was alive with sound. She was being pursued. She was no longer quietly stalked, she was being pursued.

She lost her bearing and spun in a circle. She started to run again and realized then that the sounds were growing louder. She was racing toward the beast that was pursuing her in the night.

Suddenly she screamed, throwing up her arms to cover her face as she dashed from the trees and straight into the path of a running horse.

The horse reared as its rider jerked back with ferocity. The animal went up high on its hind legs and then crashed over backward into the brush. Someone swore furiously as the animal stumbled up. Skye screamed again as the horse went thrashing by her into the woods. She turned to run again herself.

It was not over; it had not ended. Blindly she turned to run, aware that the forest was still alive, that she was still being pursued. Recklessly, desperately she ran. The branches touched upon her hair like spidery fingers, pulling it. Tree roots seemed to come alive beneath her feet, reaching out to trip her.

And clouds fell over the moon. As if the very heavens laughed at her, dark clouds covered the moon and cast her into deeper, greener darkness.

Then a shrill cry to split the very earth burst from her as hands seized upon her. She was falling, falling hard upon the earth in the darkness, fighting wildly and desperately against the thing that stalked her in the night.

"Skye!"

She couldn't register her own name, nor did the man above her mean anything to her at all. She beat out and kicked at him vigorously, unaware that he swore softly, irritated and alarmed. She knew only that she was losing the battle. He straddled her hips, pinning her to the earth, and then he captured her flailing hands, and they were pinned down to the earth, too.

She screamed in terror and frustration, thrashing even as she was held.

"Skye!"

The clouds drifted away from the moon just as he said her name again. Spiderwebs seemed to fall away from her vision, and reason came slowly back to her.

Roc Cameron, taut and solid, straddled her. She stared at him, and slowly, slowly exhaled. It was no beast, just the man who claimed to be her husband. She might have been better off with a tusked boar, she thought briefly, but that thought quickly faded. She might fear his temper upon occasion, but it was so different than her absolute terror of the darkness.

"Skye!" he repeated, and she went very still, swallowing tightly, staring at him.

"What in God's name were you doing?" he demanded.

"Me!" she cried. "You stalked me, you scared me to death, you—"

"You, madame, nearly killed yourself running into my mare. After not only having deserted me, but having stolen my finest mount in the process."

"I didn't mean to steal him. I would have returned him."

"And yourself?"

"I am not yours."

"You are."

"That's debatable."

"I say that it is not," he told her softly.

She opened her mouth to argue with him anew, but at that very second another treacherous cloud chose to close over the moon. Darkness fell upon them and all that she could see was the startling silver flame of his eyes. She started to shiver.

He lifted away from her and she was stunned to find herself clinging to him. He freed himself from her grasp. "Hold, my love. I will build a fire."

He was true to his word, and prepared with a striker and flint. She sat shivering by a tree while he gathered up tinder and logs and arranged them to his satisfaction. He struck hard with his flint upon the striker and drew sparks, and in seconds his tinder had caught, and soft flames began to rise, higher and higher. His face was caught in those flames, and then the glow fell over them both and lit up the darkness of the forest.

He had changed to come for her, she noted. He looked like a woodsman. Gone was the elegance of his customary attire, and even the more casual garb he sometimes wore upon his ship. Tonight he was clad in simple buckskin and cotton with a homespun cotton shirt beneath his jacket. His hair was still queued, but he had eschewed his wig. Despite his clean-shaven cheeks, she had never seen him look more like the Silver Hawk than he did that night, alone with her in the forest.

She started to shiver all over again, but then it had little or nothing to do with fear. She hugged her knees to her chin and watched him, her eyes wide with the night.

He came over to her and drew her gently close. She protested his touch, then gave in to it, leaning against him.

"Why did you come after me?" she asked him. "I would have been all right—"

"All right? Like hell, madame! I found you because Storm came tearing out of the woods. You're not even heading in the right general direction!"

"That's because I got lost. I would have found—"

"You were in sheer terror before you ever came thrashing into my horse. And now we're both stuck out here because that stupid mare will run like the blazes home and Storm will break his tether to follow her back. Leave it to a fool stallion to go racing after a female."

"Just as you run after me?"

He gazed at her sharply. She was too weary, and still trembling too fiercely, to seek a fight. He smiled slowly. "Just as I race after you, milady." He paused, finding a tousled tendril of her hair to smooth back. "Why did you run?"

"I had to," she murmured simply.

He left her standing, finding another log to set upon the fire. For the longest time he was still, tall before her. She had tried to escape him, but now he was her barrier against the night, and she was glad of him there. She spoke softly. "I—I needed to find my father."

He cocked his head for a moment, listening to something. Then he came back beside her. "I am worried about your father myself. I would have taken you first thing tomorrow morning to Williamsburg by carriage."

"Tomorrow morning," she murmured uneasily.

He reached out, touching her cheek. "You were in such horror of me that you were willing to brave the darkness rather than my touch?"

A flush came to her features. She drew her face from his finger, lowered her eyes. "No . . . I . . . no."

"Then?"

"I—I—"

"You're lying."

"I'm not. I don't know what to say to make you understand. I—I don't hate you."

"Well, we've nothing here," he murmured, drawing to his feet once again. "I brought food in my saddlebags, but that is gone now. We can snare something if you like. And there is water nearby. I can hear the brook."

"You can?" She tilted her head, listening. She could hear nothing.

He nodded. "Trust me, madame. I was not bred to the city. I can hear the water plainly."

"How close?"

"Very close."

He reached down to her. "Come on. I'll show you."

She rose as he helped her. Despite herself, she looked longingly to the fire.
"Don't worry," he told her. "We will not let the flames get too far behind us.
You will see the light."

She cocked her head with disbelief, a rueful smile tugging at her lips.
"Couldn't we . . . walk toward Williamsburg?" she asked him.

He shook his head. "It would take us hours and hours afoot, and with these
clouds, it is a dark night indeed."

"You intend that we should stay here—in the forest?"

"We will be safe. The fire will burn throughout the night."

They had left the fire behind then, but he was right, she could still see its glow.
He wouldn't leave it too far, she thought; he would not risk the forest in flames.
He knew his way here, just as he did upon the sea.

"Hold up," he told her softly, stopping before her. He had her hand. She
came around beside him and saw that the flames and the moonglow just touched
upon the water. It made a slight bubbling sound as it ran toward the river.

"Oh!" she murmured, thinking that it looked delicious. She knelt down by
the water's edge and cupped handfuls of the clean clear liquid to drink. He came
to his knees beside her, throwing it over his face, drinking as deeply as she.
When Skye was done, she fell away from it, lying upon the mossy slope. It was all
right. The moon was freed from the clouds. Stars shone. She could feel the
coolness of the brook, and the warmth of the fire.

And he was with her. She was not alone.

Not alone at all. He lay at her side upon an elbow and idly chewed upon a
blade of grass. He watched her intently, she knew. He dropped the blade of grass
and touched her cheek. She did not draw away.

"Why the darkness?" he asked her softly.

She flushed. "No one knew of it at all," she murmured. "Except for Father
and Mattie, and Gretel, my housemaid at school."

"Why?" he persisted.

She shook her head, lowering her lashes and flushing. "It's so silly really. Not
silly, but frustrating that I cannot get over it. It isn't a reasonable fear. It closes in
upon me and I begin to panic, and then I have no control at all."

"Why are you so afraid?"

She hesitated a moment longer and then sighed. After all that she had brought
upon him, she probably owed him something so simple as an explanation.
"Father owns a lot of land," she said. "He had property up in the northern
country."

"Iroquois country?" he asked her.

She nodded. "I was very young then. No more than five. My mother was
supposed to have been very beautiful. She was no great lady, but a colonial tavern
wench, and my father defied his own parents and tradition to marry her, she
swore that she would love him all her life, and follow him to the ends of the
earth." She hesitated a moment. "She was warmth and beauty and energy. I will
never forget her."

"You loved her very much."

"Yes. Yes . . . well, she followed Father when he came to see this northern land in Iroquois country. Father was out with his surveyor; Mother and I were in a little cabin alone. We had only one servant with us, and Mother was singing and humming, as happy as a sparrow not to have to remember her manners and that she was a lady. Then suddenly she quit humming, and she shoved me into a little trapdoor where they stored wine and ale in the summer to chill it. It was very small, and it was black, and it was made of earth, and the smell of dirt was stifling."

She hesitated, gasping for breath, finding it difficult to breathe all over again. She hated the weakness, hated to betray it to anyone, but he knew about it. Her father had married her to him without her consent. He had surely warned him about the darkness, and had Theo not told him, she knew that this man would have discovered it on his own.

"What happened?" he persisted.

She shook her head. "She warned me not to make a sound. Then I heard noises as if the whole place had caved in, and then I heard her screaming. I peeked out. I saw the Indians coming for her. Perhaps they wouldn't have hurt her; perhaps she fought too desperately. I fell back against the earth, terrified at the sight of them. They were painted; a war party. I didn't see anymore. I just kept hearing the screams. Then they found the trapdoor. One of them was looking in at me, laughing. He was bald and painted with a thatch of hair, and his hands were covered with blood when he reached for me. Father came back and shot him. He fell on top of me, and the door closed and we were locked in the darkness together with his blood streaming over the both of us. I suppose that it wasn't that long before Father dragged us out, but it seemed like forever."

"And they killed your mother?"

She shook her head. "She took her own life rather than let them capture her," she whispered. "She—she loved Father. That's why I cannot understand why—" She broke off, not wanting to say anything bitter when he was being so decent to her, and when she was pouring out her heart to him.

"You can't understand why he forced you to marry me?"

"I can't understand why he would force me to marry anyone." She stared up at him hopefully. She had never really spoken to him before, not with any sincerity. Not as a possible friend. "Roc, please tell me, this thing cannot be legal!"

He shook his head. He seemed almost sad, as if she had his sympathy. "It is legal," he said. She fell back against the earth. "Why is it so horrid. I am not a monster."

"I did not say that you were. I just—" She hesitated. "I cannot make you understand."

He was quiet for long moments. She heard the brook as it gently danced alongside them. She felt the fire, warm against the flesh on her face. She was absurdly comfortable, and not at all afraid of the night anymore. He was there, beside her.

"Tell me, did you fall in love with my rogue cousin?"

"Of course not!" she argued, jumping up. "He—he was a pirate. I—I told you—"

"Ah, yes. He was cruel and horrible and forceful. You must despise him terribly." The same cloud that came to cover the moon dropped enigmatic shadows upon his eyes. He looked up at her curiously. Words caught in her throat. "Of . . . course."

He smiled suddenly, reaching out to her. "Come back here. Lie down. It's comfortable upon the earth, and I will just hold you until morning."

"I—I—" she stuttered, but she had no choice, for he wound a foot about her ankle and jerked upon it and she came sprawling down to the earth. She sputtered in protest, but he halfway rolled atop her, laughing, and then he pulled her against him upon the soft mosses. "It's all right," he said softly. Her head rested upon his shoulder. His hands held her close to his body. His long hard frame curved around her back, like a living wall of security.

She smiled, curiously thrilled by the words. She didn't need to face him, and so she closed her eyes.

"Umm," she murmured. "You were ready to hand me right over to a pirate for being trouble."

"You are trouble," he agreed.

She did not dispute him. She closed her eyes, and slept in the wilderness, content to do so with him near.

———

As daylight came, she dreamed, and yet it was real. There were sun rays breaking through the leaves and trees, and she could hear the tinkle and melody of water.

The lagoon . . .

She lay by the water, with the Silver Hawk. She could feel the warmth of the sun and breathe the fragrance of the earth.

She could feel her lover's hands upon her, stirring and provocative as they had always been. She could feel the heat of his breath at her nape and the tender stroke of his fingers over her breasts. She could feel the length of his body, hard and as hot as molten steel.

She lay there in her web of melody and sound and sensation, a dreamer in her distant paradise. His hand shifted, slipping beneath her shirt. His fingers stroked a fantastic dance upon the bare flesh of her thigh, and formed over the soft tender curve of her derriere. She murmured, and she would have turned to him to cast her arms around him, but he held her still. His touch was no longer gentle but demanding as his hands latched firmly upon her hips. Then she gasped, startled by the searing steel rod of his sex thrusting deeply into her. "Shh!" his whisper came to her, and he held her tight. The world erupted into life and vibrance and sweet fury. He moved against her with the force of the wind and waves, with the driving, undaunted tempest of a storm at sea. It swept her by surprise, but it enwrapped her completely in its splendor. It raged within and around her, and it left her crying out softly, reaching for the sunlight, reaching ever higher for a grasp of rapture. It exploded upon her, as sweet as silken drops of sugarcane, filling her limbs, her body, her very center with warm liquid ecstasy. She trembled and felt him, groaning and shuddering, and holding her fast one last moment as his body surged into hers, seeming to touch the length and breadth of her in one sweep of magic.

Then he fell still. His hand rested upon her naked thigh, exposed beneath her skirts.

She opened her eyes and heard the delicate sound of the brook. She looked up and saw the trees, and she felt his limbs entangled with hers still, the life and pulse of him within her still. . . .

He withdrew from her, and she felt him adjust his breeches; she felt the buckskin next to her naked rump.

It was no dream.

She turned with fury to face her husband. His eyes were open, lazy silver daggers that touched upon her with satisfaction and pleasure and masculine triumph.

"Oh!" she screamed, wrenching free her skirts from beneath him, struggling and scrambling to her feet to right her clothing. He rested upon an elbow, completely and respectably clad. "How could you!" she sputtered.

The cloud fell over his eyes. "How could I, madame? Indeed, how have I waited this long?"

"But you knew—" She broke off.

"I knew what?"

"You knew that I wanted no part of you!"

"Oh?" His casual air left him as he sprang to his feet, lithe and agile as a cat. His hands upon his hips, he faced her. "I beg your pardon, wife. I did not hear you scream in protest, nor feel your hands upon me in any fight. Would you like to know what I did hear, what I did feel? Just this, milady. Soft sweet moans coming from your lips. The jut and rhythmic sway of your hips against my own. A lush sweet cry of pleasure escaping from your lips."

"You did—not!" Skye protested furiously.

He arched a brow in stunned surprise. "This was deadly force?"

"Yes!" she cried too quickly. His eyes instantly narrowed and his voice took on the gravel of demand.

"Is this something like the force that the awful and despicable pirate used against you?"

She gasped aloud and stepped forward, slapping with all the strength that she could muster. He allowed her hand to fall across his face, but then he swept her hard against him, threading his fingers into her hair with a cruel grip and setting his lips upon hers with fire and determination. She struggled and squirmed and fought him and he held her still to his pleasure, coercing in his touch as well as demanding, filling her with his fire until it burned between the two of them and she went limp in his arms, lacking the power to fight him any longer.

He broke away from her and his tongue just teased her lips, then his mouth fell against her eyelids in a gentle touch. He lifted her chin and whispered, "The next time, milady, I will make sure that there is no mistaken identity on your part beforehand. The kiss will come first. And you will face me with your eyes open, and you will whisper my name."

"There will not be a next time!" she cried.

"I say that there will be."

She shook her head, no longer fighting his hold, but suddenly and fiercely close to tears. "I cannot make you understand!"

"No, you cannot, I fear, my love."

"Don't you see!" she demanded desperately, and the tears did spill over her lashes. He frowned, as serious as she, taut and straight with tension. "What?" he demanded.

She wrenched away from him, turning aside, and spoke in a broken whisper. "I will not be able to bear it, and neither should you, if I—if I carried a child now. I would not know if it belonged to the pirate or the lord, and still, sir, I should love it! And you would despise me . . . don't you see?" she repeated.

He was silent for a long, long time. She turned at last, and was stunned by the anguish that seemed to touch his features.

The look was quickly gone. He reached out to her, and then his hand fell away. He sighed, then bowed to her.

"Milady, I will not disturb you again," he said quietly, and then he turned away from her. "Come on. Williamsburg should not be more than a few hours' walk by daylight."

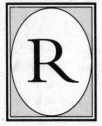

13

ROC CAMERON PAUSED LONG ENOUGH TO DRINK deeply by the spring, dousing his head in the cold waters. Skye longed to sink within the water, but she did not, sipping it in silence and cooling her heated face with several splashes of it.

He waited for her quietly. The fire had long since died away, but he kicked the scattered ashes, dusted his hat upon his breeches, and proceeded toward the road. She followed him in silence. Even when they came upon the main road, she hovered slightly behind him. Exhaustion seemed to weigh heavily upon her heart. She could not forget the night, or the dark secrets she had given away during the length of it. Nor could she forget the morning. She knew him better than she had known him before, and still she did not know him at all. Perhaps she could escape him still, and perhaps she didn't really want to escape him at all. He intrigued her, and fascinated her, and he could evoke wild fires within her. If she could just forget the man who had come before him . . .

But that didn't matter now. He had admitted that he was worried about her father, too. They did not head back toward his estate, but hurried along the road to Williamsburg.

She paused to pluck a pebble from her shoe. He waited for her, frowning. "Do I walk too fast?"

She shook her head. "No." Then she admitted softly, "Perhaps, just a little."

His dark lashes fell over his eyes for a moment, then he reached for her hand and took it within his own. "We needn't travel so swiftly," he said, and started out again. They had not moved far then when he paused once more. She looked at him curiously. "There's a carriage coming. Mine, I hope."

It was his carriage. It came around a corner and Skye saw the family crest upon the doors. She looked at Roc and he offered her a rueful smile. "I should hope that they would have come looking for us. I can almost guarantee that Storm followed that mare all way home."

Perhaps Storm had followed the mare, but now he obediently trailed behind the carriage. Peter sat by the coachman; he leaped down from the driver's seat as he saw the two of them, his face splitting into a relieved grin. His affection for his master was so apparent that Skye felt her heart warm and shimmer slightly. There was, perhaps, much about the man to draw affection. His voice could ring with steel and he could command with the finest of captains. He was a seaman of worthy measure. He knew his own mind and seemed determined to his own will.

And he was young and striking, with his silver-eyed charm and reckless ways.

He could make her laugh, she thought, and he could also make her tremble with excitement and desire.

"Milord, milady! And glad I am to see the two of you!" Peter called out, hurrying to them. "When those horses came back with the dawn, we were deeply worried."

"No harm done anywhere, Peter," Roc said. "Minor spills and mishaps, but we're most heartily glad to see you, too. Peter, we've a need to reach Williamsburg, and quickly."

"Yes, milord." He opened the door of the lovely teal carriage for them. "Williamsburg, and quickly!" he cried to the driver, who nodded gravely to Roc beneath his low-brimmed hat.

Skye paused, wondering if she hadn't seen the man before. Then she forgot him as Roc urged her into the carriage with a prodding hand upon her derriere. She moved in quickly and sat, gnawing upon her lower lip. He sat in his own corner, ignoring her then. When she glanced his way, she saw that his eyes were dark and brooding and a finger of fear touched upon her heart. He was worried, too.

"What's wrong?" she asked him. "Where could Father be?"

"At home, perhaps? Thinking that we should come to him?"

She shook her head. "You know that isn't so. Where could he be?"

"I honestly don't know."

He reached out as if he meant to take her hand and squeeze it with assurance. He stiffened his fingers instead, and his hand fell flat. "We shall see soon enough."

The carriage stopped in another few minutes and Peter came around to the door. "We're on the outskirts of the city, sir. Am I to go direct to the governor's house, or Lord Kinsdale's?"

"Lord Kinsdale's," Skye said over Roc's shoulder. She glanced his way as he watched her. "Just in case Father is there."

She parted the drapes as the carriage set to motion again. Her heart leaped. Williamsburg had changed. They were passing the Bruton parish church, and it had been built anew. They turned, and she saw the governor's mansion, complete now, rising at the end of the broad greenway with grace and elegance.

Children were playing, men were hawking their wares. Slaves were working in the gardens, and upon a pile of bricks before a white house a fifer was idly playing a tune. She sat bolt upright. There, halfway down the street, lay her own home. Two-storied, whitewashed, brick-trimmed, with a picket fence about the small yard.

The coachman knew his way. He drew up before the house. Skye didn't wait for anyone to come to her. She leaped down from the carriage and tore through the fence, ran up past the steps, past the flower beds, and burst through the doors.

"Father!"

She heard footsteps from the parlor and headed that way. A tall black woman with strong handsome features came hurrying toward her. "Mattie!" she said with pleasure.

"Skye!"

They came together with a fierce hug. "Child, child, child, it is so good to see you! Safe and sound and home at last. Your father was so very worried about you—"

"Where is Father?" Skye asked hopefully, pulling away. Mattie was looking over her shoulder to the parlor door. Roc stood there now, watching them.

"Lord Cameron," Mattie murmured, bobbing him a small curtsy.

"Mattie," he acknowledged her. He stepped on in. He was comfortable in her parlor, Skye thought with a touch of resentment. "Where is Lord Kinsdale?" he asked also.

"It's a terrible thing, Lord Cameron!" Mattie said. She pulled away from Skye and walked to the elegant rosewood liquor cart and poured out something. Skye assumed it was a brandy for her.

Mattie walked straight past her and handed the glass to Roc. He nodded his thanks and drank down the brew. She looked at Skye. "I'll get tea on right away, and something for you to eat."

"Mattie!" Skye wailed.

Mattie shook her head miserably. "He's gone run off and been captured by those louts, he has!"

"What?" Skye gasped, looking quickly to Roc.

"The *Silver Messenger* come into the river about a week ago. You know your father, Skye. He went about ranting and raving and saying that he had to come for you himself. Well, he's so anxious to go off to sea to find you or meet you or just wear off steam, that he decides to hire himself a new captain out of one of the taverns. Turns out he hires himself a pirate! It's the government down in Carolina, that's what Spotswood says it is. Those slimy sea creatures go into North Carolina, then slip on up here. When we catch 'em, we hang 'em! It's just that we don't catch them all. . . ."

Skye fell into one of the elegant little Louis XIV chairs before the fireplace. She covered her face with her hands, remembering the carnage when the *Silver Messenger* had first been taken by the pirates. A great trembling shook her, and silent tears began to fall down her cheeks. He was all that she had in the world.

No, she had a husband.

A stranger . . .

She needed her father. She loved him, and she needed him desperately. The old fool! Why had he left?

He had come for her. He had wed her to Roc Cameron, but he hadn't even trusted in Roc. He had been impulsive—like she was herself. He had cast care and reason to the wind.

"Has there been a ransom demand as yet?" Roc asked.

Skye looked up hopefully.

Mattie shook her head. "A man come back off of the *Silver Messenger,* a decent man, I assume, for he went to the governor with his tale. The ship is taken, and Lord Kinsdale is prisoner in the hold, and that is all I know for the moment."

A sob escaped Skye. Mattie sank down by her, taking her into her arms. "Don't fret, they won't hurt him, I'm certain. The governor has ships out—"

Skye leaped up. "The governor. Perhaps he knows more!"

She swept past Mattie and Roc Cameron and came out to the street again. She was travel-stained from her night in the woods and tears made dirty tracks down her cheeks, but she didn't care. She ran down the length of the palace green, near hysteria. She loved Theo; she adored him. Even when they disagreed, he would puff up his cheeks and eventually see things her way. Even if he had cast her into marriage against her will . . . He had worried about her unduly, all of these years. He had wanted a fine house for her, a bastion against the world. He hadn't even wanted her to travel to England, but his position had meant that she should be well trained in the fine arts of feminity, and so he had given in.

"Skye!"

She paused, leaning against a tree. She didn't stop because she had been summoned, she stopped to gasp for breath. Roc was coming behind her.

"Skye, wait!"

She turned around and ran again, approaching the gates to the mansion. Armed guards stood before them. They blocked her way with their brown Besses when she would have burst through the gate. "I have to see the lieutenant governor!" she cried.

"And who might you be, miss?" one asked her skeptically.

Hands fell upon her shoulders. Roc had caught up with her. "Lord and Lady Cameron, and it is most urgent."

"Oh, milord! It is you. Lieutenant Governor Spotswood is in." The guards moved away. "He was preparing to ride to your estate this very morning, milord."

"Well, then, we have saved him some trouble," Roc murmured. His hands remained fast upon her shoulders and he steered her through the gate. His words sizzled angrily against her earlobe as he bent to whisper to her. "Now, milady, I know that you are upset, and in private I have promised you certain concessions, but if you think to burst away from me like that again, I'll take a horsewhip to you." To emphasize his words, his hand fell hard upon her rear anatomy.

She gasped in surprise and fury. The guards all turned their way. Roc smiled charmingly. "Horsefly!" he said.

"Horsefly, my—"

"Come, love. We're far from properly attired to visit the lieutenant governor, but it seems now that we shall visit anyway!"

Even then the front doors opened and Spotswood's butler bowed low in greeting. "The lieutenant governor will see you upstairs, Lord Cameron." If the butler thought anything of their strange attire, he did not betray it. As Roc pushed her through the entryway she suddenly gasped, looking at the layout of the mansion, at the arms upon the walls, at the size of the hall and the stairway.

"What?" Roc demanded tensely.

"Bone Cay," she murmured.

"What?" he repeated suspiciously.

"Bone Cay. The—the Silver Hawk's house there. It greatly resembles this one."

He fell silent. Skye did not glance his way. Maids were polishing the floor. The butler hesitated, awaiting them.

"Come along," Roc murmured, urging her forward.

Upstairs they came straightaway to the grand reception room with the fine leather wall covering that was of such pride to Spotswood. The lieutenant governor was at tea, finely dressed and wigged and ready for his day. He stood, expecting them, a fine porcelain cup in his hands. "Ah, Skye, my dear!"

He set his cup upon a table and hurried toward her, taking both her hands tight in his and studying her anxious eyes. "I am so sorry, dear, to greet you after these years with such sorry news!"

"Is there nothing else that you know, sir?" she asked.

Lieutenant Governor Spotswood looked over her head to Roc. Irritated, Skye squeezed his hands. "Sir, please . . . !"

He squeezed her hands in turn, and his gaze returned to hers. "I believe that he is alive and well, my dear. I told him that he should wait patiently and all would prove to be well. But he could not be patient, he determined to set to sea, and set to sea he did, with a rogue for his captain."

"Do you know the pirate's name, sir?" Roc asked.

Spotswood nodded slowly. "A seaman managed to escape the ship and swim to shore. He came instantly to my house, bringing the news."

"And?" Roc persisted.

"The man's name is Logan. Captain Logan. We hear tell that he has sailed with Hornigold and Vane. Do you know anything of him?"

"Logan!" Skye cried. Logan, she repeated inwardly, feeling the blood rush from her face. Logan, cruel, reckless, careless—and hating her greatly, she was certain. What would he do to her father?

She shivered, remembering the hook upon the man's arm where his hand should have been. She remembered his narrow face, and his total lack of mercy. She remembered his fury when the fight had broken out, and how he had demanded her as his prize.

"You know this pirate?" Spotswood said to her intensely. She looked into his eyes again and nodded. She trusted him; he would do what he could. Some found him controversial; Skye had always cared for him greatly. He had been born in Tangier, on the east coast of Africa, when his father had been stationed there for the Crown. He was an adventurer himself, she thought, a man quick to rise to a challenge, determined, and vigorous.

"I know—Logan," she murmured. She was striving for control but a huge sob shook her anyway. "I am afraid that he will kill Father."

"Tea!" the lieutenant governor said. "You must have some tea, and something to eat. Then a long wash with hot water, and a good night's sleep. Sleep will make the world look brighter."

"I must do something!" she cried.

"Perhaps—" Spotswood began, but Roc cut him off with a startling fury. "Sir! Would you cast the girl into danger all over again when she has just been brought from it? I will take the *Lady Elena* and go after this Logan."

His hand was upon Skye's shoulder again. He pressed down, causing her to sit. "My love, you will do nothing! You may remain here in Williamsburg, or you may return to Cameron Hall, but you will not set sail again." He bowed low to them both. "Sir! I am going to order my servants home, to see that the *Lady Elena* is readied for sail."

"I shall see to breakfast, Petroc," the lieutenant governor called after him. He smiled to Skye. "It will work out, Skye, I am quite certain."

Her troubled eyes fell upon his. "Sir! You do not know this Logan. I have seen the man."

"Have you?"

"On the island of New Providence."

"Hmmph! That den of iniquity will soon be no more. There will be proper government there, and soon, I swear it!" He handed her a cup of tea and winked. "There's a touch of honey and whiskey in the brew, Skye. Steadies the hands, on an occasion such as this. So you know Logan."

"Yes!"

"As fierce a man as the Silver Hawk?"

Skye lowered her eyes, shaking her head. "A far, far different man than the Silver Hawk! Logan is cruel and horrid and the Hawk—"

"Yes, my dear, tell me. I am boundlessly interested in these rogues!"

"Logan is cruel," she repeated simply. "The Hawk is not."

"They say that Logan is sailing the islands and shoals of the inland waters just south of our own colony, in North Carolina. It might take one rogue to find another." He came close to her suddenly, coming down upon one knee and looking past her shoulder to the hallway. He was anxious, Skye realized, that her husband not return.

"They say that your Silver Hawk is in Virginia."

She gasped, winding her fingers into her shirt. "So—why—why haven't you seized him, arrested him. Surely, you plan on hanging the man!"

"Too slippery, my dear. I cannot come near him, not as yet. I haven't the force, or the power. He could well disappear into the night, and that would be that. But I have heard rumors that there is a tavern near Jamestown way, but on the peninsula, by the waterfront. All manner of rogues congregate there, milady! I have heard that the Silver Hawk is among them, just arrived last night."

"Why are you telling me this?" Skye whispered. Suddenly, like Spotswood, she was looking over her shoulder, lest her husband should return. Her heart began to beat quickly. A startling new hope began to build within her.

Lord Cameron was a worthy seaman.

The Silver Hawk was . . . indomitable.

"You were his captive for many days?" Spotswood said.

She nodded, feeling that the blood was drained from her face.

"And he was gentle with you?"

"Er—yes," she murmured.

"Then perhaps you could pay the one rogue to go after the other! Let him help us first, then he can hang in his own time!"

"Sir—"

"Shush! Your husband is returning."

He is not my husband! she longed to shout, but he had once told her that she could not change truth by denying it.

And she was also shivering and trembling within, besieged by a tremendous guilt. He had been honorable in all things. Perhaps not. There had been last night. Last night he had not been so honorable; he had been a man, and the man who claimed to be her husband. He had touched her and awakened her, and maybe it hadn't been his fault that she had dreamed of another, and that their images had combined.

She could not go to the Silver Hawk. She was Lord Cameron's wife. She could not seek out a rogue. . . .

But her heart was beating frantically. When Roc Cameron left her, she knew that she would ride herself, and try to find the pirate king. Her father's life was at stake.

Roc Cameron's long strides beat against the hardwood floor. Spotswood called to a servant and asked that a meal be served to them there. Roc came behind Skye. "I have sent Peter homeward. I will find your father, Skye. I swear it. I will bring him home safely, no matter what the trial and cost. Believe in me."

Skye thought that Spotswood watched them with a curious light to his eyes. She flushed, for Roc's declaration had been passionate, and his touch upon her was tender. She didn't know quite what Spotswood knew about their relationship, but she found herself looking uneasily to her lap. She meant to betray her husband.

"When will you leave, Petroc?" Spotswood asked him.

"I'll see Skye settled in her home tonight, and ride out in the morning."

"The morning!" Skye cried.

Roc's silver eyes fell to hers. "Yes. What is the matter with that?"

"Just that—just that you should leave earlier! You should leave today. Perhaps Logan takes Father further and further away. Time is of the essence—"

"Skye, they can only load and arm and supply the ship so quickly. I will see you safe this evening, leave by the dawn, and sail with the tide. It will be all right, I swear it."

Food was brought to them. Spotswood began to question her sharply about the time she had spent in New Providence. There was little she could tell him. Her time there had been so brief. Yet both men listened to her with rapt attention, and when she caught her husband's eyes upon her, they were bright with a startling fire.

What could she do? she wondered in dismay. If he would not leave, then she could not escape him to find the Silver Hawk!

When the day waned to twilight, Roc rose and told Spotswood that they would take their leave. Skye nervously arose with him. He took her hand and bowed to Spotswood. Skye murmured something, aware that the lieutenant governor was watching her. He thought that she should go for the Silver Hawk. That's why he had told her what he had.

He would gladly hang the Hawk, but later!

She nibbled nervously upon her lower lip as Roc led her from the governor's mansion and outside to the palace green. His hand was upon hers and she trembled, torn between guilt and a growing affection, and a slowly rising desperation that he should leave her.

"What is the matter with you?" he asked her suspiciously.

She shook her head, lowering it. "I am worried about my father."

He paused, catching her shoulders, drawing her close. "You mustn't worry!" he told her kindly. "You mustn't. I swear that I shall not fail you."

She smiled, startled to feel that tears were hovering on her eyes. He held her against him. She heard the sound of the children playing, of the leaves rustling over their heads. It seemed so peaceful, and he held her so gently. As a husband might. As a lover.

She inhaled and exhaled quickly, pulling away. "I'd like to get home. I'd like to have a bath."

"Of course," he told her.

By nightfall she was up in her own room and in her own deep tub with a froth of French rosewater all about her. She leaned back her head and breathed deeply and felt steam rise above her.

He was across the hallway from her. In one of the guest bedrooms. She had not told him that he must go there; he had chosen the room. He had said that he would not disturb her, and he was a man of his word.

A man of his word, and more.

The steam about her seemed to swirl within her. She remembered his whisper, and his touch, and it seemed that the very heat of the steam swept deep inside of her. She flushed, wanting to forget. It was so wrong to feel this way. It had to be, after what she had come to feel for the Hawk.

She was going after the man to help her—and never to come close to him again. She could not do so. She was married to Lord Cameron. Truth, whether she denied it or not.

And truth . . . because in the fireglow and green darkness of the forest, he had taken her into his arms, and their marriage had been consummated there. She would never escape it now.

Not her marriage . . .

She had to escape her husband. That night, she had to escape him. How? she wondered desperately.

She shivered, despite the heat of the water. She could not betray him so. He had been too decent to her.

She had to leave, and leave that very night!

She never quite knew her intention when she stood in her bath, the scented rosewater dripping from her, to reach for her bathtowel. It was a huge cotton sheet of material that smelled freshly of the sun. She wrapped it around herself and stepped into the hallway. Downstairs, she could hear Mattie humming softly. But no one would ever disturb her up the stairs. Mattie would come if she called. If not, Skye knew, she would be left undisturbed.

She clutched the towel to her breasts. For long moments she stared at the door, then she knocked upon it. She did not wait for an answer, but shoved it open and entered into his room.

He had been lying upon the bed. As she entered, he bolted up.

He had bathed, earlier, Skye knew. He had gone out to the barn, and they had brought him pails of warm water there. He was barefoot and bare-chested, and clad only in a pair of soft bleached buckskin breeches. He looked at her, startled, reaching for a linen shirt that lay across the bed. His action amused her some-what. He had been so ready to touch her in the night, to make intimate demands upon her. Then he shielded his own chest with a startling modesty.

His actions did not help her cause, she thought, and she was already rueing the rash impulse that had brought her here.

"What is it?" he asked her. The room was dim, his voice was husky. Strange, but the lack of brightness did not bother her here. She felt safety, knowing that he was near. No . . . she felt very alive, knowing that he was near. She dared not admit that it had been easy, easy to come here.

The damage was done! she cried inwardly. It had been done last night. And if this ever ended well, then she would be his wife in all truth, and she would make it up to him, God help her!

She stepped closer. "I . . ."

"What?" He came out of the bed. She remembered briefly from the fleet seconds in which she had seen them bare that his shoulders were broad and fine and his skin bronzed and sleek. She remembered his touch, and the strength and demand of it, and she wondered briefly if she hadn't discovered him to be very fine, and if she hadn't lost a corner of her heart to his raw demand and vehe-ment, sometimes tender care. Perhaps she had. In the dim light she found that she had no voice, and she could not think of the words she wanted to say.

"You're trembling," he murmured.

It was not without some astonishment that he said the words, for he was amazed that she should be there.

He had been a fool to touch her last night. He should keep a far greater distance than he did. But when she had lain so close to him, and when his hands had found her nakedness in the night and her soft moan had been his response, he had cast caution to the wind. He had never meant to take her. Her distress this morning had struck deep into his heart, and he had never felt more the knave.

But now she was here.

Fresh from her bath. Her eyes wide and luminous and nearly teal in their glazed color. Her features so fine and delicate and so hauntingly feminine that the sight of her trembling lips brought a rush of heat stabbing into his groin. Desire rose, and pulsed hard against his breeches, and still she stood there, silent.

He strode around the bed to the side table where he had brought a bottle of

Mattie's best dark rum. He poured out a portion and came before her, bringing the glass to her lips. She swallowed, and winced slightly as the fire of the rum rode through her.

"I . . ."

"Yes?"

"If it is truly your desire . . ."

He waited, but her voice had trailed away. "Yes?" he prompted softly.

She took another sip of the rum, moistening her lips. Her hair spilled all about her, touched by candlelight. It glowed with the red fury of fire, it cascaded like sunlight. He longed to thread his fingers through the length and mass of it. He longed to feel the fiery tendrils fall softly over his naked shoulders and chest. . . .

"Yes?" he repeated.

"You have been very kind."

"Have I?"

She was still faltering. "I appreciate all that you have done for me."

"You are my wife," he said softly, standing back to watch her curiously. The length of him had come alive. The pulse and need rushed to fill his limbs, and his heart, and his soul. Warnings called out to him, and he ignored them. Let her speak! Let her come to him, or run, for he could not bear to keep his hands from her a moment longer. He wanted to rip away the towel and drink the sweet scent of rose dust from her flesh.

"That's what I'm trying to say."

"What?" he demanded sharply.

"I've been trying to say that . . . if it is your desire despite all that has happened . . . if you wish to have me for your wife, then, milord, I am yours."

Her words hung softly upon the air for long moments as he tried to believe them. This sweet wild thing, this creature of temper and beauty and tempest, was coming to him.

She lifted her arms and dropped the towel that covered her. She stepped from it and stood before him in naked perfection, her flesh so gently kissed by the glow of the candlelight that touched the room. She was exquisite. Her hair did not touch his shoulders, but streamed over her own. Her breasts rose with coral peaks, full and tantalizing, beneath the caress of her swirling gold locks. Strands of red and gold cascaded all the way to her waist, and curled over the curve of her hips and buttocks.

He caught his breath. For one long moment he was unable to move.

Then he cried out hoarsely, casting the rum glass into the fireplace and sweeping her into his arms. He carried her swiftly to the bed and laid her upon it. The candles glowed on the table. He looked down at her and her eyes were passionate slits, teal and shadowed by the lush fringe of her lashes. Her lips were damp and parted as if they awaited his. As if they invited his touch . . .

But he did not bring his mouth to hers. Not then.

His lay low against her, fascinated to touch her. His hands curved over her breasts while his tongue teased the taut skin of her abdomen. Slight sounds escaped her, and he continued to touch. He rose against her to bring her breast deep into his mouth, and he withdrew to watch the nipple harden and the color deepen. He stroked the length of her, and felt the surge of her body, and still he did not touch her lips. She reached for him, but he eluded her, and buried his face against the sweetness of her body again. He moved lower and lower again, taking all of her with his sweeping caress. He parted her thighs and heard a startled sob escape, but he gave her no quarter that night; he longed to seek from her all that she had to give. He watched her for a moment, and her eyes were closed. They opened slowly, and when they met his, he lowered himself between her legs. He teased her inner thigh and stroked her flesh with the searing heat of his tongue. She gasped, writhing to escape so great an intimacy, but she was his, and he knew it. He touched her with that sweet stroke where and how he would, and her fingers curled into his hair while a breathless series of whispers and sobs and incoherent words tore from her lips. He brought her to the very brink of passion and then cast her over the edge, savoring the constriction of her beautiful form, and at long last, coming to her lips, there to swallow down the cries of pleasure that rose.

He did not hesitate a moment, but untied his breeches and drove deep within her welcoming warmth. She lay still, just trembling from all that had been before. He moved against her with the care of a master artist, seeking to elicit all emotions, all desires, and all needs. And when she rose again to the sure blaze of sensation, he at last gave over to his own desperate need. Hungry and afire, he took her with a fierce and driving force, and it seemed that the sun rose in his heart and vision, only to burst and explode all around him. There was no woman like her. None with her slender, provocative form, none with the perfect fullness of her breasts, not with her wild blaze of hair, her startling teal eyes.

No woman could love as she, caress a man so, part her lips so. Drive him to absolute heights with the thrust and sway of her hips, with her whispers, cries that touched the wind, that brought him to heaven.

She created . . . paradise.

She was his wife. She had said it. He had claimed her.

And he loved her. Deeply, and forever.

He fell beside her, pulling her close. For long, long moments they were silent. They were together, softly trembling with aftershocks of the explosion of the sun.

At long last he gently moved his hand over her bare breast, watching a golden curl fall from it. She buried her head against his throat and reached out a finger tentatively to touch his shirt.

"You're still dressed!" she whispered reproachfully.

He hesitated. "Umm," he said noncommittally. He saw his own fingers upon her flesh and he drew them away, holding her tightly. He should not even let her see his hands so, he thought. A smile teased her lips. Of all women to fear the darkness!

Darkness could hide so many sins.

He drew up the covers, but she was watching him pensively. She seemed very nervous. He leaned against her, and a shudder swept through him. He was about to leave her again. It might have been easier if she hadn't come so close to him. If she hadn't given him, freely, and willingly, this ecstasy.

He touched her lip. He stared into her beautiful eyes, and he remembered how he had fought the very idea of marriage.

This was no cross-eyed bride.

She was everything to him. She had been, from the very beginning.

"I love you," he told her.

She inhaled sharply, her eyes widening. Then they widened even further, and she whispered, "I—I think I love you, too."

"You think?"

She twisted away. He longed to pull her tight again. He knew that she was remembering a different man, a pirate, in a faraway paradise of her own.

He hated himself at that moment.

He longed to speak to her.

But he could not.

He pressed his lips against her hair and held silent for long moments. Then he whispered again, "I do love you, Skye Kinsdale Cameron. You have become my very life, and I swear, my love, I vow myself to you, now and forever."

She lay silent. He turned away with a sigh, tying up his breeches. He rose from the bed and walked over to the table, picking up the rum bottle and swallowing down a long draft.

They would have this night, he determined. He would have to leave her in the morning, and by God, he would return with her father. She would be his wife then, in every way, for every day and month and year that came to follow.

But until then, he would have this night.

Something like a sob seemed to escape her. He turned around and saw that she was rising, too. Naked and graceful and beautiful and sleek, she walked his way. Her head was lowered. She came to stand in front of him. Her hands fell upon his chest. She leaned against him, kissing him, letting the wet warmth of her tongue blaze through the linen of his shirt.

"I will honor you, I swear it!" she cried softly.

He frowned, for her tension was so great, then his frown faded, for the lap of her tongue against his flesh was so arousing. Her fingers moved against his shoulder, her body was flush against his. She had indeed given herself to him that night, in so many ways.

In so many ways . . .

He moved to sweep his arms around her, but she slipped away and idly picked up the rum bottle.

"I'll get you a glass, love," he murmured.

She shook her head, and her teal eyes were luminous with a glaze of tears. "It will not be necessary," she said.

She slipped back into his arms. She drew him down to her embrace, finding his lips with parted mouth, meeting him with a wild abandon that swept away his very thoughts. . . .

Then a shattering pain burst upon his skull.

Darkness came in upon him, and wavered back. Liquid spilled over him as he crashed down to his knees. He managed to look up, and into her eyes. He saw the broken rum bottle in her hands, and he managed to swear at her in a single gasp.

"Bitch!"

Then he fell, heavy and flat. She cried out, but stepped aside, and his weight came down full upon the floor as the blackness of oblivion came surely to claim him.

14

OC CAME BACK TO CONSCIOUSNESS VERY slowly.

Pale light flickered by his eyes.

He smelled like the scurviest of taverns. He moved his hand, and winced, feeling broken glass beneath.

Then he heard a soft chuckle and saw a handsomely buckled shoe with a well-turned masculine calf attached to it. He groaned aloud, allowing his eyes to fall closed once again.

"Come on, my boy, up, up!"

Wincing, he sat, and cast Spotswood an angry glare. "What are you doing in my room? And why is it—sir—that you seemed to have known that you would find me in this state."

"Truthfully, Petroc, I did not know how I would find you at all, but it was imperative that I see you now, so I came as quickly as I saw your wife leave."

"Leave!"

He bolted up, shaking his head, desperate to clear it. "Blast that wench! I have chased her over half the seaboard and through forest and glen, and I swear, sir, that I am about to keep the lady in chains. Dammit, where has she gone now?"

"Why, to find the Silver Hawk, of course," Spotswood said complacently.

"What?"

"I believe that I've sent the young lady off to find the Silver Hawk. In fact, I know that I have."

"Why!" Roc exploded incredulously. "Damn you, sir, but what have you done to me now?"

"Petroc, wait, listen!" Spotswood pleaded vehemently. "We've worked at this for years now, and you must know the rationale of what I've done. A tremendous favor, and that's the God's own truth, sir, and I swear it. Think—"

"Think!" Roc groaned and clutched his head and sank down to the bed. "Think, eh? Sir, it has been bad enough. I returned from my last adventure with the woman who is my wife, afraid to put my hands upon her, afraid to come too near her! Now you think that I must go out and change roles again! Her husband was going for her father! I was going, I would have sailed today with my legal and legitimate crew and a ship that docks safely upon the James—"

"Robert Arrowsmith has the Hawk's sloop ready and waiting on the river. You need only don your whiskers—"

"Don them! They were real last time." Roc rubbed his clean-shaven chin, gritting his teeth. He'd had time to grow a fine set when sailing for New

Providence and the Tortugas in the hopes of claiming the *Silver Messenger* and his bride. This time he would have to play with theatrical hair and sticking gums. He didn't care for the idea, but in one respect, the lieutenant governor was right —it might be far better for the Silver Hawk to set sail against Logan than for Lord Petroc Cameron to do so. No other pirate would come to his assistance if they knew him as Lord Cameron, but if a battle or skirmish came about some-place, he might find assistance as the Silver Hawk. Everyone knew about the "relationship" between the two men, and therefore it was easy enough to play the act before men and women who did not come too close—

Playing an act before one's wife . . . one's mistress, one's lover . . . was nearly impossible.

He had envied the Hawk. Until this very evening, he had longed to be his alter ego once again, the man who could freely shed his clothing before Skye and not fear that she'd find some scar upon him that would tell her beyond a doubt that he was, indeed, his own "cousin"—the sea slime, the scourge of the seas, the rogue.

The man to whom she had willingly and so sweetly given her love.

He stood up suddenly, his temper soaring. The wretched little adventuress. She'd seduced him to betray him—him! her lawfully wedded husband—to go off to find a rogue. Perhaps the acting would not be so heinous after all.

"You, sir, sent her after the Hawk?" he inquired darkly of Spotswood.

"It was necessary, Petroc."

"Alexander, did it occur to you that you might have warned me?"

Spotswood shrugged, a twinkle in his eye. "Petroc, I didn't think that a mere wisp of a girl could take you by such complete surprise. I was most interested in the results myself. When I remembered how you fought the marriage vows—to that poor cross-eyed lass!—I thought that surely, the man will be strong against this, his despised baggage of responsibility. Then lo and behold, the great Lord Cameron of the Camerons of Tidewater Virginia falls prey to a trick older than time."

"Hmm." Roc crossed his arms over his chest and nodded laconically to Alexander's amusement. Perhaps he did deserve the man's laughter.

Skye deserved a lot more.

And she was going to get it.

"You've put me in a horrible position, you know."

"Alas, Petroc, this has been in the works these four years now!"

"I should have told her the truth," Roc murmured.

"You can't. Not yet. Not until you return safely to these shores. Not until you can make her understand. You promised me to uphold the secret, Petroc. I need you! I need the Silver Hawk. It is my only way of knowing what goes on in the Caribbean, and down in North Carolina, beneath my own nose. You cannot tell her yet."

"I didn't intend to tell her—not yet," Roc murmured. What role was she going to play herself this time? The Silver Hawk was longing to touch her again. Touch her . . . as she touched and seduced him this night.

Lord Cameron was dying to throttle his beautiful bride, the lady willing to trick and seduce him to seek assistance from another.

"You need to hurry," Spotswood said. "I let her slip away just as I came. She'll take some time to question some of the men in the town taverns, then they'll send her down to the river's edge, and to the Blackhorse."

"The Blackhorse? Why, 'tis full of river rats!"

"Umm. And a place where the Silver Hawk has been seen before, and may appear again. I'll send down. Peter should be below with the Silver Hawk's apparel." He paused, looking back. "It really was necessary, Petroc. You do know as well as I that the Silver Hawk will command the respect of the rogues in the area. They will not come together against him, while they might pool all their resources to send Lord Cameron down to the bottom of the sea."

"Yes, it was necessary." He touched his temple and winced. "I'm not sure about the headache, though, sir. Perhaps you could have warned me, and she could have just slipped out unnoticed."

Spotswood lowered his head, a subtle smile playing on his lips. "I don't know. Maybe the way she left was necessary, too."

He turned around and left.

Roc crossed his arms over his chest, pensively awaiting Peter's arrival with the things he would need.

Maybe her departure had not been necessary, but perhaps it had been well worth the price of a headache. She had come to him, and she had given the promise of a sweet tomorrow. . . .

Right before she had clunked him on the head to leave him.

Maybe it really wasn't such a bad thing that she was going to see the Silver Hawk again after all. They had a bit of reckoning to do, all three of them: the Silver Hawk, Lord Cameron—and Skye, Lord Cameron's lady.

"He's going to catch up with you any minute, young woman. Any minute!" Mattie moaned. She looked over her shoulder, past the lamplit main street and toward the palace green. Mattie was absolutely convinced that Skye had dragged her on a fool's mission. Any minute indeed her young mistress's husband—enraged husband, now, surely—would come tearing out of that house and down the street, seeking his wayward bride. Mattie did not want to be in the path of his anger, nor did she think that Skye really wanted to meet his fury, either.

"Mattie, that's why we need to hurry!" Skye said. "Now come along."

Mattie groaned and hurried along beside her Skye. It had been her choice to come. She wasn't happy about Lord Cameron lying on the floor in a pool of rum, but she hadn't been able to endure the idea of Skye running off alone. She had practically raised the girl, and Skye's years in London hadn't lessened the affection they shared.

Skye was heading on toward the next tavern on the street. This one wasn't as reputable as the others where they had gone to seek information, but Mattie still felt as if they were safe. This was Williamsburg. It was Lieutenant Governor Spotswood's city, and there would surely be some good men about to know that

Lady Skye Kinsdale had been married to Lord Petroc Cameron—and that to touch her or cause her harm could well mean death at that man's able hands.

Mattie hurried along beside Skye against the quiet of the night. As they approached the tavern, a shadow stepped out from the trees by the side of it. Mattie gasped, pulling Skye back against her side. "Lady Cameron!" a voice called softly.

"Sh! Don't give no stranger in the shadows your name!" Mattie warned her.

"Yes!" Skye said, stepping closer.

The shadow backed away, lifting a hand.

"No closer, milady. No closer."

"Then what do you want?"

"I hear you've been prowling about tonight, asking what ships lie in the James, seeing if any man knows about a pirate. A rogue ship, out in the river."

"Yes! Do you know about her?" Skye stepped forward again in her excitement. The man blended against a tree. The streets were always lit well by lamps, but the trees afforded such deep secretive shadows that the lamps could help little against the night.

"Stay where you are!" the voice commanded.

"Let's get out of here!" Mattie urged her in a whisper. "Let's go home. Please, child! You can be the fine lady wife, kneel down by his side, and pretend it was an accident—"

"An accident!" Skye whispered in turn. "I struck him over the head with a rum bottle—by accident?" She shook her head. "Mattie, no! I must find the Silver Hawk. He can save Father."

"Hey!" called the man from the shadows. "Are we negotiating here or are we not!"

"We're talking—" Skye said quickly, coming forward.

"Stand still!"

"I'm standing still," Skye promised, stopping. Mattie hovered unhappily just behind her. The breeze stirred, sweeping unease along her spine.

"I'll tell you where to find the Silver Hawk."

"Where?" Her heart thundered quickly. Perhaps she was on a fool's errand. She was coming to know Roc Cameron well, and he would not take kindly to her betrayal. Maybe she should run back and throw herself upon her husband's mercy. Maybe it would be much, much better than leaving the one man behind to seek out a rogue and enter into a world of tempest and temptation. She clenched her jaw, realizing anew that she was coming to love her husband. To love the man that she had betrayed. She had to move forward. Her father was out there, Logan's prisoner.

She almost screamed aloud with the thought, and she cast her guilt from her shoulders with a shrug. "Where!" she cried out to the man in the shadows.

"Not so fast, milady. You wear an emerald around your neck. I will have it."

"What?" Skye murmured. Her fingers came to her throat and she realized that she still wore the emerald pendant she had found among her things at Bone Cay.

She had worn it the first night that she had been with the Silver Hawk. She had worn it when she had cast aside all else, all clothing, all inhibitions. . . .

Her fingers closed around the pendant. She carried gold to give to the Silver Hawk. She could afford to give this man the pendant.

She snatched it from her throat and started to cast it forward. "Wait!" the voice cried. "Come forward, and drop the pendant."

"No!" Mattie called out. She stepped forward, taking the pendant from Skye. "I'll drop it, and if this man is a reputable liar and thief, then he'll have his pendant and you'll have your information, child."

Skye would have protested casting Mattie into danger, but Mattie gave her no chance to do so. She hurried forward to the tree and cast the pendant down as the shadow slunk back. Mattie sniffed her opinion of the man loudly, and came back to Skye.

A hand reached down and scooped up the emerald.

"The Blackhorse Tavern. It's south on the river. Speak softly and subtly, and you'll find the Silver Hawk." The shadow turned from the tree and went racing toward the rear of the tavern. Skye followed after him and found him leaping atop a sleek bay horse. "Wait! Wait, please! I still don't where this tavern is! I—I haven't followed the waterfront that often—"

She stopped, gasping. She recognized Robert Arrowsmith, the Silver Hawk's first officer aboard his pirate ship. "Robert!"

"Milady!" He doffed his hat to her, then swore. "Come! Come with me now!"

She didn't have time to agree or disagree. He urged his mount quickly forward and reached down to her, sweeping her up before him on his mount even as the bay pranced and prepared to bolt.

"Skye!" Mattied shrieked, coming after her.

"Tell her it's all right," Robert warned her.

"Mattie! It's fine. He's a—friend."

Mattie's tense and worried features as they rode into the night gave Skye a second seizure of guilt for the evening. Mattie would understand, surely. Mattie loved Theo Kinsdale as much as Skye did. But she would worry. She would worry horribly.

And worse. She would go back to the house and arouse Lord Cameron and then Roc would come riding for her. She swallowed as the wind lashed against her face. It was going to be dark along the road.

She couldn't fear the darkness, for there were worse dangers in the offering that night. Roc Cameron might well come for her, determined to kill the Silver Hawk. And if he did, it might well be her own fault—because she had told her husband that she was no innocent bride and that the Hawk had behaved in a foul and abusive way and seized her innocence away. . . .

She couldn't think about it. Robert would take her to the Hawk, and when she reached him, she would explain that they had to run, and quickly. He was a fool for being in Virginia anyway. Governor Eden of North Carolina might suffer pirates, but Lieutenant Alexander Spotswood of Virginia did not. The Hawk had to flee Virginia, and since he did, he might as well seek out Lord Theo Kinsdale and reap the benefits of the gold that Skye would so gladly pay.

The gold only! she thought with vehemence.

Gold . . . and nothing of herself

She shivered, remembering the day not so long ago when she had lain in the pirate's arms beneath the sun. When she had felt his dark beard brush her naked flesh along with the searing rays of the sun. It was so easy to remember.

Easy to remember the first night, the very first night. He had warned her. . . .

And she had walked into his arms anyway, of her own free will.

That was before! she vowed to herself. Before she had come to know Petroc Cameron. Before she had discovered that she could love him. Before this very night, even, when she had come to him knowing that she would leave him, and determined to love him first. It was before the soaring splendor of his passion.

She trembled suddenly, and it was not the darkness of the night that brought her fear. Robert rode behind her, and though the lamps of the city were fading behind them, the moon was very high. There was light.

And she was learning not to fear the darkness, to fight the panic of it. Roc Cameron had done that for her, she thought. He had drawn the venom of the past from her soul. She had spoken about it to him, and she wasn't afraid. Roc had taken the words from her, while the Silver Hawk had taught her that there could always be a beacon against the darkness of the night.

The Silver Hawk . . .

She loved her husband.

She had fallen in love with the pirate king first, and though his memory had faded away only to combine with that of the man she had legally wed, she was both dreading and anticipating her meeting with the pirate. What would his memories be?

What would his demands be?

Could she sell her soul to come to him again, if that should be his price?

"Are you cold?" Robert whispered behind her.

She shook her head. "No. I am—I am anxious to see the Hawk. Are you certain you know where he is?"

"Yes."

She hesitated, thinking how kind Robert had always been to her. He was here in Virginia, and she had to be glad. But she dreaded the future for him. "Robert, you shouldn't be here!"

"The Hawk dares anything."

"The Hawk is not in Williamsburg."

Robert chuckled softly. "Sometimes it is necessary to come close to the flame of the fire, lady. Surely, you know that."

"You came to Williamsburg to spy," she accused him.

"Aye, milady, I did."

"If they catch you, they'll hang you."

"They'll never catch the Silver Hawk."

"But—"

"I am Robert Arrowsmith here, milady, good citizen of His Majesty's colony of Virginia. I am safe." He hesitated. "Are you all right? We are almost there, another twenty minutes."

They no longer galloped, but Robert moved the horse along at a quick trot. The moon beat strongly upon the road, but she was touched. Even Robert considered her fear of the darkness.

"I am fine," she murmured, twisting to seek out his eyes. "But my husband might come after me. Robert, I would not have him come upon you. . . ."

"Is his temper so bad then?"

"He would slay a pirate, surely."

"But you would defend me?"

"I would, for you were always kind."

"And tell me, milady, what of the Hawk himself? Would your husband seek to slay him, or await a hanging?"

She started to shiver again. She could not imagine the Silver Hawk and Lord Cameron coming together. One of them would die, and she would not be able to endure the outcome of it.

"Hurry, Robert! Race the night, for we must get the Hawk and leave Virginia. We must!"

"We!"

"Yes! My father—"

"I know about your father, milady. But there will be no 'we.' I'll talk to the Hawk with you on your behalf, and I know that he will set sail. But he will not take you. You will go home."

She would not go home. She could not go home, not now. But she didn't tell Robert that—it was something she would have to worry about later.

Robert turned his mount eastward toward the river, nudging the animal's ribs, and sweeping them into a fast lope once again. She liked Robert so much! Skye thought. She felt warm with him, and assured that he would carry her to the Hawk.

Even if he had stolen her emerald!

It was all right. It was all right to race with him through the night, leaning low against the flying mane of his bay horse, feeling the wind and the gentle wash of the glowing moon upon her. It would be all right. . . .

"There! We're coming up on the Blackhorse now!" Robert said, reining in. "Stay with me, milady, do you understand?"

Skye nodded. She was glad of his presence, for she did not like the appearance of the tavern.

It stood just off the waterway and the docks, a rickety place with broken windowpanes and faulty steps. Dim, misty light issued from the open doorway and windows, and raucous laughter could be heard.

Robert dismounted from the horse, reaching up to help her down. Skye drew the hood of her navy mantle close over her forehead and slipped her hand through his arm as he led her toward the doorway.

It was not a place for a lady.

It was a complete den of iniquity, she thought, and her heart hammered somewhat as she thought of the Hawk. How dare he come here when she might need him! It was not a place where any decent woman would want to be.

"Milady?" Robert said to her, watching her curiously.

"Shall we?" she murmured.

He helped her up the rickety steps and through the open front doorway, and there they paused.

The main rooms were heavy with smoke and they stank of ale. Even the standing room by the bar was crowded, and all manner of men—and women— were there. The smell of humanity was terrible here. The men were old and young, but all of them had a look of dust and dirt about them; they were neither clean shaven, nor did they seem to have a decent beard among them. One fellow at the bar wore an eye patch and a white queued wig, but his wig was askew and his brawny shoulders seemed about to split the shoulders of his elegant mustard frockcoat. A stolen coat, no doubt, Skye thought.

Nearby at one of the tables a group of seamen in linen shirts and caps frolicked with a single, buxom, dark-haired wench. One fellow slipped his hand straight into her bodice while she kissed another, then laughed uproariously. She bit into the coins handed to her by the both of them, then laughed, and kissed them each, in turn.

Robert cleared his throat.

"The Silver Hawk is here?" she said.

"Aye, milady. He is a pirate, you know."

She thought that Robert's eyes were twinkling. "A pirate, a rogue, and he'll hang!" she agreed. She cried out as one of the men from the rough wood table rose, grinned a drunken grin, and lunged toward her. Robert stepped forward and his fist shot out and the man fell flat to the floor. "She's come to see the Hawk!" he warned the others. "Make way—she's here for the Hawk!"

Men and wenches stepped aside and Robert led her through the path of them toward a dark and narrow stairway in the rear. Skye felt eyes boring into her. The men coveted her gold, or her person, Skye thought. The women would have gladly robbed her blindly of her clothing.

But Robert was at her back. And he had announced that she had come for the Hawk. None of them would touch her.

"This is awful!" she muttered.

Robert passed ahead, catching her hand. She saw his eyes, and he flashed her a smile. "As I said, milady, the Hawk is a pirate."

"Umm. And welcome to his ways."

"You mustn't be . . . jealous, milady."

"Jealous! I assure you, sir, I am not jealous!"

"Umm, well, begging your pardon, milady, it did seem at the end that you and the Hawk had settled . . . er . . . well, certain of your difficulties. But you must remember, and I warn you kindly, that he is a rogue and a fiend."

"Oh, is he? Thank you for the warning, Robert. I might not have noted that on my own!"

They had come to the top of the stairs. Robert smiled, and with a broad shrug he cast open the door there. He prodded Skye into the murky light of the room, then closed the door behind her.

Slowly, her eyes adjusted to the light in the room. She heard a soft giggle, then she stared with amazement and a slow simmering rage.

Robert had brought her to the Hawk, all right!

"Lady Kinsdale! Why, no, 'tis Lady Cameron, is it not?"

She stood dead still, collecting her wits and control as she stared at the Hawk. He lay bare-chested atop the bed, with a beautiful redheaded wench curled nearly atop him. The girl watched her with amusement; the Hawk watched her with interest. His hand rested lightly atop the redhead's hair, and he seemed not at all distressed to have been found so by Skye.

"Aye, 'tis Lady Cameron," she murmured, pushing away from the door. If the sea slime meant to unnerve her, he would be surprised. She would never let him know that her insides were afire, that she had thought that he had come to care for her because he had taken her with such passion and such fire. . . .

She was not jealous! He was a fiend, a beast, a pirate! Robert had warned her.

But she had spent all that time on the road here wondering what she should do if he demanded her love in payment for service. Demanded her love! The rogue had a string of women in every port.

The sheets were drawn to his waist. He folded his hands over them and cocked his bearded face to the side. "Far be it from me to question a lady, madame, but what are you doing in such a place? Did you miss me so, then? Were you anxious to come back?" He didn't wait for an answer, but teased the redhead at his side. "If Lady Cameron is anxious, then you must hurry away, Yvette."

"I've come on business!" Skye snapped.

"Oh. Oh!" He pretended that it was a very grave matter, narrowing his eyes. Skye shivered suddenly, fiercely. Now she shivered because his resemblance to her husband was so great. Cousins! They were near to being twins. If she had not seen the both of them at the same time on the day that she sailed away from Bone Cay, she could easily think that they were one.

Well, the Silver Hawk had been bred on the wrong side of the Cameron covers. She had seen the portraits now at Cameron Hall. This Cameron had the eyes, if not the name.

"Sir—" Skye began, but he interrupted her, turning to the redhead.

"Yvette, love, this is business." He gave her an affectionate pat on the rump, and Yvette arose, dragging one of the covers along with her. She wrinkled her nose Skye's way.

"That's business, Hawk? Eh, is she paying you then, love, for the servicing?"

Skye nearly gasped, but determined that Yvette was a whore, and she was a lady. She smiled sweetly instead and strode very calmly for the washbowl. Within a blink of an eye, she had tossed the contents of it over Yvette's red head. The girl cried out in shock and rage.

"Eh, Hawk—stop her, or I will!"

Yvette lunged across the bed for her. The Hawk reached out for Yvette, capturing her wrists. Sodden, she fell against him and he laughed. "I cannot kiss and tell, Yvette, but if Lady Cameron needs a word with me, then for"—his silver gaze shot to Skye—"then for old times' sake, I must listen."

"You're a very scurvy son-of-a-bitch, sir," Skye said sweetly. She watched as Yvette arose, looked her way with menace, then smiled to the Hawk.

"See you later, love."

"You'll see him on a gibbet, I'm sure," Skye said pleasantly. Her eyes remained upon him. Yvette slammed the door.

The Hawk smiled deeply and patted the now empty spot on the bed beside him. "Care to join me?"

"Never."

"Ah, Lady Cameron, but you lie!" he taunted her, his silver gaze wide. "I can make you want me, you know."

Skye lifted her brows with imperious disdain. "No, you cannot, Captain Hawk. I do not come where refuse has lain."

"Refuse?"

"Trash, rank trash."

"Do you refer to the girl—or to me. Wait, wait, don't answer that. She must be rank trash, since I am merely sea slime."

Skye carefully ignored him, remaining very straight, her eyes smoldering. "I have come on business—"

"Wait," he interrupted her sharply, his gaze narrowing upon her. He sat up further, winding his arms around his legs as he watched her. "We have not finished with this first business yet."

"Aye, sir, but we have finished!" she insisted softly.

"I remember the very day that you left me, madame. The warmth and the woman. Where has she gone? Where is the warmth."

"Iced over, I'm afraid, Captain. Now if you would just—"

"You would not lie where refuse had been," he repeated pensively. "So you will not crawl in beside me because another has warmed my bed, is that it?"

"Time is of the essence here!" Skye said irritably. "All right, no, you stupid, stinking, stupid knave, I would not so dirty myself. Are you satisfied? May we get on with it?"

He shook his head, his eyes insistent upon hers. "You didn't mention your husband, madame. Isn't marital life bliss? I had thought to hear you cry that you could not betray him—not that you would not play where another lass had tarried."

She inhaled sharply, hating him with her whole heart. He had thought of words that should have come to her lips, should have been wafted there on wings from her very soul.

She stayed stiff and still and silent, praying that she showed no emotion. "My reasons, Captain Hawk, do not matter. Let's let it remain sufficient that it shall not come to pass."

"Skye, Skye," he continued mildly, casting off his sheets to rise from the bed stark naked. Skye tightened her jaw and turned about, determined not to see him. He was taunting her, he wanted reaction, and so help her, she would not give it to him.

She had to react; she had no choice. He came around behind her, catching the hood from her head and pulling it back to display the length of her hair. "You're forgetting, Lady—Cameron, that I am a pirate. And we all know what pirate's do to their women!"

Skye emitted a sharp sound of displeasure, stepping quickly away from him. Fear crept along her spine. She spun around, desperately wondering how to elude him. She moved to the left and he smiled slowly, his hands upon his hips, everything about him bold and brash. Like a cat with prey he stalked and played with her. "Bastard!" she hissed.

"Sea slime!" he corrected.

She turned about again and he followed her. He no longer played. He caught hold of her arm and sent her flying to the bed, then sprawling down upon it. She cried out, flailing at him wildly. He ignored her flying fists and feet, leaping roughly astride her and pinning her there.

His eyes were alive with silver sparks. "Alas, I am a pirate. And you, my love, are in my power once again. And now that I have you here . . . ah, I retaste every sweet morsel of all that ever lay between us."

"Quit this and get up!" Skye insisted with bravado.

"I am a pirate, madame! Forceful and brutal. I can wrench you into my arms—"

"You have already done that!"

"I repeat! I can wrench you into my arms and force you beneath me. Brutally, terribly, I can ravage and rape you. Isn't that what one expects of a pirate?"

Her eyes went very wide as she desperately tried to read his mind and his reason. His naked body was a blaze of fire against her, burning through her cloak and gown, corset and bone and petticoats. She didn't want to tremble beneath him, but she was afraid. She didn't think that she had ever seen him this fierce, this taut. This demanding, seeking something of her. She swallowed tightly, looking up at the living steel of his eyes, feeling the force of his muscle and flesh against her, the wrought-iron pressure of his fingers lacing around her wrists.

He did mean to rape her, she thought. He was not the man she had known at all. He meant to have her, and brutally.

Just as she told Roc that it had been . . .

"Stop it! Please, stop it!" she whispered to him. She trembled from head to toe.

Some of the fever left his eyes. He bent low against her. His lips brushed hers, his beard and mustache teased the softness of her flesh. She would have twisted away but his kiss was so gentle, so light, baby's breath. Then he stared down at her again.

"You must listen to me, please!" Skye said. She wanted to hate him so thoroughly. She could never let him touch her again, but she despised herself as well. When he came near, there was warmth, there was fire. She felt alive.

She loved her husband! she cried to herself. But her husband was so very like this man.

"Talk."

He still sat above her, impervious to his lack of dress. Skye sought out his eyes. "I need your help. And my—my husband could be right behind us."

"Oh?"

"My father is missing. He isn't missing—I mean, I know where he is. He was anxious to see me, and when the *Silver Messenger* returned here, he outfitted her with a new captain. It turned out to be Logan. Logan has my father. Please, I need you."

"I've heard about it," he told her.

"Then . . . ?"

"You say that you think that your husband might well be on his way after you?"

"Yes."

"Why. Where did you leave him?"

"What does that matter to you? I tell you that time is of the essence."

"I am curious. If you want my help, answer my questions."

"You haven't told me if I will get your help or not!"

"Talk!"

"Oh, you are a fool anyway! Spotswood will hang you if he finds you here."

"And your husband will slay me."

"Of course!"

"I might well slay him." He fell down by her side, rested upon an elbow, staring at her with fascination again. She rose quickly, leaping out of the bed, returning his glare.

"Don't be so certain, Captain Hawk. I have seen him in action, and he is a bold, brave fighter."

"Oh?" His brows shot up with surprise. "I thought you were determined to rid yourself of the excess baggage of your betrothed—your husband, that is—the moment you touched shore."

"None of this is your concern."

He smiled, enjoying her, enjoying himself. He rolled over, staring up at the ceiling. "So, madame, it was not so awful then. You lay with him and came back to me, furious that I should have another in my bed. Were your expecting my undying devotion. Should I have pined away while you slept with my illustrious cousin?"

Skye snatched up his black breeches from the floor and tossed them along with his boots upon his naked belly. He grunted from the pain and stared up at her, still smiling.

"Your temper, love! Marriage had not improved it."

"Are you going to help me or not?"

"I don't know. I'm still thinking about it."

"I will pay you."

"Of course, you will pay."

"I have gold."

He cast his legs over the side of the bed and slipped into his breeches. Standing, he tied them, then sought about for his hose. His bronze chest glimmered in the candlelight, rippling muscle defined and fascinating.

He sat again in a chair before the mantel and donned his hose and boots and buckled his black knee breeches. Skye watched him in silence all the while. She waited. Then, exasperated, she repeated herself. "I have gold! Are you going to help me or not?"

He stood and found his light linen shirt upon the foot of the bed. He drew it over his head, then looked at her with a slow lazy grin and a long, cunning assessment. "I have a lot of gold already, madame. I am not just a raping, plundering, murdering sea-sliming pirate, but I am a very successful raping, plundering, murdering, sea-sliming pirate. I don't really need your gold."

"You have to help me!"

"Why?"

"Because, because . . ."

"Because you're a damsel in distress?" he suggested. He came toward her, taking her hands, keeping his eyes upon her as he kissed both sets of her knuckles. "Ah, because I was the first lover you had ever known! Women have soft spots for such things, don't they?"

She jerked her hands away from him and lashed out at him. He caught her fists and, laughing, drew her against him. He held her tight and met her eyes.

"Let go of me!" she said.

"You came to me."

She didn't know if he referred to the night now, or if he talked about that night in a different lifetime in his paradise at Bone Cay. The night when the tropical breezes had swept through the windows.

"Please, let go of me." She hesitated. "Whether you help me or not, you mustn't stay around here, don't you know that? Spotswood—Spotswood knows that you are here."

"Does he?" The Hawk seemed unalarmed.

"Yes. He'll hang you."

"I do not need gold."

"Please, you must—"

"Ah, yes. I must."

"And you must hurry. My husband—"

"Why, madame, didn't you go to your husband with this request? You told me yourself that he was brave and bold and competent."

"But he is not a pirate!"

The Hawk's lashes fell over his silver eyes, hiding his thoughts from her. "Not a pirate, you say?"

"No," she murmured.

His arms tightened around her. "But what if he were?"

"He is not! You can find Logan, I know that you can. Roc could fight him, but he could not negotiate. He could not draw upon support from others in a battle. Please . . ."

He still held her too tight. She could feel the length of him, hard, determined.

"I do know where Logan is," he murmured.

"What?"

"I know where he is. I heard of it when I arrived here."

"Then—oh, my God, please! Help me."

A slow, cynical smile curved into his lip. "For payment, madame, always for payment."

"Of course, I told you, I have gold—"

"And I have told you, I do not want your gold."

"Then—"

"I want you, milady."

Skye gasped. "But—"

"You, milady. I have named my price. I will have you. Just as I had you upon Bone Cay. Scented softly from the bath, sweet and seductive, your hair a sunset blaze about your naked shoulders, and most of all . . . your will agreeable to the act, your heart and body not just willing, but eager."

"I—I can't!"

He smiled and released her, turning away. "That is my price, and my final offer. Take it or leave it."

She stamped a foot furiously against the ground. "I cannot pay such a price! I'm—I am married now."

"Now you think of such a thing!" he said. "You were married at the very time we lay together before."

"I did not know it then."

"You knew you were betrothed."

"What does it matter! I cannot pay this price."

He shook his head, still smiling, as he picked up his black frockcoat and pulled it around his shoulders. He found his scabbard and buckled it around his waist. He set his hat atop his head and found his pistol to shove into his waist.

He tipped his plumed hat to her.

"Then, adieu, milady. I will take your advice and vacate the premises." He strode past her toward the door.

"No!" Skye cried out.

He turned around and arched a brow to her slowly.

"I'll—I'll pay."

"You will?" He waited. "And what of your ardent husband?"

"It is none of your concern! I said that I will pay."

"Perhaps it is every bit my concern."

"What?"

"Never mind," he said swiftly. He strode back into the room and took her hand. He turned it over and planted a kiss on it. Then his eyes met hers. "Our bargain is made, milady."

"Yes."

"I will collect upon the payment, come what may."

"Yes." Silver chills raced along her spine. She had made a bargain in hell, she thought.

What of her ardent husband?

She couldn't think of him now, couldn't believe in him or dare to believe in love. Her father's life was at stake. Was another night spent in the arms of a pirate a small enough price for life?

No . . . for it was betrayal now.

The Hawk was staring at her, as if his silver eyes read her thoughts, and her very soul. He kissed her forehead, then took her hand.

"Come, lady. Our deal is made, and our bargain sealed. I will deliver. . . ."

"And then payment will be made."

15

HE SILVER HAWK CAST OPEN THE DOOR TO THE hallway. "Robert! Robert Arrowsmith." he called.

Robert could not have been far away, for he came instantly to the door. "Aye, Captain?"

"Give the order to our own men below that we must get to the longboats and onto the ship. We sail out tonight."

"Aye, sir!"

"And when the warning is given, come back to me. You may escort Lady Cameron back to wherever it is that you found her. Deliver her to the lieutenant governor with my compliments and suggest that he might wish to keep her somewhere out of harm's way."

"As you wish, sir," Robert agreed.

"What!" Skye cried out.

"Go," the Hawk told Robert. Robert saluted, and left them. The Hawk turned back to look at Skye. "You're not coming, milady. You know that you cannot possibly come. You must go back to your husband and your home."

"My father—"

"I will find your father. I will give you my word."

"But—"

"I will not put your life at risk again. Were your father not so impulsive as to seek you when others were better at the task, we would not be here now. There is danger aboard a pirate ship. You should know that well."

"Not when one is under the captain's protection!"

"But you know very well that one captain can be killed and another man take his place. You know full well that the sea can rage, and cannons fire. I will not take you with me."

"But . . . but what about your reward, Captain Hawk, your payment?"

He shrugged. "I have given you my promise that I will find your father and restore him to you. I will take your word that you will give payment, when payment is due. Your promise will be sufficient."

"My promise—"

He came back to her, a curious smile curving his lips. She didn't think to walk away; she was touched by the silver fire in his eyes and the wistful curl of his mouth beneath the mustache and beard. "You made a promise to me once before," he said softly. "Do you remember?"

She started to shake her head, suddenly frantic to be free from him. Sweet warmth filled her.

She might have stayed with him. Once, if it had not been for her love for Theo, she might well have cast caution and society and propriety to the wind. She might well have stayed with him upon his paradise while the world be damned. She had cared so very deeply. And now with his touch upon her . . .

"Do you remember? Darkness had fallen and you defied me and all danger to escape the night. And you promised me anything, anything at all that I could desire. To give to me all. You later retracted the promise—you had given it to a pirate. But you did not retract, in truth, and I will never forget the time that you gave me the innocence, the trust."

"You never forget?" she whispered. "Except when you bed with whores?"

"Never even then," he replied. "You tell me, milady, do you think of me when you bed with your husband?"

She pulled from him quickly, lowering her head. She had made new vows in her heart. She had sworn that when this danger was over, she would never fight her legal lord and husband again. She would live with him at Cameron Hall, and love him for all of her life.

If he wanted her still, after what she had done. Perhaps this time he would not forgive her.

Her heart seemed to tear within her chest and she wondered if he could understand what she had done. She was afraid to return, she realized, and she wondered not only who she loved the more, the pirate or the lord, or, at the moment, who she feared the more. In the whole of her life no man had had such power over her; now she was storm-tossed between two men, ever battling, and seldom leaving the fray without some wound.

"I love my husband," she said softly.

"What?"

He came up to her, spinning her around to see her face. His gaze was as sharp as his snapping voice, full of demand. Her eyes widened with surprise at his manner, but just then the door burst open again. Robert Arrowsmith had returned. "The men are heading to the longboats and await you. We'd best hurry. It seems that someone has spied a group of the lieutenant governor's militia coming our way. I can leave the lady in their care, and find you as you sail."

"Fine," the Hawk said. He turned, captured her hand elegantly, and kissed it with courtly finesse. "Milady, I stand forever at your service. My promise is my vow, as I am sure that yours shall be."

His eyes sought hers quickly, and then he was gone. She was left to Robert's care.

"We should leave now, and quickly," he told her. "The word is out that Spotswood's men approach. This place is coming alive with scurvies afraid of capture and hanging. I must leave in safety, and see to my own continued life, if you don't mind."

She shook her head, certain that she never wanted Robert Arrowsmith to hang. She dreaded returning to Williamsburg, and even more she dreaded returning to her husband. Perhaps there was some way to explain why she had rendered him unconscious, but she was certain that she could not make him understand a promise such as the one she had made to the Silver Hawk.

She could never explain it. But then, neither would she ever be able to forget it.

"Milady?"

Robert offered her his arm and she took it and they hurried toward the stairs together. Once there, they were brought up sharply.

The Hawk's men were gone, but many another knave was not. They awaited Robert standing in a circle at the foot of the stairs. He paused, shoving her behind him.

One fellow with a gold tooth and straggling dark hair stepped forward, grinning broadly. "Why, 'tis Mr. Arrowsmith of the Silver Hawk's sloop, is it not? Alas, while the Hawk's away . . ."

"What do you want, Fellows?" Robert demanded darkly.

Fellows lifted his hand, rubbing his thumb together with his forefinger. "What is it that we always want, good Master Robert? Gold, son, and that's a fact." Jeering, he pointed a finger behind Robert toward Skye. Nervously she pulled her hood further down upon her forehead. "There's rumor in the common room that the Hawk was visited by a lady . . . and that the lady was none other than the Cameron bride. She's a pretty thing, ain't she? Nay, lads, more than pretty. She's a beauty true and rare, and that's a fact. She's a ticket out of here to any man. She's a very fortune in gold—"

"Let me by, Fellows. She's been given the Hawk's safe passage, and that's a fact."

Fellows cocked his head. "Why, the Hawk's gone, Master Robert. 'E's gone after Logan, so I 'ear, and this time, I daresay, they will kill each other at last. I fear the Hawk no longer."

"Don't you, then?"

The voice thundered across the room and all assembled at the foot of the stairs turned quickly to the doorway. The Hawk wasn't gone at all, not yet. He was standing in the doorway with his greatcoat over his shoulders and his sword drawn. He lifted his hand, beckoning to Fellows. "Come, sir, let's discuss this with our steel, shall we?"

"Get the girl!" Fellows bellowed out.

It was quickly apparent that he did not intend to battle the Hawk, not when a roomful of men stood between them. Some loathsome young man with filthy hands and rum-coated breath lunged toward Skye. She screamed, hurrying up toward the top of the stairs. Robert came against the young man, not reaching for his sword but jabbing his fist into the lad's jaw. The young man went down, and then Robert drew his sword.

"Get her out!" the Hawk raged to Robert across the room.

Robert shoved her upward. They were quickly pursued. Robert dueled with agility and grace, but he had no less than three opponents at a time.

"I need a sword, Robert!" Skye called.

"A sword, milady?"

He lunged at an opponent. The man gasped, clutching his skewered middle. He fell forward, and his sword fell to his feet.

Skye could not take the time to look upon the ugly death with horror. She plucked up the enemy's sword and swept her skirts behind her, anxious to parry their attackers along with Robert.

"Me! My hearties, 'tis me you must fight!" the Hawk cried, coming further and further into the room, battling all who came his way with a startling ferocity and trying to draw opponents from Robert and Skye.

He was strong, Skye thought, yet his brilliance at swordplay lay in his grace. No sword could touch him, for he could leap above the steel. No man could surprise him, for he would suddenly soar atop a wooden table and leap down upon his attacker.

"Come!" Robert urged her.

They fought to the top of the stairway. The Hawk fought his way closer and closer to them, and then he was suddenly beside them, his steel bathed in blood. They entered into the hallway, then he pushed open the door to the room where they had been. He shoved her inside, then Robert, then entered himself.

"The bed!" he roared to Robert.

Between them they shoved the bed against the door. Swords and knives hacked against it. It would burst open soon, Skye thought, in a bare matter of seconds.

The Hawk was already across the room and to the window. He picked up the hearth chair and sent it shattering against the murky panes. He jerked the dirty drapes down and wrapped them quickly about his wrist, shoving aside the broken glass. Then he turned to her. "Come on."

"What?" she demanded incredulously. "We're on the second floor, Captain Hawk. You—you and Robert can jump. I cannot!"

"You can!" Robert assured her. "You will be all right. It's our only chance. It—"

"Oh, for the love of God, Robert! We have to go!"

Skye screamed as the Hawk suddenly strode to her and swept her up and brought her straight to the window. He did not pause, nor could she begin to fight his movement or his speed.

He meant to kill her! He meant to cast her straight out of the window!

He did just that, tossing her instantly. She screamed for all that she was worth as she fell and fell into the night, then her scream was silenced and her breath was swept away as she landed hard upon a stack of hay. A body fell near hers, and then another. She tried to scramble up. She couldn't breathe. She couldn't believe that she was alive.

Skye pushed herself up at last.

"Go, Jacko!" the Hawk called out.

And Skye fell again, flat on her back, as the hay wagon that held her jerked forward. She tried to struggle up again, but the ride was rickety and so swift she could barely move. Fingers curled around hers. "Lie still!"

The wagon came to a halt. The Hawk and Robert leaped down, then their driver, Jacko. The Hawk reached for Skye, lifting her up, and she recognized Jacko from her days aboard the pirate ship. He bowed to her with a broad grin. " 'Evening, milady!"

They stood upon the dock. Skye could hear the lap of the water. "My God, how did you know to double back?" Robert demanded of the Hawk.

"I didn't like the look on some of the men's faces as I left," the Hawk said briefly. "Jacko here thought to borrow the wagon and head around back to the windows, for which I am eternally grateful."

"We have to move," Jacko said. "Any minute now they shall discover the room empty, and the bulk of our men have headed out. They'll have to run themselves, with the militia coming. We've got to reach the ship, and quickly, Captain."

"What about Lady Cameron?" Robert asked.

The Hawk looked her up and down and then issued an exasperated sigh. "She comes with us. We've no choice. I cannot send her back, even with the militia coming. There are no guarantees." He caught Skye's arm and jerked her up against him. "Madame, I have said it before, and I say it again. You are trouble!"

She jerked away, her fingers still tight about the sword she had plucked from the slain ruffian. "You pirated my ship, Captain Hawk! Bear that in mind, sir! Had you lived an honest life, we'd have never met!"

"That thought could, indeed, make a cutthroat repent, milady. I shall bear it in mind. Now, let's go!"

He stepped toward her and she was afraid of some fight, but he merely swept her up into his arms and took another step with balanced precision into the darkness beneath them. She muffled a cry of alarm, for they had merely come down into the longboat, and Jacko and Robert were following them. The men quickly picked up oars, and they slid away, silently, into the night.

The Hawk leaned toward her suddenly. She was shivering; she had grown very cold despite her cloak.

"Milady, I dare not light a lamp. Will you be all right."

She nodded. His eyes remained fixed on hers.

Suddenly the soft sound of the oars dipping against the water was drowned by the shouts and fury that emanated from the tavern. "Company comes!" Jacko laughed.

"Ah, and I fear too late!" Robert said, pleased. Skye quickly looked back toward the land. The rogues from the tavern were spilling out to the stretch of land before the docks. They raced for their boats, but even as they sought the water, an explosion of shots was heard on the air.

"The militia," Robert murmured.

"They'll be taken?" Skye whispered.

"Aye, lady. Those known for their deeds will face trial and hang. There will be a few of the notorious among them. Those not known by face or name will be set free."

"The Silver Hawk would be known," she whispered.

"Aye, lady, the Silver Hawk would be known." He offered her a wry grin, and she trembled inside. Freedom had loomed before him while death had lain behind him and he had still come back. He had come back for her.

"Will we make it?" she said.

He lifted his oar. "The ship lies just ahead."

"You thrive on danger!" she accused him.

"Ah, but I do appreciate my neck, my love!" he assured her.

They fell silent again. Skye looked back. Horses raced along the shoreline. Boats were slipping into the river, men fought fiercely on land. Shots rang out; steel clanged.

The light began to fade in the distance, and the noise, too.

They knew the river here well, these pirates, Skye thought. They navigated in the near darkness. Silence and darkness enveloped them. Skye began to shiver.

The Hawk ceased to row. His hand stretched out to hers, his fingers entwined over them. "It is all right," he assured her softly. His warmth swept into her. She nodded and swallowed. Her throat was dry. Her heart was wretched.

"It will not be so long," he promised her.

It was long. She knew that his ship could not have been so close, that he must have hidden her carefully in some inlet. Still it seemed that they traveled long and hard before they at last saw a beacon in the night.

"The ship," Robert murmured.

"Aye, she awaits us," the Hawk said. "Is Mr. Fulton at the helm, ready to set out?"

"Aye, Captain. That he is."

The longboat moved up by the ship. The ladder was cast over the portside, and the Hawk helped Skye to her feet. Shivering, she clung to the rope rigging and climbed.

He was quickly topside with her, then Robert, then Jacko.

"Take Lady Cameron to quarters," the Hawk said.

"Wait!" Skye cried. Did he think to take her into his cabin again? She had to make him understand that he could not.

"I cannot wait!" he cried impatiently. "I'm captain here, madame, and I sail at your request, hounded my the militia on your behalf. Robert, take her!"

He turned away, heading toward the helm. Robert seized hold of her arm, and she knew that no matter how the man cared for her, he would obey the Hawk.

"Milady, come, please."

He tugged upon her arm, gently, then more insistently. "Now, milady."

"Damn. Damn him!" she cried out, hoping that her fury would reach the Hawk. But he had already dismissed her. He stood atop the platform and shouted out his orders. The anchor was drawn; men were rushing to the rigging to hoist sails.

Robert led her along to the Hawk's own cabin. She bit her lip. He opened the door and thrust her inside.

The fire burned in the stove. Lamps were lit. Warmth and light surrounded her.

The cabin had not changed. Not a bit, since she had been within it last.

"I cannot stay here!" she cried to Robert.

But he ignored her and pulled the door closed behind her. She heard him slide the bolt outside, and she knew that there was no fighting the circumstances.

She fell down upon the bunk, exhausted. It had to be nearly dawn, and there wasn't a thing in the world that she could do at the moment.

She dropped her sword, doffed her cloak, and stretched out upon the bed. Her mind raced and her heart ached and fits of trembling seized her again and again.

At last she stood up and went straight to the Hawk's liquor supply. She downed a good portion of rum, recorked the bottle, and staggered back to the bunk. She fell down upon it again.

And that time, she slept.

In the morning she awoke alone.

She had feared the Hawk throughout the night, but he had not come near her. As she rose, she realized miserably that she did not fear his force, but her own response.

Robert came, quiet and subdued, bringing her breakfast and water with which to wash. He watched her intently. "It was not your fault," he told her. "The Hawk's not pleased at all that you're with us, but don't be alarmed by him, it was not your fault."

"Thank you, Robert."

He smiled to her encouragingly. "Robert, if a pardon comes through, is there any possibility that you will forswear your ways and sign loyalty to the king?"

She thought that his smile deepened, but he quickly lowered his lashes and she could not see his eyes any longer. "I will do whatever the captain does, madame."

"Is your loyalty so fierce, then?"

"It is." He hesitated. "He nevers betrays a trust, milady. He has said that he will lay down his life for you—he will do so then. I will lay down my life for him. That is how we all feel, all of us sailing with him. And that is why he is feared and respected." He paused, as if he longed to go on. Then he shrugged. "The door is open, milady, you are welcome topside."

"Wait, Robert!" she pleaded. He stopped, and it was her turn to pause as a crimson flush climbed over her face. "Robert, where did he sleep last night?"

Robert's gaze swept over her, and he smiled secretively. "In the officers' quarters, milady. Is there any other way in which I may serve you now?"

In the officers' quarters . . .

He had given her his cabin in privacy. Was he waiting to collect his payment, the honorable rogue to the very end? The thought made her shiver, and then she remembered her husband left lying upon the floor, and she wondered where Lord Cameron had spent the night. A fierce surge of trembling rose within her and she had to sit down upon the bunk. Roc . . . could he forgive all of this? Would he disown her, or beat her? Or both. Such behavior would lie well within his rights for all that she had done.

And gave promise to do in the future.

She didn't know who she hated the most then, Lord Cameron or the Hawk. She didn't know who she feared more.

And she still didn't know who she loved more.

"All you all right, milady?" Robert asked anxiously.

"I'm—I'm fine, Robert. Thank you."

"There's nothing I can do?"

She shook her head slowly. When he was gone, she picked at the food that he had brought her, then she quickly washed, brushed her hair, and came topside.

The sails were mostly drawn in, and they traveled slowly and very close to shore. Dangerously close, Skye thought. She could see land to the starboard side. She looked to the carved platform and to the helm and saw that the Hawk was there, navigating his own ship that day.

Skye smiled to the men she passed upon the deck, and they smiled in turn or tipped their hats. Once, she had been in terror of these men, she thought. Now they were her allies.

Her friends.

She couldn't dwell upon such curious twists of fate. She hurried by them and up the platform.

The Hawk was in a black open-necked shirt and black breeches and his dark head was bared to the day. He nodded to her gravely when she came his way.

"Did you sleep well, milady?"

She nodded. "Did you?"

"Alas, I whiled away the night in dreams."

"I thank you for that, Captain Hawk," she said softly. He glanced to her, then looked up toward the crow's nest.

"Jacko!"

"Aye, Captain?"

"Is she clear?"

"As clear as fine crystal, Captain!"

"Robert! Mr. Arrowsmith!"

"Aye, Captain!" Robert was quickly with him, bounding up the steps of the platform from the far deck.

"Take the wheel, sir, if you please."

"As you please, Captain!" Robert agreed.

The Hawk stepped away, offering Skye his arm. She hesitated, then took it, glancing wryly toward Robert. "I wonder if His Majesty's ships of the Royal Navy work so smoothly," she murmured.

"I wonder," the Hawk agreed pleasantly. He led her starboard side, where the sea breeze touched her face and lifted her hair. "I've a few lady's things aboard," he told her. "We had not anticipated your arrival, and so little was prepared.

What I have will be sent to you by afternoon." He leaned against the rail, watching her intently. "I know your penchant for bathing, milady, and would not deny you the pleasure."

She flushed slightly and turned to stare out at the coastline. "I want nothing of your ill-gotten gain, Captain," she told him.

"Who says that what I offer is ill-gotten gain?"

She glanced at him sharply, and then her color deepened. "I want nothing belonging to your whores, either, Captain, thank you."

He smiled, staring out on the water silently, not touching her. "Milady, I promise you, what I send belongs to no whore."

"Then—"

"Certain of my men are married, milady. Though their wives' finery might not be to your standards, still, certain . . ." He paused, his eyes meeting hers with a devilish light. "Certain intimate apparel will be clean and neat and surely acceptable."

Even his silver eyes seemed to touch and stroke her, she thought. She should be far away from him. Far, far away.

She stared across to the shore. "Tell me, Captain, do you intend to let me wear this clean and neat clothing on my own?"

"Milady?"

"Are you—" Her lips were dry, and she was breathless, and they merely stood together and spoke. If only she could forget the past. If only the slightest brush of his arm against hers did not evoke memories of tempest.

"Are you going to leave me in peace, Captain? Your cabin, sir, have you given me that as my own?"

He took a long time answering. When she looked to him at last, he was studying her very seriously. "Until it is time to do otherwise."

"What do you mean?"

"When we've found and taken your father, milady. Then I will return. It will be most difficult for you to keep your promise to me if I am bedded elsewhere."

She did not reply but tore her eyes from his to survey the shore. "With my father on board?" she queried softly.

"You're worried about your father—and not your husband?"

"My husband is not aboard," she murmured miserably.

"Ah . . . so that makes it all right to be an adulteress?"

"Stop it!" she hissed desperately. "Nothing makes it all right!"

"No, it doesn't, does it?" he murmured. He turned her around by the shoulders. She tried to jerk free from his touch, but he would not allow her to go. She stared up at him, her eyes glazing with tears.

"I need your help!" she insisted bitterly. "I had no choice. My father—"

"Aye, your father," he muttered darkly. "And still I tell you, milady, that your husband would have gladly fought and died rather than let you pay this price."

"His blood cannot be payment for my request."

"Aye, milady, for his blood has become your blood, as surely as yours is his. God alone knows how he will feel this time!"

"What do you mean?" she cried, wrenching away from him at last.

"Well, milady, I assume you must have admitted something." The sweep of his eyes told her clearly and boldly that he spoke of her lack of innocence when she entered into her marital bed. "What did you say? That it was fear? Loneliness? Desperation, a bid to save your very life! This time . . . perhaps you need not tell him that you bartered with what was his, that you offered yourself in payment. You can tell him that I am a pirate, a cutthroat, a ravaging rapist, and that I dragged you down before you had a chance to think." He reached out for her again so suddenly that she nearly screamed. His fingers threaded cruelly into the hair at her nape, and he dragged her close. "Maybe he'll be so enraged he'll beat you to within an inch of your life. I wonder what I would do, milady, if you were my wife, under such circumstances. I'd kill the man, that is for certain."

She kicked him savagely, taking him by surprise. He howled with outrage as her foot came in wild contact with his shin, then he jerked harder upon her hair, pulling her flush against him. He gritted his teeth. "Pirates, milady. We are allowed to be savages, remember? But I do wonder just how savage your fine aristocrat of a husband might turn out to be when he hears of this latest maneuver on your part! But then, you told me that you loved him, didn't you?"

"Let me go!" she cried frantically. "He is my concern." Aye, Roc was her concern, just as the Hawk was her concern. And at the moment, he was the man to fill her heart and her thoughts, for she was so completely his prisoner. From head to toe she was flush with the man, achingly aware of the heat of his muscles, the strength of his hands and arms, the fire in his groin. It occurred to her fleetingly then that she knew him more thoroughly still than she did Petroc Cameron, for this one she had seen boldly in the nude, while her husband had seduced her and been seduced in return while never quite shedding his clothing.

Warmth blazed through her as she struggled to be free.

"Captain!"

"Aye!" He released her instantly, striding the deck to come back upon the platform by the helm. It was Jacko calling to him from atop the crow's nest.

"I see ships ahead, far right into the inlet."

"Pirates?"

"Aye, sir! I see Teach's flag atop the one. They're drawing it in, I believe."

"Safe harbor on the islands!" Robert Arrowsmith seemed to growl.

Skye hurried after the Hawk to the platform. "Where are we?" she demanded.

"My glass!" the Hawk demanded. He leaped for the mast and began to shimmy up the length of it. Skye watched his dexterity with perplexity and annoyance, then turned to Robert. "Robert! Where are we? What is going on, here?"

"A party, milady."

"A party!"

"A pirate fete upon a North Carolina island. A number of men have gathered here. Teach just took some incredible prize and enhanced his reputation a thousand times over. We believe he has a certain immunity here, in this area of North Carolina. So do some of the others."

Skye gasped. "So Eden of Carolina has been bribed by the pirates!"

"So goes the rumor."

"But why have we come . . . ?" she began, but even at the last, her voice trailed away. "Logan! The Hawk thinks that Logan has come here with my father!"

"Precisely, Lady Cameron."

Skye fell silent and hurried back to the railing, looking starboard side. She realized that the Hawk was calling down orders to Robert Arrowsmith, and that Robert was then calling out commands to the crew. The sails were drawn in tighter and the ship began to shift. Skye thought that the Hawk meant to sail straight into the land, and she nearly turned to scream that they were insane. But just when she would have done so, she saw the narrow channel leading inland. It was a fair space ahead of the other pirate ships.

They were going to hide, she thought. Hide, until the Hawk could get a fair layout on the land—and its inhabitants.

She was right in her assumptions.

Turning about again, she saw that the order had been given to bring down the longboats.

Then a moment later, in the midst of all the activity, the Hawk was striding back toward her. He was fully armed now, she saw, with his cutlass in his scabbard, a knife in a sheath at his boot, and a brace of pistols shoved into his waistband.

"Go back to the cabin," he told her curtly. "Stay out of sight."

He started to turn away. "Wait!" she cried to him, catching hold of his arm. "Please, don't leave me here—"

"Damn you, stay out of sight!" he told her, his eyes narrowing. "You little witch! Don't you remember the last time, girl? If you hadn't been so determined to escape, Logan might well never have known that you existed!"

And he might not have kidnapped her father. The words went unsaid. Skye stepped back as if she had been stung, but she did not cease her argument, for it was the same as his.

"Please, don't leave me here! It is because—" she hesitated, then continued, "it is because of my very foolish determination at that time that I beg you to bring me along."

He hesitated, and she knew that he recalled how Logan had come to the ship when it had been weak and unguarded.

"Damn it!" he swore. "Damn it! Aye, come along, then! But you heed my words and warnings at all times, and so help me, if you prove to be trouble, I will lash you to a tree! Robert! Get the lady's cloak."

"Robert! And my sword, please!" Skye added.

The Hawk stared at her. He did not refuse her request. "Come, lady," he said at last, as Robert brought her things. "We'll take the first boat."

His touch was far from gentle as he handed her down the ladder to the longboat from the deck. He was not leaving the ship as unguarded as he had in New Providence, but at least twenty-five of his men were accompanying them.

He did not row, but balanced forward, looking ahead. Jacko and Robert and two others were in their boat, rowing steadily. Skye sat tense and silent, watching as they came to land.

When they did, the Hawk asked no by-your-leave, but plucked her up in his arms and thrashed through the water with her in his arms. She smiled suddenly as he carried her, taut and distant, over the sand to the secrecy and shadows of the brush. He glanced down, startled by her gaze.

"Once," she whispered, "you said that I wasn't even worth a fair price in gold. But you are risking your life for one night in my arms. Should I be flattered, Captain Hawk?"

"Perhaps I value my life less than gold. Perhaps that is a pirate's way."

"I, sir, do not value your life as less!"

She thought that he would be pleased. He stiffened like cold steel and fell to his knees to dump her angrily upon the sand. His men milled behind them but he spoke in a heated whisper anyway.

"What of your life, lady—and all that is of value to your husband?"

She straightened herself, longing to slap him. He knew her intent, for he quickly caught her wrist, and together they rolled across the sand. Breathlessly she shoved against him.

He paused at last. They had come beneath the shadow of spidery trees, on a bed of pines. He rose over her. He cupped her chin in his hands and bent down to kiss her. She tried to twist away. Her resistance was to no avail. His lips found hers. His tongue ravaged them, demanding that they part to him. He was merciless, savage, demanding. She could scarce breathe. She twisted and kicked.

But she could not move, nor could she deny the wild abandon that snaked traitorously into her veins. He brought her alive with fire, with liquid heat. She could fight no more. She tasted his lips and tongue and the deep recesses of his mouth, tears coming to her eyes. She felt his hands upon her, sweeping along her thigh, cupping her breast.

Then at last he broke away. He started to swear at her furiously, incoherently, but then his words broke away. He gently smoothed the tear from her cheek with his forefinger, then he drew her to her feet.

"You will wait here with Robert, do you understand me? I am looking today, nothing more. I may, perhaps, leave you ashore tonight, and enter into the festivities with you safely out of sight and far, far from harm's way. Stay with Robert and my men, and take care. Do you understand me?"

She nodded. He turned and, shouting orders, left her. She waited until he was long gone, then she came over and joined Robert, who sat idly by the shore. Others of the men had stayed behind, too. Five of them. To protect her, Skye thought.

By Robert's side, she suddenly burst into tears. He set his arm around her like a brother, drawing her close. Miserably, awkwardly, he tried to comfort her. "I've tried to tell him. Ah, Skye, I've tried, I'm so sorry. . . ."

"What?" she managed to gasp out. "Tell him what?"

"To leave you be," he whispered. "You don't understand. You can't possibly understand. He . . . never mind. It will be all right. Trust me, milady, trust me, please."

She fell silent and stayed by his side.

Later he rose, looking upward with agitation. "What is it?" Skye demanded.

"Clouds. Storm clouds. I don't like them."

Skye looked up herself. Even as she did so, it seemed that the day darkened. The breeze picked up.

"We should get back," Robert said.

"We can't leave him! We can't leave the Hawk!" Skye protested.

"We won't be leaving him. I'll take you back, and he can come with the others in one of the longboats."

A sudden, brilliant flash of lightning rent the sky. Thunder followed it like a clash of heavenly swords. "Come on!"

Robert dragged her to her feet. Skye whirled around as the other men rose, hurrying toward them.

The rain began to fall.

"We head to the ship in one boat!" Robert cried. He reached for Skye's hand. A second bolt of lightning came, and thunder followed, and the very heavens seemed to open up upon them. "Come, Skye!" Robert grabbed her hand, and they started racing down the beach. Then suddenly she stopped, and she slammed hard against him. "Hawk!"

Skye pushed sodden tendrils of hair from her face to stare ahead of herself. He was indeed coming back. Running along before the main group of his men, he reached them. He spoke quickly to Robert. "They're here all right, a full party of them. Logan, Teach, a fine baker's dozen of others. We'll move in tomorrow. For now, let's hie from here. This storm promises to be fierce!"

He reached behind Robert, finding Skye's hand and pulling her along. He lifted her and shoved her into one of the longboats. Robert and two men crawled in behind them and shoved them away from the shore.

The Hawk ignored Skye, rowing hard with the others. Lightning flashed, thunder cracked, and she flinched. At the shoreline she could see the waves swelling and the trees and bracken bending low to the strength of the wind. She shivered. In a matter of moments, it seemed, a true tempest had swirled upon them.

"Damn!" Robert swore. "I cannot hold her steady!"

"Pull together!" ordered the Hawk.

Skye turned around. She could see the ship, and it still seemed far ahead of them. The ferocity of the waves seemed to push them ever closer toward the shore.

"Take care of the rocks!" the Hawk cried, but he had barely voiced the words when a terrible rending sound was heard. Skye didn't know what had happened at first. The sound seemed part of the horror of the storm, like the crack of thunder, like the high scream of the wind. "Signal the others!" the Hawk cried.

Skye stared at him and saw the power he set to the oars, trying to hold the small boat steady. She looked to her feet. Water rushed in upon them. They had struck a rock. They were sinking, she realized.

"Fulton has seen us!" Robert cried. "He's circling back."

"Dive in, we'll take less water, and I'll stay with Skye to the last!" the Hawk shouted. "She cannot make it far in these skirts!"

"I can't leave you—"

"You'll drown us if you stay! It will come right, Robert, if we don't take any more water! Tyler, Havensworth, dive now, and reach Fulton, and bring him around for us!"

Seeing the wisdom of his words, his men quickly obeyed his orders. Skye gasped, her hand coming quickly to her mouth, for it instantly seemed that the wild sea swallowed them over. Grayness prevailed.

Then she saw Robert's head as he broke out of the waves. Then she saw the two other men, and that they could survive; they were swimming hard toward another boat.

She glanced down to her feet again. The water was rising high. She looked to the Hawk. He was staring at her.

"Ready?" he asked.

She lifted her chin with a smile of bravado. "I am afraid of the dark, not the water!" she told him. A slow smile curved into his features. He reached out to her.

"Come then, my love!"

She took his hand. The rescue boat was almost next to them, but Skye realized that they had to jump and swim—else risk the damaged boat crashing with the one that would save them. With her fingers entwined with the Hawk's, she dove over the side.

She was instantly dragged down. The water was cold, heavy, and dark. Her lungs hurt and she tried to kick her way back to the surface. She was so very heavy.

There was a jerk upon her hand. The Hawk was dragging her up. Her face broke the surface. Still, she could scarce breathe. The rain beat against her savagely, the wind screamed and tore at her, stealing away what breath she could gasp in.

"Swim!" the Hawk commanded.

A giant wave crashed down upon her. Their hands were torn apart. Skye felt as if she were lifted by a giant icy hand and tossed about. She was heavy, so heavy! Wildly, desperately, she broke the pull of the sea.

Salt water stung her eyes and filled her mouth as she gasped for air. She strained to see, and horror engulfed her. The longboat seemed to be miles away. Miles and miles away.

And the Hawk was next to it, clinging to it. He could crawl right over to safety, while she . . .

Water rose and crashed over her head again. She started going down. Her lungs were going to burst. Searing pain swept through them. She realized that she was about to die, to drown, to sink down to the sea bed in a swirl of bone and petticoats and skirts, and lie there to be food for sharks and other fishes. Life, sweet tempest that it was, would be over. Death could not be so hard. Not so painful as the agony that came to her lungs. Not so terrifying as the sea green darkness and the cold that was enveloping her. They said that a drowning man saw his life flash before his eyes. What of a drowning woman?

A drowning woman saw her lover's face, she thought, but her air was all but gone, and she did not know if she saw her husband or the Hawk before her. . . .

Pain awoke her just before she opened her mouth to breathe in gallons of the water. Fingers entwined in her hair, dragging her up and up. She broke the surface and through the darkness and gray and pelting of the rain, she saw the Hawk.

"Swim!" he commanded her furiously.

"I cannot! My petticoats—"

"Shut up!"

He was holding her against him, treading the water with a fury and coming at her with a knife. If she had had breath, she would have screamed. He meant to slay her so that she would not drown, she thought incredulously.

But he did not slay her. His knife did not cut into her flesh, but severed away her clothing. Her skirts and petticoats fell, and her legs were free, and she could tread water herself. "Get rid of your shoes!" he shouted.

She reached down and gulped in some water. He spun her around, digging into her hair again, but holding her face above water. She managed to shed her shoes. She realized that he was already swimming, his fingers dragging her along by the hair.

"I can manage!" she cried. Twisting, she began to go with the water. He wasn't fighting the current or the waves. He was allowing the rush of the storm to cast them toward the shore.

Hope surged within her, but then it died. She was tiring so quickly! And it took them so long. The shoreline seemed so close, and then a gray wave would crash over her, and it would seem miles away again. She started to flag. He caught her by the hair again.

"Stop!" she cried. The cold was numbing. It made her want to die. "Stop, you're hurting me. I can't make it. Go on!"

"I'll hurt you like you can't imagine if you don't stop fighting me!" he swore. His fingers were grasping her, biting cruelly into her. They laced through her hair, and he was swimming hard again. She ceased trying to fight him. The rain was all around her, as gray as the sky, as dark as the sea. There was no difference between them. Sky and rain and sea were one, and they were imprisoned by them all.

"There. Hold on!" the Hawk demanded.

She didn't know if she held on or not. The darkness encompassed her. She went limp. She sank beneath the waves. The shore was just ahead of them. She saw that. Then the world was dark.

She came to moments later because she was flat in the sand, and he was straddled over her, his mouth on hers, forcing air into her lungs. She gasped, and breathed on her own. Her eyes flew open.

"We're alive!" she cried.

"We're alive," he said simply. He crashed down beside her. She realized that she could no longer feel the rain. He had brought them into the shelter of a small cove with overhanging rock and ledge.

She could think no more that night. She closed her eyes, and slept.

The sun, hot and beautiful upon her damp body, awoke her. Skye rolled, dazed, to her side. She looked about, and she saw the Hawk. He was still out, sprawled not ten feet away from her. Desperately pleased to see him with her and alive, she crawled the distance to him. If he slept, she could dare to wake him with a tender kiss. This morning, she could not feel guilt or shame.

Yet before she could touch him, she paused. A frown furrowed her brow as she stared down at his face.

Half of his beard had been sheared away. His mustache, too. Bits and pieces of hair clung to his flesh in a very odd manner.

She reached out and touched the hair. It came away in her grasp. It was fake. His beard was fake. He was really clean shaven. And with the beard gone to display the contours and angles of his face, he looked even more like Petroc Cameron. In fact, he looked exactly like Petroc Cameron.

She stared at him, and the truth slowly, slowly dawned upon her. She stood, forgetting their wild fight for life and death, forgetting everything as rage seared into her heart, blinding her to the entire world.

"Bastard!" she shrieked, and she awoke him not with a kiss, but with a wild and savage kick to the midsection.

16

ESPICABLE BASTARD! SCURVY KNAVE. WORSE than a sea slime, worse than the densest pile of—of rat dung! You should be sliced to ribbons, disemboweled! Skinned alive, inch by scurvy inch!"

He was dreaming, Roc thought. The storm and the roiling waves were all about him still and he was dreaming that some Harpy had come flapping around above him to torture him awake.

No . . . he was not dreaming.

It was Skye.

She was railing against him, hollering like a shrew, and tugging upon him, too. His sword . . . she was stealing his sword from his sodden leather scabbard!

Reeling from the pain in his gut, straining to come awake and to terms with the morning, Roc realized slowly that it was indeed Skye, she was standing over him, her left hand upon her hip, her right hand brandishing his sword, and a bit too close to his extremities, at that. Her eyes flashed like sapphires in the sun, she was as tense as steel. She stood disheveled, her hair a wild blaze about her, her skirts torn and shredded, her feet bare. If she weren't so enraged, he would have smiled. She was in a sorry state, except that, even so, she was more captivating than ever. Her legs were bare to her thighs, her breasts strained against the damp material of her bodice, and she might have been some pagan creature from a far barbaric time.

He stared at her blankly. She hissed some other ungodly name his way, and her toe landed hard against his midsection again. His own temper bubbled and soared and skyrocketed with him, exploding like some witch's brew.

He groaned, and she kicked him anew!

He pushed up from the sand in amazement.

"Skye! What the hell is the matter with you?"

"You!" she told him.

Then he touched his face. Half of the beard was there; half of it was gone. He muttered out an expletive and pulled away the remaining false whiskers, wincing as he did so. He was weary. His head was splitting and he ached from head to toe and she was standing there abusing him verbally—and physically—with a vengeance.

"Get up!" she commanded him, bringing the point of his own sword close against his jugular. His eyes narrowed with a flash of anger as he came slowly to his feet, facing her. "I should dice you into tiny pieces, and save the hangman his efforts. My God, the things that you did to me!"

"The things that I did to you!"

"Oh, Captain-Lord-Cameron-Hawk! How could you! How dare you! Hanging will be far too good a fate for you!" She started walking forward in her vehemence, and with that razor-honed blade so close to his throat, he had no choice but to back away from her along the sand. He'd never seen her this angry. He didn't know if she would or wouldn't use it.

"Give me the sword, Skye."

"Give *you* the sword? You must be out of your mind."

"You don't want me to kill me—"

"Kill you!" Her brows shot up eloquently. "Kill you? Oh, my dear captain! I'm longing to kill you, but torture comes first! I should love to see you stew in boiling oil, or perhaps have your fingers and toes and other protrusions chopped off, one by one—"

"Madame—" he began warningly.

"No! Let's see, *who* shall I kill, Lord Cameron? No, my legal husband, a member of the peerage, no . . . 'tis the pirate I should kill. Captain Hawk. The scurvy knave, the rogue, the—"

"Your lover, Lady Cameron?" he inquired with a long, taunting drawl. She hesitated and he continued, daring to put his fingers upon the cold steel and move it away from his throat and bear slowly down upon her in turn. Once more they moved across the sand, with his voice rising in deep angry tones. "Ah, yes! Captain Hawk, the Silver Hawk. That dastardly villain who so crudely and brutally *raped* you upon your first meeting. That was the description of what came between us, wasn't it? Is that what you told your husband, milady, when you threw yourself so completely upon his mercy when trying to disavow your marriage?"

They came against a palm tree. She gasped, startled, as her back hit it. Then her jaw locked and the sword whistled as she smoothly retrieved the blade from his touch. The edge just drew a thin line of blood against his thumb and he made a furious sound like a growl. It did not daunt her in the least. The blade was next to his throat once again.

"You son-of-a-bitch! You *were* cruel and brutal when you seized that ship! You and your announcements that the crew were free to take Tara and Bess . . . but that I was yours! Thrusting me into that dark chamber, seizing my clothing—"

"I thrust you into my cabin because I wanted you safe from the crew. They are good men and loyal, but a captain always needs to take care. And I seized your clothing because they were damp and you might well have gotten pneumonia."

"I might have had some choice in the matter."

"Give me the sword, Skye."

They had come back center on the sand. They circled one another very warily.

"And on that island—" she began.

"What on that island? What? Go ahead, tell me! Was I cruel on the island, brutal? Ah, yes, that's where I forced you into my arms."

"You did force me—"

"Never, lady, and hence your wrath against me! My God, I had the patience and restraint of a saint—"

"Of a saint!"

"Of a saint. And I warned you time and again, and still you came to me. Vixen, you came to me."

"You knew about—you knew about the marriage!" she charged him.

"Yes, I knew. Of course, I knew. 'Tis my wife I came to rescue."

"And 'twas your wife you seduced?" she snapped.

A slight flush of color touched his cheeks. "I didn't intend to."

"Oh!" She stamped her foot against the sand and prodded the sword further against him. "You slimy, seafaring bastard! You went running from my house to bed another woman, knowing that I would come after you! Don't you ever, ever think to touch me—"

"There was no other woman."

"Liar! We both saw her; her hair was red—"

"I hired her, merely to irritate you." The words were a mistake. Her hand shook. The steel touched him ever more closely. "Skye, give me back my sword!"

"Never! When I give you this steel, Captain Cameron-Hawk, you are going to feel it beyond a doubt."

"There was no woman. But you—you, my love, my dear, darling devoted wife—"

"I never claimed to be a devoted wife!" she spat out. "I was forced to be a wife, just as I was forced to be a pirate's possession!"

"Ah, but the wife didn't mind going off to make a bargain with a pirate. Promises, my love, remember!"

"You are the most despicable man ever!" she hissed.

He ducked down, seeking to retrieve his sword. She sent it slashing dangerously through the air and he quickly danced back a step, circling her. *"Me, milady! Me?"*

"You! This double life of yours! Well, I promise you, sir, they will hang you just as high as the Silver Hawk, even knowing that you are Lord Cameron! You were supposedly my father's friend! And you stole his ship anyway. I should slice you from groin to neck for that alone."

"Oh, so that's it, lady! The hurt is sexual indeed! Slice him to pieces and make sure you damage the man!"

" 'Tis your heart I'd like on a platter!"

"Is it, milady? I seized your father's ship from One-Eyed Jack, lady," he reminded her tensely. "I seized you from him and his band of murdering cutthroats!"

"And you took me to Bone Cay!" Tears were suddenly stinging her eyes, and she didn't want him to see them. She blinked them back furiously and kept moving, watching him very warily at all times. She *should* kill him. She should kill the pirate Silver Hawk right then and there. He would deserve it.

"Give me the sword, Skye!"

"No!"

Suddenly he drew his long knife from the sheath at his calf. He smiled, his eyes glittering silver. "Then slay me," he told her.

"Stop it!" she commanded as he feinted toward her with the short broad blade. Hers was by far the better weapon, and she *did* know how to use it. "Stop it or I shall have to kill you!"

"Come, come, love! Aye, the temptation is great for me!" He dove toward her. She reeled back, slicing at his blow, and their steel clanged together loudly. She swirled around, ready for the next attack. He was coming at her now with a new vengeance. "I should catch you now and beat you silly, madame, redden your aristocratic and sashaying derriere—"

"It's been done before!" she reminded him, her teeth gritted.

"Ah, but the pirate had the pleasure, and not Lord Cameron. Not the injured husband."

"Injured husband!" She was so startled and incensed that she stood still. He lunged, and she was forced to leap back, just barely parrying his blow. "Injured husband indeed!"

"Injured husband. Seduced so sweetly by his angelic and long-suffering wife, just so that she could viciously render him unconscious with a liquor bottle!"

"I had to—"

"You had to! Ah, yes, render Lord Cameron senseless so that you could run off into the arms of another man. To promise to bed him as happily and givingly as a lark for services rendered!"

"Oh, how dare you!" she shouted, and for the moment, she had the advantage again. She moved across the sand in a flurry, and the air cried out with the force of swords and steel as she backed him far across the beach to palm tree again. "How dare you! Fine! You hired a whore just to lie naked with you in a bed to taunt me!"

"Aye!" he cried. "And you were distressed that the Silver Hawk had lain with another woman—not that he asked you to be the *adulteress* to come to him!"

"You bastard, you deserved it! I asked you to leave me be as my good and strong and loyal husband—I warned you about the other man and the fact that I could . . . that I could carry the Hawk's child. But you! You waited until I slept, and then you seduced me, after all that I had said—"

"Exactly, milady! Those words mattered until you meant to leave me for the Hawk—then *you* came and seduced *me!* What of your morals then, eh, Lady Cameron?"

"How dare you—" she began again, but he saw his chance. He had unnerved her, and her grip was slack. He surged forward, catching the tip of his sword with tremendous force. The reverberation of it traveled down the steel and she cried, dropping the blade.

"I dare whatever I please, milady!" he assured her. "You are my wife, remember?"

She stared at him in fury and looked to the sword upon the ground.

They dove for it together.

Skye grappled desperately in the sand to reach the blade. His long bronzed fingers closed over it first, tossing it aside. She tried to reach it. He cast himself against her and they went rolling across the sand. When they came still again, he swiftly straddled her, pinning her beneath him, pinning her to the ground. She writhed and fought against his strength, squirming and kicking, and succeeding only in making the sand fly. Eventually she was gasping for air, and still his prisoner, exhausted and beaten. She stared at him defiantly. "You *will* hang, sir!"

He cocked his head inquiringly. "And will you come to the spectacle, my love? Will you watch, and perhaps shed a tear or two?"

"I've nothing to say to you. You're a rogue."

"And you're a cunning, manipulative seductress, so which of the two of us is more at fault?"

"You!"

"Milady, I—"

"You! You knew all the while what was going on! You led me on time and time again, and taunted me on purpose. You knew that my soul was in agony and you—"

"Agony! When were you in agony, my love?"

"Oh, never mind! Just get off of me now, and leave me—"

"Get off of you! Well, love, this is typical. There I lay, sleeping deeply after having saved your life, plucking you from the cruel and icy fingers of the sea! Then you come up with your very tender toes and nearly dislocate the whole of my rib cage. You take a sword to my throat, and nearly slice open my veins. Now I am on top again, and so we should quit the fight. Well, no, milady, it does not work that way. I owe you, remember? I owe you for nearly splitting my skull with that bottle, for leaving me to nearly drown in a pool of rum. For trying to sever from my body various protrusions. It is *not* over! You will talk to me, and you will listen—"

"I will not listen!" she snapped. "Ever, ever again! I will be free from you, and so help me, I *will* see you hang! All of those innocents you have fooled! Lieutenant Governor Spotswood believing in you so deeply! How could you! Lord Cameron! You had everything that you could have wanted! But you had to be a pirate anyway. Robbing, stealing, plundering—"

"Raping?" he suggested nonchalantly.

Skye cried out an oath and tried to fight him again. Tears stung her eyes as she writhed and scrambled beneath him. She had so little of her gown left, it was awful. Her shift and shorn petticoats rose about her and she felt his damp thighs clamped hard against her bare hips. She went still, staring at him. He smiled slowly, a devil's taunting, promising, sensual grin. Her heart sank. She could not deny his looks, his appeal. She could not deny the rippling, muscled strength of his arms, or the trembling that seized upon her when he stared at her that way, so very aware of her skirt climbing, and of the distress it caused her.

The silver glitter in his eyes was as wicked as the rogue's curl of his smile. With tension all about him, he leaned toward her. "A pirate's life, ah, yes, milady! The rogue's way. I'm fond of it, yes, I am! Take what a man will, love where he desires, have what he wants! It's a good life, it is! Surely, I will hang for it—and certainly, I will hang, too, for the deceit I played on you!"

She gasped suddenly, staring at him, twisting again with new vigor. "You *are* a —a despicable sea slime! *Oh!* Lord Cameron never doffed his clothes, not even to make love, because you were afraid I would know, that I would find some little mark, that—oh!"

"Yes, it was difficult," he said nonchalantly. "Most difficult. I couldn't have you in the dark—not with your fears, love. That's why the pirate tried so hard not to touch you."

"The pirate touched me again and again!"

He shrugged. "Yes, well, the part of Lord Cameron inside the pirate's clothes didn't want to think that his beloved wife would fall into the arms of another man."

"I didn't know that I was anyone's wife!" she spat out. "Oh, you bastard! You cannot put this on me!"

He leaned low against her, his eyes still wickedly alive, his smile near to a taunting, sensual sneer. "I can do whatever I will, milady. I am a pirate, remember?"

She shook her head furiously. "You will never have me again."

"You are still my wife."

"I disavow you!"

"It isn't that simple."

"So help me, sir, if you ever touch me again, it *will* be rape!"

"Ah, but my lady," he murmured, "you forget so much! The dread pirate Hawk has already taken you by force, why not again? Your words, milady, not mine. And Lord Cameron surely owes his bride the thrashing of her life. Then there is the main thing, and that is your father. You were willing to sell your . . . er, virture—or what was left of it—to find him first—"

"Oh!" she flared, twisting anew. Her skirt climbed completely and she was bare to the waist and they both knew it. He arched a single brow tauntingly.

"You do make things easy, love. Shall I beat you first, and make love to you— excuse me, that's force you into my arms, I mean—second? Or the other way around? Promises, promises! I am supposed to find your father, you know, for the sweet promise of your willing—and eager—arms."

"Someone should really skewer you through!" Skye announced.

"Should they? Tell me, then, what happened to this tempest inside of you? What of the gentle feelings you bore the Hawk for being tender in the dark? What of the truth that you whispered to Lord Cameron in the forest about your fears? What, lady, of the sweet seduction you played in that room? You told the pirate Hawk that you loved your husband. What of those words?"

She narrowed her eyes carefully, her heart hammering inside her chest with a fierce beat. "Lies, sir. Lies. And that is all!" she said flatly. "Issued about the one man to avoid the other, sir, and that is all."

He shook his head and lowered it against hers. But he wasn't laughing anymore. His features were tense and serious, his eyes were dark, shadowed smoke. "So you care nothing for either man, milady, is that what you're saying?"

"Aye, I care deeply! To see them hang, as one and the same!"

His fingers tensed around hers, his mouth tightened grimly, and for a moment Skye was truly frightened. He had had his fill of her, and he was finished. Perhaps he would play the pirate in truth and slit her throat. Or perhaps his role would be that of the grievously injured husband, and he would strike her where she lay. Thunder touched his features, anger, deep and sure. She did hate him; she despised him for all that he had done.

But she had fallen in love with a man, too. With tenderness, with caring, with flashing silver eyes, and with startling courage against all odds. She had fallen in love with flesh and blood, and she had lain in paradise, be that paradise an island, or a bower within the woods, or a bed upon a soft mattress with white silky sheets. He would hang; and she never be able to bear it.

She closed her eyes, and waited for his blow.

It never came. He released her and came to his feet, and caught her hands and none too gently dragged her up before him. "I am in love with you," he told her softly.

"Love!" she cried. "What can you know of or mean by love, after what has been done!"

"I'd have died to save you any number of times."

"You risk your life each time you sail!" she retorted. "You chose your course in life! You risk your throat every time you step upon the shore of New Providence!"

"What of your father?" he demanded curtly.

"What do you mean?" she asked, faltering.

"You wanted me to find your father."

"Yes, and I still expect you to do so!"

"Under the same conditions."

"What?" Skye cried out.

He didn't reply right away. He asked her another question instead. "What if I could prove myself to you, milady?"

"I don't know what you're talking about."

"What if I could explain my deeds?"

"You shall never explain your deeds to me. And you will hang, eventually, I know it. Lord Cameron or no."

His eyes flashed with renewed anger. "One day, milady, so help me, I will see that you rue those words. For now, however, we will return to the business at hand. The pirate is better suited to finding your father, so the pirate I will remain. You may have my cabin to yourself, milady. But the bargain stays the same. When your father is found and rescued, you had best come to me laughing, your hair draping your shoulders, your clothing at your feet."

"Bastard!"

"Are we agreed?"

"I hate you!"

"Hate me, love me, have it as you will. Until I do hang, madame, you are mine!"

A sudden noise, the cocking of a pistol, sent them both flying around. Skye gasped softly, for they were no longer alone upon the sand.

Logan was there. Captain Logan.

Logan, with two of his henchmen at his side, standing before them.

"I beg to differ with you, Hawk!" Logan announced. "I intend to take her. The lady will be mine."

Roc drew Skye around behind him in an instant, holding her there. He watched Logan very warily, for the man had two pistols aimed straight toward him.

Roc's sword and knife lay in the sand. His pistols were lost to the sea and his powder was sodden anyway. He had nothing, nothing at all with which to fight.

"Move away from the lady, Hawk!"

Behind him, Skye shivered. There was no help; no help anywhere at all. Logan had all the power, and he knew it. He was elegantly dressed in a crimson velvet coat and high black boots, and his hat bore a dashing plume. Skye wondered from where he had pilfered his finery, then she did not care. His lip was curled in an evil grin, and he scratched his chin with the hook he wore for a hand.

He would kill the Hawk, she thought. With the greatest pleasure and relish, he would kill the Hawk, probably ripping him open from groin to gullet with the very hook he wore because of the Hawk's prowess with the sword.

The henchmen with him were not so dandified. They were both young men, in their early twenties perhaps, one blond, one dark. They were both barefoot, in knee breeches with no hose, and in coarse cotton shirts. They were both smiling, too, glad of this confrontation.

Logan's smiled deepened. "Dear, dear, how have we come to find you here? And engaged in this oh, so touching scene!" He laughed to his companions. "Methinks that the lady is no creature of ice! She comes in this fight to the pirate, knowing him so, so well! It seems that the Hawk did teach the lady the finer points of love, which is well enough—I shall enjoy her the more."

"You'll never touch her, Logan!" the Hawk snapped.

"Oh, I think I will," Logan replied pleasantly. "Damn you, Hawk, but you have always been a cocky bastard. The lady is behind you, and you are unarmed, and I have here six pistols and three swords at my disposal. I knew that the girl would have to come if I had her father, and that you would have to come after the girl. I hadn't expected you to fall so easily into my hands, but then the weather was helpful, was it not? And then you two were so engaged with your private affairs that you mightn't have heard the sound of a cannon explosion. Ah, dear lady! But you have done what I never could, you stole the Hawk's guard away. Thank you, my dear. I do appreciate that, and I will be happy to show you just how much!"

"No . . . !" Skye started to cry, but then she was stunned when Roc turned around and slapped her hard across the face. His strength was so great that she went crashing down to the sand, the breath knocked from her, her flesh burning.

"Shut up!" he hissed down to her. Then he turned his attention to Logan. "Take her—you want her so badly. Take her, have done with it!"

"How rude, Hawk! I *shall* take her. Your ruse will not work."

"Over my dead body, only, shall you have her!"

"That will be fine," Logan chortled.

Roc shook his head. Skye's mind continued to swim. She wanted to kill him; she abhorred the thought of Logan.

She could not begin to understand the brutality of Roc's attack.

"She's just a woman, Logan!" Roc called out. "Mine, because I took her. But she's no better or worse than any other. Having her will give you little pleasure!"

"I'll decide on that!" Logan said. "What is this, anyway! I do intend to shoot you and have her. When I tire of her, the others may have her. You will be dead. What will it matter to a corpse?"

"If you kill me, you'll never have the treasure that One-Eyed Jack took off of the Spaniard."

Logan hesitated, his eyes going very narrow against his cadaverous features. "What are you talking about?"

"Don't play games with me, Logan. Jack pirated the Spaniard, *Doña Isabella* out of Cartagena! Everyone knew about it. They talked about it on the islands for months. Why do you think I was so determined to go after the *Silver Messenger?* To take a single merchant sloop? You'd be daft, man! It was Jack I wanted, Jack that I was after. Oh, Logan, you speak of death! Jack died slowly, I tell you! He *had* taken the *Doña Isabella,* and buried all that Spanish gold. Gold that you can't even begin to imagine, Logan."

"The *Doña Isabella?* With the—the Inca gold?"

Roc smiled slowly, folding his hands over his chest. "Aye, Logan, and that's a fact. I'm the only man alive who knows where to find it."

"How do I know that?" Logan demanded.

"I'm telling you that it is so."

Skye stared up at him. She didn't know if it was the truth or not. She didn't know anything at all about him anymore. She was aware only that her choices now lay between two different hells.

Roc wanted Logan to think that she didn't matter so much to him, that she was something to be owned and used, and abused if the mood so struck him. He wanted to save his own life. He was, beyond a doubt, a scurvy bastard.

But, so help her! She could not stand the thought of Logan. What was happening?

Logan cocked his head, staring at Roc. "What is then, a play for time? I keep you alive to take me to this treasure of Jack's—then I slay you anyway. I take the girl, and I find my entertainment, then I ask Spotswood or Lord Cameron for the ransom on them both, the lady and Lord Kinsdale. Any way that one looks at it, Hawk. I win."

Roc shook his head slowly. "You don't take the girl. She's mine."

"What good will she do a corpse?"

"She's mine. She stays with me. We head on to the meeting here in North Carolina across the island and we go to someone to mediate."

"Mediate!" Logan protested.

"Aye, mediate. Blackbeard."

Logan started to laugh. "You'd give her over to Blackbeard?"

Roc shrugged. "If rumor has it right, he's fourteen young wives. He's women enough."

"They say that he's the fiercest murderer of us all."

"They say—but I know the man. He'd never harm her. And if he swore to me that he'd see her safe back to Virginia, then that is exactly what he would do."

Logan hesitated. "I won't—"

"It's the only way, Logan. It's absolutely the only way that you're going to have the pleasure of killing me and acquiring the treasure, too."

"It's too risky, Captain," the dark-haired man murmured to Logan.

"Risky! What, have you become a coward, Logan? We live at risk, we thrive on risk. Aye, come on, and it is a challenge! I dare you, Logan, take the chance!"

"Send her over to me!" Logan demanded.

Roc came over to Skye, reaching down for her. She lowered her eyes, not about to touch his hand. He had gone insane. She had been there when he had dueled with One-Eyed Jack. The pirate had died cleanly in the fight. There had never been any discussion about gold whatsoever.

Or was there gold? Did he know of it some other way? Had he come after One-Eyed Jack and the *Silver Messenger* because he *had* wanted a bigger prize? Because he needed Jack dead? She didn't know. Her head was still reeling, and she didn't trust him, not in the least.

And still, she was in love with him. Even with her face still stinging, even as she wondered about his double life, certain that he would hang. She did love him. . . .

She started to scramble to her feet on her own, but he wrenched her up and held her close to him. "No. I will not send the girl to you. We do it my way. She's mine."

Logan hesitated a long time. "I *will* kill you when we get that treasure. If you're telling me the truth, Hawk, I will shoot you clean and simple. If you've lied to me, then I'll have you staked out, and I'll rip your flesh from your body inch by inch with my hook. Savor that, Hawk. And pray that you find that treasure." He pocketed his pistols.

"I haven't lied to you."

Logan shrugged. "Then keep the girl. Enjoy her until your death." He smiled suddenly, watching Roc. "You've lost your beard, sir. Was that to please this lady?"

"It was hot," Roc said. "I do nothing to please anyone, Logan, and you know that."

" 'E looks an awful lot like the other one now," the dark-haired pirate said, eyeing Roc up and down.

"What other one?" Logan demanded.

Roc tensed; Skye felt it as his arms tightened around her.

" 'E looks like the high-and-mighty lord, like his kinsman, Cameron."

"You've seen Cameron?" Logan said sharply.

"At a distance, aboard his ship." The dark-haired fellow grinned. "Eh, Logan! 'E's trying to look like her husband; he's trying to be a gentleman."

Logan cackled, bending over. Roc's fingers tightened on Skye's arm. "Not a word!" he warned her. "Not a word!"

"I should let him skewer you!" she hissed.

"Then think, milady, of what he will do to you!" Roc warned softly. Icy trails sped along her back. He was right. Whatever her anger, he was right.

"And don't he look pretty, minus the whiskers!" Logan said at last. "Didn't work, though, eh, Captain? Not from what I heard. The lady ain't too pleasured to be with you!"

"She's pleasured enough."

"Then come on," Logan said, his eyes riveted on the both of them suspiciously. "We go to Teach, and we sign our agreements. Don't you go against me, not a hair, Hawk. I'll shoot her down where she stands if you betray me, and that will be a fact."

"I won't betray you, not on this."

"Then walk!" Logan commanded.

Roc turned, seeing the direction that Logan indicated. Skye pulled back.

"Where's my father?" she demanded of Logan. "Is he alive? Have you harmed him?"

"He's alive, and his dignity is ruffled, and perhaps he has a bruise or two. That's it, milady. Now, if you will please? There's a feast going on behind those dunes, and we'll be a part of it this night. Move, Hawk."

"I'm not going anywhere," Skye insisted.

"What?" the Hawk demanded.

"Bring me my father. I'm going to sit right here until you prove to me that he's alive."

Logan looked to Roc. "Get her moving, Hawk. Or we'll end it here and now."

"If you kill my father," Skye cried, "then I will not care."

"Move her!" Logan ordered.

Roc dipped low, striking her in the midriff with his shoulder and tossing her over. "Stop it!" she railed, beating against his back. "Stop it, put me down, don't you see that he'll kill you anyway! We have to——"

"We have to shut up!" Roc roared to her. He spun around, searching out Logan. "Lead the way, damn you, will you, please!"

Logan, cackling, stepped forward. He started out walking and Roc followed. Skye continued to protest, rising against him, until he slammed down hard on her rump portion. The action did not hurt her so much, but it reminded her that she was very poorly clad, and that her position was very precarious.

Life had become precarious.

But she didn't trust Logan, and she was certain that Roc had gone mad. He didn't intend to hand her over to Logan, but he did intend to hand her over to Teach, to Blackbeard, while he went off to get killed by Logan himself. It was insanity.

She fell silent as they walked along the dunes. It seemed that they walked forever and ever. The water, though, was always at their side. Pirates needed water, she thought. The land was death; the water was their salvation, their escape.

What was Roc planning . . . ?

"Hear the music?" Logan asked suddenly. He spoke to Roc, who grunted. Skye strained to hear, and the sounds of a fiddle came surely her way. The music grew louder and louder as they walked.

Then she pushed against Roc's shoulder and saw that they had come to a small shanty village. Sparse, crooked buildings made carelessly of thatch and logs lay about a beach where dozens of longboats had been drawn.

Dozens of spits had been set up on the beach. Joints of beef and pork turned and roasted upon the spits, along with numerous fowl and venison. Huge kegs lay about; kegs of ale, Skye thought.

There was a platform in the center of the shantytown. Edward Teach, Blackbeard, with his chinful of illustrious whiskers, sat there as if he sat upon a throne. Before him stood the fiddlers, tapping their toes to the music.

And upon the platform, a woman danced.

She was black-haired, with a lithe slim figure, a startling grace, and a full, firm bosom that rose high against her cotton blouse. She was barefoot and laughing, and she danced like a young doe, like a healthy young animal. The men watched her and cheered.

She was not the only woman there. Others sprawled about with men, leaning against kegs, falling beneath the platform, sitting on the porches of the shanties.

Logan stood behind Roc and smiled at Skye as she lay high against her husband's shoulders.

"The ball, milady, the pirates' grand ball! Welcome. We do not often dare to come so brazenly together on the mainland, but then certain figures of power in North Carolina have been known to turn deaf ears to the sounds of our musicians! Isn't it grand? Not many silks, not many satins, and the petticoats are limited, but we do enjoy ourselves! Welcome!"

There was something about his eyes so hideous that she shivered.

Roc spun around to face Logan. "Remember," Logan warned him. "You play anything other than straight with Blackbeard, and I will shoot and kill this girl who means so little to you!"

"I'll play it fair. Go."

"You go. I'll follow behind with my pistol cocked and aimed for the lady's back. And don't forget. A good number of the men you see about will be off of my ship."

"I'll remember," Roc said. He started to walk. Skye clung to him. Drunken men pointed their way. Some laughed. Some called out. "It's the Hawk! It's the Hawk, and 'e's brought a lady here, can you imagine." Chortles rose up, ringing upon the air. "Damme, but the man would dare anything, anything at all."

"My pistol's aimed at her back, remember!" Logan said.

Roc kept walking. As they neared the platform, Blackbeard's attention was drawn to them, and he leaped to his feet. "What? Ho, there, it's the Hawk, is it not? Aye, and with the lass I was ever so charmed to meet as of late!" His big, bellowing voice rose over the music and over the sounds of the dance. Blackbeard pulled his pipe from his mouth and reached for Roc's hand. "Welcome! We'd thought you'd avoid this place, since you don't much care for the Carolinas, sir! Do you see my Carlotta? My latest 'wife'—she dances for me now. Sit and watch, enjoy. Now there's some warm blood for you, me boy!"

Logan stepped around Roc. "We've come for you to be mediator. The Hawk is my prisoner. He's to take me to a treasure, if you see the girl home. We've agreed it, sworn upon it."

Roc set Skye down upon her feet. Blackbeard gave her a captivating smile. "Lady Kinsdale—no, Cameron, I've heard. Anyway, my lady, you're most welcome here! A flower among us dregs of humanity, and I do mean it!"

"Teach, will you swear to me to see her home?" Roc demanded.

"With my blood. You carry out your bargain, and I'll see her home. I've no wish to hurt a woman, sir, of that you are well aware."

"But *he* comes with me!" Logan cried. "I want it agreed in blood!"

"Raise your arm!" Blackbeard commanded to Roc.

Roc lifted his arm. Blackbeard took his knife and Skye could not help but cry out as the pirate slashed her husband's arm. A trail of blood oozed out. Roc did not protest; he didn't say a word. Blackbeard slashed his own arm and placed it next to Roc's. "Sealed in blood. You owe Logan, and by my honor, I owe you. Now tell me, Hawk, how did you let this scurvy piece of dog meat get the best of you?"

"There's no excuse, Teach. He just did."

Blackbeard swirled around to Skye. "Come, sit with me, we'll drink together.

"I've no wish to drink with you or any of your kind!" Skye spat out.

"A feisty one, yes, I do say!" Blackbeard laughed. He leaned low against her. "Girl, I'm all the hope you've got here, do you understand?" He raised his voice then. "Hawk! You come, too."

"He's my prisoner, bound by blood—" Logan began.

"Yes, but this is my party, my pirate's ball, and I'll not have you leaving with my guests, not tonight. Hawk, you play out your devil's bargain in the morning, and God and Satan be with you both! For now, come with the girl, and watch my beloved dance!"

He pulled the two of them along to join him on his platform. Skye was dragged down beside him on the one side and Roc on the other. The fury of the music increased to a tempestuous tempo. The girl danced ever more swiftly.

A mug was pressed into Skye's hands. She looked into the drunken eyes of a middle-aged, buxom woman with her bodice torn in two. The woman smiled and started to laugh. "Dearie, dearie, a lady! We've a lady among us! Let us take her, Blackbeard, and she'll not be a lady much longer, I'll warrant."

The woman reached for Skye, tearing at her bodice, Skye screamed, trying to draw away. Her chair fell over. Her head cracked against the platform, and she was dazed.

"No!" There was another sound of thunder as a second chair fell back. Roc was on his feet. He came to stand before her, his booted feet planted hard, his hands upon his hips. "She's mine; she's mine this night, and she's Blackbeard's promise of safe conduct when this night is over. No one touches her. No one but me. She's mine, and 'tis my night, and I'll have her in peace from the lot of you scurvies and whores!"

He bent down and lifted her from the floor. "No!" she whispered in desperation.

He barely glanced her way but turned to Blackbeard. "This is your party, Captain Teach! I'm your guest this night, and would request quarters, sir, if I may!"

The pirate Blackbeard laughed and nodded. "Aye, Captain Hawk! If it's a dead man you're to be, you should have this night! Every man gets a last request before the gallows!"

"Wait!" Logan protested. "I did not say—"

"Tomorrow, Logan, you may take the Hawk. Your prisoner, sir! Tonight, he gets his last request!"

Blackbeard indicated a building fifty yards from the platform on the beach. Roc leaped down from the platform with her in his arms and began striding toward the waterfront shanty. Pirates and their doxies applauded and laughed.

"She's a tough one, Captain!"

"Aye, there, lad, feisty but fun!" Roc agreed. Skye hit him, slapping him just as hard as he had slapped her against the cheek. She was just barely aware of the guffaws rising from the pirates sprawled about them with their half-clad drunken whores.

"Take her, Captain!"

Roc, staring at her with fire in his eyes, quickly replied, "I intend to, lad, I intend to!" He lowered her down. Skye screamed, shocked and alarmed as she fell hard upon the sand. He bounded down upon her, seizing her hair in a rough grip, holding her still to his pleasure as he ravaged her lips with his mouth, all the while raking his hands over her breasts.

Laughter arose, whistles and catcalls. He leaped up, jerking her back to her feet, then forcefully into his arms. "I intend to this very minute, lads!" he cried.

"No . . . !" she gasped. Her lips were swollen and bruised and she had never seen such reckless disregard in him before. She gritted her teeth and beat against him in a sudden, desperate fear.

"No!"

"Shut up! Damn you, shut up!"

His eyes lit upon hers, silver and hard. "Open your mouth again and I swear you shall learn something of brute force this very night!"

Skye opened her mouth. She shivered uncontrollably but fell silent to the warning in his eyes.

And Roc dashed up the steps to the shanty and kicked open the door. She was alone again with him, with the pirate, with the lord. With her lover, with her husband.

Alone . . .

With the very devil himself . . .

17

OC KICKED THE DOOR CLOSED AND SET SKYE down. For a second she remained perfectly still, for shadows fell all around them, and she was frightened of a terrible darkness falling.

Darkness did not come. It was barely afternoon, she thought. She spun around, stared at Roc, and moved away from him, running quickly to the wall, setting her back against it.

He glanced her way with a certain disdain and fell against the door himself, sinking down before it. His eyes closed wearily, then shot open and stared at her with immense displeasure. He pointed a finger at her. "You! You little bitch! You're going to get us both killed!"

Skye stared at him wide-eyed. "Me! You've lost your mind!"

"I am grabbing at straws to keep us going—"

"*Straws!* There is no treasure!" she hissed.

His lashes fell briefly over his eyes. "That's my problem. I want you out of here. Blackbeard may be many things, but his reputation for cruelty has been deliberately exaggerated. He will keep his word to me. Tomorrow he will see that you are delivered back to Virginia, where you belonged in the first place."

"Then Logan takes you!" she exclaimed.

The anger faded from his eyes and a slow smile touched his lips. "Will you care then, love? You were waiting to attend my hanging, remember? What difference will it make? Alas, you won't get to witness the deed, but the end result will be the same."

"Don't!" Skye murmured.

"Don't what, milady?"

Skye didn't reply. She shook her head and backed against the far wall herself, staring at him. He could not die! And she could not trust herself to speak. She lowered her head, swallowing tightly against the tears that burned hotly behind her eyes. She looked about the room. Sand dusted the floor; there was a plain wooden table with a single candle in a brass holder and two rickety chairs beneath it, and against the far wall was a bed of straw with a gray blanket thrown haphazardly upon it.

"Elegant accommodations," Roc murmured with a certain humor, "but the best that Blackbeard has to offer, I'm afraid. He's a man who falls in love often enough; he's glad to give us the night."

She didn't respond to his words but jumped back up and pushed away from wall and came to kneel down before him. "This is insane! What are you doing? We must escape from here somehow!"

"We?" He arched both brows. She wasn't a foot away from him. Her hair trailed in sunset tendrils over her shoulders and her breasts pushed against the fabric of her bodice and her eyes were earnest and sparkling with emotion. He longed to touch her, but he did not. He allowed his hands to dangle idly over his kneecaps. "We? My love, there is no need for you to escape. Your safety is guaranteed. In certain matters, there is no man you can trust so thoroughly as a rogue such as Blackbeard."

"I can't go back without you!"

"Why ever not? You'll miss a hanging, of course, but you'll live anyway, I'm sure."

"Stop it! Stop being so—nonchalant!"

"What would you have me be?"

"Concerned! Sir, you are to die!"

He sighed deeply. The temptation was too great. He reached out and fingered one of the silky soft curls. Not even the seawater could damage the softness of her hair.

She did not wrench away from him. He went further, and stroked his knuckles over her cheek. "Will you care?" he asked her softly. "This morning you were anxious to see me boiled in oil! Skinned alive. Ah, yes, that is what Logan promised, I think, if I did not lead him to the treasure."

"And there is no treasure!" she said desperately.

"What makes you so sure?"

"I was there the day you killed Jack!"

"Ah, yes, of course. Thank God Logan wasn't about," he muttered.

"Then there is no treasure!"

He shrugged. "Oh, there is a treasure. There really was a *Doña Isabella* that sailed out of Cartagena, and it was supposedly laden with a new cache of Indian gold. And rumor has it that Jack did seize her, steal the cargo, and scuttle the ship. The treasure is supposedly buried somewhere."

"But you haven't the faintest idea of where!" Skye moaned.

He was still smiling at her. Smiling ridiculously. There was sensual silver laughter and tenderness in his eyes; his touch against her was gentle and provocative. His fingertips just moved across her flesh. She wanted to hold him, to cling to him. He had lied to her, he had used her, he had made a fool of her, and he was leading a despicable life, but she loved him. She could fight it; she could deny her heart. But she could not change the emotion deep inside.

"You do care!" he whispered.

"I don't—"

"You do!" he insisted, and then his touch was not so light as he reached out, sweeping her hard and full into his arms. He kissed her again, but this kiss was no hard seizure as it had been outside; this kiss was fierce and demanding but infinitely tender. His lips fell upon her with consuming desire, his tongue teased her mouth, grazed her teeth, sought deep, honeyed recesses. He held her with tenderness, too. His arms were ever ardent, but gentle. His hand cupped her cheek, his fingers trailed her throat as he held her to his kiss. His hands molded her breast, and her waist, and then he broke away, gasping for breath, holding her close. He did love her, too, she thought. He was a rogue, a terror. Demanding, autocratic as the pirate, and as the lord, but his will was fierce and could not be broken, only altered by his own choice, and perhaps, just perhaps, gentled by love.

His eyes probed hers feverishly. "You *do* care!" he repeated.

She moistened her lips, lowering her lashes. She only dared whisper so much upon this occasion. "If I am with child, sir, I'd just as soon he have a living sire."

His smile deepened. "Ah. So that is why you have not betrayed me!"

"Betrayed you?" She lay against his arm, grateful for the curious moment of peace.

"To Logan. He still does not know that Lord Cameron and the Silver Hawk are one and the same."

She swallowed hard, not caring to be reminded of the fact herself. She shrugged. "What difference does it make? He plans to kill the Hawk. He would be only too pleased, I'm sure, to discover that he has killed Lord Cameron, too."

He carefully set her down and stood, pacing the room, his hands upon his hips. "It makes a great deal of difference. If Blackbeard were to know—"

"Your crew is all in on this, I imagine?" Skye interrupted curtly. Robert! Robert Arrowsmith had known all along that her husband and her lover were one and the same. All of them!

And still, there wasn't a single man among his crew she would like to see dangle from a noose!

He paused, casting her a frown, then nodding. "Yes, they all know both of my identities. But these fellows here, they do not. And, thank God, you did not see fit to inform them."

"I'm not a fool."

"You were acting like one out there."

"Because he's going to kill you! Then he'll probably kill my father, too, for good measure!"

Roc shook his head. "Your father is worth too much."

"Oh? Amazing, the pirate Hawk let me go for not so much as a farthing! Perhaps my father is worthless as well."

"The pirate Hawk let you go for not so much as a farthing, my love, to show you not that you were worthless, but rather worth far much more than gold and silver to him."

She stared at him incredulously. Then she saw the tug at the corner of his lip and she came quickly to her feet, hands on her hips, defying him. "You are a liar, sir!"

"All right, so I was deathly afraid of your self-importance becoming exaggerated beyond all measure. I knew that you would return home and discover yourself married and that you would try every trick and wile in the world to escape your husband. And I, milady, was already deeply in love, and not about to let you go."

"You're still a liar!" she accused him.

"And if I'm not?"

"If—you're not?" she whispered.

"What if it's true? What if I really do love you, Skye Cameron? Can you spare just a touch of emotion for an old friend, an old lover?"

She whirled around, not wanting to meet his eyes. "You know that I would be distressed to see you die."

"Ah, for a child. But what about yourself?" He came behind her, setting his hands upon her shoulders. "A child would be nice," he whispered. "An heir to Cameron Hall . . . when I am skinned alive and then shot dead and left for the carrion!"

"Stop it!" she hissed, but she did not turn around.

"Come here!" he told her.

She held still.

"Skye, come here," he repeated, and she did not know what drew her around, but she did turn. And she came to him, too, standing before him, not touching him, but looking up into his eyes. She did not know what emotion was betrayed in her, but he touched her shoulders and bent to touch her lips very lightly. Then he kissed her forehead and drew her against him.

"You do care!" he assured her.

She laid her palms against his chest and pushed him from her and looked at him gravely. "I care, yes, Roc, I care! But I cannot accept you, or what you've done. I've no desire to see you hang, but I wonder at the innocents you've robbed and plundered, and what has created the whole empire you rule at Bone Cay. But for now, I do not think that I can leave you—"

"There is no question that you will leave me," he said harshly. "I will have you safe."

"I don't want you to die! And Logan will kill you, and heinously so, when he discovers there is no treasure!"

He shrugged. "Perhaps I will find treasure. Accidents do happen."

"That would be a miracle!" Skye murmured.

"My men are out there, you know."

Her eyes widened. She had forgotten that, a fact so important that it *was* nearly a miracle. Roc's ship—rather, the Hawk's ship—lay somewhere out on the other side of the island. Unless the storm had torn her to shreds. But Skye was certain that the Hawk and his pirate crew had weathered much worse.

"They'll rescue you—us!" she said happily. "They'll come in here and . . ." Her voice trailed away. He was looking at her sadly.

His crew could not just sail in, she realized. There were many captains here, at Blackbeard's pirates' "ball." More men than the Hawk's crew could possibly meet with any chance of victory.

And it would still leave her father as Logan's prisoner. An enraged Logan, at that.

"There is no miracle to be had!" she whispered brokenly.

"Yes, perhaps there is," he said.

There was a sudden hammering upon the door. "Who is that?" Skye murmured with alarm.

"I don't know. Get over there, on the bed," Roc said swiftly.

"What?" she demanded, frowning.

"Damn you, milady, must you question everything? Get over there!"

She must not have responded quickly enough to suit him, for she found herself flying forcefully across the room and landing hard upon the straw bedding. He was quickly down beside her, gathering her into his arms. Alarmed and furious at his treatment, she struggled against him, kicking out madly. "Damn you, you have lost your mind!" she cried.

His hand landed hard over hers. "Shut up!" he ordered her. "Come in!" he called out.

Outraged, she struggled against him. The door opened and one of the pirates' doxies stood there, dark hair spilling over her enormous breasts, her eyes dark and flashing and her very red lips curled in amusement as she watched Skye struggling.

"Leave her, Hawk!" The girl laughed. "I could provide far more entertainment than this one!"

He shook his head and smiled broadly. "She loves me, Leticia. Honest—she loves me truly. Right, love?" Skye tried to bite his hand. He laughed, a pirate's laugh, and she realized that she was inadvertently playing right along with his ruse.

Leticia shrugged. "Every man to his choice, Captain! But remember if you tire of her . . . you need only call my name." She walked more fully into the room. Roc regretfully pulled himself up from Skye, but dragged her along with him. He held her close, his hand nonchalantly over her breast. She was a possession here, and safe because he had claimed her as his, an *important* possession.

And one he chose to allow to live on beyond him.

"I came to see if you are hungry." She smiled beguilingly and Skye thought that she was really very pretty with her large breasts, trim waist, and dark eyes. Leticia. Roc knew her, he knew her by name. No, the Hawk knew her. Skye wondered just how well the Hawk knew her, and she felt ill. This was insane. She loved him. She despised him. She could not bear his death, and yet she hated this untenable position.

"Hungry . . . for food," Leticia murmured.

"Ravenous," Roc told her.

"I will bring something." She came very close to them both, kneeling by the bedding. She watched Skye with a searing curiosity. Skye raised her chin and the dark-haired woman chuckled huskily. "Ice fires can burn hot, so they say," she murmured, and laughed again. Then her voice lowered and she spoke very softly to Roc alone. "Blackbeard wants to see you. Alone. He thinks that the two of you should talk."

"Does he?" Roc said.

Leticia nodded fervently. "He hates Logan. Always has hated him. You know that."

Roc shrugged. "But Blackbeard is on his honor here. We came to him as a mediator between us."

Leticia tossed back her dark hair. "Blackbeard is his own law, and his own honor. He will do what he chooses, and that will be the honorable thing. If men say that it is cruel and treacherous, he will be glad of it. He savors what they say, as you know well enough. If a man fears the terror of Blackbeard's wrath, he is quick to lay down his arms. You must understand that power, Hawk!"

Roc nodded gravely. "All right. I'll speak with him."

Leticia looked to Skye with amusement. "Not now. I've not come to interrupt anything!" She laughed again. "Later. When darkness has fallen, then I'll come, and I'll bring you to him."

"All right," Roc agreed. Leticia smiled, and whirled around like a young doe to leave them. When the door closed behind her, Skye elbowed Roc with all of her might. She was gratified to feel him release her and grunt painfully.

"Damn you, Skye Cameron!" he swore to her, staggering to his feet.

"Damn me! You tossed me about like so much baggage, and seized hold of me in front of that—that woman! I am not your whore, Captain, and I—"

"Yes, you are," he told her, his tone sharp with warning. He came over to her and she started to back away, but he caught her arm and wrenched her against him. "Here, milady, you are my whore, a cherished whore, and therein lies your safety. So go ahead, scream and fight and lash out, it makes no difference. You will obey me here, or sorely regret it, I promise."

She ground down hard on her teeth, wishing she could think of something horrible enough to say to him. He released her, and as he did, there came a subtle tap on the door again. Leticia slipped back in. "Food, Captain Hawk. And"—she paused, turning to Skye and curtsying with mock respect—"of course, for you, too, Lady Cameron! The finest, of course. The very finest."

Skye inclined her head toward the woman. "Thank you," she said softly. Her gentle tones seemed to confuse Leticia. She stared at Skye a moment longer, then shrugged and turned back to Roc, setting the tray she carried upon the table. "From Blackbeard's own supply of dark rum, Captain. And for the lady—" She glanced Skye's way quickly again. "For the lady he sends Burgundy off of the French packet *St. Louis*. And there's roast meat and bread, and all the very best cuts, I assure you!"

"Thank you very much, Leticia," the Hawk said. He offered her a wry, grateful smile. Skye felt her stomach twist, for in the midst of all this, he was still a strikingly handsome man, charismatic as the Hawk, charismatic as Lord Cameron.

She lowered her head slightly. Then she lifted her eyes, realizing that the woman was still watching her. "Thank you, Leticia," she repeated. Leticia did not say anything to Skye. She nodded to her, then looked to Roc. "I'll be back when the others are in drunken stupors, when I can bring you to Blackbeard."

She left them. Roc looked to Skye; then, every inch the gentleman, he pulled out her chair for her. He helped her into it before taking the wine from the tray and pouring out a pewter mug of it for her. He sat down himself, lifting a red cloth from the food and then looking to the rum flask provided for him. "Dark Caribbean," he murmured, and drew deeply on it. "It's a fine brew," he told Skye.

"A fine brew!" she exclaimed. "At a time like this—"

"At a time like this," he muttered. "I'm sure that it's an exceptionally fine brew." He drew on it deeply, eyeing her with wary, narrowed eyes.

She didn't look at him but at the tray of food. The meat did smell delicious. Roc set down the rum flask and skewered her a piece of beef with a table knife, setting it upon her plate. "Eat," he told her.

"I can't eat—"

"I'm sure that you can. We haven't had a bite in a day, and I'm famished, if you are not."

He took a rib bone and plowed into it with gusto. Skye watched him and realized that she was starving. It was not so difficult to enjoy the pirate's feast before her. The beef was succulent and delicious and flavored with salt and peppercorns.

The wine, too, was good.

Skye sipped it, watching Roc. "What does this mean?" she asked him. "With —Leticia."

He shrugged. "It means that Blackbeard wants One-Eyed Jack's treasure."

"But there is no treasure."

"There *is* a treasure."

"But not a treasure that you can find!" she wailed.

He set down his food and drank deeply from the rum flask again. "There is a treasure, milady, and that for the moment shall suffice."

"And that for the moment shall suffice!" Impatiently she stood, and her chair fell behind her. "Don't you take that tone with me, Lord Hawk, or whoever you would be today! I am in this, too—"

"And you do not know the rules!" He was up as well, coming around the table to her. She was suddenly drawn into his arms. His fingers raked into her hair and he drew her head back, searching her eyes. "You do not know the rules, my love; you have only your reckless courage, and that will not serve us now! For the love of God, milady, pay heed to me!"

His hold upon her was so very tight. She smiled very slowly, sensually, wistfully. "It is just, sir, that in truth, I would not see you killed."

He stared at her intently, then he drew her to him, burying his head against her throat, emitting some deep-felt sound of passion.

"Skye, Skye," he murmured, "my brave, beautiful love! God! That I could but have you safely away from here this very moment!"

"But I am not away!" she whispered. "And I cannot see you go."

He lifted her up then into his arms. His eyes locked with hers and he strode with her to the crude straw mattress upon the floor with its scanty blanket. He laid her there with tenderness, coming beside her. His mouth covered hers. His kiss ran passionate, and deep, and it ignited her fears and her desires, and she knew that she wanted to cling to him forever. She could not let him go. She wanted him. She wanted to make love to him. She wanted to hold on to the splendor and glory of all that raged between them. She had not forgiven him. . . .

But she had not fallen out of love with him, either, and it seemed that every second now death came closer to their doorway.

He pulled away from her. He saw her eyes, wide and teal and steady upon his. Her lips parted slightly, damp with his kiss. She offered her arms out to him again and he groaned, holding her close.

"I want to make love to you," he whispered. "I want to lie down by crystal waters, with the fragrance of flowers, with the sun overhead burning down upon our flesh, or with the moon offering a gentle glow. I want to give you a soft mattress and silken sheets, or an Eden of sweet earth. I want to love you, and not upon this bare and ugly straw. . . ."

She touched his hair and stroked it from his face. She met his eyes with her smile wistful, her gaze both damp and aflame. "It is Eden, it is paradise," she told him with all of her heart. "Where you are, dear sir, it is paradise, for that is what you create inside of me, within my soul."

He caught her fingers, and kissed them. He met her eyes again. "I do love you, milady. With all of my heart, I love you. As Lord Cameron, as the Silver Hawk, as any man, myself, I love you, and I will do so until my dying day."

She touched his face. His fingers dropped to her bodice and he pulled upon the delicate satin strings until her breasts fell free to his touch. He savored them with his touch, with the sweet intensity of his teeth and tongue and lips. His hands ravaged her thighs, teasing, stroking. He entered into the core of her, and once his touch came so intimately to her, the fires within her soared, and she arched against him, desperate for more of the splendor that churned its fine sweet storm throughout the length of her.

He was the Hawk, he was her husband, and there was no fear any longer that the one might be recognized as the other.

He stood, and shed his clothing, and came back down beside her, stripping away what remained of her gown.

Shadows fell more deeply. Night was falling. Skye did not fear the darkness. He was with her. His hands were upon her. His kiss seared her flesh, and made her warm.

She rose on a wind of fate and glory, desire lapping against her flesh, the fever of it entering her fingers and her lips. She bathed his shoulders with her kiss, she raked his spine with her nails.

She whispered to him of her longing. Of the thing that swirled inside of her. Of the way that she needed him, needed him so desperately to appease the yearning. . . .

And it was paradise. There was no coarse straw, no sandy blanket, no shanty walls around them. The scent of the earth was with them, the music of their heartbeats rose.

Her flesh was silk, and his was splendor. The sun was in his fingertips, spiraling warmth that caressed her naked flesh. Rays that fell against her spine and stroked and rounded her hip, rays that entered intimately, deep, deep within her. . . .

She no longer whispered, she cried out. She strained against him with urgency, her hips undulating to the demanding rhythm of his thrust, her limbs locked around him. She soared and swept ever higher into Eden, then she called out his name, shuddering as the force of his seed racked her again and again. She felt the absolute constriction of his body, the explosion within her, and then she fell softly. Eden was gone, but she drifted on clouds, and those clouds left her sadly satiated and deeply in love upon the raw straw and the sandy blanket. It didn't matter. His arms were still around her. He held her. He stroked her hair.

And that was the paradise of it. Distant and far, as paradise might seem.

"If something does happen—"

"Shush!" she told him, rolling to cover his lips with her fingers.

He drew her hand away and cradled her to his chest, massaging his fingers through the hair at her nape. "Listen to me, Skye, I beg you. I do not believe that it is so simple to conceive an heir, and yet I tell you now that if I have a prayer tonight, it is that you might already carry my child."

"Roc—"

"No, please. I am an eternal optimist, my love—and an eternal rogue, I suppose you might say. I will fight Logan with whatever I might have until the very end. But in case—"

"Roc—"

"No! Listen to me!" Passionately, intently, he rolled her beneath him, demanding that she heed him. "You promise me this, milady, whatever else may come, whatever else may be. If we have created a child, swear to me that you will hold well to his or her heritage."

"Roc—"

"Cameron Hall. The land. The estate."

"Stop it, please!" Skye cried. "You speak of bricks and a handful of earth when—"

"No, lady, no!" he protested gravely. "It is not land, not brick. It is the Tidewater, it is a—dream! It is where my forebears came to live, to find their destinies. It is everything that I am, milady. It is my family. It is the future, and it is the past. There is honor there in the way that we have lived, in the Eden that we have carved from the earth. Promise me that come what may, you will preserve it!"

He was so very tense! Death lay all around them in the shanty, in the night, and he was desperate that she keep his land. She wanted to protest again, but she could not. "I promise."

"A promise you will keep, love."

"I have kept every promise that I have ever given you!" she whispered passionately.

He kissed her lips. "So you have."

"I vow it, Roc. With all of my heart, I vow it," she swore.

He ruffled her hair, falling down beside her, cradling her closer. "It is always beautiful there," he murmured.

She smiled beside him. "Always. The days are not too hot because of the river."

"And winter is never too cold, because of the river."

"The grass is green and blue and rich."

"And the fields are verdant."

He kissed her forehead. "There's an old oak there, down by the river, secluded by other trees and the gardens. The water rushes by almost silently. The leaves are shields against too much sunlight. There are pines there, too, and the earth is moist and soft and giving. It is, I think, Eden, here on earth."

"Is it?" Skye murmured.

"It is. My father used to take my mother there. He told me once. When she died, he told me how she had loved to come there, and how she had laughed. And what great difficulty he'd had convincing her that none could see her if she shed her clothes. And she said then that they were like Adam and Eve in the garden, and he promised her that there were no serpents in his Eden."

"Only wickedly seductive Camerons!" Skye murmured.

His arms tightened about her, then he suddenly bolted up.

"What is it?" Skye demanded.

He didn't answer her, but drew the blanket around her. He reached for his breeches just as a quick knock sounded, and was still stepping into them even as the door opened. Leticia slipped quietly into the room.

Skye held the blanket close to her breast, watching as Leticia drew a finger to her lips, beckoning for Roc to come with her. Skye thought that the woman looked at her curiously where she lay silent upon the straw, but she could not tell. Shadows filled the room.

"I'll be back!" Roc promised her softly. Skye watched him go to the woman and whisper something to her. He glanced Skye's way. "She'll come back to light the candle."

Skye smiled, catching her lower lip between her teeth as she fell back against the straw. She watched them leave, then she closed her eyes, shivering.

It had not been a frightening place when he had been with her.

It had, for a time, been created a paradise.

But he was gone now, and it had become a shanty, chilled by sea breezes, covered in sand, barren and stark.

Skye rolled upon her stomach and rested her head upon her arm, exhausted and yet keenly aware that she couldn't be so, that she needed desperately to think. This was a world of madness. She could be safe from it, but Roc would sail away to certain death, and she could not let him. And Logan still held her father. It was the worst nightmare she might have ever imagined.

Skye was dimly aware that the door opened again. She wasn't worried. Leticia was coming back to light the candle. Skye was so deeply enmeshed in her worries that little could have moved her then, for she knew that she could not leave Roc, not ever; she hadn't known that she had taken vows when she did, but there was but one thing that could part them, and that was death.

Her father! Where did Logan have him? If Blackbeard decided to help them, Logan would still have her father. . . .

She frowned suddenly, aware that no candle was being lit, that Leticia was murmuring no words to her, mocking or other. She started to spin around but halted as something cold and steel touched upon her bare back.

"Be very still, my dear."

Skye froze instantly. It was Logan. He spoke softly in the night, but the evil and menace in his tone was unmistakable.

The cold steel skimmed along her naked back from her nape to the small of her spine. Logan chuckled softly. "Once I had fingers, milady, and now you feel what is there, a hook for a hand, fashioned of metal. There is ice where once there was warmth. And still, it is an interesting caress, is it not? Feel my touch, lady. Brood upon it, if you will."

She bit down on the flesh inside her jaw, trying hard not to scream as she felt the hook skim over her again. He touched her with the curve of the hook until he came to the end of her spine, then he teased her flesh with the rough edge of the hook, a touch that hinted of drawn blood any second.

He did not want her blood, she realized. He wanted the Hawk's blood. He only wanted her because she was the Hawk's.

"Have you enjoyed your evening, my dear? Your last night with Captain Hawk. It's a pity that he cannot be trusted. He did try to buy your freedom, but I'm afraid that I can't let that be. If Blackbeard takes you, then I've nothing left to use against him. Blackbeard is a greedy man. And this time, he cannot have it all. Turn around. Look at me."

"No!"

He caught her arm with his good hand and wrenched her over. She would have fought him in a frenzy, but his hook landed instantly against her throat and she went still, staring at him with hate and venom afire in her eyes.

Then she realized that he was not alone. Two of his men stood silently, just inside the door. How many of them were behind it? Would Roc come back and stumble into a trap? She needed to scream, she needed to warn him, she needed to call help. She didn't know Logan's intentions, but she had to warn Roc that he was here.

Logan chuckled huskily, drawing her attention back to his face. She met his eyes once again, and drew breath to scream.

"Don't! Don't do it!" The point of the hook lay against her jugular. Slowly, her breath escaped her. She could not scream.

He smiled slowly and idly drew the curve of his hook down the length of her throat to her collarbone, then taunting, a curious caress indeed, over the rise of her breast. The hook continued downward, dislodging her blanket, leaving her bare to his assessment. She bit down ever harder upon her lip to keep from panic. A scream rose and bubbled in her throat, but as his eyes returned to hers, she knew that he would not hesitate to slit her open with the weapon he wore upon his severed wrist.

"That's right, love, quiet!" he whispered, and laughed. Something of regret passed over his eyes. "Milady, how I'd like you now, this very minute, alive and attuned to sensation by the most unique and tender stroke of my adoring . . . fingers. I'd like your Hawk to enter into his room and find you touched and filled by his dearest enemy. Alas! What a pity that I cannot do so."

Relief escaped her in a long gasp. His smile, however, was not reassuring.

"Nay, lady, first I must take you to my ship. You are so concerned for your father, eh? Well, now, perhaps we should let the old man watch, too. That's where we shall capture the Hawk for real, milady. And when we see that he is coming, that is when I shall have you, in bold light, upon the deck. You'll feel the true kiss of this steel, my love, and he'll know that I'll use it against you in truth when I am done."

"Perhaps he will not come," Skye said.

"I think that he will."

"But he won't. You've seen him with me. He demands things because that is his way, but I'm nothing to him, not really. He's women everywhere, what is one more, or one less?"

Logan sat back on his haunches, his eyes alight with a leering humor. His hook raked around the fullness of her breast as he answered, "Lady, you are worth your weight in gold. That was long ago decided. You are worth even more to me. He will live to rue the day that he caused me to wear this hook. Now, get up!"

He stood, and reached down with his good hand, wrenching her to her feet. His eyes assessed the length of her in the shadows, and she had never felt more violated. From the doorway, she felt his men, staring at her, too.

She jerked her hand free. "I cannot come like this!" she told him. "Let me dress." She bent down to retrieve the tattered remnants of her dress. Logan's foot fell upon the material. "We haven't time," he said harshly. "Morgan, toss her the cloak."

A woolen garment fell her way. Skye retrieved it quickly, grating her teeth as she quickly slipped the scratchy wool cape around her shoulders. She drew it close about her and stared at Logan again, waiting.

He bowed deeply to her. "My dear?"

She passed him by. The two men at the doorway stepped aside, opening the door for her. They were all behind her.

Skye quickly stepped out the doorway of the little shanty.

Fires still burned upon the sand, warmth against the night and the sea breezes. There was no music, though, no one danced. Men and women still lay sprawled about, but they lay in sleep, some snoring, some dead to the world in drunken stupors.

Logan, she thought, had no more than the two men with him. They were all behind her.

She hurried down the few steps to the sand, screamed as loudly as she could, and started to run.

"Catch her, you fools!" Logan shouted.

She didn't know where to go, nor did it matter. She couldn't possibly have navigated a course in the darkness.

And it was dark. Away from the fires, the night closed in. The sky met the sea, and the wilderness beyond the beach. There were more shanties, more ramshackle and makeshift homes and buildings.

Roc would be within one, she thought. Bargaining with Blackbeard.

But where?

She couldn't pause to determine that fact, she had to run. "Help me! Help me! Someone, for the love of God, help me!" she shrieked.

There were various stirrings about, but few heeded her cries.

The pirates were accustomed to hearing pleas for mercy—and equally accustomed to ignoring them, Skye thought bleakly.

She whirled around. Logan's men were almost upon her.

She was losing time, racing around the shanty buildings on the beach. They could trap her that way. They were trying to do so right then, she thought. "Take her! Take her from the left!" one of them cried, and another waved, running around to encircle the building.

Skye screamed again, and turned to flee toward the beach.

Her legs flying, she raced past the platform where Blackbeard had held his pirates' court that day. She went onward, seeing that a startled Leticia stood upon the steps to the shanty where she had spent the day. "Tell the Hawk!" Skye screamed.

Leticia jumped back and Skye realized that the men were almost upon her. She tore on down the beach, her lungs afire, her heart thundering, her calves cramping mercilessly. She could hear the sound of the waves rushing up on the beach, beckoning to her. Their dark invitation called to her.

The sea! she thought.

The night was frightening, the darkness unimaginable, but it might well be her only hope. If she could strike out and shed the cape, she could swim. She didn't know if her strength would hold out against the currents, but she had no other choice. She had only to pass the shadows of twin palms and plunge into the waves to find freedom.

Suddenly a figure stepped out from the palms. She could not stop running, her momentum was so great.

She collided with Logan. She screamed; his arms came around and they fell hard into the sand together. They rolled and she kicked and fought desperately.

"Logan!"

The thunder of the Hawk's voice interrupted their wild fight. Logan looked up, and Skye tried to dislodge him again. He was wiry and strong. He had his hook, and he carried a sharp and lethal knife. He caught her about the waist with his arm, dragging her to her feet. He stared back toward the fires of the night.

Skye, sobbing for breath, tossed back her hair. He was there, the Hawk was there, feet wide apart, his hands on his hips, defying Logan. A sword dangled now from his scabbard. There was a lineup of men behind him, Blackbeard among them.

"Let her go!" Roc demanded.

Logan laughed. With his good hand he pulled open her cape, placed the blade squarely against her heart, upon her bared flesh.

"I've warned you, Hawk. Back off, or she will die!"

"Let her go!" Roc demanded again. "This fight is between us. It is between men! Don't drag the girl in!"

"Ah, because she's a part of you, eh, Hawk? Like my hand was a part of my body? Severed now! Back off, Hawk, and I mean it! My knife shivers with the beat of her heart. I'll slice it out for you, Hawk, so help me God! You want her back so badly? I'll slice her heart from her body, and hand to you, sir, still beating."

"What the bloody hell is this?" Blackbeard demanded. "Now, Logan, you were with me, we were all agreed upon the details! I got the girl, and you took the Hawk."

"You're a slimy, scurvy backstabber, Edward Teach, and that's what you are!" Logan called out.

"Now, sir, I take offense at that!" Blackbeard bellowed.

"Take all the offense that you want. I'm leaving in me boat with the girl. If one of you makes a move, it's her heart, and that's a fact. Are we understood?"

No one moved. Least of all Skye. The razor-sharp edge of his blade just scratched her flesh and she felt faint. He meant it. Logan would carve out her heart without a moment's thought.

"You move now!" he ordered her harshly. He jerked her, dragging her toward the water's edge. She heard the sound of oars and knew that Logan's longboats awaited them.

"I'll be on me deck!" Logan called out to the Hawk. "You want her alive, you row out alone. I'll be waiting to see you, Hawk. I'll be waiting right on the deck, and she'll be with me. She'll be right in my arms. You come, and she lives!"

Seawater, cold with the night, rose over Skye's ankles. They backed against Logan's longboat. His men were in it, she saw from the corner of her eye. The two who had come after her, and another two, who had probably remained with the boat, ready and awaiting his command. Logan was no fool; neither did he know the slightest thing about mercy.

"Hawk! Don't come! He'll kill us both!" Skye cried. Then she gasped, for the steel came hard and cold and deadly against her.

Logan spoke against her ear. "Get in! And not another word, and not a move. I'll cut you yet, my pretty!"

Stumbling, Skye stepped into the longboat with Logan still behind her. He dragged her down before him with the blade of the knife still tight against her breast.

"Shove off!" Logan commanded, and the longboat shot into the dark.

For several seconds, Skye could still see the Hawk. He stood on shore, tall and formidable, his legs arrogantly apart, his feet firm upon his sand, his fingers knotted upon his sword.

He could not come for her! They would both die. She was certain of it.

Good-bye, my love, she thought. And you are my love, in every way.

Suddenly she wished that she could go back, just for a few hours. Just long enough to tell him that she did love him, that she didn't care about the past, that the future was what needed forging. No matter what he had been, she would hold her silence unto the grave, and she would live with him and love him in his Tidewater paradise forever, for as long as they both should live. He was everything to her, everything in life.

"There she is, the ship!" Logan cried. His arm tightened around Skye. "No diving, my love, no swimming this night! No tricks, no fun, and I am in no mood for games! Climb aboard now, and know that my knife urges you upward."

Skye grated her teeth and gripped the ladder. Logan's men had crawled up before her, and Logan himself was behind her. She looked longingly back to the sea.

Logan's knife prodded her rump. "No swimming, my love. Remember, we've been this road before!"

Arms reached down for her and his men dragged her aboard. She landed in a heap upon the deck, the cloak drawn around her. Logan crawled over the railing and looked down at her, smiling.

"Here we are, my love, alone at last. Well, not alone." He lifted an arm, indicating the many men of his crew, pirates in all manner of dress, some in the rigging, one climbing to the crow's nest, one at the helm, and gunners as ease, their breeches and shirts blackened by powder.

Logan took a step toward her. "But alone enough. Away from the Hawk." He reached out his good hand to her. "Come. Come on, milady. Take my hand. You see, love, you and I are going to await the good Hawk. We're going to await him together."

18

N THE WHOLE OF HER LIFE, SKYE HAD NEVER been so frightened. No darkness surrounded her now, but rather Logan's ship was ablaze with lanterns against the darkness of the night, and of the sea. Perhaps it seemed that the very creature of her nightmares had stepped forth from the darkness to meet her in the light, and the face of fear was far uglier in light than it could ever be in shadow. Logan threatened all that mattered in life. He threatened her father, he threatened Roc, and he very definitely threatened her person, and did so at that very moment.

She stared at his hand. She knew that she would never take it.

"Get up!" he bellowed. "Come—to me!"

She hesitated. Then she leaped to her feet with speed and agility, racing past Logan across the deck.

"Stop her!" Logan ordered. "She'll jump!"

She would have jumped; it was her whole intent. She would rather face a shark or any monster of the blue depths than face Logan.

But his men were quick and agile, too. She had just reached the railing when her cloak was seized from behind, and she was dragged back, spinning into the arms of a black-toothed hearty. He laughed, enjoying her discomfort. Skye faced him, and carefully smiled in return. She was thrust against him. She inhaled the filth of his body and the reek of rum upon his breath, but she endured the horror for the sake of freedom. He did not know just how far she was willing to go to achieve her freedom, and so he was totally unprepared when she drew his sword from the scabbard at his side.

"Damme!" the man swore.

"Fool!" Logan raged. "Seize her, take her! She cannot best you all! By God, I thought I had men on this ship!"

She could not best them all, Skye knew that. But she spun away from the pirate who had stopped her plunge into the sea and backed herself to the railing again. The pirates surged toward her, but they were forced to take care. She parried their steel swiftly and desperately, aided by Logan's next bellowed order.

"I need her alive! Idiots! What good will she be against the Hawk if she lies dead!"

Two of her attackers backed away. Skye eyed them warily, and they watched her like sharks, waiting for her to blink, to drop her guard for a single second.

"Ahoy, Captain Logan!" someone cried. "A ship approaches!"

Logan's attention was temporarily distracted. "The Hawk!" he called, savoring the words.

"Nay, sir, I think not. Or perhaps it is! 'Tis Blackbeard, sir, I can see him standing toward the bow!"

"Then the Hawk is with him!" Logan said. "I need the girl! Now!"

Skye was already crawling up atop the railing. She screamed when she was caught by the hair and thrown down hard to the deck. She looked up, gasping for breath. It was Logan himself. She still held her sword. She lifted it in a definite threat.

"You want to fight, little girl?" he demanded. "All right, then, we will fight! Toss me my sword, gents! Someone toss me my sword."

A blade swirled through the air and landed at his feet. Skye feinted toward him as he reached for the weapon, but he was quick, and he was good. He lunged toward her, and it was all that she could do to evade the heavy thrust.

"Milady, have to!" Logan cried. He attacked and she parried, and he attacked again, and she parried once again. His men backed away now as they fought, and she thought that she knew why. Logan didn't believe that she could really kill him. She was good, very good. But she didn't have his strength or stamina, and if he kept a fair distance, he would eventually wear her down.

She could not let him do so.

He smiled at her as they fought. "Milady! Your cleavage is showing!"

She smiled in turn, aware that the cloak gaped open, then it spun and flew as she fought. She could not seek modesty now. Logan hoped to unnerve her with that ruse.

"Does it, sir?" she inquired, undaunted. Their swords clashed hard and the momentum brought them together, face-to-face. He reached out as if to touch her with his hook and she cried out, flinging herself away. She leaped toward the mainmast, and kept it to her back. When Logan charged, she quickly sliced the air.

She caught him in the cheek. A thin stream of blood appeared against his flesh. He paused, wiping it away with the back of his sleeve, then staring at the blood that stained his sleeve. His eyes shot back to Skye's with undimmed hatred.

"Little girl, you play rough. But I will play however you want, and lady, you will wish that you were dead!" He thrust toward her hard and she screamed, ducking. His sword sliced into the masthead, dropping rigging, and Skye screamed again, rushing over to the side of the boat. Blackbeard was coming. He would be there any second.

She could not believe that she was waiting for the infamous Blackbeard to save her, but she was. If he would just arrive while she still held her own, the pirates could all engage in battle, and she would be free.

But her father would not. Where was he? Somewhere aboard the ship? She prayed that she could help him, but she could hardly help herself.

"Hold her, seize her, take her!" Logan ordered, and suddenly they were all coming after her again.

She held her own. She fought valiantly, and she fought well, and she was certain that no lad could have lasted longer. But the sailors were already upon her. While she parried the one, the next was striking. She was forced further and further along the deck to the stern, and then she parried and turned to leap but found that her way was blocked. Logan was there, and his sword was ready this time. He cast the point hard against her throat.

"Drop the sword," he ordered her.

"I'd—I'd rather die!" she managed to cry, even though she shivered and quaked with the fear of it. She wanted so desperately to live!

"Fine. Drop the sword, or I will slice you from head to toe. And when I am done, I will drag the old man up here on deck, and while you bleed slowly to death, I will hack him into little pieces before you."

"And you will never have the Hawk."

"One day I will have him. It is inevitable."

"You will never have the treasure."

"Is there a treasure, my dear?"

"Of course!"

"I think not."

"There is—"

"Drop the sword."

"Logan! Captain Logan!"

The call came from the longboats, far below the railing. It was Blackbeard's voice. The pirate had arrived at last. Too late.

"Drop it!"

Skye did not respond, and Logan surged forward with a fury. He caught her blade with his, and it fell flat to the deck. He wrenched her to him by her hands, hurrying over the fallen rigging to reach the portside of his ship and the new arrivals. "Blackbeard, you common traitor! Get away!" Logan roared.

"Now, Captain Logan, that's not atall nice, sir, not atall nice! Now I've come in good faith—"

"You've come for more treasure, you greedy viper, and that's that. You'd kill me, you'd kill the Hawk, you'd kill your own mother's every living son or daughter for more treasure!"

"Yer hurtin' me, Logan, yer hurtin' me deep!" Blackbeard called out sarcastically.

Slammed against the railing with Logan behind her, Skye could see that longboats were arriving with men by the dozen. Her heart caught in her throat, then suddenly soared. Against the lantern glare and the darkness, she could see Robert Arrowsmith. The Hawk's own men had arrived. There would be a mighty battle here, indeed.

"Where's the Hawk?" Logan raged.

"Not with me!" Blackbeard called.

"He'd best be. It's the Hawk I want. If I don't get him, I kill the girl, and that's that. Stay out of it, Blackbeard. This is no business of yours."

"Now Logan—"

"Shut up!"

In a fury, Logan turned around, thrusting Skye toward one of his burliest men. The man caught her hard, sweeping his arm around her and dragging her across the deck again. He held her against the railing while Logan looked down to Blackbeard. "I want the Hawk. I don't know what he's playing but I want him now. Don't think to storm the ship. Hans has Lady Cameron, and he has a blade at her heart now, and he'll kill her quicker than you can blink. Get the Hawk before me, and get him now."

"Now, Logan!"

"I'm done!" Logan thundered. "Man, I am done, and she is nearly dead!"

Nearly dead . . .

And that she was, Skye thought, for the man with his arms about her was huge, well over six feet, and each of his arms was greater in circumference than her own waist. His arm was clamped around her, holding her tight against him. And as Logan spoke, he drew out his dagger and smiled as he moved the cold steel between the valley of her breasts. His hold was so tight she could scarcely breathe. He would smother her before he could stab her, she thought. And yet she was afraid. Deathly afraid.

"He'll come!" someone called out. "Don't fear, lady, the Hawk will come!"

And then silence reigned. There was nothing, nothing but the night, nothing but the darkness and the eerie glow of the lanterns, and the sound of the water lapping against the ship at night.

"He'll come!" Logan laughed, casting back his head. "She'll die!"

His laughter faded, and the silence continued. Logan strode over to her furiously. He plucked up a piece of her golden-russet hair and fingered it slowly. "Pray, lady! Pray now, pray deep, for if I do not soon see his face before me, you will swiftly die!"

He dropped the lock of her hair. He stroked the length of her cheek and he jerked open her cloak, drawing the palm of his hand slowly down to cup her breast. Skye moved to fight him but Hans jerked her back, his hold as secure as rock.

"Blackbeard!" Logan called. "Can you hear me?"

"Aye, Logan!"

"Tell him—tell the Hawk that her hair is satin and her flesh is velvet. Tell him that her breasts are lush and firm and ripe. Tell him that I'm touching her."

Skye spat at him. He started, and wiped his cheek. He stared at her and smiled and she cried out, for he viciously caught and twisted her breast. "Next time, milady, it will be the hook!" he warned her.

He smiled, and his touch lingered, and she barely dared breathe, nor could she move. Logan tired of staring at her. He strode back across the deck. Silence held the night once more. Silence . . .

She heard something. It was nothing, she told herself. It was just water lapping against the hull of Logan's ship. It was nothing, nothing at all.

But then she managed to cast her gaze behind Hans, and she was glad then that she was so nearly smothered, for she could not gasp out in startled surprise.

He was coming . . . he *had* come. To save her. The Hawk.

He had crawled up along the hull of the ship, barefoot and bare-chested, his knife between his teeth. He silently leaped over the edge of the starboard hull, landing with the softest thud upon the wooden deck. Hans started to turn, his knife still taut against her breast.

But Hans turned too late. He dropped his hold on Skye to defend himself against the Hawk. Roc attacked quickly, catching the bulky Hans right in the rib cage. Hans didn't get to say a word. The breath left him with a soft *whooshing* sound, and he crumpled to the deck.

That was when Logan turned.

"Hawk!"

"Aye, 'tis me, Logan! Here, where you have her!" Roc cried. He grabbed Skye, throwing her behind him to the rigging. "Climb!" he ordered her. "Climb high!"

She obeyed him, clinging to the rigging for dear life. She paused, and looked back.

Roc had found the sword Logan had forced her to discard. He held to the rigging, balancing as he fought with speed and fury, knees bent, the whole of him as agile as a dancer. "Come, fellows! You'd fight a mere girl and threaten her life as one, come, take me on, too."

Steel clashed. He parried forward, he allowed himself to be thrust back, only to surge forward with a whole new force again. Men fell before him. One sailor leaped over the side; Roc caught his midriff with the sword and the fellow screamed as he crashed into the water.

"Come, Logan!" Roc cried out. "It's you and me, isn't it? Isn't that what this melee is about? Come, sir, let us have at it again."

"Sir!" Logan stormed. "As you wish it! And understand that there will be no mercy for you!"

The sounds of a score of cries, battle cries, suddenly burst through the night as Blackbeard and his men and the Hawk's crew climbed aboard Logan's ship, all of them entering into the fray. Skye, climbing high atop the rigging, looked down and saw the fight. She saw Robert Arrowsmith and Fulton, fighting finely, their swords flashing, bringing about victory. Then she gasped softly, for she saw young Davie, too, and she was stunned.

Roc had taken the innocent lad aboard a pirate ship! she thought, but then her thoughts gave way, and her attention was riveted back to the pirates fighting below her.

Logan and the Hawk.

This was, she knew, a duel, and a duel to the death. Neither man would leave this fray until one of them lay bleeding life away upon the decks.

Pray God that it would be Logan dead, Skye thought!

"You bastard, hold still!" Logan shouted. "Then I may skewer you through!"

"Skewer me? Why, sir, it seems that you cannot touch me!"

Logan bellowed at Roc's words, leaping forward. Roc caught hold of the rigging and swung clear of the man's lunge, turning swiftly to renew his own attack.

"She was sweet and wonderful!" Logan taunted, backing away.

"What?" Roc demanded quickly.

"I touched her, I had her, all of her. I held her taut and I let her scream, but I had her, deep and sweet and sure—"

"Lying bastard!" Roc roared, surging forward. It was the advantage Logan wanted. He lifted his sword to crack it down upon Roc's shoulder with all of his might. Just at the last second, Roc dropped down and back, spinning about, reappearing on the other side of the mainmast.

"I'll have your ears!" Logan called. "I'll slice your ears and your toes and your privates, and I'll stuff them down your own throat, and you'll choke to death on your own flesh, knave!"

"You'll have to best me to do it, rogue!" Roc retorted.

Logan looked up suddenly. He smiled, seeing Skye perched high upon the rigging. He suddenly lifted his sword and brought it hacking down hard upon the ropes.

"No!" Roc bellowed.

Skye screamed as the rope sagged and the wood beams could be heard to crack and shiver. She held tight, afraid to climb upward, afraid to climb down.

Someone knocked over a lamp. A fire caught in the forward section.

"So help me, by God, by the very devil! This night will be the end of you, Hawk!" Logan screamed.

"Abandon the bloody ship!" a voice raged out.

Skye's heart sank. Her father!

"Roc!" she screamed. He paused, his gaze still warily upon Logan as he listened to her. "My father, Roc! He's aboard! He'll burn to death aboard this bloody death trap."

He looked up at her, and smiled slowly. He looked out to the sea, then over to Logan. Logan started to laugh. "Ah, the Hawk is in trouble at last, is he? Save the girl, save the man—or slay me, and save his own hide!"

"Do you mind a bit of a swim, love?" Roc murmured.

She shook her head, frowning, having no idea of what he meant to do. Suddenly he lifted his own sword and hacked with a swift clean blow against the rigging. She couldn't help but scream and hold tight as the mast seemed to sway and tottered with her and the rigging, then started plunging toward the sea.

She fell . . . fell and fell and fell, and felt the cold embrace of the water. She plunged downward, downward into darkness at first. There was nothing, nothing but the cold, nothing but the darkness. Her lungs were near bursting. She closed her eyes against the darkness, kicked with all her strength, and went shooting back up to the surface of the water again.

It seemed that all of the ship was ablaze. Men were screaming; men were leaping into the water. The night was alive with light, with activity, with shouts, and still, with the clang of steel.

Skye grabbed on to a floating log. The cloak had been dragging her down but she clung to it once she had the log; it seemed to offer her a certain warmth, sodden as it was. Or maybe the fire was warming up the water, she didn't know.

Perhaps her heart and soul had gone so cold that she could not feel any ice external to herself. Her father and her husband remained aboard the ship, and it burned with an ever-wilder frenzy.

"Scurry, men! If you would. By God, see! There's enemy sails afloat!" someone called out.

More cries broke out in the night. Longboats broke away in the night, but Skye didn't try to reach any of the pirates. She would wait. She would hold tight to her log and . . . pray.

"Lady Cameron! Lady Cameron!" someone shouted to her.

She turned about, and a gasp formed and froze upon her lips.

Lieutenant Governor Alexander Spotswood was sitting forward in a longboat, reaching out a hand to her.

"I—I can't—" she began.

"Child, look who I have with me!" Spotswood demanded.

She looked past him. Lord Theodore Kinsdale peeked around the lieutenant governor's shoulder, his eyes rheumy with tears, his mouth breaking into a hearty smile.

"Father!" she cried.

"Help the lass, help her!" Spotswood demanded.

Spotswood's sailors reached into the sea for her. Skye flushed, and the men politely turned aside as she tried to adjust the sodden cloak and find a seat within the longboat. Theo's ferocious hug nearly upset all of the boat, and she found herself held warmly in her father's arms. She shivered and chattered insanely. Someone pressed a bottle to her lips. The brew threatened to burn her mouth.

"Drink it!" she was ordered.

She swallowed. Then she swallowed more deeply. The shivering at long last seemed to subside. "More!"

She swallowed more. The world was hazy around her. Maybe some of the rough edges of pain were eased.

"Bless God and the saints above us!" Theo muttered.

Skye pulled back. Her father—her dear, fastidious father—was torn and disheveled, from his unpowdered hair to his filthy mustard breeches and snagged stockings. He smelled like an animal hold and he was every bit as sodden as she, but she cried out and hugged him again, because he was alive and well. "Father! Oh, Father! Why did you come for me! I was safe; you could have been safe! And now . . ." Her voice trailed away. In her relief to see her father, she had momentarily forgotten the Hawk.

"I had to come, you're my life, my only child. You are everything to me!" Theo reminded her.

"Oh, Father! I do love you. But now—"

"The Hawk!" Theo said.

"My God!" she breathed.

"My God, indeed!" Spotswood murmured, and he turned to her. "There, milady. I see him there, still aboard the ship!"

She strained to see past the fire and the smoke and she saw that the lieutenant governor spoke the truth. The figures of two dueling men could be seen, outlined clearly like black silhouettes against the fiery furnace of the blaze. They feinted forward, and they feinted back.

Theo placed his hand upon her shoulder. " 'Tis the Hawk," he murmured. "He tossed me overboard to the boats below with that vile Logan a-breathing right down his shoulder."

"He'll best Logan. He has to win, Skye. You understand that?"

She didn't understand anything. She screamed suddenly, leaping up, for the pirate ship exploded, bursting in the night. But just as it happened, the silhouettes were still stark and visible. And one of them drew back his sword with a fierce and mighty swing, and sent it flying like a headsman across the other's throat. And even as the explosion rent the air, sending both silhouettes flying into the dark and waiting water of the night, she could see a severed head go flying from a torso.

She screamed and screamed, clutching her throat. The explosion had killed the other man, surely! It was an inferno, and they were scarcely far enough away themselves not to feel the horrid heat of the blaze.

"Skye!" Spotswood called to her. "Dammit, child, sit, will you? Skye!"

Their boat tipped, and capsized.

And for the life of her, she could not care. She wanted to sink at that moment into the darkness. Life, she thought, had been darkness until he had lifted her from it. She wanted no part of the light, if she could not share it with him.

"Daughter!"

"Skye Cameron, come over here!"

Whether she wanted life or no, she was going to be forced to live. The sailors righted the boat; her father grabbed her. When the boat was righted, they dragged her up. They all sat shivering.

Another explosion rent the pirate ship. The fire crackled high in the night, and then it began to fade. It would burn for hours, Skye thought, but never so brightly as now. By morning, the fire would be gone.

Spotswood inhaled and exhaled. "All right, men. I see no other of ours in the waves. Head toward the *Bonne Belle.*"

"No! We can't leave!" Skye protested.

"My dear, there are other boats about."

"No man could have survived that explosion!" one of the sailors said. He whispered, but Skye heard him.

"Now, now. The Hawk is known to be a survivor. Perhaps he has gone on with his pirate friends, and maybe that is best," Spotswood said.

No, Skye thought. The sailor had been right. No man could have survived the explosion. Not unless he had leaped clear when the ship went to splinters.

Oars lapped the water. Theo pulled her close to him again and Skye rested her head on her father's shoulders.

"Damn child, if I'm not quite a mess!" Spotswood murmured, very unhappily wringing out his wig. "I'm not even supposed to be here—this is North Carolina territory, you know. Not supposed to be here—I'm *not* here! If any man ever says it, I will deny it! Blimey, but you have given us a good soaking girl."

She couldn't respond. Theo took her face tenderly between his hands. "Did he hurt you, Skye? Are you well, are you fine? I was so terrified for you; all I could think of all the time was how very afraid you must be of the darkness."

"I'm not afraid of the dark, Father," she whispered, and she squeezed his hand. He loved her, and that was why he had come for her. She had to understand that. She had been willing to sell her own soul for Theo's sake, and she was grateful beyond measure that he was alive. "I'm not afraid of the dark, not anymore."

"There she is, right ahead, the *Bonne Belle*. And not too far from our own waters at that!"

The longboat came alongside the ship the *Bonne Belle*. "Captain, lower the ladder if you will!" Spotswood called out. "I've Lady Cameron and Lord Kinsdale safe and sound and with me!"

A cheer went up. Skye was helped up the ladder and over the edge, and she tried to smile to the young man who helped her so intently. She fell against the railing, though, and as her father and Spotswood crawled up behind her, she turned about to stare out to the sea, out to the night.

"Peter! Bring your mistress a dry blanket, and quickly!" Spotswood called out.

Peter! Skye whirled around and, indeed, Peter was there, rushing to her with a dry, warm blanket. He set it about her shoulders. "My lady, are we grateful to see you!"

"Peter!" She forgot protocol and hugged him fiercely, then looked to Spotswood. Spotswood shrugged.

"I already told you, dear—I am not here this evening. The *Bonne Belle* is another of your husband's ships."

"Oh!" she cried, then she turned back to the water again, and she started to shake and cry in earnest, tears cascading down her cheeks. She couldn't bear it. She just couldn't. She loved him too deeply, for all his sins, because of all his sins. He had always been there for her. He had risked his life time and again to save hers. He had come to her in darkness, and in light, and all that mattered now was that he was gone, and that life held no meaning.

"Skye!"

She heard her name as a rasping whisper, calling out to her from the fog of anguish that covered her heart. It was not real, she thought, but she turned slowly, and then her heart started to leap. *He was there.* Standing before her, drenched and dripping over the deck, barefoot and bare-chested still. He held no weapons, but faced her with his palms out, his heart within his silver eyes. He was alive.

"Roc!" she screamed his name in gladness, hurtling toward him, throwing herself against him. She cried his name again and again, holding close to him. She clutched his face between her hands and she showered him with kisses, his forehead, his lips, his cheeks, his sea-wet bare chest and shoulders. His arms folded around her. He pulled her close, holding her wet and sleek to his heart. His fingers combed through her sodden hair.

"Skye . . . beloved . . ."

His mouth covered hers, and the warmth of a summer day exploded within her. He was alive! He was warm, he was real, he was with her, beside her upon the deck of the *Bonne Belle.*

"Really!" Theo Kinsdale groaned. "They're barely clad, between the two of them."

"Theo!" Spotswood reprimanded him. "Have a heart, sir! They are duly wed, and I might remind you, it was all your doing. Give them a moment's peace, then I shall part them myself."

A moment's peace . . .

Skye didn't hear the words. She was in her own world.

In paradise . . .

Touching him, feeling him, convincing herself with all of her senses that he was truly alive. Then he broke away from her, and she saw his face, stripped of his beard. His hair unpowdered, wet and trailing down his back. His shoulders sleek and bronze and rippling with muscle.

And Spotswood was here. The lieutenant governor! He would know—just as she knew!—that the Hawk and Lord Cameron were one and the same. And there would be no escape now. No escape at all. Roc had survived Logan and the fire just to hang!

"No!" she gasped in horror, staring at him.

"Skye—" he murmured.

"All right, my dear young friends," Spotswood said, coming toward them. "I'm afraid I must interrupt you now—"

"No! No!" Skye cried. She held her husband tightly. "You don't understand! You mustn't take him—"

"But, my dear, I must—"

"No!" she cried.

"Skye . . ." Roc murmured.

But it was suddenly too much for her. She fought for reason; she fought for light. Darkness was overwhelming her. She clung to her husband, and his arms came around her. But it was not enough. She fell into his arms, and the world closed in darkness around her.

"My God, what's happened to her!" Theo demanded, pushing forward.

"Nothing, Theo, nothing. And it seems that the lad has her well in hand. She's fainted, Theo, and that's all. And for the night that the poor thing has endured, it seems little enough!"

"I will take her to bed," Roc said softly.

"But—" Theo sputtered.

"They're married, Theo!"

Theo tried with dignity to adjust his ragged clothing. "Quite right, Alexander, quite right. It's just that . . ."

"Quite right, and that's that!" Alexander said. "Lord Cameron! I need a word with you as soon as she's settled."

When she woke up, it was light. The sun streamed in upon her and she rose up, amazed to discover that she was home.

Home. Cameron Hall.

She was dressed in a soft blue nightgown with lace at the collar and the cuffs and hem. Her hair was dried and soft and she was comfortable. She had been out a very long time.

She lay upon her husband's bed, and the very sight of it brought her up, amazed. "Roc!" she cried out his name, but he was not with her, and she had known that he would not be. Spotswood would have arrested him for piracy by now. They would take him to the jail in Williamsburg, and as soon as the court met, they would try him.

And hang him.

"Oh, no!" She leaped out of the bed, and she was amazed that she could have been out so long, and so completely. It was the liquor they had made her drink, she thought. Her head was still pounding. She pushed up from the bed, and she stared about the room. How ironic! Now, at long last, she slept in her husband's handsome bed. But he was not with her. The sun streamed into this place that he loved so much, and she was alone with it. She let her hand fall to her abdomen, and she thought of all the time that had passed since she had first encountered the Hawk, and she trembled. He had wanted an heir. Perhaps that was what she had left. Perhaps she could live to give him that which he had so desired, the son to carry on his name in this all-important land. "Please God, let it be that it is so!" she whispered.

Then she spun around, determined. She would not let the father hang so quickly, she could not! Her father would help her. Theo would testify that the Hawk had saved his life during the fire. There would be enough men to stand for the Hawk, oh surely.

She had to find her father, or the governor, or Peter, or someone. Ignoring her state of undress, she tore out of the bedroom and along the hallway with the portraits of the Cameron lords and ladies. She paused, and her heart beat fiercely. "I shall not let you down, I swear it! I will save him, I promise. I did not want to come here, that is true, but it's my blood, too, now, you see. I think I'm to have his child, and besides, you see . . . I love him. With all my heart. He is my life, and this land is his passion, and therefore, it is mine."

She was talking to portraits, she realized. But the Camerons looked down upon her, and she thought that they smiled their encouragement. The men with their silver eyes, the women with their knowing warmth and soft beauty.

She turned away from the portraits and ran down the elegant stairway. From the grand hallway she burst into the office.

Spotswood and her father were there. They were seated quite comfortably, lighting pipes, sipping coffee—out of fine Cameron cups.

Skye strode to the desk, facing Spotswood. "Where is he? I demand to know." She spun around. "Father, you make him tell me where my husband is! I want to see him now. You may arrest him, but you'll not hang him. I'll fight you. I'll fight you both tooth and nail until we are all nothing but blood. Father! He saved your life!"

"I know that, daughter—"

"And Alexander! You were all willing and eager for the Hawk to do your dirty work. The government of Virginia cannot interfere with the government of North Carolina, and so you didn't mind seeing him attack other pirates in Carolina waters. Now I'm telling you, I demand to know where he is."

Theo looked at Alexander, and Alexander looked at Theo. The lieutenant governor shrugged. "By the river, I believe. He mentioned a certain spot. It's quite lovely and private. Down past the docks, beyond the graveyard. You'll not see him if you don't run down the slope by the old oaks."

"What?" Skye murmured. "But—"

"Find him. Speak with him."

Skye backed away from the desk. They had both gone mad, but Roc was out there somewhere. She could see him and touch him. She could cling tightly to him and tell him that there would be an heir to Cameron Hall. She could love him, before they could take him.

She stared at her father and the lieutenant governor, then she whirled around and raced out of the house.

"Milady!" Peter called to her, startled that she should be running out in her night attire. She ignored him. She burst from the house and into the day and down the slope. She saw the docks before her, and the family graveyard to the right, and she kept running upon the soft green grass. Her feet were bare, and she stumbled, but she didn't care. She had to reach him.

"Roc!" she screamed. She raced far past the graveyard, and by the mound of oaks.

She saw him then. He was clean and bathed and handsomely dressed in fawn breeches and buckled shoes and a deep red frockcoat. His dark hair was un-powdered, but neatly queued. He rested a hand against a pine tree, and he looked out to sea.

Until he heard her call. He turned about, and his eyes came alight with a silver blaze, and his lazy, slow, sensual smile curved his lips. Perhaps he would have reached out to her. She didn't know. She tripped and went stumbling down the slope of grass there, and fell at last into his arms.

"Skye!"

Her force nearly knocked them both over. He swept her into his arms, and down then upon the ground, in a bed of pine needles. He cradled her gently and searched her eyes while her fingers fell tenderly upon his clean-shaven cheeks. She gasped for breath, then kissed him. He arched his brow and brought his palm against her thundering heart. "My love—" he murmured.

"Aye, Roc, and I do love you!" she gasped. "I'll not let them have you!"

"Them?" he inquired.

She could smell the sweet pine needles beneath her and the cleanliness of the river air. She felt both the sun and the shade of the trees, the birch and the oaks and the pines. She felt the searing warmth and sweet fire of the man, the silver blaze within his eyes. She held tightly to him. This was indeed his Eden. It was where his parents had come. It was a garden where a man could love a woman, and a woman love a man, far from the cares of the world.

"Oh, Roc!" she whispered. "We are, I think, I'm almost sure—"

"What?" he demanded, his arms tightening around her.

"We're—we're going to have a child." His arms came like steel, warm and loving, and she spoke on quickly. "I don't know whether Lord Cameron or the Hawk has fathered the babe, but Roc, I will raise him, I swear it, come what may! Yet I swear, my love, too, that I haven't given up on his sire as yet—"

"I should hope not!" Roc said indignantly. "Oh, my love, a babe, really?" The tenderness in his voice tore into her heart. It brought tears to her eyes.

"Really, I believe. Now, Roc—"

His kiss cut off her words. It was deep and sweeping and sensual, and it enveloped and enwrapped her in splendor and warmth. It filled her with sweet longing and desire, and left her trembling in his arms. When he rose above her, the tenderness was still with him. "My dear lady, bless you. With all of my heart, madame, I do love you. You believe that now, don't you?"

"Yes, I believe you!" she whispered. He smiled, and reached to her gown, tugging upon the laces at the bodice. The material fell away and he lowered his head against her, taking her nipple deeply into his mouth and laving it with his teeth and tongue.

"Roc!" she cried out, tugging upon his hair. "Stop, please, we must talk. . . ."

He spoke huskily against her flesh. "We've a lifetime to talk!"

"No!" She tugged fiercely upon him, drawing him back up to face her. He was a handsome devil, she thought. Handsome, strong, seductive. She could not bear life without him now! "No, Roc, now listen to me. We must think. We must find you legal representation, the very best. And witnesses, the proper witnesses."

He was nuzzling her breast once again. Sensations blazed into her, but she fought them all fiercely. "Roc, this is serious!"

He groaned.

"Roc, they'll hang you!"

His eyes fell upon her, wicked and silver, and hungry like a gray wolf's.

"If I am a condemned man, then love me, wife!"

"Roc! You mustn't—you must listen to me. Roc—"

"Have you ever seen such a glorious place?" he murmured, and again he spoke against her flesh. He edged her gown from her shoulders, and his words and kisses fell against them, then he moved lower as he stripped her completely in the bower of pines. "It is Eden. Feel the breeze, love, upon your flesh. Like my touch, I swear it. Gentle always, soft sometimes, with heady passion at others. Feel where the air touches you where my lips have just lingered, the coolness against the heat. Hear the birds, my love? Sweet and never strident. Smell the earth, the verdancy, the flowers. Never so good as the sweet scent of you, never so provocative, yet always enticing. . . ."

"Stop!" she pleaded, catching his dark hair as he teased her belly with the hot tip of his tongue. Swallowing, seeking breath, she dragged him to her. She pressed her lips passionately to his, then drew away. Tears glazed her eyes. "I cannot! I will not let them hang you!"

His lashes fell, dark over his eyes. "They are not going to hang me, love."

"What?" she cried. "Oh, Roc! You must not be overconfident because you are Lord Cameron!"

He paused then, and cradled her in his arms. He ran his palms over her naked breasts tenderly, and he thought that he had never seen her more beautiful, more gentle, than at this moment. The trees rocked their branches above. Her night-gown hovered in a soft blue swirl about her hips while the beauty of her throat and breasts and torso were bared to his eyes. Her hair cascaded all about her, sunlight, sunset. Her eyes were all teal, liquid with her love for him.

He had never felt more humble, and he trembled. He had never known what love could be. Now, it was his. It was more precious that life, limb, earth, or country. She was life. His life. Their child grew within her. Their future stretched before them. He had loved the land before; now it was everything. Now it would be shared.

"My God!" he whispered, and his fingers shook as he smoothed away her hair. "Skye, I love you. I cannot say it deeply enough. I love you."

"I love you!" she whispered, and the tears still stung her eyes.

He smiled, holding her tight, cherishing and savoring the soft feel of her naked chest as he held her against his body. "I'm not going to hang, my love, because the lieutenant governor has been in on it all the time."

"What!" Stunned, she broke away from him. He was reminded of the daring temptress who had fought him so fiercely on the deck of the *Silver Messenger,* the very first day he had seen her.

He nodded slowly, watching her flashing eyes. "I was asked to be a pirate, milady. I stole nothing. I tried to learn the plans of the real rogues at their hideaways, and I captured ships, but only my own ships, or imaginary ships, or ships that I captured from other pirates to send on home."

"But—but—"

He lifted his hands. "Spotswood would deny it, of course. He is a servant of the Crown. But several years ago I had a ship taken and my crew was butchered, and I could not help but want to seek revenge. Alexander and I spent a night drinking and . . . the Silver Hawk was born."

"But the place on Bone Cay—"

"I own it. The Camerons have owned it for at least fifty years."

"Oh!"

"Love, I'm sorry! I could not tell you. You already despised the man you were to marry, and I had sworn to Alexander that I would never divulge the truth to anyone."

"But Robert—"

"Robert Arrowsmith has always been one of my best friends. I have given him a plot of land connecting ours. He is going to become a gentleman planter now."

"What of Mr. Soames and Señor Rivas and—"

He shrugged. "They like the Caribbean. And I have no intention of giving up my island. It holds wonderful memories for me, and can be fine to visit in the winter. The pardon you spoke of before has come through. Men in authority have gone to take control of New Providence. The Silver Hawk will seek a pardon, turn his property over to his deserving cousin—Lord Cameron—and then disappear into the pages of history."

"Then you won't—you won't set sail again?" she whispered.

"Alas, no, my love. My pirating days are over. Jack is gone, and Logan is gone. One day Spotswood will have Blackbeard, but I haven't the heart for that fight, and the lieutenant governor has decided that my usefulness to the Crown is over. I am a changed man, love! I swear it!"

"Oh!" she gasped.

He stroked her cheek, and laid her down upon the pines. "I love this place," he whispered. "I want our son to grow here. I want it to be the finest estate in all Tidewater Virginia."

"Ummm," she murmured.

"Say something!" he implored her. "Will you mind so very much that the Hawk is not to hang?"

She shook her head. She stretched her arms around him and drew him close, loving the masculine hardness of his body as it pressed against hers on their bed of pines. "I'm glad he's not to hang," she whispered. "And since he is not . . ."

"Since he is not?"

"Then I demand that he love me here, in this Eden. Perhaps he is of no more use to the Crown, but his lady shall always demand his time, and his energy."

"Ah, but the Hawk will be gone! 'Tis Lord Cameron who will give you his life and his love and his passion."

She laughed with sweet delight and raked her fingers through his dark hair, drawing him close. "Perhaps. But perhaps my legal lord will always be the valiant pirate Hawk in my heart. And perhaps I will always lie with him now, forever, in this Eden."

"Perhaps . . ."

"And then, perhaps, it matters not at all, for I love the man, you see. Whether he is the Hawk or the lord, the rogue or the noble gentleman, I love him. And would have him love me now."

He smiled to her, and caught her lips, and rose above her, his eyes—silver eyes, dancing eyes, rogue's eyes—alight with his passion.

"Gladly, milady, gladly," he assured, and set forth with fire and passion and tenderness to prove to her the bold beguiling truth of his ardent assurance.

Epilogue

LYING BENEATH THE OAKS, SKYE WAS HALF-asleep when Roc came upon her. He smiled down at his wife, for she looked beautiful and pure and childlike, with her hair all tousled about, and at the same time mature, for she was huge with their child—the babe was due any day.

"My love!" he murmured, sitting down beside her.

She jerked up and he laughed, smoothing back her hair. " 'Tis just me," he assured her, and drew her close. He kissed her forehead. "No one is allowed in Eden with Eve except for Adam, you know."

She smiled, and stretched lazily and then leaned against him, as content as a kitten. "How are things in Williamsburg? How is Father?" she asked. "What of the pirates?"

"Your father is fine and feisty as always," he said. "The pirates . . ." He sighed. Spotswood had managed to get his hands on Blackbeard at last. There had been a battle at Ocracoke Island last fall, and Blackbeard had fallen.

His head, it was rumored, had been severed and hoisted up on the bow of Lieutenant Maynard's ship for all to see. "Woe to all pirates!" was the message.

Well, Blackbeard had been a rogue and caught at it, and perhaps he had rightfully deserved to die, Roc thought. But in his own dealings with him, he had seen Blackbeard maintain a curious honor, and so he was sorry for the end of it in a way.

Skye squeezed his hand. "At least he was not captured and taken prisoner with the others!"

Men *had* been taken. They had been sent to the Williamsburg jail, and they had been tried on March 12. All but one gentleman—who had been able to prove himself a guest and no more on Blackbeard's ship, the *Adventurer*—had been sentenced to hang.

"Aye. Well, it's over now."

"Is it?" Skye asked him.

He nodded, looking out to the James that swept by them, the very life of their land, their property, their estate, their future.

Their children's future. Their destiny.

"Yes," he said, drawing his wife close. "I think that it is over. I told you once that the Crown created pirates—Sir Francis Drake was a fine example. We warred with Spain, so the kings and queens cried, 'Rob them blind!' Then men began to forget that they should pirate only foreigners, the enemy. The islands gave the rogues bases. Now Woodes is cleaning up New Providence, and Ocracoke will never welcome pirates again. An age is coming to an end. The age of piracy. Maybe that was our age, my love. When the settlers arrived here last century, they had to survive against the Indians. They had to hold fast to the land. For us, it was the menace of the pirates. We had to endure, and survive. Who knows now what the future, what our children shall face? It's all to God, isn't it? Fate. And we can only pray that each generation will endure."

Skye touched his cheek. She started to smile, started to speak. "Oh!" she cried instead.

"What is it?"

She sighed, and flushed, and smiled again. "It's quite all right. I mean, I think that it's some time yet."

"What?"

"Well, you remember, I met *you* when the age of pirates was flourishing! And you were an absolutely irresistible and ravishing pirate. And—"

"Skye!"

"Well, I believe it's time for a certain ravishment or seduction—whichever it was!—to bear fruit."

"The babe!"

"Yes!"

"Oh!"

He leaped to his feet and drew into his arms. He groaned slightly. "Well, you're not as light as air at the moment!" he apologized.

"And I can walk perfectly well!"

"Not on your life, my love."

He carried her to the house, and up the stairs, and to the bed they shared. Mattie was there, and Tara and Bess, and Peter hovered by the door with Davey and some of the others ready to run and fetch whatever might be required. Davey was sent for the doctor, then Mattie expelled Roc, too. "It's a long, long time!" she assured him.

He paced the portrait gallery, and then he went out walking again, and he came down to the cemetery, and looked out over the tombstones. He walked over to those belonging to Jamie and Jassy, and he touched the cold stone, and he smiled. "I *am* mad!" He laughed aloud. "But it all came out so very well." He paused. "Life is good. It is Eden. I—I thank you for this place."

He decided that he *was* mad, smiled again, and turned around. He came back to the house, and he paused by the beautiful portrait of his great-great-grandmother, then he walked on again and went to his office down the stairs.

Robert Arrowsmith arrived, and drank with him.

He had several snifters of brandy, and smoked several pipes.

Then he heard one cry, and then another, and he glanced toward Robert, and he tore up the stairs, two at the time. He burst into the room, where Mattie was just swaddling the babe. Roc looked at her expectantly. Mattie smiled and handed him the squirming bundle.

"A . . . ?" he inquired.

"What else, Lord Cameron? A boy."

"A boy! Wonderful. But don't you what-else-me, Mattie! A girl would have been just as welcome!"

"Well, sir . . ."

"What?"

"I'm glad to hear that, for the second is a little girl, wee and fine and golden-haired."

"Two!"

"Twins, Roc!" Skye called from the bed. He hurried over to her. She was pale, but she smiled beautifully, and the happiness that radiated from her was glorious. He knelt down beside her and he kissed her hand. Mattie brought their son over, while Bess carried over their scarcely bathed daughter.

They inspected their infants, hesitant, curious, laughing. Adoring the infants, more deeply in love than ever with one another. Mattie and the girls left them alone. The babies fussed, and Skye, laughing and awkward, tried to nurse them both. Roc helped, trading infants while she traded breasts, and together they laughed again, until he saw that her eyes were closing, and that she was exhausted.

"I'll call for Mattie and Tara," he assured her, kissing her forehead.

She nodded sleepily, and he called to the servants, and then it was Mattie's turn to cluck proudly over the newborns. Roc came back beside his wife and sat down, cradling her hand. She was nearly asleep. Clean and bathed and beautiful after the ordeal, she was again sweetly innocent and pure to him. It was hard to recall her as the passionate vixen who had come to his arms to create their marvelous new additions, but he knew that he would meet the vixen again. He kissed her forehead. Her eyes fluttered open, teal, beautiful.

"I'll let you sleep. I'll send a message to your father. I'm sure he can be here by tonight."

She nodded, and squeezed his hand. He kissed her again and stood. Her eyes opened again, devilish slits. "Make sure you tell *them* we have twins," she whispered.

"Them."

She winked. "Jamie and Jassy. I think that they'd like to know."

He laughed, and said indignantly, "My love, one day our children's children will live here. In the world we work to build year by year."

"And one of our great-great-great-grandchildren, a handsome lad, a rogue with dancing silver eyes, will come by us, and whisper of what has come!" she said.

"Vixen!" he teased her, and kissed her again.

"It takes one to love a rogue," she assured him demurely.

And he laughed, and it turned out that he didn't leave so quickly after all, for she was not so tired that she could resist being taken into his arms and giving him a kiss of infinite tenderness and passion and promise.

A kiss . . . to the future.

Love

Not

A Rebel

NORTH AMERICAN
WOMAN
3

Prologue

BETRAY NOT THE HEART!

Cameron Hall
Tidewater Virginia
June 1776

MANDA!"

The door to the bedroom burst open just as she heard the distant thunder of the cannon upon the sea. Amanda leapt up from her bedcovers and dreams to streak across the polished floor to the full-length windows. There were ships in the harbor. Flying the British colors.

Danielle stood behind her. Another cannon boomed; Amanda saw the explosion of black powder upon the sea.

"It's Lord Dunmore! Aiming at the house!" Amanda gasped. She swung around to see that Danielle was watching her, her dark eyes condemning.

"Aye, 'Highness.' He's come for revenge against Cameron—no matter what service you've offered him."

Amanda's eyes flashed in offense at Danielle's blunt words while fury reigned in her heart. She had fulfilled her part of every bargain she had ever made with the royal governor. And still he was threatening Cameron Hall. After fleeing Williamsburg, he had asserted his royal vengeance from the sea, destroying so much of the coast! And now he was here.

Fear struck her heart. He knew! He knew about the weapons and powder that had been brought to the dock. He knew . . .

But *she* had not told him! She would never have gone so far. There had not been anything left to threaten her with, and she could not have done so . . . not now. Not against . . . Eric.

"Amanda—"

"Shush! I have to act quickly!"

Amanda ran to her wardrobe. "Help me!" she commanded Danielle sharply. She stepped from her nightgown, her fingers trembling as she tried to tie the knots of her corset.

Danielle came at last behind her. "What do you intend to do?"

"Send the slaves and servants and workers into the forest. I'll go out and speak with Dunmore—"

"And if your father is with him? Or Lord Tarryton?"

"God's blood!" she swore in panic, as no lady should. But the events of the last two years of her life had prevented her from being the lady she might have been.

She stared hard at Danielle before the woman could offer reproach. "Stop! I cannot think—"

"You should have thought before taking on the role of spy, milady!" Danielle told her woefully.

"Leave off, mam'selle!" Amanda commanded her. She chose a shift and gown and quickly pulled them over her head, then stumbled into her garters and stockings. She gazed across the room to the now-empty bed and shivered in sudden fear of what was to come. What had she done? Should she be praying for British defeat or victory at this moment?

She didn't dare think. "My shoes," she murmured, sliding her feet into a pair of black leather slippers with rhinestone buckles. "Now, Danielle—" she began, but broke off. A British officer was standing in her bedroom doorway. Lord Robert Tarryton. She realized instantly that he had ridden in while the attack had been staged upon the sea.

"Hello, Amanda." He paused for a moment, looking her over from head to toe, then taunted, "Ah, Highness! You are a sight. I feel that I have waited a long time to claim you."

"You cannot *claim* me," she told him flatly, despising him.

She stood warily watching the man. He was handsome, with light hair and light eyes and beautiful lean features. Once she had thought him the most beautiful man she had ever seen. Then she had come to notice that there was a twist to his smile which marred his good looks, for there was a hint of cruelty to it.

Alas, she had discovered the truth of the man too late.

"We've come for you," he said.

Her heart quickened with horror. "I will not go with you."

"What? The Tory princess is suddenly casting her fate with the rebels? Don't be a fool. They say that Cameron knows you alerted us. Take care, lady! My touch would be ever more gentle than his!" Robert spoke swiftly as he moved into the room. He looked from the elegant bed to the wardrobe and the tables and the graceful length of the windows, and his jaw twisted further with some inner rage. The essence of the man who owned the room remained. And something of his power. Perhaps it disturbed Robert, Amanda thought.

It had often disturbed her.

"Eric knows!" She gasped suddenly. "But I did not betray—"

"Lady, you did. We are here. And I *have* come for you!" he told her with sudden fury.

Her mouth went dry as he came toward her. Danielle tried to block his way, and he shoved the Acadian woman to the side. In seconds he was before Amanda. She struggled with him, tearing her fingers down his cheek. He laughed as he caught her fingers, twisting them brutally. "Don't play your games, Highness. You called, and I am here."

"No!" She gasped, horrified. *She* was the one who had been betrayed. She knew that the arms had been stored at the docks, but she was no longer Highness! She had told no one.

She struggled furiously against him but he held her firmly in a viselike grip. Danielle lay on the floor where she had fallen, her eyes closed.

"You've killed her!" Amanda cried, trying to escape him. "God, how I hate you, loathe you—"

"The crone lives," Robert replied. "Let's go! Warn your people to get out. We're firing the house."

"I'll never come with—" Amanda began, then she realized what he'd said. *We're firing the house. Firing the house. Cameron Hall.* "No!" With a rage of energy she flung herself against him, tearing at his flesh again. His cheek bled as she fought for the house, bricks and chimneys and walls that suddenly seemed so desperately dear to her. "No, you can't burn the hall, you can't—"

He caught her fingers, his face white with fury except for the blood-red scratches her nails had left. "I have to fire the house," he said. "But . . ."

"But?" She cast back her head.

"Walk out of here with me. Come aboard the *Lady Jane,* your husband's *seized* ship, of your own free will, and I will see that the fires are set small, and that your people can come back and quickly put them out."

She stared at him in anguish, thinking quickly. She knew that she had little choice. He could drag her away screaming anyway.

"I'll walk," she said, fighting the tears that threatened to fill her eyes. They could not burn the house! They couldn't! She jerked away from him as he pressed a handkerchief to his face and prodded her forward.

The stairway was filled with the servants. Amanda swallowed hard and looked at them all—Pierre, Margaret, Remy, Cassidy. "You all must go outside quickly. They plan to burn the house."

"Look at 'er—the Tory bitch!" Margaret cried out.

Amanda's face went ashen. Robert stepped forward to strike the woman.

"No!" Amanda called.

He turned back to her, smiling, offering her an elbow. "Highness?"

She bit her lip and took his arm. Amanda didn't turn back as he led her down the stairs. Remy spit at her, but she stiffened her shoulders, remaining silent. She was a Tory. That was the truth. But the rest of this was some bitter irony. At the door she pulled away from Robert and turned back to the servants. "Get out. Get out, please! They'll—"

"This is a house of wicked rebellion against God's own anointed King of England! Leave it or die in the flames of hell!" Robert shouted, pulling her along.

But on the porch he paused, conferring with one of his lieutenants. The young man cast her a leering gaze, then nodded to his superior.

"The house, lady, will survive. The docks will not," Robert stated.

She could smell fire. One of the tobacco warehouses was ablaze. When the shed with the powder went, there would be explosions everywhere.

Robert dragged her along to his horse. The sun was shining high overhead and a multitude of birds were singing. The grassy slope had never appeared more green. But the fresh river air was polluted already by the acrid smell of smoke.

Amanda could see far down the hill that Lord Dunmore had come in, that his men were rowing from his ships to the *Lady Jane,* at berth on the dock.

"Mount with me, lady. We will ride," Robert whispered in her ear. Her stomach roiled. That she had loved him once she could scarcely believe. She shoved away from him and leapt upon his mottled gray stallion. He followed behind her. In seconds they were racing down to the dock. Her hands were cold, but no colder than her heart. She had gone numb.

They came to a halt. Robert reached for her, lifted her down.

Suddenly a cannon boomed out on the river. The men in British navy uniforms who were milling about the *Lady Jane,* preparing her for sail, twirled around to see the new angle of attack.

"God's blood!" Robert swore. Dazed, Amanda stared out to the river. Ships were appearing. Ships that did not fly the colors of the British Crown.

"He's come!" Amanda gasped. He should have been in New York, or in New Jersey. Far, far away.

"Aye, he's come. And what will he do if he finds you? Hang you? Highness, you'd best pray that we are victorious! Now come!"

Robert set his arm about her, practically lifting her from her feet. Amanda seemed to skim the ground until they reached the *Lady Jane,* ready now to sail. They raced up the gangplank and aboard.

Captain Jannings, one of Lord Dunmore's men, bowed to her regretfully. "Highness! We are under attack. Fear not, I will see you into Lord Dunmore's hands, and then you shall be safely whisked away to England!"

Tears stung her eyes. Once she would have begged to hear those words. Now she had no choice. Her dreams had burned away in the fires that had raged on land.

Cameron Hall would remain standing. Yet from the moment the British had come for the arms stored in warehouses along the docks, she herself had been doomed. The truth would not matter now.

A cannon exploded near the ship. A man screamed as a shard of steel cut into his flesh. Battle was engaged, and they weren't even out into the open water.

The young captain raced to the fore, putting his glass to his eye. "Be damned, but it is *Cameron* riding the ship! Gunners, to your weapons. Sergeant, call the orders to fire!"

Robert grabbed her hand and hurried her toward the aft of the ship where the captain's large cabin commanded a fine view of the sea. He threw open the door and shoved her inside.

Then he followed her, closing the door behind him. His eyes were bright with the excitement of battle, with the pleasure of winning. "He will die, Amanda. I swear it."

She felt as if she would faint. Cannon boomed again, and even as they stood there, the room seemed to fill with the black soot of powder and fire. "You'll never kill him!" she vowed.

"I'll kill him, I swear it." Two steps brought Robert to her. She struggled as he swept her into his arms. "I'll kill him, and I'll have you naked beneath me while the blood still runs warm from his body."

She lashed out at him, and he started to laugh. "Pray to the saints that it is so, lady, for he knows of this treachery, and *he* will kill *you*!"

She shoved her knee into his groin with all of her strength. He staggered back. Amanda gripped the wall, ready to do battle again. But the door was thrown open and a uniformed Highlander stepped in. "Lord Tarryton! You are needed, your Grace. Milady! I am here to die for your protection! Lieutenant Padraic McDougal at your service."

Robert gritted his teeth against the pain and cast her a glance that promised sure revenge. Then he straightened, ever the military man, and exited the cabin. The Highlander nodded to her, closing the door and standing guard beyond it. Amanda clamped her hands over her ears as the cannon boomed again.

They would all die.

She raced to the velvet-draped windows and looked out to the water. A ship called the *Good Earth* was almost upon them, coming about with grappling irons. Men were leaping from the rigging to come aboard the *Lady Jane.*

Eric's ship.

His ship, which the British had taken . . .

And now she was on board. He would never believe her innocent!

With a cry of anguish she rose, determined to have none of it. They could not have traveled too far from shore yet. She needed to reach the deck and be quit of them all. Robert would betray her. He would never take her to Lord Dunmore, never see her safely to England.

And Eric would . . .

Kill her.

She hurried to the cabin door. Beyond it she could hear the sound of clashing steel. Still she threw the door wide open, but then she halted in horror at all that she saw.

Battle had come hand to hand, and to the death. Even as she stood there, the captain fell dead, skewered by a blade in the hands of a mountain man. Amanda stepped aside as two boys, fighting with ropes and fists, crashed down before her. She nearly slipped in a pool of blood that oozed from the throat of a bearded redcoat. She looked forward, and her heart caught in her throat.

Eric was there.

On the bow of the *Lady Jane,* his rapier drawn, he and Robert were cast heavily into the fray. Both men knew their swordplay, yet no man was so subtle, so swift, as Eric Cameron. He moved forward suddenly, pushing Robert back, his black crackling silver beneath the sun despite the mist and smoke that hung over the deck. He was talented and dramatic, provoking Robert to angry lashes, taunting him then as he flecked his sword against his opponent's chin. His left hand remained behind his back as he moved again with speed and grace, demanding that Lord Tarryton cast down his sword.

"God's blood, someone take this man!" Robert screamed.

Five of Dunmore's finest navy men turned at Tarryton's call for help, daring opponents as they sprang forward.

She heard Eric's reckless laughter. He lived on the edge now, and enjoyed it. He cared nothing for danger for they had attacked his very home. They had attacked her! Amanda thought.

But he would not see it that way.

Her hand fluttered to her throat as she watched him fight. Silently she screamed as men thrust and parried. Not knowing what she did, she dipped low to the deck, grabbing up a sword.

Robert Tarryton had turned. Amanda watched as he leapt to the rigging by the mainmast, then catapulted into the sea.

"So you'd give fight, eh?"

A cheerful young man in West County buckskins and a bloody shoulder stood before her. She looked down at the sword in her arm. It was covered with blood too. She wanted to scream. She wanted to cast the sword down and back away screaming. She'd never seen bloodshed like this before. War had always been distant; battle something one heard of in glorious accounts that didn't mention the cries of the dying. She shook her head, but the lad had grown serious. "Milady, if you must give battle, then I shall engage you so!"

"Highness!" someone yelled out. "The woman must be Highness!"

Amanda held up her weapon in terror. She didn't want to kill the man, nor did she want to die in a pool of blood, there upon the *Lady Jane*. "No, I shall not fight or surrender!" she claimed, thrusting the sword forward in warning so that the lad fell back. Then she turned and raced blindly back toward the captain's cabin. Men streamed after her.

She raced through the door, breathless, slamming it closed behind her. Her Highlander was there, rushing forward to meet the enemy, carrying his loaded Brown Bess. He never lifted the weapon. A sword was thrust through his heart, and he came crashing down at Amanda's feet. "Dear God, no!" she cried, falling to his side, trying to staunch his wound.

It was over, she realized. There was silence on the deck.

But the echo of the shots had barely ceased, the ring of steel had just gone silent, when the door to the captain's cabin burst open, the wood shuddering as if it would splinter into a million fragments. A man stood there, towering in the doorway, framed by the combination of sea mist and black powder that swirled upon the deck. He was exceedingly tall, broad shouldered, lean in the hips, legs firm upon the deck. He stood silent and still, and yet from her distance, Amanda felt the menace of his presence, felt the tension hot upon the air.

Amanda's mouth went dry. She didn't know whether to exult in his surviving, or damn him for not dying.

She did not scream, nor even whisper a word. She looked up quickly from where she knelt at Lieutenant McDougal's side, still trying in vain to staunch the flow of blood that poured forth from his chest. McDougal was dead. There was really no more that she could do for him.

And she had to face the man in the doorway.

Amanda grabbed the lieutenant's Brown Bess, staggering up with the heavy and awkward five-foot gun. McDougal could help her no more, and she had never needed protection so desperately. She stared at the doorway, at the man who had come for her. Although she was determined to fight, still she trembled, for the look in his eyes made her heart shudder, as if a blade had cut cruelly into the very depths of her.

Cameron. Lord Eric Cameron. Or Major General Lord Cameron now, she thought, near hysteria.

"Eric!" she whispered his name.

"Highness," he said. His voice was deep and husky, sending shivers down her spine. Watching her, he removed a handkerchief from his frock coat and wiped clean the blade of his sword. She braced herself as he kept his eyes upon her and sheathed his sword at his side.

"How intriguing to see you," he murmured. "You, milady, should be tending the home fires. And as I am a special adjutant to General Washington, I should be with him. But how could I be when I received an urgent request from Brigadier General Lewis, commander of the Virginia militia, warning me that our arms and my very home were in danger. That we had all been betrayed."

"Eric—"

"Lord Dunmore, Virginia's gallant royal governor—who now decimates her coast—was driven from Williamsburg in the summer of 1775, but as you know so well, Highness, he took to the sea, and from H.M.S. *Fowey,* he descended upon the towns, harrying them in the name of the king. He always seemed to know so much of what was going on! Then on New Year's Day this year he burned Norfolk to the ground with the seventy big guns of his fleet, and he continued to haunt the Tidewater, attacking my very home, milady."

"If you would listen to me—"

"No, Amanda. I listened to you for too long. I kept believing that some sense of honor would keep you silent, even if we did not gain your loyalty. And now, well I know the full truth of it." Eric spoke so softly. Still she felt the sizzling heat and tension behind his words, the energy behind his quiet stance. "Put down the gun," he warned her.

Dread filled her. She had chosen her course. If she was not guilty now of the treachery he suspected, she had still chosen her own side in the conflict. She held her head high, trying not to show her fear. Once it might have been a game. Like chess. Check, and check again. But even when they had played and he had allowed her to seek certain advantages, the warning had been there. Nay, the threat, for he had told her that she would pay if he ever caught her betraying him.

And now that she was innocent at long last, she'd been caught!

He stood there so tall and unyielding. As the powder and mist faded, she saw him so much more clearly. His taut white breeches defined the rugged muscle and sinew of his thighs and the navy frock coat with the epaulets upon the shoulders emphasized the breadth of them. His hands were gloved, but she knew them well. Knew their tenderness, and their strength.

It was the power of his eyes that held her now. Those startling, compelling eyes. Silver and indigo steel, they stared at her with such fury that she nearly forgot that she held the loaded gun. Amanda could barely hold the unwieldy weapon, but she couldn't let him see that. She couldn't falter; she could never surrender.

She wanted to cry out. She wanted desperately to remind him that she had never turned her back on England, that she had always been a loyalist, and could only follow her heart, as he had followed his. But he was not angry because of her beliefs. He was angry because of all that he believed she had done.

"I am innocent of this!" she told him heatedly.

His brow arched with polite interest. "You are innocent—Highness?"

"I tell you—"

"And I tell you, milady, that I know full well you are a British spy and the notorious 'Highness,' for I oft fed you misinformation that found its way to Dunmore's hands. You betrayed me—again and again."

She shook her head, swallowing against the fear that closed about her throat. He spoke with dispassion, but a fire burning beneath his words brought terror to her heart. She had never seen him like this. When she had despised him, he had been determined and patient. When she had been cold, he had been an inferno. He had been there for her, always, no matter what scandalous truth he discerned, he was ever there, a ferocious warrior to wage her battles. She had known how to take care; she had feared for her heart should she lose it to him.

And now that she was cast into that desperate swirl of love and abandon, she was lost indeed. All that was left was the tenacious grip with which she tried to cling to some semblance of dignity and pride. She had to be strong; she needed to remember how to fight.

Yet it was terrible to think that she must find the wit and reason to battle him now. Never had he seemed more a pillar of strength, filling the doorway, taller than all other men in his boots and cockaded hat, striking with his hard handsome features, his dark hair queued but unpowdered, his stance so confident yet so fierce. And so determined.

"Give it to me, Amanda," he repeated. Low and husky and deep, his voice seemed to touch her. To sweep over her flesh. Assured, commanding, touched by the rawness of the colonial man, yet with a trace of his Oxford education, he was a contradiction. In a land the British often considered to be peopled by criminals, Eric Cameron was one of their own, but with all the strengths and rugged power of the colonial. He knew the strategy of war, and he knew, too, the skill of hand-to-hand combat. He had learned how to fight from master generals—and from the blood-thirsty Iroquois and Shawnee. He was like the country, made of muscle and sinew, wild and untamed, no matter how civil his manner, no matter that they called him "lord."

"Amanda!" He moved toward her.

"Get away from me, Eric!" she warned him.

He shook his head, and in his eyes she saw the depth of his anger. She wanted to throw down the gun, to back away. All was lost this day.

"Now, Amanda! I warn you that my temper is brittle indeed. I almost fear to touch you, lest I strangle the light from those glorious eyes! I'll take the gun."

"No!" Her voice was barely a whisper. "Let me by you. Let me go. I swear that I am innocent—"

"Let 'Highness' go? Why, milady! They would hang me for the very act!"

His words were light; they were followed by a long determined stride in her direction. She backed away as he lunged for her with the finesse of the fencer. "No!" she cried. "I'll shoot you, Eric, I swear it—"

"And I do believe you, milady!" he countered, approaching her nonetheless, a mocking light of challenge in his eyes. "Shoot me, then, if you dare, milady! But take heed that your weapon be loaded!" He moved like lightning, catching the gun by the barrel, sending it flying across the room. The firing mechanism snapped; the gun went off, sending the bullet into the wall.

He stared at her, hard. And then he smiled slowly, bitterly. "It *was* loaded, milady. And aimed upon *my heart.*"

She had never seen his eyes colder. Never seen his lip curl with such disdain.

She faced him, thinking frantically. She needed to turn, to run. There had to be somewhere else to go. If she could reach the door, she could escape the ship. No other man would seek to stop her. She could cast herself into the Chesapeake Bay. Eventually she could reach the shore. Dunmore's ships were lost to her, Robert had kidnapped her just to desert her to her fate, but if she could swim to the shore, she could eventually make it north and find General Howe's troops. If she could just escape Eric this night! He would offer her no mercy, not this time. She knew that as she saw the cold and wary eyes.

"And now, Highness . . ."

"Wait!" Amanda swallowed hard. She feared that she would faint as a rush of memory swept over her, leaving her hot and trembling. She knew so much about him. She knew the searing hellfire of his passion, and she knew the ice of his fury. Just as she knew the gentle sweep of his fingers . . . and the relentless power of his will and determination. He could step forward now and break her neck and be done with it, and by silver-blue rapier blades of his eyes that struck upon her now, it seemed that that was what he longed to do.

God! Deliver me from this man I love! she prayed in silence.

"Wait for what, milady? Salvation? You shall not find any!"

She stared at the gun, broken upon the floor. He had seized it with such power that the heavy stock had shattered. She glanced at him one more moment, then she burst into motion, determined to run, to risk any factor, just to escape him.

She was not quick enough. His arm grabbed her, his fingers winding into her hair. She screamed with the pain of it and panicked as she was brought swirling back into his arms. She fought his hold, squeezing her arms between them, pummeling his chest. Tears of desperation stung her eyes. She tried to kick him and quickly earned his wrath. He caught her wrists and wrenched them hard behind her back, and through it all she felt the simmering liquid heat of his body, bold and vibrant and recalling echoes of the past. She cried out as he pulled upon her wrists, and went still at last, pressed against him, tossing back her head to meet his eyes.

With one hand he held her wrists at the small of her back while he placed his left palm against her cheek and slowly stroked it. "So beautiful. So treacherous. But it is over now. Surrender, milady."

She met his gaze. Something of all that had lain between them touched her heart and seemed to skyrocket. Just the touch of his strength against her seemed explosive. Once love had flamed so fiercely and so strong! But their battles had been as passionate, and now she did not know what tempest ruled the blood that flowed within them and the air that churned about them. Her eyes burned with tears, but she could not give in now. Be it love, be it hate, what burned between them demanded that she not falter now. She shook her head and dared to offer him a rueful, wistful smile. "No surrender, my lord. No retreat, and no surrender."

Footsteps echoed upon a stairway and a second man came to a halt behind him. He was young, barely beginning to grow whiskers, and his eyes widened at the sight of her. "We've found her! Highness! She gave the ship and the intelligence to the British."

"Aye, we've found her," Eric said softly, and still his eyes bored into hers, with what thoughts she could not fathom. She did not look away, even with the young officer watching them. Then Eric muttered an oath and cast her from him. She nearly fell, but caught herself, and stood tall, backed against the paneling. She braced herself with her hands, and thought, How peculiar. The sea was so very calm she could scarcely feel the ship rock, and the room was alive with storms.

The young man suddenly let out a soft whistle as he watched her. "No wonder she played our men so false so easily!" he murmured.

Eric Cameron felt everything inside of him tighten like a vise at the man's words. She was still beautiful. More beautiful than ever. She was flush against the wall, cornered, yet still defiant. She was a perfect picture of femininity, of grace. So delicate and glorious as she stood, her breasts rising from her bodice with each breath, her flesh pale, as perfect as marble. She wore green silk with an overskirt and bodice of golden brocade. Her throat and shoulders were bare, and her hair was worn in soft ringlets that curled just over her shoulders. She was as cool and smooth as alabaster as she returned his stare, her eyes as green as the gown, her hair a startling and beautiful contrast with the shades of the silk and brocade. It was deep, deep red, sometimes sable, sometimes the color of the sunset, depending on the light.

He wanted to wrench her hair from the pins, he wanted to see it tumble down. He did not want to see her so silent, so beautiful, so still, so regal. Damn her. Her eyes defying him, even now.

"Aye," he said quietly. "It was easy for her to play men falsely."

"I wonder if they will hang her," the soldier said. "Would we hang a woman, General?"

Amanda felt a chill of fear sweep over her, and she swallowed hard to keep tears from rising to her eyes. She could see it. She would hear the drums beat. Hanging. It was a just punishment for treason. They would lead her along. They would set the rope around her neck, and she would feel the bristle of the hemp against her flesh.

Dunmore had sworn that he would have Eric hanged, were he ever to get his hands upon him. But Eric had never cared. Amanda wondered what fever it was that could fill a man with such haunting loyalty to a desperate cause. It was a passion that made him turn his back on his estates in England, risk his wealth and title and prestige and even his life. He had everything, and he was willing to cast it aside for this rebel cause of his.

She had risked her life upon occasion for her cause. Indeed, her very life might well stand on the line now.

The young officer stared at her still. He sighed softly again. "Milord, surely you *cannot* have her hanged!"

"Nay, I cannot," Eric agreed ironically, the silver and steel of his eyes upon her, "for she is, you see, my wife."

The man gasped. Eric turned to him impatiently. "Tell Daniel to set a course for Cameron Hall. Have someone come for this lieutenant. The Brits must be buried at sea; our own will find rest at home." He turned back to Amanda. "My love, I shall see you later." He bowed deeply to her, and then he was gone, the young officer on his heels. Two men quickly appeared, nodding her way in silence, and carefully picked up the body of the slain Highland lieutenant.

Then the door closed. Sharply.

He was gone. Eric was gone. The tempest had left the room, and still she was trembling, still she was in fear, and still she didn't know whether to thank God or to damn him. They had been apart so long, and now the war had come to them, and the battle was raging in her very soul.

Amanda cast herself upon the captain's bunk, her heart racing. Through the sloop's handsome draperies and the fine paned windows she could see the distant shore, the land they approached.

Cameron Hall. Rising white and beautiful upon the hill, the elegant manor house itself seemed to reproach her. It looked so very peaceful! The British had set their fires, but Robert had spoken the truth about the blazes. Obviously those fires had been put out with very little difficulty.

No dark billow of smoke marred the house or the outbuildings. Only the warehouses on the dock seemed to have burned with a vengeance. They were not so important. It was the house that mattered, she thought. She loved the house, more than Eric himself did, perhaps. It had been her haven in need. And in the turbulent months that had passed, she had strode the portrait gallery, and she had imagined the lives of those women who had come before her. She had seen to the polishing of their silver, she had taken tender care of the bedding and furnishings they had left behind.

A chill swept through her suddenly.

He wasn't going to hang her. What was he going to do with her? Could she vow that she would not leave the house, that she would take no more part in the war? She could never, never have set fire to the house. But he would never believe that now.

She closed her eyes and heard the orders to dock. She imagined the men, pulling in the *Lady Jane*'s sails, furling them tightly as the ship found her deep-water berth. She heard the fall of the plank, and the call of victory as men walked ashore.

The patriots had needed that victory! The British were heading toward New York, and Washington hadn't enough troops to meet them properly. The colonials were up against one of the finest fighting forces in the world.

Oh, couldn't he see! she thought in anguish. The British would win in the end, and they would hang Eric! They would hang him and George Washington and Patrick Henry and the Adamses and Hancock and all those foolish, foolish men!

The door opened again. Amanda sprang up. Her heart seemed to sink low in her chest. Frederick had come for her, the printer from Boston. Eric had saved his life once, and she knew Frederick would gladly die for him now.

"Where is Eric?" she demanded.

"Your husband will be with you soon enough, milady," Frederick said. "He has asked me to escort you to the house."

"Escort me?"

"Milady, none of us would seek to harm you." He was quiet for a moment. "Even if you are a spy."

"Frederick, please, I—"

His anguished eyes fell upon hers. "Oh, milady! Cameron Hall! How could you have betrayed his very home?"

"I did not, Frederick," she said wearily.

"Then—"

"I have no defense," she told him.

"Milady, I will take your word."

"Thank you." She did not tell him that her husband would not do so. She lowered her eyes quickly, feeling that tears sprang to them. If he had condemned her, if he had spoken with fury or wrath, it would have been easier.

"Come now," he said.

"Where are you taking me?" she asked him.

"Nowhere but to your own home, milady."

Amanda nodded to Frederick and swept through the cabin's narrow doorway. She climbed the ladder to the deck. As she came topside to the early-evening air, the chatter of the men died down, and one and all, they stared at her. They paused in their motions of cleaning the *Lady Jane*'s guns or in tying her sails. They were not navy but a ragtag outfit of militia men. She knew the men from the western counties by their buckskin fringed jackets, and she knew some of the old soldiers by the blue coats they wore, leftovers of the French and Indian Wars. Still others were clad differently, and she knew that they were the uniforms of the counties they had come from. Some were friends, and others were strangers.

She tried to steady herself to walk before them, and yet it did not seem that they condemned her too harshly. Someone began to whistle an old Scottish ballad. Then one by one they all began to bow to her. Confused, she nodded her head in turn as Frederick led her from the ship. She walked the plank to the dock.

The small coach awaited them. Pierre was driving. He did not look her way. Amanda walked to the coach and hoisted herself up, Frederick close behind her. She looked back to the ship. The old captain in a green rifleman's outfit saluted her.

She glanced quickly to Frederick. "I don't understand," she murmured.

Seating himself beside her, Frederick smiled. "All men salute a brave enemy in defeat."

"But they must hate me."

"Yes, some of them. But most men respect a fallen enemy who fights true to his or her heart. And those who do know the secret of 'Highness' might well wish that you had chosen your husband's side."

"I cannot help where my heart lies!"

"Neither can any man, milady," Frederick said. He was silent then. Pierre cracked the whip over the horse's head, and the wheels jolted over the rough path.

Amanda pulled back the curtain and stared up the expanse of verdant sloping ground to the mansion.

From the large paned windows to the broad porches, the house exuded the charm of the Tidewater. Amanda loved it; she had loved it from the moment she had first seen it. From the sweeping, polished mahogany stairway to the gallery with its fascinating portraits of the Camerons, she loved every brick and stone within the place.

The coach came to an abrupt halt. Pierre opened the door, still refusing to look at her. She wanted to strike him. She wanted to scream that none of it had been her fault.

He would not understand. She had left with Robert.

Amanda leapt from the carriage and started for the house, ignoring the servant. Frederick was quickly beside her, walking with her up the steps. He wasn't merely delivering her to the front door, she realized.

Frederick cleared his throat. "Lord Cameron will come to his chambers, milady."

Amanda looked at him and nodded. She thought about attempting to fly past him, to race into the woods that fringed the fields. She would never make it, she knew. Some of these people might still believe in her, and some of them loved her. But they loved her husband more.

And their cause was the cause of liberty, and not her own.

"Thank you, Frederick," she said, sweeping up her skirts and heading for the stairway. As she walked she heard his footsteps behind her.

She looked down and saw that the silk was stained with the Highland lieutenant's blood. She smelled of cannon fire and black powder.

She passed by the portraits in the gallery and felt as if they all, the Camerons who had come before her, stared down at her with damning reproach. I did not do this thing! she longed to cry out. But it was senseless. She was damned. She saw her own portrait and wondered if Eric would not quickly strike it from the wall. What other Cameron bride had ever betrayed her own house?

Finally Amanda stepped into the master chamber. Frederick closed the doors, and she was alone.

A rise of panic swelled within her breast. It hadn't been long ago that she had lain in the bed, dreaming. Spinning fantasies of the time when her husband would return.

Now she knew that he would return very soon, and she hadn't a fantasy left to believe in.

A soft cry of misery escaped her. She couldn't bear waiting for him, not here. Too many memories rested here. Memories of storms and fire and passionate upheaval, memories of laughter.

She had come here, determined to despise him. But from the first, her eyes had fallen upon his every movement. In the deepest anger she had watched him rise, watched him dress, or stand bare-chested before the windows, and even then, in the very beginning, some sweet secret thrill had touched her heart when she looked upon him, for he had been so fiercely fine, and he had wanted her with such blind, near-ruthless determination. He had wanted her so . . .

Once upon a time.

But now . . .

Her gaze fell upon the handsome bed that sat atop a dais. Beautifully carved of dark wood, draped in silk and brocade, it had always seemed a place of the greatest intimacy and privacy. She drew her eyes from the bed and looked up at the Queen Anne clock upon her dressing table. Nearly six. Night was coming at last.

But not Eric.

Amanda began to pace the room, too nervous to dwell on the future, too frightened to recall the past.

Darkness came.

Cassidy, Eric's ebony-black valet, came to the room, knocking before entering. He looked at her sadly.

"What? Have you come to hang me too, Cassidy?"

He shook his head. "No, Lady Cameron. Perhaps there was more than the eyes could see." He was her friend—but Eric's first.

Still, she smiled. "Thank you."

"I've brought wine and roasted wild turkey," he told her. He moved back into the hallway and returned, bearing with him a heavy silver tray. "And Cato and Jack are bringing up water for the hip bath."

"Thank you, Cassidy," she told him. She smiled awkwardly at him. His accent was wonderful, with traces of Eric's own enunciation, as acquired at Oxford. He was in white and black, very much a lord's gentleman. He was born a slave and had become a free man here.

She was no longer free, she realized.

She was a prisoner in her own room in her own house. More than any slave the Camerons had ever owned, she was a prisoner here. The slaves were allowed to earn their freedom if they chose. She would not have that luxury.

Cassidy said no more to her, but set the tray down upon the table. Jack and Cato, in the red, white, and green Cameron livery, came with water, and the bath was dragged out. She waited until the hip bath was halfway filled with the steaming water and then thanked the men. Her fight was not with them. Margaret might well call her a Tory bitch, but perhaps the others understood that life was far more complex than any neat little label.

"Where is Lord Cameron?" she asked Cassidy.

"Involved with affairs, milady. They plan to follow on the heels of Lord Dunmore and see that he is pushed from our coast once and for all."

Affairs . . . so he might not come back to her at all. She might spend day after day in this room, awaiting her sentence. She cleared her throat. "Is he . . . is he coming back, do you know? Or am I perhaps to be turned over to some Continental official?"

"Oh, no. Lord Cameron will come."

His words were not reassuring.

She wished that she *had* been dragged before some Continental court. Any man would deal with her more gently than her husband, she thought.

"May I see Danielle?"

"I am sorry, milady."

"Is she all right?"

"Yes, she is well."

Cassidy bowed to her and left with the others. The door closed. She heard a key twist, locking her in, and she sank down at the table and tried to eat. The food was delicious but she had no appetite so she sipped wine and stared at the darkness beyond the windows.

At length she realized that the bath water was growing cold and that the charred smell of her clothing and hair was distasteful. Glancing at the door, she felt her numbness leaving her as she wondered if her husband would return.

He could be gone for days, she reminded herself.

She finished the wine for courage, then shed her rich gown, hose, corset, and petticoats and stepped into the water. The warmth was delicious. She sank beneath the water to soak her hair, and scrubbed it thoroughly, as she scrubbed her flesh.

She could not wash away her fear or her thoughts. What would Eric think if he knew that she had bargained with Robert Tarryton to save the house? He would not believe it, or worse. He would think that she had sought to leave with Tarryton.

The evening was cool. Rising from the tub, Amanda folded a huge linen towel about herself and shivered, wishing that she had asked Cassidy for a fire. She walked to the window and pulled back the drapes. Down the slope by the docks she could see tremendous activity. Half the militia was camped out on their property, so it seemed.

God, give me courage! she prayed. And if you cannot, please let me disappear into the floorboards.

God did not answer her prayer.

She started, hearing a sound, and whirled around. Eric was there. He had come, opening the door in silence, standing there now in silence, watching her. Their eyes met. He turned and closed and locked the door, then leaned against it, his eyes fixed on hers once again. His tone was soft, its menace unmistakable.

"Well, Highness, it has come. Our time of reckoning."

Amanda's heart slammed against her breast. She wanted to speak but words failed her.

He awaited her reply, and when there was none, a crooked mocking smile curled his lip, and he walked toward her, dark, towering, and determined.

"Aye, milady, our time of reckoning at last."

A time of reckoning.

It had been coming a long while. A long, long while. Ever since he had first set eyes upon her that long-ago night in the city of Boston.

It had all begun then. The tempest of war.

And the tempest that lay between them. . . .

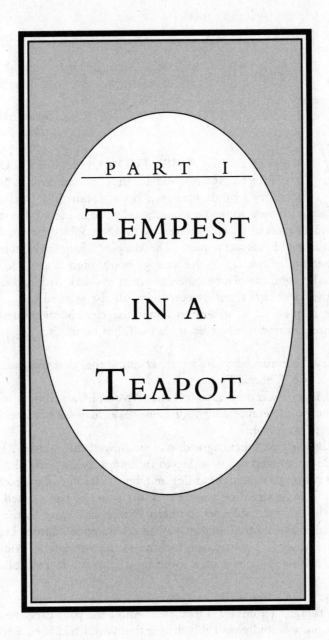

PART I

TEMPEST

IN A

TEAPOT

1

 HISKEY, ERIC?" SIR THOMAS SUGGESTED.

Eric Cameron stood by the den window in Sir Thomas Mabry's handsome town house. Something had drawn him there as soon as the contracts had been signed. He stared out at the night. An occasional coach clattered by on the cobbled streets, but for the most part, the night was very quiet. The steeples of the old churches shone beneath the moonlight, and from his vantage point, high atop a hill, Eric could see down to the common. The expanse of green was dark with night, cast in the shadow of the street lamps, and as peaceful as all else seemed.

Yet there seemed to be a tension about the city. Some restlessness. Eric couldn't quite describe it, not even to himself, but he felt it.

"Eric?"

"Oh, sorry." He turned to his host, accepting the glass that was offered to him. "Thank you, Thomas."

Thomas Mabry clicked his glass to Eric's. "Milord Cameron! A toast to you, sir. And to our joint venture with your *Bonnie Sue*. May she sail to distant shores —and make us both rich."

"To the *Bonnie Sue*!" Eric agreed, and swallowed the whiskey. He and Sir Thomas had just invested in a new ship to sail to far-distant ports. Eric's stores of tobacco and cotton went straight to England, but with some of the recent trouble and his own feelings regarding a number of the taxes, he had wanted to experiment and send his own ships to southern Europe and even to the Pacific to acquire tea and some of the luxuries he had once imported from London.

"Interesting night," Thomas said, looking to the window as Eric had done. "They say that there's to be a mass meeting of citizens. Seven thousand, or so they say."

"But why?"

"This tea thing," Thomas said irritably. "And I tell you, Parliament couldn't be behaving more stupidly over this than if foolishness had been a requisite for representatives!"

Amused and interested, Eric swallowed most of his drink. "You're on the side of the rebels?"

"Me? Well, that hints of treason, eh?" He made a snorting sound, then laughed. "I tell you this. No good will come of it all. The British government gave the British East India Company a substantial rebate on tea shipped here. It's consigned to certain individuals—which will shove any good number of local merchants right out of business. Something will happen. In this city! With agitators like the Adamses and that John Hancock . . . well, trouble is due, that it is!"

"This makes our private venture all the more interesting," Eric pointed out.

"That it does!" Thomas agreed, laughing. "Well, we shall get rich or hang together then, my friend, and that is a fact."

"Perhaps." Eric grinned.

"Well, now that we've discussed business and the state of the colony," Sir Thomas said, "perhaps we should rejoin the party in the ballroom. Anne Marie will be quite heartbroken if you do not share a dance."

"Ah, Sir Thomas, I would not think to break the lady's heart," Eric said. He had promised his old friend's daughter that they would not tarry on business all night, that he would come back to the ballroom and join her. "Of course, her dance card is always filled so quickly."

Sir Thomas laughed and clapped him on the shoulder. "But she has eyes only for you, my friend."

Eric smiled politely, disagreeing. Anne Marie had eyes that danced along with her feet. She was ambitious, and a flirt, but a sweet and honest one. Eric was wryly aware of his worth on the marriage mart. His vast wealth would have made him highly eligible even if he had been eighty, his family pedigree would have stood him well had he rickets, black teeth, and a balding pate. He was not yet thirty, he had all his teeth, and his legs were strong and very straight.

Perhaps Anne Marie would catch him one day. He simply was not of a mind to be caught at the moment.

A tapping on the door was quickly followed by an appearance by the lady herself. Anne Marie was a soft blonde with huge blue eyes and a coquette's way with a fan. She smiled her delight at him and slipped her hand through his arm. "Eric! You are coming now, aren't you?"

"Let him finish his whiskey, daughter!" Sir Thomas commanded.

"I shall do so quickly," he promised Anne Marie. He swallowed down the amber liquid, smiling as she pouted.

Suddenly his smile faded as his gaze was caught by a flash of color beyond the open door. A strange sense of the French déjà-vu seemed to seize him as he caught first an impression, nothing more. Then the dancers in the hall swept by again. As a gentleman shifted to the left, he saw the girl who had so thoroughly caught his attention. Her gown was blue, deep, striking blue, with a full sweeping skirt and a daring décolletage trimmed with red ribbons and creamy lace. Against that blue, tendrils of her hair streamed down in a rich and elegant display of sable ringlets. They curved about her naked shoulders and over the rise of her breasts, enhancing her every breath and movement. Her hair was so very dark . . . and then, with a shift of light, it wasn't dark at all, but red as only the deepest sunset could be red.

His gaze traveled at last from her breast to her face, and his breath caught and held. Her eyes were the most startling, purest emerald he had ever seen, fringed by dark lashes. Her features were stunning, perfectly molded, lean and delicate, with a long aquiline and entirely patrician nose, high-set cheekbones, slim, arched brows. All that hinted of something less than absolute perfection was the wideness of her mouth, not that her lips were not rose, were not formed and defined beautifully, but they held something that cold marble perfection could not, for the lower lip was very full, the top curved, and the whole of it so sensual that even within the innocent smile she offered her partner, there could be found a wealth of sensuality. She wore a tiny black velvet beauty patch at the side of her cheek, very near her ear, and that, too, seemed to enhance her perfection, for her ears were small and prettily shaped.

There was something familiar about her. Had he seen her before? He would have remembered a meeting with her. From this moment onward he would never forget her. He had not moved since he had seen her, had not spoken, yet he had never felt more startlingly alive. He had lived a reckless life, mindful of his inheritance, but fiercely aware of his independence, and women—virtuous and not so virtuous—had always played a part within it.

He had never known anyone to affect him so. To render him so mesmerized, and so very hot and tense and . . . hungry, all at once.

"Eric? Are you with us?" Anne Marie said, annoyed.

Thomas Mabry laughed. "I believe he's just seen a friend, my dear."

"A friend?" Eric managed to query Thomas politely.

"Lady Amanda Sterling. A Virginian, such as yourself, Eric. Ah, but she has spent most of the past years at a school for young ladies in London. And perhaps you have been at sea on those ships of yours when the young lady has been in residence."

"Ah, yes, perhaps," Eric replied to his host. So the woman was Lady Amanda Sterling. They had met, but it had been years before. Still, it was an occasion that neither of them should have forgotten. There had been a hunt. She had been a mere child of eight upon a pony and he had been longing for the very mature and beautiful upstairs maid at their host's manor. Young Lady Amanda had jostled her pony ahead of his and the result had been disaster with both of them being thrown from their mounts. And when he had chastised her, she had bitten him. He hadn't given a fig about Lord Sterling and had paddled her there and then. She had raged like a little demon, the child had.

The child had grown.

"Eric, may we dance?" Anne Marie prodded sweetly. "I promise an introduction. Father, do remind me from now on not to have parties when Mandy is our guest, will you?"

Thomas laughed. Eric joined in, and Anne Marie grinned prettily. Eric gathered his wits about him and reached politely for her arm. "Anne Marie, I am honored."

He led her out to the floor, and they began to dance. Anne Marie gave him a lazy smile as he swept her expertly about the floor, seeking out the woman who had seized his attention. He saw her again. Saw her laugh for her partner, saw the devil's own sizzle in her eyes. He thought that he recognized something of himself within that look. She would not be governed by convention, she would demand her own way, and fight for it fiercely.

The sound of her laughter came to him again and he felt a reckless fever stir within him. Come hell itself, and time be damned, he would have to have that woman.

Who was the man who caused her laughter, he wondered.

Anne Marie, watching him indulgently, answered the question that he did not ask. "That's Damien Roswell—her cousin," she said sweetly.

"Cousin?" He smiled. His hand tightened upon hers.

Anne Marie nodded sagely. "But—and this is a grave 'but,' I must warn you! —the lady is in love."

"Oh?"

Love so often meant nothing. Girls of Amanda Sterling's tender young age were in and out of love daily. Their fathers seldom let the affairs go past fluttering hearts and dreams.

Yet her eyes were wild, deep with laughter and secrets and passion. He smiled, thinking she was one lass who should probably be wed and quickly—to an appropriate person, of course.

"And he loves her," Anne Marie warned.

"Who is 'he'?"

"Why, Lord Tarryton. Robert Tarryton. 'Tis said that he has adored her for years, as she has adored him. She will become eighteen in March, and it is believed that he will ask Lord Sterling for her hand then. It is a perfect match. They are all loyal Tories, landed and wealthy. You're frowning, Eric," Anne Marie warned him.

"Am I?" Tarryton. He knew the man, if vaguely. The old Lord Tarryton had been a good Indian fighter, but Eric didn't think that this young Tarryton could hold a candle to his lamented father. Their properties were not so far apart that they had not met upon occasion, nor did the social organization of Virginia allow for much secrecy in private life.

There were rumors in very high places that Lord Tarryton was seeking a union with the widowed Duchess of Owenfield. As the lady was young and childless, dispensations could be made to give the title to Lord Tarryton.

"Aye, you're frowning! And you're very fierce when you do so. You take my breath away, you cause me quite to shiver and make me wonder what woman would dare to wish that you might court her!"

He grinned at Anne Marie's sweet dramatics and thought that they would always be the very best of friends. He started to assure her that she would dare anything she chose when he found himself staring over her shoulder instead.

Amanda Sterling had ceased to dance. Her young escort was whispering earnestly to her near the door. She kissed his cheek, then watched as he retrieved his cloak and hat and discreetly disappeared into the night.

She stood still a minute. Then she, too, hurried toward the door, procuring a huge black hooded cape from the halltree, and then rushed out into the night.

"What the—"

"What's the matter?"

"Why, she's just departed."

"Amanda!" Anne Marie cried in distress. "Oh, how could she! If Lord Sterling returns . . ."

Eric glanced at her sharply. She was very pale, not acting at all. "He is about on business this night. Perhaps he will not come back—he sometimes stays gone." She paused, her eyes wide. Eric realized that Anne Marie was trying to tell him that Lord Sterling frequented the area brothels and left his daughter in Sir Thomas's care.

"If he comes back?"

"It is just that he is so . . ."

"I know Sterling," Eric said, waiting for more.

"I'm just always afraid that he shall—hurt her."

"Has he ever?"

"Not that I know of. But the way he looks at her sometimes . . . his own daughter. I do not envy her, no matter what her wealth or title. I pray that Robert marries her soon!"

Eric kissed her cheek. "I'm going out. I'll find her," he assured Anne Marie. She still gazed at him anxiously. "Wait up for me," he advised her softly. "I'll come back, I promise."

He offered her an encouraging smile and swept by her. He, too, went to the door after retrieving his cloak and his hat. He turned to Anne Marie and waved, and exited the house.

As soon as he was on the streets, he could almost feel the tension on the air and beneath his feet. This night, Boston was alive. He wondered just what was going on.

He called to the Mabry groom, and his horse was quickly brought to him. "Do you know anything about what is going on?"

Dark eyes rolled his way. "They say it's a tea party. A tempest in tea, Lord Cameron. Dark days is a-comin', milord! You mark my words, dark days is a-comin'!"

"Perhaps," Eric agreed. He nudged his mount forward. It was true, something was afoot tonight. He could hear men walking, men calling out.

Damien Roswell had gone into the night. And Lady Amanda Sterling had followed. Just what route might she have taken in these dangerous times? He nudged his mount on, determined to find her.

Frederick Bartholomew shivered as he hurried along the street. The night was cold, and a mist fringed the harbor, floating about the city lanterns, making the ships that sat in the harbor and at dock look ghostly.

It had been a quiet night . . . but now it was about to explode.

Frederick could see the great masts of the proud sailing ships that ventured forth from England to her colonies rise high against the night sky, seeming to disappear into the darkness and the clouds. The cold winter's water lapped softly against the sides of the ships. A breeze stirred, lifting the mist of winter, swirling about cold and certain, and still so quiet.

Then the peace of the night was broken. A shout rang out.

"Boston Harbor's a teapot tonight!" a fellow shouted.

Then their footsteps began to thunder. Dozens of footsteps, and the night came alive.

We must be a curious sight, he thought. There were fifty or so of them, streaming out of the mist and out of the darkness and through the cold of winter, toward the harbor ships. At first glance they would appear to be Indians, for they were half naked, bronzed, darkly bewigged, and painted, as if in warpaint.

They were at war, in a way, but they were not Indians, and it was not death they sought to bring to the ships, unless it was the death of tyranny.

They rowed out to the three British ships riding in the harbor and streamed upon them.

Frederick stood in the background then.

The head "Indians" were polite as they demanded the keys to the tea chests from the captains.

"All right, men!" came the command.

Frederick still remained in the distance, watching as his friends apologized when they knocked out the guards. Then he joined in; they all set to their tasks, dumping the contents of 340 chests of tea into the sea. Fires burned high against the darkness and the mist. The men went about their task with efficiency, unmolested, for it was unexpected by the British and condoned by the multitude of the citizens of Boston.

Frederick Bartholomew, printer by trade, quietly watched the tea fall into the sea. Beside him, one of his friends, Jeremy Duggin, chortled. "A fine brew we're making, strong and potent!"

"And sure to bring about reprisals," Frederick reminded him.

Jeremy was silent for a moment. "We'd no choice, man. We'd no choice at all. Not if we intended to keep the British out of our pockets."

"Lads! Hurry now. Swab down the decks, see that all is left shipshape! We've not come to cause real injury to the captains or the men—the tea has been our business, and that is all. Now hurry!"

The older men in the crowd had planned the action. The younger ones had carried it out with glee. Many of the boys were college students from Harvard. For some it was a prank, a lark.

Others saw what the future might bring, but all carried out the work, and to a man, they cleaned the ships when they were done.

The keys were politely returned to the captains.

"Away!" someone called. "Our deed is done. Let's flee! The troops will be out soon enough."

"Come then, Jeremy!" Frederick called. They were both oiled and slick, wearing buckskin breeches and vests. Frederick was starting to shiver violently. Out on the water, it was viciously cold.

"Aye, and hurry, man!" Jeremy said.

They climbed down to the small boats that would bring them to the dock. "A teapot she is! The harbor is a teapot tonight! She steams, she brews! And what comes, soon, all men will soon see."

It was one of their leaders shouting then, passionately, heartfully.

The British fighting force was estimated to be one of the finest in the world. If it came to war . . . Frederick thought.

If they were caught . . .

There were so many of them. The entire port of Boston had been with them, except for the British troops and the minority of loyalists.

The Indians reached dry land again. They were making little secret of their actions, marching to the grand old elm, the Liberty Tree. They would not hang for their deeds this night. The governor could not see that they all hanged! If the king had thought that Boston rebelled before, let him see the people after a heinous act like that!

"Back home, me lads! And a deed well done!" one of the leaders called.

Frederick tensed, for he was not done with his night's work. As the others began to drift away, returning to their homes or heading for their chosen taverns, Frederick stood waiting by the tree.

Two men soon appeared before him, one another printer, a man named Paul Revere, and one the wealthy and admired John Hancock. Hancock was a cousin of the well-known patriot Samuel Adams, but it was the seizure of his ship *Liberty* by the British that had turned him so intensely toward the cause of the patriots. He was a handsome man, richly dressed in gold brocade and matching breeches. "Have you come by the arms, Frederick?" Hancock asked him.

Frederick nodded.

"We still hope it'll not come to conflict, but the Sons of Liberty must now begin to take precautions," Revere warned him. Frederick himself had become involved because of Paul Revere. He had begun as an apprentice in the older man's employ. Now they were both kept busy printing pamphlets and flyers for the cause of freedom.

"They come from Virginia, sir. A good friend travels to the western counties and gets French weapons from the Indians there," Frederick said nervously. This was not like their tea party—this could be construed as high treason. "The wagon is down the street, near the cemetery."

"Good work, Frederick. And your Virginian is a good friend, indeed. Go ahead now, and the West County men will follow quietly behind you. If you see a redcoat anywhere, take flight. Sam has said that we've had a leak and that the Brit captain Davis knows we're acquiring arms. Go quickly, and take care."

Frederick nodded. He was anxious to return home. He believed passionately in his cause, but he believed, too, in the love he shared with his young wife and in the future he sought for his infant son. He'd tried to explain to Elizabeth that it was for the future that he had come out this night. They were a free people. They had won the right to representation in 1215 when the barons had forced King John of England to sign the Magna Carta. They were good Englishmen, even if they were colonists. It was not the idea of taxes they minded so much—it was the idea of taxation without representation.

No one really thought that it might come to war.

And yet, already, there were whispers of bloody, horrible conflict, of American fields strewn with blood . . .

He didn't dare think of blood, not now. He still had to make it to the wagon, and then home.

He hurried along the street, turning corners, moving in silence. He knew that he was followed, and he took care to allow the West County Sons of Liberty easily keep tempo with his gait and yet keep hidden.

At last he passed the cemetery. In the cold mist of the night, the sight of the weathered tombstones made him shiver. He was almost upon the simple wagon that held the French armaments. His breath came quickly. Before him he could see the shadowed figure of his contact. The figure saluted sharply, then hurried away to disappear into the cemetery.

Frederick's feet seemed to slap against the cobblestones.

He passed the wagon by and exhaled heavily. He was almost home. Suddenly he heard a flurry of footsteps. He turned about. There was a woman running down the street in a huge sweeping cape.

"Damien?" a female voice called.

Frederick's heart began to pound. She was not following anyone named Damien, she was following him! He ducked around a corner into a lamplit street and started to run across it, then he paused. There was a sentry out. A sentry in a red coat.

"Halt!" the soldier cried.

Never—come death or all of hell's revenge, he could not halt.

He streaked across the road. Then he heard the woman calling out. "No! Oh, no!"

A Brown Bess was fired, but though he did not pause to look, Frederick was certain that the woman had caused the sentry to lose the precision of his aim. He was struck, but in the shoulder. He barely suppressed a scream as the bullet tore into him.

He clasped the injury with his good hand and sagged against a brick building. He could hear the sentry arguing with the woman, and he could hear the delicate tones of the woman's voice. Who was she, and why was she saving him?

He closed his eyes and thanked God for that small favor, but when he tried to open his eyes again, he discovered that he could barely see. He was falling, falling against the building and toward the mud beneath him.

He heard the sound of hoofbeats.

There was a horse pounding down the street. Frederick tried to push away from the wall. He had to find a place to hide, and quickly.

He staggered into the road. Looking up, he could see the spire of the Old North Church rising out of the mist. Or was the mist in his eyes? He was falling.

He would never see Elizabeth again. He would never cradle his infant son in his arms again. Was this, then, the price of liberty? Death and bloodshed? He would never see her face again. He would never see her smile, he would never feel the tender caress of her lips against the heat of his skin.

The rider was upon him. Frederick threw up his arms as a great black stallion reared before him. "Whoa, boy, whoa!" a man called out, and Frederick staggered back. The massive animal came to a rigid halt, and the rider leapt from his back.

Frederick fought to stand but slumped to the ground instead. The man coming toward him was tall and towering, and wearing a fine black greatcoat trimmed with warm fur. He wore fine boots over impeccable white breeches and a crimson frock coat. His shirt was smocked and laced. Dimly Frederick realized that he was not just a man of means, but a man with an aura of confidence and the assured and supple movement of a well-trained fencer or fighter. Dressed in his buckskin and paint, he had come across a member of the nobility.

Now he would not even die in peace. He would be dragged into prison, tried by a puppet jury, condemned by the king to be shot or hanged by the neck until dead.

"What in God's name—" the stranger began.

"Aye, in God's name, milord, for the love of God, kill me quick!" Frederick cried.

As he reached out, trying to ward off an expected blow, he saw the stranger's face. It was a striking face, composed of steel-fire eyes, a hard jaw, and strong cheekbones. He was dark-haired and wore no wig. His very presence was menacing, for he was not just tall but extremely well muscled for all that he gave the appearance of a certain leanness.

"Hold, boy, I've no mind for murder in the streets!" the stranger said, a touch of humor upon his lips. "You're no Indian, and that's a fact. I can only determine that you were in on the trouble at the harbor. Is that it?"

Frederick remained stubbornly silent. He was doomed anyway.

"Ah . . . perhaps there is even something worse," the stranger murmured.

"Search this way!" came a shout from the street. "I'm sure I've seen one of them!"

"Wait!" Frederick could hear the woman's frantic voice. The stranger stiffened, hearing it too. He seemed puzzled.

"Redcoat coming," the man murmured. "We'd best get you out of here, boy. I've business to attend to, but still . . . I'm wondering how badly you've been hurt. Now first . . ." He took off his cloak and wrapped it around Frederick.

"I'm not a boy. I'm married and I've got a child."

"Well, you're one up on me then, lad. Come on, then, take my shoulder, we'll have to move quick."

"You'll turn me in—"

"And leave your wee babe an orphan? No, man, the British will have their revenge for this night—a blind man would know that. But I can't see why your life should be forfeit."

Frederick was not a small man, but his strange deliverer swept him up into his arms and quickly slung him over saddle on the flanks of the black stallion. He mounted the horse behind Frederick and then paused briefly again. "I dare not go back by Faneuil Hall. We'll have to move westward."

Breathing desperately against the pain in his shoulder, Frederick swallowed hard. "My house, milord, is just down the street."

There. He had done it. He had told this man where he lived. He might be bringing danger down upon Elizabeth and the baby. He might have sealed their fate.

"Point me onward, and I will see you home."

But before Frederick could do so, the sentry rounded the corner with the woman in the cloak following close beside him. "Sir! A man is lost, I tell you, and you must give up this ridiculous manhunt to help me!" the feminine voice cried.

The sentry stood dead still staring down the cobbled street to where Frederick sagged atop the horse. Frederick's rescuer stepped forward. "Amanda!"

Frederick could see that she stared at him blankly, but perhaps the sentry did not fathom the look. The man stepped forward, drawing her toward him. "My betrothed, Officer. Her father would be horribly distressed if he knew that she was roaming the streets. He would charge me with negligence, and . . . well . . . My friend, have a heart. Were you to report this, my lovely prize might well be snatched from my very hands."

"What? Your betrothed—" she began in protest.

"Yes!" he snapped, narrowing his eyes. "She has lapses!" the man said quickly, and he caught hold of her with force, pulling her against him in a fine semblance of desperate affection. Frederick heard his urgent and commanding whisper. "If you wish your Damien well, you will shut your mouth now!"

She went stiff, but still. "Take the lady, milord, and save me some time and strength!" the soldier complained. "I'm looking for a dangerous, armed rebel. I followed his trail—who is that up on your horse?" he said with sudden sharp suspicion.

"My friend has partied too heartily this night. We've been at the home of Sir Thomas Mabry, and well . . . young fellows do imbibe too freely upon occasion. Isn't that right, Mandy?"

She went very stiff, but agreed. As she smiled to the sentry, Frederick saw that she was very beautiful. "It was quite a party, Officer," she murmured.

"There's parties all about tonight, so it seems!" The sentry saluted the man. "Milord, then, if you've things in hand, I'll be on my way."

"Quite right! Thank you."

The sentry moved on. His footsteps fell upon the cobblestones, then faded away.

"Who are you, sir, and what do you think you're doing?" the woman hissed. "Where's Damien? And what do you know about him?"

"I only know, mam'selle, that you were about to lead the king's men straight to him."

"And what difference would that make?" she demanded heatedly.

"I don't know, nor can I care. This man needs help."

"Help! He's been shot! Oh, my God! He's one of the rabble, one of the dissidents—"

"He's a bleeding human being, milady, and you'll help him since you're here! Then I'll see you home!"

"I don't need you to see me anywhere—"

"You do need me, milady. And I need you at the moment. Come, let me put my arm about your shoulder and sing. That should see us as far as this poor man's place. Frederick! You must lead us, for I don't know where we're going."

There was no choice. Frederick told him the number of his house, and they hurried onward. They could still hear the soldiers running blindly about the streets. The night was coming more and more alive as news of the night's deed spread quickly from house to house.

Soldiers passed them again. The man cast his head against the woman's shoulder and stumbled, singing. "Stop it, you lout!" the woman cried.

"Ah, Mandy, love, drunken lout—it's a drunken lout I am. 'Scuse me, Officer!" He stumbled, looked about sheepishly, and pulled the woman against him again, but led the horse along with perfect direction. The soldiers snickered—and left them alone.

Frederick could almost hear the woman's teeth grate, and if he didn't hurt so badly, he'd be laughing. What were they doing with him, he wondered, for they were aristocrats, the two of them. Alive in a sea of the Sons of Liberty.

It was a patriot's city! Frederick thought proudly, and then he wondered again at the man who carried him homeward. He winced. This man was a lord.

But his accent sounded a bit . . . colonial. It was cultured, it wasn't a northern accent, it had a softer slur to it. Maybe there was hope. Why, George Washington, a growing power in Virginia, was friends with Lord Fairfax, a man of importance very loyal to the crown. The time would come when a man had to choose sides. It would come soon.

The man reined in on the horse quickly as they stopped before the house. Frederick didn't realize how weak he was until he was lifted bodily from the black stallion. "Help me!" the man demanded quickly of the girl. She complied, seething, helping as Frederick fell from the horse into the man's arms.

Quickly, competently, the man brought him to his door and knocked upon it.

Elizabeth came and opened the door. Frederick tried to rise against the stranger's shoulder. He saw her face, saw her soft gray eyes widen with alarm, but then she responded ably, drawing them into the small but comfortable home where they lived.

"Frederick!" she cried when the door was closed against the night.

"He's taken a shot in the shoulder, and he drifts in and out of consciousness," the stranger was explaining. His voice quickened. "We need to pluck the bullet out—he's probably got a broken arm and collar bone, but ma'am, first, we need to wash away the paint, in case of a visitor."

"The paint!" The girl gasped.

Elizabeth gaped at the strangers for a moment. The girl was stunning, well dressed, beautiful. There was no doubt of the man's prestige and power, for though his clothing was not overly elegant, the cut and quality were unmistakable.

"Let's lay him down, shall we?" the man said softly.

"Oh, oh! Of course!" Elizabeth agreed.

Frederick drifted in and out of reality as they laid him out and bathed him. He was offered a bottle of home-distilled whiskey, and he drank it deeply. Then the man was digging into his shoulder for the bullet and Elizabeth, with tears in her eyes, was clamping her hand over his mouth and begging him to silence.

"Let me," the girl said suddenly. Elizabeth and the man stared at her. She shrugged. "I've some skill."

"How?" the man asked her.

She shrugged dispassionately. "My father has been shot upon occasion," she said. She smiled at Frederick and brought the blade of a knife against his flesh.

Frederick passed out cold.

Eric watched with a cool assessing gaze as Lady Amanda Sterling removed the bullet from the young man's shoulder. Her touch was both gentle and expert, and she murmured that it was best that he had lost consciousness, for he would feel no pain. "There's no break in the shoulder, I'm quite certain." She glanced at Elizabeth who stood by, wringing her hands upon her apron, tears in her eyes. "Cleanse the wound with alcohol, and I'm sure that all will be well."

Elizabeth Bartholomew fell down upon her knees, grasping Lady Sterling's hands. "Thank you! Oh, thank you—"

"Please!" Amanda Sterling's beautiful face flushed to a soft rose. "Don't thank me! God alone knows how I have come here, and I intend to leave now. This is a bed of traitors—"

"You are good, lady! So kind—"

Amanda Sterling, her hood fallen back, her hair glistening a glorious red in the firelight, pulled Elizabeth to her feet. "Please don't. I'm leaving, and I—"

"Lady Sterling would not dream of betraying you," Eric said firmly. Amanda glanced at him quickly. He saw the fury and defiance in her startling emerald eyes, but she did not deny his words.

"Warn your husband that he is a traitor against the king," she said to the woman.

"But you will not turn us in."

"No." She hesitated a moment. "No, you've my word, I shall not turn you in."

Eric stepped forward, taking her arm. "I'll be back," he told Elizabeth. "I shall return Lady Amanda—"

"I can return well enough on my own—"

"The Sons of Liberty are on the streets, milady, as well as British soldiers—as well as some common rapists and thieves ready to take advantage of the situation. I promised Anne Marie that I would find you, and for her, I shall return you."

He set his hand upon her with a force she could not deny. She seemed to sense the implacable determination in his words, so she merely stared at his hand, gritted her teeth, and agreed. "Fine."

She swept around, then paused, looking back to Elizabeth. The young wife now knelt by her husband with such a look of love and anxiety in her eyes that even Lady Sterling seemed to soften. "Keep him well," she murmured, and exited quickly to the streets.

Eric followed her, catching her arm when she would have walked ahead. She spun about, staring at him with her chin and nose regally high. He smiled. "Did you ride?"

"No, I—"

His voice deepened harshly. "You have been walking all this distance on a night like this? What an idiot! You could have been robbed of that splendor, stripped naked, raped, killed!"

"You are crude!"

"You are a fool."

She tried to wrench her hand from his hold. He had already released her to set his hands about her waist and throw her up atop his horse. Before she could protest he was mounted behind her. Her back went very stiff. "How do I know that you are not about to rob, rape, or knife me, sir?" she demanded coolly.

"Because I am worth far more than you are, I prefer my women warm, willing, and talented, and murder simply isn't among my decadent hobbies." He nudged his horse into a canter. She twisted her face against the chill of the night, shivering as she raised her voice so that he might hear her.

"You may take me back to the Sir Thomas's, milord, but it will do you no good. I must find Damien."

Eric hesitated. He had an idea where young Roswell might be, if he was in any way involved with the dissidents. He reined in so sharply that she crashed back against him. The sweet scent of her hair teased his nostrils and the shocking warmth of her body lay flush against his.

"Milord—" She gasped, but he ignored her, nudging his heels against his mount's flanks and leading the animal toward the left.

"We'll find Damien then," he said.

They rode through the streets until they came to a tavern. The street was very quiet there, the light within was dim. Eric dismounted. "Don't move!" he ordered her. Then he turned and entered the tavern.

A multitude of men were there, engaged in soft and quiet conversation. There were no drunks about, just working men in their coarse coats and capes and tricorns, huddled about the meager warmth of the fire. At his entrance, all eyes turned to him. Several faces went pale as the quality of his clothing was taken into account.

Someone rushed forward—the barkeeper, he thought. "Milord, what is it that we can do—"

"I need a word with Mr. Damien Roswell."

"Milord, he is not—"

"I am here, Camy." The handsome young man who had partnered Amanda in the dance stepped forward. He stretched out his hand. "You're Lord Cameron. I've heard much about you."

Eric arched a brow. "Have you?"

"Why were you looking for me?" Damien asked carefully.

Eric cleared his throat. "I am not. A lady is."

"Amanda!" He gasped. "Then she knows . . ."

"She knows nothing. But perhaps you should come along."

Damien nodded instantly. He and Eric exited the tavern together without a backward glance.

From atop Eric's horse, the girl cried out. "Damien! You had me so worried!" She leapt down gracefully and ran forward.

"Amanda! You shouldn't have followed me."

"You are in trouble, off on your own," she said worriedly.

Eric stepped back on the porch of the tavern, watching the two together. Damien turned to him. "Thank you, milord. Thank you most fervently. If I can ever be of assistance to your—"

"I'll let you know," Eric drawled calmly. He tipped his hat to Lady Amanda. "Good evening, milady."

"Milord," she said stiffly. Had she been a cat, he thought, her back would have been arched, her claws unsheathed. He had not made much of an impression. He smiled deeply anyway, feeling as if he burned deep inside. He did not mind her manner, and he was willing to wait. She did not know it as yet, but she would see him again. And again. And in the end, he would have his way.

He swept his hat from his head and bowed low, then mounted his horse.

"Who was that arrogant . . . bastard?" he heard her demand of her cousin.

"Mandy! I'm shocked. What language!" Damien taunted.

"Who was he?"

"Lord Cameron. Lord Eric Cameron, of Cameron Hall."

"Oh!" She gasped. "Him!"

So she, too, had remembered their meeting long ago. Eric smiled and led his mount into the darkness of the streets. They would meet again.

2

WHEN FREDERICK CAME TO, HE WAS STILL ON THE sofa, he could hear the fire crackling and burning in the hearth, and he could feel its warmth.

There was a certain commotion at the door. Elizabeth and the man were both standing there, talking to the redcoat before them.

"I assure you, Sergeant," the man was saying, "that I know nothing about any tea party at the harbor, nor do I know anything about any smuggled and hidden arms. And I assure you that this young lady knows nothing of it either. Indeed, I would appreciate some discretion here. I visited here earlier with a lady friend. You know how difficult a certain privacy can be. Then I returned, for I'd hoped to convince the Bartholomews to move down to Virginia to take positions at Cameron Hall, but Frederick's printing business has been quite a success."

"He prints traitorous garbage!" the sergeant insisted, then he added quickly, "Lord Cameron, sir, that is."

"What? Is the man not still a free Englishman with rights! Come on, man, what has this to do with anything? I'm telling you, Sergeant, yes, we've been having a tea party. Elizabeth and I were sipping a warm berry brew when you so rudely interrupted us. I wish privacy now. I have been harassed quite enough for the night, as have these good people, I am quite sure. Am I understood?"

"Oh, quite, milord, yes!" The sergeant snapped to a salute. "Yes, milord. Good night, milord."

Milord. Milord Cameron. Frederick smiled. He had heard of the man. He had fought, leading a band of Virginians, in the French and Indian Wars. He sat on the Governor's Council in Virginia. He was immensely wealthy, with estates in the colonies, the islands, and in England. But he had stood in the line of battle again and again, defying bullets, so they claimed. He could do more than shoot Indians, he could speak their language. He was powerful, yes, and by God, he was a member of an elite peerage, but he was an American, too, so it was sworn. Virginia was not Massachusetts, the seeds of discontent were not so fully sown there as here, but she was a great colony, creating great statesmen.

This man sat on the Governor's Council instead of in the House of Burgesses. The Councilmen were appointed for life, a great honor. He should be loyal to the Crown. And still, Frederick realized, Lord Cameron had saved *his* life.

The door was shut and bolted. Elizabeth fell against the door, trembling. "I shall faint—"

"You mustn't madam, I beg of you!" he said, and drew her up.

562

"You've saved us once again. Oh, milord, our lives are yours! Whatever you wish—"

"I wish a long, potent drink!" Eric laughed. "And a word with your husband."

Elizabeth nodded and glanced worriedly toward Frederick. Then she hurried toward the kitchen, and Eric approached Frederick. He pulled up a chair and straddled it, and stared at the printer. "I want to know about it. I want to know about tonight."

"But you must know—"

"I know nothing. I'm a Virginian. I'm here on business, and I stumbled upon you."

Frederick inhaled and exhaled. The man was tough, and he wanted answers.

"We didn't want it to happen—"

"Don't tell me that. The trouble has been brewing here since the Boston 'Massacre' in 1770."

Frederick exhaled. The Boston Massacre had actually been a street fight. About fifty citizens, infuriated by the soldiers within the city, had attacked a British sentinel. Captain Preston, the British officer in charge, had brought more soldiers, and they had fired into the crowd. Three people were killed, eight were wounded, and two of the wounded later died. A town meeting had been called, and the British had agreed to let the captain stand trial for murder. John Adams and Josiah Quincy had been his defense counselors, and he had been acquitted of murder—it couldn't be proven that he had ordered his men to fire into the crowd. Two soldiers were found guilty of manslaughter, and they were branded on their hands and dismissed from the service. Speechmakers and politicians, eager to keep sentiment high against the British, had termed the event the Boston Massacre.

"We did not intend this!" Frederick insisted. "Milord," he added quietly. Then he lifted his chin. "Ask around, among your friends, and you will discover the truth. The British offered the British East India Company a rebate for tea sold in America. The tea was to be consigned to certain individuals. There would have been a monopoly on the tea, and our local merchants would have been put out of business. It was a government move to enforce the tea tax, milord, can you understand? The Committee of Correspondence refused to permit these tea-laden ships to land, and we appealed to Governor Hutchinson to let the loaded ships return to England. The governor refused. There was a meeting, a huge meeting at the Old South Meeting House. We went to the governor again, and again he refused to receive the mass of people." Frederick lowered his head. "At a signal from Sam Adams, we boarded the ships and dumped the tea."

Eric was silent for several long seconds. "There are going to be repercussions, you know."

"Of course."

"We move ever farther and farther away," Eric murmured. "God, how it hurts. But of course, they don't want to hang you for your part in this tea party. They want to hang you for smuggling arms to use against the Crown. So—tell me. What of these arms?"

Frederick started. "Arms?"

"You are guilty. Of storing arms."

Frederick wet his lips nervously with his tongue. He knew all about the arms. There was no sense denying it. "We are not planning anything. The arms are not to be kept in Boston. I should not tell you more."

"You're right—you should not. Not now."

Frederick looked at the man, and he tried to rise. But Eric wasn't looking his way, he was staring into the flames. The fire caught the curious color of his eyes. They had seemed dark, indigo. Now they looked like steel. They burned with startling, silver flames. He was lost in thought, but Frederick could not read those thoughts.

"Tell me, is a man—a Virginian—named Damien Roswell involved in any of this?"

Frederick inhaled sharply. "Milord, turn me in if you would, but I will not give you names—"

"Never mind. You have given me what I want."

Elizabeth came, and offered Lord Cameron a glass of whiskey. Lord Cameron flashed her a quick smile, and Frederick was somewhat startled by his wife's reaction. She flushed deeply, and her eyes fell over the length of him as he straddled his chair. Even at rest he was laden with energy. There was a pulse about him. In silence he spoke of tempest and passion. His eyes portrayed intelligence, fire, and wisdom; his mouth betrayed a great sensuality and an undaunted love of life.

"You'll not turn me in now, will you?" Frederick whispered. Lord Cameron looked his way, and the printer realized that the man was not ten years his senior, he was hardly thirty, if he was that.

"I'd hardly bring you here, act out such outrageous performances, and lie to a soldier to turn you in," he said.

"What of—what of the lady who saved my arm?"

He shook his head slowly, his eyes clouding over. "No. You have nothing to fear from the lady. Not for this night's work."

"She is so kind—"

"She is not so kind, my friend. But though she refuses to face it, she has a stake in all that has occurred. You will be safe from all that she knows."

Frederick nodded, then spoke to him in blunt amazement. "You're a lord, sir. You've a great deal at stake here."

"I have promised you that I will not turn you in. And my word is seldom doubted, sir!"

"Oh, bless you, milord! Again and again!" Elizabeth cried passionately, and she fell to her knees.

Eric smiled, touched her hair, and looked at Frederick. "You've far more at stake than I have, lad. You have this lovely woman, and you have her love, and you have your son. What you possess now is precious. You must take care with your decisions in the future."

"My son is the future, sir, and it is for him that I make my decisions. I am not a lord, I have no memory of a motherland, nor did my father, or his father."

Eric laughed, rising. "Dear sir! I'll have you know that my ancestors settled the Hundred when Jamestown was still in its infancy." He was silent for a moment. "Our blood has been shed for this land, my father and my father's father and his before him, all lie cradled in Virginia earth." He shrugged, and Frederick saw more than the strength and severity of the man, he saw his humor and his youth and all that was charismatic and powerful in his lazy smile. "Perhaps I do have much at stake, for I do love my land, and I would fight, and die gladly, to hold it."

"Who would you fight, milord?" Frederick asked.

"God knows, lad. God alone knows. Perhaps we should all pray for peace. Elizabeth, may I have my greatcoat, please?"

Elizabeth brought his coat and set it over his shoulders. He started for the doorway.

"Milord!" Frederick said, imploring him back.

Eric turned. Frederick offered him his hand. "I thank you, Lord Cameron. I am your servant, for all of my life."

Cameron shook his hand. "My name is Eric. And it is good to have friends, Frederick. I shall remember that I have friends here."

"Aye, milord—Eric. And that you do. The very best of friends."

With a smile, Eric turned and strode out of the house and into the night. Elizabeth sank down by her husband's side, and together they watched as he closed the door. She trembled slightly, but he said no word to her, and they both knew that their lives had been strangely touched. Greatness had descended upon them, and had done so with mercy.

————

Eric mounted Joshua, his great stallion, but pulled in on the reins.

The last of the soldiers' footsteps had gone still, and the night was coming quiet again. Cold and quiet and touched with mist. The spires of the churches rose high against mist and darkness to touch the heavens, and the city lamps were burning low. There was quiet all about.

There would never be quiet again, Eric thought. This particular tea party would be known about from the length and the breadth of the country, and its cry of rebellion would stretch across the Atlantic Ocean. In his pursuit of Lady Sterling he had seen the tea floating in the harbor, and he felt both a horrible, wrenching pain and a startling excitement. They were a new people. A new breed of men. They would be given the rights and liberties of English men by the English government, or, by God, they would forge their own liberties.

I have become a dissident this night! he thought. But maybe he had not, maybe the seeds of dissatisfaction had been sown in him long ago, perhaps during the French and Indian Wars, or the Seven Years War, as it was known on the Continent.

War. It could come to war again. . . .

No one wanted to speak of war. Even the worst of the radicals were careful not to speak of it.

Eric sighed deeply. It didn't matter. The whisper was on the wind, and it was growing louder and louder. Virginia's ties to England were firm and fast. The Virginian Patrick Henry spoke passionately about reform and against illegal representation. But not even he spoke aloud about war.

Eric glanced toward the printer's house and smiled ruefully to himself. The lad and his young bride were so in love, and so passionate, and so ready to die for a cause. He knew their feelings, though, for he would die, and gladly, for his land. Frederick's question was a good one.

Just who would he battle?

He thought of Lady Sterling, of the passion in her eyes when she warned Elizabeth that her husband was a traitor. Her mind was set! She was loyal to the Crown. Still, Eric knew instinctively that Frederick was in no danger from her. She did not know that her cousin Damien was procuring arms for the Sons of Liberty, but she suspected something. And because fear for him lurked within her breast, she would keep quiet, no matter what her loyalties. Poor lass! Her heart was due to be shattered. That fool Tarryton was destined to betray her, and her own kin was already embroiled in rebellion!

There was nothing more for him to do that night.

Eric rode back to Thomas Mabry's. The house was very quiet, but he knocked softly upon the door. Anne Marie opened it quickly, her eyes wide and brilliant. She had been awaiting him, it was obvious.

"Lady Amanda returned safely?"

Anne Marie nodded, catching his arm and pulling him inside. "She is sleeping, and thank God! Lord Sterling did return; he is anxious to get home tomorrow. And Amanda is expected by her aunt in South Carolina within the next few weeks. If she had not been here, God knows what would have happened! He wouldn't have let her go, and I fear for her when she is at home."

Eric frowned. "But why? What would he do to her? The girl is his child, his own blood."

Anne Marie poured him a whiskey. "Eric, something about it chills me! She does not see the danger. She tosses her head in the air and ignores it all." She hesitated. "Just as she ignores trouble. With—with Damien." Anne Marie cast him a quick glance. "She loves him, passionately, you see. And that is her way, her nature. When she loves like that, she is reckless and daring and so defiant! Oh! How I do go on! But I wanted to thank you, Eric, with all of my heart."

He kissed her cheek tenderly. "It is ever a pleasure to serve you, Anne Marie," he told her.

She smiled. "I just wish that you could love me!"

He started to speak, to protest. She smiled and placed a finger against his lip. "You do not, so don't deny it! And I would settle for no less than a man who did love me, milord, so there!'' Her smile was only slightly saddened by the mist in her eyes.

"Anne Marie, you are a priceless treasure, and I will never allow you to settle for less than a man who adores you and will know all that he holds." He finished the drink and handed her the glass, then started for the door.

"Where are you going?" she asked him.

"Back to my lodgings. Then—home."

"Home! But it is so late. You mustn't start to Virginia now!"

"Nay, lass! 'Tis morning. A new day. A very new day," he added reflectively.

"You should stay—"

"I must go."

She walked him out. He took his reins from the post and mounted his horse and smiled down to her, saluting. "I shall see you soon. Give your father my regards!"

"Yes, Eric! And—thank you. Thank you, so much!"

He waved and started to ride. The light was coming. Boston was about to burst into activity.

It suddenly seemed urgent that he head for home as quickly as he could.

He wanted to stand upon his own acres, feel the breeze from the James River. God, how he loved that land. The land had always been his mistress, his heart's desire. He smiled ruefully, though, thinking that he envied Frederick his son. Perhaps it was time that he married, for Cameron Hall needed heirs. And he craved a son who would learn to love the land as he did.

Maybe it was not his sudden interest in an heir that led his thoughts, he warned himself ruefully. Maybe it was the memory of Lady Sterling. She, who carried within her soul the passion of this very night, all the fire and the tempest and the spark of raw excitement that seemed so very necessary to him.

Pausing beneath a streetlamp, he smiled. He remembered the girl she had been. Passionate, aristocratic, haunting even then. She had been so young, but already those emerald eyes had carried a dazzle and a fury to match. She'd had a soft, vixen's laughter, and a will of steel. It had been years since he had first seen her, but tonight he could remember the encounter vividly. He'd been so furious, and she'd been so very indignant, calling him boy, and assuring him after his first warning that she was Lady Amanda Sterling, and that no one ever spanked her.

No one had previously, he told her, but the situation was about to be rectified. She had warned him imperiously that her father would have him lashed, but he didn't care. She had so very nearly killed them both, he had still been tense and frightened because she had so nearly been crushed.

He had paddled her good and hard, but she had cried out only once, and when he had released her, she had promised him that he would die very slowly and rot, she would see to it. He had offered to tell her father about the entire event himself, and she walked off furiously, her eyes flashing, her chin in the air.

But she had never told her father about the occasion. She would have gotten into trouble as well as he, Eric was certain.

She had changed. The lady had definitely grown.

Take care, friend, he warned himself. She was becoming a fascination. And this was a dangerous time to find oneself falling beneath the spell of Lady Sterling. Very soon it could come to war.

No. It would not come to war. No one wanted war.

It did not matter. For the time he was going home. He would make inquiries about Lord Sterling's daughter—she had not seen the last of him. If Tarryton meant to marry the Duchess of Owenfield, he had best forget his interest in Amanda Sterling. And if it were all bald rumor, then Tarryton had best be prepared to fight for the lady, for Eric did indeed plan to have her.

Tension filled him as he nudged the stallion back into motion. Repercussions were sure to come, swift and serious. There had been a tea party that night, and the guests were destined to pay. Where were men of good reason? There was an answer to this new trauma, surely, there must be an answer.

And yet, as he rode toward his room by the common to gather his things for the long ride home to Virginia, Eric felt a new rustle upon the winter wind.

As he reined in on the stallion, he felt it all around him. He knew that the events of the night had forever changed him, and that there were things he could not deny.

There was that movement, a whisper on the wind. And the whisper grew louder . . . the whisper of war.

Eric rode on, unaware that his next meeting with Lord Sterling's daughter would indeed cause him as much turbulence as the dangerous deeds of the night.

3

Tidewater Virginia
June 1774

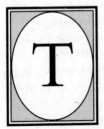HERE HAD NEVER BEEN A MORE BEAUTIFUL summer's night, Amanda was convinced of it. Oriental lanterns had been lavishly strewn about the estate in all shades of soft colors. The breeze was soft and cool for the season, the flowers were all in full bloom, and the magnolias were casting their delightful scent upon the air. Summer was hot, but not tonight. Tonight everything was peaceful and beautiful and the sea breeze whispered gently.

There was no hint of dissent or trouble to mar the night, she thought, and then she was annoyed with the very thought, just as she was nearly sick to death of the continual talk of separation from the Crown. Had the men of Virginia, of the colonies, forgotten that the dear motherland had come to their defense against the French and Indians in the horrible war? Taxes had paid for that defense. They could not expect the Englishmen at home to cover their expenses here! The people of the colonies had opposed the Stamp Act, and that had been repealed.

Now they were fighting over tea. Ever since that night when the Bostonians had decided to dump endless chests of English tea into Boston Harbor, people talked of nothing but tea. And to punish the citizens for the act, the British had closed the port of Boston. And Virginia—so far away from Boston—was becoming embroiled in the whole matter. Tension was a constant emotion among the people, something almost tangible in the air.

Amanda did not want to be interested in politics, but she had a keen, sharp mind and she knew all the basics of the current problem simply because it seemed that everyone was beginning to speak of it. And of course, she had been in Boston on the very night when the tea had been dumped, and everyone always wanted to know her opinion of what had happened. She could never say that she didn't give a damn about the tea—Damien's involvement in the matter worried her. When she thought of her cousin, it was with irritation for the trouble he seemed bent on causing her. And when she became irritated with Damien, she became further irritated because she was forced to remember Lord Cameron. The audacity of the man! He had involved her in something that smelled despicably of treason, and he had never given her a chance to protest. He had set his hands upon her and ordered her about, and despite her outrage, she'd

569

had to go along with him because of Damien. She didn't know what he was involved in, but she was afraid.

She shivered and looked down at her hands. Cameron could have turned Damien in as well as the young printer. But he hadn't. And so they all shared a filthy little secret. The thought of it made her grow warm and tremble, but she inhaled quickly and gained control of herself. She hadn't seen the man in these many months. Pray God, she would never see him again. And when Damien came tonight, she would warn her foolish cousin to keep his nose clean—and out of politics. She would take care to keep silent on the subject tonight. Her father disapproved of her knowledge of it, and tonight she would strive to please him with her silence—except when she spoke discreetly with Damien!

Nigel Sterling had taught her often enough that a woman's place was to be beautiful and soothing, a wife of virtue would be a notable woman adept at the finer arts who was also able to manage her husband's estates.

But he was wrong, in a way. For men all about, in all phases of life, were appealing to their wives and sisters and mothers to help boycott tea. Ladies were forming societies where they worked on homespun materials and garments and where they drank home-grown herbal teas. Their opinions and assistance were proving frightfully important.

"No more tea!" she whispered aloud. On this night, this magic night, when the future might well dangle before her in glazed and golden magnificence, she would curb her thoughts. This was her night. Robert had said that he needed to talk to her, that he needed to see her alone when they had met so briefly at tea earlier in the week—with her father present.

It was her night, a beautiful night, and she didn't want to think about politics, or the frightfully willful Bostonians, or even the foolish things being done by the Virginia House of Burgesses—and she especially did not want to worry about Damien or the dark and fierce Lord Cameron who had been so terribly rude and outrageous.

From the second-floor balcony of Sterling Hall she gazed down on the drive. She felt the kiss of the soft breeze and inhaled the subtle scent of the flowers. She was delighted. It was a perfect night. The musicians would soon be warming up in the gallery above the dance hall, the guests would arrive, and men and women in the height of elegance would swirl to the dances. Beautiful women would arrive in velvets and silks and satins and brocades, their hair powdered, their faces, perhaps, adorned with tiny hearts or moons, drawn in with a kohl pencil or made of velvet or silk patches. Their hair would be high, their bodices would be daringly low, and their conversation would be light and musical. Handsome men would arrive too. And they, too, would be dressed in the height of fashion. They would wear silk or satin knee breeches, fine hose, silver-buckled shoes, and elegant shirts all cuffed and collared in lace. It was her first week home from visiting her aunt in South Carolina, her first party of the summer season, and it was going to be a magical night.

Fine carriages, all marked with prestigious family coats-of-arms, were beginning to arrive. They moved down the oak-shaded drive in the moonlight. Lord

Hastings was first, she saw, her father's old friend. She knew his carriage, even in the shadows, for it was drawn by four white stallions with braided tails and manes.

Everyone would arrive soon.

Lord Robert Tarryton would arrive.

At the thought of his name, Amanda sucked in her breath and fought a wave of dizzying sensation. Yes, Lord Robert Tarryton would arrive. He would find her on the dance floor . . .

No, no, no. She would let him arrive first, and then she would go down. She would make a grand entrance on the broad curving stairway that led to the entry. She would walk slowly and innocently, but she would pause in the middle of the stairway, and she would look out across the sea of faces, and she would find that he was looking for her, only for her. Perhaps she would allow her hand to flutter to her throat, and, of course, her heart would be pounding mercilessly.

He would be the most elegant man present. Tall, and with his soft blue eyes and near-platinum hair. Lean and nonchalant, he would wear mustard brocade, she was nearly certain, for the color so enhanced his masculine beauty.

His eyes would touch hers . . .

And she would know that this night was indeed the night, the most beautiful of all summer nights—no, the most beautiful of all nights.

He would thread his way through the crowd to her, and he would capture her hand, and soon she would be on the dance floor with him. But his need to speak would be great, and he would sweep her away, out to the garden, into the maze. And she would run behind him laughing; all the way to the statue of Venus, and there he would set her upon the bench and fall down upon one knee and beg her to be his wife. She would smile, and clasp him to her to breast, and—

"Amanda! Amanda! We've guests arriving! Come down here immediately."

Her dream dissolved in a shimmer of gray ashes as her father called her harshly.

"Yes, Father!"

"I'm going down; the guests are already filing in. Amanda!"

"I'm coming, Father!" she called in return. She swallowed down a touch of pain that he should always be so brusque with her. She was his only child, and though he provided for her in all things, he never displayed the slightest affection. She wondered sometimes if he despised her for not having been born a son, or if he despised her for bringing about her mother's death with her birth. She didn't know, and she learned over the years to harden her own heart and not to care. Danielle had been with her always, and Danielle showered affection upon her. Harrington, the butler and head of the staff, was proper in public and affectionate in private. At least she knew what caring was.

And now . . .

Now there was Robert. Lord Robert Tarryton. And she believed that he intended to ask her to be his wife this very night. She was so in love with him.

There had been other men in her life. In fact, she thought with a rueful smile, there had been many. She was accomplished, she was beautifully clad, and she was her father's daughter. Dozens of the most influential young men had called themselves her suitors, and she had laughed with them and flirted with them, but she had never given her heart away and, for all of his coldness, her father had never forced her hand. Even when John Murray, Lord Dunmore, the royal governor of the colony, had teasingly suggested that she was of an age, her father had shrugged and said that she had a mind of her own, she was not quite eighteen, and there was plenty of time for marriage.

She did have a mind of her own, and she enjoyed life. Before leaving the Colonies for her schooling in London, she had ridden with Sir Henry Hershall, sipped spiked lemonade on the balcony swing with the Earl of Latimer's second son, Jon, and played golf with the Scottish commander of Lord Newberry's Highlanders. And even Robert she had teased mercilessly until she had returned home in November last year and discovered that she was in love with him, wonderfully in love, at last.

"Amanda!"

"I'm coming, Father!"

She rushed from the balcony, and through her room to the hallway, and from there, to the top landing of the winding stairway. Once there she paused, breathing deeply.

The great hallway below was already filling with guests. She hurried down a few steps and then paused again. This was her grand entrance. She was supposed to move slowly and demurely. She inhaled again, resting her fingers delicately on the bannister. She felt her heart beat. Robert should just be arriving. She should glance to the entryway and find him, and his eyes should be upon her.

Perhaps he had already arrived. She quickly gazed out over the room, smiling to friends. The dream was too real, and so she looked on to the entryway.

A man was just entering, handing his gloves and hat to Harrington, smiling and offering the man a word.

Suddenly he looked up, just as if he had sensed that she was there. She discovered his eyes upon hers.

Just as she had imagined . . .

Except that the man was not Lord Robert Tarryton.

It was her nemesis—Lord Eric Cameron.

God! What right did he have to be there? In her very house? Yet she stared at him, unable to draw her gaze from his.

His hair seemed very dark, almost black that night. He had not worn a wig and he had not bothered to powder it. He seemed exceptionally tall, towering in the doorway. His eyes, she thought, were even darker than before, indigo blue, with just that touch of taunting silver. He was dressed fashionably enough in a frock coat of royal blue, and white laced shirt, and breeches in a light-blue silk. His hose was white, and his shoes were adorned with silver buckles. Somehow he still didn't look quite civilized. Perhaps it was the way he wore his hair, defying fashion. Perhaps it was the structure of his face. He was tanned, as if he spent much time outdoors, and his features were bold and strong, his cheekbones were high and his chin was quite firm and squared. His mouth was full and wide, and as his eyes met hers, she thought that perhaps his very smile gave him the look of something just a bit savage, for his lip curved with a slow and leisurely ease that caused little shivers to race down her spine.

She realized that her hand had fluttered to her throat, and then she decided angrily that it was his eyes that gave him such an uncivilized appearance, for they danced then with startling silver humor as if he knew that he had somehow affected her, somehow caused her breath to catch. And she couldn't even seem to look away from him.

And neither did he look away from her.

Eric Cameron stood in the entry and stared up at the girl, his hostess, and he was both amused and entranced.

He saw in her eyes the same little vixen with the dark red hair and emerald eyes who had bit him with such certainty and vengeance all those years ago.

He almost pitied Lord Tarryton, if the man hadn't made sure to tell her the truth as yet. Eric had heard word from the governor himself that if Tarryton had not jumped with joy at the prospect of the young duchess, he had been quick to covet the title and property that came with her. Yet from the look of Amanda this evening, he surmised that she did not know. She had dressed to entrance a lover, but the excitement in her eyes was a greater attraction than any lace or velvet could create. Eric thought that she might well be aware of her femininity and her assets, she had confidence, but he wondered if she knew just how beautiful she was, standing upon the landing, her fingers trailing delicately over the bannister and brought softly against her throat. She was a woman of medium height, but so slim and delicate that she appeared somewhat taller than she really was. Her neck was long and graceful, and her breasts rose provocatively high and round against the embroidered bodice of her white gown.

Her hair was truly her glory that night. It was flame and it was dark, a deep auburn that framed the ivory of her perfect complexion, in ripples and waves. It was caught high above one ear with a golden comb just to tumble and cascade over the opposite shoulder like a deep burning fire.

Everything about her that night was glorious. Her beauty was startling. Her face was such a fine oval, like something exquisitely carved. Her cheeks just now burned with a touch of pink. Her eyes were deep green, like the land at its most verdant, Eric thought. He smiled slowly. Flame hair, green eyes. And though she stood motionless, he felt her vitality. She would fight, he thought, for what she wanted.

She raised her chin slightly. She was determined to look away. Her will had not lessened a bit, nor, it seemed, had she had occasion to learn much about humility.

She had been looking for a man, Eric thought with amusement. And most obviously he was not that man. Tarryton. She did not know that she been cast aside for riches.

He bowed to her deeply. When she barely acknowledged him, he realized that she was still furious about the night in Boston. He hadn't had much choice about his actions, but it was unlikely that she would ever understand or forgive him. She arched a delicate brow, caught up her skirts, and hurried on down the stairway. The perfect hostess, she began to greet her guests. She offered her cheek for the most delicate of kisses, she regally offered her hand to those she knew less well, and men and women flocked to her, eager to greet her.

"Why, Mandy, Mandy, dearest! Don't you look just heavenly!" someone gushed to her. Eric looked through the crowd. It was Lady Geneva Norman, one of the richest heiresses in the area with countless estates in England. She was a beauty in her own right, but Eric had never found her any more than amusing and he was careful to keep his distance from her—she was a cunning witch who delighted in trouble and in dangling her worth before her suitors. She would, Eric thought, acquire a husband, for not many a man could forget that life was a harsh game that must be played well.

He was grateful then for his own position, for he was not dependent upon making a fortunate marriage. His forefathers had acquired some of the finest land in Tidewater Virginia, and he retained estates in England he had seen but once. He could play Geneva's game. He could delight in her bald humor and her coquetry and laughter, and he did not need to feel the sting of her temper at all, for he had nothing at stake. He could enjoy her beauty and walk away.

His land in the colonies and his estates in England gave him so very much.

Of course, those estates might not remain his for long, he realized solemnly. Not if he continued with his present course of action. Ever since Boston, he had become more and more deeply involved with men whom the Crown would call questionable associates.

Some of his friends were calling it suicide, but he could not turn back. He believed in what he was doing.

"Lord Cameron!" a voice bellowed, and Eric saw that his host, Lord Nigel Sterling, had come up before him, reaching for his hand. He thought briefly of the things that Anne Marie had told him about the man. Still, Amanda did not seem to show any signs of abuse.

"Eric, my man, I've been most anxious to talk to you. I've been hearing the most fearful rumors."

Eric took Lord Sterling's profferred hand and smiled. "Rumors? How intriguing. I shall be interested in hearing them."

"Come with me, and we'll take a brandy into my office. I would have a word with you in private," Sterling said.

Eric shrugged and smiled, looking over his host. He was a squat man with heavy jowls and beady brown eyes. How he could have taken part in the creation of the thing of beauty upon the stairs, Eric did not know. Nor was he particularly fond of the man's personality. He was forceful, rude, and often abrasive, a great believer in his own nobility. Still, he was Eric's host this evening, and if they had been prone to great dissent when they had sat together in the Governor's Council, by every rule of polite behavior, Eric owed him a moment of his time.

"As you wish, Nigel. But I warn you, it will not change anything."

"Come, I'll take my chances."

They moved through the room. Eric nodded to some of his male friends and acquaintances and bowed to the ladies as he followed. He could already hear whispers as he did so. He smiled more deeply. So much for polite society. He had become a black sheep already.

"Ah, my dear! Amanda, there you are. Have you met Lord Cameron? Ah . . . yes, of course, you have, but that was years ago. Amanda was in a young ladies' school in England for several years, and since then she has been in South Carolina with relatives. Do you remember my daughter, Lord Cameron?"

"We met recently, Nigel. At Thomas Mabry's, in Boston."

"What? Oh, so you were at Mabry's fête that evening, were you?"

"Yes." Eric kept his eyes upon Amanda. She was flushed, despite her determination to ignore his knowing smile.

"Yes, Papa, Lord Cameron was there."

Eric took her hand and bowed over it deeply, just brushing the back of it with his lips. He felt the pulse race at her wrist. As he raised his head, he looked into her eyes, those passionate, telltale eyes, and he moved his thumb slowly over the delicate blue veins that he could just see beneath the surface of her porcelain skin.

"It was a night I shall not forget," he said pleasantly.

Her eyes widened slightly. She nearly snatched her hand away, but then she spoke softly and with poise. "Lord Cameron. How nice to see you again."

It was anything but nice for her to see him again, he thought, somewhat amused and somewhat sorry. She was even lovelier up close. So much of her beauty lay in her love for life, something vital and warm that seemed to sweep about her in a golden light. Well, she was passionately against him, he realized.

"Milady." He bowed to her. These were passionate times. He was determined in his own course of action, and it was natural that tempers and spirits would soar high.

"Save a dance for Lord Cameron, my dear," her father said. "Come, Eric, please, so that I may have my word with you."

Eric bowed to Amanda once again, then followed Sterling toward the doorway to his office.

Cameron! Amanda thought, watching his broad back disappear in the wake of her father. Cameron!

He had come to taunt her! On this magical night, he had come here! Well, he had nothing on her! If he ever dared to implicate Damien, she would call him a traitor in no uncertain terms! He laughed at her, she saw it in his smile, he dared her with every glance!

She tightened her jaw, thinking that the man had really changed little. He had always been less than cavalier, supremely confident and assured. So *arrogant*. She would never forget the day of the hunt. Perhaps she *had* been too eager to catch the fox, but he'd had no right to spank her. She hadn't thought that he would dare, but he would dare anything, she had learned. Perhaps it had been as much his fault. He had been about seventeen, and eager to return to one of Lord Hastings's pretty chambermaids. She'd already heard his name whispered in various households. His appeal was legendary.

Oh! Cameron was a traitor. Just two weeks ago he had stood up in the governor's chambers, a member of the prestigious council, an honor set upon one for life, and he had suggested that perhaps he should resign because he disagreed with various actions being taken. Everyone had been speaking about it. The governor had refused to accept his resignation, demanding that he think it all through. The colony had been abuzz with it! Last night Robert had talked of it, calling the man a fool and a traitor. It was amazing that he hadn't been arrested on the spot, hanged, boiled in oil, or drawn and quartered.

Well, perhaps nothing so dramatic. And perhaps it was true that the governor would be hanging men from dawn to dusk if he had to start with the men who had spoken so in the lower house, the House of Burgesses. But Cameron was not a member of that society. He was a lord. His duty was to support his king and his governor.

It was said that he had given a fine speech with a wonderful elocution—learned at Oxford, so she had heard—and agreed to wait, but suggested that time would make little difference. His heart was with the men who had gone to Bruton Parish Church for their day of prayer—just as his heart was with the men who had dumped the tea into the sea. His heart was not with many of the decisions being made, and therefore he did not think that he could serve the governor to the best of his abilities.

He was listening to radicals. Men like Patrick Henry. He was far more interested in the lower House of Burgesses than he was in the goings-on of his own council chambers. He met with radicals at the various taverns in Williamsburg. He was dangerous.

"There goes the most arresting man in the colonies," a soft voice mused behind her.

Amanda swirled around to see Lady Geneva standing behind her, batting her fan, her dark eyes following Lord Cameron.

"Cameron?" Amanda said incredulously.

Geneva nodded knowingly. "Lord Cameron," she said, as if she tasted the name as she spoke and found it very pleasing. Her gaze shot to Amanda again. "He's dashing, don't you think? Bold, a rebel. He bows down before no man. All heads turn when he enters a room. Don't you feel it? The tension . . . why, darling, the very heat! Oh, but I do just feel ignited!"

A sizzle of warm rushing liquid seemed to trail down the length of Amanda's spine with Geneva's words and she shivered, remembering how it felt to have her eyes locked with his, to feel his lips against her flesh. She shook her head, though, denying the sensation. She didn't even want to think about the man, she wanted to find Robert.

"Lord Cameron is a traitor and nothing more. And I can't even imagine why Father would want him here."

"He might prove to be an invaluable friend one day," Geneva said. "He is trusted by the radicals, and, oddly enough, he is even trusted by those very men he spurns. Your father is no fool, my pet. I'm sure he intends to stay very good friends with Lord Cameron."

"And you, Geneva, do you intend to become very good friends with Lord Cameron?"

"Ah"—Geneva laughed— "the little tigress shows her claws! Me? Ummm. I am good friends with him. I don't know about a lifetime commitment, for I like balls and pageants, I love royalty, I adore the finer things in life. Our fierce and proud Lord Cameron is casting his path in a different direction. He might well come to hang one of these days, and should he not, he might well find his bed to be one of hay. And still, I have danced with the man. I've felt his arms around me, and sometimes I do wonder if lying with him in a bed of hay might not be preferable to lying with any other man upon silk. But don't worry, pet—the competition is still wide open."

"You needn't worry, Geneva," Amanda said sweetly. "You've no competition from me. I've no interest whatsoever in a traitor to the Crown."

Geneva batted her fan prettily, smiling to someone across the room. "Because of Lord Tarryton, I believe?"

"Believe what you wish," Amanda told her, but Geneva was very smug, obviously ready to tell a secret that she was finding most amusing.

"I know things, Amanda. I'll tell them to you if you like."

"All right, Geneva. Tell me what you will."

"Lord Tarryton is engaged to marry the Duchess of Owenfield back in England. She's a widow and as her dear departed husband left no heirs, young Robert will gain the title of Duke of Owenfield."

"I don't believe you!" Amanda gasped, so stunned at the news that she could not pretend nonchalance.

"Then ask Robert," Geneva said sweetly. "Excuse me, dear, will you? Men are flocking to your father's study, and I'm quite certain they'll have Lord Cameron on the cooking spit, searing him away. I should love to see him defend himself."

Geneva hurried toward the hallway door. She bypassed it, excusing herself to various people to escape out the open doorways at the back of the hall. She would walk around the terrace to the floor-length windows and find a seat upon one of the swings, out of sight, and therefore able to listen in on the conversation.

Amanda looked around the room. She didn't see Robert anywhere. She had to find him and speak with him. Geneva was lying. Robert loved her, and though she couldn't give him a new title, she did come with a rich dowry. There was no reason they should not marry. They were Virginians, both of them. He couldn't wish to live across the sea. . . .

And yet Geneva's words had left her with a set of chills, for the woman had not teased or taunted, she had simply stated what she knew and disappeared, eager to chase Lord Cameron.

Amanda sighed, determined to follow.

It was not so easy, for she was stopped by young men and older women, and as her father's hostess, she was obliged to be polite to their guests. Finally, though, she managed to escape down the hall while the musicians played a minuet.

Outside, Amanda did not see Geneva, but as she moved near the open windows, she felt her heart suddenly pound, for Robert was inside the study with her father, Lord Cameron, and Lord Hastings.

"You turn your back on us, Cameron, when you do such things!" Lord Hastings was saying.

Seated before her father's desk, Cameron set down his brandy glass. Then he rose, setting his thumbs into the waistband of his breeches, and faced Hastings.

"Lord Hastings, I beg to differ. The House of Burgesses determined that a day of prayer for our sister city would not be out of order. Tell me, sir, who is it that we offend with prayer!"

"You were not obliged to attend!" Robert said fervently.

Cameron arched a dark brow at him, turning to face him. "No, sir, I was not obliged to attend, I did so because I desired to do so. The British closed the port of Boston—"

"The British! *We* are the British!" her father proclaimed.

"There is no land I would claim with more ardor as my mother country than Britain, sir, but I am not, I fear, British. I am a Virginian. I am his Majesty's subject, but I cling to my rights as his subject. I attended a day of prayer—"

"Boston is not our sister city. Not when she behaves as she does!" Hastings exclaimed.

"To feel so, sir, is indisputably your prerogative," Cameron said, bowing deeply. He turned then toward his host. "Lord Sterling, I cannot apologize for what I feel to the depths of my heart. There was nothing wrong with prayer. Lord Dunmore has now dissolved the House of Burgesses, and yet I fear her members will only meet with more regularity. They have elected representatives to their Continental Congress, and I fear that the way to peace must soon be found or else—"

"Damn it, Cameron! You're a fine soldier, a wealthy man, and we all admire you. But you're talking treason again!" Sterling thundered, pounding upon his desk.

"I have spoken no treason, sir. But beyond a doubt, our difficulties with the mother country must be solved. I offered to give up my place on the council, sir, because I know how my opinions distress you all. I shall continue to offer my own absence if you feel that you cannot tolerate my opinions, although I hope that I speak with reason. And now, gentlemen . . ."

His voice suddenly trailed away. Amanda realized that he saw her staring in at him, listening to the conversation—and searching about the room. She quickly ducked behind one of the pillars but kept her eyes upon the man. He smiled, bowing his head, yet she saw the laughter in his eyes and the rueful curve of his lip and the devil's own humor at her expense. He knew that she was looking for Robert, she thought.

Damn the traitor. And then she didn't care, because Robert had seen her too. Lord Cameron quickly recovered his poise and continued speaking. Robert did not do so well. A gentle smile touched his features and he started toward the floor-length windows.

"Robert—" her father began with a frown.

"Ah, sir, I was just feeling the need for a bit of air myself," Eric Cameron said. "Shall we break, milords?"

He gave the men no opportunity to protest, but bowed sharply to them all and quickly departed the room.

"Well, I never—" her father began, but Robert interrupted him hastily.

"Sir, it is frightfully hot in this room. Excuse me, Lord Sterling, Lord Hastings."

He bowed his way out. Amanda quickly ducked back around the pillar and hurried to the doors leading out from the hallway. She could hear the musicians clearly there, playing a Virginia tune. Men and women swayed in one another's arms and parted to a far different tone and beat from the minuet. They laughed and touched and their eyes danced as they participated in the more energetic reel.

Amanda searched for Robert, and yet her eyes rested upon one couple on the floor.

Lord Cameron had found Geneva. Well and good for them both, they deserved one another! Amanda thought, and yet she paused, for they were enchanting together. He so tall and dark as he bent over her blond beauty, pulling her close. She so full of laughter, her eyes those of a cat, feline and feminine. One could almost feel the heat between them.

Hers was a finer love, she assured herself. And Geneva was a liar. Robert was not going to marry another woman.

Geneva whispered something to Lord Cameron. The two of them disappeared together.

Amanda looked again for Robert, and at last she saw him hurrying toward her down the hallway and through the doors. She was so glad to see him, and so glad to be alone, that she threw her arms around him and came upon her toes to kiss his lips. For a moment he was still, then his arms swept around her and he held her tightly. His lips eagerly sought hers, indeed, he hungered for more, smoothing back her hair, passing the barriers of her lips with his tongue.

She drew away from him, not so alarmed by his ardor as she was by their nearness to the party.

"Amanda, for the love of God, let me touch you! Last night we were not alone a second, your father was always there!" he cried, but she silenced him, pressing her fingers against his lip.

"Let's go into the maze," she urged him. Catching his hand, she hurried down the back steps, pulling him along. She knew the maze, she had played within it as a child, and now, with fingers entwined with Robert's, she scampered quickly into the very heart of the foliage. The night was warm with the softest of breezes. The high foliage rustled in the breeze and the flowers, in summer bloom, caught silver light from the moon and lay around them abundantly in a dazzling display of color.

"Amanda!" Robert called to her, but she laughed, winding around a cherry hedge and coming to the statue of Venus with its tinkling waterfall and fountain.

The statue was beautiful, draped in marble as if Venus lived, an innocent virgin. Twin cupids played by her head with the long tendrils of her marble hair, and a wrought-iron loveseat awaited those who came to the Venus garden in the maze.

Breathless, Amanda fell into the seat. "Oh, Robert!" she whispered delightedly. "Now! We're alone at last!"

There was a curious rustling sound, and she frowned, then determined that it was nothing more than the wind in the bushes. She smiled up at her lover, adoring his lean and poetic features, and reached for his hand.

"Come sit by me. I have to speak with you."

"Amanda, I have to kiss you."

"Robert! Sit!"

He did so and she curled against him, resting her head upon his shoulder. He bent down slowly to her, very slowly. Then his lips found hers, and the kiss was rich and deep and sweet. She moved her hand against his cheek, and she felt his fingers against her own. Then he gripped her tightly against him. She felt the power of his heart. And she felt his fingers, fervently wandering upon the bodice at her breast, seeking the rise of bare flesh.

Some inner warning sounded and she realized that she was not behaving like a lady. She was in love. She just wanted to touch him, and to be held in turn, and to believe in their future together.

She had to pull away. He was growing reckless with his kisses, and with his hands, and although it was private in the Venus garden in the midst of the maze, she knew that she was tempting the man too far.

"My love, please!" She gasped, capturing his straying fingers and bringing them to her lap. He still didn't quite seem to hear her. Breathing heavily, he stared at her. He tried to lift his hand to touch her, but she held tight. "Robert—"

"I have to have you!"

"I love you, and our time will come. Robert—"

"But I need you now. I need to feel your lips and I need to touch your flesh, I need to be with you. I am a man, my God, can't you understand that!"

"Oh, Robert, I long for you too, but we must wait. Surely you understand. My father . . ." No, it wasn't her father, not really. It was her upbringing. She was Lord Sterling's daughter, of Sterling Hall, and even if she was in love, and loved in turn, she had to wait. Until the words were spoken. Until they were joined before God.

"Come to me, love. Feel my lips, my kiss. . . ."

She was startled when he drew her back into his arms with an alarming force. They had teased and laughed a dozen times together, and it had never been like this. Her frown alone had stopped his ardor before, while now her harried fingers had no power at all against his touch.

"Robert!" Leaping to her feet, she escaped him. He stood quickly, coming behind her, gently holding her shoulders. His voice was harsh when he spoke to her.

"Amanda, come, we've played this game again and again. Surely you must feel it, you must ache and crave as I do, you long for consummation of this desire as deeply as I! And I would die for your touch, for your kiss, and still you play the tease, and you taunt and torture me. We are not children any longer. I cannot stand it!"

She swung around, heartfully sorry and somewhat alarmed. She didn't want what he wanted, not desperately at all. Marriage was not the same for men as it was for women. She liked to be close, and she liked to be loved. The rest, she was certain, would have to come with time.

"We cannot, Robert. Not until we are married."

"Married!"

She knew the moment he repeated the word that Geneva had not lied to her. She need not feel guilty for a single thing she might have done to Robert, Lord Tarryton. Pain spilled through her. She wanted to fall to the ground, and she wanted to scream, and she very nearly wanted to die.

"It's true!" She gasped, backing away from him. "You're to marry some duchess for her estates!"

"Amanda—" He reached for her, his misery written clearly upon his face. "Amanda, I love you. I have no choice. It doesn't have to make any difference between us."

"You have no choice!" she cried. "Oh, you dreadful, despicable, cowardly bastard! How dare you!" She slapped him as hard as she could across the face.

He gasped, staring at her, his eyes narrowing. "I have no choice!"

"Don't you ever come near me again. Ever."

"I am no coward, milady. You wait until your father has chosen for you, lady, and then tell me how to fight what we are honor-bound to do!"

"Honor bound! You say you have no choice," Amanda retorted. "You say *no*, milord, and that is that! But you don't wish to say no, do you? Ah, that's right. You'll be a duke. Well, so be it then. Marry the duchess for a title. I hope that it will be well worth the price of your soul and my heart."

"Damn you, Amanda!" Robert cried, and he reached for her, dragging her hard against him. "You've no right! And you wait! You will be promised to a man like Lord Hastings, a man with three chins and four stomachs, and then you shall be sorry that you taunted me so! I love you, and you will not forget me. You will see. And for now, my God, you've played the bitch and the tease—"

"How dare you—" she began, her voice low and husky and shaking with emotion and pain.

"You've led me on! You've taunted and teased with your eyes, you've driven me near madness with your touch, and now you tell me that I shouldn't come near you—"

"Let me go!"

"I'll not! I'll have tonight what you've offered from the start, and when you're forced into a wretched marriage, then you'll understand. It will happen. The day will come, and your father will force you into wedlock with some monster, an old goat perhaps, and then you'll come to me. You'll know the world is not perfect, no fairyland, milady."

"Let me go!"

He did not. His lips came down upon hers, hard and suffocating. She slammed against his chest, to no avail. He was making her dizzy, and she wondered how long she could fight. And she couldn't believe that she had to fight, that love had turned to nightmare, that her dreams were being shattered one by one, here in the Venus garden, beneath the summer moon.

"No!" she cried out, wrenching from his lips, horrified when his fingers latched hard upon the velvet ties to her bodice. Desperate, she twisted in his arms, certain that she had not lost as yet and determined to kick him into agony. But just as she freed herself enough to strike he leapt forward and she fell hard upon the ground, the breath knocked from her. He jumped down upon her and started to speak.

"Amanda—"

His word was cut cleanly from his lips as he was grasped from behind and lifted high and tossed into the bushes. Stunned, Amanda gazed past her fallen foe to see the tall man standing before her, watching Robert where he had fallen, with immense distaste.

Cameron. Lord Cameron!

"How dare you!" In a rage, Robert was up and on his feet. Bellowing like a wounded bull, he lunged forward.

Cameron sidestepped him neatly, then delivered a hard chop upon his nape, sending Robert down into a heap at his feet. Robert groaned, then staggered up again.

"You! What right have you here! None at all. This is a private affair!"

"Oh?" Cameron said, not even breathing hard. He crossed his arms slowly over his chest and his eyes fell upon Amanda. "I don't think that there is anything between the two of you anymore, do you?"

"It's none of your business!" Robert repeated.

"I'm afraid that it is. She asked you to let her go—I heard her."

"This is none of your affair!"

Amanda's cheeks blazed despite herself. She could not believe that she had been dragged into this horrible and humiliating position. She longed to skewer both men through.

"You . . . bastard!" she breathed.

"Amanda—" Robert began.

"Robert, you're a mewling coward, and I hate you, I swear it."

Robert glanced at Eric Cameron and took a sudden, wild swing at the man. It was almost pathetic, the ease with which Cameron caught the flailing arm and twisted it.

"Well, Milord Tarryton," Cameron said softly, "I can well believe that the lass has elicited a fire in your loins, and I do believe that she could tease and tempt a man to hell and back again. But still, she said no. And you, sir, are considered an aristocrat. Hardly the manners one should expect, eh?"

Amanda gasped enraged that he should speak of her so—and witness so much of her humiliation. She couldn't be grateful to him. She swallowed hard and took a step toward him. "Lord Cameron . . ." She kept her voice soft and quiet, demure. Ladylike. "You! You again! You are the plague of my life!" she charged him softly.

Then she slapped him.

His features went rigid but he barely blinked. "Once, milady, you may take that liberty. Don't take it again. As to you . . ." He shoved Robert forward. "The night, milord, is over."

Robert's head bowed. "I still say that it's none of your affair!"

"But that, sir, is point two. The lady's behavior is every bit my concern, as is her welfare. Tonight, Lord Tarryton, we have sparred and played. Touch her again, and I might well determine to kill you."

"What?"

"I am that horrible, wretched, monster man she will be forced to marry, Lord Tarryton. The old goat. I have asked her father for her hand, and he has most graciously agreed." He bowed to Amanda. "Truly, mam'selle, you are about to find me the plague of your life!"

4

DON'T BELIEVE YOU!" AMANDA GASPED, stunned. And of course, it had to be a lie. Still reeling from the impact of Robert's words and actions, she was afraid that she was going to be sick. She hurt, as she had never hurt before. Her sense of betrayal was already complete, yet now she was discovering that not only Robert but her father had turned from her. It could not be true. Her father had not let her go her way so freely and so far to turn her over to a rebel! She backed away from him, shaking her head. "Sir, you are a liar!"

He arched a brow and though he maintained a pleasant enough countenance, his silver-blue eyes narrowed sharply. He didn't like being called a liar, no matter how nonchalantly he stood. "No, I am not, milady," he said softly, and his gaze rested upon Robert. "Lord Tarryton, my warning stands. And as you are a man affianced, perhaps you should be casting your attentions upon your future bride." He paused, pointing a finger at Robert. "Go. Now."

"Amanda," Robert said, appealing to her. "We can discuss this later—"

"Discuss this!" she cried. "No, Lord Tarryton, we will never discuss—this. Or anything else, for that matter. You fool! I loved you!" she whispered.

"Amanda, I do love you, I tried to tell you—"

"Lord Tarryton!" Eric snapped. "This is a touching scene indeed, but under the circumstances . . ."

There was a deadly note of menace in Eric's voice. Robert stiffened and walked past Amanda and Eric without another word. Amanda listened to his footsteps falling upon the earth as he disappeared, then she spun around on Cameron.

"I'm sorry that you were hurt. I'm afraid that Lord Tarryton's engagement has been common knowledge for quite some time now," he told her. "I suppose you hadn't heard the news at your aunt's."

"I am not hurt, Lord Cameron," she lied. She wanted to die on the spot from the humiliation and the pain she was experiencing. She hated him. She hated him more than she hated Robert, because he'd witnessed her humiliation.

"Lady Sterling—"

She did not want his help or his compassion. She wanted to be alone, she wanted to rage and cry in private. "Get away from me, sir, for you are far more heinous a man than he. You've no right here, you've no business here—"

"I do beg your pardon, Lady Sterling." Now he sounded cool and dangerous. "I did not intend to spy upon you, but I heard your cries of distress and assumed that you wanted assistance."

"Assumed—"

He sat down on the bench before the Venus statue, idly watching her. "Tell me, did I interrupt you rather than rescue you?"

It took several seconds for the meaning of his words to sink into her mind. And when she grasped their full meaning, she was furious. In a sudden rage, she flew at him, but he stood immediately, catching her arms, securing them behind her back and pulling her very close. She struggled against him wildly, determined to free herself at any cost. Desperate, she tried to kick him. He slipped a foot against her ankle and she started falling. He deftly preceded her to the ground, rolling beneath her so that when she fell, his body took the brunt of the force. Then he rolled swiftly, and she was caught beneath him again, staring up at him exhausted but ever more furious, yet her breath coming so quickly that she could not speak. She gritted her teeth and he laughed, but there was an edge about the sound and she wondered just how amused he was. "I warned you," he told her quietly. "You struck me once. I will not allow you to strike again."

"Don't you dare laugh at me."

"Why, milady, I wouldn't dream of doing so."

"Let me go!"

"Are we understood?"

"Lord Cameron, I am quite certain that I shall never understand you!"

"Perhaps you should make an effort to do so."

"Get off me."

"Milady, your every wish is my command."

He leapt to his feet, but she found no freedom, for his hands were upon her own, drawing her up against him.

She tossed back her head, staring up him, longing to do serious battle again, yet painfully aware that she could not win. Praying for composure, she held still with her chin high, her hair tumbling and rippling down her back and seeming to burn like a slow flame in the moonlight. Her eyes sizzled and she spoke as softly as he, with every bit as much of an edge.

"I'm demanding, Lord Cameron, that you let me go. Or perhaps you imagine that I'm really dying to remain in your arms too? Can I dare hope that some other man is otherwise engaged elsewhere in this maze and will come to my rescue?"

He laughed, and it was an open, honest sound. It brought back strange feelings to her, causing a cascade of warmth to rush through her. Geneva's words came back to her. *The most arresting man in the colonies.* And she felt his arms acutely. They were strong arms, well muscled, like the steel of a blade. His body was hard and vital, and his thigh was pressed tightly against her own. Her breath came quickly, and she longed to escape him.

"Milady," he told her, "you have not lost one bit of your aristocratic hauteur. You had quite an abundance of it as a child, you know."

"And you were a very rude child, and now you are a very rude adult, Lord Cameron. You're not only a traitor, you're a brute."

"This is a subject, mam'selle, with which I think that you should take extreme care."

"Your activities—"

"I am no traitor but a man of convictions. And a brute, milady? For seeking to save myself from your very tender touch? Alas, I should stand still, and allow those feminine claws of yours to draw blood. That is what you seek tonight, isn't it? Blood, milady?"

"You're sadly mistaken. I seek no vengeance upon anyone."

Still, he held her close. His fingers wound tight around her wrists, and his words whispered like the breeze against her lips. She could almost feel the brush of his lips. The lace of his shirt and the satin of his surcoat lay against her bare flesh where the mounds of her breasts rose daringly above her bodice, and she was uncomfortably aware of the feel and texture of the fabric and of the warmth of the man beneath it.

"Tarryton is a fool."

"How dare you judge him!"

"Any man who would cast aside such exquisite beauty for mere wealth is a fool."

"You've no right to judge him!"

"Ah, but he didn't exactly cast you aside. He meant to have love *and* money."

She tried to kick him again. He dragged her down upon the bench, laughing again. "Careful, milady! I'm striving not to be a brute, but the role of knight is difficult to play when you are so determined to cause me pain."

"You are causing *me* great pain!" she retorted. Drawn upon his lap, she was in a very awkward position. He held her hands still, and though his touch was easy, she was still his prisoner. There was no doubting that.

"I'm so sorry. As I said, my wish is really only to fulfill your desires."

"Oh, you lie!"

"But I don't lie, milady!"

"I'll never, never marry you, so any point you wish to make between us is quite moot."

"Alas! You crush me!" he said with mock despair.

He was not in the least crushed or broken, but every bit amused. Things had not changed at all. He still viewed himself the adult, the master of the world, and her but a child playing willfully within his realm.

Except that now he touched her differently. He held her tightly. And she was all too aware of that hold. The scent of flowers was all around them and the moonlight played over his striking face, which reminded her of the fine statues in the Venus garden. His features were like those of Mars, or Apollo, hard cast and striking, as was his smile. She wanted to wrench away from him, and then again, she was struck with the startling and dizzying desire to learn more about him. She trembled already. If he touched her lips with his own the way that Robert had done, just what was it that she would feel?

"Let me go," she said swiftly. "Now."

His smile deepened. He knew, she thought with sudden panic. He knew exactly what she was thinking, and he was both amused and challenged. He was holding her ever closer, but now just one of his hands secured her wrists and the other moved upward to her cheek.

"I could scream!" she threatened in a whisper.

"Scream," he suggested.

But she did not. The softest little whimper escaped her as his lips touched hers. They brought with them an incredible heat that consumed her. There was no hesitance about him, just sweeping determination and power. He offered no subtlety, he asked nothing, but demanded, his tongue plunging against the crevice of her lips with an intimate surge, breaking through the barrier of her teeth and sweeping her mouth with deep and sensual effrontery. She felt the breath of him and the scent of him, and she was filled with everything that was intimate about the man. She freed her hand to fight him, and found that her palm fell against the breast of his frock coat, and she was achingly aware of even the feel of the material there. She was trembling. She should be fighting now for dear life and honor, yet she was locked in his embrace, and could not begin to find the power to pull away. His kiss was an invasion, a subtle rape of her mouth, and yet his touch was so overwhelming that she could do nothing but absorb the sensations. Tears stung her eyes, for she was somehow aware that the magic of the night was over. Innocence was gone. She had fallen in love, she had believed in a man, and she had believed in love. And she had been spurned. And now she was discovering that she could still be touched, that she could feel, that she could rage and despise a stranger and still fall prey to the demand of a kiss, to tremble and shake in the arms of the enemy. . . .

She pulled away from him at last, gasping and horrified. Her fingers flew to her swollen lips, her arms wrapped protectively about her chest. "St-stop!" she charged him. She rose and backed away, hating him and hating Robert with all of her heart. She would never, never love anyone again, she vowed silently. And certainly not this man who now watched her with such striking curiosity in his silver eyes. He did not breathe hard, he did not shake or tremble. He was, at least, no longer amused, for his gaze was hard and grave upon her.

"Stop!" she repeated, still shaking. "You are in truth no better than he!"

"Ah, but I am, you see," he said softly as he stood. "I can offer you an honest proposal of marriage, and he cannot."

"Marriage!"

"Yes, marriage. The legal type of arrangement."

She ignored the taunt. "You are a rebel, a rogue, and a backwoods adventurer, sir, and I cannot begin to take such an idea even remotely seriously. You are the last man that I should ever wish to marry. You thought that you could frighten me and bully me in Boston; well, you cannot do so here! You must know what I feel for you, and I cannot begin to wonder what it is that you can possibly feel for me."

He laughed. "Your father took my offer very seriously. And as for my feelings, why, I am enchanted."

She flushed and stared up at the stars. "You are no better than Robert. You are ruled by lust."

She saw the hint of his smile. "Lust? Your word, milady, and so I will admit to a fair amount of it. But perhaps I see more. A heart that drums a different beat, eyes that dare the very devil."

"And are you the devil? So goes your reputation, Lord Cameron."

"No devil, lady. Just a man in lust."

Amanda moved back, hugging her arms more tightly about herself, wondering if his agreement with her father could possibly be true. All of Virginia's society, or their society at least, was up in arms against Lord Cameron. Although Cameron Hall was a magnificent estate, and he owned endless acres of cotton and tobacco and produce, and had a pedigree that went back to the Dark Ages, dissension was in the air, and he was turning his back on his own kind to join up with rebels.

"I don't believe you!" she whispered again, but she said it more quietly. "My father did not—agree to a marriage!"

"Milady, I do not lie," he told her. He walked toward her, and she wanted to turn and run. She hated to be a coward, but at that moment she wanted to run, and still she could not. It was not courage at all that kept her still, it was something about the way he looked at her.

He stopped several feet before her and reached out gently. She thought that he was going to sweep her into his arms again, but he did not, and for the life of her, she did not know if she was relieved or disappointed. She could not breathe properly, and it seemed that the very masculine scent of him was not just around her, but part of her, and that she would never forget it or forget his power. He touched just her cheek, his knuckles running over the softness of it, his hand then falling to his side. "But neither shall I force the issue. If you are adamantly opposed to me, milady, then the matter is solved. However, I do suggest that you think carefully before accepting Lord Tarryton's . . . proposition."

Heedlessly she tried to strike him again. He was quick, catching her hand before it could land upon him. He turned her wrist slowly, drawing a finger over the valley of her palm, then pressing his lips against it. Her breath came in a rush and her heart pounded and again. She wanted nothing more than to escape him and the sensations of his touch.

"I told you, milady, you may not strike me again."

She smiled very sweetly. "Being a loyalist's mistress might be preferable to a life as a traitor's wife."

"Really? I think that you're sadly mistaken. About yourself, Lady Sterling, if nothing else. Young Tarryton is a boy, playing at a man's games. He isn't for you. He'll never be for you. He desires you, perhaps he even loves you. But he hasn't the courage to fight for you, milady, and in the end you would be sadly disappointed."

"Oh, I see. I'd never be disappointed in you, I presume?" she challenged him sarcastically.

"No," he said. "You would not be disappointed in me. Had I set out to seduce you, milady, it would never have come to attempted rape, and in the outcome, I promise that you'd have been mine."

She opened her mouth to protest with outrage, but she never spoke. He did touch her again then, hard and sure. He drew her against him and his lips found hers. She whimpered and pounded furiously against his chest, but he paid her no heed, and he gave her no quarter. His mouth closed upon hers with swift, searing hunger and his tongue penetrated deeply against her protest, filling her with a warmth that consumed all thought and reason. She whimpered and pressed herself against him, feeling dizzy and almost falling. But it didn't matter, for as he continued to kiss her, he held her weight with ease. She thought briefly that he would never let her fall, and she realized that the overpowering heat that exploded throughout her emanated from some searing center of her being that had come alive tonight. It was unlike anything she had ever imagined before, this hot excitement that stirred her blood and swept from her lips to her breasts, and from her breasts to some secret place within her, near the juncture of her thighs, wickedly deep within her.

And then, abruptly, he released her, a negligent smile upon his lips. "You should marry me, milady, because I do believe that I could promise never to disappoint you."

"I would fight you all of my life!" she exclaimed out, and then realized that it was she who still clung to him. She needed the support.

"You would fight me, but you would not be disappointed by me. Now, milady, if you'll excuse me, I shall leave you to your own devices, since you are so capable." He let her hand fall and bowed deeply to her, turning about to leave the maze.

Shaking, Amanda determined to have the last word. "You are a traitor, Lord Cameron! A traitor to the king, a traitor to your own kind!"

He turned back around, bowing deeply. "As you would have it, milady. Far be it that I should argue with your gentle tongue."

He turned again and was gone.

Amanda sank down upon the bench, feeling the pressure of her tears come rushing to her eyes. She pressed her hands against them, determined not to cry. She was trembling still. He had awakened things inside of her, things she had never dared to dream of. . . .

And things she now despised.

She hated him. She had hated him in Boston, and she hated him now! How dare he come upon her so highhandedly again. He had known about Robert— dear God, all the world had known about Robert, all the world but she!

She touched her swollen lips, and all that she could remember was Eric Cameron's touch. Yet it was true, the magic was gone, love was gone, and her belief in things beautiful and good and right was gone. Innocence had been cruelly slain, she thought, and then, despite her best intentions, tears did start to fall down her cheeks. Robert! How could he? How could he speak of his longing and desire for her and then tell her that yes, he did intend to marry the Duchess of Owenfield?

How could he suggest that she become his mistress?

Amanda wiped the tears from her cheeks and forced herself to stand and smooth down her gown. She dusted bits of leaves from her skirt and swallowed hard and touched her fingers to her hair.

She had to go back. She had to lift her head and smile and return to the house and be her father's most gracious hostess, and she had to laugh and dance and be certain that no one ever knew what had taken place in the Venus garden.

"Amanda!"

Hearing her name called, she leapt to her feet and forced a smile to her lips.

"Damien!" she called in response to that well-loved voice. She knew her cousin would quickly be upon her, for he knew the maze as thoroughly as she did. They had often played there as children. "Damien!"

He came through the last row of hedges, bewigged and handsome, looking fabulously elegant. He knew his appearance was quite proper and perfect, and he paused by the Venus statue to pose for her quickly. "The ultimate gentleman, the lord of leisure!" he said, then he laughed and raced toward her, and she threw herself into his arms.

"Damien! You're back. I thought that you were staying in Philadelphia with your brother and that the two of you had been larking about from Boston to New York. And it frightens me when you and he are apart for I am ever afraid of what trouble you will find!"

He shook his head, and it seemed for a moment that sober thoughts clouded his dark handsome eyes. "I am ever quick to avoid trouble!" he vowed to her, then laughed. "I heard that Lord Sterling was hosting a ball, and I came quickly, thinking that my dear sweet cousin might need me."

Amanda pulled away from him, watching his eyes. Then she sighed softly. "So you knew too. All the world knew about Robert and this Duchess of Owenfield except for me, and, therefore, I made the most horrible fool of myself." If she wasn't careful, she'd start crying again.

"Amanda, he's not worthy of you," Damien told her swiftly. Setting an arm about her shoulder, he led her to sit down on the bench.

She smiled up at him lovingly. "Perhaps not, but I loved him, Damien. So what do I do now?"

"Forget him. There will be other men to offer for you, to love you—"

"Well, I've had the offer!" she said, and laughed bitterly. "But not the love. It was quite astounding. Lord Cameron appeared on the scene and offered himself."

"Cameron!" Damien repeated, startled.

"Aye, the traitor. My night is beset by betrayal, so it seems, for Father had told him yes!"

Damien stood, hooking his thumbs into his waistband as he paced before her. He swung around and looked at her. "He's been quite the bachelor, Mandy. You know that. Mamas have thrown their daughters at him for some time now, and he has never shown the least interest. You are deeply honored, you know."

"You like him!" Amanda accused. "You were good friends in Boston, or so it seemed, but, Damien, you must take the greatest care! You know that the man is a traitor."

Damien hesitated a long time, looking at her. "No, I do not know him as a traitor, cousin."

Amanda gasped, leaping up to catch hold of his shoulder. "You can't mean that! I . . . I know that he is guilty of evil deeds, I have seen him in action. And he follows the words of fanatics, of fools—"

Damien shook his head, watching her sadly. "I do not believe that these men are fanatics or fools, Mandy." She stared at him blankly, and he suddenly gripped her hands with excitement. "In Philadelphia I met with the writer and printer Benjamin Franklin. I—"

"Benjamin Franklin? The newspaper man? The fellow who puts out that *Poor Richard's Almanac?*" Franklin lived in Pennsylvania; his yearly book on weather and forecasts and sayings was like a bible to men from Georgia to Maine, and even up into the Canadian colonies.

"Yes, Franklin. Benjamin Franklin. He's considered a great man these days there, a wise man indeed."

"He prints insurrection, I take it."

"You'd love him, Mandy."

"Oh, Damien! You frighten me. I do not like the company you keep. Franklin wants war."

"No! No man wants war. But if you listen to these people, you'll come to understand."

"Understand what? We are English. We must pay taxes for English defense! Come, Damien, think on it. Without our fine English soldiers, what would we have done during the French and Indian Wars? Our militia was sad and pathetic! Scant defense!"

"Not so scant!" Damien protested. "Why, it was only what our colonials learned about Indian warfare that saved us then. George Washington was a volunteer with the British regulars when General Braddock was overtaken by the French and Indians, and it was young Washington who saw the troops back to Virginia. And Robert Rogers's rangers out of Connecticut were so adept and disciplined that they became part of the regular British army."

"British reinforcements saved us in the end, and it was a horrible and long bloody war. Without the Crown forces we would have been lost, and you know it."

He looked at her. "A Continental Congress is due to meet in Philadelphia this September to protest the closing of the port of Boston and other 'intolerable' acts."

Mandy exhaled. "I am so tired of this endless talk of war."

Damien laughed. "Cousin, you weren't even born when the French and Indian Wars broke out in 1754. And you were a babe of eight when it ended in sixty-three, so tell me, what makes you such an expert?"

She lowered her head suddenly, remembering that it had been in 1763, when the last of the campaigns had begun, that she had first seen Eric Cameron. Lord

Hastings had called a hunt just before some of the Virginia relief troops were due to leave. There'd been no reason for young Cameron to go, but his father had already been killed in the fighting and his grandfather had not denied him the right to fight if he chose. He had been young, disdainful, and ardent, she remembered. Determined to fight. Assured, poised . . .

Abysmally rude to her.

She shook her head. Well, he had come back, and he had been given some officer's commission. Even though his grandfather hadn't allowed him to leave with one, he'd earned it on his own.

Mandy shivered. She couldn't understand war, and although she'd been very young during the French and Indian Wars, she could still remember the tears of the women who had lost husbands, the sons who had lost fathers, the girls who had lost their lovers. And there had been greater tragedy before her birth, when the war had just begun, for the Acadians from Nova Scotia—Frenchmen who had loved their land and stayed with it when it had gone from French rule to British in a previous treaty—were no longer trusted. They were cruelly exiled from their lands and cast upon the shores of Maine and Massachusetts and Virginia. Although some were able to make it into the French Louisiana Territory, many had been forced to seek some livelihood among the hostile English and Americans. There were still Acadians at Sterling Hall, even though her father despised them. She had heard it rumored that her father had slain an Acadian, although it had been at her birth, and she had never known whether it was true or not. She pitied the women, and the beautiful little children, and she had always done her best to be kind to the Acadians who remained with them. Indeed, Danielle was Acadian.

And still men went to war.

They had gone before, and it seemed now that they were growing eager to do battle again, that they might soon be eager to stand before flaring muskets, to allow themselves to be brutally ripped and torn and maimed.

"I'm not an expert on war, Damien, and I don't want to be," she assured him. "And I'm very worried about you."

"No! Ah, cousin, please, for the love of God, don't worry about me. This is Damien. I land on my feet, always. Remember that."

"I'll keep it in mind when they hang you."

"They'll not hang me. And they'll not hang your new betrothed either, love."

"Betrothed!"

"You said that Lord Cameron proposed—"

"Proposed? No, I did not say that. He burst upon Robert and me with an announcement that Father had agreed to his suggestion that he and I marry. But then . . ."

"Then what?"

"He was quick to assure me that he did not want me without my consent." She paused, looking at Damien. "Why would Father do such a thing so suddenly, though? Father is an ardent loyalist. Could it be true?"

"Zounds—"

"Damien, don't swear."

"Me! Why, Mandy, when you've the mind, you swear like a seaman!"

"Don't be absurd. Ladies don't swear. But if I were to swear, I wouldn't do silly things like turn the words around. I should say, 'God's body!' and that would be that!"

"Tarnation! So you would, Mandy!"

"Damnation—and be done with it!" she said.

"If you weren't such a lady, that's exactly what you'd say!" Damien murmured with mock solemnity. But then he frowned in earnest. "Who knows anything about your father? He's never much liked me, and that's a fact."

Amanda frowned. It was true. Damien was the child of her mother's younger brother, and her father had tolerated him, keeping up the pretense of family, but had never shown him any affection. Michael, Damien's elder brother, very seldom came near Sterling Hall. He would not pretend to tolerate his uncle, and though Amanda loved Michael dearly, she seldom saw him now for he had moved to Pennsylvania.

"Surely Father does love you—" Amanda began awkwardly, but Damien interrupted her, waving a hand in the air.

"Cousin, I do not mean to be cruel, but I wonder if he even loves you. Never mind, how callous of me. What a horrible thing to say. And still, let's head into the house, shall we? He was asking about you, and I'd hate to bring his wrath down upon the two of us. And—"

"And what?" Amanda asked quickly as her cousin paused.

"And you need to dance, love. You need to dance and laugh and appear as if you're having the time of your life."

"Oh!" The blood drained from her face as she remembered that she had been rejected and humiliated. She tossed back her hair, adjusting the comb over her ear. "Am I all right, Damien?"

"All right? You are entirely beautiful. And we shall kick up our heels and make fools of the lot of them!" He caught her hand and led her quickly through the maze. "Remember when we were children? I loved this place so. You were going to marry a prince, or a duke at the very least. And I was going to kidnap the most glorious Indian maiden and strike out to conquer the world."

Gasping as she hurried to keep up with his pace, Amanda laughed. But there was pain to the laughter, just as there was pain to growing up. Dreams were like clouds, created only to be shattered by violent, unexpected storms.

She stopped short, just outside the entrance to the maze. She could see the lanterns swaying brilliantly upon the porch, and she could see the silhouettes of their guests through the windows, elegant men, beautiful women with their coiffures piled high and their skirts most fashionably wide. Growing up. It was suddenly very frightening, and she had never felt so old as she did this night. Life was still a game, but it was for higher stakes, and she suddenly shivered.

"It's all going to change again, isn't it, Damien?"

"Who knows what the future holds?" he answered her with a shrug. "Come, hold my hand, and we'll slip right onto the dance floor."

They scampered up the steps and over the broad porch together, slipping into the house at the end of the hallway. It wasn't to be quite so easy as they had planned, for Amanda's father was there, watching them as they arrived.

"Damien!" he said sharply. "I would have a word with you now. And you, girl—" He paused, his voice low and grating as he stared at her coldly. "You I will deal with later!"

"Ah, Lady Sterling!" A voice interrupted. She spun around, recognizing the deep resonant sound. It was Eric Cameron. He bowed to her father. "Alas, your charming daughter and I shall not wed, sir, but she did promise me this dance just minutes ago."

"Minutes ago—"

"But of course, sir. May I?" He smiled at Lord Sterling and caught Amanda's hand, swirling her out to the center of the hall where couples were just forming for a reel. The musicians started up and she could not move at first. His silver gaze lit upon her and a daring smile touched his lips.

"Dance, Lady Amanda. You've got it in you, I know that you do. Toss your head back with that glorious mane of hair and cast one of your dazzling smiles upon me. Laugh, and let the whole of the world go to hell. They are whispering about you, and your scandalous behavior, rushing into the maze with an engaged man. Gossips and old hags. Let them know that you don't give a halfpenny about their opinions."

"What makes you think that I have ever cared about their opinions?" she countered. His hands touched hers, and suddenly they were swirling to the music.

"Perhaps you don't. But you do care about your pride."

"Do I?"

"Immeasurably."

"Enough so that I should not be dancing with a known rabble-rouser?"

"Rabble-rouser? Ah, milady, I've not nearly the eloquence necessary to sway the populace!"

"They talk of you from here to the nether regions, Lord Cameron. How can you say that?"

"You haven't heard the real speech masters, milady. They rouse the heart, and that is where change lies, madame. Not in arms, and not even in bloodshed. Change lies within the very heart and soul of the people."

"So you do seek war."

"No one seeks war."

"You are infamous."

"Perhaps, but as I said, I haven't the eloquence to move worlds, milady."

She shivered suddenly, not knowing why. He was scarcely a humble man, yet his words caused her to feel chills.

Someone walking over her grave. . . .

Or perhaps a warning. As if she would live to see the day when she would depend desperately upon his eloquence and his ability to sway the masses.

Never. He was the traitor.

"You are a liar, a knave, and a scoundrel."

He laughed, lowering his head near hers, and she realized that all the room was watching them. "Am I all that, milady? Pity, for I felt that you fit so very well with me. And of course, I'm even daring to believe that you might realize it one day—once your heart recovers from its bruising."

"I shall survive, but I shall never discover that I fit well with you, milord." She smiled sweetly, and they swirled with an ever greater vigor about the floor. His eyes never left hers, and with each step she felt more fully the heat of the summer's night, the sizzle of fire, as if lightning storms raged outside. His confidence in himself was outrageous, yet even thinking of his kiss, of his touch upon her, caused her breath to catch, her heart to thunder, and she realized there was one thing about him she could not resist—he was exciting. He infuriated her, and if she cared for nothing else, she did long to show him that she would never be beaten.

"Ah . . . careful, smile sweetly! Lady Geneva has her eyes upon us."

"Perhaps she is jealous. Didn't you recently share a dance with her?"

"Recently, yes. But I've never proposed marriage to her."

"I see. But perhaps you have made other proposals to Lady Geneva?"

"The green eyes of jealousy, love?"

"I'm not your love, and my eyes are green by birth, milord."

"Lady Geneva makes her own proposals," he told her softly, and she almost wrenched from his hold, for she knew then that they had been lovers, and she was furious that she should be so bothered by the thought.

"I'm quite exhausted. May we cease this mockery?"

"Alas, no! Chin up, eyes bright, 'tis be damned with the world, remember?"

" 'Tis be damned with you, sir, and if you'll excuse me—"

"Ah, but I won't."

And he did not. He held her close, and she was captured with the dance. Swirling and spinning, they passed by the other dancers, her hair and her gown flying out about her, making her a vision of beauty and fire in the night, on the arms of the tall, dark man. He twirled her from the dance floor out onto the porch, and then he had her laughing, for he did not quit then, but deftly brought her leaping down the steps and onto the lawn. Once there, he continued to swirl her beneath the moonlight. She cast back her head, smiling, for he was right about one thing. She longed to throw all caution to the wind, to show the gossips that she would do as she pleased, that she was not spurned and she knew no pain. He saw her smile, and some knowing glint came to his eyes.

"A temptress and a hell-raiser, milady? Shall we show them that life is to be lived to the fullest and that passion is its own master?"

"You are a hell-raiser. I am no temptress."

"Ah! I beg to disagree!"

"Do you, sir? Amazing, but I do not see you begging at all."

He smiled. "A matter of speech, milady."

"Humility is surely your greatest virtue."

"However you would have it, Lady Sterling, however you would have it."

And then suddenly they were dancing no more. They stood beneath the moonlight. His mouth was hard and unsmiling. His eyes were as piercing as a silver blade as they stared down into hers.

"There are whispers upon the wind, Amanda. Harsh whispers. Should you need me, know that I will be there."

"I will not need you!" she promised. But perhaps that was not so true, for even though the night was warm she was already shivering, and despite the entire debacle of the evening, she longed to cast herself into his arms and feel their warmth and security about her. And yet, she thought, for all the lightness of his words, this man would be no gentle master, but one determined upon his own cause. A woman who loved him was bound to be mastered by that iron will and determination.

No! she thought. I shall never lose my heart or my soul to one such as he! The pain that she felt this night was one thing. She realized that being entrapped by the fierce passion of this man could cause an anguish she could not begin now to fathom. The strange sensations touched her like mist, making her feel uneasy and hot. The strange tingling seized her body once again, dangerously touching places that it should not.

"You—you cannot love me, you don't even know me!" she cried.

"I know a great deal about you," he told her, and he smiled again. "And don't forget—I am in lust with you."

"You wish to best me! That is all. I have not fallen amorously into your arms, as others do too easily. You like to win, before you step upon your conquests. Well, you shall not win against me, sir."

"Perhaps not. I'll consider it a challenge well met." He was silent for a moment, then he indicated someone over his shoulder. "It's an interesting evening. Your lost love is consoling himself, I see."

"What?" Amanda swung around, stunned to see that Robert had come to the porch.

With Geneva. And they were close together in an intimate embrace. She had cast her arms about his neck. Her head was back and her laughter was throaty. And then she was kissing him.

Amanda gave not a thought to the night, the world, or propriety. Blindly she cast arms about the man before her and came up high on her toes to press her length against him. Instinctively she arched against him, curling her fingers into his hair and then pressing her lips against his. Tentatively she pressed her tongue against his teeth.

And then the world seemed to explode. His mouth gave way, and he was not in her arms, but she was in his. She was barely upon her feet, swirling in the moonlight again, and his tongue raked her mouth as if it invaded the very soul of her and reached with his searing liquid fire to touch her heart. He laid his hand upon her breast, and something moved in her to that touch, something that pulsed with curiosity.

With desire.

"Oh . . ." She gasped against him, when his mouth lifted from hers at last.

He held her still, swept off her feet, in his arms. She stared up at him in the darkness and saw his slow rake's smile just touch the corner of his lips as he spoke seriously. "Did that suffice for what you wished, milady? I do believe you've struck fairly in return. The poor dear fellow is on the porch. I'm afraid he's just about ready to trip over his tongue. Shall I release you and ease his agony? Or do you wish to heap more torture upon him? I am ready to oblige you in any manner you choose."

"Oh! Oh, you bastard!" She gasped. "Set me down! This instant."

He started to do so. Instantly. She nearly fell flat and managed to save herself only by clinging to his neck.

"Lord Cameron—"

"Yes, love. What is it now? I never seem to be able to please you."

"That's because I absolutely despise you."

"Ah, then I shall look forward to the kisses you will give when you've discovered that you love me."

"Kisses! I shall spit upon your carcass when they've hanged you!"

"Shh! Careful, he's coming close. With Geneva upon his heels. Ah, and there is Lady Harding! Amazing how many of your father's guests have discovered that they need a bit of fresh air. Slowly now, slide down against me." He carefully set her down. She was against him still, yet it was a very proper position, with his arm just about her as he escorted her in the moonlight. She stared at him furiously, but she didn't fight him. She didn't want to face her father with any more whispers of scandal raging about her.

"You will be made to pay one day," she promised him pleasantly.

"To pay? Why, milady, I have desired to do nothing the whole night long except to ease you from any difficulty you encountered. You do have a vengeful streak within your delicate soul. Perhaps, when we are married, I shall have to beat it from you."

She started to jerk from him and she saw the laughter in his eyes. "Perhaps I shall marry you, just before they tighten your noose. I understand that your property is very fine."

"You must visit it. Come to Cameron Hall any time, milady. Or if you're in Williamsburg, you must be my guest, whether I am in attendance or not. I shall leave word with Mathilda that you are welcome any time. Ah . . . here comes your father. He is looking for us, I think."

He raised a hand. Nigel Sterling stood upon the porch, his hand stuck into his frock coat. He saw Eric Cameron's wave and started down the steps.

Amanda did not like the speculative look within her father's eyes. She did not like his glance upon her, colder than usual.

"There you are, my dear, Eric."

"The night was captivating. Not nearly so captivating as your daughter, yet the combination of loveliness was one that I could not resist. Forgive me."

"You are forgiven for being young and enamored, Lord Cameron—if not for other things," Nigel said. He smiled cordially, but when he gazed at Amanda, she still felt the coldness. "Our guests are beginning to leave, Mandy. Perhaps you will be so kind as to see them on their way?"

"Of course, Father. Excuse me, Lord Cameron."

He reached for her hand, kissed it. She waited until his eyes rose to hers and she mouthed sweetly, "Good-bye."

"I'm not leaving—yet," he returned, arching a brow rakishly.

She pursed her lips, turned about, and fled for the house. Her father remained talking a moment longer, then he followed her, standing by the door while Amanda took a position at the landing of the stairway, by the bannister.

The Hastings and the Hardings were leaving, and Amanda called Danielle to fetch their hats and accessories. She was thanked for a wonderful time, and she kept her sweet smile in place, wondering if the ladies were pitying her—or if they were eager to rush home to discuss her scandalous behavior. It didn't matter. She kept her chin up and her laughter light. No one would ever know just how devastated she had been.

Mrs. Newmeyer left next, thanking her and Lord Sterling for the sumptuous buffet. Smiling graciously, Amanda realized she hadn't even glanced at the buffet table.

Then Robert was before her, his eyes pained as they stared into hers—as if he was the one who had been betrayed. He managed to draw her aside as her father was caught in a discussion nearer the door.

"My God, how could you!" Robert whispered heatedly.

"How could I?"

"I saw you in his arms. It was indecent."

"Indecent! Robert, he asked me to marry him. You asked me—no! You sought to force me into something that was indecent!"

"He'll never marry you," Robert said harshly.

"Oh?"

"It's a lie. It's a ploy. He's disgustingly wealthy, and you are perhaps an heiress, but nowhere near as wealthy as he. He couldn't possibly be serious. You're not—"

"I'm not as disgustingly wealthy? Robert, take your hands off me. Contrary to your belief, not every man longs to awaken with wealth alone on the pillow beside him. Now leave me be."

Robert stiffened and turned sullen. Although the pain of betrayal and shattered dreams was still with her, she was startled by the discoveries she was making. She did not like this side of him.

"You won't marry him. He's a bloody patriot."

"Patriot? I believe the word might well mean many things. And I do intend to marry him."

A slight cough interrupted them. Amanda swung around to see Lord Cameron. His eyes were alight with amusement and mockery. "Good night, my love," he said, purposely turning her away from Robert. "I shall return very soon—to discuss the wedding plans, of course."

She longed to kick him but she didn't dare. Robert was still before her. She forced herself to smile. "Good night. My love," she added.

He bowed deeply. At the door he paused, speaking with her father.

In a fury, Robert swung about and left too.

There were more guests bidding her good night. She longed to escape to her room, but she held her ground and maintained her smile.

Damien was the last to leave for his home, an hour north of his uncle's estate. She kissed him and agreed to ride to Williamsburg with him soon. Then Damien said good night to her father.

"Yes. Good night, young man."

They shook hands, and Amanda thought that Damien had been right—her father did not like him. She clenched her hands behind her back, wishing that he would not be so obvious.

The door closed. Danielle stood quietly before Lord Sterling, lowering her eyes. "Is there anything else, sir?"

Her voice still held a hint of a French accent, and Amanda thought that even that annoyed her father. He looked at Danielle distastefully, even though she was a wonderful servant. She managed the household staff and slaves, and did so very well, and still Lord Sterling never had a good word for her.

Amanda thought that Danielle stayed because of her. She wasn't sure. Danielle's husband and brother had died in the cargo hold of the ship that had brought them to Virginia from Port Royal, Nova Scotia. Her tiny daughter had died in that same hold.

"No. You are dismissed."

Danielle turned to leave. Lord Sterling quickly shifted his gaze from his servant to his daughter, and the cold distaste remained in his eyes.

"And for you, girl."

"What is it, Father?" Amanda said wearily.

"Come here."

She was somewhat surprised by his tone, but too weary to fight him. She strode across the room to stand before him.

"Yes?"

She was stunned when his hand lashed out at her, catching her across the face with such violence that she fell to her knees, her head reeling. She screamed out in her surprise and pain. Danielle, barely out of the room, heard her cry and came rushing toward her.

"Stop!" Lord Sterling commanded Danielle. "It will be a whipping for you. You are dismissed."

Danielle paused, then continued forward. Crawling to her knees, Amanda raised a hand to stop her. "I'm fine. Danielle, *tu peux t'en aller maintenant.*" she urged her in French.

Her father seemed to hate even the language. His eyes darkened further with displeasure as he stared down at her. "Don't you ever go against my word. I made arrangements. You broke them."

"What?" Amanda said, amazed.

"Lord Cameron has informed me that he is not interested in a marriage that is not desirable to you. I will make the arrangements for your life—you will not."

"No!" she cried. This night, which she had hoped would be a night of magic, had turned into a nightmare. "You cannot make me marry, Father! I do not believe this. I—"

"Don't worry. Lord Cameron no longer wants you."

"You cannot make me marry anyone!"

"When I so choose, you will marry. You will not disobey me, or else you will learn the persuasion of the lash. Now go to your room. Get out of my sight."

She stood, facing him, feeling her cheek swell while tears rushed to her eyes. "I—I hate you!" she whispered to him.

And to her amazement, he smiled. With pleasure. "Hate me to your heart's content. But you bear my name, and you will obey me. Now go to your room."

She turned and fled up the stairway. More than anything in the world, she wanted to escape the sight of him.

When she reached her room, she slammed and locked the door and leaned against it, gasping for breath.

Then she burst into tears and fell on her bed. What sin could she have committed that was so grave that she should deserve the agony of all that had happened this night?

Magic had died.

And even in her misery she was dimly aware that the nightmare was just beginning.

The world was changing, her whole world was changing. Winds of change were sweeping over the land, and no one, no one at all, would be able to stand against them.

5

 OR SEVERAL WEEKS AMANDA MANAGED TO STAY
clear of her father, just as he stayed far away from her. It helped
that he was gone on business for a time, but even when he
returned, she had no difficulty avoiding him. He dined in his
room; she dined in her own.

It was a miserable time for her as she accepted the fact that not only had she
been betrayed by the man she had so foolishly loved, but her own father did not
care for her at all. All of her life she had thought he was being stern for her own
good, but now she realized he hated the very sight of her.

Then she was plagued by thoughts of Eric Cameron. Despite her rude refusal
of his proposal, he had willingly allowed her to use him to taunt Robert when
she'd had an opportunity to salvage some of her pride. She had not heard a word
from him since the party, and as the days passed, she realized that she would not.
His promise that he would come by to discuss the wedding had been for Robert's sake.

Yet she had expected him. He was not a man to give up what he wanted, and
he had said that he wanted her. Maybe he hadn't wanted her badly enough. She
told herself that it was definitely well and good, but when she lay awake at night,
flushed and tossing, it was Eric Cameron she was remembering, the audacity of
his touch and laughter, the bold command of his eyes. He knew too much, she
thought, and she tried to tell herself that she referred to Boston—and to Damien.
But it wasn't true. He knew too much about her. He knew her far too well.

Her days passed easily enough despite her expectation and dread that Eric
would come—and her startling disappointment that he did not. Her pride was
doubly wounded, nothing more. She just wished that she did not feel such
peculiar flashes of heat and unease when she thought of his eyes upon her, when
she remembered the force of his hold, the caress of his lips.

Still, her father's cruelty ravaged her soul. If home had not been such a
pleasant place to be, she would have thought about running away. She did start
wondering where she could go if she ever felt desperate enough to leave. She
could go back to Boston and stay with Anne Marie, but if her father wished to
wed her to some distasteful stranger, he would come for her, and Sir Thomas
would dutifully hand her over. She had just returned from her father's sister's
plantation in South Carolina. And while she loved her aunt and her cousins, she
knew that if her Aunt Clarissa were pressed to side with either her or her father,
she would choose her father.

Then there was Philadelphia, where Damien's brother Michael lived, but both

601

Philadelphia and Boston seemed to be such hotbeds of rebellion right now that they did not seem to be safe places to visit. Thinking over her own position, she realized that she was very strongly a loyalist herself and that she did not want to live among rebels.

Then, too, she loved her home. She loved Virginia, she loved the soft flowing river. She loved the summer warmth and the flowers and the beauty of the land, and she loved the accents of the people. She loved Sterling Hall, the singsong of the slaves in the field, the melodic murmurs of the Acadians on the household staff and in the laundry.

Walking out beyond the oaks that lined the walkway before the house, Amanda suddenly panicked, remembering that her father had mentioned sending her to England when she had first returned from South Carolina. She hadn't protested emphatically then, for she had thought that he meant to protect her because he loved her. Now she knew that he merely wanted her out of the way, set upon a shelf until he was able to use her as pawn to his advantage. Her heart quickened. She would not go to England. She would weather the storms of discontent until reason prevailed.

She stared down the slope of ground in the back of the house, leading toward the river. Sterling Hall was self-sufficient. There was a huge smokehouse, the laundry, the stables, the barn, the carriage house, the cooper's, the blacksmith's, and the shoemaker. Beyond those buildings lay the slave quarters, and the larger houses for the free servants, and far beyond those lay the lands and the homes of the tenant farmers. Her father did very well here. The land was rich, and the fields were filled with the very best tobacco. Her father gave it no thought himself; he never dirtied his hands, nor did he keep his own books. He hunted, danced, and indulged in politics, drank hard, and played hard. Amanda knew that he had a mistress in Williamsburg, and she had also heard that he slept with one of their young mulatto slaves.

On her fifteenth birthday she had struck Damien in a fury when he had told her about it. But then, when she had asked Danielle if it was true, she had been appalled, for Danielle had not been able to deny the accusations.

She had known that her father was not a terribly nice man. She had just never realized how he really felt about her. Maybe she had always sensed it, though. And maybe that was why she had fallen so desperately in love with Robert.

Robert. At the thought of him, she felt the same gnawing pain in her middle. She had been so desperately in love. She had imagined a life with Robert, waking beside him, laughing in his arms, taking great pride in the fact that their home was known far and wide in all the colonies for its grace and beauty. She had never dreamed of a different house—it had always been Sterling Hall. She had never imagined her father's death—he had just been gone, and Robert had been lord of Sterling. They had laughed and played by the river, and she had even indulged in fantasies about making love. The water would ripple by them and the moon would be full up above, or else the sun would beat down upon their daringly naked flesh, but it would be all right, because they would love one another so deeply. She had never really thought too terribly much about the act of making love, not until . . .

Her thought trailed away, and then she flushed furiously, grateful that she was alone with her awful realization.

She had never, never thought about the act itself until she had been with Eric Cameron in the maze. Never, never before that night had she felt anything like that physical excitement, like a hot river sweeping through her, awakening her flesh.

"Oh! Will he forever plague me?" she whispered aloud, and pressed her hands against her cheeks. They were flaming. He had sworn that he would plague her, she recalled, but she had not thought that it could be in this manner! She didn't want to think about Eric Cameron, she hated him almost as much as she hated her father this morning. She wanted to hate Robert, but love died a very hard death, and so she hated Eric all the more venomously. For all that he had witnessed, for all that he had caused—and for the horribly shameful way that he made her feel.

She wasn't going to think about him, that was all. Not now, not ever again. And as much as she loved Sterling Hall, maybe it was time to leave for an extended vacation. Then she wouldn't have to hear the rumors and whispers when Robert married his duchess.

"Amanda! Amanda!"

She swung around. Danielle was on the porch steps, wiping her hands on her apron, waving to her. Frowning, Amanda waved in return and then hurried toward the house. Danielle's dark eyes were anxious. *"Ma petite,* your father is looking for you. He is in his study. You must go now."

Amanda stiffened. She had no desire to see her father, but such a summons would be difficult to ignore. He had total power over her; he could beat her if he chose, he could send her away. And her only recourse would be to run away.

She squared her shoulders. "Thank you, Danielle. I will see Father now."

She smoothed down her cotton skirt and composed herself as she walked down the hallway to his office. She knocked on the door, then waited for him to bid her to enter. When he did, she came in and stood before his desk in silence, waiting. An open ledger book lay before him, and he finished with a group of sums before looking up. When he did, his eyes were as cold as lead. He looked her up and down distastefully.

"Make ready for a trip."

"What?" she said. "I don't wish to leave—"

"I care nothing for your wishes. I am going to Williamsburg. The governor has asked that I come. And he has especially asked that you come too. You will do so."

Her heart took flight. He was not attempting to send her out of the country. She just wished that they would not be traveling together.

"Fine. When do we leave?"

"This afternoon. Be ready by three."

That was it. He turned his attention back to his ledger. Amanda turned around and left his office. Danielle was out in the hall, her deep, beautiful dark eyes full of anxiety again.

"It's all right," Amanda told her. "We are leaving this afternoon. For Williamsburg."

"Am I going with you?"

"I didn't think to ask. Yes, you must come. It's the only way I shall be able to—"

"To what?" Danielle prompted her.

"To bear being near him," Amanda said quietly, then she turned around and hurried for the stairs.

At three she was waiting in the hallway. Timothy and Remy, two of the house slaves, had carried down her trunks. She was dressed in white muslin with a tiny print of maroon flowers and an overcoat of the same color in velvet. The overcoat fell in fashionable loops over her wide-hipped petticoats, then fell gracefully in a short train down the back of her skirt. She wore her delicate pearled pumps and a wide-brimmed straw hat decorated with sweeping plumes. Danielle, behind her, wore a smaller hat and a soft gray cotton dress, but even she had given way to fashion in her choice of petticoat. She was still very beautiful, Amanda thought of Danielle. After all these years.

Her father appeared, looked her over curtly, gave the servants last-minute instructions, and then ordered her into the carriage. He looked at Danielle for a long moment and then shrugged. "No French," he told her as she climbed up into the carriage. "I won't hear any of that gibberish, do you hear me?"

"Yes, milord," Danielle said simply. Her eyes were lowered as they entered the carriage, and a chill shot through the Amanda as she watched the exchange. She was suddenly certain that her father had used Danielle, just as he had used his mistress in Williamsburg, and just as he used the mulatto slave girl. She felt hot and ill, and wished desperately that she would not have to face him for the next several hours as they traveled.

It was a miserable journey, the whole of it passing in near silence. Her father read his paper, scowling constantly. Danielle stared out the window. There had been rain, and the road was pockmarked and heavily grooved. Like the others, Amanda sat in silence. She stared out the window, eager to arrive, eager to be rid of her father's presence. Not until they neared Williamsburg and passed the College of William and Mary to come down Duke of Gloucester Street and turn onto Market Green did she begin to feel the least bit pleased to have come. Then she leaned back, thinking that her father would be completely occupied, she would be free to shop, to visit friends, to forget some of what happened, and to plan for her own future.

They halted before the governor's palace. Servants were quick to help them from the carriage and to attend to their luggage. Amanda and her father were ushered into the entrance hallway while Danielle was taken to the servants' quarters on the third floor. Amanda did not look at her father while they waited, but stared at the impressive weaponry displayed with artistic grandeur upon the walls.

"Ah, Lord Sterling!"

She turned around as John Murray, Earl of Dunmore and the governor of Virginia, came toward them. Lord Dunmore was a tall, striking man with red hair and amber brown eyes and a fiery temperament to match his coloring. Amanda had always liked him. He was imperious but vivid and energetic, and generally kind and most often wise in his dealings with his elected government officials. It was only recently that he seemed to have completely lost his temper with the officials.

He was impeccably dressed in yellow breeches, fawn hose, and a mustard frock coat. His hair was powdered and queued, and his hand, when he took Amanda's, was as soft as pigskin. He smiled at her as he kissed her hand. "Lady Amanda, but you have grown to be a true beauty! You grace our very presence. The countess will be so sorry that she missed you!"

"Thank you, milord," she murmured, retrieving her hand. "Is your wife not here?"

"She is not feeling well this afternoon." He smiled with pleasure. "We are expecting a child, as you might have heard."

"I had not, milord, but I am delighted, of course."

She stepped back, aware that his true interest was in her father, which was fine. She wanted to escape them both.

"Nigel, you old goat, you're looking fit."

"And so are you, John."

"Come along. I've had tea served in the garden."

John Murray took Amanda's hand, slipping it through his arm. He chatted about the summer roses and about the weather as they walked through the vast and expansive ballroom to reach the gardens out in the rear. They walked along a path of beautiful hedges, and came at last to a manicured garden. At a table places were set with huge linen napkins and silver plates. Lord Dunmore's butler waited to serve them.

Amanda sat, and thanked the man when her tea was poured. She nibbled at a meat pie and realized she could barely eat when her father was near.

"Isn't it a glorious day?" John Murray demanded, and she agreed. She listened and responded politely, and wondered when they would clear their throats and indicate that their coming conversation might be lengthy and of little interest to a young lady.

They never came to that point. She was sipping a second cup of tea and watching a bluebird, wishing that she could fly away as easily as it could, when she realized that both men were silent and staring at her. She flushed and set down her teacup. "I'm so sorry. I was wandering."

"Ah, milady, it's quite all right. It is a beautiful day. And a young woman's fancy must not be confined to a garden with two older men, eh? I've heard that Lord Cameron asked for your hand in marriage, young lady," Dunmore said.

She flushed again and lifted her chin without glancing her father's way. "I believe he asked Father permission to court me, milord."

"You turned him down."

"I—" She hesitated a minute, feeling her father's eyes boring into her. She smiled sweetly. "Milord, I hear that he is in sympathy with certain men of whom I do not approve. His politics are quite different from my own."

"His politics! Nigel, do you hear that!" Dunmore laughed. "Why, young lady, you mustn't worry yourself with politics!"

She smiled. He was still chuckling, but the men exchanged glances again and again. A prickling of unease crept along her spine. Dunmore moved toward her. "Did you know, Amanda, that he is one of the wealthiest men in Virginia? He owns endless acres. He is titled, he is deeply respected. He is young, striking, and known for his courage, honesty, and valor. Perhaps he is noted for a certain hardness, determination, and temper, but his anger is aroused, they say, only under the greatest duress. He is considered a most illustrious marriage prospect and has been approached by nobility and royalty, as well as by the most affluent of private citizens. He has politely eluded all of these offers—then shocks us all with a proposal for you. Not that you are wanting in any physical way, indeed, my dear, you are surely one of the loveliest creatures in all of his Majesty's realm. But you are not royalty. Your father's holdings in Europe are meager. Therefore one would think that Lord Cameron is quite enchanted by your beauty and your beauty alone. You should feel quite honored, milady."

Honored. She remembered the way he had taken her into his arms, the way she had felt. And she remembered the way Robert had seemed to cower before him, and she felt ill.

She remained silent, and Lord Dunmore spoke again. "His teeth are excellent, and one of my maids told me the other day that he had the most manly handsome face and fascinating eyes she had ever seen. Would you mind explaining to me, milady, your aversion to the man?"

"I—" She paused, completely unprepared for the intimate conversation. This should be between her father and her, and no one else. She couldn't have even told her father, though, that her aversion was her love for another. She could have also told them both that Lord Cameron did not want her anymore, that he manipulated her like a puppet on a string, and that she would never be able to endure his laughter or the mocking knowledge in his eyes.

"I cannot say, milord," she answered at last, smiling. "What is there in one that we do or do not love? Who can say?"

Dunmore leaned back, nodding. "Your father has the right to say, child," he reminded her. "And at the moment . . ." His voice trailed for a moment. "Eric Cameron is one of my most able commanders. I will lead men out west to fight a Shawnee uprising very soon, and Eric will be my right hand. He can summon more men for a fighting force in less time than it takes to gather the militia. He is a very important man to me."

"I imagine that he is, milord," Amanda agreed carefully. She cast her lashes down and gazed toward her father, wondering where the conversation was leading. John Murray did not play idle games. He was a powerful man who spent his time wisely and well.

Her father remained silent. He just watched her, his eyes very small and narrow and speculative.

"Do you love England, my dear? Do you honor your king?" Lord Dunmore asked suddenly, staring at her as if she were a culprit.

"Of course!" She gasped, startled by the turn of conversation.

"So I thought!" he said proudly. He leaned toward her again. "Lady Amanda, I have a task to ask of you."

Her fingers started to shake. Dread filled her.

"As I've said, Lord Cameron is to leave very soon for the west. The Indians are giving our people severe trouble, and they must be stopped. Cameron and I will be together in this venture, I know—he has given me his word."

Eric Cameron was leaving. That was wonderful. But what on earth could they want of her then?

"Until such a time, I would like you to see him."

"I beg your pardon, milord?"

"For me, for England, Lady Amanda. It is also your father's will. See him. Become his friend. Pretend that you might consider his proposal."

She didn't realize that she was standing until she heard her teacup shatter upon the ground. "Oh, no! I can't. I really can't. I'm sorry, I do love England, milord, and I will be loyal to the death if need be, but I cannot—"

"He spends his time at a tavern with a number of hotheads. Men who might be arrested soon enough for their politics. I want to know if he is still loyal to the Crown. And I want to know what plans are being made by these so-called patriots."

"But milord! Men speak openly of their opinions. I believe Lord Cameron is a traitor, but then, by the law, so are hundreds of men. Lord Dunmore—"

"Please. Other men may have opinions. Not Lord Cameron. Too many men will follow him blindly, and, my dear, if he is guilty of stockpiling arms against the king, then he is a traitor in black and white, and must be stopped."

"But . . . I—I can't stop him!"

Dunmore leaned back. It was her father's turn to speak at last. He stood up, facing her coldly. "You can, Amanda. And you will."

"Father—"

"You see, Lord Dunmore has on his person an arrest warrant for your cousin Damien."

"What?" She gasped. He stared at her, smiling. He was enjoying himself, she realized. He really enjoyed seeing her hurt and shocked, and he enjoyed using her. Her ears seemed to roar. She could smell the flowers, and she could hear the chatter of birds on the air. The day was so very beautiful.

And so awful.

She looked at the governor, and she knew that it was true. "What crime has Damien committed?" she asked hollowly. She tried very hard not to scream in panic, for they didn't need to tell her much. She had suspected him of foolish deeds for a long, long time. She had followed him in Boston because she had been so afraid of his activities. She didn't think that he had dumped tea into the harbor, but he had left the party so determinedly. . . .

"Damien Roswell is guilty of a number of crimes, dear. We know that he has smuggled arms and armaments and that he has possessed and propagated numerous pieces of seditious literature."

"Seditious literature! Why, Lord Dunmore. You would have to hang half of the colony—"

"I can prove that he has been smuggling arms, Amanda," Dunmore said softly. His tone was truly unhappy. Then he fell silent, and in those seconds Amanda felt her blood run cold. She could not bear it if harm were to come to her cousin, no matter how foolish his behavior. "His crime," Dunmore continued softly, "is treason, we have him dead to rights. But Damien is a small fish, and knowing how dear he is to you, we are loath to make him a scapegoat for the sharks."

She sank back to her seat again. They couldn't be serious, but they were. She lifted her chin, determined that she could be as cold as her father. She would never forgive him now. She hated him with all her heart.

"What do you want?"

"The truth about Cameron. What he intends to do, what he has done. I have to know if he will turn his back on me if the trouble with the radicals becomes too serious."

"If I get you the information you want—"

"Then I destroy the warrant for your cousin."

"I don't mind—I don't mind being a spy, milord. I don't mind serving England, and I am a loyal Tory. But milord, if you'll just ask something else of me—"

"I need you, Lady Amanda."

"But Lord Cameron is no fool!" she said uneasily.

"Yes, I realize that. The man is my friend, even if we are destined to be enemies. You'll have to be convincing. Tarnation, girl! I must know if he is loyal to me or not!"

"You—you are both blackmailing me!" she cried.

Lord Dunmore rose. He was not happy with the situation, she knew. He didn't like what he was asking her to do.

But her father was delighted with it. She knew then that it had all been her father's doing.

"Think about it. Your service would be greatly appreciated," Dunmore said. He rested his hand upon her shoulder. "The decision is still yours, my dear. I'll leave you to think." He walked away, and she was alone with her father. She stared at him for several long moments, listening to the chirp of the birds, feeling the sun and the breeze against her cheeks. Then she spoke with softly yet with venom.

"I hate you. I will never forgive you for this," she told him.

He rose, coming so close to her that she nearly leapt to her feet to run. He caught her chin and held it in a painful grip. "You'll do as you're told. I have waited all these years for you to be of some use, I have let you live the life of a lady, and now you will obey me. You will give me a place of prominence with the king. And if you do not, Damien will hang. Do you understand?"

She jerked free of his touch, trying to hide the tears that burned behind her eyes. "As I told Lord Dunmore, Eric Cameron is no fool! He knows that I despise him!"

"You must change his mind."

"He will not trust me."

"Convince him."

"What would you have me do, prostitute myself?"

Nigel Sterling curled his lip into a smile. "If necessary, my dear, yes."

She gasped, leaping up again, clutching her skirts. "You're a monster!" she told him. "No father would ask this of a child!"

His smile tightened. "I am a monster, but you are the spawn of a whore," he told her softly. "Use your heritage."

She gasped aloud, stunned. Then she cried, "No! How dare you! You cannot say that about my mother!" Furious, she leapt toward him.

He was no small man. He caught her in a cruel grip and held her very tight. She felt ill. His breath touched her face, his eyes raked over her, and that hateful smile remained.

"It would delight me to take a bullwhip against you. I can do that, as well as see that Damien hangs." He paused, staring into her eyes with an assurance that he did not threaten her idly. "Perhaps you should get ready for an evening out. Damien is here, in Williamsburg. I've told him that we are coming, and I've assured him he has my permission to take you for a ride this evening. You should get dressed. I expect him by seven. Such a young lad. Many will cry to see him hang, I am certain. Don't make the mistake of warning him. He is a dead man if you do."

Nigel released her and walked away, leaving her alone in the garden.

The scent of the summer flowers rose high all around her. The birds continued to chirp, the breeze to flutter the foliage. She sank down on the garden seat, her fists clenched in her lap, and feared that she would be sick.

Somewhere inside the mansion the countess was lying back on her bed with a smile upon her lips. She probably dreamed of her child, and when that child was born, both she and Lord Dunmore would cherish it, and plan a future for the babe with love and care.

What had gone so horribly awry in her life that her own father could despise her so? Label her mother a whore, and send her out to play a harlot's game?

She brought her knuckles to her mouth and bit down hard upon them, silently damning Damien for his foolish ways. But Damien loved her, honestly, with his soul and his heart. She had so little of value in life, of love sincere and untainted.

They were casting her to Lord Cameron. Casting her to the very wolf. Wolf? Aye, he was that! But if he had wanted her—even to devour her!—he would have come to her to do so. What could she do? Her father could not know how crude or harsh the words had been between them. He could not understand that it would be dangerous indeed for her to suddenly appear to have a change of heart.

She rose slowly and turned back toward the mansion. It had to be nearly seven now.

She did not mind serving England, there was so much that she would have done gladly for Lord Dunmore!

But this . . .

She started to shake, and so she walked faster. She was still shaking when she entered the mansion and hurried up the stairs to the guest room she had been given. She knew she had to wash and dress, but she threw herself on the bed, still shaking.

She remembered Eric Cameron's face, the strength of his features, the laughter in his eyes and then the hardness.

And then she knew why she shook so badly. She had said it, and it was the truth. The man was no fool. And if he suspected her of betraying him, if he caught her . . .

She swallowed hard, and she knew that she was afraid. Very, very afraid.

––––––––

A hush fell over the crowd as Eric entered the public room of the Raleigh Tavern. It was known to be a place where men of different minds gathered, and Eric was looked upon with a certain distrust, for he was a lord, and it was expected that his allegiance was with the king. After all, he had great estates in England to consider.

Men, mostly planters and farmers, some merchants and shopkeepers, looked about, nodded his way respectfully, then looked nervously back to their meals or their ale. In turn he bowed, then ignored their suspicious gazes. He strode in, doffing his tricorn and cape and taking a table near the rear door.

The owner rushed forward to greet him. "Lord Cameron, come to visit with us for a spell, eh? Well, it's honored we be, and that's a fact."

"Is it? Tell me, is Colonel Washington about?"

The man went red in the face. "Well, now, I don't know—"

"It's all right" came a laughing voice. Washington himself was looking in from the hallway that led to the private rooms. He was a tall man, broad-shouldered, with dark hair—graying now—neatly queued at his nape. "He's my friend, and he's come to see me. Eric! Come along, will you? I've some people eager to meet you."

Eric rose, nodded to the innkeeper, and followed the colonel down along the hallway. Washington was a good many years his senior, a man hailing from the Fredericksburg area and now living closer to the coast at Mount Vernon, when he managed to be home these days. Mount Vernon was a beautiful plantation, and much like his own, Cameron Hall. Both homes had large main hallways and graceful porches with a multitude of windows facing the water in order to take advantage of the river breezes. Washington loved his estate, his lands, his horses, everything about home. But he had always been an ambitious man as well as a smart one. Eric shared his love of botany and respected his business sense. They were both heavily invested in the Ohio and Chesapeake Canal, and eager to see more westward expansion across the mountains. Washington had married a very prosperous Williamsburg widow, Martha Custis, and though it had been whispered at the time that she was a somewhat dowdy little thing, she apparently offered him the warmth and domesticity that he needed. Eric knew Martha well and liked her very much. She had the touching ability to listen, to weigh a man's words carefully, and to respond with a gentle intelligence.

Following his friend down the hallway, Eric thought that George had aged rapidly in the last year. He and Martha had had no children of their own, but he had doted on his stepchildren, and last year his stepdaughter, Patsy, had died. The loss had taken its toll upon the man.

Perhaps all these whispers about war were good after all. They kept George's mind busy.

But then so did his estate. He had inherited Mount Vernon, his brother's property, after his sister-in-law and niece had both passed away. The property was his passion, as Eric could well understand. He felt that way about Cameron Hall. He never tired of studying the house, of adding on, or improving, just as he never tired of the land, moving crops, studying the growth of his vegetables, experimenting with growth cycles. The men had met in Williamsburg a few years after the French and Indian Wars. As they discussed the differences between the colonial and British soldiers, they had both reached the sad conclusion that the Crown did not treat the colonials at all well. Ever since his adventures in Boston on the eve of the tea party, Eric had joined Washington and members of the House of Burgesses more frequently in their conversations. Many men did not trust him as yet. Many others did.

In 1769 Lord Botetourt, then governor of Virginia and a popular and well-liked man, had made enemies when he dismissed the Virginia legislature because of the representatives' protest of the Stamp Act. Eric had been young then, a new member of the Upper House, and his voice had had little effect upon the decision. Eric had maintained his position—and his opinion, and eventually, the situation had evened out. The Stamp Act had been repealed.

Now the legislature had been dissolved again. During the first dissolution there had been a strained period between Eric and many of his more radical friends, but this time, he had offered to resign from the Governor's Council—an unprecedented event. Eric was walking a dangerous fence, and he was well aware of it. His ancestor Jamie Cameron had carried over a title, and because of that, Eric should be a staunch loyalist, a Tory to the core. But something about his meeting with young Frederick Bartholomew that night in Boston had changed him. There was danger in the air, but there was excitement as well. It seemed to Eric that it was becoming a time of great men and a time of change. He had heard Patrick Henry speak on several occasions, and though many people considered him a brash and foolish rabble-rouser, Eric found him to be amazingly eloquent, and more. Henry believed in his principles, and he was not afraid to risk his life or material possessions or position to speak out.

This was the New World. Cameron's own family had been living in Virginia since the early 1600s. But that was less than a score of decades. When compared with the age of the mother country, Virginia and the other colonies were young, raw, and exciting. Eric had attended Oxford; he had seen the Cameron estates in England, he had traveled to France and Italy and many of the German principalities, and he had learned that he loved no land as much as he did his own. Because of the very rawness, the newness, the excitement. Men and women traveled ever westward, seeking expansion, seeking a dream.

He didn't even like to think it, and yet Eric was convinced that the time was coming when the colonies would break away from England. And though even the supposed hotheads who met at the taverns decried the possibility of war, it was becoming increasingly evident that a split was looming before them.

"Come on in here," Washington said, opening the door to one of the smaller parlors. "It is just Thomas, Patrick, and myself tonight. I'm preparing to leave."

"Leave?"

"Our First Continental Congress meets in September."

"Oh. Of course. There are seven of us representing Virginia. Peyton Randolph, Richard Henry Lee, Patrick Henry, Richard Bland, Benjamin Harrison, Edmund Pendleton, and myself."

"A noble assembly," Eric complimented.

Washington grinned. "Thank you."

They entered the private room. Patrick Henry and Thomas Jefferson were both sitting before the fire. Henry leapt to his feet first. "Ah, Lord Cameron. Welcome!"

Eric walked across the room and shook his hand. He admired the man. His speeches were incredible, his energy was undauntable, and his passion for his cause was contagious. Henry, opposing the Stamp Act, had spoken openly about the severity of the friction between the king and the colonies a very dangerous time. "Caesar had his Brutus, Charles the First his Cromwell, and George the Third—"

He'd been forced to pause, for there had been such staunch cries of "Treason!" But then he had gone on.

"George the Third may profit by their example. If this be treason, make the most of it!"

He was from the western counties, and to many he was a crude man, rough and rugged. His clothing was not cut to eastern standards. He was intriguing, Eric thought, capable at times of a brooding temperament, but still possessed of a fascinating fire that brought men rallying to his cause.

Jefferson was a quieter man, calmer, far more elegant in his dress and manner. But as time passed, he was becoming every bit as passionate.

"Eric, sit, have a brandy," Jefferson encouraged him. There seemed to be a twinkle in his eye. He looked older too, Eric thought. As the political situation grew more and more grave, they were all aging rapidly.

"Thank you. I shall be delighted," Eric said. He drew his chair to the fire with them, accepting a glass from Washington. "How are you, gentlemen?"

"Well enough," Jefferson said. "I have heard that you are about to leave with Governor Lord Dunmore's militia for the west to suppress the Shawnee uprising."

Eric nodded. It hadn't really been decided until tonight, but it seemed like the proper move for him. "It's an easy decision, isn't it?" he inquired softly. "I was asked to lead some men against a common enemy. Here it's difficult to decide."

Washington stared at him hard. "My friend Lord Fairfax is preparing to return to England. Perhaps you should do the same."

Eric smiled slowly and shook his head. "No. I cannot 'return' to England, sir, for I did not come from England. I am a Virginian."

The three exchanged glances. Jefferson smiled again. "I've heard rumors that a certain brash lord arrived in the nick of time to save an injured, er—Indian—in Boston. Have you heard this rumor?"

"Shades of it, yes," Eric said.

"Take heed, my friend," Washington warned him.

"Tell me—was there proof of the rumor?"

"Not a whit of it!" Henry replied, pleased.

Eric leaned forward, feeling the warmth of the fire, hearing the snap and crackle of it. "I tell you, the three of you, that you must take heed. There are more rumors about. Thomas Gage has been sent as governor of Massachusetts, and the king has ordered him to arrest Sam Adams and John Hancock."

"They shall have to find them to arrest them, right?" Henry said. He rose and walked to the fire, tense with energy. He leaned against the mantel, then swung around to look at Eric. "God knows the future now, for none of us can read it, Lord Cameron. Yet if—"

"When," Jefferson said softly.

"If it comes to that point, Lord Cameron, I shall hope that a man of your wit and wisdom chooses to cast his lot with us. Yet even I would have difficulty in your position. I have watched the members of our house weigh their thoughts, and it is a difficult process indeed."

"Perhaps war will still be averted," Eric said.

Washington, who was careful with his language, swore beneath his breath. "Every man among us has hoped that a force of arms be our last resort! And so we continue to pray. But, Eric! Think back on the war. I resigned my commission because they demoted me—for being a colonial. This has long simmered and brewed."

"They repealed the Stamp Act and came back at us with the Townshend Acts, further restricting our freedoms. We thought of ourselves as Englishmen—but those thoughts faded as we were denied the rights of Englishmen," Jefferson said.

"The Townshend Acts were repealed—" Eric said.

"Except for a tea tax," Jefferson reminded him complacently.

"And they were repealed," Henry said vehemently, "merely because Lord North discovered that it cost more to collect the taxes than they were worth!"

They all laughed, and then their laughter ceased abruptly as there was a rap upon the door. Washington quickly rose to answer it. The innkeeper stood there.

"There's a woman here," he said.

"A woman?"

"Lady Sterling. She is looking for Lord Cameron."

"Cameron!" Washington swirled around, looking at Eric who was about to light his pipe. He arched his brow and shrugged. A slow, curious and rueful smile appeared on Washington's face.

"Truly one of Virginia's great treasures," Jefferson said.

"The daughter of Lord Sterling," Patrick said, his tone indicating the care one should take with such a man.

"Mmm, yes," Eric murmured. "You see, gentlemen, I did ask Lord Sterling's permission to court the young lady, but alas, her heart lay elsewhere and she rather adamantly turned me down."

"But she is here now. A young lady in a tavern—her reputation shall be forever tarnished!" Washington mused.

"Alone?" Eric asked the innkeeper. "Surely not!" He flashed Washington a wicked smile. "I rather like a slightly tarnished reputation, sir."

"She is escorted by her cousin, Mr. Damien Roswell," the innkeeper said.

The men all exchanged sharp glances. Eric shrugged and looked pleasantly at the innkeeper. "Then tell her that I shall be with her immediately. My every wish is to serve her."

The door closed and the innkeeper left them.

"Damien Roswell is an ardent patriot," Henry said. "One who moves in ways that may well be more practical than the rest of us, at the moment."

"More treasonous ways, the king might well say. I hope the young man has the good sense to take care with his cousin," Jefferson agreed.

Watching Eric, Washington shrugged. "Perhaps she is fond of him and fond of his policies after all."

Eric remembered her expertise in removing the bullet from the young printer's shoulder in Boston. He remembered, too, her fury at her position—following his lead because she was afraid. For Damien.

She was not seeing things their way. Not at all. "Perhaps she is after something," Eric said.

"Well, you'll have to see the young lady to find out, won't you?" Henry suggested.

"Spy upon the spy?" Jefferson laughed, but his eyes were grave.

"There's nothing for her to discover," Eric said.

"Is that true?" Washington asked him. "There are some who believe, Lord Cameron, that you are more deeply involved than anyone."

"Men believe almost anything these days," Eric said evenly.

"Still, take care," Washington warned him. "I speak as your friend, Eric, and a man who would see you well."

Eric sat, drumming his fingers against the wooden arm of his chair. "Perhaps you are right. Thank you for the warning, but I always take care. Perhaps I can discover certain truths about the lady—with certain lies of my own." He stood again and bowed. "And, gentlemen, it will be fascinating, this road of discovery. I am looking forward to it immensely."

They laughed. "I bid you good luck at the Congress," he added.

"And we bid you Godspeed against the Indians," Jefferson said.

Eric grinned and left them. Outside the door, he paused for a moment before heading toward the public room and his unexpected meeting with Lady Sterling.

His smile faded, his eyes went hard. He remembered her hatred for him, and he knew that nothing had changed between them. She thought to use him.

Well, she was welcome to try.

Then he remembered the way that she had looked when he had seen her upon the stairs, and he recalled the way that she had felt in his arms. He tasted anew the nectar of her lips, saw the fire of her eyes, and felt the perfection of her body pressed to his. He had meant to have her, in his own time, in his own way. He had not forgotten for a single moment the excitement of wanting her, the ache she had created within him, nor the raw and relentless determination he would use in his careful pursuit . . .

But now she was there. And not because of any ardent desire, he was certain. She was playing with fire.

Aye, she played with fire, he thought. But it was her choice, and her game, and by God, he would play it.

And win.

PART II

THE
RELUCTANT
SPY

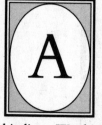MANDA WAS VERY BEAUTIFUL THAT NIGHT. ERIC saw her long before she saw him, for she was seated at a table with Damien and she was speaking earnestly with her cousin. Her eyes betrayed some deep emotion that was soft and spellbinding. Watching her, Eric realized that he envied her cousin. She loved Damien. And in that moment, as she sat in the flickering firelight, he thought that he would gladly sell his soul and be damned if she would just gaze upon him once so warmly.

He knew he was being a fool and reminded himself that he barely knew the little hellion, but it didn't matter. He hadn't needed to know much once he had seen her, once he had touched her.

He was in lust, so he had said. Perhaps that, too, was true. He had been careful to wait, biding his time. He had not expected her to seek him out, and yet here she was. With Damien. He wondered what she knew of her cousin's activities. No matter how her heart bled for England, she would never endanger young Roswell.

She had turned down his proposal of marriage, but now she was back. Deviously. What a pity. Her soft smile for him would be a lie. She had come to wage battle, else she never would have stepped foot inside this tavern.

Her beauty was her weapon, and she was not averse to using it, nor did she lack the confidence, he thought, to know the very power of it.

She wore green, a fetchingly casual gown with a heavier brocade bodice that tied with delicate ribbons over her breasts. It was a color that highlighted the evocative depths of her eyes, emphasizing the emerald dazzle of them. The night was warm, but she carried a light shawl, and it draped about her elbows, exposing her upper arms. Her hair had been swept up high in ringlets, and the sleek length of her neck was bare and inviting.

Every eye in the tavern was on her, of course. She looked like a thread of gold in a coat of coarse linen. There weren't many women in the place, and not one of them could hold a candle to her striking splendor.

He felt himself grown warm, watching her, and it occurred to him that many a man was drooling in his beer. Eric quickly grew annoyed. She shouldn't be here. Even escorted by her cousin, she should not be out as she was now. She was an innocent, yet there was something about her that was more than evocative. He thought of Helen of Troy and of a face that could launch a thousand ships. Amanda Sterling had that same kind of power; she created tension and emotion. Lust, perhaps, but longing and a haunting yearning too. With a smile she could tempt a man to any act; with a promise she could be deadly trouble.

Be forewarned, my friend, he told himself. And yet still his own confidence was great. He was older. Wiser, he assured himself. He saw the danger and therefore could elude it.

"Lady Sterling, Damien," he said, moving forward. Damien rose, Amanda remained seated. She offered Eric her hand and one of those smiles for which a man could be led to kill. He kissed her gloved fingers, glanced Damien's way, and took a seat beside Amanda.

" 'Tis good to see you, lad," he told Damien.

"And you, sir."

"And your fair cousin, of course," he said, looking at Amanda. "And yet, milady, I'm very curious. What has brought you here? I had the distinct impression that you did not wish to see me again."

"Did you?" she said, her voice distant and soft. "You were mistaken." She seemed to shudder slightly, then her smile returned to her features, and she grew animated and her eyes glowed like jewels. Her cheeks were just touched with the rose of a flush, her lips seemed as red as wine, and at that moment Eric did not think that he had ever seen a woman more alluring. He did not just yearn for her with his loins—though that urge lay very strong within him—but he ached to possess her in all ways, to run his fingers through her hair, to feel those eyes upon him with trust and innocence and their touch of the siren too. He wanted to hold her against him, to watch the rise and fall of her breast, to feel the whisper of her words against his cheek.

"Was I mistaken?" he asked her.

She nodded. "I came to apologize. You caught me at a frightful disadvantage. I am grateful, of course. And I'm so very sorry that I was rude. Please, do forgive me."

"What else could I do, milady?" he replied.

"Pardon me, milady, milord," Damien complained softly. "I am here too, you know."

Eric laughed, looking at Damien. He liked the young man very much. He was bold and brash and witty, and yet, beneath it all, he was determined—and talented. Damien had already cast his glove into the fray. Roswell, he had learned, was dealing very closely with the Bostonians. Most men were still eager to negotiate. Damien ran with a crowd that seemed collectively certain that it would come down to a force of arms. Even though Washington spoke carefully, Eric was certain that he, too, thought it would come to bloodshed.

"A thousand pardons, sir. But I'm afraid my keenest interest is in your cousin, Damien. Curious, isn't it, that a lady should seek out a man in a tavern for an apology."

She still had her temper, he saw, even if she was trying to hide it. Her lashes were lowered, but he saw the flash in her eyes. When she lifted her head, she was smiling again. "Is it shocking behavior that I should be here? Why, all manner of good men and women come to this place, so I am told. The rooms, they say, are of a far more pleasant nature at Mrs. Campbell's Tavern, but the food here is fine, the drink palatable, and the company . . . most respectable."

"Perhaps. But for a lady of your affluence?"

"But there is a lord of your affluence here."

"And there lies the difference, Amanda," he told her flatly.

She flushed slightly but picked up a pewter tankard of ale, which she sipped and smiled. "Ours is a wonderful new world, isn't that what they say? I am fascinated by it." Her lashes rose and fell, her smile was compelling. She was flirting with him. Her fingers fell over his like butterfly wings.

He caught her fingers with his own. "You are a loyalist to the core, Amanda," he told her flatly.

She tried to maintain a smile while she struggled to free her fingers from his grasp. "Milord! Do you mean to say that you are not? Have you then repudiated the king? I had not heard that the staunchest rebels had yet gone so far!"

Only in whispers. But things were moving so quickly. Throughout the colonies, throngs of people had attacked shopkeepers who had failed to respect the boycotts on British goods. Few men or women had been injured, but the goods had been destroyed. And there had been no reprisals. It was all like a gigantic wind, sweeping around them. Rebellion was close at hand.

And he was going off to fight Indians in the west, at Lord Dunmore's request.

He did not need to answer Amanda because Damien was already doing so. Leaning forward, her cousin spoke to her heatedly. "Amanda, hush! God alone knows who may listen to our words these days! Lord Cameron said nothing about having repudiated the king. Indeed, he is the king's good servant, leaving his own hearth and risking his own life, limb, and health and fortune to go forth and meet the Shawnee."

"You should watch for your own life and limb, cousin," Amanda warned softly.

Damien sat back, staring at her. "What are you talking about?"

She knew exactly what she was talking about, Eric thought. The night became ever more interesting.

"Nothing," she replied, and turned from her cousin, a charming smile on her lips. "It is whispered that this is where it all takes place."

"It . . . all?" Eric queried her innocently.

"The clandestine meetings. The speeches, the—"

"The rebellion, that's what she means."

She pouted sweetly. "Amusing, Damien. But so very exciting," she told Eric. What a wonderful liar she was, he thought. But it didn't matter.

"And are you fascinated, Lady Sterling?"

"Incredibly."

"Is that a loyalist hobby?"

"No, milord, merely a growing interest in politics," she said. "Mob rule can be so very intriguing."

"Oh?"

"Yes. We hear about the glorious cause of rights for Englishmen, the demand for self-government, how very ill the poor colonist is treated. But those same brave men raided the home of Lieutenant Governor Hutchinson in Boston, and he was a man very much opposed to the Stamp Act!"

"Madness against an innocent man," Eric murmured.

"I beg pardon, sir?" Damien said.

"Oh, the lieutenant governor's words," Eric said. "Yes, it's true. Mob rule can turn very ugly. I daresay that the man did not understand just how incensed the people were about the Stamp Act."

"The 'Sons of Liberty,' " Amanda said sweetly with only a touch of mockery to her tone.

"Ah, the study of those sons fascinates you, remember!"

"Of course."

She looked around the room. Eric was aware that she was looking for the men rumored to be at the root of the Virginia dissension.

He rose, bowing to her deeply. "Lady Sterling, Damien, I was on my way out. Perhaps, if you are still interested in political discussion, you would be good enough to accompany me to my town house."

"What!" Amanda exclaimed, startled.

He suppressed a smile at her discomfiture. "I was leaving, milady. But you are most welcome to accompany me. You, milady, and Damien too, of course."

"I'd love to," Damien said quickly. "Mandy?"

"I—I—" She hesitated, staring at him. Then she found her smile again. "I'm sure you can't be so willing to forgive my bad manners that you would want me in your very home."

"My dear Lady Sterling, you would always be welcome in my home. Indeed, you—and your father, of course—are more than welcome to be my full-time guests at any time."

"That would not be necessary," she said, maintaining a sweet smile. "We are guests of Lord Dunmore."

"Ah, so you are residing at the palace, and I offer my most humble abode. I'm quite sure Lady Dunmore has you in the comfortable guest room on the second floor. It is spacious, and so beautifully appointed. I could offer nothing so grand."

"Milord, it is a charming room he has given me, yes. You know the palace well."

"I have been a guest there often myself," he said softly. "And I regret that you are not my guest for your stay in Williamsburg." He smiled charmingly himself. It was good to know exactly where the lady was staying—and might be found, if necessary. "And, milady, it is incredibly easy to forgive you. Please, my carriage is outside. Yours can follow."

Damien was enthusiastic, and Amanda seemed to realize that she had little choice. Eric retrieved his cape and hat and led the two outside. His carriage, with the Cameron coat-of-arms emblazoned on the doors, did await them. The driver started to hop down from his seat, but Eric waved a hand to him. "It's all right, Pierre. I shall get the steps. We're going home."

"*Oui,* Lord Cameron," the man replied.

Eric opened the door and dropped the steps, then ushered Amanda up and into the carriage. He breathed in the scent of her hair as she passed him. Did she always smell so sweet and so good, like tender flowers on a sunny day?

"Damien, after you," he said. He watched the young man climb into the carriage, then followed behind him.

After Eric climbed up and tapped on the carriage roof, the horses started off. His town house wasn't far from Raleigh Tavern.

"You're near to the governor's palace, aren't you?" Damien inquired.

Eric nodded. "Near enough."

"Prime, prime property!" Damien applauded.

Eric laughed. "It belonged to my paternal grandmother."

Damien leaned forward. "There's a rumor that your grandfather was a pirate," he said excitedly.

Eric arched a brow politely. "Is there?"

"Yes. I've heard tell that he was a rogue, spying on the very likes of Blackbeard for the governor. Tell me, do you know anything about the treasure?"

Eric laughed. "I'm afraid not, Damien. He did play a pirate, but he pirated only his own ships. Any gold he claimed was his own, and to the best of my knowledge, he knew nothing about any of Blackbeard's treasure."

"Blackbeard's head was severed," Damien told Amanda excitedly, "and set upon a spike as a warning to all pirates. Then the men of his crew who had been taken were tried here, and all but one was hanged."

"Perhaps you should look to your own neck, cousin!" she warned again, then paled, seeing Eric's eyes upon her. She inhaled and exhaled quickly, and Eric smiled, seeing her discomfort. He didn't know quite what was going on, but she hadn't planned on going to his town house.

Soon the carriage drew to a halt. Pierre hopped down and opened the door, and Eric quickly climbed down then reached up for Amanda. His hands slipped around her waist, and he set her down slowly, loath to let her go. Her eyes were on his, very wide, and dusky green in the moonlight. He almost felt sorry for her then. Except that he longed for her, more deeply each time he saw her, and he knew that she was using him. It was a good thing that his ego was substantial, he thought. Her disdain was sometimes so apparent in her gaze.

"Do you like the boxwoods?" he asked her, leading her along the walk as Damien followed. "My housekeeper grows them. I'm afraid that I'm not in residence often enough to do the plants here justice."

"And where are you?" she asked.

"Why, at Cameron Hall, of course," he said, opening the door. As they entered, a tall lean woman with her hair knotted beneath a mob cap came hurrying into the hallway.

"Lord Cameron, I was not expecting you so early," she said, taking his hat and cape.

"Mathilda! I promised that I should be home nice and early!" he said quickly. "This is Lady Sterling, Mathilda, and her cousin, Damien Roswell."

Mathilda bobbed quickly to them both. Amanda murmured a greeting, looking about the hall. The Cameron wealth was evident in the fine wall covering, in the display of weapons, in the polished furniture. There was a maple cabinet in the hallway that had to be worth an apprentice artisan's entire first year of pay. There were silver candlesticks set about, and, looking up the stairway, she noted that the upper hallway was lined with oil paintings.

"This way, Lady Sterling," Eric murmured.

She was led into his study, a warm room with claw-footed, brocade upholstered chairs, a massive oak desk, a standing globe of the world, endless bookshelves, and a marble mantel. She felt his hand at the small of her back, and she longed to scream out. His touch could not be forgotten. Although he was perfectly polite, the lordly gentleman to the core, she felt that he was watching her with sizzling curiosity. He knew, she thought, and the very idea made her shiver. He was leading her along, waiting to pounce upon her like a wildcat.

She had no choice. Damien was her cousin, her friend. If he had gone astray, she had to help him. There was nothing that Lord Cameron could know. She was befriending him, and that was all. There was nothing that she could learn from him. They had not joined his friends—they had left the tavern. And now she was in his home.

"Sit, milady!" he said cordially, inviting her into one of the beautifully upholstered chairs. She did so and tried to smile again. The effort was weak.

"It's a wonderful house," Damien said admiringly.

"Thank you. Damien, a brandy? Lady Sterling, I would offer you tea, except that I have chosen to boycott its usage."

"I'd love a brandy," she said sweetly.

"Would you!" Damien laughed.

"Yes," she said, maintaining her smile but warning him with her eyes. She wanted twenty brandies. She wanted to pretend that she was far, far away and that she hadn't been blackmailed into this trickery.

Lord Cameron had one dark brow arched as he looked her way. He didn't say a word though, but poured out three brandies from a snifter on his desk. He brought her a delicate glass, setting it into her fingers. His eyes touched hers, and when their fingers met, she was suddenly beset with shivers again. He was clad darkly this evening. His breeches and his frock were navy, as was his surcoat, and only the white lace of his shirt showed at his throat to lighten the effect. It was somewhat somber garb, and it became him well, with his hair so very dark and his eyes so hauntingly silver-blue. They probed the soul, she thought, and she tried to look away. He seemed to tower over her as he stood by her chair, not releasing the brandy but watching her endlessly, seeking some answer.

"Thank you," she said, taking the glass. He smiled and moved away, offering

Damien his brandy. Damien thanked him quickly and studied the books that lined the cases. He strode to the globe and spun it around, fascinated.

"You are quite blessed, Lord Cameron," Damien said. This beautiful town house, and I understand that Cameron Hall is magnificent."

"Thank you, I think it is." Eric told him as he watched Amanda steadily. She wanted to look away from him, and she discovered that she could not. He was darkly satyrish this evening, and it was almost as if he had some mysterious power over her.

It was nonsense, she convinced herself.

"Do you play chess, Lady Sterling?"

"Yes."

"Play me."

Was it the game he referred to? It was difficult to tell when he stared at her with such probing eyes. She shrugged. "If you wish."

He rose and went over to a small table with the board built onto it. The fine ivory pieces were kept in little pockets at the side.

Eric set up his men and looked at Amanda. They had drawn their chairs close, and she felt his presence all the more keenly. "Your move," he told her.

She brought forth a pawn. He followed suit. She moved in silence; he moved again. Her gaze fell upon his hands. His fingers were long, his nails clipped and neat. They were intriguing hands, bronzed from the sun, large, long, and tapered. The palms were not smooth but callused, as if he often engaged in manual labor.

She looked up and found that he was watching her, that it had long been her turn. She paled and foolishly moved a second pawn. He took it with his knight, and she was helpless to fight back.

"In love and war—and chess—milady, it is dangerous to forget the object of the attack for even a moment."

"You're giving me advice?" she said. "We have hardly begun the game. Perhaps, milord, you will find yourself on the defensive much sooner than you think."

"I had not realized that I was on the offensive."

"Are you playing to win?" she murmured.

He smiled, very slowly, his gaze silver and searing while he rested back in his chair. "I always do win, Lady Sterling."

"Always?"

"Always," he assured her nonchalantly.

She tore her eyes from his and concentrated on the game. Damien watched in silence.

They moved quickly for a few minutes. They were both on the offensive, and they both played with skill. Amanda lost a knight and a rook, but in turn she took a knight and bishop and two pawns. Soon the game began to slow down as they both took greater care with each move, trying to weigh what would come after the next immediate turn.

"Long-range planning," Damien said lightly.

Eric's eyes met his over Amanda's head. "Mmm. It can take a long, long time to win a game. Hours. Days, even. Alas, I haven't many days left."

"Alas!" Damien sighed. "I was so looking forward to seeing your Cameron Hall."

"Were you? Well, sir, you've a standing invitation. I shall be gone, and I don't know when I shall return, but my home is your home."

"Milord, I thank you sincerely!" Damien said.

"My pleasure." Eric looked over the board and maneuvered his knight in a position to set Amanda into checkmate on the next turn.

She saw his move and countered it, saving her king. The rescue, however, cost her a bishop.

"Ah! Take care, milady. I am stripping away your defenses. One by one."

"I am not beaten, milord."

"I should hope not, milady. You would not be a worthy opponent if you did not fight until the very end."

She was shivering again. They weren't talking about chess, not at all. And Damien was blithely innocent to it all.

They played for an hour and had reached a stalemate when Damien drew away Eric's attention. "I am fascinated by your books, Lord Cameron!" Damien said.

"Are you? I noticed you looking at the thesis on animal husbandry. I've another matching volume on botany. Would you like to borrow them?"

"Yes, I would, very much," Damien said.

"Come then, I believe the volume is upstairs. Amanda, will you excuse us, please?"

"Of course," she murmured quickly. Her heart was beating hard and she could not wait for them to leave the room. When they were gone, she leapt to her feet. On sudden inspiration she raced around the desk and tried the top drawer, impatiently searching through the papers there. There were bills and receipts. He had written a note to buy Mathilda's daughter a toy for her birthday. He had a list of stores in his wine cellar. There was nothing, nothing, indicative of any treason.

She started to sink into his chair, then she paused and wrenched open a side drawer. There was a letter there, postmarked from Boston.

They were coming back down the stairs. Amanda inhaled and exhaled deeply, then stuffed the letter into one of the pockets in her skirt. Then she closed the door quickly and raced back to her chair.

"I'm sure you'll enjoy the volume tremendously," Cameron was saying. "If you love the land."

"Very much. Almost as much as I love horses," Damien said cheerfully.

"You sound like a friend of mine, Colonel Washington. He is enamored of horses and forever experimenting with botany."

"I am in good company!" Damien replied, and Amanda winced. Good company for a hanging! she thought, but then it didn't seem to matter too much then for her heart was hammering and she could scarcely breathe. She imagined that any minute Eric would wrench her to her feet and his hands would fall brutally upon her until he managed to find the letter. And then his long fingers would curl around her neck.

"Amanda, I should get you back. Your father will be worried." And more cruel than usual. Damien did not say it, but Amanda sensed the thought behind his words.

"To the governor's palace, then," she said as Eric gazed at her. Why did it always look as if he knew so much more behind those silver eyes?

The governor's palace—she would stay at such a place, or with friends. A lady of her standing seldom sought lodging in a public place. It was probably scandalous that she had gone as she had tonight to the tavern. She didn't care much about her reputation, though. It had mattered only when love had mattered, and now she had been betrayed. She would never love again, she still bore the bitter scars of Robert's betrayal, and so her reputation didn't mean a thing.

Eric smiled, taking her hand. She wished that she could wrench away from him. He seemed to do so much more than touch her hand. The heat from his fingers coursed through her. "It has been a pleasure, milady. I'm sorry that you are established with Lord Dunmore. As I said, I would have gladly offered you this residence. Or Cameron Hall, had you use for it."

Amanda smiled, pulling her hand back. She had to get away. She was hot and shaking, and she could feel his letter in her pocket. "Thank you," she told him.

She turned about and started for the door. Mathilda came to see them out, and Eric walked them down the road to where Damien's small carriage awaited them with his old Negro driver. Thomas was sleeping, and Amanda was pleased to see the gentle way her cousin awakened him. There was so much good in Damien. How could he be a traitor!

"Let me help you, milady." While Damien spoke to Cato, Eric Cameron lifted her up and set her into the carriage. She felt his hands upon her waist and then she felt them brush her skirt. Her eyes widened with fear. She quickly tried to hide her eyes, lowering her head and her lashes. Then she raised them again, composed, her heart beating furiously.

Damien still spoke with the driver. Eric looked in at her, a twisted smile upon his lips. "One would think, Lady Sterling, that my touch aroused you."

"What?"

"Arouse, milady. You do know the meaning of the word."

"Lord Cameron, how dare—"

"Lady, I have seldom seen such wide eyes. And there—at your throat—a pulse beats with ardent fury." He came closer to her. "One might think that you longed to be kissed again."

"You think—wrongly."

"What?" he demanded. "Your heart does not clamor for a lover's touch. Then one would think that you were hiding something from me. That you were a thief, with stolen goods within your pockets."

"Don't—be ridiculous," she managed to reply.

His smile deepened. "Then your apology tonight was sincere."

Her breath came too quickly, causing her breasts to rise in rapid succession, pressing provocatively against the ribbon-laced bodice of her gown. Soft swirls of radiant ringlets framed her face and cast shadows against the emerald of her eyes. She gripped the seat, unaware that her fear gave her added beauty, that she enticed, even as she angered the man.

"My apology was most sincere," she said, desperate to raise her chin, to defy him.

"I am glad," he told her. With that he stepped into the carriage and sank down beside her. With the length and breadth of her she felt his form beside her own, heated, tense. She opened her mouth to protest, but no sound came to her. He reached out and touched her cheek, stroking downward upon it, bringing his fingers around to the nape of her neck. She nearly closed her eyes, for the sensations were so sweet, as if she were suddenly drugged by the nearness of the man. It was the brandy. Burning, swirling throughout her body. She could not protest, she could sit and feel and nothing more.

His lips hovered just above hers. "I am very, very glad," he murmured, "for I should hate it, milady, were I to discover you false."

Amanda could not answer for several seconds. She fought for reason, for words. "I offer you friendship," she whispered. She could not pull away from him. She felt the curious combination of force and tenderness in his hold upon her. She remembered his hands. Strong hands. He could break a man's neck, if he chose. Or a woman's.

She was being foolish. He would not harm her. No matter how she betrayed him.

Or would he?

She swallowed, trying to keep her eyes innocently upon his, desperate, for his letter lay within her pocket. There was steel in his eyes. He would not forgive or forget if he was betrayed. Perhaps he would not harm her, and yet, if he discovered the truth about her, she was certain that she would regret her actions for the rest of her life.

Take your hands from me! she wanted to cry. She longed to leap from the carriage and to race all the way to the governor's palace. She could not do so. His hold remained firm, just as his eyes continued to compel her. His mouth came ever closer to her own. He brushed her cheek with his lips, touched her earlobe, and she felt unable to break away, unable to fight the raw, sensual power. His face rose over hers again, his eyes entering into her naked soul. She moved toward him then, wanting more. Wanting just to taste . . . Her lips parted as she drew breath. No breath came to her, for his kiss closed down upon her lips.

She tasted brandy and the heat of his mouth. What she had initiated, he finished. His tongue swept with sensual insinuation deeply into her mouth. His fingers stroked first her face and then her breasts.

She could not breathe. She could feel only the flow of the brandy within her, and it was like a liquid fire. It was like the man, entering into all of her, making her burn with a sweet and startling desire to feel more, to know more.

"Mandy—" Damien began, and then he halted, clearing his throat.

Eric Cameron lifted his lips from hers, smiling. He set her gently back upon the seat and leapt down from the carriage facing Damien with no apology. His dark hair was somewhat tousled, slashing over his forehead. She could well see him as the pirate his ancestor had been, she thought, and then she realized that her fingers were at her lips and that she was trembling.

And that the warmth and desire were still with her. She didn't even understand desire, she thought with pain and fury, and yet it was something there, living deep inside of her. And this dark traitor had awakened it.

A whore. Her father had called her a whore like her mother.

She didn't believe it. She would never believe it.

He watched her. Damien was still, and she was silent, and it seemed that even long moments passed before Eric spoke to her again. "I have asked for your hand, lady. The offer still stands, should you need me."

She managed to form words. "I cannot marry you."

"And still, Amanda, I tell you, if you need me, I will be there. I will suffer your disdain, I will marry you knowing that you love another. Just don't seek to betray me."

"Betray you, sir? Pray, tell me what is there that I might betray?"

"Any man can be betrayed."

"I do not betray you," she lied smoothly.

"Good," he told her. But he did not smile, and the look of steel remained about his eyes. He turned to Damien. "I will offer no excuse, Damien, for I would marry her, if she would have me."

Damien didn't jump to her defense. He looked from Amanda to Eric. "Why?" he asked politely.

Amanda and Eric both stared at him. "I'm sorry, Mandy," Damien said. "But you were so very rude to him, from what you say yourself. And you've hardly been an angel this evening. Lord Cameron, I know that the world can be yours, so I am simply curious. Why?"

"Damien!" Mandy warned.

Eric laughed. "Aye, lad, she's cruel and abrasive, but she's truly the most beautiful creature I've ever seen."

"But you cannot love me! You've admitted as much," Amanda murmured desperately. No, he did not love her, but she felt the attraction more and more herself this evening. She might despise him for what he was, for what he knew of her, for all he had witnessed of her soul, but he fascinated her! She was drawn to his touch, she wondered more and more about the way his hands might roam, the places his lips might kiss. She reddened with horror. "You can't just . . ."

He chuckled softly again, and the tone of it made her burn, as did the husky sound of his voice when he spoke. "Amanda, I can. Ah, lady, perhaps I do not love you. You most certainly do not love me. But as you boldly pointed out at our last meeting, lust can rule a man's heart and soul and mind, and lady, you have driven me to distraction. I do desire you, with a fever scarce kept under control. Watch your kiss, lady, lest it go too far."

"My kiss!" she cried.

"You do wound me to the soul. You kissed me tonight, do you recall?"

"Damien, can we please go?"

"Mm . . . surely," Damien agreed, but he was grinning.

"Damien, now!"

Damien leapt up into the carriage. Amanda stared straight ahead, determined not to so much as glance Eric Cameron's way again. She looked down to her lap, feeling a fierce burning inside her. She could not bear these feelings. She had loved Robert, she had been deeply in love. And she had never felt like this with him, so what could it be? Her father's words returned to haunt her. She was a whore's daughter. . . .

Her heart rebelled. She had seen the portraits of her beautiful mother, seen her gentle smile, the intelligence in her eyes. She couldn't have been a whore. Amanda had never known her, but she could not believe such a thing.

"I remain your faithful servant, milady!" Cameron said.

Grinning, Damien waved to him and tapped on the carriage. Thomas clipped the reins, and they started down the street. They were very close to their destination.

The carriage swayed and she felt she was going to be sick. She stared across in the shadows at Damien, aware that he was watching her.

"He is twice the man Robert Tarryton is," Damien said softly.

Longing to pull his hair out, Amanda let loose with a startling oath. "Damien, don't you dare say such a thing to me! After all that he has said and done that you have seen or heard!"

"He has been honest," Damien said quietly. "Which you are not, cousin," he added.

She longed to rail at him and barely managed to hold back her words. "Leave me be, Damien."

"Amanda," he said softly.

"What?"

"I love you, you know," he reminded her.

She exhaled. "Oh, Damien! I love you too."

He reached across the dark carriage and squeezed her hand as Cato drove up around the driveway to the front door of the palace. "I'll deliver you to your father, and then Cato and I shall retire for the evening." He lifted her from the carriage and set her upon her feet, grinning. "I shall face my uncle the ogre with you!" he said dramatically.

"I will be all right," she assured him.

He shrugged. "Come."

The door was already being opened by a servant in handsome livery. They entered the hall and Amanda saw her father coming down the stairway, hurrying toward them.

"I've brought her home, Uncle, well and in good time, I pray," Damien said.

Nigel Sterling nodded curtly to Damien. "Fine. You may call upon her again, nephew."

Damien quirked a brow at Amanda, then wished her good night and made a hasty retreat.

When the door closed behind him, the servant discreetly disappeared and Amanda faced her father alone.

"Well?"

She shrugged. "Lord Cameron intends to leave on the governor's behalf to the west country to fight the Shawnee."

"He does intend to go?"

"Yes, definitely. Dunmore knew that already."

"Did Cameron introduce you to his acquaintances?"

"No."

"Then you failed! He did not—"

"He asked me to marry him again, Father," she said coldly, "so I did not fail."

Sterling fell silent, stroking his chins. She returned her father's stare and felt distinctly uneasy. He hated her and she was quickly learning to hate him.

She felt the letter in her pocket. She had brought it to turn over to her father. Yet she could not do so. Not until she had read it herself.

"When he comes back, you'll see him again."

She smiled. "I understand that the Shawnee are fierce and merciless. Perhaps he will not return."

"Then there will be no worry on the matter, and we will decide a different future for you." He smiled pleasantly. "Lord Hastings has been a widower for some time now. He would be delighted to take you in marriage."

Lord Hastings was well over sixty with a girth the size of an elephant's and a penchant for whipping his slaves.

She shivered and stood staring at her father, despising him with ever greater ferocity. She had never been afraid to be near him before, and now she realized that she dreaded the days to come. He would sell her to any man, and do so with relish.

"We'll go home in the morning," Sterling said. "You may go to bed. And Damien will be safe. For the time being."

She trembled, fearing the sudden brutality of his smile. Without knowing what she was saying, she started to talk.

"Lord Cameron offered me the hospitality of his home while he is gone fighting, Father. I thought that I should go."

"You will not—" Sterling began, but then he broke off, smiling again. "Yes. Yes, you shall go. And while he is gone, you can search his belongings for his correspondence. We could capture the whole core of this rebellion and hang them all like the traitors they are if we can bring proof of high treason into court!"

"There is no high treason, Father, don't you see that! The man is Lord Dunmore's friend—"

"No. No man has friends right now, girl. Bear that in mind. Friendship will not matter—blood will not matter."

Amanda felt a chill sweep over her. Her father turned away, heading for the stairs. "Tell him that you will marry him. You won't have to do so, but the promise alone will open doors for you."

"Father—"

"And think of it, my dear," he said, holding the newel post and turning back to her. "Such a move will salvage your pride. Robert Tarryton's fiancée has arrived from England. They are to be married in the middle of October. It will look so much better to the world if you are betrothed to Lord Cameron."

He started up the stairs again, murmuring to himself. "Perhaps you should marry him. If he is innocent, he is a man of the greatest prestige. And if he is guilty they will hang him, and his property will fall to you."

The chill swept around Amanda, settling deeply into her heart. "I cannot marry him!" she cried, racing after her father.

He paused and looked down at her. "You will do as you are told," he said, and kept walking.

She gritted her teeth, longing to run away, into the night. She didn't care what happened to her, as long as she could escape him.

But then Damien would hang.

She waited until he had disappeared, then she tore up the stairs herself and slammed into her room. She fell upon the bed, breathing heavily.

Then she remembered the letter in her pocket, and she slipped her fingers into it, anxious to read the correspondence.

Her fingers faltered, and her heart began to slam. She had his life in her hands.

And before God, she didn't know if she wished the letter to prove him a traitor or no. Pulling it from her pocket at last, she began to shiver. Even as she smoothed out the envelope, she felt again the fever of his kiss, the touch of his hands. Yes! She could condemn him. She had to! She was a loyalist; he was a patriot.

And it might well be Damien's life against his.

She rolled over and looked at the envelope. There was a name and address in the corner. Frederick something of Boston.

With shaking fingers, she reached inside.

The envelope was empty.

She lay back on the bed, and she began to laugh. She laughed until she cried.

And then she sobered with a gasp. She had spoken in haste.

And now she was condemned to play this torturous game still further. She was to go to his home; she was to make promises that she would never keep.

By God, she could not . . .

By God, she had to.

7

HERE WAS A SOFT TAP ON AMANDA'S DOOR. SHE hastily stuffed the envelope back into her pocket and rose, hurrying to the door. "Yes?" she called softly.

"C'est moi, Danielle."

Amanda quickly opened the door and Danielle, dressed in sober blue with an immaculate white pinafore, slipped into the room. She had taken her hair down, and it streamed in dark folds down her back.

She touched Amanda's cheek. "You had a nice evening, *ma petite?*"

"It was . . . fine," Amanda lied. She forced a smile that probably did not fool the woman in the least. "You know how I love Damien."

Danielle nodded and crossed the room to a large wardrobe in the corner, opened it, and brought out one of Amanda's nightgowns. It was soft silk, trimmed with Flemish lace at the throat and bodice and sleeves. "Lord Sterling does buy for you the best," Danielle murmured. "You have fought with him again?"

Amanda shrugged. "Not really. It is as it always is."

"No. It is worse now. He sees you growing up." She was quiet for a moment, her dark eyes luminous. "I should have killed him years ago!"

"Danielle!" Amanda gasped. "No, you cannot even think such a thing! They would hang you for it. And perhaps—perhaps not even God would forgive you."

Danielle moved the silk against her cheek. "God would forgive me," she said. She looked at Amanda, troubled. "That they should hang me, perhaps that is better than what he will do to you!"

Amanda was shaking again and she didn't like it.

"He is my father. He would not really hurt me." But she couldn't help it; the shivers remained with her. She couldn't forget the way that Nigel had called her mother a whore and suggested that she was just like her.

Danielle opened her mouth to say something, but then she closed it and helped Amanda out of her gown. Left in her stockings and corset and petticoats, Amanda hugged her arms about herself. "What was my mother like, Danielle?"

"Beautiful," Danielle said softly. "Her eyes were the color of the sea, her hair was as radiant as a sunset. Her smile made others smile, and she was both gentle and passionate. And beautiful." She hesitated, taking a petticoat as Amanda stepped from it. "You are her very image, Amanda. And that is why . . ."

"Why what?"

Danielle shook her head. "She was so very kind to me, and to Paul."

"Paul?"

"My brother. He died before you were born." Danielle untied the ribbons of Amanda's corset, then slipped the nightgown over her head. Amanda murmured her thanks, then sat on the bed to remove her shoes and stockings and garters from beneath the gown, watching Danielle as she returned her things to the wardrobe and trunks.

"I can never forget," Danielle continued. "It was so horrible. We Acadians, we were farmers in Nova Scotia. When the British took over the French rule, we vowed to serve the English king. But then war broke out again, and the French feared that we would fight with the British, while the British feared that we would take up arms with the French. And so they simply stole our land and exiled us from the place of our birth. We lived in a little town called Port Henri. It had been named for our great-grandfather. We reclaimed the marshland, we had many cattle, we fished the Bay of Fundy. Then the British gathered us at Port Royal and told us that we must leave. We were huddled into ships like slaves, and the captains made money on the misery they inflicted upon us. They made their coin, whether we lived or died. *Mon Dieu!* Day after day, the human waste and sickness gathered upon us. They would not let us out of the hold . . . except for Marie d'Estaing, for the captain raped her again and again. She began to look forward to his violence, for she told me that it was better than smothering in the hold with the smell and the worms. She died before we came to port. I was barely alive when our ship came to Williamsburg. Your mother demanded that your father take some of us in, and he was forced to oblige her. So Paul and I had a home."

Amanda rolled up one of her stockings, her fingers clenching against the pain and injustice done to Danielle's people. Many who had lived had not been accepted upon the colonial shores, and they had left again, searching for a homeland with the French, to the west.

Danielle exhaled slowly, then sucked in her breath. "I'm sorry. This is long ago. In 1754. Before you were born."

"But my mother was there. And she was kind. She was good then, Danielle. She was good and kind and beautiful."

Danielle nodded. "She was very good. Has someone told you otherwise?"

Amanda shook her head hastily. She knew that the pain her father caused her would hurt Danielle even worse. "I just wanted to hear about her from you, that is all."

"Then good night, *ma belle jeune fille*," Danielle said softly. She kissed Amanda's head and hurried to the door. Then she swung back suddenly. "How long are we staying?"

"I—I don't know," Amanda replied. "Maybe not long. We have been invited to see Lord Cameron's estate on the James. Perhaps we shall do so."

Danielle's eyes widened with pleasure. "We may go there?"

"Yes."

"Away from your father?"

"Yes."

Danielle nodded, pleased. "Lord Cameron is a far better man than the other you loved, Amanda."

Robert. His memory tugged at her heart, even if she had forced it to grow cold. She had dreamed too often of his golden head beside her own upon a pillow. She still had visions of little children, their little children, laughing and running about the house on Christmas day.

"Goodnight, Danielle," she said, more abruptly than she had intended. The woman stiffened, and Amanda immediately regretted her harsh tone. She raced over and hugged her. "I'm sorry, Dani. It's just that—I loved him, you see. And Lord Cameron—" She paused, shivering. "He might well be a traitor."

"Tell me, *petite,* what is a traitor but a man with a different cause? The British exiled me from my homeland. They took everything. The French were not there for me. I was Acadian, lost. And now I listen to the people on the streets and I know."

"You are a Virginian."

"I am an American," Danielle said with quiet dignity, and she smiled. "Who can ever say? If one wages war and is victorious, he is a hero, *c'est vrai*? If he wages war and loses, then he is a traitor, it is so simple."

Danielle pulled away from Amanda for a moment, studying her eyes. "Whatever else Lord Cameron may be, Amanda, he is a man who would be true to his own honor, and if he loved you, he would never betray you, as others have done." Danielle smiled, and then left.

Amanda watched after her, then she locked the door with the key and went back to the bed. She stared at the candle on the bedside, then snuffed out the flame, swearing. "Damn! He is a traitor, and a rogue, and so help me, I will use him as is necessary!"

She crawled beneath the covers, still shivering. It was not so cold a night, but the fire in the hearth was very low, and there was an autumn snap in the air. It was definitely the cold, she assured herself, that brought about her shivers, and nothing else.

She closed her eyes and prayed for sleep to ease her soul. No matter how she tried, though, she could not drift into slumber. She was haunted by visions of the day, of her father in the governor's delightful rose garden, calling her mother a whore. Calling *her* a whore. Threatening her. And then her father's face faded away, and she saw Eric Cameron before her with his steely eyes, watching her, knowing . . . something. Chess pieces moved before her. Gravely he leaned toward her. "Checkmate, milady. Checkmate."

She jerked up suddenly. She must have dozed, because she had now awakened. She didn't know why; she didn't know what she had felt.

The fire had gone down to almost nothing, and the window was open—she could see the drapes flowing soft and white into the room. She could have sworn that the window had been closed when she had lain down.

She tossed her covers aside and set her bare feet upon the floor, then hurried to the window. The moon was sending down shafts of light and the breeze was picking up. The drapes swirled, and the soft silk of her gown rose against her legs, rippling around her.

She sensed a shadow in the room. She turned about, but the moonlight had blinded her, and now she could not see. But she wasn't alone; she could feel someone else there.

"Who—who is it!" She gasped. She wanted to scream, but the words came out in a whisper.

There was a sudden motion. She saw the dark silhouette as it approached her, and she inhaled to scream. A hand fell across her lips. She kicked viciously and contacted human flesh, but then she was swept up high and tossed down hard upon the bed. Dazed, she tried to roll away, and she was wrenched back as the dark shadow fell upon her. She twisted, freeing her knee and her mouth. She gasped, but again no sound managed to escape, for a hand fell back down upon her, firmly clamping down upon her jaw and mouth, and she felt forceful arms lock tight around her. Wildly she clutched at the fingers that held her, raking them with her nails. Her hands were quickly caught and she was pushed down deeply into the bed. The attacker was still behind her, a leg cast over her, his one arm beneath her as his fingers stifled her breath and words, his other arm around her like an iron band, his hand beneath her breast, holding her taut and hard against his body.

"Shush," he whispered. Warm breath, scented with a pleasant masculine combination of brandy and good pipe tobacco, swirled against her cheek. She tried to bite, but she could not, she was held too tightly. She tried to squirm away, and she realized with horror that her movement brought the hem of her gown high up, baring her legs, and tugged the bodice of her gown even lower. She could feel his fingers upon the fullness of her breasts through the flimsy lace of the gown.

"Lady, I mean it, not a whisper. And be still."

She went dead still, not to be obedient, but with shock. It was Lord Cameron!

With the realization she panicked. She tried to kick and thrash again. He swore with no heed for her fair sex, then wrested her beneath him, his thighs taut about hers, his hand now a brutal clamp upon her mouth, and the length of him leaned low and close to her. She had no breath; she feared that she would faint. She could see his eyes flashing in the curious combination of the dying fire's glow and the moonlight, and there was no love, and no humor, within them now.

"Be still," he warned her again, staring into her eyes, daring her to defy him. Slowly he moved his hand.

"Get off me! I shall scream to high heaven!" she warned him.

"Yes, that's quite what I'm afraid of," he told her. She gasped then, for she realized that he now had a knife in his hand. He had slipped it from a sheath at his calf while he spoke. He lay the blade low between the valley of her breasts. She inhaled raggedly, fought for courage, then stared into his eyes again.

"You wouldn't do it. You wouldn't take a knife against an innocent woman."

"But you're not an innocent woman," he told her.

He knew. He had seen her take the envelope. Fear rushed through her. "You would not slay me, I know it. And I will scream. I find you despicable! How dare you come in here. I will scream, and my father will see that you hang—"

"Your father very well may wish to see me hang at some point, but I'd wager it would not be now. And what happened to the sweet apology you offered me earlier this very eve?" he demanded. "I warn you again, lady—" He paused, letting her feel the cold blade of the knife. "You shall be greatly distressed."

"You've broken into my room—into the governor's palace!" She smiled suddenly, lifting her chin. He wouldn't hurt her, and she knew it. She opened her mouth to scream, heedless of the consequences.

His fingers slapped back over her mouth. The blade of the knife moved swiftly in seconds, and she discovered that although her flesh remained unharmed, her garment was in shreds, and her breasts were spilling free from the silk and lace bodice. "Lady, I will wrest you from this place stark naked if you are not silent, and that is a promise. I will parade you down the streets of Williamsburg, and there are enough people here to enjoy it, for Tories such as yourself are not gaining much popularity these days."

"You wouldn't—"

"Don't ever tempt me too far. There are many things that I would like to do."

"You bas—" she began.

"No, no, milady. You are forewarned. Take care."

"I'll not—"

"You will!" His hand clamped hard upon her again, but she gave it no heed. She wasn't about to take care. She surged against him with all of her strength, seeking to kick him. She thrashed violently against him, flailing and twisting in a fury.

Eric didn't fight back. He just held her, letting her arch, writhe, and twist. Her efforts were almost amusing to him, she realized. He had only to maintain his grasp upon her wrists, and the power of his body hold did the rest.

While she . . .

She had managed only to wrest herself closely against him, leaving her legs as naked as her breasts.

"Be still!" he warned again.

Amanda fell silent, a blush scorching all of her flesh, for she was already half naked and he was studying her at his leisure. She tried to twist away from him, but his hold upon her wrists was firm. She went still at last, aware that the ruffles of his shirt hung down upon the bareness of her nipples and breasts, and that her position was precarious indeed. Always with him she was wrested and beaten, so it seemed. She moistened her lips, horrified to realize their position. She thought of his hands, should they move. Should they touch her. She thought of the feel of his lips upon hers, and she wondered what the sensation would be if they moved lower against her, brushing her shoulder blades, closing upon her breasts. She felt the hardness of his thighs against her hips, the pressure of his manhood against the near-naked territory at the apex of her thighs, and suddenly she was truly silent, no longer wishing to defy him, desperate only that he should move away from her.

She shook her head. His fingers eased from her swollen lips. "I shall not scream! I shall not. I swear it."

He watched her for a long, hard moment. Then he sat back. She was still his prisoner, still captive between his muscular thighs.

"What do you want?" she whispered.

"Many things," he told her casually, "but at the moment, I want my letter returned."

Amanda stiffened, then forced herself to relax, offering him a wide-eyed smile. "Why ever would you think—"

"I don't think, I know. And by God's blood, lady, cease the dramatics with me, for though you do bat your lashes prettily, you are a liar and we both know it. I want my letter now. Or you shall forfeit something else."

She was seething with fury, hating him for his crude and quick ability to see through her. She gritted her teeth. "Truly, Lord Cameron, your behavior is not civilized!"

"If it was civilized, I would not be here. I am pretending nothing, Amanda. I am no gentleman, and no fool, so do be warned and take heed for the future. I want my letter."

"I—I don't have it anymore."

His fingers closed harshly upon her shoulders, wrenching her up against him with such violence that she cried out in pain. He thrust her back down again, heedless of the pain, his lips very near to hers as he spoke. "I may well lose my own neck over you one day, Lady Sterling, but I'll not have other men endangered because of your treachery. Where is the envelope?"

"I gave it to my father."

"You're lying!" he snapped so quickly that she gasped and trembled and bit her lip in an effort to stay still. She had forgotten his knife. It lay against her cheek now. He stroked her face with it.

"You would not use that," she challenged him.

"Perhaps not." His eyes were very dark but glittering still in the night. "Perhaps I would use other means to reach my end."

She didn't know what he meant, only that the warning was very real. She didn't want to discover what lay beneath it. "It's—it's in the pocket of my gown."

If he was dying with desire for her, he certainly betrayed no emotion then. He was off her in a second, dragging her from the bed. His hat had fallen to the floor in their scuffle and now he swept it up atop his head. Stumbling, she tried to draw her gown together. She hurried to the wardrobe with him two steps behind her. She could barely open the door, and when she found the dress, he pushed her aside, reaching into the fashionable pocket hidden within the skirt. He found the envelope and thrust the dress back inside, and closed the door.

"Why did you take it?"

"Because—because you're a traitor. And you have to get out of here. Now."

"Oh? And you intend to prove that I'm a traitor?"

"No!" she cried with horror. "I just . . . I . . ."

"Pray, do go on."

"You get out of here! Before I do choose to scream!"

But he didn't move. He was watching her very closely. She clasped the gown closely about her, backing away. Something about him was exceptionally fierce in the strange shadowland of the bedroom, and yet she no longer felt the explosion of anger about him. He stepped toward her, towering in his tricorn and cape.

"Why didn't you give this to your father?" he demanded.

"I—I never had a chance."

"You're lying."

"All right. I wanted to read it myself. But as you see, there is no letter. If fact . . . why are you here, if there is no letter?"

He turned around, striding across the room to her bed. He sat on it, watching her carefully. "There is a name upon it," he told her. She shivered, feeling the silver touch of his eyes, even in the shadows.

"Frederick's name. The printer from Boston. The Indian tea-ditcher, right?" She swallowed quickly, not liking his eyes as they fell upon her. "You've got the envelope. Now go."

He shook his head. "I haven't quite decided what to do about you."

"About me?" she exclaimed. She tilted her head back, defying him.

"You went through my personal belongings; you stole my property."

"If you're not out of here in two seconds, I promise that I will scream until the entire British army is in here."

He leaned back more comfortably. "Nice lads. Some of them are my friends." He shrugged, then rose up from the bed and approached her with slow, menacing steps. She was nearly against the door. She had nowhere else to run. And yet she had not managed to scream.

"If you do scream," he promised her softly, "I shall offer your father my gravest apologies, but I shall tell him that you seduced and coerced me to this room, and then I shall be broken-hearted, of course, wondering just how many men you have led astray." He set a hand against the wall, his teeth flashing whitely as he smiled.

Amanda stared at him, furious and appalled.

"He knows I—"

"Despise me? Ah, but Lady Sterling! You came after me this evening! With apologies sweeter than wine tripping off your fair tongue."

"Yet—" She broke off. Both were silent as they heard footsteps coming down the hallway outside.

His knife flashed suddenly before her face. "Behave!" he warned her. "A word, and someone will die!"

He turned and seemed to disappear. Amanda stared into the shadows after him, uncertain as to whether he had slipped out the window or perhaps into the dressing room beyond her own.

There was a sharp pounding on her door. She stood behind it, her mouth dry. "Who is it?"

"Your father. Open the door."

She hesitated, then threw open the door. She stayed there, blocking his entry to the room. "What is it?" she asked quietly.

He pushed past her and went on in, lighting a candle with a wick from the fire, then looking about. He went over to her, staring at her intently. "I heard voices."

"Did you?"

He cuffed her on the side of the head, a silent blow that still sent her reeling down to the bed. She jumped back to her feet, loathing him, trying to pull the torn shreds of her bodice together. He walked over to her, staring closely. He lifted a finger to talk to her as his eyes narrowed. "You'll not play the harlot, not on my time, girl. A whore breeds a whore, but you'll serve me and do my purpose before playing elsewhere."

She stood still, her teeth clenched, her shoulders squared, and she prayed that Eric Cameron was gone. She could not bear him witnessing another scandalous scene, yet if he was near, he could not miss hearing the words.

She was a fool, she thought. If she shouted out and screamed and cried, she could tell the truth! But Cameron's words were true. With her father's appraisal, it would appear that she had asked him here. She spoke softly. "There is no one here, Father. I am alone. Please leave me, so that I can sleep."

"There is no one here?"

"No."

"Don't play games with me. I have ordered you to bestow your charms on Lord Cameron, and you will obey me."

She inhaled sharply, looking into the shadows. Please God, she thought, let him be gone, let him be gone.

Her father suddenly came close to her. She felt uneasy as his eyes raked over her. They seemed to have a strange, hungry light about them. He touched her chin, lifting it up, and he stared down at her breasts, so ill concealed in the gown. His finger ran down her throat to the deep valley between the mounds. "What happened?"

"I twisted in my sleep. I have rent the seam, nothing more. I will fix it."

"It is a beautiful gown on you, daughter. I have kept you well clad."

"You have," she acknowledged bitterly.

His hand hovered closer until she thought that she was going to throw up. She cried out, backing away from the door. His eyes narrowed as if he would grab her and wrench her away, and for the first time she was physically afraid of him as a man. He made her feel unclean.

She threw open the door quickly. If he came toward her again, she would scream. The governor was a good Englishman who might stoop to a little bribery or blackmail, but if she screamed hysterically, he would at least see that she was left alone. Her father would not dare abuse her before Lord Dunmore.

"Good night, Father," she said.

Sterling stared at the door then stared at her, a pulse ticking at the base of his throat. He swallowed hard and walked by her, but paused in the doorway, holding the door open. "It's not over between us, my daughter. We will return to our own home."

He closed the door sharply. Amanda fell against it, leaning her forehead upon it, ready to cry.

Then a sudden movement alerted her and she twirled around.

Eric Cameron hadn't left at all. He had hidden, motionless and silent, beyond the dressing-room door. Now he was standing there before her, watching her, his face somewhat hidden by shadow, and yet she felt both the fury and the pity within it. She didn't want his pity.

"I wanted to kill him," he said furiously.

She arched a brow, startled. Even in the darkness she could sense the tension about him. He was more enraged with her father than he was with her.

"He is my father," she said, shrugging. She could not bear that he should see her pain.

"The more he should be slain for what he does to you."

As regally as she could manage, she swept her gown about her. "My God, can't you please get out of here too?"

He strode toward her, taking her shoulders, and stared into her eyes. Some furious war waged in the very cobalt of his eyes. "So, you were ordered to apologize to me!"

"You've found your letter, now please go."

"I warn you now, milady," he said very softly, "I will not be betrayed again. Why didn't you tell him that I was here?"

"You promised to kill someone if I did."

"And you believed me?"

"What difference does it make?" she snapped scathingly. "You would have said that I'd asked you here."

"And he would have believed me, wouldn't he?"

She didn't answer. She didn't want to see his piercing silver-blue eyes anymore, or feel the strength of his hands upon her. She wanted to be left alone.

"Answer me!"

He could rise so quickly from gentleness to sharp, demanding anger! "Yes! He would have believed you. He—he despises me," she admitted softly. Then she jerked back away from him. "For the love of God, will you leave me alone?"

"I did not start this thing, lady, but I would finish it," he said softly. She didn't understand his meaning, and it worried her. His tension seemed to have increased and he paced the floor, as if he were suddenly loath to leave her.

She trembled. "You know what I have done—"

"I know that he is willing to sell. And I am willing to buy."

"My father—"

"You must be taken from him."

Amanda felt the heat and fury of his words, though they were spoken softly. She shook her head, protesting. "You don't understand! I do find you a traitor! Whatever I did—"

"You are a fool. It is best for me, milady, to have my eyes upon you. I will speak with him, and warn him that I don't want my bride bruised, battered—or touched in any way."

"I'll never marry you."

"Little idiot. No one can make you marry. I am offering you an escape, and God alone knows why. No woman is that beautiful," he murmured. "Yet you are," he said softly. "Beautiful, and cold. And yet I have seen the passion in you. I've even felt it. Why do you pretend so fiercely that it isn't so?"

"Because I hate you, Lord Cameron!" she cried. She hated that he could make her tremble so easily, to grow hot and flushed, and breathless as if she were what her father accused her of being . . .

A whore.

"Never mind! If you would just—"

"But I will not 'just' anything," he assured her huskily. Then he came around to her again, and it did not seem that he felt her resistance when she tried to free herself from his hold.

"You will come tomorrow. You cannot wait any longer, do you understand me?"

"I don't know what you're talking about!"

"I will leave the invitation with Lord Dunmore. If they are eager to hang me, I must give them the rope. Whatever his mind, he is a decent man. I will speak with your father. A betrothal will give you freedom. You will come out to Cameron Hall tomorrow—"

"You are mad!" she cried. "I stole your letter, and you know that I hate you, but you would have me anyway! And what makes you think that I would come?"

"The fact that I will be quickly gone and that you will have the place to yourself."

She fell silent. She knew that she would go. She longed so desperately to escape her father.

Cameron doffed his hat to her. "You should marry me, and quickly, you know. I could well be skewered through by a Shawnee arrow."

"I don't believe that I should have such wonderful good luck," she retorted.

His teeth flashed in a dangerous smile and he reached out suddenly, pulling her gown back in place. The silk had slipped from her fingers, and she had been standing before him, proud and bare. She swore softly, brushing his hand aside, but not before she felt the stroke of his fingers, warm and taunting. "You may have to marry me soon. For the sake of your good name."

"I haven't a good name left at all, Lord Cameron. And I don't give a fig," she said regally.

His laughter was soft and husky, but then it faded, and the silver-blue eyes that fell upon her held pity and tension. "You don't need to fear me."

"Don't I?" she inquired sweetly, now holding the remnants of her bodice together very firmly. She smiled, her teeth grating, as she awaited his answer.

"You should fear those around you, lady. Come on your own accord, milady, else I shall find a way to rescue you from yourself."

"I don't know what you mean."

"And I pray that you need not discover the truth of my words," he warned her. Then he bowed deeply. "Adieu, milady."

He twirled around and was gone. The breeze rustled through the open window, and she wondered briefly how he did not break his neck, or a leg at the very least. Then she wondered, too, about the British guard assigned to the governor's palace. She should hear shouts any second. Eric would be arrested, strung up.

She raced to the window, her heart hammering in her breast. She looked down into the yard below but saw nothing but the shadows of the night and, beyond, the foliage of the governor's gardens and mazes. Cameron was uncanny. For his great height and the breadth of his shoulders, he could move swiftly, and silently.

Damien once told her that many men who had fought in the French and Indian Wars had come home like that. Still soldiers.

Still savages.

He was no savage, she assured herself. But he was swift to anger, and she had already aroused him.

The letter was gone, in his hands.

Her tongue felt dry; her breath came quickly. Though she was afraid of Lord Cameron, still she knew that if the invitation was true, she would travel to Cameron Hall in the morning.

She dared not remain with her father, and Lord Cameron was right about one thing. A betrothal would buy her freedom.

———

The next day had turned to a beautiful sun-streaked twilight when Amanda first saw Cameron Hall. She didn't know when Eric had gone to talk to the men, but she listened in silence when her father told her that she was betrothed and when Lord Dunmore told her that Pierre, with the Cameron carriage, would be waiting for her and Danielle whenever she was ready.

Lord Cameron would be leaving any day, but he wanted her to accustom herself to his home in his absence. The wedding date, in these troubled times, must be set later.

Her father caught hold of her arm just before she entered the carriage. "You will make yourself at home. You will search his desk and his papers, and you will find the truth. Anything, anything you find—letters, names, addresses—we must have. Do you understand?"

"He'd probably kill you, Father, if he knew what you were about," she said flatly.

"You're still my daughter, mine to command," Sterling reminded her roughly. "And I can have you dragged home whenever I choose. Then there is your cousin. You think on it, girl." He released her arm. Then he smiled and stared at her, and the same unease that had touched her the night before filled her with dread. She didn't think that she could ever bear to be in a room with him alone again.

"If you touch me, he'll kill you," she said bitterly, and then she was startled by the fear she saw in her father's eyes. For a man who had been badgering his prospective son-in-law about his political views not a month previous, suddenly he seemed very wary and cautious.

Sterling stepped away from her, and she was glad. Danielle was already in the carriage.

Lord Dunmore had already turned his mind to the matters of the day, and it was her father who stood before the gates of the palace to watch the carriage turn along the green. He did not wave, and Amanda was relieved. She leaned her head back against the carriage and was glad of the respite. It would be a three-hour drive down the peninsula to Lord Cameron's home.

From the moment she first set eyes on the place, she felt a peculiar stirring in her blood. A mist was just rising as the carriage turned down the long winding drive. Great oaks sheltered the drive, and the mist caught within their branches and leaves. Then suddenly the trees parted and the house could be seen, rising high upon a hill on a waving lawn of emerald-green grasses. It was a huge place, made of brick, with a great porch surrounding the whole of it and great white Doric columns adding grace and elegance to the symmetry of the architecture.

"*Mon Dieu,*" Danielle murmured, pulling back the carriage draperies to better study the house. Her eyes were bright as she smiled at Amanda. "This is a house, *mais oui!*"

Amanda tried to smile, but she felt butterflies in her stomach. The whole of the plantation was impressive. As they rounded the drive, she could glimpse the neat rows of outbuildings all on a path and surrounded by vegetable and flower gardens. The gardens seemed to stretch out forever, just as the main house seemed almost to glitter beneath the sun and reach upward to the heavens. It was an illusion of the mist, she thought, and yet she couldn't deny that it was beautiful. To the far left she could see the fields, and already there were a multitude of men at left. From this distance, slaves and white tenant farmers all seemed to blend together as they bent at their tasks. Far beyond she could see a rise of trees as the land sloped down to the river, and she could just make out some of the dock buildings that lay directly behind the house and far down the slope. Lord Cameron was at a distinct advantage with his property sitting on the river and with his own dock and deep harbor.

Danielle's eyes were flashing happily. "It will be good here, *ma chérie*. It will be good. This lord is very wealthy, and he will marry you and keep you far from your papa."

Amanda shivered suddenly, despite the grace and beauty that surrounded her, and she didn't know if it had been Danielle's mention of her father or of Lord Cameron. She was escaping the one to come to the other. He knew that she was a fraud, yet it was his fraud that they were now perpetuating. She had never lied about her own political beliefs. He knew she considered him a traitor. He had been furious to hear that her apology the other night had been forced upon her, but he'd already known that she had been spying on him.

She could never marry him. Even if nothing had ever happened between them, if she had not fallen in love with Robert, if her heart had not been twisted by her father's dark corruption, she was still, in her heart, and always, a loyalist. They were English; they were English people, with English laws, and she was proud of that heritage. At the school for young ladies, she had learned she loved London. America was still raw and wild, but her people belonged to one of the most cultured and greatest nations on earth. To her, he was a traitor.

"There he is! Lord Cameron awaits us!" Danielle said happily.

Amanda was not so happy. She swallowed sharply as she held open the curtain. He was awaiting them on the steps to his house. He was in white breeches and stockings, boots, and a navy frock. As usual, his shirt was finely laced and impeccable, his hair was unpowdered but neatly queued. As the carriage clattered along the stone drive, Amanda admitted that he well fit the regal house, for his bearing was fine.

The carriage came to a halt. Pierre came scampering down from the driver's seat. Lord Cameron called out something to him, and Pierre laughed, then helped Danielle from the carriage.

"Welcome, Danielle," Cameron said. He took the woman's hand in both of his own. "Welcome to Cameron Hall."

Flustered, Danielle smiled and Lord Cameron kissed her hand.

"Merci, merci!" Danielle murmured, blushing and flustered. She was so happy, Amanda thought. And perhaps she had the right, for Nigel Sterling had never treated her with anything that resembled kindness.

He had always hurt her, Amanda thought, paling. Then she saw Eric's eyes on her, and she flushed. He had known that she would come. And she had.

He took her hand. "And, my love, to you my warmest welcome. I hope that you shall be very happy here. And safe."

Safe? she wondered. Could she be safe from him?

With both of her hands within his own, he pulled her close. He kissed her cheeks and then slowly released her, studying her eyes. "Pierre, find Thom if you would, and see to Lady Sterling's trunks, please."

"Mais oui," Pierre agreed, grinning and turning toward the house.

Amanda found herself looking at the carriage with its coat-of-arms and then to Eric Cameron. He was so comfortable here, so affluent, and yet it seemed that he was willing to risk it all.

"Shall we go in?" he asked her.

She nodded, and then she realized that she hadn't spoken a word yet. "Yes, of course."

"Come, Danielle, I think that you'll enjoy a bit of a tour too."

"Merci—thank you," she said quickly. Nigel Sterling hated her to speak French. He hated the fact that Amanda had mastered the language so easily.

But Lord Cameron did not mind at all. He smiled kindly, and in those seconds

Amanda felt a curious thrill sweep through her, for his smile had made him arresting indeed, charming and youthful.

It was only when he was crossed that the laughter left him and the tension settled in.

She had already crossed him.

Large double doors painted white were opened behind them and he was no longer gazing her way. "The land, my love, was originally called the Carlyle Hundred. It was granted to my many times great-grandfather by James the First. He was a Jamie himself, and he and his wife Jassy built this place. They were here when the Powhatans massacred the settlers in 1622, but they survived to lay the cornerstones and build the hall."

He had led her through the doors, and now they stood in a grand and massive hallway. Opposing double doors opened to the river behind them, and a gentle breeze blew through the hallway. A grand stairway stood at center, and a door led off in either direction to the wings of the house. The bannister was polished mahogany, the walls were covered with European silks, and the ceilings had beautifully crafted moldings. A man in crimson livery similar to Pierre's came hurrying down the stairs. "Ah, here is Richard. Richard, Lady Sterling, and her maid, Mademoiselle Danielle."

White-haired and lean, Richard bowed. "At your service, milady, mam'selle. Milord Cameron, shall you desire anything now?"

"Blackberry tea in the library in an hour, Richard, if you would be so good. I had thought that I would show milady and mam'selle their rooms, and give them time to refresh themselves from the ride."

"Very good, milord," Richard said, and bowing, he left them.

Lord Cameron led them on up the wide and graceful stairway. At the landing they came upon a portrait gallery. Amanda found herself stopping before the first portrait, startled. A dark-haired man in seventeenth-century dress stared out at her with Eric Cameron's silver-blue eyes. Beside him was the portrait of a beautiful blond woman with crystal eyes.

"Jamie and Jasmine," Lord Cameron told her. "Rumor has it that she was a tavern wench, but he was so enamored of her that he would have her no matter what her birth."

Amanda stared at him and flushed, feeling the piercing power of his eyes. "Are all Cameron men so determined?"

"Yes," he said flatly. "Ah, here, Jamie's grandson, another Jamie. And his Gwendolyn. They sheltered numerous Roundheads when Cromwell ruled and King Charles the First lay headless in his grave. Virginia has always been a loyalist colony."

"So what has happened?" Amanda asked him.

"Time changes eternally, Lady Sterling. Seeds, once sown, often flourish, and the seed of liberty has fallen here."

"So you are a traitor."

"What words, lady! I am about to travel with Lord Dunmore to face the West County savages! What traitorous work is that?"

She smiled serenely, and he laughed huskily. "Alas, I can imagine your very thoughts. You see a Shawnee hatchet riding high upon my temple. Mam'selle, that you could be so cruel!"

He mocked her, she knew, but his fingers felt like steel about her own, tense and powerful. He raised her hand to his lips and kissed it. Just the very light brush of the hot moisture of his lips made her blood seem to sizzle and flow, her knees grow weak. A flush came to her features because she knew that he evoked forbidden things within her, and it should not be. And still she stood, captured in a curious hold as he turned her hand, touching his kiss against her palm. A pulse leapt through her. His eyes rose to hers and she felt suddenly dizzy. "Please . . ." she whispered, dismayed by the note of desperation in her voice.

He let go of her hand and moved down the gallery to another portrait. He was, she thought, well versed in this game they were playing. He was making the rules. She could not allow him to do so. "Here, my lady! This is a favorite portrait of mine. Petroc Cameron, and here, his wife. Roc was rumored to be a pirate, and to have captured and seduced his own bride."

"A Cameron tradition?" Amanda inquired pleasantly.

He paused, looking into her eyes. "He pirated for the Crown."

"So 'tis *rumored*."

"He was my grandfather, and he raised me, for my father was killed fighting the French. I know the truth about him and his beloved, for I heard it from their very lips. They aged in beauty and in love, and never seemed to change to one another. He was the pirate; I daresay that she did the taming. But they taught me much of the true values in life, and I am grateful."

He turned away from her, walking on with Danielle at his heels. Amanda paused, suddenly aching. She'd never known what it was like to watch someone age with love, to learn any of life's true values. She'd known coldness, betrayal, and brutality.

She looked again at the portraits, and wished that these people had been her own family. She wanted this background, she wanted the very beautiful people to look down upon her, with love.

Amanda trembled and feared that she would cry. It was so very senseless. She was there to escape her father. Bless the warring Shawnees, they would take Lord Cameron away, and she would have peace.

"Milady?"

He was politely waiting for her now.

She hurried along. He threw open a door on the southern side of the passage. She stepped into a huge room with a mahogany sleigh bed and Persian carpets on the polished wood floor. Huge grand windows opened to a river view, and there was a massive fireplace to warm one, a fine carved table with two elegant French brocade chairs to face the windows. It was a room fit for a princess, finer than the governor's room at the palace.

"Will this suffice?" he asked her.

She nodded, then lowered her head. He had turned to speak with Danielle. "Mam'selle, you are just down the hall, there."

The open door awaited her and Danielle smiled, thanked him, and hurried forward with delight. Amanda still had her head down but she could feel him near her, the very crisp clean fabric of his clothing, the pleasant scent of good tobacco and brandy and leather, and something subtle, something with which he apparently bathed. And there was his own scent, vibrantly masculine. She moistened her lips and turned to him. He was watching her, his hands folded behind his back, his eyes unreadable.

"Where is your room, Lord Cameron?" she asked him.

He arched a brow politely, then smiled. "Through the wardrobe, Lady Sterling." He watched with amusement as she paled, then added, "You have a key, of course."

"Of—course."

"But then, one wonders why you are so interested. Are you concerned about my whereabouts, or my belongings?"

"I'm not concerned—"

"You are, so please, spare us both, and quit lying. Search to your heart's content, but take care. If I find you too close to my bed, I might be tempted to believe that you wish to lie upon it. Pride, my love, dies hard."

"I imagine, for yours is monstrously large."

"Perhaps with just cause."

"You do flatter yourself."

"Do I? I think not. I do believe that I know you better than you know yourself, and therefore I am at an advantage."

She opened her mouth to protest, but he gave her no chance. He bowed and turned away, then paused at the door.

"Richard will come to escort you to tea. You'll need to meet Cassidy, my valet, and let's see, Margaret will furnish you and Danielle with anything you need. From then on, milady, you shall be on your own. And, my lovely little spy, it will be quite fascinating to see where your—delicate—steps do lead you."

"Never too close!" she called after him. "Never so close as to be . . ."

"Caught?" he inquired pleasantly. His eyes leisurely drifted to her, and he smiled. "You are in check already."

"I do not concede the game!"

"Ah, trust me. You will."

He turned then and was gone.

8

MANDA DID NOT TAKE LONG TO INSPECT HER room, though a high excitement had risen in her, just being there. She loved the gracious manor, the view of the river beyond her windows, the exquisite sense of freedom. She didn't understand it. She was there under false pretenses, playing a dangerous game with a dangerous man. But she was far away from Nigel Sterling, and at the moment that seemed enough.

A pitcher had been filled with clean fresh water and a bowl and towel and sponge had been left for her arrival. She washed quickly, smoothed her hair with the silver-handled brush upon the dressing table, and quickly turned for the door. She hesitated just a moment. There was a door at the far rear of the room. She couldn't resist it.

A key was set within the lock. She had the ability to lock him out of the room. She smiled and then twisted the key. Then she pushed open the door and entered his room.

Here, too, long windows looked out on the sloping lawn and down to the river and the docks and warehouses. The sun streamed in beautifully, the river breeze lifted the light curtains under their heavier velvet backers. His bed seemed huge; it was four-postered, and hewn of a wood as dark as the man. But the room was not at all dark. It was exceptionally large and, though masculine by nature, it also had a sweeping elegance, as if it would welcome the partnership of a woman. The mantel was large also, with fine molded woodwork. Candles in elegant silver holders awaited the fall of night as did beautiful glass lamps. A small cherrywood table sat before the windows, catching the fall of the sun. A large braided rug added warmth to the polished wood floor, and the armoires and dressing tables that rimmed the walls were even finer than the furnishings she had seen in his Williamsburg town house. There also seemed to be a scent on the air. A scent of fine Virginia tobacco, rich leather, and a touch of men's cologne. It was a haunting scent, arresting.

Like the man.

Amanda felt color rise to her cheeks and she quickly exited the room, forgetting that she was supposed to be a spy of sorts and that spies do not flush and retreat when they fall upon the very core of their search. Still, she hurried into her own room and closed the connecting door between the rooms, breathing deeply. Irritation rose high within her. Her father was such a fool! Damn his fascination with Cameron. What man these days did not wonder what the next years would bring? But, of course, it was true, she knew. Cameron was in sympathy with the rogues, saving the fellow in Boston, meeting with the burgesses in the Apollo Room at the Raleigh Tavern. But she had heard that Colonel Washington himself had been dismayed at the events in Boston, saying that the destruction of property could not be justified. But even with the House dissolved Washington was still engaged in meetings, and he had been elected to attend the Continental Congress. And Lord Fairfax, loyalist to the core, called Washington a great man, a pride of the Crown. Life was in a whirlwind. Nothing was as simple as black and white anymore.

She pushed away from the door, wondering if she was trying to excuse Eric Cameron within her own mind. She told herself that it could not be true, yet she was suddenly running away from herself and toward her next meeting with the man.

She did literally run, past the pictures in the wide gallery and to the sweeping stairway. Once she reached the upper bannister she paused, for a man was waiting for her at the foot of the stairs. He was as tall as Cameron and so black as to be ebony. He stood as straight as an arrow, and he was dressed in a handsome uniform that enhanced his startling color. He was regal, she thought, and wondered that such a word could come to her in reference to a slave.

She struggled for breath as he bowed deeply. "Lady Sterling, I am Cassidy, Lord Cameron's valet. I shall take you to him now, and if ever I can be of assistance, you must let me know."

Amanda nodded, startled by the man's exquisite speech. She held herself with dignity as she descended the stairs. He said no more but walked along the large main hall until he came to a set of double doors. He opened them and moved discreetly to the side. "Lady Sterling, Lord Cameron."

Amanda entered the handsome parlor. Eric was waiting for her by the mantel, this one made of fine smoke-gray marble. Persian rugs lay scattered over the floorboards, the walls were covered in a fine silk cloth, and there were deep window seats toward the rear of the room. A tea cart with a silver server and delicate porcelain cups was parked before a richly upholstered French sofa.

"Do sit down, Amanda," he welcomed her, nodding to the black man. "I see you've met Cassidy."

"Yes," Amanda said, nervously taking a seat near the edge of the sofa. She smiled at Cassidy. He reminded her of his master. He appeared to be exceptionally strong, a man who could be of great value in the fields. Her father would never have had him as a house servant.

Cassidy bowed deeply and left them.

Amanda turned back to Eric to find that he was studying her intently, his silver-blue eyes brooding. She wondered if she hadn't been a fool to come. She loved the house, she loved the excitement, she loved the freedom. But she didn't know at all what she felt for the man anymore. He tempted her like the original sin of Eden, and that temptation burned into her, for her father's words were never far away. She could not believe that her beautiful mother had been a whore, but when Eric Cameron came near her, she was forced to wonder at the blood that simmered within her.

"So that is Cassidy," she murmured. "He looks more like a prince than a house slave."

"I believe he would have stood in line to be a Nubian prince. And he is not a slave. He earned his freedom. He remains with me by choice, and earns wages."

"How . . . interesting," she murmured. She had difficulty meeting his gaze so she lowered her eyes quickly, wondering what he read within them. "So this is berry tea, milord? How intriguing."

"No. It is horrible. But one gets used to it."

"Shall I pour?"

"Please do."

Her hands were shaking. She gritted her teeth and willed her fingers to cease their trembling. She lowered her head to her task, but when the curious berry tea was within a cup, she almost cried out, for when she raised her lashes he was before her, hunched down upon the balls of his feet and looking at her. He wasn't a foot away. She hadn't heard him move, hadn't realized he was so near.

His teacup clattered within its saucer. She swallowed, noting his remarkable eyes and the pulse that beat a wicked rhythm against his throat.

"You startled me." She gasped.

He rescued his cup, setting it down, his eyes never leaving hers.

"Marry me," he told her.

"I cannot!" she whispered desperately.

He caught her hands and came up beside her on the sofa. A rueful smile curled his lip even as the tension remained in his eyes. "There is no reason that you cannot. There is every reason that you should."

"I do not love you!"

"Ah, so you are still in love with that fop."

"Fop! Robert Tarryton—"

"Is a fop, by God's body, I swear it. Still, no man but Robert Tarryton will ever convince you of that. He is due to wed within the week. And your father is a dangerous man."

"My father!" She flushed, fully aware that he was telling the truth and fully aware of him as he sat beside her. She had never felt more alive, she thought, more attuned to every fiber of feeling within herself. Her flesh burned with greater sensitivity, her heart beat as if it were touched. She was drawn . . . she frightened. His very passion on her behalf could well stand against her. He excited her beyond reason, he scared her to the depths of her soul. A pact with him would be like a pact with the very devil.

She shook her head, losing both breath and reason. She didn't want tea or sustenance of any kind. She discovered that she was fascinated only with the long dark fingers that curled over hers. His thumb brushed again and again over her flesh, stirring strange fires and causing truth and wisdom to sweep away.

"Your father will not let you play this game long, though I am not certain of what game he plays himself. If you do not set a date to wed me, he will seek another for you. There was talk, you are aware, of betrothing you to Lord

Hastings, a man almost thrice your age and—I've got it from very reputable sources—a man who snores with the vehemence of the west wind."

She couldn't help but laugh at Eric's bold description of the man. He moved closer to her, drawing a finger provocatively over her cheek, then defining the breadth of her lower lip with the same sensual touch, his eyes following his movement. "I am not as young as Tarryton, and I admit to a scar or two upon my back and at my side, but I swear that my teeth are all mine and quite good, I've kept to one chin, and I do bathe with frequency. I am wealthy, landed, and I come with this house, a stable full of horses, and fields full of tobacco and grain. Marry me. And—I have it from very reputable sources—I do not snore." She laughed again, but his eyes grew darker as they seemed to possess her own. "I promise to be an excellent lover."

"Oh!" She gasped, but laughter still mingled with her indignity. He had broken into her very bedroom and forced her down upon her bed. What brazen words he offered now could not cause her more outrage. "You, sir, are the most egotistical man I have ever met! Tell me, sir, does that piece of information come from reputable sources too?"

"I'm sure I can arrange for references, milady, should you require them."

"Lady Geneva?" she inquired sharply.

"I do believe you're jealous. Marry me," he insisted. "And do so quickly. Before I leave. Then, if the Shawnee split my head, you shall have safety and peace."

"I cannot marry you so fast—"

"Ah! You will consider it then."

She couldn't help smiling again. The world faded away when he was before her so vehemently, so adamantly. And she did feel safe. As if no man—not even her father—would dare to come against her. "You're forgetting something."

"What?"

"I am a loyalist. That is not my father's voice, nor Lord Dunmore's, but my own. I fear the radicals and what is to come. And you, sir, are a patriot."

"You are welcome to be a loyalist."

"And your wife?"

"Yes. You may follow your convictions, just so long as you take no steps to betray me."

Amanda inhaled sharply. How could she make such a promise when she had been cast into his arms for that very purpose? She looked down to where his hands lay over hers. His palms were rough from work he must have chosen to take on himself. Perhaps they were a soldier's hands, roughened by his hold upon his horse's reins. She didn't know. She only knew that the roughness against the soft flesh of her hand was somehow good. She drew her eyes back to his, and she was suddenly very frightened, and not so much of the man as by the depths of the feelings that stirred within her. If he kissed her now, she would want to explore that touch.

Like a whore . . . like the whore her father claimed her to be. Her mother's daughter.

Some darkness must have fallen over her eyes for Eric frowned, watching her. "What is the matter?"

"Nothing. Nothing!" she cried. She leapt to her feet, shaking her head. "I can't marry you. I can't. We—we're on different sides. It's impossible. If you want me to leave—"

"Leave!" He stood, watching the sudden torment that constricted her features. "Leave?" He smiled slowly. "Why, of course not. I should not want to cast you to Lord Hastings with his four-score chins. My God, what a travesty that would be!"

Amanda almost smiled; she could not. She turned around and fled the room, to race up the stairs. She entered her room. Her trunks had arrived, and a servant would come to hang her clothing on the hooks in the armoire and to set her hose and undergarments into the drawers of the dresser. But no one was there now. Night had come. A fire had been lit in the hearth to burn away the dampness. The windows were open to the river. She walked toward them and looked out on the night. Slowly her heart ceased to beat its rampant rhythm. As she stared at the James, a sense of peace settled over her. She was safe here. Eric Cameron might taunt and tease her and discard propriety, break into the governor's palace and perhaps even manhandle her. But he would never force her to do anything against her own will. He would not strike her in anger, and he would not use her for his own cause. It was almost like being loved. She smiled to the night, then changed into a cool cotton nightgown. So mellow had she become that she dropped her stockings, garters, shoes, corset, shift, and gown upon the floor with no thought and curled into the comfortable bed to sleep. She did not dream, and she did not hear the knocking upon her door later when Danielle came to see if she would have supper.

Nor did she hear the connecting door open when the clocks about the house were striking midnight.

Eric stood and looked down on her as she slept. The dying firelight lay gently upon her face, and she looked very young. Fragile and vulnerable. Anger rose within him as he thought of Nigel Sterling, and he wondered how any man could so mistreat a daughter, especially one so beautiful and proud as this. He wanted to touch her, but he did not allow himself to do so. He did not want to wake her, and so he just watched her, the ache to possess her tempered by the very innocence of her appearance. She evoked so many things within him. From the moment he had seen her dancing at Thomas Mabry's in Boston, he had wanted her with an urgent fever. From the night he had touched her in the garden, he had wanted her forever with something that burned and sizzled inside of him. But from the time he had seen her with her father, he had wanted to protect her with all of his heart. Her loyalty to the Crown was so very fierce! If she could but love a man so fiercely, then he would gladly lay down his life for her and smile in the dying.

He reached out but did not allow his hand to fall. He smiled and felt the cool breeze ripple over him, and then he turned to go back to his own room. The game had changed, if subtly so.

In the morning when Amanda walked into the dining room, Eric was nowhere about. The girl he had mentioned, Margaret, a fresh-faced farm lass with
bright dark eyes and bouncing black curls, came to inform her that his lordship
was about seeing to the mustering of his Tidewater troops. Margaret left then,
and Thom served her—coffee that morning, rather than the berry tea—delicately seasoned fish and fresh-baked bread. When she was finished with the meal
she decided to explore beyond the house. After exiting by the rear, she started
down a path that led by the outbuildings, the smokehouse, laundry, bakehouse,
kitchen, the cooper's and the blacksmith's, and the barns and stables. Men and
women stopped in their work to look her way curiously, then quickly bowed or
curtsied to her. She smiled to all she met in turn, wondering how many of the
blacks were slaves and how many were freemen. Nor were the servants all black,
and not just within the house. A white woman who spoke with a soft French
accent was directing the smoking of a butchered hog. There were numerous
Acadians here, she thought, and she was happy, for Danielle would be pleased to
meet so many of her own people.

Just as she thought of Danielle she came upon the stables. To her surprise she
saw Danielle there, deeply engrossed in conversation with a tall white man.
Amanda hurried forward, then paused. The two were speaking French very
quickly. And furtively. They whispered, they gesticulated.

Amanda instinctively slipped behind the wall of the barn and looked at the
man. He was very handsome, perhaps forty years old, with dark hair and sensitive
light eyes, eyes that haunted his face and gave it much of its appeal. His features
were fine. He almost had the look of a scholar about him, except that he was tall
and well muscled, and wore the plain breeches and hardy hose and shoes of an
outdoors worker. He did not seem to be the blacksmith, which made Amanda
wonder at his work.

"Lady Sterling."

Startled—and caught in the act of spying upon the servants—Amanda swung
around. Cassidy was there, towering over her. He seemed to glisten beneath the
sun.

"Aye, Cassidy!" she said, annoyed and embarrassed.

He betrayed no emotion at all. "Lord Dunmore has come to look over Lord
Cameron's troops. Your father has accompanied him, along with Lord Hastings."

"I shall come right away, Cassidy." She fell into step beside him but he
quickly let her precede him. She fell back, determined to be on her guard.
"Then Lord Cameron has returned?"

"He has. They await you in the parlor."

"Thank you."

She walked ahead again. When she came around the trail, she could see that
the rear yard was filling with canvas tents. Men were arriving, camping out on
the open lawn. A captain drilled a company of foot soldiers near the river while
others sat about on crates or on the ground, cleaning their rifles, drinking from

tins, laughing with one another. She could not make out faces or men, but she estimated that at least fifty men had come, and they seemed to be dressed in the buckskin clothing that was associated with the West County men. She paused again and waited pointedly for Cassidy.

"Who are all these men? They are not regular militia."

"No, Lady Sterling. They are troops raised by Lord Cameron—tenants, farmers, a few artisans. And many cousins."

"Cousins?"

"Distant, perhaps. Half of the men out there are Camerons. They own property, some estates, near here, all on the old Carlyle Hundred grounds. The first lord and lady had several children, and since that was well over a hundred years ago, you can imagine that their descendants are many."

"Of course," Amanda murmured.

"Milady, they're waiting."

She had hardly fled her father and he was upon her again like a vulture. She did not answer Cassidy but hurried up the back steps to the hall and went from there straight to the parlor. The men were all there, her father and Lord Hastings with his "four-score chins," Lord Dunmore and Eric himself. Lord Dunmore was striking as usual with his flashing brown eyes and elegant apparel. Eric wore navy breeches and a white cotton shirt. Her eyes were drawn to his, a habit that seemed more and more customary as time wore on.

"Ah, Amanda, my dear!" Her father drew her close and kissed her cheek. She wanted to scream and refuse his touch. However, she managed to hold her ground and escape him, allowing the governor to take her hand and bow low over it.

"I've come to see how Eric is managing to gather men. I did not believe he could summon so many," Lord Dunmore said.

"Only half have arrived as yet, John. The others will come by the end of the week, I believe. We shall be ready to travel very soon."

"Good. Lewis has his West County men out on the frontier; we'll come at the Shawnee in a pincer movement and settle this once and for all," the governor stated.

Glancing at Eric, Amanda didn't think he believed that things would be settled once and for all, but he didn't say so. Instead he announced, "I believe that our meal is ready to be served. Gentlemen, Lady Amanda, shall we?"

Eric would have taken her arm, she thought, except that she stood before Lord Hastings, and the old man hooked his arm into her own, smiling down at her with his little beady dark eyes. "May I, milady?"

"Ah . . . of course," she murmured, and so she was escorted into the dining room on his arm. She was very grateful when he released her and they all took their seats about the table.

The dining room took up almost the entire left side of the house. The table was long, able to seat at least twenty, but this afternoon the five of them were gathered at the far end. Upon the walls were several displays of arms, and a large family crest sat high above the fireplace. There were sideboards on all four sides of the rooms, and deep window seats where Amanda imagined guests could relax and socialize before and after the meal. Perhaps the ladies gathered by the fire in the plush seats when the men exited the room for their brandy and pipes.

She drew her eyes from the room to realize that Lord Dunmore was watching her. She flushed and asked after his countess's health.

"She is quite well, thank you."

"I had not heard that she was ill," Eric commented, frowning.

"Not ill, soon to create a new Virginian," the governor said.

"Ah, then to your fair lady's health!" Eric murmured, lifting his glass of Madeira. About the table the toast was repeated and they all sipped wine. Thom and Cassidy served the meal of delicious wild fowl and summer squash and pole beans. Amanda was somewhat forgotten as Dunmore heatedly discussed tactics with Eric.

Eric calmly disagreed on many points. "I have fought the Indians before, Governor. They are not cowards, and their practices are not so different from our own at times. The white men on the frontier take scalps as often as the Indians. The Indians themselves are fierce fighters who were never taught to stand in neat lines. They attack from the brush, they attack in darkness, and they must never, never be taken lightly as simple savages. Especially not the Shawnee."

Amanda shivered, suddenly aware that she did not want Eric Cameron falling beneath a Shawnee's scalping knife. He was leaning back quite calmly and comfortably in his chair, dauntless, she thought, yet aware. She set down her fork, paling.

"Gentlemen! Our conversation is distressing the lady!" Lord Hastings protested.

"Is it?" Eric, amused, was looking her way. "I do apologize most deeply, Amanda."

She smiled, standing quickly. "I do believe I could benefit from some fresh air. If you gentlemen will just excuse me. . . ."

They all stood, but she gave none the chance to protest, sweeping quickly from the dining room and out into the hall. She raced out to the front porch and stared down the endless drive before the house.

"Lady Amanda!"

She turned, truly distressed to discover that Lord Hastings had followed her. She tried to smile as he waddled to her, panting. She backed away from him, but he reached for her hands. "Are you unwell?" he asked.

"No, no, I'm so sorry that you left the meal—"

"I'm so sorry that you were distressed. Yet perhaps, my dear, it is best that you realize that young Cameron may not return." He clicked his tongue unhappily against his cheeks.

"Oh, I . . . I'm sure that Eric will return. He's fought the Indians before. He will take care."

"Still . . . my dear, I hope that you do not think of me unkindly."

"No . . . of course not, Lord Hastings. I shall never forget all the wonderful hunts at your estate when I was a child."

"You are a child no more, Amanda. And you must not be worried for the future. I would have you know now that if Eric does not return from the front, I will be there for you. I know that I am an old man, but I am one who is humbly and deeply in love with you. I have spoken with your father and if anything does not go as planned, well, then he has agreed that I should be your husband." She tried not to gaze at him in horror, but a light in his beady dark eyes made her feel as if she would spew her meal all over his fine silk shirt. She swallowed hard, gaping at him. Then she realized that the other men were coming out on the porch, Eric between her father and the governor.

"How . . . kind," she told Lord Hastings. She felt cold, sick, imagining his fleshy hands upon her. She would die first, she thought.

"How very, very kind, but . . . you see, we, er, we cannot wait. We cannot wait—"

"Cannot wait for what?" her father boomed out.

She moistened her lips. Eric was watching her, amused once again. She ignored his look, smiled regretfully at Hastings, then hurried past him and slipped her arm through Eric's. "We—we have agreed that we cannot wait for Eric to return. We're going to be married right away."

"What? But there are just days before we are due to leave for the frontier—" the governor protested.

"Yes, yes, of course," Eric murmured, his cobalt eyes falling upon her with a sizzle. "And we should have spoken earlier, Amanda, we should have told them right away." His eyes remained upon hers, daring her. "Alas, it is the very thought that I could die that has prompted us to this measure. I would leave an heir behind if I could."

"But you cannot marry so quickly—" Sterling began.

"Your pardon, sir! Lord Dunmore can give us a special license, and the service can be quiet and performed at Bruton Parish within the week."

"It's quite inappropriate—" Nigel began.

"I like it," the governor said. His Scots burr sounded for just a moment and his brown eyes sparkled. "I like it very well. We shall marry our little loyalist to this doubtful fellow and keep him in line, what do you say?"

They all laughed. The tension lay far beneath the comment, and at the moment, it was ignored by them all.

"Perhaps, under these circumstances, Amanda should return with me to Williamsburg," Sterling said.

"No!" Eric retorted. So quickly that it was almost rude. He softened his speech, smiling. "Gentlemen, we should all spend the night here and go into town tomorrow."

"Splendid!" the governor agreed.

He clamped his hand on Sterling's shoulder. "A good match, Nigel. Come, let's imbibe upon your son-in-law's spirits and toast to your future grandchildren!"

Lord Dunmore led Sterling back toward the house. Lord Hastings looked from the older men to the young people, then sighed and headed toward the house. When they were alone at last, Amanda struggled to free herself from Eric's hold. He did not release her. She tossed back her head to stare into his eyes.

"I'm delighted," he murmured. "What brought on this sudden ardor upon your part? Have you discovered if not love, then lust for me at last?"

"Don't be absurd. I've discovered . . . I've discovered Lord Hastings's four-score chins," she retorted.

His smile deepened. A dimple showed against his cheek and his eyes were touched by a silver glitter born of the very devil. "You have cast yourself into this. You will not renege?"

She swallowed, shaking her head. She could not breathe. "No. No, I will not renege."

"You needn't say that as if you were going to your execution."

"That is how I feel."

He threw back his head and laughed, then he lifted her chin with his finger, searching out her eyes. "You are mistaken. I will prove to you that it will be fun."

"Fun!" She shivered. "It cannot be fun. Not for a wife."

"But it will be," he promised her. His eyes seemed to pour down upon her with fierce and unyielding promise. His fingers stroked over her throat and then his lips touched down on hers. Her eyes closed and she felt as if demons set fire throughout her, causing a cascade of searing liquid to dance against her limbs. Then his lips left hers and touched down upon the arch of her throat, and the sensations increased. She swallowed suddenly, tearing away. Puzzled, he caught her hand and pulled her back. Color blazed in her cheeks.

"What in God's name is wrong with you?" he demanded.

"It isn't—right!" She gasped.

Angrily he held her against him, lifting her chin once more to meet the tumult in her eyes. "Not right? Lady, you are not a harlot I have chosen for the night. We are to marry."

She lowered her lashes. "Let me go, please! We are not married as yet."

He did not let her go. "Tomorrow we will be. And when the words are said and you are my wife, don't think that you can turn to me and trust in my honor to leave you be. I am taking a wife because I desire one. You do understand that."

"Yes!" She wrenched free from him and turned and ran down the steps. He started to follow her and then paused, then turned to reenter the house.

———

That night Amanda was too nervous to remember the dark-haired man with whom Danielle had been having her curious animated conversation. She paced the room endlessly, having preferred supper on a tray to the gentlemen's company that evening. She walked back and forth telling Danielle that she was insane, but that she did not know what else to do. Danielle was quiet, but Amanda did not even notice.

She ceased her pacing when a knock came on the door at about eight o'clock.

She did not answer it—her father opened the door and stepped into the room. He took one look at Danielle and said curtly, "Go." The woman glanced toward Amanda but obeyed him quickly enough.

He closed the door behind Danielle. "So you are going to marry him tomorrow."

"Yes, Father. It's what you want, isn't it?"

"Yes. But I want you to remember that even if you are his wife, you remain my daughter."

"Meaning?"

"You will do as I say."

She smiled, glad of her coming marriage for one reason. Eric Cameron could protect her from anything. "He is a forceful man. He might disagree."

"He cannot save Damien Roswell's neck from the hangman."

She paled, her pleasure cleanly erased. Sterling kept talking, ignoring her. "Damien is accompanying Lord Cameron to the front, did you know that? No, I did not suppose so. Perhaps one of them will die. It will be interesting to see."

He turned to leave her. "Don't forget how very much of your future I still hold, my dear, dear child."

The door closed. Amanda sank down on the bed, shaking.

Eric Cameron could not protect her from everything.

In the morning Danielle came to her very early. Amanda dressed numbly. Danielle had chosen a soft blue-gray gown for her with pearls stitched into the lacing. She did not bind or cover Amanda's hair, but let it stream down upon the gown like a ripple of dark fire. When Amanda was ready, she walked down the stairs. The servants were lined up on the stairs. A glass was raised to her, and she was welcomed among them as Lady Cameron. She thanked them but had gone so pale that she could not manage a smile.

She remained numb for the long drive back to Williamsburg. She and Danielle rode alone, for Eric had gone in with the others even earlier to make the arrangements.

Danielle was pleased about the marriage, if distressed about the rush. "There should have been time for a wedding gown, for the church to properly announce the ceremony. But it is good, *mais oui,* it is good. You will be out of that monster's clutches forever!"

"That monster," Amanda knew, was her father. But Danielle was wrong. She was not out of his clutches.

In Williamsburg she was taken to the governor's palace. His countess very kindly and enthusiastically helped her freshen up from the journey. She chatted very happily about her wedding day, and apologized for the indisposition that had kept her from entertaining Amanda on her last visit. "I do hope that John was gracious."

"Very gracious," Amanda agreed. He had threatened her cousin's life—graciously.

But then the countess offered her a stiff brandy. "A gentleman's drink perhaps, but for the prewedding tremors, a lady's drink as well!"

Amanda drank a lot of it. It seemed to be one way to endure the ceremony.

Despite the haste of the wedding, the Bruton Parish Church was quickly filled. Many of the men who had been in town for the dissolved House—who would soon be attending the Continental Congress—came to see Lord Cameron take his bride. As she walked down the aisle on her father's arm, Amanda noted that it was a curious assembly indeed. The governor laughed and joked with the very men whose meeting he had so recently dissolved. Lady Geneva had come, and squeezed her hand as she passed by. Colonel Washington was there, she saw, nodding to Eric with a pleased grin on his sober countenance. She did not see Damien, and that worried her, as he had been invited. Actually, everything worried her.

She was going to pass out, she thought. But she could not. Nigel Sterling passed her hand over to Eric, and the reverend stepped forward to tie their wrists together with white ribbon.

And then he began to speak.

Amanda did not hear his words. She felt the heat of the small church, and she heard the muffled whisperings of the people in the pews. She felt Eric standing beside her, and she heard the clear, well-modulated tones of his vows. Then she heard a pause, and she forced herself to speak even as she wondered at the words she said. She swore to love, honor, and obey.

Suddenly the reverend was smiling and suggesting that Eric might kiss his bride. Then his lips were upon hers, and fierce as she had never felt them before. The breath was robbed from her body and very nearly her life. It was not so different from any other of his demanding kisses except that it seemed ever more so. It was not a taunt . . . it was a possession, she thought.

There was a cry, and Lady Geneva surged forward, laughing, kissing her, then kissing her groom with something a little less than propriety. But that didn't seem to matter, for the peculiar assemblage was in a joyous mood. Dunmore kissed her deeply, then others in the council, and then members of the House of Burgesses.

There were so many people around her. Unable to breathe and feeling terribly trapped, she finally managed to escape through the crowd and exit the church into the cemetery. There she leaned against the cold wall, closing her eyes and breathing deeply. She opened her eyes to discover that Washington had followed her. Tall, with soft blue-gray eyes, he smiled her way ruefully. "Are you all right, Lady Cameron?"

Cameron. It was her name now, she thought. She opened her mouth to answer the man, but no words would come, and she knew that her eyes were wary. She nodded.

Washington smiled at her. "If I can ever help you, please do not hesitate to come to me. I see your husband coming. I wish you long life and happiness, milady, and I hope that you will visit us at Mount Vernon. We shall all pray for peace."

"Yes, we will pray for peace!" she agreed. The trees rustled over their heads, and for a moment they smiled at one another and shared something. Then the moment was broken, for Damien had discovered her.

He flashed Washington his rogue's smile, then kissed his cousin warmly. "Felicitations, Lady Cameron!"

"Damien! I did not see you!"

"I was in the church. I would not have missed it!" He swept her off her feet and swirled her around, then he suddenly paused, laughing. "Uh-oh. Lord Cameron! Well, er, here she is! Your bride!"

He thrust Amanda into Eric's arms. So she wouldn't be dropped between the two men, she curled her arms around her husband's neck and met his gaze. He smiled down at her, and the tenderness in his smile warmed her. She offered a tentative smile in turn, and then he was laughing at something someone was saying, and then agreeing that the wine and ale were flowing freely at his town house.

It wasn't much of a walk to the town house. Eric carried her all the way there with a score of wellwishers behind them. She remembered little more of the afternoon, for despite his smile she was very, very nervous and so she kept her glass of Madeira filled and refilled, perhaps far too often. She thought that they would party into the night, but the wellwishers were still in abundance when Eric came to her, sweeping her into his arms again. Panic seized her as she felt his arms close around her.

"What—"

"We're going home."

"Home?"

"Cameron Hall."

"But—" she said, then fell silent, for she was glad of it. The long drive would delay their time alone together, the time that she was dreading, that now held her in pure terror. She had sold herself today, to a devil or a traitor, she knew not which. She had done so with open eyes, yet now she was afraid.

"Speech!" someone shouted out, and Eric gave one, waxing on eloquently about love—and then Shawnees, ending with an apology that all must be so quick since the darned Shawnees didn't care a whit about his love. Laughter followed them out to his carriage. He deposited her inside first, then climbed in beside her. Danielle would follow in her own coach.

Amanda closed her eyes as the horses clattered down the street, afraid to acknowledge the man beside her. He shifted suddenly, and her eyes flew open, for she was afraid that he meant to take her into his arms. He did not. He watched her from the shadows of the carriage. "It will be a long drive. You've been, er, imbibing quite freely. Perhaps you should try to sleep."

"Ladies do not imbibe," she told him.

"Nor do they swear, and Damien tells me that you could put a cattle drover to shame."

Lowering her lashes, she flushed and informed him that it was very rude of him to say so. He laughed and slipped an arm about her, drawing her upon his lap. She looked up at him in the shadows, ready to protest, then felt his fingers smoothing back her hair. "Rest, Amanda."

She did so. She fell asleep and did not waken until he had lifted her from the carriage and carried her up the stairs. Then her eyes widened with renewed panic, for this was it, she was home. She wondered where he would carry her. He took her past the portraits and into his room, and lay her down upon the huge bed there. He straightened then. "I will send Danielle to you, her coach has arrived behind us, I am sure."

He left her and she sprang up. A steaming hip bath awaited her by the fire. She began to pace, ruing the fact that she had slept away many of the effects of the wine.

The door opened. Danielle came in and hugged her quickly. Amanda stepped back, wringing her hands. "I can't do this!"

"There, there, love, you can!" Danielle protested. She turned her about and unhooked Amanda's gown, sliding it down from her shoulders. Amanda stepped from it.

"I can't breathe."

"It's your corset." Danielle pulled away her shift, then untied her corset. It didn't help. She still couldn't breathe. Danielle had to lead her to the bed to sit down so that she could remove her shoes and hose and garters. Then she shivered desperately as the breeze hit her naked flesh.

"Come, into the hip tub before you catch your death!" Danielle chided.

Amanda found herself in the bath smelling the sweet scent of rosewater. She sank back as Danielle lifted her hair carefully away from the water. The woman dropped her a round ball of French soap and a cloth, and Amanda automatically picked them up and sudsed the cloth, then her body. Then she started to shiver. Danielle handed her a little glass.

"Brandy."

"Oh, thank God!"

She nearly inhaled the liquid. "Again!" she begged Danielle, gasping. Danielle refilled her glass, and she swallowed it down quickly again. Then she was furious with herself. She was behaving like such a coward. Just who did he think that he was, terrifying her so? He had wanted the marriage. She just wasn't ready for this side of it. He would understand. She would make him.

She scrubbed herself to a glow then stood and grabbed for the towel Danielle offered her. Then she stood shivering as Danielle dropped a shear silk and lace gown over her head. The night was cool, despite the fire. She did not shake with fear, she absolutely assured herself.

"Bonsoir, ma petite!" Danielle told her, kissing her cheek tenderly.

"You're leaving!" Amanda gasped.

"But of course," Danielle said, shaking her head. But she had not left when the door suddenly opened, and Eric appeared.

His dark hair was damp, as if he had bathed elsewhere. He was clad in a long velvet robe that tied at his waist and fell nearly to his ankles. A smattering of dark hair showed at the neck of the robe where it lay open against his chest. Amanda discovered herself staring at his chest and losing the strength to stand.

"Pardonnez-moi!" Danielle said quickly.

"Bonsoir, Danielle," he said, his eyes locked on Amanda.

Danielle left them and the door closed behind her. Amanda moistened her lips and cleared her throat. She discovered herself backing toward the windows. "Eric . . ."

"Yes?" He was walking toward her. He had the grace of a wildcat and the same sure stride of determination.

"I . . . uh . . . I can't."

"Can't?"

"I can't go through with this."

"Oh?" He paused, his smile polite. "What do you mean, can't?"

"I . . ." She looked down at her gown. Horror filled her as she realized that the gossamer gown delineated the rouge crests of her nipples and the red-gold triangle at the juncture of her thighs. She drew her eyes quickly back to his, wishing that she could snatch the curtains from the walls to cover herself. He was coming toward her again. She shook her head.

"Eric, I beg of you, be a gentleman and understand . . ."

He paused again, as if carefully weighing his decision. "No."

"No!"

He shook his head and kept coming for her. "I told you yesterday what I would expect. You gave me your word that you would not renege."

"I didn't intend to renege. I swear it. Eric, please try to understand. I don't know you—"

"By the end of the night, my love, you will know me very well."

"Eric, honest to God, I would like to! I can't—"

He caught her arm and pulled her hard against him. Beneath the robe she felt the pulse and vitality of his body, for her gown lay as nothing but mist between them. She felt his male shaft, rising. She looked into his eyes and saw the darkness within them and the silver glitter of his laughter as he lowered his head to whisper against her lips.

"But you can, my love. Honest to God, you can." He lifted her into his arms. "Now, if you don't mind, Amanda, I'd just as soon have no more of the deity on my wedding night." He tossed her down into the softness of the bed. Even as she struggled to rise she heard his laughter, then his weight was upon her, bearing her ever farther downward into the depths of the bed.

9

HE FELT AS IF SHE WERE IMMERSED WITHIN lightness and magic and clouds, and yet at the same time Amanda keenly felt everything about her. She felt the rush of the river wind and the warmth and flicker of the candles and the fire. And she felt the hard-muscled body and heat of the man on top of her, barely clad in the robe, and nearly naked against her. But even as she brought her arms against his chest, she felt the simple fascination of touching him there, of feeling the dark, crisp hair with her fingertips, of knowing the ripple of sinew and muscle beneath it. When she looked up she saw that he was smiling, no, laughing.

"Don't you dare gloat and laugh at me!" she cried, but his smile deepened and his laughter was haunting, as was the silver-blue decadence in his eyes. He planted a kiss upon her forehead, for she was powerless to move, and then his lips brushed her cheeks and her mouth, causing her to ache for more. His words fell softly against her flesh, and they, too, were a curious caress. "I'm not laughing at you, my love, and if I gloat, well, then you will have to forgive me."

"I forgive you nothing!" she retorted, meeting his eyes in the candlelight that made a devil's flame of them. It was best to meet his eyes. She did not dare look upon him. It was enough that she felt him.

"No, you would not!" he whispered. "Nor would you give up any fight, and yet you are, my little hawk, suddenly a sparrow in this bed."

"Sparrow!" She surged hard against his chest. A gasp escaped her as she saw that he had purposely goaded her to action, that pressing against him only served to accent all that was male and relentless, all that was hard and unyielding about him. Her fingers closed over his arms. As she felt the tension and size of the muscle there, she knew that she would never dislodge him. Despite herself she began to tremble. She moistened her lips to speak, but that was when he chose to kiss her at last. His tongue penetrated into the far recesses of her mouth, touching her as if he entered into her soul. Each movement was so slow, and so filling, and each robbed her of more breath, each made her tremble with a greater fever. His face rose above hers in the darkness, and he smiled, tracing his finger over the wetness of her lips. "So the hawk returns. You are never afraid, Amanda. Why fear me now?"

"I do not fear you," she whispered.

"And you must not," he told her. "I have not lied to you. Life is meant to be lived, to be enjoyed, my love, aye, even here! And I promise you, I will teach you that it is so."

"If you would do this tonight, it will be rape, and I swear that I will never forgive you."

"It will not be rape."

"It will!" she cried in sudden panic, slamming a fist between them, seeking any way to fight his weight and strength. In a burst of desperate new energy she thrust against him with all her strength, her knee connecting with his masculine anatomy.

At first she didn't comprehend what she had done.

He was suddenly still and taut, his features harsh, pained. At first all she realized was that he had eased his hold upon her. She slammed hard against him again, managing to escape his hold.

Before she could roll off the bed, she felt a hard tug upon her gown. The material ripped down her side as she cried out and tried to rise. She rolled and fell to the floor.

His foot landed hard upon her gown and she looked up into his face. He was furious. And he was reaching down for her. "Amanda, my love, you are a true bitch."

"No," she whispered. She didn't know if she denied his words, or the things yet to come between them that night. "No!" she breathed again, frantically trying to tug her gown free. She could not endure him towering over her so, and she couldn't cease her trembling. She realized then that she had really hurt him and she was suddenly afraid. She had been a fool. She should have continued to try to reason with him.

"I did not mean to hurt you!" she cried.

"Oh? Was that your idea of a gentle, wifely caress? Then, my dear, you are sorely in need of instruction."

She did not like the look upon his face at all, he had not forgiven her. "Eric—"

"Get up, Amanda!" He reached down a hand to her.

She stared at it, and knew that she could never take it.

She ripped free from the patch of gown beneath his foot, rose, and tore across the room. She spun around to face him again with her back to the wall. With almost casual strides he pursued her, pausing there, not touching her, but imprisoning her by placing his hands upon the wall on either side of her head. He smiled. "We spoke of this. Nothing, nothing, my love, will change the course of this night. Be it whatever it shall be."

She gasped, startled, and tried to strike out as he swiftly pulled her into his arms. She kicked and writhed, but he carried her back to the bed and cast her down upon it. She tried to rise, but he was on top of her, catching her wrists and holding them high above her head with one hand.

"We will be man and wife this night," he promised her savagely.

Then he captured her cheek with his free hand, and he kissed her. Kissed her thoroughly, passionately, open-mouthed, stealing her breath and strength and reason, and shattering her will with the reckless plunder of his tongue. She did not know how long the kiss went on between them. When he took his lips from hers, his eyes were passionate, his words were harsh. "You're my wife, Amanda. Your commitment to lie with me in this bed was made when you spoke your vows to me, and, lady, you may not now change your mind!"

She stared at him, knowing that she would fight him no matter what his words, yet wondering at the fierce new pounding in her heart. She hated him.

Yet . . . she might even want him.

He released her wrists, placed his palms over hers, and threaded her fingers with his own, holding them steady by the sides of her head. Her hair flamed out over their entwined fingers, radiantly red in the firelight. He smiled again as she stared at him, her eyes wide and emerald in that same haunting light.

He had never wanted her more, never needed her with such a frightening urgency. He had sworn to himself that he would go gently; he had not expected her to fight so viciously, nor had he expected the anger that would cause him to treat her so. Nor had he expected to feel a surge so strong within himself that it could not be denied. She had said that it would be rape.

Grimly he determined that it would not be so, and yet he knew that one way or another, he would have her. There was no way that he would let her go this night. No way that she would not sleep beside him, his wife in fact, his marriage consummated.

He spoke to her on a tense breath of air. "I will not take you, madame, until you give me leave. But you will not stop me from seeking that permission."

Her fingers curled tightly against his. "I will never give my leave to you."

"Be still, you are not to deny my kiss, my touch . . ."

A denial did form on her lips, but it never found voice. His mouth touched down upon hers, then wandered with abandon, effortlessly, slowly. His lips teased her flesh and her earlobes. She stared at the ceiling as his kisses covered her throat, hovering ever closer to the lace and gossamer of her gown where it fell low against her breasts. She felt his sex, engorged and hot against her thighs, and she ignored the heat and trembling within her own body and hoped that, pray God, it would be over swiftly.

But it was not. His own desires did not seem to affect his easy leisure, and as his hot breath swirled against the lobe of her ear, some sweet stirring took root and found life within her. She closed her eyes and gasped, for his hands were moving with the same lazy purpose as his lips. He lay his palm against her breast and his fingers closed over the mound, his thumb playing against the nipple. She twisted with the startling sensation, burying her face against his throat, a choking sound escaping her as his lips followed the movement of his hand upon her right breast, closing hotly about her nipple, teasing the swollen bud mercilessly. He repeated the evocative act upon her left breast, as if he would not leave that mound cold and forsaken. When he was done with the taunting play she was nearly limp against him, determined never to see his face again, for she was aware of the surge of her body against his. She felt his fingers upon her naked thigh, drawing her gown high above her hip. She twisted against him, trying to capture his hand, to prevent its wandering over her. The tear in the gown gave him such easy access to her flesh, and she felt the rough stroke of his palm so acutely upon her naked hip and belly. She writhed to free herself from him, but he did not seem to notice.

Impatience seized him when the gown caught beneath his own weight and he swore, destroying the rest of the garment as he rended the delicate fabric to pieces in a single movement. "Damn you!" Amanda swore, her eyes upon his, wide with anger and alarm, her protest frantic. "You've ruined the gown—"

"My love, God rot the gown!" he said flatly, pulling the remnants of silk from her body and the bed. Amanda grasped for the disappearing fabric, then found herself entirely naked and captured by his arm and his thigh. She was amazed at the emotion that welled within her, the fury, the fear . . . and the tense excitement. "You'd said you'd not take me until I gave you leave!"

"You, love, have not held to your part of the bargain."

"My part! I want no part of this!"

"You do, Amanda. You are flesh and blood, lady. You are ripe and I shall prove to you that married life is no hardship. Lie still, lady, and let me touch you. Better yet, do not lie still, but twist and writhe beneath me, press yourself against me," he ordered her, his eyes hard and demanding upon hers.

She felt what his words implied. Felt his body with the length of her own. Completely naked beneath him, she tried to whisper words to disavow him. She wanted to fight him so badly, and yet she was so suddenly still. His leg was cast upon hers, powerful, muscular, she could not escape him if she chose. She did not know if she chose. There was a rushing all about her, a startling fire within her. She felt it as she saw his naked thigh draped upon her own beneath the rising hem of his robe. She felt it deep within her stomach, and deeper still, at the juncture of her thighs. Hot and frantic, it coiled tighter and tighter and she both dreaded and eagerly anticipated his touch.

She swallowed sharply and he watched the length of her throat, watched where her heart showed its frantic beat against the swan's column.

"Eric—"

"Be still!" he commanded her. He pressed his lips against the pulse at her throat, moving his hands upon her, his fingers stroking the length of her with a hunger he could not deny. He touched her thighs and allowing his touch to brush the striking red triangle at the apex of her thighs, and he went onward to explore her belly and waist, the deep valley between her breasts. Her fingers curled over his shoulders, her nails digging heedlessly into his flesh.

Suddenly he drew up, casting his robe aside.

When he stared down upon his wife, her eyes were closed, her lush lashes dark above her cheeks, her lips parted, her breath rushing from them. Her breasts rose in swift and beautiful agitation. He found himself pausing for the simple pleasure of seeing her body before he lowered himself to touch it again. The tendrils of her hair lay like laps of flame upon the pillow, like liquid fire, spilling into him, haunting him. The fever that had seized him the first time he had seen her in

Damien's arms came home to him then, causing him to tremble with the prospect of his longing. He hurriedly sank back down, afraid of breaking the spell that lay upon her, so fragile was her consent to his will. She was his wife; he could have her as he pleased, and no man could gainsay him. He wanted more.

He caught her shapely limbs, parting them and lying between them so that her eyes opened with alarm. A gasp escaped her and her eyes closed as a word of protest tore from her. With a wicked smile he cast his hands beneath her buttocks, lifting her hips. He buried his face within the fascinating texture of the tempting sable-red triangle, his tongue ravaging her with a shocking, seductive invasion. Her fingers tore into his hair, she writhed, she cried out.

"Nay . . . !"

"Aye, my love," he murmured, his breath hot against her delicate flesh. She could not fight the weight of his shoulders, nor would he show mercy now.

"My God, 'tis wicked—"

"God, madame, has blessed our union. And love, lady, is wicked and beautiful, as it will be between us."

She gasped again, but the sound of it was lost in a cry, for he curled his fingers within those that tugged upon his hair, and he had his way with leisure and purpose, finding the sweet bud wherein her own desire lay, touching upon her very innocence. She thrashed upon the bed, seeking to escape him, seeking then to know more of him. He felt the change within her as he ruthlessly captured her sensuality, felt the surge of her body, tasted the nectar of her warmth as she writhed against him, seeking release from all that he had nurtured within her. Frantic whimpers fell from her lips, and her hips undulated in an ever-growing rhythm. Then she stiffened, straining, crying out, and the sweetness of climax exploded from within her. He lost no time but rose above her, the full weight of his body wedged between lovely length of her thighs. "Madame, would you stop me?" he demanded.

She lay silent, her eyes closed. He leaned low against her, demanding more emphatically, "Amanda! Shall I have my wife this night?"

Her lips parted just slightly. He lay his palm against her breast, bringing his words to the hollow of her throat. "Amanda—"

"Yes!" It was a pained whisper that tore from her throat. Then she cried out, her eyes opening for a moment of emerald anguish, then closing again as her arms wound around him. She could not meet his gaze, he knew, and he did not care, not at that moment. He gritted his teeth, his muscles clenching, demanding that despite his state of desperation, he take his wife with care. He moved against her, the tip of his shaft coming into the contact with the barrier of innocence. A cry of pain and protest rose to her lips no matter how he had prepared her; he closed over that cry with his kiss and entered into her like silk and steel. Her nails dug into his flesh again, her head fell back. He moved slowly, so slowly, until she had taken all of him into her, whispering assurances all the while. Her eyes remained closed, her face pale, but once she had accepted him, he began to move. He fought the wave of stark dark desire that seized him and brought his rhythm to her slowly. He had proven that passion dwelled within her, he need only ignite it again.

He touched her as he moved, stroking her breasts, her cheeks, her breasts again. He touched her lips with his own and seared her with his kiss. Her lips parted, a soft moan escaped her, and then triumph seized him, for she was moving again. Moving with his thrust and surge, undulating, like a wave of fire, beneath him.

Somewhere in the tempest that followed he allowed himself the sheer pleasure of having her at last, of burying himself within the beauty of her molten sheath. All the reckless abandon that he had denied himself burst forth, and he took her in raw, blinding desire, his tension and energy relentless, then finding fruition in a volatile combustion that cast him shuddering deep, deep within her time and time again. The pleasure was so great that he saw blackness as the veil of release first lifted from him, then, in alarm, he stiffened against her. He exhaled, feeling the trickle of sweat seep down his chest, and then he exhaled again, feeling that she still lay, wracked with tremors, beneath him. He held her tight, kissing her forehead, then pulling back to see how the moon and the firelight fell over her sleek body.

Her hair was entwined about them both. She did not open her eyes until he touched her cheek, then they came wide upon him, and she groaned, trying to twist away in some new horror. Alarmed and impatient, he dragged her back. "Madame, what—"

She bent her head against him, whispering fervently, "It is not right! Oh, God, what you have done to me—"

"I am baffled, love. What have I done that no other husband, young Tarryton or multichinned Hastings, would not?"

"It isn't that!" she whispered.

"Is it me? Forgive me, milady, but I thought that I caused you as little pain as possible. Nay, call me an egotist as you are so wont to do, and yet still, I would swear I caused pleasure."

"Oh!"

She almost turned from him. He caught her shoulders and lay her back, crawling above her and demanding now that she meet his eyes. "What is it?"

She moistened her lips. "It is not you. It is me!"

He sank back, careful to keep his weight upon his haunches. "You . . ."

She closed her eyes. He had never imagined such a look of bleak misery. "Milord," she said hollowly, "only a woman of a different variety should . . . feel so."

The last he did not even hear, for the whisper had grown so soft upon her lips. "Who told you that?" he demanded so harshly that her eyes flew open again.

"It's the way—you must be horrified."

"No, milady, it is not the way of anything, and I am not horrified but delighted. You are my wife. Warm and fascinating in my bed, and I confess, I am evermore enchanted. If I am horrified, it is because I must leave you so soon."

Her eyes were so wide, so very vulnerable then. What was it that she had feared so greatly? He wanted then to protect her so fiercely from all the hurts of the world. He swept her into his arms, whispering to her fervently, "Tell me! What has done this to you!"

"I cannot tell you!" she whispered, but she did not press away from him. Rather she curled close, her small hands knotted but against his chest, her head bowed beneath his chin. He inhaled the fragrance of her hair, and he swore then, to himself alone, that he would love her until the day that he died, defend her against all odds.

He stroked back her hair. "Shh . . . I will not ask you again. When you can trust me, tell me. Until then, believe me when I say that you are more exquisite than I dared dream, that I am well pleased." He hesitated a moment. "I did promise that it would be enjoyable."

She shuddered suddenly and he laughed, running his finger around her ear. "Well, madame, is it not enjoyable?"

"That's a terrible thing to ask me, sir!"

"Then I will show you again!" he swore, and swept her beneath him. Her eyes went very wide, but then a smile curved her lips. He kissed her.

And he loved her again, bringing her once more to an exquisite peak of pleasure and finding that agony and ecstasy again himself. Exhausted and spent, she lay against him, and he held her tight, his hand below the sweet curve of her breast. He thought that she slept when she whispered to him.

"Milord?" Her voice was soft and pale and lazy.

"Aye, love?"

"Indeed . . . I do suppose that one might call this . . . enjoyable."

He smiled, and he allowed his eyes to close. He did not think that he had ever slept so deeply, or so well.

———

In the days that followed Amanda came to wonder that she had ever thought to refuse Eric. He was demanding, voracious, unexpected, and always exciting, and most of all, he lived up to his promise that life should be lived and that it could be enjoyable. There was an exceptional energy about him in those days when he knew he would leave so soon. Awaking to discover that he was down with the troops, she would take great care with her dress, and start down the stairs only to discover that he had finished with drilling for the day and was running up the stairs even as she began to descend them. No protest stilled him then, and she would be swept into his arms, laughing, and all her careful detail to her appearance would be for naught since it seemed to take him less than seconds to disrobe her.

They rode over his acreage and the land of the original Hundred and she met many of the landowners and planters, artisans and merchants who made their homes near Eric's. They were always welcomed warmly and, though tea was no longer served and more and more women were dressing in homespun, there seemed to be little talk of politics then, and much more discussion of homes and estates and repair and planting. Many men were eagerly working their prize horses, for racing was a prime diversion of the Tidewater aristocrats, and nothing ceased their talk of good horseflesh.

Despite the seemingly endless troops camped out on the lawns of Cameron Hall, Eric saw to it that he showed Amanda their immediate realm. As they walked down to the cemetery one afternoon, he told her tales of a great-great-aunt who had married a Pamunkee Indian and whose several times great-grand-children were the half-dozen blue-eyed, blond Clark children they had met on a nearby estate the day before. They left the cemetery and he walked her on toward the river until she found herself in a pine-arbored copse. She could feel the river's breeze there, and distantly she could hear the fife and bugle of the men who marched and drilled upon the hill. Eric drew her into his arms, and before she could protest the wicked determination in his arms, she found herself lain upon the soft pine-strewn earth, looking up into a dazzle of sunlight that wavered with the motion of the tree branches. He laid his hands upon the laces of her gown and she gasped, protesting with outrage that they could not. She continued to protest, but his arguments were fast, his hands faster still, and before she knew it she was naked upon the raw, sweet-smelling earth, laughing and arguing in one, and then unable to laugh or argue for the passion that blazed there between them was shocking and intense, bursting upon them like the radiance of the dappled sun rays. And when they lay still the river breeze swept sensually over their dampened bodies, adding something of the feel of an intimate Eden to the place. She shivered, and he warmed her with his body. She stroked his cheek and he caught her hand, bringing it down against him, teaching her to hold and stroke the bold arousal the breeze and her nearness had wrought. She did not think to argue then, for his kisses filled her as deeply as the shaft of his body, and the warmth and liquid fire that burned into her mingled from the force of his mouth and that of his loins. Twilight came, and with it the cool of the night, before they roused themselves at last, dressed, and returned to the house.

That night they had their first argument as man and wife, yet there was nothing new in the gist of it.

Damien arrived to serve with Eric, commissioned a captain to command one of the companies he himself had raised. Amanda, delighted to see him, greeted him in the parlor. He was all enthusiasm for the cause, but he was even more enthusiastic about the events taking place in Williamsburg and beyond. Washington had returned to Mount Vernon, so Damien said, and Patrick Henry and Edmund Pendleton had stopped there before all three men headed for the Philadelphia Continental Congress. Rumors were running rampant that no gentle words for the Crown would be spoken.

Eric stood by the mantel as Damien spoke, lighting his pipe from the fire with a wick. He was silent as Damien went on. "Things are about to change. Mark my words, milord, I daresay that the very men who govern our colonies will all be looking over their shoulders to see to the sheriffs with arrest warrants!"

"I daresay that it would be quite difficult for a handful of soldiers to arrest the whole congress," Eric told him.

"It will depend on which way many hearts lie, won't it, sir? It will depend on where the power lies. If the militia leaders side with the Crown—or the patriots."

"Stop it, Damien!" Amanda commanded him. "You are talking about treason."

"Mandy, Mandy, do stop with this treason nonsense! The will of the people must prevail." Damien leaned forward on his seat. "Lord Cameron, it will be interesting indeed to travel west once again. When the Shawnee are subdued, treaties might be made that could be of grave importance later. And the French arms to be purchased on the coast are often in abundance—"

"Damien!" she snapped, rising from her chair and staring at Eric. "Make him stop this, Eric."

Eric's dark brows shot up. "Amanda, I cannot make him stop his mind from working—"

"You are his commander, Eric! I demand that you stop this talk of arms and war this very second."

"Amanda, this is my home," Eric reminded her, "and though I would do my utmost to give you any request, milady, I will not accept a demand."

She twirled about in a fury and exited the room, slamming the door with a vehemence that the servants could not miss. When Danielle came to her, saying that dinner was being served, she refused to dine and asked for a tray. She ordered a bath be brought up but not to the master bedchamber, rather to the one that adjoined it, the one with the locking door. Fuming and incensed, she locked herself in with a cup of warmed Madeira and the steaming water. She settled back, swearing that her husband would find himself duly chastised when he thought to be so crude to her.

Yet that was not to be the case. She had barely adjusted her long hair and lain back, the steam delightfully easing the pain from her, when the locked connecting door shattered and banged open upon its sagging hinges. His eyes dark and furious, his features those of a stranger's, Eric stood there. She gaped, then hastily closed her mouth in a fury of her own. "The lock meant that I did not wish you to enter!" she warned him heatedly.

"You married me, milady. I will enter where I wish."

His strides brought him quickly to her. In panic she rose, wet and streaming, ready to fight him with all of the fire of the worry and fear within her. "Stop it, Eric, don't you dare come near me, I am telling you—"

Her breath was swept from her as his arms came about her. He lifted her from the water, giving no thought to his fine brocade waistcoat and silk shirt. She struggled against him, wanting to hurt him, then suddenly wanting to escape him as she saw the light that her fight had brought to his eyes. "No!" she breathed, slamming hard upon his chest, yet he bore her down anyway, lying over her as he brought her atop the bed where she had thought to find her privacy. "I shall claw you to ribbons!" she warned him desperately.

"If you do so, Amanda, make sure it is with wifely passion, with cries of ecstasy upon your lips."

"Oh!" she cried, and tried to slam her knee against him, but he shifted his weight, and the gaze he gave her then shot daggers into her heart. "You fool, you will get Damien hanged and yourself hanged and I will not let you do this to me!"

He held her head between his hands and looked angrily into her eyes. "Politics will not enter into the bedroom," he told her firmly.

"I am a loyalist and you knew it when you married me, and you said that you'd not deny me my beliefs!"

"I do not deny you your beliefs, but I swear, lady, by all that is holy, you will not bring them to bed, and you will not slam doors or think to make a stricken, gelded fool of me because of them. Do you understand me?"

She thought for a moment, straining against him, her teeth gritted. Then she shouted out a vehement "No!"

His eyes darkened. She thought that he meant to strike her, his teeth were so tightly clenched. "Let me up!" she demanded in fear and fury.

"Madame, I will not!"

He dragged her hands up high over her head and held them easily despite her struggles and curses. His lips covered hers, trailed the valley between her breasts, then fondled the rouge crests, watching her eyes as he did so. She found that gaze upon her and knew that he read more within their depths than she wanted him to know. Suddenly, savagely, she twisted free from his hold, slamming her fists against his chest. She sought to roll free from him, but he threaded his fingers through her hair, dragging her back beneath him. His eyes sought hers again with war within them. He held her still, and his mouth captured hers. She thumped her fists against his shoulders, but he ignored the pain, demanding more and more with his lips and tongue. His hands stroked her sides and buttocks, and thighs, and his knee wedged them apart. He kissed her, and touched her, his kiss consuming, his touch ever more evocative. His lips parted from hers and she spoke his name, desperately trying to remember her argument. His kiss moved over her throat, to her collarbone, to her breast, and the passion of her fight became a flame of desire deep within her. Perhaps the need was even heightened by the torment of emotion. He did not disrobe, but adjusted his breeches and had her there with a startling fever and vengeance, and as he spent himself within her, she thought that she had passed over some strange line between what she had been before . . . and what she would be as his wife. Something indelible poured into her along with his seed that evening. She did not understand it. She whispered that she hated him even as her arms wound around him, she cried against him even as her body was wracked with the sweet shudders of ecstasy. The battle had receded between them, she thought. But it was far from over.

She felt his fingers upon her cheeks and only then did she realize that tears had escaped her. He was quickly up, guarded and hard, but anxious too. "Did I hurt you?"

She shook her head, trying not to meet his eyes.

"Amanda!"

"No! No, you did not hurt me."

He rolled from her, his back to her, then stood, adjusting his clothing. "Come down to the meal. There will be no talk of arms, and I swear that I will keep my eye upon your cousin."

"And smuggle arms yourself!" she whispered.

"What?"

"Nothing! Please, leave it be, nothing!"

"Come down then, and we shall close the subject."

"I—I cannot!" she whispered. "My God, all of the house will have heard that door shatter."

He reached for her hands, pulling her tight against him. His smile was suddenly wicked and taunting and challenging. "I did not suggest that you should slink down in shame, milady. Rather, my love, you should do so with laughter on your lips, your chin as high as ever, your glance one of the greatest disdain."

She pulled away from him. "The meal will be quite cold, I am certain."

"Dress, or I shall dress you myself."

She swore, she called him every name that would come to her tongue, but when he moved toward her, she determined that she would choose her gown, and do as he suggested. He helped her with corset and with her hooks despite the stiffness of her back, and when she was duly clad, he insisted that she sit so that he could comb out her hair. His fingers lingered on her shoulders as her hair fell down upon them. In the mirror she saw his hands upon her flesh, bare for the gown lay low upon her bosom, and she saw how very dark and masculine and large they were, and yet felt how very tender their brush upon her could be. She shivered, meeting his eyes in the mirror, and he smiled, with what emotion she did not know. "Lady, none could deny your beauty, nor the boldness of your spirit. Come, take my hand. You do grace this ancient hall and will, I expect, continue to do so. Even if they do decide to hang me."

She stood, shivers upon her heart, for even in the very depth of this battle, she knew then that she could not bear to see him hanged.

They started down the stairway together. Thom and Cassidy met them at the doors of the dining room. As they neared the pair, Eric suddenly laughed, as if he and Amanda shared some great joke, and he whispered against her ear. She turned to him, and a smile formed upon her lips, and she knew that the act had been very well executed. No one would wonder at the goings-on of the master and mistress, they were newlyweds, and prone to take their time.

She did not forgive Damien though. Not until the hour grew late, and she rose, begging that they continue to talk, but forgive her, for she was exhausted. Then she hugged her cousin fiercely, because she was afraid for him.

"Forgive me!" he whispered to her sorrowfully. "We have chosen different paths." He had never seemed older to her, or more serious or grave.

She said nothing, but turned away, not offering her cheek to her husband. There were no servants about to witness the act.

But when she went upstairs, she did not seek out a separate bed. She lay within the one they shared, and for a long while she remained awake, tormented by all that lay between them. Her eyes closed, and the hour grew very late. The fire dimmed, and she slept.

She awoke slowly, with the feel of his lips against her spine. She did not think at first but rather felt the delicious slow motion of his hands over her hip, stroking down upon her buttocks. His lips and tongue moved with rich and languorous ease over the silky flesh of her shoulders and back. Then she felt his body, bare and heated and rigid, thrust against her own. She started to twist, but he whispered against her ear, "Amanda. I leave with the morning light."

He drew her against him, kissing her nape, her throat, her shoulders. His hands fondled her breasts while he thrust into her from behind. The urgency touched her. Love was bittersweet, but something she would not deny. She did not want to think of the nights ahead.

"I do not retreat—"

"Nor surrender!" he agreed, but the words were meaningless, for she had given in to him that night, though his fervent words and his fierce cries of pleasure gave her some sense that perhaps she had not lost at all, that indeed perhaps he held the strength, but she held her own curious power.

The next morning when Amanda awoke she saw Eric standing before the window while the draperies rustled in the wind. Her muscles constricted tightly for she saw that he was dressed in a buckskin jacket with fringe and rugged leather leggings and high boots. She looked at him with confusion. It was so very early. But then she remembered that it had to be early, he was riding out this morning. He knew that she had awakened; he turned to her and walked back to the bed where she lay, sitting beside her. His gaze fell over her where she lay, and he reached out to touch her cheek. Cascades of her hair fell wildly over his fingers, and he smiled with a touch of bitter irony. "How very hard it is to leave you so. I sit here about to cast all honor and right to the wind and tell Dunmore that I cannot risk my neck for my soul is in chains."

She flushed, listening to his words. His thumb moved over her cheek and she was tempted to grab hold of his hand and beg him not to leave her, not when he had just taught her so very much about life and . . . was it love? she wondered. She had hated him so fiercely, feared him, needed him, and now she did not dare judge the seed of emotion that stirred so desperately in her heart. They had lived the days since their marriage in a fantasy, and now the world was intruding upon them. But in those days she had come to find an ever greater fascination in the strong planes and angles of his face, in the curve of his lip, in the light of his eyes. She had lain upon the bed with her lashes low, her eyes half closed, and she had watched the effortless grace of his body as he had dressed or undressed. She had touched the scars upon his shoulders and she had learned which he had sustained in the closing days of the French and Indian Wars, and which he had obtained as a child playing recklessly upon the docks. He did not love her, he had told her once, and she had labeled the emotion as lust. Were that what it was, then the same spellbound fever held her. She wanted to touch him, and so she reached out and laid her palm against his freshly shaven cheek. Then she dropped her covers, rising to kiss him, to breathe into that kiss the truth that she would miss him with all of her heart, that she would pray until the day that he returned that God keep him safe.

His lips parted from hers and he caught her palm, kissing it softly. His brow arched with humor but with tenderness too. "Dare I take this to mean that you will not be too disappointed if the Shawnee leave my scalp intact, despite all that occurred last night?"

She nodded, suddenly afraid to speak. She had loved once and had discovered then that love brought betrayal. Her own father had turned from her.

"Take care, my love. Take the greatest care," he told her.

"God watch you, Eric," she whispered.

"Tell me, what are your feelings of this marriage into which you so desperately plunged? Is it better to endure my temper than Lord Hastings's chins?" he asked, his lips still moving just above her own, the warmth of his words entering into her.

"I am not . . . displeased," she said, unable to meet his eyes. "Except upon occasion. What of you?" she demanded, looking at him at last.

"I knew what I wanted, madame, from the very moment that I saw your face," he told her.

His lips brushed hers. "Betray not my heart, Amanda, that is all that I ask." He rose and then was gone.

For long moments she lay in the bed, feeling the tingle of his kiss upon her lips. Then she cried out and leapt to her feet, throwing open her armoire to find a heavy white velvet dressing gown. She quickly hooked the garment about her and tore down the stairs. Thom stood in the hallway with a silver tray and a very traditional stirrup cup upon it. "May I?" she begged him, awaiting no answer but running out to the porch steps in her bare feet.

Eric was mounted upon his huge black stallion at the front of a disciplined line of troops. Amanda, her hair like a stream of wildfire against the white velvet, ran down the steps to her husband's side. The officers who had been shouting out orders fell silent, and Eric turned from his study of the men behind him to see her before him.

That was how he would remember her in the long nights to come. Proud and wild with tousled flaming hair, a soaring spirit with her emerald eyes, pagan with her bare toes showing upon the earth, exquisite as the white velvet outlined her body. She handed him the cup, and a cheer went up that warmed his soul and tore upon his heart.

He drank the whiskey and set the cup upon the tray. "Godspeed to all of you!" she cried, and again a chant rose, a cheer for the lady of Cameron Hall.

And he thought that he just possibly detected tears within the emerald beauty of her eyes.

Eric leaned down and kissed his wife's lips. Then he rode forward, toward the west.

10

TWO DIVISIONS CAME AGAINST THE SHAWNEE that fall, marching toward the Ohio River. Lord Dunmore led his men from the northern part of the valley. Eric was not with him. It had been decided that he would take a number of his old Indian fighters and accompany General Andrew Lewis, a man Eric highly respected, one of Washington's stalwart colleagues from the campaign against the Frenchman Duquesne. Lewis led his men by way of Fort Pitt while the governor's men came through the Great Kanawha Valley.

The western militia were an interesting breed of men. The majority of the men were clad in doeskin, and many of them had taken or displayed an Indian scalp upon occasion. In the Virginia Valley, life was still raw, and men eked out their livings. The Indians had a name for Lewis's men; they called them the Long Knives, an acknowledgment of their prowess with the weapons.

But they weren't after just any Indians. As Eric rode with Lewis, the general explained much of a situation that had not changed. "We encroach upon the land. Hostiles kill white settlers, then the settlers turn around and they don't seem to know if they're after a Delaware, or Cherokee, a Shawnee, or another. Inevitably they kill an Indian from a friendly tribe and then that tribe isn't so friendly anymore. A lot of trouble started with the establishment of trading posts out here—greedy men selling so much liquor that they create a savage out of any man. But now we're going after Cornstalk, and there ain't any man alive could call that man anything but a savage when he fights. You mark my words. The Delaware and Cherokees themselves, they tremble at the name Cornstalk."

"So I have heard," Eric agreed. Cornstalk was a powerful voice among the Indians. He was trying to form a confederacy of all the Ohio tribes.

Lewis looked up at the sky. "Dunmore could be in some difficulty for this one," he advised Eric. "The territory might well be Canada—according to the Quebec Act. If not, it's still disputed between Virginia and Pennsylvania."

"He is determined to fight the Shawnee, and that is that."

"Didn't you get enough of Indian fighting back when the wars were going on?"

"I was asked to raise men."

"There ain't been a war whoop heard in the Tidewater region, not in a long, long time. Well, if we meet up with Cornstalk, we'll hear plenty."

Eric learned the truth of that statement at Point Pleasant where they found the

Shawnee under Cornstalk. Tension raced high throughout the forces as the commanders conferred, but the Shawnee were the first to attack.

And Eric heard the war whoops, blood-curdling, savage, just as Lewis had said. The Indians appeared like painted devils, glistening in the sunlight, attacking with their cries. Yet above the roar of those cries and above the roar of his own orders, Eric heard Cornstalk. The Shawnee warrior, painted generously himself, cast his voice out over his people like that of God—or Satan. His men spurred forward, unafraid of steel or bullets, unafraid of death itself.

The militia fought well. Men stood their ground, and did not falter or fall back against the onslaught of the savage fighters. War whoops rose from the white men, and hand-to-hand combat came quickly. Eric was unhorsed when a Shawnee warrior fell atop him from a tree. As he rolled in the mud, he saw the brave raise his knife against him. Eric latched his wrist about the warrior's, aware that his life lay at stake. He strained against the Indian's slick muscles, and just as the blade neared his throat, Eric found the burst of energy to send the Indian flying. He did not waste time, but leapt upon the Indian, bringing his own blade swiftly home within his enemy's chest. A gurgle of blood rose on the brave's mouth, then his dark eyes glazed over and Eric was quickly up on his feet again, wary for his next opponent. One of his men, a distant Cameron cousin, hurried his horse to him. "Down the lines, sir, we have to hold here!"

They did hold, but Eric fought even as he shouted new orders, and the hours passed by slowly and painfully. Still he heard the haunting shouts of Cornstalk, and he realized that the Shawnee were still coming.

Then darkness came at last, and the Shawnee slipped away across the Ohio, shadowy silhouettes in the night. The militia had taken the day. But even as he realized that there were no more opponents to fight, Eric looked about the darkened field before him. Men lay everywhere.

"All right! We've got to tend to our wounded," he called sharply. Then it all came home to him, the horrible cries of the dying, the screams of pain that had not ceased. He began to hurry, hearing from one sergeant that two hundred of their own number lay dead, entwined with the glistening bodies of their enemies.

It took well into the night to sort the living from the dead, to bring what aid they could to the wounded and the dying. He was anxious to find Damien, whom he hadn't seen since very early in the day. He did not want to return home without his wife's cousin. Amanda had, he thought, very specifically entrusted his life to Eric, and she would expect the young man to survive.

Dismay and despair claimed him as he searched the men. At last he found Damien on a stretcher with a surgeon examining a bloody head wound. He grinned at Eric. "Knocked me for a loop, it did! I thought I was dead. But it's hard to keep a good man down, eh, sir?"

"Aye, Damien, it's hard to keep a good man down," he agreed.

He went past the tents of the men, conferred with Lewis who wanted to start building a fort the next morning, then hurried onward to his own canvas shelter. He had a bottle of good Caribbean rum with him and as he cast himself down upon his pallet, he was glad of the liquor. Home seemed a distant place now. All that danced before his eyes were the bodies of the Shawnee. He saw red, the color of blood, and it colored everything.

A chill shook him. He had come very close to death himself. Once he had fought so haphazardly and with undauntable courage. He had been a lad then. He had not seen himself as being mortal. Age had taught him that all men die, and age had even allowed him to accept the prospect of his own death. Now he was fiercely determined not to die.

He smiled, because even here, even in this wilderness with the stench of oil and blood so strongly with him, he could close his eyes and see her face. "I will not die, madame, to thwart you, love, if for no other reason!" His hands shook, and so he drank more deeply from the rum bottle. His marriage had brought more to him than he had dared hope, but the idyll of their days had been rudely marred by the quarrel before he left. There was more going on than he could see, though he could not pinpoint what. She despised him for being a "traitor," yet she laughed in his arms and she came alive when he reached for her. The line between love and hate was thin indeed. He wondered on what side of the line her true emotions lay. He had taken her from her father—and from Lord Hastings—and for that she seemed pleased enough. But still there was something there, something that he did not trust. He almost imagined that Sterling held something over his daughter, but he did not know what it could be.

He shrugged, tossing over, praying that he could sleep. He did not. He tossed again and wondered what went on back in the Tidewater. He did not want to stay in the west any longer. Men were meeting in Philadelphia, things were happening, his wife was home—alone—and he was caught up in this wretched battle against the redskins. Robert Tarryton would have married his duchess by now. He wondered if Amanda had attended the wedding, and he wondered how she fared at Cameron Hall.

His heart quickened suddenly. Maybe she had conceived an heir for him. A son . . . a daughter. A child to teach to love the land, to ride, to plant, to stand by the river and learn to read the wind.

She did not love him, he thought, and he wondered if she still carried any feelings for Robert Tarryton. The thought angered him, and he breathed deeply, tossing again. She did not need to love him to conceive an heir. And if she ever went near Tarryton . . .

She would not. She had a fierce pride and would surely keep her distance—if only to make Tarryton pay.

Then he wondered if Tarryton was haunted at night like this, lying awake, wondering about Amanda. No, he could not wonder so fiercely, for he had never known the explosion of heaven that it was to possess her. To touch her and fall . . . in love.

He smiled bitterly in the darkness. Love would be a very dangerous weapon in her hands. He had to take care that he not give her the chance to use it.

He tossed again, and remembered her eyes, then the rise of her breasts, the rose color of her nipples, the fragile ivory beauty of her skin. He wanted to go home.

It simply wasn't to be. In the morning they started a crude fort. When the fort was done they rode north again against the Shawnee across the Ohio. They met with Dunmore's forces.

There, finally, the governor announced that they should disperse and return to their homes.

The militia were angry, for they were so close to ending more of the fray. General Lewis was in sympathy with his men, Eric thought, but he was a commander, and a Virginian, and his opinions were certainly not clear to those around him.

He asked Eric to accompany him as they backtracked home. Eric bit down hard upon his desire to return as rapidly as possible to Cameron Hall and agreed that he would do so.

———

She should have been delirious with joy, Amanda chastised herself as she sat in the arbor by the river, her shoes and stockings cast aside, her bare toes wiggling in the cool grass. Above her the trees danced and swayed and the sun fell down upon her with the same curious dappled light that had touched them both when she had come here with Eric. It seemed so long ago. The weeks had become months, and summer had given way to fall, and now it was November.

She had everything that she had wanted. She had her freedom, she had the run of this magnificent estate, and in Eric's absence, her every wish was considered to be law. It had not been difficult to slip into the role of mistress here for there was not much that differed from Sterling Hall. Though the estate would have run quite competently in Eric's absence with or without her, she loved involving herself and she had tried to enter into the management of the hall unobtrusively. She had earned Thom's mistrust when he had discovered her assiduously going over the books, but then she had been careful to praise him lavishly with her very best smile, and then point out where they could perhaps reduce an expenditure here or there and use the savings to improve upon the house.

She had been shocked to learn from Danielle that she had an enemy within the house. Young Margaret whispered in the servants' quarters that the lady of Cameron Hall was looking to its future because she was looking forward to its master's demise. Amanda was horrified and longed to either slap Margaret's round little cheeks or send her packing. She did neither, determined that she would not betray her fury. A servant's sly whisperings should not distress her, and she determined that no one would ever see her upset.

When one of the mares went into labor for a late foal, she heard the news and instantly headed down to the stables. The dark-haired Frenchman who had whispered with Danielle was there. His name was Jacques Bisset. An Acadian, he was the estate manager, responsible for the running of the acreage and the groves and the stables just as Thom was responsible for the running of the house and Cassidy was responsible for everything regarding Eric's personal needs.

She did not have much occasion to come across him, and at the stables he did not seem pleased to see her, though he treated her with courtesy. She ignored his manner and spoke to him in French, asking after the mare, demanding to know if he thought that they would lose the horse or not.

He informed her curtly that the birth was breech, and that so far he had not managed to turn the foal.

"Well, sir, my hands are much smaller than yours. Perhaps I shall have better luck," she informed him.

Aghast, he stood blocking her way to the stall. *"Mais, non,* Lady Cameron, you must not come in here at this time—"

"I must do as I choose, Monsieur Bisset," she told him, but at his look she could not resist a wicked smile, then she laughed and tried to ease his tormented soul. "Really. We had fine Arabs and bred many racehorses at Sterling Hall. And my father was never about and seldom cared about what I did—" She paused, dismayed at her own words. She ignored him and moved past him, heedless of her gown, of her safety, of anything. She spoke softly to the troubled mare, then plunged in. To her delight she was able to shift the foal about, and though the birth still took several long hours and she was exhausted and a mess when it was over, Amanda was delighted. The beautiful little filly with a blaze upon her forehead had a fine broad chest and stupendous long legs. She and Jacques laughed with delight as the filly tried to stand, then managed to teeter up. When she smiled at Jacques she saw that the laughter faded from his eyes and that he gazed at her with sorrow and remorse. Her own laughter faded, and a ripple of unease washed over her. She was not afraid of him, rather he fascinated her. And she was determined to discover why he had argued with Danielle. Perhaps the two were falling in love, she thought. The idea dazzled her. She would be delighted if this curious marriage of hers brought happiness to Danielle.

She teased Danielle about it from her bath, but to her surprise, the woman quickly lost her temper, emphatically denying a love interest.

"Come now! He has the most gorgeous eyes, Danielle," Amanda said. "Huge and green and rimmed by those dark, dark lashes. And his features are so fine and fair. It looks as if he were sculpted by a master artist, planes and coloring all put together so beautifully. You should marry, Dani! You should."

"Cease to taunt me, *ma petite!* There can be no marriage, ever!"

"But, Danielle—"

"He is my brother!"

"Brother!" Amanda gasped, astounded. "But—but you told me that your brother was dead!"

"I thought that he was dead," Danielle said, folding and refolding Amanda's towel in her agitation. "I did not know that he lived until I came here."

"Then we must—"

"We must do nothing! Amanda, I beg of you, never mention it. Never, never mention that my brother lives."

Startled, Amanda stared at her maid. Danielle dropped the towel and came to kneel by the tub. "Please—"

"Danielle, calm down. I would never do anything to hurt you, you know that. I don't understand your distress, but—oh, no, Danielle, he wasn't a criminal, was he?"

"I swear, no. Yet you must keep the secret. He did not know these many years himself who he was—"

"What?"

"He nearly died. He very nearly died. But Lord Cameron's father found him and kept him alive, and he never did know from whence he came, nor could he remember his circumstances."

"Until—he saw you?" Amanda said.

"*Oui, oui.* You must keep his secret safe. He has been Jacques Bisset these many years, and he must stay so, please!"

"Tell me—"

"I can tell you no more! If you bear me any love at all—"

"You know that I love you dearly and that if you wish it, your secret is safe."

Danielle hugged her, soaking herself. Amanda fell silent but her curiosity was definitely piqued. She was determined to discover the truth.

Lying in the grass and feeling the breeze upon her, she reflected that she should be very happy. She had never, never been so free. She had done very well for the estate; her time and her life were her own. She had come to Cameron Hall just for this freedom, then she had married Eric to achieve it. But curiously, it did not taste so sweet as she had imagined. She could not believe that there had ever been a time when she had hoped that Eric Cameron might fall before the Shawnee. She did not want to miss him, but she did. She remembered all that he had done to her there in the grass, and she colored feverishly with the explicit memories. She was anxious about his return and prayed each night that God would keep him safe.

She was falling in love with him, she realized, and then she rose, fiercely annoyed with herself. Last month she had dressed in her finest to attend Robert Tarryton's wedding to his duchess, and she had smiled and offered him best wishes without a flutter of emotion. It helped that the Duchess of Owenfield was lank and skinny with horrible jutting teeth and limp brown hair. Amanda had felt fiercely sorry for the young woman, but she was still not certain that she could befriend her. She was just glad to realize that her heart had grown cold, that watching Robert marry meant nothing, and that feeling him kiss her cheek meant even less. And still, she did not want to love again. Love was a wretched emotion that left one vulnerable and weak and entirely miserable. She wanted no part of it. But there was more to love. It came whether asked or nay, and she had fallen beneath her husband's spell.

Sudden agitation came to her as she watched the river. She reached for her hose, pulling them on too quickly, snagging one. News had reached her that the parties had split, that Eric was traveling with General Lewis. She had even received a letter after they had fought a battle on the Ohio. Pierre, who had ridden into Williamsburg for a copy of the *Virginia Gazette,* had told her that the governor was back. That had quickened her heart, but then her hopes sank for she learned that Eric was not with the governor.

She turned and raced back to the house, suddenly hungry for more information. Running inside, she shouted for Thom. When the butler came to her, she smiled winningly. "Thom, please call Pierre and tell him that I'll have the carriage and that we'll go to Williamsburg tonight. I'll have my trunks ready within the hour. Have you seen Danielle?"

"Aye, she's gone to the laundry. I'll send her to you immediately, Lady Cameron."

He didn't seem to approve of her trip, she knew from his deep frown, but he had no power to stop her. She smiled radiantly. "I won't be gone long. I—I'd like to know more about my husband's whereabouts, if I can discover some news."

He nodded, but she still didn't think that he was pleased. She tossed her hair back. She had married for this freedom, and it was hers and not to be denied her. "Thank you, Thom," she told him brightly, and turned to hurry upstairs to pack.

Danielle did not seem any happier about her proposed trip, but Amanda ignored her as well. It would be fun to stay at the town house, to walk the streets, to visit the shops.

"And see your father!" Danielle warned her.

Folding a shift, Amanda paused, her heart fluttering. No. She had still not obtained freedom. She was still afraid of the power he held over Damien's life, and therefore over her.

"I hate him!" she whispered.

Danielle did not chastise her. She merely closed a trunk, opened the door, and called down to Thom, asking for help.

By nightfall Amanda had reached the town house. Though she was certainly surprised, Mathilda quickly made her welcome, asking her into the parlor while a room was freshened for her.

"The city is wild these days, milady! Every corner has an orator, every coffee-house is full of conversation."

"What has happened?" Amanda asked.

"Why, 'tis the men back from the Continental Congress. Now they have formed an association. Measures are not so voluntary now. We are to strictly boycott British goods, to band together to do so. And there will be committees to see that the rules of the association are carried out. We are even to call off the Dumfries races, if you can imagine the good men of Virginia doing so!"

Amanda could not, but she was careful of what she said before her husband's housekeeper. "Whatever shall come of it?"

"Well, 'tis rumored that the governor is quite irate, and that he is. Him with his grand Scots temper! He's holding quiet, but you know that the assembly is prorogued until spring, I think that he is quite distressed that the burgesses would come in spouting all this rebellion and that there could be war on the very streets!"

A small black woman came to the doorway, bobbing toward Amanda and informing her that her room was ready. Exhausted, Amanda rose, determined to get a good night's sleep, then explore the mood of the city herself in the morning. "Have you heard anything of Lord Cameron?" she asked his house-keeper.

"Why, yes, I have. You needn't fret any longer, child, for they say that the fighting is all over. And he handled himself splendidly, riding at the front of his troops and meeting those red devils without so much as a blink. He's heading back, taking a route through Richmond. He'll be here soon enough, even if he is waylaid. By Christmas."

Christmas still seemed a long, long way off. Amanda thanked the woman, then hurried upstairs. She realized that it was Eric's room that had been prepared for her. She ran her fingers over his desk, tempted to delve within the drawers. That's what she was supposed to be doing, searching his belongings. But she had no heart for it. She was haunted by the presence of him that seemed to live in the room. When she disrobed and stretched out on the bed, she moved her hands over the coolness of the sheets, and her body burned and she tossed about with a certain shame. She wanted him there. She even knew exactly what she wanted him to be doing.

She lay awake at least an hour before she sat up suddenly, furious. He hadn't written to tell her that he was well; his one missive had been while he was traveling. The servants knew more than she did.

Fuming, she tossed and turned, the slow burn of anger simmering within her. But it wasn't the anger that kept her awake, she realized. It was the longing.

———

She had barely come downstairs in the morning when she heard the cheerful tones of Lady Geneva Norman's voice. She stiffened, remembering that she was certain that Geneva and Eric had been lovers at some time, then she gave the matter no more thought. When she reached the landing, Geneva, splendid in silk and brocade, hugged her tightly. "Marriage does become you, Mandy, darling, even if you stole away the inestimable Lord Cameron!" She lowered her voice. "Father told me that you had come in last night. Do let's get out on the streets and see what is happening today!"

Intrigued to see what was happening, Amanda hugged Geneva in return, wondering if she wasn't a terrible hypocrite. "Fine, let's head out."

"There's a wonderful new little coffee house off of Duke of Gloucester Street. Come, we'll see the rabble!"

"I'd love to see the . . . rabble," Amanda agreed, and so they were off.

It was fun just to be back in Williamsburg, to feel as light and free as she did, to look in the shop windows and study the fashions and hats and jewelry.

"Homespun is the rage," Geneva said, wrinkling her nose.

And it was.

They stopped to buy a copy of the *Virginia Gazette*. As they did so, there was a sudden commotion ahead of them. Amanda rushed forward as she heard a woman scream, then she saw that a crowd had formed around the steps to a shop door. A man had apparently walked into the store, removed bolt after bolt of fabric, and tossed them into the center of the road. He stamped on them and the material sank into the road, soaked by mud and excrement.

"Stop him!" Amanda cried, rushing forward. She was accustomed to people giving way for her; but now no one moved. The restless mob of people ringing the shop held tight.

"Ye'll find no peace in this town, Mrs. Barclay, you'll not, not with English goods in your store!" someone called out.

The shopkeeper backed away. Pushing against the crowd, Amanda shouted in fury. "That is destruction of private property! Would you be a people ruled by the force of a mob!"

A few people turned to her, shamefaced. More and more of them looked at her defiantly.

"Dear girl, committees keep an eye upon the articles of the association, but then this type of thing will happen. I find it entirely exciting myself!"

Amanda, hearing the voice, swung around with pleasure despite the words. "Damien!" she cried. She almost hugged him, then backed away laughing as she looked him up and down. He was clad in the buckskins of the West County men, and he looked very provincial and entirely fierce. She had never imagined it of her cousin who did so love his finery. "Damien! You are home, alive and well!"

"I am. A slight gash to the temple, but I'm quite fine now."

"Oh, Damien! Poor dear! Is—is Eric with you?"

"Oh. No, I'm sorry. I, er, traveled ahead of him. He has been held up on General Lewis's request. He will come soon enough, though." Smiling, Damien bowed to his cousin's companion. "Lady Geneva. This is indeed a pleasure."

Amanda expected Geneva to lift her delicate chin with scorn at Damien's appearance, but the woman did just the opposite. She came up on her toes, caught his hands, and kissed his cheek. "Damien. You're with us again. Thank God. We were on our way to the coffeehouse. Will you join us?"

"I wouldn't dream of leaving a Tory like Amanda on her own, Lady Geneva. I fear that trouble might find her."

"Trouble! These people are acting like rabble! And they pride themselves so fiercely on being Virginians, the descendants of free enterprise rather than the cast-off dregs of society or poor religious dissenters!" Amanda cried.

Damien laughed. "That's true, love, we Virginians do keep our noses in the air. But we're sniffing rebellion these days, and that's the way that it is. Come, let's have that coffee, shall we?"

He slipped an arm within each of theirs and they hurried on down to the side street and then to the coffeehouse. The place was filled, but the harried owner still came forward quickly and politely, eager to serve. Even as he brought them steaming cups of coffee and morning pastries, conversation rose around them.

Then one young man was up—a student at William and Mary, Amanda was certain—and began to weave an eloquent tale of the trouble in the colonies. "We are, by the grace of God, free Englishmen! And we shall have the rights of free Englishmen, we will not grant Parliament the right to take men from our colony to England to stand trial for the crime of treason, or for any crime!"

"Here, here!" Boisterous shouts rang out. Amanda felt a chill settle upon her.

"You would think that we were at war!" she whispered.

She did not like the look that Damien gave her. Then he excused himself to speak with some men behind them. A tall, bulky fellow from the cabinet maker's shop approached Amanda, rubbing the rim of his hat nervously.

"You're Lady Cameron, eh, mum?"

"I am, yes."

"I just wanted to tell you that I served under your husband at Point Pleasant. I never served beneath a finer commander nor a braver man. I'm pleased to be his servant, should he ever require."

"Thank you," Amanda murmured, moving forward anxiously. "Can you tell me more?"

The room had fallen strangely silent, and it seemed that the men and the women in the coffeehouse had all turned to look at her. A cup was raised and the young man who had spoken insurrection shouted out. " 'Tis Lady Cameron! A toast to our hero's wife. Madame, you should have been there, and yet you should not, for the blood did run deep."

Suddenly everyone wanted to talk to her. Many of the men there had served in Dunmore's Indian campaign. One young fellow came before her to give a description of her husband in battle. "Why, one of those Shawnees a-come straight at him, leaping down from his horse. I was certain that our Lord Cameron had seen his last blessed light of day, but suddenly he throws off the savage, and God bless me, but if he didn't slice the fellow faster than a cow could sneeze!

"And he was upon his feet again in an instant, never used a musket at all, did he, but fought hand to hand with savages, and shouting orders all the time, even when we came up knee deep in our own dead. He wouldn't allow no scalpin' though, and when we moved north, he wouldn't allow no killing of squaws or chillun, even if we did try to tell him that little savages grew up to big 'uns."

Amanda smiled. "My husband has many relatives with Pamunkee blood. Maybe that ruled his thinking."

"Maybe it did! How is his lordship?"

She tightened her smile but managed to maintain it. "I believe him well."

"Ah, well, no message, but I expect as you'll hear from him any day now."

Another toast was raised to her. Geneva seemed to love all of it. Her eyes sparkled and she clapped with delight. Amanda had been so eager for news, but knowing that despite the bloody battles he had fought, Eric was alive, and heedless of her feelings, a simmering fury brewed within her. She ceased to listen to the men as Geneva flirted and laughed and chatted. Then she realized that she could hear the muted voices of the men behind her—and Damien.

"I have managed . . . a cache of a hundred . . . fine French rifles, I managed to trade soon after Point Pleasant with some Delaware."

Someone said something and Damien's voice lowered. There was an argument over price. Amanda felt her face burn as she listened. "Fine. We shall secrete them in the Johnsboro warehouse after dark. The place is abandoned. If there is trouble, no man shall have property confiscated or face the threat of removal to England."

Damien! she wanted to shout. She had to tell him that Dunmore knew him to be an arms smuggler. Perhaps then he would cease his foolish and dangerous activities.

She rose suddenly, startling Geneva. "I wish to leave. Excuse me."

She brushed past the men who had surrounded her and hurried out to the street, trying to breathe deeply. Damien came upon her quickly. "Amanda—"

"Damien! You are an idiot!"

He twisted his jaw. "Amanda, you are the fool," he said irritably. "All of America is up at arms—"

"But they do not practice treason!"

"What is treasonous here? To want to protect oneself?"

"They are on to you, Damien!"

He backed away from her. "Who?"

She did not answer for Geneva appeared suddenly before them, laughing indignantly. "Fine friends! Leave me to the rabble."

"Geneva, never." Damien bowed deeply over her hand. "I shall consider it my first duty and greatest pleasure to see you both home."

They walked back to the Cameron town house first. Amanda kissed Damien and gave him a fierce glance, and she thought that he would come back.

But as night fell he did not return. Anxious, she paced the downstairs. Then she tried to read, and when she did she found the book on botany that Eric had lent to Damien that summer. A gasp escaped her when a small map fell from the book. She stared at it for a long while, thinking it was merely a pattern for planting boxwoods. Yet there were curious symbols on it. Then her blood ran very cold, for she realized that some of the curious markings referred to money and some of them referred to powder and arms.

She sat back, shaking. Eric was a traitor beyond a shadow of doubt. He was involved more deeply than she had ever imagined.

The map was exactly the proof that her father had demanded she find.

She held the map, then thoughtfully went upstairs and slipped it down into the bottom of one of her jewel cases. Then she went downstairs, put the book back into the shelf, and returned to her room, to curl up beneath the covers of her bed.

———

Two days later her father appeared at the town house. She was in the parlor, poring over the *Virginia Gazette* and trying to assimilate everything that had occurred since the Continental Congress. Reading between the lines, she was certain that Governor Dunmore had to be grateful that he had disbanded the

Virginia Assembly, for it seemed that the members of the convention had come back breathing the fire of insurrection. Thankfully they would have to let some of the fires die down before they came together to meet again. It was frightening.

And, she thought, every man who had attended the convention and set his signature to many of the agreements had to be aware that he courted the charge of treason. But still, she had seen what had happened in the streets of Williamsburg. It might very well be the loyalists who were in danger if all of the colony began to rise in this rebellion. That is . . . until English troops arrived. British troops were admired the world over for their discipline and ability. Once troops descended down upon the colony . . .

She shivered, sipped some of the berry tea, winced, then realized that the taste of it was actually growing palatable to her.

Then Lord Sterling arrived.

It was Danielle who opened the door. From the parlor, Amanda heard her father enter, and she rose, planning to go to the entry to meet him. But he did not give her the chance. He stormed into the parlor. Danielle followed him, announcing him softly.

"Go. I'll speak with my daughter alone!" Nigel snapped.

She hadn't seen him in quite some time, yet even as the door closed quietly behind Danielle, they made no pretense of greeting one another with warmth. Amanda watched him with open hostility.

"Good morning, Father. If you've come for my husband—the suspected traitor—he has not yet returned from the western front where he fought for the governor." She smiled sweetly. "Would you have some tea, father? Something stronger? Tell me, to just what do I owe this . . . pleasure?"

"Damien Roswell," Sterling answered flatly, tossing his tricorn down upon the sofa. He walked over to the fire to warm his hands, smiling as he watched her face. "Ah, you're not so cocky now, girl."

She knew that she had paled. She raised her head, eyeing him coldly. "You wouldn't dare see that an arrest warrant was served upon him now. The colony would be up in arms. If he was transported to England for some trial—"

"If he disappeared in the night none would be the wiser, eh?"

"Dunmore would never condone this."

"You're mistaken. Dunmore is a nervous man, with Peyton Randolph spouting off about natural law and seeking elections for the Virginia Conclave. Aye, who would notice the disappearance of one eager young lad?" Her father lost his pretense of a smile. He stared at her hard. "I'd do him in myself easily enough. I've killed before, girl, don't you doubt it. I'll kill again if need be. This is my path to royal favor, and I will have it!"

Chills riddled Amanda and she longed to go to the fire, just to feel some warmth. But Nigel Sterling was by the fire, and she would not take a step near him.

"My husband would kill you."

"So—you've turned on England, joined the rabble."

"I am loyal to the Crown."

"Then give me something—or else I swear that Damien Roswell will not live to see the morning sun. One way or other, lady, I will see that he dies. And don't deceive yourself about the state of this colony. Prompt and forceful action from London will quell this rebellion before it begins."

She paused, staring at him. She believed him. He would kill Damien, or seize him and see him transported to Newgate. It might not be legal, but her father still had the power to see it done.

He started moving toward her. "Don't come near me!" she warned, and he stood still, smiling again.

"Give me something! If you love the Crown, serve it!"

She thought quickly, her heart seeming to fall. She remembered the conversation in the coffeehouse, and it occurred to her that she could save Damien, serve the Crown indeed, and be sure, too, that no foolish young swain died in the serving. "There is a cache of arms," she blurted out.

Sterling's eyes glistened with pleasure. "Where?"

"On—on the river. At the Johnsboro warehouse."

Sterling smiled, collecting his hat. "If you've told me the truth, girl, you've bought yourself Christmas. Good day, daughter."

He left. For an endless moment Amanda could not move. She was so cold that she didn't think that even the warmth of the fire could help her now. She didn't feel that she had helped the cause of England. She felt as if she had betrayed not just the patriots . . .

But Eric.

She moved across the room to the brandy decanter, poured herself a liberal portion, and swallowed it down quickly. Then she repeated the action, and at long last some semblance of warmth, of life, poured back into her.

But that night when she slept she was haunted by the faces of the young men in the coffeehouse. They marched on her with fixed bayonets upon their muskets, with eyes of condemning fire, with features frozen into cold masks. They marched upon her and she backed away with a silent scream. And then they stopped, breaking apart, for a new man to make his way among them. She heard the sure purpose of his boots ringing as they fell against the ground, and then she saw his face, and it was Eric's, and it was as cold as a winter's wind, as devoid of love or passion. Like shimmering steel his eyes gazed upon her, and then he reached out to touch her, his fingers winding tightly about her. . . .

She screamed, thrashing about, for the dream was so real. Then she realized that it was no dream, she fought a real man, and that Eric was above her, truly with her, his eyes a curious glistening silver but his lip curled into a smile.

"Shush! My God, lady, what is this greeting? I reach to touch you, ready to die for the time and distance between us, and you treat me like a monster!"

She went still, the fear subsiding, yet remaining to haunt her, as it would forever. "Eric!" She gasped. And she reached up to touch his face. His hair was damp, he was naked as he sprawled atop her, and she realized that he must have come home, found her there, bathed elsewhere, and come to her. He was no dream, nor did he look upon her coldly or with disdain. His eyes were alight with fire, his body was hotter than flame, the length of him seemed to tremble against her with startling fervor. She moistened her lips, gazing at him, and she cried out, forgetting anger, forgetting everything. "Eric!" she cried his name again. She placed her hands on the clean-shaven sides of his face and pulled him to her, almost swooning as she tasted the warmth and hunger of his kiss. She drew away from him then, trying to speak, trying to recall her anger and not her fear.

"You did not write!"

"I had little time."

"I worried—"

"Did you?" He paused, staring down at her, his eyes alight against the dim glow of the fire, a dark brow arched in a satyr's mask against rugged angles of his face. Then he lay low against her and whispered with searing desire against her lips. "Forgive me this night, for I can bear the distance no more!"

His hands closed upon her gown, material ripped, and she felt the startling deliciousness of his body against hers. His hands, his teeth, his lips were everywhere. They moved upon her with wanton abandon, with wild demand. Soft moans escaped her as she discovered her body caught by his heat, alive in every way, her flesh begging to be touched, and the spiral of desire within her soaring. She arched her breasts to his lips, dug her fingers into his hair, and gasped and writhed as his fingers delved within the woman's core of her, teasing the sable-red triangle at the juncture of her thighs, mercilessly finding the tiny bud of deepest sensation. Where he stroked and teased with his touch he followed with his tongue's bold caress, sweeping the nectar from her until she surged against him, begging senselessly for she knew not what. He towered above her full of laughter, but she pushed him from her, crawling atop him, lashing him with the soft stroke of her hair as she rubbed the length of her body low over his. She kissed his chest and stroked his buttocks and thighs, nipping his flesh, lapping it with tiny kisses, and moving upward again. Gently, tenderly, wickedly, she stroked and teased him, then went on with her hair a shower about them both to lap and stroke and lick and tease the very shaft of him, so softly that it was torment, then with a sizzling force that brought forth a torrent of shudders and groans from his lips. Then the very force of his hands was upon her as he lifted her, catching her eyes, meeting them, then thrusting into her with deep, shocking passion that still seemed to burn her from the inside out, impale her until she was fused with him. His eyes held hers as he thrust, and thrust again, and sobs of sweet hunger and desperation fell from her lips. He held her steady and they rode the night and the stars and the painful distance between them and the shimmering passion that was explosive and primitive and so very undeniable.

She thought that she had died when she fell against him at last. Though she gasped for breath and lay slick and spent and awed and exhausted, his touch was upon her again, his fingers idly upon her breasts, her buttocks; his lips seared her shoulders, his hands stroked the slope of her buttocks.

"Eric . . ." she whispered his name, and she twisted, thinking that there were things to say. But even as she gazed at him the heat went cool within her.

Even now her father was seeing that the rebels' arms were seized. And that the man who touched her so fervently now might well wind his fingers about her throat if he only knew. She reached out to touch his damp, dark-haired chest, and she felt the shudder and violent ripple of muscle there and her throat constricted. "Eric—"

He rolled over, sweeping her beneath him with a sudden savage movement. His eyes touched deep into hers, dark and tempestuous, relentless. A hoarse cry escaped him and he buried his face against the fiery cascade of her hair and her throat. "Love me tonight!" he demanded of her raggedly. "Do nothing but love me this night!" he repeated, and his lips found hers, moving against them voraciously, then finding the sensitive spots at her ear, coming to the pulse as her throat, sweeping to secure the hardened bud of her breast with hunger and magic. She exhaled on a gasp, feeling the excitement rise in her again, the promise of the exquisite peaks of ecstasy.

There was nothing that she could say to him, and in moments she did not remember that there were things that she wanted to say to him.

He demanded that she love him; that night, she did.

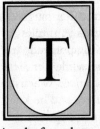HAT CHRISTMAS SEASON WAS ONE OF THE HAPPI-
est times of Amanda's life, or would have been, had the threat
of what was to come not hung over them so surely. For the
first few days of her husband's return, Amanda waited anxiously for what would happen. But Virginia itself seemed quiet then.

They stayed in Williamsburg long enough for a round of parties, many in
celebration of Lord Dunmore's newborn baby daughter. The *Virginia Gazette*
wrote of the blessed event. Throughout the coffeehouses where the students
were still preaching sedition, cups were still raised to the countess and her baby.

Snow began to fall toward the end of the month, and that was when Eric
determined that it was time to return home. Amanda was glad to go; she missed
Cameron Hall.

Their homecoming was wonderful. Amanda and Eric sat together in the
coach, bundled beneath a blanket, while Pierre drove. Eric taught her a few of
the bawdier tunes he had learned traveling with the western militia, and she
blushed and laughed, accused him of making up things as he went along, and he
assured her that he did not, and held her closer in the warmth of the blanket. All
along the road the snow fell in soft, delicate flakes. The forests were frosted with
it, the trees glistened, and when the snow had stopped falling, the sky was not
wintry gray but crystal blue, and the sun melted the very top layer of snow to ice,
and the world about them seemed to be a dazzling, crystal palace.

At Cameron Hall they were greeted warmly by the servants. Danielle, who
had gone ahead, stood beside Jacques Bisset on the steps as they arrived. Thom
had come down with a silver welcoming tray full of wassail drinks, and Cassidy
stood beside him, ready to serve. Margaret and the cook and several grooms
stood by, and when Pierre opened the carriage door there was a cheer to greet
them. Amanda drank deeply of the warm, sweet wine, and when it came time to
face her husband at the table for their evening meal, her eyes were softly glazed,
her lips curved, her manner most gentle and bemused.

Watching his wife, Eric became sorely frightened, for it shook him to the
bone to realize how much he loved her. So much about her had changed since
they'd met. She laughed so easily, her emerald eyes bore for him the sparkle that
he had once so envied when she cast it upon another man. This night she wore
velvet, deep forest-green velvet, the fur-trimmed bodice falling very low off her
shoulders and molding handsomely over her breasts. Delicate flame-deep curls
curved in fascinating tendrils over the alabaster crescents of her breasts as they
rose almost indecently high against the gown. She barely touched her food, but

smiled throughout the evening. They ate by candlelight, and he noted things he might not notice otherwise. The crystal of the candle holders seemed to shimmer with greater colors, the silver of their goblets was dazzling, the white linen laid out upon the table was impeccable, soft as the snowdrifts that had followed them home. But nothing was more outstanding than the color of her eyes, nor the sweep of her lashes, nor the curve of her smile, the sound of her laughter. When they had finished with the meal he swept her from her chair, mindless of the green velvet dress, mindless of the servants who discreetly disappeared, and with drama and finesse he walked her up the stairs. And all the while her arms curled around his neck, her eyes met his with a fascinating radiance. When he came to their room he sat her down upon the fine bed they shared, and he knelt down before her, slipping off her black satin pumps. He looked up and saw something in her eyes that he had not caught before, as if the moon had cast strange shadows upon them, and in that moment he shuddered suddenly. She had married him under duress; they had never once exchanged words of love, though they whispered often and fervently enough of passion.

She reached out, touching his face, a cry upon her lips. "What is it?" she whispered.

He shook his head, searching out her eyes still, then setting his fingers upon the laces to her bodice. The sweet, fascinating scent of her rose to sweep around him like a haunting caress. Her breasts spilled forward and he rested his cheek against them, then found her eyes again. "I just wonder, lady, will you always be so gentle, so tender, with your love?"

"Always!" she whispered, stroking his dark hair and holding him close to her.

He rose with her, bearing her downward, velvet, fur, and all. The dress fell away from the perfection of her upper body and her hair streamed free and wild upon her nakedness. He pressed his lips to hers and wondered at the curious fever and fear that gripped him that night. "You have spun magic webs upon me, Amanda. Webs of silk and steel, so soft and yet so strong. With a word from your lips, I would long for death; for the brush of your fingers upon me, love, I would move mountains. Forever, lady, I am yours."

She returned his stare, curious at his whimsy, of which he was capable, but not so often given. He was customarily a man who took what he wanted, even when what he wanted was his wife. But this night the words played easily upon his lips, just as his fingers stroked her slowly, without the demand, without the solicitation. It was her eyes he delved now, raking and searching, and still the easy mist and magic of his words lay with them, and the soft mood that had come from the wassail drinks wrapped sweetly about her. She touched him and vowed to him, "I will love you sweet and tender always, my lord."

He stroked her cheek with his forefinger, tracing the pattern of her lips. "Betray not the heart, Amanda. Of all in life, that is the greatest sin."

She parted her lips to protest, but that was when she lost her easy lover, when he seized her with passion and demand. The words were lost to her as the mist swirled away and the startling reality of sensation touched and ravaged her. Through it all he was ruthless in what he would take from her, and yet he was also a tender lover. No hands more gentle could ever touch a woman, no fingers could stroke upon her or touch her most intimate secrets with greater sensitivity. No whispers more driving could caress her ears; no lips could touch the whole of her with greater thoroughness or greater determination to elicit and evoke sensation. They rode the wind, and the wind danced within them, bringing them to erotic peak upon peak, and in the end she was sated, sleeping upon crystal snowdrifts of the mind, cocooned in both beauty and warmth.

In the morning Amanda discovered him at the small table within their room, sipping coffee as he read the latest issue of the *Virginia Gazette*. He was fully attired in plain clothing, navy breeches, a white cotton shirt with no lace or frills, a wool surcoat, and his high boots. His greatcoat lay over a chair by the door, and she knew that he meant to travel over his land. He would spend time with Jacques, and he would see each and every one of his tenants, and she knew that if any one of them was in need, he would see to it that they ate well for Christmas. The holiday was upon them; there would be a great party here for landowners and tenants and servants alike. It was tradition. He had told her about it earlier.

He sensed that she was awake and he looked at her, smiling though his eyes were grave. Amanda smiled in return, rising, sweeping the sheet about her as she came to stand behind him. He swallowed more coffee, indicating an article. "Some of Dunmore's navy men raided a warehouse on the coast. The Johnsboro warehouse. There were all manner of French weapons being stored there."

She was glad that she stood behind him. Her fingers clenched and she shivered painfully. Her eyes would have given her away, for they widened in fear and dismay. She could not speak.

But her husband did not suspect her. He shook his head. "At least no one was killed or injured. No one knows where the guns came from—'tis an abandoned place. Thank God. I am sick to death of seeing men die."

He set his cup down and rose and kissed her absently. "I am off. Perhaps you would like to ride with us tomorrow."

She nodded, unable to find her voice. He was watching her again. "There is no reason that you should not, is there?" he asked her.

"I—I don't know what you mean," she managed to gasp.

He looked her carefully up and down. "I mean," he said softly, "there is no sign of a child for us as yet, is there?"

"Oh!" Relief flooded through her. She shook her head, blushing. "No . . . no."

He kissed her again and turned away, picking up his civilian tricorn. Then he turned back with a wicked smile and he drew her into his arms, and kissed her with the fever and shockingly intimate surge and sizzle that had first taught her the stirrings of desire. Her knees went weak and her heart came to thunder against her ears, and fear and unease were gone. She fell against him, and when he raised his lips, she met his eyes with an emerald smile that was secure and dazzling . . . and ever tender.

He smiled. "I am about to forget the day."

"There is always the night."

"There is nothing like the moment."

"My lord, how could I dare to argue with you?"

He started to laugh, and she did not know where the breathlessness would lead, but there was a discreet tap on the door and Eric broke from her regretfully.

The next day she did ride with him, plowing through the snow when they were inland, shivering against the breeze when they came upon the river. Winter was coming upon them full force, but despite the cold and the harshness, she enjoyed herself tremendously. She loved the tenant farms with their thatched roofs and wattle-and-daub walls, their central rooms with spinning wheels and hearths and kitchens all in one. They were, above all, homes of warmth and laughter, filled with the melody of the voices of children. Jacques accompanied them wherever they visited. Amanda found him more curious each time she saw him. He was so strikingly good-looking with his dark-fringed light eyes and fine features. Every bit the Frenchman in dress and manner, but an Acadian still, and wary of both the peoples who turned from him. He watched her too, she thought. But it did not distress her. It warmed her.

Christmas came. Religious services were humbly observed, then it was time for the people to celebrate, and they all drew to Cameron Hall. There was mistletoe to dangle from the doorways, and the house was decorated with holly and wreaths and ribbons. Fires crackled brilliantly, musicians played the old European tunes and the livelier colonial music too. The lord and lady of the house took part in all the festivities. Amanda danced with the very proper Thom, with the round little cook, with a very shy and blushing groom. She was laughing, delighted to catch her husband's approving eye across the room, when suddenly there was a pounding on the door. Eric, leaning against the bannister in the hallway, waved away Thom and Cassidy and started for the door himself. He opened it and stepped back, welcoming their new guests.

"Well, well!" boomed her father's voice. "Daughter!"

Nigel Sterling walked into the room, Lord Hastings and Lord Tarryton, the Duke of Owenfield, with his new lady duchess following behind him.

The music died, the servants ceased to shriek with laughter, and a curious quiet fell upon the room.

"Hello, Father," Amanda greeted him coolly. Her fingers were trembling. She could not forget that the weapons had been seized, that she was lying to the man with whom she had fallen in love. Dear God, why on this day! she prayed in silence, but he was already upon her, taking her hands, brushing her cheek with his cold kiss. Thom was quickly there to take coats and hats; she greeted Lord Hastings and Robert and his duchess, and quickly suggested that they retire to the dining room where there was still warm food and a blazing fire. She saw that Eric watched her, carefully, and she wondered at his thoughts.

There was a scuffle as she led their new guests toward the dining room. Startled, Amanda twirled around. She was shocked to see Eric standing there with his arm locked about Jacques Bisset's throat, holding him despite the fact that the muscled Frenchman was straining to break free. Eric smiled despite his determined fight. "Do go on, my love. I'll be right with you."

"But, Eric—"

"Our guests, Amanda."

Confused, she nevertheless hurried forward to escort their new guests to the dining room. As she closed the doors, she could see that Danielle had come over to talk swiftly to the man she had claimed as her brother. Amanda could not catch the words. With a sigh, she gave up. She turned about, facing those who had come. Her father watched her with his ever-calculating eyes; Lord Hastings with his ever-lecherous eyes; Robert with a startling lust; and Anne, the Duchess of Owenfield, with her soft brown doe's eyes, ever frightened and timid.

"Anne, you must have some of our Christmas grog!" Amanda said cheerfully. "And the rest of you must try this too. Father, I know you prefer your whiskey, but this is a wonderful concoction with a trace of whiskey in it." She didn't wait for a reply, but played the grand hostess, pouring from a silver decanter that sat atop a small pot of burning oil to keep the contents warm. She placed a stick of cinnamon in each drink. By then Eric had come into the room, looking only slightly worse for the curious tussle.

"Welcome," he said to the group, taking Anne's hand in the best manner of the Virginia aristocrat. He kissed her fingers and smiled at the young woman—a trifle more gently than he smiled at her, Amanda thought, but then she realized that he was very sorry for the timid woman married to Robert. "Duchess, it is indeed a pleasure to have you here. I'm so sorry I missed your wedding. I understand it was quite the occasion of the decade." His eyes sparkled. "Tell me, do I detect something special here already?"

"Quite." Robert had the grace to hold his wife's shoulders and pull her against him. "We are expecting our first child."

"Oh! How wonderful!" Amanda said, raising her glass to the pair. "A toast to the two of you, and to a healthy, happy babe."

"Here, here!" Eric agreed, and he lifted his glass to the pair. "To a healthy, happy babe! Come, lady, be warmed by the fire."

Eric was wonderful with Anne, light and warm, making her feel very much at home. But the conversation did not stay light long; Nigel Sterling brought up the fact that Williamsburg was alive with gossip about the conclave that was already being planned. "The time is coming, and coming fast, when a man will have to make up his mind! He will either be the king's servant or his enemy."

Eric waved a hand in the air, but Amanda noted that her husband's eyes were glittering with tension. She knew to beware of him in such moods; she doubted if her father would see the danger or heed it. "Nigel, I have just recently returned from service at Dunmore's request," Eric stated. "I met the Indians upon our borders while politicians argued. Why do you tell me this?"

"Because, sir, you should abhor these proceedings! You, with your strength and power and your influence, you should be out there fighting the hotheads, not joining them!"

"Or leading them!" Robert suggested sharply.

It was out—it was almost an accusation of treason.

Amanda stood, bursting in between them. "I'll not have it!" she announced, lifting her chin imperiously. "This is my house, and it is Christmas, and every man here shall behave with propriety for the occasion, or leave. This is not a tavern, and you'll not act like it! Are we all understood? Nigel, you are my father, and as such you are welcome here, but not to reap discord!"

There was silence for several long seconds. Amanda realized that Eric was looking at her and that his temper had faded. His eyes were glistening with laughter.

"Amanda—" Sterling began.

Eric rose. "You heard my wife. We've quite a traditional Christmas here and we are delighted to have you, but only in the Christmas spirit. Come along. We've excellent musicians, quite in the spirit of the holiday. Come, Lady Anne, 'tis a slow tune. If your husband will allow, I will gladly lead you gently to it." The group returned to the party.

Robert nodded distractedly. As soon as Eric had taken Anne to the dance floor, he swept his arms about Amanda. He held her too close. Trying to ignore him and the pressure of his arms, she danced focusing her attention on the music and the movement of her feet. The fiddler was wonderful and the plaintive tunes of the instrument, joined by the soft strains of flute and harp, were haunting. Or they could be . . . if she did not feel Robert's arms about her.

"Marriage becomes you, Amanda. You are more beautiful than ever."

"Thank you. And congratulations. You are to be a father."

"No child yet, eh? Tell me, do you sleep with the bastard?"

"With the greatest pleasure," she replied sweetly. She felt his hands quicken upon her so that she was in pain; he nearly snapped her fingers.

"You're lying," he told her.

"No woman could find a more exciting lover."

"You have not forgiven me yet. But you love me still, and I can warn you now, the time is coming when you will run to me."

"Oh? Is it?"

"The British soldiers will descend upon this town very soon, and men the likes of your husband will be burned in the wake."

She wanted to retort something horrible to him, but she did not have the chance. Her father touched his shoulder, and despite Robert's irritated expression, he was forced to relinquish his hold upon her. She was no more pleased to be held by her father, but she had little choice.

"You did good work, daughter," he told her softly. Her heart leapt uneasily. "The arms were stashed where you said."

"Then we are even."

"There is no such thing as even. You will serve me when I demand that you do."

"You're a fool, Father. It will not be so easy! Haven't you begun to understand anything yet? There are arrest warrants abounding in Boston—and no one to see them carried out. The people are turning away from this mess that men like you are causing!"

He smiled. "Don't forget, daughter, that I do not make idle threats. When I need you again, you will obey me."

He halted, turning her over to Lord Hastings. Amanda, wretchedly miserable from her father's words, tried to smile and bear the man. She was certain that he drooled upon her breast, and by the time the music came to a halt at last she was ready to scream and go racing out into the snow. She excused herself and raced outside to the back porch, desperate for fresh air, be it frigidly cold.

The river breeze rushed in upon her. She touched the snow on the railing and rubbed it against her cheeks and the rise of her breasts, and then she shivered, staring out at the day. It was gray now, and bleak. And it had been such a beautiful, shimmering Christmas.

"Amanda."

She turned around, startled. Eric had come outside. His arms were covered in naught but the silk of his shirt, but he didn't seem to notice the cold. The wind lifted a dark lock of his hair and sent it lashing back against his forehead. He walked toward her, pulling her into his arms. "What is going on here?"

"What?" she cried.

"Why has he come?"

"Father? Because it is Christmas."

He kept staring into her eyes, and as he did so, the biting cold seemed to seep into her, wrapping around her very heart. Now was the time. She should throw her arms around him; she should admit to everything.

She could not. For one, there was England. Above everything, she could not turn upon her own beliefs.

And there was Damien. She could not risk his life.

She moistened her lips and wondered desperately what would happen if it did come to war. She was Eric Cameron's wife; and she knew beyond the shadow of a doubt that he would cast aside everything for his own beliefs. Would he so easily cast her aside? And what of her? Perhaps she dared not utter the words, for they were painful ones, but she did love him. Deeply. More desperately than she had ever imagined.

It was terrifying.

"He has come," she whispered, "to make me wretched."

Eric's arms tightened upon her. "And Tarryton?"

"Robert?" she said, startled.

"I saw the heat and the passion in your eyes when you spoke with him. Tell me, was it anger, or something else?"

"Anger only. I swear it."

"Would God that I could believe you."

She pulled away from him, hating him at that moment.

"You never pretended to love me," he reminded her. He kept walking toward her, and he was a stranger to her then. He caught her arm and pulled her back to him.

"He is a married man expecting a child!" Amanda lashed out.

"And you are a married woman."

"That you could think—" she began, then she exploded with a violent oath and escaped him, running past him and back into the house. The party was dying down. The servants were no longer guests, but they hurried about to pick up glasses and platters and silver mugs that had been filled with Christmas cheer. Amanda had assumed that her father and the others were staying; they were not. They took their leave soon after, telling her they meant to make Williamsburg before nightfall. Eric had come in quietly behind Amanda. He bid them all farewell cordially, ever the lord of his castle.

Amanda escaped him, rushing up to bed. She dressed in a warm flannel gown and sat angrily before her dressing table, brushing her hair.

A few minutes later the door burst open. Eric, who obviously had imbibed more than was customary, stood there for a moment, then came in and dropped down upon their bed. He tore off his boots, his surcoat, and his shirt, letting them fall where they would. Amanda felt his eyes upon her. He watched her every movement even as she tried to ignore him.

"Why is it, Amanda, that we are not expecting a child?" he asked at last.

Her brush went still as the tense and brooding question startled her motionless. Then she began to sweep the brush through the dark red tresses again. "God must know, for I do not."

He leapt up, coming behind her. He took the brush from her fingers and began to work it through her hair. The tendrils waved softly against his naked chest as he worked. She sat very still, waiting.

"You do not do anything to keep us from having a child, do you?" he asked.

"Of course not!" She gasped, trembling. Then she rose and spun around on him. "How can you suggest such a thing! 'Tis you—you marry me, and then leave me!"

His eyes softened instantly and he drew her against him. "Then you do not covet him, do not lie awake dreaming that the duchess should die, that perhaps . . ."

"My God! How could you think such a heinous thing of me!" she cried, outraged. She tried to jump to her feet and leap by him. He caught her and shoved her back to the chair, and suddenly she discovered that she was not just furious, but hungry for the man. She teased her hair against his bare midriff, soft sounds forming in her throat. She touched him with just the tip of her tongue, lathing his hard-muscled flesh until she felt the muscles ripple and tremble. She loosened his breeches and made love to him there until he shouted out hoarsely, wrenching her up and into his arms. He entered into her like fire, and the passion blazed steep and heady and wild. Crying, throbbing, sobbing, she reached a shattering climax. She felt the volatile shuddering of his body atop her own, and she shoved him from her, curling away, ashamed. He tried to draw her back. She stared into the night, amazed that she could be so angry, hate him so fiercely, and be so desperate for his touch.

"Amanda—"

"No!"

"Yes," he said simply. He drew her back and kissed her forehead. His soft husky laughter touched her cheek. "Perhaps you will better understand me after this night," he murmured. "Anger, passion, love, and pain. Sometimes they are so very close that it is torment. I have wanted you in fury, in deepest despair, when wondering if I am a fool, when despising myself for the very weakness of it. That is the nature of man."

She curled against him, glad that he did not laugh at her. He sighed softly, his breath rustling her hair. "If the world could just stay as it is. . . ."

His words faded away. For the first time since he had come home she guiltily remembered the map she held in the bottom of one of her jewelry cases. A shudder ripped through her. His arms tightened about her. "Are you cold?" he asked.

"No," she lied. She was suddenly colder than she had ever been, even with his arms about her.

She determined to change the subject of their changing world. "What was that with Jacques today? You never told me; what a very curious incident."

"Oh. Well, he wanted to kill your father. I stopped him."

Amanda wrenched around, certain that he was fooling her. She glanced at his handsome features in the darkness, and she saw that though he smiled, he was very serious. The firelight played upon his bronze and muscled chest as he lay with his fingers laced behind his head. "Why does he want to kill my father?"

"Heaven knows. Or, perhaps, everyone knows," he said quietly. He reached out and touched her chin very gently. "I have wanted to kill him upon occasion. He is not a very nice man."

Amanda flushed and her lashes fluttered above her cheeks. Eric reached out for her, pulling her back into the snug warmth of his arms. "You are not responsible for your father," he said briefly, dismissing the entire situation.

"You did not punish Jacques?"

"Punish Jacques? Of course not. He is a very proud man. He is not a slave or an indentured servant of any type—he could up and leave at a second's notice. And I need him."

She smiled in the darkness, thinking that he did tease her then. "How did you calm Jacques, then?"

He was quiet for a long time. "I told him that I wanted to kill Nigel myself," he said at last. His arm held heavily around her when she tried to rise. "Go to sleep, Amanda. It has been a long day."

She lay still beside him, but she did not sleep.

———

They traveled into Williamsburg to welcome in the New Year of 1775. The governor hosted a party, and despite the political climate, it was attended by all important men, be they leaning toward the loyalist side or the patriot. Watching the illustrious crowd that had come for the festivities, Amanda felt a tightening in her breast. It was, she thought, the last time that she should see all these people so, Damien laughing and sweeping Geneva about the floor, then bowing very low to the governor and his lady. The music was good, the company was sweet, but the mood was such that she clung to her husband's arm and remained exceptionally silent. Damien brought her to the floor and she chastised him for not appearing for Christmas. But the young man was very grave, almost cold. She wanted to box his ears, for she wouldn't be in her present predicament at all if it weren't for him. I should have let them hang you! she nearly shouted, but then her father appeared, asking for the dance, and Damien demurely handed her over to her father.

"I need something more," Sterling told her.

"What?"

"British troops are moving with greater frequency into Boston, and I suspect help here. There isn't going to be any help for Virginia if I can't get more information."

"I haven't any more! Eric has just come home; it has been winter."

"Find something."

"I won't do it."

"We shall see," he told her softly, and left her standing alone on the dance floor. She quickly fled over to the punch bowl, but the sweet-flavored drink was not spiked. Robert Tarryton found her there.

"Looking for something stronger, love?"

"I'm not your love."

He sipped the punch himself, assessing her over the rim of his glass. Her hair was piled into curls on top of her head, her shoulders were just barely covered with the fringe of the mink that trimmed her gown. "The time is coming. There's to be a Virginia Convention in March. In Richmond. The delegates are hiding from the governor."

"They can hardly be hiding when Mr. Randolph approached the governor himself about the elections."

He smiled. "Your husband has been asked to be there."

"What? But it will be closed sessions, surely—"

"Nevertheless, madame, I have it from the most reputable sources that he has agreed to be there." He bowed, smiling deeply. "The time is coming, Amanda . . ." he whispered. Then he, too, slipped away into the crowd.

Glancing across the room, Amanda saw that Eric was heavily involved in conversation with a man she knew to be a member of the House of Burgesses. Feeling doubly betrayed, Amanda retrieved her coat and headed for the gardens. A tall handsome black man in impeccable livery opened the door for her, and she fled out into the night. She wandered aimlessly, for the flowers were dead, and the garden was barren and as wintry as her heart. She had never deceived herself, she tried to reason. Eric was a traitor, she had known it. She had despised him for it. She had never thought that she could learn to love a traitor so dearly.

But what would she do while the world crumbled?

As she came around to the stables, she suddenly heard a strange commotion among the horses and grooms. For a moment she was still, and then she hurried over to see what was happening. An older man with naturally whitened hair was instructing a few boys on how to make a fallen, saddled mount stand. The horse was down, sprawled upon the ground in a grotesque parody of sleep.

"What has happened?" Amanda cried.

The older man, wiping a sheen of sweat from his face despite the winter's cold, looked her way quickly, offering her a courteous bow. "Milady, we're losing the bay, I'm afraid. And I canna tell ye why! 'Tis a fine young gelding belonging to Mr. Damien Roswell, and of a sudden, the horse is taken sick as death!"

The boys had just about gotten the mount to its feet. Beautiful dark brown eyes rolled suddenly. They seemed to stare right at Amanda with agony and reproach. Then the horse's legs started to give again. The eyes glazed over, and despite the best efforts of the grooms, the beautiful animal crashed down dead upon the hard, cold ground.

Amanda started to back away. A scream rose in her throat. It was Damien's horse. Dead upon the ground. It was a warning of what might soon befall Damien if she did not obey her father.

"Milady—" someone called.

She heard no more. Just as the horse had done, she crashed to the ground, oblivious to the world around her.

———

When she came to, she was being lifted in her husband's arms. His silver blue eyes were dark as cobalt then, upon her hard with suspicious anxiety. She closed her eyes against him, but held tight to him. "I'll take you inside—"

"No, please, take me home."

There was a crowd around them, Damien among them. She did not want to see her cousin's concerned face, and so she kept her eyes closed. Eric announced that she just wanted to go home, and then he was carrying her to their carriage. Inside he was quiet, and he did not whisper a word. When they reached the town house he carried her upstairs, asking that his housekeeper make tea, the real tea that had come from China aboard his own ship. Danielle came to help Amanda from her gown and into a warm nightdress, clucking with concern over her. Amanda kept saying dully that she was all right. But when she was dressed and in bed Eric himself came with the tea. She did not like the very suspicious and brooding cast to his eyes, so she kept her own closed. But he made her sit up, made her sip the tea, and then demanded to know what had happened.

"The horse. It—it died."

"There's more to it than that."

Amanda flashed him an angry glare. "If Geneva or Anne or the governor's lady had passed out so, you and every man there would have assumed it was no sight for a lady to see!"

"But you are a lady created of stronger stuff. You are not so sweet—or so insipid—a woman, and hardly such a delicate . . . lady."

She lunged at him in a flash of temper, very nearly upsetting the whole tea tray. He rescued it just in time, his eyes narrowing upon her dangerously.

After setting the tray upon the dresser, he turned to her. "Amanda—"

She came up upon her knees, challenging him. "What of you, milord?" she demanded heatedly. "I was fascinated to hear that you were traveling to Richmond!"

She had taken him by surprise; he seemed very displeased by it, and wary. "I see. You managed to slip away with your old lover long enough to discern that information. You are a wonderful spy."

"I am not a spy at all!" she insisted, beating upon his chest. "While you, milord, are a—"

He caught her wrists and his eyes sizzled as he stared down at her. "Yes, yes, I know. I am a traitor. What happened with Damien's horse, Amanda?"

She lowered her eyes quickly, tugging to free her wrists. She did not want to tell him that Damien, and he himself, stood in line to die in the same agonizing manner as the horse.

"I'm tired, Eric."

"Amanda—"

A lie came to her lips, one she would live to regret, one she abhorred even as she whispered it. "I'm not feeling well. I think that I might—that I might be with child."

His fingers instantly eased their hold upon her. He lay her back upon the bed, his eyes glowing, his features suddenly young and more striking than ever. His whispers were tender, his touch so gentle she could barely stand it.

"You think—"

"I don't know as yet. Just please . . . please, I am so very tired tonight!"

"I shall sleep across the hall," he said instantly. He touched her forehead with his kiss, then her lips, and the touch was barely a breath of the sweetest tenderness. He rose, and her heart suddenly ached with a greater potency than it thundered as she watched him walk across the hall.

She lay there for long hours in wretched misery, then she rose, and quickly dressed. With trembling fingers she reached for her jewelry case and found the map that had been in the botany book. She needn't tell anyone where she had found it. On the floor of some tavern, perhaps.

Silently she crept from the room and down the stairs, and then out into the night.

She brought her hand to her lips, nearly screaming aloud, when a shadow stepped from behind a tree, not a half block from the house. Nigel Sterling his arms crossed over his chest, blocked her way.

"You have something for me, daughter? I was quite sure that you would."

She thrust the map toward him. "There will be no more, do you hear me? No more!"

"What is it?"

"I believe that it points out stashes of weapons about the Tidewater area. Did you hear me? I have done this. I will do no more."

"What if it comes to war?"

"Leave me alone!"

She turned to flee.

Sterling started to laugh. Even as she ran back toward the town house, she heard him wheezing with the force of his laughter.

She didn't care right then. She had appeased him for the next few months at least. And God alone knew what would happen then.

She hurried back up the steps of the town house, opened the door, and closed it behind her. Her lashes fell wearily over her eyes with relief, then she pushed away from the door, ready to start up the stairs.

She paused, her throat closing, her limbs freezing, the very night seeming to spin before her. But blackness did not descend upon her now. She could see too clearly, she was too acutely aware of the man who stood on the stairs, awaiting her. He wore a robe that hung loosely open to his waist, his sleekly muscled chest with its flurry of dark hair naked to her view and strikingly virile. His fingers curled about the bannister as if they would like to wind so about her throat. His eyes were like the night, black with fury, and his words, when he spoke, were furiously clipped.

"Where were you?"

"I—I needed air."

"You needed rest before."

"I needed air now."

"Where were you?"

"A gentleman, even a husband, has no right to question his lady that way!"

"It has been established that I am no gentleman, you are no lady. Where were you?"

"Out!"

His steps were menacing as he came toward hers. She backed into the hallway, trying to escape his wrath. "You can't force me to tell you!" she cried out. "You cannot force me . . ." Her words trailed away as he neared her. Blindly she struck out, afraid to trust his rage. He ignored her flailing hands and ducked low, sweeping her over his shoulder.

"No! You cannot make me—stop this instantly! One of the servants will hear us . . . will come . . . stop!"

His hand landed forcefully upon her derrière. "I don't give a pig's arse if the servants do come, and perhaps I cannot force you to tell me why you prowl the streets. But while you do so, madame, I shall be doubly damned if I shall be cast from my own bedroom!"

She pounded against his shoulder to no avail. A quick and vicious fight followed when they reached their chamber, but then his lips touched hers, and she remembered his words. Anger . . . it was so close to passion, so close to need. She wanted to keep fighting. She could not. The fire was lit, in moments it blazed. She never did betray her mission, nor did it matter. Despite all that soared between them, she lost something that night.

By morning Eric was gone. He left a letter telling her that he was headed for the convention and that she was to go home. She would do so with little fuss, he suggested, because certain of the servants would see that she did so by her own power or theirs.

The note was not signed "Your loving husband," "Love, Eric," or even "Eric." Warning words were all that were given to her. "Behave, Madame, or else!"

With a wretched cry she threw her pillow across the room and then she lay back, sobbing. All that she had discovered, she realized, was lost. Love had been born, it had flourished . . . and then it had foundered upon the rocky shores of revolution.

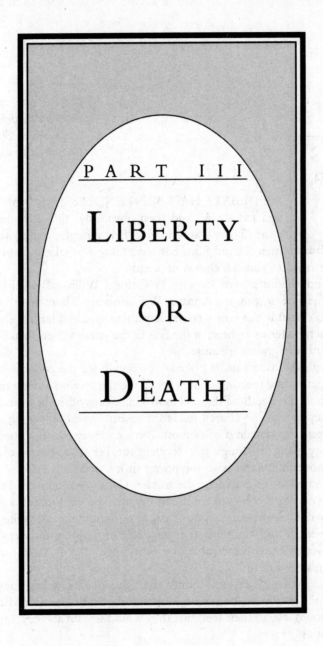

PART III

LIBERTY

OR

DEATH

12

 HE DEBATE HAD BEEN ENDLESS, HOT AND HEAVY and passionate, and then, curiously, the delegates fell silent again. There was resistance, Eric thought, quietly watching the men around him, but something was taking form here today that was destined to cast the course of a nation.

Richmond, the little town founded by Colonel William Byrd II in 1733, did not boast the fine accommodations of Williamsburg. There were not so many taverns, and certainly the inns were far less numerous, and far less elegant. Yet it seemed much better to be here, at the falls of the James River, than in Williamsburg, beneath the governor's nose.

The town itself hadn't had a place large enough for the conclave to convene, so the delegates were meeting in the church. To the loyalists among the populace —who sensed the depth of the rebellion going on within hallowed halls—the fact that they met in the church made the assembly an obscene one.

And despite the warnings of caution, Patrick Henry had the floor again, the West County giant, the rough but eloquent speaker who seemed to possess the ability to move mountains with the power of his words.

"It is in vain, sir, to extenuate the matter. Gentlemen may cry Peace! Peace! But there is no peace. The war is actually begun. The next gale that sweeps from the north will bring to our ears the clash of resounding arms! Is life so dear, or peace so sweet, as to be purchased at the price of chains and slavery? Forbid it, Almighty God! I know not what course others may take, but as for me, give me liberty, or give me death!''

The tenor of his voice, the sound, the substance of words, rang and rang against the day, with startling, dizzying, almost blinding passion. Eric thought that men would leap to their feet, that they would scream and cry from the force of the emotion.

But there was silence. Men appeared stunned by the boldness and the honesty of the words.

Henry looked around the assembly, then sat.

And still his words were met by silence as they seemed to echo and echo through the church. Then slowly a few delegates rose to oppose him, but then

Richard Henry Lee was on his feet, speaking up for Henry's resolution, and then Thomas Jefferson asked for recognition. Jefferson was a damned good writer but not much of an orator. Still, when he rose, and spoke for Patrick Henry's resolves, a peculiar eloquence touched him. Tall, with his flaming red hair neatly queued, he gestured awkwardly, but still, his words, his manner, touched many men. Eric could feel it in his own heart; he could see it in other men's eyes.

When the gentlemen at last broke for the day, it was resolved that they would form committees.

It was resolved that troops would be raised for Virginia's defense.

And it was known that within the next few days, the vote would be cast for the delegates to travel to Philadelphia a second time.

Eric, leaving the church at Washington's side, was quiet as he heard the words spoken by Patrick Henry repeated again and again. They were whispered at first, but then the whispers rose.

Two years ago they would have all claimed his words treason. But now only the staunch loyalists thought so.

"He shall go down in history," Washington commented.

Eric grinned as they carefully moved through the early-spring muck, heading for one of the local taverns.

"I imagine he shall," Eric agreed.

Washington stopped suddenly, leaning against a tree that had just sprouted soft green leaves. He turned and looked at Eric intently. "It will be war, you know."

"Yes, I think it shall."

"What will you do?"

Eric twisted his jaw, watching his own friend levelly. "I think, George, that over the years I have more than proven my loyalty to Virginia."

"Your loyalty is not in question. But you have grave interests. I've spoken with many dear friends who are planning to return to England. Fairfax and Sally . . . they are going soon. Many friends."

Eric nodded grimly. "I've spoken with a few cousins who are leaving. I've an appointment tonight with a distant Cameron relation. I'm selling him property I have in England and I'm buying up the land that he has bordering my own."

"You are lucky to be able to make such arrangements." Washington watched him intently. "What of your wife?"

Eric did not mean to stiffen so abruptly and so completely, and give away so much of himself. "I don't know what you mean," he said too quickly. Life had moved fast and furiously in the last few months. Momentous things were happening. He was caught in the wild winds of change, and he was eager to ride them. He had steered his mind from thoughts of Amanda by day, but she had haunted him every night, and along with the pain and the longing had come bitterness. He would never be able to trust her. What in God's name had she been doing, running into the night? Meeting with an influential Tory—or with a lover? Or perhaps the lover and the Tory were one and the same. His anger at her had been so great he hadn't dared to stay with her.

She had lied about the child. She had known something about the death of Damien's horse. She was betraying him with every breath she took.

"What do you mean, 'What of my wife'?" he queried coldly.

"Eric, I'm your friend. It's just that it is well known that Lady Cameron's sympathies have not changed—"

"She is suspected of something?" Eric asked flatly.

"Eric, I do not try to offend you—"

"George, you do not offend me. But Amanda is my wife. She will support me."

"But—"

"Or else," Eric said, squaring his jaw stubbornly. "I will take care of her."

"What if—"

"I will take care of her, George. You've my solemn vow on that. If it becomes necessary, I will see that she is removed."

Washington looked at him, then sighed softly. "I pray, my friend, that you can. I for one could not. But come, let's have a drink together, while we still can. I've a feeling that things that have so far crawled will take off with a mad gallop soon."

Twenty minutes later they were all within the tavern at a table, he and George, Richard Henry Lee, Patrick Henry, and a few others. An elderly gentleman, Pierre Dupree, from north of the Richmond area, had joined them. And yet, as the men drank and laughed and teased and tried to take harbor from the growing sense of tension they themselves were creating, Eric noted that Dupree was watching him and paying little attention to the true firebrands who were the root of revolution.

Dupree, white-haired, impeccably dressed in mustard breeches and crimson coat, could down his fair share of whiskey. As the others flagged and begged leave to retire for the night, Dupree remained. Finally Washington rose, and all that remained in the dimly lit place at the table were Eric—and Dupree.

"Well, my young *ami*," Dupree murmured, "perhaps another drink?"

The candle burned low upon their table. Slumped back in his chair, Eric grinned, feeling lighter than he had for some time. "Monsieur Dupree, you have studied me so seriously. You have waited for so long. Why?"

The old man offered him a Gaelic shrug. "Curious, monsieur. And with no right to be so."

"Curious?" Surprised, Eric raised his pewter tankard and downed a long swallow of whiskey. "I admit to being baffled, monsieur. Tell me, what is it you wish to know?"

"I don't wish to offend you."

Eric smiled. "Don't offend me, sir, merely speak."

Dupree inhaled deeply. "Perhaps I can be of service to you, and that is what really draws me."

"Then I am grateful. Please, tell me what this is all about."

Dupree plunged in then, quickly and somberly, his words so soft that they did not carry in the empty room. "I understand that Amanda Sterling is now Lady Cameron."

Eric's reaction was instantaneous. Again he felt the stiffening of his muscles, the razor pain that touched him. The loneliness, the bitterness. He wanted his wife. He wanted her with him, beneath him, crying out softly in hunger and need. He wanted to strike her and walk away from her.

"She is my wife." He did not realize that his eyes had narrowed darkly, that any semblance of a smile had fled his features, that his words came out in a growl. "If you've something to say, then do so, for I tire and I lose my patience quickly!"

"It is a delicate matter—"

"Delicate be damned. If you would speak, do so. If not, leave me in peace!"

"There is a story—"

"Then tell it!"

Dupree had hesitated, but the man was no coward. He did not balk at Eric's anger, but plunged in quickly. "Years and years ago I knew her mother."

"My wife's mother?"

"Yes. She was beautiful. So beautiful. Light and elegant, with the sun in her eyes, in her words, in her every movement. She was passion, she was energy, she was vitality! Remembering her gives me back my youth. She was so alive."

Like Amanda, Eric thought. Always the flames in her eyes, the heat in her soul, the passion for life itself.

"Go on." Again, the short words came as a growl.

Pierre Dupree moved closer. "I came to Williamsburg often in those days. I was a Frenchman born on Virginia soil, loyal to the King of England. But when I knew that Acadians were arriving in Williamsburg, desperate for homes, I had to come. I had to help those men who spoke my language. You understand?"

Eric merely nodded. Dupree went on. "I was Lenore's friend. She trusted me. She—she came to me for advice."

"About what?" Eric demanded.

"Well, she was kindness itself, you must remember. She saw the suffering; she saw the loss and confusion of the people. When the ships came laden with the exiled Acadians, Lenore demanded that her husband take some of them on. Perhaps it was not so great a kindness. I'm assuming you know Nigel Sterling."

Again Eric nodded gravely, saying nothing, giving nothing. Dupree did not need his approval. He continued. "She never should have married him. Never. Sterling was always everything pompous and cruel in a man, despite his property, despite his title, despite his claim to wealth. He coveted glory, and greater titles, at the expense of all else. He did not deserve a woman like Lenore."

"Pray, sir! The good woman is long dead and buried. And freed from Nigel Sterling. So of what do you prattle?"

"She came to me, sir, because she was going to bear a child. A child who did not belong to Nigel Sterling, but to a handsome young Frenchman. To an Acadian, that is, sir. To the man Sterling had taken on as hired help."

Eric inhaled sharply, watching the man ever more intently.

Dupree saw that his words had sunk home. "She was in love. Deeply in love. Oh, it is easy to imagine. There was Sterling, hard, unbending—cruel. And there was the handsome Frenchman with light eyes and ebony hair and the kindest touch upon her! He loved her, I am certain. Who could not love Lenore? And yet when she came to me, I saw nothing of love and everything of scandal. I told her that she must not sin again, that she must give Sterling the child as his very own son or daughter, that for her sake—and for the very life of her lover!—she must never let Sterling know." He sighed, shaking his head. "I was so very wrong! She should have fled with the Frenchman, she should have run to New Orleans with him. She might have found happiness. Instead . . ."

"Instead! What the hell happened, Dupree? Damn you, man, finish this thing now that you have started!"

"I know nothing for fact," Dupree said regretfully, looking into his whiskey. "All I know is what was whispered of the Acadians. Sterling discovered her. He damned her, he fought with her. She tumbled down the stairway and was delivered too soon of her daughter. And as she lay abed, dying, bleeding to death, he swore to her that he would kill her lover. And he promised her that he would use her daughter and see that she paid for every sin her mother had ever committed. And when Lenore lay dead at last, he found the young Frenchman and beat him to death and buried him in some unmarked grave."

"My God," Eric breathed at last. He didn't want to believe the man's words. The accusations were too horrid.

But he could not disbelieve him. He had seen Nigel Sterling with his daughter. He had seen how he had treated her.

Did that mean that he had committed murder, though? Would he sink so very low?

His heart lurched suddenly, seeming to tear, to split assunder. God! He wanted to believe in her. He wanted to love her, to give her everything. What hold did Sterling have upon her?

He wanted her. He wanted her then to hold and cradle and keep and assure. He wanted to make certain that no one could hurt her again. That Nigel Sterling could never again reach her.

He jolted up suddenly, thinking of his own man, Jacques Bisset.

Jacques—who had seen Nigel and who had flown into a raving fury, determined to kill the man. . . .

Jacques, who had been found when Eric had been just a boy. Found on the roadside, barely alive, unconscious, barely breathing. Jacques, who had never known who he was, or from where he had come. All that he had known was that he was a Frenchman. Striking, with laughing dark eyes, fine features, full, sensual lips . . .

"Her father."

"Your pardon, my lord?"

Eric shook his head vehemently. "Nothing—"

Suddenly Dupree's light eyes clouded over and he looked very grave. "Lord Cameron! You must not believe that you have been tricked or defrauded! No one knows of this . . . oh, I am so distressed now. I had not realized that you might now despise your wife for being the love child of her mother and not the legitimate issue of Lord Sterling. Oh, please, you mustn't despise her for this—"

"I assure you, sir, that I will never despise her for this." He might be furious with her for any number of other reasons, but for being Jacques's daughter rather than Sterling's, he could only applaud her.

"Sir! I brought you this secret because I owed the girl's mother. I have been plagued with guilt for years; I have worried about *la belle jeune fille,* and I beseech you—"

"And I assure you, Monsieur Dupree, that your secret about my wife's birth shall remain my secret now. I do ask your permission, though, to tell the truth to Amanda, if I ever feel that it will be to her benefit to know."

"Tell a lady that she is a love child? I cannot see where this would please one raised as she!"

"Bastard, actually," Eric suggested with a trace of humor. "Still, Monsieur Dupree, the news might please her. At some later date. If that time comes . . . ?"

Dupree lifted his hands in a typical French gesture. "She is your wife, Lord Cameron. You must know her very well."

Not half as well as I would like, Eric thought. "Thank you, *merci,*" he said aloud. Dupree rose then and left him at the round oak table. Eric downed the rest of his whiskey and sat there as the candle died, pensively watching the dying flicker of the flame.

Then he rose quickly, called for writing materials, and set about carefully to write to his wife.

He had not forgiven her; he did not know if he could. But he loved her, and he wanted her. Jacques and the servants had been keeping a steady eye upon her, but she was his responsibility. His temper had somewhat cooled. It was time to see her again.

———

He never knew quite what she would do.

The convention ended on March 27; Eric had returned to Williamsburg, where he had bade Amanda to meet him.

He did not go immediately to his town house, but stopped by the Raleigh for ale to cool his parched throat—and for a hot bath out in the privacy of one of the storerooms with only a lad who couldn't begin to comprehend Eric's determination to totally immerse himself more than necessary. He could have gone home and enjoyed bathing in far more luxury, but didn't want to greet Amanda with the dust and mud of travel upon him. There was too much between them now, far too great a gulf. And he was far too eager to see her.

"Damn her!" he muttered aloud, through the steaming bath cloth that lay over his face.

"Your pardon, my lord?" the serving boy said with confusion.

He laughed softly, a dry sound, and removed the cloth. He grinned to the boy. "Nothing, lad. Just take your time before you marry, son, and even then, take more time!"

The boy grinned. Eric popped the cloth back upon his face, and she was there again before him. Amanda.

Many times he lay awake at night and cursed himself. The world was exploding, he was living in a time of drastic revolution and change. He was central to many of the things happening, and despite that, he spent his nights and often his days in anguished thought and dream and nightmare regarding his wife. He did love her so much. And that was the rub. It was bitter, bitter gall to wonder at the emotion she bore him, to never know for certain what was hidden beneath the sweep of her lashes, within the beautiful color of her eyes. There was always that which she held away from him, always that which she seemed to deny him with thought and stoic determination. He had walked away from her in anger, but he had been the one to pay the price. Now, knowing more about her, he wanted to try to find the truth within her heart and mind once more.

And still, he reflected, there was the matter of a man's pride. He had, upon occasion, betrayed himself for her. He swore silently that he would never betray Virginia, or the colonies, or his men for her.

The steam had grown cold. He called for a towel and his clothes, dressed quickly, tipped the serving lad, and headed for the street and his horse. He was but minutes from the town house.

And when he arrived, he sat on his horse for several long moments. He wondered if she had even obeyed his summons to come here. His words had been curt, demanding her appearance. His pride had forged his words.

The moon, soft and glowing, rose high over him. The first of the spring roses were just beginning to blossom in the garden, and vines were curling around the latticed trellises upon the porch. The light of a gas lamp glowed softly from within the parlor, and suddenly, even as he watched, even as his heart and body quickened, he saw her silhouette. Slim, graceful, she moved across the room, leaving it. And then, seconds later, she was at the front door, opening it.

"Eric?"

He dismounted from his horse, patted its rump, and let the animal amble forward to graze on the small stretch of lawn before the house. The horse would make it to the stables by itself. He watched her where she stood upon the porch, awaiting him. It was spring, and a soft breeze rose, and her gown looked like spring, soft white and lace with delicate blue flowers upon it. Her hair was swept up demurely, but strands escaped it, like drifting curls of flame, touching her cheek, dusting across her shoulders. He could not see her eyes for the shadow, but he prayed that there had been a welcome in her voice.

He did not respond to her; he did not need to. The streets were lit with gas lamps and the moon itself was giving off a majestic glow. He started slowly along the path, seeking her eyes. She did not move. He came to the steps, and still she did not move, and then he stood before her, and he smelled the lush sweet scent of her hair and of her flesh. And he felt the racing tenor of her heart, saw the pulse thump erratically against her throat, and he wanted to sweep her into his arms and up the stairway right then. But then he forced himself to wonder if she trembled with pleasure at his return, or if she trembled with some secret fear or excitement due to some new espionage. Her beautiful eyes were so very wide, so anxious, almost as if she loved him, welcomed him. . . .

He allowed his eyes to travel over her and touch her, though he forced his itching fingers to remain still. "You are here," he said simply.

She stepped back, her shoulders squared, her eyes suddenly as hard as diamonds. "You commanded that I come, my lord. You commanded that I retire to Cameron Hall, and so I did. Then you commanded that I come back here, and so I have."

He caught her chin, lifting it, and his lip curled into a slow, cynical smile. "I commanded you to tell me what you did running about in the middle of the night too, and you defied me in every way imaginable."

She snatched her chin from his grip, attempting to turn about. "If you have ordered me here simply to argue—"

"I have not, madame," he said sharply, catching her arm, spinning her back about so that she faced him again. Her breasts rose provocatively with her agitation. A silken skein of hair fell like a burning cascade over her shoulder, loosened by the force of his touch. He clamped down hard upon his teeth, grateful that his breeches were tight, hating the fever that rushed through him, the desire that seemed to override both common sense and pride every time he touched her.

"Listen to me, my love!" he commanded her heatedly, coming closer against her, feeling the startling warmth of her body touch and inflame his. "There will be no argument. You're my wife. You will not disappear by night again, or by day, for that matter. There are men out there who might gladly hang you—"

"And there are men out there who might gladly hang you!" she retorted, her eyes flashing. She tugged her arm away from him. "Must we squabble in the very street?" she demanded in a tense whisper.

He laughed, startled by her hauteur. "No! By all means, let's do go in. I'd much rather squabble in our own bedchamber!"

A bright flush covered her cheeks but she did not reply to that, and he wondered if she hadn't missed him in some small way. She opened the door, entering before him. She headed for the parlor, but he caught hold of her hand, pulling her back. Her eyes came wide upon his as he indicated the stairway. "I said that I'd rather squabble within my own bedchamber. That way, madame."

She clenched her teeth. Her eyes snapped beautifully and he did not think that he could stand much more. She was going to defy him and deny him, he thought, but then she spun about in a regal fury and began to take the stairs swiftly. She burst into the bedroom. The door started to slam on him as he arrived behind her, but he caught it with his hand before it could do so and followed her in, then closing the door tightly behind him, and leaning against it. She stared at him for a moment, then spun around again to sit at her dressing table, removing the pins from her disheveled hair, brushing it with a high level of energy.

There was a sudden rapping upon the door. Eric turned impatiently and opened it. Mathilda stood there anxiously. "Oh! Lord Cameron! I hadn't realized that you had come home. I heard the commotion and I was worried about my lady—"

"Ah, Mathilda! Thank you for your concern, but as you see, it is unnecessary. I am home and all is well."

"And glad to see you, I am, my lord—"

"Thank you, Mathilda." He quickly steered her around, away from the door. "Perhaps we'll dine later."

"Oh!" Mathilda flushed crimson, realizing that her master wanted to be alone with his wife. "Oh, of course!"

Eric closed the door once again to discover Amanda staring at him with a flush nearly as bright as Mathilda's and the fire of battle naked in her eyes. "How could you be so crude!" she accused him.

"Crude? Lover, I have not yet begun."

She spun back to her mirror, and her brush tore through her hair. "Spoken like a true patriot!" she hissed.

Swift steps brought him behind her. She leapt to her feet, spinning about to face him. "Don't you dare come home like a strutting cock!" she warned him, her eyes ablaze with fury and passion. "I am tired of being ordered about and dragged here and there at your whim. Don't you dare touch me!"

"Dare touch you!" he exclaimed, his fingers gripping tightly into the back of the chair she had so recently vacated. "Madame, I shall do far more than dare to touch you. And if you keep up with your present attitude toward my return, I shall be sorely tempted to deal with you as I did when you were a child."

Her eyes widened and he could almost see her temper soar as she remembered that time when they had first met, when Eric had dragged her over his knee in the midst of the fox hunt. He took a step toward her and she seized her brush from her dressing table, hurtling it toward him. Eric ducked just in time.

Amanda knew she had gone too far when she saw the dark cast to his expression as his eyes met hers again. She hadn't meant this, this awful fight, it was just that she was always afraid, it seemed. And he goaded her so.

What she had wanted was him, but she had gone too far now to admit that. She straightened her shoulders. She needed time. "Eric, let's leave this be. I've things to do, we can cool down, we can talk later—"

"I don't want to talk, Amanda," he snapped.

"You're being crude again!" she charged him.

"And I don't want to cool down."

"Don't you take another step toward me."

He did, and she looked quickly for a second object to throw. She found a book set upon the chair by the fire and hurled it so quickly that she found her mark, catching him right in the temple.

He swore furiously. Even as she cried out, he had grasped her wrist. "No, Eric, no!" she gasped, but he was not to be waylaid. Within seconds he was in the chair, and she was strung over his lap, and his palm was descending deftly upon her posterior. Outraged, she cried out. Desperately she freed herself from his hold, falling to the floor at his feet and staring at him with wrath nearly choking away her words.

"Now, madame—" he began.

"You must be insane. After what you've done! This is neither the time nor the place—"

"It is precisely the place, and the time," he stated flatly.

It was not. She was quickly on her feet. Her eyes met his and she realized that he was still every bit as furious as she was. She decided on a hasty retreat, streaking toward the bedroom door. He was there beside her, slamming it closed. She stepped quickly away as he remained there, his back to the door. "The time, and the place, love. You'll note, our bed lies there, my love, awaiting us."

"I've no intention of joining you in bed. No intention, do you understand me?"

"Then the floor shall be just fine."

He was already in motion. Even as she turned to flee a second time, his hands were upon her arm, jerking her around and into his arms. Gasping, she tried to kick him. She was off balance so, and he quickly swept her up, bearing her down to the floor. She found herself staring into his eyes, startled by the depth of the passion within them. "I have missed you deeply," he breathed to her.

"Bastard!" she snapped back with soft venom. "I will not—" she paused, moistening her lips. "I will not make love with you here on the floor." His lips were above hers. He smiled slowly. Her heart was thundering. He would surely strike her, or kiss her. He did not. Instead, he straddled her, and began to untie the ribbons to her bodice. She lay still, feeling his fingers move upon her, knowing how deeply she had missed him.

"I think that you'll make love anywhere I demand," he said.

"Oh!" Furious, she slapped his hands away. He laughed dangerously and warned her, "Make love, my lady, or take the risk of further interrogations!"

"Eric Cameron—" she began.

But then he did kiss her, and in moments she didn't feel the floor, she felt the warmth and heat of the man and fire escalating between them. His hands were upon her, beneath her shirt and petticoats, finding naked flesh. She did not know what seized her there, she knew only that the flames of anger and passion were combining with her and that she could no longer fight him. He was quickly wedged between her thighs. His hand cupped her mound, his fingers stroked into the moist heat of her body even as his lips caught hers, searing her with another kiss. She felt him wrestle with his breeches, and then it was the steel shaft of his masculinity within her, and fevered winds quickly rose to rock the world between them. Desperately she rocked with him and clung to him, felt the pounding, pulsing rhythm, the need rising so high and sweet that it was nearly anguish. And then it burst upon her, so shattering, so strong, and filled with honeyed sweetness, that the world itself swung to darkness for long, long moments.

Then she kept her eyes closed as she tried to breathe slowly once again. She felt Eric shift from her, and she felt his eyes upon her. Then she felt his lips touching hers. Softly. So softly. She opened her eyes and met his. There was a certain sorrow within them.

He rose, lifting her up into his arms, and setting her down at the dressing table. She met his eyes in the mirror. He found her brush on the floor and stroked it through the sable strands of her hair.

"Why do we fight so?" he asked her.

She shook her head, unable to answer.

"Let me be tender," he whispered softly.

He was going to make love to her again, she realized.

And she wanted him to do so. She still hungered for him. Hungered for him greatly.

He stroked his knuckles over her cheeks, then over her shoulders where they were bared. So gently now. His fingers stroked softly lower to the ribbons of her bodice, and those he finished untying. He slipped the straps of her shift from her shoulders, and pressed down upon the mounds of cotton and muslin until the gown and garment fell to her waist, baring her breasts to him in the mirror. She did not move, but continued to meet his gaze. His fingers closed over her breasts, molding them, cupping them. Then he flicked his thumbs upon her nipples, stroked around the aureoles, and delicately, softly, caressed the pebbled crests again. She moaned low and softly and with just a touch of desperation. Her eyes closed at last and her head fell back against his torso. And still, he saw, in the shimmering image of the mirror, the beauty of her. The fullness, the lushness of her breasts beneath his hands, the ivory gleam and perfection of her flesh, the startling fall of her hair against the slender column of her throat. He bent down, finding her lips, and kissed her. She tasted of everything sweet and intoxicating in life. Her lips trembled beneath his and parted.

He straightened and came around before her upon one knee. Her eyes wide and dilated, she looked down upon him.

"I'll never ask you again where you went from the town house, Amanda," he told her. "But I'll never let you leave again. Do you understand me?" She nodded very slowly. Something about the way she looked at him swept the last of the anger from his being. He cried out in sudden frustration, rose, and pulled her to her feet against him. "You needn't fear him, Amanda, do you understand me? You needn't fear Nigel Sterling!"

Dismay filled her eyes. Her head fell back. Eric rushed on. "Dammit, don't you understand me? You can never go to him again, never go near Tarryton again, or I shall be forced to kill one of them, can't you understand that? Amanda! I am your husband, I will protect you. You needn't fear Sterling or Tarryton!"

A soft sob escaped her and she tried to bury her face against him, but he could not allow her to do so. He caught her shoulders and shook her slightly. "Do you understand me, Amanda?"

"Yes! Yes!" she cried out, and tried to jerk free. He held her tight and his lips descended upon hers. They were bruising and forceful and even cruel to hold on to hers . . . but then she went still in his arms, soft and warm and giving, and his tongue bathed her mouth where he had offered force, and his lips became gentle and coercive, and then so soft that she was hungrily pressing against him for more.

And her fingers were upon his frock coat, shoving it from his shoulders. And soft and subtle, they were upon the buttons of his shirt, and then the stroke of her nails was delicate and exquisite upon his naked flesh.

He brought his hands against her flesh, shoving her gown and garments to the floor. He plucked her up and lay her upon the bed in her stockings and garters. She watched him in the soft candle glow as he divested himself of his clothing. When he came down beside her, she wrapped him in her arms.

They made love slowly that second time. So slowly. Exchanging sultry kisses and soft caresses, and then urgent whispers. She made love to him sweetly, and more savagely, and Eric reveled in her every touch. Desire, volatile and explosive, rose high within him. He thrust into her with his very being, so it seemed.

It was exquisite, it was a tempest. It drew everything from him and returned everything to him. But when it was over and he held her naked form close to him while the candle upon the dressing table faded out, he again decried himself for loving her so deeply. No matter how sweetly, how wantonly she made love to him, she held something back. He had yet to touch her soul.

Yet to touch the truth.

She moved slightly against him. He held her closer. "Are you cold?"

"No."

"Hungry?"

"No," she replied again.

He rose slightly upon an elbow, enjoying the beautiful slope and angle and shadow of her back and derriere in the near-total darkness.

He watched her in the darkness, then came back beside her. Her eyes were more than half closed as exhaustion claimed her. He softly stroked the flesh of her arm, then lay down beside her again and very gently took her into his arms. He wanted to apologize again; he could not. He held her for a long while, then whispered to her softly, "Amanda, trust in me. Dear God, trust in me, please."

She did not reply. He didn't know if she truly slept, or if she simply didn't have an answer for him.

In the days that followed Eric gave Amanda news about the convention, warning her that the time was coming close when they might be facing armed conflict. A summons came from the governor, which Eric quickly answered. Lord Dunmore was fuming. He had been furious that he had been ignored when he had issued a proclamation that all magistrates—and others—should use their utmost endeavors to prevent the election of delegates to the Second Continental Congress.

Amanda was sure that Dunmore would be furious with Eric, but he did not balk from the summons. What went on in the interview, she did not know, but she was certain that the total rift between them was begun that day.

When he returned to the town house, she ran down the stairs to the parlor to meet him. "What happened?" she asked anxiously.

He set his gloves and plumed tricorn upon the table, and looked her way. "It will come to war, Amanda. I wonder, will you be with me, or against me?"

"I—I can't deny my loyalties!" she told him, begging him with her eyes to understand. She was grasping at straws, she thought. He had caught her slipping from the house. He knew that she had lied about thinking she might be with child.

She had betrayed him, and he knew it, and he would not trust her, or love her, again.

He nodded, looking at her, looking past her. "Let your heart lie where it will. But follow my commands, my love!" he warned softly.

She did not answer, but fled up the stairs.

Several nights later, just as dawn came on April 20, Amanda lay beside him, naked, content, secure within his arms. She had not known until he had returned just how bitterly she had missed him. She loved just being held, just sleeping with the fall of his bronze arm upon her. She liked to awaken and see the angle of his jaw; she thrilled to the striking planes of his face, to the crisp mat of dark hair upon his chest, to the rugged texture of his hard-muscled and masculine thighs entangled with her own.

Shouts in the street suddenly startled her. She started to rise, half asleep, confused. Beside her, Eric bolted up and strode quickly to the window.

"What is it?" she asked.

"I don't know. A crowd. A huge crowd." He found his breeches and stumbled into them. He threw open the window and shouted down to the street. "My good man! What goes on down there."

"The powder! The arms. The bloody redcoats marines came in off the *Fowey* in the James and stole our supplies from the magazine! We're not a-goin' to take it, Lord Cameron! We can't!"

"Son of a bitch!" Eric muttered. He grabbed his shirt and boots. Clutching the sheet, Amanda stared at him.

"They'll march on the palace!" she said.

He cast her a quick glance. "Bloodshed here and now must be avoided!" he said, but she didn't think that he was really talking to her, but rather thinking aloud. He reached for his frock coat and she leapt from the bed at last.

"Eric—"

"Amanda, go back to sleep."

"Go back to sleep!" she wailed, but he was already leaving her, closing the door behind him.

She watched him go, then quickly dressed and followed him out.

When she left the house, she knew that she was followed. Jacques Bisset had followed her every move since Eric had left her in January. She didn't mind. She was fascinated by the man, and she always felt safe with him behind her.

And she'd had no more demands from her father since she had given him the map.

It was not difficult to follow Eric. The roar and pulse of the crowd could be heard and felt from afar. Amanda hurried toward the Capitol. It seemed that the whole population of Williamsburg had turned out in a fury.

Someone shouted, "To the palace!"

Stepping back against a building, Amanda inhaled sharply. The cry was going up on the air. The mob seemed to seethe, the people within it angry, impassioned, ugly in their reckless force.

"Stop, stop!" a voice called out.

Amanda climbed upon shop steps to see. It was Peyton Randolph. Carter Nicholas was at his side, Eric was behind him.

The noise from the crowd dimmed. Randolph began to speak, advising the people that they might defeat their own purpose. They needed to issue a protest drafted in the Common Hall.

Carter Nicholas echoed the warnings, and then Eric spoke, urging everyone to caution.

Slowly the crowd dispersed.

Jostled in the sudden stream of humanity, Amanda was startled when she was suddenly clutched from behind and turned around to meet her husband's angry eyes. "I told you to go back to sleep!"

"But, Eric—"

"Damn you, Amanda, I am trying to avoid the shedding of your dear Tory Dunmore's blood. Jacques is taking you back to Cameron Hall. Today. I want you out of this!"

She tried to protest, he wasn't about to allow it.

And by noon she was on her way home.

———

News trickled to her slowly at Cameron Hall. She listened avidly to the servants, and she eagerly awaited the news in the _Virginia Gazette._

The people drafted a demand to know why the governor had taken their weapons. Dunmore replied that he had been concerned about a slave insurrection and had removed the powder for safety's sake.

Eric arrived exhausted one evening to tell her that meetings had been taking place elsewhere. Randolph and Nicholas had managed to keep the people of Williamsburg under control, but the people of Caroline County had authorized the release of gunpowder to the volunteers gathered at Bowling Green. Edmund Pendleton, however, chairman of that committee, would not allow action until he heard from Peyton Randolph.

Fourteen companies of light horse had gathered in Fredericksburg, and they were ready to ride on the capital. On April 28 the reply from Randolph reached those ready to fight—he requested caution. While there was any hope of reconcilation, it was necessary to avoid violence.

The people had ridden home. The message had been tactfully written, and men such as the Long Knives were quieted.

"Thank God!" Sitting in the elegant parlor at Cameron Hall, Amanda turned anguished eyes on her husband and fervently whispered the sentiment.

Eric, worn and dusty from riding, stared at her with a curious look in his eyes.

"There is more," he told her.

She rose, her hands clenched in her lap. "What? You—you've been in Fredericksburg. You would have ridden on the capital!"

He did not answer the question. "Amanda, shots were fired in Massachusetts. At Lexington and at Concord. The British went after the arms stored there, and the colonists—the 'minutemen'—fought them every step of the way back to Boston."

"Oh, no!" So blood had been shed after all, not in Virginia, but in Massachusetts.

"Patrick Henry marched with forces toward Williamsburg, but Dunmore added sailors and marines to the palace, and dragged cannon out upon the lawn. An emissary came out on May second to pay for the powder that had been taken."

"You were with Patrick Henry!" she gasped.

"I was a messenger, Amanda—"

"How could you—"

"I can caution reason on both sides, my lady!" he snapped, and she fell silent. "That is not all."

She stared at him, extremely worried by his tone of voice.

"Amanda, Patrick Henry has been branded a rebel." He hesitated briefly. "And so have I," he continued very quietly. "I suspect that within a number of days there might well be an arrest warrant out for me."

"Oh, no!" Amanda gasped. She stared at him, her husband, tall, dark, striking and ever commanding, and in that moment she didn't care about the world. England could rot, and Virginia could melt into the sea, she did not care. "Oh, Eric!" she cried his name, and flew across the room, hurtling herself against him. He caught her in his arms and held her tight.

There were no more words between them. He carried her upstairs, and he made love to her gently and with tenderness. With that same tenderness he held her against the night, brushing a kiss against her forehead as the dawn broke.

His eyes were dark and serious as they searched hers. He lay half atop her, smoothing her hair from her forehead.

"Men are already beginning to return to England. Loyalists who believe that this breech cannot possibly be closed again. I ask you, Amanda, do you stay with me of your own accord?"

"Yes! Yes!" she told him, burying her face against his throat. "Yes, I will stay with you."

He held her in silence. "Do you stay for me, or for England?"

"What?"

He shook his head. "Never mind. I am a man labeled rebel for a moment, not that I think that Dunmore has the power to do anything about it. There are very long days ahead of us." He was silent again. "Long years," he whispered. "Come, love. A rebel dare not lie about too long. I've much I would get done about here in case—"

"In case?" she demanded anxiously.

His eyes found hers again. "In case I should have to leave quickly."

13

Y THE END OF THE WEEK, ERIC AND AMANDA stood on the dock and waved good-bye as some of their friends and neighbors—some of them bearing the Cameron name—set sail for England. Amanda cried softly, but though Eric said nothing, he felt the sense of loss keenly himself.

He did not have to worry about Governor Dunmore's branding of him as a rebel. Dunmore had fled the governor's palace and was trying to administer the government of Virginia from the decks of the naval ship *Fowey,* out in the James River.

Lord Tarryton, Anne, and their newborn daughter went with him. Amanda heard nothing from her father, and so she assumed that he, too, had fled.

Amanda worried endlessly, because Eric discovered that Damien was in Massachusetts, and he had been there at Concord and at Lexington. The Massachusetts men had played a cunning game with the British. In Boston, they had arranged a signal to warn the people when the British tried to come inland to seize their arms. Lanterns were hung in the Old North Church:— "one if by land, two if by sea." The printer Paul Revere had ridden hard into the night to give the warning. Midway through the journey, he had been stopped by soldiers, but the cry was taken up by a friend and the men were forewarned. Shots were fired on April 19, 1775, and many felt the revolution was thus engaged.

In the days that followed, Eric was seldom with Amanda. He had been asked to raise militia troops, and he was doing so. News trickled back to the colonials from Philadelphia where the Continental Congress sat. George Washington had been appointed general of the Continental forces, and he had been sent to Massachusetts to take charge of the American troops surrounding the city of Boston. It was rumored that British troops were about to march on New York City. Most members of Congress had been escorted by large parties of armed men—to protect them from the possibility of arrest. Ethan Allen, commissioned by Connecticut, and Benedict Arnold, authorized by Massachusetts, had marched on Fort Ticonderoga. The British garrison, caught by surprise, had capitulated immediately. Congress had been elated to hear tales that the Brits had been so surprised that they had not had time to don their breeches.

The fort was very important, Eric explained to Amanda, because it commanded the gateway from Canada. It was vital to the control of Lake Champlain and Lake George, principal routes to the thirteen colonies.

In June a battle was fought at Bunker Hill. The people were vastly cheered, it was rumored, because the colonial forces had met the British—and they had held their own. Defeated only because they had run out of ammunition, they had fought bravely and gallantly, even if they were rough and ragtag.

On July 3, on Cambridge Common, George Washington took command of the forces, and the Continental Army was born.

By the end of August Virginia's leaders had returned from Philadelphia. Patrick Henry appeared at Cameron Hall, and when Amanda saw him, she knew that things had really come to a head. Henry had been commissioned the colonel of the of the first Virginia regiment, and as such, he was commander-in-chief of the colony's forces.

He met with Eric alone in the parlor. When Amanda saw him leave the house, she tore down the stairs. She found Eric standing before the fire, his hands folded behind his back, his expression grave as he watched the flames.

He did not turn around, but he knew that she was there. "George has asked that I come to Boston. Congress has offered me a commission, and I am afraid that I must go."

No . . .

The word formed in her heart but did not come to Amanda's lips. He was going to accept the commission and go, and she knew it.

She turned around and fled up the stairway, then threw herself on the bed. She didn't want him to go. She was afraid as she had never been afraid before.

She had not realized that he had followed her until she felt his hands upon her shoulders, turning her to him. He touched the dampness that lay upon her cheek, and he rubbed his finger and thumb together, as if awed by the feel of her tears.

"Can this be for me?" he asked her.

"Oh, stop it, Eric! Please, for the love of God!" she begged him.

He smiled, handsomely, ruefully, and he lay beside her, wrapping her within his arms.

"Perhaps I shall not be gone so very long," he told her.

She inhaled and exhaled in a shudder against his chest, breathing in his scent, feeling the rough texture of his shirt against her cheeks. She hated it when he was gone. She had yet to learn to tell him of her feelings, she could only show them, letting the fires rise and the passion ignite between them. But not even the intensity of that heat had dissolved the barriers that had lain between them since he had caught her returning to the town house that night in Williamsburg. She did not have his trust. She felt him watch her often, and she knew that he wondered just how seriously she had betrayed him in the past and just how far she might go in the future. She could not let down the wall of her pride and beg him to forgive—it would do no good, she knew. He would still look at her the same way. And yet, when they were together at Cameron Hall, life was good, despite the tempest of the world. There was planting to be done, meat to be smoked, a household and estate to run. There were intimate dinners together, evenings when she sat quietly with a book or embroidery while he pored over maps and his correspondence. There were times when he talked to her, when his eyes glowed so fiercely and his words came so eloquently that she was nearly swept into the storm of revolution herself.

And yet she had not lied to him, ever. Her loyalty had always lain with the Crown. She had never wanted to betray him, and she did not want to turn from him now. She was afraid for him. Dunmore might be attempting to rule from a ship now, but the British fighting force was considered the finest in the world. More troops would arrive. They would cut down the men outside Boston, they would take New York.

"They will hang you if they get their hands upon you!" she told him, swallowing back a sob.

He shrugged. "They must get their hands upon me first, you know." He stroked her cheek and her throat. "There are some, you know, my love, who think that—were you a man—you might be a prime prospect for a hanging yourself."

She said nothing, aware that she was safe among any of the rebels because of their respect for Eric. Suddenly she felt a rise of chills, wondering what might become of her if he ever withdrew his protection.

"Aren't you ever afraid?" she whispered.

"I am more afraid of leaving you than I am of arriving at a battlefront," he told her. But he was smiling, and his smile seemed tender. She thought that in that moment, he believed in her. Perhaps he even loved her.

She searched out his eyes anxiously. "You mustn't worry about me at all. You must give all of your attention to staying alive!"

He laughed softly, ruffling her hair, catching a long strand between his fingers. "One might almost think that you care," he said.

She could not answer him. She wrapped her arms around him, and kissed him, teasing his lips with her tongue, taking his into her mouth, touching him again provocatively with her own. A soft low groan escaped him, and he rose, meeting her eyes, his own afire. "This is what it should be, always then. There's so little time. So let's be decadent with it, my love. Let's stay here, locked within our tower, and die *la petite mort* again and again in one another's arms."

She smiled, arrested and aroused by his charm. Then they both started at some sound by the door. Eric frowned and rose, and strode quickly to the door, throwing it open.

There was no one there. He closed the door and slid the bolt. Then he turned to her. He pulled his shirt from his breeches, slowly unbuttoned the buttons, and cast the white-laced garment to the floor. Propped on an elbow, Amanda watched him. Eric pulled off a boot, then another, then faced her, his hands on his hips. "Well, wife, you could be accommodating me, you know."

She laughed, so pained that he was leaving, so determined to hold tight to the moments they had left. Her lashes fell in a sultry crescent over her cheeks and she stared at him with lazy sensuality. "My dear lord Cameron, but I am too thoroughly enjoying this curious show! Why, 'tis scarce midday, and you seem to think—" She broke off, gasping, for he had taken a smooth running leap onto the bed, pinning her down with a mock growl.

"Conniving wench!" he accused her. His fingers curled into hers, his lips locked upon them. When the kiss was ended she no longer felt like laughing, but met his eyes with the hunger and the wonder fierce within her own. He rolled to shed his breeches, her gown was quickly cast aside, and they were then upon their knees together, eyes still meeting, a leisure seizing them again. They stroked one another softly, their knuckles upon naked flesh, running the gamut from shoulders to thighs. It was she who cried out first, and he who swept her down. But the day was long, and there was not to be a minute of it in which they were not touching in some manner. Hunger seized them, slow, sweet need. They each teased and taunted with lazy abandon, and each was caught in the tempest when the taunt and fever swept from one form to the other.

Morning did come. Amanda awoke to find her husband's eyes upon her. For a moment she thought that she saw an anguish in their depths, but then the look was gone, and he was nothing but very grave as he stared at her. He touched her cheek and warned her, "Amanda, take care in my absence. Do not betray me again. Betray not the heart, my love. For I could not forgive you again."

She pulled the covers closely about her. "How would I betray you!" she cried. "Patriots hold Virginia now!"

"But Governor Dunmore is in a ship out upon the James, not so very far at all, my love. Not so very far." He sighed, curling a lock of her hair with his finger. "Amanda, I have claimed that I am your husband, that you will go where I beckon. But I am telling you now, if you would leave me, do so. Do so now with my blessing. I can set you on a ship out to meet the governor today, before I ride myself."

"No!" she cried quickly.

"Can this mean that you have taken on the patriots' cause?" he asked her.

She colored and shook her head. "No, Eric. I cannot lie to you. But . . . neither would I leave you."

"Then dare I take this to mean that you offer me some small affection at last?"

She cast him a quick glance and she thought that he teased her, his eyes seemed so aflame with mischief. She flushed furiously. "You know that I . . ."

"Mmm," he murmured, and it sounded hard. "I know that you are probably glad to be with me—the rebel—rather than within your father's care. I can hardly take that as a compliment, madame."

"Eric, my God, don't be so cruel at a time such as this—"

"I am sorry, love. Truly, I am sorry," he muttered. She seemed so earnest. Her hair spilled in a rich river of dark flame all about her. The white sheet was pulled high upon her breast and the eyes that beheld his were dazzling with emotion, perhaps even the promise of tears.

He pulled the sheet from her and crawled over her. "One more time, my love. Pour yourself upon me, let your sweetness seep into me, one more time. For the cold northern nights ahead, breathe fire into my soul. Wife, give yourself to me."

Her arms wrapped around him. She gave herself to him as she never had before, and indeed, he felt as if he left something of himself within her, and took from her a flame, a light, that might rise in memory to still the tremors of many a night ahead.

And yet that, too, came to an end, and he was forced to realize that he must rise.

She remained abed, cocooned within the covers, as he called for a bath. When he was done, she bathed herself, and then she helped him to dress. She helped to buckle his scabbard, and when that was done she closed his heavy cloak warmly about him. He caught her to him, and as the seconds ticked by he pressed his lips to her forehead.

Then he broke away and left the room. She followed him slowly down the stairs and out to the porch where he was mounting his horse, a party of five of his volunteers ready to accompany him. She offered him the stirrup cup.

"Will you pray for me?" he asked her curiously.

"Yes, with every fiber of my being!" she whispered.

He smiled. "I will find Damien for you. And I will correspond as regularly as I can. Take care, my love," he told her. He bent and kissed her. She closed her eyes and felt his lips upon her own, and then she felt the coldness when his touch was gone.

At last he rode away, and she stood on the porch and waved until she could see him no more. Then she turned and fled up the stairs and back to her room.

But the room, too, had grown cold. She started to cry, and then she found that she was besieged by sobs. They seemed to go on and on forever. But then her tears dried, and she told herself with annoyance that she must pull herself together. Her fears were irrational. Eric would come home, and nothing would go wrong. They would ride out the storm; they would survive.

He would come home . . .

And when he did, she would find a way to earn his trust again. She would find a way to tell him that she loved him.

———

Eric had been gone two weeks when Cassidy came to her in the parlor to tell her that she had a visitor. Cassidy's manner made her frown and demand, "Who is it?"

He bowed to her deeply. "Your father, my lady."

"My father!" Stunned, she stood, knocking over the inkwell she had been using as she worked on household accounts. Neither she nor Cassidy really noted the spill of ink.

"Has he come—alone?" she asked. The coast was dangerous for Nigel Sterling now. He had been out on the river, the last she heard, with Lord Dunmore—and Robert Tarryton.

"His ship rests at the Cameron docks. A warship."

She understood why Sterling hadn't been molested upon his arrival. Biting nervously into her lower lip, she shrugged and sank slowly back to her chair. She had no choice but to see her father. She wondered if Cassidy realized it.

"Show him in," she told Cassidy.

He cast her a quick, condemning glance. He didn't understand.

Anger rose quickly within her. Couldn't Cassidy, and the others, understand that she simply wanted to save the house?

They hadn't managed to fight Sterling and his warship!

She wasn't going to beg Cassidy to believe in her or understand her. She stared at him and waited. He turned sharply on his heel and left the room. A few moments later her father entered. He came into the room alone, but even as he stepped in, she heard a commotion beyond the windows. Amanda hurried to one of the windows and looked out. A troop of royal navy men were assembling on the yard.

She turned around to stare at her father.

"What are you doing here?"

"Ever the princess, eh, daughter? The supreme lady. Not 'Welcome, Father,'' or 'How are you, Father?' but 'What are you doing here!' Well, your highness, first I shall have some of your husband's fine brandy." He walked to a cherrywood table to help himself from the decanter. Then he sat comfortably across the desk from her. "I want more information."

"You must be mad—"

"I could burn this place to the ground."

"Burn it!"

"Your husband's precious Cameron Hall?" Sterling taunted.

"He'd rather that it burned than that I give anything to you."

"Why, daughter! You've fallen in love with the rogue." Sterling set his glass sharply upon the desk, eyeing her more closely. "Then let's up the stakes here, Highness. I have Damien. I'll torture him slowly before I slit his throat if you don't cooperate."

She felt the blood rush from her face. The pounding of her heart became so loud that it seemed to engulf her. "You're lying," she accused him. But it had to be true. It had been so long since she had heard from her cousin.

Sterling sat back confidently. "The fool boy was in Massachusetts, harrying the soldiers straight back into the city of Boston. He was captured—he was recognized as kin of mine. Out of consideration for my service to the Crown, the officer in charge thought that the dear boy—my kin, you realize—should be given over to me. I greeted him like a long-lost brother—before tossing him into the brig." Sterling stared at her, smiling, for a long while.

"How—how do I know that you really have him?" Amanda managed to ask at last.

Sterling tossed her a small signet ring across the desk. She picked it up and pretended to study it, but she knew the ring. And she knew her father.

"What do you want out of me?" she demanded harshly.

"Information. About troop movements. About arms."

"But I don't know—"

"You could find out. Go into Williamsburg. Sit about the taverns. Listen. Write to your dear husband, and bring me his letters."

"You're a fool, Father. Even if I wanted to spy for you, I could not. The servants suspect me to begin with. They follow me everywhere."

"Then you had best become very clever. And you needn't worry. I will find you. Or Robert will find you."

"Robert!"

"Yes, he's with me, of course. He's very anxious to see you. The duchess has returned to England with her child, and he is a lonely man. Anxious for a tender mistress."

"You are disgusting. You thrust me to my husband against my will, and now you would cast me—despising him!—back to Robert. What manner of monster are you, Father?"

He rose, his smile never faltering. "Highness, I would hand you over to all the troops from England and beyond, and gladly."

She stood, wishing she dared to spit in his face. "When do I get Damien?"

"You don't get him! You merely keep him alive."

"No! That is no bargain. I will not be blackmailed forever."

"Why, daughter! I thought that you were loyal to the Crown!"

"I am! I was! I can no longer betray my husband—"

"Your husband!" Sterling laughed, then shook his head. "Why, daughter, you are a whore. Just like your dear mother. Lord Cameron keeps you pleased 'twixt the thighs, and so you would suddenly be loyal to a new cause!"

She slapped him as hard as she could. He sobered quickly, catching her wrist, squeezing it hard. "Pray that if your fine, rebel-stud Cameron catches you at this, daughter, I will take you away. Despise Tarryton if you would now, Amanda, but you'd be better off in his hands than in Cameron's once he discovers you!"

She jerked her hand free. "If I ever leave Virginia, I will go to Dunmore—"

He knew that she would do anything to save Damien. "Daughter—Highness! —I shall see you again soon. Very soon."

He smiled, and turned around and left her. She heard new orders shouted outside, and the sounds of the men and their armament as they marched back down to the docks. Amanda sank back into her chair and she closed her eyes. She didn't hear the door open, but she sensed that she wasn't alone. She opened her eyes and discovered that Cassidy was standing before her. Pierre, Richard, Margaret, and Remy all stood silently behind him.

"What?" Amanda cried, startled and alarmed. They stared at her so accusingly!

"They left," Cassidy said. "They didn't burn us or threaten us."

"Of—of course," Amanda said. She let her face fall into her hands. "It was my father. He—he just wanted to see if I wanted to leave with him, that is all."

Five pairs of eyes stared at her. She didn't like the defiance in young Margaret's. Or was she imagining the look? The blue-eyed, dark-haired Irish maid looked as if she were about to pick up a musket and go to war herself. And Remy, older, dark as the satin night, with Cameron Hall as long as anyone could remember, staring at her with such naked suspicion!

She wanted to scream at them all. She was mistress here in Eric's absence. They were the servants!

But they were right. She was about to betray them all.

"Have you all nothing to do!" she charged them wearily. "If you are at leisure, I am not. I have accounts!"

Slowly their lashes flickered downward. One by one they turned to leave her. When the door closed, she rested her face on her arms and damned her cousin Damien a thousand times over. She damned him for being a patriot, then she damned him for being brave, for being a fool—and then she damned him for being the one person who had always loved her unquestioningly and who had made her love him so fiercely in return.

Then her heart began to thunder anew, and she wondered what she could discover that she could give to her father that would cause the least peril among all men, the patriots and the redcoats.

And to her husband.

———

Perched atop Joshua on the heights overlooking the city of Boston, Eric was cold, bitterly cold. It was winter, and there was a very sharp bite to the wind, a dampness that seemed to sink into the bones and settle there.

Sieges were long and tedious, but Eric had come to admire the men of New England who ringed the city. They had already met the gunfire and the bloodshed of the war, but they held strong, despite the hardships, the cold, the monotony. It had been feared by some that the northern men might not take to the idea of their commander being a Virginian, a southerner, but not many people had questioned his military experience, and it seemed now that the colonies had really banded together at last to stand against a common tyranny.

"Major Lord Cameron!"

Eric turned, lifting a hand in a salute and smiling as he saw Frederick Bartholomew hurrying toward him. The young printer had come a long way since the day he had run through the streets, wounded and desperate. He had been commissioned a lieutenant. Just as Washington had found certain men indispensable to him, Eric had discovered quickly that Frederick was a man he could not do without. Though the siege itself was tedious, military life was often hectic for him. There were the endless meetings with Washington and Hamilton and the others, the continuous necessity of communications, the need to gather information about his ships, and his desperate need to know at all times what was happening in his native Virginia.

Frederick waved an envelope in his hand. "A letter from your wife, my lord!"

Eric leapt off Joshua's back, grinning good-naturedly as a chant went up from the men ringed about him. "Thank you, Frederick," he told the young printer, taking the letter. He didn't mind the camaraderie of the men, but he did want to be alone with the correspondence.

His nights were miserable. He lay awake and worried, and he slept and dreamed. He dreamed of Amanda with her fiery hair wrapped about his flesh, her eyes liquid as they met his, her kiss a fountain of warmth that aroused and enwrapped him. But then his dreams would fade and he would hold her no more, she would be dancing away in the arms of another man, and her eyes would catch his again, and the laughter within them would tell him clearly that she had played him for a fool all along.

Eric led Joshua away from the siege line, back to an empty supply tent. He sat at the planked table there with his back against the canvas and ripped open the letter. His heart quickened as she wrote that her father had come to Cameron Hall with a warship, but that he had simply left and gone back to join Dunmore when she had told him that she was going to stay.

Her letter went on, but she wrote no more of her father. Instead she wrote about the military state of Virginia, the fish being brought in and the smoking going on, about the repairs done to the mansion, about the cold. It could have been a warm letter. Yet it was stilted somehow, as if there were something she wasn't saying.

As if she were lying to him . . .

Eric cursed softly. If only he could trust her!

"Trouble, my friend?"

He started, looking to the entrance to the tent. George Washington had come upon him. As he entered the tent, he swept off his plumed and cockaded hat and dusted the snow from his cloak. Then he sat across from Eric. Alone together, neither man bothered with military protocol.

"You've a letter, I understand."

"A personal letter."

George hesitated. "There's a rumor, Eric, that someone in Virginia is supplying the British with helpful information. Areas to raid for salt and produce. Information that has helped Dunmore create such fear all along the coast."

Eric shrugged. "We all know of his burning Norfolk. That could not possibly have been caused by a spy!"

Washington was quiet for a long time. Then he leaned across the desk. "I trust your judgment, my friend. I trust your judgment."

He left without saying any more. Eric sat back, then rose and called for Frederick. He asked for writing supplies to form his reply to his wife. When the printer returned, Eric sat to his task.

He closed his eyes for a moment, shivering. He had wanted her to come to Boston for Christmas. Washington, however, had specifically requested that he not do so, promising that he could return home in the spring.

Eric exhaled, then he began to write. Very carefully. False information that might look like it could be invaluable to the British.

He finished the letter and sealed it with his signet. Then he called to Frederick again to see that his correspondence moved south as quickly as possible.

When the letter was gone he stared out at the snows of winter, feeling as if they swirled about his heart and soul. "Damn you, Amanda!" he said softly.

———

As soon as winter turned to spring, Amanda decided on another trip into Williamsburg. She announced her intentions to travel with just Pierre and Danielle, but when she came downstairs on the morning when she was to leave, she wasn't surprised to discover that Jacques Bisset was dressed and mounted and ready to ride behind her coach.

"Jacques! I did not ask you to accompany me," she told him.

He looked at her strangely, and replied as he had every time Amanda had left Cameron Hall after Eric had departed in the fall. *"Pardonnez-moi,* but Lord Cameron has charged me to guard you, and that I will."

To guard her. It was a lie. He was to watch her and discover if she betrayed her husband or his cause, Amanda knew. It didn't matter. There was really no way for him to discover anything of what she was doing, and she liked Jacques, liked him very much. She nodded slowly. "Fine," she said softly. "I will feel ever so much safer if you are along."

Danielle stepped into the coach and sat across from her. Amanda smiled wearily. The coach jolted, and they were on their way. The road was slushy with spring rains, and the day was still chill. Amanda shivered again as she looked out the window, back to the house.

She loved Cameron Hall even more fiercely than Eric, she thought, for she spent so much time there. Her portrait and his had now joined the others in the gallery. It was her home.

"You're thinking that you should take care, eh?" Danielle questioned her.

Amanda cast her a quick glance. "Danielle, I do not know what you're talking about."

Danielle exhaled impatiently. Amanda ignored her. She swallowed tightly, closing her eyes. It seemed that so very much distance lay between her and Eric now. Miles . . . and time. She had missed him so much when he had first gone. In the days that followed, she had tossed and turned through the cold lonely nights. But then her father had come, over six months ago now, it was then that the distance had settled in, then that she had grown cold, then that she had begun to feel that things were so very horrible they might never be righted.

Amanda opened her eyes and saw that Danielle was still staring at her reproachfully. The Acadian woman started to speak.

"I'm very tired," Amanda said quietly, and the other woman remained silent. Leaning back against the coach, Amanda realized that she was very afraid of Eric now. She would never be able to make him understand. She wasn't always sure she understood herself. In her desire to give information that would keep Damien alive and avoid bloodshed at the same time, she had resorted to using information from Eric's letters to her. Small things. Casual paragraphs on supplies of salt, herbs, fruits that the navy needed to avoid the plaguing diseases on the ships. She had only discovered major troop movements once, and then, it seemed, her information coincided with something the governor had learned himself. She tried not to think about battles, but she knew that it was war. Men were going to die.

Eric would never forgive her.

Somewhere during the journey she must have slept. She awoke to discover that they had come to the town house, that it was night. The door to the coach opened, starting her awake.

"We're here, Amanda," Danielle said to her.

Amanda hurried toward the house. She walked up the steps, pulling off her gloves, calling to the housekeeper at the same time. "Mathilda, I've come!" She twisted the knob, found that the door was open, and walked on into the house. "Mathilda!" she called again, walking on through to the parlor. She tossed her gloves absently upon the desk, thinking idly of that first night here when she had begun her game of chess with Eric. He had been right. She had been in check all the time.

A sound suddenly startled her and she looked across the room. Her heart leapt to her throat and caught there, and she had to clutch the desk to steady herself.

Eric was there, an elbow leaned upon the mantel, a snifter of brandy in his hand. He looked wonderful in his tight white breeches, deep-blue frock coat, white laced shirt, and high boots, his lips curved in a slowly lazy smile as she realized his presence at last.

"Eric!" Her hand fluttered to her throat.

"Amanda!" He tossed his snifter into the fire, heedless of the cracking of the glass, of the hiss and steam and ripple as the alcohol sent the flames rising high. In seconds he was across the room, and she was in his arms. In seconds she was achingly aware of him, of the scent of him, of the texture of his face, the ripple of his muscles, the rough feel of his fabric, the intoxicating feel of his lips. She felt as if she were sinking into clouds, rising into acres of heaven. It had been so long since he had touched her. . . .

She was going to fall. It didn't matter. Not at that moment. He was kissing too hungrily. When her trembling caused her to slip, he lifted her into his arms. Then she forgot her fears again as his fingers moved through her hair, and she found a simple fascination in the way that it sprang beneath her fingers. She was barely aware that they moved upstairs, she was desperate to touch more of him, to feel more of his kiss. And then, in the darkness, there was nothing but the feel and the warmth and the sex of the man, and the throbbing pulse of an ancient music, wrapping them in a world where words meant nothing. She tried to speak, whispering his name with wonder. She didn't know how he was there, but he was, glistening muscle rippling beneath her fingers, his lips feverishly upon her, upon her body, upon her breasts. The night seemed to come alive with the ragged harmony of their heartbeats, with the pulse that pounded between them, with the fever and flames that leapt and crackled and caused beautiful colors to explode even within the darkness. . . .

The night . . .

It remained alive with the beauty, and the hunger, and when passion was sated, it was still not time for words, for they needed just to touch, to hold one another, to relish something that had become exceedingly precious just to be wrenched away.

It was morning before they talked. Before Amanda worried again. Before Eric was able to explain his presence. He was still in bed, leaning against the frame, his fingers laced behind his head. Amanda had risen at last and sat before the dressing table, trying to detangle the wild mass of her hair.

"It ended. The siege ended. St. Patrick's Day brought an Irish surprise. The Brits had evacuated Boston."

Amanda met his eyes in the mirror. "I'm glad for you, Eric."

"But not for the Brits, eh?"

She shrugged.

"Well, Amanda?"

"Eric, I am trying very hard to be a neutral."

He leapt up from the bed. She felt as if she were being stalked by a tiger as he walked up behind her. "Are you, Amanda? Are you really?"

His hands were upon her shoulders. She prayed that he would not feel the way that she shook, and yet she was not lying when she spoke. "Yes! I swear that I would be neutral now, if I could."

Some passion must have touched her voice, for though he still seemed frustrated, he seemed to believe her too. He stalked back to the bed, then stretched out upon its length, casual, bold, and brazen, and catching her heart all over again. "I have heard that some of the things I told you in my letters came to be discovered."

Fear clutched her heart like an icy hand. "Much of what you have told me has been common knowledge!"

"Aye, that it has. But since I have come home, I have realized that many a good Virginian politician and military man is alarmed by the rumor that a spy rests closely among us. A woman spy, my love. They are calling her 'Highness.' Actually, her fame had even reached Boston. Washington thinks that it might be you."

His voice was cool, ironic. Her heart thundered drastically and she could scarcely breathe. She shook her head. "Eric—"

"You have never denied being a Tory, my love."

He sprang to his feet and moved up behind her. He set his hands on either side of her head and stroked her cheeks and her throat. How easily his fingers could wind about her throat!

"I am your wife," she reminded him, her eyes falling.

"But are you innocent?"

She met his eyes again in the mirror. "Eric!" she told him passionately and sincerely, "By God, I swear that in any matter of choice, I would never seek to hurt you!"

"Or my cause?"

"Or—or your cause!" she swore softly.

"Am I a fool to believe in you, Amanda?"

She shook her head, unable to speak. Her hair moved against his naked belly and he bent over her, finding her lips. He spoke just above them in a whisper. "Don't ever let me catch you, lady!" he warned huskily, then kissed her. He pulled away.

"Oh! God!" he said suddenly. "How could I have forgotten, when it is so very important! I have seen Damien!"

"What?"

She nearly screamed the word, spinning around. Eric grinned, pleased. "Yes, well the Brits had him, but he managed to escape. He had some friendly guards and they shared some ale. He managed to swim his way to some flotsam, and then he was picked up by a colonial ship. He was delivered to Baltimore and hurried back to Boston. I was able to see him just before I left."

"He's—free?" Amanda asked.

"Yes—free as a bird."

She screamed out something incomprehensible, then jumped to her feet and hurtled herself upon his naked form, bearing them both back down to the bed. He grunted and groaned, and then laughed. She showered him with kisses that caused his groaning to take on a different timbre. Laughter faded and they made love again, desperately again, until they were exhausted and glistening and unable to find words for they could not find breath. And yet finally Amanda managed to speak again. "Eric, how long do you have?"

He exhaled unhappily. "Less than a week. And so much is happening here! I've already heard that when the Virginians meet again, they plan to declare the land a commonwealth—to vote for independence! Before it is even done in the Continental Congress! History, my love, in the making, and I shall be back in New York, for that is where Washington believes they will attack next. We must plan a defense for the city."

Less than a week. So little time between them. So much that might be discovered. . . .

But Damien was free.

She twisted in his arms suddenly, smiling. "I shall never betray you, Eric!" she promised him. She almost continued. She almost told him that she loved him, but some dark shadow in his eyes held her back. He did not really believe her. He did not trust her. He was not saying as much, but it was true. He was watching her, and now she was going to have to prove that she was loyal to him, if a Tory still at heart.

"See that you don't," he warned her. She lay still against him. In a while, she realized that he slept. There were new lines about his eyes, about his mouth. Battle was taking its toll upon him.

She rose, needing to leave him to sleep, and reflect upon her new good fortune.

She dressed quickly and hurried out of the room. A pair of boots rested before one of the bedroom doors. Someone had traveled with Eric, she realized. One of his men. More danger, she thought, her heart beating fiercely.

She hurried on down the stairs and slipped into the parlor. There she knelt down before the desk and drew open the door.

And then she felt the knife against her throat, brought around her from behind. She froze.

"Good day, Lady Cameron" came a husky voice. It was the tall black man. Her father's emissary.

She forced herself to speak. "You're a fool. My husband is home. Williamsburg is run by colonials. All I need do is scream, and they will hang you—"

"Ah, but your blood will rise in a pool long before that moment, and as I'm quite sure Lord Cameron might be surprised, there is a chance that his blood might also stain the floor. Think carefully, Lady Cameron . . ." The knife came so tightly against her throat she could barely speak.

And still, she was determined on her own freedom. "Damien is free, and I am done, 'Highness' no more! Kill me if you will, but tell my father he will get nothing more from me!"

"We were afraid that you had heard of your cousin's escape, my lady. Your father sends this message—if he comes to Cameron Hall again, it will be to burn the wretched mansion to the ground. And Lord Tarryton wants you to know that if he comes, you will be his prisoner, his mistress. He is most anxious."

"If they come anywhere near Cameron Hall," she said, "they will die!"

He did not reply. A second later she no longer felt the knife against her throat. With a soft rasping cry she leapt to her feet, spinning around.

He was gone. The man was gone. The window was open, the spring breeze was rushing in. She ran to it but could see nothing.

She sank into a chair and sat there, motionless, feeling the breeze. She should tell Eric. She should admit everything that had happened, she should explain that it was all because of Damien.

She should, if she could just find the courage!

But it was over now. All over. She never had to play the spy again. Never. Eric need never know. And if she told him, he might despise her, he might never forgive her. . . .

Later Mathilda came and served her breakfast. She discovered that the boots belonged to Frederick, who had accompanied Eric, and she sat and drank coffee with him.

Eric slept most of the day. And when he came down, and his eyes fell dark and brooding, upon her, she knew that she could say nothing. It was finished. It had to be. She prayed with all her heart that it should be so.

Unless . . . unless the British did come to Cameron Hall.

They did not stay in Williamsburg long. General Charles Lee, a highly respected military man and an Englishman who had cast his lot with the colonies, was in Virginia to oversee militia troops. He was learning that the Virginia political machine was very competent and that he would do best to work with the local leaders. Eric was interested in seeing Lee and other of his friends and acquaintances, but he was most interested in returning home to Cameron Hall.

They rode the estate there, and Amanda was delighted when he applauded her various efforts to keep things moving smoothly. It was still spring, and cool, but they came to the little cover by the river, and they laid their cloaks there and made love beneath the rippling branches of the trees overhead.

Amanda still agonized over telling him the truth of what she had done, yet she was not sure that she could make him understand, and since Damien was free, no one could coerce her again.

And Eric watched her. When she would move about the house; she would catch his eyes upon her. When they rode, when they lay down to sleep together, and sometimes even when he held her. If she awakened with her back to him, she would sense that he leaned upon an elbow, watching the length of her, and she would turn and would discover it to be true, and the shadows would fall over his eyes again.

On his fifth day home the *Lady Jane* sailed brilliantly past Dunmore's ships and came in to her home berth. She had just returned from Italy, so Eric told Amanda. But when she awoke that night, Eric was not beside her. She caught a sheet about her and hurried to the window to see the activity down by the docks.

"Spying, my love?"

The question startled her. She spun around to find Eric in a simple white shirt, tight breeches and boots, his hands on his hips, framed in the doorway of her room. He strode over to stand beside her. She tried not to allow her pulse to leap. "I was looking for you. I awoke, and you were gone."

He nodded, his eyes heavy-lidded and half shielded beneath his lashes. His hands rested on her shoulders and he pulled her against him.

"The real cargo was arms, wasn't it?" she whispered.

"And powder," he agreed.

She spun around to face him, her head tilted back. "If you so mistrust me, why on earth tell me the truth?"

"You are hardly a fool. I could not convince you that I unloaded leather goods and wine by night, could I?"

He turned away, sitting at the foot of the bed, stripping off his boots, shirt, and breeches. He glanced around to see her still standing by the window, hurt by his tone of voice.

Even if she was still a spy, she would never betray Cameron Hall. He had to know that.

"Come to bed, Amanda. There is something left of the night," he told her.

She walked slowly back to the bed. She sat upon her own side, still swathed in sheets, and she watched how the moonlight played upon his shoulders and chest. He was more bronzed than ever, more tightly muscled. He stretched out beside her, and despite her anger with him, she wanted to touch him. But she didn't want to make a first move.

She didn't have to.

He emitted some impatient sound and reached for her. She cried out softly, allowing the sunset and fire of her hair to sweep over the naked length of him, and then she nipped delicately upon the flesh of his chest, at his nipples, his throat. He caught her tightly to him, sweeping her beneath him, and they made love as if in a tempest, as if a storm guided them, and perhaps it was true. Time was their enemy; they had so little of it. They were strangers in the long months between his visits, and in this maelstrom they thought, perhaps, to find one another again.

And still, when they lay spent and quiet, she knew that he watched her. His fingers moved slowly off the slope of her shoulder to her hip, and he watched her, pensive, distant.

"Lord Dunmore is dangerous," he said at last. "Some men are afraid that he intends to sail to Mount Vernon and kidnap Martha Washington."

"Surely he wouldn't dare!" she murmured.

She felt him shrug. "I am afraid, too, that he might come here."

"Because of the arms?"

Eric was silent for just the beat of a second. "But the governor knows of no arms, my love."

She swung around, facing him. "I would never betray this hall, Eric, never!"

"But who, then, is 'Highness'?" he asked her.

She shook her head, lowering it against his chest. "I would never betray my very home!" she promised him.

"Pray, lady, that you do not," he whispered, and he held her close. She said nothing, and she luxuriated in his warmth. But it wasn't enough. She was shivering, and she was afraid.

When he left, he was gone so very long. Days passed and the weeks passed and then months.

"You tremble," he told her.

"With the cold."

"But I am holding you."

"But you will leave," she told him desolately.

She couldn't see his eyes in the darkness. He stared down at her, and the depths of his feelings for her were on the tip of his tongue. He loved her so deeply. Her beauty, her fire. He loved the way that she came to him now, so naturally, so givingly. She made love with passion and with laughter, and in the midst of it, her eyes were ever more beautiful. And yet . . .

They could be ever treacherous.

She held so much in her hands now. She knew about the arms and weaponry stored at the docks. If she betrayed them now . . .

She would not! he thought with anguish. She would not!

14

SHE WOULD NOT BETRAY HIM! BAH!

That was his thought two months later when he sat in Washington's large white canvas tent in New York and stared at his old friend. The general had just written him orders, commanding him to take a ship south. His old friend and partner, Sir Thomas— now Colonel Sir Thomas—had managed to have their ship, the *Good Earth,* brought down from Boston.

"For one," Washington told him, "Congress has now sanctioned privateering. Whatever damage you may do upon the sea will be appreciated."

It was late May, and they had spent the last weeks preparing earthworks and trenches for the attack they knew was to come upon New York. Brooklyn Heights and Manhattan had been fortified and manned, and Congress had ordered Washington to hold New York. The colonials were aware that the British general Howe was due to sail south for New York from Halifax, Nova Scotia. His brother, Admiral Richard Howe, was to sail from England with reinforcements. The ragtag colonial army—in trouble now as many enlistments came to an end and the men yearned to return home—would be hard put to meet the British menace. They all knew it. Despite the victories in Virginia and the Carolinas, they desperately needed to hold the north. Benedict Arnold was losing his tenacious hold of the area outside of Quebec, and General Burgoyne had arrived with reinforcements. It was a tense time for the colonials.

And in the midst of this, Eric was sitting before Washington, hearing a confiscated message that warned Lord Dunmore of the arms and powder stored in the warehouses at Cameron Hall. There was also an urgent appeal from General Lewis of the Virginia militia that Eric come with all haste to seek to oppose an expected attack from the sea.

His hands felt cold. In the heat of coming summer, he felt as if icy fingers stroked him up and down the back in cruel mockery. He had given Amanda the benefit of every doubt. He had known that she had once practiced treachery, but he had believed her when she had sworn herself to him. He was ever the fool. The greater her passion, it seemed, the greater the betrayal. While he dreamed of the nights they had lain together, tortured himself with images of her hair curled about his naked flesh, her eyes as bright as emerald seas, her breasts full and rich within his hands and the scent of her so sweetly intoxicating it invaded even a dream . . .

He was alone with Washington. The general watched him sadly, reaching into his private stock of whiskey to offer Eric a drink.

"You were last home at the end of March?"

Eric nodded. He pulled the confiscated correspondence—signed "Highness" —toward him, then he swore violently.

"Perhaps you judge too quickly," Washington warned him.

Eric shook his head. His next words were harsh, and as cold and ruthless as he felt. "On the contrary, General, I have dragged my feet, and I may cost us much because of it!"

He stood, swallowing down the last of his whiskey, then saluted sharply. "With your leave, then, I will sail south."

"What will you do?"

"Thrash Dunmore, Sterling, and Tarryton!"

Washington stood, offering his outstretched hand. "Take care, Eric. I'm afraid that you must look for the worst. The attack isn't expected for a few days, but Dunmore is in Virginia waters. Eric, I'm trying to tell you that you may reach your home to find it burned to the ground."

"I may."

"And your wife—"

"I swear, I shall see to her."

"Eric—"

"I know that she is dangerous. I will see to her. I intend to send her to France under heavy guard."

Washington shook his head. "Perhaps she is not guilty."

"You are the one always warning me about her! The evidence points cleanly to her!"

"Perhaps, perhaps not. Perhaps she deserves a fair trial."

Eric stood, ready to exit, ready to sail. "Sir, she has already received her fair trial!" he said angrily.

He took his orders and left Washington, promising to return at the earliest possible moment. After returning to the headquarters house he had chosen in lower Manhattan, he summoned Frederick and asked for a sound crew for the ship. "Virginians, West County men, if you can. I don't care if they've ever sailed before. No one on earth is more accurate with a long rifle than a West County Virginian."

"You'll need swordsmen for hand-to-hand combat," Frederick warned him.

"Give me some men from the Carolina regiment. They're seamen, and they've all learned their swordplay well."

When Frederick left him Eric nearly bent over double, ready to scream. With all his will he tried to cast a dark shield of control over his temper, and yet he could not get her out of his mind for a moment. "I would never betray this hall, Eric. Never!" The passion of her words returned to haunt him again and again.

Sweet, sweet mockery that he could not bear. How had he believed her? He knew her!

He wanted to curl his fingers around her throat and throttle her. He wanted to tear her limb from limb. He wanted to rip that glorious hair from her head. . . .

And he wanted to take her into his arms, brutally, perhaps, but he wanted her, beneath him, to shake her, to have her, until she realized at long last that her battle was over, that she could never defy him again.

As he gathered the last of his personal belongings for the trip, there was a soft rapping upon his door. He strode across the room with its rough wood table and simple cot and threw open the door, his features surely displaying the tension of his mood. To his surprise it was Anne Marie Mabry, Sir Thomas's daughter, who stood there.

Anne Marie had come a long way from that night in Boston. She had organized many of the women's protests, the boycotting of British goods, and she had been engaged to marry a young man who had lost his life in Boston. She was no longer the coquette but a beautiful, mature young woman with a soft smile and a winning way. She had followed her father to war and was considered quite an angel by the men.

And I could not have chosen her for a wife! Eric charged himself bitterly. A woman sworn to the same cause as I, and one who is gentle, with guileless blue eyes and a tender smile.

Yet even with the thought, he knew that he could not have turned back and he knew, too, in that moment, that whatever came, he loved Amanda still. If he caught her, he would deal with her as was necessary, but he would not cease to love her. He had been ignited by the magic in emerald eyes and flame-dark hair, and no one else could ever touch him so deeply again.

"Anne Marie, come in," he said stiffly. "There's little here to offer you, though there is coffee in the pot. A fire can heat it quick enough. Or there is brandy—"

"Eric, please, I haven't come for coffee or brandy." She hesitated. "I've come to ask you to think slowly and carefully before you do irreparable harm!"

He paused, staring at her with surprise and a certain amount of amusement. "Anne Marie, they are planning on burning down my home, a house with a cornerstone set in the late 1620s! They will seize weapons and arms meant for the use of the Virginia militia and this very army. And, Anne Marie, they know that the weapons are there because my wife—the very mistress of that hall!—has told them!" His temper rose as he spoke. Too late he realized that his long strides were bearing him harshly down upon her and that he nearly had her cornered.

"By God!" he roared, casting his hands into the air. "I'm sorry, Anne Marie. But leave this be."

He walked to the side table and poured himself a brandy. Undaunted, Anne Marie hurried to his side. "Eric, I have heard rumors about all this too! Servants' gossip, but often the truest source. Amanda has not been away from Cameron Hall since you left her."

"Then someone else there is her accomplice."

"Eric, she is my friend. I know her well—"

"Anne Marie, I caught her red-handed one night. And I let it go. That was my mistake. I should have beaten her with a horse crop that night and sent her to France!"

"Eric!" Anne Marie cried. "I know you too. You could have done no such thing—"

"It might have been the right thing," he said coolly. "Anne Marie, I have to leave. I want to catch the tide."

"Oh, Eric," she said miserably, "I've done nothing useful here at all. Listen to me, please. Perhaps she was a spy. But she wouldn't have turned against her own home! Someone else is using her past against her, can't you see that?"

"I can see, Anne Marie, that Amanda has always had every opportunity to talk to me. If she was threatened, I would have defended her. I would have protected her and fought for her against any man, or any menace. She chose another course. Now, if you'll be so good as to excuse me—"

She blocked his path. Her eyes were liquid with appeal and misery. "Oh, Eric!" she murmured again, and she came up on tiptoe to kiss him.

He didn't know what overcame him. Maybe it was just the bitter pain of betrayal, but when her lips touched his, he seized upon her. He did not give her the sisterly kiss she had offered but parted her lips and delved deep within her mouth, as a lover might. And she responded. Just as a lover might. Her lips parted sweetly, she welcomed him, her arms wrapped around him. Moments passed in blindness, and then he realized that he could not take from Anne Marie what he was seeking in another. He could not use Anne Marie, because she was too good a woman. And she had always cared for him; he had known that. She was his friend, and the daughter of one his best friends. Shamed, he drew his lips from hers and slowly released her from the band of his arms. He wanted to apologize. Her eyes were upon his, and they both knew his mistake.

Before he could utter a word, a furious sound at the door interrupted them. Startled, Eric looked to the door to see that Damien Roswell was there, tall, straight, outraged.

"My lord Cameron, I came to see if you needed any assistance, but I see that you are well tended."

He didn't owe Damien any explanations. His young friend was rash and hot blooded, and he'd nearly spent years as a British prisoner because of it.

"I am on my way now," Eric said curtly.

"Damien, you must understand—" Anne Marie began.

"Oh, I understand!" Damien said with a dry laugh. "He's still a Brit in his own way, still 'Lord' Cameron. Just like Henry the Eighth! Down with the one, up with the next! Were you planning on killing Amanda, or just divorcing her, Lord Cameron?"

"Whatever I did, Damien, she would deserve," Eric said smoothly.

"I'm going to sail with you."

"No, you are not."

"You might—"

"Damien, for the love of God! Washington will not let you go! Can't you understand how serious a situation this has become?"

"If you hurt her, Cameron," Damien swore, raising a tightly clenched fist, "revolution be damned! I will kill you, I swear it!" It looked as if there were tears in his eyes. Eric's heart seemed to tighten with agony. He did not want to do battle with Damien. Again he damned Amanda with all of his heart.

"Damien—" he began.

But Damien was gone. Eric stood alone in the rough little room with Anne Marie.

"It's all right. I'll explain to him," Anne Marie promised.

"It isn't all right, and it never shall be," Eric muttered. He swept up his hat, and bowed low to Anne Marie. "Take care."

"Eric, go gently!" she cried.

But he did not reply. He felt as if he were a tempest of seething emotions, and he did not trust himself to speak.

On the morning of the twenty-fifth, Eric and his crew met one of Dunmore's fleet, a small warship called the *Cynthia*. Because the Continental forces were desperate for ships, they took care not to sink her. They suffered damage to the *Good Earth's* mainmast, but nothing major, and they managed to take the *Cynthia* with little effort. Her crew were sent to the brig, and a skeletal crew of colonials was left to sail her into a patriot port where she could be reoutfitted and sent into colonial service.

On the morning of the twenty-eighth they sailed the James. Through the glass Eric could see that fires burned at Cameron Hall. The *Lady Jane* was just leaving her berth.

Was his wife aboard her? Eric wondered.

He shouted orders to the gunners. The cannons were aimed and loaded by their gun crews, and he held his hand high. "Fire!" he commanded, bringing his hand down. It was his own damn ship he was bombarding!

And it might be his own wife he was about to kill! Would she be aboard? Aye, he thought bitterly, she would! The house was still standing, he could see it upon the far distant lawn. The warehouses were ablaze. Nothing could be salvaged from them.

And the ship, his ship, the *Lady Jane*. She was coming about, ready to fire in turn.

"Gunners, we'll take it again. They weren't prepared for us—they were barely into the river. One more strike and we come along broadside. We'll grapple her and board!"

Powder filled the air, and already visibility grew bad. He shouted his order to fire once again. The *Good Earth* vibrated and trembled, and the balls shuddered into the water, and into the wood and canvas and decking of the *Lady Jane*.

The water between them seemed to froth in shades of gray. They came closer and closer, the wheel ably handled by a West County captain. There was a massive shuddering as the ships came together.

Eric raised his sword, let out a battle cry, and leapt from the one deck to the other. Swinging from the rigging, leaping from the railing, his men followed suit.

They met the British at close combat, hand-to-hand fighting, swords and dirks drawn, their long rifles used perhaps once or twice. Fury guided Eric. It was his ship. By God, he would reclaim her!

He had just dispatched a young, talented Highlander when he saw Robert Tarryton across the ship, by the bow. Dodging and avoiding the others, he grinned with reckless abandon at this new opponent, his mortal enemy.

"Cameron, you bastard!" Tarryton charged him, parrying his first thrusts easily enough.

Their swords met high and clashed, and came low and clashed, and they were cast tightly together.

"She's with me, you bastard!" Tarryton whispered heatedly. "You thought to make a fool of me and take her from me time and again, but she's with me. I've got your ship, and I've got your wife, and I intend to make good use of both!"

Anger caused a shudder to wrack the whole of his body. Robert Tarryton made a lunge that nearly skewered him. Fool! Eric charged himself in silence, aware that the man meant to unnerve him in any way that he could. With cunning, sweeping strokes of his sword, he began to move forward, quickly. Tarryton parried his thrusts, but Eric saw the fear that slipped into his features. He was the better swordsman, and he knew it.

And he was going to kill Tarryton.

"You've nothing, Tarryton, nothing at all," he replied, and proved it with a quick slash that caught the man in the chin, humiliating, damning.

Tarryton backed quickly away and Eric discovered that he could follow at his leisure. Tarryton was now the one unnerved. He touched his chin and felt the blood.

Eric grabbed hold of the rigging and leapt upon the foreward rail for a new assault. And it was then that he saw Amanda.

She had come from the captain's cabin, and she stood among a sea of men, exquisite in green, her hair caught by the sun, a burning cascade that rippled and fell down the length of her back. She seemed both alien and natural to the deck and the turmoil that abounded upon it, tall, proud, and beautiful, her head lifted to the wind, her eyes seeking those around her. His wife. The traitor.

She was there, undeniably, she was there. She has cast her fate with Tarryton at long last. He was probably taking her on to London, now that her usefulness at Cameron Hall had come to an end.

Never, my love, he vowed silently. Unless I am dead and buried in this sea, you will never be with Tarryton, I will see to that!

But just at that moment, Tarryton made another lunge toward him. Eric parried the blow swiftly and retaliated with fury and vengeance. His temper was under control now, cold and lethal. Tarryton seemed to realize that.

"Lay down your sword, Tarryton!" he demanded.

"God's blood! Someone take this man!" Tarryton cried.

It was more than he should have expected, Eric thought dryly, for Lord Robert Tarryton, His Grace the Duke of Owenfield, to fight his own battle. At his call, five navy men sprang forward, their rapiers raised.

"I will kill you one day, Tarryton," Eric vowed pleasantly.

But Tarryton had already turned away, and Eric couldn't give him much attention, for his opponents were able. Frederick sprang forward, taking on one of the men. Eric dispatched one eager lad with a lightning thrust to the abdomen. The next he caught in the chest, and the last two disappeared into the fray.

He heard a loud splash, and he realized that Tarryton was lost to him now. The *Lady Jane* was coming under the control of the patriots, and Tarryton was not going to stay to assist his failing men.

"Highness!"

The cry was going up, Eric realized. The ship was being won, and the men were becoming aware of Amanda—and that she must be the notorious "Highness" who had betrayed Virginia again and again.

He had to reach her himself first. Frederick knew her identity, as did other friends. But not the others. And he meant for no other man to take her or touch her. She was his.

There was a sword in her hand! he realized with both fear and fury. Damned fool, would she fight them even unto death? Was she so reckless and so determined that she would kill men that she would risk her own life?

"By God, love, I will throttle you!" he vowed to himself.

She thrust her sword forward in warning, and turned to run. Eric gave chase, shouting to his men to secure the deck.

Would she throw herself into the sea? No, in panic she was running back to the captain's cabin, so it seemed. Some engagement was taking place there, a Highlander gave battle to his one of his men, and was duly silenced, falling back into the cabin. "I shall take this!" Eric called to his men.

She was within that cabin.

He reached the cabin door and burst it open with a powerful slam of his boot.

And he saw her there, cradling the fallen Highlander in her arms. Her eyes rose to his, ever emerald. Defiant . . . maybe just a little fearful. His name left her lips on a whisper, and then she staggered to her feet, dragging the Highlander's heavy Brown Bess along with her.

"Highness," he muttered in return, cleaning his sword to keep his hands steady, fitting it back into his scabbard. He didn't know what he said to her then, something that meant nothing, something about the state of the war. And something about his fury to be here now, because his wife was a traitor.

She tried to interrupt him—he would not allow her to do so. He tried so desperately to keep control of his temper. He didn't want to touch her. He would kill her . . . or he would rape her, there aboard the ship with all his men about.

"I am innocent of this!" she cried at last. The denial tore into his heart. By God, she had been there—with Tarryton.

Control, he thought! And he arched a brow politely. "You are innocent—Highness?"

"I tell you—"

"And I tell you, milady, that I know full well you are a British spy and the notorious 'Highness,' for I oft fed you misinformation that found its way to Dunmore's hands. You betrayed me—again and again!"

She was holding the Brown Bess on him. Her eyes were in tempest, her hair was a beautiful fall about her. She was his wife, and he had lain with her night upon night, and she was holding the lethal weapon on him. "Give it to me, Amanda!" he demanded furiously. "Amanda!"

"Get away from me, Eric!"

Fury filled him and threatened to burst. "Now, Amanda! I warn you that my temper is brittle indeed. I almost fear to touch you, lest I strangle the light from those glorious eyes. I'll take the gun!"

"No! Let me by you. Let me go. I swear that I am innocent—"

"Let 'Highness' go? Why, milady! They would hang me for the very act." Now! He had to take the weapon from her now! Fiercely he strode to her. She moved away as he lunged.

"No! I'll shoot you, Eric, I swear it—"

"And I do believe you, milady!" he retorted bitterly. Aye, she would shoot him! And be free . . .

"Shoot me, then, if you dare, milady!" he challenged her. "But take heed, madame, that your weapon be loaded."

"Aye, 'tis loaded, Eric!" Was she trying to warn him? God! He wanted to believe in the tears that stung her eyes, in the warnings she tried to issue. He could not!

He caught the gun by the barrel and sent it flying across the room. The damned thing exploded. He spun around, staring at her coldly. "It *was* loaded, milady. And aimed upon *my heart!*" She would have killed him. His own wife, she would have killed him. "And now, Highness . . ."

"Wait!"

"Wait for what, milady? Salvation? You shall not find any."

She stared at him a long moment, her green eyes still liquid, as if she would shed tears. Lying tears. And still, she was so beautiful, her breasts heaving, the pulse ticking at her throat. Her face so very fine that he longed to feel the lines beneath the stroke of his fingers. . . .

Suddenly, like a doe, she leapt into action, trying to sweep past him. He took a step and seized her, catching her hair. She screamed out in pain and he swirled her back into his arms. She pummeled, kicked and fought wildly, and he felt the warmth of her against him, felt the rise of her breasts, the span of her hips, and so help him, all that he could remember for a fleeting moment was the laughter they had shared. Laughter, and sweet tender moments by the slow-moving river.

She nearly caught his chin with her flailing fists. He caught her wrists savagely and wound them back together at the small of her back. She tossed back her head to meet his eyes. "So beautiful," he told her. "So treacherous. But it is over now. Surrender, milady."

She smiled suddenly, and it was a smile that caught his heart, slow and nearly tender, and oh so wistful. She brought back all the years that gone between them, all the tempest, and all the precious moments of peace. "No surrender, my lord," she said softly. "No retreat, and no surrender."

It was then that they were interrupted by one of the young Carolina lieutenants. The man came to a halt behind Eric and excitedly spouted, "We've found her! Highness! She gave the ship and the intelligence to the British."

His eyes remained locked with hers. "Aye, we've found her." Fury gripped him. He no longer dared touch her. With an oath he cast her from him. She nearly fell against the back paneling and steadied herself there, ever tall and ever proud, and so damned dignified and beautiful despite it all!

The lieutenant whistled softly. "No wonder she played our men so false so easily!"

How bitter those words!

"Aye," he said quietly. "It was easy for her to play men falsely."

"I wonder if they will hang her," the soldier said. He seemed very perplexed, anxious. "Would we hang a woman, General?" He hesitated a moment. Eric barely noticed, for still his gaze was caught by his wife's brilliant green eyes, ever wider now. Was she afraid at last? Did she feel the itch of hemp about her throat?

"Milord, surely you *cannot* have her hanged!"

He smiled ironically, feeling her warmth, even now remembering that the very sun itself seemed to live in her kiss, in the glory of her hair, in the splendor of her arms.

"Nay, I cannot," he agreed, adding quietly, "for she is, you see, my wife."

The young man gasped. Eric knew that he dared not stay there now, his temper fraying so quickly and so visibly. He would deal with Amanda later, on his own territory.

On territory familiar to them both.

"Tell Daniel to set a course for Cameron Hall," he ordered. "Have someone come for this lieutenant," he said, referring to the Highlander. Apparently this man had fought and died—to protect Amanda from him! "The Brits must be buried at sea; our own will find rest at home."

He turned back to Amanda. "My love, I shall see you later." He bowed deeply to her and then strode from the cabin as quickly as he could. He did not stop by the wheel, he walked straight to the tip of the bow and stood against the wind, feeling the wash and spray of the surf as it flooded over him.

The deed, at least, was done. The arms and munitions were probably all lost, but the *Lady Jane* was his again.

And Amanda was his again.

His fingers itched. He remembered Tarryton, and his words, and a staggering pain gripped his gut as he wondered what was true and what was not.

They had been married more than two years. She was his wife! His, and no part of that bastard Tarryton. He should cast her from him, he should demand a divorce. . . .

He could no more divorce her than he could cut away his own right hand. He shouldn't touch her.

He couldn't wait to get his hands upon her. He needed time. Time to steady himself, time to prove the victor indeed. And there were things to be done. He had to find General Lewis, and join with him to make the final plans for hunting down Lord Dunmore.

He closed his eyes and leaned back against the rigging. In time, Daniel came to him to tell him that they were nearly docked.

"See that Frederick takes my wife home and that the servants are made aware that she is not to leave. I will ride immediately to find the troops. Our own men may stay aboard, or set tents upon the lawn, as is their choice."

"Aye, sir!"

Eric stayed where he was when Frederick went for Amanda. He watched from his vantage point as the man led her across the deck, and to the gangplank. And he watched, his heart pierced as if by fire, as she was saluted as a worthy foe.

Damn her. Damn her a thousand times over.

When the carriage disappeared with her within it, he strode off the ship himself. A horse was quickly supplied to him, and Daniel was ready to ride beside him.

They didn't have far to hunt for General Lewis, his old friend from the Indian days. Lewis had been heading along the peninsula, and now he was eager to point out Dunmore's position.

"We'll chase him to his anchor off of Gwynn's Island. We'll see that he and his pirating fleet are sent far away for good!" Lewis swore vehemently.

"We'll join my men with the militia in the morning then, General," Eric agreed. "I'll ride back now to my men."

"Lord Cameron!" Lewis stopped him.

Eric, halfway out of the brigadier general's tent, paused beneath the flap. "Aye?"

"I would have you know that there is no proof as to the identity of the spy," the general said quietly.

"No proof?"

Lewis cleared his throat unhappily. "Well, news of your victory aboard the *Lady Jane* traveled even more swiftly than you did, my lord. The battle was witnessed from the shore, and the rumor is, of course, that your wife was aboard and that the men seemed to recognize her as 'Highness.' Bear in mind, sir, that some thought as how Dunmore would have liked to have kidnapped Mrs. Washington. Perhaps your lady was taken quite the same."

Eric nodded, not believing a word of it. His "lady" had already lifted a Brown

Bess against him. God knew what surprises she might have waiting for him within their room.

"I thank you for your concern, General Lewis. My wife will soon be leaving for France, where she will be safe from either side."

He saluted and left then, nodding to Daniel. He mounted his horse, with Daniel behind him, and he started off for home. Seconds later he was galloping across Virginia fields, more than anxious to reach his home.

At the steps he dismounted. Pierre was there to take his mount, to greet him enthusiastically. "What happened here?" he demanded of his good servant. "The truth, Pierre. The truth of it."

Pierre shrugged unhappily. "I don't know the whole truth of it, my lord. Danielle was struck and has just regained consciousness, and she swears your lady innocent."

"Danielle would swear her innocent were she caught in the king's own arms!" Eric exclaimed.

Pierre shrugged unhappily. "She meant no harm to any of us. That monster Tarryton would have struck young Margaret, but Lady Cameron would not allow it."

"But she went with Tarryton easily enough herself."

Pierre lowered his head. "So it seemed," he admitted softly.

"That is all I need for now, Pierre," he said. "I want her taken to France tomorrow, as soon as I have left. I shall leave the *Good Earth* here for that purpose. You will go with her, and Cassidy—"

"Cassidy thinks that he should be serving you, milord."

"If he can keep my wife from mischief and harm, he will be serving me."

"And Danielle?"

"Aye," Eric said after a moment. "Danielle may accompany her."

"How long shall we stay?"

"Till hell freezes over, so it seems!" Eric muttered. Then he sighed. "I don't know as yet. You will go to the Comte de la Rochelle, who is with the court at Versailles. When this thing is solved, I will come for my lady and the rest of you."

"Aye, my lord. And Cameron Hall?"

"Richard will remain here. He knows the place even better than I. He has kept things running so well."

"If I may, milord, Lady Cameron has kept things running so well."

"Then, Pierre, it shall not run so well, but there is nothing else that I can do. Is everything clear?"

"Aye, milord."

"Good night then, Pierre."

"Good night, milord."

Eric started up the stairs to the house. Upon entering his home he saw the scorched walls and places where the fires had been beaten out. The faint smell of smoke still lay about the place, but very little had been harmed.

He looked up the stairs and hesitated, his fingers winding into fists by his side.

Then he started up the steps, and when he reached his own door he paused again.

Control . . . he warned himself.

He silently opened the door and stepped within the room.

Instantly his eyes fell upon her. Passion and desire combined with raw fury to sweep all his thoughts of a cold and distant reunion aside.

Steam still rose softly from a bath, but she was no longer within it. She stood by the window, her form draped in a towel, her features grave as she gazed upon the lawn, her hair high and sable and fire and gloss in a cascade of curls. She turned to him, her eyes wide and emerald and startled. There was an innocence, a vulnerability, to the way she clutched her towel to her breast. As if she held her innocence against him, as if they were strangers, never man and wife.

You are my wife! he vowed in silence.

Her eyes met his, clouded and wary. He turned and closed and locked the door, then leaned against it. His anger and desire joined to make his voice tremble with menace as he spoke to her.

"Well, Highness, it has come. Our time of reckoning at last."

He waited for her reply, for her denial, for her cry of innocence.

A smile curled his lip. He could no longer remain still; he could not bear the distance. A searing tempest all took root within his soul, and he took his first, ruthless step toward her.

"Aye, milady, our time of reckoning at last."

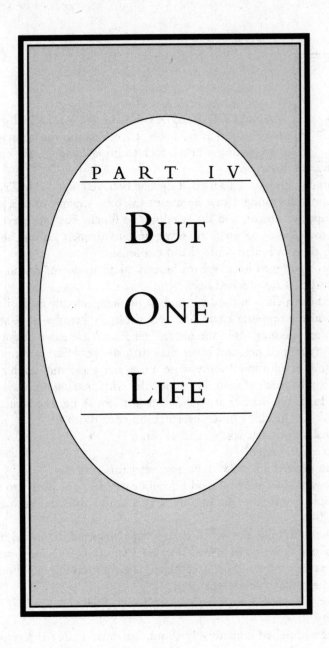

PART IV

BUT

ONE

LIFE

15

MANDA STARED AT ERIC WORDLESSLY, UNABLE to believe that he could have become the stranger standing there with the brutal lock to his jaw and the icy expression in his eyes.

She wanted to cry out so badly that she had betrayed no one. As Eric strode on into the room, she thought that he meant to come straight to her, to wind his fingers around her throat, and she tried not to flinch. His eyes were dark now. They had that ability to go from silver gray to deepest cobalt, and now, by candlelight, they were dark indeed and fathomless.

He did not come to her. Perhaps he was afraid to do so. Afraid of what he might do to her if he touched her.

He pulled out a chair at the table and sat, wincing slightly as he lifted his foot to set it upon the opposite chair. She could scarcely breathe as he stared at her relentlessly, and neither could she move. Her fingers clenched about the snowy towel that enwrapped her, and other than that, she could do nothing but return his stare. He poured himself some wine, using her glass, and cast his gaze upon the tray of barely touched food. He sipped the wine, staring her way once again. "Is there a knife you harbor at your breast, my love?" he asked softly.

She shook her head. "I have never desired your death."

"No? That's not what you've said at times."

"I've spoken in anger."

"And you leveled a musket upon my heart this very day."

"I never wanted to kill you! And I do not carry a knife. Were I to desire your death, I would not be fool enough to carry a knife. You could too easily use it against me."

"Ah." She didn't like the way that he softly whispered the sound, nor did she like his manner as he continued. "Because you are weak, and I am stronger. Amanda, you do have the most exceptional talent for crying out about femininity the moment that you are cornered."

"I am not cornered. I am innocent."

"Innocent?"

Her fingers clutched convulsively about the towel before she realized that it did seem she hid some weapon at her breast. She did not reply quickly enough and he suddenly and violently stood. This time there was no hesitation as he strode across the room toward her. His walk was so filled with menace that she gasped, seeking to elude him, but he was upon her too quickly, wrenching her arms from their taut wrap. The linen towel fell to her feet, her hair streamed damp red streamers down her back and over her shoulders, and but for that she was left naked before his gaze.

And his eyes went darker still.

She longed to reach for the towel quickly, to retreat, but they had now taken their battle farther than they had ever gone, and she could not play the coward. She lifted her chin and spoke mockingly instead. "No blade, milord, as you can see." She waited, condemning him with her eyes. Then she did begin to slowly bend to retrieve her towel. "If you'll excuse me—"

"If I'll excuse you? Madame, do you think that I intend to engage in some drawing-room conversation. No, my love, that is the point here. I am done with excusing you!" he thundered out vengefully. His hands were upon her shoulders, wrenching her up to face him. His fingers lay upon her naked flesh, biting and cruel, and he drew her hard against him. Fire burned brightly within his eyes as they tore into hers. "I knew from the beginning that you followed the Crown, and I even knew that you were Dunmore's spy, and that didn't matter to me, lady. When we married I had you watched and followed, not so that you could not give away the information you had been given, but because I feared for your safety."

Her face went pale. He nearly ceased in his tirade. He could not. He had missed her too long. And she had played him false when he had believed that if not her love, her loyalty to the very house she called home would have kept her true. He was too shaken to cease. Too shaken to take his hands from her. He clenched her shoulders even more tightly. "My God, lady, if there is an excuse, tell it to me now!"

"I didn't do it!"

"You lie!"

"I do not!"

She brought her fists up between them to beat against him, but he swung her around and she stumbled, falling to her knees before him. She cast her hair back again, fighting tears. There had been so many times when she had deserved his wrath! She had fought him and hated him at every turn, but not now. Now she was in love with him, and, innocent, she had no defense.

"There is nothing that I can say!" she cried out to him. "Cast me before your courts, hang me for a traitor if you will, but by God, leave me be—"

"Leave you be!" He hunched down before her. His ruffled shirt was torn and powder smudged, his waistcoat and frock coat both showed signs of the day's wear. "I am called back from service in New York because my wife is planning my very doom! Handing my very property to the enemy! My God, you might very well have set fire to the house with your very own hand!"

"No!"

"You might have sailed the ship!"

She couldn't believe that there seemed to be no mercy, no reason in him at all. And still, she was desperate to make him understand. "I did not fire the house! Eric, I pleaded that they not burn the manor. I said that I would go if only—"

"Stop it!" he hissed, and his hand lashed out in a fury, stopping just short of her cheek. "You did what?"

"I said that I would go along willingly if they did not burn the house! And it didn't burn, Eric! It—"

"Bitch!" He swore to her, low and trembling. "You went with him willingly! Into Tarryton's arms! You forget how we met, my lady wife!" he charged her scathingly. "That you would need bargain with Robert Tarryton! The army lies languishing and I need run to capture my own wife, the Brit's courtesan!"

"How dare you!" she cried, near tears of anguish and fury. She could not fight. Not even the truth stood in her defense. Rising, she lashed out at him. The fight had been simmering and brewing between the two of them, and he was glad of it. He seized her arm and dragged her up to him. In panic she struggled against him. She had never seen this dark rage take hold of him, and it terrified her. "Let me go! Eric, you're hurting me, let go of me, Eric!"

He flung her hard on the elegant bed and fell atop of her, his thumbs and forefingers caressing her temples as he stared down at her.

"I've wondered. I've lain awake nights, and I've wondered if you were here, alone, in this bed. I agonized over leaving you so, yet I believed that you had vowed yourself into this marriage and that you would honor the promise sworn between us. I've faced bullets and steel time and again, and never have I sweat as I did nights, lady, torturing myself with visions of you as I have found you this night, sweet and fragrant from the bath, your flesh like alabaster, your heart beating that pulse to your veins. I've tried not to think that Tarryton might find his way to you, that his hands might close over your breasts, as mine do now."

"I never betrayed you with any man!" she cried out, and she felt as if her teeth chattered harshly within her mouth. "I cannot bear Robert now! You know that—"

"I do not know that. I know that you walked out of this house with him this morning—willingly."

"The servants—"

"The servants would not lie."

"But I . . ."

"You what, milady?" he asked scornfully.

The words fled from her; she could not whisper them. I love you. They echoed within her skull, but she could not say them. They came too late, and they would not be believed.

"I did not do this!" she cried, and his lip curled in disbelief.

"I wanted to kill Tarryton—and you," he told her. "From the time that I was summoned here, I felt an almost primal desire to draw torment and blood."

"Eric—"

"Fear not, milady. I do not intend to go so far."

"Eric, please—"

"Please what?"

"Let me up!"

He hated her at that moment, she was certain. Almost as much as she hated him for the disbelief and mockery in his eyes. And still he lay against her bare flesh, pinning her against the bed that they shared as man and wife. Love and hate . . . the emotions were close indeed. Though she thought she despised him desperately and burned to be free of him, she was filled by a greater need, to feel him close again, his hands and lips upon her, caressing, demanding.

"You're forgetting that you're my wife," he reminded her. "And that I am a soldier, returned from the front."

"I am forgetting nothing! We are bitter enemies, milord, and no matter how I try, you refuse to believe me."

"You speak of war again. You chose to fight this particular battle. Well, I won, madame. You lost. And you are my wife."

"Your despised wife! Eric, for the love of God—"

"For the love of God, lady, no. I will not free you this night. If it is war, madame, then know the truth of it. If we shall win this fight, then I am a hero. If the king is victorious, then I am a traitor indeed. But this night, lady, I am the conqueror, and the rewards of conquest are as old as time."

Anguish and tempest struck her anew. She could not surrender, not to his touch, not even to the ardent fever that swept about them both like a relentless tide. She had not seen him in so long. It had been more than two months. Two months in which she had done her best to be a Cameron wife, to cherish and nurture the land and the hall, to stand fast against any enemy. And then . . .

After everything, the British ships had appeared that morning and Robert had come to her bedchamber. And now everything that she had ever feared in Eric had been unleashed. He hated her with a passion, she could feel it in his touch each time his fingers brushed her or curled around her. His temper was on a taut string, barely held from total explosion.

But not even the bitter fire of his anger nor his absolute mockery could still the things he evoked in her when he came too close. Dear God! That she could go back to a time when she had despised him! But that time was gone. And now she longed to forget this day, this horrid, horrid day. She longed to embrace him. She hadn't tasted in so long the sweetness and decadence of once-forbidden pleasures, felt his lips, his hands upon her. But she could not give to him now. Not when she knew so little of his mind, when his fury was so sharp, so blinding.

She parted her lips to speak, but she did not. She saw the wrath of his gaze and fell silent, unable to read his thoughts.

They were easy to fathom, he could have told her. But he hadn't told her what others dreams had kept him awake at night. Dreams of her, as he saw her now. Her eyes so green, shadowed and shaded by the rich sweep of her lashes as they fell over the emerald orbs, fluttering open again. Even now her hair dried in tendrils both deep, dark sable and flaming red, depending how the locks curled or waved or lay upon her flesh.

He moved his hand to her cheeks, tracing the excellence of her features, the high set of her bones, the slight heart shape of the face, accented by the widow's peak at her temple and the sweeping richness of her hair. Her lips were beautifully shaped, naturally rose, the lower lip full and the curve of the whole evocatively sensual. At rest she was exquisite, as a statue was exquisite. Her flesh was like marble in its perfection, from the slope of her shoulders and rise of her breasts to the shapely curves of her hips and calves. In motion she was more than beautiful, for she was energy and tension and passion, and her eyes were haunted with what emotion ruled her thoughts, always exciting, always eliciting his own passion, be it yearning need or a cyclone of fury.

And now . . . now her lips lay parted beneath his. Her breasts rose and fell with each whisper of her breath, and the length of her perfection lay beneath him. Theirs had never been a soft or quiet relationship, yet he had never thought it would come to this. He knew he would take her that night by any force, rather than see tomorrow come without the memory of the night.

His mouth came closer. Their eyes met at just a breath of space.

"No! We will not—do this!" Amanda managed to protest. "Not like this! Not when you do not love me!"

"Love, madame? When did that enter into your priorities? Certainly not when you married me. Not when you discovered maps within my library to give your father. Not when you betrayed this very house."

"But I did not! Oh, Eric, you fool! Listen to me! Perhaps I am guilty of giving away past . . . secrets. You don't understand! They held Damien—"

"What?" he demanded sharply.

She swallowed. "My father had Damien. He always threatened me with Damien. First he swore that he would have him arrested and hanged. And then he did have him, Eric. The horse! Remember at the governor's palace on New Year's? Damien's horse died, and I knew that Father wouldn't hesitate to do the same to a man. And then they actually held Damien! They were threatening me—"

"I see. But Damien has been freed for some time now, milady."

"And that is what I am telling you! There is another spy out there, and it isn't me!"

He smiled. "A pretty tale," he told her.

"Eric, please—"

"Amanda, I do not please, milady! But before God, I swear it! I have missed you."

"Oh!" she cried, then gasped and swore in fury, surging against him to escape him, feeling him ever more pressed against her body. Little was hid by the tightness of his breeches. Her eyes widened as she felt the strength of him. She shuddered violently, hating him and hating herself all the more because she did not care about pride or reason, only that he held her, even if it was all a lie.

"We cannot!"

"But you are my wife."

"Who betrayed you, so you say."

"It does not matter. Not now. Not tonight."

"No! Eric!" She was very close to tears. "Not after today. My God, let me up!" She surged against him anew, trying to dislodge him, to free herself by any means. Darkness seemed to surround her in a rise of mist like the steam of a summer's sun. She felt his hardness against her again, pulsing, vivid, and it seemed as if a thousand pagan drums began to beat within her heart and core and blood. She fought him, and she fought herself, but he held her firm, his eyes ever upon her until she blushed radiantly even as she choked and swore and struggled. "Eric! No!"

He smiled, and his gaze was taunting, provocative. "Ah . . . Mandy! Don't you seek forgiveness?"

She went very still and moistened her lips.

"What?" She gasped.

"Perhaps I will."

She watched him for a moment, but she didn't trust him. He leaned against her, imprisoning her hands. "You cast yourself upon Tarryton, why not me? We even have the sanctity of marriage upon us, my love."

"I never cast myself upon Tarryton!" she swore. She tried to kick him. He laughed, for his weight was well upon her, and he was in no danger. Fury filled her. "You want me to beg your forgiveness in this manner!"

"It is a way to start," he commented dryly. But his eyes were silver and blue flame and a vein ticked rampantly against his throat. She caught her breath, but then her heart fell again and she defied.

"Then you would call me a whore!" she retorted. "Giving in for—for what I might get in turn."

"The words are yours," he said.

"Oh! Never! Eric—"

"Shh! The words do not matter, truth does not matter, nay, not even love! You are my wife, and I have been away too long, and, lady, this thing between us is ever fierce, and I will not be denied."

His lips pressed against hers with searing hunger, stealing away her words. She tried to twist her head, but his hands were powerful upon her head, holding her still to his leisure. She felt the heady fullness of his tongue as he played against the barriers of her lips and teeth and filled her mouth, seeking and giving, bringing a rush of heat to rise within her. She tried to push against him, but he caught her hands, and laced his fingers with hers, pinning them to her sides. She tossed and turned and writhed, and felt the fires burning ever more brightly, more fervently about her. She sank into the heat, into the desperate rise of passion, where thought knew no place and the heart and hunger ruled all.

She loved him. Pride be damned, for it was lost, cast along with dignity upon the shores of emotion, for come what may, in truth she could not deny him, nor herself.

Her hand was free. He stroked her open palm with his fingers, and then his hands moved over her, trembling, and yet with sureness and relentless hunger. He cupped her breast, and explored her hip, and his lips left her mouth to trail against her throat and breasts. She gasped with the startling pleasure as he took the rosebud of one crest within his mouth, teasing with his teeth and bathing it again and again with the lavish sweep of his tongue. Her hands were upon him, she realized. Her fingers fell upon his shoulders, and she felt the ripple of his muscle beneath the fabric of his uniform. She threaded her fingers into his dark hair and marveled at the texture of it. And still he moved against her.

"Give to me, my wife, my love!" His whispers coursed her ears and the heat of them filled her with heightened excitement. "Fill me with your beauty, with the magic of the night. . . ."

The threat of war receded, and battle was forgotten. The night breeze rushed in with its scent of river salt, caressing her flesh where he did not, but nothing else of the world could touch her. It had been too long since they had lain like this, lovers entwined. She closed her eyes, and he moved against her. He shifted his weight and stroked her abdomen and her hip and the flame trail of his kiss followed along. The stroke of his lips and teeth and tongue fell again and again upon her. She tried to thread her fingers into his hair, to somehow capture the heat and flow of passion, but it was far beyond her. She trembled at his touch, she moved as he manipulated her, feathering his fingers down the length of her spine, gently nipping against the rise of her buttocks, lying her back down again to bathe her breasts anew with the hot liquid tempest of his mouth. He rose then, and she watched him with half-slit eyes, certain that he would cast aside his uniform and come to her. And she would watch him as he shed his clothing, and came back to her, walking with his particular grace and determination, almost like a wildcat assured of his every movement.

He did not cast aside his clothing then, but caught her foot and delicately teased the arch and heel and toes. Then his tongue ran a straight trail down her calf and along her inner thigh, and even as she gasped he wedged the hardness of his shoulders there and delved his kiss into the very center and secret place of her most haunting desire. She bit her lip, longing to cry out. She tugged upon his hair and her head began to thrash. Sweet waves of ecstasy wracked her, sweeping through her body like waves upon the shore. She fought him, yet her head tossed upon the pillow and wild cries escaped her as her body surged of its own accord against her. He led her on and on, and when she thought that she could stand no more, he was gone again.

And this time it was to shed his clothing.

Naked, he came back to her. His shaft as hard as steel, he thrust within her, and was welcomed by the warm encompassing sheath of her body. The waves began again, they came to crest and build and crest again with each stroke of his body. He rose high above her and his eyes met hers, dark with passion, or with anger, she knew not which. Did he make love . . . or hate? She did not know. But the passion could not be denied. It stormed upon them, and music of their every breath and whisper and cry. It made the air a silken cloud, it made the night a bit of magic in a world gone destitute of fantasy. Still his eyes held her, and still he stroked within her, urgency filling him. The waves coming upon her seemed to rise and shatter and sprinkle down again in tiny flakes of silver rapture. Again and again climax seized her, and she shuddered and trembled and shook in his arms. He thrust again with vehemence, and she felt the startling heat and liquid as his seed rushed into her, filling her.

He touched her cheek and tenderly kissed her lips, then he fell from her, coming to her side.

Moments of silence passed. Then she started to speak, and he touched his finger to her lips. "No. Not now. Not tonight."

"Eric!" she cried. "Please listen. I—I love you!"

Tension filled him, the muscles of his arms tightened and bulged and his features constricted until they were taut and anguished. She thought that he would strike her then, or that his fingers would wind around her throat and crush away her air.

"By all the saints, madame, play your games no more this night!" he swore violently.

"But it is no game, no ploy, no taunt!" she insisted, challenging his anger. "Eric!" She choked upon his name, tears rising to her eyes.

He exhaled, forcing his body to ease, and he shook with a sudden venom. "Would God that I could believe you!" he said, his voice low, harsh.

"Please . . ."

"No! No more tonight! If you would give love, lady, then prove love."

And so she fell silent, and in seconds he let out a hoarse cry, pulling her close once again. And after the breeze had come in to gently cool the heat that had remained so slick and damp upon their flesh, he kissed her upper arm and then began to make love to her again. This time she touched him in turn. Freely. Allowed herself to stroke the hard muscles of his arms and chest, the lean sinew of his hips, the tightness of his buttocks. She teased and seduced, taking him into her hands, sweeping her hair over his naked flesh and touching him with the tip of her tongue, with her kiss, the lash and lave of her tongue. . . .

When the tremors of ecstasy faded next, he held her. And in the darkness and quiet of the night, sleep, deep and dreamless, came to them both.

When she awoke, he was dressed again. A new white shirt, clean white breeches, his doublet and his frock coat in blue and red, his cockaded military hat upon his head. He stood by the window, as if he waited for her to awake.

She knew instantly that things had changed, that the night was over. She drew the covers against her breasts, and she stared at him. He turned slowly toward her. The eyes that fell upon her were the eyes of a stranger, deep, dark, and distant.

"You're leaving," she said.

"We're going after Lord Dunmore. You knew that."

"Yes," she whispered. "Am I—am I to be a prisoner here?"

He shook his head. For a moment the beginnings of elation filled her. If they had time . . . if they just had time, perhaps there could be a separate peace between them. Perhaps she could explain that her heart had not changed, but that she was no longer fighting. She was his wife and would take his side. She could even learn to be a patriot.

"Then I am free," she said.

"No."

"What?"

He moved across the room, picking up his saber, his musket and dirk. "You are going to France."

"France! No, Eric, I will not—"

"You will."

Stunned, she swept the covers around her and tried to leap from the bed. She stumbled within her swath of sheets. He caught her, and her eyes, in tempest, met his. "Eric, I beg of you, leave me here. I did not betray you and I'll not—"

"Alas, I cannot believe you," he told her softly.

"But you said that I—" She broke off, and his brows raised expectantly. His lip curled as he awaited her words.

She flushed furiously. "You said—"

"You have my forgiveness. Just not my trust."

"I will not go to France, I'll escape to England!" she threatened, afraid of the tears that burned behind her lids. He was casting her away, she realized.

"No, you will not. You will not be alone," he promised her.

"Eric—"

"No! Don't beg, plead, or threaten! This once, my love, you will obey me." He hesitated, and his words were bitter when he spoke again. "In France, my love, you can cause us no more harm. I suggest that you dress. Your escort will be here any minute."

"My escort?"

"Cassidy, Pierre—Jacques Bisset."

Bisset. She would never escape him to run to England. She knew that. Jacques had never forgotten what the English had done to the Acadians. Nor did he forgive. He was a better guardian than a father might be.

"You cannot do this!" she charged him. Her fingers curled about his arms and she shouted with fear and fury. "Eric, please! Listen to me. I did not do this! You are a fool if you will not believe me. You will be hurt, because the person who did give out this information will betray you again." He ignored her, moving about. Fear rose, and desperation, and before she knew it, she was shouting in fury, severing anything that remained between them. "Oh, you bastard! I will hate you, I will never forgive you!"

"Cheer up. Dunmore may reach me yet."

"You should die by the hangman's rope!"

"Should I? Will you cry—since you do love me so much?"

"Oh, Eric! Please! Don't send me away!"

He swept her up into his arms and redeposited her upon the bed. He looked into the tearful liquid emerald of her eyes, and for the life of him, he wanted to recant.

His heart hardened. Cameron Hall could have burned to the ground. She had gone with Tarryton. By her own admission, she had gone with the man. More than anything in the world, he wanted to believe that she loved him. He wanted to believe her innocent.

But he could not trust her. He had done so before, and he had been betrayed. Time and time again she had betrayed him. Other lives were at stake.

He smiled, then bent down and kissed her lips. He had to leave, but he could not resist. He cupped her breast with his fingers and felt the anguish of longing burst upon him. He kissed her long and slowly, and stroked her flesh as if he could memorize with his hands as well as his mind.

Then he rose and gazed down upon her ruefully. *"Au revoir, my love."*

He turned and walked to the door. She was on her feet again, flying after him. "Eric!"

He closed the door. He heard the thud of her hands against it and then he heard her curses. He stiffened as he listened to the words upon her lips. Then he heard her fall against the door. And he heard the anguish of her tears.

He squared his shoulders and wondered how he would bear it, knowing that she was in France. At least she would be far away from Tarryton. And she would be safe. Bisset would see to that. He leaned against the wall in anguish.

He straightened at last, breathing deeply. Then he walked down the hallway, down the long portrait gallery. He paused, looking up at his ancestors, at the men and women who had carved out this Eden from the raw wilderness.

The fires of war were burning brightly in his Eden.

He turned and walked again. Lewis would be awaiting him and his men. They had to break the British menace, and he had to return to Washington soon. The Congress was meeting; any day the colonies would declare for freedom.

And he would risk all in that struggle.

But he would not lose! he swore, and he paused, looking back to the bedroom. Poignant, wistful pain swept into his heart. If only she were with them! If only she did love him.

In the gallery he stared at the portraits. Theirs were the last ones. Her hair was swept up in ringlets and fashionable curls, her beautiful eyes had been caught in all the majesty of their color. Her smile was one that could make a man willing to die in any manner for a mere whisper from her lips.

He was beside her, in the very uniform he wore now.

Lord and Lady Cameron of Cameron Hall, one of the finest properties in Tidewater Virginia! he thought with some bitter irony. They graced the gallery as finely as any of his illustrious ancestors, when they might well be the very fall of the house. Was he the first Cameron to sell his soul for love, his birthright for some vague dream of new country?

Amanda . . .

He had not left the house, and already his blood warmed and his muscles tensed and tightened when he thought her name and conjured before his eyes a vision of the woman he had left behind. He was tempted to turn back, but he could not. There were battles to be waged. In Philadelphia men were busy writing the words for the Declaration of Independence. Thomas Jefferson was drafting the document, he had heard. The Virginians were very proud of that fact, just as they were proud that many of the ideas were coming from words penned for Virginia by George Mason.

The British would hang him, he thought, if they ever got their hands upon him. Dunmore, his old friend, would hang him higher than any other.

He looked up at the portraits again and smiled wryly. "What do you say, monsieurs? Am I a fool? Casting this heritage to the winds of war?" Perhaps not, he thought, his smile deepening. His forebears had left behind a safe and guarded world to strike out into a wilderness. They would understand that he gambled all in a dream of liberty and honor. Even if his wife did not.

He turned, fighting the urge to go back to touch her just once again. He left the portraits behind and hurried down the stairs. Cassidy waited for him at the front door, holding his mount.

"There's a flagon of whiskey in your saddlebag," Cassidy told him.

"For breakfast, eh, Cassidy?"

Cassidy grinned. "Thought you might be needing it."

Eric agreed. "Aye, that I might. But I'll have to get the troops moving first. Wouldn't do to show them a drunken example, eh, Cassidy?"

"No, sir, it wouldn't do at all."

Eric mounted upon his horse and looked down to Cassidy. "You'll go with her to France?"

"Wherever you send me, milord, I will go."

Eric stretched out his hand and took Cassidy's dark one. "Thank you. And Pierre. And see that Jacques sails with her too; that is very important. He will let no harm come to her."

Cassidy nodded. "Jacques will guard her with his life. His loyalty to her is deep seated."

"It should be," Eric murmured.

"Milord?"

He hesitated, looking down at Cassidy. "I believe that she is his daughter," he said quietly, then grinned at Cassidy's dumbfounded expression. "Say nothing."

"No!" Cassidy agreed. "You mean Lord Sterling—"

"Is a monster," Eric agreed, but said nothing more on the subject. If there was a God, and if there were a multitude of battles, surely Sterling would be taken home to his eternal rest before it was all over. "I will come as soon as I can. God alone knows when that will be. If I am killed—"

"Lord Cameron, please!"

He waved a hand impatiently in the air. "It is only a matter of time before independence and war are proclaimed. Virginia will set herself free before the others, I believe. Death is a fact of life, and very much one of war. If I am killed, care for my lady still, Cassidy, for I love her."

"Always, milord," Cassidy assured him, his dark eyes grave and misted.

Eric saluted quickly and rode away toward the fields where the troops were encamped.

He did not turn to look back at the house.

He did not dare. If he saw her face in the window, he would not be able to ride away.

16

URING THE FIRST FEW DAYS OF JULY, ANDREW
Lewis took command of the troops gathered on the mainland
elevation that fronted Gwynn's Island, where Dunmore had
brought his fleet. Charles Lee had reported him as living cat-
erpillarlike off of the land, stripping it bare, taking everything.

Lewis fired the first shot himself.

It was later reported that the first cannon shot ripped into the governor's
cabin, the second killed three of his crew, and the third wounded Dunmore in
the leg and brought his china crashing down upon him.

It was a complete rout. Those who could do so fled. Eric wondered briefly if
either Nigel Sterling or Robert Tarryton had been killed or wounded in the fray,
but there was no way of knowing. Nor did it matter, he tried to tell himself. The
threat was gone.

Or was it?

By night he often lay awake, and when he slept, he kept remembering
Amanda's face and her eyes, and her whispered, desperate words of innocence.
She entered into his dreams, and she tortured him. His anger had kept him from
listening to her, but now, with Dunmore far from Virginia shores, he wondered
if he shouldn't have listened.

News arrived from South Carolina that was exciting and uplifting to the
colonial soldiers—Admiral Sir Peter Parker's squadron had attacked the pal-
metto-log fortification on Sullivan's Island, the key to the harbor defenses at
Charleston. Under Colonel William Moultrie, amazing damage was done to the
British fleet. The ships limped away, with British general Sir Henry Clinton
determined to rejoin Howe at New York.

With Dunmore bested, Eric was due to return to Washington's side, but he
decided to return home instead. There was a slight possibility that Amanda had
not sailed as yet. And he was suddenly eager to listen to her again. Desperate. He
had said horrible things to her, made horrible accusations, and many had been
driven by simple fear and fury.

He rode hard, leaving Frederick in the dust. But when he reached the long
drive to the house, his heart sank. Beyond the rise he could see that the *Good
Earth* was no longer at her berth; Amanda had indeed sailed.

He reached the house and threw open the door anyway, but only Richard and
the maids were there to greet him. The house seemed cold and empty in the
dead heat of July. He slowly climbed the steps to the gallery, and he felt the
emptiness close around him. She had come to be so much a part of the house.

The scent of her perfume remained to haunt him, almost like an echo of her voice, a sweet and feminine whisper that taunted and teased. It was best! In France she would be safe—and the colonies would be safe from her!

No words, no logic, mattered. His world was cold, his house was nothing but masonry and brick and wood without her.

"Lord Cameron!"

He swung around and looked down the stairs. Frederick had come bursting into the room. "Lord Cameron! Independence! The Congress has called for independence! A declaration was read in Philadelphia on the sixth day of July, and it's beginning to appear in the newspapers all over the country! Lord Cameron, we've done it! We've all done it! We're free and independent men!"

Aye, they had done it. Eric's fingers wound around the railing of the gallery balcony as he stared down at the printer. They'd already been fighting over a year, but now it was official. They could never go back now. Never.

They were free.

A fierce trembling shook through him. He was suddenly glad that he had heard it here, in Cameron Hall. Despite the emptiness. He knew again what was so worth fighting for, worth dying for.

He hurried down the stairs. "Richard! Brandy, man, the best in the house! The Congress has acted at last! My God, get the servants, get everyone. A toast! To . . . freedom!"

Worth fighting for . . .

By the time Eric returned to New York and Washington's side, he had come to realize just what the words meant. The British commander Howe had already landed 32,000 troops on Staten Island. Half of the Continental Army of 13,000, under General Putnam, was sent across Long Island. The remaining half remained on Manhattan.

The Battle of Long Island took place on August 27. Howe landed 20,000 of his troops on Long Island between the twenty-second and twenty-fifth of the month, then turned Putnam's left flank.

Eric rode back and forth between the divisions with intelligence and information. He had never so admired Washington as he did when the general determined to evacuate Long Island. The brilliant operation took place between the twenty-ninth and thirtieth.

It was a bitter fall. In early September, Sergeant Ezra Lee attacked the British fleet in the *American Turtle*—a one-man submarine created by David Bushnell. The operation was mainly unsuccessful, but the *Turtle* created tremendous alarm and gave a burst of amusement and renewed vigor to the American forces.

But from there, things became ever more grim. On September 12 the Americans decided to abandon New York. On the fifteenth, American troops fled as the British assaulted them across the East River from Brooklyn. On the sixteenth, at the Battle of Harlem Heights, although Washington managed to slow Howe, Washington's communications were threatened, and he was forced to pull back.

Eric was in George's tent at the end of the month poring over maps of New York and New Jersey when a message arrived. He watched the general's face, then he saw the shoulders of his giant friend slump and his face turn ashen. "They have caught my young spy," he said.

Eric thought back quickly. Washington had asked a highly respected group from Connecticut, the Rangers, to supply a man to stay in New York to obtain information on the Brits' position. A young man named Nathan Hale had volunteered on the second call, and he had gone in pretending to be a Dutch schoolmaster.

Washington rubbed his temple fiercely. "He couldn't have been more than twenty-one. He was betrayed. Howe condemned him to hang." He exhaled on a long note, looking at his sheet of correspondence again. "He gave a speech that impressed them all, ending it like this—listen, Eric, it's amazing—'I only regret that I have but one life to give for my country.' One life. My God."

"It is war," Eric said quietly after a moment.

"It is war. We will lose many more," Washington admitted. "But this young Hale . . . that such courage should be cruelly snuffed from life!"

Cruel, yes, Eric thought, riding with his troops the next day. Cruel, but something more. Nathan Hale's words were being whispered and shouted by all men. In death Nathan Hale had given an army an inspiration. He had gained immortality.

By night the smell of powder seemed to penetrate Eric's dreams. With his eyes opened or closed, he saw lines and lines of men, heard the screams of men and horses alike, saw the burst of cannon and heard its terrible roar. But sometimes, when the black powder faded, he would see Amanda. And she would be walking toward him through the mist and death and carnage, and her eyes would be liquid with recrimination.

They had hanged Hale, the British. Traitors are usually hanged, and that is the way that war goes.

But what if she hadn't lied? What if her days as spy had ended? What if someone else played them all false?

Groaning, he would awaken. And with his eyes open to the dawn, he knew that he would ride and fight again—and lead men unto death.

On October 28 they fought the Battle of White Plains. The Americans fought bravely and valiantly, and with a startling skill and determination. Eventually the British regulars drove them off the field. Waving his blood-soaked sword in the air, Eric shouted the order to retreat to the men under his command.

Anne Marie and Sir Thomas were often his consolation then. Anne Marie continued to follow her father to war. On the field she loaded weapons, supplied water, and tended to the wounded. When conditions permitted, Eric ate with the two, and when the meal was over, he would often sit with Anne Marie. One night, as they walked beneath the trees, she turned into his arms. She rose up on her toes and kissed him. He responded, as he had before, his heart hammering, his body quickening. She drew his hand to her breast, and he touched her softness, but then he folded her hands together, drew away from her her, and gently touched her cheek. "I'm a married man, Anne Marie. And you are too fine a woman to be any man's mistress."

"What if I do not care?" she whispered.

He exhaled slowly and felt her eyes upon him in the darkness.

She smiled. "I am too late, Lord Cameron, so it seems." She teased him, her smile gentle. "When you were wild and reckless and seemed to collect women, I was seeking a ring about my finger. And now I would have nothing more but a few nights with a hero in my bed, and it really wouldn't matter if I were the most practiced whore on the continent. Eric, go after your wife. Bring her home. I do not believe that she would have betrayed you so completely."

He folded her hands together. "Anne Marie, I cannot. Perhaps I should not come anymore—"

She pressed her finger to his lips. "No. Don't take away your friendship. I need you and Damien."

"Ah! My bloodthirsty young cousin-in-law. He is still scarcely speaking to me; he does so under orders only. But he is a fine young man—"

"And in love, didn't you know?"

"No, I did not," Eric told her.

Anne Marie dimpled prettily. "With Lady Geneva. I suppose it began long ago in Williamsburg. Now he pines for her when he cannot travel south. I believe she will come north to be with him."

"Really? Geneva does love her comforts."

"You know her so well?"

"I did," he murmured. "Well, perhaps she has caught patriot's fever herself. Only time will tell."

"Only time." Anne Marie kissed him chastely upon the cheek. "Go for your wife, Eric."

"I cannot," he said, and in such a manner that she knew their talk had come to the end. She saw the twist of his jaw and the ice in his eyes, and she fell silent.

———

In November Fort Washington, on northern Manhattan overlooking the Hudson, fell. Twenty-eight hundred Americans were captured. And the Americans were forced to evacuate Fort Lee, in New Jersey, with the loss of much badly needed material.

The Americans began their retreat into New Jersey, southward. Charles Lee was left behind to cover the retreat. He and four thousand men were captured near Morristown.

Washington paled at the news. Furious, he refrained from swearing. He led the remaining three thousand men of the Continental Army southward and crossed the Delaware into Pennsylvania. Congress fled from Philadelphia to Baltimore, and Washington was given dictatorial powers.

Eric changed into buckskins and slipped behind the lines to discover the British position. He kept remembering Nathan Hale, and he prayed that he could be as heroic as the younger man should he be captured. The British would dance at his hanging, he was certain.

But he was able to gain information easily enough. Howe, confident of a quick final victory in the spring, had gone into winter quarters, the bulk of his men in New York and southern New Jersey.

As Christmas neared, Eric sat with other commanders and watched as Washington paced the ground and pointed at the maps. "We are desperate, gentlemen. Desperate. Our army has been sheared to threads, those men who remain with me talk constantly of the fact that their enlistment periods are up. Now, I have a plan . . ."

His plan was risky, desperate, dangerous—and brilliant, Eric thought. On Christmas night they recrossed the Delaware, nine miles north of Trenton, with 2,400 men, during a snowstorm. The cold was bitter, the wind was horrid, the water was ice. Eric felt his face chafed, he felt the numbing sting as the water rose from the tempest-tossed river in a spray to strike him. But in the pale light ahead he saw Washington standing at the bow of his boat. All of the men saw him. They crossed in safely.

At dawn they fell on the Hessian garrison at Trenton.

Victory was complete. Drunk, stunned, and hungover, the mercenaries fighting for the British tried to rise from their beds, but the colonials were all over them. Eric had little need to shout orders, for his troops moved with swift efficiency, and the attack was a complete surprise. When it was all over, of fourteen hundred Hessians, a thousand had been captured, thirty had been killed, and the Americans had lost only two men frozen to death and five wounded. Most important, perhaps, was the booty they captured, a good supply of small arms, cannon, and other munitions.

That night the small band celebrated. Within twenty-four hours, however, danger threatened again. The British general, Lord Cornwallis, was moving quickly. By January 2, he faced the American position with 5,000 men while another 2,500 awaited an order join him from Princeton.

"There is no way to fight this battle," Washington said. "Campfires . . ." he muttered.

"We leave them burning?"

"We leave them burning."

They slipped away by night. On January 3, battle cries went up as they came upon the British regulars who were marching to join Cornwallis. The battle was fierce, and furious, and when it was over, the Americans were victorious. They hurried on to Princeton and captured vast supplies of military equipment, then hastened away to Morristown.

That night they again celebrated.

"They will tout you as one of the most brilliant commanders ever," Eric told Washington.

"Unless I lose a few battles. Then I shall be crucified."

"My God, no man can do more than you have done!"

The general smiled, stretching out his feet. "Then until the spring, I shall be a hero. Cornwallis is abandoning his positions in western New Jersey because we have cut his communications. It is time we dig in for winter ourselves." He hesitated. "I have some letters for you."

Eric was a mature man, a major general, a man who commanded hundreds of men, who shouted orders in the field, who never flinched beneath powder or sword. He was, in fact, growing old with the damned war. And yet now he felt his fingers tremor, his palms go damp. "From my wife?"

Washington shook his head. "No, but from France. One from your man, Cassidy. Another from Mr. Franklin."

"Franklin!"

"Mmm. Poor Ben. He's been sent there by Congress to woo the French into assisting our cause. Seventy years old is Ben. And quite the rage of Paris, they are saying. A good choice by Congress, so it seems. The ladies are all charmed by his sayings and his wit and even his spectacles. Even the young queen is impressed by him."

"He is an impressive man," Eric muttered as he ripped open the letter from Cassidy and scanned it quickly. Things were well, the voyage had been smooth, they were living in the shadow of the royal party at Versailles. Everything was wonderful, so it seemed, and yet Cassidy urged him to come. He looked at the letter and realized that it had been written in September. He frowned at Washington.

"The letter went to Virginia before it reached me," Washington said.

Eric nodded, then ripped open the second letter. Worded in the most polite and discreet tones, Benjamin Franklin informed him that he was about to become a father. " 'Seems a pity that the child cannot be born upon American soil as you are so firm and kind and staunch a father of our land, but nevertheless, sir, I thought that the news would delight you and as it seems from her conversation your lady is not disposed to write, I have taken this upon myself . . .' "

The letter went on. Eric didn't see the words. He was standing, and he didn't realized it.

All the months, all of the longing, all of the wonder. And now Amanda was going to have a child and she was all the way across the Atlantic Ocean. And Franklin was right. There was no way that the child could be born on American soil. He tried to count, and he couldn't even manage to do that properly. He had last seen her in June. He had seen her in March . . . but no, he would have known by June. What was nine months from June?

"Eric?" Washington inquired.

"She's . . . she's having a child. At last," Eric said, choking on the words.

"At last?" Washington's brows shot up. "My dear fellow, you were married what—two years?"

"Three now," Eric corrected him. "I had thought that we could not, I . . ." His voice trailed away. He knew that no matter how dearly Washington had loved his adopted stepchildren and stepgrandchildren, he had wanted his own child. Washington bore no grudge against other men and loved Martha dearly, yet Eric felt suddenly awkward. It was the surprise, the shock. He sank back to his chair and he remembered that he had accused her of being Tarryton's mistress. And he had sent her away in raw fury, God alone knew what she would feel for him, if she wouldn't have rejoiced in betraying him in France. No! he assured himself in anguish. She was not alone. Jacques Bisset was with her, Jacques who surely knew that no matter what he had said or done, he loved her. . . .

"God!" he said aloud.

Washington sat back, studying him. "It is winter. I can foresee no action for some time to come. Perhaps I can send you with letters for the French to Paris myself. If . . . if you can find a ship that will sail."

Eric grinned suddenly. "I can find a ship to sail. My own, George. I shall take the *Lady Jane*. And I will make it up to you. I will capture a British ship with a multitude of arms, I swear it."

Washington leaned over his desk. "I will start on the necessary papers."

"Lady Cameron!"

Amanda was seated in one of the small gardens off the *tapis vert,* or "green carpet," the broad walk in the center of the gardens at the Palace of Versailles. She had gone there to be alone, but she knew the low, well-modulated voice very well now, and as was usual, she felt a smile curve her lip. It was Ben Franklin, and he was huffing a bit with the exertion of walking. He wasn't a young man, of course, but he didn't really act like an old man at all. His eyes were young, she decided, as young as his thoughts and ideas and dreams.

"I'm here, Mr. Franklin!" she called, and he came around a newly planted rose bush to meet her.

"Ah, there you are, my dear!"

"Sit—if there is room!" Amanda encouraged him. She was so very large now, she felt as if she were taking up the entire garden seat with her bulk. He smiled brightly and did so.

"How are things going?" she asked him.

"Ah, *pas mal!*" he said, "Not bad, not bad. And yet not so good either. I think that the French are our friends. Individual counts and barons support me, and I believe that eventually the king and his ministers will fall in for us. I believe the queen is all for me."

"Marie Antoinette? She is quite smitten, sir, I would say!" Amanda teased him. Of course, it was true. The queen was as taken with Benjamin Franklin as all the other ladies seemed to be.

Franklin sighed. "Not that I'm at all sure she even knows what I'm asking for! Alas, they're just children, you see. The king is scarce a boy of twenty-three, and the queen—oh! But then you are barely that yourself, milady! My apologies. It's just that when you reach my age, well . . ."

"There was no offense at all taken, Mr. Franklin. Besides, they say that Louis tries very hard, that he is thoughtful and considerate, but not a very talented ruler as yet. Perhaps he will become so in time. My goodness, I should hope so. This palace itself is so magnificent—and so huge!"

Versailles was huge and beautiful, and under other circumstances, Amanda might have loved it. But she lived with too much bitterness inside of her to truly enjoy the magnificence with which she lived.

She had not believed that Eric should be able to ride away from her so easily—and yet he had. She had watched him from their window when he had ridden, and he had not so much as looked back.

And even then she had thought that he would turn around. That he would come back to her. But he did not. As soon as the necessary repairs had been done to the ship, Cassidy had told her that they would be leaving on the *Good Earth*. She had been delighted to discover that Danielle had recovered fully from her injury at Tarryton's hands, and would accompany her, but she still could not believe that she was being escorted off her own property.

She shivered suddenly. The story of the valiant Nathan Hale had reached France, and she could not forget that had she been a man and captured by some man other than her husband, she might well have swung from a rope herself. Except that she was innocent!

Innocent . . .

She had remembered her innocence during the whole long ocean voyage. She had remembered it when she had first started to get sick upon the open sea, and she had been so wretchedly sick that she had thought it a pity Eric wasn't there. He would have thought her duly punished if he could have just seen the green shade of her face. She didn't normally react so to ships, perhaps it was a just punishment for trying to save her cousin's ungrateful throat!

But then, slowly, she had begun to realize that it was not the sea making her so wretched. It probably took her longer to discover than it should have, but her mind was ever active, and she felt as if her heart bled daily. Sometimes she was furious with a raw, scarce-controlled passion; sometimes her anger was cold, something that made her numb. She swore that she would never forgive Eric, never. Then she missed him all over again and wondered if he lived and if he was well. Then she thought that he deserved to rot for what he had done to her, but then that thought would flee her mind, and she would pray quickly that God would not let him die because of her careless thoughts.

They had nearly reached France by the time she realized, with some definite shock, that she was going to have a child. Joy filled her. No amount of anger or hatred could stop the absolute delight that filled her body, heart, and soul. She had been so afraid that they never would have a child. Eric had even accused her of trying not to have one. And now, when all between them seemed severed forever . . .

She was going to have a child. An heir for Cameron Hall.

Should the hall survive the war. For it was war now. The colonies were thirteen united states, and it was full-scale war.

And in the midst of their own personal warfare and battle, a child had at last been conceived. She hugged the knowledge to herself at first, but by the time they at last stepped from the *Good Earth* to French soil, Danielle had guessed her secret. Danielle wanted her to write to Eric immediately, but Amanda could not do so. She was thrilled with the child and determined that she would do nothing to risk the babe's health whatsoever, but the bitterness was alive within her, and she would not write. She would not have him send for the child. He could not have their babe so easily. When he determined to sail for her, then he would find out about the child.

Perhaps there was more, too, she realized, trembling. He had accused her of adultery with Robert. She could not believe that he meant his words, but then she had never seen Eric so angry, so cold, as he had been that last time. She could not forgive him. She swore to herself that she hated him.

But it was, of course, a lie, and she prayed nightly that he had not been killed. News came daily to the French court. Even if it was old by the time that it reached there, Amanda thrived on all that she heard. Virginia, Manhattan, Long Island, New Jersey, Pennsylvania—and Trenton. She heard about them all. General Washington's maneuvers of the last days of December and early January were being characterized as some of the most brilliant in military history. And Eric was always with Washington, so it was always possible to know how he fared. Fine, and well, she was always told. A Virginia horseman to match any, he was usually seen mounted atop his beautiful black horse, Joshua, and always at the forefront of action. He had survived every confrontation.

So far.

It was nearly spring. The first days of March were upon them. Snows would be thawing in Pennsylvania and New York, and it would be time for men to go to war again.

He could die, she thought. He could die without ever knowing that he had a child. And he would have one soon. Any day, perhaps any hour.

"You look cold," Franklin chastised beside her. "You should not be out here, Lady Cameron, and certainly not alone."

"Oh, I'm not alone, Mr. Franklin. A man of your acute vision must have observed that I am never alone! No, sir, my husband's man, Cassidy, is with me now. And if you will note later, sir, there will be a handsome Acadian man near me, and there is my maid, of course, and my sponsor here, the Comte de la Rochelle."

Franklin nodded and patted her hand. "Well, my dear, there was a rumor, you know, that you were sympathetic to the British."

Her eyes widened. A sudden burst of emotion hurtled past her walls of cool defense. "Rumors! Sir, shall I admit all to you now?" He was her friend, she realized. One of the best friends she had ever had. She knew why he was loved. It wasn't for the things he said, though they were charming—it was the way that he listened, the way he really heard what she had said. The elderly Comte de la Rochelle was very kind, and it was in his apartments in the far wing of the palace where she stayed, but it had not been until Ben Franklin arrived that she had felt comfortable. From the start he had sought to meet with her, he had come to her after his appointments with the ministers, and she had discovered in him a new meaning to revolutionary fever. Until the middle of 1775 he had been eager for reconciliation with Britain, but then he had seen that the desire for independence lay deep in the very hearts of the people. "Once the tide reaches the heart, milady, then no man can change that tide!" he had told her. She had believed him, and she quickly came to see through his eyes. By New Year's day she had realized that she was not just a Virginian but an *American*. She might have been a loyal British subject once, but she was an American now. What that truly meant, she knew, she had yet to discover.

"Amanda, admit to me—"

"Well, sir, there was some truth to rumor," Amanda said softly. Agitated, she rose. She stared back at the palace and caught her breath. Versailles. It was more than half a mile long, she had been told, with two enormous side wings. Once it had been the sight of a small hunting lodge, but Louis XIV had planned a very grand palace, and begun work upon it in 1661. He had hired the best architects, sculptors, and landscape gardeners. His successors had added to it, and now the palace boasted hundreds of rooms, marble floors, hand-painted ceilings, and the most beautiful gardens and landscaping that could be imagined. The king and queen and their retainers lived in such splendor and opulence that it was hard to imagine. They were like children, masters of this fairyland.

She looked from the beauty of the palace, rising against the sun, to Mr. Franklin, and she smiled. He was so plain and simple beside it all, his hose a dull mustard, his breeches blue, his surcoat a dark maroon, and his heavy cloak black. A civilian tricorn sat over the bald spot atop his head, and his hair, snowy white and gray, tufted out from either side. His face was wrinkled and jowled and reddened from cold and wind, but within were those eyes of his, soft blue beneath his spectacles, seeing and knowing all. And he was so much more impressive than the men of the court in their silks and satins and ungodly laces. And the women! Some wore their hair teased and knotted a good foot atop their heads. They called much of it Italian fashion—the most outlandish of it. Thus the term "macaroni." It was used in the song that was becoming very popular called "Yankee Doodle." This impressive fellow was far from "macaroni" fashion! Her smile slowly faded. Neither could they ever accuse her husband of being so. He had never even bent to fashion so far as to powder his hair. His shirts were laced, but never ostentatiously so. And when he moved about the estate he usually wore plain wool hose and dark breeches and a shirt that opened at his throat to display the bronze flesh of his throat and chest and the profusion of dark hair that grew short and crisp upon it . . .

"I was not guilty!" she swore suddenly. "Would God, sir, that you at least would believe me! I was free, can you understand? They had blackmailed me with my cousin, but once I knew he was free, they had nothing else to use against me. I gave away nothing!"

"There, there, now!" Franklin was on his feet. He caught her hands and brought her back to the bench, sitting again. "You must be careful. Mustn't upset the babe! Why, I remember my own dear children's birth . . . I've a son who is still with the British, my dear, so trust me, I do understand. Most men understand. This war is a fragile thing! If you say you are innocent, then I believe you."

"That simply?"

"Well, of course. I do believe that I know you rather well."

She started to laugh. "My husband should have known me well."

Franklin sighed. "He is a good man, Lady Cameron. I've known him long and well too, and you must see things as he did. His name is an old and respected one. It was risked, and he believed that it was by your hand. He fights a war, he marches to battle daily. You have mentioned to me that you do not correspond. I implore you, madame, when the babe is born, you must write to him."

She withdrew her hands quickly. Eric could die! He could ride into battle with his musket and his sword, and he could falter and fail. Exhaustion could overtake him, and his great heart could stop. She could not bear it if he were to perish!

But he had exiled her, cast her away. God knew, he was probably planning divorce proceedings this very moment. She had sworn that she would not forgive him. Her heart had grown cold.

But he could die. . . .

The thought was suddenly so painful that she doubled over. She couldn't breathe.

"Lady Cameron?" Franklin said anxiously.

She shook her head. "It's all right. It's all right. It's quite faded now."

He nodded, watching her anxiously still. When she seemed to have recovered, he smiled. "I've a confession of my own, dear. The moment I arrived here, I wrote to your husband."

"What?" She gasped in dismay.

"I had to, my dear. Lady Cameron, I was sent to England last, and while I waited there at the order of my country, my own dear wife departed this world. Life is short, and wisdom ever so hard to gain, and too oft gained to late. Forgive me—"

"Oh!" Amanda interrupted him. The sharp, blinding pain had seized her again. It was not worry, she realized then. She had gone into labor.

She rose, gasping. "Mr. Franklin—"

"It's all right!" he assured her, on her feet. "A first labor takes hours and hours, Amanda. Hours and hours—"

"Oh! But the pains are coming so quickly."

"Well, then maybe this labor will not be hours and hours! Oh, dear, this is not my forte—"

"Lady Cameron!"

She swung around. Both Cassidy and Jacques were hurrying up to her. She smiled. "See," she told Franklin. "I never am alone."

But she was glad that she was not alone, for the next pain doubled her over. She thought that she would fall, but she was scooped up into strong arms. She looked up and she saw Jacques's dear face, and she smiled and touched his cheek. "Thank you," she murmured.

He did not smile, but searched out her eyes. She was glad of his strength, for the palace was so very big, and her chambers were at the far end of it. They left the gardens and traveled long hallways. Finally Jacques burst open a set of molded double doors; they had reached the apartments of the Comte de la Rochelle. The elderly French statesman was sitting before the fire, warming his toes, when they entered.

"My dear—" he began, but he saw Jacques's face and moved quickly instead. "Danielle! The lady's time has come! Be quick, I shall send for the physician!"

Jacques carried her into the beautiful room that had been assigned her. Danielle was already running in before him, sweeping back the fine damask bedcurtains and the spread. Jacques set Amanda down. Suddenly she did not want him to go. She squeezed his hand. He touched her forehead and smiled to her, and in softly spoken French he promised her a beautiful son. Then he left. Danielle urged her to sit up and started tugging on her silk and velvet gown.

"I can help—" Amanda assured her, but the pain attacked her savagely again, and this time, it was so sudden that she could not help but cry out.

"Hold to the bed frame!" Danielle advised her. "Ah, *ma petite*! It will be much worse before it will be better!"

Danielle was so very right. For hours the pain came at short intervals. At first Amanda felt that she could bear it—the result would be her child, the babe she so desperately craved. Someone to hold and to love and to need her.

Then the pain became intense, and so frequent that she began to long for death. She swore, and she cried, and some point she didn't know what she was saying. Exhausted, she drifted to a semisleep in the few minutes between the pains. She dreamed of Eric Cameron, coming toward her in his boots and breeches and open shirt. He had loved her once, she thought. His eyes had danced upon her with silver and blue desire, and his mouth had turned into a sensual curl when he had touched her. He had held her against so much danger, but she hadn't trusted in the strength of his arms. He was speaking to her, accusing her of things.

"You have done something. You have done something to deny me a child." She protested. She promised that she had not. But he accused her anew, the silver lights of laughter and desire gone from his gaze. "Betraying bitch!" But there is a child now! she tried to tell him. He already had the baby; he held it high and away from her. "My son returns with me, my son returns with me—"

A savage pain, just like the thrust of a knife, cut across her lower back and wound around to her front.

"Easy, *ma petite,* easy!" It was Danielle who spoke, Amanda realized dimly.

Amanda screamed, trying to rise to consciousness. Her eyes were wild, her hair was soaked and lay plastered about her head. A cool cloth fell upon her forehead, smoothing back her hair. "No!" she screamed the word. "He cannot have my baby, the lying, treacherous bastard shall not take the baby away—"

"Amanda, if you mean me, my love, I've no intention of taking the babe away. If you'll only be so good as to deliver him to us."

Her eyes flew wide. She had to be dreaming still. He was there, standing above her. It was Eric with the damp sponge, cooling her brow, smoothing back her hair. She stared at him in distress and amazement. He could not be there. He despised her so, and now he was seeing her thus! Wretched and in anguish and so much pain. And though he spoke softly, she thought that there was bitterness in his voice. And coldness, like an arctic frost.

"No," she whispered, staring at him.

"Aye, my love," he retorted, his devil's grin in place, silver and indigo glittering in his gaze. He was nearly dressed as in her dream, wearing ivory hose and navy breeches, his frock coat and surcoat both shed, the laced sleeves of his shirt shoved high upon his muscled arms, his hair neatly queued back from his face.

"Please, don't be!" she hissed, and she did not know if she wanted him gone because she was angry still, or because she was so afraid that she could never attract him again.

His glance moved toward the foot of the bed, and she realized that, of course, they were not alone. She followed his gaze and saw Danielle and the French physician. She swallowed tightly. Again a pain seized, swift and sure and barely a minute from the one before it. She cried out pitifully, unable to hold back. Danielle whispered feverishly to Eric.

"It's over twenty-four hours. I do not see how she bears it."

"It is time now," the French physician said. "She must find the strength to bear down."

Eric's arms came around her. "Go away!" she begged him.

"He has said that you must push, Amanda. I'll help you."

"I do not want your help—"

"But you shall have it! Now do as you are told."

It was not so hard, for an overwhelming desire to do so came to her. Nor would Eric let her quit. When she would have fallen back he pressed her forward, his voice full of command. "Push, madame!"

"I am not among your troops, Major General!" she retorted, and then she was gasping and unable to say more, and they let her fall back at last.

"Come, come! A little Cameron head has nearly entered into the world!"

"Again, Amanda—"

"Eric, please—"

"Push!"

She did so, and that time she was rewarded with the sweetest sense of relief. The child emerged from her body and the physician exclaimed with delight, slapping the tiny form. A lusty cry was heard, and Danielle called out, "A girl! *Une petite jeune fille, une belle petite jeune fille*—"

"Oh!" Amanda gasped. She had been so very happy, so thrilled and excited. But then pain had seized her again, and she was suddenly terrified that she was going to die.

"What is it?" Eric demanded harshly.

"The pain—"

The Frenchman severed the birth cord, Danielle took the squalling baby girl. Eric gripped her hand, staring at her. "You are not going to die, my love. I have not finished with you," he promised her.

She wanted to answer him, but she could not. The urge to push had come upon her again.

"*Alors!* There are two!" The doctor laughed.

"Push!" Eric commanded her again. She could not. She was so exhausted she might well have been dead. He lifted her up, forced her to press forward.

"*Bon! Bon!*" the doctor exclaimed, nodding to Eric. Eric let her fall back, cradling her shoulders. She closed her eyes. She could remember the security of those arms. Once he had held her against the world. And now they were very much strangers. They were enemies to a greater extent than they had ever been. But he was there, holding her. Because he wanted their child. . . .

But she had a daughter, and she was so grateful! The baby was alive and well and—

"A boy, Lord Cameron!" The doctor laughed. "A boy, small, a twin, but all his fingers and toes are there! He will grow! His color is good. He is fine."

A son. She had a daughter and a son. Her eyes closed. They had said that they were healthy. Twins. Two . . . and both alive and well and with good color. She wanted to see them so badly. She couldn't begin to open her eyes.

"Amanda?"

She heard Eric's voice. She felt his arms, but she could not open her eyes.

"My lord Cameron, you have gotten her through, but she has lost much blood, and the time, you see. I still have work to do with her, and then she must sleep. My lord, Danielle has the girl. If you insist upon helping, take your son."

"My son. Aye, gladly, sir! I will take my son!"

She heard Eric say the words, and then she heard no more.

She must have slept a very long time, and very deeply, for when she awoke she was bathed and clean and wearing a soft white nightgown and her hair was dried and tied back from her face with a long blue ribbon. She awoke hearing a fretful crying. She opened her eyes, a smile on her face as she reached out for her infants.

Danielle was with her, she saw, smiling grandly as she walked over to the huge draped bed with the two bundles. "Your daughter, milady, or your son?" Danielle teased affectionately.

"I don't know!" Amanda laughed, delighted. They were both screaming away. She decided to let them scream for a moment, removing their bundling, checking out the tiny bodies. "Oh, how extraordinary!" She laughed, for her baby daughter had a thatch of bright red hair and the little boy was very dark. Both had bright blue eyes at the moment. She checked them both swiftly, counting fingers and toes. "Oh, they are perfect!"

"A little small, so we must take care. Lord Cameron was anxious to leave, but the size of these two has slowed even him down."

"Leave!" Amanda gasped.

"We're going home," Danielle said.

"We—all of us?"

"Mais oui! What else?"

Amanda exhaled slowly, afraid to speak her fears. No husband would have taken his infants—and not his wife. Not even Eric.

Yet that did not heal the distance between them.

"You must try to feed both. Jeannette Lisbeth—the queen's woman—says that you can hold both. . . ." Danielle came to her and adjusted the babies in her arms and her gowns. Amanda cried out with a little squeal of delight as her twins latched upon her breasts, tugging, creating a glowing sensation within her.

"They are so very small, however shall I manage?" She rested her chin atop one downy head, and touched a little cheek with her finger. "Oh, Danielle! Now I am so afraid. There are so many awful diseases—"

"Shush, and enjoy your children, *ma petite.* God will look after us all!"

Amanda smiled at Danielle's statement. She took delight in the infants, touching them, smiling. But then she stiffened, startled and wary, when the door suddenly opened without a knock. She would have quickly drawn her gown together except that she could not.

Eric had come. He was really there. Tall, elegant this morning in dark brocade and snow-white hose and silver-buckled shoes. She wanted to tell him that she was glad he was alive; glad he had come. But she could not. The breach between them was too great. She had told him that she loved him once, and he had called her a liar. She would not make the mistake again.

And yet his eyes fell instantly to her breasts where the babies feasted noisily. He seemed to drag them back to hers.

"You might have knocked," she told him coolly.

"I might have," he agreed smoothly, "except that a man should not be required to knock upon his wife's door." He glanced at Danielle. "Mam'selle, if you would . . . ?"

"Danielle!" Amanda wailed.

But Danielle was gone. Eric approached the bed. The little girl's mouth had gone slack. Her eyes were closed. Eric reached for her, swathing her in the blanket, setting her with care and skill upon his shoulder. His large bronzed hand looked mammoth against the child.

He glanced her way. "I do believe that they are supposed to burp this way."

Amanda nervously closed her gown, setting her infant son upon her own shoulder, patting the little back. She kept watching Eric, but he paid her little heed, giving his attention to their daughter. He did not look at her when he spoke at last. "I should like to call her Lenore."

"That was—"

"Your mother's name, yes. Does that suit you?"

"Yes," she said softly. "And—our son?"

"Jamie," he said huskily. "A Jamie Cameron began life in a new land. This Jamie Cameron will begin life in a new country."

"The war has not been won," Amanda observed.

His eyes fell upon her coldly. She lifted her chin, not wanting to fight, not knowing how not to do so. "And with what you said to me when we last met, I had doubts you would claim them as your own," she murmured.

She held her breath, awaiting his answer. She so desperately wanted him to disclaim his words, to vow some small word of love to her.

His eyes stayed upon her. "As this is March eleventh, I daresay the timing is quite right since our last—encounter."

Tears stung her eyes. She refused to shed them. "I wish that they were not yours!" she lied softly.

He stiffened, his back to her. "Ah, my dear wife! And you claimed to love me so the last time that we met!" She was silent. He turned to her. He set the baby down carefully in one of the cradles that had been brought and came to stand beside her. She nearly flinched when he reached down to touch her hair. He did not miss her reaction. He picked up his son even though a sound of protest escaped her. "The lad sleeps," he said. With Jamie Cameron set in his cradle, Eric came back to her again.

He reached into his frock coat and produced a small velvet box. He withdrew a ring from it and took her hand. She tugged upon her fingers but he held fast. A second later a stunning emerald surrounded by diamond chips was set upon her third finger. "Thank you," he said very softly, and it was the tone of voice that could set her heart to shivering, her very soul to trembling. She wanted so badly to reach out and stroke his face. No matter how tender his words, she dared not. "I did not mean to be so crude. I do, however, live sometimes for the day when I might meet Lord Tarryton once again. You forget, I discovered you once within his arms."

A smile escaped her. "And rescued me from them, if I recall."

"Yes, but I admit, I cannot forget that you loved him, and fears have often tormented my dreams. But I thank you for my children—healthy twins were far more than I dared dream. I would that they had been born at home—"

"You sent me here."

"Aye, and I would bring you home now. But, Amanda, you must swear to me that you will no longer betray my cause."

"I did not betray your cause—"

"I ask you for the future."

She lowered her head, feeling the urge to burst into tears. He still did not believe her. He had always been there for her, even in the midst of childbirth! But he did not believe her, and she knew of no way to heal their breach.

"I will not betray you, I swear it," she said softly.

His knuckles rested upon her cheek. He opened his mouth as if to speak. She turned her head aside. "This is a travesty of a marriage, is it not? When you loved me, I did not love you. Then I loved you—and you did not love me. There is nothing now, is there?"

His hand fell and he walked away from the bed. She heard the door open, and yet he hesitated. "Aye, there is something," he said. Her eyes rose to his. Cobalt fire, they fell upon her, and touched her flesh and blood and entered deeply inside of her. "For you are mistaken. I have loved you since I first laid eyes upon you, milady, and I have never ceased to love you."

The door closed. She was alone.

17

T WAS SEVERAL DAYS BEFORE AMANDA SAW ERIC again. Although she pondered his words endlessly when she was awake, it seemed that she was often exhausted in those first days. Danielle assured her that producing live, healthy twins was no easy task and that she deserved her rest. And in those days, countless gifts came to her, from the Comte de la Rochelle, from Benjamin Franklin, and even from the young king and queen. Marie Antoinette sent her Flemish lace christening gowns, as beautiful and opulent as the Palace of Versailles. While she was still abed, the twins were taken to be baptized, in an Episcopal ceremony, although the French royal court was devoutly Catholic. Though no one dared say it to Amanda, infant mortality was high, and so the ceremony was quickly arranged. Danielle stood as godmother to both infants, while Amanda was delighted to have Ben Franklin stand as their godfather.

By the end of a week she was feeling much stronger, and though she had been offered a young wet nurse by the court, she was determined to care for both of her babies herself. It was trying but greatly rewarding, and she could not forget for a moment how deeply she had feared that she would never have children.

Now she had two, precious beings who still brought her to awe. She never tired of searching over their little bodies, of counting fingers and toes, of studying their eyes and their hair and their noses and chins, trying to decide just whom they resembled. "I shall show you some of your ancestors!" she promised. "There's a huge gallery with rows and rows of Camerons! You shall see, and then we shall decide!"

They were way too young to smile, but still, she thought that Jamie, especially, watched her with very grave eyes. His father's eyes. They already had a tendency to look cobalt at times, silver at others.

She had her infants . . . and she had Eric. And he had even said that he loved her, that he had always loved her. But could it be enough? He had come for her—but she was certain that he still did not trust her.

And he stayed away from her. He came to see his new son and daughter, she knew, for Danielle always informed her. But he did not wait to see her when she wakened. She didn't know where he slept at night, but there Danielle assured her too. He was across in the comte's room, and the comte was in his eldest son's quarters. And Eric was not often around, Danielle continued, because he had been entrusted by Congress and General Washington to take messages to the French ministers. He also spent hours with Mr. Franklin.

They would leave for home on the first of April. Eric would arrive in time to fight during summer and fall—if the fledgling country survived so long. Sometimes it terrified her that she would be bringing her children home to a land of bloodshed.

The twins were a full two weeks old when she awoke to find Eric in her room, rocking one cradle while seriously observing Lenore. Amanda felt her eyes upon him and he turned to her. A misty shield covered any emotion, but his expression seemed as grave as Jamie's was often wont to be.

"We still leave on the first of April. I hope that is convenient for you."

She nodded, wishing that he had not caught her so unaware. Her hair was tousled, her gown was askew, slipping down from her shoulder. She had wished so badly that she might be more dignified, more perfect, more beautiful. He had said that he loved her. And they were so distant still, strangers who met between the explosions of cannon balls and the clash of steel.

She slipped out of bed and went to him, touching his arm. "Eric, maybe we shouldn't go back."

"What?" He swung around, amazed, staring at her hand where she touched his arm. Her hand fell.

"I was just thinking—maybe we should stay here. In France. We could survive. We would not need so very much—"

"Have you lost your very mind!" he asked her.

She backed away from him, shaking her head. "I am afraid! Look at the strength of the British army. They can keep sending men and more men! They have Hessians and Prussians and all other kinds of mercenaries. The colonies—"

"The United States of America," he corrected her very softly, his jaw twisting.

"We cannot pay our own troops!" she exclaimed. "Eric, if we should lose the war—"

"We?"

"Pardon?"

"You said 'we,' my love. Are you part of that 'we'? Have you changed sides, then?"

She exhaled, mistrustful of the tone of his voice. She felt at such a disadvantage, clad in the sheer silk gown, tousled by the night, barefoot. Eric towered over her in his boots. He was dressed fully in his uniform with his cockaded and plumed hat pulled low over his eyes, his breeches taut about his muscled thighs, his spring cloak emphasizing the breadth of his shoulder. She trembled slightly. He would not come to her now—indeed, he did not seem interested in her— but she wished suddenly and desperately that she could sweep away the time and the anger and the hatred and rush into his arms, just to be held.

She forced a cool and rueful smile to her features. "You have called me a traitor. Well, sir, if I was for the British, then I was not a traitor at any time, unless that time should be now. Am I for the colonies now—excuse me, the United States of America? Yes, I am. And no thanks to you, Lord Cameron. You haven't the gifts of persuasion that Mr. Franklin so amply possesses. I should very much like to see the Americans win. It's just that—"

"That you doubt that they can, is that it?"

She flushed and lowered her head slightly. "I have never known quite what it was to love with the need to protect until these last few days. I am afraid."

Eric was quiet for several seconds. "As far as I know, madame, the British have yet to make war on children. I have to go back. You know that. You've known where I stand, and just how passionately, from the very beginning."

"And you knew where I stood," she reminded him softly.

"I just never thought—" He broke off, shaking his head.

"What!" Amanda demanded heatedly. She knew what. He had never thought that she would take it so far as to betray her home. "I have told you that I did not—"

"Let's not discuss it—"

"If we cannot discuss it, then we've nothing at all to discuss!" she cried.

He stiffened. For a brief moment she thought that his thin control upon his temper would snap, that he would wrench her into his arms, that he would demand her lips as he had been so quick to do in the past. She prayed silently that he would touch her.

He did not. He bowed deeply to her. "I leave you to the care of our children, madame. Remember that you must soon be ready to travel."

———

It was not so difficult to leave behind Versailles, no matter how beautiful it was. Amanda had never really entered into the inner circle of the court, but she had made friends, and she would miss them. Most of all, though, she would miss Ben Franklin, who would stay on in France until his mission was completed. He hugged her warmly when the party bundled into the coaches that would take them to the port.

"Ah, I do long for home! But then, my dear, I am too old to be a soldier, so this is how I must serve. God with you and yours in all your endeavors!"

She was going to cry, Amanda thought. Mr. Franklin had offered her a quiet and steady friendship when her world had been awry, and she would always love him for it. She kissed his cheek impulsively and climbed up into the coach with Danielle and the twins. One of the babies was thrust into her arms, and she sat back, listening as Franklin said his good-byes to Eric, giving him the last of his communications homeward to Washington, the Congress, and his daughter.

Amanda heard the crack of the whip, and she realized she was leaving Versailles for good. It hurt to leave Mr. Franklin and the comte, who had been kind, but that was the only pain. A raw excitement was already burning in her heart. She was very eager to go home. The soft whisper of the river already seemed to sound in her blood. She could feel the salt against her face, the heat of the summer's day; she could see the leaves in the autumn, falling with their beautiful and brilliant colors upon the leaves and the water. She could see the stables and the smokehouse and smell Virginia ham. Please God, she thought, let it be there when we return! Let Cameron Hall still stand!

It would stand, she thought. Eric had told her that the British were threatening the north—they had been, at least, away from southern shores.

He did not ride in the carriage with her, but chose to ride a horse alongside. Nor, even during the long journey to reach the water, did he tarry with her long. When they stopped for an evening meal and a bed for the night, he ordered her a room and had food sent to her and Danielle and the twins. It was Jacques who saw to her welfare most often. And each time Jacques approached, he stopped to admire the twins, never touching the pair but watching them with such a poignancy about his eyes that her heart seemed to catch in her throat. Amanda would wonder what tragedy had touched the man's past to cause such a look in the eyes.

By the fifth of April they were upon the open seas, heading for home with a steady wind. Amanda and the twins had been given the captain's cabin. She assumed that Eric had chosen to take the first mate's berth and that the first mate was in with his fellow officers. She felt very well this trip and was eager to walk the decks. Unfortunately, the crew aboard the ship was composed of many of the same men who had discovered her last June with a sword in her hand. While none of them seemed to harbor her any ill will, Amanda still felt awkward around them. Eric was captaining his own ship and, once again, keeping his distance from her. She tried to remind herself that he did not trust her and that she had every right to despise him for his treatment. But again she could not forget that he had said he loved her, and she could not rid herself of the pain of the estrangement. She wondered about him by night. She lay awake and she wondered about his life, the life she had never known, the life of a soldier. She knew that women followed the armies, some for love and some for money, and she wondered how he had spent his time, if he had managed to forget her frequently in the arms of another. She hated the thoughts. They tormented her again and again.

It anguished her, too, that now, when things should be so very fine between them, he drew a greater distance from her daily. He might have claimed that he loved her, but any man who could so thoroughly ignore his wife must have some interest elsewhere. Determined to taunt him, she took to spending her time on deck. Jacques was her friend and would always listen to her, and Frederick, who had accompanied Eric, seemed quite adept with the sea for a printer-turned-soldier. One evening she had managed to gather quite a group about her as she described some of the very outlandish fashions of the French and Italians at Versailles. Then someone started singing:

> "Yankee Doodle went to town,
> A-riding on a pony,
> Stuck a feather in his cap,
> And called it macaroni!"

They were all laughing when Frederick suddenly sobered. Amanda looked past the group of men to see that her husband was standing before them, dark and towering and very silent. In the night his eyes were ebony and condemning and she was glad of it, for she was ready for a fight.

"My love, I hear whimpering from the cabin. Shouldn't you be about the babes?"

"But they sleep, my love, I am quite certain," she returned.

"I say that I have heard crying, and I ask, milady, that you see to it," he said harshly, his eyes narrowing.

The air, the night, seemed charged. This time it seemed that all these men who so loved and admired her husband were on her side. Amanda came to her feet, smiling sweetly. "Please, please, gentlemen, do forgive my husband's horrid lack of manners. I quite often do myself."

With that she swept by Eric, hoping that traces of perfume would haunt his clothing where the silk of her own touched him. She even hoped that she had soured his temper, but he did not follow her. In dismay she realized that the next days followed as the first had done. They were halfway across the ocean, and still, except for an occasional meal with Frederick and Jacques and others in attendance, he did not speak with her all.

The twins were her delight. The sea air seemed to do wonders for them, and when the days were warm, Amanda brought them to the deck. The crew, hardy hands one and all, acted like fools before the babes, clucking, making faces, vying for attention. Amanda, holding Lenore, laughed at one mate's antics and looked up, searching for Eric. She discovered him not far away, his eyes upon her, pensive and dark. She flushed. He did not look away. "Isn't she clever, Eric? I could swear that Lenore smiles already, and it has nothing to do with bubbles in the belly!"

He smiled at last. "Aye, my love. She is clever indeed. Like her mother."

Amanda did not know what the comment meant, and so she turned away.

Soon they were approaching Virginia. Eric often ordered her curtly below-decks then, for he was wary of British schooners. Frederick told her that they had battled and seized two British warships on their trip to France. "His lordship hoped to catch on to that Lord Tarryton or Sterling, but alas . . ." His voice trailed away as he remembered that Nigel Sterling was her father. "Begging your pardon, my lady, but they did invade Cameron Hall—"

"There is no pardon necessary, Frederick. Two ships! You battled two ships?"

"Aye, lost only three of our crew, one wounded, two dead, and sent them packing down to Charleston with skeleton crews in place. Lord Cameron promised General Washington that he would take a ship or two, he did, that's how he gained the time to come to France. And he won't be wanting to have any run-ins with the Brits now, not with you and the little lad and lass aboard!"

Amanda thanked him for the information. She knew that they would make Virginia by the next night. That evening when the twins slept she left them in Danielle's care and went atop the deck, seeking out Eric. She saw him at the rail, staring out at the sea and the stars and the night, a tall, rugged silhouette against the velvet patina. Inhaling sharply, she touched her hair, stiffened her spine, and walked softly toward him. She had not quite reached him when he spun around, his hand reaching for his sword. He relaxed when he saw her, and she realized that he was ever ready for a fight now that the war had become a part of his living.

"What is it, Amanda? You should be below. The night is cool, and we are in dangerous waters."

"Virginia is not so dangerous. You have said so yourself—that is why you are allowing me to return."

"Tell me what you want, and get below."

"For one, my lord, I am not one of your servants to be ordered about!"

His lip curled with a trace of amusement. "You are my wife, and still suspected by many to be a traitor, and therefore your position is more precarious than that of any of my servants."

"Then perhaps, Lord Cameron, I will not care to live in your abode!"

"What?"

She shrugged extravagantly. "Sterling Hall still stands, I do believe. I can take my children and go home."

"The devil you will, madame—"

"Lord Cameron!"

Eric's words were interrupted as the lookout shouted down from the crow's nest. "Lord Cameron! Warship off to the left, sir! She's flying England's colors."

"Be damned!" Eric swore, spinning around. "Frederick, the glass! Gunners, to your stations. Can you see her up there, mate? How many guns is she carrying?"

"Six portside, milord!"

"I can take her," Eric muttered. "I don't dare run, she'll follow us home." He spun around, suddenly aware of his wife again. "Get to the cabin, Amanda."

"Eric—"

"For the love of God, will you go? Our children are there!"

She started to speak again, but then closed her mouth and turned quickly. She had barely scampered into the cabin when the roar of a cannon was heard.

"Take Jamie, please!" Amanda said to Danielle. Lenore was already awake and whimpering. Amanda swept her daughter into her arms. Seconds later the ship shivered and trembled.

"We've been hit!" Danielle called.

Amanda hurried to the window, drawing back the small velvet drapes. A ship was just coming along hard broadside. A cannon boomed again. Amanda gasped. A direct shot had hit the ship that was almost upon them. The force of the explosion and fire sent her flying back. She landed hard, trying to protect Lenore as she fell on the floor.

There were screams and horrible shouts. The British ship was going down, but those crewmen who had survived the blast were coming aboard. Amanda closed her eyes against the clang of steel and the sound of musket shot. She huddled on the bed, holding Lenore tight. How long could it go on, the horrid, horrid war! How many times could Eric fight—and himself survive?

Eventually the sound of battle began to die down. Amanda walked toward the cabin door, trying to hear. There was nothing. She hurried back to Danielle, thrusting Lenore into her arms along with Jamie. "I'll be back."

"Amanda, you come back in here! You were surely told—"

"Danielle, shush, please!"

It didn't matter, Amanda was already out the door. She paused, choking as powder filled her lungs. As she hurried along the deck, she stepped over the bodies of fallen men, redcoats and patriots alike. She rushed on, suddenly horribly frightened. There was so much silence!

When she came around to the helm, she heard the fighting again at last. It was down to one-to-one combat, the British navy men highly visible in their colors. She looked frantically about for Eric. He was engaged with a young sergeant. Suddenly another man came up behind him. Eric swung around in time to avoid the blow to his back, but the second opponent had caught his sword, and the silver rapier went flying down to his feet.

Amanda screamed, then raced forward. "Amanda!" She heard the roar of his voice as he stepped toward her, grasping the helm rail, staring down the steps to her. He didn't seem to care that he could be skewered at any moment, his concern was for her.

She caught his bloodied sword up in her hands and raced toward him. He clutched it from her hands, his eyes meeting hers. Then he thrust her behind him and set to dueling his opponents once again. He seemed to move on clouds, agile and able, always a superior swordsman. And always he kept her behind him, until he leapt forward suddenly, catching the sergeant with a quick thrust, then slicing the second man as he rebounded from the first. With a groan the second man slumped to the ground.

Eric looked from the men to her. He touched her cheek, wondering. "I told you to go to the cabin."

"I did go to the cabin."

He smiled. "Madame, you were supposed to stay within it."

"I might have saved your life."

"Indeed, my lady, perhaps you did."

"Lord Cameron!" Frederick called, limping over to them. "The English ship is sinking, and there are live men afloat out there."

Eric's eyes remained upon Amanda's. He smiled. "We must pick them up. They go to the brig, Frederick, but by all means, we must pick up the living!"

Frederick turned to go about his task. "Will you go back to the cabin now?" Eric asked her.

She nodded, smiling, and turned around.

———

That night was so very different from that long-ago June day when she had been forced to accompany Robert Tarryton. Now she was heartily cheered by all of the ship. The maids and servants and craftspeople and artisans hurried down to greet the ship, eager for a glimpse of the Cameron heir. Eric held the twins up high, one in each arm, and accepted the congratulations of his servants, slaves, and dependents. A coach awaited them. Amanda returned to the house alone—Eric had the business of the British prisoners to deal with and more. Her heart caught as they approached the house, and then she seemed to grow warm, and tears burned her eyes. She loved the place so very much! She hoped that it would not be awkward there, that enough of the people knew her and loved her well enough to understand that she had not betrayed them.

"My lady!" Richard, too excited to be staid, came running down the steps, eager to snatch away one of the twins. "Two! Two! Why, we'd no idea. Of course, we'd no idea at all until Lord Cameron sent word. I do declare, milady, but the lad looks like his father did! Just alike. And with a mat of hair upon his head too! But then, who knows, we cannot tell until the wee ones have grown a bit, eh, madame? But you must be weary, come, come along now!"

Amanda smiled, following Richard. When she entered the hallway she saw that Margaret was standing on the stairway, very still and very white. The servant lowered her head and hurried down the steps. "I'll leave, milady. I needed me wages, so I waited here working, but I'll leave—"

"Margaret, you needn't leave. No one need leave. You thought that I had betrayed this hall—I can only swear to you that I did not. If you believe in me, you are welcome to stay."

Margaret was crying. "Thank you. Thank you, milady. May I tell the same to Remy?"

Remy had actually spat at her. Amanda ground her teeth. How could she condemn the servant when her husband still did not believe in her?

"Yes," she said softly. "Remy may stay."

Before Margaret could start thanking her again, Amanda hurried on up the stairs. Richard came along, and Danielle with Lenore. Richard showed her to the nursery—the room that had once been hers had been cleverly converted with a basin and drawers suitable for the blankets and tiny garments of a babe, and a beautiful bassinet with mosquito netting draped about it. "There's two, milady, you needn't fret! There's been twins before, there will be twins again, I daresay! We'll have the second down in no time."

"That's fine. I shall take both babies in with me for a while," Amanda assured Richard.

"Yes, milady. And may I say welcome home. We've missed you, we have!"

She smiled. "Yes, Richard, you may say so. Thank you."

Amanda brought the twins in with her to nurse, and when they had become sated and slept, she called for Danielle. By then both bassinets were ready. The two women set the babes to sleep for their first night in their own home.

When she returned to her own room, she discovered that Richard had sent her a steaming tub, with French soap and huge snowy towels and a silver tray filled with wine and plate of ham swimming in honey and raisin sauce with fresh green beans and summer squash. She smiled with gratitude, then she shivered slightly, remembering how like that last night things seemed.

Still, she sipped the wine and sank into the bath. There had been no such luxury over the nine weeks it had taken them to return. When she finished she stepped out of the tub and wrapped herself in the towel, drying her hair before the fire. Then, with her towel swept around her, she sat at her dressing table and started to brush out her hair.

And it was then that he entered the room. In his boots, breeches, and open-necked shirt, he stepped into the room and closed the door. Amanda turned slowly around to meet his gaze. He strode slowly across the room until he came to her. Then he lowered himself upon one knee before her and touched her shoulders. His hands moved slowly over and around her breasts, and the towel fell away. She caught her breath, wishing that she were not so eager for him. But firelight danced in his eyes, and in her own, and with a poignant ache she realized that it had been a year since he had touched her. She could not protest what she desired with all of her heart, and if things were not perfect between them, she was still his wife. And she was here once again, in the room they shared. No matter what his words, no matter how he fought her, she could see and feel the heat of the desire about him, and instinctively she knew that he had never wanted another woman as he wanted her.

"Perhaps I should go," he told her. "Maybe I've no right to be here, madame."

She swallowed, alarmed at the strength of the sensations that swept through her at the simple soft stroke of his fingers upon her swollen breasts, rolling lightly over the dusky rose of her nipples, stroking again the underflesh.

"I have waited for you," she told him solemnly.

"And I have been the worst fool in the world, and if you had sent me away, lady, God help me, there is no way that I could have gone."

He stood and scooped her up into his arms. When he lay her down upon the bed, he paused and looked over the length of her. An soft explosion, a curse, a cry, escaped him, and then he was upon her. He had never touched her with such care, with such tenderness. His touch stirred her, his kiss aroused and awoke her, and as his lips and fingertips and tongue traveled and caressed the length of her, whispers, then moans, escaped her. He drew her ever upward, and when she thought that she would cry out and beg that she could bear no more, he would gently ease her just slightly downward again, his tongue delving soft and vulnerable flesh.

And when he came to her she did cry out, shuddering, holding tight, winding her limbs about him. The need to be with him was so great, the strength of his body so shocking, that she nearly whispered all that she felt. She almost told him that she loved him. But just in time, she bit back the words, and she cried out her longing instead and he dove and swept within her, becoming the world, searing her soul, taking all of her, and bringing everything of life, and just a little bit of death.

———

There was no time for them. Perhaps that was the most bitter fact that she seemed always to have to face. Eric was gone all the next day, seeing to the estate, the planting, the horses, the building, the repairs. They did not even have dinner together, but Amanda waited, and when he came to her, she welcomed him with her body silken, her arms eager to close about him. They made love until it was nearly dawn, holding tight.

In the morning it was time for him to leave again. It was the middle of June, and Eric had been away from the war a long time. Virginia was peaceful enough, but the British offensive was moving in the northern states, and there had already been several battles.

As usual, Amanda stood on the steps, ready to watch Eric ride away. He was upon Joshua, ever the excellent horseman, exceedingly handsome in his uniform with his plumed hat, high boots, his hair still damp. Amanda approached him with the stirrup cup, for it was tradition now, and as he returned the cup to her, she met his eyes with her own wide and grave upon his. "I never did betray this hall, Eric," she told him.

He leaned down to kiss her lips. "Care for them, Amanda. For the twins. And if anything happens to me, fight for this place. With whatever you have. It is their heritage."

He kissed her again. Tears flooded her eyes, and she stepped back. He was riding away to war again, and though he might love her, he still did not trust her. He did not believe her, and he was telling her that if the war was lost, she was to keep Cameron Hall by any means available—including a plea to the British should the master of Cameron Hall be hanged.

She watched the horses ride away. "I do love you," she whispered aloud. But there was no one to hear.

———

In December she sat upon the rail at the paddocks watching Jacques put the yearlings through their paces. Danielle came running down the pathway from the house, waving her arms frantically. As she leapt off the fence, alarmed, Amanda quickly felt her worried frown slip into an incredulous smile.

Damien was coming close behind Danielle.

Amanda let out a shriek of pure pleasure and raced madly along the dirt path until she pitched hard into her cousin, crying and laughing, shouting his name, crying and laughing all over again. He scooped her up and swung her around and held her close, and at last he set her down.

"My God, how are you here?" she demanded.

"One furlough in how many years?" he teased. Then he sobered. "There aren't many furloughs these days," he said grimly, and her heart thundered hard.

The war was not going well, she thought. "Come on into the house. Look at me, I am a disaster!"

"They say you run one of the finest estates in Virginia," Damien said dryly.

Amanda shrugged, walking up the back steps to the house. "Come into the parlor and have a brandy." He was looking ragged, she thought. His brass buttons were not shining, his boots barely seemed to have soles, and his coat was nearly threadbare. "Damien! I cannot believe it!" she cried, and hugged him all over again.

In the parlor she served him brandy and felt his eyes upon her. Seated casually in a chair before the fire, he lifted his snifter to her. "Amanda, you are thin and lithe and more beautiful than ever. Your features are ever more delicate and refined. You thrive, cousin, even as a matron."

"Matron!"

"Well, you are a wife and mother of two. And I am most eager to see my new relations. God knows, there are few enough of us!"

"The twins will be down soon, Damien. Danielle will bring them when they awake. Tell me, what is happening? How is—how is Eric?"

Damien leaned forward, frowning. "The war? Let's see. A young lad named Alex Hamilton is Washington's secretary now, and doing a damned good job of it. He knows money better than any of those fools in Congress. What else. Ah— we've another young man, a Frenchman. The Marquis de Lafayette. He is a volunteer who rides to death with a smile upon his face—and does wonders for our cause. General Washington is wonderfully impressed with him, and I must admit, so am I. The war, let's see. There have been so many battles! The British meant to split the colonies, you know. Right down the Mohawk Valley. They did not manage that. In April they attacked Danbury—Benedict Arnold held them back. Burgoyne took Ticonderoga in July, but I am very proud to say that he surrendered on the seventeenth of this month. General Arnold again, with some fine help from Morgan's riflemen. We lost the Battle of Hubbardton, we won the Battle of Bennington. The Battle of Brandywine—your husband was magnificent at that one. Riding that giant stallion of his . . . few men are better with a sword. Still, Howe very skillfully turned the American right, forcing Washington back toward Philadelphia. General Howe—with the help of his brother, Admiral Howe—has taken Philadelphia now. This winter, cousin, the British will sit in the splendid homes of Philadelphia. Washington is moving his forces to Valley Forge."

"But Eric—"

"Eric is alive and well," Damien said irritably.

Amanda sat back, surprised. "Damien, you used to be so fond of Eric yourself! What has happened?"

Distraught, Damien rose and stood before the fire, watching the flames. "I did not care for his treatment of you," he said simply.

Amanda sighed, clutching the arms of her chair. "Damien, I was betraying him."

Shocked, Damien turned around. "What?"

She didn't want to distress him further, but she had to tell him the truth. "Not when the British came to destroy the supplies here, someone else is guilty of that, and someone will betray the Virginians again unless Eric does believe me and look elsewhere. But, Damien—" She hesitated just a second and then plunged onward. "Damien, Father used to blackmail me with you."

"Me!"

"They knew all along that you were running arms from western Virginia to Boston and Philadelphia. First he promised to arrest you and see you hanged. He killed your horse, Damien. Don't you remember? In Williamsburg."

"Oh, my God!"

Amanda didn't look at him. "Then you were his prisoner. He promised me that there were all manner of things he could do to you."

"Oh, Amanda!" He came to her, kneeling down, taking her hands into his. "My God, I am so sorry! I did not know! How could you risk so much for me?"

She touched his cheek. "Get up, Damien. I love you, remember? We have always had each other, and besides, it is all over now."

He stood and walked back to the fire, and she realized that he was hesitating. "It isn't really over," he said at last.

"What do you mean?"

"I mean that you should be with your husband this winter."

"But—"

"Martha always comes to stay with George when he settles into his winter quarters. And you—you need to come."

"I haven't been asked," Amanda said stiffly. "I don't think that he believes me yet." She sighed. "I know that he does not completely trust me, no matter how far it seems that we have gone. God knows, I might betray something were I to be there!"

"You need to be there!" Damien persisted.

"Why?"

Damien stuttered and then cleared his throat. "Anne Marie is there."

"Anne Marie Mabry?"

"She has followed her father to war. And she cooks often for Eric. And—"

"And what?" Amanda demanded.

Damien lifted his arms and dropped them. "I don't know. But you need to be there."

She felt as if giant icy fingers gripped her heart and squeezed, and then she felt an awful fury rip through her. How dare he judge her when he . . .

Anne Marie had always cared for Eric. Always. Amanda had known that the night she had first met him.

The cold, and then the heat, settled over her. She tried to breathe deeply. If he meant to have another woman, she told herself, he would do so. She could not walk with him everywhere.

She could not force him to love her.

But she could discover the truth of it, and if he was determined to have Anne Marie, then he would not have her at home waiting eagerly for his return!

"I—I think that I will accompany you to Valley Forge, Damien. When you're ready to go."

He smiled. "That's my darling, daring cousin. What of the babes?"

How could she leave them? Danielle would care for them. They were old enough now to eat food, and though it would hurt her, she would find a wet nurse. They would be well. She would be the one to be empty without them.

"They will be fine here," she assured Damien softly.

He smiled again. "Well then, I am glad that you will ride with me. We should leave within the week. I've some business in Williamsburg . . . and then there's Lady Geneva."

"Lady Geneva?"

"Cousin, even I was destined to fall in love."

"With Geneva!"

"And why not?"

Why not, indeed? Geneva was beautiful, sensual, and perhaps just right for Damien. "No reason. How long has this been going on?"

"Affairs of the heart move slowly in wartime, Mandy. And sometimes quietly. This, as you call it, has been going on for several years now."

Amanda started to laugh. Damien cast her a hard warning glare and she laughed all the harder.

"Amanda—"

"I am delighted, Damien. Absolutely delighted. And a week will be fine. I need time to leave the twins and time to gather supplies to go. I cannot imagine that they are overly endowed with food and blankets for the winter."

"Hardly," Damien said dryly, then smiled. "Laugh away at me, then, cousin, if you will! I shall be eager to see the show once we arrive."

Amanda sobered quickly. He winked her way, taking full advantage of his own turn to be amused. He lifted his brandy glass.

"To the winter at Valley Forge!"

Neither of them was quite aware yet of what those words would mean.

18

AMANDA HAD KNOWN THAT THINGS WERE GOING badly. She knew that General Washington had gone to Valley Forge from his defeat at Germantown, and Damien had warned her that the men were in bad shape.

But once Damien had identified himself and they entered into the compound —she, Damien, Geneva, and Jacques Bisset—Amanda was still stunned by the appearance of the men and the encampment.

Snow rose everywhere, piled high, part of the biting cold of the winter. The soldiers' homes were crude log buildings that they had constructed themselves. Smoke billowed from makeshift chimneys, windows were covered with canvas or paper. There didn't seem to be a leaf or a straggling bush left alive anywhere; about the emcampment there were only the barren and naked branches of tall trees, skeletal, deathlike.

Yet the camp was not so appalling as the men. As Damien flicked the reins and the horse dragged the cart onward, they passed hundreds of men. Lined up along the trail, some waved, some saluted, and some just stared. They huddled in frayed blankets, shivering, staying close to one another. Amanda's eyes fell toward the ground and she gasped, despairing to see that many had no shoes, but stood in the snow with their feet bound in rags.

"My God!" she breathed, and tears stung her eyes. "Dear God, but perhaps surrender would be better than this!"

No retreat, no surrender. The words rose in her heart. They had always been there, between her and Eric. And now they seemed appropriate for the ragtag army. They had come this far. Surely they were weighed down heavily with despair.

Damien exhaled behind her. "Washington endures this place day after day while there are those in Congress trying to tear him down. I've never seen a man so willing to suffer with his subordinates, so touched by all that he sees." He flicked the reins again. "There, up ahead, are the command quarters. I see your husband's ensignia. There lies your home, Amanda."

"And what of mine?" Geneva asked sweetly from the rear.

Amanda swung around to grin at her old friend. Geneva had been eager to come. She had sworn that she could cure many a man of whatever ailed him. But looking about the complex, she did not seem so assured.

"My dear lady, I shall see that you have the finest accommodations in the place!" Damien assured her.

"See that you do," Geneva replied sweetly. Amanda could feel the sparks flying between them. She glanced at Jacques and grinned, then lowered her head, still smiling. They were both so strong-willed and determined upon their own way. Perhaps they deserved one another.

Damien pulled in on the reins. As he did so, Amanda saw Eric appear in the doorway of one of the huts. He was striking as he stood there, very tall in the shadows. But even his uniform seemed ragged, his boots were shined but worn, the brass upon his frock coat was heavily tarnished. His face was lean and hard, perhaps more arresting than ever, taut with character, his eyes very blue against the bronze of his features. But they were not welcoming eyes. They did not touch her with warmth, but with reserve.

She had thought to run to him, to find herself swept off her feet. Suddenly she could not run. Her heart was caught in her throat. Eric remained still, and Jacques helped her down from the wagon.

"Lady Cameron!"

Thankfully, Washington had stepped out from around her husband, a petite, rounded woman in a mob cap coming behind him. "Lady Cameron, as your husband seems tongue-tied, I must welcome you to Valley Forge. Martha, have you ever met Eric's wife? I hadn't thought so, well, you must do so now. Lady Cameron—"

"Amanda," she breathed quickly.

Many had speculated that George had married the widow Martha Custis for her money alone—there had been many more attractive and younger women available to him at the time. Amanda realized instantly what Washington had seen in the woman. As the older woman welcomed her with a kiss and hug, Amanda was enveloped by an overwhelming sense of warmth. There was a kindness in her light eyes that was unmistakable. She attracted just like the comforting heat of a fire.

"Damien, you rascal, you disappear and return with two beautiful young ladies!" Washington called. "Lady Geneva, welcome. Good God, Cameron, shouldn't we have them in out of the cold. And you too, Monsieur Bisset. Do come on in. All that we have is yours, however meager that may be!"

"We've brought supplies from Cameron Hall," Amanda said softly. She thought of the meat and grain and coffee and tobacco in the barrels and chests aboard the wagon, and she thought of the thousands of men here. It would hardly make a dent.

"Amanda?"

Eric reached out a hand to her at last, stepping forward. His fingers curled around hers and he drew her close, kissing her coolly upon the cheek. He asked her quickly about the twins and she said that they were well. Then he led her inside, and she instantly stiffened.

Anne Marie was there, standing by a coffeepot that heated over the hearth fire.

"Amanda!" Anne Marie came forward, kissing her swiftly on the cheek. Amanda tried to smile in return. Damien and Geneva and the Washingtons were entering, and it seemed that everyone was talking at once. Anne Marie hugged her.

"So you have been fighting this war with the men, have you?" Amanda asked sweetly.

"I've followed Father from the very beginning," Anne Marie agreed. "I should say, since he decided to cast in with the patriots. I'd no real idea for the longest time just which way we were meant to go."

"This is a horrible place to be," Washington said suddenly, softly. "Horrible. I've eleven thousand men here. Of that number, almost three thousand are without shoes or are half naked, and Congress tells me there is nothing to be given my men, nothing to be done. Ah, ladies, you should not be here."

"Oh, posh!" Mrs. Washington protested. "If I did not see you, Mr. Washington, in your winter quarters, why, then I should have no husband at all."

"I wonder if I do have one at all," Amanda said sweetly. The company about them laughed; Eric did not.

"Well, we've something of a stew to eat tonight," Anne Marie said. "Please, everyone, sit. We'll have something."

Amanda felt acutely uncomfortable, a guest in her husband's living quarters, while Anne Marie was the very comfortable hostess. She held tight to her temper, noting as she sat that a woman's cloak was upon the crude peg by the door and that there seemed to be other signs of constant feminine occupation of the hut, such as the lace dusters on the table sills. The main room consisted of the hearth, a large raw center table, and some poorly crafted chairs. There was a doorway leading to a second room. It was cracked open and Amanda could see a rope bed within it, covered it by a thin green blanket. There were trunks and a desk within the bedroom too, but everything seemed sparse and empty and cold.

She caught Eric's eyes. A trace of amusement flickered across them, as if he thought that she had surveyed her surroundings and found them entirely lacking. As if she were wishing that she had not come.

Well, she was not. Reckless and irritated, she tossed back a stray curl and bent her head to listen to General Washington as he spoke, assuring Damien had they had come from hard times before. "And curious pieces of luck have been ours, as if God does smile upon us now and then. Monsieur Bisset, did you know that we barely reached Trenton? We did so by a play of card, can you imagine? Colonel Johann Rall was playing poker on Christmas Eve, and was so engrossed that when a messenger handed him a warning that we were launching a surprise attack, he merely shoved it into his pocket. The note was discovered only after the attack, when the colonel lay dead."

"One might say," Damien joked, "General, that you were the one holding the full house."

"Ah, yes. But how fickle is life, eh?"

"How fickle indeed," Geneva murmured.

"You see," Mrs. Washington said, rising to ladle out the stew, "God is on our side. We've only to wait and see!"

She was a determined woman, determined to make the night go smoothly. Baron Von Steuben, another volunteer to the American cause, arrived, and was fed, and explained some kind of a military tactic to the men. The hour grew late.

Mrs. Washington told Geneva that they had an extra room where she might sleep while other arrangements were being made, and people began to leave. "I guess Jacques and I get the floor out here, eh, Lord Cameron?" Damien asked. There was still that edge to his voice.

"It's the best I have to offer," Eric replied, his tone cool in return.

"I must get back," Anne Marie said.

"I will escort you," Eric told her. He didn't glance toward Amanda as he took his great cloak from the peg. Anne Marie said good-bye to Amanda, then walked out into the cold wind. It buffeted her. Amanda gritted her teeth as she saw Eric reach for the woman instantly, catching her arm.

What went on here? She wanted to be reasonable, and logical, but he spent years calling her a liar and traitor, while he had always had another woman right behind him while he went to war.

And now Jacques and Damien were both in the main room, and unless she chose to cast aside her pride totally and have an argument that would draw them all in, she had no choice but to smile and say good night sweetly and walk into her husband's bedroom. She wanted to throw something—and preferably right at Eric!

She removed the blanket from his bed and sat down by the fire, drawing the blanket around her. Twenty minutes later she heard the door open and then slam closed, and then she heard Eric speaking softly with Jacques. She smiled, hoping that he imagined her eagerly awaiting him. He would find things far different.

But she never knew what he imagined. The door opened and he stood there, pulling off his gloves. His eyes fell upon her with little surprise. Coming in, he closed the door softly and leaned against it.

"So you rode in winter wind all this way to come and sleep upon a cold dirty hearth," he said at last.

She rose to her knees, holding the blanket about her, nudging a log with a crude iron poker. "No, my lord Cameron. I did not come all this way to do so— but rather I arrived here and found it the expedient thing."

He swore impatiently and crossed the floor to her, catching her hands and dragging her to her feet. "What are you talking about?" he demanded harshly.

"Anne Marie," she said flatly.

His lip curled slightly. "Ah."

"Ah! And that is all that you have to say?"

"What can I say? I'm sure that Damien has sliced me to ribbons on that matter, quite competently."

Amanda jerked from his touch. Cold, she swallowed and forced herself to raise her chin. "You've nothing to say in defense."

"I've much to say. I've never touched her—all right, that's not exactly true. I kissed her once. When I had been told that you had sold out my inheritance and my marriage. And once again, quite innocently, before I left for France." He leaned against the wall, crossing his arms over his chest, watching her. "Of anything else, I am innocent."

"Damien—"

"Damien is ever loyal to you, and he has not forgiven me the first."

Her knees were trembling. She was afraid that she would completely lose her temper, that she would cry out in frustration and anger and pain. She could not tell if he was telling the truth or not, she knew only that they had been apart again and he was not glad to see her. "I don't believe you," she whispered.

"Amanda, my God—" He took a step impatiently toward her. She raised a hand against him and despite herself, her voice was high and close to tears.

"You've never believed me, Eric. Well, this time, my lord, I am afraid that I do not believe you! Don't touch me."

"Amanda—"

"I mean it, Eric!"

He went still, his eyes narrowing. "Am I to be punished then, dear wife? Denied your charms and my rights?"

"My lord Cameron, I'm well aware that your life was far from empty before I entered into it—"

"Regretfully entered into it."

"You had an affair with Geneva!"

He seemed slightly surprised, but shrugged, and she felt ill and jealous and couldn't help but imagine that he was lying. He and Sir Thomas had been partners, and he and Anne Marie . . .

"Amanda, I can hardly be blamed—"

"You had a wicked reputation, Eric!" she reminded him.

He laughed softly. "Amanda, my God, we are talking about years ago—"

"I don't believe you!"

"Well, I will be damned! Amanda, come here!"

"No! I don't want you touching me tonight!" she vowed heatedly.

She heard the grate of his teeth and then he smiled very slowly. "Ah, yes, I am supposed to take care because your cousin and your—because Damien and Jacques sleep outside the doorway. Well, Amanda, don't fool yourself. If I wanted—if I chose, Amanda!—I would seize upon you here and now, and that would be that, and I would not give a damn if the whole of the camp was aware of it."

He took two long steps toward her. A scream nearly tore from her as his hands landed firmly upon her and she was lifted up and tossed upon the narrow bunk. "Oh, you bastard!" she hissed to him.

But he backed away from her then and bowed deeply. "You may have the bed. And you shall have things, milady, just as you wish them. You needn't sleep on the floor. I shall find another place to lay my head!"

With that he slammed out of the room. Amanda watched him, then she turned over and cried softly into the pillow. There would never be a good time for them, she thought. Never more than brief moments when passion drew them together. She could not even grasp at the straws anymore. . . .

She had come here. And she was alone.

———

Walking out in the cold snow, Eric quickly determined that he had been a fool. When he thought that Damien had sown the seeds of discontent and suspicion so thoroughly over such a rather sad incident, he felt fury fill him. And when she had pulled away from him, as if his touch made her shudder like something that crept and crawled upon the earth, he had known that he had to walk away. Walk away, when he had thought of nothing but lying down beside her, with her naked flesh beneath him. . . .

He groaned aloud and paused in the night, patting the nose of the packhorse that had drawn the cart from Cameron Hall. The horses had been unharnessed, but the crates still remained unpacked. He looked over the wagon and smiled. They were desperate at Valley Forge. They spent the days and nights drilling—and foraging for food. There were so many men to feed. They deserted daily. He did not blame them. He didn't know how many times he had wanted to leave the bitter cold of Pennsylvania and ride back to the Tidewater where winter was ever so much milder. Where his home and children awaited him. Where a well-crafted fire and decent food could be had. Home, to Amanda, to a chance at their marriage.

And now she was here, and like an ass, he had walked away from her. His fingers wound into fists. Damn her! He had spent bitter-cold, lonely nights alone again and again. She had been in his dreams forever and ever, and now . . .

Now he was too proud to go back. "Damn her!" he whispered. And then he sobered. She thought that he had been cold. That he hadn't wanted her, that he had, perhaps, been having an affair with Anne Marie.

She didn't understand. There were many men who still did not trust her. Rumor from Virginia had reached the whole of the army, and Nigel Sterling's daughter was still known as a Tory—whether she had truly changed her coat or not.

And that he did not know if he could believe himself.

He grated his teeth hard and swore out loud, his breath creating a mist upon the night. He wasn't going back. Not until she asked him.

Or not until his slender hold upon sanity did break, and he swept her heedlessly into his arms.

———

A week later Amanda was working in the huge sickbay, bringing water to the countless men down with smallpox. It was terrifying just to see the men stretched out before her—there were so many men ill, thousands of them.

She wiped her brow, offered a Connecticut rifleman an encouraging smile, and moved on to the next bed. Hands suddenly slipped about her waist and a whisper touched her ear. "Well, cousin, he is not sleeping with the illustrious Anne Marie. Her father came home from his foraging expedition the same night that you arrived, and I know Sir Thomas Mabry very well. Nothing illicit is taking place in that hut!"

Amanda swung around in dismay. "Damien, I did not ask you—"

"Oh? You're not curious as to where your husband is sleeping?"

"No, I'm not!" Amanda lied.

Damien made a *tsk*ing noise at her. She sighed impatiently, noted that one of her patients was burning up, and hurried back to the barrel to moisten a towel for his forehead. "Damien, I'm busy here."

Damien leaned against a support pole. "Well, the last three days he has been out foraging. And I think that I know where he was before then."

"Oh?"

"But then, you're not interested."

She kicked him as hard as she could in the shin. "Damien—"

"With Von Steuben. Von Steuben is brilliant—I think that he might whip us into a viable fighting force after all. Well, if enough of us live. But Eric knows Indians—and the Brits have half the Mohawk tribes on our tails. So they've much to talk about, you see."

"I see," she said, then she paused, because she knew where her husband was at that moment—standing just inside the doorway, watching her with Damien.

"Ah, Major General Lord Cameron!" Damien said quickly. He saluted sharply and disappeared through the sickbay. Amanda watched him, winding his way through the endless makeshift cots and the various women and doctors who moved about the room. Then she felt a rough hand upon her arm. She swung around once more to find that Eric had come to her, his expression was grim.

"What are you doing in here?"

"Why, I'm trying to help—" she began.

"These men have smallpox!" he reminded her.

She smiled. "I had it. Damien and I both had it as children, and they say that if you survive—" She paused. "What are you doing in here?"

"Trying to get you out."

A man groaned on his pallet. "Lord Cameron! Eh, sir, we're about ready to ride again, eh?"

The man was feverish; his eyes were bleary, but they had touched upon Eric with something like adoration. And Eric patted the man's shoulder, heedless of disease, and assured him with a smile. "No, Roger, we're not ready to ride. Not until spring. But Von Steuben is waiting for you, have no fear. He'll drill you to the ground once you're up and about. I promise you, lad."

The sick man laughed. His eyes rolled, then fell shut. "My God, I think he's died!" Amanda said miserably.

Eric felt the man's heart, then touched his forehead. "No, he's just breathing easy again. Von Steuben may get his hands on the boy yet."

He straightened, staring at Amanda. She wanted to say something to him, anything to bring him back. But words would not come. She couldn't apologize —he owed her the apologies, and he would never see it, and never admit it.

And he was standing in the smallpox ward!

"Get out of here, Eric!"

"Come with me. I want to talk to you."

She sighed and looked around. There were many women in the room. Wives, sisters, daughters—and lovers and whores. The officers' ladies, the poor privates' women, some in velvet and lace, and some in homespun. Tears suddenly stung her eyes, and she realized that in a way, that was what it was all about. The colonies had joined, and the people had joined. If the war was won, it would be a new land indeed, with a new society and new look at life. Here a man could aspire to greatness no matter his birth. A blacksmith could fight alongside the landed gentry. The country would belong to all of them, the wives, the sisters, the daughters, the lovers and the whores.

"Amanda?"

"I'm coming." She untied her apron and hurried out of the sickbay with Eric. The weather had not improved. The wind came scurrying furiously about her and she shivered. Eric quickly swept his greatcoat about her and headed her toward the open stables. She felt his arm about her, her heart quickening as she walked.

He drew her into the stable. Not far from them a smithy's fire burned and hammering could be heard as a harness was repaired. Amanda leaned against the rough wooden wall, watching Eric, waiting.

"What?" she demanded.

He smiled. "Do you know where Howe's men are spending their winter?" She stiffened. "In Philadelphia."

"Mmm. Twenty-eight miles from here. Some of our men were discovered foraging and taken prisoner. God knows, maybe they'll fare better with the Brits than they do here, but most men still count the cost of freedom high."

"Why are you telling me this!" she exclaimed.

"Because someone is getting information through to the British."

She gasped, astounded. She'd barely been away from the place, except to ride out with Damien one afternoon. Her voice was low and trembling with fury when she spoke. "I do not believe that you would dare to accuse me again!"

"Amanda—"

She shoved at his chest as hard as she could, feeling tears well behind her eyes. "Don't! Don't speak to me, don't come near me, don't you throw your foul accusation at me anymore! Damn you!"

She ran away from him, ignoring his voice as he shouted to her to come back. She didn't care who saw them, she didn't care who heard. She was certain that most of the camp knew that he spent his nights away from his wife anyway.

Gasping, she tore back to their hut. Jacques was within, sitting on a bench, cleaning muskets. He looked up sharply when she entered.

"What is it, milady?"

She shook her head. The tears spilled onto her cheeks anyway. "Oh, Jacques! How can he be so blind! I have done everything that I can and still . . ."

She rushed to the bench, glad of the arm he set about her to comfort her. He had been with her so long. Always so quiet, and always there. No matter what the tempest of her life, she felt that she had a defender. He whispered gentle words in French to her, soothing words. Suddenly the door burst open. Eric had followed her home.

And there she was, in Jacques's arms. She wondered if he wouldn't fly into a rage at that and accuse her of more awful things.

But to her amazement, he was absolutely silent. Jacques didn't even pretend to move away from her—he stared at Eric over her head.

And Eric didn't say a word. He closed the door and left.

———

That night she lay awake in bed, cold despite her flannel gown and the rough blanket and the fire. Her teeth chattered miserably. Suddenly she heard a commotion in the outer room, the door bursting open, voices rising, then falling.

Then there was silence.

And then the door to the bedroom seemed to shatter open upon its hinges. Eric stood in the doorway in his high boots and heavy cloak and plumed hat. She sat up instantly, afraid and wary. He was drunk! she thought. But he was not. "Tell me that you are innocent," he said, his voice low and husky.

"I am innocent," she replied, her eyes wide and challenging and level upon his.

He smiled and strode firmly into the room. She leapt from the bed, backing away to the fire. "Eric! Damn you! Don't you think that you can come swaggering in here—"

"I do not swagger, my love. I stride."

"Well, you cannot stride—"

"Ah, my love, but I can!"

And he could. He was before her, catching her wrist, spinning her into his arms. She protested, crying out, swearing as the best of the soldiers might, and pummeling his chest. He laughed, ignoring her efforts, and swept her up into his arms. Her fight, however, off-balanced him, and they crashed heavily down upon the bed together. "Eric Cameron—"

"Shush up and pay attention, Amanda." She had no choice. His sinewed thigh was cast heavily over her hips and his hands were taut upon her wrists. His words touched her lips, warm, soft, beguiling. The tone of his voice was deep and quiet and richly masculine, reaching deep inside of her. "I believe you. I believe that you are innocent. Now, listen to me, love, and listen this once, for I shall not make a habit of explaining. I am innocent, too, of all charges. I admit, there were times when I would have bedded another woman if I could have for the sheer loneliness of this life. Yet I could not, you see. There is no other woman with a cascade of rich silken hair the color of fire, and no other woman anywhere to charm the soul with the steady gaze of emerald eyes, the velvet caress of her voice. I have never faltered once, Amanda. From the night that I first saw you, I wanted you and no other. It shall never change. No matter what I have believed, I have wanted you. And I have loved you. Now, lady, if you would, cast me out again. Into the snow."

A slow, sensual smile curved lazily into her lips. "If I cast you out, will you go?"

"No."

She sighed extravagantly. "I did not think so."

"So?"

"Let go of my wrists."

"Why?"

"Because I cannot touch you this way."

His hold upon her eased. Her fingers trembled as she rubbed her knuckles against his cheek, then arched high against him, winding her arms about him as she found his lips with her own. She hungered for his kiss, playing with his tongue, bringing it deeper and deeper into her mouth, as if she drew upon other sexual parts of his body, intimating all that she would do. A dry, hoarse sound tore from him, and he returned the kiss aggressively, his lips caressing and consuming hers, his tongue demanding hers hotly within his mouth, his hands feverishly upon her face and within her hair. Then he tore away from her, casting aside his cape and his boots. He all but tore his frock coat away, and stumbled from his breeches to descend heavily upon her again, his hands feverish as they immediately set upon her calves and then her naked thighs, shoving the gown up high on her. She laughed, delighted at his eagerness, but when his lips touched hers again, she was determined to arouse him even as he stirred the most frantic and glorious yearnings within her. She stroked the magnificent muscled breadth of his back, and she brought her hands low against his ribs, and over the tightness of his buttocks. She teased his abdomen with the stroke of her fingers, and then she closed her fingers around his shaft, trembling with sweet pleasure at his cry and mammoth shudder at her evocative touch. She stroked and teased, gently caressed, and brought about a rougher rhythm, and then caressed with the greatest tenderness again. But then she found her fingers entwined with his and the length of his body was thrust between her thighs. His mouth formed over her breast, and all of the heat and hardness was thrust within her, and ecstasy seemed to flourish and grow and to boundless heights.

Snow fell outside; the wind was bitter, and its cry was harsh upon the winter's night. But none of it mattered to her that night. He rose high above her, his face contorted with his passion, his eyes a deep blazing blue upon hers. She did not allow her lashes to flutter, but as the sensations swept through her with chaotic abandon, she moistened her lips and dared to whisper to him again.

"I love you, Eric. I love you."

He fell against her, cradling her head, his fingers and palms upon her hair, her cheeks. His lips found hers and whispered above them, "Say it again."

"I love you." Tears stung her eyes. "I love you, I swear it, with all of my heart, I love you."

He groaned, and he whispered again that he loved her. And when everything exploded between them, he whispered it again, and then he held her in his arms and they both watched the fire, and she told him that she had loved him for a very long time—even when she had hated him—and he laughed, and they made love again, and she didn't think that anything, ever, had been as good.

It was very late when she finally slept.

Somewhere, in the middle of the night, she awoke. Puzzled, she wondered why. The fire still burned. Their door lay slightly ajar, and the outer room appeared to be empty, despite the shadows. Some noise had disturbed her, she thought. She didn't move. They slept naked and entwined. Her husband's broad shoulders were slightly bared, and she drew the blanket more tightly about him. Then she slept again.

———

Later, much, much later, she awoke. She had been dreaming, she realized, and she had been soundly asleep. It was late, for the sun was out and almost brightly so, especially for winter. She had slept the morning away, she thought, and she had awakened now only because someone was frantically calling her name.

"Amanda! Amanda, for the love of God, wake up!"

Her eyes focused at last. It was Geneva, her beautiful eyes wide and frightened, her hair tumbling down about her shoulders. "Amanda, come on, wake up. You must come with me right away. Eric has been hurt."

"What!"

Stunned, stricken, Amanda sat up. The covers began to fall and she caught them to hide her nakedness.

"Eric has been hurt. He went out with a foraging party and he was hit by mistake. I think that his leg is broken. Damien is arranging for a conveyance to bring him back. But he wants you. Now. Oh, Amanda, come on!"

"Oh, dear God!" Terrified, Amanda sprang from the bed and hurriedly searched for her clothing. Her trembling caused her trouble as she tried to pull on her hose, but at last she managed. She forced herself to be calm enough to dress. She ignored her hair, letting it fall down her back in tangles.

Hurt . . . hurt. He had been wounded. Men died when they were wounded. Men died when they were wounded because infection and disease spread so rapidly. No! No, God, please, no, after all of their years together they had finally come to really love one another, to trust one another, to need one another. She could not lose him now. He had fought in endless battles, and always with courage, and always so selflessly. He could not die.

"Geneva, how bad is he?" she asked anxiously, reaching for her cloak.

"I don't know yet. I just know that he wants you. Come on now, hurry!"

They ran out to the snow. Two horses were waiting. "Where's Damien?" Amanda asked anxiously.

"Getting a wagon. Amanda, let's go. Before it's too—"

"Oh!" Amanda cried out. She wondered if Washington knew, or Frederick, or any other of his close friends or fellow officers. They wouldn't let him die if they knew. They would not let him die, she was certain!

"Geneva, perhaps I should get someone else!"

"Damien is doing that! Amanda, there is no one else about now. We have to hurry!"

"Oh, God, yes!"

She leapt upon the scrawny horse Geneva had brought for her even as Geneva gracefully catapulted upon her own mount. In seconds they were racing through the camp.

"Hey!" someone called. "Wait! Where—"

"We haven't time!" Geneva responded.

She whipped her horse into a mad gallop. Amanda followed suit, and they were quickly beyond the gates and frantically plowing through the snow. Geneva managed to find something of a trail that had been trampled down, and the floundering horses found their footing again. Amanda was glad, for it seemed that they raced forever. The wind whipped her cheeks and the cold was so bitter that she could no longer feel her fingers about the reins, or her toes in the stirrups. Her heart thundered with fear.

Away from the camp, they slowed for a while. "We need to hurry!" Amanda cried then.

"It's far. The horses won't make it. We'll let them rest a bit, then race them again."

And so they plodded along. Anxiety grew and swelled within Amanda's heart. She did not move a foot that she did not pray again, pray for her husband's life.

They began to race again. There seemed to be nothing, nothing before them, just the endless white of the snowdrifts, just the skeletal leaves of the barren trees. The camp even seemed far behind them. Very far. So far that it seemed like a miniature village, a child's toy, and not a place where grown-up men suffered and died.

"Geneva, how far? Where is he? Have we missed him."

"No, no!" Geneva shouted back.

They kept racing. Suddenly, ahead, Amanda saw an embankment of fir trees. Rich and green, they covered the landscape.

"Just ahead!" Geneva called.

"Thank God!" Amanda shouted in reply. She forced her tired horse to draw close beside Geneva's. "There? In the woods?"

Geneva nodded, her lashes falling over her beautiful eyes to form crescents on her cheeks. "Yes, Amanda, in the woods."

The woods . . .

The thicket of green pines suddenly came alive. Horsemen came bounding out from both directions, horsemen wearing the bright red colors of a British cavalry unit.

Amanda drew her horse quickly to a halt, determined to turn back and flee as quickly as possible. "Geneva, the British! We've got to escape! It's the damned redcoats—"

"There is no escape! Look around. We're surrounded."

They were surrounded. There was no direction in which she could escape.

"The British—"

"I know," Geneva said quietly.

Stunned, Amanda stared at her friend. Then she understood. "It's you. You're Highness—I never really was! You called Robert and Father to Cameron Hall, you've been sleeping with my cousin for whatever information you could gain. You—you whore!"

"Tsk, tsk, Lady Cameron!"

Amanda swung her nag of a horse around as a rider approached her. Well clad, well fed, sitting his horse very well, it was Robert Tarryton. "What a horrid thing to say to an old friend!" he taunted Amanda.

"Traitor!" Amanda snapped to Geneva, spitting toward the ground.

"Traitor! Ah, no, milady. Geneva is not the traitor—you are. You should be frightened. We hang traitors, you know. Ah, but a lovely lady? Maybe not. You're much too useful. You see, my love, with you my prisoner, I just might get your husband at last. And maybe a few more of your illustrious patriots. Eh, love? I might even manage to pick off the entire Continental Army."

"Never. You'll never beat them, Robert. Never."

"They are dying. They are beating themselves."

"No. You don't understand, do you? It isn't guns—it isn't even in battles. The revolution is in the heart of the people, and you can never take the heart, Robert. Not you, not Howe, not Cornwallis, not King George."

"Brave words, Amanda. Let's go. I'm willing to bet that I can nab a victim or two for the hangman. Hurry back, Geneva. It's time now to bring Lord Cameron for his lady."

They had led her here with lies. They would bring Eric out in the same manner.

She couldn't let it happen.

She dug hard into the flanks of her horse, wrenching the reins around. The animal shrieked out and reared up. Amanda slashed the reins about, catching Robert across the face with length of them as he tried to lunge for her. He faltered as leather stips whipped his face and Amanda's horse bolted, then lunged forward.

"Get her!" Tarryton commanded.

She tried. The valiant little horse tried. But ten horsemen were bearing down on her. A red-coated rider suddenly jumped forward. Caught in his arms, she was brought down, down into the snow with the soldier firmly upon her. Flakes were in her mouth and nose and eyes. Coughing, she fought for breath.

Then rough hands were upon her as Robert Tarryton dragged her to her feet. When she stood he slapped her hard. "Bitch!" he accused her with a quiet smile. Then he wrenched her forward to where his own mount waited. He set her swiftly upon it and mounted in a leap behind her.

His whisper was chilling against her. "I'm just wondering, Amanda, whether to settle my score first with your husband—or with you. We do have a score to settle, milady, and I've imagined endless ways of just how it will be settled!"

"He'll kill you!" Amanda promised on a whisper.

Tarryton broke into dry laughter. He lashed his horse's haunches pitilessly. "No, he'll kill you. You've always been a traitor to him. And here's just another occasion of your treachery. Before I hang him, Amanda, love, I will be sure to let him know that you have been very cleverly planning his demise for the longest time!"

19

ERIC HAD JUST RETURNED TO THE HUT AFTER extensive drilling of the troops with Von Steuben when he heard his name called hysterically from outside. That the place seemed very empty and cold without Amanda about added to his feeling of icy anxiety as he hurried to open the door.

Geneva was practically falling from one of the broken-down old nags that had toughly survived the winter. Damien was rushing over from the blacksmith's to catch her as she fell.

"Damien, oh, thank God! And Eric!"

"What's happened?" Damien demanded.

"Bring her in," Eric urged. "Out of the cold."

In seconds Geneva was inside, sipping brandy, a blanket wrapped about her shoulders. "She insisted that we search for food. Amanda. She thought that we could contribute to the men by scouring the country ourselves. Then she fell . . . Eric, she's alive but I think that her leg is broken. She needs you desperately."

Cold . . . she was lying out in the cold, shivering, hurt, probably in horrid pain. There was a storm coming too. If the snows came on too densely, they might never find her, she might perish in her attempts to prove herself a loyal patriot . . .

"Dear God!" he whispered aloud, and then he was in motion. "Damien, tell Frederick to arrange for a wagon. Geneva, can you tell me where she is? How to reach her? Frederick will need you to guide him, and I must get to her with blankets and brandy. The cold is so very bitter!"

"Of course, of course—" Geneva said, rising.

But then the door swung open. Jacques Bisset stood in the doorway, towering and dark, a mask of fury upon his face as he stared at Geneva.

"The woman is lying," he said flatly.

"What?" Eric demanded sharply.

"The woman is lying."

"How dare you!" Geneva gasped. "Eric! Damien! You are not going to listen this—this—frog servant! And take his word over mine?"

There was something in her tone of voice that Eric didn't like at all. He smiled slowly, leaning back against the wall. "I have known Jacques most of my life, Geneva. He has never lied to me. Jacques, tell me quickly, what is the truth of this?"

"I followed them. Lady Geneva came here and urged Amanda with her. I followed them when they rode out into the snow. I kept my eye upon it all when they were ambushed by a troop of redcoats. It was planned, Lord Cameron. It was a planned kidnapping."

Eric felt as if his heart were catapulting to his gut and there lay bleeding. His mouth dry, he demanded, "Who, Jacques? Who has taken her?"

"Tarryton. Lord Robert Tarryton. She was lured to your side, and now you are being lured to hers. I didn't know what to do! I could not bear to leave her with them, alone in the snow, yet I could not help her unless I came back to warn you. She is the bait, Lord Cameron. The bait to lure you to your death." He hesitated, staring at Geneva. If eyes could kill, Eric thought, Geneva would have been lying in blood, slain with daggers through the core of her heart.

Damien backed away from the woman. The fire burned low in the little hut, smoke and soot seemed heavy on the air. Then he took a step toward her. She backed away from him, toward the wall.

"It's a lie!" she cried out. "He's lying and I don't know why! I can't begin to understand—"

"I can!" Eric interrupted harshly. He strode past Damien, wrenching Geneva around by the shoulders. "It was you. You were the one to see to it that Nigel Sterling and Robert Tarryton knew about the arms kept at Cameron Hall. It was you."

"No!"

"Yes," Damien said softly. "I told her. I told her while we lay in bed. The bloody whore!" he exclaimed.

Geneva spat at Damien. He cracked her furiously across the cheek with his open palm. Screaming, she cowered on the floor. "Eric, make him stop—"

"What do we do with her, Eric?" Damien asked, his jaw still twisted savagely, his fingers knotting into fists. "God forgive me, and Eric, would that you could forgive me too! The grief that this woman has caused us all with her treachery, and the fool that I was to believe in her!"

Eric caught hold of Geneva's wrists and dragged her back to her feet. "How many men has Tarryton got with him?"

"Twenty thousand," she said defiantly.

He smiled. "Lie like that again, Geneva, and I will give you far greater injury than Damien has managed thus far. In fact . . ."

He paused, smiling at Damien. "Did you ever realize just how vain our dear Lady Geneva is? Her face is her life. Jacques—I know that this will give you great pleasure. Bring the fire poker. We wouldn't be so heathen as to threaten the lady's life—just her beauty."

Geneva's eyes grew wide with disbelief. Damien grabbed her shoulders, turning her toward Jacques. The tall Acadian approached her smiling, the poker in his hand, the end of it burning red from its recent thrust into the fire. He drew it closer and closer to her cheek, just below her eyes. She fought Damien's hold furiously. "Eric, you're bluffing! I know that you are bluffing! You will not—" She broke off, screaming, as the heat nearly singed her lashes. "You would not do this!" she cried.

"Well, not usually, no," Eric agreed. "But I love my wife, Geneva, and by heaven and hell, I will have the truth from you now to get her back!"

The poker moved closer. "All right! All right!" Geneva cried out. "They've barely a hundred. General Howe is enjoying his winter in Philadelphia, there are countless balls and teas and he is living quite well. This was Sterling's idea. He wants you—and Robert wants Amanda. They've taken Robert's company and no more. They knew that you would run recklessly to her aid, and they would take whoever accompanied you, a minor coup. Yet a major blow to the Americans and a warning to would-be patriots when the noble Lord Cameron was hanged!"

Eric ignored her biting sarcasm. "What is he planning? Where does he have my wife?"

"There's . . . there's a house. Ten miles from here. It's surrounded by pines. I was supposed to bring you to the pines. The British cavalry were to take you there."

"Jacques, take her to General Washington. He must decide her fate. Damien, call Frederick, have him rouse company A of my Virginia troops. Then come back, and I'll explain my plan."

"Company A!" Geneva laughed. "You're talking about twenty men. They'll all die, you fool."

"Dear Geneva, I did not ask for your opinion! Jacques, for the love of God, get her out of here!"

He wondered if he should have spoken. Jacques wrenched hard on her arm, practically throwing her out into the snow. He heard Geneva exclaim in pain and outrage, but then she was silent, and he was certain that she dared speak no more. She couldn't understand Jacques's absolute fury; she was only aware that the Acadian would just as soon kill her as look at her.

"I caused it, Eric. I caused it all," Damien said, ashamed. "Can you forgive me?"

"I was the one who was blind," Eric said harshly. "I refused to see until it was too late. Let's get Amanda back. That is all that matters."

"They won't hang her, I don't believe that they'll hurt her. Although Tarryton . . ." Damien's voice trailed away. They both knew what Tarryton would do.

"I've always risked the hangman's noose," Eric reminded him. "And she is my life. Without her, not even the future has meaning. Now listen, I think I know how to do this without losing a single man."

———

To Amanda, the house seemed almost obscenely elegant after the time she'd spent in the wretched hovels at Valley Forge. The fireplace was marble, the ceilings were elegantly molded, and the walls were covered with handsome leather. A rich carpet covered highly polished floorboards, and she sat in a plush wingback chair, a snifter of brandy in her fingers.

Night was coming. Shadows fell upon the snow beyond the windows.

Amanda's fingers curved so tightly around her glass that the fragile stem nearly broke.

Robert Tarryton was returning. She heard his footsteps on the floorboards outside the door.

He threw the door open and swaggered in, pausing at the desk to pour himself a shot of whiskey. He smiled pleasantly to her as he took a seat on the edge of it. "I'm so sorry to have neglected you."

Amanda ignored him, staring out the window. How long would it have taken Geneva to have ridden back? How long until Eric came riding for her? Any time now. He would come at any time. And he would be either shot down by the troops surrounding the house, or captured to swing from the rope already tossed over a tree out back. The rope had been the first torture Robert had used against her. He had dragged her out back and rubbed it against her cheek, and he had told her what happened to a man's body functions when the rope tightens about his throat.

Then he brought her here, thrust her into the chair, and left her to arrange his murderous trap. She hadn't been alone long. Her father had appeared to offer her brandy. He had assured her that he would listen to delight to every one of her screams when Tarryton returned. "With pleasure, with delight! I had imagined that you would have suffered with Cameron. I intended that you should, but then, like a fool, you fell in love with the bastard. It doesn't matter. You will suffer now."

"Why!" she had demanded furiously. "Why? What in God's name did I ever do to you?"

"You were born, girl. Born of a whore whom I will never forget. This is my revenge. I pray that there is a god, and that there is an afterlife, so that she can look down and see you suffer!"

Then Sterling had left her too. When she had tried to escape through the window, she had discovered it nailed shut. And beyond it walked a sentry, watching her every move.

Now Robert moved across the room, glancing out the window. He ran his hand over the handsome mahogany of the window seat. "They'll have him any minute. They'll have your husband any minute now. I've ordered that he should be brought here first. I want him to see you before he dies."

"You cannot just hang him so! You must have a trial. You—"

"Want to bargain for his life, Amanda?"

She caught her breath, afraid to hear more, desperate to do so. "You haven't got him yet."

"Ah, but I will." He left the window and walked toward her, smiling as she shrank back in the chair. He grabbed hold of her bodice and wrenched it, tearing fabric. She caught his hand, screaming, clawing at his flesh. He drew her up, laughing as her gown gaped open, laughing still as she wildly clawed for his face. Her nails gouged him and the laughter left his face. "When I have him, bitch, he's going to suffer a long, long time before he dies. I can have the rope set so that he dangles and dangles and slowly chokes to death!" He caught hold of her hands, forcing her back toward the fire, nearly snapping her fingers with the force of his hold. When he pressed her against the wall he smiled again. "Nice house, eh? Of course, your Continentals had pretty well stripped it of food and supplies before we came. Seems the owners must have deserted some time ago. You should see the bedroom. There are silk sheets on a huge bed with the softest mattress you've ever touched. You're used to luxury, though. That's why I thought maybe it should be right here. On the floor, against the wall. You shouldn't be taken in luxury like a lover—no, because you turned on me. You teased and taunted and beckoned—and then you turned on me. So I'm going to have you like a whore. Just like a whore. Right here, and right in front of your husband."

She screamed, twisting her face, praying for death as he reached into her torn bodice and wrapped his fingers around her breast. "I'm going to do this right in front of him—"

Tarryton broke off at a knock on the door. He did not take his hands off of Amanda but called sharply, "Come in!"

She tried to fight him again, kicking, twisting, shoving. But then the fight left her, and she went numb with fear and horror.

Two men with hats low upon their brows dragged Eric into the room. His shirt was bloodied, his hat was gone, his frock coat torn from him. He stood before her, tall and defiant, his eyes deadly, his arms locked behind his back by the men who held him.

"Eric! Welcome!" Robert said. "I was just talking with your wife. No, let's be honest here, we're among old friends. I was just enjoying your wife."

Eric swore violently.

"You're going to hang, Cameron. Within seconds. You're going to hang, and I'm going to watch you, and I'm going to make Mandy watch too."

"You're a dead man, Tarryton."

"No, sir. You're a dead man."

"No!" Amanda cried out. She looked from Eric's passionate, hate-filled gaze to Robert. "Don't kill him. I'll do anything. Anything at all. Please—"

"Amanda!" Eric roared.

"I'll trade my life for his, anything!"

"You won't have that opportunity. How much of your wife do you want to see, Cameron? One last glance of at her throat, at her breast? At my hand upon her—"

"You are dead, Tarryton! Now!" Eric thundered.

Eric shook off the arms holding him and slipped a sword from the scabbard of one of the men beside him. When the redcoat raised his head, Amanda gasped. He was no enemy, but Frederick.

Tarryton dropped hold of Amanda, screaming for his guards. Instantly men flooded along the hallways. Something hurtled through the window, rolling upon the floor. It was Damien. He leapt to his feet, sword in his hand, his knees bent, ready for the fight.

Men flooded in. Amanda stood flat against the wall, holding her dress together at the bodice, still stunned as Robert and Eric set to deadly combat before her. They parried with a clash of steel, they backed away, they met as tight as dancers again, steel clenched together in a battle of strength and wills. Robert fell back, tossing a chair into Eric's path. Eric leapt over the obstacle. His fury led him. Coming before Robert, he thrust toward him with a shuddering blow. Robert's sword flew high in the air, landing at Amanda's feet. She knelt down and grabbed it. Eric held the tip of his sword against Robert's throat. "How dearly I would love to run you through! But what a prize you would be for General Washington!"

"Amanda, get their small arms!" Damien called to her suddenly. Damien, Frederick, and the young captain with them had bested the British guards. Two men lay dead, and two stood still and silent while Damien and Frederick held their swords upon them. Amanda ran to do as she had been beckoned. With her back to the empty doorway, she suddenly felt cold steel against her own neck.

"My, my, gentlemen! What a ruckus over naught!" came a pleasant voice.

Nigel. Nigel Sterling. Her father was behind her again, his arm wrapped about her, his small dagger digging into her throat. Damien looked to Eric, who stared cold and frozen at Sterling.

Robert Tarryton laughed and shoved the sword from his throat, rubbing the sore spot where the tip had dug into his flesh. "Cameron, you will hang! Unless I can find a way to crucify you!"

"But one life to give for your country, eh, Cameron? And one life to give for your wife," Sterling said pleasantly. "No swordsman could take you, Cameron. Seems it was only love and beauty needed to down you all the while. Eh, my dear daughter? Well, perhaps we shouldn't play around here any longer. Lord Cameron must be hanged and quickly, and, my dear daughter, I intend to see that you thoroughly enjoy the spectacle—"

Suddenly Sterling went silent. Amanda could not turn to see behind him, but she heard the strong voice with the deep tenor that spoke next, the voice with the trace of French within it, cool and furious and ruthless. "Take your hands off of her, you filthy pig!"

It was Jacques Bisset.

"I'll kill her. I'll rip open her throat without a thought," Sterling ground out. And he would. Amanda could feel the chill of the steel, closer and closer against her throat, so sharp, so cold, cold like death. . . .

"Pig!" Jacques swore in French. Then, to Amanda's amazement, the grip on her went lax. She stepped forward, desperately rubbing her throat, then crying out as she watched her father fall. His eyes were wide—his arms, at the last, reached out to her. Blood-soaked, he fell against her. Horrified, she moved away. She saw Jacques then, standing behind Sterling's fallen body. Tall and immobile, his dark eyes devoid of emotion. He looked at her. Emotion returned to him. "He had to die."

"Bloody bastard—" Tarryton suddenly roared. He lunged forward, trying to capture Eric's sword. Eric barely flicked his wrist, and then Robert had fallen too. He had thrust himself upon the blade.

"It was your choice to die!" Eric murmured, drawing back his sword. He looked to Amanda, reaching out a hand to her with an awkward smile. "We've got to go, we've got to hurry—"

A new thunder of footsteps on the hallway floor alerted everyone to his meaning. The troops from the pines were coming back, trying to ascertain what had happened.

"Amanda! Out the window!" Eric urged her. She ran to him. He caught hold of her waist and lifted her through the shattered pane. He paused upon the windowsill, then together they fell into the deep snow below them, rolling and rolling. She heard Damien behind them, and then Frederick and the captain. "Run!" Eric urged her, dragging her to her feet. "Run!" He held her hand. The snowdrifts were so high! The British were behind them, and he was pulling her onward and onward. Bitter cold assailed her, the snow rose to her waist, and walking, much less running, was nearly impossible.

"Eric!" she screamed, falling. He fell down with her. They had hit an embankment again, and they were rolling and rolling. Tears stung her eyes and fell icily to her cheeks as they ceased to roll at last, as he rose over her, meeting her eyes. She clutched his shoulders, and she returned his anguished stare. "Oh, Eric! There is but one life! And if it is over, dear God, I would have you know, my one life I would gladly give for you—"

"For you," he agreed, smiling, "and this country."

She kissed him fervently. If the British were about to come, she would seize this last sweet taste of his lips.

"One life . . . to spend with you. No matter how brief, no matter how long, it has been a fire of warmth and splendor."

"Amanda, I love you."

"I love you!"

"Amanda, it isn't over."

"What?"

"I've troops waiting in the forest. I wanted the men to follow us. Indeed, my love, we've got to walk again. We've got to reach the men."

"Oh! You made me say all of those things—"

He smiled, tenderly, handsomely. The rogue, the gentleman, his eyes touched her with a love she could not deny. "But weren't they true? But one life, my love, and freely, eagerly, would I give it to you!"

She laughed. She wrapped her arms around him. "Oh, Eric! It was Geneva—"

"I know."

"Poor Damien!"

"He is a rugged lad. He will survive."

"My father is dead."

Eric hesitated, then he stood, dragging her to her feet. Up the ledge, they could hear the clash of steel. A musket exploded in a volley, then several others answered as if in reply. Eric grasped Amanda's hand. "Come on, I'm getting you up on a horse and out of here."

"I'm not leaving without you!" She panted, following him up the snow-covered decline.

"You'll do what—"

He broke off. They had reached the top of the crest just in time to see that it was over. At least twenty of the redcoats lay dead in the snow. Others were disappearing behind the trees, running. Damien was letting loose with a wild Virginia battle cry.

Eric walked out into the snow and surveyed the scene. "The boots, lads. We need their boots for our own. Then, if we can break through the ground, we'll bury the dead. Frederick! Take my lady back to camp, please."

"But, Eric—" she started.

He caught her shoulders and kissed her lips. "Please, Amanda. If you wait, Damien, Jacques, and I will be back as soon as possible. It's time we all had a talk."

Her eyes widened. He was very serious. Her curiosity and wonder were so great that she could not think to argue any longer.

"All right," she agreed. "But you all hurry!"

She turned about, thanking Frederick for his coat as he slipped it around her shoulder and then taking his arm.

"I didn't think that she'd ever leave!" Damien said. "Feisty little wench, eh?"

Amanda was about to swirl around to tell her cousin what she thought of him, but her husband was answering him already.

"Patriots are like that," Eric said casually.

"Aye, you're right, my lord! Aye, you are right!" Damien agreed. They laughed together. Amanda did not look back. When Frederick set her up atop a horse, he was smiling, and she smiled in return.

———

The men returned to Valley Forge within a few hours. Amanda sat at the table in the hut and stared at the three of them, Eric, Damien, and Jacques, as they stood before her, something like errant schoolboys.

Eric cleared his voice to speak, but then Jacques stepped forward. "I killed your father, Amanda."

"He meant to kill me, Jacques," she said quietly. "He—he meant it. He always despised me."

Then Jacques went silent. Eric cleared his throat again. "Amanda, Nigel wasn't your father."

"What?" Astonished, she leapt to her feet.

"But—"

Damien slipped an arm about her, coming down upon his haunches by her side as he led her to sit again. "Didn't you ever wonder that a man could be so cold to his own flesh and blood? I had heard the rumors, of course, but—I remember your mother, Amanda. Just vaguely. She was always so kind and so sweet, and so—"

"Giving," Jacques interrupted him. He looked at Amanda, but he seemed to see beyond her, to another time and another place. "She was beautiful and gentle and sweet, and her voice was like a nightingales, and she cared for everyone about her, be they slave or freedman, worker or gentry. She—she bought my indentured time when I arrived from Nova Scotia."

He paused, hesitating a long moment. His dark eyes fluttered over Amanda. "I fell in love with her," he said, his voice cracking. "And she fell in love with me. We meant to slip away to Louisiana, but he caught us. He left me for dead. I was taken in by Lord Cameron's grandfather, and over the years my body healed, but it wasn't until Danielle arrived that I remembered all that my life had been."

Amanda discovered that she couldn't breathe. She tried to form words. "What —what do you mean?"

"Amanda," Eric said, speaking quietly at last. "Jacques is your father."

There was silence. Dead silence, then Jacques started to speak, his French mingling with his English in his eagerness. "I could not tell you, I did not even tell Lord Cameron, I was so afraid that you would be horrified to know that you were not the daughter of a great lord but the child of a common laborer, a man who worked the land. But I saw, *mon Dieu*! I saw what he did to you, and I had vowed that I would kill them. *Mais, ma petite,* not even then did I mean to tell you, but your husband insisted—I am so sorry. I have loved you greatly from afar, and my life has been made rich just to see you, just to be privileged to touch my grandchildren, to live in the shadow cast by the bounty of the hall. . . ."

Amanda felt numb. So very numb! He was watching her with such anguish, and Eric was staring at her, and Damien . . .

She leapt to her feet, throwing her arms around Jacques. With a glad cry, she showered his cheeks with kisses. "My father! *Mon père!* Oh, thank God, thank God! Eric, how could you have known, how could have guessed and not told me!"

"Well, I—"

"You are not so horrified then?" Jacques asked her, his hands trembling as he held her.

"Horrified? Horrified! Oh, no, I am so thrilled and so very proud! My father was not some monster who lived to take revenge upon me because my mother could not bear his touch! He is tall and handsome and brave and wonderful, and he loves me. He loves me! Oh, Eric, isn't that what matters the most?"

Eric, relieved and greatly pleased, leaned back against the mantel, grinning. "Oh, of course, Amanda." It was both wonderful and poignant to watch the tears hovering in her eyes, to see the wonder upon her face. And Jacques. The Acadian who had always been there for her, loving her, never thinking to speak the truth, when the truth might have caused her pain. "Love—and the man," Eric agreed. "We're fighting for a new world here. For rights, where it is the measure of a man that matters, and nothing more. And I would say, Monsieur Bisset—as a man who has known you since he wore knee breeches—that there is no man of finer measure, or greater measure. No man whom I would rather call father-in-law."

Eric reached out for Jacques's hand. Jacques looked from his daughter's red head to the hand outstretched to him. Their hands met. Then Eric cleared his throat and smiled at Damien, who was staring on delightedly. "Maybe we should give them a few minutes."

"Maybe we should."

Neither Jacques nor Amanda noticed as they left. Amanda was crying, tears of joy. "Danielle! Danielle is my aunt! Oh, how delightful. I cannot wait to see her again."

Eric left her alone until very late, and then returned to the hut. The main room was empty, and so Eric hurried on into the bedroom.

Amanda was there, and for a moment he thought that she slept, she was so very still. He walked over to the narrow bed and discovered that her beautiful emerald eyes were open, that they had a dreamlike quality to them. Her lips were slightly parted in a beautiful rose smile and her hair was splayed about her in ripples of sable and fire, sweeping over the bare and naked beauty of her ivory shoulders. He knelt down by her. As her eyes focused on him, her smile broadened.

"Hello," he said.

"Hello," she returned.

"So . . ."

"Oh, Eric!" She wrapped her arms around him and held him close. "Thank you! Thank you for so much! You've not only given me love, but you've given me our beautiful children, and our home, and now you've even given me a father!"

He chuckled softly. "Well, I can't really take credit for all of that—"

"And you've given me a country, Eric. Today I knew it. I knew it so thoroughly! I knew that I would die for you, and then I discovered that I would die for this cause too. I understand everything that meant so much to you, what it was worth fighting for, worth dying for. . . . It's meant to be, Eric! Not a land for titled hogs such as Nigel Sterling, but for men like my real father. Quiet, dignified, determined to wrest the very best from the land. To give to it. Oh, Eric! I cannot tell you how happy I am! You cannot imagine what it was like to wonder how a parent could hate you so fervently! And he's wonderful, isn't he? Jacques is wonderful!"

"Yes, love, he is wonderful."

Her smile faded. "What of Geneva?"

"They'll hold her in Baltimore until they can see to it that she's shipped off to England."

"It was her all along!"

"Well—almost all along," Eric said.

Amanda flushed. "All right, I was guilty, somewhat. But you sent me to France because of her! You—"

"I most humbly beg your forgiveness, my love."

"Really? You?" She smiled. "I cannot imagine you humble at all. Nor begging."

"Well, maybe not."

She wrapped her arms around him. "But the words sounded sweet anyway."

"Would you like to hear more words that sound sweet?"

"Mmm . . ."

He stood up, cast aside his cloak, and quickly stripped down. He ripped away the blanket and she was cold, but then his body settled over hers, and she thought that she had never know such sweet and beautiful warmth. He caught her face between his hands and began kissing her.

"It's over," she whispered between trysts with his lips.

He paused, looking down at her very seriously. "Amanda, it is far from over."

"The war. It seems so very grim, doesn't it? Dark and grim and frightening. But for us, my love, it is over. Our war is over."

Eric smiled. "Aye, love, our war is over. No matter what time and distance should take from us again, we can never really be parted because we have found our peace. Love—and trust."

She smiled. "Love—and trust."

He started to kiss her again. She caught hold of his shoulders and forced his eyes to hers. "Did you really love me from the very beginning?"

"Mmm."

"Liar!"

"Well, I coveted you with all of my being. How is that?"

"You said—"

He twined his fingers with hers, bracing her hands tightly at the sides of her head. "Amanda!" he wailed.

"All right!" She closed her eyes. She felt the pulse of his body naked against hers, the heat, the wonder of muscle and sinew and hard masculinity. She wondered if it was all right to pray, to thank God, in the midst of such sweet splendor.

She opened her eyes. "I do surrender!" she promised him.

"You do?" Silver mischief rode his eyes like clouds dancing in the night. "Then, my love, I gladly conquer all."

"Eric!"

His laugh warmed and roused her, his breath taunted her ear wickedly. "Love, I surrender all that I am, my heart and my soul, this night! Life has been tempest, and will be again, but through any of my rages and storms, my love, you will know: I have surrendered."

She sighed, and she felt his kiss.

Thank you, dear God, for all of it! For giving me Jacques as my father . . . She felt his hands upon her breast, his fingers stroking her thigh.

Thank you for the twins . . .

His kiss stroked her shoulder, her abdomen. His flesh against hers was so erotic she could scarcely think, scarcely breathe.

Thank you, God, for this man . . .

She gave up. His touch upon her was flagrantly bold and intimate, daring, defying. A Cameron touch.

"Amanda . . ." he whispered her name.

She gave himself entirely over to his touch. "My love, let the tempest swirl, the rages fly, I care not! Just so long as you love me, that is all I could ever crave."

"And that is all that I shall ever do," he vowed.

And with himself, his warmth, his need, his love, he set forth to prove his words in every way.

Epilogue

HERE WAS A SOFT FALL OF SNOW UPON THE ground, but Amanda had seen the lone rider coming slowly down the path and she had instantly recognized the huge black horse. Knowing the animal, she was certain that the bundled rider had to be her husband.

"He's home!" she called joyously to Danielle. She left the window and went racing past the pictures in the gallery, and then down the long curving staircase, and to the front doors. Richard and Cassidy both went to the hallway to watch her; Jacques, whittling by the fire in the parlor, just smiled.

Amanda ignored the fall of the soft light flakes that fell upon her face and gown, and she ran on. Eric saw her. He reined in on Joshua and slipped down from his mount. He patted the animal on the haunches, and Joshua trotted off on his own. He knew the way home to the stables. Just as Eric could reach home by himself now. Home. God, it had been a long war.

"Eric!"

He started running too. The distance between them shortened, and then he could see her face clearly. So chiseled and exquisite, the years had never seemed to cost her anything. Maybe her beauty had always really been in the emotion in her eyes. He could see them. Emerald, dancing, moist with tears, moist with love.

"Amanda!"

They came together. He caught her up high in his arms and twirled her around. Mist rose between as they breathed in the cold. Her hands were icy; she wore no gloves.

"It's done, then?"

He nodded. It had really been done for some time. The fighting had gone on after that awful winter at Valley Forge, but Von Steuben's drilling had changed the army. They had become an awesome force. And though the British had managed to take Charleston, the south had hung on through the efforts of men like Francis Marion, the renowned "Swamp Fox," and through the talents of men like Nathanael Greene and Daniel Morgan. Finally, in '81, the war had returned to Virginian soil.

Benedict Arnold, Washington's once-trusted general, had been heavily involved. Arnold had married a Tory girl named Margaret Shippen when he took command of Philadelphia. Perhaps she had been the one to turn his heart.

Maybe he had been disgruntled over his military progress—several times Congress had neglected him when promoting brigadier generals to major generals. No one really knew. But in the end it was discovered that he had communicated with the British for sixteen months. In 1780 he was in command of West Point, and he planned to surrender the fort to the British general Sir Henry Clinton. His treachery was discovered when British major John Andrew was captured carrying a mesage from Arnold about the surrender.

The news had aged Washington, Eric knew. But West Point had been saved. They hadn't caught Arnold, though. They had burst in on Peggy, and she had put on what Eric dryly considered to be one of the finest performances of the war. Clad in a frothy nightgown, she had cried and played at madness. Washington, ever the gentleman, had dealt gently with the distraught female.

Arnold had escaped to New York.

The British Major Andre, Arnold's comrade, liked and respected by both sides, a gallant man to the very last, was hanged by the patriot forces. It was a sad occasion. And as a British officer, Arnold had entered Virginia to burn Richmond. With Phipps he went about further destruction and marched south to join forces with Cornwallis. Lafayette was sent to Richmond, and then Von Steuben was also sent to Virginia. Cornwallis arrived in Petersburg in May to take command of the British forces in Virginia. In a well-planned ambush near Jamestown Ford, Cornwallis caught General Anthony Wayne's brigade by surprise, but the Americans rallied, fought bravely, counterattacked, and then retreated in good order. By August Cornwallis was moving to Yorktown.

It had been a frightening time for both Amanda and Eric as the British moved so close to home. But the British sidestepped Cameron Hall, coming very near, but never touching the property. Eric had ordered Amanda to leave—she had not. She had sent the twins north with Danielle, but she and Jacques had stayed, burying the silver, the plate, and, most important, the portraits in the hall. Eric had managed to arrive just in time to find her dirty-faced, tramping down the last of the soil cover over the cache they had made to the west of the house.

With Washington's consent and approval, Eric joined his forces with the Virginia militia, Washington himself was in New York, conferring with the French general Rochambeau. They knew that the French Admiral de Grasse was in the West Indies. De Grasse offered his services, and Washington knew that if they could concentrate the sea strength with the land force, he could beat Cornwallis. By September the Americans had Yorktown under siege. Amanda had been with Eric at the end. Cornwallis, hoping to receive reinforcements from Clinton, retired to his inner fortifications, allowing the American siege equipment to bombard him.

Benjamin Franklin's efforts had more than paid off. The French had entered the fray in 1778, and at Yorktown, Virginia, Franco-American forces stormed two of the redoubts, and new batteries were established. No one would ever forget waiting through that night! The cunning of the operations, the care, the secrecy, the darkness, the hand-to-hand combat!

On October 17 Cornwallis opened negotiations for surrender. Washington gave him two days for written proposals, but it was to be total surrender. No one had forgotten or forgiven how ignominiously the British had forced the Americans from Charleston.

Cornwallis, however, was determined not to surrender to Washington. Pretending illness, he had his second in command turn over his sword. The British and Hessians stacked their arms. Rather aptly, to the tune of the "World Turned Upside Down," with the American flag rising in the breeze, the troops marched by in surrender. Amanda stood beside Eric as it happened, and he knew that they felt the same thing, that their hearts beat in unison.

The United States of America was, at last, a reality. It was all over but the paper signing. It had been hard and brutal and often terrifying, but now the world was theirs.

But the "paper signing" had taken some time. The Treaty of Versailles had come about by the beginning of 1783, but Congress had taken until April 15 to ratify it, and not even then had Eric been able to come home for good.

Only now . . .

He stood back from Amanda and smiled. "The last of the British left New York, and George said his final good-byes to his officers at Fraunces' Tavern on December fourth. There were tears in his eyes. And in mine, Amanda, I am quite certain. In it all, my love, I would say that his courage and determination kept us going when little else did."

Amanda held his cheeks between her hands and kissed him. "He is a hero, an American hero," she agreed. "But then, so are you, my love, and you are home at last! For good, forever!"

He nodded and swept her hungrily into his arms again, his fingers threading through the rich length of her hair. It had been ten years, he reflected, ten years since that Christmastime in Boston when the harbor had turned into a teapot. Ten long years. His own dark head was beginning to turn gray, but Amanda's hair was still a cascade of flame, as evocative as her smile, as beautiful as her eyes.

It had been some fight to keep her, he reflected. Just as it had been some fight to earn the independence that was now theirs. And of course, once the fight was won, there was still so much to learn. Marriage was like an odyssey in which they stumbled and learned, and this new country would be an odyssey, and they would have to stumble and learn. And yet his wife, looking at him now with her emerald eyes and her tender smile, was all the more precious to him for the tempests they had endured.

And this great country they had forged would have to endure tempests too and yet be all the greater for it.

"You're freezing!" he said suddenly, feeling her hands. He swept his coat from about himself and set it upon her shoulders.

"Christmas dinner is almost on the table and the hall is festooned with holly and ribbons," Amanda said. She smiled.

"Father! Father!"

He looked toward the house. The twins were on the steps with Danielle and Jacques behind them. Six years old now, they were dressed for Christmas, young

Jamie handsome in a stylish frock coat, buckled shoes, and fine knee breeches, and Lenore a picture of her mother, a dazzling redhead already in a beautifully laced gown.

He glanced at Amanda. "They've grown too quickly, and I've missed so much of it."

She smiled ever more sweetly as the twins came running down the path. He had been home briefly in September, yet they seemed to have grown since then.

"I think," Amanda told him, "that you're going to have a second chance at watching growth."

Lenore and Jamie both pitched into his arms. Kissing and hugging them, he didn't quite catch her words. As he scooped up a child in each arm, he stared at her suddenly.

"What?"

"Well, I haven't the faintest idea of whether it will be twins again or not, but by June, my love, you should get your chance to watch a little Cameron grow."

"Really?"

"Really!"

He managed to kiss her exuberantly with the twins between them.

"Alors!" Danielle shouted from the porch. "Come in! *Il fait froid!"*

"Run, little ones," Eric told the twins, setting them upon the ground again. He set his arm about Amanda and they walked toward the house.

Dinner was a joyous occasion. And when the twins had been tucked up in bed, it was still a warm and wonderful night, for all of the household had gathered in the parlor, family and servants, and Eric tried to speak lightly of some of what had happened. "Think of it! We've 'cocktails' now! They say the mixture of spirits and sugar and bitters was born in a tavern in 1776, when barmaid Betsy Flannagan gave a tipsy patron a glass with the brew stirred up by a cockfeather! And we've ghost stories galore. They say a buxom young woman named Nancy Coates fell madly in love with Mad Anthony Wayne, and cast herself into the river when she discovered him returning to Fort Ticonderoga with a society girl. They say that Nancy still haunts the fort, that she walks about bedraggled and wet and calls for Anthony by the light of the moon."

Amanda arched a brow to him in disbelief. Then she leaned toward him, whispering softly, "There is a woman here, alive and well, who haunts your hall, calling your name! Eric! Eric! See there? That woman is going up to bed now and shall wait to haunt you, should you come soon enough."

He laughed aloud. Amanda was up, pausing by Jacques, kissing the top of his head. "Good night, Father, good night, all!" Gracefully she swept from the parlor.

"Well, then!" Eric rose. "I'll say my good nights too. Jacques, Danielle, Cassidy, Pierre—Richard."

Richard stopped him, standing in the doorway. "Lord Cameron, it is good to have you home, sir. Good to have you home!"

Eric nodded. "Thank you. Thank you, all of you."

He left the parlor and he started up the stairs, and when he came to the picture gallery, he paused. He looked at all the noble faces staring down at him, and he smiled rather wistfully. "Well, milords, I think that I am home for good. There is still the forging of a country to take place. And I'm not so sure that I'm 'Lord' Cameron anymore. That title came from the estates in England. But I am still Eric Cameron, gentleman of Virginia. I rather like that. I hope that you all understand."

They would, he thought. They had forged the land, and now he was hoping to forge the new country. They didn't seem too distressed as they stared down upon them.

"I really don't know what the future will bring," he continued. "There's going to be so much to do to unite thirteen very different states. Why, Patrick Henry told me that being governor here in Virginia was a nightmare at first, for laws were so difficult to form, and because they must be made so very carefully. And so I wonder at the future. I promise you, though, this hall with survive—"

"Eric. Oh, Eric . . ."

He heard her voice, coming from the bedroom. Soft and sweet and most certainly—haunting. Very haunting. His grin deepened as he looked at the portraits. Particularly at the portrait of his wife. Ever challenging, ever lovely, her sweet smile as haunting as the tone of her voice.

He bowed low to the portraits. "My lords, I'm afraid that the future will have to wait. I, Eric Cameron, gentleman of Virginia, am most earnestly interested in the present!"

And with that he turned about and hurried down the hall, into the bedroom and into her arms. This was the present, and together they had earned their freedom, their peace, and their home . . .

And the splendor of the night together.

Indeed, the future could now wait!

ABOUT THE AUTHOR

HEATHER GRAHAM is a bestselling author whose novels include the highly regarded Civil War trilogy *One Wore Blue, And One Wore Gray,* and her *New York Times* bestseller *And One Rode West.*